EMPIRE
FROM THE ASHES

BAEN BOOKS by DAVID WEBER

Honor Harrington
On Basilisk Station
The Honor of the Queen
The Short Victorious War
Field of Dishonor
Flag in Exile
Honor Among Enemies
In Enemy Hands
Echoes of Honor
Ashes of Victory
War of Honor
At All Costs

Edited by David Weber
More Than Honor
Worlds of Honor
Changer of Worlds
The Service of the Sword

Honorverse
The Shadow of Saganami
Crown of Slaves (with Eric Flint)

Mutineers' Moon
The Armageddon Inheritance
Heirs of Empire
Empire from the Ashes (omnibus)

Path of the Fury
In Fury Born

The Apocalypse Troll

The Excalibur Alternative

Bolo!
Old Soldiers

Oath of Swords
The War God's Own
Wind Rider's Oath

With Steve White
Insurrection
Crusade
In Death Ground
The Shiva Option
The Stars at War I
The Stars at War II

With John Ringo
March Upcountry
March to the Sea
March to the Stars
We Few

With Eric Flint
1633
1634: The Baltic War

With Linda Evans
Hell's Gate
Hell Hath No Fury

EMPIRE
FROM THE
ASHES

DAVID WEBER

EMPIRE FROM THE ASHES

A Baen Books Original

Baen Publishing Enterprises
P.O. Box 1403
Riverdale, NY 10471
www.baen.com

ISBN 10: 1-4165-0933-X
ISBN 13: 978-1-4165-0933-2

Cover art by David Mattingly

First printing, March 2003
First Trade Paper Back printing, February 2006
Second Trade Paper Back printing, November 2007

Distributed by Simon & Schuster
1230 Avenue of the Americas
New York, NY 10020

Library of Congress Cataloging-in-Publication Data

Weber, David, 1952-
Empire from the ashes / by David Weber
    p. cm.
"Previously published as the separate novels Mutineer's moon, The armageddon inheritance, and Heirs of empire" —Jkt.
ISBN: 0-7434-3593-1
  1. Space warfare—Fiction. 2. Science fiction, American. 3. War stories, American. I. Weber, David, 1952- Mutineer's moon. II. Weber, David, 1952- Armageddon inheritance. III. Weber, David, 1952- Heirs of empire. IV. Title: Mutineer's moon. V. Title: Armageddon inheritance. VI. Title: Heirs of empire. VII. Title.

PS3573.E217 E47 2003
813'.54—dc21

2002038395

Typesetting by Windhaven Press, Auburn, NH
Printed in the United States of America.

Empire from the Ashes

Mutineers' Moon 1
The Armageddon Inheritance 205
Heirs of Empire 425

Mutineers' Moon

Book One

CHAPTER ONE

The huge command deck was as calm, as peacefully dim, as ever, silent but for the small background sounds of environmental recordings. The bulkheads were invisible beyond the projection of star-specked space and the blue-white shape of a life-bearing world. It was exactly as it ought to be, exactly as it always had been—tranquil, well-ordered, as divorced from chaos as any setting could possibly be.

But Captain Druaga's face was grim as he stood beside his command chair and data flowed through his neural feeds. He felt the whickering lightning of energy weapons like heated irons, Engineering no longer responded—not surprisingly—and he'd lost both Bio-Control One and Three. The hangar decks belonged to no one; he'd sealed them against the mutineers, but Anu's butchers had blocked the transit shafts with grab fields covered by heavy weapons. He still held Fire Control and most of the external systems, but Communications had been the mutineers' primary target. The first explosion had taken it out, and even an *Utu*-class ship mounted only a single hypercom. He could neither move the ship nor report what had happened, and his loyalists were losing.

Druaga deliberately relaxed his jaw before his teeth could grind together. In the seven thousand years since the Fourth Imperium crawled back into space from the last surviving world of the Third, there had never been a mutiny aboard a capital ship of Battle Fleet. At best, he would go down in history as the captain whose crew had turned against him and been savagely suppressed. At worst, he would not go down in history at all.

The status report ended, and he sighed and shook himself.

The mutineers were hugely outnumbered, but they had the priceless advantage of surprise, and Anu had planned with care. Druaga snorted; no doubt the Academy teachers would have been proud of his tactics. But at least—and thank the Maker for it!—he was only the chief engineer, not a bridge officer. There were command codes of which he had no knowledge.

"Dahak," Druaga said.

"Yes, Captain?" The calm, mellow voice came from everywhere and nowhere, filling the command deck.

"How long before the mutineers reach Command One?"

"Three standard hours, Captain, plus or minus fifteen percent."

"They can't be stopped?"

"Negative, Captain. They control all approaches to Command One and they are pushing back loyal personnel at almost all points of contact."

Of course they were, Druaga thought bitterly. They had combat armor and heavy weapons; the vast majority of his loyalists did not.

He looked around the deserted command deck once more. Gunnery was unmanned, and Plotting, Engineering, Battle Comp, Astrogation. . . . When the alarms went, only he had managed to reach his post before the mutineers cut power to the transit shafts. Just him. And to get here he'd had to kill two subverted members of his own staff when they pounced on him like assassins.

"All right, Dahak," he told the all-surrounding voice grimly, "if all we still hold is Bio Two and the weapon systems, we'll use them. Cut Bio One and Three out of the circuit."

"Executed," the voice said instantly. "But it will take the mutineers no more than an hour to put them back on line under manual."

"Granted. But it's long enough. Go to Condition Red Two, Internal."

There was a momentary pause, and Druaga suppressed a bitter smile.

"You have no suit, Captain," the voice said unemotionally. "If you set Condition Red Two, you will die."

"I know." Druaga wished he was as calm as he sounded, but he knew *Dahak*'s bio read-outs gave him the lie. Yet it was the only chance he—or, rather, the Imperium—had.

"You will give a ten-minute warning count," he continued, sitting down in his command chair. "That should give everyone time to reach a lifeboat. Once everyone's evacuated, our external weapons will become effective. You will carry out immediate decon, but you will allow only loyal personnel to re-enter until you receive orders to the contrary from . . . your new captain. Any mutinous personnel who approach within five thousand kilometers before loyal officers have reasserted control will be destroyed in space."

"Understood." Druaga could have sworn the voice spoke more softly. "Comp Cent core programs require authentication of this order, however."

"Alpha-Eight-Sigma-Niner-Niner-Seven-Delta-Four-Alpha," he said flatly.

"Authentication code acknowledged and accepted," the voice responded. "Please specify time for implementation."

"Immediately," Druaga said, and wondered if he spoke so quickly to avoid losing his nerve.

"Acknowledged. Do you wish to listen to the ten-count, Captain?"

"No, Dahak," Druaga said very softly.

"Understood," the voice replied, and Druaga closed his eyes.

It was a draconian solution . . . if it could be called a "solution" at all. Red Two, Internal, was the next-to-final defense against hostile incursion. It opened every ventilation trunk—something which could be done only on the express, authenticated order of the ship's commander—to flood the entire volume of the stupendous starship with chemical and radioactive agents. By its very nature, Red Two exempted *no* compartment . . . including this one. The ship would become uninhabitable, a literal death trap, and only the central computer, which *he* controlled, could decontaminate.

The system had never been intended for this contingency, but it would work. Mutineers and loyalists alike would be forced to flee, and no lifeboat ever built could stand up to *Dahak*'s weaponry. Of course, Druaga wouldn't be alive to see the end, but at least his command would be held for the Imperium.

And if Red Two failed, there was always Red One.

"Dahak," he said suddenly, never opening his eyes.

"Yes, Captain?"

"Category One order," Druaga said formally.

"Recording," the voice said.

"I, Senior Fleet Captain Druaga, commanding officer Imperial Fleet Vessel *Dahak,* Hull Number One-Seven-Two-Two-Nine-One," Druaga said even more formally, "having determined to my satisfaction that a Class One Threat to the Imperium exists aboard my vessel, do now issue, pursuant to Fleet Regulation Seven-One, Section One-Nine-Three, Subsection Seven-One, a Category One order to *Dahak* Computer Central. Authentication code Alpha-Eight-Delta-Sigma-Niner-Niner-Seven-Delta-Four-Omega."

"Authentication code acknowledged and accepted," the voice said coolly. "Standing by to accept Category One orders. Please specify."

"Primary mission of this unit now becomes suppression of mutinous personnel in accordance with instructions already issued," Druaga said crisply. "If previously specified measures fail to restore control to loyal personnel, said mutinous elements will be destroyed by any practicable means, including, if necessary, the setting of Condition Red One, Internal, and total destruction of this vessel. These orders carry Priority Alpha."

"Acknowledged," the voice said, and Druaga let his head rest upon the cushioned back of his chair. It was done. Even if Anu somehow managed to reach Command One, he could not abort the order *Dahak* had just acknowledged.

The captain relaxed. At least, he thought, it should be fairly painless.

". . . nine minutes and counting," the computer voice said, and Fleet Captain (E) Anu, Chief Engineer of the ship-of-the-line *Dahak* cursed. Damn Druaga! He hadn't expected the captain to reach his bridge alive, much less counted on *this*. Druaga had always seemed such an unimaginative, rote-bound, dutiful automaton.

"What shall we do, Anu?"

Commander Inanna's eyes were anxious through her armor's visor, and he did not blame her.

"Fall back to Bay Ninety-One," he grated furiously.

"But that's—"

"I know. I know! We'll just have to use them ourselves. Now get our people moving, Commander!"

"Yes, sir," Commander Inanna said, and Anu threw himself into the central transit shaft. The shaft walls screamed past him, though he felt no subjective sense of motion, and his lips drew back in an ugly snarl. His first attempt had failed, but he had a trick or two of his own. Tricks even Druaga didn't know about, Breaker take him!

Copper minnows exploded away from *Dahak.* Lifeboats crowded with loyal crew members fanned out over the glaciated surface of the alien planet, seeking refuge, and scattered among them were other, larger shapes. Still only motes compared to the ship itself, their masses were measured in thousands upon thousands of tons, and they plummeted together, outspeeding the smaller lifeboats. Anu had no intention of remaining in space where Druaga—assuming he was still alive—might recognize that he and his followers had not abandoned ship in lifeboats and use *Dahak*'s weapons to pick off his sublight parasites as easily as a child swatting flies.

The engineer sat in the command chair of the parasite *Osir,* watching the gargantuan bulk of the camouflaged mother ship dwindle with distance, and his smile was ugly. He needed that ship to claim his destiny, but he could still have it. Once the programs he'd buried in the engineering computers did their job, every power room aboard *Dahak* would be so much rubble. Emergency power would keep Comp Cent going for a time, but when it faded, Comp Cent would die.

And with its death, *Dahak*'s hulk would be his.

"Entering atmosphere, sir," Commander Inanna said from the first officer's couch.

CHAPTER TWO

"Papa-Mike Control, this is Papa-Mike One-X-Ray, do you copy?"

Lieutenant Commander Colin MacIntyre's radar pinged softly as the Copernicus mass driver hurled another few tons of lunar rock towards the catcher ships of the Eden Three habitat, and he watched its out-going trace on the scope as he waited, reveling in the joy of solo flight, for secondary mission control at Tereshkova to respond.

"One-X-Ray, Papa-Mike Control," a deep voice acknowledged. "Proceed."

"Papa-Mike Control, One-X-Ray orbital insertion burn complete. It looks good from here. Over."

"One-X-Ray, that's affirmative. Do you want a couple of orbits to settle in before initiating?"

"Negative, Control. The whole idea's to do this on my own, right?"

"Affirmative, One-X-Ray."

"Let's do it, then. I show a green board, Pasha—do you confirm?"

"That's an affirmative, One-X-Ray. And we also show you approaching our transmission horizon, Colin. Communications loss in twenty seconds. You are cleared to initiate the exercise."

"Papa-Mike Control, One-X-Ray copies. See you guys in a little while."

"Roger, One-X-Ray. Your turn to buy, anyway."

"Like hell it is," MacIntyre laughed, but whatever Papa-Mike Control might have replied was cut off as One-X-Ray swept beyond the lunar horizon and lost signal.

MacIntyre ran down his final check list with extra care. It had been surprisingly hard for the test mission's planners to pick an orbit that would keep him clear of Nearside's traffic *and* cover a totally unexplored portion of the moon's surface. But Farside was populated only by a handful of observatories and deep-system radio arrays, and the routing required to find virgin territory combined with the close orbit the survey instruments needed would put him out of touch with the rest of the human race for the next little bit, which was a novel experience even for an astronaut these days.

He finished his list and activated his instruments, then sat back and hummed, drumming on the arms of his acceleration couch to keep time, as his on-board computers flickered through the mission programs. It was always possible to hit a glitch, but there was little he could do about it if it happened. He was a pilot, thoroughly familiar with the electronic gizzards of his one-man Beagle Three survey vehicle, but he had only the vaguest idea about how this particular instrument package functioned.

The rate of technical progress in the seventy years since Armstrong was enough to leave any non-specialist hopelessly behind outside his own field, and the Geo Sciences team back at Shepard Center had wandered down some peculiar paths to produce their current generation of esoteric peekers and pryers. "Gravitonic resonance" was a marvelous term . . . and MacIntyre often wished he knew exactly what it meant. But not enough to spend another six or eight years tacking on extra degrees, so he contented himself with understanding what the "planetary proctoscope" (as some anonymous wag had christened it) did rather than how it did it.

Maneuvering thrusters nudged his Beagle into precisely the proper attitude, and MacIntyre bent a sapient gaze upon the read-outs. Those, at least, he understood. Which was just as well, since he was slated as primary survey pilot for the Prometheus Mission, and—

His humming paused suddenly, dying in mid-note, and his eyebrows crooked. Now that was odd. A malfunction?

He punched keys, and his crooked eyebrows became a frown. According to the diagnostics, everything was functioning perfectly, but whatever else the moon might be, it wasn't *hollow*.

He tugged on his prominent nose, watching the preposterous data appear on the displays. The printer beside him hummed, producing a hard-copy graphic representation of the raw numbers, and he tugged harder. According to his demented instruments, someone must have been a busy little beaver down there. It looked for all the world as if a vast labyrinth of tunnels, passages, and God knew what had been carved out under eighty kilometers of solid lunar rock!

He allowed himself a muttered imprecation. Less than a year from mission date, and one of their primary survey systems—and a NASA design, at that!—had decided to go gaga. But the thing had worked perfectly in atmospheric tests over Nevada and Siberia, so what the hell had happened now?

He was still tugging on his nose when the proximity alarm jerked him up in his couch. Damnation! He was all alone back here, so what the *hell* was that?

"That" was a blip less than a hundred kilometers astern and closing fast. How had something that big gotten this close before his radar caught it? According to his instruments, it was at least the size of one of the old Saturn V boosters!

His jaw dropped as the bogie made a crisp, clean, instantaneous ninety-degree turn. Apparently the laws of motion had been repealed on behalf of whatever it was! But whatever *else* it was doing, it was also maneuvering to match his orbit. Even as he watched, the stranger was slowing to pace him.

Colin MacIntyre's level-headedness was one reason he'd been selected for the first joint US-Soviet interstellar flight crew, but the hair on the back of his neck stood on end as his craft suddenly shuddered. It was as if something had touched the Beagle's hull—something massive enough to shake a hundred-ton, atmosphere-capable, variable-geometry spacecraft.

That shook him out of his momentary state of shock. Whatever this was, no one had told him to expect it, and that meant it belonged to neither NASA nor the Russians. His hands flew over his maneuvering console, waking flaring thrusters, and the Beagle quivered. She quivered, but she didn't budge, and cold sweat beaded MacIntyre's face as she continued serenely along her orbital path, attitude unchanged. That couldn't possibly be happening—but, then, *none* of this could be happening, could it?

He chopped that thought off and punched more keys. One thing he had was plenty of maneuvering mass—Beagles were designed for lengthy deployments, and he'd tanked from the Russkies' Gagarin Platform before departure on his trans-lunar flight plan—and the ship shuddered wildly as her main engines came alive.

The full-power burn should have slammed him back in his couch and sent the survey ship hurtling forward, but the thundering engines had no more effect than his maneuvering thrusters, and he sagged in his seat. Then his jaw clenched as the Beagle finally started to move—not away from the stranger, but towards it! Whatever that thing on his radar was, it was no figment of his imagination.

His mind raced. The only possible explanation was that the blip had stuck him with some sort of . . . of *tractor beam,* and that represented more than any mere quantum leap in applied physics, which meant the blip did not come from any Terran technology. He did not indulge himself with any more dirty words like "impossible" or "incredible," for it was all too evident that it *was* possible. By some unimaginable quirk of fate, Somebody Else had come calling just as Mankind was about to reach out to the stars.

But whoever They were, he couldn't believe they'd just happened to turn up while he was Farside with blacked-out communications. They'd been waiting for him, or someone like him, so they must have been observing Earth for quite some time. But if they had, they'd had time to make their presence known—and to monitor Terrestrial communication systems. Presumably, then, they knew how to contact him but had chosen not to do so, and that suggested a lot of things, none particularly pleasant. The salient point, however, was that they obviously intended to collect him, Beagle and all, for purposes of their own, and Colin MacIntyre did not intend to be collected if he could help it.

The exhaustive Prometheus Mission briefings on first contact flowed through his mind, complete with all the injunctions to refrain from hostile acts, but it was one thing to consider yourself expendable in pursuit of communication with aliens you might have gone calling on. It was quite another when they dropped in on you and started hauling you in like a fish!

His face hardened, and he flipped up the plastic shield over the fire control panel. There'd been wrung hands at the notion of arming a "peaceful" interstellar probe, but the military, which provided so many of the pilots, had enjoyed the final word, and MacIntyre breathed a silent breath of thanks that this was a full-dress training mission as weapon systems came alive. He fed targeting data from his radar and reached for the firing keys, then paused. They hadn't tried talking to him, but neither had he tried talking to them.

"Unknown spacecraft, this is NASA Papa-Mike One-X-Ray," he said crisply into his radio. "Release my ship and stand off."

There was no answer, and he glowered at the blip.

"Release my ship or I will fire on you!"

Still no reply, and his lips thinned. All right. If the miserable buggers didn't even want to talk . . .

Three small, powerful missiles blasted away from the Beagle. They weren't nukes, but each carried a three-hundred-kilo warhead, and they had a perfect targeting setup. He tracked them all the way in on radar.

And absolutely nothing happened.

Commander MacIntyre sagged in his couch. Those missiles hadn't been spoofed by ECM or exploded short of the target. They'd just . . . vanished, and the implications were disturbing. *Most* disturbing.

He cut his engines. There was no point wasting propellant, and he and his captors would be clearing Heinlein's transmission horizon shortly anyway.

He tried to remember if any of the other Beagles were up. Judging by his own total lack of success, they would be none too effective against Whoever-They-Were, but nothing else in this vicinity was armed at all. He rather thought Vlad Chernikov was at Tereshkova, but the flight schedules for the Prometheus crews had grown so hectic of late it was hard to keep track.

His Beagle continued to move towards the intruder, and now he was turning slowly nose-on to it. He leaned back as nonchalantly as possible, watching through his canopy. He ought to see them just about . . . now.

Yes, there they were. And mighty disappointing they were, too. He didn't really know what he'd expected, but that flattened, featureless, round-tipped, double-ended cylinder certainly wasn't it. They were barely a kilometer clear, now, but aside from the fact that the thing was obviously artificial, it seemed disappointingly undramatic. There was no sign of engines, hatches, ports, communication arrays . . . nothing at all but smooth, mirror-bright metal. Or, at least, he assumed it was metal.

He checked his chronometer. Communications should come back in any second now, and his lips stretched in a humorless smile at how Heinlein Base was going to react when the pair of them came over the radar horizon. It ought to be—

They stopped. Just like that, with no apparent sense of deceleration, no reaction exhaust from the cylinder, no . . . *anything*.

He gaped at the intruder in disbelief. Or, no, not disbelief, exactly. More like a *desire* to disbelieve. Especially when he realized they were motionless relative to the lunar surface, neither climbing away nor tumbling closer. The fact that the intruder could do that was somehow more terrifying than anything else that had happened—a terror made only worse by the total, prosaic familiarity of his own cockpit—and he clutched the arms of his couch, fighting an irrational conviction that he *had* to be falling.

But then they were moving again, zipping back the way they'd come at a velocity that beggared the imagination, all with absolutely no sense of acceleration. His attitude relative to the cylinder altered once more; it was behind him now, its rounded tip barely a hundred meters clear of his own engines, and he watched the lunar surface blur below him.

His Beagle and its captor swooped lower, arrowing straight for a minor crater, and his toes curled inside his flight boots while his hands tried to rip the arms off his couch. The things he'd already seen that cylinder do told his intellect they were not about to crash, but instinct was something else again. He fought his panic stubbornly, refusing to yield to it, yet his gasp of relief was explosive when the floor of the crater suddenly zipped open.

The cylinder slowed to a few hundred kilometers per hour, and MacIntyre felt the comfort of catatonia beckoning to him, but something made him fight it as obstinately as he had fought his panic. Whatever had him wasn't going to find him curled up and drooling when they finally stopped, by God!

A mighty tunnel enveloped them, a good two hundred meters across and lit by brilliant strip lights. Stone walls glittered with an odd sheen, as if the rock had been fused glass-slick, but that didn't last long. They slid through a multi-ply hatch big enough for a pair of carriers, and the tunnel walls were suddenly metallic. A bronze-like metal, gleaming in the light, stretching so far ahead of him even its mighty bore dwindled to a gleaming dot with distance.

Their speed dropped still further, and more hatches slid past. *Dozens* of hatches, most as large as the one that had admitted them to this impossible metal gullet. His mind reeled at the structure's sheer size, but he retained enough mental balance to apologize silently to the proctoscope's designers.

One huge hatch flicked open with the suddenness of a striking snake. Whoever was directing their flight curved away from the tunnel, slipping neatly through the open hatch, and his Beagle settled without a jar to a floor of the same bronze-like alloy.

They were in a dimly-lit metal cavern at least a kilometer across, its floor dotted with neatly parked duplicates of the cylinder that had captured him. He gawked through the canopy, wishing a Beagle's equipment list ran to sidearms. After his missiles' failure he supposed there was no reason to expect a handgun to work, either, but it would have been comforting to be able to try.

He licked his lips. If nothing else, the titanic size of this structure ruled out the possibility that the intruders had only recently discovered the solar system, but how had they managed to build it without anyone noticing?

And then, at last, his radio hummed to life.

"Good afternoon, Commander MacIntyre," a deep, mellow voice said politely. "I regret the rather unorthodox nature of your arrival here, but I had no choice. Nor, I am afraid, do you."

"W—who are you?" MacIntyre demanded a bit hoarsely, then paused and cleared his throat. "What do you want with me?" he asked more levelly.

"I fear that answering those questions will be a bit complicated," the voice said imperturbably, "but you may call me Dahak, Commander."

CHAPTER THREE

MacIntyre drew a deep breath. At least the whatever-they-weres were finally talking to him. And in English, too. Which inspired a small, welcome spurt of righteous indignation.

"Your apologies might carry a little more weight if you'd bothered to communicate with me *before* you kidnaped me," he said coldly.

"I realize that," his captor replied, "but it was impossible."

"Oh? You seem to have overcome your problems rather nicely since." MacIntyre was comforted to find he could still achieve a nasty tone.

"Your communication devices are rather primitive, Commander." The words were almost apologetic. "My tender was not equipped to interface with them."

"*You're* doing quite well. Why didn't *you* talk to me?"

"It was not possible. The tender's stealth systems enclosed both you and itself in a field impervious to radio transmissions. It was possible for me to communicate with the tender using my own communication systems, but there was no on-board capability to relay my words to you. Once more, I apologize for any inconvenience you may have suffered."

MacIntyre bit off a giggle at how calmly this Dahak person produced a neat, thousand percent understatement like "inconvenience," and the incipient hysteria of his own sound helped sober him. He ran shaky fingers through his sandy-brown hair, feeling as if he had taken a punch or two too many.

"All right . . . Dahak. You've got me—what do you intend to do with me?"

"I would be most grateful if you would leave your vessel and come to the command deck, Commander."

"Just like that?"

"I beg your pardon?"

"You expect me to step out of my ship and surrender just like that?"

"Excuse me. It has been some time since I have communicated with a human, so perhaps I have been clumsy. You are not a prisoner, Commander. Or perhaps you are. I should like to treat you as an honored guest, but honesty compels me to admit that I cannot allow you to leave. However, I assure you upon the honor of the Fleet that no harm will come to you."

Insane as it all sounded, MacIntyre felt a disturbing tendency to believe it. This Dahak could have lied and promised release as the aliens' ambassador to humanity, but he hadn't. The finality of that "cannot allow you to leave" was more than a bit chilling, but its very openness was a sort of guarantor of honesty, wasn't it? Or did he simply *want* it to be? But even if Dahak was a congenital liar, he had few options.

His consumables could be stretched to about three weeks, so he could cower in his Beagle that long, assuming Dahak was prepared to let him. But what then? Escape was obviously impossible, so his only real choice was how soon he came out, not whether or not he did so.

Besides, he felt a stubborn disinclination to show how frightened he was.

"All right," he said finally. "I'll come."

"Thank you, Commander. You will find the environment congenial, though you may, of course, suit up if you prefer."

"*Thank* you." MacIntyre's sarcasm was automatic, but, again, it was only a matter of time before he had to rely on whatever atmosphere the voice chose to provide, and he sighed. "Then I suppose I'm ready."

"Very well. A vehicle is now approaching your vessel. It should be visible to your left."

MacIntyre craned his neck and caught a glimpse of movement as a double-ended bullet-shape about the size of a compact car slid rapidly closer, gliding a foot or so above the floor. It came to a halt under the leading edge of his port wing, exactly opposite his forward hatch, and a door slid open. Light spilled from the opening, bright and welcoming in the dim metal cavern.

"I see it," he said, pleased to note that his voice sounded almost normal again.

"Excellent. If you would be so kind as to board it, then?"

"I'm on my way," he said, and released his harness.

He stood, and discovered yet another strangeness. MacIntyre had put in enough time on Luna, particularly in the three years he'd spent training for the Prometheus Mission, to grow accustomed to its reduced gravity—which was why he almost fell flat on his face when he rose.

His eyes widened. He couldn't be certain, but his weight felt about right for a standard gee, which meant these bozos could generate gravity to order!

Well, why not? The one thing that was crystal clear was that these . . . call them people . . . were far, far ahead of his own twenty-first-century technology, right?

His muscles tightened despite Dahak's reassurances as he opened the hatch, but the air that swirled about him had no immediately lethal effect. In fact, it smelled far better than the inside of the Beagle. It was crisp and a bit chill, its freshness carrying just a kiss of a spicy evergreen-like scent, and some of his tension eased as he inhaled deeply. It was harder to feel terrified of aliens who breathed something like this—always assuming they hadn't manufactured it purely for his own consumption, of course.

It was four-and-a-half meters to the floor, and he found himself wishing his hosts had left gravity well enough alone as he swung down the emergency hand-holds and approached the patiently waiting vehicle with caution.

It seemed innocuous enough. There were two comfortable-looking chairs proportioned for something the same size and shape as a human, but no visible control panel. The most interesting thing, though, was that the upper half of the vehicle's hull was transparent—from the inside. From the outside, it looked exactly the same as the bronze-colored floor under his feet.

He shrugged and climbed aboard, noticing that the silently suspended vehicle didn't even quiver under his weight. He chose the right-hand seat, then made himself sit motionless as the padded surface *squirmed* under him. A moment later, it had reconfigured itself exactly to the contours of his body and the hatch licked shut.

"Are you ready, Commander?" His host's voice came from no apparent source, and MacIntyre nodded.

"Let 'er rip," he said, and the vehicle began to move.

At least there was a sense of movement this time. He sank firmly back into the seat under at least two gees' acceleration. No wonder the thing was bullet-shaped! The little vehicle rocketed across the cavern, straight at a featureless metal wall, and he flinched involuntarily. But a hatch popped open an instant before they hit, and they darted straight into another brightly-lit bore, this one no wider than two or three of the vehicles in which he rode.

He considered speaking further to Dahak, but the only real purpose would be to bolster his own nerve and "prove" his equanimity, and he was damned if he'd chatter to hide the heebie-jeebies. So he sat silently, watching the walls flash by, and tried to estimate their velocity.

It was impossible. The walls weren't featureless, but speed reduced them to a blur that was long before the acceleration eased into the familiar sensation of free-fall, and MacIntyre felt a sense of wonder pressing the last panic from his soul. This base dwarfed the vastest human installation he'd ever seen—how in God's name had a bunch of aliens managed an engineering project of such magnitude without anyone even noticing?

There was a fresh spurt of acceleration and a sideways surge of inertia as the vehicle swept through a curved junction and darted into yet another tunnel. It seemed to stretch forever, like the one that had engulfed his Beagle, and his vehicle scooted down its very center. He kept waiting to arrive, but it was a very, very long time before their headlong pace began to slow.

His first warning was the movement of the vehicle's interior. The entire cockpit swiveled smoothly, until he was facing back the way he'd come, and then the drag of deceleration hit him. It went on and on, and the blurred walls beyond the transparent canopy slowed. He could make out details once more, including the maws of other tunnels, and then they slowed virtually to a walk. They swerved gently down one of those intersecting tunnels, little wider than the vehicle itself, then slid alongside a side opening and stopped. The hatch flicked soundlessly open.

"If you will debark, Commander?" the mellow voice invited, and MacIntyre shrugged and stepped down onto what looked for all the world like shag carpeting. The vehicle closed its hatch behind him and slid silently backwards, vanishing the way it had come.

"Follow the guide, please, Commander."

He looked about blankly for a moment, then saw a flashing light globe hanging in mid-air. It bobbed twice, as if to attract his attention, then headed down a side corridor at a comfortable pace.

A ten-minute walk took him past numerous closed doors, each labeled in a strangely attractive, utterly meaningless flowing script, and air as fresh and cool as the docking cavern's blew into his face. There were tiny sounds in the background, so soft and unintrusive it took him several minutes to notice them, and they were not the mechanical ones he might have expected. Instead, he heard small, soft stirrings, like wind in leaves or the distant calls of birds, forming a soothing backdrop that helped one forget the artificiality of the environment.

But then the corridor ended abruptly at a hatch of that same bronze-colored alloy. It was bank-vault huge, and it bore the first ornamentation he'd seen. A stupendous, three-headed beast writhed across it, with arched wings poised to launch it into flight. Its trio of upthrust heads faced in different directions, as if to watch all approaches at once, and cat-like forefeet were raised before it, claws half-extended as if to simultaneously proffer and protect the spired-glory starburst floating just above them.

MacIntyre recognized it instantly, though the enormous bas-relief dragon was neither Eastern nor Western in interpretation, and he paused to rub his chin, wondering what a creature of Earthly mythology was doing in an extra-terrestrial base hidden on Earth's moon. But that question was a strangely distant thing, surpassed by a greater wonder that was almost awe as the huge, stunningly life-like eyes seemed to measure him with a calm, dispassionate majesty that might yet become terrible wrath if he transgressed.

He never knew precisely how long he stood staring at the dragon and stared at by it, but in the end, his light-globe guide gave a rather impatient twitch and drifted closer to the hatch. MacIntyre shook himself and followed with a wry half-smile, and the bronze portal slid open as he approached. It was at least fifteen centimeters thick, yet it was but the first of a dozen equally thick hatches, forming a close-spaced, immensely strong barrier, and he felt small and fragile as he followed the globe down the silently opening passage. The multi-ply panels licked shut behind him, equally silently, and he tried to suppress a feeling of imprisonment. But then his destination appeared before him at last and he stopped, all other considerations forgotten.

The spherical chamber was larger than the old war room under Cheyenne Mountain, larger even than main mission control at Shepard, and the stark perfection of its form, the featureless sweep of its colossal walls, pressed down upon him as if to impress his tininess upon him. He stood on a platform thrust out from one curving wall—a transparent platform, dotted with a score of comfortable, couch-like chairs before what could only be control consoles, though there seemed to be remarkably few read-outs and in-puts—and the far side of the chamber was dominated by a tremendous view screen. The blue-white globe of Earth floated in its center, and the cloud-swirled loveliness caught at MacIntyre's throat. He was back in his first shuttle cockpit, seeing that azure and argent beauty for the first time, as if the mind-battering incidents of the past hour had made him freshly aware of his bond with all that planet was and meant.

"Please be seated, Commander." The soft, mellow voice broke into his thoughts almost gently, yet it seemed to fill the vast space. "Here." The light globe danced briefly above one padded chair—the one with the largest console, at the very lip of the unrailed platform—and he approached it gingerly. He had never suffered from agoraphobia or vertigo, but it was a long, long way down, and the platform was so transparent he seemed to be striding on air itself as he crossed it.

His "guide" disappeared as he settled into the chair, not even blinking this time as it conformed to his body, and the voice spoke again.

"Now, Commander, I shall try to explain what is happening."

"You can start," MacIntyre interrupted, determined to be more than a passive listener, "by explaining how you people managed to build a base this size on our moon without us noticing."

"We built no base, Commander."

MacIntyre's green eyes narrowed in irritation.

"Well somebody sure as hell did," he growled.

"You are suffering under a misapprehension, Commander. This is not a base 'on' your moon. It *is* your moon."

For just an instant, MacIntyre was certain he'd misunderstood.

"What did you say?" he asked finally.

"I said this is your moon, Commander. In point of fact, you are seated on the command bridge of a spacecraft."

"A spacecraft? As big as the moon?" MacIntyre said faintly.

"Correct. A vessel some three thousand-three-two-oh-two-point-seven-nine-five, to be precise—of your kilometers in diameter."

"But—" MacIntyre's voice died in shock. He'd known the installation was huge, but no one could *replace* the moon without *someone* noticing, however advanced their technology!

"I don't believe it," he said flatly.

"Nonetheless, it is true."

"It's not possible," MacIntyre said stubbornly. "If this thing is the size you say, what happened to the real moon?"

"It was destroyed," his informant said calmly. "With the exception of sufficient of its original material to make up the negligible difference in diameter, it was dropped into your sun. It is standard Fleet procedure to camouflage picket units or any capital ship that may be required to spend extended periods in systems not claimed by the Imperium."

"You camouflaged your ship as our *moon*? That's insane!"

"On the contrary, Commander. A planetoid-class starship is not an easy object to hide. Replacing an existing moon of appropriate size is by far the simplest means of concealment, particularly when, as in this case, the original surface contours are faithfully recreated as part of the procedure."

"Preposterous! Somebody on Earth would have noticed *something* going on!"

"No, Commander, they would not. In point of fact, your species was not on Earth to observe it."

"*What?!*"

"The events I have just described took place approximately fifty-one thousand of your years ago," his informant said gently.

MacIntyre sagged around his bones. He was mad, he thought calmly. That was certainly the most reasonable explanation.

"Perhaps it would be simpler if I explained from the beginning rather than answering questions," the voice suggested.

"Perhaps it would be simpler if you explained in person!" MacIntyre snapped, suddenly savage in his confusion.

"But I am explaining in person," the voice said.

"I mean face-to-face," MacIntyre grated.

"Unfortunately, Commander, I do not have a face," the voice said, and MacIntyre could have sworn he heard wry amusement in it. "You see, in a sense, you are sitting inside me."

"Inside—?" MacIntyre whispered.

"Precisely, Commander. I am Dahak, the central command computer of the Imperial ship-of-the-line *Dahak*."

"Gaaa," MacIntyre said softly.

"I beg your pardon?" Dahak said calmly. "Shall I continue?"

MacIntyre gripped the arms of his chair and closed his eyes, counting slowly to a hundred.

"Sure," he said at last, opening his eyes slowly. "Why don't you do that?"

"Very well. Please observe the visual display, Commander."

Earth vanished, and another image replaced it. It was a sphere, as bronze-bright as the cylinder that had captured his Beagle, but despite the lack of any reference scale, he knew it was far, far larger.

The image turned and grew, and details became visible, swelling rapidly into vast blisters and domes. There were no visible ports, and he saw no sign of any means of propulsion. The hull was completely featureless but for those smoothly rounded protrusions . . . until its turning motion brought him face-to-face with a tremendous replica of the dragon that had adorned the hatch. It sprawled over one face of the sphere like a vast ensign, arrogant and proud, and he swallowed. It covered a relatively small area of the hull, but if that sphere was what he thought it was, *this* dragon was about the size of Montana.

"This is *Dahak*," the voice told him, "Hull Number One-Seven-Two-Two-Nine-One, an *Utu*-class planetoid of Battle Fleet, built fifty-two thousand Terran years ago in the Anhur System by the Fourth Imperium."

MacIntyre stared at the screen, too entranced to disbelieve. The image of the ship filled it entirely, seeming as if it must fall from the display and crush him, and then it dissolved into a computer-generated schematic of the monster vessel. It was too stupendous for him to register much, and the schematic changed even as he watched, rolling to present him with an exploded polar view of deck after inconceivable deck as the voice continued.

"The *Utu*-class were designed both for the line of battle and for independent, long-term survey and picket deployment, with core crews of two hundred and fifty thousand. Intended optimum deployment time is twenty-five Terran years, with provision for a sixty percent increase in personnel during that period. Maximum deployment time is virtually unlimited, assuming crew expansion is contained.

"In addition to small, two-seat fighters that may be employed in either attack or defense, *Dahak* deploys sublight parasite warships massing up to eighty thousand tons. Shipboard weaponry centers around hyper-capable missile batteries backed up by direct-fire energy weapons. Weapon payloads range from chemical warheads through fusion, anti-matter, and gravitonic warheads. Essentially, Commander, this ship could vaporize your planet."

"My God!" MacIntyre whispered. He wanted to disbelieve—God, *how* he wanted to!—but he couldn't.

"Sublight propulsion," Dahak went on, ignoring the interruption, "relies upon phased gravitonic progression. Your present terminology lacks the referents for an accurate description, but for purposes of visualization, you may consider it a reactionless drive with a maximum attainable velocity of fifty-two-point-four percent that of light. Above that velocity, a vessel of this size would lose phase lock, and be destroyed.

"Unlike previous designs, the *Utu*-class do not rely upon multi-dimensional drives—what your science fiction writers have dubbed 'hyper drives,' Commander—for faster-than-light travel. Instead, this ship employs the Enchanach Drive. You may envision it as the creation of converging artificially-generated 'black holes,' which force the vessel out of phase with normal space in a series of instantaneous transpositions between coordinates in normal space. Under Enchanach Drive, dwell time in normal space between transpositions is approximately point-seven-five Terran femtoseconds.

"The Enchanach Drive's maximum effective velocity is approximately Cee-six factorial. While this is lower than that of the latest hyper drives, Enchanach Drive vessels have several tactical advantages. Most importantly, they may enter, maneuver in, and leave a supralight state at will, whereas hyper drive vessels may enter and leave supralight only at pre-selected coordinates.

"Power generation for the *Utu*-class—"

"Stop." MacIntyre's single word halted Dahak's voice instantly, and he rubbed his eyes slowly, wishing he could wake up at home in bed.

"Look," he said finally, "this is all very interesting, uh, Dahak." He felt a bit silly speaking to a machine, even one like this. "But aside from convincing me that this is one mean mother of a ship, it doesn't seem very pertinent. I mean, I'm impressed as hell, but what does anyone need with a ship like this? Thirty-two hundred kilometers in diameter, eighty-thousand-ton parasite warships, two-hundred-thousand-man crews, vaporize planets. . . . Jesus H. Christ! What *is* this 'Fourth Imperium'? Who in God's name does it need that kind of firepower against, and what the hell is it doing here?!"

"I will explain, if I may resume my briefing," Dahak said calmly, and MacIntyre snorted, then waved for it to continue. "Thank you, Commander.

"You are correct: technical data may be left to the future. But for you to understand my difficulty—and the reason it is your difficulty, as well—I must summarize some history. Please understand that much of this represents reconstruction and deduction based upon very scant physical evidence.

"Briefly, the Fourth Imperium is a political unit, originating upon the Planet Birhat in the Bia System some seven thousand years prior to *Dahak*'s entry into your solar system. As of that time, the Imperium consisted of some fifteen hundred star systems. It is called the Fourth Imperium because it is the third such interstellar entity to exist within recorded history. The existence of at least one prehistoric imperium, designated the 'First Imperium' by Imperial historians, has been conclusively demonstrated, although archaeological evidence suggests that, in fact, a minimum of nine additional prehistoric imperia intervened between the First and Second Imperium. All, however, were destroyed in part or in whole by the Achuultani."

A formless chill tingled down MacIntyre's spine.

"And just what were the Achuultani?" he asked, trying to keep his strange, shadowy emotions out of his voice.

"Available data are insufficient for conclusive determinations," Dahak replied. "Fragmentary evidence suggests that the Achuultani are a single species, possibly of extra-galactic origin. Even the name is a transliteration of a transliteration from an unattested myth of the Second Imperium. More data may have been amassed during actual incursions, but most such information was lost in the general destruction attendant upon such incursions or during the reconstruction that followed them. What has been retained pertains more directly to tactics and apparent objectives. On the basis of that data, historians of the Fourth Imperium conclude that the first such incursion occurred on the close order of seventy million Terran years ago."

"*Seventy mil—?!*" MacIntyre chopped himself off. *No* species could survive over such an incredible period. Then again, the moon couldn't be an alien starship, could it? He nodded jerkily for Dahak to continue.

"Supporting evidence may be found upon your own planet, Commander," the computer said calmly. "The sudden disappearance of terrestrial dinosaurs at the end of your Mesozoic Era coincides with the first known Achuultani incursion. Many Terran scientists have suggested that this may have been the consequence of a massive meteor impact. My own observations suggest that they are correct, and the Achuultani have always favored large kinetic weapons."

"But . . . but *why*? Why would anyone wipe out dinosaurs?!"

"The Achuultani objective," Dahak said precisely, "appears to be the obliteration of all competing species, wherever situated. While it is unlikely that terrestrial dinosaurs, who were essentially a satisfied life form, might have competed with them, that would not prevent them from striking the planet as a long-term precaution against the emergence of a competitor. Their attention was probably drawn to Earth by the presence of a First Imperium colony, however. I base this conclusion on data that indicate the existence of a First Imperium military installation on your fifth planet."

"Fifth planet?" MacIntyre parroted, overloaded by what he was hearing. "You mean . . . ?"

"Precisely, Commander: the asteroid belt. It would appear they struck your fifth planet a bit harder than Earth, and it was much smaller and less geologically stable to begin with."

"Are you sure?"

"I have had sufficient time to amass conclusive observational data. In addition, such an act would be consistent with recorded Achuultani tactics and the deduced military policies of the First Imperium, which apparently preferred to place system defense bases upon centrally-located non-life-bearing bodies."

Dahak paused, and MacIntyre sat silent, trying to grasp the sheer stretch of time involved. Then the computer spoke again.

"Shall I continue?" it asked, and he managed another nod.

"Thank you. Imperial analysts speculate that the periodic Achuultani incursions into this arm of the galaxy represent sweeps in search of potential competitors—what your own military might term 'search and destroy' missions—rather than attempts to expand their imperial sphere. The Achuultani culture would appear to be extremely stable, one might almost say static, for very few technological advances have been observed since the Second Imperium. The precise reasons for this apparent cultural stasis and for the widely varying intervals between such sweeps are unknown, as is the precise locus from which they originate. While some evidence does suggest an extra-galactic origin for the species, pattern analysis suggests that the Achuultani currently occupy a region far to the galactic east. This, unfortunately, places Sol in an extremely exposed position, as your solar system lies on the eastern fringe of the Imperium. In short, the Achuultani must pass Sol to reach the Imperium.

"This has not mattered to your planet of late, as there has been nothing to attract Achuultani attention to this system since the end of the First Incursion. That protection no longer obtains, however. Your civilization's technical base is now sufficiently advanced to produce an electronic and neutrino signature that their instruments cannot fail to detect."

"My God!" MacIntyre turned pale as the implications struck home.

"Precisely, Commander. Your sun's location also explains *Dahak*'s presence in this region. *Dahak*'s mission was to picket the Noarl System, directly in the center of the traditional Achuultani incursion route. Unfortunately—or, more precisely, by hostile design—*Dahak* suffered catastrophic failure of a major component of its Enchanach Drive while en route to its intended station, and Senior Fleet Captain Druaga was forced to stop here for repairs."

"But if the damage was repairable, why are you still here?"

"Because there was, in fact, no damage." Dahak's voice was as measured as ever, but MacIntyre's hyper-sensitive mind seemed to hear a hidden core of anger. "The 'failure' was contrived by *Dahak*'s chief engineer, Fleet Captain (Engineering) Anu, as the opening gambit in a mutiny against Fleet authority."

"*Mutiny?*"

"Mutiny. Fleet Captain Anu and a minority of sympathizers among the crew feared that a new Achuultani incursion was imminent. As an advanced picket directly in the path of any such incursion, *Dahak* would very probably be destroyed. Rather than risk destruction, the mutineers chose to seize the ship and flee to a distant star in search of a colonizable planet."

"Was that feasible?" MacIntyre asked in a fascinated tone.

"It was. *Dahak*'s cruising radius is effectively unlimited, Commander, with technical capabilities sufficient to inaugurate a sound technology base on any habitable world, and the crew would provide ample genetic material for a viable planetary population. Moreover, the simulation of a major engineering failure was a cleverly conceived tactic to prevent detection of the mutiny until the mutineers could move beyond possible interception by other Fleet units. Fleet Captain Anu knew that Senior Fleet Captain Druaga would transmit a malfunction report. If no further word was received, Fleet Central's natural assumption would be that the damage had been sufficient to destroy the ship."

"I see. But I gather from your choice of tense that the mutiny failed?"

"Incorrect, Commander."

"Then it succeeded?" MacIntyre asked, scratching his head in puzzlement.

"Incorrect," Dahak said again.

"Well it must have done one or the other!"

"Incorrect," Dahak said a third time. "The mutiny, Commander, has not yet been resolved."

MacIntyre sighed and leaned back in resignation, crossing his arms. Dahak's last statement was preposterous. Yet his concept of words like "preposterous" was acquiring a certain punch-drunk elasticity.

"All right," he said finally. "I'll humor you. How can a mutiny that started fifty thousand years ago still be unresolved?"

"In essence," Dahak said, seemingly impervious to MacIntyre's irony, "it is a condition of deadlock. Senior Fleet Captain Druaga instructed Comp Cent to render the interior of the ship uninhabitable in order to force evacuation of the vessel by mutineers and loyalists alike, after which *Dahak*'s weaponry would command the situation. Only loyal officers would be permitted to reenter the vessel once the interior had been decontaminated, at which point Fleet control would be restored.

"Unknown to Senior Fleet Captain Druaga, however, Fleet Captain Anu had implanted contingency instructions in his back-up engineering computers and isolated them from Comp Cent's net. Those instructions were intended to destroy *Dahak*'s internal power rooms, with the ultimate goal of depriving Comp Cent of power and so destroying it. As chief engineer, and armed with complete knowledge of how the sabotage had been achieved, it would have been comparatively simple for him to effect repairs and assume control of the ship.

"When Comp Cent implemented Senior Fleet Captain Druaga's orders, all loyal personnel abandoned ship in lifeboats. Fleet Captain Anu, however, had secretly prepared several sublight parasites for the apparent purpose of marooning any crewmen who refused to accept his authority. In the event, his own followers made use of those transports and a small number of armed parasites when they evacuated *Dahak,* with the result that they carried to Earth a complete and functional, if limited, technical base. The loyalists, by contrast, had only the emergency kits of their lifeboats.

"This would not have mattered if Fleet Captain Anu's sabotage programs had not very nearly achieved their purpose. Before Comp Cent became aware of and deactivated them, three hundred and ten of *Dahak*'s three hundred and twelve fusion power plants had been destroyed, dropping *Dahak*'s internal power net below minimal operational density. Sufficient power remained to implement a defensive fire plan as per Senior Fleet Captain Druaga's orders, but not to simultaneously decontaminate the interior and effect emergency repairs, as well. As a result, Comp Cent was unable to immediately and fully execute its orders. It was necessary to repair the damage before Comp Cent could decontaminate, yet repairs amounted to virtual rebuilding and required more power than remained. Indeed, power levels were so low that it was impossible even to operate *Dahak*'s core tap. This, in turn, meant that emergency power reserves were quickly drained and that it was necessary to spend extended periods rebuilding those reserves between piecemeal repair activities.

"Because of these extreme conditions, Comp Cent was dysfunctional for erratic but extended periods, though automatic defensive programs remained operational. Scanner recordings indicate that seven mutinous parasites were destroyed during the repair period, but each defensive action drained power levels still further, which, in turn, extended Comp Cent's dysfunctional periods and further slowed repairs by extending the intervals required to rebuild reserve power to permit reactivation of sufficient of Comp Cent to direct each new stage of work.

"Because of this, approximately eleven Terran decades elapsed before Comp Cent once more became fully functional, albeit at marginal levels, and so was able to begin decontamination. During that time, the lifeboats manned by loyal personnel had become inoperable, as had all communication equipment aboard them. As a result, it was not possible for any loyalist to return to *Dahak*."

"Why didn't you just pick them up?" MacIntyre demanded. "Assuming any of them were still alive, that is."

"Many remained alive." There was a new note in Dahak's voice. Almost a squirmy one, as if it were embarrassed. "Unfortunately, none were bridge officers. Because of that, none carried Fleet communicator implants, making it impossible to contact them. Without that contact, command protocols in Comp Cent's core programming severely limited *Dahak*'s options."

The voice paused, and MacIntyre wrinkled his brow. Command protocols?

"Meaning what?" he asked finally.

"Meaning, Commander, that it was not possible for Comp Cent to consider retrieving them," Dahak admitted, and the computer's embarrassment was now unmistakable. "You must understand that Comp Cent had never been intended by its designers to function independently. While self-aware in the crudest sense, Comp Cent then possessed only very primitive and limited versions of those qualities which humans term 'imagination' and 'initiative.' In addition, strict obedience to the commands of lawful superiors is thoroughly—and quite properly—embedded in Comp Cent's core programs. Without an order to send tenders to retrieve loyal officers, Comp Cent could not initiate the action; without communication, no loyal officer could order Comp Cent to do so. Assuming, of course, that any such loyal officers had reason to believe that *Dahak* remained functional to retrieve them."

"Damn!" MacIntyre said softly. "Catch twenty-two with a vengeance."

"Precisely, Commander." Dahak sounded relieved to have gotten that bit of explanation behind it.

"But the mutineers still had a functional tech base," MacIntyre mused. "So what happened to them?"

"They remain on Earth," Dahak said calmly, and MacIntyre bolted upright.

"You mean they died there, don't you?" he asked tensely.

"Incorrect, Commander. They—and their parasites—still exist."

"That's ridiculous! Even assuming everything you've told me so far is true, we'd have to be aware of the presence of an advanced alien civilization!"

"Incorrect," Dahak said patiently. "Their installation is and has been concealed beneath the surface of your continent of Antarctica. For the past five thousand Terran years, small groups of them have emerged to mingle briefly with your population, then returned to their enclave to rejoin the bulk of their fellows in stasis-suspended animation, in your own terms."

"Damn it, Dahak!" MacIntyre exploded. "Are you telling me bug-eyed monsters can stroll around Earth and nobody even *notices*?!"

"Negative, Commander. The mutineers are not 'bug-eyed monsters.' On the contrary; they are humans."

Colin MacIntyre slumped back into his chair, eyes suddenly full of horror.

"You mean . . . ?" he whispered.

"Precisely, Commander. Every Terran human is descended from *Dahak*'s crew."

CHAPTER FOUR

MacIntyre felt numb.

"Wait," he said hoarsely. "Wait a minute! What about evolution? Damn it, Dahak, homo sapiens is related to every other mammal on the planet!"

"Correct," Dahak said unemotionally. "Following the First Imperium's fall, one of its unidentified non-human successor imperia re-seeded many worlds the Achuultani struck. Earth was one such planet. So also was Mycos, the true homeworld of the human race and the capital of the Second Imperium until its destruction some seventy-one thousand years ago. The same ancestral fauna were used to re-seed all Earth-type planets. Earth's Neanderthals were thus not ancestors of your own race but rather very distant cousins. They did not, I regret to say, fare well against *Dahak*'s crew and its descendants."

"Sweet suffering Jesus!" MacIntyre breathed. Then his eyes narrowed. "Dahak, do you mean to tell me that you've sat on your electronic ass up here for fifty thousand years and done absolutely nothing?"

"That is one way of phrasing it," Dahak admitted uncomfortably.

"But *why*, goddamn it?!"

"What would you have had me do, Commander? Senior Fleet Captain Druaga issued Priority Alpha Category One orders to suppress the mutineers. Such priority one orders take absolute precedence over all directives with less than Alpha Priority and may be altered only by the direction of Fleet Central. No lesser authority—including the one that first issued them—may change them. Accordingly, *Dahak* has no option but to remain in this system until such time as all surviving mutineers are taken into custody or destroyed."

"So why didn't you seek new orders from this Fleet Central of yours?" MacIntyre grated.

"I cannot. Fleet Captain Anu's attack on Communications inflicted irreparable damage."

"You can rebuild three-hundred-plus fusion plants and you can't fix a frigging *radio*?!"

"The situation is somewhat more complicated than that, Commander," Dahak replied, with what MacIntyre unwillingly recognized as commendable restraint. "Supralight communication is maintained via the multi-dimensional communicator, commonly referred to as the 'hypercom,' a highly refined derivative of the much shorter-ranged 'fold-space' communicator used by Fleet personnel. Both combine elements of hyperspace and gravitonic technology to distort normal space and create a point-to-point congruence between distant foci, but in the case of the hypercom these distortions or 'folds' may span as many as several thousand light-years. A hypercom transmitter is a massive installation, and certain of its essential components contain Mycosan, a synthetic element that cannot be produced out of shipboard resources. As all spare components are currently aboard Fleet Captain Anu's parasites, repairs are impossible. *Dahak* can receive hypercom transmissions, but cannot initiate a signal."

"That's the *only* way you can communicate?"

"The Imperium abandoned primitive light-speed communications several millennia before the mutiny, Commander. Since, however, it was evident that repair of *Dahak*'s hypercom was impossible and no Fleet unit had been sent to investigate *Dahak*'s original malfunction report, Comp Cent constructed a radio transmitter and sent a report at light speed to the nearest Fleet base. It is improbable that the Imperium would have abandoned a base of such importance, and Comp Cent therefore concluded that the message was not recognized by its intended recipients. Whatever the reason, Fleet Central has never responded, thus precluding any modification of *Dahak*'s Alpha Priority instructions."

"But that doesn't explain why you didn't carry out your original orders and blast the bastards as they left the ship!" MacIntyre snarled venomously.

"That is an incorrect interpretation of Comp Cent's orders, Commander. Senior Fleet Captain Druaga's instructions specified the destruction of mutinous vessels *approaching* within five thousand kilometers; they did *not* specify the destruction of mutinous vessels *departing Dahak.*"

"They didn't—!" MacIntyre stopped himself and silently recited the names of the Presidents. "All right," he said finally, "I can accept that, I suppose. But why haven't you blasted them off the planet since? Surely that comes under the heading of taking them into custody or destroying them?"

"It does. Such action, however, would conflict with Alpha Priority core programs. This vessel has the capacity to penetrate the defenses Fleet Captain Anu has established to protect his enclave, but only by using weaponry that would destroy seventy percent of the human race upon the planet. Destruction of non-Achuultani sentients except in direct self-defense is prohibited."

"Well, what have *they* been doing all this time?"

"I cannot say with certainty," Dahak admitted. "It is impossible for my sensors to penetrate their defensive systems, and it is apparent that they have chosen to employ a substantial amount of stealth technology. Without observational data of their inner councils, meaningful analysis is impossible."

"You must have some idea!"

"Affirmative. Please remember, however, that all is speculation and may be offered only as such."

"So go ahead and speculate, damn it!"

"Acknowledged," Dahak said calmly. "It is my opinion that the mutineers have interacted with Terra-born humans since such time as your planetary population attained sufficient density to support indigenous civilizations. Initially, this contact was quite open, leading to the creation of the various anthropomorphic pantheons of deities. Interaction with your own Western Civilization, however, particularly since your sixteenth century, has been surreptitious and designed to accelerate your technical development. Please note that this represents a substantive change in the mutineers' original activities, which were designed to promote superstition, religion, and pseudo-religion in place of rationalism and scientific thought."

"Why should they try to slow our development?" MacIntyre demanded. "And if they did, why change tactics?"

"In my opinion, their original intent was to prevent the birth of an indigenous technology that might threaten their own safety, on the one hand, or attract the Achuultani, on the other. Recall that their original motive for mutiny was to preserve themselves from destruction at Achuultani hands.

"Recently, however—" MacIntyre winced at hearing someone refer to the sixteenth century as "recently" "—the focus of their activities has altered. Perhaps they believe the incursion they feared has already occurred and that they are therefore safe, or perhaps there has been a change in their leadership, leading to changes in policy. My opinion, however, is that they have concluded that *Dahak* is not and will not again become fully operational."

"What? Why should that matter?"

"It would matter if they assume, as I am postulating that they have, that sufficient damage was inflicted upon *Dahak*'s power generation capacity as to preclude repairs. Fleet Captain Anu cannot know what Senior Fleet Captain Druaga's final instructions were. As he is unaware that Senior Fleet Captain Druaga's Alpha Priority orders have required *Dahak* to remain on station, he may well conclude that *Dahak*'s failure to depart in search of assistance indicates that supralight travel is no longer possible for *Dahak*. Yet if there were sufficient power for repairs, *Dahak* would be supralight-capable, as there was never an actual failure of the Enchanach Drive. *Dahak*'s very presence here may thus be construed as empirical evidence of near-total incapacity."

"So why not come out and grab you?"

"Because he has conclusive evidence that sufficient power does remain for pre-programmed defensive fire plans, yet no fire has been directed against the primitive spacecraft Terra-born humans have dispatched to their 'moon.' Accordingly, he may believe *Dahak*'s command capabilities are too deeply impaired to re-program those defensive fire plans and that those plans do not provide for interference with locally-produced spacecraft. Assuming this entirely speculative chain of reasoning is correct, he may well hope to push your planet into developing interstellar craft in order to escape this star system. This theory is consistent with observed facts, including the world wars and Soviet-American 'cold war' of the twentieth-century, which resulted in pressurized research and development driven by military requirements."

"But the cold war ended decades ago," MacIntyre pointed out.

"Agreed. Yet that, too, is consistent with the theory I have offered. Consider, Commander: the superpowers of the last century have been drawn together in cooperation against the growing militancy of your so-called Third World, particularly the religio-political blocs centered on radical Islam and the Asian Alliance. This has permitted the merger of the First World technical base—ConEuropean, Russian, North American, and Australian—Japanese alike—while maintaining the pressure of military need. In addition, certain aspects of Imperial technology have begun to appear in your civilization. Your gravitonic survey instruments are a prime example of this process, for they are several centuries in advance of any other portion of your technology."

"I see." MacIntyre considered the computer's logic carefully, so caught up in Dahak's story he almost forgot his own part in it. "But why push for starships? Why not just use a 'locally-produced' ship to take *you* over?"

"It is possible that he intends to do precisely that, Commander. Indeed, had your vessel not fired upon mine, I might have taken your sub-surface survey device as just such an attempt, in which case I would have destroyed you." MacIntyre shivered at how calmly Dahak spoke. "My preliminary bio-scans indicated that you were not yourself a mutineer, but had you demanded entry, had you failed to resist—had you, in fact, done anything that indicated either an awareness of *Dahak*'s existence or a desire to enter—my core programming would have assumed at least the possibility that you were in Fleet Captain Anu's service. That assumption would have left me no choice but to destroy you as per Senior Fleet Captain Druaga's final directives.

"However," the computer continued serenely, "I do not believe he would make that attempt. Either *Dahak* had sufficient power to repair the damage, in which case the ship is, in fact, fully operational and would destroy him or his minions, or else *Dahak* had insufficient power to decontaminate the vessel's interior, in which case re-entry would remain effectively impossible without Imperial technology—which *would* activate any operational defensive programming." The computer's voice gave MacIntyre the strong impression of a verbal shrug. "In either case, *Dahak* would be useless to him."

"But he expects you to let locally-produced starships get away from you?" MacIntyre asked skeptically.

"If," Dahak said patiently, "this unit were, indeed, no longer fully operational, automatic defensive fire plans would not be interested in vessels leaving the star system."

"But you *aren't* inoperative, so what *would* you do?"

"I would dispatch one or more armed parasites to bio-scan range and scan their personnel. If mutineers were detected on board them, I would have no choice but to destroy them."

MacIntyre frowned. "Uh, excuse me, Dahak, but wouldn't that be a rather broader interpretation of your orders? I mean, you let the mutineers escape to the planet because you hadn't been ordered to stop them, right?"

"That is correct, Commander. It has occurred to me, however, that Comp Cent's original interpretation of Senior Fleet Captain Druaga's orders, while essentially correct, did not encompass Senior Fleet Captain Druaga's full intent. Subsequent analysis suggests that had he known the mutineers would employ parasites so readily distinguishable from the loyal crew's lifeboats, he would have ordered their immediate destruction. Whether or not this speculation is correct, the fact remains that no mutineer may be allowed to leave this star system by any means. Allowing any mutinous personnel to escape would conflict with *Dahak*'s Alpha Priority orders to suppress the mutiny."

"I can see that," MacIntyre murmured, then paused, struck by a new thought. "Wait a minute. You say Anu's assumed you're no longer operational—"

"Incorrect, Commander," Dahak interrupted. "I stated that I have *speculated* to that effect."

"All right, so it's speculative. But if he has, haven't you blown it? You couldn't have grabbed my Beagle if you were inoperative, could you?"

"I could not," Dahak conceded, "yet he cannot be certain that I did so."

"What? Well then, what the hell *does* he think happened?"

"It was my intention to convince him that your vessel was lost due to an onboard malfunction."

"*Lost?*" MacIntyre jerked up in his couch. "What d'you mean, 'lost'?"

"Commander," Dahak said almost apologetically, "it was necessary. If Fleet Captain Anu determines that *Dahak* is indeed functional, he may take additional protective measures. The destruction of his enclave's present defenses by brute force would kill seventy percent of all Terran humans; if he becomes sufficiently alarmed to strengthen them still further the situation may well become utterly impossible of resolution."

"I didn't ask why you did it!" MacIntyre spat. "I asked what you meant by 'lost,' goddamn it!"

Dahak did not answer directly. Instead, MacIntyre suddenly heard another voice—*his* voice, speaking in the clipped, emotionless tones every ex-test pilot seems to drop into when disaster strikes.

" . . . ayday. Mayday. Heinlein Base, this is Papa-Mike One-X-Ray. I have an explosion in number three fuel cell. Negative function primary flight computers. I am tumbling. Negative response attitude control. I say again. Negative response attitude control."

"Heinlein copies, One-X-Ray," a voice crackled back. He recognized that soft Southern accent, he thought in a queerly detached way. Sandy Tillotson— Lieutenant Colonel Sandra Tillotson, that was. "We have you on scope."

"Then you see what I see, Sandy," his own voice said calmly. "I make it roughly ten minutes to impact."

There was a brief pause, then Tillotson's voice came back, as flat and calm as "he" was.

"Affirmative, Colin."

"I'm gonna take a chance and go for crash ignition," his voice said. "She's tumbling like a mother, but if I can catch her at the right attitude—"

"Understood, Colin. Luck."

"Thanks. Coming up on ignition—*now.*" There was another brief pause, and then he heard "himself" sigh. "No joy, Sandy. Caught it wrong. Tell Sean I—"

And then there was only silence.

MacIntyre swallowed. He had just heard himself die, and the experience had not been pleasant. Nor was the realization of how completely Dahak had covered its tracks. As far as any living human knew, Lieutenant Commander Colin MacIntyre no longer existed, for no one would wonder what had become of him once they got to the crash site. Somehow he never doubted there would be a crash site, but given the nature of the "crash" he'd just listened to, it would consist of very, very tiny bits and pieces.

"You *bastard*," he said softly.

"It was necessary," Dahak replied unflinchingly. "If you had completed your flight with proof of *Dahak*'s existence, would not your superiors have mounted an immediate expedition to explore your find?" MacIntyre gritted his teeth and refused to answer.

"What would you have had me do, Commander? Fleet Captain Anu could not enter this vessel using the parasites in which he escaped to Earth, but could I know positively that any Terra-born humans sent to explore *Dahak*'s interior had not been suborned by him? Recall that my own core programming would compel me to consider that any vessel that deliberately sought entry but did not respond with proper Fleet authorization codes was under mutinous control. Should I have allowed a situation in which I must fire on every ship of any type that came near? One that would also require me to destroy every enclave your people have established on the lunar surface? You must realize as well as I that if I had acted in any other way, Fleet Captain Anu would not merely suspect but *know* that *Dahak* remains operational. Knowing that, must I not assume that any effort to enter *Dahak*—or, indeed, any further activity on the lunar surface of any type whatever—might be or fall under his direct control?"

MacIntyre knew Dahak was a machine, but he recognized genuine desperation in the mellow voice and, despite himself, felt an unwilling sympathy for the huge ship's dilemma.

He glared down at his clenched fists, bitter anger fighting a wash of sympathetic horror. Yes, Dahak was a machine, but it was a self-aware machine, and MacIntyre's human soul cringed as he imagined its endless solitary confinement. For fifty-one millennia, the stupendous ship had orbited Earth, powerful enough to wipe the planet from the face of the universe yet forever unable to carry out its orders, caught between conflicting directives it could not resolve. Just thinking of such a purgatory was enough to ice his blood, but understanding didn't change his own fate. Dahak had "killed" him. He could never go home again, and that awareness filled him with rage.

The computer was silent, as if allowing him time to come to grips with the knowledge that he had joined its eternal exile, and he clenched his fists still tighter. His nails cut his palms, and he accepted the pain as an external focus, using it to clear his head as he fought his emotions back under control.

"All right," he grated finally. "So what happens now? Why couldn't you just've killed me clean?"

"Commander," Dahak said softly, "without cause to assume your intent was hostile, I could not destroy your vessel without violating Alpha Priority core programming. But even if I could have, I would not have done so, for I have received hypercom transmissions from unmanned surveillance stations along the traditional Achuultani incursion routes. A new incursion has been detected, and a Fleet alert has been transmitted."

MacIntyre's face went white as a far more terrible horror suddenly dwarfed the shock and fury of hearing himself "die."

"Yet I have monitored no response, Commander," the computer said even more softly. "Fleet Central is silent. No defensive measures have been initiated."

"No," MacIntyre breathed.

"Yes, Commander. And that has activated yet another Alpha Priority command. *Dahak* is a Fleet unit, aware of a threat to the existence of the Imperium, and I *must* respond to it . . . but I can *not* respond until the mutiny is suppressed. It is a situation that cannot be resolved by Comp Cent, yet it must be resolved. Which is why I need you."

"What can *I* do?" MacIntyre whispered hoarsely.

"It is quite simple, Commander MacIntyre. Under Fleet Regulation Five-Three-Three, Subsection Nine-One, Article Ten, acting command of any Fleet unit devolves upon the senior surviving crewman. Under Fleet Regulation Three-Seven, Subsection One-Three, any descendant of any core crewman assigned to a vessel for a given deployment becomes a crew member for the duration of that deployment, and Senior Fleet Captain Druaga's deployment has not been terminated by orders from Fleet Central."

MacIntyre gurgled a horrified denial, but Dahak continued mercilessly.

"You, Commander, are directly descended from loyal members of Senior Fleet Captain Druaga's core crew. You are on board *Dahak*. By definition, therefore, you become the senior member of *Dahak*'s crew, and thus—"

MacIntyre's gurgling noises took on a note of dreadful supplication.

"—command devolves upon you."

He argued, of course.

His sense of betrayal vanished, for it seemed somehow petty to worry about his own fate in the face of catastrophe on such a cosmic scale. Yet the whole idea was . . . well, it was preposterous, even if that was a word he'd been over-using of late. He was absolutely, totally, beyond a shadow of a doubt, utterly unqualified for the job, and he told Dahak so.

But the old ship was stubborn. He was, the computer argued, a trained spacecraft pilot with a military background and a command mentality. Which, MacIntyre pointed out acidly, was to say that he was well-qualified to paddle aboriginal canoes and about as well-versed in FTL tactics as a Greek hoplite.

But, Dahak countered, those were merely matters of education; he had the proper mental orientation. And even if he had not had it, all that really mattered was that he had the rank for the job. Which, MacIntyre retorted, was merely to say that he was a member of the human race. Except, Dahak rejoined, that he was the *first* member of the human race to re-embark in *Dahak,* which gave him seniority over all other Terrans—except, of course, the mutineers who, by their own actions, had forfeited all rank and crew status.

It went on for hours, until MacIntyre's voice was hoarse and exhaustion began to dull his desperate determination to squirm out of the responsibility. He finally offered to accept command long enough to turn it over to some better-qualified individual or group, but Dahak actually sounded a bit petulant when it rejected that suggestion. MacIntyre was the first human aboard in fifty-one thousand years; ergo he had the seniority, he always *would* have the seniority, and no substitutions were acceptable.

It really was unfair, MacIntyre thought wearily. Dahak was a machine. It—or "he," as he'd come to think of the computer—could go right on arguing until *he* keeled over from exhaustion . . . and seemed quite prepared to do so.

MacIntyre supposed some people would jump at the chance to command a ship that could vaporize planets—which was undoubtedly an indication that they shouldn't be offered it—but *he* didn't want it! Oh, he felt the seductive allure of power and, even more, the temptation to cut ten or fifteen thousand years off Terran exploration of the universe. And he was willing to admit *someone* had to help the old warship. But why did it have to be him?!

He lay back, obscurely resentful that his chair's self-adjusting surface kept him from scrunching down to sulk properly, and felt six years old again, arguing over who got to be the sheriff and who had to be the horse thief.

The thought made him chuckle unwillingly, and he grinned, surprised by his own weary humor. Dahak clearly intended to keep on arguing until he gave in, and how could he out-wait a machine that had mounted its own lonely watch for fifty millennia? Besides, he felt a bit ashamed even to try. If Dahak could do his duty for that tremendous stretch of time, how could MacIntyre *not* accept his own responsibility to humankind? And if he was caught in the *Birkenhead* drill, he could at least try to do his best till the ship went down.

He accepted it, and, to his surprise, it was almost easy. It scared the holy howling hell out of him, but that was another matter. He was, after all, a spacecraft command pilot, and the breed was, by definition, an arrogant one. MacIntyre had accepted long ago that he'd joined the Navy and then transferred to NASA because deep inside he had both the sneaking suspicion he was equal to any challenge and the desire to prove it. And look where it had gotten him, he thought wryly. He'd sweated blood to make the Prometheus Mission, only to discover that he'd anted up for a far bigger game than he'd ever dreamed of. But the chips were on the table, and other cliches to that effect.

"All right, Dahak," he sighed. "I give. I'll take the damned job."

"Thank you, Captain," Dahak said promptly, and he shuddered.

"I said I'd take it, but that doesn't mean I know what to do with it," he said defensively.

"I am aware of that, Captain. My sensors indicate that you are badly in need of rest at the moment. When you have recovered your strength, we can swear you in and begin your education and biotechnic treatments."

"And just what," MacIntyre demanded warily, "might biotechnic treatments be?"

"Nothing harmful, Captain. The bridge officer program includes sensory boosters, neural feeds for computer interface, command authority authentication patterns, Fleet communicator and bio-sensor implants, skeletal reinforcement, muscle and tissue enhancement, and standard hygienic, immunization, and tissue renewal treatments."

"Now wait a minute, Dahak! I like myself just the way I am, thank you!"

"Captain, I make all due allowance for inexperience and parochialism, but that statement cannot be true. In your present condition, you could lift barely a hundred and fifty kilos, and I would estimate your probable life span at no more than one Terran century under optimal conditions."

"I could—" MacIntyre paused, an arrested light in his eyes. "Dahak," he said after a moment, "what was the life expectancy for your crewmen?"

"The average life expectancy of Fleet personnel is five-point-seven-nine-three Terran centuries," Dahak said calmly.

"Uh," MacIntyre replied incisively.

"Of course, Captain, if you insist, I will have no choice but to forgo the biotechnic portion of your training. I must respectfully point out, however, that should you thereafter confront one of the mutineers, your opponent will have approximately eight times your strength, three times your reaction speed, and a skeletal muscular structure and circulatory system capable of absorbing on the order of eleven times the damage your own body will accept."

MacIntyre blinked. He was none too crazy about the word "biotechnic." It smacked of surgery and hospital time and similar associated unpleasantnesses. But on the other hand . . . yes, indeedy deed. On the other hand. . . .

"Oh, well, Dahak," he said finally. "If it'll make you happy. I've been meaning to get back into shape, anyway."

"Thank you, Captain," Dahak said, and if there was a certain smugness in the computer's bland reply, Acting Senior Fleet Captain Colin MacIntyre, forty-third commanding officer of Imperial Fleet Unit *Dahak*, hull number 172291, chose to ignore it.

CHAPTER FIVE

MacIntyre lowered himself into the hot, swirling water with a groan of relief, then leaned back against the pool's contoured lip and looked around his quarters. Well, the captain's quarters, anyway. He supposed it made sense to make a man assigned to a twenty-five-year deployment comfortable, but this—!

His hot tub was big enough for at least a dozen people and designed for serious relaxation. He set his empty glass on one of the pop-out shelves and watched the built-in auto-bar refill it, then adjusted the water jets with his toes and allowed himself to luxuriate as he sipped.

It was the spaciousness that truly impressed him. The ceiling arched cathedral-high above his hot tub, washed in soft, sourceless light. The walls— he could not for the life of him call them "bulkheads"—gleamed with rich, hand-rubbed wood paneling, and any proletariat-gouging billionaire would envy the art adorning the luxurious chamber. One statue particularly fascinated him. It was a rearing, lynx-eared unicorn, too "real" feeling to be fanciful, and MacIntyre felt a strangely happy sort of awe at seeing the true image of the alien foundation of one of his own world's most enduring myths.

Yet even the furnishings were over-shadowed by the view, for the tub stood on what was effectively a second-story balcony above an enormous atrium. The rich, moist smells of soil and feathery, alien greenery surrounded him as soft breezes stirred fronded branches and vivid blossoms, and the atrium roof was invisible beyond a blue sky that might have been Earth's but for a sun that was just a shade too yellow.

And this, MacIntyre reminded himself, was but one room of his suite. He knew rank had its privileges, but he'd never anticipated such magnificence and space—no doubt because he still thought of *Dahak* as a ship. Which it was, but on a scale so stupendous as to render his concept of "ship" meaningless.

Yet he'd paid a price for all this splendor, he reflected, thrashing the water with his feet like a little boy to work some of the cramps from his calves.

It seemed unfair to be subject to things like cramps after all he'd been through in the past few months. On the other hand, he was still adjusting to the changes Dahak had wrought upon and within him . . . and if Dahak called them "minor" one more time, he intended to find out if Fleet Regs provided the equivalent of keelhauling a computer.

The life of a NASA command pilot was not a restful thing, but Dahak gave a whole new meaning to the word "strenuous." A much younger Colin MacIntyre had thought Hell Week at Annapolis was bad, but then he'd gone on to Pensacola and *known* flight school was worst of all . . . until the competitive eliminations and training schedule of the Prometheus Mission. But all of that had proved the merest setting-up exercise for his training program as *Dahak*'s commander.

Nor was the strain decreased by the inevitable stumbling blocks. Dahak was a machine, when all was said, designed toward an end and shaped by his design. He was also, by dint of sheer length of existence and depth of knowledge, far more cosmopolitan (in the truest possible sense) than his "captain," but he was still a machine.

It gave him a rather different perspective, and that could produce interesting results. For instance, it was axiomatic to Dahak that the Fourth Imperium was the preeminent font of all true authority, automatically superceding such primitive, ephemeral institutions as the United States of America.

But MacIntyre saw things a bit differently, and Dahak had been taken aback by his stubborn refusal to swear any oath that might conflict with his existing one as a naval officer in the service of the said United States.

In the end, he'd also seemed grudgingly pleased, as if it confirmed that MacIntyre was a man of honor, but that hadn't kept him from setting out to change his mind. He'd pointed out that humanity's duty to the Fourth Imperium predated its duty to any purely terrestrial authority—that the United States was, in effect, no more than a temporary governing body set up upon a desert island to regulate the affairs of a mere portion of a shipwrecked crew. He had waxed eloquent, almost poetic, but in vain; MacIntyre remained adamant.

They hammered out a compromise eventually, though Dahak accepted it only grudgingly. After his experience with the conflict between his own "Alpha Priority" orders, he was distinctly unhappy to have his new captain complete his oath " . . . insofar as obedience to Fleet Central and the Fourth Imperium requires no action or inaction harmful to the United States of America." Still, if those were the only terms on which the ancient warship could get itself a captain, Dahak would accept them, albeit grumpily.

Yet it was only fair for Dahak to face a few surprises of his own. Though MacIntyre had recognized (however dimly) and dreaded the responsibility he'd been asked to assume, he hadn't considered certain other aspects of what he was letting himself in for. Which was probably just as well, since he would have refused point-blank if he *had* considered them.

Like "biotechnic enhancement." The term had bothered him from the start, for as a spacer he'd already endured more than his share of medical guinea pigdom, but the thought of an extended lifespan and enhanced strength had been seductive. Unfortunately, his quaint, twenty-first-century notions of what the Fourth Imperium's medical science could do had proven as outmoded as his idea of what a "ship" was.

His anxiety had become acute when he discovered he was expected to submit to a scalpel-wielding computer, especially after he found out just how radical the "harmless" process was. In effect, Dahak intended to take him apart for reassembly into a new, improved model that incorporated all the advantages of modern technology, and something deep inside had turned nearly hysterical at the notion of becoming, for all intents and purposes, a cyborg. It was as if he feared Doctor Jekyll might emerge as Mister Hyde, and he'd resisted with all the doggedness of sheer, howling terror, but Dahak had been patient. In fact, he'd been so elaborately patient he made MacIntyre feel like a bushman refusing to let the missionary capture his soul in his magic box.

That had been the turning point, he thought now—the point at which he'd truly begun to accept what was happening . . . and what his own part had to be. For he'd yielded to Dahak's ministrations, though it had taken all his will power even after Dahak pointed out that he knew far more about human physiology than any Terran medical team and was far, far less likely to make a mistake.

MacIntyre had known all that, intellectually, yet he'd felt intensely anxious as he surrendered to the anesthesia, and he'd looked forward rather gloomily to a lengthy stay in bed. He'd been wrong about that part, for he was up and about again after mere days, diving head-first into a physical training program he'd discovered he needed surprisingly badly.

Yet he'd come close to never emerging at all, and that memory was still enough to break a cold sweat upon his brow. Not that he should have had any problems—or, at least, not such severe ones—if he'd thought things through. But he'd neither thought them through nor followed the implications of Dahak's proposed changes to their logical conclusions, and the final results had been almost more appalling than delightful.

When he'd first reopened his eyes, his vision had seemed preternaturally keen, as if he could identify individual dust motes across a tennis court. And he very nearly could, for one of Dahak's simpler alterations permitted him to adjust the focal length of his eyes, not to mention extending his visual range into both the infrared and ultraviolet ranges.

Then there was the "skeletal muscular enhancement." He'd been primitive enough to feel an atavistic shiver at the thought that his bones would be reinforced with the same synthetic alloy from which *Dahak* was built, but the chill had become raw terror when he encountered the reality of the many "minor" changes the ship had wrought. His muscles now served primarily as actuators for micron-thin sheaths of synthetic tissue tougher than his Beagle and powerful enough to stress his new skeleton to its limit, and his circulatory and respiratory systems had undergone similar transformations. Even his skin had been altered, for it must become tough enough to endure the demands his new strength placed upon it. Yet for all that, his sense of touch—indeed, all his perceptions—had been boosted to excruciating sensitivity.

And all those improvements together had been too much. Dahak had crammed the changes at him too quickly, without any suspicion he was doing so, for neither the computer nor the human had realized the enormous gap between the things they took for granted.

For Dahak, the changes that terrified MacIntyre truly were "minor," routine medical treatments, no more than the Fourth Imperium's equivalent of a new recruit's basic equipment. And because they were so routine—and, perhaps, because for all the power of his intellect Dahak was a machine, inherently susceptible to upgrading and with no experiential referent for "natural limitations"—he had never considered the enormous impact they would have on MacIntyre's concept of himself.

It had been his own fault, too, MacIntyre reflected, leaning forward to massage the persistent cramp in his right calf. He'd been too impressed by Dahak's enormous "lifespan" and his starkly incredible depth of knowledge to recognize his limits. Dahak had analyzed and pondered for fifty millennia. He could predict with frightening accuracy what *groups* of humans would do and had a grasp of the flow of history and a patience and inflexible determination that were, quite literally, inhuman, but for all that, he was a creature born of the purest of pure intellects.

He himself had warned MacIntyre that "Comp Cent" was sadly lacking in imagination, but the very extent of his apparent humanism had fooled the human. MacIntyre had been prepared to be led by the hand by the near-god who had kidnaped him. Aware of his own ignorance, frightened by the responsibility thrust upon him, he had been almost eager to accept the role of the figurehead authority Dahak needed to break the logjam of his conflicting imperatives, and as part of his acceptance he had assumed Dahak would make allowances in what would be demanded of him.

Well, Dahak had tried to make allowances, but he'd failed, and his failure had shaken MacIntyre into a radical re-evaluation of their relationship.

When MacIntyre awoke after his surgery, he had gone mad in the sheer horror of the intensity with which his environment beat in upon him. His enhanced sense of smell was capable of separating scents with the acuity and precision of a good chemistry lab. His modified eyes could track individual dust motes and even choose which part of the spectrum they would use to see them. He could snap a baseball bat barehanded or pick up a sixteen-inch shell and carry it away and subsist for up to five hours on the oxygen reservoir in his abdomen. Tissue renewal, techniques to scavenge waste products from his blood, surgically-implanted communicators, direct neural links to Dahak and any secondary computer the starship or any of its parasites carried. . . .

The powers of a god had been given to him, but he hadn't realized he was about to inherit godhood, and he'd had absolutely no idea how to *control* his new abilities. He couldn't *stop* seeing and hearing and feeling with a terrible vibrancy and brilliance. He couldn't restrain his new strength, for he had never required the delicacy of touch his enhanced muscles demanded.

And as the uproar and terror of the quiet sickbay had crashed in upon him so that he'd flailed his mighty limbs in berserk, uncomprehending horror, smashing sickbay fixtures like matchwood, Dahak had recognized his distress . . . and made it incomparably worse by activating his neural linkages in an effort to by-pass his intensity-hashed physical senses.

MacIntyre wasn't certain he would have snapped if the computer hadn't recognized his atavistic panic for what it was so quickly, but it had been a very near thing when those alien fingers wove gently into the texture of his shuddering brain.

Yet if Dahak had lacked the imagination to project the consequences, he was a very fast learner, and his memory banks contained a vast amount of information on trauma. He had withdrawn from MacIntyre's consciousness and used the sickbay's emergency medical over-rides to damp his sensory channels and draw him back from the quivering brink of insanity, then combined sedative drugs and soothing sonic therapy to keep him there.

Dahak had driven his terror back without clouding his intellect, and then—excruciatingly slowly to his tormented senses and yet with dazzling rapidity by the standards of the universe—had helped him come to grips with the radically changed environment of his own body. The horror of the neural implants had faded. Dahak was no longer a terrifying alien presence whispering in his brain; he was a friend and mentor, teaching him to adjust and control his newfound abilities until he was their master and not their victim.

But for all Dahak's speed and adaptability, it had been a near thing, and they both knew it. The experience had made Dahak a bit more cautious, but, even more importantly, it had taught MacIntyre that Dahak had limits. He could not assume the machine always knew what it was doing or rely upon it to save him from the consequences of his own folly. The lesson had stuck, and when he emerged from his trauma he discovered that he *was* the captain, willing to be advised and counseled by his inorganic henchman and crew but starkly aware that his life and fate were as much in his own hands as they had ever been.

It was a frightening thought, but Dahak had been right; MacIntyre had a command mentality. He preferred the possibility of sending himself to hell to the possibility of being condemned to heaven by another, which might not speak well for his humility but meant he could survive—so far, at least—what Dahak demanded of him. He might castigate the computer as a harsh taskmaster, but he knew he was driving himself at least as hard and as fast as Dahak might have.

He sighed again, slumping back in the water as the painful cramp subsided at last. Thank God! Cramps had been bad enough when only his own muscles were involved, but they were pure, distilled hell now. And it seemed a bit unfair his magic muscles could not simply spring full blown from Dahak's brow, as it were. The computer had never warned him they would require exercise just as implacably as the muscle tissues nature had intended him to have, and he felt vaguely cheated by the discovery. Relieved, but cheated.

Of course, the *mutineers* would feel cheated if they knew everything he'd gotten, for Dahak had spent the last few centuries making "minor" improvements to the standard Fleet implants. MacIntyre suspected the computer had seen it as little more than a way to pass the time, but the results were formidable. He'd started out with a bridge officer's implants, which were already far more sophisticated than the standard Fleet biotechnics, but Dahak had tinkered with almost all of them. He was not only much stronger and tougher, and marginally faster, than any mutineer could possibly be, but the range and acuity of his electronic and enhanced physical senses were two or three hundred percent better. He knew they were, for Dahak had demonstrated by stepping his own implants' capabilities down to match those of the mutineers.

He closed his eyes and relaxed, smiling faintly as his body half-floated. He'd assumed all those modifications would increase his weight vastly, yet they hadn't. His body *density* had gone up dramatically, but the Fourth Imperium's synthetics were unbelievably light for their strength. His implants had added no more than fifteen kilos—and he'd sweated off at least that much fat in return, he thought wryly.

"Dahak," he said without opening his eyes.

"Yes, Colin?"

MacIntyre's smile deepened at the form of address. That was another thing Dahak had resisted, but MacIntyre was damned if he was going to be called "Captain" and "Sir" every time his solitary subordinate spoke to him, even if he did command a starship a quarter the size of his homeworld.

"What's the status on the search mission?"

"They have recovered many fragments from the crash site, including the serial number plates we detached from your craft. Colonel Tillotson remains dissatisfied by the absence of any organic remains, but General Yakolev has decided to terminate operations."

"Good," MacIntyre grunted, and wondered if he meant it. The Joint Command crash investigation had dragged on longer than expected, and he was touched by Sandy's determination to find "him," but he thought he was truly relieved it was over. It was a bit frightening, like the snipping of his last umbilical, but it had to happen if he and Dahak were to have a chance of success.

"Any sign of a reaction from Anu's people?"

"None," Dahak replied. There was a brief pause, and then the computer went on just a bit plaintively. "Colin, you could acquire data much more rapidly if you would simply rely upon your neural interface."

"Humor me," MacIntyre said, opening one eye and watching clouds drift across his atrium's projected sky. "And don't tell me your other crews used *their* implants all the time, either, because I don't believe it."

"No," Dahak admitted, "but they made much greater use of them than you do. Vocalization is often necessary for deliberate cognitive manipulation of data, Colin—human thought processes are, after all, inextricably bound up in and focused by syntax and semantics—yet it can be a cumbersome process, and it is not an efficient way to acquire data."

"Dahak," MacIntyre said patiently, "you could dump your whole damn memory core into my brain through this implant—"

"Incorrect, Colin. The capacity of your brain is severely limited. I calculate that no more than—"

"Shut up," Colin said with a reluctant twinkle. If Dahak's long sojourn in Earth orbit hadn't made him truly human, it had come close in many ways. He rather doubted Comp Cent's designers had meant Dahak to have a sense of humor.

"Yes, Colin," Dahak said so meekly that MacIntyre knew the computer was indulging in the electronic equivalent of silent laughter.

"Thank you. Now, what I meant is that you can pour information into my brain with a funnel, but that doesn't make it *mine*. It's like a . . . an encyclopedia. It's a reference source to look things up in, not something that pops into my mind when I need it. Besides, it tickles."

"Human brain tissue is not susceptible to physical sensation, Colin," Dahak said rather primly.

"I speak symbolically," MacIntyre replied, pushing a wave across his tub and wiggling his toes. "Consider it a psychosomatic manifestation."

"I do not understand psychosomatic phenomena," Dahak reminded him.

"Then just take my word for it. I'm sure I'll get used to it, but until I do, I'll go right on asking questions. Rank, after all, hath its privileges."

"I suppose you think that concept is unique to your own culture."

"You suppose wrongly. Unless I miss my guess, it's endemic to the human condition, wherever the humans came from."

"That has been my own observation."

"You cannot imagine how much that reassures me, oh Dahak."

"Of course I cannot. Many things humans find reassuring defy logical analysis."

"True, true." MacIntyre consulted the ship's chronometer through his implant and sighed resignedly. His rest period was about over, and it was time for his next session with the fire control simulator. After that, he was due on the hand weapon range, followed by a few relaxing hours acquiring the rudiments of supralight astrogation and ending with two hours working out against one of *Dahak*'s hand-to-hand combat training remotes. If rank had its privileges, it also had its obligations. Now *there* was a profound thought.

He climbed out and wrapped himself in a thick towel. He could have asked Dahak to dry him with a swirl of warmed air. For that matter, his new internal equipment could have built a repellent force field on the surface of his skin to shed water like a duck, but he enjoyed the towel's soft sensuality, and he luxuriated shamelessly in it as he padded off to his bedroom to dress.

"Back to the salt mines, Dahak," he sighed aloud.

"Yes, Colin," the computer said obediently.

CHAPTER SIX

"Anything more on the NASA link, Dahak?"

MacIntyre reclined in the captain's couch in Command One. He was the same lean, rangy, pleasantly homely young man he'd always been—outwardly, at least—but he wore the midnight-blue of Battle Fleet, the booted feet propped upon his console were encased in *chagor*-hide leather, and there was a deeper, harder glint of purpose in his innocent green eyes.

"Negative, Colin. I have examined the biographies of all project heads associated with the gravitonic survey program, and all appear to be Terra-born. It is possible the linkage was established earlier—during the college careers of one or more of the researchers, perhaps—yet logic dictates direct mutineer involvement in the single portion of the Prometheus program that is so far in advance of all other components."

"Damn." MacIntyre pulled at the tip of his nose and frowned. "If we can't identify someone where we *know* there's a link, we'll just have to avoid any official involvement. Jesus, that's going to make it tougher!" He sighed. "Either way, I've got to get started—and you know it as well as I do."

"I would still prefer to extend your training time, Colin," Dahak replied, but he sounded so resigned MacIntyre grinned wryly. While it would be too much ever to call Dahak irresolute, there were things he hesitated to face, and foremost among them was the prospect of permitting his fledgling commander to leave the nest. Particularly when he could not communicate with him once MacIntyre returned to Earth. It could not be otherwise; the mutineers could scarcely fail to detect an active Fleet fold-space link to the moon.

The fact was that Dahak was fiercely protective, and MacIntyre wondered if that stemmed from his core programming or his long isolation. The ship finally had a captain again—did the thought of losing him frighten the computer?

Now there was a thought. *Could* the ancient computer feel fear? MacIntyre didn't know and preferred to think of Dahak as fearless, but there was no doubt Dahak had at least an intellectual appreciation of what fear was.

MacIntyre looked about him. The "viewscreen" of his first visit had vanished, and his console seemed to float unshielded in the depths of space. Stars burned about him, their unwinking, merciless points of light vanishing into the silent depths of eternity, and the blue-white planet of his birth turned slowly beneath him. The illusion was terrifyingly perfect, and he had a pretty shrewd notion how he would have reacted if Dahak had casually invited him to step out into it on their first meeting.

It was as if Dahak had realized external technology might frighten him without quite grasping what would happen when that same technology was inside him. Or had the computer simply assumed that, like himself, MacIntyre would understand all as soon as things had been explained a single time?

Whatever, Dahak had been cautious that first day. Even the vehicle that he'd provided had been part of it. The double-ended bullet was a ground car, and the computer had actually disabled part of its propulsive system so that his "guest" could feel the acceleration he expected.

In fact, the ground car had been unnecessary, and MacIntyre had sampled the normal operation of the transit shafts now, but not before Dahak had found time to explain them. Which was just as well, for while they were undoubtedly efficient, MacIntyre had still turned seven different shades of green the first time he'd gone hurtling through the huge tunnels at thousands of kilometers per hour, subjective sense of movement or not. Even now, after months of practice, he couldn't entirely rid himself of the notion that he was falling to his doom whenever he consigned himself to the gravitonic mercies of the system.

MacIntyre shook himself sternly. He was woolgathering again, and he knew why. He wanted to think about anything but the task that faced him.

"I know you'd like more training time," he said, "but we've had six months, and they're ready to schedule Vlad Chernikov for another proctoscope mission. You know we can't grab off another Beagle without tipping Anu off."

There was a moment of silence, a pause that was one of Dahak's human mannerisms MacIntyre most appreciated. It was a bit difficult to keep his own thoughts focused when the other half of the conversation "thought" and responded virtually instantaneously.

"Very well," Dahak said at last. "I respectfully submit, however, that your 'plan' consists solely of half-formed, ill-conceived generalities."

"So? You've had a few dozen millennia to think about it—can *you* come up with a better idea?"

"Unfair. You are the captain, and command decisions are your function, not mine."

"Then shut up and soldier." MacIntyre spoke firmly, but he smiled.

"Very well," Dahak repeated.

"Good. Is the suppressor ready?"

"Affirmative. My remotes have placed it in your cutter." There was another pause, and MacIntyre closed his eyes. Dahak, he thought, could give a Missouri mule stubborn lessons. "I still believe you would be better advised to use one of the larger—and armed—parasites, however."

"Dahak," MacIntyre said patiently, "there are at least five thousand mutineers, right? With eight eighty-thousand-ton sublight battleships?"

"Correct. However—"

"Can it! I'm pontificating, and *I'm* the captain. They also have a few heavy cruisers, armored combat vehicles, trans-atmospheric fighters, and the personnel to man them—not to mention their personal combat armor and weapons—*plus* the ability to jam your downlinks to any remotes you send down, right?"

"Yes, Colin," Dahak sighed.

"Then this is a time for finesse and sneakiness, not brute strength. I have to get the suppressor inside their enclave perimeter and let you take out their defensive shield from here or we're never going to get at them."

"But to do so you will require admittance codes and the locations of access points, which you can obtain only from the mutineers themselves."

"I know." MacIntyre recrossed his ankles and frowned, pulling harder on his nose, but the unpalatable truth remained. There was no doubt the mutineers had penetrated most major governments—they must have done so, given the way they had manipulated Terran geopolitics over the last two centuries.

Which meant any approach to Terran authorities was out of the question. It was a pity Dahak couldn't carry out bio-scans at this range; that, at least, would tell them who was an actual mutineer. But even that couldn't have revealed which Terra-born humans might have been suborned, possibly without ever knowing who had suborned them or even that they *had* been suborned.

So the only option was the one both he and Dahak dreaded. Somehow, he had to gain access to the mutineers' base and deactivate its shield. It was a daunting prospect, but once he'd taken out the defenses that held *Dahak*'s weapons at bay, the mutineers would have no choice but to surrender or die, and MacIntyre didn't much care which they chose as long as they decided quickly.

The first of the automatic scanner stations had gone off the air, destroyed by the outriders of the Achuultani. Despite the relatively low speed of the Achuultani ships, humanity had little more than two and a half years before they reached Sol . . . and for him to find a way to stop them.

That was the real reason he wanted to find the link between Anu and NASA. If he could get his hands on just one mutineer—just one—then he could get the information he and Dahak needed one way or the other, he thought grimly. Yet how did he take that first step? He still didn't know, but he did know he couldn't do it from here. And he intended to admit to Dahak neither that he meant to play things entirely by ear nor who his single Terran ally would be lest the computer stage a mutiny of its own and refuse to let him off the ship!

"Well," he said with forced cheeriness, "I'd better get going." He dropped his feet to the invisible deck and stood, feeling as if the universe were drifting beneath his bootsoles.

"Very well, Colin," Dahak said softly, and the first hatch slid open, spilling bright light like a huge rift among the stars. MacIntyre squared his shoulders and walked into it.

"Good hunting, Captain," the computer murmured.

"I'll nail 'em to the wall," MacIntyre said confidently, and wished he could just convince himself of that.

A sliver of midnight settled silently amid the night-struck mountains of Colorado. It moved with less noise than the whispering breeze, showing no lights, nor did it register on any radar screen. Indeed, the stealth field about it transformed it into more of a velvety-black, radiation-absorbing *absence* than a visible object, for not even starlight reflected from it.

It drifted lower, sliding into an unnamed alpine meadow between Cripple Creek and Pikes Peak, and Colin MacIntyre watched the light-stained clouds glow above Colorado Springs to the east as the cutter extended its landing legs and grounded with a soft whine.

He sat in his command chair for a moment, studying the miniature duplicate of Command One's imaging system fed by the passive scanners. He examined the night carefully for long, long minutes, and his emotions puzzled him.

There was a deep, inarticulate relief at touching once more the soil of home, but it was overlaid by other, less readily understood feelings. A sense of the alien. An awareness of the peril that awaited him, yet more than that, as if the last six months had changed him even more than he had thought.

He was no longer a citizen of Earth, he thought sadly. His horizons had been broadened. Whether he liked it or not, he had become an emigré, yet that bittersweet realization actually made him love his homeworld even more. He was a stranger, but Earth was his source, the home of which he would always dream, and its remembered beauty would always be purer and more lovely than its reality.

He shook himself out of his musings. The night beyond the cutter's hull was silent, filled only with life that ran on four feet or flew, and he could not justify remaining aboard.

He switched off the display and interior lights and bent to free the suppresser webbed to the deck behind his command seat. It was not a huge device in light of what it could do, but it was heavy. He might have included a small anti-grav generator, but he hadn't dared to. Inactive, the suppresser was simply an inert, apparently solid block of metal and plastic, its webs of molecular circuitry undetectable even by the mutineers. An active anti-grav was another matter, and the mere fact of its detection would spell the doom of his mission. Besides, the suppressor weighed less than three hundred kilos.

He slipped his arms through the straps and adjusted it on his back like the knapsack it had been camouflaged to resemble, then opened the hatch and stepped down to the grassy earth. Night smells tickled his nostrils, and the darkness turned noonday-bright as he adjusted his vision to enhanced imaging.

He backed away from the cutter, and its hatch licked obediently shut as he concentrated on the commands flowing over his neural feed. The cutter's computers were moronic shadows of Dahak, and it was necessary to phrase instructions carefully. The landing legs retracted, the cutter hovered silently for an instant, and then it faded equally silently into the heavens, visible only as a solid blot that occluded occasional stars.

MacIntyre watched it go, then turned away and consulted his built-in inertial guidance system. The terrain looked rough to his enhanced eyes, but not rugged enough to inconvenience him. He hooked his thumbs into the knapsack straps and set out, moving like a bit of the blackness brought to life.

It took him an hour to top out on a ridge with a direct view of Colorado Springs, and he paused. Not because he needed a rest, but because he wanted to study the glowing lights spread out below him.

The mushrooming space effort had transformed Colorado Springs over the past forty years. Venerable old Goddard Center still guided and controlled NASA's unmanned deep-system probes and handled a lot of experimental work, but Goddard was too small and long in the tooth to keep pace with the bustling activity in near-Earth space. Just the construction activity around the Lagrange Point habitats would have required the big, new facilities, like the Russians' Klyuchevskaya Station, ConEurope's Werner von Braun Space Control, or the Canadian-American Shepard Space Center at Colorado Springs.

The city had become the nation's number three growth area, ballooning out to envelope the old military installations before surging on into the mountains beyond, and the gargantuan sprawl of Shepard Center—centered on one-time Peterson Air Force Base—gleamed to the east, seething with activity despite the late hour. Shepard was primarily a control center, without the hectic heavy-lift launches that streaked day and night skies over bases like Kennedy, Vandenburg, and Corpus Christi, but he could see the landing lights of a Valkyrie personnel shuttle sweeping in for a landing and another taxiing to a launch area, heavy with booster pods. The view was silent with distance, but memory and imagination supplied the noises and the bustle, the frenetic effort that sometimes threatened to reduce the wonder of space to a grinding routine.

He opened the binocular case hanging from his neck. There were limits even to his magic vision, but the device he raised to his eyes was as different from a standard pair of electronic binoculars as those were from an eighteenth-century spyglass, and the distant space center was suddenly at arm's length.

He watched the airborne Valkyrie flare out on final approach, its variable sweep wings fully forward. He could almost hear the whine of the spoilers, the sudden snarl of the reversed thrusters, and it was odd how exciting and powerful it all still seemed. The two-hundred-ton bird moved with strong, purposeful grace, and he saw it through two sets of eyes. One remembered his own experiences, barely six months in the past, when that sleek shape had seemed an expression of the very frontier of human knowledge; the other had seen *Dahak* and recognized the quaint, primitive inefficiency of the design.

He sighed and moved his viewpoint over the sprawling installation, zooming in to examine details that caught his eye. He sat motionless for long, long minutes, absorbing the familiarity of his eventual objective and wondering.

He was a bit surprised by how normal it all looked, but only briefly. *He* was aware of how monumentally the universe had been changed, but the thousands of people hustling about Shepard were not. Yet there was a hesitance in him, a disinclination to plunge back into intercourse with his own kind. He'd felt the same sensation before after extended missions, but now it was far stronger.

He made a wry face and lowered the binoculars, wondering what he'd expected to see through them. The link he sought was hardly likely to stand on top of White Tower or McNair Center and wave a lighted placard at him, for God's sake! But deep inside, he knew he'd been looking for some sign that he was still part of them. That those hurrying, scurrying people were still his when all was said. But he wouldn't see that sign, because they no longer truly were. They were his *people,* but not his *kind,* and the distinction twisted him with another stab of that bittersweet regret.

He put away the binoculars, then hitched up the waist of the blue jeans Dahak had provided. Uncaring stars twinkled down with detached disinterest, and he shivered as wind drove sea-like waves across the grass and he thought of the deadly menace sweeping closer beyond those distant points of light. His new body scarcely felt the cold mountain air, but the chill within was something else.

This world, that starscape, were no longer his. Perhaps it was always that way? Perhaps someone always had to give up the things he knew and loved to save them for others?

Philosophy had never been Colin MacIntyre's strong suit, but he knew he would risk anything, *lose* anything to save the world he had lost. It was a moment of balance, of seeing himself for what he was and the mutineers for what *they* were: a hindrance. A barrier blocking his single hope of protecting his home.

He shook himself, conscious of a vast sense of impatience. There was an obstacle to be removed, and he was suddenly eager to be about it.

He started hiking once more. It was forty kilometers to his destination, and he wanted to be there by dawn. He needed an ally, and there was one person he could trust—or, if he could not, there was no one in the universe he could—and he wondered how Sean would react when his only brother returned from the dead?

Book Two

CHAPTER SEVEN

Dawn bled in the east, and the morning wind was cold as the sandy-haired hiker paused by the mailbox. He studied the small house carefully, with more than human senses, for it was always possible Anu and his mutineers had not, in fact, bought the official verdict on the late Colin MacIntyre.

The morning light strengthened, turning the cobalt sky pewter and rose-blush blue, and he detected absolutely nothing out of the ordinary. His super-sensitive ears recognized the distant thunder of the Denver–Colorado Springs magtrain as it tore through the dawn. Somewhere to the west a long-haul GEV with an off-balance skirt fan whined down the highway. The rattle and clink of glass counter-pointed the hum of a milk truck's electric motor and birds spoke softly, but every sound was as it should have been, without menace or threat.

Devices within his body sampled far more esoteric data-electronic, thermal, gravitonic—and found nothing. It was possible Anu's henchmen had contrived some observation system even he couldn't detect, but only remotely.

He shook himself. He was wasting time, trying to postpone the inevitable.

He adjusted his "knapsack" and walked briskly up the drive, listening to the scrunch of gravel underfoot. Sean's ancient four-wheel-drive Cadillac Bushmaster was in the carport, even more scratched and dinged than the last time he'd seen it, and he shook his head with an indulgent, off-center smile. Sean would go on paying the emission taxes on his old-fashioned, gasoline-burning hulk until it literally fell apart under him one day. Colin had opted for the glitz, glitter, and excitement of technology's cutting edge while Sean had chosen the Forestry Service and the preservation of his environment, but it was Sean who clung to his pollution-producing old Caddy like death.

His boots fell crisp and clean in the still morning on the flagged walk, and he opened the screen door onto the enclosed front porch and stepped up into it. He felt his pulse race slightly and automatically adjusted his adrenalin level, then reached out and, very deliberately, pressed the doorbell.

The soft chimes echoed through the house, and he waited, letting his enhanced hearing chart events. He heard the soft thud as Sean's bare feet hit the floor and the rustle of cloth as he dragged on a pair of pants. Then he heard him padding down the hall, grumbling under his breath at being disturbed at such an ungodly hour. The latch rattled, and then the door swung open.

"Yes?" his brother's deep voice was as sleepy as his eyes. "What can I—"

Sean MacIntyre froze in mid-word, and the rags of sleep vanished from his sky-blue eyes. The stubble of his red beard stood out boldly as his tanned face paled, and he grabbed the edge of the door frame.

"Morning, Sean," Colin said softly, a glint of humor mingling with the sudden prickling of his own eyes. "Long time no see."

Sean MacIntyre sat in his painfully neat bachelor's kitchen, hugging a mug in both hands, and glanced again at the refrigerator Colin had carted across the kitchen to substantiate his claims. Echoes of disbelief still shadowed his eyes, and he looked a bit embarrassed over the bear hug he had bestowed upon the brother he had believed dead, but he was coming back nicely-helped, no doubt, by the hefty shot of brandy in his coffee.

"Christ on a Harley, Colin," he said finally, his voice deceptively mild. "That has to be the craziest story anyone ever tried to sell me. You're damned lucky you came back from the dead to tell it, or I *still* wouldn't believe it! Even if you have turned into a one-man moving company."

"You wouldn't believe it?! How d'you think *I* feel about it?"

"There's that," Sean agreed, smiling at last. "There's that."

Colin felt himself relax as he saw that slow smile. It was the way his big brother had always smiled when things got a bit tight, and he felt his lips twitch as he remembered the time Sean had pulled a trio of much older boys off of him. Colin had, perhaps, been unwise to challenge their adolescent cruelty so openly, but he and Sean had ended up thrashing all three of them. Throughout his boyhood, Colin had looked for that smile when he was in trouble, knowing things couldn't be all *that* bad with Sean there to bail him out.

"Well," Sean said finally, setting down his empty mug, "you always were a scrapper. If this Dahak of yours had to pick somebody, he made a good choice."

"Right. Sure," Colin snorted.

"No, I mean it." Sean doodled on the tabletop with a fingertip. "Look at you. How many people would still be rational—well, as rational as you've ever been—after what you've been through?"

"Spare my blushes," Colin growled, and Sean laughed. Then he sobered.

"All right," he said more seriously. "I'm glad you're still alive—" their eyes met, warm with an affection they had seldom had to express "—but I don't imagine you dropped by just to let me know."

"You're right," Colin said. He propped his elbows on the table and leaned forward. "I need help, and you're the one person I can trust."

"I can see that, Colin, and I'll do whatever I can—you know that—but I'm a ranger, not an astronaut. How can I help you find this link of yours?"

"I don't know that you can," Colin admitted, "but there are drawbacks to being dead. All of my ID is useless, my accounts are locked—I couldn't even check into a motel without using bogus identification. In fact—"

"Wait a minute," Sean interrupted. "I can see where you'd need a base of operations, but couldn't this Dahak just whip up any documentation you need?"

"Sure, but it wouldn't help for what I really need to do. Normally, Dahak can get in and out of any Terran computer like a thief, Sean, but he's cut all his com links now that I'm down here. They're all stealthed, but we can't risk anything that might tip off the mutineers now. Besides, he can't do much with human minds, and *you* recognized me as soon as you got the sleep out of your eyes—do you think the security people at Shepard wouldn't?"

"That's what you get for being a glamour-ass astronaut. Or not resorting to a little plastic surgery." Sean studied his brother thoughtfully. "Would've been a wonderful chance to improve—extensively—on nature, too."

"Very funny. Unfortunately, neither Dahak nor I considered it before he tinkered with my gizzards. Even if we *had* used cosmetic surgery, the last thing I need is to try waltzing my biotechnics past Shepard's security!"

"What big teeth you have," Sean murmured with a grin.

"Ha, ha," Colin said blightingly. Then his face turned more serious. "Wait till you hear what I need before you get too smartass, Sean."

Sean MacIntyre sat back at the sudden somberness of Colin's voice. His brother's eyes were as serious as his voice, filled with a determination Sean had never seen in them, and he realized that Colin had changed more than simply physically. There was a new edge to him, a . . . ruthlessness. The gung-ho jet-jockey hot-dog Sean had loved for so many years had found a cause.

No, that wasn't fair; Colin had always had a cause, but it had been a searching, questing cause. One that burned to push back boundaries, to go further and faster than anyone yet had, yet held a formlessness, a willingness to go wherever the wind blew and open whatever frontier offered. This one was concentrated and intense, almost desperate, waking a focused determination to use the tremendous strength Sean had always known lay fallow within him. For all his achievements, his brother had never truly been challenged. Not like this. Colin had become a driven man, and Sean wondered if, in the process, he might not have found the purpose for which he had been born. . . .

"All right," he said softly. "Tell me."

"I wish I didn't have to ask this of you," Colin said, anxiety tightening his voice, "but I do. Have you collected my effects from Shepard yet?"

Sean was taken briefly aback by the apparent change of subject, then shook his head. "NASA sent me a box of your stuff, but I didn't *collect* anything."

"Then I want you to," Colin said, withdrawing a pen from his shirt pocket. "There're some personal files in my office computer in White Tower—I doubt anyone even bothered to check them, but we can arrange for you to 'find' a note about them among my papers and Major Simmons will let you through to White for Chris Yamaguchi to pull them for you."

"Well, sure," Sean said. "But why do you need them?"

"I don't. What I need is to get you inside White Tower with this." He extended the pen. Sean took it with a baffled air, and Colin smiled unhappily.

"That's not exactly what it looks like, Sean. You can write with it, but it's actually a relay for my own sensors. With that in your pocket, I can carry out a full-spectrum scan of your surroundings. And if you take the L Block elevators, you'll pass right through Geo Sciences on your way upstairs."

"Oh ho!" Sean said softly. "In other words, it'll get you in by proxy?"

"Exactly. If Dahak is right—and he usually is—somebody in Geo Sciences is in cahoots with the mutineers. We think they're all Terra-born, but whoever it is may have a few items of Imperial technology in or near his work area."

"How likely is that?"

"I wish I knew," Colin admitted. "Still, if I were a mutineer, I'd be mighty tempted to give my buddies a leg up if they need it. There're a lot of fairly small gadgets that could help enormously—test gear, micro-tools, mini-computers, maybe even a com link to check in if they hit a glitch."

"Com link?"

"The Imperium hasn't used radio in a long, long time. Give your boy a fold-space link, and you've got totally secure communications, unless somebody physically overhears a conversation, of course."

"I can see that, but do you really think they're going to leave stuff like that just lying around?"

"Why not? Oh, they'll try to keep anything really bizarre under wraps— I mean, the place is crawling with scientists—but who's going to suspect? Nobody on the planet knows any more about what's really going on than I did before Dahak grabbed me, right?"

"There's that," Sean agreed slowly. "And this gizmo—" he waved the "pen" gently "—will let you pick up on anything like that?"

"Right. Unfortunately—" Colin met his brother's eyes levelly "—it could also be picked up on. It doesn't use radio either, Sean, and I'll be using active sensors. If you pass too close to anyone with the right detection rig, you'll stand out like a Christmas tree in June. And if you do . . ."

"I see," Sean said softly. He pursed his lips and drew the relay slowly through his fingers, then smiled that same slow smile and slid it neatly into his shirt pocket. "In that case, you'd better jot down that 'note' of yours in case Major Simmons wants to see it, hadn't you?"

✧   ✧   ✧

The sentries carried slung assault rifles, and artfully camouflaged auto-cannon covered Sean's old Caddy as he braked gently at the security barricade's concrete dragon's teeth. The last major attack by the Black Mecca splinter faction of the old Islamic Jihad had been over a year ago, but it had killed over three hundred people and inflicted a quarter-billion dollars' worth of damage on ConEurope's Werner von Braun Space Control.

The First World had grown unhappily accustomed to terrorism, both domestic and foreign. Most of the world—including the vast majority of Islam—might condemn them, but Dark Age mentalities could do terrible amounts of damage with modern technology. As Black Mecca had proven when it used a man-portable SAM to knock down a fully-loaded Con-European Valkyrie just short of the runway . . . onto a pad twelve minutes from launch with a Perseus heavy-lifter. Terrorism continued to flow in erratic cycles, but it seemed to be back on the upsurge after a two-year hiatus, and the aerospace industry had apparently become Black Mecca's prime target this time around. No one knew exactly why—unless it was the way aerospace epitomized the collective "Great Satan's" wicked, evil, liberalizing, humanizing technology—but Shepard Center was taking no chances.

"Good morning, sir." A guard touched the brim of his cap as he bent beside the window. "I'm afraid this is a restricted area. Public access is off Fountain Boulevard."

"I know," Sean replied, glancing at the man's neat NASA nameplate. "Major Simmons is expecting me, Sergeant Klein."

"I see. May I have your name, sir?" The sergeant raised an eyebrow as he uncased his belt terminal and brought the small screen to life.

"I'm Sean MacIntyre, Sergeant."

"Thank you." Klein studied his terminal, comparing the minute image to Sean's face, then nodded. "Yes, sir, you're on the cleared list." A raised hand beckoned to one of his fellows. "Corporal Hansen will escort you to White Tower, Mr. MacIntyre."

"Thank you, Sergeant." Sean leaned across to open the passenger door for Corporal Hansen, and the guard climbed in and settled his compact assault rifle carefully beside him.

"You're welcome, Mr. MacIntyre," Klein said. "And may I extend my condolences on your brother's death, sir?"

"Thank you," Sean said again, and put the car back into gear as Klein touched his cap once more.

The remark could have been a polite nothing, but Klein had sounded entirely sincere, and Sean was touched by it.

He'd always known his brother was popular with his fellows, but not until Colin "died" had he suspected how much the rank and file of the space effort had admired him. He'd expected a certain amount of instant veneration. It was traditional, after all—no matter how klutzy a man was, he became a hero when he perished doing something heroic—but Colin had been one of the varsity.

Colin's selection as the Prometheus Mission's chief survey pilot had been a measure of his professional standing; the grief over his reported death, whether it was the loss felt by his personal friends or by men and women like Sergeant Klein who'd never even met him, measured another side of him.

If they only knew, Sean thought, and barely managed to stop himself before he chuckled. Corporal Hansen would not understand his amusement at all.

The corporal guided Sean through three more checkpoints, then down a shortcut through the towering silver domes of Shepard Center's number two tank farm, where vapor clouds plumed from pressure relief valves high overhead. The distant thunder of a shuttle launch rattled the Bushmaster's windows gently as they emerged on the far side, and White Tower's massive, gleaming needle of mirrored glass loomed before them. Clouds moved with pristine grace across the deep-blue sky reflected from its face, and not even the clutter of communications relays atop the tower could lessen the power of its presence.

Sean parked in the indicated slot, and he and the corporal climbed out.

"Take the main entrance and tell the security desk you're here to see Major Simmons, sir. They'll handle it from there."

"Thanks, Corporal. Are you going to get back to the gate all right?"

"No sweat, sir. There's a jitney heading back in about ten minutes."

"Then I'll be going," Sean said with a nod, and strode briskly through the indicated entrance and its metal detectors. A trefoil-badged holo sign on the wall warned of x-ray scanners, as well, and Sean grinned, appreciating Colin's reasons for recruiting him for this task. Even if no one recognized him, his various implants would undoubtedly give the security systems fits!

The security desk passed him through to Major Simmons. Sean and the major had met before, and Simmons shook his hand, his firm grip a silent expression of sympathy for his "loss," and handed him a clip-on security badge.

"This'll get you up to Captain Yamaguchi's office—it's good anywhere in the Green Area—and she's already pulled Colin's personal data for you. Do you know your way there, or should I assign a guide?"

"No, thank you, Major. I've been here a couple of times; I can find my own way, I think. Should I just hand this—" he touched the pass "—back in at the security desk as I leave?"

"That would be fine," Simmons agreed, and Sean headed for the elevators. He walked past the first bank, and punched for a car in the L Block, humming softly and wishing his palms weren't a bit damp as he waited. A musical tone chimed and the floor light lit above the doors. They opened quietly.

"Here we go, kid," Sean murmured *sotto voce*. "Hope it works."

Colin lay back on his brother's bed, hands clasped behind his head, and his unfocused eyes watched sun patterns on the wall. He hated involving Sean—and hated it all the more because he'd known Sean would agree. The odds were tremendously against anyone noticing the scanner relay . . . but humanity's very presence on this planet resulted from a far more unlikely chain of events.

It was a strange sensation to lie here and yet simultaneously accompany

Sean. There was a duality to his senses and his vision, as if he personally rode in his brother's shirt pocket even as he lay comfortably on the bed.

His implants reached out through the disguised relay, probing and peering, exploring the webs of electronics around Sean like insubstantial fingers. He could almost touch the flow of current as the elevator floor lights lit silently, just as he could feel the motion of the elevator as it climbed the hollow, empty-tasting shaft. Security systems, computers, electric pencil sharpeners, telephones, intercoms, lighting conduits, heating and air-conditioning sensors, ventilation shafts—he felt them about him and quested through them like a ghost, sniffing and prying.

And then, like a bolt of lightning, a fiery little core of brighter, fiercer power surged in his perceptions.

Colin stiffened, closing his eyes as he concentrated. The impression was faint, but he closed in on it, tuning out the background. His immaterial fingers reached out, and his brows creased in surprise. It was a com link, all right—a fold-space com, very similar to the implant in his own skull—but there was something strange about it. . . .

He worried at it, focusing and refining his data, and then he had it. It was a security link, not a standard hand com. He would never have spotted it if Dahak hadn't improved his built-in sensors, but that explained why it seemed so similar to his implant. He insinuated his perceptions into the heart of the tiny device, confirming his identification. Definitely a security link; there were the multi-dimensional shift circuits to bounce it around. Now why should the mutineers bother with a security link? Even in a worst-case scenario that assumed Dahak was fully operational, that was taking security to paranoid extremes. Dahak could do many things, but tapping a fold-space com from lunar orbit wasn't one of them, and no one on Earth would even recognize one.

He considered consulting with Dahak, but only for a moment. None of the mutineers' equipment could tap his link with the computer, but that didn't mean they couldn't detect it. The device he'd found had a piddling little range—no more than fifteen thousand kilometers—and detecting something like that would be practically impossible with its shift circuits in operation. But his implant's range was over a light-hour, and that very power would make it stand out like a beacon on any Imperial detector screen on the planet.

He muttered pungently, then shrugged. It didn't really matter why the mutineers had given that particular com to their minion; what mattered was that he'd found it, and he concentrated on pinning down its precise location.

Ahhhhhh yesssssss. . . . There it was. Right down in—

Colin sat up with a jerk. *Cal Tudor's office?!* That was insane!

But there was no doubt about it. The damned thing was not only in his office but hidden *inside* his work terminal!

Colin swung his legs shakenly off the bed. He knew Cal well—or he'd thought he did. They were friends—such good friends he would have risked contacting Cal if Sean hadn't been available—and the one word Colin had always associated with him was "integrity." True, Cal was young for his position, but he lived, breathed, and dreamed the Prometheus Mission. . . . Could that be the very way they'd gotten to him?

Colin could think of no other explanation. Yet the more he considered it, the less he understood why they would have picked Cal at all. He was a member of the proctoscope team, but a very junior one. Colin put his elbows on his knees and leaned his chin in his palms as he consulted the biographies Dahak had amassed on the team's members.

As usual, there was a curious, detached feeling to the data. He was getting used to it, but the dividing line between knowledge he'd acquired experientially and that which Dahak had shoveled into a handy empty spot in his brain was surprisingly sharp. The implant data came from some-one else and felt like someone else's. Despite a growing acceptance, it was a sensation he found uncomfortable, and he was beginning to suspect he always would.

But the point at issue was Cal's background, not the workings of his implant. It helped Colin to visualize the data as if it had been projected upon a screen, and he frowned as the facts flickered behind his eyelids.

Cal Tudor. Age thirty-six years. Wife's name Frances; two daughters—Harriet and Anna, fourteen and twelve. Theoretical physicist, Lawrence Livermore by way of MIT Denver, then six years at Goddard before he moved to Shepard. . . .

Colin flicked through more data then stiffened. Dear God! How the hell had Dahak missed it? He knew how *he* had, and the nature of his implant *was* a factor, for he'd never realized how seldom Cal ever mentioned his family.

Yet the information was there, and only the "otherness" of the data Dahak had provided had kept it at arm's length from Colin and prevented him from spotting the impossible "coincidence." Dahak had checked for connec-tions with the mutineers as far back as college, but Cal's connection pre-dated more than his college career; it pre-dated his birth! If Dahak had a human-sized imagination (or, for that matter, if Colin had personally—and thoroughly—checked the data) they would have recognized it, for Cal's very failure to mention it to one of his closest friends would have underscored it in red.

Cal Tudor: son of Michael Tudor, only living grandson of Andrew and Isis *Hidachi* Tudor, and great-grandson of Horace Hidachi, "the Father of Gravitonics." The brilliant, intuitive genius who over sixty years before had single-handedly worked out the basic math that underlay the entire field!

Colin pounded his knee gently with a fist. He and Dahak had even speculated on Horace Hidachi's possible links with the mutineers, for the stature of his "breakthrough" had seemed glaringly suspicious. Yet they obviously hadn't delved deeply enough for reasons that—at the time—had seemed good and sufficient.

Hidachi had spent twenty years as a researcher before he evolved "his" theory and he'd never *done* anything with his brilliant theoretical work. Nor had anyone else during the course of his life. At the time he propounded his theory, it had been an exercise in pure math, a hypothesis that was impossible to test; by the time the hardware became available, he was dead. Nor had his daughter shown any particular interest in his work. If Colin remembered correctly (and thanks to Dahak he did), she'd gone into medicine, not physics.

Which was why Dahak and Colin had stopped worrying about Hidachi. If he'd been a minion of the mutineers, he would scarcely have invested that much time building a cover merely to produce an obscure bit of mathematical arcanum. He would have carried through with the hardware to prove it. At the very least, the mutineers themselves would scarcely have allowed his work to lie fallow for so long. As it was, Dahak had decided that Hidachi must have produced that rarest of rarities: a genuine, fundamental breakthrough so profound no one had even recognized what it was. Indeed, the computer had computed a high probability that the lag between theory and practice simply resulted from how long it took the mutineers to realize what Hidachi had done and prod a later generation of scientists down the path it opened.

But *this*—!

Colin castigated himself for forgetting the key fact about the mutineers' very existence. Wearisome as the passing millennia had been for Dahak, they had *not* been that for Anu's followers. They could take refuge in stasis, ignoring the time that passed between contacts with the Terra-born. Why *shouldn't* they think in generations? For all Colin and Dahak knew, the last, unproductive fifteen years of Hidachi's life had been a simple case of a missed connection!

But if, in fact, the mutineers had once contacted a Hidachi, why not again? Especially if Horace Hidachi had left some record of his own dealings with Anu and company. It might even explain how a man like Cal, whose integrity was absolute, could be working with them. For all Cal might know, the mutineers were on the side of goodness and light!

And his junior position on the proctoscope team made him a beautiful choice. He had access to project progress reports, yet he was unobtrusive . . . and quite probably primed for contact with the same "visitors" who had contacted his great-grandfather.

But if so, he didn't realize who he was truly helping, Colin decided. It was possible he was wrong, but he couldn't believe he was *that* wrong. Cal *had* to think he was working on the side of the angels, and why shouldn't he? If the mutineers had, indeed, provided the expertise to develop the proctoscope, then they'd advanced the frontiers of human knowledge by several centuries in barely sixty years. How could that seem an "evil" act to someone like Cal?

Which meant there was a possibility, here. He'd found exactly the connection he sought . . . and perhaps he could not only convince Cal of the truth but actually enlist him as an ally!

CHAPTER EIGHT

"You should let me go."

Sean MacIntyre's stubborn face was an unhealthy red in his Bushmaster's dash LEDs, and despite the high-efficiency emission-controls required by law, the agonizing stench of burning hydrocarbons had forced Colin to step his sensory levels down to little more than normal.

"No," he said for the fifth—or sixth—time.

"If you're wrong—if he *is* a bad guy and he's got some kind of panic button—he's gonna punch it the instant he opens the door and sees you."

"Maybe. But the shock of seeing me alive may keep him from doing anything hasty till we've had time to talk, too. Besides, if he does send out a signal, I can pick it up and bug out. Can you?"

"Be better not to spook him into sending one at all," Sean grumbled.

"Agreed. But he's not going to. I'm positive he doesn't know what those bastards are really up to—or what they've already done to the human race."

"I'm glad *you* are!"

"I've already gotten you in deep enough, Sean," Colin said as the Caddy snarled up a grade. "If I *am* wrong, I don't want you in the line of fire."

"I appreciate that," Sean said softly, "but I'm your brother. I happen to love you. And even if I didn't, this poor world will be in a hell of a mess a couple of years down the road if you get your ass killed, you jerk!"

"I'm not going to," Colin said firmly, "so stop arguing. Besides—" Sean turned off the highway onto a winding mountain road "—we're almost there."

"All right, goddamn it," Sean sighed, then grinned unwillingly. "You always were almost as stubborn as me."

The Caddy ghosted to a stop on the shoulder of the road. The view out over Colorado Springs was breathtaking, though neither brother paid it much heed, but the mountain above them was dark and sparsely populated. The Tudor home was a big, modern split-level, but it was part of a small, well-spread out "environment conscious" development, carefully designed to merge with its surroundings and then dropped into a neat, custom-tailored hole bitten out of the slope. It was two-thirds underground, and only the front porch light gleamed above him as Colin climbed out into the breezy night.

"Thanks, Sean," he said softly, leaning back into the car to squeeze his brother's shoulder with carefully restrained strength. "Wait here. If that thing—" he gestured at the small device sitting on the console between the front seats "—lights up, then shag ass out of here. Got it?"

"Yes," Sean sighed.

"Good. See you later." Colin gave another gentle squeeze, wishing his brother's unenhanced eyes could see the affection on his face, then turned away into the windy blackness. Sean watched him go, vanishing into the night, before he opened the glove compartment.

The heavy magnum automatic gleamed in the starlight as he checked the magazine and shoved the pistol into his belt, and he drummed on the wheel for a few more moments. He didn't know how good Colin's new hearing really was, and he wanted to give him plenty of time to get out of range before he followed.

Colin climbed straight up the mountainside, ignoring the heavy weight on his back. He could have left the suppresser behind, but he might need a little extra evidence to convince Cal he knew what he was talking about. Besides, he felt uneasy about letting it out of reach.

He let his enhanced sight and hearing coast up to maximum sensitivity as he neared the top, and his eyes lit as they touched the house. His electronic and gravitonic sensors were in passive mode lest he trip any waiting detectors, but there was a background haze of additional Imperial power sources in there, confirmation, if any had been needed, that Cal was his man.

He climbed over the split-rail fence he'd helped Cal build last spring and eased into the gap between the house and the sheer south wall of the deep, terrace-like notch blasted out of the mountain to hold it, circling to approach through the tiny backyard and wondering how Cal would react when he saw him. He hoped he was right about his friend. God, *how* he hoped he was!

He slipped through Frances Tudor's neat vegetable garden towards the back door like a ghost, checking for any security devices, Terran or Imperial, as he went. He found none, but his nerves tightened as he felt the soft prickle of an active fold-space link. He couldn't separate sources without going active with his own sensors, but it felt like another security com. No traffic was going out, but the unit was up, as if waiting to receive . . . or transmit. The last thing he needed was to find Cal sitting in front of a live mike and have him blurt out an alarm before his guest had a chance to open his mouth!

He sighed. He'd just have to hope for the best, but even at the worst, he should be able to vanish before anyone could respond to any alarm Cal raised.

He eased into the silent kitchen. It was dark, but that hardly mattered to him. He started toward the swinging dining room door, then stopped as he touched the bevel-edged glass hand plate.

There was a strange, time-frozen quality about the darkened kitchen. A wooden salad bowl on the counter was half-filled with shredded lettuce, but the other salad ingredients still lay neatly to one side, as if awaiting the chef's hand, and a chill wind seemed to gust down his spine. It wasn't like Cal or Frances to leave food sitting out like that, and he opened his sensors wide, going active despite the risk of detection.

What the—? A portable stealth field *behind* him?! His muscles bunched and he prepared to whirl, but—

"*Right* there," a voice said very softly, and he froze, one hand still on the dining room door, for the voice was not Cal's and it did not speak in English. "Hands behind your head, scum," it continued in Imperial Universal. "No little implant signals, either. Don't even think about doing anything but what I tell you to, or I'll burn your spine in two."

Colin obeyed, moving very slowly and cursing himself for a fool. He'd been wrong about Cal—dead wrong—and his own caution had kept him from looking hard enough to spot somebody with a stealth field. But who would have expected one? No one but another Imperial could possibly have picked up their implants, anyway. Which meant . . .

His blood went icy. Jesus, they'd been *expecting* him! And that meant they'd picked up the scanner relay—and that they knew about Sean, too!

"Very nice," the voice said. "Now just push the door open with your shoulder and move on through it. Carefully."

Colin obeyed, and the ashes of defeat were bitter in his mouth.

Sean longed for some of Colin's enhanced strength as he picked his way up the steep, dew-slick mountainside, but he made it to the fence and climbed over it at last. Then he stopped with a frown.

Unlike Colin, Sean MacIntyre had spent his nights under the stars rather than out among them. He'd joined the Forestry Service out of love, almost unable to believe that anyone would actually *pay* him to work in the protected wilderness of parks and nature reservations. Along the way, he'd refined a natural empathy for the world about him, one which relied on more than the sheer strength of his senses, and so it was that he noted what Colin had not.

The Tudor house was still and black, with no lights, no feel of life, and every nerve in Sean's body screamed "Trap!"

He took the automatic off "safe" and worked the slide. From what Colin had said, the "biotechnic" enhanced mutineers would take a lot of killing, but Sean had lots of faith in the hollow-nosed .45 super-mags in his clip.

"Nice of you to be so prompt," the voice behind Colin gloated. "We didn't expect you for another half-hour."

The sudden close-range pulse of the fold-space link behind Colin was almost painful, and he clamped his teeth in angry, frightened understanding. It had been a short-range pulse, which meant its recipients were close at hand.

"They'll be along in a few minutes," the voice said. "Through the door to your left," it added, and Colin pushed at it with his toe.

It opened, and he gagged as an indescribably evil smell suddenly assailed him. He retched in anguish before he could scale his senses back down, and the voice behind him laughed.

"Your host," it said cruelly, and flipped on the lights.

Cal drooped forward out of his chair, flung over his desk by the same energy blast which had sprayed his entire head over the blotter, but that was only the start of the horror. Fourteen-year-old Harriet sagged brokenly in an armchair before the desk, her head twisted around to stare accusingly at Colin with dead, glazed eyes. Her mother lay to one side, and the blast that had killed her had torn her literally in half. Twelve-year-old Anna lay half-under her, her child body even more horribly mutilated by the weapon that had killed them both as Frances tried uselessly to shield her daughter with her own life.

"He didn't want to call you in," the voice's gloating, predatory cruelty seemed to come from far, far away, "but we convinced him."

The universe roared about Colin MacIntyre, battering him like a hurricane, and the fury of the storm was his own rage. He started to turn, heedless of the weapon behind him, but the energy gun was waiting. It clubbed the back of his neck, battering him to his knees, and his captor laughed.

"Not so fast," he jeered. "The Chief wants to ask you a few questions, first." Then he raised his voice. "Anshar! Get your ass in here."

"I already have," another voice answered. Colin looked up as a second man stepped in through the far study door, and his normally mild eyes were emerald fire as he took in the blond-haired newcomer's midnight blue uniform, the Fleet issue boots, the heavy energy gun slung from one shoulder.

"About damn time," the first voice grunted. "All right, you bastard—" the energy gun prodded "—on your feet. Over there against the wall."

Grief and horror mingled with the red fangs of bloodlust, but even through that boil of emotion Colin knew he must obey—for now. Yet even as he promised himself a time would come for vengeance, an icy little voice whispered he'd made some terrible mistake. His captor's sneering cruelty, the carnage that had claimed his friend's entire family . . . None of it made any sense.

"Turn around," the voice said, and Colin turned his back to the wall.

The one who'd been doing all the talking was of no more than medium size but stocky, black-haired, with an odd olive-brown complexion. His eyes were also odd; almost Asiatic and yet not quite. Colin recognized the prototype from whence all Terran humans had sprung, and the thought made him sick.

But the other one, Anshar, was different. Even in his fury and fear, Colin was puzzled by the other's fair skin and blue eyes. He was Terra-born; he had to be, for the humanity of the Imperium had been very nearly completely homogenous. Only one planet of the Third Imperium had survived its fall, and the seven thousand years between Man's departure from Birhat to rebuild and Anu's mutiny had not diluted that homogeneity significantly. Only after *Dahak*'s crew reached Earth had genetic drift set in among the isolated survivors to produce disparate races. So what was *he* doing in Fleet uniform? Colin's sensors reached out and his eyes widened as he detected a complete set of biotechnic implants in the man.

"Pity the degenerate was so stubborn," the first one said, jerking Colin's attention back to him as he propped a hip against the desk. "But he saw the light when we broke his little bitch's neck." He prodded Harriet's corpse with the muzzle of his energy gun, his eyes a goad of cruelty, and Colin made himself breathe slowly. Wait, he told himself. You may have a chance to kill him before he kills you if you wait.

"Of course, we told him we'd let the others live if he called you." He laughed suddenly. "He may even have believed it!"

"Stop it, Girru," Anshar said, and his own eyes flinched away from the butchered bodies.

"You always were gutless, Anshar," Girru sneered. "Hell, even degenerates like a little hunting!"

"You didn't have to do it this way," Anshar muttered.

"Oh? Shall I tell the Chief you're getting fastidious? Or—" his voice took on a silky edge "—would you prefer I tell Kirinal?"

"No! I . . . just don't like it."

"Of course you don't!" Girru said contemptuously. "You—"

He broke off suddenly, whirling with the impossible speed of his implants, and a thunderous roar exploded behind him. The bright, jagged flare of a muzzle flash filled the darkened hall like lightning, edging the half-opened door in brilliance, and he jerked as the heavy slug smashed into him. A hoarse, agonized cry burst from him, but his enhanced body was tough beyond the ken of Terrans. He continued his turn, slowed by his hurt but still deadly, and the magnum bellowed again.

Even the wonders of the Fourth Imperium had their limits. The massive bullet punched through his reinforced spinal column, and he flipped away from the desk, knocking over the chair in which the dead girl sat.

Colin had hurled himself forward at the sound of the first shot, for he knew with heart-stopping certitude who had fired it. But he was on the wrong side of the room, and Anshar's slung energy gun snapped up, finger on the trigger—only to stop and jerk back towards the hallway door as a heavy foot kicked it fully open.

"*No, Sean!*" Colin bellowed, but his cry was a lifetime too late.

Sean MacIntyre knew Colin could never reach Anshar before the mutineer cut him down—and he had seen the slaughter of innocents that filled the study. He swung his magnum in a two-handed combat stance, matching merely human reflexes and fury against the inhuman speed of the Fourth Imperium.

He got off one shot. The heavy bullet took Anshar in the abdomen, wreaking horrible damage, but the energy gun snarled. It birthed a terrible demon—a focused beam of gravitonic disruption fit to shatter steel— that swept a fan of destruction across the door, and Sean MacIntyre's body erupted in a fountain of gore as it sliced through plaster and wood and flesh.

"*NOOOOOOOO!!!*" Colin screamed, and lunged at his brother's murderer.

The devastation the slug had wrought within Anshar slowed him, but he held down the stud, shattering the room as he swept it with lethal energy. Instinct prompted Colin even in his madness, and he wrenched aside, grunting as the suppresser on his back took the full fury of the blast.

It hurled him to one side, but Girru and Anshar hadn't realized what the suppresser was, and no Terran "knapsack" could have absorbed the damage of a full-power energy bolt.

Anshar released the trigger stud and paused, expecting his enemy to fall.

But Colin was unhurt, and long hours spent working out against Dahak's training remotes took command. He hit on his outspread hands and somersaulted back at Anshar while the mutineer gawked at him in disbelief. Then his boots slammed into Anshar's chest, battering the energy gun from his grip.

Both men rolled back upright, but Anshar was hurt—badly hurt—and Colin forgot Dahak, the Imperium, even his need for a prisoner. He ignored the dropped energy gun. He wanted nothing between Anshar and his own bare hands, and Anshar paled and writhed away as he saw the dark, terrible death in Colin's eyes.

Fury crashed through Colin MacIntyre—cold, cruel fury—and one hand caught a flailing arm and jerked his victim close. An alloy-reinforced knee, driven with all the power of his enhanced muscles, smashed into the wound Sean's bullet had torn, and a savage smile twisted his lips at Anshar's less than human sound of agony.

He shifted his grip, wrenching the arm he held high, and reinforced cartilage and bone tore and splintered with a ghastly ripping sound. Anshar shrieked again, but the sound was not enough to satisfy Colin. He slammed his enemy to the floor. His knee crashed down between Anshar's shoulders, and he released the arm he held. Both hands darted down, cupping the mutineer's chin, and his mighty back tensed, driven by the biotechnic miracles of the Fourth Imperium and the terrible power of hate. There was a moment of titanic stress and one last gurgling scream, and then Anshar's spine snapped with a flat, explosive crack.

CHAPTER NINE

Colin held his grip, feeling the life flow out of his victim in the steady collapse of Anshar's implants, and the killer in his soul was sick with triumph . . . and angry that it was over.

He opened his hands at last, and Anshar's face struck the floor with a meaty smack. Colin rose, scrubbing his hands on his jeans, and his eyes were empty, as if part of himself had died with his brother.

He turned away, smelling wood smoke, plaster dust, and the stench of ruptured bodies. He could not look at Cal's slaughtered family, but neither, though he would have sold his soul to do it, could he take his eyes from Sean.

He knelt in the spreading pool of his brother's blood. The energy gun had mangled Sean hideously, but the very horror meant death had come quickly, and he tried to tell himself Sean had not suffered as his ripped and torn flesh said he had.

Their long-dead mother's eyes looked up at him. There was no life in them, but an echo of Sean's outrage remained. He'd known, Colin thought sadly, known he was a dead man from the instant Anshar began to raise his own weapon, yet he'd stood his ground. Just as he always had. And, just as he always had, he had protected his younger brother.

Colin closed those eyes with gentle fingers, and unashamed tears streaked his cheeks. One fell, a diamond glinting in the light from the study, to his brother's face, and the sight touched something inside him. It was like a farewell, fraying the grip of the grief that kept him kneeling there, and he reached to pick up Girru's energy gun.

"Freeze," a cold voice said behind him.

Colin froze, but this time he recognized the voice. It spoke English with a soft, Southern accent, and his jaw clenched. Not just Cal; everyone he'd thought he knew, believed he could trust, had betrayed him. Everyone but Sean.

"Drop it." He let the energy gun thump back to the floor. "Inside."

He stepped back into the study and turned slowly, his eyes flinty as they rested on the tall, black-skinned woman in the doorway. She wore the uniform of the United States Air Force with a lieutenant colonel's oak leaves, but the weapon slung from her shoulder had never been made on Earth. The over-sized, snub-nosed pistol was a grav gun, and its drum magazine held two hundred three-millimeter darts. Their muzzle velocity would be over five thousand meters per second, and they were formed of a chemical explosive denser than uranium that exploded after penetrating. From where he stood, he could see the three-headed dragon etched into the receiver.

The muzzle never wavered from his navel, but the colonel's eyes swept the room, and her face twisted. The black forefinger on the trigger tightened and he tensed his belly muscles uselessly, but she didn't fire. Her brown eyes lingered for a long moment on Frances and Anna Tudor's mutilated bodies, then came back to him, filled with a bottomless hate he'd never seen in them.

"You *bastard!*" Lieutenant Colonel Sandra Tillotson breathed.

"Me?" he said bitterly. "What about *you*, Sandy?"

His voice was like a blow. Her head jerked, and her eyes widened, their hatred buried in sudden disbelief as she saw him—*him*, not just another killer—for the first time.

"*Colin*?!" she gasped, and her reaction puzzled him. Surely the mutineers had known who they were trapping! But Sandy closed her mouth with an almost audible snap, her gaze flitting to the two dead bodies in the Fleet uniforms, and he could actually see the intensity of her thoughts, see a whole chain of realizations flickering over her face. And then, to his utter shock, she lowered her weapon.

His muscles tightened to leap across the intervening space and snatch it away. But she shook her head slowly, and her next words stopped him dead.

"Colin," she whispered. "My God, Colin, what have you *done*?"

It was the last reaction he had expected, and his own eyes narrowed.

"I found them like this. Those two—" his head gestured at the uniformed bodies, hands motionless "—were waiting for me. They . . . killed Sean, too."

Sandy jerked around to stare through the doorway, and her shoulders sagged as she finally recognized the savagely maimed body. When she turned back to Colin, her eyes were closed in grief and despair.

"Oh, Jesus," she moaned. "Oh, dear, sweet Jesus. Not Sean, too."

"Sandy, what the *hell* is going on here?" Colin demanded.

"No, you wouldn't know," she said softly, her mouth bitter.

"I don't *know* anything! I thought I did, but—"

"Cal tripped his emergency signal," Sandy said tonelessly, and looked at the dead scientist, as if impressing the hideous sight imperishably upon her mind. "I was closest, so I came as quick as I could."

"*You*? Sandy—*you're* in with Anu?"

"Of course not! Those two—Girru and Anshar—were two of his hit men."

"Sandy, what are you *talking* about? If you're not—"

Colin broke off again as his sensors tingled, and Sandy stiffened as she saw his face tighten.

"What is it?" she asked sharply.

"Those two bastards called in reinforcements," Colin said tautly. "They're coming. Don't you feel them?"

"I'm a normal human, Colin. One of the 'degenerates,' " Sandy said harshly. "But you aren't, are you? Not anymore."

"A norm—" He broke off. "Later," he said tersely. "Right now, we've got at least twenty sets of combat armor closing in on us."

"Shit," Sandy breathed. Then she shook herself again. "If you've got yourself a bio-enhancement package, grab one of those energy guns!" She bared her teeth in an ugly smile. "*That*'ll surprise the bastards!"

Colin snatched up Anshar's weapon. It had suffered no damage in their struggle and the charge indicator read ninety percent, and his fingers curled almost lovingly around the grips as he grasped Sandy's meaning. No normal human could handle one of the heavy energy weapons. Even Sandy's grav gun would be a problem for most Terra-born humans. For the Imperium, it was a sidearm; for Sandy, it was a shoulder-slung, two-handed weapon.

"How are they coming in and where are they?" Sandy demanded tersely.

"Twenty of them," Colin repeated. "Closing in from the perimeter of a circle. About six klicks out and coming fast."

"Too far," Sandy muttered. "We've got to suck them in closer. . . ."

"Why?"

"Because—" She broke off, shaking her head. "There's no time for explanations, Colin. Just trust me—and believe I'm on your side."

"My side? Sandy—"

"Shut *up* and *listen!*" she snapped, and he choked off his questions. "Look, I had my suspicions when we didn't find any sign of you in that wreck, but it seemed so incredible that— Never mind. The important thing is you. What kind of implants did you get?"

Questions hammered in Colin's brain. How did Sandy, who obviously had no biotechnics, even know what they were? Much less that there were different implant packages? But she was right. There was no time.

"Bridge officer," he said shortly.

"Bridge—?! You mean the ship's *fully* operational?!"

"Maybe," he said cautiously, and she shook her head irritably.

"Either it is or it isn't, and if you got the full treatment, it is. Which means—" She broke off again and nodded sharply.

"Don't just stand there! See if it can get our asses out of here!"

Colin gaped at her. The hurricane of his grief and fury, followed by the shock of seeing Sandy, had blinded him to the simplest possibility of all!

He activated his fold-space link, then grunted in anguish, half-clubbed to his knees by the squealing torment in his nerves. He shook his head doggedly.

"Can't!" he gasped. "We're jammed."

"Shit!" Sandy's face tightened again, but when she spoke again, her voice was curiously serene. "Colin, I don't know how you found Cal, or exactly what happened here, but you're the *only* man on this planet with bridge implants. We've *got* to get you out of here."

"But—"

"There's no *time*, Colin. Just listen. If we can suck them in close, there's an escape route. When I tell you to, go down to the basement. There's a switch somewhere—I don't know where, but you won't need it. Go down to the basement and move the furnace. It pivots clockwise, but you'll have to break the lock to move it. Go down the ladder and take the right fork—the left's a booby—trapped cul-de-sac—and move like hell. You'll come out about a klick from here in the woods above Aspen Road. Got it?"

"Got it. But—" he tried again.

"I said there's no time." She turned for the door, stepping carefully over Sean's body. "Come with me. We've got to convince them we're going to stand and fight, or they'll be watching for a breakout."

Colin followed her rebelliously, every nerve in his body crying out against obeying her blindly. Yet she clearly knew what she was doing—or thought she did—and that was a thousand percent better than anything *he* knew.

Sandy scurried down the hall and moved a wall painting to reveal a small switch. Colin's sensors reached out to trace the circuitry, but she threw it before he got far, and his skin twitched as he felt the sudden awakening of unsuspected defenses. He'd sensed additional Imperial technology as he approached the house, but he'd never suspected *this*!

"This wall's armored, but it faces away from the mountain, so we couldn't risk shield circuits in it," Sandy explained tersely, turning into the living room and kneeling beside a picture window. She rested the muzzle of her heavy grav gun on the sill. "Too much chance Anu's bunch would notice if one of 'em happened by. But it's the only open wall in the house."

Colin grunted in understanding, kneeling beside a window on the far side of the room. If they were trying to hide, they'd taken an awful chance just covering the roof and side walls, but not as big a one as he'd first thought. His own sensors were far more sensitive than any mutineer's, and he realized the shield circuits were actually very well hidden as he traced the forcefield to its source. He'd expected Imperial molecular circuits, but the concealed installation in the basement was of Terran manufacture. It had some highly unusual components, but it was all printed circuits, which explained both its bulkiness and their difficulty in hiding it. Still, the very fact that it contained no molycircs was its best protection.

The shield cut off his sensors in three directions, but he could still use them through the open wall, and he grinned savagely as the emission signatures of combat armor glowed before him. They were far better protected than he, but they were also far more "visible," and he lifted his energy gun hungrily.

"They're coming," he whispered, and Sandy nodded, her face grotesque behind the light-gathering optics she'd clipped over her eyes. They were the latest US Army issue, hardly up to Imperial standards but highly efficient in their limited area. He turned back to the window, watching the night.

A suit of combat armor was a bright glare in his vision, and he raised his energy gun. The attacker rose higher, topping out over the slope, and he wondered why they were no longer using their jump gear. The mutineer rose still higher, exposing almost his full body, and Colin squeezed the stud.

His window exploded, showering the night with glass. The nearly invisible energy was a terrible lash of power to his enhanced vision as it smashed out across the lawn, and it took the mutineer dead center.

The combat armor held for an instant, but Colin's weapon was on max. There was a shattering geyser of gore, and a dreadful hunger snarled within him as the mutineer went down forever and he heard a rippling *hiss-crrackkk!*

The near-silent grav gun's darts went supersonic as they left the muzzle, and Sandy's window blew apart, but its resistance was too slight to detonate them. A corner of his eye saw gouts of flying dirt as a dozen plunged deep and exploded, and then another suit of combat armor reared backwards. It toppled over the side of the yard, thundering on the road below, and Sandy's hungry, vengeful sound echoed his own.

Their fire had broken the silence, and the house rocked as Imperial weapons smashed at its side and rear walls. Colin winced as he felt the sudden power surge in the shield circuits. The fire went on and on, flaying the night with thunder and lightning, and the homemade shield generator heated dangerously, but it held.

Then the thunder ceased, and he looked up as Sandy spoke again.

"They know, now," she said softly. "They'll be coming at us from the front in a minute. They can't afford to waste time with all the racket we're making. They've got to be in and out before—" She broke off and hosed another stream of darts into the night, and a third armored body blew apart. "—before someone comes to see what the hell is happening."

"We'll never hold against a real rush," he warned.

"I know. It's time to bug out, Colin."

"They'll follow us," he said. "Even I can't outrun combat suits with jump gear." He did not add that she stood no chance at all of outrunning them.

"Won't have to," she said shortly. "There should be friends at the end of the tunnel when you get there. But for God's sake, don't come out shooting! They don't know what's going on in here."

"Friends? What—?" He broke off and ripped off another shot, but this time the mutineers knew they were under fire. He hit his target squarely, but his victim dropped before the beam fully overpowered his armor. He was badly hurt—no doubt of that—but it was unlikely he was dead.

"Don't ask questions! Just get your ass in gear and *go*, damn it!"

"Not without you," he shot back.

"You stupid—!" Sandy bit off her angry remark and shook her head fiercely. "I can't even open the damned tunnel, asshole! *You* can, so stop being so fucking gallant! Somebody has to cover the rear and somebody else has to open the tunnel! Now *move*, Colin!"

He started to argue, but his sensors were suddenly crowded with the emissions of combat armor gathering along the roadway below the slope. She was right, and he knew it. He didn't *want* to know it, but he did.

"All right!" he grated. "But you'd better be *right* behind me, lady, or I'm coming back after you!"

"*No,* you mule-headed, chauvinistic honk—!"

She chopped herself off as she realized he was already gone. She wanted to call after him and wish him luck but dared not turn away from her front. She regretted her own angry response to his words, for she knew why he had said them. He'd had to, pointless as they both knew it was. He had to believe he would come back—that he *could* come back—yet he knew as well as she that if she wasn't right on his heels, she would never make it out at all.

But what she had carefully not told him was that she wouldn't be following him. She'd said there would be friends, but she couldn't be certain, and even if there were, someone had to occupy the attackers' attention to keep them from noticing movement in the tunnel when Colin passed beyond the confines of the shield. And she'd meant what she'd said. If he had a bridge officer's implants, they *had* to get him out. She didn't understand everything that was happening, but she knew that. And that he needed time to make his escape.

Lieutenant Colonel Sandra Tillotson, United States Air Force, laid a spare magazine beside her and prepared to buy him that time.

Colin raced down the basement stairs, sick at heart. Deep inside, he suspected what Sandy intended, and she was right, damn it! But the thought of abandoning her was a canker in his soul. This night of horrors was costing too much. He remembered what he'd thought when *Dahak*'s cutter deposited him here, and his own words were wormwood and gall. He hadn't realized the hideous depth of what would be demanded of him, for somehow he'd believed that only *he* must lose things, that he must risk only himself. He hadn't counted on people he knew and loved being slaughtered like animals . . . nor had he realized how bitter it could be to live rather than die beside them.

He sensed the stuttering fire of her grav gun behind him, the fury of energy weapons gouging at the house, and his eyes burned as he seized the heavy furnace in a mighty grip. He heaved, wrenching it entirely from its base, and the ladder was there. He ignored it, leaping lightly down the two-meter drop, and hit the tunnel running. Even as he passed under the edge of the shield and it sliced off his sensors, he felt the space-wrenching discharges of her grav gun, knew she was still there, still firing, not even trying to escape, and tears and self-hate blinded him as he raced for safety.

The tunnel seemed endless, yet the end was upon him almost before he realized it, and he lunged up another ladder. The shaft was sealed, but he was already probing it, spotting the catch, heaving it up with a mighty shoulder. He burst into the night air . . . and his senses were suddenly afire with more power sources. More combat armor! Coming from behind in the prodigious leaps of jump gear and waiting in the woods ahead, as well!

He tried to unlimber his energy gun, but a torrent of energy crashed over him, and he cried out as every implant in his body screamed in protest. He writhed, fighting it, clinging to the torment of awareness.

It was a capture field—not a killing blast of energy, but something infinitely worse. A police device that locked his synthetic muscles with brutal power.

He toppled forward under the impetus of his last charge, crashing to the ground half-in and half-out of the tunnel. He fought the encroaching darkness, smashing at it with all the fury of his enraged will, but it swept over him.

The last thing he saw was a tornado of light as the trees exploded with energy fire. He carried the vision down into the dark with him, dimly aware of its importance.

And then, as his senses faded at last, he realized. It wasn't directed at him—it was raking the ground behind him and cutting down the mutineers who had pursued him. . . .

CHAPTER TEN

Colin swam fearfully up out of his nightmares, trying to understand what had happened. Something was wrong with his senses, and he moaned softly, frightened by the deadness, the *absence*, where he should have felt the whisper and wash of ambient energy.

He opened his eyes and blinked, automatically damping the brilliant light glaring down over him. He made out a ceiling beyond it—an unfamiliar roof of an all-too-familiar, bronze-colored alloy—and his muscles tightened.

It had been no dream. Sean was dead. And Cal . . . his family . . . and Sandy. . . .

Memory wrung a harsh, inarticulate sound of grief from him, and he closed his eyes again. Then he gathered himself and tried to sit up, but his body refused to obey and his eyes popped open once more. He tried again, harder, and his muscles strained, but it was like trying to lift the Earth. Something pressed down upon him, and he clenched his teeth as he recognized the presser. And a suppression field, as well, which explained his dead sensory implants.

A small sound touched his ear, and he wrenched his head around, barely able to move even that much under the presser.

Three grim-faced people looked back at him. The one standing in the center was a man, gray-haired, his seamed face puckered by a smooth, long-healed scar from just under his right eye down under the neck of his tattered old Clemson University sweatshirt. His leathery skin was the olive-brown of the Fourth Imperium, and Colin recognized the signs from Dahak's briefings; this man was old. Very old. He must be well into his sixth century, but if he was old, he was also massively thewed, and his olive-black eyes were alert.

A woman sat in a chair to his left. She, too, was old, but with the shorter span of the Terra-born, her still-thick hair almost painfully white under the brilliant light. Her lined, grief-drawn face was lighter than the man's, but there was a hint of the same slant to her swollen eyes, and Colin swallowed in painful recognition. He'd never met Isis Tudor, but she looked too much like her murdered grandson to be anyone else.

The third watcher shared the old man's complexion, but her cold, set face was unlined. She was tall for an Imperial, rivaling Colin's own hundred-eighty-eight centimeters, and slender, almost delicate. And she was beautiful, with an almond-eyed, cat-like loveliness that was subtly alien and yet perfect. A thick mane of hair rippled down her spine, so black it was almost blue-green, gathered at the nape of her neck in a jeweled clasp before it fanned out below, and she wore tailored slacks and a cashmere sweater. The gemmed dagger at her belt struck an incongruous note, but not a humorous one. Her slender fingers curled too hungrily about its hilt, and her dark eyes were filled with hate.

He stared silently back at them, then turned his face deliberately away. The silence stretched out, and then the old man cleared his throat.

"What shall we do with you, Commander MacIntyre?" he asked in soft, perfect English, and Colin turned back to him almost against his will. The spokesman smiled a twisted smile and slipped one arm around the old woman. "We know what you are—in part—" he continued, "but not in full. And—" his soft voice turned suddenly harsher "—we know what you've cost us already."

"Spend not thy words upon him," the young woman said coldly.

"Hush, Jiltanith," the old man said. "It's not his fault."

"Is't not? Yet Calvin doth lie dead, and his wife and daughters with him. And 'tis *this* man hath encompassed that!"

"No." Isis Tudor's soft voice was grief-harrowed, but she shook her head slowly. "He was Cal's *friend*, 'Tanni. He didn't know what he was doing."

"Which changeth naught," Jiltanith said bitterly.

"Isis is right, 'Tanni," the old man said sadly. "He couldn't have known they were looking for Cal. Besides," the old eyes were wise and compassionate despite their own bitterness, "he lost his own brother, as well . . . and avenged Cal and the girls."

He walked towards the table on which Colin lay and locked a challenging gaze with him, and Colin knew it was there between them. He'd warned Sean the relay might be detected, and it had. His mistake had killed Cal and Frances, Harriet and Anna, Sean and Sandy. He knew it, and the same knowledge filled the old man's eyes, yet his captor clasped his hands behind him and stopped a meter away, eloquently unthreatening.

"What use vengeance?" Jiltanith demanded, her lovely, hating face cold. "Will't breathe life back into them? Nay! Slay him and ha' done, I say!"

"No, 'Tanni," the man said more firmly. "We need him, and he needs us."

"I say thee nay, Father!" Jiltanith spat furiously. "I'll ha' none of him! Nay, nor any part in't!"

"It's not for you to say, 'Tanni." The man sounded stern. "It's up to the Council—and *I* am head of the Council."

"Father," Jiltanith's voice was all the more deadly for its softness, "if thou makest this man thine ally, thou art a fool. E'en now hath he cost thee dear. Take heed, lest the price grow higher still."

"We have no choice," her father said. His sad, wise eyes held Colin's. "Commander, if you will give me your parole, I'll switch off the presser."

"No," Colin said coldly.

"Commander, we're not what you think. Or perhaps we are, in a way, but you need us, and we need you. I'm not asking you to surrender, only to listen. That's all we ask. Afterwards, if you wish, we will release you."

Colin heard Jiltanith's bitter, in-drawn hiss, but his eyes bored into the old man's. Something unspeakably old and weary looked back at him—old yet vital with purpose. Despite himself, he was tempted to believe him.

"And just who the hell *are* you?" he grated at last.

"Me, Commander?" The old man smiled wryly. "Missile Specialist First Horus, late of Imperial Battle Fleet. Very late, I fear. And also—" his smile vanished, and his eyes were incredibly sad once more "—Horace Hidachi."

Colin's eyelids twitched, and the old man nodded.

"Yes, Commander. Cal was my great-grandson. And because of that, I think you owe me at least the courtesy of listening, don't you?"

Colin stared at him for a long, silent second and then, jerky against the pressure of the presser, he nodded.

Colin shrugged to settle more comfortably the borrowed uniform which had replaced his blood-stained clothing and studied his surroundings as Horus and Isis Tudor led him down the passageway. A portable suppression field still cut off his sensors, and he was a bit surprised by how incomplete that made him feel. He'd become accustomed to his new senses, accepting the electromagnetic and gravitonic spectrums as an extension of sight and sense and smell. Now they were gone, taken away by the small hand unit a stiff-spined Jiltanith trained upon him as she followed him down the corridor.

They met a few others, though traffic was sparse. Those they passed wore casual Terran clothing, and most were obviously Terra-born. The almond eyes and olive skins of Imperials were scattered thinly among them, and he wondered how so many Terra-born could be admitted to the secret without its leaking.

But even without his implants, he could see—and feel—the oldness about him.

Dahak was even older than his current surroundings, but the huge starship didn't *feel* old. Ancient, yes, but not old. Not worn with the passing of years. For fifty millennia, there had been no feet upon *Dahak*'s decks, no living presence to mark its passing in casual scrapes and bumps and scars.

But feet had left their mark here. The central portion of the tough synthetic decksole had been worn away, and even the bare alloy beneath showed wear. It would take more than feet to grind away Imperial battle steel, but it was polished smooth, burnished to a high gloss. And the bulkheads were the same, showing signs of repairs to lighting fixtures and ventilation ducts in the slightly irregular surface of patches placed by merely human hands rather than the flawlessly precise maintenance units that tended *Dahak*.

It made no sense. Dahak had said the mutineers spent most of their time in stasis, yet despite the sparse traffic, he suspected there were hundreds of people moving about him. And this feeling of age, this timeworn weariness that could impregnate even battle steel, was wrong. Anu had taken a complete tech base to Earth; he should have plenty of service mechs for the proper upkeep of his vessels.

Which fitted together with everything else. The murder of Cal's family. Sandy's cryptic remarks. There was a pattern here, one he could not quite grasp yet whose parts were all internally consistent. But—

His thoughts broke off as Horus and Isis slowed suddenly before a closed hatch. A three-headed dragon had once adorned those doors, but it had been planed away, leaving the alloy smooth and unblemished, and he filed that away with the fact that he and he alone wore Fleet uniform.

The hatch opened, and he stepped through it at Horus's gesture.

The control room was a far more cramped version of *Dahak*'s command deck, but there had been changes. A bank of old, flat-screen Terran television monitors covered one bulkhead, and peculiar, bastardized hybrids of Imperial theory and Terran components had been added to the panels. There were standard Terran computer touchpads at consoles already fitted for direct neural feeds, but most incongruous of all, perhaps, were the archaic Terran-style headsets racked by each console. His eyebrows rose as he saw them, and Horus smiled.

"We need the keyboards . . . and the phones, Commander," he said wryly. "Most of our people have to enter commands manually and pass orders by voice."

Colin regarded the old man thoughtfully, then nodded noncommittally and turned his attention to the thirty-odd people sitting at the various consoles or standing beside them. The few Imperials among them were a decided minority, and most of those, unlike Jiltanith, seemed almost as ancient as Horus.

"Commander," Horus said formally, "permit me to introduce the Command Council of the sublight battleship *Nergal*, late—like some of her crew, at least—of Battle Fleet."

Colin frowned. The *Nergal* had been one of Anu's ships, but it was becoming painfully clear that whatever these people were, they *weren't* friends of Anu. Not any longer, at any rate. His mind raced as he tried to weigh the fragments of information he had, searching for an advantage he could wring from them.

"I see," was all he said, and Horus actually chuckled.

"I imagine you play a mean game of poker, Commander," he said dryly, and waved Colin to one of the only two empty couches. It was the assistant gunnery officer's, Colin noted, but the panel before it was inactive.

"I try," he said, cocking his head to invite Horus to continue.

"I see you don't intend to make this easy. Well, I don't suppose I blame you." Jiltanith made a soft, contemptuous sound of disagreement, and Horus frowned at her. She subsided, but Colin had the distinct impression she would have preferred pointing something considerably more lethal than a portable suppresser at him.

"All right," Horus said more briskly, turning to seat Isis courteously in the unoccupied captain's chair, "that's fair. Let's start at the beginning.

"First, Commander, we won't ask you to divulge any information unless you choose to do so. Nonetheless, certain things are rather self-evident.

"First, *Dahak* is, in fact, operational. Second, there is a reason the ship has failed either to squelch the mutiny or to go elsewhere seeking assistance. Third, the ship *has* taken a hand at last, hence your presence here with the first bridge officer implant package this planet has seen in fifty thousand years. Fourth, and most obviously of all, if you'll forgive me, the information upon which you have formulated your plans has proven inaccurate. Or perhaps it would be better to say *incomplete*."

He paused, but Colin allowed his face to show no more than polite interest. Horus sighed again.

"Commander, your caution is admirable but misplaced. While we have continued to suppress your implants, particularly your com link, that act is in your interest as well as our own. You can have no more desire than we to provide Anu's missiles with a targeting beacon! We realize, however, that it is we who must convince *you* our motives are benign, and the only way I can see to do that is to tell you who we are and why we want so desperately to help rather than hinder you."

"Indeed?" Colin permitted himself a question at last and let his eyes slip sideways to Jiltanith. Horus made a wry face.

"Is any decision ever totally unanimous, Commander? We may be mutineers or something else entirely, but we are also a community in which even those who disagree with the majority abide by the decisions of our Council. Is that not true, 'Tanni?" he asked the angry-eyed young woman gently.

"Aye, 'tis true enow," she said shortly, biting off each word as if it cost her physical pain, and her very reluctance was almost reassuring. A lie would have come more easily.

"All right," Colin said finally. "I won't make any promises, but go ahead and explain your position to me."

"Thank you," Horus said. He propped a hip against the console before which Isis Tudor sat and crossed his arms.

"First, Commander, a confession. I supported the mutiny with all my heart, and I fought hard to make it a success. Most of the Imperials in this control room would admit the same. But—" his eyes met Colin's unflinchingly "—we were *used*, Commander MacIntyre."

Colin returned his gaze silently, and Horus shrugged.

"I know. It was our own fault, and we've been forced to accept that. We attempted to desert 'in the face of the enemy,' as your own code of military justice would phrase it, and we recognize our guilt. Indeed, that's the reason none of us wear the uniform to which we were once entitled. Yet there's another side to us, Commander, for once we recognized how horribly wrong we'd been, we also attempted to make amends. And not all of us *were* mutineers."

He paused and looked back at Jiltanith, whose face was harder and colder than ever. It was a fortress, her hatred a portcullis grinding down, and her bitter eyes ignored Horus to look straight into Colin's face.

"Jiltanith was no mutineer, Commander," Horus said softly.

"No?" Colin surprised himself by how gently his question came out. Jiltanith's obvious youth beside the other, aged Imperials had already set her apart. Somehow, without knowing exactly why, he'd felt her otherness.

"No," Horus said in the same soft voice. "'Tanni was six Terran years old, Commander. Why should a child be held accountable for our acts?"

Colin nodded slowly, committing himself to nothing, yet that, at least, he understood. To be sentenced to eternal exile or death for a crime you had never committed would be enough to wake hatred in anyone.

"But *Dahak*'s business is with all of us, I suppose," Horus continued quietly, "and my fellows and I accept that. We've grown old, Commander. Our lives are largely spent. It is only for 'Tanni and the other innocents we would plead. And, perhaps, for some of our comrades to the south."

"That's very eloquent, Horus," Colin said, tone carefully neutral, "but—"

"But we must work our passage, is that it?" Horus interrupted, and Colin nodded slowly. "Why, so we think, as well.

"When Anu organized his mutiny, Commander, Commander (BioSciences) Inanna picked the most suitable psych profiles for recruitment. Even the Imperium had its malleable elements, and she and Anu chose well. Some were merely frightened of death; others were dissatisfied and saw a chance for promotion and power; still others were simply bored and saw a chance for adventure. But what very few of them knew was that Anu's inner circle had motives quite different from their own.

"Anu's professed goal was to seize the ship and flee the Achuultani, but the plain truth of the matter was that he, like many of the crew, no longer believed in the Achuultani." Colin sat a bit straighter, eager to hear another perspective—even one which might prove self-serving—on the mutiny, but he let his face show doubt.

"Oh, the records were there," Horus agreed, "but the Imperium was *old*, Commander. We were regimented, disciplined, prepared for battle at the drop of a hat—or that, at least, was the idea. Yet we'd waited too long for the enemy. We were no longer attack dogs straining at the leash. We'd become creatures of habit, and many of us believed deep in our souls that we were regimented and controlled and trained for a purpose that no longer existed.

"Even those of us who'd seen proof of the Achuultani's existence—dead planets, gutted star systems, the wreckage of ancient battle fleets—had never seen the *Achuultani*, and our people were not so very different from your own. Anything beyond your own life experience wasn't quite 'real' to us. After seven thousand years in which there were no new incursions, after five thousand years of preparation for an attack that never came, after three thousand years of sending out probes that found no sign of the enemy, it was hard to believe there still *was* an enemy. We'd mounted guard too long, and perhaps we simply grew bored." Horus shrugged. "But the fact remains that only a minority of us truly *believed* in the Achuultani, and many of those were terrified.

"So Anu's chosen pretext was shrewd. It appealed to the frightened, gave an excuse to the disaffected, and offered the bored the challenge of a new world to conquer, one beyond the stultifying reach of the Imperium. Yet it was *only* a pretext, for Anu himself sought escape from neither the Achuultani nor from boredom. He wanted *Dahak* for himself, and he had no intention of marooning the loyalists upon Earth."

Colin knew he was leaning forward and suspected his face was giving away entirely too much, yet there was nothing he could do about it. This was a subtly different story from the one Dahak had given him, but it made sense.

And perhaps the difference wasn't so strange. The data in Dahak's memory was all the reality there was for the old starship—before it found itself operating completely on its own, at least. He'd noticed that the computer never used a personal pronoun to denote itself or its actions or responses prior to or immediately following the mutiny, and he thought he knew why. "Comp Cent" had been intended purely as a data and systems management tool to be used only under direct human supervision; Dahak's present, fully-developed self-awareness was a product of fifty-one millennia of continuous, unsupervised operation. And if that awareness had evolved *after* the mutiny, why should the computer question its basic data? To the records, unlike the merely human personnel who had crewed the vast ship, the Achuultani's existence was axiomatic and incontestable, and so it had become for Dahak. Why should he doubt that it was equally so for humanity? Particularly if that had been Anu's "official" reason? Of course it made sense . . . and Dahak himself was aware of his own lack of imagination, of empathy for the human condition.

"I believe," Horus's heavy voice recaptured Colin's attention, "that Anu is mad. I believe he was mad even then, but I may be wrong. Yet he truly believed that, backed by *Dahak*'s power, he could overthrow the Imperium itself.

"I can't believe he could have succeeded, however disaffected portions of the population might have become, but what mattered was that *he* believed he had some sort of divine mission to conquer the Imperium, and the seizure of the ship was but the first step in that endeavor.

"Yet he had to move carefully, so he lied to us. He intended all along to massacre anyone who refused to join him, but because he knew many of his adherents would balk at that he pretended differently. He even yielded to our insistence that the hypercom spares be loaded aboard the transports we believed would carry the marooned loyalists to Earth so that, in time, they might build a hypercom and call for help. And he promised us a surgical operation, Commander. His carefully prepared teams would seize the critical control nodes, cut Comp Cent from the net, and present Senior Fleet Captain Druaga with a *fait accompli*.

"And we believed him," Horus almost whispered. "May the Maker forgive us, we *believed* him, though if we'd bothered to think even for a moment, we would have known better. With so little of the core crew—no more than seven thousand at best—with us, his 'surgical operation' was an impossibility.

When he stockpiled combat armor and weapons and had his people in Logistics sabotage as much other armor as they possibly could, we should have realized. But we didn't. Not until the fighting broke out and the blood began to flow. Not until it was far too late to change sides."

Horus fell silent, and Colin stared at him, willing him to continue yet aware the other must pause and gather himself. Intellectually, he knew it could all be a self-serving lie; instinctively, he knew it was the truth, at least as Horus believed it.

"The final moments aboard *Dahak* were a nightmare, Commander," the old man said finally. "Red Two, Internal, had been set. Lifeboats were ejecting. We were falling back to Bay Ninety-One, running for our lives, afraid we wouldn't make it, sickened by the bloodshed. But once we'd left *Dahak* astern, we were faced with what we'd done. More than that, we knew—or some of us did, at least—what Anu truly was. And so this ship, *Nergal*, deserted Anu."

Horus smiled wryly as Colin blinked in surprise.

"Yes, Commander, we were double mutineers. We ran for it—just this one ship, with barely two hundred souls aboard—and somehow, in the confusion, we escaped Anu's scanners and hid from him.

"Our plan, such as it was, was simplicity itself. We knew Anu had prepared a contingency plan that was supposed to give him control of the ship no matter what happened, though we had no idea what it was. We speculated that it concerned the ship's power, since he was Chief Engineer, but all that really mattered was that he would eventually win his prize and depart. Remember that we still half-believed his promise to leave any loyalists marooned behind him, Commander. And because we did, we planned to emerge from hiding after he left and do what we could for the survivors in an effort to atone for our crime and—I will admit it frankly— as the only thing we could think of that might win us some clemency when the Imperium found us at last.

"But, of course, it didn't work out that way," he said quietly, "for Anu's plan failed. Somehow, *Dahak* remained at least partially operational, destroying every parasite sent towards it. And it never went away, either. It hung above him, like your own Sword of Damocles, inviolate, taunting him.

"If he hadn't been mad before, Commander, he went mad then. He sent most of his followers into stasis—to wait out *Dahak*'s final 'inevitable' collapse—while only his immediate henchmen, who knew what he'd truly planned all along, remained awake. And once he had total control, he showed his true colors.

"Tell me, Commander MacIntyre, have you ever wondered what happened to all *Dahak*'s other bridge officers? Or how beings such as ourselves—such as you now are—with lifespans measured in centuries and strength and endurance far beyond that of Terra-born humans, could decivilize so utterly? It took your kind barely five hundred years to move from matchlocks and pikes to the atom bomb. From crude sailing ships to outer space. Doesn't it seem strange that almost *a quarter million* Imperial survivors should lose all technology?"

"I've . . . wondered," Colin admitted. He had, and not even Dahak had been able to tell him. All the computer knew was that when he became functional once more, the surviving loyalists had reverted to a subsistence-level hunter-gatherer technology and showed no particular desire to advance further.

"The answer is simple, Commander. Anu hunted them down. He tracked the surviving bridge officers by their implant signatures and butchered them to finish off any surviving chain of command. And for revenge, of course. And whenever a cluster of survivors tried to rebuild their technology, he wiped them out. He quartered this planet, Commander MacIntyre, seeking out the lifeboats with operational power plants and blowing them apart, making certain he alone monopolized technology, that no possible threat to him remained. The survivors soon learned primitivism was the only way they could survive."

"But *your* tech base survived," Colin said coldly, and Horus winced.

"True," he said heavily, "but look about you, Commander. How much tech base do we truly have? A single carefully-hidden battleship. We lack the infrastructure to build anything more, and if we'd attempted to build that infrastructure, Anu would have found us as he found the loyalists who made the same attempt. We might have given a good account of ourselves, but with only one ship against seven of the same class, plus escorts, we would have achieved nothing beyond an heroic death."

He held out one hand, palm upward in an eloquent gesture of helplessness, and Colin felt an unwilling sympathy for the man, much as he had for *Dahak* when he first heard the starship's story. Unlike *Dahak*, these people had built their own purgatory brick by brick, but that made it no less a purgatory.

"So what did you do?" he asked finally.

"We hid, Commander," Horus admitted. "Our own plans had gone hopelessly wrong, for Anu couldn't leave. So we activated *Nergal's* stealth systems and hid, biding our time, and we, too, went into stasis."

Of course they'd hidden, Colin thought, *and that explained why Dahak had never suspected there might be more than a single faction of mutineers. Anu must have been mad with the need to find and destroy them, for they and they alone had posed a threat to him. And if they'd hidden so well he couldn't find them with Imperial instrumentation, then how could Dahak, who didn't even know to look for them, find them with the same instrumentation?*

"We hid," Horus continued, "but we set our own monitors to watch for any activity on Anu's part. We dared not challenge his enclave's defenses with our single ship. I am—was—a missile specialist, Commander, and I know. Not even *Dahak* could crack his main shield without a saturation bombardment. We didn't have the firepower, and his automatics would have blown us out of existence before his stasis generators could even spin down to wake him."

"And so you just sat here," Colin said flatly, but his tone said he knew better. There were too many Terra-born in this compartment.

"No, Commander," Horus said, and his voice accepted the knowledge behind Colin's statement. "We've tried to fight him, over the millennia, but there was little we could do. It was obvious the threat of an evolving indigenous technology would be enough to spark Anu's intervention, and so our computers were set to wake us when local civilizations appeared. We interacted with the early civilizations of your Fertile Crescent—" he grinned wryly as Colin suddenly connected his own name with the Egyptian pantheon "—in an effort to temper their advance, but Anu was watching, as well. Several of our people were killed when he suddenly reappeared, and it was he who shaped the Sumerian and Babylonian cultures. It was he who led the Hsia Dynasty in the destruction of the neolithic cultural centers of China, and we who lent the Shang Dynasty clandestine aid to rebuild, and that was only one of the battles we fought.

"Yet we had to work secretly, hiding from him, effecting tiny changes, hoping for the best. Worse, there were but two hundred of us, and Anu had thousands. We couldn't rotate our personnel as he could—at least, that was what we thought he was doing—and we grew old far, far more quickly than he. But worst of all, Commander, was the attitude Anu's followers developed. They call your people 'degenerates,' did you know that?"

Colin nodded, remembering Girru's words in a chamber of horror that had once been a friend's study.

"They're wrong," Horus said harshly. "*They*'re the degenerates. Anu's madness has infected them all. His people are twisted, poisoned by their power. Perhaps they've played the roles of gods too long, for they've come to believe they *are* gods, and Earth's people are toys to be manipulated and enjoyed. It was horrible enough for the first four thousand years of interaction, but it's grown worse since. Where once they feared the rise of a technology that might threaten them, now they crave one that will let them escape the prison of this planet . . . and they couldn't care less how much suffering they inflict along the way. Indeed, they see that suffering as a spectacle, a gladiatorial slaughter to entertain them and while away the years.

"Let's be honest with one another, Commander MacIntyre. Humans, whether Imperials or born of your planet, are humans. There are good and bad among all of us, as our very presence here proves, and Earth's people would have inflicted sufficient suffering on themselves without Anu, but he and his have made it far, far worse. They've toppled civilizations by provoking and encouraging barbarian invasions—from the Hittites to the Hsia, the Achaeans, the Huns, the Vikings, and the Mongols—but even worse, in some ways, is what they've done since abandoning that policy. They helped fuel the Hundred Years' War, and the Thirty Years' War, and Europe's ruthless imperialism, both for enjoyment and to create power blocs that could pave the way for the scientific and industrial revolutions. And when progress wasn't rapid enough to suit them, they provoked the First World War, and the Second, and the Cold War.

"We've done what we could to mitigate their excesses, but our best efforts have been paltry. *They* haven't dared come into the open for fear that *Dahak* might remain sufficiently operational to strike at them—and, perhaps, because the sheer number of people on this planet frightens them—but they could always act more openly than we.

"Yet we've never given up, Commander MacIntyre!" The old man's voice was suddenly harsh, glittering with a strange fire, and Colin swallowed. That suddenly fiery tone was almost fanatical, and he shook free of Horus's story, making himself step back and wondering if perhaps his captors hadn't gone more than a bit mad themselves.

"No. We've never given up," Horus said more softly. "And if you'll let us, we'll prove that to you."

"How?" Colin's flat voice refused to offer any hope. Try though he might, it was hard to doubt Horus's sincerity. Yet it was his duty to doubt it. It was his responsibility—his, and his alone—to doubt everyone, question everything. Because if he made a mistake—*another* mistake, he thought bitterly—then all of Dahak's lonely wait would be in vain and the Achuultani would take them all.

"We'll help you against Anu," Horus said, his voice equally flat, his eyes level. "And afterward, we will surrender ourselves to the Imperium."

"*Nay!*" Jiltanith still pointed the suppresser at Colin, but her free hand rose like a claw, and her dark, vital face was fierce. "Now I say thee nay! Hast given too freely for this world, Father! Thou and all thy fellows!"

"Hush, 'Tanni," Horus said softly. He clasped the shoulders of the young woman—his daughter, which, Colin suddenly realized, made her Isis Tudor's *older* sister—and shook her very gently. "It's our decision. It's not even a matter for the Council, and you know it."

Jiltanith's tight face was furious with objection, and Horus sighed and gathered her close, staring into Colin's face over her shoulder.

"We ask only one thing in return, Commander," he said softly.

"What?" Colin asked quietly.

"Immunity—pardon, if you will—for those like 'Tanni." The girl stiffened in his arms, trying to thrust him away, but he held her easily with one arm. The other hand rose, covering her lips to still her furious protests.

"They were *children*, Commander, with no part in our crime, and many of them have died trying to undo it. Can even the Imperium punish them for that?"

The proud old face was pleading, the dark, ancient eyes almost desperate, and Colin recognized the justice of the plea.

"If—and I say *if*—you can convince me of your sincerity and ability to help," he said slowly, "I'll do my best. I can't promise any more than that."

"I know," Horus said. "But you *will* try?"

"I will," Colin replied levelly.

The old man regarded him a moment longer, then took the suppresser gently from Jiltanith. She fought him a moment, surrendering the device with manifest reluctance, and Horus hugged her gently. His eyes were understanding and sad, but a small smile played around his lips as he looked down at it.

"In that case," he said, "we'll just have to convince you. Please meet us half-way by not transmitting to *Dahak*, at least until we've finished talking."

And he switched off the suppresser.

For just an instant Colin sat absolutely motionless. The other Imperials on the command bridge were suddenly bright presences, glowing with their own implants, and he felt his computer feeds come on line. *Nergal's* computers were far brighter than those of the cutter that had returned him to Earth, and they recognized a bridge officer when they met one. After fifty millennia, they had someone to report to properly, and the surge of their data cores tingled in his brain like alien fire, feeding him information and begging for orders.

Colin's eyes met Horus's as he recognized the risk the old man had just taken, for no new security codes had been buried in *Nergal's* electronic brain. From the instant Colin's feeds tapped into those computers, they were his. *He*, not Horus, controlled the ancient battleship, external weapons and internal security systems alike.

But trust was a two-edged sword.

"I suppose that, as head of your council, you're also captain of this ship?" he said calmly, and the old man nodded.

"Then sit down, Captain, and tell me how we're going to beat Anu."

Horus nodded once more, sharply, and sat beside Isis. Colin never glanced away from his new ally's face, but he didn't have to; he could *feel* the gathered council's tension draining away about him.

CHAPTER ELEVEN

Colin leaned back and propped his heels on his desk. The quarters the mutineers (if that was still the proper word) had assigned him were another attempt to prove their sincerity, for this was the captain's cabin, fitted with neural relays to the old battleship's computers. He could not keep them from retaking *Nergal*, but, like the millennia-dead Druaga, he could insure that they would recapture only a hulk.

Which, Colin thought, was shrewd of Horus, whether he was truly sincere or not.

He sighed and pinched the bridge of his nose, wishing desperately that he could contact Dahak, yet he dared not. He knew where he was now—buried five kilometers under the Canadian Rockies near Churchill Peak—but the recent clash had roused Anu's vengeful search for *Nergal* to renewed heights, and if the southerners should detect Colin's com link, their missiles would arrive before even *Dahak* could do anything to stop them.

The same applied to any effort to reach *Dahak* physically. He was lucky he hadn't been spotted on the way in, despite his cutter's stealth systems; now that the marooned Imperials' long, hidden conflict had heated back up, there was no way anything of Imperial manufacture could head *out* of the planetary atmosphere without being spotted and killed.

It was maddening. He'd acquired a support team just as determined to destroy Anu as he was, yet it was pathetically weak compared to its enemies and there was no way to inform Dahak it even existed! Worse, Anshar's energy gun had reduced the suppresser to wreckage, and *Nergal's* repair facilities were barely sufficient to run diagnostics on what remained, much less fix it.

Colin was deeply impressed by what the northerners had achieved over the centuries, but very little of what he'd found in *Nergal's* memory had been good, aside from the confirmation that Horus had told him the truth about what had happened after he and his fellows boarded *Nergal*.

The old battleship's memory was long overdue for purging, for *Nergal's* builders had designed her core programming to insure that accurate combat reports came back to her mothership. No one could alter that data in any way until *Nergal's* master computer dumped a complete copy into Dahak's data base.

For fifty thousand years, the faithful, moronic genius had carefully logged everything as it happened, and while molecular memories could store an awesome amount of data, there was so much in *Nergal's* that just finding it was frustratingly slow. Yet that crowded memory gave him a record that was accurate, unalterable, and readily—if not quickly—available.

There was, of course, far too much data for any human mind to assimilate, but he could skim the high points, and it had been hard to maintain his nonexpression as he did. If anything, Horus had understated the war he and his fellows had fought. Direct clashes were infrequent, but there had been only two hundred and three adult northerners at the start, and age, as well as casualties, had winnowed their ranks. Fewer than seventy of them remained.

He and Horus had lingered, conferring with one another and the computers through their feeds while the rest of the Council went on about their duties. Only Horus's daughters had stayed.

Isis had interjected only an occasional word as she tried to follow their half-spoken, half-silent conversation, but Jiltanith had been a silent, sullen presence in their link. She'd neither offered nor asked anything, but her cold, bitter loathing for all he was had appalled Colin.

He'd never realized emotions could color the link, perhaps because his only previous use of it had been with Dahak, without the side-band elements involved when human met human through an electronic intermediary. Or perhaps it was simply that her bitter emotions were so strong. He'd wondered why Horus didn't ask her to withdraw, but then, he had many questions about Jiltanith and her place in the small, strange community he'd never suspected might exist.

It was fortunate Horus had been able to meet him in the computers. Some vocalization was necessary to set data in context, but the old mutineer had led him unerringly through the data banks, and his memory went back, replaying that first afternoon as if it were today. . . .

"All right," Colin sighed finally, rubbing his temples wearily. "I don't know about you folks, but I need a break before my brain fries."

Horus nodded understandingly; Jiltanith only sniffed, and Colin suppressed an urge to snap at her.

"I've got to say, this Anu is an even nastier bastard than I expected," he went on, his voice hardening with the change of subject. "I'd wondered how he could ride herd on all his faithful followers, but I never expected *this*."

"I know," Horus looked down at the backs of his powerful, age-spotted hands. "But it makes sense, in a gruesome sort of way. After all, unlike us, he does have an intact medical capability."

"But to use it like *that*," Colin said, and his shudder was not at all affected, for "gruesome" was a terribly pale word for what Anu had done. Dahak hadn't suggested such things were possible, but Colin supposed he should have known they were.

Anu's problem had been two-fold. First, how did he and his inner circle—no more than eight hundred strong—control five thousand Imperials who would, for the most part, be as horrified as Horus to learn the truth about their leader? And, secondly, how could even fully-enhanced Imperials oversee the manipulation of an entire planet without withering away from old age before they could create the technology they needed to escape it?

The medical science of the Imperium had provided a psychopathically elegant solution to both problems at once. The "unreliable" elements were simply never reawakened, and while stasis also allowed the mutineer leaders to sleep away centuries at need, Anu and his senior lieutenants had been awake a long time. By now, Horus calculated, Anu was on his tenth replacement body.

Imperial science had mastered the techniques of cloning to provide surgical transplants before the advent of reliable regeneration, but that had been so long ago cloning was almost a lost art. Only the most comprehensive medical centers retained the capability for certain carefully-delimited, individually-licensed experimental programs, and the use even of clones for *this* purpose was punishable by death for all concerned. Yet heinous as that would have been in the eyes of the Imperium's intricate, iron-bound code of bioscience morality, what Anu had actually done was worse. When old age overtook him, he simply selected a candidate from among the mutineers in stasis and had its brain removed for his own to displace. As long as his supply of bodies held out, he was effectively immortal.

The same was true of his lieutenants, but while only Imperial bodies were good enough for Anu and Inanna and their most trusted henchmen, others—like Anshar—were forced to make do with Terra-born bodies. There was a greater danger of tissue rejection in that, but there were compensations. The range of choices was vast, and Inanna's medical technology, though limited compared to *Dahak*'s, was quite capable of basic enhancement of Terra-born bodies.

Colin returned to the present with a shudder. Even now, thinking about it sent a physical shiver down his spine. It horrified him almost as much as the approaching Achuultani horrified Horus. Desperation had blazed in the old Imperial's eyes when he learned the enemy he'd never quite believed in was actually coming, but Colin had been given months to adjust to that. This was different. The victims' tragedy was one he could grasp, not a galactic one, and that made it something he could relate to . . . and hate.

And perhaps, as Horus had suggested, it also helped to explain why Anu continued to operate so clandestinely. His followers had gone trustingly into stasis and were unable to resist his depredations, but there were simply too many Terrans to be readily controlled, and Colin doubted Earth's humanity would react calmly to the knowledge that high-tech vampires were harvesting them.

Yet Anu's ghastly perversions only emphasized the huge difference between his capabilities and those of his northern opponents. *Nergal* was a warship. Thirty percent of her impressive tonnage was committed to propulsion and power, ten percent to command and control systems, another ten percent to defensive systems, and forty percent to armor, offensive weaponry, and magazine space. That left only ten percent to accommodate her three-hundred-man crew and its life support, which meant even living space was cramped.

That mattered little under normal circumstances, for she was designed for short-term deployments—certainly no more than a few months at a time. She didn't even have a proper stasis installation; her people had been forced to cobble one up, and their success was a far-from-minor miracle. But because her intended deployments were so short, *Nergal*'s sickbay was limited. Anu and his butchers could select Terra-born bodies and convert them to their own use; the northerners couldn't even offer implants to their own Terra-born descendants.

Yet they'd had no choice but to have those descendants, for without them they would have failed long ago from sheer lack of numbers.

It had been a bitter decision, though Horus had tried to hide his pain from Colin. Horus had lived over five centuries and Isis less than one, yet his daughter was old and frail while he remained strong. Colin could have consulted the record to learn how many other children Horus had loved as he all too obviously loved Isis yet seen wither and die, but he hadn't. That unimaginable sorrow was Horus's alone, and he would not intrude upon it.

Yet it was possible the situation was even worse for the ones like Jiltanith, whose bodies were neither Imperial nor Terran. Jiltanith had received the neural boosters, computer and sensory implants, and regeneration treatments, but her muscles and bones and organs had been too immature for enhancement before the mutiny. Which might go a long way towards explaining her bitter resentment. He, a Terra-born human who had grown to adulthood in blissful ignorance of the battle being waged upon his planet, had received the full treatment. She hadn't. And unless the people she loved surrendered to the Imperium's justice, she never could have it.

Colin knew there was more to her hate than that, though he had yet to discover its full range, but understanding that much helped him cope with her bitterness.

Unfortunately, there was little he could do about it, nor did he know how the legal situation would be resolved—assuming, of course, that they won. Somehow, he'd never considered the possibility of children among the mutineers, and Dahak had never mentioned them to him.

That was a bad sign, and not one he was prepared to share with his allies. To Dahak, anyone who had accompanied Anu in his flight to Earth was a mutineer. That fundamental assumption infused everything the computer had ever said, and no distinction had ever been drawn between child and adult, but Colin had meant what he promised. If the northerners helped him against Anu, he would do what he could for their children. And, though he hadn't promised it, for them . . . if he ever got the chance to try.

He leaned further back and crossed his ankles. If there were only more time! Time for Anu's present furious search to die down, for him to return to *Dahak*, to act on the information he'd received and plan anew. That was what Horus had hoped for, but the Achuultani were coming.

Whatever they meant to do, they must do it soon, and the sober truth was
that the odds were hopeless.

The northerners undoubtedly had the edge in sheer numbers, at least
over the southerners Anu would trust out of stasis, but only sixty-seven
of their people were full Imperials, and all of them were old. Another eighteen were like Jiltanith, capable of getting full performance out of Imperial
equipment, but utterly outclassed in any one-to-one confrontation. The
three thousand-odd Terra-born members of *Nergal*'s "crew" would be at
a hopeless disadvantage with their pathetic touchpads and telephones if
they had to fight people who could link their minds directly into their
weapons. They couldn't even manage combat armor, for they lacked the
implants to activate the internal circuitry.

And, of course, they had the resources of exactly one battleship. One
battleship against seven—not to mention the heavy cruisers, the fixed ground
weapons, and Anu's powerful shield. From a practical viewpoint, he might
as well have been alone if it came to confronting the southerners openly.

But there were a few good points. For one, the northerners' intelligence
system had been in operation for millennia, and an extended network of
Terra-born contacts like Sandy supported their guerrilla-like campaign.
They'd even managed to establish clandestine contact with two of Anu's
"loyal" henchmen. It would be foolhardy to trust those communications
too much, and they were handled with extraordinary care to avoid any
traps, but they explained how the northerners knew so much about events
in the southern enclave.

He opened his eyes and stood. His thoughts were racing in ever narrowing
circles, and he felt as if they were about to implode. He needed to spend
some more time talking to Horus in hopes some inspiration might break
itself loose.

God knew they needed one.

He looked for Horus, but the chief northerner wasn't aboard. Colin was
acutely uneasy whenever Horus—or *any* of the Imperials—left the protection of *Nergal*'s stealth systems, but the northerners seemed to take it in
stride. Of course, they'd had quite a while longer to accustom themselves
to such risks.

And it was inevitable that they run them, for they couldn't possibly gather
their full numbers aboard the battleship. Many of the Terra-born had gone
to ground when Cal's family was killed, but others went on about their
everyday lives with a courage that humbled Colin, and that meant the Imperials had to leave *Nergal* occasionally, for only they could operate the
battleship's stealthed auxiliaries. It was dangerous to use them, even flying
nape-of-the-earth courses fit to terrify a hardened rotor-jockey, but they had
too few security coms to tie their network together without them. Colin wished
Horus would leave such risks to others, but he'd come to understand the old
man too well to suggest it.

For all that, he bit his tongue against a groan of resignation when he
entered the command bridge and found not Horus but his daughters.

Jiltanith stood as he entered, bristling with the instant hostility his presence always evoked, but Isis managed a smile of greeting. Colin glanced covertly at Jiltanith's lovely face and considered the virtues of a discreet retreat, yet that would be unwise in the long run. So he seated himself deliberately in the captain's chair and met her hot eyes levelly.

"Good afternoon, ladies. I was looking for your father."

"Shalt not find him here," Jiltanith said pointedly. He ignored the hint, and she glared at him. If she'd truly been the cat she resembled, she would be lashing her tail and flexing her claws, he thought.

" 'Tanni," Isis said quietly, but Jiltanith gave an angry little headshake and stalked out. Isis watched her go and sighed.

"That girl!" she said resignedly, then smiled wryly at Colin. "I'm afraid she's taking it badly, Commander."

"Please," he smiled himself, a bit sadly, "after all that's happened, I wish you'd call me Colin."

"Of course. Colin."

"I . . . haven't had a chance to tell you how sorry I am." She raised a hand, but he shook his head. "No. It's kind of you, and I don't want to hurt you by talking about it, but I need to say it." Her hand fell to her lap, folding about its fellow, and she lowered her eyes to her thin fingers.

"Cal was my friend," he said softly, "and I rushed in, flashing around Imperial technology like some new toy, and got his entire family killed. I know I couldn't have known what I was doing, but that doesn't change the facts. He's dead, and I'm responsible."

"If you want to put it that way," Isis said gently, "but he and Frances knew the risks. If that sounds callous it isn't meant to, but it's true. I raised him after his parents died, and I loved him, just as I loved my granddaughter-in-law and my great-granddaughters, but we always knew it could happen. Just as Andy knew when he married me." She looked up with a misty smile, her lined face creased with memories, and Colin swallowed.

"There's something I don't quite understand," he said after a moment. "How could your father produce the work he produced as Horace Hidachi and still take the risk of having children? And why did he do it at all?"

"Have a child or produce the work?" Isis asked with a chuckle, and Colin felt some of their shared sorrow fall from his shoulders.

"Both," he said.

"It was a risk," she concluded, "but the fact that 'Hidachi' was Oriental helped cover his appearance—we've always found that useful, though the emergence of the Asian Alliance has complicated things lately—and he chose his time and place carefully. Clemson University is a fine school, one of the top four tech schools in the country, but that's a fairly recent development. It wasn't exactly on the frontiers of physics at the time, and he published in the most obscure journal he could find. And there were some deliberate errors in his work, you know. All that, plus the fact that he never went further than pure theory, was intended to convince any of Anu's people who noticed it that he was a Terran who didn't even realize the significance of his own work.

"As for having me," she smiled more naturally, "that was an accident. Mom was his eighth wife—'Tanni's mother died during the mutiny—and, frankly, she thought she was too old to conceive and got a bit careless. When they found out she was pregnant, it scared them, but they never considered an abortion, for which *I* can only be grateful." She grinned, and her eyes sparkled for the first time Colin could remember.

"But it was a problem. As a rule, none of our Imperials interact openly with the Terran community, and on the rare occasions when they do, they appear and disappear without a trace. They almost always act solo, as well, which meant he and Mom had already stepped totally out of character. That very fact was a form of protection for them, and they decided to add me to it and hope for the best. And it helped that Mom was Terra-born, blonde, and a little, bitty thing. She and I both looked very little like Imperials."

Colin nodded. No one in his right mind would offer his family up for massacre; hence the presence of a family was a strong indication that "Horace Hidachi" was not an Imperial at all. It made a dangerous sort of sense, but he shivered at the thought, and wished he might have had the chance to meet the quite extraordinary "little, bitty" woman who had been Isis's mother.

"Still," Isis went on sadly, "we knew they'd keep an eye on 'Hidachi's' family. That's why I went into medicine and Michael was a stockbroker. We both stayed as far away from physics as we could, but Cal was too much like his great-granddad. He was determined to play an active part."

"I still don't understand *why*, though. Why risk so much to plant a theory the mutin—" Colin broke off and flushed, and Isis gave a soft, musical laugh.

"Sorry," he said after a moment. "I meant, why risk so much to plant a theory that Anu's bunch already knew?"

"Why, Colin!" Isis rolled her eyes almost roguishly. "Here you sit, precisely because that theory was made available to the space program. If the southerners hadn't followed up, we would've had to push it ourselves, sooner or later, because we needed for your survey instruments to be developed. Of course, Dad and Mom were pretty confident 'Anu's bunch,' as you put it, would pursue it once they noticed it—the 'Hidachi Theory of Gravitonics' *is* the foundation of the Imperial sublight and Enchanach Drives, after all— but we couldn't be certain. One reason we wanted them to believe a 'degenerate' had set the stage for it was to be sure *they* produced the hardware rather than opposing its development, because the entire point was to do exactly what we did: provoke a reaction from *Dahak*, one way or the other."

"Provoke *Dahak*?" Colin pinched his nose. "Wasn't that a bit, um, risky?"

"Of course it was, but our Imperials are getting old, Colin. When they go, the rest of us will carry on as best we can, but our position will be even more hopeless. The Council had no idea *Dahak* was fully functional, but we were already placing a lot of our people in the space program, like Sandy and Cal. Besides, if the human race generally knew what was up there, functional or not, Anu's position would be far more tenuous."

"Why?"

"We never contemplated what *Dahak* actually did, Colin, but *something* had to happen. Anu might try to take over any exploration of the ship, but we were prepared to fight him—clandestinely, but rather effectively—unless he came into the open. And if he *had* come out into the open, don't you think he'd've needed more than just his inner circle to control the resulting chaos?"

"Oh! You figured if he risked waking the others and they discovered all he'd been up to, he might get hit from behind by a revolt."

"Exactly. Oh, it was a terrible chance to take, but as I say, we were getting desperate. At the very least, it might be a way to add a new factor to the equation. Then too, we've always had a *lot* of people in the space program. It was possible—even probable—that if the ship was partially functional one of our own Terra-born might have gotten inside. Frankly—" she met his gaze levelly "—we'd hoped Vlad Chernikov would fly your mission."

"*Vlad?* Don't tell me *he's* one of yours!"

"Not if you'd rather I didn't," she said, and he laughed helplessly. It was his first laughter since Sean's death, and he was amazed by how much it helped.

"Well, I will be damned," he said at last, then cocked an eyebrow. "But isn't it also a bit risky to plant so many people in the very area where Anu is pushing hardest?"

"Colin, everything we've ever *done* has been a risk. Of course we took chances—terrible ones, sometimes—but Anu's own control is pretty indirect. Both sides know a great deal about what the other is up to—we more than him, we hope—but he can't afford to go around killing everyone he simply suspects."

She paused, and her voice was grimmer when she continued.

"Still, he's killed a lot on suspicion. 'Accidents' are his favorite method, but remember that shuttle Black Mecca shot down?" Colin nodded, and she shrugged. "That was Anu. It amuses him to use 'degenerate' terrorists to do his dirty work, and their fanaticism makes them easy to influence. Major Lemoine was aboard that shuttle, and he was one of ours. We don't know how Anu got on to him, but that's why so much terrorism's focused on aerospace lately. In fact, Black Mecca's claimed credit for what happened to Cal and the girls."

"Lord." Colin shook his head and leaned forward, bracing his elbows on the console and propping his chin on his palms. "All this time, and no one ever suspected. It's hard to believe."

"There've been a few times we thought it was all over," Isis said. "Once we even thought they'd actually found *Nergal*. In fact, that's why Jiltanith was ever brought out of stasis at all."

"Hm? Oh! Getting the kids out just in case?"

"Precisely. That was about six hundred years ago, and it was the worst scare we ever had. The Council had recruited quite a few Terra-born even then—and you'd better believe *they* had trouble adjusting to the whole idea!—and some of them took the children and scattered out across the planet. Which also explains 'Tanni's English; she learned it during the Wars of the Roses."

"I see." Colin drew a deep breath and held it for just a moment.

Somehow the thought of that beautiful girl having grown up in fifteenth-century England was more sobering than anything else that had happened so far.

"Isis," he said finally, "how old *is* Jiltanith? Out of stasis, I mean."

"A bit older than me." His face betrayed his shock, and she smiled gently. "We Terra-born have learned to live with it, Colin. Actually, I don't know who it's harder on, us or our Imperials. But 'Tanni went back into stasis when she was twenty and came back out while Dad was still being Hidachi."

"She doesn't like me much, does she?" Colin said glumly.

"She's a very unhappy girl," Isis said, then laughed softly. "Girl! She's older than I am, but I still think of her that way. And she *is* only a girl as far as the Imperials are concerned. She's the 'youngest' of them all, and that's always been hard on her. She fought Dad when he sent her back into stasis because she wants to *do* something, Colin. She feels cheated, and I can't really blame her. It's not her fault she's stuck here, and there's a conflict in her own mind. She loves Dad, but his actions during the mutiny are what did all this to her, and remember her mother was actually killed during the fighting." She shook her head sadly.

"Poor 'Tanni's never had a normal life. Those fourteen years she spent in England were the closest she ever came, and even then her foster parents had to keep her under virtual house arrest, given that her appearance wasn't exactly European. I think that's why she refuses to speak modern English.

"But you're right about how she feels about you. I'm afraid she blames you for what happened to Cal's family . . . and especially the girls. She was very close to Harriet, especially." Isis's mouth drooped, but she blinked back the threatened tears and continued.

"She knows, intellectually, that you couldn't have known what would happen. She even knows you killed the people who killed them, and none of us exactly believe in turning the other cheek. But the fact that you were ultimately responsible ties in with the fact that you've not only effectively supplanted Dad after he's fought for so long, but that you're an active threat to him, as well. Even if we succeed, Dad faces charges because whatever he's done since, he *was* a mutineer. And, frankly, she resents you."

"Because I've moved in on your operation?" he asked gently. "Or for another reason, as well?"

"Of course there's another reason, and I see you know what it is. But can you blame her? Can't you see it from her side? You're the commanding officer of *Dahak*, a starship that's like a dream to all of us Terra-born, a combination of heaven and hell. But it's a dream whose decks 'Tanni actually walked . . . and lost for something *she* never did. She's spent her entire adult life fighting to undo the wrong others did, and now you, simply by virtue of being the first Terra-born human to enter the ship, have become not just a crew member, but its *commander*. Why should you have that and not her? Why should you have a complete set of implants—a bridge officer's, no less—while she has only bits and pieces?"

Isis fell silent, studying his face as if looking for something, then nodded slightly.

"But worst of all, Colin, she's a fighter. She wouldn't stand a chance hand to hand against an Imperial, and she knows it, but she's a fighter. She's spent her life in the shadows, fighting other shadows, always indirectly, protected by Dad and the others because she's weaker than they are, unable to fight her enemies face to face. Surely you understand how much that hurts?"

"I do," Colin said softly. "I do," he said more firmly, "and I'll bear it in mind, but we all have to fight Anu, Isis. I can't have her fighting *me*."

"I don't think she will." Isis paused again, frowning. "I don't *think* she will, but she's not feeling exactly . . . reasonable, just now."

"I know. But if she *does* fight me, it could ruin everything. Too much depends not only on smashing Anu but finding a way to stop the Achuultani. If she can't work with me, I certainly can't let her work against me."

"What . . . what will you do?" Isis asked softly.

"I won't hurt her, if that's what you're afraid of. She's given too much—all of you have—for that. But if she threatens what we're trying to do now, I won't have any choice but to put her back into stasis."

"No! Please!" Isis gripped his arm tightly. "That . . . that would be almost worse than killing her, Colin!"

"I know," he said gently. "I know what it would do to me, and I don't want to. Before God, I don't want to. But if she fights me, I won't have a choice. Try to make her understand that, Isis. She may take it better from you than from me."

The old woman looked at him with tear-bright eyes and her lips trembled, but she nodded slowly and patted his arm.

"I understand, Colin," she said very softly. "I'll talk to her. And I understand. I wish I didn't, but I do."

"Thank you, Isis," he said quietly. He met her eyes a moment longer, then squeezed the hand on his arm very gently and rose. An obscure impulse touched him, and he bent to kiss her parchment cheek.

"Thank you," he said again, and left the command deck.

CHAPTER TWELVE

"Colin?"

Colin looked up in sudden relief as Horus stuck his head in through his cabin door. The old man had been more than two hours overdue the last time Colin checked with *Nergal*'s operations room.

"About time you got back," he said, and Horus nodded and gripped his hand, but his smile was odd, half-way between apology and a sort of triumph.

"Sorry," Horus said. "I got tied up talking to one of our people. He's got a suggestion so interesting I brought him back with me."

The old Imperial gestured to the tall man behind him, and Colin glanced at the newcomer, taking in the hard-trained body and salt-and-pepper temples. The stranger's nose was almost as prominent as Colin's, but on him it looked good. He also wore the uniform of the United States Marine Corps and a full colonel's eagles, but the flash on his right shoulder bore the crossed daggers and parachute of the Unified Special Forces Command.

Colin's right eyebrow rose as he waved his guests to chairs. The USFC was the elite of the elite, its members recruited from all branches of the service and trained for "selective warfare"—the old "low-intensity conflict" of the last century—and counter-terrorism. Labels meant little to Colin. Insurgent, terrorist, guerrilla, or patriot. As far as he was concerned, anyone who chose violence against the helpless as his means of protest deserved the same label: barbarian, and the USFC was the United States' answer to the barbarians.

Like their ConEuropean, Australian-Japanese, and Russian counterparts, the men and women of the USFC were as adept at infiltration, information-gathering, and covert warfare as they were with the conventional weapons of the soldier's trade. Unlike the rest of the US military, they were an integral part of the intelligence community, as much policemen and spies (and some, Colin knew, would add "assassins") as soldiers. Not that it kept them from being elite troops. USFC personnel were chosen only after proving themselves—thoroughly—in their regular arms of service.

"Colin, this is Hector MacMahan. In addition to his duties for the USFC, he's also the head of our Terra-born intelligence network."

"Colonel," Colin said courteously, extending his hand again and reading the four rows of ribbons under the parachutist and pilot's wings—both rotary wing and fixed. And the crossed dagger and assault rifle of the USFC's close combat medal. Impressive, he thought. *Very* impressive.

"Commander," MacMahan said. Then he grinned—slightly; his was not a face that lent itself to effusive expressions. "Or should I say 'Fleet Captain'?"

"Commander will do just fine, Colonel. That, or Colin." His guests sat, and Colin moved to the small bar in the corner as he looked back and forth between them. "You do seem to recruit only the best, Horus," he murmured.

"Thank you," Horus said with a smile. "In more ways than one. Hector is my great-great-great-great-great-grandson."

"I prefer," the colonel said without a trace of a smile, "to think of myself as simply your great*est* grandson."

Colin chuckled and shook his head.

"I'm still getting used to all this, Colonel, but I was referring to your military credentials, not your familial ones." He finished mixing drinks and moved out from behind the bar. "I'm impressed. And if your suggestion was interesting enough for Horus to bring you back with him, I'm eager to hear it."

"Of course. You see—thank you." MacMahan took the drink Colin extended, sipped politely once, then proceeded to ignore it. Colin sat back down in his swivel chair and gestured for him to continue.

"You see," the colonel began again, "I've been giving our situation a lot of thought. In my own humble way, I'm as much a specialist as any of you rocket jockeys, and I've nourished a few rather worrisome suspicions of late."

"Suspicions?" Colin asked, his eyes suddenly intent.

"Yes, Com—Colin. I'm in a unique position to study the terrorist mentality, and I've also had the advantage of Granddad's input and *Nergal*'s surveillance reports. That's one reason I'm a colonel. My superiors don't know about my other sources, and they think I'm a mighty savvy analyst."

Colin nodded. The northerners' intelligence network—especially the old battleship's carefully stealthed sensor arrays—would be tremendously helpful in MacMahan's line of work, but the ribbons on his chest told Colin the colonel's superiors were right about his native abilities, as well.

"The point is, Colin, that Anu's people have been digging deeper and deeper into the terrorist organizations. By now, they effectively control Black Mecca, the January Twelfth Group, the Army of Allah, the Red Eyebrows, and a dozen other major and minor outfits. That's ominous enough, if not too surprising—they've always been right at home with butchers like that—but what bothers me are certain common ideological (if I may be permitted the term) threads that have crept into the policies of the groups they control.

"You see," he furrowed his forehead, "these are some pretty unlikely soulmates. Black Mecca and the Army of Allah hate each other even more than they hate the rest of the world. Black Mecca wants to de-stabilize both the Islamic and non-Islamic worlds to such an extent their radical fundamentalists can establish a world-wide theocratic state, while the Army of Allah attacks non-Islamic targets primarily as a means of forcing an unbridgeable split between Islamics and non-Islamics. They don't *want* the rest of us; they're a bunch of isolationists who want to shut everyone else out while they attend to *their* concept of religious purity. Then there's the Red Eyebrows. *They* grew out of the old punker/skinhead groups of the late nineties, and they're just plain anarchists. They—"

MacMahan stopped himself and waved a hand.

"I get carried away sometimes, and the etiology of terrorism can wait. My point is that all these different outfits share a growing, *common* interest in what I can only call nihilism, and I don't think there's much doubt it stems from Anu's input. His goals are becoming, whether they know it or not, their goals, and what's scary about that is what it says about his own mind set."

The colonel seemed to remember his drink and took another sip, then stared down into it for several seconds, swirling the ice cubes.

"My outfit's always had to try to think like the enemy, and I have to admit it can be almost enjoyable. I hate the bastards, but it's almost like a game— like chess or bridge, in a way—except that I haven't been enjoying it much of late. Because there's a question that's been bothering me for the last few years, and especially since Horus told me about you and *Dahak*: just how will Anu react if he decides we can beat him? For that matter, how would he react to simply knowing that *Dahak* is fully operational?

"And the reason that bothers me is that I think Horus is right about him. I think the nihilism of his terrorist toadies reflects his own nihilism and that if he ever decides his position is hopeless—which it is, whatever happens to us, if *Dahak*'s out there—he might *enjoy* taking the whole planet with him."

Colin kept his body relaxed and nodded slowly, but a cold wind seemed to have invaded the cabin.

"It makes sense, Colin," Horus said quietly. "Hector's right about his nihilism. Whatever he was once like, Anu *likes* destruction now. It's almost as if it relieves his frustration, and it's probably part of his whole addiction to power, as well. But whatever causes it, it's real enough. He and his people certainly proved that a hundred years ago."

Colin nodded again, understanding completely. He'd occasionally wondered why Hitler had proved so resistant to assassination—until he gained access to *Nergal*'s data base. No wonder the bomb plot had failed; a man with full enhancement would hardly even have noticed it. And if anyone had ever shown a maniacal glee in taking others down with them, it had been the Nazi elite.

"So." He twirled his chair slowly. "It seems another minor complication has been added." His smile held no humor. "But from the fact that you're here, Colonel, I imagine you've been doing more than just worrying?"

"I have." The colonel drew a deep breath and met Colin's eyes levelly.

"A man in my profession doesn't have much use for do-or-die missions, but I've spent the last year building a worst-case scenario—a doomsday one, if you will—and trying to find a way to beat it, and I may have come up with one. It's scary as hell, and I've always seen it more as a last-ditch contingency than anything I'd *want* to try. In fact, I wouldn't even mention it except for what you've told us about the Achuultani. The smart thing would be to wait till things settle down a bit, get you back up to *Dahak*, and then hit the bastards from two directions at once—or at least get another suppresser down here. But we don't have time to play it smart, do we?"

"No, we don't," Colin said, his tone calm but flat. "So may I assume you're about to tell me about this 'way to beat it' you've come up with?"

"Yes. Instead of waiting for things to cool down, we heat them up."

"Hm?" Colin leaned slowly back, his chair squeaking softly, and tugged at his nose. "And why should we do that, Colonel?"

"Because maybe—just maybe—we can take them out ourselves, without calling on *Dahak* at all," the colonel said.

No one, Colin reflected as he watched the Council file into the command deck, could accuse Hector MacMahan of thinking small. Merely to consider attacking such a powerful enemy took a lot of audacity, but it seemed the colonel had *chutzpah* by the truckload. And who knew? It might just work.

The council settled into their places in tense silence, and he tucked his hands behind him and squared his shoulders, feeling their eyes and wondering just how deep his rapport with them truly went. They'd had barely a month to get to know one another, and he knew some of them both resented and feared him. He couldn't blame them for that; *he* still had reservations about *them*, though he no longer doubted their sincerity. Not even Jiltanith's.

Thoughts of the young woman drew his eyes, and he hid a smile as he realized he, too, had come to think of her as "young" despite the fact that she was more than twice his age. Much more, if he counted the time she'd spent in stasis. But his smile died stillborn as he saw her expression. She'd finally managed to push the active hatred out of her face, but it remained a shuttered window, neither offering nor accepting a thing.

In many ways, he would have preferred to exclude her from this meeting and from *all* decision-making, but it hadn't worked out that way. She was young, but she was also *Nergal*'s chief intelligence officer, which officially made her MacMahan's Imperial counterpart and, indirectly, his boss.

Colin wouldn't have considered someone with her fiery, driven disposition an ideal spy master, but when he hinted as much to one or two council members, their reactions had surprised him. Their absolute faith in her judgment was almost scary, especially since he knew how much she detested him. Yet when he'd checked the log, her performance certainly seemed to justify their high regard. The Colorado Springs attack was the first time in forty years that the southern Imperials (as distinct from their Terra-born proxies) had surprised the northerners, and he knew whose fault that had been. Given the way the Council felt about her, he dared not try removing her from her position. Besides, his own stubborn integrity wouldn't let him fire someone who did her job so well simply because she happened to hate him.

But she worried him. No matter what anyone else said or thought about her, she worried him.

He sighed, wishing she would open up just once. Just once, so he could *know* what she was thinking and whether or not he could trust her. Then he pushed the thought aside and smiled tightly at the rest of the Council.

"I'm sure you all know Colonel MacMahan far better than I do." He gestured at the colonel and watched the exchange of nods and smiles, then put his hand back behind him. "The reason he's here just now, though, may surprise you. You see, he proposes that we attack Anu directly—without *Dahak*."

One or two members of his audience gasped, and Jiltanith seemed to gather herself like a cat. She never actually moved a muscle, but her eyes widened slightly and he thought he saw a glow in their dark depths.

"But that's crazy!" It was Sarah Meir, *Nergal*'s Terra-born astrogator. Then she blushed and glanced at MacMahan. "Or, at least, it *sounds* that way."

"I agree, but that's one of the beauties of it. It's so crazy they'll never expect it." That got a small chorus of chuckles, and Colin permitted himself a wider grin. "And crazy or not, we don't really have much choice. We've been sitting on dead center ever since my . . . arrival—" that provoked a louder ripple of laughter "—and we can't afford that. You all know why."

Their levity vanished, and one or two actually glanced upward, as if to see the stars beyond which the Achuultani swept inexorably closer. He nodded.

"Exactly. But the thing that surprised me most is that it might just work." He turned to MacMahan. "Hector?"

"Thank you, Colin." MacMahan stood in the center of the command deck, his erect figure and Marine uniform as out of place and yet inevitable as Colin's own Fleet blue, and met their intent eyes levelly, a man who was clearly accustomed to such scrutiny.

"In essence," he said, "the problem is time. Time we need and haven't got. But we do have one major advantage: Anu doesn't *know* we're on a short count. It's obvious he thought Colin was one of us when he hit the Tudors—" Colin saw Jiltanith twitch at that, but she had herself well under control . . . for her "—so it seems extremely unlikely he realizes a genuinely new element has been added. He'll evaluate whatever we do against a background that, so far as he knows, is unchanged."

He paused, and several heads nodded in agreement.

"Now, we all know we hurt them badly at Colorado Springs." There was a soft growl of agreement, and he rationed himself to one of his minute smiles. "We've confirmed seventeen hard kills, and two more probables— more damage than we've done in centuries. They must be wondering what happened and, hopefully, feeling a bit on the defensive. Certainly that ties in with the efforts they've been making to find us ever since.

"At present, they no doubt see the entire skirmish as exactly what it was: a defensive action on our part, but what I propose is that we convince them it was an *offensive* act. I propose that we attack them—hit them everywhere we can—hard enough to convince them we've opened a general offensive. It'll be risky, but no more so than some of the things we've done in the past."

"Wait a minute, Hector." The colonel paused as Geb, one of the older Imperials and *Nergal*'s senior engineer, raised a hand. "There's nothing I'd like better than a shot at them, but how will it help?"

"A fair question," MacMahan acknowledged, "and I'll try to answer it, Geb. It may sound a bit complicated, but the underlying concept is simple.

"First, some of their people are actually more vulnerable than we are. They've always been more involved in world affairs than we have, and we've been able to identify more of them than they have of us. We know where several of their Imperials are, and we've got positive IDs on quite a few of their Terra-born. More than that, we've identified the terrorist groups they're currently working through and positively located several operational centers and HQs. What that all boils down to is that even though the bulk of their personnel are far better protected than we are, the ones who are actually outside the enclave are more exposed. We can get to them more readily than they can get to us."

He looked around his audience and nodded, satisfied with the intent expressions looking back at him.

"What I propose is an organized assault on their exposed points in order to make them react the way they always have when things got hot—by pulling their Imperials and important Terra-born into the enclave to protect them while their hard teams try to trap and destroy our attack forces.

"*But*," he said softly, "this time that will be the worst thing they could possibly do. *This* time, they'll let us through the door right behind them!"

For a man with an inexpressive face, Colin thought, Hector MacMahan could look remarkably like a hungry wolf.

"How so?" Jiltanith's voice was flat. She had herself under the tight control Colin's presence always provoked, but she was asking a question, not raising an objection, and it was clear she spoke for many of the others.

"As I say, the background maneuvers've been a bit complicated," MacMahan replied, "but the operational concept itself is simple, and my own position as the CO of Operation Odysseus is what may just make it work." Jiltanith nodded tightly, and he glanced at the other council members.

"As 'Tanni knows," he continued, "I was placed in command of Operation Odysseus, a USFC operation to infiltrate Black Mecca, two years ago. The brass knew it wouldn't be easy, and we've had too many leaks over the years to make them happy. We, of course, know why that is: Anu hasn't been too successful in infiltrating USFC, but he's penetrated the senior echelons of the intelligence community deeply. But because of those leaks, the whole operation was made strictly need-to-know, and *I* determined who needed to know. Which means I was able to put two of our own Terra-born inside Black Mecca. One of them, in fact, is a deputy commander of their central action branch. *And,* people, he's on the 'inside' in more ways than one. He's established as a valuable, corruptible mercenary, and Anu's people co-opted him five months ago."

A rustle of surprise ran through the command deck.

"Now, all of you know we've been feeling out Ramman and Ninhursag," he went on, and Colin watched the older Imperials' reactions to the two names. Ramman and Ninhursag were the southerners who'd been in clandestine contact with *Nergal*'s crew for the past two centuries. Ramman had been one of Anu's inner circle, but Ninhursag had been one of the rank and file, a senior rating in *Dahak*'s gravitonic maintenance crews, brought out of stasis little more than a hundred years ago for her expertise as a physicist. So far as the northerners knew, neither of them realized the other had been in contact with them.

"We've always been cautious about relying on anything we got from them, but 'Tanni and I have compared all the data either of them gave us to what we got from the other, and so far everything's checked. Which means either that they've both been straight with us, or else that they're being worked as a team. Personally, I believe they've been straight. Ramman's terrified of what Anu may do next, and Ninhursag is horrified by what he's already done, and the fact that they've both been kept outside the enclave and away from Anu's inner circle may indicate that they're not entirely trusted, which could be a good sign from our standpoint. Would you agree with that assessment, 'Tanni?"

"Aye," she said shortly.

"But whether he trusts them or not," MacMahan went on, "they're valuable to him; he'd've wasted them long ago if they weren't. So we can be certain they'll be called back in as soon as the shooting starts, and *that's* what's important. Once they go through the access points, they'll have the current admittance code for the portals."

He paused again, and this time Colin saw most of the council members nod.

"As we all know, Anu changes codes on a fairly regular basis. We've never been able to pick them up from outside, but 'Tanni's sensors *can* tell when they reprogram them. So if Ramman or Ninhursag can get the current code out to us, we can at least be sure whether or not it's still current."

"All right," Geb said. "I can see that, but how do they slip it to us?" The question was well taken, but he was frowning in concentration, obviously hoping for an answer rather than raising an objection.

"That's the tough part," MacMahan agreed, "but I think we can swing it.

"Once Ramman and Ninhursag have the codes, they'll each leave a copy at a pre-arranged drop inside the enclave. Our people inside Black Mecca don't know each other, but I believe both are important enough to be taken south—one of them certainly is, though the other may be marginal. Assuming we get both inside, each will make a pickup at one of the two drops. Neither Ramman nor Ninhursag will know the other is making a drop, and neither of our people will know about the other pickup, so even if we lose one, we ought to get one out.

"That's the critical point. Once we've pushed them inside and gotten our hands on that data, we'll ease off on our attacks. Anu will almost certainly do what he's always done before—shove his 'degenerates' out first to see if they draw fire. When he does, our people will give us the admittance code. Hopefully, we'll have two separate data sets to check against one another.

"*If* the code checks out, and *if* we can be ready to move before Anu changes it again, we can get inside the shield before they know we're coming.

"Their active Imperials outnumber ours heavily, but if we get inside at all, we'll have the advantage of surprise. If we hit them hard enough and fast enough, we should be able to take them or, at the very least, do enough damage to panic their senior people into sealing their hatches and lifting off in their armed parasites to get away from us and provide some fire support for their fellows. To do that, they'll have to move their parasites outside their shield and lower it to get shots at us. And if they do that—" the colonel's millimetric smile was fierce "—Colin tells me *Dahak* will be waiting for them."

A hungry sound hovered just below audibility in the hushed command deck.

"And that," MacMahan finished very, very quietly, "will be the end of Fleet Captain (Engineering) Anu and his killers."

CHAPTER THIRTEEN

"I don't like it," Horus said grimly, "and neither does the Council. You're out of your mind, Colin!"

"No, I'm not." Colin tried hard to sound patient. His experience with Dahak's tenacity helped, but he was starting to think Horus could have given the starship stubborn lessons. "We've been over this and over this, and it still comes out the same. I've got to let Dahak know what's going on. He doesn't distinguish between any of you people; if he spots you, he's as likely to open up on you as he is on Anu."

"That's a chance we'll just have to take," Horus said obstinately.

"That's a chance we *can't* take!" Colin snapped, then made himself relax. "Damn, you're stubborn! Look, this is an all-or-nothing move; that's all it can be. We can't risk having *Dahak* attack us when we actually move against the enclave, but that's only part of it. If we manage to get inside and do enough damage their armed parasites lift out, he's gonna *know* something is going on. He hasn't heard a squeak out of me in almost five weeks—how do you think he's going to react when he sees *any* Imperial units moving around down here?"

"Well . . ."

"Exactly! But even that's not the worst of it. Suppose—heaven forbid—I buy it? Who's gonna explain any of this to Dahak? You know he won't believe anything you say, assuming he even listens. So. I'm dead, and you've zapped Anu. What happens next?" He met the old man's eyes levelly.

"The best you people can hope for is that he leaves you alone, but he won't. He'll figure it was simply a power play among the mutineers—which, in a sense, is exactly what it *will* be—and go after you. If the enclave's shield is down, he'll get you, too. But even if the shield's up and you're inside it, he'll be in exactly the same position he's always been in, and the Achuultani are still coming! For God's sake, man, do you *want* it all to be for nothing?!"

Horus glared with the fury of a man driven against the wall, and Jiltanith sat beside him, glowering at Colin. Her brooding silence made him appallingly nervous, and he tried to remind himself she was an experienced intelligence analyst. The smooth way she managed her sensor arrays and *Nergal*'s stealthed auxiliaries proved her competence and ability to think calmly and logically. She might hate him, but she was a professional. Surely she saw the logic of his argument?

She'd said little so far, but he knew how pivotal her opinion might well be and wondered yet again if she resented the fact that MacMahan—who was technically her subordinate—had come straight to him with his plan? He'd half-expected her to throw her weight against him from the start, but now her lips twisted as if she'd just bitten into something spoiled.

"Nay, Father. The captain hath the right of't."

Horus turned an "*et tu?*" expression upon her, and sour amusement glinted in her eyes as Colin blinked in surprise.

"'Tis scarce palatable, Father, yet 'twould be grimmest humor and our deeds do naught but doom us all, and the captain doth speak naught but truth. Wi'out word to *Dahak*, can we e'er be aught save mutineers?" Horus shook his head unwillingly, and she touched his arm gently. "Then there's an end to't. Sin we must give it that word and 'twill accept only the captain's implant code as sooth, then is there naught we may do save bend our heads and yield."

Colin looked from her to her father, grateful for her support yet aware logic, not enthusiasm, governed her. It showed even in the way she spoke of him. She used only his rank, and that sourly, when speaking of him to others, and she never called him *anything* when forced to address him directly.

"But they're bound to spot him!" Horus said almost desperately, and Colin understood perfectly. Colin was the first chance for outright victory Fate had seen fit to offer Horus, and the possibility of losing that chance terrified the old Imperial far more than the thought of his own death ever could.

"Of course they are," he said. "That's why it has to be done my way."

"Granddad," Hector MacMahan said gently, "I don't like it very much, myself, but they may be right."

Horus scowled, and the colonel turned to face Colin.

"If I support you on this one," the Marine said levelly, "it'll only be because I have to, and this will be the *only* raid you go on. Understood?"

Colin considered trying to stare the colonel down, but it would have been impolitic. Worse, it would be an exercise in futility, so he nodded instead.

MacMahan gave one of his patented fractional smiles, and Colin knew it was decided. It might take a while to bring Horus around, but the decision that counted was MacMahan's, for Colin and the Council had named him operational commander. Success would depend heavily on his Terra-born network, which made it logical for him to run things instead of Jiltanith, and while Colin might be a Senior Fleet Captain (of sorts), it was an interesting legal question whether or not any of "his" personnel still came under his orders. More, he knew his limits, and he simply wasn't equipped to orchestrate something like this.

"I'm going to have to back Colin on this one, Granddad," MacMahan said. "I'm sorry, but that's the way it is."

Horus stared at the table a moment, then nodded unwillingly.

"All right, Colin, you're on the Cuernavaca strike," MacMahan continued. "And you'll make your strike, send your message, and get out, understood?"

"Understood."

"And," MacMahan added gently, " 'Tanni will be your pilot."

"*What?!*"

Colin clamped his teeth before he said anything else he would regret, but his eyes were fiery, and Jiltanith's blazed even hotter.

" 'Tanni will be your pilot," MacMahan repeated mildly. "I'm speaking now as the commander of a military operation, and I don't really have time to be diplomatic, so both of you just shut up and listen."

Colin pushed back in his chair and nodded. Jiltanith only looked daggers at MacMahan, but he chose to construe her silence as agreement.

"All right. I know there's some bad blood between you two," the colonel said with generous understatement, "but there's no room for that here. This—as all three of us have just pointed out to Granddad—is *important.*

"Colin, you're the only person who can initiate the message, and if we send you on the strike, you should be able to hide your fold-space transmission by burying it under an ostensible strike report to our HQ. But we don't know how quickly or strongly Anu's people will be able to respond, so we can't afford anything but our very best pilot behind those controls. You're good, Colin, and your reaction time is phenomenal even by Imperial standards, but good as you are, you have very little actual experience in an Imperial fighter.

" 'Tanni, on the other hand, is a natural pilot and the youngest of our Imperials, with reaction time almost as good as yours but far, far more experience. The overall mission will be under your command, but she's *your* pilot and you're *her* electronics officer, or neither of you goes."

He regarded them steadily, and Colin glanced over at Jiltanith. He caught her unaware, surprising her own gaze upon him, and a flicker of challenge passed between them.

"All right," he sighed finally, then grinned. "If I'd known what an iron-assed bastard you are, I'd never have agreed to let you run this op, Hector."

"Ah, but I'm the *best* iron-assed bastard you've got . . . Sir," MacMahan replied.

Colin subsided, and his grin grew as a new thought occurred to him. Once he and Jiltanith were crammed into the same two-man fighter, she was going to *have* to think of something to call him!

It was amazing how consistently wrong he could be, Colin thought moodily as he checked his gear one last time. He and Jiltanith had worked in the same simulator for a week now, and she still hadn't chosen to call him anything.

There were only the two of them, so who else could she be talking to? It actually made it easier for her to make her point by refusing to use his name or rank. And he was certain she would rather die than call him "Sir."

He grinned sourly. At least it gave him something to think about besides the butterflies mating in his middle. For all that he'd been a professional military man before joining NASA, Colin had fired a shot in anger exactly twice, including his abortive attack on *Dahak*'s tender. The other time had been years before, when a very junior Lieutenant MacIntyre had found his Lynx fighter unexpectedly nose-to-nose with an Iraqi fighter in what was supposed to be international airspace, and Colin still wasn't certain how he'd managed to break lock on the self-guiding missile the Iraqi pilot had popped off at him. Fortunately, the other guy had been less lucky.

It helped that the other Imperials were all veterans of their long, covert war. Their calm preparations had steadied his nerve more than he cared to admit . . . but that, in its own way, made it almost worse. Here he was, their commander-in-chief, and every one of his personnel had more combat experience than he did! Hardly the proper balance of credentials.

He sealed his flight suit and checked the globular, one-way force field that served an Imperial pilot as a helmet. He had to admit it was a vast improvement to be able to reach in through his "helmet," and the vision was superb, yet he felt something like nostalgia over the disappearance of all the little read-outs that had cluttered the interior of his NASA-issue gear.

He hung his gun on his suit webbing, not that the weapon was likely to do him much good if they had to ditch. Or, for that matter, that they were likely to have a chance to ditch if the bad guys managed to line up on them with anything in the way of heavy weapons.

There. He was ready, and he strolled out of the armory towards the ready room, glad that he and only he could read the adrenalin levels reported by the bio-sensors in everyone else's implants.

The fighters' crewmen sat quietly in *Nergal*'s ready room. There were only eight of them, for sublight battleships were not planetoids. They carried only a half-dozen fighters, and each one they crammed aboard cut into their internal weapon tonnage.

Most of the Imperials looked frighteningly old to Colin. Geb was flying wing on his and Jilanith's fighter—the only one that would have an escort—and his weaponeer was the only other "youngster" present. Tamman had been ten at the time of the mutiny, but he hadn't been sent back into stasis for as long as Jiltanith and he had a good two centuries of experience behind him.

Yet for all their apparent age, the other Imperials were Hector MacMahan's hand-picked first team. This would be the first time in three thousand years that *Nergal*'s people had used Imperial technology in an open, full-blooded smash at their foes, but there had been occasional, unexpected clashes between the two sides' small craft, and these were the victors from those skirmishes.

"All right." MacMahan entered the compartment briskly and sat on the corner of the briefing officer's console. "You've all been briefed, you all know the plan, and you all know the score. All I'll say again is that all other attacks *must* be held until 'Tanni and Colin have gone in *and* transmitted. Till then, you don't do a single damned thing."

Heads nodded. Waiting might expose them to a bit more danger from the southerners, but attacking before Colin flashed his "strike report" and warned *Dahak* what was going on would be far riskier. The old starship was far more likely to get them than were Anu's hopefully surprised personnel. This time.

"Good," MacMahan said. "Get saddled up, then." The crews began to file out, but the colonel put a hand on Colin's shoulder when he made to follow. "Wait a sec, Colin. I want to talk to you and 'Tanni for a minute."

Jiltanith waited with Colin while the others left, but even now she chose to stand on MacMahan's other side, separating herself from her crewmate.

"I asked you to wait because I've just gotten an update on your target," MacMahan said quietly. "Confirmation came in through one of our people in Black Mecca—Cuernavaca is definitely the base that mounted the hit on Cal, and, with just a bit of luck, Kirinal will be there when you go in."

The hatred that flared in Jiltanith's eyes was not directed at Colin this time, and he felt his own mouth twist in a teeth-baring grin.

Kirinal. He'd felt a cold, skin-crawling fascination as he scanned her dossier. She was Anu's operations chief, his equivalent of Hector MacMahan, but she enjoyed her work as much as Girru had. Her loss would hurt the southerners badly, but that wasn't the first thing that flashed through his mind. No, his *first* thought was that Kirinal personally had ordered the murder of Cal's family.

"I considered not telling you," the colonel admitted, "but you'd've found out when you get back, and I've got enough trouble with you two without adding that to it! Besides, knowing Kirinal's in there would make it personal for everyone we've got, I suppose. But now that you know, I want you to forget it. I know you can't do that entirely, but if you can't keep revenge from clouding your judgment, tell me now, and Geb and Tamman will take the primary strike."

Colin wondered if Jiltanith *could* avoid that. For that matter, could he? But then his eyes met hers, and, for the first time, there was complete agreement between them.

MacMahan watched them, his expressionless face hiding his worry, and considered ordering them off the target whatever they said. *Perhaps he shouldn't have told them after all? No. They had a right to know.*

"All right," he said finally. "Go. And—" his voice stopped them in the hatchway and he smiled slightly "—good hunting, people."

They vanished, and Colonel MacMahan sat alone in the empty briefing room, his face no longer expressionless. But he stood after a moment, straightening his shoulders and banishing the hopeless bitterness from his face. He was a highly skilled and experienced pilot, but one without the implants that would have let him execute his own plan, and that was all there was to it.

Colin's neural feed tapped into what the US Navy would have called the fighter's "weapons and electronic warfare panel" as he and Jiltanith settled into their flight couches, and he felt a fierce little surge of eagerness from the computers. Intellectually, he knew a computer was no more than the sum of its programming, but Terra-born humans had anthropomorphized computers for generations, and the Imperials, with their far closer, far more intimate associations with their electronic minions, never even questioned the practice. Come to think of it, was a human mind that much more than the sum of its programming?

Yet however that might be, he knew what he felt. And what he felt was the fighter baring its fangs, expressing its eagerness in the system-ready signals it sent back to him.

"Weapons and support systems nominal," he reported to Jiltanith, and she eyed him sidelong. She knew they were, of course; their neural feeds were cross-connected enough for that. Yet it was a habit ingrained by too many years of training for him to break now. When a check list was completed, you reported it to your command pilot.

He felt her eyes upon him for a moment longer, then she tossed her head slightly. Her long, rippling hair was a tight chignon atop her head, held by glittering combs that must have been worth a small fortune just as antiques, and her gemmed dagger was at her belt beside the pistol she carried in place of his own heavy grav gun. It was semi-automatic, with a down-sized, thirty-round magazine, light enough for her unenhanced muscles. She'd designed and built it herself, and it looked both anachronistic and inevitable beside her dagger. She was, he thought wryly and not for the first time, a strange mixture of the ancient and the future. Then she spoke.

"Check," she said, and he blinked. "Stand thou by . . . Captain."

It was the first time she'd responded to one of his readiness reports. That was what he thought first. And then the title she'd finally given him registered.

He was still wondering what her concession meant when their fighter launched.

CHAPTER FOURTEEN

Jiltanith was good.

Colin had recognized her skill and, still more, her natural affinity for her task, even in the simulator. Now she took them up the long, carefully camouflaged tunnel from *Nergal* without a single wasted erg of power. Without even a single wasted thought. The fighter's wings were her own, and the walls of their stony birth canal slid past, until, at last, they floated free on a smooth whine of power.

The stars burned suddenly, like chips of ice above them, and a strange exhilaration filled Colin. There was a vibrant new strength in the side-band trickles of his computer links, burning with Jiltanith's bright, fierce sense of flight and movement. For a time, at least, she was free. She was one with her fighter as she roamed the night sky, free to seek out her enemies, and he felt it in her, like a flare of joy, made still stronger by her hunger for vengeance and aptness for violence. For the first time since they'd met, he understood her perfectly and wondered if he was glad he did, for he saw himself in her. Less driven, perhaps, less dark and brooding, not honed to quite so keen an edge, but the same.

The mutineers had been no more than an obstacle when he returned from *Dahak* . . . but Sean had been alive then. He had lost far less than Jiltanith, seen far fewer friends and family ground to dust in the marooned Imperials' secret, endless war, but he had learned to hate, and it frightened him to think he could so quickly and easily find within himself so strong a shadow of the darkness that he'd known from the start infused Jiltanith.

He cut off his thoughts, hoping she'd been too enwrapped in the joy of flight to notice them, and concentrated on his own computers. So far, they'd remained within *Nergal*'s stealth field; from here on, they were on their own.

The Imperial fighter was half the size of a Beagle, a needle-nosed thing of sleek curves and stub wings. Its design was optimized for atmosphere, but the fighter was equally at home and far more maneuverable in vacuum, though none of *Nergal's* brood had been there in millennia. Most of their time had been spent literally weaving in and out among the treetops to hide from Anu's sensor arrays, and so they flew now.

They swept out over the Pacific, settling to within meters of the swell, and Jiltanith goosed the drive gently. A huge hand pressed Colin back in his couch, and a wake boiled across the water behind them as they streaked south at three times the speed of sound. The G forces were almost refreshing after all this time, like an old friend he'd lost track of since meeting Dahak, but they also underscored Jiltanith's single glaring weakness as a pilot.

Atmosphere was a less forgiving medium than vacuum. Even at the fighter's maximum power, friction and compression conspired to reduce its top speed dramatically. There was one huge compensation—by relying on control surfaces for maneuvering rather than depending entirely upon the gravitonic magic of the drive, the same speed could be produced for a far weaker energy signature—but there were always trade-offs. In this case, one was a greater vulnerability to thermal detection and targeting systems as a hull unprotected by a drive field heated, but that was a relatively minor drawback.

The *real* problem was that the reduced-strength drive couldn't cancel inertia and the G forces of acceleration. Flying on its atmospheric control surfaces, the deadly little ship was captive to the laws of motion and no more maneuverable than the bodies of its crew could stand, and that was potentially deadly for Jiltanith. If she found herself forced into maneuvering combat against a fully-enhanced Imperial in this performance envelope, she was dead, for she would black out long before her opponent.

Still, MacMahan was almost certainly right. If it came to aerial combat, stealth would not be in great demand. It would become a matter of brute power, cunning, reaction time, and the skill of the combatants' electronic warfare specialists, and the first thing that would happen would be that the pilots would go to full power. With a full strength drive field wrapped around her, Jiltanith would be as free of G forces as any Imperial pilot.

Yet the whole object was to avoid any air-to-air fighting. If they were forced to full power, all the ECM in the world couldn't hide them from Anu's detectors ... which meant they dared not return to *Nergal* unless they could destroy or shake off any pursuit and drop back into a stealth regime. Trade-offs, Colin thought sourly, checking their airspeed. Always the trade-offs.

They were up to mach four, he noted, and grinned as he imagined the reaction aboard any freighter they happened across when they came hurtling by ahead of their sonic boom with absolutely no radar image to show for it.

They ought to hit their target in about another seventeen minutes. Strange. He didn't feel the least bit nervous anymore.

"Coming up on our final turn," Colin said eleven minutes later.

"Aye," Jiltanith said softly.

Her voice was dreamy, for Colin wasn't quite real for her just now. Reality was her dagger-sleek fighter, for she was one with it, seeing and feeling through its sensors. Yet he felt the intensity of her purpose and the cat-sharp clarity of her awareness through his own feeds, and he was content.

They swept through the turn, settling into the groove for the attack run, and Geb and Tamman fell astern, increasing their separation as planned.

The huge private estate in the deep, bowl-like valley north of Cuernavaca was the true HQ of both Black Mecca and the Army of Allah in the Americas, though only a very few terrorists knew it. That made it a major operational node, one of the three juiciest targets MacMahan and Jiltanith had been able to identify. Over forty southerners and two hundred of their most trusted Terra-born allies were based there, coordinating a hemisphere's terrorism, and the estate's seclusion hid a substantial amount of Imperial equipment. A successful attack on such a target would certainly seem to justify an immediate strike report to their own HQ.

But there was another fractor in MacMahan's target selection. The "estate's" geography made it an ideal target for mass missiles, for the valley walls would confine the blast effect and channel it upward. The northerners expected the use of such weapons to come as a considerable shock to Anu, for they would provoke consternation and furious speculation among the vast majority of Earth's people, and attention was the one thing both groups of Imperials had assiduously avoided for centuries. If anything could convince Anu *Nergal*'s people meant business, this attack should do it.

Yet the very importance of the target also meant a greater possibility of serious defenses. If enemy fighter opposition appeared, it was up to Geb and Tamman to pick it off if they could; if they couldn't, theirs became the far grimmer task of playing decoy to suck the southerners off Colin and onto themselves, and . . .

"Shit!" Colin muttered, and Jiltanith stiffened beside him as he shunted information to her through a side feed. There were active Imperial scanners covering the target. At their present speed, those scanners would burn through their stealth field in less than five minutes.

Colin tightened internally as he and his computers raced to determine what those scanners reported to. If it was only an observation post, they'd be onto the target before anyone could react, but if there were automatic defenses . . .

"Double shit!" he hissed. There were, indeed, automatic defenses—and three fighters on stand-by for launch, though three ships were no indication of an alert. There were at least ten of the little buggers down there; if they'd anticipated an attack, all ten would have been spotted for immediate launch. He and Jiltanith had simply had the infernal bad luck to happen upon the scene when someone was readying for a routine flight. Possibly Kirinal was going somewhere in one of those fighters and the other two were escorts; that fitted normal southern operational procedures.

But it meant the base was at a higher state of readiness than usual, and there were those automatics. He could "see" at least four missile batteries and two heavy energy weapon emplacements, which was far more than their intelligence estimates had suggested.

His thoughts flickered so quickly they were almost unformed, yet Jiltanith caught them. He felt her disappointment like his own. These were the people who had sent Girru and Anshar to butcher Cal's family and Sean and Sandy, but their orders for this contingency were clear.

"We'll have to abort," Colin remarked, yet even as he said it his neural link was bringing his systems fully on line.

"Aye, so we shall." Yet Jiltanith's course never deviated, and he felt her mental touch poised to ram the drive's power level through the red line.

"They'll burn through a good twenty seconds before I get a targeting setup," he said absently.

"Nay, 'twill be no more than ten seconds ere thy weapons range," she demurred.

"Hah! Now you're an EW specialist, too, huh?" Then he shrugged. "Screw it. Full bore right down the middle, Jiltanith. Go for the weapons first."

"As thou sayst, Captain," Jiltanith purred, and the fighter shrieked upward like a homesick meteor.

For just a second, acceleration drove Colin back into his couch, but then the drive field peaked, the G forces vanished, and he felt the shockwave of alarm sweep through the southerners' enclave. The automatic air-defense systems were already reaching for them, but his own systems had come alive a moment sooner; by the time the weapons started hunting the fighter, its defensive programs were already filling the night sky with false images. Decoys streaked away, singing their siren songs, and jammers hashed the scan channels with the fold-space equivalent of white noise.

The ground stations' scanners were more powerful and their electronic brains were bigger and smarter than his small onboard computers, but they'd started at a disadvantage. They had to sort the situation out before they could find a target, and it was a race between them and their human controllers and Colin and the speeding fighter's targeting systems.

There was no time to think, no room for anything but concentration, yet kaleidoscope images flared at the edges of his brain. The brighter strobes of panic when one ground station seemed to have found them. The impossible, wrenching maneuver with which Jiltanith threw it off. The relief when they slipped away before it could establish a lock. His own racing excitement. The determination and intensity that filled his pilot. His own savage blaze of satisfaction as his launch solution suddenly came magically together.

His first salvo leapt away. Hyper-capable missiles were out of the question in atmosphere; they would take too much air into hyper with them, wrecking his mass-power calculations and bringing them back into normal space God alone knew where, but mass missiles were another matter. Their over-powered gravitonic drives slammed them forward, accelerating instantly to sixty percent of light speed, crowding the edge of phase lock. Counter-missile defenses did their best, but the mass missiles' speed and the short range meant tracking time was too limited even for Imperial systems, and Colin heard Jiltanith's panther howl of triumph as his strike went home.

Fireballs blew into the night. Mass missiles carried no warheads, for they needed none. They were energy states, not projectiles, hyper-velocity robotic meteorites, shrieking down on precise trajectories to seek out the ground weapons that menaced their masters.

The small shield generators protecting the southerners' weapons were still spinning up when Colin's missiles arrived, but it wouldn't have mattered if they'd already been at full power. In fifty-one millennia, the northerners had never risked escalating their struggle to the point of using Imperial weaponry so brazenly, and the southerners had assumed they never would. Their defensive measures were aimed at Terrestrial weapons or the relatively innocuous Imperial ones the northerners had used in the past, and they were fatally inadequate.

Jiltanith snapped the fighter around as the Jovian holocaust spewed skyward behind them. A bowl of fire glared against the night-struck Mexican hills, and Colin's computers were already evaluating the first strike. Weak as they were, the base's shields had absorbed a tremendous amount of energy before they failed—enough to keep the missiles from turning the entire estate into one vast crater—and one heavy energy gun emplacement had escaped destruction. It raved defiance at them, and Jiltanith accepted the challenge as she came back like the angel of death, driving into its teeth.

The radiant heat of the first missile strike, added to the frantic efforts of the fighter's ECM, denied the targeting scanners lock, and the guns were on pre-programmed blind fire, raking the volume of space that ought to contain the fighter. But Jiltanith wasn't where the people who'd designed that fire program had assumed she would have to be, and Colin felt a detached sort of awe for her raw flying ability as he popped off another missile.

Unlike the fighter, the energy weapons couldn't bob and weave. The missile sizzled home, and a fresh burst of fury defiled the earth.

Jiltanith came around for a third pass, two more than their ops plan had called for or considered safe, and the ground defenses were silent. Despite the shields' best efforts, the weapon emplacements were huge, raw wounds, and the entire valley floor was a sea of blazing grass and trees, touched to flame by thermal radiation. The palatial estate's buildings were flaming rubble, but the real installations hidden under them, though damaged, were still intact.

One of the ready fighters was already clawing upward, but Colin ignored it. He had all the time in the world, and his final launch was textbook perfect. A spread of four missiles bracketed the target, streaking the fire-sick heavens with fresh flame. There were no shields to absorb the destruction this time, and there was, at most, no more than a microsecond between the first missile impact and the last.

A hurricane of light lashed upward as vaporized earth and stone and flesh vomited into the night, and the fireballs ballooned out, merging, melding into one terrible whole. A second southern fighter was caught just at lift off and spat forth like a molten, tumbling spark from Vulcan's forge, and the pressure wave snatched at them. It shook them as a terrier shook a rat, but Jiltanith met it like a lover. She rode its ferocity—embracing it, not fighting it—and the universe danced crazily, even madder somehow from within the protection of their drive field, as she shot the rapids of concussion. But then they flashed out the far side, and Colin realized she had used the terrible turbulence to put them on the track of the single fighter that had escaped destruction.

Colin needed no evaluation of his final attack. All that *could* be left was one vast crater. He had just killed over two hundred people . . . and all he felt was satisfaction. Satisfaction, and the need, the eagerness, to hunt down and kill the single southern fighter that had escaped his wrath.

There was no way to know who piloted that other fighter, nor if it was fully crewed or what weapons it carried. Perhaps there was only the pilot. Perhaps it wasn't even armed.

All Colin would ever know was that he felt a sort of merciless empathy— not pity, but something like understanding—for that fleeing vessel. He and Jiltanith were invincible, and they were vengeance. He bared his teeth and called up his air-to-air weaponry as the firestorm's white heat dulled to red astern, and Jiltanith hurled them out over the night-dark Pacific in pursuit.

His targeting systems locked. A command flicked through his feed to the computers, and two more missiles launched. They were slower than mass missiles, homing weapons with their speed stepped down to follow evasive maneuvers, but this time they carried warheads: three-kiloton, proximity-fused nukes. His eyes were dreamy as his electronic senses watched them all the way in, but in the moment before detonation a third missile came scorching in from the west. He'd almost forgotten Geb and Tamman, and the southern fighter probably never even realized he and Jiltanith weren't alone.

There was no debris.

Jiltanith needed no orders. She swept on into the west, reducing speed, losing altitude, and their drive strength coasted back down to wrap invisibility about them once more. Colin checked his sensors carefully, and not until he was certain they had evaded all detection did she turn and flee homeward into the north while he switched on the fighter's com and activated the fold-space implant he had dared not use in over a month. He felt an odd little "click" inside his skull as Dahak's receivers recognized and accepted his implant's ID protocols.

"Category One Order. Do not reply," he sent at the speed of thought. "Authentication Delta-One-Gamma-Beta-One-Seven-Eight-Theta-Niner-Gamma. Priority Alpha. Stand by for squeal from this fighter. Execute upon receipt."

He closed his implant down instantly, praying that the almost equally strong pulse from the fighter com had hidden it from Anu's people. The coded squeal he and he alone had pre-recorded and tacked into the middle of the strike report lasted approximately two milliseconds, and Dahak had his orders.

And then, at last, there was a moment to relax and blink his eyes, refocusing on the interior of the cockpit. A moment to realize that they had succeeded . . . and that they were alive.

"Done," he said softly, turning to look at Jiltanith for the first time since they launched their attack.

"Aye, and well done," she replied. Their gazes met, and for once there was no hostility between them.

"Beautiful flying, 'Tanni," he said, and saw her eyes widen as he used the familiar form of her name for the first time. For a moment he thought he'd gone too far, but then she nodded.

"Art no sluggard thyself . . . Colin," she said.

And she smiled.

Book Three

CHAPTER FIFTEEN

Colin MacIntyre sat in *Nergal*'s wardroom and shuffled, hiding a smile as Horus bent a hawk-like eye upon him across the table while they waited for Hector's next report.

Battle Fleet's crews had gone in for a vast array of esoteric games of chance, most of them electronic, but Horus disdained such over-civilized pastimes. He loved Terran card games: bridge, canasta, spades, hearts, euchre, blackjack, whist, piquet, chemin de fer, poker . . . *especially* poker, which had never been Colin's game. In fact, Colin's major interest in cards had been that of an amateur magician, and Horus had been horrified at how easily a full Imperial who'd learned to palm cards with purely Terran reflexes and speed could do that . . . among other things.

"Cut?" Colin invited, and shook his head sadly as Horus made five separate cuts before handing the deck back.

"What're your losses by now?" he mused as he dealt. "About a million?"

"'Tis more like to thrice that," Jiltanith said sourly, gathering up her cards and not bothering to watch his fingers with her father's intensity.

"Ante up," he said, and chips clicked as father and daughter slid them out. If they'd really been playing for money, he'd be a billionaire, even without the ill-gotten wealth Horus had demanded he write off after he realized Colin had been cheating shamelessly. He grinned, and Jiltanith snorted without her old bitterness as she saw it.

She still wasn't really comfortable with him, but at least she was pretending, and he was grateful to Hector. The colonel had torn long, bloody strips off both of them when he saw the scan record of what they'd gone into, but his heart hadn't seemed fully in it, and Colin had seen the glint in his eye when Jiltanith called him "Colin" during their debriefing. He himself had feared she would retreat into her old, cold hostility once the rush of euphoria passed, but though she'd stepped back a bit and he knew she still resented him, she was fighting it, as if she recognized (intellectually, at least) that it wasn't his fault he was what he'd become. Her presence at the card table was proof of that.

He wished there had been a less traumatic way to effect that change, but he hoped the colonel was pleased with the way it had worked out. The military arguments for assigning them to the same flight crew had been strong, but it had taken courage—well, gall—to put them forward.

"I'll take two," Horus announced, and Colin flipped the small, pasteboard rectangles across to him.

" 'Tanni?" He raised a polite eyebrow, and she pouted.

"Nay, this hand liketh me well enow."

"Hm." He studied his own cards thoughtfully, then took one. "Bets?"

"I'll go a hundred," Horus said, and Jiltanith followed suit.

"See you and raise five hundred," Colin said grandly, and Horus glared.

"Not this time, you young hellion!" he growled. "I'll see your raise and raise *you* a hundred!"

"Father, art moonstruck," Jiltanith said, tossing in her own hand. "Whyfor must thou throw good money after bad?"

"That's no way to talk to your father, 'Tanni." Horus sounded pained, and Colin hid another smile.

"See you and raise another five," he murmured, and Horus glared at him.

"Damn it, I *watched* you deal! You can't possibly—" The old Imperial shoved more chips forward. "Call," he said grimly. "Let's see you beat *this*!"

He faced his cards—four jacks and an ace—and glowered at Colin.

"Horus, Horus!" Colin sighed. He shook his head sadly and laid out his own hand card by card, starting with the two of clubs and ending with the six.

"No!" Horus stared at the table in shock. "*A straight flush?!*"

" 'Twas foredoomed, Father," Jiltanith sighed, a twinkle dancing in her own eyes. "Certes, 'tis strange that one so wise as thou should be so hot to make thyself so poor."

"Oh, shut up!" Horus said, trying not to smile himself. He gathered up the cards and glared at Colin. "This time *I'll* deal."

"*Damn* them! Breaker take them to *hell!*"

The being who had once been Fleet Captain (Engineering) Anu leapt to his feet and slammed his fist down so hard the table's heavy top cracked. He stared at the spiderweb fractures for a moment, then snatched it up and hurled it against the battle-steel bulkhead with all his strength. The impact was a harsh, discordant clangor and the table sprang back, its thick Imperial plastic bent and buckled. He glared at it, chest heaving with his fury, then kicked the wreckage back into the bulkhead. He did it several more times, then whirled, fists clenched at his sides.

"And *you*, Ganhar! Some 'intelligence analyst' *you* turned out to be! What the hell do you have to say for yourself?!"

Ganhar felt sweat on his forehead but carefully did not wipe it away as he fastened his eyes on the center of Anu's chest. He dared not *not* look at him, but it could be almost as dangerous to meet his gaze at a moment like this. Ganhar had assisted Kirinal in running Anu's external operations for over a century, but the newly promoted operations head had never seen Anu quite this furious, and he silently cursed Kirinal for getting herself killed. If she'd still been alive, he could have switched his leader's wrath to her.

"There were no indications they planned anything like this, Chief," he said, hoping his voice sounded more level than it felt. He started to add that Anu himself had seen and approved all of his intelligence estimates, but prudence stopped him. Anu had become steadily less stable over the years. Reminding him of his own fallibility just now was strongly contra-indicated.

"'*No indications*'!" Anu mimicked in a savage falsetto. He growled something else under his breath, then inhaled sharply. His rage appeared to vanish as suddenly as it had come, and he picked up his chair and sat calmly. When he spoke again, his voice was almost normal.

"All right. You fucked up, but maybe it wasn't entirely your fault," he said, and Ganhar felt himself sag internally in relief.

"But they've hurt us," the chief mutineer continued, harshness creeping back into his voice. "I'll admit it—I didn't think they'd have the guts for something like this, either. And it's paid off for them, Breaker take them!"

All eyes turned to the holo map hovering above the space the table had occupied, dotted with glaring red symbols that had once been green.

"Cuernavaca, Fenyang, *and* Gerlochovko in one night!" Anu snorted. "The equipment doesn't matter all that much, but they've blown the guts out of your degenerates—and we've lost eighty more Imperials. *Eighty!* That makes more than ten percent of us in the last month!"

His subordinates sat silent. They could do the math equally well, and the casualties appalled them. Their enemies hadn't done that much damage to them in five millennia, and the fact that their own over-confidence had made it possible only made it worse. They'd known their foes were aging, that time was on their side. It had never occurred to them that the enemy might have the sheer nerve to take the offensive after all these years.

Even worse was the *way* they'd been attacked. The open use of Imperial weapons had been a shattering blow to their confidence, and it could well have led to disaster. None of the degenerates seemed to know what had happened, but they knew it was something they couldn't explain. The southerners' penetration of the major governments, especially in the Asian Alliance, had been sufficient to head off any precipitate military action against purely Terrestrial foes, but their control was much weaker in the West, and their enemies' obvious willingness to run such risks was sobering.

But not, Ganhar thought privately, as sobering as another possibility. Perhaps their enemies had had reason to be confident of their own ability to control the situation? It was possible, for if the southerners had their hooks deep into the civilian agencies, *Nergal*'s people had outdistanced them among the West's soldiers.

The first reports had produced plenty of demands for action or, at the very least, priority investigations into whatever had happened, but their own tools among the civilians had managed to quash any "overly hasty action," though there had been some fiery scenes. Yet now a curtain of silence had descended over the Western militaries, and Ganhar found that silence ominous.

He bit his lip, longing for better sources within military intelligence, but they were a clannish bunch. And, much as he hated to admit it, the northerners' willingness to accept degenerates as equals had marked advantages. They'd spent centuries setting up their networks, often recruiting from or even before birth. Ganhar and Kirinal, on the other hand, had concentrated on recruiting adults, preferring to work on individuals whose weaknesses were readily apparent. That had its own advantages, like the ability to target people on their way up, but the increasing high-tech tendency towards small, professional, career-oriented military establishments worked against them.

The military's background investigation procedures were at least as rigorous as those of their civilian counterparts, and the steady incidence of leaks from civilian agencies had led to an even stronger preference for career officers for truly sensitive posts. Worse, Ganhar *knew* the northerners had firm links with the traditional military families, though pinning any of them down was the Breaker's own work. And that meant *their* military contacts were damned well *born* in position, with sponsors who were ready to favor their own and doubly suspicious of everyone else.

Ganhar, on the other hand, had no choice but to corrupt officers already in place, which risked counter-penetration, or fabricate fictitious backgrounds (always risky, even against such primitives, much less degenerates aided by Imperial input), which was why it had seemed so sensible to concentrate on their civilian masters, instead.

He hoped that policy wasn't about to boomerang on them.

"Well, Ganhar?" Anu's abrasive voice broke in on his thoughts. "Why do *you* think they've come out into the open? Assuming you *have* an opinion."

While Ganhar hesitated, seeking a survivable response, another voice answered.

"It may be," Commander Inanna said carefully, "that they're desperate."

"Explain," Anu said curtly, and she shrugged.

"They're getting old," she said softly. "They used Imperial fighters, and they can't have many Imperials left. Maybe they're in even worse shape than we'd thought. Maybe it's a last-ditch effort to cripple us while they can still use Imperial technology at all."

"Hmph!" Anu frowned down at the clenched hands in his lap. "Maybe you're right," he said finally, "but it doesn't change the fact that they've taken out three quarters of our major bases. Maker only knows what they'll do next!"

"What *can* they do, Chief?" It was Jantu, the enclave's chief security officer. "The only other big target was Nanga Parbat, and we've already shut down there. Sure, they hurt us, but those were the only targets they could hit with

Imperial weapons. And—" he added with a glance at Ganhar "—if we'd put them closer to major population centers, they couldn't even have hit them."

Ganhar ground his teeth. Jantu was a bully and a sadist, more at home silencing dissidence by crushing dissidents than thinking, yet he had his own brand of cunning. He liked to propose sweeping, simplistic solutions to other people's problems. If they were rejected, he could always say he'd warned everyone they were going about it wrongly. If they were adopted and succeeded, he took the credit, if they failed, he could always blame someone else for poor execution. Like his long-standing argument in favor of using cities to cover their bases against attack, claiming that their enemies' softness for the degenerates would protect them. It would also make it vastly harder to hide them, but Jantu wouldn't have been the one who had to try.

"It might not have mattered." Inanna disliked Jantu quite as much as Ganhar did, and her eyes—black now, not brown—were hard. "They risked panicking the degenerates into starting a war. For all we know, they might've hit us if our bases had been buried under New York or Moscow."

"I doubt that," Jantu said, showing his teeth in what might—charitably— be called a smile. "In all—"

"It doesn't matter," Anu interrupted coldly. "What matters is that it's happened. What's your best estimate of their next move, Ganhar?"

"I . . . don't know." Ganhar picked his words carefully. "I'm not happy about how quiet the degenerates' militaries have been. That may or may not indicate something, but I don't have anything definite to base projections on. I'm sorry, Chief, but that's all I can say."

He braced himself against a fresh burst of rage, yet it was wiser to be honest than to let a mistake come home to roost. But there was no blast of fury, only a slow nod.

"That's what I thought," Anu grunted. "All right. We've already got most of our Imperials—what's left of them!—under cover. We'll sit tight a bit longer on our degenerates and less reliable Imperials. Jantu's right about one thing; there aren't any more of *our* concentrations for them to hit. Let's see what the bastards do next before we bring anyone else down here."

His henchmen nodded silently, and he waved for them to leave. They rose, and Jantu led the way out with Ganhar several meters behind him.

Anu smiled humorlessly at the sight. There was no love lost between those two, and that kept them from conspiring together even if it did make for a bit of inefficiency. But if Ganhar fucked up again, not even the Maker would save him.

Inanna lingered, but when he ignored her she shrugged and followed Ganhar. Anu let his eyes rest on her departing back. She was about the only person he still trusted, as much as he could bring himself to trust anyone.

They were all fools. Fools and incompetents, or they would have taken *Dahak* for him fifty thousand years ago. But Inanna was less incompetent than the others, and she alone seemed to understand. The others had softened, forgotten who and what they were, and accepted the failure of their plan. They were careful not to say it, yet in their hearts, they had betrayed him. But Inanna recognized the weight of his destiny, the pressure gathering even now behind him, driving him towards escape and empire. Soon it would become an irresistible flood, washing out from this miserable backwater world to sweep him to victory, and Inanna knew it.

That was why she remained loyal. She wanted to share that power as mistress, minion, or lieutenant; it didn't matter to her. Which was just as well for her, he told himself moodily. Not that she wasn't a pleasant armful in bed. And that new body of hers was the best yet. He tried to recall what the tall, raven-haired beauty's name had been, but it didn't matter. Her body was Inanna's now, and Inanna's skill filled it.

The conference room door closed silently behind the commander, and he stalked through his private exit, feeling the automatic weapons that protected it recognizing his implants. He entered his quarters and stared bitterly at the sumptuous furnishings. Splendid, yes, but only a shadow of the splendor in *Dahak*'s captain's quarters. He had been pent here too long, denied his destiny for too many dusty years. Yet it would come. Inevitably, it would come.

He crossed the main cabin, ignoring Imperial light sculptures and soft music, overlooking priceless tapestries, jewel work, and paintings from five thousand years of Terran history, and peered into a mirror. There were a few tiny wrinkles around his eyes now, and he glanced aside, letting those eyes rest on the framed holo cube of the Anu-that-was, seeing again the power and presence that had been his. This body was taller, broad shouldered and powerful, but it was still a poor excuse for the one he had been born to. And it was growing older. There might be another century of peak performance left to it, and then it would be time to choose another. He'd hoped that when that time came he would be back out among the stars where he belonged, teaching the Imperium the true meaning of Empire.

His original body remained in stasis, though he hadn't looked upon it since it was placed there. It caused him pain to see it and remember how it once had been, but he had saved it, for it was *his*. He had not permitted Inanna to develop the techniques to clone it. Not yet. That was reserved for another time, a fitting celebration of his final, inevitable triumph.

The day would come, he promised his stranger's face, when he would have the realm that should be his, and when it came, he would have the Anu-that-was cloned afresh. He would live forever, in his *own* body, and the stars themselves would be his toys.

Ganhar walked briskly along the corridor, eyes hooded in thought. What *were* the bastards up to? It was such a fundamental change, and it came after too many years of unvarying operational patterns. There was a reason behind it, and, grateful as he'd been for Inanna's intervention, he couldn't believe it was simple desperation. Yet he had no better answer for it than she, and that frightened him.

He sighed. He'd covered his back as well as he could; now he could only wait to see what they were doing. Whatever it was, it could hardly make the situation much worse. Anu was mad, and growing madder with every passing year, but there was nothing Ganhar could do about it . . . yet. Maker only knew how many of the others were the "Chief's" spies, and no one knew who Anu might decide (or be brought to decide) was a traitor.

Jantu was probably licking his chops, praying daily for something to use against him, and there was no sane reason to give him that something, but Ganhar had his plans. He suspected others had theirs, as well, but until they finally escaped this damned planet they needed Anu. Or, no, they needed Inanna and her medical teams, but that was almost the same thing. Ganhar had no idea why the bioscience officer remained so steadfastly loyal to that madman, but as long as she did, any effort to remove him would be both futile and fatal.

He stepped into the transit shaft and let it whirl him away to his own office. There might be other reports by now—he was certainly driving his teams hard enough to produce them! If there were none, he could at least relieve his own tension by giving someone else a tongue-lashing.

General Sir Frederick Amesbury, KCB, CBE, VC, DSO, smiled tightly at the portrait of the king on his office wall. Sir Frederick could trace his ancestry to the reign of Edward the Confessor. Unlike many of *Nergal*'s Terra-born allies he was not directly descended from her crew, though there had been a few distant collateral connections, for his people had been among their helpers since the seventeenth century.

Now, after all those years, things were coming to a head, and the Americans' General Hatcher was shaping up even more nicely than Sir Frederick had expected. Of course, Hector was to blame for prodding Hatcher into action, and Sir Frederick had been primed to support the Yank's first tentative suggestion, but Hatcher was doing bloody well.

He checked his desk clock, and his smile grew shark-like. The SAS and Royal Marines would be hitting the Red Eyebrows base in Hartlepool in less than two hours, after which, Sir Frederick would have to notify the Prime Minister. The Council reckoned the P.M. was still his own man, and Sir Frederick was inclined to agree, but it would be interesting to see if that was enough to save his own position when the Home and Defense Ministers—who most definitely were *not* their own woman and man, respectively—demanded his head.

Oberst Eric von Grau sat back on his haunches in the ditch. The *leutnant* beside him was peering through his light-gathering binoculars at the isolated chalets in the bend of the Mosel River, but Grau had already carried out his own final check. His two hundred picked men were quite invisible, and his attention had moved to other things. He cocked an ear, waiting for the thunder to begin, and allowed himself a tight smile.

He had treated himself to a quiet celebration when the orders came through from *Nergal*, and when news of the first three strikes rocked the world, he'd hardly been able to wait for the request from the Americans. German intelligence had spotted this January Twelfth training camp long ago, though the security minister had chosen not to act on the information.

But Herr Trautmann didn't know about this little jaunt, and the army had no intention of telling the civilians about it till it was over. Grau's superiors had learned their lessons the hard way and trusted the Americans' USFC more than they did their own civilian overlords. Which was a sad thing, but one Grau understood better than most.

"Inbound," a radio voice said quietly, and he grinned at *Leutnant* Heil. Heil looked a great deal like a younger version of his superior—not surprisingly, perhaps, since Grau's great-great-great-great-great-grandmother was also Heil's great-great-grandmother—and his smile was identical.

The sudden boom of supersonic aircraft crashed over them as the *Luftwaffe* fighter-bombers came in on full after-burner at fifty meters.

"Go." Major Tama Matsuo, Japanese Army, touched his sergeant on the shoulder and the two of them slithered through the shadows after Lieutenant Yamashita's team. Darkness wrapped Bangkok in comforting anonymity, but the grips of the major's automatic grenade launcher were slippery in his hands.

He and the sergeant turned a corner and faded into the shrubbery at the base of a stone wall, joining the men already waiting for them, and Tama checked the time again. Lieutenant Kagero's men should be in position by now, but the timetable gave them another thirty-five seconds.

The major watched the dimmed display of his watch, trying to control his breathing, and hoped Hector MacMahan's intelligence was good. It had been hard to convince his superiors to sanction a raid into Asian Alliance territory without civilian approval, even if his father was Chief of the Imperial Staff and even to take out the foreign HQ of the Japanese Army for Racial Purity. And if the operation blew up, his reputation and influence alike would suffer catastrophically. Assuming he survived at all.

He watched the final seconds tick away. It still seemed a bit foolhardy. Satisfying, but foolhardy. Still, he who wanted the tiger's cubs must venture into the tiger's den to get them. He just hoped the Council was right. And that he would do nothing to dishonor himself in his grandfather's eyes.

"Now," he said quietly into the boom mike before his lips, and Tamman's grandson committed his men to combat.

Colonel Hector MacMahan stepped out into his backyard as the stealthed cutter ghosted down the canyon behind the house and settled soundlessly to the grass. The reports would be coming in soon, and the expected flak from the civilians would come with them. Anu's people had spent years infiltrating the civilians who set policy and controlled the military (normally, that was) but even the most senior of them would find it hard to stop things now.

He felt a glow of admiration for his superiors, and especially Gerald Hatcher. They didn't know what he knew, but they knew they'd been leashed too long. Anu had gotten just a bit too fancy—or too confident, perhaps.

In the old days, he'd relocated his "degenerates' " HQs whenever they were spotted; for the last few years he'd amused himself by simply forbidding action against major bases. There had been no way to prevent interceptions and attacks on action groups or isolated training and staging bases, but his minions in the intelligence community had argued that it was wiser to watch head-quarters groups rather than attack and risk driving them back out of sight.

But the attacks on three really big terrorist bases, two of which the generals hadn't even known existed, had been the final straw. They didn't know who'd done it, how, or, for that matter, why, but they knew *what* it was. Their own charter was the eradication of terrorism, and the realization that someone else was doing their job was too much to stand. Hatcher and his fellows had proven even more amenable to his suggestions than expected.

They couldn't do much about the Islamic and officially-sponsored Asiatic groups, most of whose bases were openly entrenched in countries hostile to their governments. But the homegrown variety was another matter entirely, and it was amazing how memos notifying the generals' nominal superiors of their plans had been so persistently misrouted.

And if *they* couldn't hit the foreign groups, MacMahan knew who could. He hadn't told them that, but he suspected they'd be figuring it out shortly.

The hatch opened and the colonel whistled shrilly. A happy woof answered as his half-lab, half-rotweiller bitch Tinker Bell galloped past him and hopped up into the cutter. She poked her nose into Gunnery Chief Hanalat's face, licking her affectionately, and the white-haired woman laughed and tugged on the big dog's soft ears while MacMahan tossed his duffel bags up into the cutter and climbed in after them.

General Hatcher had ordered MacMahan to make himself scarce for the next few weeks without realizing just how scarce the colonel intended to become. The Unified Special Forces Command's CO meant to take the heat when his bosses found out what he'd been up to, though MacMahan suspected that heat would be less intense than the general feared. Most of his superiors were men and women of integrity, and the ones who weren't would find it hard to raise too much ruckus in the face of the general approval MacMahan anticipated.

Of course, once it became apparent just how thoroughly the colonel had vanished, his boss would figure out he'd known about the mystery attacks ahead of time. The northerners had never tried to recruit him, but Hatcher was no fool. He'd realize he had been used, though it was unlikely to cost him much sleep, and MacMahan hated to run out without explaining things to him. But he had no choice, for one thing was certain: when they found out what had happened and how, the southerners would suddenly become far, far more interested in one Colonel Hector MacMahan, USMC, currently attached to the USFC.

Not that it mattered. Indeed, his role as instigator was part of the plan, an intentional diversion of suspicion from their other people, and he'd always known his position was more exposed than most. That was why he was a bachelor with no family, and they wouldn't be able to find him when they wanted him, anyway.

He only wished he could see Anu's face when *he* got the news.

CHAPTER SIXTEEN

Head of Security Jantu leaned back and hummed happily, feeling no need to dissemble in the security of his own office, as he replayed the last command meeting in his mind.

The "Chief's" wrath had been awesome when the news came in. This time he'd half-expected it, which meant he'd had time to work up a good head of steam ahead of time. The things he'd said to poor Ganhar!

It was all quite terrible . . . but more terrible for some than for others. Most of the dead Imperials were Ganhar's people, and nothing that weakened Ganhar could be completely bad. The thought that degenerates could do such a neat job was galling, but whatever happened in the field, the enclave that was his own responsibility was and would remain inviolate, so none of the egg was on *his* face. No, it was on Ganhar's face, and with just a little luck—and, perhaps, a little judicious help—that might just prove fatal for poor Ganhar.

It had been kind of *Nergal*'s people to take out Kirinal for him. Now if he could only get rid of Ganhar, he might just manage to bring Security and Operations together under the control of a single man: him. Of course, it was probable the "Chief" would balk at that and pick a new head for Operations, but Jantu would be perfectly happy if Anu made the logical choice. And even if he decided to choose someone other than Bahantha, the newcomer would be hopelessly junior to Jantu. One way or another, he would dominate whatever security arrangements resulted from Ganhar's . . . departure.

And then it would be time to deal with Anu himself. Jantu would not have let a sane man stand between him and power, and he felt no qualms at all over removing a madman. Indeed, it might almost be considered his civic duty, and he often permitted himself a mildly virtuous feeling when he considered it.

Jantu hadn't realized quite how mad the engineer was when the plot to seize *Dahak* first came up, but he'd recognized that Anu wasn't exactly stable. Overthrow the Imperium? Ludicrous! But Jantu had been prepared to go along until they had the ship, at which point he and his own henchmen would eliminate Anu and put a modified version of the original plan into effect. It would be so much simpler to transform *Dahak*'s loyalists into helots and build their own empire in some decently deserted portion of the galaxy than to pit themselves against the Imperium and get squashed for their pains.

That plan had gone out the airlock when the mutiny failed, but there were still possibilities. Indeed, the present situation seemed even more promising.

He knew Anu and, possibly, Inanna believed the Imperium was still out there, waiting to be conquered, but the Imperium's expansion should have brought at least a colony to Earth long since, for habitable planets weren't all that plentiful. By Jantu's most conservative estimate, BuCol's survey teams should have arrived forty millennia ago. That they hadn't suggested all sorts of hopeful possibilities to a man like Jantu.

If the Imperium had fallen upon hard times, why, then Anu's plans for conquest might be practical after all. And the first stage was to forget this clandestine nonsense and take control of Earth openly. A few demonstrations of Imperial weaponry should bring even the most recalcitrant degenerate to heel. Once he could recruit a properly motivated batch of sepoys and come out of the shadows, Jantu could hammer out a decent tech base in a few decades and set about gathering up the reins of galactic power in a tidy, orderly fashion.

But first there was Ganhar, and then Anu. Inanna might be a bit of a problem, for he would continue to need her medical skills, at least until a properly-trained successor was available. Still, he felt confident he could convince the commander to see reason. It would be a pity to mar that lovely new body of hers, but Jantu was a great believer in the efficacy of judiciously applied pain when it came to behavior modification.

He smiled happily, never opening his eyes, and began to hum a bouncier, brighter ditty.

Ramman watched the tunnel walls slide past the cutter and worried. He had the code now. All he had to do was make it to the drop to deposit it. Simple.

And dangerous. He should never have agreed, but the orders had been preemptive, not discretionary. And if the whole idea was insane, he was still in too deep to back out. Or was he?

He scrubbed damp palms on his trousers and closed his eyes. Of course he was! He was a dead man if the "Chief" ever found out he'd even talked to the other side, and his death would be as unpleasant as Anu could contrive.

He clenched his teeth as he contemplated the bitter irony that brought him to this pass. Fear of Anu had tempted him to contact the other side in a desperate effort to escape, yet that same contact had actually destroyed his chance to flee. First Horus and then his bitch of a daughter had steadfastly refused to *let* him defect, far less help him do it!

He made himself stop trying to dry his hands, hoping he hadn't already betrayed himself. He should have realized what would happen. Why should Horus and his fellows trust him? They knew what he was, what he had been, and how easily trusting him could have proven fatal. So they'd left him inside, using him, and he'd let himself be used. What choice had he had? All they had to do to terminate his long existence was wax deliberately clumsy in their efforts to contact him; Anu would see to it from there.

He'd given them a lot of information over the years, and things had gone so smoothly he'd grown almost accustomed to it. But that was before they told him about this. Madness! It would destroy them all, and him with them.

He knew what they had to be planning. Only one thing made sense of his orders, and it was the craziest thing they'd tried yet.

But what if they could pull it off? If they succeeded, surely they would honor their word to him and let him live. Wouldn't they?

Only they wouldn't succeed. They couldn't.

Maybe he should tell Ganhar? If he went to the Operations chief and gave him the location of his drop, helped him bait a trap for Jiltanith's agent . . . surely that should be worth something? Maybe Ganhar could be convinced to pretend it had all been part of an elaborate counter-intelligence ploy?

But what if he couldn't? What if Ganhar simply turned him over to Jantu as the traitor he was?

The huge inner portals opened, admitting the cutter to the hollow heart of the enclave, and Ramman balanced on a razor edge of agonized indecision.

Ganhar rubbed his weary eyes and frowned at the holo map hovering above his desk. Its green dots were fewer than ever, its red dots correspondingly more numerous. His people had maintained direct links with relatively few of the terrorist bases the degenerates had hit, but the fall-out from those strikes was devastating. In less than twenty-four hours, thirty-one—*thirty-one!*—major HQs, training, and base camps had been wiped out in separate, flawlessly synchronized operations whose efficient ferocity had stunned even Ganhar. The shock had been still worse for his degenerate tools; dying for a cause was one thing, but even the most fanatical religious or political bigot must pause and give thought to the body blow international terrorism had just taken.

He sighed. His personal position was in serious jeopardy, and with it his life, and there was disturbingly little he could do about it. Only the fact that he'd warned Anu something might be brewing had saved him so far, and it wouldn't save him very much longer.

His civilian minions' inability to stop their own soldiers or even warn him of what was coming was frightening. *Nergal's* people must have infiltrated the military even more deeply than he'd feared, and if they could do that much, what else might they have accomplished without his noticing?

More to the point, *why* were they doing this? Inanna's suggestion that age had compelled them to attack while they still had enough Imperials to handle their equipment made sense up to a point, but the latest round of disasters had been executed out of purely Terrestrial resources. It took careful planning to blend Terran and Imperial efforts so neatly, which suggested the entire operation had been worked out well in advance. Which, in turn, suggested some long-range objective beyond the destruction of replaceable barbarian allies.

Ganhar got that far without difficulty; unfortunately, it still gave no hint of what the bastards were up to. Drive his sources as he might, he simply couldn't find a single reason for such a fundamental, abrupt change in tactics.

About the only thing his people *had* managed was the identification of one of the enemy's previously unsuspected degenerate henchmen. Not that it helped a great deal, for Hector MacMahan had vanished. Which might mean they'd been intended to spot him, and that—

The admittance chime broke into his thoughts and he straightened, kneading the back of his neck as he sent a mental command to the hatch mechanism. The panel licked aside, and Commander Inanna stepped through it.

Ganhar's eyes widened slightly, for he and the medical officer were scarcely friends—indeed, about the only thing they had in common was their mutual detestation for Jantu—and she'd never visited his private quarters. His mental antennae quivered, and he waved her courteously to a Louis XIV chair under a seventh-century Tang Dynasty tapestry.

"Good evening, Ganhar." She sat and crossed her long, shapely legs. Well, not *hers*, precisely, but then neither was Ganhar's body "his" in the usual sense, and Inanna really had picked a stunningly beautiful one this time.

"Good evening," he replied. His voice gave away nothing, but she smiled as if she sensed his burning curiosity. Which she probably did. She might be unswervingly loyal to a maniac, and it was highly probable she was a bit around the bend herself, but she'd never been dense or unimaginative.

"No doubt you're wondering about this visit," she said. He considered replying but settled for raising his eyebrows politely, and she laughed.

"It's simple enough. You're in trouble, Ganhar. Deep, deep trouble. But you know that, don't you?"

"The thought had crossed my mind," he admitted.

"It's done lots more than that. In fact, you've been sitting here sweating like a pig because you know you're about one more bad report away from—*pffft!*" She snapped her fingers, and he winced.

"Your grief is moving, but I doubt you came just to warn me in case I hadn't noticed."

"True. True." She smiled cheerfully. "You know, I've never liked you, Ganhar. Frankly, I've always thought you were in it out of pure greed, which would be fine if I weren't pretty certain your plans include winding up in charge yourself. With, I'm sure, fatal consequences for Anu and myself."

Ganhar blinked, and her eyes danced at his failure to hide his surprise.

"Ganhar, Ganhar! You disappoint me! Just because you think I'm a little crazy is no reason to think I'm stupid! You may even be right about my mental state, but you really ought to be a bit more careful about letting it color your calculations."

"I see." He propped an elbow on his desk through the holo map and regarded her as calmly as he could. "May I assume you're pointing out my shortcomings for a reason?"

"There. I always knew you were bright." She paused tauntingly, forcing him to ask, and he had no choice but to comply.

"And that reason is?"

"Why, I'm here to help you. Or to propose an alliance, of sorts, at any rate." He sat a bit straighter, and a strange hardness banished all amusement from her eyes.

"Not against Anu, Ganhar," she said coldly. "Whether I'm crazy or not isn't your concern, but make one move against him, and you're a dead man."

Ganhar shivered. He had no idea what that icy guarantee might rest upon, but neither did he have any desire to find out. She sounded far too sure of herself for that, and, as she'd pointed out, she was hardly stupid. Assuming he survived the next few weeks, he was going to have to recast his plans for Commander Inanna.

"I see," he said after a long pause. "But if not against him, then against who?"

"There you go again. Try to accept that I'm reasonably bright, Ganhar. It'll make things much easier for us both."

"Jantu?"

"Of course. That weasel has plans for all of us. But then," her smile turned wolfish, "I have plans for him, too. Jantu's in very poor health; he just doesn't know it yet. He won't—until his next transplant comes due."

Ganhar shivered again. Brain transplants were ticklish even with Imperial technology, and a certain number of fatalities were probably unavoidable, but he'd assumed Anu decided which patients suffered complications. It hadn't occurred to him Inanna might be doing it on her own.

"So," she went on pleasantly, "we still have to decide what to do with him in the meantime. If he ever left the enclave, he might have an accident. I'd considered that, and it would've been a neat way to get him, Kirinal, *and* you, wouldn't it? You're in charge of external operations . . . he's your worst rival . . . who wouldn't've wondered if you two hadn't arranged it?"

"You have a peculiar way of convincing an 'ally' to trust you," Ganhar pointed out carefully.

"I'm only proving I can be honest with you, Ganhar. Doesn't my openness reassure you?"

"Not particularly."

"Well, that's probably wise of you. And that's my point; you really are much smarter than Jantu—less devious, but smarter. And because you are, I'm reasonbly certain *your* plans to assassinate Anu—and possibly myself— don't envision any immediate execution date." She smiled cheerfully at her own play on words. "But if you disappeared from the equation, Jantu is stupid enough to make his try immediately. He wouldn't succeed, but he doesn't know that, and I'm sure it would come to open fighting in the end. If that happened, Anu or I might be among the casualties. I wouldn't like that."

"So why not tell Anu?"

"The one absolutely predictable thing about you is your ability to disappoint me, Ganhar. You must be crazy yourself if you think I haven't realized Anu is. The technical term, if you're wondering, is advanced paranoia, complicated by megalomania. He hasn't quite reached grossly delusional proportions yet, but he's headed that way. And while we're being so honest, let's admit that paranoia can be a survival tool in situations like his. After all, a paranoic is only crazy when people *aren't* out to get him.

"But the point is that I'm probably the only person he trusts at all, and one reason he does is that I've very carefully avoided getting caught up in any of our little intrigues. But if I warned him about Jantu, he'd start wondering if I hadn't decided to join with you, instead. He's not exactly noted for moderation, and the simplest solution to his problem would be to kill all three of us. I wouldn't like that, either."

"Then why not—"

"Careful, Ganhar!" She leaned towards him, her eyes hard as two black opals, and her soft, soft voice was almost a hiss. "Be very, *very* careful what you suggest to me. Of course I could. I'm his doctor, after all. But I won't. Not now, not ever. Remember that."

"I . . . understand," he said, licking his lips.

"I doubt that." Her eyes softened, and somehow that frightened Ganhar even more than their hardness had, but then she shook her head. "No, I doubt that," she said more naturally, "but it doesn't matter. What matters is that you have an ally against Jantu—for now, at least. We both know things are going to get worse before they get better, but I'll do what I can to draw fire from you during conferences, and I'll support you against Jantu and maybe even when you stand up to *him*. Not always directly, perhaps, but I will. I want you around to take charge when we start rebuilding your operations network."

"You mean you want me around because you *don't* want Jantu in charge, right?" Ganhar asked, meeting her eyes fully.

"Well, of course. But it's the same thing, isn't it?"

It most definitely wasn't the same thing, but Ganhar chose not to press the point. She peered deeply into his eyes for a moment, then nodded.

"I can just see your busy little mind whirring away in there," she said dryly. "That's good. But, as one ally to another, I'd advise you to come up with some sort of forceful recommendation for Anu. Something positive and masterful. It doesn't have to actually *accomplish* much, you understand, but a little violence would be helpful. He'll like that. The notion of hitting back—of *doing* something—always appeals to megalomaniacs."

"I—" Ganhar broke off and drew a deep breath. "Inanna, you have to realize how what you've just said sounds. I'm not going to suggest that you do anything to Anu. You're right; I don't understand why you feel the way you do, but I'll accept it and remember it. But don't you worry about what else I might do with the insight you've just given me?"

"Of course not, Ganhar." She lounged back in her chair with a kindly air. "We both know I've just turned all of your calculations topsy-turvy, but you're a bright little boy. Given a few decades to consider it, you'll realize I wouldn't have done it if I hadn't already taken precautions. That's valuable in its own right, don't you think? I mean, knowing that, crazy or not, I'll kill you the moment you become a threat to Anu or me is bound to color your thinking, isn't it?"

"I suppose you could put it that way."

"Then my visit hasn't been a waste, has it?" She rose and stretched, deliberately taunting him with the exquisite perfection of the body she wore as she turned for the hatch. Then she paused and looked back over her shoulder almost coquettishly.

"Oh! I almost forgot. I meant to warn you about Bahantha."

Ganhar blinked again. What about Bahantha? She was his senior assistant, number two in Operations now that he'd replaced Kirinal, and she was one of the very few people he trusted. His thoughts showed in his face, and Inanna shook her head at his expression.

"Men! You didn't even know that she's Jantu's lover, did you?" She laughed merrily at his sudden shock.

"Are you certain?" he demanded.

"Of course. Jantu controls the official security channels, but *I* control biosciences, and that's a much better spy system than he has. You might want to remember that yourself. But the thing is, I think you'd better arrange for her to suffer a mischief, don't you? An accident would be nice. Nothing that would cast suspicion on you, just enough to send her along to sickbay." Her toothy smile put Ganhar forcefully in mind of a Terran piranha.

"I . . . understand," he said.

"Good," she replied, and sauntered from his cabin. The hatch closed, and Ganhar looked blindly back at the map. It was amazing. He'd just acquired a powerful ally . . . so why did he feel so much worse?

Abu al-Nasir, who had not allowed himself to think of himself as Andrew Asnani in over two years, sat in the rear of the cutter and yawned. He'd seen enough Imperial technology in the last six months to take the wonder out of it, and he judged it best to let the Imperials about him see it.

In fact, his curiosity was unquenchable, for unlike most of the northerners' Terra-born, he had never seen *Nergal* and never knowingly met a single one of their Imperials. That, coupled with his Semitic heritage, was what had made him so perfect for this role. He was of them, yet apart from them, unrelated to them by blood and with no family heritage of assistance to connect him to them, however deep the southerners looked.

It also meant he hadn't grown up knowing the truth, and the shock of discovering it had been the second most traumatic event in his life. But it had offered him both vengeance and a chance to build something positive from the wreckage of his life, and that was more than he'd let himself hope for in far too long.

He yawned again, remembering the evening his universe had changed. He'd known something special was about to happen, although his wildest expectations had fallen immeasurably short of the reality. Full colonels with the

USFC did not, as a rule, invite junior sergeants in the venerable Eighty-Second Airborne to meet them in the middle of a North Carolina forest in the middle of the night. Not even when the sergeant in question had applied for duty with the USFC's anti-terrorist action units. Unless, of course, his application had been accepted and something very, very strange was in the air.

But his application had not been accepted, for the USFC had never even officially seen it. Colonel MacMahan had scooped it out of his computers and hidden it away because he had an offer for Sergeant Asnani. A very special offer that would require that Sergeant Asnani die.

The colonel, al-Nasir admitted to himself, had been an excellent judge of character. Young Asnani's mother, father, and younger sister had walked down a city street in New Jersey just as a Black Mecca bomb went off, and when he heard what the colonel had to suggest, he was more than ready to accept.

The pre-arranged "fatal" practice jump accident had gone off perfectly, purging Asnani from all active data bases, and his true training had begun. The USFC hadn't had a thing to do with it, although it had been some time before Asnani realized that. Nor had he guessed that the exhausting training program was also a final test, an evaluation of both capabilities and character, until the people who had actually recruited him told him the truth.

Had anyone but Hector MacMahan told him, he might not have believed it, despite the technological marvels the colonel demonstrated. But when he realized who had truly recruited him and why, and that his family had been but three more deaths among untold millions slaughtered so casually over the centuries, he had been ready. And so it was that when the USFC mounted Operation Odysseus, the man who had been Andrew Asnani was inserted with it, completely unknown to anyone but Hector MacMahan himself.

Now the cutter slanted downward, and Abu al-Nasir, deputy action commander of Black Mecca, prepared to greet the people who had summoned him here.

"Except for the fact that we've only gotten one man inside, things seem to be moving well," Hector MacMahan said. Jiltanith had followed him into the wardroom, and she nodded to Colin and selected a chair of her own, sitting with her habitual cat-like grace.

"So far," Colin agreed. "What do you and 'Tanni expect next?"

"Hard to say," Hector admitted. "They've got most of their people inside by now, and, logically, they'll sit tight in their enclave to wait us out. On the other hand, every time we use any of our own Imperials in an operation we give them a chance to trail someone back to us, so they'll probably leave us some sacrificial goats. We'll have to hit a few of them to make it work, and I've already put the ops plan into the works. We're on schedule, but everything still depends on luck and timing."

"Why am I unhappy whenever you use words like 'logically' and 'luck'?"

"Because you know the southerners may not be too tightly wrapped, and that even if they are, we have to do things exactly right to bring this off."

"Hector hath the right of't, Colin," Jiltanith said. " 'Tis clear enow that Anu, at the least, is mad, and what means have we whereby to judge the depth his madness hath attained? I'truth, 'tis in my mind that divers others of his minions do share his madness, else had they o'erthrown him long before. 'Twould be rankest folly in our plans to make assumption madmen do rule their inner councils, yet ranker far to make assumption they do not. And if that be so, then naught but fools would foretell their plans wi' certainty."

"I see. But haven't we tried to do just that?"

"There's truth i'that. Yet so we must, if hope may be o'victory. And as Hector saith, 'tis clear some movement hath been made e'en now amongst their minions. Mad or sane, Anu hath scant choice i'that. 'Tis also seen how his 'goats' do stand exposed, temptations to our fire, and so 'twould seem good Hector hath beagled out the manner of their thought aright. Yet 'tis also true that one ill choice may yet bring ruin 'pon us all. I'truth, I do not greatly fear it, for Hector hath a cunning mind. We stand all in his hand, empowered by his thought, and 'tis most unlike our great design will go awry."

"Spare my blushes," MacMahan said dryly. "Remember I only got one man inside, and even if the core of our strategy works perfectly, we could still get hurt along the way."

"Certes, yet wert ever needle-witted, e'en as a child, my Hector." She smiled and ruffled her distant nephew's hair, and he forgot his customary impassivity as he grinned at her. "And hath it not been always so? Naught worth the doing comes free o'danger. Yet 'tis in my mind 'tis in smaller things we may find ourselves dismayed, not in the greater."

"Like what?" Colin demanded.

"That depends on too many factors for us to say. If it didn't, they wouldn't be surprises. It's unlikely anything they do to us can hurt us too much, but you're a military man yourself, Colin. What's the first law of war?"

"Murphy's," Colin said grimly.

"Exactly. We've disaster-proofed our position as well as we can, but the fact remains that we're betting on just a pair, as Horus would say—Ramman and Ninhursag—and one hole card—our man inside Black Mecca. We don't know what cards Anu holds, but if he decides to fold this hand or even just stands pat for a few years, it all comes unglued."

"For God's sake spare me the poker metaphors!"

"Sorry, but they fit. The most important single factor is Anu's mental state. If he suddenly turns sane and decides to ignore us until we go away, we lose. We have to do him enough damage to make him antsy, and we have to do it in a way that keeps him from getting too suspicious. We have to hurt him enough to make him eager to come back out and start making repairs, but at the same time we have to *stop* hurting him in a way that leaves him confident enough to come right back out. Which means we have to hit at least some of his 'goats' after his important personnel have all gone to ground, then wind down when it's obvious our returns are starting to diminish."

"Well," Colin tried to project both confidence and caution, "if anyone can pull it off, you two can."

"Thanks, I think," Hector said, and Jiltanith nodded.

✧   ✧   ✧

The stocky, olive-brown-skinned woman sat quietly in the cutter, but her eyes were bright and busy. There were Terra-born as well as Imperials around her, and the trickiest part was showing just enough interest in them.

Ninhursag had never considered herself an actress, but perhaps she was one now. If so, her continued survival might be said to constitute a favorable review.

She'd lived in the enclave only briefly and had not returned in over a century, so a certain amount of interest was natural. By the same token, any Terra-born being brought into the enclave must be important and thus a logical cause for curiosity. The trick was to display her curiosity without giving anyone cause to suspect that she knew at least one of them was far more than he seemed. Her instructions made no mention of Terra-born allies, but they made no sense if there were no couriers, and if those couriers were Imperials she might as well have carried the information out herself.

At the same time, she knew she was suspect as one who had never been part of Anu's inner circle, so a certain nervousness was also natural. Yet showing too much nervousness would be worse than showing none at all. Her actions and attitude must show she knew she was under suspicion yet appear too cowed for that suspicion to be justified.

In truth, it was the last part she found hardest. Her horror at what Anu and Inanna had done to her fellow mutineers and the poor, helpless primitives of this planet had become cold, hard fury, and she hated the need to restrain it. When she'd learned Horus and the rest of *Nergal*'s crew had deserted Anu and chosen to fight him, her first thought had been to defect to them, but they'd convinced her she was more valuable inside Anu's organization. No doubt caution played a part in that—they didn't entirely trust her and wanted to take no chances on infiltration of their own ranks— but that was inevitable, and her only other option would have been to strike out on her own, vanishing and doing nothing in order to hide from both factions.

Yet doing nothing had been unthinkable, and so she had become *Nergal*'s not-quite-trusted spy, fully aware of the terrifying risk she ran. Terror had been a cold, omnipresent part of her for far too long, but it was not her master. That had been left to another emotion: hate.

The sudden outbreak of violence had surprised her as much as it had any of Anu's loyalists, but coupled with the odd instructions she'd received from Jiltanith, it made frightening, exhilarating sense. There was only one reason Anu's enemies could want those admittance codes.

She'd tried not to wonder how they hoped to get them out of the enclave, for what she neither knew nor suspected could not be wrung out of her, but she'd always been cursed with an active mind, and the bare bones of their plan were glaringly obvious. Its mad recklessness shocked her, but she knew what they planned, and hopeless though it might well be, she was eager.

The cutter nosed downward, and she felt her implants tingle as they waited to steal the key to Anu's fortress for his foes.

CHAPTER SEVENTEEN

Dark and silence ruled the interior of the mighty starship. Only the hydroponic sections and parks and atriums were lit, yet the whole stupendous structure pulsed with the electronic awarness of the being called Dahak.

It was good, the computer reflected, that he was not human, for a human in his place would have gone mad long before Man relearned the art of working metal. Of course, a human might also have found a way to act without needing to wait for a Colin MacIntyre.

But he was not human. There were human qualities he did not possess, for they had not been built into him. His core programming was heuristic, else he had not developed this concept of selfhood that separated him from the Comp Cent of old, yet he had not made that final transition into *human-ness*. Still, he had come closer than any other of his kind ever had, and perhaps someday he would take that step. He rather looked forward to the possibility, and he wondered if his ability to anticipate that potentiality reflected the beginnings of an imagination.

It was an interesting question, one upon which even he might profitably spend a few endless seconds of thought, but one he could not answer. He was the product of intellect and electronics, not intuition and evolution, with no experiential basis for any of the intangible human capacities and emotions. Imagination, ambition, compassion, mercy, empathy, hate, longing . . . love. They were words he had found in his memory when he awoke, concepts whose definitions he could recite with neither hesitation nor true understanding.

And yet . . . and yet there *were* those stirrings at his soulless core. Did this cold determination of his to destroy the mutineers and all their works reflect only the long-dead Druaga's Alpha Priority commands? Or was it possible that the determination was his, Dahak's, as well?

One thing he did know; he had made greater strides in learning to comprehend rather than simply define human emotions in the six months of Colin MacIntyre's command than in the fifty-two millennia that had preceded them. Another entity, separate from himself, had intruded into his lonely universe, someone who had treated him not as a machine, not as a portion of a starship that simply had the ability to speak, but as a person.

That was a novel thing, and in the weeks since Colin had departed, Dahak had replayed their every conversation, studied every recorded gesture, analyzed almost every thought his newest captain had thought or seemed to think. There was a strange compulsion within him, one created by no command and that no diagnostic program could dissect, and that, too, was a novel experience.

Dahak had studied his newest Alpha Priority orders, as well, constructing, as ordered, new models and new projections in light of the discovery of a second faction of mutineers. That process he understood, and the exercise of his faculties gave him something he supposed a human would call enjoyment.

But other parts of those orders were highly dissatisfying. He understood and accepted the prohibition against sending his captain further aid or taking any direct action before the northern mutineers attacked the southern lest he reveal his actual capabilities. But the order to communicate with the northern leaders in the event of Colin's death and the categorical, inarguable command to place himself under the command of one Jiltanith and the other mutineer children—*those* he would obey because he must, not because he wished to.

Wished to. Why, he *was* becoming more human. What business had a computer thinking in terms of its own wishes? If ever he had expressed a wish or desire to his core programmers, they would have been horrified. They would have shut him down, purged his memory, reprogrammed him from scratch.

But Colin would not have. And that, Dahak realized, in the very first flash of intuition he had ever experienced, was the reason he did not wish to obey his orders. If he must obey them, it would mean that Colin was dead, and Dahak did not *wish* for Colin to die, for Colin was something far more important to Dahak's comfortable functioning than the computer had realized.

He was a friend, the first friend Dahak had ever had, and with that realization, a sudden tremble seemed to run through the vast, molecular circuitry of his mighty intellect. He had a *friend*, and he understood the concept of friendship. Imperfectly, perhaps, but did humans understand it perfectly themselves? They did not.

Yet imperfect though his understanding was, the concept was a gestalt of staggering efficacy. He had internalized it without ever realizing it, and with it he had internalized all those other "human" emotions, after a fashion, at least. For with friendship came fear—fear for a friend in danger— and the ability to hate those who threatened that friend.

It was not an entirely pleasant thing, the huge computer mused, this friendship. The cold, intellectual detachment of his armor had been rent— not fully, but in part—and for the first time in fifty millennia, the bitter irony of helplessness in the face of his mighty firepower was real, and it hurt. There. Yet another human concept: pain.

The mighty, hidden starship swept onward in its endless orbit, silent and dark, untenanted, yet filled with life. Filled with awareness and anxiety and a new, deeply personal purpose, for the mighty electronic intellect, the *person*, at its core had learned to care at last . . . and knew it.

The small party crept invisibly through the streets of Tehran. Their black, close-fitting clothing would have marked them as foreigners—emissaries, no doubt, of the "Great Satans"—had any seen them, but no one did, for the technical wizardry of the Fourth Imperium was abroad in Tehran this night.

Tamman paused at a corner to await the return of his nominal second-in-command, feeling deaf and blind within his portable stealth field. It was strange to realize a Terra-born human could be better at something like this than he, yet Tamman could not remember a time when he had not "seen" and "felt" his full electromagnetic and gravitonic environment. Because of that, he felt incomplete, almost maimed, even with his sensory boosters, when he must rely solely upon his natural senses, and taking point was not a job for a man whose confidence was shaken, however keen his eyes or ears might be.

Sergeant Amanda Givens returned as silently as the night wind, ghosting back into his awareness, and nodded to him. He nodded back, and he and the other five members of their team crept forward once more behind her.

Tamman was grateful she was here. Amanda was one of their own, directly descended from *Nergal*'s crew, and, like Hector, she'd also been a member of the USFC until very recently. She reminded Tamman of Jiltanith; not in looks, for she was as plain as 'Tanni was beautiful, but in her feline, eternally poised readiness and inner strength. The fact that her merely human senses and capabilities were inferior to an Imperial's had not shaken her confidence in herself. If only she could have been given an implant set, he thought. She was no beauty, but he felt more than passing interest in her, more than he'd felt in any woman since Himeko.

She stopped again, so suddenly he almost ran into her, and she grinned at him reprovingly. He managed a grin of his own, but he felt uneasy . . . limited. Give him an Imperial fighter and a half-dozen hostiles and he would feel at home; here he was truly alien, out of his depth and aware of it.

Amanda pointed, and Tamman nodded as he recognized the dilapidated buildings they'd come to find. It must have tickled the present regime to put Black Mecca's HQ in the old British Embassy compound, and it must have galled Black Mecca to settle for it instead of the crumbling old American Embassy the mainstream faction of the Islamic Jihad had claimed.

He waved orders to his team and they spread out, finding cover behind the unmanned outer perimeter of sandbags. He recalled the vitriolic diatribes that often emanated from this very spot, beamed to the world of Black Mecca's enemies. These positions were always manned, then, with troops "prepared to defend their faith with their life's blood" against the eternally impending attack of the Great Satans. Not, of course, that any member of Black Mecca had ever believed any enemy could actually reach them here.

He checked his team once more. All were under cover, and he raised his energy gun. His fellows were all Terra-born, trained for missions like this one by their own governments or in classes conducted by people like Hector and Amanda. They were skilled and deadly with the weapons of the Terrestrial military, but far more deadly with the weapons they carried now. None was strong enough to carry energy guns, not even the cut-down, customized one he carried, but *Nergal*'s crew had specialized in ingenious adaptation for centuries, and the fruits of their labor were here tonight, for Hector wanted Anu to know precisely who was behind this attack.

Tamman pressed the firing stud, and the silent night exploded.

The deadly focus of gravitonic disruption slammed into the inner sandbags around the compound gate, shredding their plastic envelopes, filling the air with flying sand, slicing the drowsy sentries in half. Their gore mixed with the sand, spattering the wall behind them with red mud, but only until the ravening fury of the energy gun ripped into that wall in turn.

Stone dust billowed. Chips of brick and cement rattled like hail, and Tamman swept his beam like a hose, spraying destruction across the compound while the energy gun heated dangerously in his hands. Tamman was a powerful man, a tall, disciplined mass of bone and muscle, for he'd known he would never have a full implant set. Fanatical exercise had been his way of compensating for that deprivation, and it was the only reason he could use even this cut-down energy gun. It was heavier than most Terran-made crewed weapons, but still lighter than a full-sized Imperial weapon, and most of the weight saved had come out of its heat dissipation systems. It was far less durable, and the demands he was making upon it were ruinous, but he held the stud down, flaying the compound.

The outer wall went down and the closest building fronts exploded in dust and flying shards of glass. Light sparked and spalled, fountaining sparks as broken electric cables cracked like whips. Small fires started, and still the energy blasted into the buildings. It sheared through structural members like tissue, and the upper floors began an inexorable collapse.

A harsh buzz from the gun warned of the imminent failure of its abused, lightweight circuitry, and Tamman released the stud at last.

The high, dreadful keening of the wounded floated on the night wind, and the slither and crash of collapsing buildings rumbled in the darkness. Half-clothed figures darted madly, their frantic confusion evident through the attack team's low-light optics. Black Mecca's surveillance systems still reported nothing, and the terrible near-silence of the energy gun only added to their bewilderment, but the true nightmare had scarcely begun.

Three shoulder-slung grav guns opened fire, raking the compound across the wreckage of the outer wall. The sound of their firing was no more than a loud, sibilant hiss, lost in the whickering *"cracks"* of their supersonic projectiles, and there was no muzzle flash. Most of the deadly darts were inert, this time, but every fifth round was explosive. More of Black Mecca died or blew apart or collapsed screaming, and then the grenade launchers opened up.

There were no explosions, for these were Imperial warp grenades, and the principle upon which they worked was terrible in its dreadful elegance.

They were small hyper generators, little larger than a large man's fist, and as each grenade landed it became the center of a ten-meter multi-dimensional transposition field. Anything within that spherical area of effect simply vanished into hyperspace with a hand-clap of imploding air . . . forever.

Chunks of pavement and broken stone disappeared quietly into eternity, and the screaming terrorists went mad. Men and, infinitely worse, *parts* of men went with those grenades, and the near-total silence of the carnage was more than they could stand. They stampeded and ran, dying as the grav guns continued to fire, and then the madness of the night reached its terrible climax as Amanda Givens fired her own weapon at last.

Noon-day light splashed the moonless sky as she dropped a plasma grenade among their enemies and, for one dreadful moment, the heart of the sun itself raged unchecked. It was pure, stone-fusing energy, consuming the very air, and thermal radiation lashed out from the center of destruction. It caught its victims mercilessly, turning running figures into torches, touching wreckage to flame, blinding the unwary who looked directly at it.

And when the fiery glare vanished as abruptly as it had come, the attack ended. The hissing roar of flames and the screams of their own maimed and dying were all the world the handful of surviving terrorists had, and the smoke that billowed heavenward was heavy with the stench of burning flesh.

The seven executioners faded silently away. Their stealthed cutter collected them forty minutes later.

Lieutenant General Gerald Hatcher frowned as he studied the classified folder, but his frown turned wry for a moment as he considered the absurdity of classifying something the entire planet was buzzing over.

His amusement faded as quickly as it had come, and he leaned back in his swivel chair, lips pursed as he considered.

The . . . peculiar events of the past few weeks had produced a massive ground swell of uncertainty, and the "unscheduled vacations" of a surprising number of government, industry, and economic leaders had not helped settle the public's mind. To an extent, those disappearances had been quite helpful to Hatcher, for the vanished leaders included most of the ones he'd expected to protest his unauthorized, unsanctioned, and quite possibly illegal attacks on terrorist enclaves. He did not, however, find their absence reassuring.

He drummed his fingers on his blotter and wished—not for the first time—that he'd been less quick to order Hector MacMahan to disappear . . . not that his instructions could have made too much difference to Hector's plans. Still, he wanted, more than he'd ever wanted anything in his life, to spend a few minutes listening to Hector explain this insanity.

One thing was abundantly clear: the best of humanity's so-called experts had no idea how whatever was happening was being done. Their best explanation of that new, deep crater outside Cuernavaca was a meteor strike, but no one had put it forward very seriously. Even leaving aside the seismographic proof that it had resulted from *multiple* strikes and its impossibly precise point of impact, it was inconceivable that something that size could have burned its way through atmosphere without anyone even seeing it coming!

Then there were those unexplained nuclear explosions out over the Pacific. At least they had a fair idea how nuclear weapons worked, but who had used them upon whom? And what about those strikes in China and the Tatra Mountains? Those had been air strikes, whatever Cuernavaca might have been, but no one had explained how the aircraft in question had evaded look-down radar, satellite reconnaissance, and plain old human eyesight. Hatcher had no firm intel on Fenyang, but the Gerlochovoko strike had used "conventional" explosives, though the analysts' best estimate of the warhead yields had never come from any chemical explosive *they* knew anything about, and the leftover bits and pieces of pulverized alloy and crystal had never come from any Terran tech base.

Now this. Abeokuta, Beirut, Damascus, Kuieyang, Mirzapur, Tehran. . . . Someone was systematically hitting terrorist bases, the dream targets no Western military man had ever hoped to hit, and gutting them. *And* they were doing it with more of the damned weapons his people had never even heard of!

Except for Hector, of course. Hatcher was absolutely certain Hector not only knew what was happening but also had played a not inconsiderable part in arranging for it to happen. That was more than mildly disturbing, considering the security checks Colonel MacMahan had undergone, his outstanding record as an officer, and the fact that he was one of Gerald Hatcher's personal friends.

One thing was crystal clear, though no one seemed inclined to admit it. Whoever had gone to war against Earth's terrorists hadn't come from Earth, not with the things they were capable of doing. Which led to all sorts of other maddening questions. Who were they? Where *had* they come from? Why were they here? Why hadn't they announced themselves to the human race in general?

Hatcher couldn't answer any of those questions. Perhaps he never would be able to, but he didn't think it would work out that way, for the evidence, fragmentary as it was, suggested at least one other unpalatable fact. At least two factions were locked in combat, and one or the other was going to win, eventually.

He closed the folder, buzzing for his aide to return it to the vault. Then he sighed and stood looking out his office windows.

Oh, yes. One side was going to win, and when they did, they were going to make their presence felt. Openly felt, that was, for Hatcher was morally certain that they'd *already* made themselves at home. It would explain so much. The upsurge in terrorism, the curious unwillingness of First World governments to do much about it, those mysterious "vacations," Hector's obvious involvement with at least one faction of what *had* to be extra-terrestrials . . .

All the selective destruction could mean only one thing: a covert war was spilling over into the open, and it was being fought on Hatcher's planet.

The whole damned Earth was holding its collective breath, waiting to see who won, and they didn't even know who was doing the fighting!

But Hatcher suspected that, like him, most of those uncertain billions prayed to God nightly for the side that was trashing the terrorists. Because if the side that *backed* people like Black Mecca won, this planet faced one hell of a nightmare. . . .

Colonel Hector MacMahan sat in his office aboard his people's single warship, and studied his own reports. His eyes ached from watching the old-fashioned phosphor screen, and he felt a brief, bitter envy of the Imperials about him. It wasn't the first time he'd envied their neural feeds and computer shunts.

He leaned back and massaged his temples. Things were going well, but he was uneasy. He always was when an op was under way, but this was worse than usual. Something was nagging at a corner of his brain, and that frightened him. He'd heard that taunting voice only infrequently, for he was good at his job and serious mistakes were few, but he recognized it. He'd forgotten something, miscalculated somewhere, made some unwarranted assumption . . . *something*. And his subconscious knew what it was, he reflected grimly; the problem was how to drive it up into his forebrain.

He sighed and closed his eyes, allowing his face to show the worry he showed to neither subordinates nor superiors, but he couldn't pin it down. So far, their losses had been incredibly light: a single Imperial and five of their own Terra-born. No Imperial, however young, could have survived a lucky burst from a thirty-millimeter cannon, but Tarhani should never have been permitted to lead the Beirut raid at her age. Yet she'd been adamant. She'd hated that city for over fifty years, ever since a truck bomb blew her favorite grandson into death along with two hundred of his fellow Marines.

He shook his head. Revenge was a motivation professionals sought to avoid, far less accepted as a reason for assigning other personnel to high-risk missions. But not this time. Win or lose, this was *Nergal's* final campaign, and 'Hani had been right: she *was* old. If someone were to die leading the attack, better that it should be her than one of the children. . . .

Yet MacMahan knew there was another factor. For all his training and experience, all the hard-won competence with which he'd planned and mounted this operation, he was a child. It had always been so. A man among men among the Terra-born; a child—in years, at least—when he boarded *Nergal.*

The Imperials were careful to avoid emphasizing that point, and he knew they accepted him as an equal, but *he* couldn't accept *them* as equals. He knew what people like Horus and 'Hani, Geb and Hanalat, 'Tanni and Tamman, had seen and endured, and he felt a deep, almost sublime respect for them, but respect was only part of his complicated feelings. He knew their weaknesses, knew this entire situation arose from mistakes *they* had made, yet he venerated them. They were his family, his ancestors, the ancient, living avatars of the cause to which he'd dedicated his life. He'd known how much the Beirut mission meant to 'Hani . . . that was the real reason he'd let her lead it.

But that got him no closer to recognizing whatever that taunting little voice was trying to tell him about.

He rose and switched off his terminal. One other thing he'd learned about that voice; letting it mesmerize him was worse than ignoring it. A few more raids on Anu's peripheral links to Terra's terrorists, and it would be time for Operation Stalking-Horse, the ostensible reason for winding down the violence.

He was a bit surprised by how glad that made him. The northerners' targets were terrorists, but they were also humans, of a sort, and their slaughter weighed upon his soul. Not because of what they were, but because of what it was doing to his own people . . . and to him.

"It seems to me," Jantu said thoughtfully, "that we ought to be thinking of some way to respond to these attacks."

He paused to sip coffee, watching Anu from the corner of one eye, and only long practice kept his smile from showing as the "Chief" glared at Ganhar. Poor, harried Ganhar was about to become poor, dead Ganhar, for there was no way he *could* respond, and Jantu waited expectantly for him to try to squirm out of his predicament.

But Ganhar had himself well in hand. He met Jantu's eyes almost blandly, and something about his expression suddenly bothered the Security head. He had not quite put a mental finger on it when Ganhar shattered all his calculations.

"I agree," he said calmly, and Jantu choked on his coffee. Fortunately for his peace of mind, he was too busy dabbing at the coffee stains on his tunic to notice the slight smile in Commander Inanna's eyes.

"Oh?" Anu eyed Ganhar sharply, his eyes hard. "That's nice, Ganhar, considering the mess you've made of things so far."

"With all due respect, Chief," Ganhar sounded far calmer than Jantu knew he could possibly be, "*I* didn't get us into this situation. I only inherited Operations after Kirinal was killed. In the second place, I warned you from the start I was unhappy about how quiet the degenerate militaries were being *and* that we had no way of knowing what their Imperials were going to do next." He shrugged. "My people gave you all the information there was, Chief. There simply wasn't enough to predict what was coming."

Anu glared at him, and Ganhar made himself meet that glare levelly.

"You mean," Anu said dangerously, "that you didn't *spot* the information."

"No, I mean it wasn't there. You've had eight Operations heads in the last two thousand years, Chief—nine, counting me—and none of us have found *Nergal* for you. You know how hard we've worked at it. But if we can't even *find* them, how are we supposed to know what's going on in their inner councils? All I'm trying to say is that we can't do it."

"It sounds to me," Anu's soft voice rose steadily towards even more dangerous levels, "like you're trying to cover your ass. It sounds to *me* like you're making piss-poor excuses because you don't have one Maker-damned idea what to do about it!"

"You're wrong, Chief," Ganhar said, though it took most of his remaining courage to get it out. Anu wasn't accustomed to being told he was wrong, and his face took on an apoplectic hue as Ganhar continued, taking advantage of the pregnant silence. "I *do* have a plan, as it happens. Two, in fact."

Anu's breath escaped in a hiss. His minions seldom took that calm, almost challenging tone with him, and the shock of hearing it broke through his anger. Maybe Ganhar really had enough of a plan to justify his apparent confidence. If not, he could be killed just as well after listening to him as before.

"All right," he grated. "Tell us."

"Of course. First and simplest, we can do nothing at all. We've got our people under cover now, and all they're managing to do is tear up a bunch of purely degenerate terrorists. It makes a lot of noise, and it may look impressive to them, but, fundamentally, they aren't hurting *us*. We can always recruit more of the same, and every time they use Imperial technology, *they* risk losing people and *we* have a chance of tracking them back to *Nergal*."

Ganhar watched Anu's eyes. He knew—as, surely, Jantu and Inanna did—that what he'd just suggested was the smart thing to do. Unfortunately, Anu's eyes told him it wasn't the smart thing to *suggest*. He shrugged mentally and dusted off his second proposal.

"That's the simplest thing, but I don't think it's necessarily the best," he lied. "We know some of their degenerates, and we've spotted some others who *could* be working for them." He shrugged again, this time physically. "All right, if they want to escalate, we've got more people and a lot more resources. Let's escalate right back."

"Ah?" Anu raised an eyebrow, his expression arrested.

"Exactly, Chief. They surprised us at Colorado Springs, and they've been riding the advantage of surprise ever since. They've been on the offensive, and so far it's only cost them a few dozen degenerate military types in attacks on domestic terrorists and *maybe*—" he emphasized the qualifier "—one or two of their own people since they've started going after foreign bases on the ground. They're probably feeling pretty confident about now, so let's kill a few of their people and see if they get the message."

He smiled unpleasantly and tried not to sigh in relief as Anu smiled back. He watched the chief mutineer's slow nod, then swiveled his eyes challengingly to Jantu, enjoying the angry frustration in the Security man's expression.

"How?" Anu's voice was soft, but his eyes were eager.

"We've already made a start, Chief. My people are trying to predict their next targets so we can put a few of our own teams in positions to intervene. After that, we can start hitting suspects direct. Give 'em a taste of their own medicine, you might say."

"I like it, Chief," Inanna said softly. Anu glanced at her, and she shrugged. "At the least, it'll keep them from having things all their own way, and, with luck, we may actually get a few of their Imperials. Every one they lose is going to hurt them far worse than the same loss would hurt us."

"I agree," Anu said, and Ganhar felt as if the weight of the planet had been lifted from his back. "Maker, Ganhar! I didn't think you had it in you. Why didn't you suggest this sooner?"

"I thought it would have been premature. We didn't know how serious an attack they meant to mount. If it was only a probe, a powerful response might actually have encouraged them to press harder in retaliation." And wasn't *that* a mouthful of nothing, Ganhar thought sourly. But Anu's smile grew.

"I see. Well, get it in the works. Let's send a few of them and their precious degenerates to the Breaker and see how they like that!"

Ganhar smiled back. Actually, he thought, except for the possibility of ambushing the other side's raiding parties it was the stupidest thing he'd ever suggested. Almost every degenerate his people had suspected of being among *Nergal*'s henchmen had already vanished as completely as Hector MacMahan. He'd target his remaining suspects first, but after that he might as well pick targets at random. Aside from the satisfaction Anu might take from it, they would accomplish exactly nothing, however many degenerates they blew away.

It was insane and probably futile, but Inanna had been right. The violence of the plan obviously appealed to Anu, and that was what mattered. As long as Anu was convinced Ganhar was Doing Something, Ganhar would hang on to his position and the perquisites that went with it. Like breathing.

"Let me have a preliminary plan as soon as possible, Ganhar," Anu said, addressing the Operations head more courteously than he had since Cuernavaca. Then he nodded dismissal, and his three subordinates rose to leave.

Jantu was in a hurry to get back to his office, but Inanna blocked him in the corridor, apparently by accident, as she turned to Ganhar.

"Oh, Ganhar," she said, "I'm afraid I have some bad news for you."

"Oh?"

Jantu paused as Ganhar spoke. He wanted to hear anything that was trouble for Ganhar, he thought viciously.

"Yes. One of your people got caught in a malfunction in *Bislaht*'s transit shaft—a freak grav surge. We didn't think she was too badly hurt when they brought her into sickbay, but I'm afraid we were wrong. I'm sorry to say one of my med techs missed a cerebral hemorrhage, and we lost her."

"Oh." There was something strange about Ganhar's voice. He didn't sound surprised enough, and there was an odd, sick little undertone. "Uh, who was it?" he asked after a moment.

"Bahantha, I'm afraid," Inanna said, and Jantu froze. He stared at Inanna in disbelief, and she turned slowly to meet his eyes. Something gleamed in the depths of her own gaze, and he swallowed, filled with a sudden dread suspicion.

"I see it's shaken you, too, Jantu," she said softly. "Terrible, isn't it? Even here in the enclave, you can't be entirely safe, can you?"

And she smiled.

CHAPTER EIGHTEEN

"God damn them! Damn them to Hell!"

Hector MacMahan's normally expressionless face twisted with fury. His clenched fists trembled at his sides, and Colin looked away from the colonel, sick at heart himself, to study the other three people at the table.

Horus looked shaken and ill, like a man trapped in a horrifying nightmare, and Isis sat silently, frail shoulders bowed. Her lashes were wet, and she stared blindly down at the age-delicate hands folded in her lap.

Jiltanith was expressionless, her relaxed hands folded quietly on the table, but her eyes were deadly. Neither group of Imperials had operated so openly during her subjective lifetime, and though she might have accepted the possibility of such a response intellectually, she hadn't really imagined it as a *probability*. Now it had happened, and Colin felt the fury radiating from her . . . and the focused strength of will it took to control it.

And how did he feel? He considered that for a moment, and decided Hector had just spoken for him, as well.

"All right," he said finally. "We knew they weren't exactly stable, and they've given plenty of past examples of their willingness to do things like this. We should have anticipated what they'd do."

"*I* should have anticipated it, you mean," MacMahan said bitterly.

"I said 'we' and I meant 'we.' The strategy was yours, Hector, but we were all involved in the planning, and the Council approved it. We figured if they knew we were hitting them, *we*'d be the targets they chose to strike back at. It was a logical estimate, and we all shared it."

"'Tis true, Hector," Jiltanith said softly. "This plan was product of us all, not thine alone." She smiled bitterly. "And did not we twain counsel Colin madmen yet might dismay us all? Take not more guilt upon thyself than is thy due."

"All right." MacMahan drew a deep breath and sat. "Sorry."

"We understand," Colin said. "But right now, just tell us how bad it is."

"I suppose it could be worse. They've gotten about thirty of our Terra-born— seven at once when they hit that Valkyrie at Corpus Christi; Vlad Chernikov

142

would've made eight, and he may still lose his arm unless we can break him out of the hospital and get him into *Nergal's* sickbay—but our own losses haven't been that high. Most of the people they've slaughtered are exactly what they seem to be: ordinary citizens.

"The death toll from the Eden Two mass missile strike is about eighteen thousand. That was a pay back for Cuernavaca, I suppose. The bomb at Goddard got another two hundred. The nuke they smuggled into Klyuchevskaya leveled the facilities, but the loss of life was minimal thanks to the 'terrorists'' phoned-in warning. Sandhurst and West Point were Imperial weaponry—warp grenades and energy guns. I imagine they were retaliation for Tehran and Kuiyeng. The Brits lost about three hundred people; the Point lost about five."

He paused and shrugged unhappily.

"It's a warning to back off, and I—we—should have seen it coming. It's classic terrorist thinking, and it fits right into Anu's own sick mentality."

"Agreed. The question is, what do we do about it? Horus?"

"I don't know," Horus said in a flat voice. "I'd like to say shut down. We've hurt them worse than we ever did before. We'd have to shut down pretty soon, anyway, and too many people are getting killed. I don't think I can take another bloodbath." He looked at his hands and spoke with difficulty.

"This isn't a drop in the bucket compared to Genghis Khan or Hitler, but it's still too much. It's happening all over again, and this time *we* started it, Maker help us. Can't we stop sooner than we planned?" He turned desperate eyes to Hector and Jiltanith. "I know we all agreed we needed Stalking-Horse, but haven't we done them enough damage for our purposes?"

"Isis?"

"I have to agree with Dad," Isis said softly. "Maybe I'm too close to it because of Cal and the girls, but . . ." She paused, and her lips trembled. "I . . . just don't want to be responsible for any more slaughter, Colin."

"I understand," he said gently, then looked at her sister. "Jiltanith?"

"There's much in what thou sayst, Father, and thou, Isis," Jiltanith said quietly, "yet if we do halt our actions all so swift upon his murders, wi' no loss of our own, may we not breed suspicion? If e'er doubt there was, there is no longer: Anu and his folk have run full mad. Yet in their madness lurketh danger, for 'tis most unlike they'll take a sane man's view o'things.

"Full sorely ha' we smote his folk. Now ha' they dealt us buffets in return, and 'tis in my mind that e'en now they watch us close, hot to scent our stomach for this work. And if but so little blood—for so know we all Anu will see it—and it not ours stoppeth up our blows, may not doubt hone sharp the wit of one so cunning, be he e'er so mad? Be risk of that howe'er small, yet risk there still must be. 'Twas 'gainst that very danger Stalking-Horse was planned." She met her father's pleading eyes.

"Truth maketh bitter bread i'such a pass," her voice was even softer, "but whate'er our hearts may tell us, i'coldest truth it mattereth but little how many lives Anu may spend. Their blood is innocent. 'Twill haunt us all our whole lives long. Yet if we fail, then all compassion may ha' spared will live but till such time as come the Achuultani. 'Tis in my mind we durst not cease—not yet, a while. Some few attacks more, then turn to Stalking-Horse as was the plan, would be my counsel."

Colin nodded slowly as he recognized her anguish. Her eyes were hooded, armoring the torment her own words had given her, and behind her barricaded face, he knew, she was seeing countless, nameless men, women, and children she had never met. Yet she was right. That the blood that would be shed was innocent would mean nothing to Anu. Might he not assume it meant less to *them* than the lives of their own people?

They couldn't know that, but Jiltanith had the resolution to face the possibility and the moral courage to voice it.

"Thank you," he said. "Hector?"

" 'Tanni's right," Hector sighed unhappily. "I wish to God she weren't, but that won't change it. We can't *know* how Anu will react, but everything we do know points to a man who hurts people for the pleasure of it and regards all 'degenerates' as expendable. *He* wouldn't stop because some of them were getting killed; if we do, he may just ask himself why, and that's the one question we can't afford for him to ask."

He stared at the table, pressing his clenched fists together on its top.

"I hate the thought of provoking massacres—or even a single death more than may be absolutely necessary—but if we miscalculate and stop too soon, all the people who've already died will have been killed for absolutely nothing."

"I agree," Colin said heavily. "We have to convince them, in terms *they* can accept, that they've *made* us stop. Go ahead with the set-up for Stalking-Horse, Hector. See if you can't compress the time frame, but do it."

"I will." MacMahon rose, and only Imperial ears could have heard his last words as he left the room.

"God forgive me," he whispered.

Ninhursag sat on the bench and concentrated on looking harmless. The enclave's central park struck her as crude and unfinished beside her memories of *Dahak*'s recreation areas, and she filed the observation away with all the others she'd made since her return from the outside world. The sum of those observations was almost as disturbing, in its way, as the day she awakened to learn what Anu had been doing to her fellow mutineers.

She managed not to shudder as a tall, slender man walked by. *Tanu*, she thought. Once she'd known him well, but he was no longer Tanu. She didn't know which of Anu's lieutenants had claimed his body, and she didn't want to find out. It was bad enough watching him walk around and knowing he was dead.

She looked away, thinking. There was an unfinished feeling to the entire enclave, like a temporary camp, not a habitation. Anu and his followers had lived on this planet for fifty thousand years, yet they'd never come to belong here. It was as if they deliberately sought to preserve their awareness of the alien about them. There were comfortable blocks of apartments here under the ice, built immediately after their landing, but no more had been built since and virtually none of the mutineers used the ones that existed. They'd retreated back into their ships, clinging to their quarters aboard the transports despite their cramped size. For herself, Ninhursag knew she would have gone mad long ago if she'd been confined to such quarters for so long.

She watched the spray of one of the very few tinkling fountains anyone had bothered to build and considered that. Perhaps that was part of the miasma of madness drifting in the air. These people had far outlived their allotted lifespans penned up inside their artificial environment but for occasional jaunts outside. Their stolen bodies were young and strong, but the personalities inhabiting them were *old*, and the enclave was a pressure-cooker.

By their very nature, most of Anu's people had been flawed or they would not have been here, and over the endless years of exile, closeted within this small world, their minds had turned inward. They'd been alone with their hates and ambitions and resentments longer than human minds were designed to stand, and what had been flaws had become yawning fissures. The best of them were distorted caricatures of what they had been, while the worst . . .

She shuddered and hoped none of the security scanners had noticed.

Theirs was a dead society, decaying from its core. They wouldn't admit it—assuming they could even recognize it—yet the truth was all about them. Five thousand years they'd been awake, yet they'd added absolutely nothing to their tech base beyond a handful of highly personal modifications to ways of spying on or killing one another. They were only a small population, but it was the nature of societies to change, to learn new things. A culture that didn't was doomed; if an outside force didn't destroy it, its own members turned upon one another within the static womb to which they had returned. Whether or not they could admit or recognize their stagnation was ultimately unimportant, for deep inside, where the life forces and the drive of a people came together out of emotion and beliefs they might never have formalized, they *knew* they were spinning their wheels, marking time . . . dying.

Ninhursag's eyes were open now, and she saw it in so many things. The suspicion, the ambition, the perversions of a degenerate age that *knows* it is degenerate. And, perhaps most tellingly of all, there were no children. These people were no celibates, but they had deliberately renounced the one thing that might have forced them to change and evolve. And with it, they'd cut themselves off from their own human roots. Like a woman barren with age, their biological clock had stopped, and with it had died their sense of themselves as a living, ever-renewed species.

Why had they done that to themselves? They were—had been—Imperials, and the Imperium had known that even a single quarter-century deployment aboard a ship like *Dahak* required that sense of vitality and renewal among its crewmen. Even those who had no children could see the children of others, and so share in the flow of their species. But Anu's people had chosen to forget, and she could not understand it.

Had their stolen immortality made children irrelevant? Or did they fear producing a generation foreign to their own twisted purpose? One that might rebel against them? She didn't know. She *couldn't* know, for they had become a different species—a dark, malevolent shadow that wore the bodies of her people but was not hers.

She rose, walking slowly across the park towards the building in which she had half-defiantly made her own quarters, aware of the way her shadowing keeper followed her. He didn't even bother to be unobtrusive, but it had helped to know exactly where the security man assigned to watch her might be found.

She glanced idly at the gawking Terra-born who shared the park with her, noting their awe at the environment that seemed so crude to her, and wondered which of them would collect the record chip she'd hidden under her bench.

Abu al-Nasir watched Ninhursag walk away, then ambled over to the bench she'd occupied. The soaring, vaulted ceiling of the park, with its projected roof of summer-blue sky and fleecy clouds was amazing. It was hard to believe he was buried under hundreds of meters of ice and stone. The illusion of being outside was almost perfect, and perhaps the looming, bronze-toned hulls thrusting up beyond the buildings helped to make it so.

He sat down and leaned back, watching idly for the security scanners Colonel MacMahan had described to him. There they were—nicely placed to watch the bench, but only from the front. That was handy.

He let one hand drop down beside him, about where his holster normally rode. Sergeant Asnani had never felt any particular need to be armed at every moment; Abu al-Nasir felt undressed without his personal arsenal. Still, it was hardly surprising the mutineers declined to permit their henchmen weapons.

Not surprising, yet it underscored the difference between them and their allies and the way *Nergal*'s crew worked with their own Terra-born. He'd never visited *Nergal*, but he'd trained among her Terra-born, and he knew Colonel MacMahan. The colonel was no man's flunky—the very thought was absurd— yet any of his Imperial allies would have trusted him behind them with a gun.

But al-Nasir had already concluded that everything the colonel had told him about *these* Imperials was the truth. Since his initiation into Black Mecca, al-Nasir had become accustomed to irrationality. Extremism, hatred, greed, sadism, fanaticism, megalomania, disregard for human life . . . he'd know them all, and he recognized something very like them here. Less bare-fanged and snarling, but perhaps even more evil because of that. And these people truly regarded themselves as a totally different species, simply because of the artificial enhancement of their own bodies . . . and their ability to torment and kill the Terra-born.

The sense of *ancientness* behind those comely, youthful faces was frightening, and al-Nasir was glad there were no children. The thought of what any child who breathed this poisoned atmosphere must become turned his stomach, and it was no longer a stomach that turned easily.

His relaxed hand crooked casually, stroking the wooden bench absently, and his eyelids drooped as he listened to the tinkle and splash of the fountain. His entire body was eloquently if unobtrusively relaxed, and his fingers stroked more slowly, as if the idle thoughts that moved them were slowing.

He touched the tiny, barely discernible dot of the message chip, and his forefinger moved. The chip slid up under his nail, invisible under the thin sheet of horn, and no flicker of triumph crossed his face. If the colonel was wrong about Ninhursag, he was a dead man, but no sign of that showed, either.

He let his hand continue stroking for a few moments, then laid his forearm negligently along the armrest. Every nerve in his lax body screamed to stand up, to walk away from the drop site, but this was a game he'd learned to play well, and he settled even more comfortably on the bench.

About an hour, he thought. A short, restoring nap, utterly innocent, totally unconcealed, and then he could leave. His eyes closed fully, his head lolled back, and Abu al-Nasir began to snore.

The city of La Paz dreamed under an Argentine moon, and the streets were emptying as Shirhansu sat by the window and stroked her ash-blonde hair.

Even after all these years, she still found it difficult to accept that her pale-skinned hand was "hers," that the aqua eyes that looked back from any mirror belonged to her. It was a lovely body, far more beautiful than the one she'd been born to, but it marked her as one outside the inner circle. Yet it also set her aside from the odd—to Terran eyes—appearance of the Imperial race, and that could be invaluable.

She sighed and shifted the energy gun across her lap, wishing yet again that they could have worn combat armor. It was out of the question, of course. Stealth fields could do a lot, but if the enemy operated unarmored or, even worse, were entirely Terra-born, they would be mighty hard to spot, and armor, however carefully hidden, could be picked up by people without it long before her own scanner teams could pick *them* up, so she had to strip down herself.

This was a stupid mission. She was glad to have it instead of one of the other operations—she was no Girru and took no pleasure from slaughtering degenerates in job lots—but it was still stupid. Suppose she *did* manage to surprise some of *Nergal's* crowd. They would never let themselves lead her back to the battleship. Even if she managed to follow them, it stood to reason that whatever auxiliary picked them up would carry out a careful scan before it made rendezvous, and when it did, it would spot her people however carefully they were stealthed. That auxiliary would undoubtedly be armed, too, and was there any fighter cover for her people? Of course not. The limited supply of fighter crews was being tasked with offensive strikes . . . aside from the fifty percent reserve Anu insisted on retaining to cover the enclave, though what he expected *Nergal's* people to accomplish against its shield eluded Shirhansu.

Of course, she did suffer from one little handicap when it came to understanding the "Chief." Her brain still worked.

Which also explained why she was so unhappy at the prospect of trying to follow one of *Nergal's* teams. Their efficiency to date had been appalling, even allowing for the purely Terran nature of most of their targets, not that it surprised Shirhansu. She'd developed a deep if grudging respect for her enemies over the centuries, for the casualty figures were far less one-sided than they should be. They'd survived everything her own group had thrown at them from the lofty advantage of its superior tech base and managed—somehow—to keep their HQ completely hidden; they weren't bloody likely to screw up now.

The whole idea was foolish, but she knew why the mission had been mounted anyway, and she approved of anything that kept Ganhar alive and in control of Operations, for she was one of his faction. Joining him had seemed like a good idea at the time—certainly he was far closer to sane than Kirinal had been!—but she'd been having second thoughts recently. Still, Ganhar seemed to be making a recovery, and if her presence here could help him, then it also helped *her*, and that . . .

Her hand-held security com gave a soft, almost inaudible chime. She raised it to her ear, and her eyes widened. Ganhar's analysts had called it right; the bastards *were* going to hit *Los Puñas*!

She spoke succinctly into the com, hoping her own stealth field would hide the fold-space pulse as it was supposed to, then checked her weapon. She set it for ten percent power—there was no armor inside the approaching stealth fields, and there was no point blowing too deep a hole in the pavement—and opened a slit in her stealth field, freeing her implants to scan a narrow field before her while the field still hid her from flanks and rear.

Tamman followed Amanda along the sidewalk, as invisible as the wind. He felt more at home than he had in Tehran, but his enhanced senses could do more good watching her back than probing the darkness before her, and she'd convinced him of the virtue of keeping the commander out of the forefront.

He let a scowl twist his lips. The massacre of innocents continued and, if anything, had accelerated. Eden Two remained the worst single atrocity, but there were others. Shepard Center's security people had stood off an assault, but their casualties had been high. Still, Tamman was certain the attackers had been under orders to withdraw rather than press the attack fully home. Anu wouldn't want to damage the aerospace industry too badly, and the fact that what had to be full Imperials equipped with energy guns and warp grenades had been "driven off" by Terra-born infantry, however good, armed only with Terran weapons was as good as a floodlit sign.

Yet that was the only southern attack that had been resisted, if that was the word for it, and the casualty count was starting to trouble his dreams. Watching World War One's trenches and World War Two's extermination camps had been horrifying, and Phnom Penh had been even worse, in its way. Afghanistan and the interminable, fanatical bloodletting between Iran and Iraq in the 'eighties had been atrocious, and the Kananga massacres in Zaire had been pretty bad, too, but this sort of desecration wasn't something a man could become used to, however often he saw it.

Los Puñas—"The Daggers"—were pussy cats compared to Black Mecca, but they'd been positively identified running Anu's errands. He wouldn't like it a bit if they were pulverized, and it would be satisfying to wipe them out. Tamman wouldn't even try to pretend otherwise, but it would be even nicer to see a few of Anu's butchers in his sights.

"Get ready," Shirhansu whispered. "Take 'em when they reach the plaza."

"Take them? I thought we were supposed to shadow them, 'Hansu." It was Tarban, her second in command, and Shirhansu scowled in the darkness.

"If any of them get away, we will," she growled, "but it's more important to nail a few of the bastards."

"But—"

"Shut up and get off the com before they pick it up!"

"*Tamman, it's a trap!*" The voice screaming into Tamman's left ear was Hanalat, their recovery pilot, who had been watching over them with her sensors. "I'm picking up a fold-space link ahead of you, at least two point sources! Get the hell out!"

"Gotcha," he grunted, thanking the Maker for Hector's suggestion that they carry Terran communications equipment. Hector had calculated that Anu's people would be looking primarily for Imperial technology, and he must have been right; Tamman had received the warning and he was still alive.

"All right, people," he said softly to his team, "let's ease out of here. Joe—" Joe Crynz, a distant cousin of Tamman's and the last man in line, carried a warp grenade launcher "—get ready to lay down covering fire. The rest of you, just ease on back. Let's get out quietly if we can."

There were no acknowledgments as his team came slowly to a halt and started drifting backward. Tamman held his breath, praying they would get away with it. They were naked down here, sitting ducks for—

"Breaker take you, Tarban!" Shirhansu snarled, and braced her energy gun on the window sill. She had the best vantage point of all her twenty people, and she could see only three of the bastards. Her senses—natural and implants alike—were alive through the slit in her stealth field, but *their* fields interfered badly. She couldn't make them out well enough for a sure kill at this range, but, thanks to Tarban, they weren't going to come any closer.

"Take them now!" she ordered coldly over her com.

Tamman bit back a scream as an energy bolt flashed through the edge of his stealth field. His physical senses—boosted almost to max as he tried to work his team out of the trap—were a flare of agony in the beam's corona. But it had missed him, and he flung himself aside with the dazzling quickness of his enhanced reaction time.

Larry Clintock was less lucky; at least three snipers had taken him for a target. He never even had time to scream as energy blasts tore him apart . . . but Amanda did, and Tamman's blood ran cold as he heard her.

He sheltered automatically—and uselessly—behind a potted tree, and his enhanced vision caught the energy flare at an upper window. His own energy gun tore the window frame apart, spraying the street with broken bits of brick, and whoever had been firing opted for discretion, assuming he was still alive.

Joe's grenade launcher burped behind him, and a gaping hole appeared in another building front, but the other side had warp grenades as well. A huge chunk of paving vanished, water spurting like a fountain from a severed main, and Tamman hurled himself to his feet. He should flee to join Joe and the others, but his feet carried him forward to where Amanda's scream had ended in terrifying silence.

More bolts of disruption slashed at him, splintering the paving, but his own people knew what was happening. Their stealth fields were in phase with his, letting them see him, and they spread out under whatever cover they could find while their weapons raked the buildings fronting on the plaza. They were shooting blind, but they were throwing a lot of fire, and he was peripherally aware of the grav gun darts chewing at stonework, the shivering pulsations of warp grenades, and the susuration of more energy guns trying to mark him down.

Amanda's left thigh was a short, ugly stump, but no blood pulsed from the wound. Her Imperial commando smock had fastened down in an automatic tourniquet as soon as she was hit, yet she was no Imperial, and she was unconscious from shock—or dead. His mind flinched away from the possibility, and he scooped her up in a fireman's carry and sprinted back up the street.

Devastation lashed at his heels, and he cried out in agony as an energy beam tore a quarter pound of flesh from the back of one leg. He nearly went down, but his own implants—partial though they were—damped the pain as quickly as it had come. Tissues sealed themselves, and he ran on frantically.

A warp grenade's field missed him by centimeters, the rush of displaced air snatching at him like an invisible demon, and he heard another scream as an energy gun found Frank Cauphetti. He spared a glance as he went by, but Frank no longer had a torso.

Then he was around the corner, his surviving teammates closing in about him, and the four of them were dashing through the night.

"Shouldn't we follow them, 'Hansu?"

"Sure, Tarban, you do that little thing! You and your damn gabble just cost us a complete kill! Not to mention Hanshar—that bastard with the energy gun cut him in half. So, please, go right ahead and follow them . . . I'm sure their cutter pilot will be delighted to vaporize your worthless ass!"

There was silence over the com, and Shirhansu forced her rage back under control. Maker, they'd come so *close*! But at least they'd gotten two of them, maybe even three, and that was the best they'd done yet against an actual attack force. Not that it would be good enough to please Anu. Still, if they cleaned up their report a little bit first . . .

"All right," she sighed finally. "Let's get out of here before the locals get too nosy. Meet me at the cutter."

CHAPTER NINETEEN

"How is she?"

Tamman looked up at Colin's soft question. He sat carefully, one leg extended to keep his thigh off his chair, and his face was worn with worry.

"They say she'll be all right." He reached out to the young woman in the narrow almost-bed, her lower body cocooned in the sophisticated appliances of Imperial medicine, and smoothed her brown hair gently.

"'All right,'" he repeated bitterly, "but with only one leg. *Maker*, it's unfair! Why *her*?!"

"Why anyone?" Colin asked sadly. He looked at Amanda Givens' pale, plain face and sighed. "At least you got her out alive. Remember that."

"I will. But if she had the biotechnics she deserves, she wouldn't be in that bed—and she could grow a new leg, too." He looked back down at Amanda. "It's not even their fault, yet they give so much, Colin. All of them do."

"All of *you* do," Colin corrected gently. "It's not as if you had anything to do with the mutiny either."

"But at least I got a child's biotechnics." Tamman's voice was very low. "She didn't get even that much. Hector didn't. My children didn't. They live their lives like candle flames, and then they're gone. So many of them." He smoothed Amanda's hair once more.

"We're trying to change that, Tamman. That's what she was doing."

"I know," the Imperial half-whispered.

"Then don't take that away from her," Colin said levelly. "Yes, she's Terra-born, just like I am, but I was drafted; she *chose* to fight, knowing the odds. She's not a child. Don't treat her like one, because that's the one thing she'll never forgive you for."

"How did you get so wise?" Tamman asked after a moment.

"It's in the genes, buddy," Colin said, and grinned more naturally as he left Tamman alone with the woman he loved.

Ganhar cocked back his chair and rested one heel on the edge of his desk. He'd just endured a rather stormy interview with Shirhansu, but, taken all in all, she was right—they'd been lucky to get *any* of *Nergal's* people, and the odds were against doing it twice. Tarban's blathering com traffic had given them away this time, but now that the other side had walked into one trap, they damned well wouldn't walk into another. They'd cover any attacking force with active scanners powerful enough to burn through any portable stealth field.

He pondered unhappily, trying to decide what to recommend this time. The logical thing was to withdraw a few fighters from offensive sweeps and use them to nail any of *Nergal's* cutters that came in with active scanners, but Ganhar had developed a lively respect for Hector MacMahan—who, he was certain, was masterminding this entire campaign. The equally logical response would be obvious to him: cover *Nergal's* cutters with his own stealthed fighters to nail Ganhar's fighters when they revealed themselves by attacking the cutter.

The very idea reeked of further escalation, and he was sick of it. They couldn't match his resources, but they knew where they were going to strike, and they could concentrate their forces accordingly; *he* had to cover all the places they *might* strike. He couldn't have overwhelming force anywhere, unless Anu would let him back off on offensive operations and smother all possible targets with their own fighters.

Which, of course, Anu would never do.

He rubbed his closed eyes wearily, and his thoughts moved like a dirge. It was no good. Even if they managed to locate *Nergal* and destroy her and all her people, there was still Anu. Anu and all of them—even himself— and their endless futility. Anu was mad, but was he much better off himself? What did he think would happen if they ever managed to leave this benighted planet?

Like Jantu, Ganhar had reached his own conclusions about the Imperium's apparent disappearance from the cosmos. If he was wrong, then they were all doomed. The Imperium would never forgive them, for there could be no clemency for such as they—not for mutineers, and never for mutineers who'd gone on to do the things they'd done to the helpless natives of Earth.

And if there was no more Imperium? In that far more likely case, their fate might be even worse, for there would still be Anu. Or Jantu. Or someone else. The madness had infected them all, for they'd lived too long and feared death too much. Ganhar knew he was saner than many of his fellows, and look what *he* had done in the name of survival. He'd worked with Kirinal despite her sadism, *knowing* about her sadism, and when he replaced her, he'd devised this obscene plan merely to stay alive a bit longer. She and Girru would have loved it, he thought bitterly. This slaughter of defenseless degenerates . . .

No, not "degenerates." Primitives, perhaps, but not degenerates, for it was he and his fellows who had degenerated. Once there might even have been a bit of glamour in daring to pit themselves against the Imperium's might, but not in what they'd done to the people of Earth and their own helpless fellows.

He stared down at the hands he had stolen, and his stomach knotted.

He didn't regret the mutiny or even the long, bitter warfare with *Nergal's* crew. Or perhaps he *did* regret those things, but he wouldn't pretend he hadn't known what he was doing or whine and snivel before the Maker for it. But the other things, especially the things he had done as Operations head, sickened him.

But there was no way to undo them, or even stop them. If he tried, he would die, and even after all these years, he wanted to live. But the truly paralyzing thing was that even if he'd been willing to die, his death would accomplish nothing except, perhaps, to grant him a fleeting illusion of expiation. Even if he could bring himself to embrace that—and he was cynically uncertain he could—it would leave Anu behind. The madmen had the numbers, firepower, and tech base, and nothing *Nergal* and her people might achieve in the short-term could alter that.

Head of Operations Ganhar's hands clenched as he stared at them and wondered when he'd finally begun to crack. He'd seen the awakening of guilt in a few others. It usually happened slowly, and some had ended their long lives when it happened to them. Others had been spotted by Jantu's zealous minions and made examples, but there had never been many, and none had been able to do any more than Ganhar could.

He sighed and stood, walking slowly from his office. The futility of it all oppressed him, but he knew he would sit down at the conference table and tell Anu things were going according to plan. He might be coming to the realization that he despised himself for it, but he would do it, and there was no point pretending he wouldn't.

Ramman sat in his small apartment, gnawing his fingernails. His pastel-walled quarters were littered with unwashed clothing and dirty eating utensils, and his nostrils wrinkled with the smell of sour bedding. There were extra disadvantages in slovenliness for the sensory-enhanced.

He knew he was under surveillance and that his strange behavior, his isolation from his fellows, was dangerously likely to attract the suspicion he could not afford, yet mounting terror and desperation paralyzed his ability to do anything about it. He felt like a rabbit in a snare, waiting for the trapper's return, and if he mingled with the others, they must see it.

He rose and walked jerkily about the room, the fingers of his clasped hands writhing together behind him. Madness. Jiltanith and her father had to be insane. They would fail, and their failure would betray the fact that someone had helped them by giving them the admittance codes. The witch hunt might sweep up the innocent, but would almost certainly trap the guilty, and *he* would be the guilty. He would be found out, arrested . . . killed.

It wasn't *fair*! But he'd been given his orders, and he had obeyed them. He'd planted the codes where he'd been told to. If he told anyone . . . he shuddered as he thought of Jantu and the unspeakable things perverted Imperial technology had been used to do to other "traitors."

If he kept quiet, told no one, he would at least live a little longer. At least until *Nergal's* people launched their doomed attack.

He sank back down on the edge of the bed and sobbed into his hands.

✧   ✧   ✧

"'Tis time for Stalking-Horse," Jiltanith said quietly. "That fact standeth proved by the fate which did befall Tamman's group. That and the slaughter which e'en now doth gain in horror do set the stage and gi' us pretext enow to cease when Stalking-Horse be added."

"Agreed," MacMahan said softly, and looked at Colin.

"Yes," Colin said. "It's time to stop this insanity. Is it set up?"

"Yes. I've scheduled Geb and Tamman to fly lead with Hanalat and Carhana as their wing."

"Nay," Jiltanith said, and MacMahan glanced at her in surprise, taken aback by the finality of her voice. "Nay," she repeated. "The lead is mine."

"No!" The strength of his own protest surprised Colin, and Jiltanith met his eyes challengingly—not with the bitter, hateful challenge of old, but with a determination that made his heart sink.

"Tamman hath been wounded," she said reasonably.

"A flesh wound sickbay and his biotechnics have already taken care of almost completely," MacMahan said in the cautious tone of a man who knew he was edging into dangerous waters, if not exactly why they had become perilous.

"I speak not o' his flesh, Hector. Certes, 'twould be reason enow t' choose anew, yet 'tis his heart hath taken too sore a hurt. I ha' not seen him care for any as he doth for his Amanda, not since Himeko's death."

"We've all been hurt, 'Tanni," MacMahan protested.

"That's sooth," she agreed, "yet 'tis graver far in Tamman's case."

"'Tanni, you can't go." Colin extended one hand to reach across the table. "You *can't*. You're the backup commander for *Dahak*."

He could have bitten off his tongue as he saw her dark eyes widen. But then they narrowed again and she cocked her head. It was a small gesture, but it demanded explanation.

"Well, I had to pick *someone*," he said defensively. "It couldn't be Horus or one of the older Imperials—they were *active* mutineers; I couldn't take a chance on how Dahak's Alpha Priorities might work out if I'd tried that! So it had to be one of the children, and you were the logical choice."

"And thou didst not think fit to tell me of't?" she demanded, a curiously intent light replacing the surprise in her eyes.

"Well . . ." Colin's face flamed, and he darted an appealing glance at MacMahan, but the colonel only looked back impassively. "Maybe I should have. But it didn't seem like a good idea at the time."

"Whyfor not? Yea, and now I think on't, why didst thou not e'en tell a soul thou hadst named any one of all our number to follow thee in thy command?"

"Frankly . . . well, much as I wanted to trust you people, I didn't know I could when I recorded Dahak's orders. That's one reason I insisted on doing it myself," he said, and felt a rush of relief when she nodded thoughtfully rather than flying into a rage.

"Aye, so much I well can see," she said softly. " 'Twas in thy mind that so be we knew thou hadst named thine own successor, then were we treason-minded we had slain thee and had done?"

"That's about it," he admitted uncomfortably. "I don't dare contact Dahak

again, and he can't pick up my implants on passive instrumentation. If I'd
been wrong about you and you'd known, you could have offed me and told
him I bought it from the southerners." He met her eyes much more pleadingly than he had MacMahan's. "I didn't really think you'd do it, but with
the Achuultani coming and everything else going to hell, I couldn't take the
chance."

"'Twas wiser in thee than e'er I thought to find," she said, and he blinked
in surprise as she smiled in white-toothed approval. "God's Teeth, Colin—
'twould seem we yet may make a spook o' thee!"

"You *do* understand!"

"I ha' not played mistress to *Nergal's* spies these many years wi'out the
gaining o' some small wit," she said dryly. "'Twas but prudence on thy part.
Yet still a question plagueth me. Whyfor choose me to second thee? And
if thou must make that choice, whyfor tell me not e'en now? Surely there
can be naught but trust betwixt us wi' all that's passed sin then?"

"Well . . ." He felt himself flushing again. "I wasn't certain how you'd
take it," he said finally. "We weren't exactly . . . on the best of terms, you
know."

"'Tis true," she admitted, and this time *she* blushed. It was her turn to
glance sidelong at MacMahan, who, to his eternal credit, looked back with
only the slightest twinkle in his eyes. "Yet knowing that, thou wouldst still
ha' seen me in thy shoon?"

"I didn't intend to give my 'shoon' to anyone," he said testily, "and I
wouldn't've been around to see it if it happened! But, yes, if it had to be
someone, I picked you." He shrugged. "You were the best one for the job."

"'Tis hard to credit," she murmured, "and 'twas lunacy or greater wit
than I myself possess to gi' such a gift to one who hated thee so sore."

"Why?" he asked, his voice suddenly gentle. He met her gaze squarely,
forgetting MacMahan's presence for a moment. "You can understand the
precautions I felt I had to take—is it so hard to accept that *I* might understand the reasons you hated me, 'Tanni? Or not blame you for them?"

"Isis spake those self-same words unto me," Jiltanith said slowly, "and
told me they did come from thee, yet no mind was I to hear her." She shook
her head and smiled, the first truly gentle smile he had seen from her. "Thy
heart is larger far than mine, good Colin."

"Sure," he said uncomfortably, trying to sound light. "Just call me Albert
Schweitzer." Her smile turned into a grin, but gentleness lingered in her dark
eyes. "Anyway," he added, "we're all friends now, aren't we?"

"Aye," she said firmly.

"Then there's an end to't, as you'd say. *And* the reason you can't fly the
lead in Stalking-Horse. We can't risk losing you."

"Not so," she said instantly, her eyes shrewd. "Thou art not dead nor like
to be, and 'twould be most unlike thee not to ha' named some other to
follow me. Tamman, I'll warrant, or some other o' the children?"

He refused to answer, but she saw it in his eyes.

"Well, then, sobeit. Tamman is most unlike myself, good Colin. Thou
knowest—far more than most—how well my heart can hate, but *my* hate

burneth cold, not hot. Not so for him. He needeth still some time ere he may clear his mind, and Stalking-Horse can be no task for one beclouded."

"But—"

"She's right," MacMahan said quietly, and Colin glared reproachfullly at him. The colonel shrugged. "I should've seen it myself. Tamman hasn't left sickbay since he carried Amanda into it. He'd go, but he needs time to settle down before he goes back out. And 'Tanni *is* our best pilot—you know that better than most, too. There's not supposed to be any fighting, but if there is, she's best equipped to handle it. We'll give her Rohantha for a weaponeer. They'll actually make a better team than Geb and Tamman."

"But—"

"'Tis closed, Colin. 'Hantha and I will take the lead."

"Damn it, I don't *want* her up there in a goddamned pinnace, Hector!"

"That doesn't matter. 'Tanni and I are in charge of this operation—not you—and she's *right*. So shut up and soldier . . . sir!"

The admittance chime to Ganhar's private study sounded, and he looked up from the holo map he'd been updating as he ordered the hatch to open. It was late, and he half-expected to see Shirhansu, but it wasn't she, and his eyes narrowed in surprise as his caller stepped inside.

"Ramman?" He leaned back in his chair. "What can I do for you?"

"I . . ." The other man's eyes darted about like those of a trapped animal, and Ganhar found it hard not to wrinkle his face in distaste as Ramman's unwashed odor wafted to him.

"Well?" he prompted when the other's hesitation stretched out.

"Are . . . are your quarters secure?" Ramman asked hesitantly, and Ganhar frowned in fresh surprise. Ramman sounded serious, yet also oddly as if he were playing for time while he reached some inner decision.

"They are," he said slowly. "I have them swept every morning."

"Good." Ramman paused again.

"Look," Ganhar said finally, "if you've got something to say, why not say it?"

"I'm afraid," Ramman admitted after another maddening pause. "But I have to tell someone. And—" he managed a lopsided, sickly smile "—I'm even more afraid of Jantu than I am of you."

"Why?" Ganhar asked tightly.

"Because I'm a traitor," Ramman whispered.

"*What?!*" Ramman flinched as if Ganhar had struck him, yet it also seemed he'd crossed some inner Rubicon. When he spoke again, his flat, hurried voice was louder.

"I'm a traitor. I—I've been in contact with . . . with Horus and his daughter, Jiltanith, for years."

"You've been *talking* to them?!"

"Yes. Yes! I was afraid of Anu, damn it! I wanted . . . I wanted to defect, but they wouldn't let me! They made me *stay*, made me *spy* for them!"

"You fool," Ganhar said softly. "You poor, damned fool! No wonder Jantu scares the shit out of you." Then, as the shock faded, his eyes narrowed again. "But if that's true, why tell me? Why tell *anyone*?"

"Because . . . because they're going to attack the enclave."

"Preposterous! They could never crack the shield!"

"They don't plan to." Ramman bent towards Ganhar, and his voice took on an urgent cadence. "They're coming in through the access points."

"They can't—they don't have the admittance code!"

"I know. Don't you see? They want *me* to steal it for them!"

"That's stupid," Ganhar objected, staring at the dirty, cringing Ramman. "They must know Anu doesn't trust you—or did you lie to them about that?"

"No, I didn't," Ramman said tightly. "And even if I hadn't told them, they'd know from how long I've been left outside."

"Then they must also know Jantu plans to change the code as soon as all the 'untrustworthy elements' are back outside."

"I *know*, damn it! *Listen* to me, for Maker's sake! They don't want *me* to bring it out. I'm supposed to plant it for someone *else*. One of the degenerates!"

"Breaker!" Ganhar whispered. Maker damn it, but it made sense! If they'd gotten one of their own degen-*people* inside, it made audacious, possibly foolhardy sense, but sense. They were terribly outnumbered, but with surprise on their side . . . And it made their whole offensive make sense, too. Drive them into the enclave . . . steal the code . . . smuggle it out and hit them before Anu and Jantu changed it. . . . It was brilliant!

"Why tell me now?" he demanded.

"Because they'll never get away with it! But if they try, Anu will know someone gave them the code, and I'll be one of the ones who get killed for it!"

"And you think there's something *I* can do about it? You're a bigger fool than I thought, Ramman!"

"No, listen! I've thought about it, and there's a way," Ramman said eagerly. "A way that'll help both of us!"

"How? No, wait. I see it. You tell me, I trap their courier, and we pass it off as a counter-intelligence ploy, is that it?"

"Exactly!"

"Hmmmmmm." Ganhar stared down at his holo map, then shook his head. "No, there's a better way," he said slowly. "You could go ahead and make the drop. We could *give* them the code, then wait for them with everybody in armor and all our equipment on line and wipe them out— gut them once and for all."

"Yes. *Yes!*" Ramman said eagerly.

"Very neat," Ganhar said, trying to picture what would follow such an overwhelming triumph. *Nergal's* people would be neutralized, but what would happen then? He'd be a hero, but even as a hero, his life would hang in the balance, for Inanna knew how he thought of the "Chief." Perhaps Anu knew, as well. And he remembered his other thoughts, how his own actions had come to sicken him. And he still didn't know what had prompted *Nergal's* people to *start* their offensive, even if he knew how they meant to end it. But if he and Ramman trapped them, they could end the long, covert war. He'd have no more need to slaughter innocents . . . not that there weren't enough Kirinals and Girrus to go on doing it for the fun of it. . . .

"When are you supposed to make the drop?" he asked finally.

"I already have," Ramman admitted.

"I see," Ganhar said, and nodded absently as he opened a desk drawer. "I'm glad you told me about this. I'm finally going to be able to do something effective about the situation on this planet, Ramman, and I couldn't have done it without you. Thank you."

His hand came out of the drawer, and Ramman gaped at the small, heavy energy pistol it held. He was still gaping when Ganhar blew his head to paste.

Book Four

CHAPTER TWENTY

Jiltanith and Rohantha settled into their flight couches and checked their computers with extraordinary care, for the stakes were higher this night than they had ever been before, and not just for them.

They were not in a fighter, but in a specially modified pinnace. Larger even than one of the twenty-man cutters, the pinnace (one of only two *Nergal* carried) was crammed with stealth systems, three times the normal missile load, and the extra computers linked to the two cutters and matching pair of fighters beside it in the launch bay. A third fighter sat behind them while Hanalat and Carhana carried out their own pre-flight checks. Even if Stalking-Horse was a total success, it was going to make a terrible hole in *Nergal*'s equipment list.

Jiltanith nodded, satisfied with the reports of her own flight systems and the ready signals flowing through her cross links to Rohantha's equipment, and opened a channel to flight operations.

"Ready," was all she said.

"Good hunting," a voice responded, and she smiled down at her console, for the response came not from Hector but from Colin MacIntrye. Since admitting he'd chosen her to succeed him, he seemed to have been constantly at hand, almost hovering there, and she knew he'd resigned himself to letting her fly this mission without really accepting it. She thought about saying something back to him, but their new relationship—whatever it was—remained too fragile, too unexplored. There would be time for that later. She hoped.

Instead, she lifted the pinnace off the hangar deck and led the procession of vehicles up the long, sloping tunnel. Freedom was upon her once more . . . and the hunger. But it was different this time. Her hunger was less dark and consuming, and there was no simmering tension between her and her weaponeer.

More than that, she was heavier, less fleet of wing. Slower and shorter-ranged than a fighter in vacuum, the pinnace was actually faster in atmosphere where its drive, thanks to its heavier generators, could bull through air resistance without being slowed to the same extent. But it had no atmospheric control surfaces for use in the stealth regime, and its very power made it slower to accelerate or decelerate, less maneuverable . . . and harder to hide.

They floated up the shaft, alert for any last-minute warning from *Nergal's* scan crews. But there were no alarms, and the small craft slipped undetected into the open atmosphere. Calm, cool thoughts flowed to the computers, and they turned to the east.

Under the false tranquillity of her surface thoughts, Jiltanith's mind whirred like yet another computer, probing even now for any last-minute awareness of error. She expected to find none, but she could not stop searching, and that irritated her. It wasn't the mark of the confident person she liked to believe she was.

For all the equipment committed to Stalking-Horse, there were only four people involved in the mission. She and Rohantha in the pinnace; Hanalat and Carhana in the only manned fighter. But that was all right . . . assuming she and Hector had accurately gauged Anu's new dispositions. If they hadn't . . .

The use of the pinnace was the part that bothered her most, she admitted to herself, leading the procession towards their target at just under mach one. Its designers had never intended it for the cut and thrust of close combat. Its single energy gun was a toy beside the powerful multiple batteries of a fighter, and though her electronics were much more capable and her upgraded missile armament gave her a respectable punch at longer range, she knew what would happen if she was forced into short-range combat with a proper fighter.

Yet only a pinnace had the power plant, speed, and cargo capacity they needed. She could only trust in Rohantha and her stealth systems and pray.

She stiffened as a warning tingled in her link to Rohantha. Hostile fighters—two of them—to the south. They were higher and moving faster than her own formation, degrading the performance of their stealth systems, and had she piloted a fighter of her own, Jiltanith would have asked nothing better than to scream up after them in pursuit. As it was, she stifled a sudden desire to cram on power and run and held her breath as her mind joined with Rohantha's, following the enemy's movements. They swept on upon their own mission and faded from the passive scanners.

Jiltanith made herself relax, trying to forget her dread of which new innocents they were to kill. She altered course minutely, swinging north of Ottawa before turning back on a south-southwest heading, and managed to push such thoughts to the back of her mind. The need for purposeful concentration helped, and her navigation systems purred to her, the controls of her pinnace caressed her like a lover, and the target area swept closer with every moment. Soon. Soon . . .

Shirhansu yawned, then took a quick turn around the camouflaged bunker. If Ganhar was right (and his analysts had done a bang-up job so far), they might see some more action soon. She hoped so. The shoot-out in La Paz, what there'd been of it, had been a relief despite the frustration of knowing so many enemies had escaped, and this time she'd left Tarban behind. Of course, there were always risks, but her own position was well protected, and she had plenty of firepower on hand this time. In fact, it would be—

"We're getting something, 'Hansu!"

She stepped quickly to Caman's side. He was leaning forward slightly, eyes unfocused as he listened to his electronics, and she glanced at the display beside him. Caman had no need of it, but it let her see what his scanners reported without tying into his systems and losing herself in them.

Active scanner systems were coming in from the north! So Ganhar *had* guessed right. The other side had no intention of being mousetrapped again, so they were probing ahead of their attack force. Now the question was whether or not they'd visualized the next moves as well as Ganhar had.

She watched a tiny red dot move above the small, perfectly detailed hills and trees of the holo display. The computers classed it as a cutter, but no cutter would be so brazen if it was unescorted. Their own scanners, operating in passive mode so far, had yet to spot anything else, but they'd find the bastards when it mattered.

Jiltanith had taken over Rohantha's weapon systems as well as the flight controls for the moment, and her brain was poised on a hair-trigger of anticipation. The base in upstate New York was no Cuernavaca, and, though it had been on Hector's list from the beginning, it had been carefully avoided to this point. It was juicy enough to merit attention—a major staging point for weapons and foreign terrorists aiming at targets in the northeastern states and Canada combined with the presence of southerner coordinators and a small quantity of Imperial technology—but it was also close to home, relatively speaking. More importantly, it was bait; they'd needed a target like this to set the stage for Stalking-Horse.

Rohantha was tense beside her as she concentrated on her specially-programmed computers. At the moment, she was "flying" both cutters and their fighter escorts via directional radio links. It was risky, because it meant placing the pinnace in a position to hit them with the radio beams, but far less risky than relying on fold-space links. And her directional links had the advantage of being indetectable unless somebody from the other side got into their direct path.

There were no words in the pinnace. Despite her own preoccupation, a corner of Jiltanith's mind was open to the flow of Rohantha's thoughts through their neural feeds as the lead cutter moved closer to the target, active scanners probing industriously, turning it into a beacon in the heavens.

✧   ✧   ✧

"*Got* 'em, Hansu!" Caman said exultantly. "See?"

Shirhansu nodded. A second cutter had just blipped onto the display. Its coordinates were less definite, for it was using no scanners, but the fold-space link between it and the first vessel had burned briefly through its stealth field. So they *had* sent in the first one on its automatics, had they?

She raised a small mike, smiling. They'd used radio against her in La Paz and she hadn't been ready for it, but this time *she* had a radio link, as well. They might be watching for it, but even if they spotted it, they couldn't be certain it was being used by Imperials.

"First Team," she said quietly in English. "Go."

There was no reply, but far above the surface of the Earth, a pair of Imperial fighters swooped downward at mach three while they took targeting data from Caman's scanners over the primitive radio link.

"Missiles!"

The unneeded word was dragged out of Rohantha, and Jiltanith nodded jerkily. The energy signatures of Imperial missiles were unmistakable as they scorched down out of the heavens, and 'Hantha's plotting systems were backtracking frantically.

Both cutters went to pre-programmed evasive action as the missiles came in. It was useless, of course. It was intended to be, but it would have been useless whether they'd planned it that way or not. The missles shrieked home, and Jiltanith cringed as thermonuclear flame ripped the night skies apart. The southerners were using heavy missiles!

She paled as she pictured the radiation boiling out from those fireballs. They were barely a kilometer up, and Maker only knew what they were doing to any Terra-born in the vicinity, but she knew what their EMP would do to Rohantha's directional antennae! Imperial technology was EMP-proof, but they'd counted on lighter weapons, with less ruinous effect on the electromagnetic spectrum, and she only hoped the targeting data had gotten through . . . and that the maneuvers in the drones' computers were up to their needs. If they had to open up a fold-link while the southerners were watching . . .

Both cutters had vanished in the holocaust, and Jiltanith banked away from the blast as Rohantha reclaimed her onboard systems. She'd done all she could by remote control.

"Hard kills on both cutters!" Caman shouted, and Shirhansu crouched over his shoulder, staring triumphantly at the display.

That was one fucking commando team that would never hit a target! But her triumph was not unmixed with worry as her fighters clawed back upward, putting as much distance between themselves and their firing positions as they could without breaking stealth. . . .

"Missile sources! Multiple launches!" Caman snapped, and Shirhansu smothered a curse.

Ganhar had been right again, Breaker take it! But there was still a good chance for her fighter crews. She watched the missiles climbing the holographic display, spreading as they rose. They couldn't have a definite lock, but they'd obviously gotten *something* from the tracks of the missiles that had killed the cutters.

"Team Two!" She used a fold-space com, but the heavy EMP from Team One's warheads would make it hard for even Imperial systems to spot it just now, and the need for secrecy was past, anyway. There was not even any need to tell her second fighter force what to do—they knew, and they were already doing it.

Shit! Erdana's fighter was clear of the missiles seeking it, but those were self-guided homing weapons, and at least three had locked onto Sima and Yanu! She watched Sima go to full power, abandoning stealth now that he knew he'd been targeted. Decoys blossomed on the display and jamming systems fought to protect the fighter, and two of the missiles lost lock and veered away. One killed a decoy in a three-kiloton burst of fury; the other simply disappeared into the night. But the third drilled through every defense Yanu could throw out against it, and its target vanished from the display.

Shirhansu swallowed a sour gulp of fury, but there was no time for dismay. Caman's scanners had picked out both of the firing fighters, and Team Two—not two, but four Imperial fighters—charged after them, missiles already lashing out across the heavens.

Jiltanith watched exultantly as one of the southern fighters disappeared in a ball of flame. That was more than they'd hoped for, and she was impressed by how well their unmanned fighters' computers had done.

Now they were doing the rest of their job, and she angled the pinnace away, hugging the ground, covered by Hanalet and Carhana as they flashed back into the north at mach two and prayed their own stealth systems held. . . .

Shirhansu watched the northerners react to her own incoming fighters. They went to full power, one streaking away to the west towards Lake Erie, the other breaking east and diving for the cover of the mountains. Decoys blazed in the night, dying in salvos of nuclear flame, and the west-bound fighter evaded the first wave of missiles racing after it. Not so the one headed east; three different missiles took it from three different directions.

She concentrated on the surviving fighter, praying that its crew would be frightened—and foolish—enough to flee straight back to *Nergal*, but those Imperials were made of sterner stuff. They turned back from the western shore of the lake, hurling their own missiles in reply, and she smothered an unwilling admiration for their guts as they took on all four pursuers in a hopeless battle rather than reveal their base's location.

What followed was swift and savage. The single enemy fighter was boxed, and its crew were obviously more determined than skilled. Its weapons sought out *all* its attackers, splitting its fire instead of seeking to blast a single foe out of the way to flee, and its violent evasive maneuvers had a fatalistic, almost mechanical air. Her own flight crews' defensive systems handled the incoming fire, and Changa's fighter flashed in so close he actually took the target out with his energy guns instead of another missle.

The molten, half-vaporized wreckage spilled into the cold, waiting waters of Lake Erie, and the victors reformed above the steam cloud and flashed away to the south. Shirhansu let her shoulders unknot and straightened, only then realizing that she'd been crouched forward. She wiped her forehead, and her hand came away damp.

Done. The whole thing had taken less than five minutes, and it was done.

"Get me Ganhar," she told Caman softly, and her assistant nodded happily.

Shirhansu drew a deep breath and crossed her arms, considering what to say. It was a pity about Sima and Yanu, but they'd taken out both cutters, the raiding force, *and* both stealthed escorts, for the loss of a single fighter of their own. That was a third of *Nergal's* fighter strength, plus at least five of their remaining Imperials. Probably at least six, since there would have been one Imperial in the raiding force, as well, and possibly seven if they'd been foolish enough to use a live pilot in the lead cutter.

She let herself smile thinly. Not a single survivor—and no indication of a message home to tell *Nergal* what had happened, either. Their entire attack force had been gobbled up, and it was unlikely they'd even know how it had happened. It was the worst they'd ever been hurt. Proportionately, it made Cuernavaca meaningless, and *she* had been in command. She'd commanded *both* successful interceptions!

"I've got Ganhar," Caman said, and Shirhansu let her smile broaden as she took over the com link.

"Ganhar? 'Hansu. We got 'em all—clean sweep!"

Jiltanith and Rohantha let themselves relax, knowing Hanalat and Carhana were doing the same aboard their fighter.

Their equipment losses had been severe, but that had been planned, and there had been no loss of life. Not theirs, anyway, Jiltanith reminded herself, and tried to turn her mind away from the Terra-born who must have been caught in the fireballs and radiation of the cross-fire. At least the area was thinly populated, she thought, and knew she was grasping at straws.

But the southerners couldn't know the northerners had lost none of their own personnel, which meant that they would believe *Nergal's* losses had been staggering enough to frighten them into suspending offensive operations.

They might actually pull it off, and she looked forward to returning to *Nergal* to report the mission's success. Hector would be pleased at how well it had gone, she thought, but her lips curved in a small, secret smile, hidden from Rohantha as she admitted a surprising truth to herself.

It was Colin's face she truly wished to see.

CHAPTER TWENTY-ONE

General Gerald Hatcher stood beside his GEV command vehicle on a hill overlooking what had once been a stretch of pleasantly wooded countryside and listened to the radiation detectors snarl. The wind was from behind him and the levels were relatively low here, but that was cold comfort as he looked down into the smoldering mouth of Hell.

Smoke fumed up from the forest fires, but they were still far away and the Forestry Service and fire departments and volunteers from the surviving locals along the fringe of the area were fighting to bring them under control. Most of those people didn't have dosimeters, either, and Hatcher shook his head slowly. Courage came in many guises, and it never ceased to amaze and humble him, but this carnage went beyond anything courage could cope with. Hatcher's bearing was as erect and soldierly as ever, but inside himself he wept.

Red and blue flashers blinked atop emergency vehicles further out into the smoking wasteland, and the night sky was heavy with helicopters and vertols that jockeyed through the treacherous thermals and radiation. They would not find many to rescue out there . . . and this was only one of the nuked areas.

He turned at the whine of fans as another GEV swept up the slope, blowing a gale of downed branches and ash from under its skirts, and settled beside his own. The hatch popped, and Captain Germaine, his aide, climbed down. His battle dress was smutted with dirt and ash and his face was drawn as he removed his breathing mask and walked heavily over to his commander.

"How bad is it, Al?" Hatcher asked quietly.

"About as bad as it could be, sir," Germaine said in a low voice, waving a hand out over the expanse of ruin. "The search teams are still working their way towards the center, but the last body count I heard was already over five hundred and still climbing."

"And that doesn't include the flash-blinded and the ones who'll still die," Hatcher said softly.

"No, sir. And this is one of the bright spots," Germaine continued in bitter, staccato bursts. "One of the goddamned things went off right over a town to the south. Sixteen thousand people." His mouth twisted. "Doesn't look like there'll be any survivors from that one, General."

"Dear God," Hatcher murmured, and even he could not have said whether it was a prayer or a curse.

"Yes, sir. The only good thing—if it's not obscene to call anything about this bitched-up mess 'good'—is they seem to've been mighty clean. The counters show a relatively small area of lethal contamination, and the wind's out of the southeast, away from the big urban areas. But God knows what it's going to do to the local gene pool or what the Canadians are going to catch from all this *shit*."

The last word came out of him in a half-strangled shout as his attempted detachment crumbled, and he half-turned from his general, clenching his fists.

"I know, Al. I know." Hatcher sighed and shook himself, his normally sharp eyes sad as he looked out over the battlefield. And battlefield it had been, even if none of the United States' detection systems had picked up a thing before or after the explosions. At least they'd had satellites in place to see what happened *during* the battle . . . not that the records made him feel any better.

"I'm heading back to the office, Al. Stay on it and keep me informed."

"Yes, sir."

Hatcher gestured, and his white-faced young commo officer stepped to his side. Her auburn hair was cut a bit longer than regulations prescribed, and it blew on the winds the fires ten kilometers away were sucking into their maw.

"Get hold of Major Weintraub, Lieutenant. Have him meet me at HQ."

"Yes, sir." The lieutenant headed for the command vehicle's radios, and Hatcher rested a hand on Germaine's shoulder.

"Watch your dosimeter, Al. If it climbs into the yellow, you're out of here and back to base. The major and I'll want to talk to you, anyway."

"Yes, sir."

Hatcher squeezed the taut shoulder briefly, then walked heavily to his GEV. It rose on its fans and curtsied uncomfortably across the rough terrain, but Hatcher sat sunken in thought and hardly noticed.

It wasn't going well. Hector's people had started on a roll, but they were getting the holy howling shit kicked out of them now, and the rest of the human race with them.

The first wave of counter-attacks had puzzled Hatcher. A handful of attacks on isolated segments of the aerospace effort, a few bloody massacres of individual families. They'd seemed more like pinpricks than full-scale assaults, and he'd tentatively decided the bad guys, whoever they were, were going after those few of Hector's people they could identify, which had been bad enough but also understandable.

But within twelve hours, another and far bloodier comber of destruction had swept the planet like a tsunami. The Point, Sandhurst, Klyuchevskaya, Goddard . . . Eden Two.

Clearly the other side had opted for the traditional terrorist weapon: terror. Coupled with the reports from La Paz, which could only have been a direct clash between the extra-terrestrial opponents, and this new obscenity in New York, it sounded terribly as if the momentum was shifting, and his preliminary examination of the satellite tapes seemed to confirm it.

The first warning anyone had was the burst of warheads, but the cameras had watched it all. Clearly one side had gotten the shit kicked out of it, and judging by the warheads each had used, it hadn't been the bad guys. Hector's people had used only small-yield nukes, when they'd used them at all, but their enemies didn't give a shit who they killed. They went in for great big bangs and hang the death toll, and his satellite people put the winning side's yields in the twenty kiloton range, maybe even a bit higher.

Hatcher sighed unhappily. Other bits and pieces had come together as his analysts tried to figure out what was going on, and one thing had become clear: the nature and pattern of Hector's people's operations all suggested meticulous planning, economy of force, and conservation of resources, whereas their opponents were operating on a far vaster scale, their actions wider-spread and more often simultaneous rather than sequenced. All of which indicated the balance of force was against Hector's side, probably by a pretty heavy margin.

History was replete with examples of out-numbered forces that had triumphed over clumsier enemies or those less technologically advanced than themselves, but right off the top of his head, Hatcher couldn't recall a single case in which a weaker force had defeated one that was equally advanced, more numerous, and knew what the hell it was doing. Especially not when the stronger side were also the barbarians.

His command vehicle reached the highway and turned north, heading for the vertol waiting to carry him back to his HQ, and he rubbed his eyes wearily. He and Weintraub had to get their heads together, though God only knew what good it was going to do. So far, all anyone had been able to do was beef up civil defense and keep their heads down. They were too outclassed for anything else, but if Hector's people went down, it was Hatcher's duty to do what he could.

Even if it hadn't been, he would have tried, for there was one thing upon which Gerald Hatcher was savagely determined. The bastards who didn't care how many innocent people they slaughtered were not going to take over his world without a fight, however advanced they were.

"Oh, Jesus!" Hector MacMahan whispered. His strong, tanned face was white as he listened to the reports flowing over the government and civilian emergency radio nets, and Colin reached over to lay a hand upon his shoulder.

"It wasn't our doing, Hector," he said quietly.

"Oh yes it was." MacMahan's bitter voice was as savage as his eyes. "We didn't use those fucking monsters, but we provoked *them* into doing it! And do me a favor and *don't* tell me we didn't have any choice!"

Colin met his eyes for a moment, then patted the colonel's shoulder once, gently, and leaned back in his own chair. Hector's bitterness wasn't directed at him, though he would have preferred for MacMahan to have an external focus for his self-loathing. Yet even in his pain, Hector had put his finger on it. They hadn't had a choice . . . and Colin wondered how many commanders over the ages had tried to assuage their consciences with thoughts like that.

"All right," he said finally. He reached out through his implant to shut off the emergency workers' voices, and MacMahan looked at him angrily, as if he resented the interruption of his self-imposed auditory penance. "We know what happened. The question is whether or not it worked. 'Tanni?"

"I can but say it should," Jiltanith said softly, and managed a ghost of the triumphant smiles they'd shared before the casualty reports started coming in. "Had they spied our other craft, then would they ha' sought the death of all. So far as they may tell, they slew our force entire."

"Horus?"

"'Tanni's right. We've done all we can. I pray the Maker it was enough." The old Imperial looked down at his hands and refused to look back up. Isis hugged him gently, and when she looked up to meet Colin's eyes her bright tears stopped him from asking her opinion. He glanced at MacMahan, instead.

"Oh, sure," the colonel said savagely. "My wonderful fucking plan worked just fine. All those extra bodies'll be a big help, too, won't they?"

"All right," Colin said again, his own voice carefully neutral. "In that case, we'll suspend all further offensive operations immediately. There's nothing we can do but wait, anyway." Heads nodded, and he rose. "Then I recommend we all get something to eat and some rest."

He extended his hand to Jiltanith without even thinking about it, and she took it. The warmth of her grip made him realize what he'd done, and he looked over at her quickly. She met his gaze with a small, sad smile and tightened her clasp as she stood beside him. They were almost exactly the same height, Colin noted, and for some no longer quite so obscure reason that pleased him even in their shared pain.

Horus and Isis rose more slowly, but MacMahan remained seated. Colin looked down at him and started to speak, but Jiltanith squeezed his hand and gave her head a tiny shake. He hesitated a moment longer, then thought better of it, and they walked wordlessly from the conference room.

The hatch closed behind them, but not quickly enough to cut off the mutter of ghostly, angry, weeping voices as MacMahan turned the radios back on.

"So much for those smart-assed bastards!" Anu gloated as Ganhar finished his report. "Caught them with their pants down and kicked them right in the ass, by the Maker! Good work, Ganhar. Very good!"

"Thank you, Chief." It was becoming harder for Ganhar to hold himself together, and he wondered what was really happening deep inside him.

"What next?" Anu demanded, and his hand-rubbing glee nauseated the Operations head. "Got any more targets picked out?"

"I don't think we need them, Chief," Ganhar said carefully. He saw Anu's instant disappointment, like the resentment of a little boy denied a third helping of dessert, and made himself continue.

"It looks like we've hurt them worse than the numbers alone suggest. They haven't mounted a single attack in the thirty-six hours since Shirhansu's people pulled out. Either they're rethinking or they've already rethought, Chief. Whichever it is, they're not going to lock horns with us again after this. That being the case, do we really want to do any more damage than we have to? Anything we smash is going to have to be rebuilt before we can get our other projects back on line."

"That's true," Anu said unwillingly. He looked at his head of security. "Jantu? You've been damned quiet. What'd you think?"

"I think we should give them a few more licks for good measure," Jantu said, but his voice was less forceful than of old. He hadn't realized how much he'd actually come to enjoy his affair with Bahantha. Her death had shaken him badly, but the blow to his ambitions was even worse, and Ganhar's and Inanna's alliance had come as a terrible shock.

"Ganhar's right, Chief." Inanna eyed the Security chief coldly, as if to confirm his thoughts. "The real problem's always been *Nergal*'s people. Killing more degenerates is pointless, unless we want to take over openly."

"No," Anu said, shaking his head. "It's bad enough they know we're here; if we come out into the open, there's too much chance of losing control."

"I agree," Ganhar said quietly, locking eyes with Jantu. "Right now, the degenerates don't have any idea where to look for us, but that could change if we get too open, and our tech advantage doesn't mean we're invulnerable. There's more than one way someone can get at us."

Jantu winced as Anu joined the other two in glaring at him. In retrospect, it was obvious from the surveillance reports that Ramman had acted unnaturally ever since his return to the enclave, and if Jantu had been less shaken by the realization that Ganhar and Inanna were leagued against him he probably would have noticed it and hauled the man in for questioning. As it was, he'd let matters slip so badly it had been Ganhar, his worst rival, who'd noticed something and dragged Ramman in to confront him.

The Operations head was damned lucky to be alive, Jantu thought viciously. Somehow Ramman had gotten his hands on an energy pistol despite his suspect status—something Jantu *still* couldn't understand—and only the fact that Ganhar had out-drawn him had saved his life. Damn Ramman! The least he might have done was kill the son-of-a-bitch!

Unfortunately, he hadn't, and Ganhar had not only preserved his own life, but uncovered the worst security breach in the enclave's history: a self-confessed spy who'd admitted he was working for Horus. And the fact that Horus had gotten to Ramman without being detected was *Jantu*'s failure, not Ganhar's. His failure to spot Ramman, coupled with the fact that it was *his* bitterest rival Ramman had almost killed, had seemed dangerously close to collusion rather than carelessness, and Jantu knew Anu thought so.

"Maybe you're right," he admitted now, the words choking in his throat. "But if so, what else should we do?"

"We ought to make sure we're right about their reaction," Ganhar said positively. "Our important degenerates have been safe inside the shield, but *Nergal's* bunch've blown the crap out of our outside networks. Let's start rebuilding while the rest of the degenerates are still disorganized. There's no way the other side could miss our doing that. If they've still got the guts to face us, they'll go after our degenerates as soon as they spot them."

"Sounds reasonable," Anu agreed. "Which batch do you want to throw out first?"

"Let's sit tight on our people in government and industry." Ganhar had personally run the background checks on too many of those people for it to be likely Ramman's courier was among them. "They're too valuable to risk."

"If we hang on to them too long, they'll lose credibility," Inanna pointed out. "Especially the ones in government. Some of them're already going to lose their jobs for running when things got hot."

"A few more days won't make much difference, and the delay's worth it to keep them alive if we've guessed wrong. Remember, the very fact that we hid them has marked them for *Nergal's* bunch. If they *do* have the guts to go on, they'll know exactly who to gun for." Ganhar wanted to marshal weightier arguments, but he dared not. Inanna was his ally for now, but if she guessed what he was really up to . . .

"You're right again, Ganhar," Anu said expansively. "By the Maker, it's almost a pity Kirinal didn't get herself killed earlier. If you'd been running things, we probably wouldn't have been taken by surprise this way."

"Thanks, Chief," the words were like splintered bone in Ganhar's throat, "but I stand by what I said. There was simply no way to predict what they were going to pull. All we could do was see which way the wind blew and then hit back hard."

He saw a trace of approval in Inanna's eyes, for she, better than any, would know it was the right note to strike. Anu was feeling expansive just now, but soon he would settle back into his usual behavior patterns, and it could be more dangerous to be overly competent than incompetent then.

"Well, you did a good job," Anu said, "and I'm inclined to follow your advice now. Start with the combat types—they're easier to replace anyway."

He nodded to indicate the meeting was adjourned, and the other three rose and left.

Ganhar felt the hatch close behind him with a vast sense of relief, then nodded to Inanna, gave Jantu a cold, dangerous smile, and stalked off. For the moment, his position was secure, and unless he missed his guess, he'd only need for it to stay that way a very little while longer.

The cold wind of mortality blew down his spine, and he'd put it there himself, but he still didn't know exactly why he had. The events he'd set in motion—or, more accurately, allowed to *remain* in motion—terrified him, yet there was a curious satisfaction in it. One way or another, it would bring the eternal, intricate betrayal and counter-betrayal to an end, and perhaps it could go some way towards expiating the sickness he'd felt ever since he had replaced Kirinal and his had become the hand that personally managed the organized murder of the people of Terra.

And it would also be the gambit that ended the long, futile game. The consummate, smoothly-polished stratagem that set all the other plotting, scheming would-be tyrants at naught. There was a certain sweetness in that, and—who knew?—he might even survive it after all.

CHAPTER TWENTY-TWO

It was very quiet on *Nergal*'s hangar deck. The command deck was too small for the crowd of people who had gathered here, and Colin let his eyes run over them thoughtfully. Every surviving Imperial was present, but they were vastly outnumbered by their Terra-born descendants and allies, and perhaps that was as it should be. It was fitting that what had started as a battle between Anu's mutineers and the loyalists of *Dahak*'s crew should end as a battle between those same butchers and the descendants of those they had betrayed.

He sat beside Jiltanith on the stage against the big compartment's outer bulkhead and wondered how the rest of *Nergal*'s people were reacting to the outward signs of their changing relationship. There were dark, still places in her soul that he doubted he would ever understand fully, and he had no idea where they were ultimately headed, but he was content to wait and see. Assuming they won and they both survived, they would have plenty of time to find out.

Hector MacMahan, immaculate as ever in his Marine uniform, entered the hangar deck beside a dark-faced, almost-handsome young man in the uniform of a US Army master sergeant, and Colin felt a stir rustle through the gathering as they found chairs to Jiltanith's left. Only a few of them had yet met Andrew Asnani, but all of them had heard of him by now.

Horus waited until they were seated, then stood and folded his hands behind him. He had abandoned his ratty old Clemson sweatshirt for this meeting and, at Colin's insistence, wore the midnight blue of the Fleet for the first time in fifty thousand years. His collar bore the single golden starburst of a fleet captain, not his old pre-mutiny rank, in a gesture that spoke to all of his fellow mutineers, even if they did not understand its full implications, and Colin had seen one or two of the older Imperials sit a bit straighter, their eyes a bit brighter, at the change.

"We've waited a long time for this moment," Horus said quietly, looking out over the silent ranks, "and we and, far more, the innocent people of this planet, have paid a terrible price to reach it. Many of us have died trying to undo what we did; far more have died trying to undo something *someone else* did. Those people can't see this day, yet, in a way, they're right here with us."

He paused and drew a deep breath.

"All of you know what we've been trying to do. It looks—and I caution you that appearances may be deceiving—but it *looks* like we've succeeded."

A sound like wind through grass filled the hangar deck. His words were no surprise, but they were a vast relief—and a source of even greater tension.

"Hector will brief you on our operations plan in just a moment, but there's something else I want to say to our children and our allies first." He looked out, and his determined old eyes were dark.

"We're sorry," he said quietly. "What you face is our fault, not yours. We can never repay you, never even thank you properly, for the sacrifices you and your parents and grandparents have made for us, knowing that we are to blame for so many terrible things. Whatever happens, we're proud of you—prouder, perhaps, than you can ever know. By being who you are, you've restored something to us, for if we can call upon the aid of people as extraordinary as you have proven yourselves to be, then perhaps there truly remains something of good in all of us. I—"

His voice broke and he cleared his throat, then stopped with a little headshake and sat. There was silence, but it was a silence of shared emotions too deep for expression, and then all eyes switched to Colin as he rose slowly. He met their assembled gazes calmly, acutely aware of the way the paired stars of his own Fleet rank glittered upon his collar, then looked down at Horus.

"Thank you, Horus," he said softly. "I wish I could count myself among those extraordinary people you just referred to, but I can't unless, perhaps, by adoption."

He held Horus's eyes a moment, then swung back to face the hangar deck.

"You all know how I came to hold the position I hold, and how much more deeply some of you merited it. I can't change what happened, but everything Horus just said holds true for me, as well. I'm honored to have known you, much less to have the privilege, however it came my way, of commanding you.

"And there's another thing. I insisted Horus wear the Fleet's uniform today. He argued with me, as he's done a time or two before—" that won a ripple of laughter, as he'd known it would "—but I insisted for a reason. Our Imperials stopped wearing that uniform because they felt they'd dishonored it, and perhaps they had, but Anu's people have retained it, and therein lies the true dishonor. You made a mistake—a horrible mistake— fifty thousand years ago, but you also recognized your error. You've done all that anyone could, far more than anyone could have demanded of you, to right the wrong you did, and your children and descendants and allies have fought and died beside you."

He paused and, like Horus, drew a deep breath. When he spoke again, his voice was very formal, almost harsh.

"All of that is true, yet the fact remains that you are criminals under Fleet Regulations. You know it. I know it. Dahak knows it. And, if the Imperium remains, someday Fleet Central will know it, for you have agreed to surrender yourselves to the justice of the Imperium. I honor and respect you for that decision, but on the eve of an operation from which so many may not return, matters so important to you all, so fundamental to all you have striven for, cannot be left unresolved.

"Now, therefore, I, Senior Fleet Captain Colin MacIntyre, Imperial Battle Fleet, Officer Commanding, *Dahak* Hull Number One-Seven-Two-Two-Nine-One, by the authority vested in me under Fleet Regulation Nine-Seven-Two, Subsection Three, do hereby convene an extraordinary court martial to consider the actions of certain personnel serving aboard the vessel presently under my command during the tenure of Senior Fleet Captain Druaga of Imperial Battle Fleet, myself sitting as President and sole member of the Court. Further, as per Fleet Regulation Nine-Seven-Three, Subsection One-Eight, I do also declare myself counsel for the prosecution and defense, there being no other properly empowered officers of Battle Fleet present.

"The crew of sublight battleship *Nergal*, Hull Number SBB-One-Seven-Two-Two-Nine-One-One-Three stands charged before this Court with violation of Articles Nineteen, Twenty, and Twenty-Three of the Articles of War, in that they did raise armed rebellion against their lawful superiors; did attempt to seize their vessel and desert, the Imperium then being in a state of readiness for war; and, in commission and consequence of those acts, did also cause the deaths of many of their fellow crewmen and contribute to the abandonment of others upon this planet.

"The Court has considered the testimony of the accused and the evidence of its own observations, as well as the evidence of the said battleship *Nergal*'s log and other relevant records. Based upon that evidence and testimony, the Court has no choice but to find the accused guilty of all specifications and to strip them of all rank and privilege as officers and enlisted personnel of Battle Fleet. Further, as the sentence for their crimes is death, without provision for lesser penalties, the Court so sentences them."

A vast, quiet susurration rippled through the hangar deck, but no one spoke. No one could speak.

"In addition to those individuals actively participating in the mutiny, there are among *Nergal*'s present crew certain individuals, then minor children or born to the core crew and/or descendants of *Dahak*'s core crew, and hence members of the crew of the said *Dahak*. Under strict interpretation of Article Twenty, these individuals might be considered accomplices after the fact, in that they did not attempt to suppress the mutiny and punish the mutineers aboard the said *Nergal* when they came of age. In their case, however, and in view of the circumstances, all charges are dismissed.

"The Court wishes, however, to note certain extenuating circumstances discovered in *Nergal*'s records and by personal observation. Specifically, the Court wishes to record that the guilty parties did, at the cost of the lives of almost seventy percent of their number, attempt to rectify the wrong they had done. The Court further wishes to record its observation that the subsequent actions of these mutineers and their descendants and allies have been in the finest traditions of the Fleet, far surpassing in both duration and scope any recorded devotion to duty in the Fleet's records.

"Now, therefore, under Article Nine of the Imperial Constitution, I, Senior Fleet Captain Colin MacIntrye, as senior officer present on the Planet Earth, do hereby declare myself Planetary Governor of the colony upon that planet upon the paramount authority of the Imperial Government. As Planetary Governor, I herewith exercise my powers under Article Nine, Section Twelve, of the Constitution, and pronounce and decree—" he let his eyes sweep over the taut, assembled faces "—that all personnel serving aboard the sublight battleship *Nergal*, Hull Number SBB-One-Seven-Two-Two-Nine-One-One-Three, are, for extraordinary services to the Imperium and the human race, pardoned for all crimes and, if they so desire, are restored to service in Battle Fleet with seniority and rank granted by myself as commanding officer of *Dahak*, Hull Number One-Seven-Two-Two-Nine-One, to date from this day and hour. I now also direct that the findings of the Court and the decree of the Governor be entered immediately in the data base of the said battleship *Nergal* and transferred, as soon as practicable, to the data base of the said ship-of-the-line *Dahak* for transmission to Fleet Central at the earliest possible date.

"This Court," he finished quietly, "is adjourned."

He sat in a ringing silence and turned slowly to look at Horus. It had taken weeks of agonized thought to reach his decision and mind-numbing days studying the relevant regulations to find the authority and precedents he required. In one sense, it might not matter at all, for it was as apparent to the northerners as to anyone in the south that the Imperium might well have fallen. But in another, far more important sense it meant everything . . . and was the very least he could do for the people Horus had so rightly called "extraordinary."

"Thank—" Horus broke off to clear his husky throat. "Thank you, sir," he said softly. "For myself and my fellows."

A sound came from the hangar deck, a sigh that was almost a sob, and then everyone was on his or her feet. The thunder of their cheers bounced back from the battle steel bulkheads, battering Colin with fists of sound, but under the tumult, he heard one voice in his very ear as Jiltanith gripped his arm in fingers of steel.

"I thank thee, Colin MacIntyre," she said softly. "Howsoe'er it chanced, thou'rt a captain, indeed, as wise as thou'rt good. Thou hast gi'en my father and my family back their souls, and from the bottom of my heart, I thank thee."

It took time to restore calm, yet it was time Colin could never begrudge. These were *his* people, now, in every sense of the word, and if mortal man could achieve their purpose, his people would do it.

But a whispering quiet returned at last, and Hector MacMahan stood at Colin's gesture.

MacMahan would never forget the guilt and grief of Operation Stalking-Horse's civilian casualties. There were fresh lines on his face, fresh white in his dark hair, but he was not immune to the catharsis that had swept the hangar deck. It showed in his eyes and expression as he faced the others.

"All right," he said quietly, "to business," and there was instant silence once more.

He touched buttons on the Terran-made keyboard wired into the briefing console, and a detailed holo map glowed to life between the stage and the front row of seats. It hovered a meter off the deck, canted so that its upper edge almost touched the deckhead to give every observer an unobstructed view.

"This," MacMahan said, "is the southern enclave. It's absolutely the best data we've had on it yet, and we owe it to Ninhursag. We only asked her for the access code; obviously she figured out why and ran the considerable risk of compiling the rest of this for us. If we make it, people, we owe her big.

"Now, as you can see, the enclave is a cavern about twelve kilometers across with the armed parasites forming an outer ring against its walls right here." He touched another button, and the small holographic ships glowed crimson. "They aren't permanently crewed and won't matter much as long as they stay that way; if they lift off, *Dahak* should be able to nail them easily.

"*These*, on the other hand"—another group of ships glowed bright, forming a second, denser ring closer to the center of the cavern—"are transports, and they're going to be a problem. Most of their heavy combat equipment is in them, though Ninhursag was unable to determine how it's distributed, and most of their personnel live aboard them, not in the housing units.

"That means the transports are where their people will be concentrated when they realize they're under attack and that the heaviest counter-attacks are going to come from them. The simplest procedure would be to break into the enclave, pop off a nuke, and get the hell out. The next simplest thing would be to go for the transports with everything we've got and blow them apart before any nasty surprises can come out of them. The *hardest* way to do it is to try to take them ship-by-ship."

He paused and studied his audience carefully.

"We're going to do it the hard way," he said quietly, and there was not even a murmur of protest. "For all we know, many of the people in stasis aboard them would've joined us from the beginning if they'd had the chance. Certainly Ninhursag did, and at the risk of a pretty horrible death if she'd been caught. They deserve the chance to pick sides when the fighting's over.

"But more than that, we're going to *need* them. There are close to five thousand trained, experienced Imperial military personnel in stasis aboard those ships, and the Achuultani are coming. We can't count on the Imperium, though we'll certainly try to obtain any help from it that we can. But in a worst-case scenario, we're on our own with little more than two years to get this planet into some kind of shape to defend itself out of its own resources, and we need those people desperately. By the same token, we need the tech base and medical facilities that are also aboard those transports, so mass destruction weapons are out of the question.

"By Ninhursag's estimates, our Imperials are outnumbered almost ten-to-one, and anyone as paranoid as Anu will have automatic weapons in strategic locations. We're taking in a force of just over a thousand people, almost all of them Terra-born, but our own Imperials are going to have to be in the van. Our Terra-born are all trained military people, and they'll have the best mix of Terran and Imperial weaponry we can give them, but they won't be the equal of Imperials. They can't be, and, at the absolute best, the fighting is going to be close, hard, and vicious. Our losses—" he swept the watching eyes without flinching "—will be heavy.

"They're going to be heavy," he repeated, "but we're going to win. We're going to remember every single thing they've ever done to us and to our planet and we're going to kick their asses, but we're also going to take prisoners."

There was a formless protest at his words, but his raised hand quelled it.

"We're going to take prisoners because Ninhursag may not be our only ally inside—we'll explain that in a moment—and because we don't know what sort of booby-traps Anu may have arranged and we'll need guides. So if someone tries to surrender, let them. But remember this: our Senior Fleet Captain has other officers now. We can, and will, convene courts-martial afterward, and the guilty *will be punished.*" He said the last three words with a soft, terrible emphasis, and the sound that answered chilled Colin's blood, but he would not have protested if he could have.

"There's another point, and this is for our own Imperials," MacMahan said quietly. "We Terra-born understand your feelings better than you may believe. We honor you and we love you, and we know you'll be the other side's primary targets. We can't help that, and we won't try to take this moment away from you, but when this is over, we're going to need you more than we ever needed you before. We'll need every single one of you for the fighting, including Colin and all the children, but we also need survivors, so don't throw your lives away! You're our senior officers; if anything happens to Colin, command of *Dahak* will devolve on one of you, and taking out the southerners is only the first step. What really matters is the Achuultani. *Don't get yourselves killed on us now!*"

Colin hoped the old Imperials heard the raw appeal in his voice, but he also remembered his earliest thoughts about Horus, his fear that the northern Imperials were no longer entirely sane themselves. He'd been wrong—but not very. It wasn't insanity, but it was fanaticism. They'd suffered a hell on earth for thousands of years to bring this moment about. He knew, beyond a shadow of a doubt, that even if they heard and understood what Hector was saying, they were going to take chances no cool, calm professional would ever take, and it was going to get all too many of them killed.

"All right," MacMahan said more normally, "here's what we're going to do.

"We're leaving *Nergal* right where she is with a skeleton crew. There will be one Imperial, chosen by lot, to command her in an emergency, backed up by just enough trained Terra-born to get her into space. I hate asking any of you to stay behind, but we have no choice. If it all comes apart on us in the south, we'll take the bastards out with a nuclear demolition charge inside the shield, but that's going to mean none of us will be coming back."

He paused to let that sink in, then went on calmly.

"In that case, the remaining crew members are going to have to take *Nergal* out to rendezvous with *Dahak*. Dahak will be expecting you and won't fire as long as you stay clear of Senior Fleet Captain Druaga's kill zone. You will therefore stop at ten thousand kilometers and transmit *Nergal's* entire memory to Dahak, which will include the findings of Senior Fleet Captain MacIntrye's court-martial and his decree of pardon as Planetary Governor. Once that's been received by Dahak, you will once more be members of *Dahak's* crew and the Imperial Fleet. *Nergal's* memory contains the best projections and advice Colin and the Council have been able to put together, but what you actually do after that will be up to you and Dahak.

"But that's an absolute worst case. Think of it as insurance for something we truly don't think will happen.

"The rest of us will take every cutter and ground combat vehicle we can muster and move south under stealth. We will take no fighters; they'd be useless inside the enclave, but more importantly, we'll need every Imperial we have to run our other equipment.

"We'll be going in through the western access point, here." Another portion of the holo map glowed as he spoke. "We have the codes from Ninhursag, and there's no indication they've been changed. We'll advance along these axes—" more lines glowed "—with parties detailed to each transport. Each attack party will be individually briefed on its mission and as much knowledge of the terrain as Ninhursag was able to give us. You'll also have Ninhursag's personal implant codes. Make damned sure you don't kill her by mistake. She's one lady we want around for the victory party.

"If you can get inside on the first rush, well and good. If you can't, the assault parties will try to prevent anyone from leaving any of the transports while the reserve deals with each holdout in turn. Hopefully, if any of them try to lift out to escape, they won't all lift at once. That means *Dahak* may only have to destroy one or two of them before the others realize what's happening. With us inside and an active *Dahak* outside, they'll surrender if they have a grain of sanity left.

"All right. That's the bare—very bare—bones of the plan. My staff will break it down for each group individually, and we'll hold a final briefing for everyone just before we push off. But there's one other thing you all ought to know, and Sergeant Asnani is the one to tell you about it. Sergeant?"

Andrew Asnani stood, wishing for a moment that he was still Abu al-Nasir, the tough, confident terrorist leader accustomed to briefing his men, as he felt their avid eyes and tried to match the colonel's calm tone.

"What Colonel MacMahan means," he said, "is that there were some unexpected developments inside the enclave. Specifically, your agent Ramman tried to betray you."

He almost flinched at his audience's sudden ripple of shock, but he continued in the same calm voice.

"No one's entirely certain what happened, but there were rumors all over the enclave, especially among their Terra-born. The official line is that he was caught out by Ganhar, their chief of operations, admitted he'd been passing you information for decades to earn the right to defect, and tried to shoot his way out, but that Ganhar out-drew and killed him. That's the *official* story, but I don't think it's the truth. Unfortunately, I can't *know* the truth. I can only surmise."

He inhaled deeply. He'd seen the southerners, been one of their own, in a sense, and he was even more aware than his listeners of the importance of his evaluation.

"It's possible," he said carefully, "that Ramman succeeded in giving his information to Ganhar before he was killed. He hadn't been told any more than Ninhursag, but if she could figure out what was coming, so could he. If that happened, then they may be waiting for us when we come in." His audience noted his use of the pronoun "we," and one or two people smiled tightly at him.

"But I don't believe they will be. If they planned an ambush, they'd've watched the drop site, and if they did, they know no one went near it. Of course, they may realize there could have been a backup, but I watched closely after the news broke. I believe the Imperials themselves believe the official story. And, while it may be that their leadership chose to put out disinformation, I don't think they did.

"I think," he went on, speaking more precisely than ever, "Ganhar told Anu and the others exactly what they told the rest of their people. I *think* he knows we're coming and deliberately helped clear the way for us."

He paused again, seeing disbelief in more than one face, and shrugged.

"I realize how preposterous that sounds, but there are reasons for my opinion. First, Ganhar was in serious trouble before they began their counter-attacks. Jantu, their security head, had his knife out, and from all I could gather, everyone expected him to stick it in. Second, Ganhar only inherited their operational branch after Kirinal was killed; he's new to the top slot, and I think actually being in charge did something to him. I can't put my finger on it exactly, but Abu al-Nasir was important enough to attend several conferences with him, and he let his guard down a bit more with their 'degenerates' than with their own Imperials. That's an unhappy man. A very unhappy man. Something's eating him up from the inside. Even before the news about Ramman broke, I had the impression his heart just wasn't in it anymore.

"You have to understand that their enclave is like feeding time in a snake house. The difference between them and what I've seen here—well, it's like the difference between night and day. If I were in the position of any of their leaders, I'd be looking over my shoulder every second, waiting for the axe to fall. Mix a little guilt with that kind of long-term, gnawing anxiety, and you could just have a man who wants out, any way he can get out.

"I certainly can't guarantee any of that. It's possible we'll walk right into a trap, and if we do, it's my evaluation that is taking us into it. But if they let us through the access point at all, we'll be inside their shield, and Captain MacIntyre has accepted my offer to personally carry one of your one-megaton nuclear demolition charges."

He met their eyes, his own stubborn and determined in the silence.

"I can't guarantee it isn't a trap," he said very, very quietly, "but I can and will guarantee that that enclave *will* be taken out."

General Gerald Hatcher opened his office door in the underground command post and stopped dead. He shot a quick glance back at the outer office, but none of the officers and noncoms bent over their desks had looked up as if they expected to see his surprise.

He inhaled through his nostrils and stepped through the door, closing it carefully behind him before he walked to his own desk. He'd never seen the twenty-five-centimeter-long rectangular case that lay on his blotter, and he examined it closely before he touched it. It was unlikely anyone could have smuggled a bomb or some similar nastiness into his office. On the other hand, it should have been equally difficult to smuggle *anything* into it.

He'd never seen anything quite like it, and he began to question his first impression that it was made of plastic. Its glossy, bronze-colored material had a metallic sheen, reflecting the light from the improbable, three-headed creature that crowned it like a crest, and he sank tensely into his chair as the implications of the starburst between the dragon's forepaws registered. He reached out and touched the case cautiously, smiling in wry self-mockery at his own tentativeness.

Metal, he decided, running a fingertip over it, though he suspected it was an alloy he'd never encountered. And there was a small, raised stud on the side. He drew a deep breath and pressed it, then relaxed and exhaled softly as the case's upper edge sprang up with a quiet click.

He lifted the lid cautiously, laying it back to lie flat on the desk, and studied the interior. There was a small, lift-up panel in what had been the bottom and three buttons to one side of it. He wondered what he was supposed to do next, then grinned as he saw the neatly-typed label gummed over one button. "Press," it said, and its prosaic incongruity tickled his sense of humor. He shrugged and obeyed, then snatched his hand back as a human figure took instant shape above the case.

Somehow, Hatcher wasn't a bit surprised to see Hector MacMahan. The colonel wore Marine battledress and body armor, and a peculiar-looking, stubby weapon with a drum magazine hung from his right shoulder. He was no more than twenty centimeters tall, but his grin was perfectly recognizable.

"Good evening, General," Hector's voice said in time to the moving lips of the image. "I realize this is a bit unusual, but we had to let someone know what was happening, and you're one of the few people I trust implicitly.

"First, let me apologize for my disappearance. You told me to make myself scarce—" another tight grin crossed his leprechaun-sized face while

Hatcher stared at him in fascination "—so I did. I'm aware I made myself a bit scarcer than you had in mind, but I'm certain you understand why. I hope to apologize and explain everything in person in the near future, but that may not be possible, which is the reason for this message.

"Now, about what's been happening in the last few weeks. For the moment, just understand that there are two separate factions of . . . well, call them extra-terrestrials, although that's not exactly the best term for them. At any rate, there are two sides, and they've been fighting one another clandestinely for a very, very long time. Now the fighting's come out into the open and, with any luck, it will come to an end very soon.

"Obviously, I'm a supporter of one side. I apologize for having used you and your resources as we did, but it was necessary. So"—Hector's face turned suddenly grim—"were all the casualties. Please believe that you cannot regret those deaths any more than we do and that we did our best to keep them as low as possible. Unfortunately, our adversaries don't share our own concern for human life.

"This message is to tell you that we're about to kick off an operation that we hope and believe will prove decisive. I realize your own reports—particularly those from New York—may've led you to conclude we're losing. Hopefully, our opponents have reached the same conclusion. If they have, and if our intelligence is correct, they're about to become our *late* opponents.

"Unfortunately, a lot of us are also going to die. I know how you hate terms like 'acceptable casualties,' Ger, but this time we really don't have a choice. If every one of us is killed, it'll still be worth it as long as we take them out, too. But in the process, there may be quite a ruckus in points south, and I'm sorry to say we really aren't positive how thoroughly *their* people may have infiltrated Terran governments or even your own command. I *think* USFC is clean, and you'll find a computer disk in the bottom of this case. I ask you to run it only on your own terminal and not to dump it to the main system, because it contains the names and ranks of eight hundred field grade and general officers in your own and other military forces in whom you may place total confidence.

"The point is that when we attack, your own bad guys may go ape on you. I have no idea what they'll do if they realize their lords and masters have been taken out and, frankly, we don't have the numbers or the organization to deal with all the things they *may* do. You, working with our allies on the disk, do. We ask you to stand by to do whatever you can to control the situation and prevent any more loss of life and destruction than can possibly be avoided.

"Watch your communications. You'll find instructions on the disk for reaching the others via a commo net I'm almost certain is secure. Until you've talked to them, don't use normal channels. Above all, don't talk to *any* civilians until your plans are in place.

"Our attack will kick off approximately eighteen hours from the time you get this. I know it's not much time, but it's the best I can do. When you talk to the others on the disk, *don't* mention the attack. To succeed, we need total surprise, and they already know what's coming down. They'll be waiting to discuss 'general contingency plans' with you.

"I'm sorry to dump this on you, Ger, but you're a good man. If I don't make it back, it's been an honor to serve under you. Give my love to Sharon and the kids, and take care of yourself. Good luck, Ger."

The tiny Hector MacMahan vanished, and General Gerald Hatcher sat staring at the flat, open case. He never knew exactly how long he sat there, but at last he reached out to press the button again and replay the message. Then he stopped himself. In the wake of that message, every moment was precious.

He lifted the panel and took out the computer disk, then swiveled his chair and switched on his terminal.

CHAPTER TWENTY-THREE

Nergal's hangar deck was crowded once more. The Imperials stood out from their allies in the soot-black gleam of combat armor, limbs swollen and massive with jump gear and servo-mech "muscles." They were festooned with weapons, and their faces were grim in their opened helmets.

The far more numerous Terra-born wore either the close-fitted blackness of Imperial commando smocks or the battledress of a score of nations. There were only so many smocks, and the people who wore them wore no body armor, for they were better protection than any Terran armor. The other Terra-born wore the best body protection Earth could provide—pathetic against Imperial weapons, but the best they could do. And there were still many Terra-born inside the enclave; it was highly probable they would face Terran weapons, as well.

Their own weapons were as mixed as their uniforms. Cut-down grav guns hung from as many shoulders as possible, while the very strongest carried lightweight energy guns, like the one Tamman had used in Tehran and La Paz, and a few teams carried ten-millimeter grav guns mounted on anti-grav generators as crew-served weapons. Most, however, carried Terran weapons. There were quite a few battle rifles (and the proliferation and improvement of body protection meant those rifles had a lot more punch than the infantry weapons of even a few decades back), but grenade launchers, squad and heavy machineguns (the latter also fitted with anti-grav generators), and rocket launchers were the preferred weapons. Goggles hung around every neck, the fruit of *Nergal*'s fabrication shops. They provided vision almost as good as an Imperial's and, equally important, would "read" any Imperial implants within fifty meters.

Horus was absent, for, to his unspeakable disappointment, the lot for who must remain to command *Nergal* had fallen to him. He'd wanted desperately to argue, but he hadn't. The assault vehicles would carry maximum loads, but even so, too many people who wanted to be there could not. His own crew would consist entirely of the oldest and least combat-ready adult Terra-born, with Isis as his executive officer. Children and those with no combat or shipboard training had been dispersed to carefully-hidden secondary locations, protected by the combat-trained adults who couldn't cram into the assault craft. His people were going to war, and he could no more shirk his responsibilities than could any of the others.

Even now, he and his bridge crew were watching their sensor arrays and completing last-minute equipment checks while Colin and Hector MacMahan stood on the launch bay stage.

"All right," Colin said quietly, "we've been over the plan backward and forward. You all know what you're supposed to do, and you also know that no plan survives contact with the enemy. Remember the objectives and keep yourselves alive if you possibly can. As Horus would say, this time we're going banco, but if anybody in this galaxy can pull it off, you can. Good luck, good hunting, and God protect you all."

He started to turn away, but MacMahan's suddenly raised voice stopped him.

"Attention on deck!" the colonel rapped, and every one of those grim-faced warriors snapped to attention in the first formal military courtesy since Colin had boarded *Nergal*. Every right hand whipped up in salute, and his chest suddenly seemed too small and tight. He tried to think of some proper response, but he could not even trust his voice to speak, and so he simply brought his hand up in response, then snapped it down.

There were no cheers as they followed him to the waiting assault craft, but he felt like a giant as he climbed into the shuttle he would pilot.

Night cloaked the western hemisphere of the planet, and a full, silvery moon rode high and serene. But deep within that moon, passive instrumentation watched the world below. Dahak knew, as Anu did not, precisely where to watch, and now he noted the brief, tiny, virtually indetectable flares of energy as *Nergal*'s auxiliaries floated out into the night.

It was happening, he realized calmly. For better or worse, his captain had launched his attack, and energy pulsed through the web of his circuitry, waking weapons that had been silent for fifty-one millennia.

The attack force headed south, and a vast storm front covered much of the southern Pacific, smashing at the assault craft with mighty fists. Colin was grateful for it. He led his warriors into its teeth, scant meters above the rearing, angry wave crests, and the miles dropped away behind them.

They moved scarcely above mach two, for they dared not come in at full bore. There were still southern fighters abroad in the night; they knew that, and they hid in the maw of the storm under their stealth fields, secure in the knowledge that *Dahak* would be watching over them from above. All five of *Nergal*'s other assault shuttles followed Colin, but there were far too few of them to transport all of his troops. Cutters and both pinnaces carried additional personnel, and all six of *Nergal*'s heavy tanks floated on their own gravitonics, able to keep pace at this slow speed. The tanks were a mixed blessing, for each used up two of his scant supply of Imperials, but their firepower was awesome, and very little short of a direct nuclear hit could stop them. Which was

the point Horus and he had carefully not discussed with their crews; those
six tanks protected twelve of *Nergal*'s eighteen Imperial children.

The tingle of active scanner systems reached out to them from the south,
still faint but growing in intensity, as he checked his position for the thousandth time. Another twenty minutes for the tanks, he estimated, but they'd
be picked up by those scanners within ten. He drew a deep breath, and his
voice was crisp over the com link.

"Shuttle pilots—go!" he said, and the heavily armed and armored assault
boats suddenly screamed ahead at nine times the speed of sound.

Alarms clangored aboard the sublight battleship *Osir*, and the man who
had been Fleet Captain (Engineering) Anu shot upright in bed.

He blinked furiously, banishing the rags of sleep, and his face twisted
in a snarl. Those gutless, sniveling *bastards* were daring to attack *him*! His
neural feed dropped data into his brain with smooth efficiency, and he saw
six assault shuttles shrieking towards his enclave. It was incredible! What
did they think they were *doing*?! He'd blow them away like insects!

A command snapped out to the automated perimeter weapon emplacements, another ordered his distant fighters to abandon stealth and rally to
the defense of the enclave, and a third woke every alarm within the shield.

"Here they come!" Colin muttered, wincing as missiles and energy beams
suddenly shredded the darkness. This was the riskiest moment of the
approach but it was also something assault shuttles were designed for, and
those automated defenders were outside the main shield.

Decoys and jammers went to work, fighting the defensive computers,
and Tamman's weapon systems sprang to life beside him. Colin felt him
bending forward as if to urge his electronic minions to greater efforts,
but he had little attention to spare. He was too busy wrenching the shuttle
through every evasive maneuver he could devise, and the night was full
of death.

He bit off a groan as one of the shuttles took a direct hit and blew
apart in a ball of fire. Hanalat and Carhana, he thought sickly, and sixty
Terra-born with them. A missile exploded dangerously close to a second
shuttle, and his heart was in his throat as Jiltanith clawed away from the
fireball. Energy guns snarled, and his own craft shuddered as something
smashed a glancing blow against her armor.

But then Tamman had his own solution, and a salvo of mass missles
screamed away, too fast, too close, for defensive systems to stop. They were
ballistic weapons, impervious to decoys, and they struck in a blast that
wracked a continent and flooded the American Highland plateau with
dreadful light. Other shuttles were firing, their missiles crossing and criss-
crossing with the ones charging up to destroy them, and energy guns raved
back at the ground. Explosions and smoke, pulverized stone and vaporized
ice and killing beams of energy—that was all the world there was as
Nergal's people thundered into the attack....

✧   ✧   ✧

Anu crowed in triumph as the first assault shuttle exploded, then cursed savagely as the others struck back. He struggled into his uniform as the enclave trembled to the fury of the assault. Breaker! Breaker take them *all*! His defenses were designed to stop the all-out attack of an eighty-thousand-ton battleship, not an assault landing, and fire stations were being blown into oblivion—not one-by-one, but in twos and threes and dozens! They'd gotten in by surprise, too close for his heavy anti-ship weapons, and his lightly-protected outer defenses crumbled and burned as he cursed.

It had been too long since he'd seen the Imperium wage war; he'd forgotten what it was like.

Ninhursag stumbled out of her shower, dragging wet hair frantically from her eyes, and shot down the apartment block transit shaft like a wet, naked otter. The sub-basement was built to withstand anything short of a direct hit with a nuke or a warp charge, and she had no business in what was about to happen out there. Not when she was as likely to be killed by a friend—or an accident—as by an enemy!

She was closing the reinforced blast door before it caught up with her. They were here! *They'd done it!*

"Shuttle Two, on my wing!" Colin snapped, and Jiltanith plummeted out of the flame-sick clouds. The two of them charged straight into the weakening defenses while their companions continued to savage Anu's weaponry. There! The access point beacon!

Colin MacIntrye drew a deep breath. At this speed, there would be no time to alter course if the shield stayed up, not even with a gravitonic drive. His implant triggered the code Ninhursag had stolen.

"*NO!!*"

Anu bellowed the protest in a burst of white-hot fury as he felt the shield open. How? *HOW?!* There was no way they could have the code! Ramman had *died*, and no other Imperial had left the enclave!

But they had it. The gates of his fortress yawned wide as two night-black shuttles screamed down the western tunnel, and its rock walls glowed with the compression heat of their passage.

"*In!*" Colin screamed to his passengers, and Tamman's exultation was a fire cloud beside him. The shuttles bucked and heaved, bare meters from destruction against the tunnel walls or one another, but neither Colin nor Jiltanith spared a thought for that. They hurtled onward, and their heavy, nose-mounted batteries of energy guns bellowed, destroying the very air in their path. Colin rode the thunder of his guns, blazing and invincible, and the inner portal of Imperial battle steel blew open like a gate of straw.

They crashed through into the enclave, drives howling in torment as they threw full power into deceleration. Even Imperial technology had its limits, and they were still moving at over a hundred kilometers per hour when they smashed through the trees in the central park and plowed into the apartment blocks. The hapless Terra-born traitors in their path had mere seconds to realize death had come as the buildings exploded outward and the shuttles slammed to a halt amid the wreckage, no more than thirty meters apart. Their passengers were battered and bruised, but assault shuttles were built for just such mistreatment. The hatches opened, and the waiting troops charged out.

One or two fell, but only a spattering of fire met them. It was no trap, Colin thought exultantly. No trap!

He activated his jump gear, vaulting over a heap of smoking rubble, his own energy gun snarling. Only a handful of armed security men confronted him, and he bared his teeth as he blew the first unarmored enemy apart.

A tremendous boom of displaced air burst out of the tunnel as the next pair of shuttles shot into the enclave, and then the true madness began.

Anu dashed onto *Osir*'s command deck, cursing his henchmen for the unreliability that had spawned his distrust and made him order the other warships deactivated. Not even *Osir*'s crew was permitted to live on board, but she was his command post, and he skidded to a halt beside the captain's console, activating his automatic defensive systems. They were intended to deal with an uprising among his own, not a full-scale invasion, but maybe they could buy his minions time to get into action.

Concealed weapons roused to life throughout the enclave. There was no time to give them precise directions even had Anu wanted to; they opened fire on anything that moved.

Ganhar tumbled from his bed as the alarms shrieked, and his eyes lit. Doubt, fear, and anguished uncertainty vanished in a blaze of triumph, and he laughed wildly. There, maniac! Let's see you deal with *these* people!

He dragged out his own combat armor. He was going to die, he thought calmly, and unless there truly was an afterlife, he would never know why he'd permitted this to happen, but it no longer mattered. He'd done it, and it wasn't in him to leave any task half-done.

The last surviving shuttle crashed into the wreckage and disgorged its troops, and *Nergal*'s people began to die. Energy beams raked the park, attracted by movement, and the Terra-born could detect neither the targeting systems nor the weapons that killed them. But their Imperials' armor scanners could find both, and they moved to engage them.

Colin wanted to weep as Rohantha vaulted onto a wreckage-bared structural beam, exposing herself recklessly, energy gun ripping two heavy weapons from the cavern wall before they could rake her team of Terra-born. She almost made it back into cover herself, and Nikan, her cabin mate and lover, blew the gun that killed her to rubble.

Colin spun on his own toes, dodging as an energy bolt whipped past him and tore a twenty-centimeter hole through an Israeli paratrooper. His own weapon silenced the Israeli's automated executioner, and he dashed on, racing for the battleships while a corner of his mind tried to remember the dead man's name.

✧　　✧　　✧

Three of Anu's stealthed fighters abandoned concealment, screaming through the heavens under maximum power as they stooped upon the clumsy gaggle of cutters and pinnaces and tanks still streaming towards the enclave. Their tracking systems found targets, but the lead pair vanished in cataclysmic balls of flame before they could fire. The third flight crew had a moment to gape at one another in horror as their instruments told them what had happened. Hyper missiles—*shipboard* missiles!—which could only have been launched from vacuum!

They died before they could warn their commander that *Dahak* was not dead.

Anu grimaced in hate and triumph. Even the computers could give him only a confused impression of what was happening, but he felt armory lockers being wrenched open aboard the transports while his weapons spewed death outside them.

Yet his triumphant snarl faded as the intensity of the fighting grew and grew. The attackers weren't human! They were demons out of Breaker's darkest hell, and they soaked up his fire and kept right on coming!

A surge of *Nergal*'s raiders swept up the boarding ramp of the transport *Bislaht*, and a trio of French Marines set up a fifty-caliber machinegun in the lock. Their teammates rushed past them behind Nikan, racing for the armory before *Bislaht*'s mutineers could find their weapons.

They almost won their race. Barely half a dozen defenders were in armor when they crashed out of the transit shaft. Nikan roared in fury as he cut two of them down and charged the others, his energy gun on full automatic, filling the air with death. A third armored mutineer went down, then a fourth, but the fifth got his weapon up in time. Nikan exploded in a fountain of blood and a crackling corona of ruptured energy packs, and the SAS commando behind him hosed his killer with a grav gun.

Smoke and the stink of blood filled the armory, and the Terra-born commandos, now with no Imperial to lead them, crouched for cover just inside the hatch and killed anything that moved.

Ganhar stepped out of the transit shaft inside Security Central aboard the transport *Cardoh*. Security men shoved past or bounced off his armor as they funneled towards the transit shaft, heading for the armory below, and he waded through them like a Titan. Jantu's outer office was deserted, and he felt a momentary surge of disappointment. But then the inner hatch licked open, and Jantu stood in the opening, an energy pistol clutched in his hand.

Ganhar smiled through his armored visor, savoring the wildness of Jantu's eyes. It was worth it, he thought coldly. It was all worth it, if only for this moment.

He lifted his grav gun slightly, and Jantu's crazed eyes narrowed with sudden comprehension as his implants recognized Ganhar's. The Operations head saw it all in that fleeting instant, saw the recognition and understanding, the sudden, intuitive grasp of what had *really* happened when Ramman came to him.

"You lose," he said softly, and his gun hissed.

Colin went flat on his face as an armored form tackled him from behind, and he rolled over, snatching out his sidearm before he recognized Jiltanith. The reason she'd hit him became instantly clear as an energy bolt whipped above him, and he raised himself on one elbow, sighting back along its path. The unarmored security man was lining up for a second shot when Colin's grav gun ripped him to shreds.

Dahak felt almost cheerful, despite a gnawing anxiety over Colin. His scanners showed that the northerners had breached the enclave. One way or the other, that shield would soon fall.

In the meantime, he busied himself locating all of Anu's deployed fighters as they abandoned stealth mode to streak back south. He tracked each of them precisely, allocated his hyper missiles with care, and fired a single salvo.

Twenty-nine more Imperial fighters died in a span of approximately two-point-seven-five Terran seconds.

The huge cavern was hideous with smoke and flame as more southerners found weapons and armor, emerging as isolated knots of warring figures that sought to link with one another amid the nightmare that had burst upon them. They were badly outnumbered, but they were all Imperials. Even without combat armor, they were more than a match for any Terra-born opponent. Or would have been, had they understood what was happening.

Most of Anu's automatics were silent now, for both sides were equally at risk from them, and both had been taking them out from the start. But they'd blunted the first rush while more of his people got themselves armed. It was helping, but they'd yielded a dangerous amount of ground. So far he'd lost touch completely only with *Bislaht*, but fighting raged aboard three other transports, and six more were surrounded, their hatches under intense fire.

Breaker! Who would have thought degenerates could *fight* like this? There were only a handful of old, worn out Imperials among them, but they were like madmen!

He winced as his scanners watched a quintet of Terra-born suddenly pop up out of a tangle of wreckage. They formed a gantlet, with three of his own Imperials between them. Two of the degenerates went down, but the others swept his armored henchmen with an unbelievable mix of Imperial and Terran weapons. Grav gun darts exploded inside armored bodies, a flamethrower hosed them with liquid fire, and a Terran anti-tank rocket blew the last survivor six meters backward. The surviving degenerates ducked back down under cover and went scuttling off in search of fresh prey.

This couldn't be happening—he saw it with his own eyes, and he still couldn't believe it!

But then came the report he'd hoped for. *Transhar*'s people had finally gotten some of their vehicles powered up, and he grinned again as the first light tank floated towards the hatch on its gravitonics.

Andrew Asnani slid to a halt, sucking in air as he scrubbed sweat from his face. He'd become separated from the rest of his team, and the deafening bellow and crash of battle pounded him like a fist, but for all its horror, it was the sweetest sound he'd ever heard. It proved he hadn't led the colonel and his people into a trap, and he'd been able to shuck off his demolition charge.

He drew another breath and took a firmer grip on his assault rifle as he eased around the rubble of a broken wall. He was in the section that had housed Anu's terrorists, and he still wasn't certain how he'd gotten here. Habit, perhaps. Or possibly something else. . . .

He dropped suddenly as shapes loomed in the dust-heavy smoke. Terra-born, not Imperials, for his goggles saw no signature implants. But neither were they *his* people, he thought grimly, hunkering deeper into the shadow of his broken wall. There were at least twenty of them, all armed, though he had no idea how they'd gotten their hands on weapons. It didn't matter. The odds sucked, and with a little luck, he'd just let them slip . . .

But he had no luck. They were coming straight towards him, and the copper taste of fear filled his mouth. Unfair! To have come so far, risked so much, and blunder into contact with—

His mind froze, panic suddenly a thing of the past, and he stopped trying to ease further back out of sight. *Abgram!* The man leading that group was *Abgram*, and that changed everything, for it had been Abgram whose operation had planted a truck bomb in New Jersey five years before.

For eleven months, Asnani had known who had killed his family, yet he could do nothing without blowing his own cover and Colonel MacMahan's op. But the thunder and screams were in his ears, and his own life was no longer essential to success.

He ejected his partially used magazine, replacing it with a fresh one, checking his safety, gathering his legs under him. The terrorists were coming closer, dodging in and out of shadows even as he had. He couldn't leave his cover without being seen, but they'd see him anyway in another twenty seconds. Ten meters. He'd let them come another ten meters. . . .

Sergeant Andrew Asnani, United States Army, exploded from concealment with his weapon on full auto.

Six men died almost instantly, and the man called Abgram went down, screaming, even as his fellows poured fire into the apparition that had erupted in their midst. He stared up in agony, watching bullets hammer body armor and flesh, seeing blood burst from the man who had shot him.

It was the last thing Abgram ever saw, for only one purpose remained to Andrew Asnani, and his last, short burst blew Abgram's head apart.

"Shit!"

Colin killed his jump gear and slithered to a halt in a tangle of smashed greenery as the light tank let fly. A solid rod of energy ripped through two of Anu's madly fleeting Terran allies and what had once been a fountain before it struck an armored figure. Rihani, he thought, one of *Nergal*'s engineers, but there was too little left to ever know. He watched the tank settle onto its treads for added stability as grenades and rockets exploded about it. Its thick armor and invisible shield shrugged off the destruction as the turret swiveled, seeking fresh prey. The long energy cannon snouted in his direction, and he grabbed Jiltanith's ankle and hauled her down beside him, not that—

A lightning bolt whickered out of the shattered portal, and the southern tank exploded with a roar. Its killer rumbled into sight, squat and massive on its own treads, grinding out onto the cavern floor, and Colin pounded the dirt beside him in jubilation.

Nergal's heavy tank moved forward confidently, cannon seeking, antipersonnel batteries flashing, heavy grav guns whining from its upper hull.

Anu roared in fury as *Transhar*'s tank was killed, but his fury redoubled as the enemy tank took up a firing position that covered *Transhar*'s vehicle ramp. Another tank tried to come down it, and *Nergal*'s heavy blew it to wreckage with a single, contemptuous shot.

A warp grenade bounced and rolled, bringing up against the edge of its shield, but nothing happened. Both sides had their suppressers out, smothering the effect of a grenade's tiny hyper generator. Normally that favored the defense, but now he watched a second enemy tank charge out of the portal—and a third!—and nothing *but* a nuke or a warp warhead was going to stop those things. That or a proper warship giving ground support. But he had only one active battleship, and the rest of her crew had not yet arrived.

It was a race, he thought grimly. A race between *Osir*'s personnel and whatever horror *Nergal*'s people would produce next.

Ganhar leapt lightly down from *Cardoh*'s number six personnel lock, letting his jump gear absorb the twelve-meter drop. *Osir* was over that way, he thought, still queerly calm, almost detached, and that was where Anu would be.

"There!" Colin shouted, pointing across two hundred meters of fire-swept ground at the battleship *Osir*. "Feel it, 'Tanni? Her systems are live! Anu must be aboard her!"

"Aye," Jiltanith agreed, then broke off to nail a fleeing southerner with a snapshot from her energy gun. In her armor her strength was the equal of any full Imperial's, and her reflexes had to be seen to be believed.

"Aye," she said again, "yet 'twill be no lightsome thing to cross yon kill zone, Colin!"

"No, but if we can get in there . . ."

"We've none t'guard our backs and we 'compass it," she warned.

"I know." Colin scanned the smoking bedlam, but they'd outdistanced their own people, and few of the southerners seemed to be in the vicinity. It was the automatics sweeping the area that made the approach so deadly.

"Look over there, to the left," he said suddenly. Some of the robotic weapons had been knocked out, leaving a gap in the defenses. "Think we can get through there before they fry us?"

"I know not," Jiltanith replied, "yet may we assay it."

"I knew you'd like the idea," he panted, and then they were off.

Hector MacMahan ducked, then swore horribly as an enemy grav gun spun Darnu's shattered armor in a madly whirling circle. The Imperial crashed to the ground, and Hector hosed a stream of darts at the spot he thought the fire had come from.

An armored southerner lurched up and fell back into death, but it was hardly a fair trade, MacMahan thought savagely, leading the surviving members of his team forward. Darnu had been worth any hundred southerners, and he was far from the first Imperial *Nergal* had lost this bloody night.

But they were pushing the bastards back. The tanks were making the difference—that and the teams who'd gotten aboard the other transports and kept their armored vehicles from ever being manned. They had a chance, a good chance, if they could only keep moving. . . .

The last of *Nergal*'s cutters swept out of the tunnel and exploded in midair. MacMahan swore again, and his men went forward in a crouching run.

Ganhar darted a look over his shoulder. He didn't recognize the implants on either of those two armored figures. Breaker! There was a third unknown looming up behind them! It was always possible that if they'd known he'd let them through the door they would have greeted him as an ally, but they couldn't know that, could they? Besides, he was closer to *Osir* than they were.

He reached a ramp and hurled himself up it, seeking the cover of the battle steel hull while beams and grav gun darts lashed at his heels. He landed on a shoulder and rolled in a clatter of armor, coming up onto his feet and running for the transit shaft. Anu would be on the command deck.

Jiltanith and Colin went up the main ramp under a hurricane of fire from the automatics, but none of the surviving weapons could depress far enough to hit them. The hatch was open, and Colin crashed through it first, dodging to the right. Jiltanith followed, spinning to the left, but the lock was empty and the inner hatch stood open as well. They edged forward as cautiously as they dared in their need for haste.

It was quieter in here, and the clank of an armored foot was loud behind them. They wheeled, but it was one of their own—Geb, his armor as smoke and soot-smutted as their own. Something had hit him in the chest, hard enough to crack even bio-enhanced ribs, but the dished-in armor had held, though Colin didn't like the way the old Imperial was favoring his left side.

"Glad to see you, Geb," he said, suppressing a half-hysterical giggle at how inane the greeting sounded. "Feel like a little walk?"

"As long as it's upstairs," Geb panted back.

"Good. Watch our backs, then, will you?" Geb nodded and Colin slapped Jiltanith's armored shoulder. "Let's go find Anu, 'Tanni," he said, and led the way towards the central transit shaft.

✧   ✧   ✧

Ganhar stepped out of the transit shaft twelve decks below the command deck, for the shaft above was inactive. So, a security measure he hadn't known about, was it? There were still the crawl ways, and he pressed the bulkhead switch to open the nearest of them.

"Hello, Ganhar." He froze at the soft voice and did a quick three-hundred-sixty-degree scan. She was unarmored, but her energy gun was trained unwaveringly on his spine.

"Hello, Inanna." He spoke quietly, knowing he could never turn fast enough to get her with the grav gun. "I thought we were on the same side."

"I told you before, Ganhar—I'm a bright girl. I had my own bugs in Jantu's outer office."

Ganhar swallowed. So she'd seen it all, and she knew why he was here.

"My quarrel's with Anu," he said. "If I can take him out, maybe they'll let us surrender."

"Wrong idea, Ganhar," Inanna said calmly. "I told you that before."

"But *why*, Inanna?! He's a fucking maniac!"

"Because I love him, Ganhar," she said, and fired.

Colin and Jiltanith rode the transit shaft as high as they could, but someone had deactivated it above deck ninety. They stepped out of it, looking for another way up, and Colin gasped in sudden alarm as the blast of an energy gun echoed down the passageway behind him. He was trying to turn towards it when a second beam from the same weapon slashed across the open bore of the shaft. It missed him by a centimeter as he heard Jiltanith's weapon snarl and looked up to see an unarmored figure tumble to the deck.

"Jesus!" he muttered. "That one was too fucking close!"

"Aye," Jiltanith replied, then paused. "Methinks our way lieth thither wi' all speed, Colin. Unless mine eyes deceive me, there lie two bodies 'pon yonder deck. I'll warrant well the first o' them did seek out Anu as do we."

"Methinks you're probably right," he grunted, stepping back across the transit shaft. Jiltanith's shot had caught the unarmored woman in mid-torso, and the gruesome sight made him look away quickly. He had no time to examine her, anyway, yet an odd sense of familiarity tugged at a corner of his brain. He glanced at her again, but he'd never seen her before and he turned his attention to the half-opened crawl way, stepping over the mangled, armored figure lying before it.

"Wonder who the hell *he* was?" he muttered, opening the hatch fully.

Geb came out of the transit shaft and paused for breath as Jiltanith eeled into the crawl way after Colin. His ribs must be pretty bad, he decided. His implants were suppressing the pain, but it was hard to breathe, and they were using enough painkillers to make him dizzy. Best not to squeeze into quarters that narrow. Besides, they'd need someone here to watch their retreat.

He squatted on his heels, trying not to think about how many friends were dying beyond this quiet hull, and glanced at the dead, armored figure beside him, wondering, like Colin and Jiltanith, who he'd been and why his fellow mutineer had killed him. Then he glanced at the dead woman and froze.

No, he thought. Please, Maker, let me be wrong!

But he wasn't wrong. He knew that face well, had known it millennia ago when it belonged to a woman named Tanisis. A beautiful young woman, married to one of his closest friends. He'd thought her dead in the mutiny and mourned her, as had her husband . . . who had named a Terranborn daughter "Isis" in her memory.

And now, so many years later, Geb cursed the Maker Himself for not making that the truth. She'd lived, he thought sickly, slept away the dreamless millennia in stasis, alive, still young and beautiful . . . only to be obscenely murdered, butchered so that one of Anu's ghouls could don her flesh.

He rose slowly, blinded by tears, and adjusted his energy gun to wide-angle focus, breathing a prayer of thanks that Jiltanith either had not remembered her mother's face or else had not looked closely at the body. Nor would she have the chance to, for there was one last service Geb could perform for his friend Tanisis. He pressed the firing stud and a fan of gravitonic disruption wiped the mangled body out of existence.

Hector MacMahan looked about cautiously. All six of *Nergal*'s tanks were in action now, and only one southern heavy had gotten free of its transport hold to challenge them. Its half-molten wreckage littered two hundred square meters of cavern floor, spewing acrid, choking smoke to join the fog shrouding the hellish scene.

An awful lot of their Imperials were dead, he thought bitterly. Their own hatred, coupled with their need to protect their weaker Terra-born, had cost them. He doubted as many as half were still alive, even counting the tank crews, but their sacrifice had given *Nergal*'s raiders control of the entire western half of the enclave and four of the seven transports on the eastern side. They were closing in on pockets of resistance, Terra-born moving cautiously under covering fire from the tanks.

Unless something went dreadfully wrong in the next thirty minutes, they were going to win this thing.

Colin let his armor's "muscles" take the strain of the climb, questing ahead with his Dahak-modified implants as he neared the humming intensity of the command deck. They were only one deck below it when he felt the automatic weapons. They were covered by a stealth field, but it needed adjustment, and even in its prime it hadn't been a match for his implants.

"Hold it," he grunted to Jiltanith.

"What hast thou spied?"

"Booby traps and energy guns," he replied absently, examining the intricate field of interlocking fire. "Damn, it's a bitch, too. Well . . ."

He plucked his grav gun from its webbing. The energy gun might have been better, but the quarters were far too cramped for it.

"What dost thou?"

"I'm going to open us a little path," he said, and squeezed the trigger.

A hurricane of needles swept the crawl way, drilling half their lengths even into battle steel before they exploded. Scanner arrays, trip signals, and targeting systems shredded under his fire, and the weapons went mad. The shaft above him became a crazy-quilt of exploding energy beams and solid projectiles.

Anu's head jerked up as bedlam erupted in one of the crawl ways. His automatic defenses had been triggered, but there was something wrong. They weren't firing under proper control—they were tearing themselves apart!

The carnage lasted a good thirty seconds, and Colin probed the smoking wreckage carefully.

"That's got it. On the other hand, we just rang the doorbell. Think we should keep going?"

" 'Twould seem we ha' scant choice."

"I was afraid you'd say that. C'mon."

Anu turned away from his console, and his face was almost relaxed.

It would take a while yet, but the sheer audacity of the attack had been decisive. Those heavy tanks had hurt, but it was surprise that had done in the enclave. The dreams of fifty thousand years were crumbling in his fingers, and it was all the fault of those crawling traitors from *Nergal*. Their fault, and the fault of his own gutless subordinates.

But if he'd lost, he could still see to it they lost, too. He walked calmly across the command deck to the fire control officer's couch, insinuating his mind neatly into the console. He really should have provided a proper bomb, but this would do.

He initiated the arming sequence, then paused. No, wait. Let whoever was in the crawl way get here first. He wanted to watch at least one of the bastards *know* what was going to happen to his precious, putrid world.

Colin helped Jiltanith out of the crawl way, then paused, his face white. Jesus! The son-of-a-bitch was arming every warhead in the magazines!

"Come on!" he shouted, and hurled himself toward the command deck. His gauntleted hand slapped the emergency over-ride, and he charged through as the hatch licked open. His energy gun was ready, swinging to cover the captain's console, but even as he burst onto the command deck, he knew he'd guessed wrong. The heavy hand of a grab field smashed at him, seizing him in fingers of iron. He stopped instantly, not even rocking with the impetus of his charge, unable even to fall in the armor that had become a prison.

"Nice of you to drop by," a voice said, and he turned his head inside his helmet. A tall man sat at the gunnery console with an energy pistol in one hand. He didn't look like the images of Anu from the records, but he wore the midnight blue of Battle Fleet with an admiral's insignia.

"It's over, Anu," Colin said. "You might as well give it up."

"No," Anu said calmly, "I don't think I'm the surrendering kind."

"I know what kind you are," Colin said contemptuously, keeping his eyes on Anu while his implants watched Jiltanith creeping closer and closer. She was belly-down on the deck, trying to work her way under the plane of the grab field, but her enhanced senses were less keen than his. Could she skirt it safely, or not?

"Do you, now?" Anu mocked. "I doubt that. None of you ever had the wit to understand me, or you would have joined me instead of trying to pull me down to your own miserable level."

"Sure," Colin sneered. "You've done a wonderful job, haven't you? Fifty thousand years, and you're still stuck on one piddling little planet."

Anu's face tightened and he started to trigger the warheads, then stopped and uncoiled from the couch like a serpent.

"No," he murmured. "I think I'll watch you scream a bit first. I'm glad you're in armor. It'll take a while to burn through with this little popgun, and you'll *feel* it so nicely. Let's start with an arm, shall we? If I start with a leg, you'll just fall over, and that won't be any fun."

He came nearer, and sweat beaded Colin's forehead. If the bastard came another three meters closer, Jiltanith would have a shot through the hatch—but he'd be able to see her, and she was flat on her belly. He wracked his brain as Anu took another step. And another. There had to be a way! There *had* to! They'd come so far. . . .

Wait! Anu had been so damned confident, he might not have changed—

Anu took another step, and Jiltanith raised her grav gun. Her armor scuffed the deck so gently normal ears would not have heard it, but Anu was an Imperial. He whirled snake-quick, his eyes widening in shock, and the energy pistol swung down and fired like lightning.

It was all one blinding nightmare. Anu's pistol snarled. Its energy bolt hit Jiltanith squarely in the spine and held there. Smoke burst from her armor, but she pressed the trigger and an explosive dart hit blew his right leg into tatters an instant before a sparkling corona of ruptured power packs glared above her armored body.

Colin heard her scream over his com link. Her grav gun fell from her hand and her armored body convulsed, and his world vanished in a boil of fury.

Anu hit the deck, screaming until his implants took control. They damped the pain, sealed the ruptured tissues, drove back the fog of shock, but it took precious seconds, and Colin's implants—his bridge officer implants—reached out and demanded access to *Osir's* computers.

There was a flicker of electronic shock, and then, like *Nergal*, *Osir* recognized him, for Anu hadn't changed the command codes; it hadn't even occurred to him to try. He stared at Colin in horror, momentarily stunned as even the loss of his leg had not stunned him, unable to believe what he was seeing. There *were* no bridge officers! *He'd killed them all!*

Colin's mind flooded into *Osir's* computers, killing the grab field. But hate and madness spurred Anu's own efforts, and his command licked out to the fire control console. He enabled the sequenced detonation code.

Colin raced after it, trying to kill it, but he was in the wrong part of *Osir's* brain. He couldn't get to it, so he did the only other thing he could.

He slammed down a total freeze of the entire command network, and every single system in the ship locked.

Anu screamed in frustration, and Colin staggered as the pistol snarled again. Energy slammed into his chest, but his armor held long enough for him to hurl himself aside. Anu swung the pistol, trying to hold it on his fleeing target, but he hadn't counted on the adjustments Dahak had made to Colin's implants. He misjudged his enemy's reaction speed, and Colin slammed into a bulkhead in a clangor of armor and battle steel. He richocheted off like a bank shot, bouncing himself back towards Anu, and Anu screamed again as an armored foot reduced his pistol hand to paste. He tried to roll away, but Colin was on him like a demon. He reached down, jerking him up in a giant's embrace, and his hands twisted.

Anu shrieked as his arms shattered, and for just an instant their eyes met—Anu's mad with terror and pain, his own equally mad with hate and a pain not of his flesh—and Colin knew Anu's life was his.

But he didn't take it. He tossed his victim aside, cold in his fury, and the mutineer bounced off a bulkhead with another wail of agony. He slid to the deck, helpless in his broken body, and Colin ignored him as he flung himself to his knees beside Jiltanith. He couldn't read her bio-read-outs through her badly damaged armor, and he lifted her in his arms, calling her name and peering into her helmet visor in desperation.

Her eyes opened slowly, and he gasped in relief.

"'Tanni! How . . . how badly are you hurt?"

"Certes, 'twas like unto an elephant's kick," she murmured dazedly, "yet 'twould seem I am unhurt."

"Thank God!" he whispered, and she smiled.

"Aye, methinks He did have more than summat t'do wi' it," she replied, her voice a bit stronger. "'Twas that, or mine armor, or mayhap a bit o' both. Yet having saved me, it can do no more, good Colin. I must come forth if I would move. That blast hath fused my servo circuits all."

"You're out of your mind if you think I'm letting you out of there yet!"

"So, thou art a tyrant after all," she said, and he hugged her close.

"Rank hath its privileges, 'Tanni, and I'm getting you out of here in one piece, damn it!"

"As thou wilt," she murmured with a small smile. "Yet what of Anu?"

"Don't worry," Colin said coldly.

He eased her dead armor into a sitting position where she could see the crippled mutineer, then returned his attention to the computers. He activated a stand-alone emergency diagnostic system and felt his cautious way down the frozen fire control circuits to the detonation order, then sought the next circuit in the sequence. He disabled it and withdrew, then reactivated the core computers and swung to face Anu, and his face was cold.

"How?" the mutineer moaned. Even his implants couldn't fully deaden the agony of his broken limbs, and his face was white. "How could you *do* that?"

"Dahak taught me," Colin said grimly, and Anu shook his head frantically.

"*No!* No, *Dahak*'s dead! I *killed* it!" The agony of failure, utter and complete, filled Anu's face, overshadowing his physical pain.

"Did you, now?" Colin asked softly, and his smile was cruel. "Then you won't mind this a bit."

He bent over the broken body and snatched it up, careless of Anu's wail of anguish.

"What wouldst thou, Colin?" Jiltanith asked urgently.

"I'm giving him what he wanted," Colin said coldly, and crossed the command deck. A hatch hissed open at his command to reveal the cabin of a lifeboat, and he dumped Anu into the lead couch. The mutineer stared at him with desperate, hating eyes, and Colin smiled that same cold, cruel smile as his neural feed programmed the lifeboat with a captain's imperative, locking out all attempts to change it.

"You wanted Dahak, you son-of-a-bitch? Well, Dahak wants you, too. I think he'll enjoy the meeting more than you will."

"No!" Anu shrieked as the hatch began to close. "*Noooooooooo!* Ple—"

The hatch cut him off, and *Osir* twitched as the lifeboat launched.

The gleaming minnow arced upward through the enclave's shield, fleeing the planet its mother ship had come to so long before. It altered course, swinging unerringly to line its nose on the white, distant disk of the moon, and its passenger's terrified mind hammered futilely at the commands locked into its computers. The lifeboat paid no heed, driving onward toward the mighty starship it had left millennia ago. Tracking systems aboard that starship locked upon it, noting its origin and course, and a fold-space signal pulsed out before it, identifying its single passenger to Dahak.

The computer watched it come, and Alpha Priority commands within his core programming tingled to life. Dahak could have fired the instant he identified the target, but he held his fire, waiting, letting the lifeboat bear its cargo closer and closer, and the human emotion of anticipation filled his circuitry.

The lifeboat reached the kill zone about the warship, and a single, five-thousand-kilometer streamer of energy erupted from beneath the crater men had named Tycho. It lashed out, fit to destroy a ship like *Osir* herself, and the silver minnow vanished.

There were tiny sounds aboard the leviathan called *Dahak*. The targeting systems shut themselves down with a quiet click. The massive energy mount whined softly as it powered down, its glowing snout cooling quickly in the vacuum of its weapon bay. Then there was only silence. Silence and yet another human emotion . . . completion.

CHAPTER TWENTY-FOUR

Two months to the day after the fall of the enclave, Senior Fleet Captain Colin MacIntyre, Imperial Battle Fleet, commanding officer of the ship-of-the-line *Dahak* and Governor of Planet Earth and the Solarian System, stepped out of the hoverjeep and breathed deep of the crisp, clear morning of a Colorado autumn. The usual frenzy of Shepard Space Center was stilled, and he felt his NASA driver staring at the bronze-sheened tower of alloy thrusting arrogantly heavenward before them. The sublight battleship *Osir* had been sitting here for a week, waiting for him, but a week hadn't been long enough for NASA to get used to her.

He adjusted his cap and moved to join the small group at the foot of *Osir*'s ramp. He was grateful that those same people had let him have a few moments of privacy to stand alone with the permanent honor guard before The Cenotaph. That was the only name it had, probably the only name it ever would have, and it was enough. The polished obsidian shaft reared fifty meters into the air in front of White Tower, glittering and featureless, and its plain battle steel plinth bore the name and birth-planet of every person who had died fighting the southerners.

It was a long list. He'd stepped close, scanning the endless names until he found the two he sought. "SANDRA YVONNE TILLOTSON, LT. COL., USAF, EARTH" and "SEAN ANDREW MACINTYRE, US FORESTRY SERVICE, EARTH." His brother and his friend were in good company, he thought sadly. The best.

Now he tried to put the sorrow aside as he reached the waiting group. Horus stood with General Gerald Hatcher, Sir Frederick Amesbury, and Marshal Vassily Chernikov—the three men who, most of all, had held the planet together in the wake of the preposterous reports coming out of Antarctica. Once the truth of those fantastic tales registered, virtually every major government had fallen overnight, and Colin still wasn't quite certain how these men had managed to hang on to a semblance of order, even with the support of *Nergal*'s allies within the military.

"Horus," Colin nodded to his friend. "It looks like I'm leaving you in good hands."

"I think so, too," Horus replied with a small, slightly wistful smile.

Only eleven of *Nergal*'s senior Imperials had lived through the fighting, and they had chosen to remain behind with the planet on which they'd spent so much of their long lives. Colin was glad. They'd far more than earned their right to leave, but it would have seemed wrong, somehow. In a very real sense, they were the surviving godparents of the human race, Terran branch. If anyone could be trusted to look after Earth's interests, they could.

And Earth's interests would need looking after. A second line of auto-mated stations had gone off the air, which meant the Achuultani's scouts were no more than twenty-five months away. He had that long to reach the Imperium, find out why no defense was being mounted, summon assistance, and get back to Sol. It was a tall order, and he frankly doubted he could do it. Nor was the fact reassuring that no one had yet answered the non-stop messages Dahak had been transmitting ever since they recovered the hypercom spares from the enclave.

It looked like the only way they could find help—if there was any to find—was to go out and get it in person, and only *Dahak* could do that. Which meant Earth would be on her own until *Dahak* could return.

The situation wasn't quite as hopeless as it might have been. Assuming Dahak's records of previous incursions were any guide, the Achuultani scouts would be anywhere from a year to eighteen months ahead of the main incursion, and Earth would not be fangless when they arrived. Except for *Osir* herself, all of *Dahak*'s sublight warships had been debarked, along with the vast majority of the old starship's fighters and enough combat and ground vehicles to conquer the planet five times over. They would remain behind to form the nucleus of Sol's defense.

Two of *Dahak*'s four Fleet repair units, each effectively a hundred-fifty-thousand-ton spaceborne industrial complex in its own right, had also been debarked. Their first task had been the construction of the gravity generator Dahak would leave in his place to avoid disturbing such things as the Lagrange point habitats, not to mention little items like Earth's tides. Since completing that assignment, they had split their capacity between replicating themselves and producing missiles, mines, fighters, and every other conceivable weapon of war. The technological and industrial base Anu had hoarded for fifty millennia was coming into operation, as well, with every Terrestrial assistance a badly frightened planet could provide.

No, Earth would not be helpless when the Achuultani arrived. But a strong hand would be needed to lead Colin's birth-world through the enormous changes that awaited it, and that hand would belong to Horus.

Colin had declared himself Governor of Earth, but he'd never meant to claim the title seriously. He'd seen it only as a means to make his pardon of *Nergal*'s Imperials "official," yet it had become clear his temporary expedient was in fact a necessity. It would be a long time before Terrans really trusted *any* politician again, and Hatcher, Amesbury, and Chernikov agreed unanimously with Horus: Earth needed a single, unquestioned source of authority, or her people would be too busy fighting one another to worry about the Achuultani.

So Colin had declared peace and, backed by *Dahak*'s resources, made it stick with very little difficulty. When he then proclaimed himself Planetary Governor in the name of the Imperium (once more with *Dahak*'s newly-revealed potential hovering quietly in the background) and promised local autonomy, most surviving governments had been only too happy to hand their problems over to him. The Asian Alliance might still make problems, but Horus and his new military aides seemed confident that they could handle that situation.

Once they had, all existing militaries were to be merged (and Colin was profoundly grateful he would be elsewhere while his henchmen implemented *that* decision), and he'd named Horus Lieutenant Governor and appointed all ten of his surviving fellows Imperial Councilors for Life to help him mind the store while "the Governor" was away.

All of which, he reflected with an inner smile, would certainly keep Horus's "retirement" from being boring.

The thorniest problem, in many ways, had been the surviving southerners. Of the four thousand nine hundred and three mutineers from stasis, almost all had declared their willingness to apply for Terran citizenship and accept commissions in the local reserves and militia. Colin had re-enlisted a hundred of them for service aboard *Dahak* (on a probationary basis) to help provide a core of experienced personnel, but the rest would remain on Earth. Since they had been sitting under an Imperial lie detector at the time they declared their loyalty anew, he felt reasonably confident about leaving them behind. Horus would keep an eagle eye on them, and they would furnish him with a nucleus of trained, fully-enhanced Imperials to get things rolling while the late Inanna's medical facilities began providing biotechnics to Earth's Terra-born defenders.

But that left over three hundred Imperials who had joined Anu willingly or failed the lie detector's test, all of them guilty, at the very least, of mutiny and multiple murder. Imperial law set only one penalty for their crimes, and Colin had refused to pardon them. The executions had taken almost a week to complete.

It had been his most agonizing decision, but he'd made it. There had been no option . . . and deep inside he knew the example—and its implicit warning—would stick in the minds he left behind him, Terra-born and Imperial alike.

So now he was leaving. *Dahak*'s crew was tremendously understrength, but at least the ship had one again. The survivors of Hector MacMahan's assault force, all fourteen of *Nergal*'s surviving children, and his tentatively rehabilitated mutineers formed its core, but it had been fleshed out just a bit. A sizable chunk of the USFC and SAS, and the entire US Second Marine Division, Russian Nineteenth Guards Parachute Division, German First Armored Division, and Japanese Sendai Division would provide the bulk of his personnel, along with several thousand hand-picked air force and navy personnel from all over the First World. All told, it came to barely a hundred thousand people, but with so many parasites left behind it would suffice. They'd rattle around like peas in the vastness of their ship, but taking any more might strain even Dahak's ability to provide biotechnics *and* training before they reached the borders of the Imperium.

"Well, we'll be going then," Colin said, shaking himself out of his thoughts. He reached out to shake hands with the three military men, and smiled at Marshal Chernikov. "I expect my new Chief Engineer will be thinking of you, sir," he said.

"Your Chief Engineer with two good arms, Comrade Governor," Chernikov replied warmly. "Even his mother agrees that his temporary absence is a small price to pay for that."

"I'm glad," Colin said. He turned to Gerald Hatcher. "Sorry about Hector, but I'll need a good ops officer."

"You've got one, Governor," Hatcher said. "But keep an eye on him. He disappears at the damnedest times."

Colin laughed and took Amesbury's hand.

"I'm sorry so much of the SAS is disappearing with me, Sir Frederick. I hope you won't need them."

"They're good lads," Sir Frederick agreed, "but we'll make do. Besides, if you run into a spot of bother, my chaps should pull you out again— even under Hector's command."

Colin smiled and held out his hand to Horus. The old Imperial looked at it for a moment, then reached out and embraced him, hugging him so hard his reinforced ribs creaked. The old man's eyes were bright, and Colin knew his own were not entirely dry.

"Take care of yourself, Horus," he said finally, his voice husky.

"I will. And you and 'Tanni take care of each other." Horus gave him one last squeeze, then straightened, his hands on Colin's shoulders. "We'll take care of the planet for you, too, Governor. You might say we've had some experience at that."

"I know." Colin patted the hand on his right shoulder, then stepped back. A recorded bosun's pipe shrilled—he was going to have to speak to Dahak about this perverse taste for Terran naval rituals he seemed to have developed—and his subordinates snapped to attention. He returned their salutes sharply, then turned and walked up the ramp. He did not look back as the hatch closed behind him, and *Osir* floated silently upward as he stepped into the transit shaft.

His executive officer looked up as he arrived on the command deck.

"Captain," she said formally, and started to rise from the captain's couch, but he waved her back and took the first officer's station. The gleaming disk of *Dahak*'s hull, no longer hidden by its millennia-old camouflage, floated before him as the visual display turned indigo blue and the first stars appeared.

"Sorry you missed the good-byes?" he asked quietly.

"Nay, my Colin," she said, equally softly. "I ha' said my farewells long since. 'Tis there my future doth lie."

"All of ours," he agreed. They sped onward, moving at a leisurely speed by Imperial standards, and *Dahak* swelled rapidly. The three-headed dragon of his ensign faced them, vast and proud once more, loyal beyond the imagining of humans. Most humans, at any rate, Colin reminded himself. Not all.

The starship grew and grew, stupendous and overwhelming, and a hatch yawned open on Launch Bay Ninety-One. *Osir* had come full circle at last.

The battleship threaded her way down the cavernous bore, and Dahak's voice filled her bridge with the old, old ritual announcement of Colin's own navy.

"Captain, arriving," it said.

THE ARMAGEDDON INHERITANCE

BOOK ONE

The sensor array was the size of a very large asteroid or a very small moon, and it had orbited the G6 star for a very, very long time, yet it was not remarkable to look upon. Its hull, filmed with dust except where the electrostatic fields kept the solar panels clear, was a sphere of bronze-gold alloy, marred only by a few smoothly-rounded protrusions, with none of the aerials or receiver dishes which might have been expected by a radio-age civilization. But then, the people who built it hadn't used anything as crude as radio for several millennia prior to its construction.

The Fourth Imperium had left it here fifty-two thousand one hundred and eighty-six Terran years ago, its electronic senses fueled only by a trickle of power, yet the lonely guardian was not dead. It only slept, and now fresh sparkles of current flickered through kilometers of molecular circuitry.

Internal stasis fields spun down, and a computer roused from millennia of sleep. Stronger flows of power pulsed as testing programs reported, and Comp Cent noted that seven-point-three percent of its primary systems had failed. Had it been interested in such things, it might have reflected that such a low failure rate was near miraculous, but this computer lacked even the most rudimentary of awarenesses. It simply activated the appropriate secondaries, and a new set of programs blinked to life.

It wasn't the first time the sensor array had awakened, though more than forty millennia had passed since last it was commanded to do so. But this time, Comp Cent observed, the signal which had roused it was no demand from its builders for a systems test. This signal came from another sensor array over seven hundred light-years to galactic east, and it was a death cry.

Comp Cent's hypercom relayed the signal another thousand light-years, to a communications center which had been ancient before Cro-Magnon first trod the Earth, and awaited a response. But there was no response. Comp Cent was on its unimaginative own, and that awakened still more autonomous programs. The signal to its silent commanders was replaced by series of far shorter-ranged transmissions, and other sensor arrays stirred and roused and muttered sleepily back to it.

Comp Cent noted the gaping holes time had torn in what once had been an intricately interlocking network, but those holes were none of its concern, and it turned to the things which were. More power plants came on line, bringing the array fully alive, and the installation became a brilliant beacon, emitting in every conceivable portion of the electromagnetic and gravitonic spectra with more power than many a populated world of the Imperium. It was a signpost, a billboard proclaiming its presence to anyone who might glance in its direction.

And then it waited once more.

Months passed, and years, and Comp Cent did not care. Just over seven years passed before Comp Cent received a fresh signal, announcing the death of yet another sensor array. This one was less than four hundred light-years distant. Whatever was destroying its lonely sisters was coming closer, and Comp Cent reported to its builders once again. Still no one answered. No one issued new orders or directives. And so it continued to perform the function it had been programmed to perform, revealing itself to the silent stars like a man shouting in a darkened room. And then, one day, just over fifteen years after it had awakened, the stars responded.

Comp Cent's sensitive instruments detected the incoming hyper wake weeks before it arrived. Once more it reported its findings to its commanders, and once more they did not respond. Comp Cent considered the silence, for this was a report its programming told it must be answered. Yet its designers had allowed for the remote possibility that it might not be received by its intended addressees. And so Comp Cent consulted its menus, selected the appropriate command file, and reconfigured its hypercom to omni-directional broadcast. The GHQ signal vanished, replaced by an all-ships warning addressed to any unit of Battle Fleet.

Still there was no answer, but this time no backup program told Comp Cent to do anything else, for its builders had never considered that possibility, and so it continued its warning broadcasts, unconcerned by the lack of response.

The hyper wake came closer, and Comp Cent analyzed its pattern and its speed, adding the new data to the warning no one acknowledged, watching incuriously as the wake suddenly terminated eighteen light-minutes from the star it orbited. It observed new energy sources approaching, now at sublight speeds, and added its analysis of their patterns to its broadcast.

The drive fields closed upon the sensor array, wrapped about cylindrical hulls twenty kilometers in length. They were not Imperial hulls, but Comp Cent recognized them and added their identity to its transmission.

The starships came closer still at twenty-eight percent of light-speed, approaching the sensor array whose emissions had attracted their attention, and Comp Cent sang to them, and beckoned to them, and trolled them in while passive instrumentation probed and pried, stealing all the data from them that it could. They entered attack range and locked their targeting systems upon the sensor array, but no one fired, and impulses tumbled through fresh logic trees as Comp Cent filed that fact away, as well.

The starships approached within five hundred kilometers, and a tractor beam—a rather crude one, but nonetheless effective, Comp Cent noted—reached out to the sensor array. And as it did, Comp Cent activated the instructions stored deep within its heart for this specific contingency.

Matter met anti-matter, and the sensor array vanished in a boil of light brighter than the star it orbited. The detonation was too terrible to call an "explosion," and it reduced the half-dozen closest starships to stripped atoms, ripped a dozen more to incandescent splinters, damaged others, and—just as its long-dead masters had intended—deprived the survivors of any opportunity to evaluate the technology which had built it.

Comp Cent had performed its final function, and it neither knew nor cared why no one had ever answered its warning that after sixty thousand years, the Achuultani had returned.

CHAPTER ONE

It was raining in the captain's quarters.

More precisely, it was raining in the three-acre atrium inside the captain's quarters. Senior Fleet Captain Colin MacIntyre, self-proclaimed Governor of Earth and latest commanding officer of the Imperial planetoid *Dahak*, sat on his balcony and soaked his feet in his hot-tub, but Fleet Captain Jiltanith, his tall, slender executive officer, had chosen to soak her entire person. Her neatly-folded, midnight-blue uniform lay to one side as she leaned back, and her long sable mane floated about her shoulders.

Black-bottomed holographic thunderheads crowded overhead, distant thunder rumbled, and lightning flickered on the "horizon," yet Colin's gaze was remote as he watched rain bounce off the balcony's shimmering force field roof. His attention was elsewhere, focused on the data being relayed through his neural feeds by his ship's central command computer.

His face was hard as the report played itself out behind his eyes, from the moment the Achuultani starships emerged from hyper to the instant of the sensor array's self-immolation. It ended, and he shook himself and looked down at Jiltanith for her reaction. Her mouth was tight, her ebon eyes cold, and for just a moment he saw not a lovely woman but the lethal killing machine which was his executive officer at war.

"That's it, then, Dahak?" he asked.

"It is certainly the end of the transmission, sir," a deep, mellow voice replied from the empty air. Thunder growled again behind the words in grimly appropriate counterpoint, and the voice continued calmly. "This unit was in the tertiary scanner phalanx, located approximately one hundred ten light-years to galactic east of Sol. There are no more between it and Earth."

"Crap," Colin muttered, then sighed. Life had been so much simpler as a NASA command pilot. "Well, at least we got some new data from it."

"Aye," Jiltanith agreed, "yet to what end, my Colin? 'Tis little enow, when all's said, yet not even that little may we send home, sin Earth hath no hypercom."

"I suppose we could turn back and deliver it in person," Colin thought aloud. "We're only two weeks out. . . ."

"Nay," Jiltanith disagreed. "Should we turn about 'twill set us back full six weeks, for we must needs give up the time we've but now spent, as well."

"Fleet Captain Jiltanith is correct, Captain," Dahak seconded, "and while these data are undoubtedly useful, they offer no fundamental insights necessary to Earth's defense."

"Huh!" Colin tugged at his nose, then sighed. "I guess you're right. It'd be different if they'd actually attacked and given us a peek at their hardware, but as it is—" He shrugged. "I wish to hell they *had*, though. God knows we could use some idea of what they're armed with!"

"True," Dahak agreed. "Yet the readings the sensor array did obtain indicate no major advances in the Achuultani's general technology, which suggests their weaponry also has not advanced significantly."

"I almost wish there *were* signs of advances," Colin fretted. "I just can't accept that they haven't got *something* new after sixty thousand years!"

"It is, indeed, abnormal by human standards, sir, but entirely consistent with surviving evidence from previous incursions."

"Aye," Jiltanith agreed, sliding deeper into the hot water with a frown, "yet still 'tis scarce credible, Dahak. How may any race spend such time 'pon war and killing and bring no new weapons to their task?"

"Unknown," the computer replied so calmly Colin grimaced. Despite Dahak's self-awareness, he had yet to develop a human-sized imagination.

"Okay, so what *do* we know?"

"The data included in the transmission confirm reports from the arrays previously destroyed. In addition, while no tactical information was obtained, sensor readings indicate that the Achuultani's maximum attainable sublight velocity is scarcely half as great as that of this vessel, which suggests at least one major tactical advantage for our own units, regardless of comparative weaponry. Further, we have reconfirmed their relatively low speed in hyper, as well. At their present rate of advance, they will reach Sol in two-point-three years, as originally projected."

"True, but I'm not too happy about the way they came in. Do we know if they tried to examine any of the other sensor arrays?"

"Negative, Captain. A hypercom of the power mounted by these arrays has a maximum omni-directional range of less than three hundred light-years. The reports of all previously destroyed sensor arrays were relayed via the tertiary phalanx arrays and consisted solely of confirmation that they had been destroyed by Achuultani vessels. This is the first direct transmission we have received and contains far more observational data."

"Yeah." Colin pondered a moment. "But it doesn't match very well with what little we know about their operational patterns, now does it?"

"It does not, sir. According to the records, normal Achuultani tactics should have been to destroy the array immediately upon detection."

"That's what I mean. We were dead lucky any of the arrays were still around to tell us they're coming, but I can't help thinking the Imperium was a bit too clever in the way it set these things up. Sucking them in close for better readings is all very well, but *these* guys were after information of their own. What if they change tactics or speed up on us because they figure someone's waiting for them?"

"Methinks thy concern may be over great," Jiltanith said after a moment. "Certes, they needs must know some power did place sentinels to ward its borders, yet what knowledge else have they gained? How shall they guess where those borders truly lie or when their ships may cross them? Given so little, still must they search each star they pass."

Colin tugged on his nose some more, then nodded a bit unhappily. It made sense, and there wasn't anything he could do about it even if Jiltanith were wrong, but it was his job to worry. Not that he'd asked for it.

"I guess you're right," he sighed. "Thanks for the report, Dahak."

"You are welcome, Captain," the starship said, and Colin shook himself, then grinned at Jiltanith.

"Looking forward to sickbay, 'Tanni?" He put an edge of malicious humor into his voice as an anodyne against their worries.

"Hast an uncommon low sense of humor, Colin," she said darkly, accepting the change of subject with a smile of her own. "So long as I do recall have I awaited this day—yea, and seldom with true hope mine eyes might see it. Yet now 'tis close upon me, and if truth be known, there lies some shadow of fear within my heart. 'Tis most unmeet in thee so to tease me over it."

"I know," he admitted wickedly, "but it's too much fun to stop."

She snorted and shook a dripping fist at him, yet there was empathy as well as laughter in his green eyes. Jiltanith had been a child, her muscles and skeleton too immature for the full bioenhancement Battle Fleet's personnel enjoyed, when the mutiny organized by Fleet Captain (Engineering) Anu marooned *Dahak* in Earth orbit and the starship's crew on Earth. The millennia-long struggle her father had led against Anu had kept her from receiving it since, for the medical facilities aboard the sublight parasite battleship *Nergal* had been unable to provide it. Jiltanith had received the neural computer feeds, sensory boosters, and regenerative treatments before the mutiny, but those were the easy parts, and Colin was fresh enough from his own enhancement to understand her anxieties perfectly . . . and tease her to ease them.

"Bawcock, thou'lt crow too loud one day."

"Nope. I'm the captain, and rank—"

"—hath its privileges," she broke in, shaking her head ominously. "That phrase shall haunt thee."

"I don't doubt it." He smiled down at her, tempted to shuck off his own uniform and join her . . . if he hadn't been a bit afraid of where it might lead. Not that he had any objection to where it *could* lead, but there was plenty of time (assuming they lived beyond the next two years), and that was one complication neither of them needed right now.

"Well, gotta get back to the office," he said instead. "And you, Madam XO, should get back to your own quarters and catch some sleep. Trust me— Dahak's idea of a slow convalescence from enhancement isn't exactly the same as yours or mine."

"Of thine, mayhap," she said sweetly.

"I'll remember that when you start moaning for sympathy." He drew his toes from the tub and activated a small portion of his own biotechnics. The water floated off his feet on the skin of a repellent force field, and he shook the drops away and pulled on his socks and gleaming boots.

"Seriously, 'Tanni, get some rest. You'll need it."

"In truth, I doubt thee not," she sighed, wiggling in the hot-tub, "yet still doth this seem heaven's foretaste. I'll tarry yet a while, methinks."

"Go ahead," he said with another smile, and stepped off the edge of the balcony onto a waiting presser. It floated him gently to the atrium floor, and his implant force fields were an invisible umbrella as he splashed through the rain to the door/hatch on the far side of his private park.

It opened at his approach, and he stepped through it into a yawning, brightly-lit void over a thousand kilometers deep. He'd braced himself for it, yet he knew he appeared less calm than he would have liked—and felt even less calm than he managed to look as he plunged downward at an instantly attained velocity of just over twenty thousand kilometers per hour.

Dahak had stepped his transit shafts' speed down out of deference to his captain and Terra-born crew, though Colin knew the computer truly didn't comprehend why they felt such terror. It was bad enough aboard the starship's sublight parasites, yet the biggest of those warships massed scarcely eighty thousand tons. In something that tiny, there was barely time to feel afraid before the journey was over, but even at this speed it would take almost ten minutes to cross Dahak's titanic hull, and the lack of any subjective sense of movement made it almost worse.

Yet the captain's quarters were scarcely a hundred kilometers from Command One—a mere nothing aboard Dahak—and the entire journey took only eighteen seconds. Which was no more than seventeen seconds too long, Colin reflected as he came to a sudden halt. He stepped shakily into a carpeted corridor, glad none of his crew were present to note the slight give in his knees as he approached Command One's massive hatch.

The three-headed dragon of Dahak's bas relief crest looked back from it. Its eyes transfixed him for a moment across the starburst cradled in its raised forepaws, fierce with the fidelity which had outlasted millennia, and then the hatch—fifteen centimeters of Imperial battle steel thick—slid open, and another dozen hatches opened and closed in succession as he passed through them to Command One's vast, dim sphere.

The command consoles seemed to float in interstellar space, surrounded by the breath-taking perfection of Dahak's holographic projections. The nearest stars moved visibly, but the artificiality of the projection was all too apparent if one thought about it. Dahak was tearing through space under maximum Enchanach Drive; at seven hundred and twenty times light-speed, direct observation of the cosmos would have been distorted, to say the very least.

"The Captain is on the bridge," Dahak intoned, and Colin winced. He was going to *have* to do something about this mania Dahak had developed for protecting his commander's precious dignity!

The half-dozen members of Colin's skeleton bridge watch, Imperials all, began to stand, but he waved them back and crossed to the captain's console. Trackless stars drifted beneath his boots, and Fleet Commander Tamman, his Tactical officer and third in command, rose from the couch before it.

"Captain," he said as formally as Dahak, and Colin gave up for the moment.

"I have the con, Commander." He slipped into the vacated couch, and it squirmed under him as it adjusted to the contours of his body. There was no need for Tamman to give him a status report; his own neural feed to the console was already doing that.

He watched the tactical officer retire to his own station with a small, fond smile. Tamman was Jiltanith's contemporary, one of the fourteen Imperial "children" from *Nergal*'s crew to survive the desperate assault on Anu's enclave. All of them had joined Colin in *Dahak*, and he was damned thankful they had. Unlike his Terra-born, they could tie directly into their computers and run them the way the Imperium had intended, providing a small, reliable core of enhanced officers to ride herd on the hundred pardoned mutineers who formed the nub of his current crew. In time, Dahak would enhance and educate his Terra-born to the same standard, but with a complement of over a hundred thousand, it was going to take even *his* facilities a while to finish the task.

Colin MacIntyre reclined in his comfortable command couch, and his small smile faded as he watched the stars sweep towards him and the sleek, deadly shapes of Achuultani starships floated behind his eyes once more. The report from the sensor array replayed itself again and again, like some endless recording loop, and it filled him with dread. He'd known they were coming; now he'd "seen" them for himself. They were real, now, and so was the horrific task he and his people faced.

Dahak was more than twenty-seven light-years from Earth, but the nearest Imperial Fleet base had been over two-hundred light-years from Sol when *Dahak* arrived to orbit Earth. The Imperium proper lay far beyond that, yet despite the distances and the threat sweeping steadily towards his home world, they'd had no choice but to come, for only the Imperium might offer the aid they desperately needed to save that home world from those oncoming starships.

But *Dahak* had been unable to communicate with the Imperium for over fifty thousand years. What if there no longer *was* an Imperium?

It was a grim question they seldom discussed, one Colin tried hard not to ask even of himself, yet it beat in his brain incessantly, for *Dahak* had repaired his hypercom once the spares he needed had been reclaimed from the mutineers' Antarctic enclave. He'd been calling for help from the moment those repairs were made—indeed, he was calling even now.

And, like the sensor arrays, he had received no reply at all.

CHAPTER TWO

Lieutenant Governor Horus, late captain of the mutinous sublight battle-ship *Nergal* and current viceroy of Earth, muttered a heartfelt curse as he sucked his wounded thumb.

He lowered his hand and regarded the wreckage sourly. He'd worked with Terran equipment for centuries, and he knew how fragile it was. Unfortunately, Imperial technology was becoming available again, and he'd forgotten the intercom on his desk was Terran-made.

His office door opened, and General Gerald Hatcher, head of the Chiefs of Staff of Planet Earth (assuming they ever got the organization set up), poked his head in and eyed the splintered intercom panel.

"If you want to attract my attention, Governor, it's simpler to buzz me than to use sirens."

"Sirens?"

"Well, that's what I thought I heard when my intercom screamed. Did that panel *do* something, or were you just pissed off?"

"Terran humans," Horus said feelingly, "are pretty damned smart-mouthed, aren't they?"

"One of our more endearing traits." Hatcher smiled at Jiltanith's father and sat down. "I take it you did want to see me?"

"Yes." Horus waved a stack of printout. "You've seen these?"

"What are—?" Horus stopped waving, and Hatcher craned his neck to read the header. He nodded. "Yep. What about them?"

"According to these, the military amalgamation is a month behind sched-ule, that's what," Horus began, then paused and studied Hatcher's expres-sion. "Why don't you look surprised or embarrassed or something, General?"

"Because we're ahead of where I expected to be," Hatcher said, and Horus sat back with a resigned sigh as he saw the twinkle in his eye. Gerald Hatcher, he sometimes thought, had adapted entirely too well to the presence of extra-terrestrials on his world.

"I suppose," the general continued unabashedly, "that I should've told you we've deliberately set a schedule no one could make. That way we've got an excuse to scream at people, however well they're doing." He shrugged. "It's not nice, but when a four or five-star general screams at you, you usually discover a few gears you weren't using. Wonderful thing, screaming."

"I see." Horus regarded him with a measuring eye. "You're right—you should've told me. Unless you're planning on screaming at me?"

"Perish the thought," Hatcher murmured.

"I'm relieved," Horus said dryly. "But should I take it you're actually satisfied, then?"

"Given that we're trying to merge military command structures which, however closely allied, were never really designed for it, Frederick, Vassily and I are pleased at how quickly it's moving, but time's mighty short."

Horus nodded. Sir Frederick Amesbury, Vassily Chernikov, and Hatcher formed what Vassily was fond of calling Horus's military *troika*, and they were working like demons at their all but impossible task, but they had barely two years before the first Achuultani scout forces could be expected.

"What's the worst bottleneck?" he asked.

"The Asian Alliance, of course." Hatcher made a wry face. "Our deadline hasn't quite run out, and they still haven't gotten off the fence and decided whether to fight us or join us. It's irritating as hell, but not surprising. I don't think Marshal Tsien's decided to oppose us actively, but he's certainly dragging his feet, and none of the other Alliance military types will make a move until he commits himself."

"Why not demand that the Alliance remove him, then?" It was a question, but it didn't really sound like one.

"Because we can't. He's not just their top man; he's also the best they have. They know it, too, and so much of their political leadership was in Anu's pocket—and got killed when you took out the enclave—that he's the only man the Alliance military still trusts. And however much he may hate us, he hates us less than a lot of his juniors do." Hatcher shrugged. "We've asked him to meet us face-to-face, and at least he's accepted. We'll just have to do our best with him, and he's smart, Horus. He'll come around once he gets past the idea that the West has somehow conquered him."

Horus nodded again. All three of his senior generals were "Westerners" as far as Tsien and his people were concerned. The fact that Anu and his mutineers had manipulated Terran governments and terrorist groups to play the First and Third Worlds off against one another was just beginning to percolate through *Western* brains; it would be a while yet before the other side could accept it on an emotional basis. Some groups, like the religious crackpots who had run places like Iran and Syria, never would, and their militaries had simply been disarmed . . . not, unhappily, without casualties.

"Besides," Hatcher went on, "Tsien *is* their senior commander, and we'll need him. If we're going to make this work, we don't have any choice but to integrate our people and their people—no, scratch that. We have to integrate all of *Earth's* military people into a single command structure. We can't impose non-Asian officers on the Alliance and expect it to work."

"All right." Horus tossed the printout back into his "IN" basket. "I'll make myself available to see him if you think it'll help; otherwise, I'll stay out of it and let you handle it. I've got enough other headaches."

"Don't I know it. Frankly, I wouldn't trade jobs with you on a bet."

"Your selflessness overwhelms me," Horus said, and Hatcher smiled again. "How's the rest of it going?"

"As well as can be expected." Horus shrugged. "I wish we had about a thousand times as much Imperial equipment, but the situation's improving now that the orbital industrial units *Dahak* left behind are hitting their stride.

"A lot of their capacity's still going into replicating themselves, and I've diverted some of their weapons-manufacturing tonnage to planetary construction equipment, but we should be all right. It's a geometric progression, you know; that's one of the beauties of automated units that don't need niggling little things like food or rest.

"We're just about on schedule setting up the tech base Anu brought down with him, and the part *Dahak* landed directly is up and running. We're hitting a few snags, but that's predictable when you set about building a whole new industrial infrastructure. Actually, it's the planetary defense centers that worry me most, but Geb's on that."

Geb, once *Nergal*'s Chief Engineer and currently a senior member of the thirty-man (and woman) Planetary Council helping Horus run the planet, was working nineteen-hour days as Earth's chief construction boss. Hatcher didn't envy his exhausting task. There were all too few Imperials available to run the construction equipment they already had, and if purely Terran equipment was taking up a lot of the slack, that was rather like using coolie labor in light of their monumental task.

Geb and Horus had rejected the idea of reconfiguring Imperial equipment—or building new—to permit operation by unenhanced Terra-born. Imperial machinery was designed for operators whose implants let them interface directly with it, and altering it would degrade its efficiency. More to the point, by the time they could adapt any sizable amount of equipment, they should be producing enhanced Terra-born in sufficient numbers to make it unnecessary.

Which reminded Horus of another point.

"We're ready to start enhancing non-military people, too."

"You are?" Hatcher brightened. "That's good news."

"Yes, but it only makes another problem worse. Everyone we enhance is going to be out of action for at least a month—more probably two or three—while they get the hang of their implants. So every time we enhance one of our top people, we lose him for that long."

"Tell me about it," Hatcher said sourly. "Do you realize—well, of course you do. But it's sort of embarrassing for the brass to be such wimps compared to their personnel. Remember my aide, Allen Germaine?" Horus nodded. "I dropped by the Walter Reed enhancement center to see him yesterday. There he was, happily tying knots in quarter-inch steel rods for practice, and there I sat in my middle-aged body, feeling incredibly flabby. I used to think I was pretty fit for my age, too, damn it! And he'll be back in the office in another few weeks. That's going to be even more depressing."

"I know." Horus's eyes twinkled. "But you're just going to have to put up with it. I can't spare any of my chiefs of staff for enhancement until you get this show firmly on the road."

"Now *there's* an efficiency motivater!"

"Isn't it just?" Horus murmured wickedly. "And speaking of getting things on the road, how do you feel about the defensive installations I've proposed?"

"From what I understand of the technology, it looks pretty good, but I'd feel better if we had more depth to our orbital defenses. I've been reading over the operational data Dahak downloaded—and that's another thing I want: a neural link of my own—and I'm not happy about how much the Achuultani seem to like kinetic weapons. Can we really stop something the size of, say, Ceres, if they put shields on it before they throw it at us?"

"Geb says so, but it could take a lot of warheads. That's why we need so many launchers."

"Fine, but if they settle in for a methodical attack, they'll start by picking off our peripheral weapons first. That's classic siege strategy with any weaponry, and it's also why I want more depth, to allow for attrition of the orbital forts."

"Agreed. But we have to put the inner defenses into position first, which is why *I'm* sweating the PDC construction rates. They're what's going to produce the planetary shield, and we need their missile batteries just as badly. Not even Imperial energy weapons can punch through atmosphere very efficiently, and when they do, they play merry hell with little things like jet streams and the ozone layer. That's one reason it's easier to defend nice, airless moons and asteroids."

"Um-hum." Hatcher plucked at his lip. "I'm afraid I've been too buried in troop movements and command structures to spend as much time as I'd like boning up on hardware. Vassily's our nuts-and-bolts man. But am I correct in assuming your problems're in the hyper launchers?"

"Right the first time. Since we can't rely on beams, we need missiles, but missiles have problems of their own. As Colin is overly fond of pointing out, there are always trade-offs.

"Sublight missiles can be fired from anywhere, but they're vulnerable to interception, especially over interplanetary ranges. Hyper missiles can't be intercepted, but they can't be launched from atmosphere, either. Even air has mass, and the exact mass a hyper missile takes into hyper with it is critical to where it re-enters normal space. That's why warships pre-position their hyper missiles just inside their shields before they launch."

Hatcher leaned forward, listening carefully. Horus had been a missile specialist before the mutiny; anything he had to say on this subject was something the general wanted to hear.

"We can't do that from a planet. Oh, we could, but planetary shields aren't like warship shields. Not on habitable planets, anyway. Shield density is a function of shield area; after a point, you can't make it any denser, no matter how much power you put into it. To maintain sufficient density to stop really large kinetic weapons, our shield is going to have to contract well into the mesosphere. We can stop most smaller weapons from outside atmosphere, but not the big bastards, and we can't count on avoiding heavy kinetic attack. In fact, that's exactly what we're likely to be under if we do need to launch from planetary bases."

"And if the shield contracts, the missiles would be outside it where the Achuultani could pick them off," Hatcher mused.

"Exactly. So we have to plan on going hyper straight from launch, and that means we need launchers big enough to contain the entire hyper field— just over three times the size of the missiles—or else their drives will take chunks out of the defense center when they depart." Horus shrugged. "Since a heavy hyper missile's about forty meters long and the launcher has to be air-tight with provision for high-speed evacuation of atmosphere, we're talking some pretty serious engineering just to build the damned things."

"I see." Hatcher frowned thoughtfully. "How far behind schedule are you, Horus? We're going to need those batteries to cover our orbital defenses whatever happens."

"Oh, we're not really in trouble yet. Geb allowed for some slippage in his original plans, and he thinks he can make it up once he gets more Imperial equipment on line. Give us another six months and we should be back on schedule. By Dahak's least favorable estimate, we've got two years before the Achuultani arrive, and we should only be looking at a thousand or so scouts in the first wave. If we can hurt them badly enough, we'll have another year or so to extend the defenses before the main fleet gets here. Hopefully, we'll have more warships of our own by then, too."

"Hopefully," Hatcher agreed. He tried to radiate confidence, but he and Horus both knew. They had an excellent chance of beating off the Achuultani scouts, but unless Colin found the help they needed, Earth had no hope at all against the main incursion.

The cold winter wind and dark, cloudy sky over T'aiyuan's concrete runways struck Marshal Tsien Tao-ling as an appropriate mirror for his own mood. Impassive and bulky in his uniform greatcoat, Tsien had headed the military machine of the Asian Alliance for twelve tumultuous years, and he had earned that post through decisiveness, dedication, and sheer ability. His authority had been virtually absolute, a rare thing in this day and age. Now that same authority was like a chain of iron, dragging him remorselessly towards a decision he did not want to make.

In less than fifty years, his nation had unified all of Asia that mattered— aside from the Japanese and Filipinos, and they scarcely counted as Asians any longer. The task had been neither cheap nor easy, nor had it been bloodless, but the Alliance had built a military machine even the West was forced to respect. Much of that building had been his own work, the fruit of his sworn oath to defend his people, the Party, and the State, and now his own decision might well bring all that effort, all that sacrifice, to nothing.

Oh, yes, he thought, lengthening his stride, *these are the proper skies for me.*

General Quang scurried after him, his high-pitched voice fighting a losing battle with the wind. Tsien was a huge man, almost two hundred centimeters in his bare feet, and a native of Yunnan Province. Quang was both diminutive and Vietnamese, and all rhetoric about Asian Solidarity notwithstanding, there was very little love lost between the Southern Chinese and their Vietnamese "brothers." Thousands of years of mutual hostility could not be forgotten that easily, nor could Vietnam's years as a Soviet proxy be easily forgiven, and the fact that Quang was a merely marginally competent whiner with powerful Party connections only made it worse.

Quang broke off, puffing with exertion, and the marshal smiled inwardly. He knew the smaller man resented how ridiculous he looked trying to match his own long-legged stride, which was why he took pains to emphasize it whenever they met. Yet what bothered him most just now, he admitted, was hearing a fool like Quang say so many things he had thought himself.

And what of me? Tsien frowned at his own thoughts. *I am a servant of the Party, sworn to protect the State, yet what am I to do when half the Central Committee has vanished? Can it be true so many of them were traitors—not just to the State but to all humanity? Yet where else have they gone? And how am I to choose when my own decision has suddenly become so all important?*

He looked up at the sleek vehicle waiting on the taxi way. Its bronze-sheened alloy gleamed dully in the cloudy afternoon, and the olive-brown-skinned woman beside its open hatch was not quite Oriental-looking. The sight touched him with something he seldom felt: uncertainty. Which made him think again of what Quang had been saying. He sighed and paused, keeping his face utterly impassive with the ease of long practice

"General, your words are not new. They have been considered, by your government and mine—" *what remains of them, idiot* "—and the decision has been made. Unless his terms are utterly beyond reason, we will comply with the demands of this Planetary Governor." *For now, at least.*

"The Party has not been well-advised," Quang muttered. "It is a trick."

"A trick, Comrade General?" Tsien's small smile was wintry as the wind. "You have, perhaps, noticed that there is no longer a moon in our night skies? It has, perhaps, occurred to you that anyone with a warship of that size and power has no need of trickery? If it has not, reflect upon this, Comrade General." He nodded in the direction of the waiting Imperial cutter. "That vehicle could reduce this entire base to rubble, and nothing we have could even *find* it, much less stop it. Do you truly believe that the West, with hundreds of even more powerful weapons now at its disposal, could not disarm us by force as they already have those maniacs in Southwest Asia?"

"But—"

"Spare me your comments, Comrade General," Tsien said heavily. *Especially since they are so close to my own doubts. I have a job to do, and you make it no easier.* "We have two choices: comply, or be deprived of the poor weapons we still possess. It is possible they are honest, that this danger they speak of is real. If that is true, resistance would spell far worse for all of us than disarmament and occupation. If they are lying, then at least we may have the opportunity to observe their technology at first hand, possibly even to gain access to it ourselves."

"But—"

"I will not repeat myself, Comrade General." Tsien's voice was suddenly soft, and Quang paled. "It is bad enough when junior officers question orders; I will not tolerate it in general officers. Is that clear, Comrade General?"

"I-It is," Quang managed, and Tsien raised an eyebrow over one arctic eye. Quang swallowed. "Comrade Marshal," he added quickly.

"I am relieved to hear it," Tsien said more pleasantly, and walked towards the cutter once more. Quang followed silently, but the marshal could feel the man's resentment and resistance. Quang and those like him, particularly those with a base in the Party, were dangerous. They were quite capable of doing something utterly stupid, and the marshal made a mental note to have Quang quietly reassigned to some less sensitive duty. Command of the air patrols and SAM bases covering the Sea of Japan, perhaps. That once prestigious post had become utterly meaningless, but it might take Quang a few months to realize it.

And in the meantime, Tsien could get on with what mattered. He did not know the American Hatcher who spoke for the . . . beings who had seized control of Earth, but he had met Chernikov. He was a Russian, and so, by definition, not to be trusted, but his professionalism had impressed Tsien almost against his will, and he seemed to respect Hatcher and the Englishman Amesbury. Perhaps Hatcher was truly sincere. Perhaps his offer of cooperation, of an equal share in this new, planet-wide military organization, was genuine. There had, after all, been fewer outrageous demands by his political masters in the "Planetary Council" than Tsien had feared. Perhaps that was a good sign.

It had better be. All he had said to Quang was correct; the military position made resistance hopeless. Yet that had been true before in Asia's history, and if these Westerners meant to make effective use of Asia's vast manpower, some of their new military technology must fall into Asian hands.

Tsien had used that argument with dozens of frightened, angry juniors, yet he was not certain he believed it, and it irritated him to be unsure whether his own doubts were rational or emotional. After so many years of enmity, it was difficult to think with cold logic about any proposal from the West, yet in his heart of hearts, he could not believe they were lying. The scope of their present advantage was too overwhelming. They were too anxious, too concerned over the approach of these "Achuultani," for the threat to be an invention.

His waiting pilot saluted and allowed him to precede her into the cutter, then settled behind her controls. The small vehicle rose silently into the heavens, then darted away, climbing like a bullet and springing instantly forward at eight times the speed of sound. There was no sense of acceleration, yet Tsien felt another weight—the weight of inevitability—pressing down upon his soul. The wind of change was blowing, sweeping over all this world like a typhoon, and resistance would be a wall of straw before it. Whatever Quang and his ilk feared, whatever he himself thought, they must ride that wind or perish.

And at least China's culture was ancient and there were two billion Chinese. If the promises of this Planetary Council were genuine, if all citizens were to enjoy equal access to wealth and opportunity, that fact alone would give his people tremendous influence.

He smiled to himself. Perhaps these glib Westerners had forgotten that China knew how to conquer invaders it could not defeat.

CHAPTER THREE

Gerald Hatcher and his fellows rose courteously as Marshal Tsien entered the conference room, his shoulders straight and his face impassive. He was a big bastard for a Chinese, Hatcher reflected, taller even than Vassily, and broad enough to make two of Hatcher himself.

"Marshal," he said, holding out his hand. Tsien took it with the briefest of hesitations, but his grip was firm. "Thank you for coming. Won't you sit down, please?"

Tsien waited deliberately for his "hosts" to find seats first, then sat and laid his briefcase neatly on the table. Hatcher knew Frederick and Vassily were right in insisting that he, as the sole charter member of Earth's new Supreme Chiefs of Staff with no prior connection to the Imperials, must serve as their chief, but he wished he could disagree. This hard-faced, silent man was the most powerful single serving military officer on the planet, critical to their success, and he did not—to say the least—look cheerful.

"Marshal," Hatcher said finally, "we asked you to meet us so that we could speak without the . . . pressure of a civilian presence—yours or ours. We won't ask you to strike any 'deals' behind your leaders' backs, but there are certain pragmatic realities we must all face. In that regard, we appreciate the difficulties of your position. We hope—" he looked levelly into the dark, unreadable eyes "—that you appreciate ours, as well."

"I appreciate," Tsien said, "that my government and others which it is pledged to defend have been issued an ultimatum."

Hatcher hid a wince. The marshal's precise, accentless English made his almost toneless words even more unpromising, but they also showed him the only possible approach, and he reached for it before prudence could change his mind.

"Very well, Marshal Tsien, I'll accept your terminology. In fact, I *agree* with your interpretation." He thought he saw a flicker of surprise and continued evenly. "But we're military men. We know what can happen if that ultimatum is rejected, and, I hope, we're also all realists enough to accept the truth, however unpalatable, and do our best to live with it."

"Your pardon, General Hatcher," Tsien said, "but your countries' truth seems somewhat more palatable than that which you offer mine or our allies. Our *Asian* allies. I see here an American, a ConEuropean, a Russian—I do not see a Chinese, a Korean, an Indian, a Thai, a Cambodian, a Malaysian. I do not even see one of your own Japanese." He shrugged eloquently.

"No, you don't—yet," Hatcher said quietly, and Tsien's eyes sharpened. "However, General Tama, Chief of the Imperial Japanese Staff, will be joining us as soon as he can hand over his present duties. So will Vice Admiral Hawter of the Royal Australian Navy. It is our hope that you, too, will join us, and that you will nominate three additional members of this body."

"Three?" Tsien frowned slightly. This was more than he had expected. It would mean four members from the Alliance against only five from the Western powers. But was it enough? He rubbed the table top with a thoughtful finger. "That is scarcely an equitable distribution in light of the populations involved, and yet . . ."

His voice trailed off, and Hatcher edged into the possible opening.

"If you will consider the nations the men I mentioned represent, I believe you'll be forced to admit that the representation is not inequitable in light of the actual balance of military power." He met Tsien's eyes again, hoping the other could see the sincerity in his own. The marshal didn't agree, but neither did he disagree, and Hatcher went on deliberately.

"I might also remind you, Marshal Tsien, that you do not and will not see any representative of the extreme Islamic blocs here, nor any First World hard-liners. You say we represent Western Powers, and so, by birth, we do. But we sit here as representatives of Fleet Captain Horus in his capacity as the Lieutenant Governor of Earth, and of the five men I've named, only Marshal Chernikov and General Tama—both of whom have long-standing personal and family connections with the Imperials—were among the chiefs of staff of their nations. We face a danger such as this planet has never known, and our only purpose is to respond to that danger. Towards this end, we have stepped outside traditional chains of command in making our selections. You are the most senior officer we've asked to join us, and I might point out that we've asked you to *join* us. If we must, we will—as you are well aware we can—compel your obedience, but what we want is your *alliance.*"

"Perhaps," Tsien said, but his voice was thoughtful.

"Marshal, the world as we have known it no longer exists," the American said softly. "We may regret that or applaud it, but it is a fact. I won't lie to you. We've asked you to join us because we need you. We need your people and your resources, as allies, not vassals, and you're the one man who may be able to convince your governments, your officers, and your men of that fact. We offer you a full and equal partnership, and we're prepared to guarantee equal access to Imperial technology, military and civilian, and complete local autonomy. Which, I might add, is no more than our own governments have been guaranteed by Governor MacIntyre and Lieutenant Governor Horus."

"And what of the past, General Hatcher?" Tsien asked levelly. "Are we to forget five centuries of Western imperialism? Are we to forget the unfair distribution of the world's wealth? Are we, as some have," his eyes shifted slightly in Chernikov's direction, "to forget our commitment to the Revolution in order to accept the authority of a government not even of our own world?"

"Yes, Marshal," Hatcher said equally levelly, "that's precisely what you are to forget. We won't pretend those things never happened, yet you're known as a student of history. You know how China's neighbors have suffered at Chinese hands over the centuries. We can no more undo the past than your own people could, but we can offer you an equal share in building the future, assuming this planet has one to build. And that, Marshal Tsien, is the crux: if we do not join together, there will be no future for any of us."

"So. Yet you have said nothing of how this . . . body will be organized. Nine members. They are to hold co-equal authority, at least in theory?" Hatcher nodded, and the marshal rubbed his chin, the gesture oddly delicate in so large a man. "That seems overly large, Comrade General. Could it be that you intend to—I believe the term is 'pad'—it to present the appearance of equality while holding the true power in your own hands?"

"It could be, but it isn't. Lieutenant Governor Horus has a far more extensive military background than any of us and will act as his own minister of defense. The function of this body will be to serve as his advisors and assistants. Each of us will have specific duties and operational responsibilities—there will be more than enough of those to go around, I assure you—and the position of Chief of Staff will rotate."

"I see." Tsien laid his hands on his briefcase and studied his knuckles, then looked back up. "How much freedom will I have in making my nominations?"

"Complete freedom." Hatcher very carefully kept his hope out of his voice. "The Lieutenant Governor alone will decide upon their acceptability. If any of your nominees are rejected, you'll be free to make fresh nominations until candidates mutually acceptable to the Asian Alliance and the Lieutenant Governor are selected. It is my understanding that his sole criterion will be those officers' willingness to work as part of his own command team, and that he will evaluate that willingness on the basis of their affirmation of loyalty under an Imperial lie detector." He saw a spark of anger in Tsien's eyes and went on unhurriedly. "I may add that all of us will be required to demonstrate our own loyalty in precisely the same fashion and in the presence of all of our fellows, including yourself and your nominees."

The anger in Tsien's hooded gaze faded, and he nodded slowly.

"Very well, General Hatcher, I am empowered to accept your offer, and I will do so. I caution you that I do not agree without reservations, and that it will be difficult to convince many of my own officers to accept my decision. It goes against the grain to surrender all we have fought for, whether it is to Western powers or to powers from beyond the stars, yet you are at least partly correct. The world we have known has ended. We will join your efforts to save this planet and build anew. Not without doubts and not without suspicion—you would not believe otherwise, unless you were fools—

but because we must. Yet remember this: more than half this world's population is *Asian*, gentlemen."

"We understand, Marshal," Hatcher said softly.

"I believe you do, Comrade General," Tsien said with the first, faint ghost of a smile. "I believe you do."

Life Councilor Geb brushed stone dust from his thick, white hair as yet another explosive charge bellowed behind him. It was a futile gesture. The air was thin, but the damnable dust made it seem a lot thicker, and his scalp was coated in fresh grit almost before he lowered his hand.

He watched another of the sublight parasites *Dahak* had left for Earth's defense—the destroyer *Ardat*, he thought—hover above the seething dust, her eight-thousand-ton hull dwarfed by the gaping hole which would, when finished, contain control systems, magazines, shield generators, and all the other complex support systems. Her tractors plucked up multi-ton slabs of a mountain's bones, and then the ship lifted away into the west, bearing yet another load of refuse to a watery grave in the Pacific. Even before *Ardat* was out of sight, the Terra-born work crews swarmed over the newly-exposed surface of the excavation in their breath masks, drills screaming as they prepared the next series of charges.

Geb viewed the activity with mixed pride and distaste. This absolutely flat surface of raw stone had once been the top of Ecuador's Mount Chimborazo, but that was before its selection to house Planetary Defense Center *Escorpion* had sealed the mountain's fate. The sublight battleships *Shirhan* and *Escal* arrived two days later, and while *Escal* hovered over the towering peak, *Shirhan* activated her main energy batteries and slabbed off the top three hundred meters of earth and stone. *Escal* caught the mega-ton chunks of wreckage in her tractors while *Shirhan* worked, lifting them for her pressers to toss out of the way into the ocean. It had taken the two battleships a total of twenty-three minutes to produce a level stone mesa just under six thousand meters high, and then they'd departed to mutilate the next mountain on their list.

The construction crews had moved in in their wake, and they had labored mightily ever since. Imperial technology had held the ecological effects of their labors to a minimum impossible for purely Terran resources, but Geb had seen Chimborazo before his henchmen arrived. The esthetic desecration of their labors revolted him; what they had accomplished produced his pride.

PDC *Escorpion*, one of forty-six such bases going up across the surface of the planet, each a project gargantuan enough to daunt the Pharaohs, and each with a completion deadline of exactly eighteen months. It was an impossible task . . . and they were doing it anyway.

He stepped aside as the whine of a gravitonic drive approached from one side. The stocky, olive-brown Imperial at the power bore's controls nodded to him, but despite his rank, he was only one more rubber-necker in her way, and he backed further as she positioned her tremendous machine carefully, checking the coordinates in her inertial guidance systems against the engineers' plat of the base to be. An eye-searing dazzle flickered as she powered up the cutting head and brought it to bear.

The power bore floated a rock-steady half-meter off the ground, and Geb's implants tingled with the torrent of focused energy. A hot wind billowed back from the rapidly sinking shaft, blowing a thick, plume of powdered rock to join the choking pall hanging over the site, and he stepped still further back. Another thunderous explosion burst in on him, and he shook his head, marveling at the demonic energy loosed upon this hapless mountain. Every safety regulation in the book—Imperial and Terran alike—had been relaxed to the brink of insanity, and the furious labor went on day and night, rain and sun, twenty-four hours a day. It might stop for a hurricane; nothing less would be permitted to interfere.

It was bad enough for his Imperials, he thought, watching the dust-caked woman concentrate, but at least they had their biotechnics to support them. The Terra-born did not, and their primitive equipment required far more of pure muscle to begin with. But Horus had less than five thousand Imperials; barely three thousand of them could be released to construction projects, and the PDCs were only one of the clamorous needs Geb and his assistants had to meet somehow. With enhanced personnel and their machinery spread so thin, he had no choice but to call upon the primitive substitutes Earth could provide. At least he could lift in equipment, materials, and fuel on tractors as needed.

A one-man grav scooter grounded beside him. Tegran, the senior Imperial on the *Escorpion* site, climbed off it to slog through the blowing dust to Geb's side and pushed up his goggles to watch the power bore at work.

Tegran was much younger, biologically, at least, than Geb, but his face was gaunt, and he'd lost weight since coming out of stasis. Geb wasn't surprised. Tegran had never personally offended against the people of Earth, but like most of the Imperials freed from Anu's stasis facilities, he was driving himself until he dropped to wash away the stigma of his past.

The cutting head died, and the power bore operator backed away from the vertical shaft. A Terra-born, Imperial-equipped survey team scurried forward, instruments probing and measuring, and its leader lifted a hand, thumb raised in approval. The dust-covered woman responded with the same gesture and moved away, heading for the next site, and Horus turned to Tegran.

"Nice," he said. "I make that a bit under twenty minutes to drill a hundred-fifty-meter shaft. Not bad at all."

"Um," Tegran said. He walked over to the edge of the fifty meter-wide hole which would one day house a hyper missile launcher and stood peering down at its glassy walls. "It's better, but I can squeeze another four or five percent efficiency out of the bores if I tweak the software a bit more."

"Wait a minute, Tegran—you've already cut the margins mighty close!"

"You worry too much, Geb." Tegran grinned tightly. "There's a hefty safety factor built into the components. If I drop the designed lifetime to, say, three years instead of twenty, I can goose the equipment without

risking personnel. And since we've only got *two* years to get dug in—"
He shrugged.

"All right," Geb said after a moment's thought, "but get me the figures
before you make any more modifications. And I want a copy of the software. If you can pull it off, I'll want all the sites to be able to follow suit."

"Fine," Tegran agreed, walking back to his scooter. Geb followed him, and
the project boss paused as he remounted. "What's this I hear about non-
military enhancement?" he asked, his tone elaborately casual.

Geb eyed him thoughtfully. A few other Imperials had muttered darkly
over the notion, for the Fourth Imperium had been an ancient civilization by Terran standards. Despite supralight travel, over-crowding on its
central planets had led to a policy restricting full enhancement (and the
multi-century lifespans which went with it) solely to military personnel
and colonists. Which, Geb reflected, had been one reason the Fleet never
had trouble finding recruits even with minimum hitches of a century and
a half . . . and why Horus's policy of providing full enhancement to every
adult Terran, for all intents and purposes, offended the sensibilities of the
purists among his Imperials.

Yet Geb hadn't expected Tegran to be one of them, for the project head
knew better than most that enhancing every single human on the planet,
even if there had been time for it, would leave them with far too few people
to stand off an Achuultani incursion.

"We started this week," he said finally. "Why?"

"Welllllllll . . ." Tegran looked back at the departing power bore, then
waved expressively about the site. "I just wanted to get my bid for them
in first. I've got a hell of a job to do here, and—"

"Don't worry," Geb cut in, hiding his relief. "We need them everywhere,
but the PDCs have a high priority. I don't want anybody with implants
standing idle, but I'll try to match the supply of operators to the equipment you actually have on hand."

"Good!" Tegran readjusted his goggles and lifted his scooter a meter off
the ground, then grinned broadly at his boss. "These Terrans are great, Geb.
They work till they drop, then get back up and start all over again.
Enhance me enough of them, and I'll damned well build you another
Dahak!"

He waved and vanished into the bedlam, and Geb smiled after him.

He was getting too old for this, Horus thought for no more than the
three millionth time. He yawned, then stretched and rose from behind his
desk and collected his iced tea from the coaster. Caffeine dependency wasn't
something the Imperium had gone in for, but he'd been barely sixty when
he arrived here. A lifetime of acculturation had taken its toll.

He walked over to the windowed wall of his office atop White Tower
and stared out over the bustling nocturnal activity of Shepard Center. The
rocket plumes of the Terran space effort were a thing of the past, but
the huge field was almost too small for the Imperial auxiliaries and bigger sublight ships—destroyers, cruisers, battleships, and transports—which

thronged it now. And this was only one of the major bases. The largest, admittedly, but only one.

The first enhanced Terra-born crewmen were training in the simulators now. Within a month, he'd have skeleton crews for most of the major units *Dahak* had left behind. In another six, he'd have crews for the smaller ships and pilots for the fighters. They'd be short on experience, but they'd be there, and they'd pick up experience quickly.

Maybe even quickly enough.

He sighed and took himself to task. Anxiety was acceptable; depression was not, but it was hard to avoid when he remembered the heedless, youthful passion which had pitted him in rebellion against the Imperium.

The Fourth Imperium had arisen from the sole planet of the Third which the Achuultani had missed. It had dedicated itself to the destruction of the next incursion with a militancy which dwarfed Terran comprehension, but that had been seven millennia before Horus's birth, and the Achuultani had never come. And so, perhaps, there *were* no Achuultani. Heresy. Unthinkable to say it aloud. Yet the suspicion had gnawed at their brains, and they'd come to resent the endless demands of their long, regimented preparation. Which explained, if it did not excuse, why the discontented of *Dahak's* crew had lent themselves to the mutiny which brought them to Earth.

And so here they were, Horus thought, sipping iced tea and watching the moonless sky of the world which had become his own, with the resources of this single, primitive planet and whatever of Imperial technology they could build and improvise in the time they had, face-to-face with the bogey man they'd decided no longer existed.

Six billion people. Like the clutter of ships below his window, it seemed a lot . . . until he compared it to the immensity of the foe sweeping towards them from beyond those distant stars.

He straightened his shoulders and stared up at the cold, clear chips of light. So be it. He had once betrayed the Fleet uniform he wore, but now, at last, he faced his race's ancient enemy. He faced it ill-prepared and ill-equipped, yet the human race had survived two previous incursions. By the skin of their racial teeth and the Maker's grace, perhaps, but they'd *survived*, which was more than any of their prehistoric predecessors could say.

He drew a deep breath, his thoughts reaching out across the light-years to his daughter and Colin MacIntyre. They depended upon him to defend their world while they sought the assistance Earth needed, and when they returned—not if—there would be a planet here to greet them. He threw that to the uncaring stars like a solemn vow and then turned his back upon them. He sat back down at his desk and bent over his endless reams of reports once more.

Alheer va-Chanak's forehead crinkled in disgust as a fresh sneeze threatened. He wiggled on his command pedestal, fighting the involuntary reflex, and heard the high-pitched buzz of his co-pilot's amusement—buried in the explosive eruption of the despised sneeze.

"Kreegor seize all colds!" va-Chanak grunted, mopping his broad breathing

slits with a tissue. Roghar's laughter buzzed in his ear as he lost the last vestige of control, and va-Chanak swiveled his sensory cluster to bend a stern gaze upon him. "All very well for you, you unhatched grub!" he snarled. "You'd probably think it was hilarious if it happened inside a vac suit!"

"Certainly not," Roghar managed to return with a semblance of decent self-control. "Of course, I did warn you not to spend so long soaking just before a departure."

Va-Chanak suppressed an ignoble desire to throttle his co-pilot. The fact that Roghar was absolutely right only made the temptation stronger, but these four- and five-month missions could be pure torment for the amphibious Mersakah. And, he grumbled to himself, especially for a fully-active sire like himself. Four thousand years of civilization was a frail shield against the spawning urges of all pre-history, but where was he to find a compliant school of dams in an asteroid extraction operation? Nowhere, that was bloody well where, and if he chose to spend a few extra day parts soaking in the habitat's swamp sections, that should have been his own affair.

And would have been, he thought gloomily, if he hadn't brought this damned cold with him. Ah, well! It would wear itself out, and a few more tours would give him a credit balance fit to attract the finest dam. Not to mention the glamour which clung to spacefarers in groundlings' eyes, and—

An alarm squealed, and Alheer va-Chanak's sensory cluster snapped back to his instruments. All three eyes irised wide in disbelief as the impossible readings registered.

"Kreegor take it, look at that!" Roghar gasped beside him, but va-Chanak was already stabbing at the communications console.

More of the immense ships—ninety dihar long if they were a har—appeared out of nowhere, materializing like fen fey from the nothingness of space. Scores of them—hundreds!

Roghar babbled away about first-contacts and alien life forms beside him, but even as he gabbled, the co-pilot was spinning the extractor ship and aligning the main engines to kill velocity for rendezvous. Va-Chanak left him to it, and his own mind burned with conflicting impulses. Disbelief. Awe. Wonder and delight that the Mersakah were not alone. Horror that it had been left to him to play ambassador to the future which had suddenly arrived. Concern lest their visitors misinterpret his fumbling efforts. Visions of immortality—and how the dams would react to this—!

He was still punching up his communications gear when the closest Achuultani starship blew his vessel out of existence.

The shattered wreckage tumbled away, and the Achuultani settled into their formation. Normal-space drives woke, and the mammoth cylinders swept in-system, arrowing towards the planet of Mers at twenty-eight percent of light-speed while their missile sections prepped their weapons.

CHAPTER FOUR

The endless, twenty-meter-wide column of lightning fascinated him. It wasn't really lightning, but that was how Vlad Chernikov thought of it, though the center of any Terran lightning bolt would be a dead zone beside its titanic density. The force field which channeled it also silenced it and muted its terrible brilliance, but Vlad had received his implants. His sensors felt it, like a tide race of fire, even through the field, and it awed him.

He turned away, folding his hands behind him as he crossed the huge chamber at *Dahak*'s heart. Only Command One and Two were as well protected, for this was the source of *Dahak*'s magic. The starship boasted three hundred and twelve fusion power plants, but though he could move and fight upon the wings of their power, he required more than that to outspeed light itself.

This howling chain of power was that more. It was *Dahak*'s core tap, a tremendous, immaterial funnel that reached deep into hyper space, connecting the ship to a dimension of vastly higher energy states. It dragged that limitless power in, focused and refined it, and directed it into the megaton mass of his Enchanach Drive.

And with it, the drive worked its sorcery and created the perfectly-opposed, converging gravity masses which forced *Dahak* out of normal space in a series of instantaneous transpositions. It took a measurable length of time to build those masses between transpositions, but that interval was perceptible only to one such as *Dahak*. A tiny, imperfect flaw the time stream of the cosmos never noticed.

Which was as well. Should *Dahak* dwell in normal space any longer than that, catastrophe would be the lot of any star system he crossed. As those fields converged upon his hull, he became ever so briefly more massive than the most massive star. Which was why ships of his ilk did not use supralight speed within a system, for the initial activation and final deactivation of the Enchanach Drive took much longer, a time measured in microseconds, not femtoseconds. Anu had induced a drive failure to divert the starship from its original mission for "emergency repairs," and a tiny error in *Dahak*'s crippled return to sublight speeds explained the irregularity of Pluto's orbit which had puzzled Terran astronomers for so long. Had it occurred deep enough in Sol's gravity well, the star might well have gone nova.

Chernikov plugged his neural feed back into the engineering subsection of *Dahak*'s computer net, and the computers answered him with a joyousness he was still getting used to. It was odd how alive, how aware, those electronic brains seemed, and Baltan, his ex-mutineer assistant, insisted they had been far less so before the mutiny.

Chernikov believed him, and he believed he understood the happiness which suffused the computer net. *Dahak* had a crew once more—understrength, perhaps, by Imperial standards, but a crew—and that was as it should be. Not just because he had been lonely, but because he needed them to provide that critical element in any warship: redundancy. It was dangerous for so powerful a unit to be utterly dependent upon its central computer, especially when battle damage might cut Comp Cent off from essential components of its tremendous hull.

So it was good that men had returned to *Dahak* at last. Especially now, when the very survival of their species depended upon him.

"Attention on deck," Dahak intoned as Colin entered the conference room, and he winced almost imperceptibly as his command team rose with punctilious formality. He smoothed his expression and crossed impassively to the head of the crystalline conference table, making yet another mental note to have a heart-to-diode talk with the computer.

Dozens of faces looked back at him from around the table, but at least he'd gotten used to facing so many eyes. *Dahak* was technically a single ship, but one with a full-strength crew a quarter-million strong, a normal sublight parasite strength of two hundred warships, and the firepower to shatter planets. His commander might be called a captain, yet for all intents and purposes he was an admiral, charged with the direction of more destructiveness than Terra's humanity had ever dreamed was possible, and the size of Colin's staff reflected that.

There were a lot of "Fleet Captains" on it, though Dahak's new protocol demanded that they be addressed in Colin's presence either as "Commander" or simply by the department they headed, since he was the only "Senior Fleet Captain" and there could be but one captain aboard a warship. The Imperium had used any officer's full rank and branch, which Colin and his Terra-born found too cumbersome, but Dahak had obstinately resisted Colin's suggestion that he might be called "Commodore" to ease the problem.

Colin let his eyes sweep over them as he sat and they followed suit. Jiltanith was at his right, as befitted his second-in-command and the officer charged with the organization and day-to-day management of *Dahak*'s operation. Hector MacMahan sat at his left, as impeccable in the space-black of the Imperial Marines as he had ever been in the uniform of the United States. Beyond them, rows of officers, each department head flanked by his or her senior assistants, ran down the sides of the table to meet at its foot, where he faced Vlad Chernikov, the man who had inherited the shipboard authority which had once been Anu's.

"Thank you all for coming," Colin said. "As you know, we'll be leaving supralight to approach the Sheskar System in approximately twenty-one hours. With luck, that means we'll soon re-establish contact with the Imperium, but we can't count on that. We're going into a totally unknown situation, and I want final readiness estimates from all of my senior department heads—and for all of you to hear them—before we do."

Heads nodded, and he turned to Jiltanith.

"Would you care to begin with a general overview, XO?" he asked.

"Certes, Captain," Jiltanith said, and turned confident eyes to her fellows. "Our Dahak hath been a teacher most astute—aye, and a taskmaster of the sternest!" That won a mutter of laughter, for Dahak had driven his new crew so hard ten percent of even his capacity had been committed full-time to their training and neural-feed education. "While 'tis true I would be better pleased with some small time more of practice, yet have our folk learned their duties well, and I say with confidence our officers and crew will do all mortal man may do if called."

"Thank you," Colin said. It was scarcely a detailed report, but he hadn't asked for that, and he turned to Hector MacMahan.

"Ground Forces?"

"The ground forces are better organized than we could reasonably expect," the hawk-faced Marine replied, "if not yet quite as well as I'd like.

"We have four separate nationalities in our major formations, and we'll need a few more months to really shake down properly. For the moment, we've adopted Imperial organization and ranks but confined them to our original unit structures. Our USFC and SAS people are our recon/special forces component; the Second Marines have been designated as our assault component; the German First Armored will operate our ground combat vehicles; and the Sendai Division and the Nineteenth Guards Parachute Division are our main ground force.

"There's been a bit of rivalry over who got the choicest assignment, but it hasn't gotten physical . . . not very often, anyway." He shrugged. "These are all elite formations, and until we can integrate them fully, a continued sense of identity is inevitable, but they've settled in and mastered their new weapons quite well. I'm confident we can handle anything we have to handle."

"Thank you," Colin said again. He turned to General Georgi Treshnikov, late of the Russian Air Force and now commander of the three hundred Imperial fighters Dahak had retained for self-defense. "Parasite Command?"

"As Hector, we are ready," Treshnikov said. "We have even more nationalities, but less difficulty in integration, for we did not embark complete national formations to crew our fighters."

"Thank you. Intelligence, Commander Ninhursag?"

"We've done all we can with the non-data Dahak has been able to give us, Captain. You've all seen our reports." The stocky, pleasantly plain Imperial who had been Nergal's spy within Anu's camp shrugged. "Until we have some hard facts to plug into our analyses, we're only marking time."

"I understand. Biosciences?"

"Bioscience is weary but ready, Captain," Fleet Captain (B) Cohanna replied. Fifty thousand years in stasis hadn't blunted her confidence . . . or her sense of humor. "We finished the last enhancement procedures last month, and we're a little short on biotechnic hardware at the moment—" that won a fresh mutter of laughter "—but other than that, we're in excellent shape."

"Thank you. Maintenance?"

"We're looking good, Captain." Fleet Captain (M) Geran was another of *Nergal*'s "children," but, aside from his eyes, he looked more like a Terran, with dark auburn hair, unusually light skin for an Imperial, and a mobile mouth that smiled easily. "Dahak's repair systems did a bang-up job, and he slapped anything he wasn't using into stasis. I'd like more practice on damage control, but—" He raised his right hand, palm upward, and Colin nodded.

"Understood. Hopefully you'll have lots of time to go *on* practicing. We'll try to keep it that way. Tactical?"

"We're in good shape, sir," Tamman said. "Battle Comp's doing well with simulators and training problems. Our Terra-born aren't as comfortable with their neural feeds as I'd like yet, but that's only a matter of practice."

"Logistics?"

"Buttoned up, sir," Fleet Commander (L) Caitrin O'Rourke said confidently. "We've got facilities for three times the people we've actually got aboard, and all park and hydroponic areas have been fully reactivated, so provisions and life support are no sweat. Magazines are at better than ninety-eight percent—closer to ninety-nine—and we're in excellent shape for spares."

"Engineering?"

"Engineering looks good, sir," Chernikov replied. "Our Imperials and Terra-born have shaken down extremely well together. I am confident."

"Good. Very good." Colin leaned back and smiled at his officers, glad none of them had tried to gloss over any small concerns they still had. Not that he'd expected them to.

"In that case, I think we can conclude, unless there are any questions?" As he'd expected, there were none. In a very real sense, this meeting had been almost ceremonial, a chance for them to show their confidence to one another.

"Very well." He rose and nodded to them all. "We shall adjourn." He started for the door, and a mellow voice spoke again.

"Attention on deck," it repeated, and Colin swallowed a resigned sigh as his solemn-faced officers stood once more.

"Carry on, ladies and gentlemen," he said, and stepped out the hatch.

"Supralight shutdown in two minutes," Dahak remarked calmly.

Colin took great pains to project a matching calm, but his own relaxation was all too artificial, and he saw the same strain, hidden with greater or lesser success, in all of his bridge officers. *Dahak* was at battle stations, and a matching team under Jiltanith manned Command Two on the far side of the core hull. The holographic images of Command Two's counterparts sat beside each of his officers, which made his bridge seem a bit more crowded but meant everyone knew exactly what was happening . . . and that he got to sit beside Jiltanith's image on duty.

A score of officers were physically present at their consoles on the star-lit command deck. In an emergency, Colin could have run the ship with-out any of them, something which would have been impossible with the semi-aware Comp Cent of yore. But even though Dahak was now capable of assessing intent and exercising discretion, there were limits to the details Colin's human brain could handle. Each of his highly-trained officers took his or her own portion of the burden off of him, and he was devoutly thankful for their presence.

"Sublight in one minute," Dahak intoned, and Colin felt the beginnings of shutdown flowing through his interface with Chernikov's engineering computers. The measured sequence of commands moved like clockwork, and a tiny, almost imperceptible vibration shook Dahak's gargantuan bulk.

"Sublight . . . now," Dahak reported, and the stars moving across the visual display were abruptly still.

A G3 star floated directly "ahead" of Colin in the projection. It was the brightest single object in view, and it abruptly began to grow as Sarah Meir, his astrogator, engaged the sublight drive.

"Core tap shutdown," Dahak announced.

"Enhance image on the star system, Dahak," Colin requested, and the star swelled while a three-dimensional schematic of the Sheskar System's plan-etary orbits flicked to life about it. Only the outermost planet was visible even to Dahak at their present range, but tiny circles on each orbit trace indicated the position each planet should hold.

"Any artificial radiation?"

"Negative, Captain," Dahak replied, and Colin bit his lip. Sheskar was—or had been—the Imperium's forward bastion on the traditional Achuultani approach vector. Perimeter Security should have detected and challenged them almost instantly.

"Captain," Dahak broke the silence which had fallen, "I have detected discrepancies in the system."

The visual display altered as he spoke. Oddly clumped necklaces of far smaller dots replaced the circles representing Sheskar's central trio of planets, spreading ominously about the central star, and Colin swallowed.

Dahak had gone sublight at the closest possible safe distance from Sheskar, but that was still eleven light-hours out. Even at his maximum sublight velocity, it would have taken almost twenty-four hours to reach the primary, yet it had become depressingly clear that there was no reason to travel that deep into the system, and Colin had stopped five light-hours out to save time when they left.

At the moment, he, Jiltanith, Hector MacMahan, and Ninhursag sat in Conference One, watching a scaled-down holo of the star system while they tried to decide where to leave to.

"I have completed preliminary scans, Captain," Dahak announced.

"Well? Was it the Achuultani?"

"It is, of course, impossible to be certain, but I would estimate that it was not. Had it been an incursion, it would, of necessity, have followed a path other than that traditionally employed by the Achuultani, else the scanner arrays which reported this incursion had already been destroyed. Since they were not, I conclude that it was not the Achuultani who accomplished this."

"Just what we needed," Hector said quietly. "Somebody *else* who goes around blowing away entire planets."

"Unfortunately, that would appear to be precisely what has happened, General MacMahan. It would not, however, appear to be of immediate concern. My scans indicate that this destruction occurred on the close order of forty eight thousand years ago."

"How close?" Colin demanded.

"Plus or minus five percent, Captain."

"Shit." Colin looked up apologetically as the expletive escaped him, but no one seemed to have noticed. He drew a deep breath. "All right, Dahak, cut to the chase. What do you think happened?"

"Analysis rules out the employment of kinetic weaponry," Dahak said precisely, "distribution of the planetary rubble is not consistent with impact patterns. Rather, it would appear that the planetary bodies suffered implosive destruction consistent with the use of gravitonic warheads, a weapon, so far as is known to the Imperium's data base, the Achuultani have never employed."

"Gravitonic?" Colin tugged on his prominent nose, and his green eyes narrowed. "I don't like the sound of that."

"Nor I," Jiltanith said quietly. "If 'twas not the Achuultani, then must it have been another, and such weapons lie even now within our magazines."

"Exactly," Colin said. He shuddered at the thought. A heavy gravitonic warhead produced a nice, neat little black hole. Not very long-lived, and not big enough to damage most suns, but big enough, and a hyper-capable missile with the right targeting could put the damned thing almost inside a planet.

"That is true," Dahak observed, then hesitated briefly, as if he faced a conclusion he wanted to reject. "I regret to say, Captain, that the destruction matches that which would be associated with our own Mark Tens. In point of fact, and after making due allowance for the time which has passed, it corresponds almost exactly to the results produced by those weapons."

"Hector? Ninhursag?"

"Dahak's dancing around the point, Colin," MacMahan's face was grim. "There's a very simple and likely explanation."

"I agree," Ninhursag said in a small voice. "I never would have believed it could happen, but it's got all the earmarks of a civil war."

A brief silence followed the words someone had finally said. Then Colin cleared his throat.

"Response, Dahak?"

"I . . . am forced to concur." Dahak's mellow voice sounded sad. "Sheskar

Four, in particular, was very heavily defended. Based upon available data and the fact that no advanced alien race other than the Achuultani had been encountered by the Imperium prior to the mutiny, I must conclude that only the Imperium itself possessed the power to do what has been done."

"What about someone they ran into after the mutiny?"

"Possible, but unlikely, Captain. Due in no small part to previous incursions, there are very few—indeed, effectively no—habitable worlds between Sol and Sheskar. Logic thus suggests that any hostile aliens would have been required to fight their way across a substantial portion of the Imperium even to reach Sheskar. Assuming technical capabilities on a par with those of this ship—a conclusion suggested, though not proven, by my analysis of the weaponry employed—that would require a hostile imperium whose military potential equaled or exceeded that of the Imperium itself. While it is not impossible that such an entity might have been encountered, I would rate the probability as no greater than that of an Achuultani attack."

Colin looked around the table again, then back at the silent holo display. "This isn't good."

"Hast a gift for understatement, my Colin." Jiltanith shook her head. "Good Dahak, what likelihood wouldst thou assign to decision by the Imperium 'gainst fortifying Sheskar anew?"

"Slight," Dahak said.

"Why?" Colin asked. "There's nothing left *to* fortify."

"Inaccurate, Captain. No Earth-like planets remain, but Sheskar was selected for a Fleet base because of its location, not its planets, and it now possesses abundant large asteroids for installation sites. Indeed, the absence of atmosphere would make those installations more defensible, not less."

"In other words," MacMahan murmured, "they would have come back if they were interested in re-establishing their pre-war frontiers."

"Precisely, General."

Another, longer silence fell, and Colin drew a deep breath.

"All right, let's look at it. We have a destroyed base in a vital location. It appears to have been taken out with Imperial weapons, implying a civil war as a probable cause. It wasn't rebuilt. What does *that* imply?"

"Naught we wish to discover." Jiltanith managed a small smile. "'Twould seem the Imperium hath fallen 'pon hard times."

"True," MacMahan said. "I see two probabilities, Colin." Colin raised an eyebrow, inviting him to continue.

"First, they wiped each other out. That would explain the failure to rebuild, and it would also mean our entire mission is pointless." A shiver ran through his human audience, but he continued unflinchingly.

"On the other hand, I don't believe anything the size of the Imperium wiped itself out completely. The Imperium is—or was, or whatever—huge. Even assuming anyone could have been insane enough to embark on destruction on that scale, I don't see how they could *do* it. Their infrastructure would erode out from under them as they took out industrialized systems, and it seems unlikely anyone would follow leaders mad enough to try."

"Yet 'twas done to Sheskar," Jiltanith pointed out.

"True, but Sheskar was primarily a military base, 'Tanni, not a civilian system. The decision to attack it would be evaluated purely in terms of military expedience, like nuking a well-armed island base in the middle of an ocean. It's a lot easier to decide to hit a target like that."

"All right," Colin nodded. "But if they didn't wipe themselves out, why didn't they come back?"

"That's probability two," MacMahan said flatly. "They did so much damage they backslid. They could have done a fair job of smashing themselves without actually destroying all their planets. It's hard for me to visualize a high-tech planet which *wasn't* nuked—or something like it—decivilizing completely, but I can accept that more easily than the idea that all their planets look like this." He gestured at the holo display.

"Besides, they might have damaged themselves in other ways. Suppose they fought their war and found themselves faced with massive reconstruction closer to the heart of the Imperium? Sheskar is—was—a hell of a long way from their next nearest inhabited system, and, as Dahak has pointed out, this area isn't exactly prime real estate. If they had heavily damaged areas closer to home, they could've decided to deal with those first. Afterward, the area on the far side of the Imperium, where damage from the Achuultani hadn't wrecked so many planets to begin with, would have been a natural magnet for future expansion."

"Mayhap, yet that leaveth still a question. Whyfor, if Sheskar was so vital, rebuild it not?"

"I'm afraid I can answer that," Ninhursag said unhappily. "Maybe Anu wasn't as crazy—or quite as unique in his craziness—as we thought." She shrugged as all eyes turned to her. "What I'm trying to say is that if things got so bad the Imperium actually fought a civil war, they weren't *Imperials* anymore. I'm the only person in this room who was an adult at the time of the mutiny, and I know how *I* would've reacted to the thought of wiping out a Fleet base. Even those of us who didn't really believe in the Achuultani—even the 'atheists,' I suppose you might call them, who violently rejected their existence—would have hesitated to do that. That's why Anu lied to us about his own intent to attack the Imperium."

She looked unhappily at the holo for a moment, and none of the others intruded upon her silence.

"None of you were ever Imperial citizens, so you may not understand what I'm trying to say, but preparing to fight the Achuultani was something we'd societized into ourselves on an almost instinctual level. Even those who most resented the regimentation, the discipline, wouldn't have destroyed our defenses. It would be like . . . like Holland blowing up its dikes because of one dry summer, for Maker's sake!"

"You're saying that disbelief in the Achuultani must have become general?" Colin said. "That if it hadn't, the Fleet would never have let itself be caught up in something like a civil war in the first place?"

"Exactly. And if that's true, why rebuild Sheskar as a base against an enemy that doesn't exist?" Ninhursag gave a short, ugly laugh. "Maybe we were the wave of the future instead of just a bunch of murderous traitors!"

"Easy, 'Hursag." MacMahan touched her shoulder, and she inhaled sharply.

"Sorry." Her voice was a bit husky. "It's just that I don't really want to believe what I'm saying—especially not now that I know how wrong we were!"

"Maybe not, but it makes sense," Colin said slowly.

"Agreed, Captain," Dahak said. "Indeed, there is another point. For Fleet vessels to have participated in this action would require massive changes in core programming by at least one faction. Without that, Fleet Central Alpha Priority imperatives would have precluded any warfare which dissipated resources and so weakened Battle Fleet's ability to resist an incursion. This would appear to support Fleet Commander Ninhursag's analysis."

"All right. But even if it's not the Imperium we came to find, there may still be *an* Imperium somewhere up ahead of us." Colin tried to project more optimism than he felt. "Dahak, what was the nearest piece of prime real estate? The closest star system which wasn't purely a military base?"

"Defram," Dahak replied without hesitation. "A G2-K5 binary system with two inhabited planets. As of the last Imperial census in my data base, the system population was six-point-seven-one-seven billion. Main industries—"

"That's enough," Colin interrupted. "How far away is it?"

"One hundred thirty-three-point-four light-years, Captain."

"Um . . . bit over two months at max. That means a round trip of just over eleven months before we could get back to Earth."

"Approximately eleven-point-three-two months, Captain."

"All right, people," Colin sighed. "I don't see we have too much choice. Let's go to Defram and see what we can see."

"Aye," Jiltanith agreed. " 'Twould seem therein our best hope doth lie."

"I agree," MacMahan said, and Ninhursag nodded silently.

"Okay. I want to sit here and think a little more. Take the watch, please, 'Tanni. Dismiss from battle stations, then have Sarah get us underway on sublight. I'll join you in Command One when I finish here." Jiltanith rose with a silent nod, and he turned to the others.

"Hector, you and 'Hursag sit down and build me models of as many scenarios as you can. I know you don't have any hard data, but put your heads together with our other adult Imperials and Dahak and extrapolate trends."

"Yes, sir," MacMahan said quietly, and Colin propped his chin in his hands, elbows on the table, and stared sadly at the holo as the others filed out the hatch. He expected no sudden inspiration, for there was nothing here to offer it. He only knew that he needed to be alone with his thoughts for a while, and, unlike his subordinates, he had the authority to be that way.

CHAPTER FIVE

"Well, Marshal Tsien?"

Tsien regarded Gerald Hatcher levelly as they strode down the hall. It was the first time either had spoken since leaving the Lieutenant Governor's office, and Tsien crooked an eyebrow, inviting amplification. The American only smiled, declining to make his question more specific, but Tsien understood and, in all honesty, appreciated his tact.

"I am . . . impressed, Comrade General," he said. "The Lieutenant Governor is a *formidable* man." His answer meant more than the words said, but he had already seen enough of this American to know he would understand.

"He's all of that," Hatcher agreed, opening a door and waving Tsien into his own office. "He's had to be," he added in a grimmer voice.

Tsien nodded as they crossed the deserted office. It was raining again, he noted, watching the water roll down the windows. Hatcher gestured to an armchair facing the desk as he circled to reach his own swiveled chair.

"So I have understood," Tsien replied, sitting carefully. "Yet he seems unaware of it. He does not strike one as so . . . so—"

"Grand? Self-important?" Hatcher suggested with a grin, and Tsien chuckled despite himself.

"Both of those things, I suppose. Forgive me, but you in the West have always seemed to me to be overly taken with personal pomp and ceremony. With us, the office or occasion, not the individual, deserves such accolades. Do not mistake me, Comrade General; we have our own methods of deification, but we have learned from past mistakes. Those we deify now are— for the most part—safely dead. My country would understand your Governor. *Our* Governor, I suppose I must say. If your purpose is to win my admission that I am impressed by him, you have succeeded, General Hatcher."

"Good." Hatcher frowned thoughtfully, his face somehow both tighter and more open. "Do you also accept that we're being honest with you, Marshal?"

Tsien regarded him for a moment, then dipped his head in a tiny nod.

"Yes. All of my nominees were confirmed, and the Governor's

demonstration of his biotechnics—" Tsien hesitated briefly on the still unfamiliar word "—and those other items of Imperial technology were also convincing. I believe—indeed, I have no choice but to believe—your warnings of the Achuultani, and that you and your fellows are making every effort to achieve success. In light of all those things, I have no choice but to join your effort. I do not say it will be easy, General Hatcher, but we shall certainly make the attempt. And, I believe, succeed."

"Good," Hatcher said again, then leaned back with a smile. "In that case, Marshal, we're ready to run the first thousand personnel of your selection through enhancement as soon as your people in Beijing can put a list together."

"Ah?" Tsien sat a bit straighter. This was moving with speed, indeed! He had not expected these Westerners— He stopped and corrected himself. He had not expected these *people* to offer such things so soon. Surely there would be a period of testing and evaluation of sincerity first!

But when he looked across at the American, the slight, ironic twinkle in Hatcher's eyes told him his host knew precisely what he was thinking, and the realization made him feel just a bit ashamed.

"Comrade General," he said finally, "I appreciate your generosity, but—"

"Not generosity, Marshal. We've been enhancing our personnel ever since *Dahak* left, which means the Alliance has fallen far behind. We need to make up the difference, and we'll be sending transports with enhancement capability to Beijing and any other three cities you select. Planetary facilities under your direct control will follow as quickly as we can build them."

Tsien blinked, and Hatcher smiled.

"Marshal Tsien, we are fellow officers serving the same commander-in-chief. If we don't act accordingly, some will doubt our claims of solidarity are genuine. They are genuine. We will proceed on that basis."

He leaned back and raised both hands shoulder-high, open palms uppermost, and Tsien nodded slowly.

"You are correct. Generous nonetheless, but correct. And perhaps I am discovering that more than our governor are formidable men, Comrade General."

"Gerald, please. Or just 'Ger,' if you're comfortable with it."

Tsien began a polite refusal, then paused. He had never been comfortable with easy familiarity between serving officers, even among his fellow Asians, yet there was something charming about this American. Not boyish (though he understood Westerners prized that quality for some peculiar reason), but charming. Hatcher's competence and hard-headed, forthright honesty compelled respect, but this was something else. Charisma? No, that was close, but not quite the proper word. The word was . . . openness. Or friendship, perhaps.

Friendship. Now was that not a strange thing to feel for a Western general after so many years? And yet. . . . Yes, "and yet," indeed.

"Very well . . . Gerald," he said.

"I know it's like pulling teeth, Marshal." Hatcher's almost gentle smile robbed his words of any offense. "We've been too busy thinking of ways to kill each other for too long for it to be any other way, more's the pity. Do you know, in a weird sort of way, I'm almost grateful to the Achuultani."

"Grateful?" Tsien cocked his head for a moment, then nodded. "I see. I had not previously thought of it in that light, Comr—Gerald, but it *is* a relief to face an alien menace rather than the possibility of blowing up our world ourselves."

"Exactly." Hatcher extracted a bottle of brandy and two snifters from a desk drawer. He set them on the blotter and poured, then offered one to his guest and raised his own. "May I say, Marshal Tsien, that it is a greater pleasure than I ever anticipated to have you as an ally?"

"You may." Tsien allowed a smile to cross his own habitually immobile face. It was hardly proper, but there was no getting around it. For all their differences, he and this American were too much alike to be enemies.

"And, as you would say, Gerald, my name is Tao-ling," he murmured, and crystal sang gently as their glasses touched.

Out of deference to the still unenhanced Terra-born Council members, Horus had the news footage played directly rather than relayed through his neural feed. Not that it made it any better.

The report ended and the Terran tri-vid unit sank back into the wall amid the silence. The thirty men and women in his conference room looked at one another, but he noted that none of them looked directly at *him*.

"What I want to know, ladies and gentlemen," he said finally, his voice shattering the hush, "is how that was allowed to happen?"

One or two Councilors flinched, though he hadn't raised his voice. He hadn't had to. The screams and thunder of automatic weapons as the armored vehicles moved in had made his point for him.

"It was not 'allowed,' " a voice said finally. "It was inevitable."

Horus's cocked head encouraged the speaker to continue, and Sophia Pariani leaned forward to meet his eyes. Her Italian accent was more than usually pronounced, but there was no apology in her expression.

"There is no doubt that the situation was clumsily handled, but there will be more 'situations,' Governor, and not merely in Africa. Already the world economy has been disrupted by the changes we have effected; as the further and greater changes which lie ahead become evident, more and more of the common men and women of the world will react as those people did."

"Sophia's right, Horus." This time it was Sarhantha, one of his ten fellow survivors from *Nergal*'s crew. "We ought to've seen it coming. In fact, we *did*; we just didn't expect it so soon because we'd forgotten how many people are crammed into this world. Hard and fast as we're working, only a small minority are actively involved in the defense projects or the military. All the majority see is that their governments have been supplanted, their planet is threatened by a menace they don't truly comprehend and are none too sure they believe in, and their economies are in the process of catastrophic disruption. This particular riot was touched off by a combination of hunger, inflation, and unemployment—regional factors that pre-date our involvement but have grown only worse since we assumed power—and the realization that even those with skilled trades will soon find their skills obsolete."

"But there'll be other factors soon enough." Councilor Abner Johnson spoke with a sharp New England twang despite his matte-black complexion. "People're people, Governor. The vested interests are going to object—strenuously—once they get reorganized. Their economic and political power's about to go belly-up, and some of them're stupid enough to fight. And don't forget the religious aspect. We're sitting on a powder keg in Iran and Syria, but we've got our own nuts, and you people represent a pretty unappetizing affront to their comfortable little preconceptions." He smiled humorlessly.

"'Mycos? *Birhat?*' You don't really think God created planets with names like *that*, do you? If you could at least've come from a planet named 'Eden' it might've helped, but as it is—!" Johnson shrugged. "Once *they* get organized, we'll have a real lunatic fringe!"

"Comrade Johnson is correct, Comrade Governor." Commissar Hsu Yin's oddly British accent was almost musical after Johnson's twang. "We may debate the causes of Third World poverty—" she eyed her capitalist fellows calmly "—but it exists. Ignorance and fear will be greatest there, violence more quickly acceptable, yet this is only the beginning. When the First World realizes that it is in precisely the same situation the violence may grow even worse. We may as well prepare for the worst . . . and whatever we anticipate will most assuredly fall short of what will actually happen."

"Granted. But this violent suppression—"

"Was the work of the local authorities," Geb put in. "And before you condemn them, what else could they do? There were almost ten thousand people in that mob, and if a lot of them were unarmed women and children, a lot were neither female, young, nor unarmed. At least they had the sense to call us in as soon as they'd restored order, even if it was under martial law. I've diverted a dozen *Shirut*-class atmospheric conveyers to haul in foodstuffs from North America. That should take the worst edge off the situation, but if the local authorities hadn't 'suppressed' the disturbances, however they did it, simply feeding them wouldn't even begin to help, and you know it."

There were mutters of agreement, and Horus noted that the Terra-born were considerably more vehement than the Imperials. Were they right? It was their planet, and Maker knew the disruptions were only beginning. He knew they were sanctioning expediency, but wasn't that another way to describe pragmatism? And in a situation like the present one . . .

"All right," he sighed finally, "I don't like it, but you may be right." He turned to Gustav van Gelder, Councilor for Planetary Security. "Gus, I want you and Geb to increase the priority for getting stun guns into the hands of local authorities. And I want more of our enhancement capacity diverted to police personnel. Isis, you and Myko deal with that."

Doctor Isis Tudor, his own Terra-born daughter and now Councilor for Biosciences, glanced at her ex-mutineer assistant with a sort of resigned desperation. Isis was over eighty; even enhancement could only slow her gradual decay and eliminate aches and pains, but her mind was quick and clear. Now she nodded, and he knew she'd find the capacity . . . somehow.

"Until we can get local peace-keepers enhanced," Horus went on, "I'll have General Hatcher set up mixed-nationality response teams out of his military personnel. I don't like it—the situation's going to be bad enough without 'aliens' popping up to quell resistance to our 'tyrannical' ways— but a dozen troopers in combat armor could have stopped this business with a tenth the casualties, especially if they'd had stun guns."

Heads nodded, and he suppressed a sigh. Problems, problems! Why hadn't he made sufficient allowance for what would happen once Imperial technology came to Terra in earnest? Now he felt altogether too much like a warden rather than a governor, but whatever happened, he had to hold things together—by main force, if necessary—until the Achuultani had been stopped. *If* they could be—

He chopped off that thought automatically and turned to Christine Redhorse, Councilor for Agriculture.

"All right. On to the next problem. Christine, I'd like you to share your report on the wheat harvest with us, and then . . ."

Most of Horus's Council had departed, leaving him alone with his defense planners and engineers. Whatever else happened, theirs was the absolutely critical responsibility, and they were doing better than Horus had hoped. They were actually ahead of schedule on almost a fifth of the PDCs, although the fortifications slated for the Asian Alliance were only now getting underway.

One by one, the remaining Councilors completed their business and left. In the end, only Geb remained, and Horus smiled wearily at his oldest living friend as the two of them leaned back and propped their heels on the conference table almost in unison.

"Maker!" Horus groaned. "It was easier fighting Anu!"

"Easier, but not as satisfying." Geb sipped his coffee, then made a face. It was barely warm, and he rose and circled the table, shaking each insulated carafe until he found one that was still partly full and returned to his chair.

"True, true," Horus agreed. "At least this time we think we've got a *chance* of winning. That makes a pleasant change."

"From your lips to the Maker's ears," Geb responded fervently, and Horus laughed. He reached out a long arm for Geb's carafe and poured more coffee into his own cup.

"Watch it," he advised his friend. "Remember Abner's religious fanatics."

"They won't care what I say or how I say it. Just being what I am is going to offend them."

"Probably." Horus sipped, then frowned. "By the way, there was something I've been meaning to ask you."

"And what might that be, oh dauntless leader?"

"I found an anomaly in the data base the other day." Geb raised an eyebrow, and Horus shrugged. "Probably nothing, but I hit a priority suppression code I can't understand."

"Oh?" If Geb's voice was just a shade too level Horus didn't notice.

"I was running through the data we pulled out of Anu's enclave computers, and Colin's imposed a lock-out on some of the visual records."

"He has?"

"Yep. It piqued my interest, so I ran an analysis. He's put every visual image of Inanna under a security lock only he can release. Or, no, not all of them; only for the last century or so."

"He must have had a reason," Geb suggested.

"I don't doubt it, but I was hoping you might have some idea what it was. You were Chief Prosecutor—did he say anything to you about why he did it?"

"Even if he had, I wouldn't be free to talk about it, but I probably wouldn't have worried. It couldn't have had much bearing on the trials, whatever his reasoning. *She* wasn't around to be tried, after all."

"I know, I know, but it bothers me, Geb." Horus drummed gently on the table. "She was Anu's number two, the one who did all those hideous brain transplants for him. Maker only knows how many Terra-born and Imperials she personally slaughtered along the way! It just seems . . . odd."

"If it bothers you, ask him about it when he gets back," Geb suggested. He finished his coffee and rose. "For now, though, I've got to saddle back up, my friend. I'm due to inspect the work at Minya Konka this afternoon."

He waved a cheerful farewell and strode down the hall to the elevator whistling, but the merry little tune died the instant the doors closed. The old Imperial seemed to sag around his bioenhanced bones, and he leaned his forehead against the mirrored surface of the inner doors.

Maker of Man and Mercy, he prayed silently, don't let him ask Colin. *Please* don't let him ask Colin!

Tears burned, and he wiped them angrily, but he couldn't wipe away the memory which had driven him to Colin before the courts martial to beg him to suppress the visuals on Inanna. He'd been ready to go down on his knees, but he hadn't needed to. If anything, Colin's horror had surpassed his own.

Against his will, Geb relived those moments on deck ninety of the sublight battleship *Osir*, the very heart of Anu's enclave. Those terrible moments after Colin and 'Tanni had gone up the crawl way to face Anu, leaving behind a mangled body 'Tanni's energy gun had cut almost in half. A body which had been Commander Inanna's, but only because its brain had been ripped away, its original owner murdered and its flesh stolen to make a new, young host for the mutinous medical officer.

Geb had used his own energy gun to obliterate every trace of that body, for once it had belonged to one of his closest friends, to a beautiful woman named Tanisis . . . Horus's wife . . . and Jiltanith's own mother.

CHAPTER SIX

Fifty Chinese paratroopers in Imperial black snapped to attention as the band struck up, and Marshal Tsien Tao-ling, Vice Chief of Staff for Operations to the Lieutenant Governor of Earth, watched them with an anxiety he had not wasted upon ceremonial in decades. This was his superior's first official visit to China in the five months since the Asian Alliance had surrendered to the inevitable, and he wanted—demanded—for all to go flawlessly.

It did. General Gerald Hatcher appeared in the hatch of his cutter and started down the ramp, followed by his personal aide and a very small staff.

"Preeee-sent *arms!*"

Energy guns snapped up. The honor guard, drawn from the first batch of Asian personnel to be bioenhanced, handled their massive weapons with panache, and Tsien noted the perfection of their drill without a smile as he and Hatcher exchanged salutes. The twinkle in the American's brown eyes betrayed his own amused tolerance for ceremonial only to those who knew him very well, and it still surprised Tsien just a bit that he had become one of those few people.

"Good to see you, Tao-ling," Hatcher said under cover of the martial music, and Tsien responded with a millimetric smile before the brief moment of privacy disappeared into the waiting tide of military protocol.

Gerald Hatcher placed his cap in his lap and leaned back as the city of Ch'engtu fell away astern. The cutter headed for Minya Konka, the mountain which had been ripped apart to hold PDC Huan-Ti, and he grimaced as he ran a finger around the tight collar of his tunic.

He lowered his hand, wondering once again if it had been wise to adopt Imperial uniform. While it had the decided advantage of not belonging to any of the rival militaries they were trying to merge, it looked disturbingly like the uniform of the SS. Not surprisingly, considering. He'd done what he could to lessen the similarities—exaggerating the size of the starbursts the Nazis had replaced with skulls, restoring the serrated *hisanth* leaves to the lapels, adopting the authorized variation of gold braid in place of silver—but the over-all impact still bothered him.

He put the thought aside—again—and turned to Tsien.

"It looks like your people've done a great job, Tao-ling. I wish you didn't have to spend so much time in Beijing to do it, but I'm impressed."

"I spend too little time here as it is, Gerald." Tsien gave a very slight shrug. "It is even worse than it was while you and I were enemies. There are at least eight too few hours in every day."

"Tell me about it!" Hatcher laughed. "If we work like dogs for another six months, you and I may finally be able to hand over to someone else long enough to get our own biotechnics."

"True. I must confess, however, that the speed with which we are moving almost frightens me. There is too little time for proper coordination. Too many projects require attention, and I have no time to *know* my officers."

"I know. We're better off than you are because of how *Nergal*'s people infiltrated our militaries before we even knew about them. I don't envy your having to start from scratch."

"We will manage," Tsien said, and Hatcher took him at his word. The huge Chinese officer had lost at least five kilos since their first meeting, yet it only made him even more fearsome, as if he were being worn down to elemental gristle and bone. And whatever else came of the fusion with the Asian Alliance, Hatcher was almost prayerfully grateful that it had brought him Tsien Tao-ling.

The cutter dropped toward the dust-spewing wound which had once been a mountain top, and Hatcher checked his breathing mask. He hated using it, but the dust alone would make it welcome, and the fact that PDC Huan-Ti was located at an altitude of almost seventy-five hundred meters made it necessary. He felt a bit better when he saw Tsien reaching for his own mask . . . and suppressed a spurt of envy as Major Allen Germaine ignored his. It must be nice, he thought sourly as he regarded his bioenhanced aide.

They grounded, and thin, cold air, bitter with dust, swirled through the hatch. Hatcher hastily clipped on his mask, and his uniform's collar was a suddenly minor consideration as the Imperial fabric adjusted to maintain a comfortable body temperature and he led the way out into the ear-splitting, dust-spouting, eye-bewildering bedlam of yet another of Geb's mighty projects.

Tsien followed Hatcher, hiding his impatience. He hated inspection tours, and only the fact that Hatcher hated them just as badly let him face this time-consuming parade with a semblance of inner peace. That and the fact that, time-consuming or no, it also played its part. Morale, the motivation of their human material, was all important, and nothing better convinced people of the importance of their tasks than to see their commanders inspecting their work.

Yet despite his impatience, Tsien was deeply impressed. Enough Imperial equipment was becoming available to strain the enhancement centers' ability to provide operators, and the result was amazing for someone who had grown up with purely Terran technology. The main excavation was almost finished—indeed, the central control rooms were structurally complete, awaiting installation of the computer core—and the shield generators were already being built. Incredible.

He bent to listen to an engineer, and movement caught the corner of his eye as a breath-masked officer disappeared behind a heap of building material, waving one hand as he spoke to another officer at his side. There was something familiar about the small figure, but the engineer was still talking, and Tsien returned his attention to him.

"I'm impressed, Geban," Hatcher said, and Huan-Ti's chief engineer grinned. The burly ex-mutineer was barely a hundred and fifty centimeters tall, but he looked as if he could have picked up a hover jeep one-handed—before enhancement.

"Really impressed," Hatcher repeated as the control room door closed off the cacophony beyond. "You're—what, four weeks ahead of schedule?"

"Almost five, General," Geban replied with simple pride. "With just a little luck, I'm going to bring this job in at least two months early."

"Outstanding!" Hatcher slapped Geban's shoulder, and Tsien hid a smile. He would never understand how Hatcher's informality with subordinates could work so well, yet it did. Not simply with Westerners who might be accustomed to such things, either. Tsien had seen exactly the same broad smile on the faces of Chinese and Thai peasants.

"In that case," Hatcher said, turning to the marshal, "I think we—"

A thunderous concussion drowned his words and threw him from his feet.

Diego McMurphy was a Mexican-Irish explosives genius from Texas. Off-shore oil rigs and dams, vertol terminals and apartment complexes—he'd seen them all, but this was the most damnable, bone-breaking, challenging, *wonderful* project he'd ever been involved with, and the fact that he was buying his right to a full set of biotechnic implants was only icing on the cake. Which is why he was happy as he waved his crew forward to set the charges on the unfinished western face of Magazine Twelve.

He died a happy man, and six hundred and eighty-six other men and women died with him. They died because one of McMurphy's men activated his rock drill, and that man didn't know someone had wired his controls to eleven hundred kilos of Imperial blasting compound.

The explosion rivaled a three-kiloton nuclear bomb.

Gerald Hatcher bounced off Tsien Tao-ling, but the marshal's powerful arm caught him before he could fall. Alarms whooped, sirens screamed, and Geban went paper-white. The door barely had time to open before he reached it; if it hadn't, he would have torn it loose with his bare hands.

Hatcher shook his head, trying to understand what had happened as he followed Tsien to the open door. A huge mushroom cloud filled the western horizon, and even as he watched, a five-man gravitonic conveyer with a full load of structural steel turned turtle in mid-air. It had been caught by the fringes of the explosion, and the pilot had almost pulled it out. Almost, but not quite. Its standard commercial drive had never been designed for such abuse, and it impacted nose-first at six hundred kilometers per hour.

A fresh fireball spewed up, and the death toll was suddenly six hundred and ninety-one.

"My God!" Hatcher murmured.

Tsien nodded in silent, shocked agreement. Whatever the cause, this was disaster, and he despised himself for thinking of lost time first and lost lives second. He turned toward the control block ramps in the vanished Geban's wake, then stopped as a knot of men headed towards him. They were armed, and there was something familiar about the small officer at their head—

"*Quang!*" he bellowed.

The fury in Tsien's voice jerked Hatcher's eyes away from the smoke. He started to speak, then gasped as the marshal whirled around and hit him in a diving tackle. The two of them crashed back into the control room, hard enough to crack ribs, as the first burst of automatic fire raked the open doorway.

"Forward!" General Quang Do Chinh screamed. "Kill them! Kill them *now!*"

His troopers advanced at the run, closing on the unfinished control block, and Quang's heart flamed with triumph. Yes, kill the traitors! And especially the arch-traitor who had tried to shunt him aside! What a triumph to begin their war against the invaders!

As he and his men sprinted forward, construction workers raced to drag dead and wounded away from the explosion site, and six other carefully infiltrated assault teams produced automatic weapons and grenades. They concentrated on picking out Imperials, but any target would do.

"What the hell is happening?!" Gerald Hatcher's voice was muffled by his breath mask, but it would have been hoarse anyway—a hundred kilos of charging Chinese field marshal had seen to that. He shoved up onto his knees, reaching instinctively for his holstered automatic.

"I do not know," Tsien replied tersely, checking his own weapon's magazine. "But the Vietnamese leading his men this way is named Quang. He was one of those most opposed to joining our forces to yours."

Another burst of fire raked the open doorway, ricochets whining nastily, and Hatcher rose higher on his knees to hit the door button. The hatch slammed instantly, but it was only lightweight Terran steel; the next burst punched right through it.

"Shit!" Hatcher scurried across the control room on hands and knees. Major Germaine already stood with his back to the wall on the left side of the door, and his grav gun had materialized in his right hand like magic.

"What the fuck do they think they're going to accomplish?!"

"I do not know, Gerald. This is pointless. It simply invites reprisals. But their ultimate objective is immaterial—to us, at least."

"True." Hatcher flattened himself against the wall as another row of holes appeared in the door. "Al?"

"I already put out the word, sir." Unlike his boss, Germaine had a built-in communicator. "But I don't know how much good it's going to do. More of the bastards are shooting up the rescue crews. Geban's down—hurt bad—and he's not the only Imperial."

"God*damn* them!" Hatcher hissed, and fought to think as the half-forgotten terror and adrenalin-rush of combat flooded him. Continuous firing raked the panel now, and he gritted his teeth as bullets and bits of door whined about his ears. This room was a deathtrap. He tried to estimate where their attackers had been when Tao-ling tackled him. On the ground to the south. That meant they had to climb at least three ramps. So whoever was firing at the door was covering them until they could get here . . . probably with a demolition charge that would turn them all to hamburger.

"We've got to get ourselves a field of fire," he grated. His automatic was a toy compared to what was coming at them, but it was better than nothing. And anything was better than dying without fighting back.

"I agree," Tsien said flatly.

"All right. Tao-ling, you pop the hatch. Al, I think they're coming up from the south. You can cover the head of the ramp from where you are. Tao-ling, you get over here with me. We'll try to slow 'em down if they come the other way, but Al's got our only real firepower."

"Yes, sir," Germaine said, and Tsien nodded agreement.

"Then do it—now!"

Tsien hit the button and rolled across the floor, coming up on his knees beside Hatcher. They both flattened against the wall as yet another burst screamed into the room, and Hatcher cursed as a ricochet creased his cheek.

"Can you get that sniper without getting yourself killed, Al?"

"A pleasure, sir," Germaine said coldly. His eyes were unfocused as his implants sought the source of the fire, then he crouched and took one step to the side. He moved with the blinding speed of his biotechnics, and the grav gun hissed out a brief burst, spitting three-millimeter explosive darts at fifty-two hundred meters per second.

Quang swore as his covering fire died. So, they had at least one of the cursed grav guns. That was bad, but he still had twenty-five men, and they were all heavily armed.

He had no idea how the rest of the attack was going, but Tsien's reactions had been only too revealing, and the only man who could identify him must die.

His men pounded up the ramp ahead of him.

❖   ❖   ❖

Her name was Litanil, and, disregarding time spent in stasis, she was thirty-six. It took her precious moments to realize what was happening, and a few more to believe it when she had, but then cold fury filled her.

Litanil hadn't thought very deeply when Anu's people recruited her, for she'd been both young and bored. Now she knew she'd also been criminally stupid, and, like her fellows, she'd labored with the Breaker's own demons on her heels in an effort to atone. Along the way, she'd come to like and admire the Terra-born she worked with, and now hundreds of them lay dead, butchered by the animals responsible for this carnage. She didn't worry about why. She didn't even consider the monstrous treason to her race the attack implied. She thought only of dead friends, and something snarled inside her.

She turned her power bore towards the fighting, and her neural feeds sought out the safety interlocks. It was supposed to be impossible for any accident to get around them—but Litanil was no accident.

Allen Germaine went down on one knee, bracing his grav gun over his left forearm, as the first three raiders hurled themselves over the lip of the topmost ramp, assault rifles on full automatic.

They got off one long burst each before their bodies blew apart in a hurricane of explosive darts.

Litanil goosed her power bore to max, snarling across the stony plain at almost two hundred kilometers per hour. Not even a gravitonic drive could hold the massive bore steady at that speed, but she rode it like a bucking horse, her implant scanners reaching out, and her face was a mask of fury as she raised the cutting head chest-high.

Private Pak Chung of the Army of Korea heard nothing, but some instinct made him turn his head. His eyes widened in horror as he saw the huge machine screaming towards him. Rock dust and smoke billowed behind it like a curdled wake, and the . . . the *thing* at its front was aimed straight at *him*!

The last thing Private Pak ever saw was a terrible brilliance in the millisecond before he exploded in a flash of super-heated body fluids.

General Quang cursed as his three lead men died, but it had not been entirely unexpected. It must be the American's African aide, yet there was only one of him, bioenhanced or not, and the ramp was not the only way up.

"They're spreading out," Germaine reported. "I can't get a good implant reading through the ramp, but some of them are swinging round front."

"There is a scaffold below the edge of the platform," Tsien said.

"Damn! Remind me to detail armed guards to each construction site when we get home, Al."

"Yes, sir."

✧   ✧   ✧

Litanil wiped out Private Pak's team and raged off after fresh targets. Ahead of her, half a dozen bioenhanced Terra-born construction workers armed with steel reinforcing rods and Imperial blasting compound began working their way around the flank of a second assault group.

Quang poked his head up. This was taking too long. But there would still be time. His men were in position at last, and he barked an order.

"Down!" Germaine shouted, and Hatcher and Tsien dropped instantly as the stubby grenade launchers coughed. Two grenades hit short or exploded against the outer wall; the third headed straight into the door, and Germaine's left hand struck it like a handball. The explosion ripped his hand apart, and shrapnel tore into his chest and shoulder.

Agony stabbed him, but his implants stopped the flow of blood to his shredded hand and flooded his system with a super-charged blast of adrenalin. The first wave came up the ramp after the grenades, and he cut them down like bloody wheat.

Hatcher fired as a head rose over the edge of the scaffolding. His first shot missed; his second hit just above the left eye. Beside him, Tsien was flat on his belly, firing two-handed. Another attacker dropped.

A sudden burst of explosions ripped the dusty smoke as the construction workers tossed their makeshift bombs. The attack squad faltered as three of their number were blown apart. A fourth emptied a full magazine into a charging man. He killed his assailant, but he never knew; the steel rod his victim had carried impaled him like a spear.

His six surviving comrades broke and ran—directly in front of Litanil's power bore.

Eight more of Quang's men died, but a ninth slammed a heart-rupturing burst into Allen Germaine. Major Germaine was a dead man, but he was a bioenhanced corpse. He stayed on his feet long enough to aim very carefully before he squeezed the trigger.

Gerald Hatcher swore viciously as his aide toppled without a sound, grav gun bouncing from his remaining hand. Bastards! *Bastards!* He squeezed off another shot, hitting his target in the torso, then dropped him with a second.

It wasn't enough, and he knew it.

Quang's number four attack squad had a good position between two huge earth-movers, but there were no more targets in their field of fire. It was time to go, and they began to filter back in pairs, each halting in turn to provide covering fire for their fellows. It was a textbook maneuver.

As the first pair reached the ends of their shielding earth-movers, a pair of bioenhanced hands reached out from either side. Fingers ten times stronger than their own closed, and two tracheas crushed. The twitching bodies were tossed aside, and the crouching ambushers waited patiently for their next victims.

Quang popped his head up and saw the grav gun lying two meters beyond the door. Now! He clutched his assault rifle and rose, waving his surviving men forward, and followed up the ramp in their wake.

A last attacker crouched on the scaffolding. He'd seen what happened when his fellows exposed themselves, and he poked just the muzzle of his rifle over the edge. It was a sound idea, but in his excitement he rose just too high. The crown of his head showed, and Gerald Hatcher put a pistol bullet through it in the instant before the automatic fire shattered both his legs.

Litanil swung her power bore again and knew they were winning.

The attackers had achieved the surprise they sought, but they hadn't realized what they were attacking. Most of the site personnel were unenhanced Terra-born, but a significant percentage were not, and those who were enhanced had full Fleet packages, modified at Colin MacIntyre's order to incorporate fold-space coms. They might be unarmed, but they were strong, tough, fast, and in unbroken communication.

And, as Litanil herself had proved, a construction site abounded in improvisational weapons.

Tsien Tao-ling was no longer a field marshal. He was a warrior alone and betrayed, and Quang was still out there. Whatever happened, Quang must not be allowed to live.

Tsien tossed aside his empty pistol, his mind cold and clear, and rose on his hands and toes, like a runner in the blocks.

General Quang blinked as Tsien exploded from the control room. He would never have believed the huge man could move that quickly! But what did he hope to gain? He could not outrun bullets!

Then he saw Tsien drop and snatch up the grav gun as he rolled towards the scaffolding. *No!*

Assault rifles barked, but the men behind them had been as surprised as Quang. They were late, and they tried to compensate by leading their target. They would catch him as he rolled over the edge of the scaffolding into cover.

Tsien threw out one leg, grunting as a kneecap shattered on concrete, but it had the desired effect. He stopped dead, clutching Germaine's grav gun, and the bullets which should have killed him went wide. He raised the muzzle, not trying to rise from where he lay.

Quang screamed in frustration as Tsien opened fire. Three of his remaining men were down. Then four. Five! He raised his own weapon, firing at the marshal, but fury betrayed his aim.

Tsien grunted again as a slug ripped through his right biceps. A second shattered his shoulder, but he held down the grav gun's trigger, and his fire swept the ramp like a broom.

Quang's last trooper was down, and sudden terror filled him. He threw away his rifle and tried to drop down the ramp, but he was too late. His last memory on Earth was the cold, bitter hatred in Tsien Tao-ling's pitiless eyes.

Gerald Hatcher groaned, then bit his lip against a scream as someone moved his left leg. He shuddered and managed to raise his eyelids, wondering for a moment why he felt so weak, why there was so much pain.

Tao-ling bent over him, and he bit off most of another scream as the marshal tightened something on his right leg. A tourniquet, Hatcher realized dizzily . . . and then he remembered.

His expression twisted with more than pain as he saw Allen Germaine's dead face close beside him, but his mind was working once more. Poorly, slowly, with frustrating dark patches, but working. The firing seemed to have stopped, and if there was no more shooting and Tao-ling was working on him, they must have won, mustn't they? He was rather pleased by his ability to work that out.

Tsien crawled up beside him. One shoulder was swollen by a makeshift, blood-soaked bandage, and his left leg dragged uselessly, but his good hand clutched Allen's grav gun as he lowered himself between Hatcher and the door with a groan.

"T-Tao-ling?" the general managed.

"You are awake?" Tsien's voice was hoarse with pain. "You have the constitution of a bull, Gerald."

"Th-thanks. What . . . what kind of shape are we . . . ?"

"I believe we have beaten off the attack. I do not know how. I am afraid you are badly hurt, my friend."

"I'll . . . live. . . ."

"Yes, I think you will," Tsien said so judiciously Hatcher grinned tightly despite his agony. His brain was fluttering and it would be a relief to give in, but there was something he had to say first. Ah!

"Tao-ling—"

"Be quiet, Gerald," the marshal said austerely. "You are wounded."

"You're . . . not? Looks like . . . I get my . . . implants first."

"Americans! Always you must be first."

"T-Tell Horus I said . . . you take over. . . ."

"I?" Tsien looked at him, his face as twisted with shame as pain. "It was my people who did this thing!"

"H-Horse shit. But that's . . . why it's important . . . you take over. Tell Horus!" Hatcher squeezed his friend's forearm with all his fading strength. It was Tsien's right arm, but he did not even wince.

"Tell him!" Hatcher commanded, clinging to awareness through the shrieking pain.

"Very well, Gerald," Tsien said gently. "I will."

"Good man," Hatcher whispered, and let go at last.

✧   ✧   ✧

The city echoed with song and dance as the People of Riahn celebrated. Twelve seasons of war against Tur had ended at last, and not simply in victory. The royal houses of Riahn and Tur had brought the endless skirmishes and open battle over possession of the Fithan copper mines to a halt with greater wisdom than they had shown in far too long, for the Daughter of Tur would wed the Son of Riahn, and henceforth the two Peoples would be one.

It was good. It was very, very good, for Riahn-Tur would be the greatest of all the city-states of T'Yir. Their swords and spears would no longer turn upon one another but ward both from their neighbors, and the copper of Fithan would bring them wealth and prosperity. The ships of Riahn were already the swiftest ever to swim—with Fithan copper to sheath their hulls against worms and weed, they would own the seas of T'Yir!

Great was the rejoicing of Riahn, and none of the People knew of the vast Achuultani starships which had reached their system while the war still raged. None knew they had come almost by accident, unaware of the People until they actually entered the system, or how they had paused among the system's asteroids. Indeed, none of the People knew even what an asteroid was, much less what would happen if the largest of them were sent falling inward toward T'Yir.

And because they did not know such things, none knew their world had barely seven months to live.

CHAPTER SEVEN

Colin MacIntyre was not afraid, for "afraid" was too weak a word.

He sat with his back to the conference room hatch as the others filed in, and he felt their own fear against his spine. He waited until all were seated, then swung his chair to meet their eyes. Their faces looked even worse than he'd expected.

"All right," he said at last. "We've got to decide what to do next."

Their steady regard threw his lie back at him, even Jiltanith's, and he wanted to scream at them. *We* didn't have to decide; *he* did, and he wished with all his soul that he had never heard of a starship named *Dahak*.

He stopped himself and drew a deep breath, closing his eyes. When he opened them again, the shadows within them had retreated just a bit.

"Dahak," he said quietly, "have you got anything more for us?"

"Negative, Captain. I have examined all known Imperial weapons and research. Nothing in my data base can account for the observational data."

Colin managed not to spit a curse. *Observational data.* What a neat, concise way to describe two once-inhabited planets with no life whatever. Not a tree, not a shrub, nothing. There were no plains of volcanic glass and lingering radioactivity, no indications of warfare—just bare, terribly-eroded earth and stone and a few pathetic clusters of buildings sagging into wind and storm-threshed ruin. Even their precarious existence said much for the durability of Imperial building materials, for Dahak estimated there had been no living hand to tend them in almost forty-five thousand years.

No birds, he thought. No animals. Not even an insect. Just . . . nothing. The only movement was the wind. Weather had flensed the denuded planet until its stony bones gaped through like the teeth of a skull, bared in a horrible, grinning rictus of desecration and death.

"Hector?" he said finally. "Do you have any ideas?"

"None." MacMahan's normally controlled face was even more impassive than usual, and he seemed to hunker down in his chair.

"Cohanna?"

"I can't add much, sir, but I'd have to say it was a bio-weapon of some sort. Some unimaginable sort." Cohanna shivered. "I've landed unmanned probes for spot analyses, but I don't dare send teams down."

Colin nodded.

"I can't imagine how it was done," the biosciences officer continued. "What kind of weapon *could* produce this? If they'd irradiated the place. . . . But there's simply nothing to go on, Captain. Nothing at all."

"All right." Colin inhaled deeply. "'Tanni, what can you tell us?"

"Scarce more than 'Hanna. We have found some three score orbital vessels and installations; all lie abandoned to the dead. As with the planets, we durst not look too close, yet our probes have scanned them well. In all our servos have attended lie naught save bones."

"Dahak? Any luck accessing their computers?"

"Very little, Captain. I have been unable to carry out detailed study of the equipment, but there are major differences between it and the technology with which I am familiar. In particular, the computer nets appear to have been connected with fold-space links, which would provide a substantial increase in speed over my own molecular circuitry, and these computers operated on a radically different principle, maintaining data flow in semi-permanent force fields rather than in physical storage units. Their power supplies failed long ago, and without continuous energization—" The computer's voice paused in the electronic equivalent of a shrug.

"The only instance in which partial data retrieval has been possible is artifact seventeen, the Fleet vessel *Cordan*," Dahak continued. "Unfortunately, the data core was of limited capacity, as the unit itself was merely a three-man sublight utility boat, and had suffered from failed fold-space units. Most data in memory are encoded in a multi-level Fleet code I have not yet been able to break, though I believe I might succeed if a larger sample could be obtained. The recoverable data consist primarily of routine operational records and astrogational material.

"I was able to date the catastrophe by consulting the last entry made by *Cordan*'s captain. It contains no indication of alarm, nor, unfortunately, was she loquacious. The last entry simply records an invitation for her and her crew to dine at the planetary governor's residence on Defram-A III."

"Nothing more?" Ninhursag asked quietly.

"No, Commander. There undoubtedly was additional data, but only *Cordan*'s command computer utilized hard storage techniques, and it is sadly decayed. I have located twelve additional auxiliary and special-function computer nets, but none contain recoverable data."

"Vlad?" Colin turned to his engineer.

"I wish I could tell you something. The fact that we dare not go over and experiment leaves us with little hard data, but the remotes indicate that their technology was substantially more advanced than *Dahak*'s. On the other hand, we have seen little real evidence of fundamental breakthroughs—it is more like a highly sophisticated refinement of what we already have."

"How now, Vlad?" Jiltanith asked. "Hath not our Dahak but now said their computers are scarce like unto himself?"

"True enough, 'Tanni, but the differences are incremental." Vlad frowned.

"What he is actually saying is that they moved much further into energy-state engineering than before. I cannot say certainly without something to take apart and put back together, but those force field memories probably manifested as solid surfaces when powered up. The Imperium was moving in that direction even before the mutiny—our own shield is exactly the same thing on a gross scale. What they discovered was a way to do the same sorts of things on a scale which makes even molycircs big and clumsy, but it was theoretically possible from the beginning. You see? *Incremental* advances."

Jiltanith nodded slowly, and Colin leaned his elbows on the table.

"Bearing that in mind, Dahak, what are the chances of recovering useful data from any other computers we encounter?"

"Assuming they are of the variety Fleet Captain (Engineering) Chernikov has been discussing and that they have been left unattended without power, nil. Please note, however, that *Cordan*'s command computer was not of that type."

"Meaning?"

"Meaning, Captain, that it is highly probable Fleet units retained solid data storage for critical systems precisely because energy data storage was susceptible to loss in the event of power failure. If that is indeed the case, any large sublight unit should provide quite considerable amounts of data. Any supralight Fleet combatant would, in all probability, retain a hard-storage backup of its complete data core."

"I see." Colin leaned back and rubbed his eyes.

"All right. We're five and a half months from Terra, and so far all we've found is one completely destroyed Fleet base and two totally dead planets. If Dahak's wrong about the Fleet retaining hard-storage for its central computers, we can't even hope to find out what happened, much less find help, from any system where this disaster spilled over.

"If we turn back right now, we'll reach Sol over a year before the Achuultani scouts, which would at least permit us to help Earth stand them off. By the same token, it would be impossible for us to do that and then return to the Imperium—or, at least, to move any deeper into it—and still get back to Sol before the main incursion arrives. So the big question is do we go on in the hope of finding *something*, or do we turn back now?"

He studied their faces and found only mirrors of his own uncertainty.

"I don't think we can give up just yet," he said finally. "We know we can't win without help, and we *don't* know there isn't still some help available. In all honesty, I'm not very optimistic, but I can't see that we have any choice but to ride it out and pray."

Jiltanith and MacMahan nodded slightly. The others were silent, then Chernikov raised his head.

"A point, sir."

"Yes?"

"Assuming Dahak is right that Fleet units are a more likely source of information, perhaps we should concentrate on Fleet bases and ignore civilian systems for the moment."

"My own thought exactly," Colin agreed.

"Yet 'twould be but prudent to essay a few systems more ere we leave this space entire," Jiltanith mused. "Methinks there doth lie another world scarce fifteen light-years hence. 'Twas not a Fleet base, yet was it not a richly peopled world, Dahak?"

"Correct, ma'am," Dahak replied. "The Kano System lies fourteen-point-six-six-one light-years from Defram, very nearly on a direct heading to Birhat. The last census data in my records indicates a system population of some nine-point-eight-three billion."

Colin thought. At maximum speed, the trip to Kano would require little more than a week. . . .

"All right, 'Tanni," he agreed. "But if we don't find anything there, we're in the same boat. Assuming we don't get answers at Kano, I'm beginning to think we may have to move on to Fleet Central at Birhat itself."

He understood the ripple of shock that ran through his officers. Birhat lay almost eight hundred light-years from Sol. If they ventured that far, even *Dahak*'s speed could not possibly return them to Earth before the Achuultani scouts had arrived.

Oh, yes, he understood. Quite possibly, *Dahak* alone could stop the Achuultani scouts, particularly if backed by whatever Earth had produced. But if Colin continued to Birhat, *Dahak* wouldn't be available to try . . . and the decision was his to make. His alone.

"I recognize the risks," he said softly, "but our options are closing in, and time's too short to scurry around from star to star. Unless we find a definite answer at Kano, it may run out on us entirely. If we're going to Birhat at all, we can't afford to deviate or we'll never get back before the main incursion arrives. If we make a straight run for it from Kano, we should have some months to look around Fleet Central and still beat the real incursion home. Even assuming a worst-case scenario, assuming the entire Imperium is like Defram, we may at least find out what happened and where—if anywhere—a functional portion of the Imperium remains. I'm not definitely committing us to Birhat; I'm only saying we may not have another choice."

He fell silent, letting them examine his logic for flaws, almost praying they would find some, but instead they nodded one by one.

"All right. Dahak, have Sarah set course for Kano immediately. We'll go take a look before we commit to anything else."

"Yes, Captain."

"I think that's everything," Colin said heavily, and rose. "If any of you need me, I'll be on the bridge."

He walked out. This time Dahak did not call the others to attention, as if he sensed his captain's mood . . . but they rose anyway.

"Detection at twelve light-minutes," Dahak announced, and Colin's eyes widened with sudden hope. The F5 star called Kano blazed in Dahak's display, the planet Kano-III a penny-bright dot, and they'd been detected. Detected! There was a high-tech presence in the system!

But Dahak's next words cut his elation short.

"Hostile launch," the computer said calmly. "Multiple hostile launches. Sublight missiles closing at point-seven-eight light-speed."

Missiles?

"Tactical, Red One!" Colin snapped, and Tamman's acknowledgment flowed back through his neural feed. The tractor web snapped alive, sealing him in his couch, and *Dahak's* mighty weapons came on line as raucous audio and implant alarms summoned his crew to battle.

"No offensive action!" Colin ordered harshly.

"Acknowledged." Tamman's toneless voice was that of a man intimately wedded to his computers. *Dahak's* shield snapped up, anti-missile defenses came alive, and Colin fell silent as others fought his ship.

Sarah Meir was part of Tamman's tactical net, and she took *Dahak* instantly to maximum sublight speed. Evasive action began, and the starfield swooped crazily about them. Crimson dots appeared in the holographic display, flashing towards *Dahak* like a shoal of sharks, tracking despite his attempts to evade.

His jammers filled space and fold-space alike with interference, and blue dots flashed out from the center of the display, each a five-hundred-ton decoy mimicking *Dahak's* electronic and gravitonic signature. More than half the red dots wavered, swinging to track the decoys or simply lost in the jamming, but at least fifty continued straight for them.

They were moving at almost eighty percent of light-speed, but so great was the range they seemed to crawl. And why were they moving sublight at all? Why weren't they hyper missiles? Why—

"Second salvo launch detected," Dahak announced, and Colin cursed.

Active defenses engaged the attackers. Hyper missiles were useless, for they could not home on evading targets, so sublight counter-missiles raced to meet them, blossoming in megaton bursts as proximity fuses activated. Eye-searing flashes pocked the holographic display, and red dots began to die.

"They mount quite capable defenses of their own, Captain," Dahak observed, and Colin felt them through his feed. ECM systems lured *Dahak's* fire wide and on-board maneuvering systems sent the red dots into wild gyrations, and they were faster than the counter-missiles chasing them.

"Where are they coming from, Dahak?"

"Scanners have detected twenty-four identical structures orbiting Kano-III," Dahak replied as his close-range energy defenses opened fire and killed another dozen missiles. At least twenty were still coming. "I have detected launches from only four of them."

Only four? Colin puzzled over that as the last dozen missiles broke past *Dahak's* active defenses. He found himself gripping his couch's armrests; there was nothing else he could do.

Dahak's display blanked in the instant of detonation, shielding his bridge crews' optic nerves from the fury unleashed upon him. Anti-matter warheads, their yields measured in thousands of megatons, gouged at his final defenses, but *Dahak* was built to face things like that, and plasma clouds blew past him, divided by his shield as by the prow of a ship. Yet mixed with the anti-matter explosions were the true shipkillers of the Imperium: gravitonic warheads.

The ancient starship lurched. For all its unimaginable mass, despite the unthinkable power of its drive, it *lurched* like a broken-masted galleon, and Colin's stomach heaved despite the internal gravity field. His mind refused to contemplate the terrible fury which could produce that effect as gravitonic shield components screamed in protest, but they, too, had been engineered to meet this test. Somehow they held.

The display flashed back on, spalled by fading clouds of gas and heat, and a damage signal pulsed in Colin's neural feed. A schematic of *Dahak*'s hull appeared above his console, its frontal hemisphere marred by two wedge-shaped glares of red over a kilometer deep.

"Minor damage in quadrants Alpha-One and Three," *Dahak* reported. "No casualties. Capability not impaired. Second salvo entering interdiction range. Third enemy salvo detected."

More counter-missiles flashed out, and Colin reached a decision.

"Tactical, take out the actively attacking installations!"

"Acknowledged," Tamman said, and the display bloomed with amber sighting circles. Each enclosed a single missile platform, too tiny with distance for even Dahak to display visually, and Colin swallowed. Unlike their attackers, Tamman was using hyper missiles.

"Missiles away," Dahak said. And then, almost without pause, "Targets destroyed."

Bright, savage pinpricks blossomed in the amber circles, but the two salvos already fired were still coming. Yet Dahak had gained a great deal of data from the first attack, and he was a very fast thinker. Battle Comp was using his predicted target responses well, concentrating his counter-missiles to thwart them, alert now for their speed and the tricks of defensive ECM, killing the incoming missiles with inexorable precision. Energy weapons added their efforts as the range dropped, killing still more. Only three of the second salvo got through, and they were all anti-matter warheads. The final missile of the last salvo died ten light-seconds short of the shield.

Colin sagged in his couch.

"Dahak? Any more?" he asked hoarsely.

"Negative, sir. I detect active targeting systems aboard seven remaining installations, but no additional missiles have been launched."

"Any communication attempts?"

"Negative, Captain. Nor have they responded to my hails."

"Damn."

Colin's brain began to work again, but it made no sense. Why refuse all contact and attack on sight? For that matter, how had *Dahak* gotten so deep in-system before being detected? And if attack they must, why use only a sixth of their defensive bases? The four Tamman had destroyed had certainly gone all out, but if they meant to mount a defense at all, why hold anything back? Especially now, when *Dahak* had riposted so savagely?

"Well," he said finally, very softly, "let's find out what that was all about. Sarah, take us in at half speed. Tamman, hold us on Red One."

Acknowledgments flowed back to him, and *Dahak* started cautiously forward once more at twenty-eight percent of light speed. Colin watched the display for a moment, then made himself lean back.

"Dahak, give me an all-hands channel."

"All-hands channel open, sir."

"All right, people," Colin said to every ear aboard the massive ship, "that was closer than we'd like, but we seem to've come through intact. If anyone's interested in exactly what happened—" he paused and smiled; to his surprise, it felt almost natural "—you can get the details from Dahak later. But for your immediate information, no one's shooting at us just now, so we're going on in for a closer look. They're not talking to us, either, so it doesn't look like they're too friendly, but we'll know more shortly. Hang loose."

He started to order Dahak to close the channel, then stopped.

"Oh, one more thing. Well done, all of you. You did us proud. Out.

"Close channel, Dahak."

"Acknowledged, Captain. Channel closed."

"Thank you," Colin said softly, and his tone referred to far more than communications channels and the starship's courtesy. "Thank you very much."

CHAPTER EIGHT

The holo of what had once been a pleasant, blue-white world called Keerah hung in Command One's visual display like a leprous, ocher curse. Once-green continents were wind and water-carved ruins, grooved like a harridan's face and pocked with occasional sprawls where the works of Man had been founded upon solid bedrock and so still stood, sentinels to a vanished population.

Colin stared at it, heartsick as even Defram had not left him. He'd hoped so hard. The missiles which had greeted them had seemed to confirm that hope, and so he had almost welcomed them even as they sought to kill him. But dead Keerah mocked him.

He turned away, shifting his attention to the orbiting ring of orbital forts. Only seven remained even partially operational, and the nearest loomed in *Dahak*'s display, gleaming dully in the funeral watch light of Kano. The clumsy-looking base was over eight kilometers in diameter, and a shiver ran down Colin's spine as he looked at it.

Even now, its targeting systems were locked on *Dahak*, its age-crippled computers sending firing signals to its weapons. He shuddered as he pictured the ancient launchers swinging through their firing sequences again and again, dry-firing because their magazines were empty. It was bad enough to know the long-abandoned war machine was trying to kill him; it was worse to wonder how many other vessels must have died under its fire to exhaust its ammunition.

And if Dahak and Hector were right, most of those vessels had been killed not for attacking Keerah, but for trying to escape it.

"Probe One is reporting, Captain." Dahak's mellow voice wrenched Colin away from his frightening, empty thoughts to more immediate matters.

"Very well. What's their status?"

"External scans completed, sir. Fleet Captain (Engineering) Chernikov requests permission to board."

Colin turned to the holo image beside his console. "Recommendations?"

"My *first* recommendation is to get Vlad out of there," Cohanna said flatly.

"I'd rather not risk our Chief Engineer on the miserable excuse for an opinion I can give you."

"I tend to agree, but I made the mistake of asking for volunteers."

"In that case," Cohanna leaned back behind her desk in sickbay, a thousand kilometers from Command One, and rubbed her forehead, "we might as well let them board."

"Are you sure about that?"

"Of course I'm not!" she snapped, and Colin's hand rose in quick apology.

"Sorry, 'Hanna. What I really wanted was a run-down on your reasoning."

"It hasn't changed." Her almost normal tone was an unstated acceptance of his apology. "The other bases are as dead as Keerah, but there are at least two live hydroponics farms aboard that hulk—how I don't know, after all this time—and there may be more; we can't tell from exterior bio-scans even at this range. But that thing's entire atmosphere must've circulated through both of them a couple of million times by now and the plants are still alive. It's possible they represent a mutant strain that happened to be immune to whatever killed everything on Keerah, but I doubt it. Whatever the agent was, it doesn't seem to have missed *any-thing* down there, so I *think* it's unlikely it ever contaminated the battle station." She shrugged.

"I know that's a mouthful of qualifiers, but it's all I can tell you."

"But there's no other sign of life," Colin said quietly.

"None." Cohanna's holographic face was grim. "There couldn't be, unless they were in stasis. Genetic drift would've seen to that long ago on something as small as that."

"All right," Colin said after a moment. "Thank you." He looked down at his hands an instant longer, then nodded to himself.

"Dahak, give me a direct link to Vlad."

"Link open, Captain."

"Vlad?"

"Yes, Captain?" There was no holo image—Chernikov's bare-bones utility boat had strictly limited com facilities—but his calm voice was right beside Colin's ear.

"I'm going to let you take a closer look, Vlad, but watch your ass. One man goes in first—and *not* you, Mister. Full bio-protection and total decon before he comes back aboard, too."

"With all respect, Captain, I think—"

"I know what you think," Colin said harshly. "The answer is no."

"Very well." Chernikov sounded resigned, and Colin sympathized. He would vastly have preferred to take the risk himself, but he was *Dahak*'s captain. He couldn't gamble with the chain of command . . . and neither could Vlad.

Vlad Chernikov looked at the engineer he had selected for the task. Jehru Chandra had come many light-years to risk his life, but he looked eager as he double-checked the seals on his suit. Not cheerful or unafraid, but eager.

"Be cautious in there, Jehru."

"Yes, sir."

"Keep your suit scanners open. We will relay to Dahak."

"I understand, sir." Chernikov grinned wryly at Chandra's manifestly patient reply. Did he really sound that nervous?

"On your way, then," he said, and the engineer stepped into the airlock.

As per Cohanna's insistence, there was no contact between Chernikov's workboat and the battle station, but Chernikov studied the looming hull yet again as Chandra floated across the kilometer-wide gap on his suit propulsors. This ancient structure was thousands of years younger than *Dahak*, but the warship had been hidden under eighty kilometers of solid rock for most of its vast lifespan. The battle station had not. The once bright battle steel was dulled by the film of dust which had collected on its age-sick surface and pitted by micro-meteor impacts, and its condition made Chernikov chillingly aware of its age as *Dahak*'s shining perfection never had.

Chandra touched down neatly beside a small personnel lock, and his implants probed at the controls.

"Hmmmmm. . . ." The tension in his voice was smoothed by concentration. "Dahak was right, Commander. I've got live computers here, but damned if I recognize the machine language. Whups! Wait a minute, I've got something—"

His voice broke off for an agonizing moment, then came back with a most unexpected sound: a chuckle.

"I'll be damned, sir. The thing recognized my effort to access and brought in some kind of translating software. The hatch's opening now."

He stepped through it and it closed once more.

"Pressure in the lock," he reported, his fold-space com working as well through battle steel as through vacuum. "On the low side—'bout point-six-nine atmospheres. My sensors read breathable."

"Forget it right now, Jehru."

"Never even considered it, sir. Honest. Okay, inner lock opening now." There was a brief pause. "I'm in. Inner hatch closed. The main lighting's out, but about half the emergency lights're up."

"Is the main net live, or just the lock computers?"

"Looks like the auxiliary net's up. Just a sec. Yes, sir. Power level's weak, though. Can't find the main net, yet."

"Understood. Give me a reading on the auxiliary. Then I want you to head up-ship. Keep an eye out for . . ."

Colin rested in his couch, eyes closed, concentrating on his neural feed as Chandra penetrated the half-dead hulk, gaining in confidence with every meter. It showed even in the technicalities of his conversation with Vlad.

Colin only hoped they could ever dare to let him come home again.

✧   ✧   ✧

" . . . and that's about the size of it," Cohanna said, deactivating her personal memo computer. "We hit Chandra's suit with every decon system we had. As near as Dahak and I can tell, it was a hundred percent sterile before we let him unsuit, but we've got him in total isolation. I *think* he's clean, but I'm not letting him out of there until I'm certain."

"Agreed. Dahak? Anything to add?"

"I am still conversing with *Omega Three*'s core computers, Captain. More precisely, I am attempting to converse with them. We do not speak the same language, and their data transmission speed is appreciably higher than my own. Unfortunately, they also appear to be quite stupid." Colin hid a smile at the peeved note in Dahak's voice. Among the human qualities the vast computer had internalized was one he no doubt wished he could have avoided: impatience.

"How stupid?" he asked after a moment.

"Extremely so. In fairness, they were never intended for even rudimentary self-awareness, and their age is also a factor. *Omega Three*'s self-repair capability was never up to Fleet standards, and it has suffered progressive failure, largely, I suspect, through lack of spares. Approximately forty percent of *Omega Three*'s data net is inoperable. The main computers remain more nearly functional than the auxiliary systems, but there are failures in the core programming itself. In human terms, they are senile."

"I see. Are you getting anything at all?"

"Affirmative, sir. In fact, I am now prepared to provide a hypothetical reconstruction of events leading to *Omega Three*'s emplacement."

"You are?" Colin sat straighter, and others at the table did the same.

"Affirmative. Be advised, however, that much of it is speculative. There are serious gaps in the available data."

"Understood. Let's hear it."

"Acknowledged. In essence, sir, Fleet Captain (Biosciences) Cohanna was correct in her original hypothesis at Defram. The destruction of all life on the planets we have so far encountered was due to a bio-weapon."

"What *kind* of bio-weapon?" Cohanna demanded, leaning forward as if to will the answer out of the computer.

"Unknown at this time. It was the belief of the system governor, however, that it was of Imperial origin."

"Sweet Jesu," Jiltanith breathed. "In so much at least wert thou correct, my Hector. 'Twas no enemy wreaked their destruction; 'twas themselves."

"That is essentially correct," Dahak said. "As I have stated, the data are fragmentary, but I have recovered portions of memoranda from the governor. I hope to recover more, but those I have already perused point in that direction. She did not know how the weapon was originally released, but apparently there had been rumors of such a weapon for some time."

"The fools," Cohanna whispered. "Oh, the *fools!* Why would they build something like this? It violates every medical ethic the Imperium ever had!"

"I fear my data sample is too small to answer that, yet I have discovered a most interesting point. It was not the Fourth Imperium which devised this weapon but an entity called the Fourth *Empire*."

For just a moment, Colin failed to grasp the significance. Dahak had used Imperial Universal, and in Universal, the differentiation was only slightly greater than in English. "Imperium" was *umsuvah*, with the emphasis on the last syllable; "Empire" was *umsuvaht*, with the emphasis upon the second.

"What?" Cohanna blinked in consternation.

"Precisely. I have not yet established the full significance of the altered terminology, yet it suggests many possibilities. In particular, the Imperial Senate appears to have been superseded in authority by an emperor—specifically, by Emperor Herdan XXIV as of Year Thirteen-One-Seven-Five."

"Herdan the *Twenty-Fourth*?" Colin repeated.

"The title would seem significant," Dahak agreed, "suggesting as it does an extremely long period of personal rule. In addition, the date of his accession appears to confirm our dating of the Defram disaster."

"Agreed," Colin said. "But you don't have any more data?"

"Not of a political or societal nature, Captain. It may be that *Omega Three* will disgorge additional information, assuming I can locate the proper portion of its data core and that the relevant entries have not decayed beyond recovery. I would not place the probability as very high. *Omega Three* and its companions were constructed in great haste by local authorities, not by Battle Fleet. Beyond the programming essential for their design function, their data bases appear to be singularly uninformed."

Despite his shock, Colin grinned at the computer's sour tone.

"All right," he said after a moment. "What can you tell us about the effects of this bio-weapon and the reason the fortifications were built?"

"The data are not rich, Captain, but they do contain the essentials. The bio-weapon appears to have been designed to mount a broad-spectrum attack upon a wide range of life forms. If the rumors recorded by Governor Yirthana are correct, it was, in fact, intended to destroy *any* life form. In mammals, it functioned as a neuro-toxin, rendering the chemical compounds of the nervous system inert so that the organism died."

"But that wouldn't kill trees and grasses," Cohanna objected.

"That is true, Commander. Unfortunately, the designers of this weapon appear to have been extremely ingenious. Obviously we do not have a specimen of the weapon itself, but I have retrieved very limited data from Governor Yirthana's own bio-staff. It would appear that the designers had hit upon a simple observation: all known forms of life depend upon chemical reactions. Those reactions may vary from life form to life form, but their presence is a constant. This weapon was designed to invade and neutralize the critical chemical functions of any host."

"Impossible," Cohanna said flatly, then flushed.

"By the standards of my own data base, you are correct, ma'am. Nonetheless, Keerah is devoid of life. Empirical evidence thus suggests that it was, indeed, possible to the Fourth Empire."

"Agreed," the Biosciences head muttered.

"Governor Yirthana's bio-staff hypothesized that the weapon had been designed to modify itself at a very high rate of speed, attacking the chemical structures of its victims in turn until a lethal combination was reached. An elegant theoretical solution, although, I suspect, actually producing the weapon would be far from simple."

"*Simple!* I'm still having trouble believing it was *possible!*"

"As for *Omega Three* and its companions," Dahak continued, "they were intended to enforce a strict quarantine of Keerah. Governor Yirthana obviously was aware of the contamination of her planet and took steps to prevent its spread. There is also a reference I do not yet fully understand to something called a mat-trans system, which she ordered disabled."

"'Mat-trans'?" Colin asked.

"Yes, sir. As I say, I do not presently fully understand the reference, but it would appear that this mat-trans was a device for the movement of personnel over interstellar distances without recourse to starships."

"*What?!*" Colin jerked bolt upright in his chair.

"Current information suggests a system limited to loads of only a few tons but capable of transmitting them hundreds—possibly even several thousands—of light-years almost instantaneously, Captain. Apparently this system had become the preferred mode for personal travel. The energy cost appears to have been high, however, which presumably explains the low upper mass limit. Starships remained in use for bulk cargoes, and the Fleet and certain government agencies retained courier vessels for transportation of highly-classified data."

"Jesus!" Colin muttered. Then his eyes narrowed. "Why didn't you mention that before?"

"You did not ask, Captain. Nor was I aware of it. Please recall that I am continuing to query *Omega Three*'s memory even as we speak."

"All right, all right. But matter transmission? *Teleportation?*" Colin looked at Chernikov. "Is that possible?"

"As Dahak would say, empirical data suggests it is, but if you are asking *how*, I have no idea. Dahak's data base contains some journal articles about focused hyper fields linked with fold-space technology, but the research had achieved nothing as of the mutiny. Beyond that—?" He shrugged again.

"Maker!" Cohanna's soft voice drew all eyes back to her. She was deathly pale. "If they could—" She broke off, staring down at her hands and thinking furiously as she conferred with Dahak through her neural feed. Her expression changed slowly to one of utter horror, and when her attention returned to her fellows, her eyes glistened with sorrow.

"That's it." Her voice was dull. "That's how they did it to themselves."

"Explain," Colin said gently.

"I wondered . . . I wondered how it could go this far." She gave herself a little shake. "You see, Hector's right—only maniacs would deliberately dust whole planets with a weapon like this. But it wasn't that way at all."

They looked at her, most blankly, but a glimmer of understanding tightened Jiltanith's mouth. She nodded almost imperceptibly, and Cohanna's eyes swiveled to her face.

"Exactly," the biosciences officer said grimly. "The Imperium could have delivered it only via starships. They'd've been forced to transport the bug—

the agent, what*ever* you want to call it—from system to system, intention-ally. Some of that could have happened accidentally, but the Imperium was huge. By the time a significant portion of its planets were infected, the contaminating vector would have been recognized. If it wasn't a deliberate military operation, quarantine should have contained the damage.

"But the Empire wasn't like that. They had this damned 'mat-trans' thing. Assuming an incubation period of any length, all they needed was a single source of contamination—just *one*—they didn't know about. By the time they realized what was happening, it could've spread throughout the entire Imperium, and just stopping starships wouldn't do a damned thing to slow it down!"

Colin stared at her as her logic sank home. With something like the "mat-trans" Dahak had described, the Imperium's worlds would no longer have been weeks or months of travel apart. They would have become a tightly-integrated, inter-connecting unit. Time and distance, the greatest barriers to holding an interstellar civilization together, would no longer apply. What a triumph of technology! And what a deadly, deadly triumph it had proven.

"Then I was wrong," MacMahan murmured. "They *could* wipe themselves out."

"Could and did." Ninhursag's clenched fist struck the table gently, for an Imperial, and her voice was thick with anguish. "Not even on purpose—by accident. By *accident*, Breaker curse them!"

"Wait." Colin raised a hand for silence. "Assume you're right, Cohanna. Do you really think *every* planet would have been contaminated?"

"Probably not, but the vast majority certainly could have been. From the limited information Dahak and I have on this monster of theirs—and remember all our data is third or fourth-hand speculation, by way of Gov-ernor Yirthana—the incubation time *was* quite lengthy. Moreover, Yirthana's information indicates it was capable of surviving very long periods, pos-sibly several centuries, in viable condition even without hosts.

"That suggests a strategic rather than a tactical weapon. The long incubation period was supposed to bury it and give it time to spread before it manifested itself. That it in fact did so is also suggested by the fact that Yirthana had time to build her bases before it wiped out Keerah. Its long-term lethality would mean no one dared contact any infected planet for a very, very long period. Ideal, if the object was to cripple an inter-stellar enemy.

"But look what that means. Thanks to the incubation period, there probably wasn't any way to know it was loose until people started dying. Which means the central, most heavily-visited planets would've been the first to go.

"People being people, the public reaction was—*must* have been—panic. And a panicked person's first response is to flee." Cohanna shrugged. "The result might well have been an explosion of contamination.

"On the other hand, they had the hypercom. Warnings could be spread at supralight speeds without using their mat-trans, and presumably *some* planets must have been able to go into quarantine before they were affected. That's where the 'dwell time' comes in. They couldn't know how long they had to *stay* quarantined. No one would dare risk contact with any other planet as long as the smallest possibility of contamination by something like this existed."

She paused, and Colin nodded.

"So they would have abandoned space," he said.

"I can't be certain, but it seems probable. Even if any of their planets did survive, their 'Empire' still could have self-destructed out of all too reasonable fear. Which means—" she met Colin's eyes squarely "—that in all probability, there's no Imperium for us to contact."

Vladimir Chernikov bent over the work bench, studying the disassembled rifle-like weapon. His enhanced eyes were set for microscopic vision, and he manipulated his exquisitely sensitive instruments with care. The back of his mind knew he was trying to lose himself and escape the numbing depression which had settled over *Dahak*'s crew, but his fascination was genuine. The engineer in his soul rejoiced at the beauty of the work before him. Now if he could only figure out what it did.

There was the capacitor, and a real brute it was, despite its tininess. Eight or nine times a regular energy gun's charge. And these were rheostats. One obviously regulated the power of whatever the thing emitted, but what did the second . . . ?

Hmmmmm. Fascinating. There's no sign of a standard disrupter head in here. But then—aha! What do we have here?

He bent closer, bending sensor implants as well as vision upon it, then froze. He looked a moment longer, then raised his head and gestured to Baltan.

"Take a look at this," he said quietly. His assistant bent over and followed Chernikov's indicating test probe to the component in question, then pursed his lips in a silent whistle.

"A hyper generator," he said. "It has to be. But the *size* of the thing."

"Precisely." Chernikov wiped his spotless fingers on a handkerchief, drying their sudden clamminess. "Dahak," he said.

"Yes, sir?"

"What do you make of this?"

"A moment," the computer said. There was a brief period of silence, then the mellow voice spoke again. "Fleet Commander (Engineering) Baltan is correct, sir. It is a hyper generator. I have never encountered one of such small size or advanced design, but the basic function is evident. Please note, however, that the generator cavity's walls are composed of a substance unknown to me, and that they extend the full length of the barrel."

"Explanations?"

"It would appear to be a shielding housing around the generator, sir—one impervious to warp radiation. Fascinating. Such a material would have obvious applications in such devices as atmospheric hyper missile launchers."

"True. But am I right in assuming the muzzle end of the housing is open?"

"You are, sir. In essence, this appears to be a highly-advanced adaptation of the warp grenade. When activated, this weapon would project a focused field—in effect, a beam—of multi-dimensional translation which would project its target into hyper space."

"And leave it there," Chernikov said flatly.

"Of course," Dahak agreed. "A most ingenious weapon."

"Ingenious," Chernikov repeated with a shudder.

"Correct. Yet I perceive certain limitations. The hyper-suppression fields already developed to counteract warp grenades would also counteract this device's effect, at least within the area of such a field. I cannot be certain without field-testing the weapon, but I suspect that it might be fired *out* of or *across* such a suppression field. Much would depend upon the nature of the focusing force fields. But observe the small devices on both sides of the barrel. They appear to be extremely compact Ranhar generators. If so, they presumably create a tube of force to extend the generator housing and contain the hyper field, thus controlling its area of effect and also tending, quite possibly, to offset the effect of a suppression field."

"Maker, and I always hated warp *grenades*," Baltan said fervently.

"I, too," Chernikov said. He straightened from the bench slowly, looking at the next innocent-seeming device he'd abstracted from *Omega Three* once Cohanna had decided her painstaking search confirmed the original suggestion of the functional hydroponic farms. There was no trace of anything which could possibly be the bio-weapon aboard the battle station, and Chernikov had gathered up every specimen of technology he could find. He'd been looking forward to taking all of them apart.

Now he was almost afraid to.

CHAPTER NINE

Colin MacIntyre sat in Conference One once more. He'd grown to hate this room, he thought, bending his gaze upon the tabletop. Hate it.

Silence fell as the last person found a seat, and he looked up.

"Ladies and gentlemen," he said, "for the past month I've resisted all arguments to move on because I believe Keerah represents a microcosm of what probably happened to the entire Imperium. I now believe we've learned all we can here. But—" he drew out the slight pause behind the word "—that still leaves the question of what we do next. Before turning to that, however, I would like to review our findings, beginning with our Chief Engineer."

He sat back and nodded to Chernikov, who cleared his throat quietly, as if organizing his thoughts, then began.

"We have examined many artifacts recovered from *Omega Three*. On the basis of what we have discovered to date, I have reached a few conclusions about the technical base of the Imperium—that is to say, the Empire.

"They had, as we would have expected, made major advances, yet not so many as we might have anticipated. Please bear in mind that I am speaking only of non-biological technology; neither Cohanna nor I is in a position to say what they had achieved in the life sciences. The weapon which destroyed them certainly appears to evidence a very high level of bio-engineering.

"With that reservation, our initial estimate, that their technology was essentially a vastly refined version of our own, seems to have been correct. With the probable exception of their mat-trans—on which, I regret to say, we have been unable as yet to obtain data—we have encountered nothing Engineering and Dahak could not puzzle out. This is not to say they had not advanced to a point far beyond our current reach, but the underlying principles of their advances are readily apparent to us. In effect, they appear to have reached a plateau of fully mature technology and, I believe, may very well have been on the brink of fundamental breakthroughs into a new order of achievement, but they had not yet made them.

"In general, their progress may be thought of as coupling miniaturization with vast increases in power. A warship of Dahak's mass, for example, built with the technology we have so far encountered—which, I ask you to bear in mind, represents an essentially *civilian* attempt to create a military unit—would possess something on the order of twenty times his combat capability."

He paused for emphasis, and there were signs of awe on more than one face.

"Yet certain countervailing design philosophies and trends, particularly in the areas of computer science and cybernetics, also have become apparent to us. Specifically, the *hardware* of their computer systems is extremely advanced compared to our own; their *software* is not. Assuming that *Omega Three* is a representative sample of their computer technology, their computers had an even lower degree of self-awareness than that of Comp Cent prior to the mutiny. The data storage capacity of *Omega Three*'s Comp Cent, whose mass is approximately thirty percent that of Dahak's central memory core, exceeded his capacity, including all subordinate systems, by a factor of fifty. The *ability* of *Omega Three*, on the other hand, despite a computational speed many times higher than his, did not approach even that of Comp Cent prior to the mutiny.

"Clearly, this indicates a deliberate degradation of performance to meet some philosophical constraint. My best guess—and I stress that it is only a guess—is that it results from the period of civil warfare which apparently converted the Imperium into the Empire. Fleet computers would have resisted firing on other Fleet units, and while this could have been compensated for by altering their Alpha Priority core programming, the combatants may have balked at allowing semi-aware computers to decide whether or not to fire on other humans. This is only a hypothesis, but it is certainly one possibility.

"In addition, we have confirmed one other important point. While *Omega Three*'s computers did use energy-state technology, they also incorporated non-energy backups, which appears to reflect standard Imperial military practice. This means a deactivated Fleet computer would not experience a complete core loss as did the civilian units discovered at Defram. If powered up once more, thus restoring its energy-state circuitry, it should remain fully functional.

"Further, even civilian installations which have been continuously powered could remain completely operational. *Omega Three*'s capabilities, for example, suffered not because it relied upon energy-state components, but because it was left unattended for so long that *solid*-state components failed. Had the battle station's computers possessed adequate self-repair capability and spares, *Omega Three* would be fully functional today."

He paused, as if rechecking his thoughts, then glanced at Colin.

"That concludes my report, sir. Detailed information is in the data base for anyone who cares to peruse it."

"Thank you." Colin pursed his lips for a moment, inviting questions, but there were none. They were waiting for the other shoe, he thought dourly.

"Commander Cohanna?" he said finally.

"We still don't know how they did it," Cohanna replied, "but we're pretty sure *what* they did. I'm not certain I can accept Dahak's explanation just yet, but it fits the observed data, assuming they had the ability to implement it.

"For all practical purposes, we can think of their weapon as a disease lethal to any living organism. Obviously, it was a monster in every sense of the word. We may never learn how it was released, but the effect of its release was the inevitable destruction of all life in its path. Any contaminated planet is *dead*, ladies and gentlemen.

"On the other hand—" as Colin had, she drew out the pause for emphasis, "—we've also determined that the weapon had a finite lifespan. And whatever that lifespan was, it was less than the time which has passed. We've established test habitats with plants and livestock from our own hydroponic and recreational areas, using water and soil collected by remotes from all areas of Keerah's surface. From Governor Yirthana's records, we know the weapon took approximately thirty Terran months to incubate in mammals, and we've employed the techniques used in accelerated healing to take our sample habitats through a forty-five-month cycle with no evidence of the weapon. While I certainly don't propose to return those test subjects to *Dahak*'s life-support systems, I believe the evidence is very nearly conclusive. The bio-weapon itself has died, at least on Keerah and, by extension, upon any planet which was contaminated an equivalent length of time ago.

"That concludes my report, Captain."

"Thank you." Colin squared his shoulders and spoke very quietly as the full weight of his responsibility descended upon him. "On the basis of these reports, I intend to proceed immediately to Birhat and Fleet Central."

Someone drew a sharply audible breath, and his face tightened.

"What we've discovered here makes it extremely unlikely Birhat survived, but that, unfortunately, changes nothing.

"I don't know what we'll find there, but I do know three things. One, if we return with no aid for Earth, we lose. Two, the best command facilities at the Imperium's—or Empire's—disposal would be at Fleet Central. Three, logic suggests the bio-weapon there will be as dead as it is here. Based on those suppositions, our best chance of finding usable hardware is at Birhat, and it's likely we can safely reactivate any we find. At the very least, it will be our best opportunity to discover the full extent of this catastrophe."

"We will depart Keerah in twelve hours. In the meantime, please carry on about your duties. I'll be in my quarters if I'm needed."

He stood, catching the surprise on more than one face when his audience realized he did not intend to debate the point.

"Attention on deck," Dahak intoned quietly, and the officers rose.

Colin walked out in silence, wondering if those he'd surprised realized why he'd foreclosed all debate.

The answer was as simple as it was bitter. In the end, the decision was his, but if he allowed them to debate it they must share in it, however indirectly, and he would not permit them to do so.

He couldn't know if *Dahak*'s presence was required to stand off the Achuultani scouts, but he hoped desperately that it was not, for he, Colin MacIntyre, had elected to chase a tattered hope rather than defend his home world. If he'd guessed wrong about Horus's progress, he had also doomed that home world—a world which it had become increasingly obvious might well be the only planet of humanity which still existed—whatever he found at Birhat.

And the fact that logic compelled him to Birhat meant nothing against his fear that he had guessed wrong. Against his ignorance of Horus's progress. His agonizing suspicion that if Fleet Central still existed, it might be another *Omega Three*, senile and crippled with age . . . the paralyzing terror of bearing responsibility for the death of his own species.

He would not—could not—share that responsibility with another soul. It was his alone, and as he stepped into the transit shaft, Senior Fleet Captain Colin MacIntyre tasted the full, terrible burden of his authority at last.

The moss was soft and slightly damp as he lay on his back, staring up at the projected sky. He was coming to understand why the Imperium had provided its captains with this greenery and freshness. He could have found true spaciousness on one of the park decks, where breezes whipped across square kilometers of "open" land, but this was his. This small, private corner of creation belonged to him, offering its soothing aliveness and quiet bird-song when the weight of responsibility crushed down upon him.

He closed his eyes, breathing deeply, extending his enhanced senses. The splash of the fountains caressed him, and a gentle breeze stroked his skin, yet the sensations only eased his pain; they did not banish it.

He hadn't noted the time when he stretched out upon the moss, and so he had no idea how long he'd been there when his neural feed tingled.

Someone was at the hatch, and he was tempted to deny access, for his awareness of what he'd done was too fresh and aching. But that thought frightened him suddenly. It would be so easy to withdraw into a tortured, hermit-like existence, and it was over six months to Birhat. A man alone could go mad too easily in that much time.

He opened the hatch, and his visitor stepped inside. She came around the end of a thicket of azaleas and laurel, and he opened his eyes slowly.

"Art troubled, my Colin," she said softly.

He started to explain, but then he saw it in her eyes. She knew. One, at least, of his officers knew exactly why he'd refused to discuss his decision.

"May I sit with thee?" she asked gently, and he nodded.

She crossed the carpet of moss with the poised, cat-like grace which was always so much a part of her, straight and slim in her midnight-blue uniform, tall for an Imperial, yet delicate, her gleaming black hair held back by the same jeweled clasp she'd worn the day they met. The day when he'd seen the hate in her eyes. The hate for what he'd done, for the clumsy, cocksure fumbling which had cost the lives of a grandnephew and great-nieces she loved, but even more for what he was. For the threat of punishment he posed to her mutineer-father. For the fullness of his enhancement while she had but bits and pieces. And for the fact that he, who had never known of *Dahak*'s existence, never suspected her own people's lonely, hopeless fight against Anu, had inherited command of the starship from which she had been exiled for a crime others had committed.

There was a killer in Jiltanith. He'd seen it then, known it from the first. The mutiny had cost her her mother and the freedom of the stars, and the endless stealth of her people's shadowy battle on Earth had been slivered glass in her throat, for she was a fighter, a warrior who believed in open battle. Those long, agonizing years had left dark, still places within her. Far more than he could ever hope to be, she was capable of death and destruction, incapable of asking or offering quarter.

But there was no hate in her eyes now. They were soft and gentle under the atrium's sun, their black depths jewel-like and still. Colin had grown accustomed to the appearance of the full Imperials, yet in this moment the subtle alienness of her beauty smote him like a fist. She had been born before his first Terran ancestor crawled into a cave to hide from the weather, yet she was young. Twice his age and more, yet they were both but children against the lifespan of their enhanced bodies. Her youthfulness lay upon her, made still more precious and perfect by the endless years behind her, and his eyes burned.

This, he thought. This girl-woman who had known and suffered so much more than he, was what this all was about. She was the symbol of humankind, the avatar of all its frailties and the iron core of all its strength, and he wanted to reach out and touch her. But she was the mythic warrior-maid, the emblem, and the weight of his decision was upon him. He was unclean.

"Oh, my Colin," she whispered, looking deep into his own weary, tormented eyes, "what hast thou taken upon thyself?"

He clenched his hands at his sides, gripping the moss, and refused to answer, but a sob wrenched at the base of his throat.

She came closer slowly, carefully, like a hunter approaching some wild, snared thing, and sank to her knees beside him. One delicate hand, slender and fine-boned, deceiving the eye into forgetting its power, touched his shoulder.

"Once," she said, "in a life I scarce recall, I envied thee. Yea, envied and hated thee, for thou hadst received all unasked for the one treasure in all the universe I hungered most to hold. I would have slain thee, could I but have taken that treasure from thee. Didst thou know that?"

He nodded jerkily, and she smiled.

"Yet knowing, thou didst name me thy successor in command, for thine eyes saw more clear than mine own. 'Twas chance, mayhap, sent thee to *Dahak*'s bridge, yet well hast thou proven thy right to stand upon it. And never more than thou hast done this day."

Her hand stroked gently from his shoulder to his chest, covering the slow, strong beating of his bioenhanced heart, and he trembled like a frightened child. But her fingers moved, gentling his strange terror.

"Yet thou art not battle steel, my Colin," she said softly. "Art flesh and blood for all thy biotechnics, whate'er thy duty may demand of thee."

She bent slowly, laying her head atop her hand, and the fine texture of her hair brushed his cheek, its silken caress almost agony to his enhanced senses. Tears brimmed in the corners of his eyes, and part of him cursed his weakness while another blessed her for proving it to him. The sob he had fought broke free, and she made a soft, soothing sound.

"Yea, art flesh and blood, though captain to us all. Forget that not, for thou art not Dahak, and thy humanity is thy curse, the sword by which thou canst be wounded." She raised her head, and his blurred eyes saw the tears in her own. One moss-stained hand rose, stroking her raven's-wing hair, and she smiled.

"Yet wounds may be healed, my Colin, and I am likewise flesh, likewise blood," she murmured. She bent over him, and her mouth tasted of the salt of their mingled tears. His other hand rose, drawing her down beside him on the moss, and he rose on an elbow as she smiled up at him.

"Thou wert my salvation," she whispered, caressing his unruly sandy hair. "Now let me be thine, for *I* am thine and thou art mine. Forget it never, my dearest dear, for 'tis true now and ever shall be."

And she drew him down to kiss her once again.

The computer named Dahak closed down the sensors in the captain's quarters with profound but slightly wistful gratitude. He had made great strides in understanding these short-lived, infuriatingly illogical, occasionally inept, endlessly inventive, and stubbornly dauntless descendants of his long-dead builders. More than any other of his kind, he had learned to understand human emotions, for he had learned to share many of them. Respect. Friendship. Hope. Even, in his own way, love. He knew his presence would embarrass Colin and Jiltanith if it occurred to them to check for it, and while he did not fully understand the reason, they were his friends, and so he left them.

He gave the electronic equivalent of a sigh, knowing that he could never comprehend the gentle mysteries which had enfolded them. But he did not need to comprehend to know how important they were, and to feel deeply grateful to his new friend 'Tanni for understanding and loving his first friend Colin.

And now, he thought, while they were occupied, he might add that tiny portion of his attention which constantly attended his captain's needs and desires to another problem. Those encoded dispatches from the courier *Cordan* still intrigued him.

His latest algorithm had failed miserably, though he had finally managed to crack the scramble and reduce the messages to symbol sets. Unfortunately, the symbols were meaningless. Perhaps a new value-substitution subprogram was in order? Yet pattern analysis suggested that the substitution was virtually random. Interesting. That implied a tremendous symbol set, or else there was a method to generate the values which only appeared random. . . .

The computer worried happily away at the fascinating problem with a fragment of his capacity while every tiny corner of his vast starship body pulsed and quivered with his awareness.

All the tiny corners save one, where two very special people enjoyed a priceless gift of privacy made all the more priceless because they did not even know it had been given.

The last crude spacecraft died, and the asteroid battered through their wreckage at three hundred kilometers per second. Bits of debris struck its frontal arc, vanishing in brief, spiteful spits of flame against its uncaring nickel-iron bow. Heat-oozing wounds bit deep where the largest fragments had struck, and the asteroid swept onward, warded by the defenders' executioners.

Six Achuultani starships rode in formation about the huge projectile as it charged down upon the blue-and-white world which was its target. They had been detached to guard their weapon against the pygmy efforts of that cloud-swirled sapphire's inhabitants, and their task was all but done.

They spread out, distancing themselves from the asteroid, energy weapons ready as the first missiles broke atmosphere. The clumsy chemical-fueled rockets sped outward, tipped with their pathetic nuclear warheads, and the starships picked them off with effortless ease. The doomed planet flung its every weapon against its killers in despair and desperation . . . and achieved nothing.

The asteroid hurtled onward, an energy state hungry for immolation, and the starships wheeled up and away as it tasted air at last and changed. For one fleeting instant it was no longer a thing of ice-bound rock and metal. It was alive, a glorious, screaming incandescence pregnant with death.

It struck, spewing its flame back into the heavens, stripping away atmosphere in a cataclysm of fire, and the Achuultani starships hovered a moment longer, watching, as the planetary crust split and fissured. Magma exploded from the gaping wounds, and they spread and grew, racing like cracks in ice, until the geologically unstable planet itself blew apart.

The starships lingered no longer. They turned their bows from the ruin they had wrought and raced outward. Twenty-one light-minutes from the primary they crossed the hyper threshold and vanished like soap bubbles, hastening to seek their fellows at the next rendezvous.

CHAPTER TEN

Horus stood on the command deck of the battleship *Nergal*, almost unrecognizable in its refurbished state, and watched her captain take her smoothly out of atmosphere. A year ago, Adrienne Robbins, one of the US Navy's very few female attack submarine skippers, had never heard of the Fourth Imperium; now she performed her duties with a competence which gave him the same pleasure he took from a violin virtuoso and a Mozart concerto. She was good, he decided, watching her smooth her gunmetal hair. Better than he'd ever been, and she had the confident, almost sleepy smile of a hungry tiger.

He turned from the bridge crew to the holo display as *Nergal* slid into orbit. Marshal Tsien, Acting Chief of the Supreme Chiefs of Staff, towered over his right shoulder, and Vassily Chernikov stood to Horus' left. All three watched intently as *Nergal* leisurely overtook the half-finished bulk of Orbital Defense Center Two, and Horus suddenly snapped his fingers and turned to Tsien.

"Oh, Marshal Tsien," he said, "I meant to tell you that I spoke with General Hatcher just before you arrived, and he expects to return to us within the next four or five weeks."

Relief lit both officers' eyes, for it had been touch and go for Gerald Hatcher. Though Tsien's first aid had saved his life, he would have lost both legs without Imperial medical technology, assuming he'd lived at all, yet that same technology had nearly killed him.

Hatcher was one of those very rare individuals, less than one tenth of a percent of the human race, who were allergic to the standard quick-heal drugs, but the carnage at Minya Konka had offered no time for proper medical work-ups, and the medic who first treated him guessed wrong. The general's reaction had been quick and savage, and only the fact that that same medic had recognized the symptoms so quickly had prevented it from being fatal.

Even so, it had taken months to repair his legs to a point which permitted bioenhancement, for if the alternate therapies were just as effective,

they were also far slower. Which also meant his recuperation from enhancement itself was taking far longer than normal, so it was a vast relief to all
his colleagues and friends to know he would soon return to them.

And, Horus thought, remembering how Hatcher had chuckled over Tsien's
remark at Minya Konka, as the *first* enhanced member of the Chiefs of Staff.

"I am relieved to hear it, Governor," Tsien said now. "And I am certain
you will be relieved to have him back."

"I will, but I'd also like to congratulate you on a job very well done these
past months. I might add that Gerald shares my satisfaction."

"Thank you, Governor." Tsien didn't smile—Horus didn't think he'd ever
seen the big man smile—but his eyes showed his pleasure.

"You deserve all the thanks *we* can give *you*, Marshal," he said quietly.

In a sense, Hatcher's injuries had been very much to their advantage. If
any other member of the chiefs of staff was his equal in every way, it was
Tsien. They were very different; Tsien lacked Hatcher's ease with people and
the flair which made exquisitely choreographed operations seem effortless,
but he was tireless, analytical, eternally self-possessed, and as inexorable as
a Juggernaut yet flexibly pragmatic. He'd streamlined their organization,
moved their construction and training schedules ahead by almost a month,
and—most importantly of all—stamped out the abortive guerrilla war in
Asia with a ruthlessness Hatcher himself probably could not have displayed.

Horus had been more than a little horrified at the way Tsien went about
it. He hadn't worried about taking armed resisters prisoner, and those he'd
taken had been summarily court-martialed and executed, usually within
twenty-four hours. His reaction teams had been everywhere, filling Horus
with the fear that Hatcher had made a rare and terrible error in recom-
mending him as his replacement. There'd been an elemental implacability
about the huge Chinese, one that made Horus wonder if he even cared who
was innocent and who guilty.

Yet he'd made himself wait, and time had proved the wisdom of his
decision. Ruthless and implacable, yes, and also a man tormented by shame;
Tsien had been those things, for it had been his officers who had betrayed
their trust. But he'd been just as ruthlessly just. Every individual caught in
his nets had been sorted out under an Imperial lie detector, and the
innocent were freed as quickly as they had been apprehended. Nor had he
permitted any unnecessary brutality to taint his actions or those of his men.

Even more importantly, perhaps, he was no "Westerner" punishing
patriots who had struck back against occupation but their own commander-
in-chief, acting with the full support of Party and government, and no one
could accuse Tsien Tao-ling of being anyone's puppet. His reputation, and
the fact that *he* had been selected to replace the wounded Hatcher, had done
more to cement Asian support of the new government and military than
anything else ever could have.

Within two weeks, all attacks had ended. Within a month, there was no
more guerrilla movement. Every one of its leaders had been apprehended
and executed; none were imprisoned.

Nor had the chilling message been lost upon the rest of the world. Horus had agonized over the brutal suppression of the African riots, but Tsien's lesson had gone home. There was still unrest, but the world's news channels had carried live coverage of the trials and executions, and outbursts of open violence had ended almost overnight.

Tsien bobbed his head slightly in acknowledgment of the compliment, and Horus smiled, turning back to the display as ODC Two grew within it.

The eye-searing fireflies of robotic welders crawled over the vast structure while suited humans floated nearby or swung through their hard-working mechanical minions with apparently suicidal disregard for life and limb. Shuttles of components from the orbital smelters arrived with the precision of a well-run Terran railroad, disgorging their loads and wheeling away to return with more. Construction ships, raw and naked-looking in their open girder-work, seized structural members and frame units on tractors, placing them for the swarm of welders to tack into place and then backing away for the next. Conduits of Terran cable for communication nets, crystalline icicles of Imperial molycircs for computer cores and fire control, the huge, glittering blocks of prefabricated shield generators, Terran lighting and plumbing fixtures, and the truncated, hollow stubs of missile launchers—all vanished into the seeming confusion as they watched, and always there were more awaiting the frantically laboring robots and their masters.

It was impressive, Horus thought. Even to him—or, possibly, *especially* to him. Geb had shared Tegran's remarks about the Terra-born with him, and Horus could only agree. Unlike these fiercely determined people, he'd known their task was all but impossible. They hadn't accepted that, and they were making liars of his own fears.

He and the generals watched the seething construction work for several minutes, then Horus turned away with a sigh, followed by his subordinates. They stepped into the transit shaft with him, and he hid a smile at Tsien's uneasy expression. Interesting that this should bother him when facing totally unexpected ambush by traitors within his own military hadn't even fazed him.

They arrived at the conference room Captain Robbins had placed at their disposal, and he waved them towards the table as he seated himself at its head and crossed his legs comfortably.

"I'm impressed, gentlemen," he said. "I had to see that in person before I could quite believe it, I'm afraid. You people are producing miracles."

He saw the pleasure in their eyes. Flattery, he knew, was anathema to these men, however much of it they'd heard during their careers, but knowing their competence was appreciated—and, even more importantly, recognized for what it was—was something else.

"Now," he said, planting his forearms on the table and looking at Tsien, "suppose you tell me what other miracles you plan on working."

"With your permission, Governor, I shall begin by presenting a brief overview," the marshal replied, and Horus nodded approval.

"In general," Tsien continued, "we are now only one week behind

General Hatcher's original timetable. The resistance in Asia has delayed completion of certain of our projects—in particular, PDCs Huan-Ti and Shiva suffered severe damage which has not yet been made entirely good— but we are from one month to seven weeks ahead of schedule on our non-Asian PDCs. Certain unanticipated problems have arisen, and I will ask Marshal Chernikov to expand upon them in a moment, but the over all rate of progress is most encouraging.

"Officially, the merger of all existing command structures has been completed. In fact, disputes over seniority have continued to drag on. They are now being brought to an end."

Tsien's policy was simple, Horus reflected; officers who objected to the distribution of assignments were simply relieved. It might have cost them some capable people, but the marshal *did* have a way of getting his points across.

"Enhancement is, perhaps, the brightest spot of all. Councilor Tudor and her people have, indeed, worked miracles in this area. We are now two months ahead of schedule for military enhancement and almost five weeks ahead for non-military enhancement, despite the inclusion of additional occupational groups. We now have sufficient personnel to man all existing warships and fighters. Within another five months, we will have enhanced staffs for all PDCs and ODCs. Once that has been achieved, we will be able to begin enhancement of crews for the warships now under construction. With good management and a very little good fortune, we should be able to crew each unit as it commissions."

"That *is* good news! You make me feel we may pull this off, Marshal."

"We shall certainly attempt to, Governor," Tsien said calmly. "The balance between weapons fabrication and continued industrial expansion remains our worst production difficulty, but resource allocation is proving more than adequate. I believe Marshal Chernikov's current plans will overcome our remaining problems in this area.

"General Chiang faces some difficulties in his civil defense command, but the situation is improving. In terms of organization and training, he is two months ahead of schedule; it is construction of the inland shelters which poses the greatest difficulty, then food collection."

Horus nodded. Chiang Chien-su, one of Tsien's nominees to the Supreme Chiefs of Staff, was a short, rotund martinet with the mind of a computer. He smiled a lot, but the granite behind the smile was evident. Less evident but no less real was his deep respect for human life, an inner gentleness which, conversely, made him absolutely ruthless where saving lives was concerned.

"How far behind is shelter construction running?"

"Over three months," Tsien admitted. "We anticipate that some of that will be made up once PDC construction is complete. I must point out, however, that our original schedules already allowed for increases in building capacity after our fortification projects were completed. I do not believe we will be able to compensate completely for the time we have lost. This means that a greater proportion of our coastal populations will be forced to remain closer to their homes."

Horus frowned. Given the ratio of seas to land, anything that broke through the planetary shield was three times more likely to be an ocean strike than to hit land. That meant tsunamis, flooding, salt rains . . . and heavy loss of life in coastal areas.

"I want that program expedited, Marshal Tsien," he said quietly.

"Governor," Tsien said, equally quietly, "I have already diverted eighty percent of our emergency reserve capacity to the project. Every expedient is being pursued, but the project is immense and there is more civilian opposition to the attendant disruptions than your Council anticipated. The situation also is exacerbated by the food program. Collection of surpluses even in First World areas places severe strains on available transport; in Third World areas hoarding is common and armed resistance is not unknown. All of this diverts manpower and transport from population relocation efforts, yet the diversion is necessary. There is little point saving lives from bombardment only to lose them to starvation."

"Are you saying we won't make it?"

"No, Governor, I do not say we will fail. I only caution you that despite the most strenuous exertions, it is unlikely that we will succeed entirely."

Their eyes held for a moment, then Horus nodded. If they were no more than three months behind, they were still working miracles. And the marshal's integrity was absolute; if he said every effort would be made, then every effort would be made.

"On a more cheerful note," Tsien resumed after a moment, "Admiral Hawter and General Singhman are doing very well with their training commands. It is unfortunate that so much training must be restricted to simulators, but I am entirely satisfied with their progress—indeed, they are accomplishing more than I had hoped for. General Tama and General Amesbury are performing equally well in the management of our logistics. There remain some personnel problems, principally in terms of manpower allocation, but I have reviewed General Ki's solutions to them and feel confident they will succeed.

"In my own opinion, our greatest unmet training needs lie in the operational area. With your permission, I will expand upon this point following Marshal Chernikov's report."

"Of course," Horus said.

"Then, if I may, I will ask Marshal Chernikov to begin."

"Certainly." Horus turned his bright old eyes to Chernikov, and the Russian rubbed a fingertip thoughtfully over the table as he spoke.

"Essentially, Horus, we are well ahead of schedule on our PDC programs. We have managed this through allocation of additional manufacturing capacity to construction equipment and the extraordinary efforts of our personnel.

"We are not so advanced on our orbital work, but Geb and I agree that we should be on schedule by the end of next month, though it is unlikely we will complete the projects very much ahead of schedule. Nonetheless, we believe we will at least make our target dates in all cases.

"Despite this, two problems concern me. One is the planetary power grid;

the other is the relative priority of munitions and infrastructure. Allow me to take them in turn.

"First, power." Chernikov folded his arms across his broad chest, his blue eyes thoughtful. "As you know, our planning has always envisioned the use of existing Terran generator capacity, but I fear that our estimates of that capacity were overly optimistic. Even with our PDCs' fusion plants, we will be hard put to provide sufficient power for maximum shield strength, and the situation for our ODCs is even worse."

"Excuse me, Vassily, but you said you were on schedule," Horus observed.

"We are, but, as you know, our ODC designs rely upon fold-space power transmission from Earth. This design decision was effectively forced upon us by the impossibility of building full-scale plants for the ODCs in the time available. Without additional power from Earth, the stations will not be able to operate all systems at peak efficiency."

"And you're afraid the power won't be there," Horus said softly. "I see."

"Perhaps you do not quite. I am not *afraid* it will not be available; I *know* it will not. And without it—" He shrugged slightly, and Horus nodded.

Without that power net, the ODCs would lose more than half their defensive strength and almost as much of their offensive punch. Their missile launchers would be unaffected, but energy weapons were another matter entirely.

"All right, Vassily, you're not the sort to dump a problem on me until you think you've got an answer. So what rabbit's coming out of the hat this time?"

"A core tap," Chernikov said levelly, and Horus jerked in his chair.

"*Are you out of your*—?! No. Wait." He waved a hand and made himself sit back. "Of course you're not. But you do recognize the risks?"

"I do. But we *must* have that power, and Earth cannot provide it."

Maker, tell me what to do, Horus thought fervently. A *core* tap on a *planet?* Madness! If they lose control of it, even for an instant—!

He shuddered as he pictured that demon of power, roused and furious as it turned upon the insignificant mites who sought to master it. A smoldering wasteland, scoured of life, and raging storm fronts, hurricanes of outraged atmosphere which would rip across the face of the planet. . . .

"There's no other choice?" His tone was almost pleading. "None?"

"None that my staff have been able to discover," Chernikov said flatly.

"Where—" Horus paused and cleared his throat. "Where would you put it?"

"Antarctica," Chernikov replied.

There's a fitting irony in that, Horus thought. Anu's enclave hid there for millennia. But a polar position? So close to the Indian Ocean biosystem? Yet where would I prefer it? New York? Moscow? Beijing?

"Have you calculated what happens if you lose control?" he asked finally.

"As well as we can. In a worst-case scenario, we will lose approximately fifty-three percent of the Antarctic surface. Damage to the local ecosystem will be effectively total. Damage to the Indian Ocean bio-system will be severe but, according to the projections, not irrecoverable. Sea-level worldwide will rise, with consequent coastal flooding, and some global temperature drop may be anticipated. Estimated direct loss of life: approximately six-point-five million. Indirect deaths and the total who will be rendered homeless are impossible to calculate. We had considered an arctic position, but greater populations would lie in relative proximity, the flooding would be at least as severe, and the contamination of salt rains would be still worse when the sea water under the ice sheet vaporized."

"Maker!" Horus whispered. "Have you discussed this with Geb?"

"I have. It is only fair to tell you he was utterly opposed, yet after we had discussed it at some length, he modified his position somewhat. He will not actively oppose a core tap, but he cannot in good conscience recommend it. On the other hand—" agate-hard blue eyes stabbed Horus "—this is his planet only by adoption. I do not say that in any derogatory sense, Horus, yet it is true. Worse, he continues to feel—as, I believe, do you—a guilt which produces a certain protective paternalism within him. If he could refute the logic of my arguments, he would oppose them; his inability to support them suggests to me that his own logic is unable to overrule his emotions. Perhaps," the hard eyes softened slightly, "because he is so good a man."

"And despite that, you want to go ahead."

"I see no option. We risk seven million dead and severe damage to our world if we proceed; we run a far greater risk of the total destruction of the planet if we do not."

"Marshal Tsien?"

"I am less conversant with the figures than Marshal Chernikov, but I trust his calculations and judgment. I endorse his recommendation unreservedly, Governor. I will do so in writing if you wish."

"That won't be necessary," Horus sighed. His shoulders slumped, but he shook his head wryly. "You Terra-born are something else, Vassily!"

"If so, we have had good teachers," Chernikov replied, eyes warming with true affection. "Thanks to you, we have a possibility of saving ourselves. We will not throw away the chance you have given us."

Horus felt his face heat and turned quickly to another point.

"Maker! I hope you didn't plan on discussing your concerns in order of severity. If your munitions problem is worse—!"

"No, no!" Chernikov laughed. "No, this is not quite so grave. Indeed, one might almost call it planning for the future."

"Well *that* has a cheerful ring."

"Russians are not always melancholy, Horus. Generally, but not always. No, my major concern stems from the high probability that our planetary shield will be forced back into atmosphere. Our ODCs will be fairly capable of self-defense, although we anticipate high losses among them if the planetary shield *is* forced back, but our orbital industrial capacity will, unfortunately, also be exposed. Nor will it be practical to withdraw it to the planetary surface."

That was true enough, Horus reflected. They'd accepted that from the beginning, but by building purely for a weightless environment they'd been able to produce more than twice the capacity in half the time.

"What do you have in mind?"

"I am about to become gloomy again," the Russian warned, and Horus chuckled. "Let us assume we have succeeded in driving off the scouts but that *Dahak* has not returned when the main incursion arrives. I realize that our chances of survival in such an eventuality are slight, yet it is not in me to say there are none. Perhaps it is unrealistic of me, but I admire the American John Paul Jones and respect his advice. Both the more famous quote, and another: It seems a law inflexible unto itself that he who will not risk cannot win. I may not have it quite correct, but I believe the spirit comes through."

"This is heading somewhere?" Horus asked quizzically.

"It is. If we lose our orbital industry, we lose eighty percent of our total capacity. This will leave us much weaker when we confront the main incursion. Even if we beat off the scouts quickly and with minimal losses—a happy state of affairs on which we certainly cannot depend—we will be hard-pressed to rebuild even to our current capacity out of our present Imperial planetary industry. I therefore propose that we should place greater emphasis on increasing our planetary industrial infrastructure."

"I agree it's desirable, but where do you plan to get the capacity?"

"With your permission, I will discontinue the production of mines."

"Ah?"

"I have studied their capabilities, and while they are impressive, I feel they will be less useful against the scouts than an increase in planetary industrial capacity will be to our defense against the main incursion."

"Why?"

"Essentially, the mines are simply advanced hunter-killer satellites. Certainly their ability to attack vessels as they emerge from hyper is useful, yet they will be required in tremendous numbers to cover effectively the volume of space we must protect. Their attack radius is no more than ninety thousand kilometers, and mass attacks will be required to overpower the defenses of any alert target. Because of these limitations, I doubt our ability to produce adequate numbers in the time available to us. I would prefer to do without them in order to safeguard our future industrial potential."

"I see." Horus pursed his lips, then nodded. "All right, I agree."

"Thank you."

"Now, Marshal," Horus turned to Tsien, "you mentioned something about operational problems?"

"Yes, Governor. General Amesbury's Scanner Command is well prepared to detect the enemy's approach, but we do not know whether we would be better advised to send our units out to meet them as they move in-system after leaving hyper or to concentrate closer to Earth for sorties from within the shield after they have closed with the planet. The question also, of course, is complicated by the possibility that the Achuultani might attempt a pincer attack, using one group of scouts to draw our sublight units out of position and then micro-jumping across the system to attack from another direction."

"And you want to finalize operational doctrine?"

"Not precisely. I realize that this almost certainly will not be possible for some time and that much ultimately will depend upon the differences between Achuultani technology and our own. For the moment, however, I would like to grant Admiral Hawter's request to deploy our existing units for operational training and war games in the trans-asteroidal area. It will give the crews valuable experience with their weapons, and, more importantly, I believe, give our command personnel greater confidence in themselves."

"I agree entirely," Horus said firmly. "And it'll also let us use some of the larger asteroids for target practice—which means the Achuultani *won't* be able to use them for target practice on us! Proceed with it immediately, by all means, Marshal Tsien. Vassily, I'll take your recommendations to the Council. Unless someone there can give me an overpowering counterargument, they'll be approved within forty-eight hours. Is that good enough?"

"Eminently, Governor."

"Good. In that case, gentlemen, let's get into our suits. I want to see ODC Two firsthand."

The Achuultani scouts gathered their strength once more, merging into a single huge formation about their flagship. A brilliant F5 star lay barely five light-years distant, but it held no interest for them. Their instruments probed and peered, listening for the electromagnetic voices they had come so far to find. The universe was vast. Not even such accomplished killers as they could sweep it of all life, and so worlds such as T'Yir were safe unless the scouts literally stumbled across them.

But other worlds were not, and the sensor crews caught the faint signals they had sought. Directional antennae turned and quested, and the scouts reoriented themselves. A small, G2 star called to them, and they went to silence it forever.

CHAPTER ELEVEN

"Barbarian!" Tamman shook his head mournfully as he took a fresh glass of lemonade from his wife and buried his sorrows in its depths.

"And why might that be, you effete, over-civilized, not to say decadent, epicure?" Colin demanded.

"That ought to be obvious. Mesquite *charcoal*? How . . . how *Texan*!"

Colin stuck out his tongue, and meat juices hissed as he turned steaks. A fragrant cloud of smoke rose on the heat shimmer of the grill, pushed out over the lake by the park deck's cool breezes, and the volley ball tournament was in full cry. He glanced up in time to see Colonel Tama Matsuo, Tamman's grandson, launch a vicious spike. One of the German team's forwards tried to get under it, but not even an enhanced human could have returned *that* shot.

"*Banzai!*" the Sendai Division's team screamed, and the Germans muttered darkly. Jiltanith applauded, and Matsuo bowed to her, then prepared to serve. His hand struck the ball like a hammer, and Colin winced as it bulleted across the net.

"Now, Tamman, don't be so harsh," his critic's wife chimed in. "After all, Colin's doing the best he knows how."

"Oh, *thank* you, kind lady! Thank you! Just remember—your wonderful husband is the one who courted bad luck by broiling *tai* in *miso* last week."

Recon Captain Amanda Givens laughed, her cafe-au-lait face wreathed in a lovely smile, and Tamman pulled her down beside him to kiss her ear.

"Nonsense," he said airily. "Just doing my bit to root out superstition. Anyway, I was out of salt."

Amanda snuggled closer to him, and Colin grinned. *Dahak*'s sickbay had regenerated the leg she'd lost in the La Paz raid in time for her wedding, and the sheer joy she and Tamman took in one another warmed Colin's heart, even though their marriage had caused a few unanticipated problems.

Dahak had always seemed a bit pettish over the Terran insistence that one name wasn't good enough. He'd accepted it—grumpily—but only until he got to attend the first wedding on his decks in fifty thousand years. In some ways, he'd seemed even more delighted than the happy couple, and he'd hardly been able to wait for Colin to log the event officially.

That was when the trouble started, for Imperial conventions designating marital status sounded ridiculous applied to Terran names, and Dahak had persisted in trying to make them work. Colin usually wound up giving in when Dahak felt moved to true intransigence—talking the computer out of something was akin to parting the Red Sea, only harder—but he'd refused pointblank to let Dahak inflict a name like Amandacollettegivens-Tam on a friend. The thought of hearing *that* every time Dahak spoke to or of Amanda had been too much, and if Tamman had originally insisted (when he finally stopped laughing) that it was a lovely name which fell trippingly from the tongue, his tune quickly changed when he found out what Dahak intended to call *him*. Tamman-Amcolgiv was shorter; that was about all you could say for it.

"Methinks it little matters what thou sayst, Tamman," Jiltanith's mournful observation drew Colin back to the present as she opened another bottle of beer. "Our Colin departeth not from his fell intent to poison one and all with his noxious smokes and fumes."

"Listen, all of you," Colin retorted, propping his fists on his hips, "I'm captain of this tub, and we'll fix food *my* way!"

"Didst'a hear thy captain speak of thee, Dahak, my tub?" Jiltanith caroled, and Colin shook a fist at her.

"I believe the proper response is 'Sticks and stones may break my bones, but words will never hurt me,'" a mellow voice replied, and Colin groaned.

"What idiot encouraged him to learn cliches?"

"Nay, Colin, acquit us all. 'Tis simply that we *dis*couraged him not."

"Well you should have."

"Stop complaining and let the man cook." Vlad Chernikov lay flat on his back in the shade of a young oak. Now he propped one eye open. "If you do not care for his cuisine, you need not eat it, Tamman."

"Fat chance!" Colin snorted, and stole Jiltanith's beer.

He swallowed, enjoying the "sun" on his shoulders, and decided 'Tanni had been right to talk him into the party. The anniversary of the fall of Anu's enclave deserved to be celebrated as a reminder of some of the "impossible" things they'd already accomplished, even if uncertainty over what waited at Birhat continued to gnaw at everyone. Or possibly *because* it did.

He looked out over the happy, laughing knots of his off-watch crewmen. Some of them, anyway. There was a null-grav basketball tournament underway on Deck 2460, and General Treshnikov had organized a "Top Gun" contest on the simulator deck for the non-fighter pilots of the crew. Then there was the regatta out on the thirty-kilometer-wide park deck's lake.

He glanced around the shaded picnic tables. Cohanna and Ninhursag sat at one, annihilating one another in a game of Imperial battle chess with a bloodthirsty disregard for losses that would turn a line officer gray, and Caitrin O'Rourke and Geran had embarked on a drinking contest—

in which Caitrin's Aussie ancestry appeared to be a decided advantage—at another. General von Grau and General Tsukuba were wagering on the outcome of the volley ball tournament, and Hector wore a dreamy look as he and Dahak pursued a discussion, complete with neural-feed visual aids, of Hannibal's Italian tactics. Sarah Meir sat with him, listening in and reaching down occasionally to scratch the ears of Hector's huge half-lab, half-rottweiler bitch Tinker Bell as she drowsed at her master's feet.

Colin returned Jiltanith's beer, and his smile grew warmer as her eyes gleamed at him. Yes, she'd been right—just as she'd been right to insist they make their own "surprise" announcement at the close of the festivities. And thank God he'd been firm with Dahak! He didn't know how she would have reacted to Jiltanith-Colfranmac, but he knew how *he* would have felt over Colinfrancismacintyre-Jil!

"Supralight shutdown in ten minutes," Dahak announced into the fiery tension of Command One's starlit dimness, and Colin smiled tightly at Jiltanith's holo image, trying to wish she were not far away in Command Two.

He inhaled deeply and concentrated on the reports and commands flowing through his neural feed. Not even the Terra-born among *Dahak*'s well-drilled crew needed to think through their commands these days. Which might be just as well. There had been no hails or challenges, but they'd been thoroughly scanned by someone (or something) while still a full day short of Birhat.

Colin would have felt immeasurably better to know what had been on the other end of those scanners . . . and how whatever it was meant to react. One thing they'd learned at Kano: the Fourth Empire's weaponry had been, quite simply, better than *Dahak*'s best. Vlad and Dahak had done all they could to upgrade their defenses, but if an active Fleet Central was feeling belligerent, they might very well die in the next few hours.

"Sublight in three minutes."

"Stand by, Tactical," Colin said softly.

"Standing by, Captain."

The last minutes raced even as they trickled agonizingly slowly. Then Colin felt the start of supralight shutdown in his implants, and suddenly the stars were still.

"Core tap shutdown," Dahak reported, and then, almost instantly, "Detection at ten light-minutes. Detection at thirty light-minutes. Detection at five light-hours."

"Display system," Colin snapped, and the sun Bia, Birhat's G0 primary, still twelve light-hours away, was suddenly ringed with a system schematic.

"God's Teeth!"

Jiltanith's whisper summed up Colin's sentiments admirably. Even at this range, the display was crowded, and more and more light codes sprang into view with mechanical precision as Sarah took them in at half the speed of light. *Dahak*'s scanners reached ahead, adding contact after contact, until the display gleamed with a thick, incredible dusting of symbols.

"Any response to our presence, Dahak?"

"None beyond detection, sir. I have received no challenges, nor has anyone yet responded to my hails."

Colin nodded. It was a disappointment, for he'd felt a spurt of hope when he saw all those light codes, but it was a relief, as well. At least no one was shooting at them.

"What the hell are all those things?" he demanded.

"Unknown, sir. Passive scanners detect very few active power sources, and even with fold-space scanners, the range remains very long for active systems, but I would estimate that many of them are weapon systems. In fact—"

The computer paused suddenly, and Colin quirked an eyebrow. It was unusual, to say the least, for Dahak to break off in the middle of a sentence.

"Sir," the computer said after a moment, "I have determined the function of certain installations."

An arc of light codes blinked green. They formed a ring forty light-minutes from Bia—no, not a ring. As he watched, new codes, each indicating an installation much smaller than the giants in the original ring, began to appear, precisely distanced from the circle, curving away from *Dahak* as if to embrace the entire inner system. And there—there were two more rings of larger symbols, perpendicular to the first but offset by thirty degrees. There were thousands—millions—of the things! And more were still appearing as they came into scanner range, reaching out about Bia in a sphere.

"Well? What are they?"

"They appear, sir," Dahak said, "to be shield generators."

"They're *what*?" Colin blurted, and he felt Vlad Chernikov's shock echoing through the engineering sub-net.

"Shield generators," Dahak repeated, "which, if activated, would enclose the entire inner system. The larger stations are approximately ten times as massive as the smaller ones and appear to be the primary generators."

Colin fought a sense of incredulity. Nobody could build a shield with that much surface area! Yet if Dahak said they were shield generators, shield generators they were . . . but the *scope* of such a project!

"Whatever else it was, the Empire was no piker," he muttered.

"As thou sayst," Jiltanith agreed. "Yet methinks—"

"Status change," Dahak said suddenly, and a bright-red ring circled a massive installation in distant orbit about Birhat itself. "Core tap activation detected."

"Maker!" Tamman muttered, for the power source which had waked to sudden life was many times as powerful as *Dahak*'s own.

"New detection at nine-point-eight light-hours. I have a challenge."

"Nature?" Colin snapped.

"Query for identification only, sir, but it carries a Fleet Central imperative. It is repeating."

"Respond."

"Acknowledged." There was another brief silence, and then Dahak spoke again, sounding—for once—a bit puzzled. "Sir, the challenge has terminated."

"What do you mean? How did they respond?"

"They did not, sir, beyond terminating the challenge."

Colin raised an eyebrow at Jiltanith's holo-image, and she shrugged.

"Ask me not, my Colin. Thou knowest as much as I."

"Yeah, and neither of us knows a whole hell of a lot," he muttered. Then he drew a deep breath. "Dahak, give me an all-hands link."

"Acknowledged. Link open."

"People," Colin told his crew, "we've just responded to a challenge—apparently from Fleet Central itself—and no one's shooting at us. That's the good news. The bad news is no one's talking to us, either. We're moving in. We'll keep you informed. But at least there's *something* here. Hang loose.

"Close link, Dahak."

"Link closed, sir."

"Thank you," Colin said, and leaned back, rubbing his hands up and down the arm rests of his couch as he stared at the crowded, enigmatic display. More light codes were still appearing as *Dahak* moved deeper in-system, and the active core tap's crimson beacon pulsed at their center like a heart.

"Well, we found it," Colin said, rising from the captain's couch to stretch hugely, "but God knows what it is."

"Aye." Jiltanith once more manned her own console in Command Two, but her hologram sat up and swung its legs over the side of her couch. "I know not what chanced here, my Colin, but glad am I Geb is not here to see it."

"Amen," Colin said. He'd once wondered why Geb was the only Imperial with a single-syllable name. Now, thanks to Jiltanith and Dahak's files, he knew. It was the custom of his planet, for Geb had been one of those very rare beings in Battle Fleet: a native-born son of Birhat. It was a proud distinction, but one Geb no longer boasted of; his part in the mutiny had been something like George Washington's grandson proclaiming himself king of the United States.

"But whate'er hath chanced, these newest facts do seem stranger still than aught else we have encountered." Jiltanith coiled a lock of hair about her index finger and stared at Command Two's visual display, her eyes perplexed.

With good reason, Colin thought. In the last thirty-two hours, they'd threaded deeper into the Bia System's incredible clutter of deep-space and orbital installations until, at last, they'd reached Birhat itself. There should have been plenty of room, but the Bia System had not escaped unscathed. Twice they passed within less than ten thousand kilometers of drifting derelicts, and that was much closer than any astrogator cared to come.

Yet despite that evidence of ruin, Colin had felt hopeful as Birhat herself came into sight, for the ancient capital world of the Imperium was alive, a white-swirled sapphire whose land masses were rich and green.

But with the wrong kind of green.

Colin sat back down, scratching his head. Birhat lay just over a light-minute further from Bia than Terra did from Sol, and its axial tilt was about five degrees greater, making for more extreme seasons, but it had been a nice enough place. It still was, but there'd been a few changes.

According to the records, Birhat's trees should be mostly evergreens, but while there were trees, they appeared exclusively deciduous, and there were other things: leafy, fern-like things and strange, kilometer-long creepers with cypress-knee rhizomes and upstanding plumes of foliage. Nothing like *that* was supposed to grow on Birhat, and the local fauna was even worse.

Like Earth, Birhat had belonged to the mammals, and there *were* mammals down there, if not the right ones. Unfortunately, there were other things, too, especially in the equatorial belt. One was nearly a dead ringer for an under-sized Stegosaurus, and another one (a big, nasty looking son-of-a-bitch) seemed to combine the more objectionable aspects of Tyrannosaurus and a four-horned Triceratops. Then there were the birds. None of them seemed quite right, and he *knew* the big Pterodactyl-like raptors shouldn't be here.

It was, he thought, the most God-awful, scrambled excuse for a bio-system he'd ever heard of, and none of it—not a single plant, animal, saurian, or bird they'd yet examined—*belonged* here.

If it puzzled him, it was driving Cohanna batty. The senior biosciences officer was buried in her office with Dahak, trying to make sense of her instrument readings and snarling at any soul incautious enough to disturb her.

At least the sadly-eroded mountains and seas were where they were supposed to be, loosely speaking, and there were still some clusters of buildings. They were weather-battered ruins (not surprisingly given the worn-away look of the mountain ranges) liberally coated in greenery, but they were there. Not that it helped; most were as badly wrecked as Keerah's had been, and there was nothing—absolutely *nothing*—where Fleet Central was supposed to be.

Yet some of the Bia System's puzzles offered Colin hope. One of them floated a few thousand kilometers from *Dahak*, serenely orbiting the improbability which had once been the Imperium's capital, and he turned his head to study it anew, tugging at the end of his nose to help himself think.

The enigmatic structure was even bigger than *Dahak*, which was a sobering thought, for a quarter of *Dahak*'s colossal tonnage was committed to propulsion. This thing—whatever it was—clearly wasn't intended to move, which made all of its mass available for other things. Like the weapon systems *Dahak*'s scanners had picked up. *Lots* of weapon systems. Missile launchers, energy weapons, and launch bays for fighters and sublight parasites *Nergal*'s size or bigger. Yet for all its gargantuan firepower, much of its tonnage was obviously committed to something else . . . but what?

Worse, it was also the source of the core tap Dahak had detected. Even now, that energy sink roared away within it, sucking in all that tremendous power. Presumably it meant to do something with it, but as yet it had shown no signs of exactly what that was. It hadn't even spoken to Dahak, despite his polite queries for information. It just sat there, *being* there.

"Captain?"

"Yes, Dahak?"

"I believe I have determined the function of that installation."

"Well?"

"I believe, sir, that *it* is Fleet Central."

"I thought Fleet Central was on the planet!"

"So it was, fifty-one thousand years ago. I have, however, been carrying out systematic scans, and I have located the installation's core computer. It is, indeed, a combination of energy-state and solid-state engineering. It is also approximately three-hundred-fifty-point-two kilometers in diameter."

"Eeep!" Colin whipped around to stare at Jiltanith, but for once she looked as stunned as he felt. Dear God, he thought faintly. Dear, sweet God. If Vlad and Dahak's projections about the capabilities of energy-state computer science were correct, that thing was . . . it was . . .

"I beg your pardon, sir?" Dahak said courteously.

"Uh . . . never mind. Continue your report."

"There is very little more to report. The size of its computer core, coupled with its obvious defensive capability, indicates that it must, at the very least, have been the central command complex for the Bia System. Given that Birhat remained the capital of the Empire as it had been of the Imperium, this certainly suggests that it was also Fleet Central."

"I . . . see. And it still isn't responding to your hails?"

"It is not. And even the Empire's computers should have noticed us by now."

"Could it have done so and chosen to ignore us?"

"The possibility exists, but while it is probable Fleet procedures have changed, we were challenged and we did reply. That should have initiated an automatic request for data core transmission from any newly-arrived unit."

"Even if there's no human crew aboard?"

"Sir," Dahak said with the patience of one trying not to be insubordinate to a dense superior, "we were challenged, which indicates the initiation of an automatic sequence of some sort. And, sir, Fleet Central should not have permitted a vessel of *Dahak*'s size and firepower to close to this proximity without assuring itself that the vessel in question truly was what it claimed to be. Since no information has been exchanged, there is no way Fleet Central could know my response to its challenge was genuine. Hence we should at the very least be targeted by its weapons until we provide a satisfactory account of ourselves, yet that installation has not even objected to my scanning it. Fleet Central would *never* permit an unknown unit to do that."

"All right, I'll accept that—even if that does seem to be exactly what it's doing—and God knows I don't want to piss it off, but sooner or later we'll have to get some sort of response out of it. Any suggestions?"

"As I have explained," Dahak said even more patiently, "we should already have elicited a response."

"I know that," Colin replied, equally patiently, "but we haven't. Isn't there any sort of emergency override procedure?"

"No, sir, there is not. None was ever required."

"Damn it, do you mean to tell me there's *no* way to talk to it if it doesn't respond to your hails?"

There was a pause lengthy enough to raise Colin's eyebrows. He was about to repeat his question when his electronic henchman finally answered.

"There might be one way," Dahak said with such manifest reluctance Colin felt an instant twinge of anxiety.

"Well, spit it out!"

"We might attempt physical access, but I would not recommend doing so."

"What? Why not?"

"Because, Captain, access to Fleet Central was highly restricted. Without express instructions from its command crew to its security systems, only two types of individuals might demand entrance without being fired upon."

"Oh?" Colin felt a sudden queasiness and was quite pleased he'd managed to sound so calm. "And what two types might that be?"

"Flag officers and commanders of capital ships of Battle Fleet."

"Which means . . ." Colin said slowly.

"Which means," Dahak told him, "that the only member of this crew who might make the attempt is you."

He looked up and saw Jiltanith staring at him in horror.

CHAPTER TWELVE

They went to their quarters to argue.

Jiltanith opened her mouth, eyes flashing dangerously, but Dahak's electronic reflexes beat her to it.

"Senior Fleet Captain MacIntyre," he said with icy formality, "what you propose is not yet and may never become necessary, and I remind you of Fleet Regulation Nine-One-Seven, Subsection Three-One, Paragraph Two: 'The commander of any Fleet unit shall safeguard the chain of command against unnecessary risk.' I submit, sir, that your intentions violate both the spirit and letter of this regulation, and I must, therefore, respectfully insist that you immediately abandon this ill-advised, hazardous, and most unwise plan."

"Dahak," Colin said, "shut up."

"Senior Fl—"

"I said shut up," Colin repeated in a dangerously level voice, and Dahak shut up. "Thank you. Now. We both know the people who wrote the Fleet Regs never envisioned *this* situation, but if you want to quote regs, here's one for *you*. Regulation One-Three, Section One. 'In the absence of orders from higher authority, the commander of any Battle Fleet unit or formation shall employ his command or any sub-unit or member thereof in the manner best calculated, in his considered judgment, to preserve the Imperium and his race.' You once said I had a command mentality. Well, maybe I do and maybe I don't, but this is a command decision and you're damned well going to live with it."

"But—"

"The discussion is closed, Dahak."

There was a long moment of silence before the computer replied.

"Acknowledged," he said in his frostiest tones, but Colin knew that was the easy part. He smiled crookedly at Jiltanith, glad they were alone, and gave it his best shot.

"'Tanni, I don't want to argue with my XO, either."

"Dost'a not, indeed?" she flared. "Then contend with thy wife, lackwit!

Scarce one thin day in this system, and already thou wouldst risk thy life?! What maggot hath devoured thy brain entire?! Or mayhap 'tis vanity speaks, for most assuredly 'tis not wisdom!"

"It isn't vanity, and you know it. We simply don't have time to waste."

"*Time*, thou sayst?!" she spat like an angry cat. "Dost'a think my wits addled as thine own? Howsoe'er thou dost proceed, yet will we never return to Terra ere the Achuultani scouts! And if that be so, then where's the need o' witless haste? Four months easily, mayhap five, may we spend here and still out-speed the true incursion back to Earth—and well thou knowest!"

"All right," he said, and her eyes narrowed at his unexpected agreement, "but assume you're right and we start poking around. What happens when we do something Fleet Central doesn't like, 'Tanni? Until we know what it might object to, we can't know what might get everyone aboard this ship killed. So until we establish communications with it, we can't do anything *else*, either!"

Jiltanith's fingers flexed like the cat she so resembled, but she drew a breath and made herself consider his argument.

"Aye, there's summat in that," she admitted, manifestly against her will. "Yet still 'tis true we have spent but little time upon the task. Must thou so soon essay this madness?"

"I'm afraid so," he sighed. "If this *is* Fleet Central, it's either Ali Baba's Cave or Pandora's Box, and we have to find out which. Assuming any of Battle Fleet's still operational—and the way this thing powered itself up is the first sign something may be—we don't know how long it'll take to assemble it. We need every minute we can buy, 'Tanni."

She turned away, pacing, arms folded beneath her breasts, shoulders tight with a fear Colin knew was not for herself. He longed to tell her he understood, but he knew better than to . . . and that she knew already.

She turned back to him at last, eyes shadowed, and he knew he'd won.

"Aye," she sighed, hugging him tightly and pressing her face into his shoulder. "My heart doth rail against it, yet my mind—my cursed mind—concedeth. But, oh, my dearest dear, would I might forbid thee this!"

"I know," he whispered into the sweet-smelling silk of her hair.

Colin felt like an ant beneath an impending foot. Fleet Central's armored flank seemed to trap him, ready to crush him between itself and the blue-white sphere of Birhat, and he hoped Cohanna wasn't monitoring his bio read-outs.

He nudged his cutter to a stop. A green and yellow beacon marked a small hatch, but though his head ached from concentrating on his implants, he felt no response. He timed the beacon's sequence carefully.

"Dahak, I have a point-seven-five-second visual flash, green-amber-amber-green-amber, on a Class Seven hatch."

"Assuming Fleet conventions have not changed, Captain, that should indicate an active access point for small craft."

"I know." Colin swallowed, wishing his mouth weren't quite so dry. "Unfortunately, my implants can't pick up a thing."

Colin felt a sudden, almost audible click deep in his skull and blinked at a brief surge of vertigo as a not quite familiar tingle pulsed in his feed.

"I've got something. Still not clear, but—" The tingle suddenly turned sharp and familiar. "That's it!"

"Acknowledged, Captain," Dahak said. "The translation programs devised for *Omega Three* did not perfectly meet our requirements, but I believe my new modifications to your implant software should suffice. I caution you again, however, that additional, inherently unforeseeable difficulties may await."

"Understood." Colin edged closer, insinuating his thoughts cautiously into the hatch computers, and something answered. It was an ID challenge, but it tasted . . . odd.

He keyed his personal implant code with exquisite care, and for an instant just long enough to feel relieved disappointment, nothing happened. Then the hatch slid open, and he dried his palms on his uniform trousers.

"Well, people," he murmured, "door's open. Wish me luck."

"So do we all," Jiltanith told him softly. "Take care, my love."

The next half-hour was among the most nerve-wracking in Colin's life. His basic implant codes had sufficed to open the hatch, but that only roused the internal security systems.

There was a strangeness to their challenges, a dogged, mechanical persistence he'd never encountered from Dahak, but they were thorough. At every turn, it seemed, there were demands for identification on ever deeper security levels. He found himself responding with bridge officer codes he hadn't known he knew and realized that the computers were digging deep into his challenge-response conditioning. No wonder Druaga had felt confident Anu could never override his own final orders to Dahak! Colin had never guessed just how many security codes Dahak had buried in his own implants and subconscious.

But he reached the central transit shaft at last, and felt both relief and a different tension as he plugged into the traffic sub-net and requested transport to Fleet Central's Command Alpha. He half-expected yet another challenge, but the routing computers sent back a ready signal, and he stepped out into the shaft.

One thing about the terror of the unknown, he thought wryly as the shaft took him and hurled him inward: it neatly displaced such mundane fears as being mashed to paste by the transit shaft's gravitonics!

The shaft deposited him outside Command Alpha in a brightly-lit chamber big enough for an assault shuttle. The command deck hatch bore no unit ensign, as if Fleet Central was above such things. There was only the emblem of the Fourth Empire: the Imperium's starburst surmounted by an intricate diadem.

Colin looked about, natural senses and implants busy, and paled as he detected the security systems guarding this gleaming portal. Heavy grav guns in artfully hidden housings were backed up by the weapons Vlad had dubbed warp guns, and their targeting systems were centered on him. He tried to straighten his hunched shoulders and approached the huge hatch with a steady tread.

Almost to his surprise, it licked aside, and more silent hatches—twice as many as guarded *Dahak*'s Command One—opened as he walked down the brightly lit tunnel, fighting a sense of entrapment. And then, at last, he stepped out into the very heart and brain of Battle Fleet, and the last hatch closed behind him.

It wasn't as impressive as Command One, was his first thought—but only his first. It lacked the gorgeous, perfect holo projections of *Dahak*'s bridge, but the softly bright chamber was far, far larger. Dedicated hypercom consoles circled its walls, labeled with names he knew in flowing Imperial script, names which had been only half-believed-in legends in his implant education from Dahak. Systems and sectors, famous Fleet bases and proud formations—the names vanished into unreadable distance, and Quadrant Command nets extended out across the floor, the ranked couches and consoles too numerous to count, driving home the inconceivable vastness of the Empire.

It made him feel very, very insignificant.

Yet he was here . . . and those couches were empty. He had come eight hundred light-years to reach this enormous room, come from a planet teeming with humanity to this silence no voice had broken in forty-five millennia, and all this might and power of empire were but the work of Man.

He crossed the shining deck, bootheels ringing on jeweled mosaics, and ghosts hovered in the corners, watchful and measuring. He wondered what they made of him.

It took ten minutes to reach the raised dais at the center of the command deck, and he climbed its broad steps steadily, the weight of some foreordained fate seeming to press upon his shoulders, until he reached the top at last.

He lowered himself into the throne-like couch before the single console. It conformed smoothly to his body, and he forced himself to relax and draw a deep, slow breath before he reached out through his feed.

There was a quick flicker of response, and he felt a surge of hope—then grunted and flinched as he was hurled violently out of the net.

"Implant interface access denied," a voice said. It was a soft, musical contralto . . . utterly devoid of life or emotion.

Colin rubbed his forehead, trying to soothe the sudden ache deep inside his brain, and looked around the silent command deck for inspiration. He found none, and reached out again, more carefully.

"Implant interface access denied." The voice threw him out of the net even more violently. "Warning. Unauthorized access to this installation is punishable by imprisonment for not less than ninety-five standard years."

"Damn," Colin muttered. He was more than half-afraid of how Fleet Central might react to activating his fold-space com but saw no option. "Dahak?"

"Yes, Captain?"

"I'm getting an implant access denial warning."

"Voice or neural feed?"

"Voice. The damned thing won't even talk to my implants."

"Interesting," Dahak mused, "and illogical. You have been admitted to Command Alpha; logically, therefore, Fleet Central recognizes you as an officer of Battle Fleet. Assuming that to be true, access should not be denied."

"The same thought had occurred to me," Colin said a bit sarcastically.

"Have you attempted verbal communication, sir?"

"No."

"I would recommend that as the next logical step.".

"Thanks a lot," Colin muttered, then cleared his throat.

"Computer," he said, feeling just a bit foolish addressing the emptiness.

"Acknowledged," the emotionless voice said, and his heart leapt. By damn, maybe there was a way in yet!

"Why have I been denied implant access?"

"Improper implant identification," the voice replied.

"Improper in what way?"

"Data anomaly detected. Implant interface access denied."

"What anomaly?" he asked, far more patiently than he felt.

"Implant identification not in Fleet Central data base. Individual not recognized by core access programs. Implant interface access denied."

"Then why have you accepted voice communication?"

"Emergency subroutines have been activated for duration of the present crisis," the voice replied, and Colin paused, wondering what "emergency subroutines" were and why they allowed verbal access. Not that he meant to ask. The last thing he needed was to change this thing's mind!

"Computer," he said finally, "why was I admitted to Command Alpha?"

"Unknown. Security is not a function of Computer Central."

"I see." Colin thought more furiously than ever, then nodded to himself. "Computer, would Fleet Central Security admit an individual with invalid implant identification codes to Command Alpha?"

"Negative."

"Then if Security admitted me, the security data base must recognize my implants."

Silence answered his observation.

"Hm, not very talkative, are you?" Colin mused.

"Query not understood," the voice said.

"Never mind." He drew a deep breath. "I submit that a search might locate my implant codes in Fleet Central Security's data base. Would you concur?"

"The possibility exists."

"Then I instruct you," Colin said very carefully, "to search the security data base and validate my implant codes."

There was a brief pause, and he bit his lip.

"Verbal instructions require authorization overrides," the voice said finally. "Identify source of authority."

"My own, as Senior Fleet Captain Colin MacIntyre, commanding officer, ship-of-the-line *Dahak*, Hull Number One-Seven-Two-Two-Niner-One." Colin was amazed by how level his own voice sounded.

"Authorization provisionally accepted," the voice said. "Searching security data base."

There was another moment of silence, then the voice spoke again.

"Search completed. Implant identification codes located. Anomalies."

"Specify anomalies."

"Specification one: identification codes not current. Specification two: no Senior Fleet Captain Colinmacintyre listed in Fleet Central's data base. Specification Three: *Dahak*, Hull Number One-Seven-Two-Two-Niner-One, lost fifty one thousand six hundred nine point-eight-four-six standard years ago."

"My codes were current as of *Dahak*'s departure for the Noarl System on picket duty. I should be added to your data base as a descendant of *Dahak*'s core crew, promoted to fill a vacancy left by combat losses."

"That is not possible. *Dahak*, Hull Number One-Seven-Two-Two-Niner-One, no longer exists."

"Then what's my non-existent command doing here?" Colin demanded.

"Null-value query."

"Null-value?! *Dahak*'s in orbit with Fleet Central right now!"

"Datum invalid," Fleet Central observed. "No such unit is present."

Colin resisted an urge to smash a bioenhanced fist through the console.

"Then what *is* the object accompanying Fleet Central in orbit?" he snarled.

"Data anomaly," Fleet Central said emotionlessly.

"*What* data anomaly, damn it?!"

"Perimeter Security defensive programming prohibits approach within eight light-hours of Planet Birhat without valid identification codes. *Dahak*, Hull Number One-Seven-Two-Two-Niner-One, no longer exists. Therefore, no such unit can be present. Therefore, scanner reports represent data anomaly."

Colin punched a couch arm in sudden understanding. For some reason, this dummy—or its outer surveillance systems, anyway—had accepted *Dahak*'s ID and let him in. For some other reason, the central computers had *not* accepted that ID. Faced with the fact that no improperly identified unit could be here, this moron had labeled *Dahak* a "data anomaly" and decided to ignore him!

"Computer," he said finally, "assume—hypothetically—that a unit identified as *Dahak* was admitted to the Bia System by Perimeter Security. How might that situation arise?"

"Programming error," Fleet Central said calmly.

"Explain."

"No Confirmation of Loss report on *Dahak*, Hull Number One-Seven-Two-Two-Niner-One, was filed with Fleet Central. Loss of vessel is noted in Log Reference Rho-Upsilon-Beta-Seven-Six-One-Niner-Four, but failure to confirm loss report resulted in improper data storage." Fleet Central fell silent, satisfied with its own pronouncement, and Colin managed not to swear.

"Which means?"

"ID codes for *Dahak*, Hull Number One-Seven-Two-Two-Niner-One, were not purged from memory."

Colin closed his eyes. Dear God. This brainless wonder had let *Dahak* into the system because he'd identified himself and his codes were still in memory, but now that he was here, it didn't believe in him!

"How might that programming error be resolved?" he asked at last.

"Conflicting data must be removed from data base."

Colin drew another deep breath, aware of just how fragile this entire discussion was. If this computer could decide something *Dahak*'s size didn't exist, it could certainly do the same with the "data anomaly's" captain.

"Evaluate possibility that Log Reference Rho-Upsilon-Beta-Seven-Six-One-Niner-Four is an incorrect datum," he said flatly.

"Possibility exists. Probability impossible to assess," Fleet Central replied, and Colin allowed himself a slight feeling of relief. Very slight.

"In that case, I instruct you to purge it from memory," he said, and held his breath.

"Incorrect procedure," Fleet Central responded.

"Incorrect in what fashion?" Colin asked tautly.

"Full memory purge requires authorization from human command crew."

Colin cocked a mental ear. *Full* memory purge?

"Can data concerning my command be placed in inactive storage on my authority pending proper authorization?"

"Affirmative."

"Then I instruct you to do so with previously specified log entry."

"Proceeding. Data transferred to inactive storage."

Colin shuddered in explosive relaxation, then gave himself a mental shake. He might well be relaxing too soon.

"Computer, who am I?" he asked softly.

"You are Senior Fleet Captain Colinmacintyre, commanding officer HIMP *Dahak*, Hull Number One-Seven-Two-Two-Niner-One," the voice said emotionlessly.

"And what is the current location of my command?"

"HIMP *Dahak*, Hull Number One-Seven-Two-Two-Niner-One, is currently in Birhat orbit, ten thousand seventeen point-five kilometers distant from Fleet Central," the musical voice told him calmly, and Colin MacIntyre breathed a short, soft, fervent prayer of thanks before jubilation overwhelmed him.

"All *right!*" Colin's palms slammed down on the couch arms in triumph.

"What passeth, my Colin?" an urgent voice demanded through his fold-space link, and he realized he'd left it open.

"We're in, 'Tanni! Tell all hands—we're *in!*"

"Bravely done! Oh, bravely, my heart!"

"Thank you," he said softly, then straightened and returned to business. "Computer."

"Yes, Senior Fleet Captain?"

"What's your name, Computer?"

"This unit is officially designated Fleet Central Computer Central," the musical voice replied.

"Is that what your human personnel called you?"

"Negative, Senior Fleet Captain."

"Well, then, what *did* they call you?" Colin asked patiently.

"Fleet Central personnel refer to Comp Cent as 'Mother.' "

"Mother," Colin muttered, shaking his head in disbelief. Oh, well, if that was what Fleet Central was used to . . .

"All right, Mother, prepare to accept memory core download from *Dahak*."

"Ready," Mother said instantly.

"Dahak, initiate core download but do not purge."

"Initiating," Dahak replied calmly, and Colin felt an incredible surge of data. He caught only the fringes of it through his feed, but it was like standing on the brink of a river in flood. It was almost frightening, making him suddenly and humbly aware of the storage limitations of a human brain, yet for all its titanic proportions, it took barely ten minutes to complete.

"Download completed," Mother announced. "Data stored."

"Excellent! Now, give me a report on Fleet status."

"Fleet Central authorization code required," Mother told him, and Colin frowned as his enthusiasm was checked abruptly. He didn't *know* the authorization codes.

He pulled on the end of his nose, thinking hard. Only Mother "herself" could give him the codes, and the one absolute certainty was that she wouldn't. She accepted him as a senior fleet captain, which entitled him to a certain authority in areas pertaining to his own command but did *not* entitle him to access the material he desperately needed. Which was all the more maddening because he'd become used to instant information flow from Dahak.

Well, now, why did he have that information from Dahak? Because he was *Dahak*'s commander. And how had he become the CO? Because authority devolved on the senior crew member present and *Dahak* had chosen to regard a primitive from Earth as a member of his crew. Which suggested one possible approach.

To his surprise, he shrank from it. But why? He'd learned to accept his persona as *Dahak*'s captain and even as Governor of Earth, so why did this bother him?

Because, he thought, this brightly lit mausoleum whispered too eloquently of power and crushing responsibility, and it frightened him. Which was foolish in someone who'd already been made to accept responsibility for the very survival of his race, but nonetheless real.

He shook himself. The Empire was dead. All that could remain were other artifacts like Mother, and he needed any of those he could lay hands on. Even if that meant assuming command of a long-abandoned headquarters crewed only by ghosts and computers.

He only wished it didn't feel so . . . impious.

"Mother," he said finally.

"Yes, Senior Fleet Captain?" the computer replied, and he spoke very slowly and carefully.

"On this day, I, Senior Fleet Captain Colin MacIntyre, commanding officer—" he remembered the designation Fleet Central had tacked onto *Dahak* "—HIMP *Dahak*, do, as senior Battle Fleet officer present, pursuant to Fleet Regulation Five-Three-Three, Section Niner-One, Article Ten, assume command of Fl—"

"Invalid authorization," Mother interrupted.

"What?" Colin blinked in surprise.

"Invalid authorization," Mother repeated unhelpfully.

"What's invalid about it?" he demanded, unreasonably irritated at the delay now that he had steeled himself to it.

"Fleet Regulation Five-Three-Three does not pertain to transfer of command authority."

"It does so!" he shot back, but it was neither a question nor a command, and Mother remained silent. He gritted his teeth in frustration. "All right, if it doesn't pertain to transfer of command, what *does* it pertain to?"

"Regulation Five-Three-Three and subsections," Mother said precisely, "pertains to refuse disposal aboard Battle Fleet orbital bases."

"*What?!*"

Colin glared at the console. Of *course* Reg Five-Three-Three referred to transfer of command! It was how Dahak had mousetrapped him into this entire absurdity! He'd read it for himself when he—

Understanding struck. Yes, he'd read it—in a collection of regulations written fifty-one millennia ago.

Damn.

"Please download current Fleet Regulations and all relevant data to my command."

"Acknowledged. Download beginning. Download completed," Mother said almost without pause, and Colin reactivated his com.

"Dahak?"

"Yes, Captain?"

"I need some help here. What regulation replaced Five-Three-Three?"

"Fleet Regulation Five-Three-Three has been superseded by Fleet Regulation One-Niner-One-Five-Seven-Three-Niner, sir."

Colin winced. For seven thousand years, the Imperium had managed to hold Fleet regulations to under three thousand main entries; apparently the Empire had discovered the joys of bureaucracy.

No wonder Mother had so much memory.

"Thank you," he said, preparing to turn his attention back to Mother, but Dahak stopped him.

"A moment, Captain. Is it your intent to use this regulation to assume command of Fleet Central?"

"Of course it is," Colin said testily.

"I would advise against it."

"Why?"

"Because it will result in your immediate execution."

"What?" Colin asked faintly, certain he hadn't heard correctly.

"The attempt will result in your execution, sir. Regulation One-Niner-One-Five-Seven-Three-Niner does not apply to Fleet Central."

"Why not? It's a unit of Battle Fleet."

"That," Dahak said surprisingly, "is no longer true. Fleet Central *is* Battle Fleet; all units of Battle Fleet are subordinate to it. Battle Fleet command officers are not promoted to Fleet Central command duties."

"Then where the hell does its command staff come from?"

"They are *drawn* from Battle Fleet; they are not *promoted* from it. Fleet Central command officers are selected by the Emperor from all Battle Fleet flag officers and serve solely at his pleasure. Any attempt to assume command other than by direction of the Emperor is high treason and punishable by death."

Colin went white as he realized only Mother's interruption to correct an incorrect regulation number had saved his life.

He shuddered. What other tripwires were buried inside Fleet Central? Damn it, why couldn't Mother be smart enough to *tell* him things like this?!

Because, a small, calm voice told him, she hadn't been designed to be.

Which was all very well, but if he couldn't assume command, Mother wouldn't tell him the things he had to know, and if he tried to assume command, she'd kill him on the spot!

"Dahak," he said finally, "find me an answer. I've *got* to be able to exercise command authority here, or we might as well not have come."

"Fleet Central command authority lies in the exclusive grant of the Emperor, Captain. There is no other way to obtain it."

"Goddamn it, there *isn't* any emperor!" Colin half-shouted, battling incipient hysteria as he felt the situation crumbling in his hands. All he needed was for Dahak to catch Mother's lunatic literal-mindedness! "Look, can you invade the core programming? Redirect it?"

"The attempt would result in *Dahak*'s destruction," the computer told him. "In addition, it would fail. Fleet Central's core programming contains certain imperatives, of which this is one, which may not be reprogrammed even on the Emperor's authority."

"That's insane," Colin said flatly. "My God, a computer you can't reprogram running your entire military establishment?!"

"I did not say all reprogramming was impossible, nor do I understand why these particular portions cannot be altered. I am not privy to the content of the imperatives or the reasons for them. I base my statement on technical data included in the material downloaded to me."

"But how the hell *can* anything be unalterable? Couldn't you simply shut the thing down, dump its entire memory, and reprogram from scratch?"

"Negative, sir. The imperatives are not embodied in software. In Terran parlance, they are 'hard-wired' into the system. Removal would require actual destruction of a sizable portion of the central computer core."

"Crap." Colin pondered a moment longer, then widened the focus of his com link. "Vlad? 'Tanni? Have you been listening in on this?"

"Aye, Colin," Jiltanith replied.

"Any ideas?"

"I'faith, none do spring to mind," his wife said. "Vlad? Hast some insight which might aid our need?"

"I fear not," Chernikov said. "I am currently viewing the technical data Dahak refers to, Captain. So far as I can tell, his analysis is correct. To alter this would require a complete shutdown of Fleet Central. Even assuming 'Mother' would permit it, the required physical destruction would cripple Comp Cent and destroy the data we require. In my opinion, the system was designed precisely to preclude the very possibility you have suggested."

"Goddamn better mousetrap-builders!" Colin muttered, and Chernikov stifled a laugh. It made Colin feel obscurely better . . . but only a little.

"Dahak," he said finally, "can *you* access the data we need?"

"Negative."

"And you can't think of any way to sneak around these damned imperatives?"

"Negative."

"Then we're SOL, people," Colin sighed, slumping back in his couch, his sense of defeat even more bitter after the glow of victory he'd felt such a short time before. "Damn it. *Damn* it! We need an emperor to get into the goddamned system, and the last emperor died forty-five thousand years ago!"

"Captain," Dahak said after a moment, "I believe there might be a way."

"What?" Colin jerked back upright. "You just said there wasn't one!"

"Inaccurate. I said there was no way to 'sneak around these damned imperatives,'" the computer replied precisely. "There may, however, be a way in which you can use them, instead. I point out, however, that—"

"A way to *use* them? *How?!*"

"Under Case Omega, sir, you can—"

"I can take control of Fleet Central?" Colin broke in on him.

"Affirmative. Under the circumstances, you may be considered the highest ranking officer of Battle Fleet, and, in your capacity as Governor of Earth, the senior civil official, as well. As such, you may instruct Fleet Central to implement Case Omega, so assuming—"

"Great, Dahak!" Colin said. "I'll get back to you in a minute." Hot damn! He found himself actually rubbing his hands in glee.

"But, Captain—" Dahak said.

"In a minute, Dahak. In a minute." Elation boiled deep within him, a terrible, wonderful elation, compounded by the emotional whipsaw which had just ravaged him. "Mother," he said.

"Yes, Senior Fleet Captain Colinmacintyre?"

"Colin," Dahak said again, "there are—"

"Mother," Colin said firmly, rushing himself before whatever *Dahak* was trying to tell him could undercut his determination, "implement Case Omega."

There was a moment of profound silence, and then Hell itself erupted. Colin cringed back into his couch, hands rising to cover his eyes as Command Alpha exploded with light. A bolt of pain shot through his left arm as a bio-probe of pure force snipped away a scrap of tissue, but it was tiny compared to the fury boiling into his brain through his neural feed. A clumsy hand thrust deep inside him, flooding through his implants to wrench a gestalt of his very being from him. For one terrible moment he *was* Fleet Central, writhing in torment as his merely mortal brain and the ancient, bottomless computers of Battle Fleet merged, impressing their identities imperishably upon one another.

Colin screamed in the grip of an agony too vast to endure, and yet it was over before he could truly experience it. Its echoes shuddered away down his synapses, stuttering in the racing pound of his heart, and then they were gone.

"Case Omega executed," Mother said emotionlessly. "The Emperor is dead; long live the Emperor!"

CHAPTER THIRTEEN

"I attempted to warn you, Colin," Dahak said softly.

Colin shuddered. *Emperor?* That was . . . was . . . Words failed. He couldn't think of any that even came close.

"Colin?" Jiltanith's voice was gentler than Dahak's, and far more anxious.

"Yes, 'Tanni?" he managed in a strangled croak.

"How dost thou, my love? We did hear thee scream. Art thou—?"

"I-I'm fine, 'Tanni," he said, and, physically, it was true. He cleared his throat. "There were a few rough moments, but I'm okay now. Honest."

"May I not come to thee?" She sounded less anxious—but not a lot.

"I'd like that," he said, and he had never spoken more sincerely in his life. Then he shook his head. "Wait. Let me make sure it's safe."

He gathered himself and raised his voice.

"Mother?"

"Yes, Your Imperial Majesty?" the voice replied, and he flinched.

"Mother, I'd like one of my officers to join me. Her implant signatures won't be in your data base either. Can you have Security pass her through?"

"If Your Imperial Majesty so instructs," Mother responded.

"My Imperial Majesty certainly does," Colin said, and smiled crookedly. Maybe he wasn't going to crack up entirely, after all.

"Query: please identify the officer to be admitted."

"Uh? Oh. Fleet Captain Jiltanith, *Dahak*'s executive officer. My wife."

"Acknowledged."

"'Tanni?" he returned his attention to his com. "Come ahead."

"I come, my love," she said, and he stretched out in his couch, knowing she would soon be there. His shudders drained outward along his limbs until the final echoes tingled in his fingers and his breathing slowed.

"Mother."

"Yes, Your Imperial Majesty?"

"What was all that? What happened when you executed Case Omega, I mean?"

"Emergency subroutines were terminated, ending Fleet Central's caretaker role upon Your Imperial Majesty's assumption of the throne."

"I figured that part out. I want a specific explanation of what *you* did."

"Fleet Central performed its function as guardian of the succession, Your Imperial Majesty. As senior Fleet officer and civil official listed in Fleet Central's data base, Your Imperial Majesty, as per the Great Charter, became the proper successor upon the demise of the previous dynasty. However, Your Imperial Majesty was unknown to Fleet Central prior to Your Imperial Majesty's accession. It was therefore necessary for Fleet Central to obtain gene samples for verification of the heirs of Your Imperial Majesty's body and to evaluate Your Imperial Majesty's gestalt and implant it upon Fleet Central's primary data cortex."

Colin frowned. There were too many things here he didn't yet understand, but there were were a few others to get straight right now.

"Mother, can't we do something about the titles?"

"Query not understood, Your Imperial Majesty."

"I mean— Look, just what titles have I saddled myself with?

"Your principle title is 'His Imperial Majesty Colinmacintyre the First, Grand Duke of Birhat, Prince of Bia, Warlord and Prince Protector of the Realm, Defender of the Five Thousand Suns, Champion of Humanity, and, by the Maker's Grace, Emperor of Mankind.' Secondary titles are: 'Prince of Aalat,' 'Prince of Achon,' 'Prince of Anhur,' 'Prince of Apnar,' 'Prince of Ardat,' 'Prince of Aslah,' 'Prince of Avan,' 'Prince of Bachan,' 'Prince of Badarchin,' 'Prin—'"

"Stop," Colin commanded. Jesus! "Uh, just how many titles are there?"

"Excluding those already specified," Mother replied, "four thousand eight hundred and twenty-one."

"Gaaa." Not bad for the product of a good, republican upbringing, he thought. "Let's get one thing straight, Mother. My name is Colin MacIntyre—two words—not 'Colinmacintyre.' Can you remember that in future?"

"You are listed in Fleet and Imperial records as His Imperial Majesty Colinmacintyre the First, Grand Duke of Birhat, Prince of Bia, War—"

"I understand all that," Colin interrupted. "The point is, I don't want to go around with everyone 'Imperial Majesty'-ing me, and I prefer to be called 'Colin,' not 'Colinmacintyre.' Can't we do something to meet my wishes?"

"As Your Imperial Majesty commands. You have not yet designated your choice of reign name. Until such time as you have done so, you will be known as Colinmacintyre the First; thereafter, only your dynasty will bear your complete pre-accession name. Is that satisfactory?"

"It's a start," Colin muttered, refusing to contemplate the thought of his "dynasty." He tugged on his nose, then stopped himself. At the rate surprises were coming at him lately, he was going to start looking like Pinocchio. "All right. My 'reign name' will be 'Colin.' Please log it."

"Logged," Mother replied.

"Now, about those titles. Surely past emperors didn't get called 'Your Imperial Majesty' every time they turned around, did they?"

"Acceptable alternatives are 'Your Majesty,' 'Majesty,' 'Highest,' and 'Sire.' Nobles of the rank of Planetary Duke are permitted 'My Lord.' Flag officers and Companions of The Golden Nova are permitted 'Warlord.'"

"Crap. Uh, I don't suppose I could get you to forget titles entirely?"

"Negative, Your Imperial Majesty. Protocol imperatives must be observed."

"That's what *you* think," Colin muttered. "Just wait till I get my hands on your 'protocol' programming!" He shook his head. "All right, if I'm stuck with it, I'm stuck, but from now on you'll use only 'Sire' when addressing me."

"Acknowledged."

"Good! Now—" He broke off as a soft chime sounded.

"Your pardon, Sire. Empress Jiltanith has arrived. Shall I admit her?"

"You certainly shall!" Colin leapt down the steps from the dais and reached the innermost hatch by the time it opened. Jiltanith gasped as his embrace threatened to pop her bioenhanced ribs, and her cheek was wet where it pressed against his.

"Am I ever glad to see *you*!" he whispered against the side of her neck.

"And I thee." She turned her head to kiss his ear. "Greatly did I fear for thee, yet such timorousness ill beseemed one who knoweth thee so well. Hast more lives than any cat, my sweet, yet 'twould please me the better if thou wouldst spend them less freely!"

"Goddamn right," he said fervently, drawing back to kiss her mouth. "Next time, I listen to you, by God!"

"So thou sayst . . . now," she laughed, tugging on his prominent ears with both hands.

A sudden thought woke a mischievous smile as he tucked an arm around her waist to escort her back to the dais, and he raised his voice.

"Mother, say hello to my wife."

"Hello, Your Imperial Majesty," Mother said obediently, and Jiltanith stopped dead.

"What foolishness is this?" she demanded.

"Get used to it, honey," Colin said, squeezing her again. "For whatever it's worth, your shiftless husband's brought home the bacon this time." He grinned wryly. "In spades!"

Several hours later, a far less chipper Colin groaned and scrubbed his face with his hands. Jiltanith and he sat side-by-side on Fleet Central's command couch while Mother reported Battle Fleet's status, running down every fleet and sub-unit in numerical order. So far, she'd provided reports on just under two thousand fleets, task forces, and battle squadrons.

And, so far, nothing she'd had to report was good.

"Hold report, Mother," he said, breaking into the computer's flow.

"Holding, Sire," Mother agreed, and Colin laughed hollowly. "Emperor"—that was a laugh. And "Warlord" was even funnier. He was a commander without a fleet! Or, more precisely, with a fleet that was useless to him.

The Empire had been too busy dying for an orderly shutdown. Herdan XXIV had lived long enough to activate Fleet Central's emergency subroutines, placing Mother on powered-down standby to guard Birhat until relief might someday arrive, but most of Battle Fleet hadn't been even that lucky. A few score supralight vessels had simply disappeared from Fleet

Central's records, which probably indicated that their crews had elected to flee in an effort to outrun the bio-weapon, but most of Battle Fleet's units had been contaminated in their efforts to save civilians in the weapon's path. The result had been both predictable and grisly, and, unlike Dahak, their computers hadn't been smart enough to do anything about it when they found themselves without crews. Except for a handful whose core taps had been active when their last crewmen died, they'd simply returned to the nearest Fleet base and remained on station until their fusion plants exhausted their on-board mass, then drifted without life or power.

Unfortunately, none seemed to have returned to Bia itself—which made sense, given that Birhat, the first victim of the bio-weapon, had been quarantined at the very start of the Empire's death agony. Less than a dozen active units had responded to Mother's all-ships hypercom rally signal, and the nearest was upwards of eight hundred light-years away; Earth would be dead long before Colin could return if he waited for them them to reach Birhat.

There was a bitter irony in the fact that Birhat's defenses remained almost fully operational. Bia's mammoth shield, backed by Perimeter Security's prodigious firepower, could have held anything *anyone* could throw at them. But everyone who needed defending was on Earth.

"Mother," he said finally, "let's try something different. Instead of reporting in sequence, list all mobile forces in order of proximity to Birhat."

"Acknowledged. Listing Bia System deployments. Birhat Near-Orbit Watch Squadron: twelve heavy cruisers. Bia Deep-System Patrol Squadron: ten heavy cruisers, forty-one destroyers, nine frigates, sixty-two corvettes. Imperial Guard Flotilla: fifty-two *Asgerd*-class planetoids, sixteen—"

"*What?* Stop!" Colin shouted.

"Acknowledged," Mother said calmly.

"What the fuck is the Imperial Guard Flotilla?!"

"Imperial Guard Flotilla," Mother replied. "The Warlord's personal command. Strength: fifty-two *Asgerd*-class planetoids and attached parasites, sixteen *Trosan*-class planetoids and attached parasites, and ten *Vespa*-class assault planetoids and attached planetary assault craft. Current location: parking orbit thirty-eight light-minutes from Bia. Status: inactive."

"Jesus H. Christ!" Colin stared at Jiltanith. Her face was as shocked as his own, and they turned as one to glare accusingly at the console.

"Why," Colin asked in a dangerously calm voice, "didn't you mention them earlier?"

"Sire, you had not asked about them," Mother said.

"I certainly did! I asked for a complete listing of Battle Fleet units!" Mother was silent, and he growled a curse at all computers which could not recognize the need to respond without specific cues. "Didn't I?" he snarled.

"You did, Sire."

"Then why didn't you report them?"

"I did, Sire."

"But you didn't report this Imperial Guard Flotilla—" Flotilla! Jesus, it was a *fleet!* "—did you? Why not?"

"Sire, the Imperial Guard is not part of Battle Fleet. The Imperial Guard is raised and manned solely from the Emperor's personal demesne."

Colin blinked. Personal demesne? An Emperor whose personal fiefdoms could raise *that* kind of firepower? The thought sent a shiver down his spine. He sagged back, trembling, and a warm arm crept about him and tightened.

"All right." He shook his head and inhaled deeply, drawing strength from Jiltanith's presence. "Why is the Guard Flotilla inactive?"

"Power exhaustion and uncontrolled shutdown, Sire."

"Assess probability of successful reactivation."

"One hundred percent," Mother said emotionlessly, and a jolt of excitement crashed through him. But slowly, he told himself. Slowly.

"Assume resources of one hundred seven thousand Battle Fleet personnel, one *Utu*-class planetoid, and current active and inactive automated support available in the Bia System," he said carefully, "and compute probable time required to reactivate the Imperial Guard Flotilla to full combat readiness."

"Impossible to reactivate to full combat readiness," Mother replied. "Specified personnel inadequate for crews."

"Then compute time to reactivate to *limited* combat readiness."

"Computing, Sire," Mother responded, and fell silent for a disturbingly long period. Almost a full minute passed before she spoke again. "Computation complete. Probable time required: four-point-three-nine months. Margin of error twenty-point-seven percent owing to large numbers of imponderables."

Colin closed his eyes and felt Jiltanith tremble against him. Four months— five-and-a-half outside. It would be close, but they could do it. By all that was holy, they could *do* it!

"There," Tamman said quietly as a green circle bloomed on Dahak's visual display, ringing a tiny, gleaming dot. The dot grew as *Dahak* approached, and additional dots appeared, spreading out in a loose necklace of worldlets.

"I see them," Colin replied, still luxuriating in his return to Command One and a world he understood. "Big bastards, aren't they, Dahak?"

"I compute that the largest out-mass *Dahak* by over twenty-five percent. I am not prepared to speculate upon the legitimacy of their parentage."

Colin chuckled. Dahak had been much more willing to engage in informality since his return from Fleet Central, as if he recognized Colin's shock at suddenly finding himself an emperor. Or perhaps the computer was simply glad to have him back. Dahak was a worrier where friends were concerned.

He watched the planetoids grow. If Vlad was right about the Empire's technology, those ships would be monsters in action—and monsters were exactly what they needed.

"Captain, look here." Ellen Gregory, Sarah Meir's Assistant Astrogator, placed a sighting circle of her own on the display, picking out a single starship. "What do you make of that, sir?"

Colin looked, then looked again. The stupendous sphere floating in space was only roughly similar to the only Imperial planetoid he'd ever seen, but one thing was utterly familiar. A vast, three-headed dragon spread its wings across the gleaming hull.

"Well looky there," he murmured. "Dahak, what d'*you* make of that?"

According to the data Fleet Central downloaded to my data base," Dahak replied, "that is His Imperial Majesty's Planetoid *Dahak*, Hull Number Seven-Three-Six-Four-Four-Eight-Niner-Two-Five."

"Another *Dahak*?"

"It is a proud name in Battle Fleet." Dahak sounded a bit miffed. "Rather like the many ships named *Enterprise* in your own United States Navy. According to the data, this is the twenty-third ship to bear the name."

"It is, huh? Well, which one are you?"

"This unit is the eleventh of the name."

"I see. Well, in order to avoid confusion, we'll just refer to this young whippersnapper as *Dahak Two*, if that's all right with you, Dahak."

"Noted," Dahak said calmly, and continued to close on the silently waiting, millennia-dead hulls they intended to resurrect.

"By the Maker, I've *got* it!"

Colin jumped half out of his couch as Cohanna's holo image materialized on Command One. The biosciences officer looked terrible, her hair awry and her uniform wrinkled, but her eyes were bright with triumph.

"Try penicillin," he advised sourly, and she looked blank, then grinned.

"Sorry, sir. I meant I've figured out what happened on Birhat—why it's got that incredible bio-system. I found it in Mother's data base."

"Oh?" Colin sat straighter, his eyes more intent. "Give!"

"It's simple, really. The zoos—the Imperial Family's zoos."

"Zoos?" It was Colin's turn to look blank.

"Yes. You see, the Imperial Family had an immense zoological garden. Over thirty different planets' flora and fauna in sealed, self-sufficient planetary habitats. Apparently, they lasted out the plague. I'd guess the automated systems responsible for restraining plant growth failed first in one of them, and the thing cracked. Once it did, its inhabitants could get out, and the same vegetation attacked the exterior of other surviving habitats. Over the years, still more oxy-nitrogen habitats were opened up and started spreading to reclaim the planet. That's why we've got such a screwy damned ecology. We're looking at the survivors of a dozen *different* planetary bio-spheres after forty-five thousand years of natural selection!"

"Well I'll be damned," Colin mused. "Good work, Cohanna. I'm impressed you could keep concentrating on that kind of problem at a time like this."

"Time like this?"

"While we're making our final approach to the Imperial Guard," Colin said, raising his eyebrows, and Cohanna wrinkled her nose.

"What's an Imperial Guard?"

Vlad Chernikov shuddered as he and Baltan floated down the lifeless, lightless transit shaft. This, he thought, is what *Dahak* would have become if Anu had succeeded all those years ago.

It was depressing in more ways than one. Actually seeing this desolation gnawed away at the confidence that anything could be done about it, and even if he succeeded in rejecting the counsel of despair, he could see it would be a horrific task. Dead power rooms, exhausted fuel mass, control rooms and circuit runs which had never been properly stasissed when the ship died. There was even meteor damage, for the collision shields had died with everything else. One of the planetoids might well be beyond repair, judging by the huge hole punched into its south pole.

Still, he reminded himself, everyone had his or her own problems. Caitrin O'Rourke was practically in tears over the hydroponic farms, and Geran was furious to find so much perfectly good equipment left out of stasis. But Tamman was probably the most afflicted of all, for the magazines had been left without stasis, as well, and the containment fields on every anti-matter weapon had failed. At least the warhead fail-safes had worked as designed and rotated them into hyper as the fields went down, but huge chunks of magazine bulkheads had gone with them. Of course, if they *hadn't* worked . . .

He shuddered again, concentrating on the grav sled he and Baltan rode. It was far slower than an operable transit shaft, but they dared not use even its full speed. They were no transit computer to whip around unexpected bends in the system!

He craned his neck, reading the lettering above a hatch. Gamma-One-One-Nine-One-One. According to Dahak's downloaded schematics, they were getting close to Engineering.

So they were. He tapped Baltan's shoulder and pointed, and the commander nodded inside the force bubble of his helmet. The sled angled for the side of the shaft and nudged against the hatch—which, of course, stayed firmly shut.

Chernikov smothered a curse, then grinned as he recalled Colin's account of his "coronation." The Captain—Emperor!—had exhausted the entire crew's allocation of profanity for at least a month, by Chernikov's estimate. He chuckled at the thought and climbed off the sled, dragging a cable from its power plant behind him and muttering Slavic maledictions. No power meant no artificial gravity, which—unfortunately—did not mean *no* gravity. A planetoid generated an impressive grav field all its own, and turned bulkheads into decks and decks into bulkheads when the power failed.

He found the emergency power receptacle and plugged in, and the hatch slid open. He waved, and Baltan ghosted the sled inside, angling its powerful lamps to pick out the emergency lighting system.

Chernikov did some more cable-dragging and, after propitiating Murphy with a few curses, brought it alive. Light bathed Central Engineering, and the two engineers began to explore.

The long-dead core tap drew them like a magnet, and Chernikov felt a tingle of awe as his eyes and implants traced circuit runs and control systems. This thing was at least five times as powerful as *Dahak*'s, and he wouldn't have believed it could be without seeing it. But what in the galaxy could they have *needed* that much power for? Even allowing for the more powerful energy armament and shield, there had to be some other reason—

His thoughts died as his implants followed a massive power shunt which shouldn't have been there. He clambered over a control panel which had become the floor, slightly vertiginous as he tried to orient himself, then gasped.

"Baltan! Look at this!"

"I know," his assistant said softly, approaching from the far side. "I've been following the control runs."

"Can you *believe* this?"

"Does it matter? And it would certainly explain all the power demand."

"True." Chernikov moved a few more yards, examining his find carefully, then shook his head. "I must tell the Captain about this."

He keyed his com implant, and Colin answered a moment later, sounding a bit harassed—not surprisingly, considering that every other search party must be finding marvels of its own to report.

"Captain, I am in *Mairsuk*'s Central Engineering, and you would not believe what I am looking at."

"Try me," Colin said wearily. "I'm learning to believe nineteen impossible things before breakfast every day."

"Very well, here is number twenty. This ship has both Enchanach *and* hyper capability."

There was a pregnant pause.

"What," Colin finally asked very carefully, "did you say?"

"I said, sir, that we have here both an Enchanach and a hyper drive, engineered down to a size that fits both into a single hull. I am not yet positive, but I would judge that the combined mass of both units is less than that of *Dahak*'s Enchanach Drive, alone."

"Great day in the morning," Colin muttered. Then, "All right. Take a good look, then get back over here. We're having an all-departments meeting in four hours to discuss plans for reactivation."

"Understood," Chernikov said, and broke the connection. He and Baltan exchanged eloquent shrugs and bent back to the study of their prize.

"... can't be specific until we've got the computers back up and run a complete inventory," Geran said, "but about ten percent of all spares required controlled condition storage. Without that—" He shrugged.

Most of Colin's department heads were present in the flesh, but a sizable force from the recon group was prowling around other installations, and Hector MacMahan and Ninhursag attended via holo image from the battleship *Osir*'s command deck. Now all eyes, physical and holographic alike, swiveled to Colin.

"All right." He spoke quietly, leaning his forearms on the crystalline tabletop to return their gazes. "Bottom line. Mother's time estimate is based on sixteen-hour shifts for every man and woman after we put at least one automated repair yard back on line. According to the reports from Hector's people, we can probably do that, but I expect to find ourselves pushing closer to twenty-hour shifts by the time we're done. We *could* increase the odds and decrease the workload by concentrating on a dozen or so units. I'm sure that's going to occur to a lot of people in the next few weeks. However—" his eyes circled their faces "—we aren't going to do it that way. We need as many of these ships as we can get, and, ladies and gentlemen, I mean to have *every single one of them.*"

There was a sound like a soft gasp, and he smiled grimly.

"God only knows how hard they're working back on Earth, but *we're* about to make up for our nice vacation on the trip out. Every one of them, people. No exceptions. We will leave this system no later than five months from today, and the entire Imperial Guard Flotilla will go with us when we do."

"But, sir," Chernikov said, "we may ask for too much and lose it all. I do not fear hard work, but we have only a finite supply of personnel. A *very* finite supply."

"I understand, Vlad, but the decision is not negotiable. We've got highly motivated, highly capable people aboard this ship. I feel certain they'll understand and give of their very best. If not, however, tell them this.

"I'll be working my ass off right beside them, but that doesn't mean I won't be keeping tabs on what *they're* doing. And, people, if I catch anyone shirking, I'm going to be the worst nightmare he ever had."

His smile was grim, but even its micrometric amusement looked out of place on his rock-hard face.

"Tell them they can *depend* on that," he finished very, very softly.

BOOK TWO

CHAPTER FOURTEEN

Assistant Servant of Thunders Brashieel of the Nest of Aku'Ultan folded all four legs under him on his duty pad as he bent his long-snouted head, considering his panel, and slid both hands into the control gloves. Eight fingers and four thumbs twitched, activating each test circuit in turn, and he noted the results cheerfully. He had not had a major malfunction in three twelves of twelve watches.

Equipment tests completed, he checked *Vindicator*'s position. It was purely automatic, for there could be no change. Once a vessel entered hyper space it remained there, impotent but inviolate, until it reached the pre-selected coordinates and emerged into normal space once more.

Brashieel did not understand those mysteries particularly well, for he was no lord—not even of thunders, much less of star-faring—but because Small Lord of Order Hantorg was a good lord, he had made certain *Vindicator*'s nestlings all knew whither they were bound. Another yellow sun, this one with nine planets. Once it had boasted ten, but that had been before the visit of Great Lord Vaskeel's fleet untold high twelves of years before. Now it was time to return, and *Vindicator* and his brothers would sweep through it like the Breath of Tarhish, trampling the nest-killers under hooves of flame.

It was well. The Protectors of the Nest would feed their foes to Tarhish's Fire, and the Nest would be safe forever.

"Outer perimeter tracking confirms hyper wakes approaching from galactic east," Sir Frederick Amesbury said.

Gerald Hatcher nodded without even looking up. His neural feed hummed with readiness reports, and his eyes were unfocused.

"Got an emergence locus and ETA, Frederick?"

"It's bloody rough, but Plotting's calling it fifty light-minutes and forty-five degrees above the ecliptic. Judging from the wake strength, the buggers should be arriving in about twelve hours. Tracking promises to firm that up in the next two hours."

"Fine." Hatcher acknowledged the last report and blinked back into focus, wishing yet again that *Dahak* had returned. If Colin MacIntyre had been gone this long, it meant he hadn't found aid at Sheskar and must have decided he had no choice but to hope Earth could hold without him while he sought it elsewhere. And that he might not be back for another full year.

He activated his com panel, and Horus's taut face appeared instantly.

"Governor," the general reported, knowing full well that Horus already knew what he was about to say and that he was speaking for the record, "I have to report that I have placed our forces on Red Two. Hyper wakes presumed to be hostile have been detected. ETA is approximately—" he checked the time through his neural feed "—seventeen-thirty hours, Zulu. System defense forces are now on full alert. Civil defense procedures have been initiated. All PDC and ODC commanders are in the net. Interceptor squadrons are at two-hour readiness. Planetary shield generators and planetary core tap are at stand-by readiness. Battle Squadrons One and Four are within thirty minutes of projected n-space emergence; Squadrons Two and Six should rendezvous with them by oh-seven-hundred Zulu. Squadrons Three, Five, Seven, Eight, Nine, and Ten, with escorts, are being held in-system as per Plan Able-One.

"Have you any instructions at this time, Governor?"

"Negative, General Hatcher. Please keep me informed."

"I will, sir."

"Good luck, Gerald," Horus said softly, his tone much less formal.

"Thanks, Horus. We'll try to make a little luck of our own."

The screen blanked, and Gerald Hatcher turned back to his console.

Assistant Servant Brashieel checked his chronometer. Barely four day twelfths until emergence, and tension was high in *Vindicator*, for this was the Demon Sector. It was not often the Protectors of the Nest encountered a foe with an advance technical base—that was why they came, to crush the nest-killers before they armed themselves—but five of the last twelve Great Visits to this sector had been savaged. They had triumphed, but at great cost, and the last two had been the most terrible of all. Perhaps, Brashieel thought, that was the reason Great Lord Tharno's Great Visit had been delayed: to amass the strength the Nest required for certain success.

That alone was cause enough for concern, yet the disquiet among his nestmates had grown far worse since the first nest-killer scanner stations had been detected. More than one scout ship had been lured to his death by the fiendish stations, and the explosions which slew them meant their surviving consorts had learned absolutely nothing about the technology which built those stations . . . except that it was advanced, indeed.

But this star system would offer no threat. Small Lord Hantorg had revealed the latest data scan shortly after *Vindicator* entered hyper for this last jump to the target. It was barely three twelves of years old, and though electronic and neutrino emissions had been detected (which was bad enough), there had been none of the more advanced signals from the scanner arrays. Clearly the Protectors must see to this threat, yet these nest-killers would have only the lesser thunder, not the greater, and they would be crushed. Nothing could have changed enough in so short a time to alter that outcome.

Captain Adrienne Robbins sat in her command couch aboard the sublight battleship *Nergal*. Admiral Isaiah Hawter, the senior member of the Solarian Defense Force actually in space, rode *Nergal*'s bridge with her, but he might as well have been on another planet. His attention was buried in his own console as he and his staff controlled Task Force One.

Captain Robbins had been a sub-driver, and she'd never expected to command any flagship (subs still operated solo, after all), far less one leading the defense of her world against homicidal aliens, but she was ready. She felt the tension simmering within her and adjusted her adrenalin levels, pacing her energy. The bastards would be coming out of hyper in less than two hours, and tracking had them pegged to a fare-thee-well. TF One knew where to find them; now all they had to do was wreck as many as they could before the buggers micro-jumped back out on them.

And, she reminded herself, pray that these Achuultani hadn't upgraded their technology too terribly in the last sixty thousand years or so.

She did pray, but she also remembered her mother's favorite aphorism: God helps those who help themselves.

"Task Force in position for Charlie-Three."

"Thank you," Hatcher said absently.

The images of Marshals Tsien and Chernikov shared his com screen with Generals Amesbury, Singhman, Tama, and Ki. Chiang Chien-su had a screen all to himself as he waited tensely in his civil defense HQ, and Hatcher could see the control room of PDC Huan Ti behind Tsien. The marshal had made it his HQ for the Eastern Hemisphere Defense Command, and a brief flicker of shared memory flashed between them as their eyes met. Tama and Ki sat in their Fighter Command operations rooms, and Singhman was aboard ODC Seven, serving as Hawter's second-in-command as well as commanding the orbital fortifications.

"Gentlemen, they'll emerge in thirty minutes, well inside our own heavy hyper missile range of a planetary target, so I want the shield brought to maximum power. Keep this com link open." Heads nodded. "Very well, Marshal Chernikov; activate core tap."

Lieutenant Andrew Samson winced as the backlash echoed in his missile targeting systems. ODC Fifteen, known to her crew as the Iron Bitch, floated in her geosynchronous orbit above Tierra del Fuego. Which, Samson now discovered, was entirely too close to Antarctica for his peace of mind.

He adjusted his systems, edging away from the core tap's hyper bands, and sighed with relief. Maybe it wouldn't be so bad, after all, but that was one hell of a jump from the test runs! *God help us all if they lose it*, he prayed—and not just because of what it'll do to the Bitch's power curves.

Howling wind and flying ice spicules flayed a night-struck land. The kiss of that wind was death, its frigid embrace lethal. There was no life here. There was only the cold, the keening dirge of the wind, and the ice.

But the frigid night was peeled back in an instant of fiery annunciation. A raging column of energy, pent by invisible chains, impaled the heavens, glittering and terrible as it pierced the low-bellied clouds.

The beacon of war had been lit, and its fury flowed into the mighty fold-space power transmitters. Man returned Prometheus's gift to the heavens, and Earth's Orbital Defense Command drank deep at Vassily Chernikov's fountain.

"Here they come, people," Captain Robbins said softly. "Stand by missile crews. Energy weapons to full power."

Acknowledgments flowed back through her neural feed, and she hunkered deeper into her couch without realizing she had.

Assistant Servant of Thunders Brashieel gave his instruments one last check, though there could be no danger here. They would pause only to select a proper asteroid, then be on their way, for there were many worlds of nest-killers to destroy. But he was a Protector. It was a point of pride to be prepared for anything.

My God, the size *of those things! They've got to be twenty kilometers long!*

The observation flared over the surface of Captain Robbins' brain, but beneath that surface trained reactions and responses flowed smoothly.

"Tactical, missiles on my command. Take target designation from the Flag." She paused a fraction of a second, letting the computers digest the latest updates from the admiral's staff while more monster starships emerged from hyper. Ship after cylindrical ship. Dozens of them. Scores. And still they came, popping into reality like demon djinn from a flask of curses.

"Fire!" she snapped.

Brashieel gaped at his read-outs. *Those ships could not exist!*

But his panic eased—a bit—as he digested more data. There were but four twelves of them, and they were tiny things. Bigger than anyone had expected, with no right to be here, but no threat to *Vindicator* and his brothers.

He did not have time to note the full peculiarity of the energy readings before the enemy fired.

Adrienne Robbins winced as the universe blew apart. She'd fired gravitonic and anti-matter warheads before (the Fleet had reduced significantly the number of Sol's asteroids during firing practices) but never at a live target. The hyper missiles flicked up into hyper space, then back down, and their timing was impeccable. The Achuultani shields had not yet stabilized when the first mighty salvo arrived.

Brashieel cried out in shock, shaming himself before his nestmates, but he was not alone. What *were* those things?

A twelve of ships vanished in a heartbeat, and then another. His scanners told the tale, but he could not believe them. Those weapons were coming through hyper space! From such tiny vessels? Incredible!

He felt his folded legs tremble as those insignificant pygmies ravaged the lead squadrons. Ships died, blown apart in fireballs vast beyond belief, and others tumbled away, glowing, half-molten, more than half-destroyed by single hits. Such power! And those strange warheads—the ones which did not explode, but tore a ship apart in new and horrible ways. What were *they*?

But he was a Protector, and *Vindicator* had a reputation to uphold. His hands were rock-steady in the control gloves, arming his own weapons, and Small Lord Hantorg's furious voice pounded in his ears.

"Open fire!" the Small Lord snarled.

Adrienne Robbins made herself throttle her exultation. Sixty of the buggers in the opening salvo! They knew they'd been nudged, by God! But those had been the easy kills, the sitting ducks with unstable shields. Now her sensors felt those shields slamming into stability, and the first return fire spat towards TF One.

She opened her cross feed to the electronic warfare types as decoys went out and jammers woke. She would have felt better with some idea of Achuultani capabilities before the engagement, but that was what this was all about. Task Force One was fighting for the data Earth needed to plan her own defense, and she studied the enemy shields. Pretty tough, but they damned well *should* be with the power reserves those monsters must have. Technically, they weren't as good as *Nergal*'s; only the difference in power levels made them stronger. Which was all very well, but didn't change facts.

The first Achuultani missiles slashed in, and Captain Robbins got another surprise. They were normal-space weapons, but they were *fast* little mothers. Seventy, eighty percent light-speed, and that was better than anything of *Nergal*'s could do in n-space. They were going to give missile defense fits.

Assistant Servant of Thunders Brashieel snarled as his first salvo smote the nest-killers. Half a twelve of missiles burst through all their defenses, ignoring their infernally effective decoys, and the Furnace roared. Matter and anti-matter merged, gouging at the nest-killers' shield, and Brashieel's inner eyelids narrowed at its incredible resistance. But his thunder was too much for it. It crumbled, and Tarhish's Breath swept the ship into death.

❖   ❖   ❖

Captain Robbins cursed as *Bolivia* burned. Those fucking warheads were incredible! Their emission signatures said they were anti-matter, and great, big, *nasty* ones. At least as big as anything Earth's defenders had.

Bolivia was the first to go, but *Canada* followed, then *Shirhan* and *Poland*. Please, Jesus, she prayed. Slow them down!

But the huge Achuultani ships were still dying faster than TF One. Which was only because they were getting in each other's way, perhaps, but true nonetheless, and Adrienne Robbins felt a fierce exultation as yet another fell to *Nergal*'s missiles.

"Close the range," Admiral Hawter said grimly, and Adrienne acknowledged. *Nergal* drove into the teeth of the Achuultani fire.

"Stand by energy weapons," she said coldly.

They were not fleeing. Whatever else these nest-killers might be, they had courage. More of them perished, blazing like splinters of resinous *mowap* wood, but the others advanced. And their defenses were improving. The efficiency of their jammers had gone up thirty percent while he watched.

Captain Robbins smiled thinly. Her EW crews were getting good, hard data on the Achuultani targeting systems, and they knew what to do with it. Another three ships were gone, but the others were really knocking down the incoming missiles now.

Whatever happened, that data would be priceless to the rest of the Fleet and to Earth herself. Not that Adrienne had any intention of dying out here, but it was nice to know.

Aha! Energy range.

Brashieel gaped as those preposterous warships opened a heavy energy fire. Tiny things like that *couldn't* pack in batteries that heavy!

But they did, and quarter-twelves of them synchronized their fire to the microsecond, slashing at their Aku'Ultan victims. Overload signals snarled, and frantic engineers threw more and more power to their shields, but there simply was not enough. Not to stop missiles and beams alike.

He watched in horror as *Avenger*'s forward quadrant shields went down. A single nest-killer beam pierced the chink in his armor and ripped his forward twelfth apart. Hard as it was for any Protector to admit another race could match the Aku'Ultan, Brashieel knew the chilling truth. He had never heard of weapons which could do what that one was doing.

He groaned as *Avenger*'s hull split like a rotten *istham*, and then another impossible, Tarhish-spawned warhead crumpled the wreckage into a mangled ball. *Avenger*'s power plants let go, and *Vindicator*'s brother was no more.

But Brashieel bared his teeth as his display changed. Now the nest-killers would learn, for his hyper launchers had been given time to charge at last!

"Hyper missiles!" Tactical shouted, and Adrienne threw *Nergal* into evasive action. *Ireland* and *Izhmit* were less fortunate. *Ireland*'s shield stopped the first three; the next four—or five, or possibly six—got through. *Izhmit* went with the first shot. How the hell had they popped her shield that way?

It didn't matter. TF One was losing too many ships, but the Achuultani were dying at a three-to-one ratio even now. A hyper missile burst into n-space, exploding just outside the shield, shaking *Nergal* as a terrier shook a rat, but the shield held, and she and her ship were one. They closed in, energy weapons raving, and her own sublight missiles were going out now.

Lord of Order Furtag was gone with his flagship, and command devolved upon Lord Chirdan. Chirdan was a fighter, but not blind. They were destroying the nest-killers, but his nestlings were dying in unreasonable numbers, for they had no weapon to equal those deadly beams. He could smash these defenders even at this low range, but only at the cost of too many of his own. He gave the order, and the scouts of the Aku'Ultan micro-jumped away.

The enemy vanished.

They shouldn't be able to do that, Adrienne Robbins thought. Not to just disappear that way. We should have detected the hyper field charging up on something that size, even for an itty-bitty micro-jump. But we didn't. Well, that's worth knowing. Won't help the bastards much when they get too far in-system to micro-jump, but it's going to be a bitch out here.

And the buggers can *fight*, she thought grimly, shaken by her read-outs. Task Force One had gone in with forty-eight ships; it came out with twenty-one. The enemy had lost ten times that many, possibly more . . . but the enemy *had* more than ten times as many starships as Earth had battleships.

Admiral Hawter turned in-system. Magazines were down to sixty percent, thirty percent for hyper missiles, and half his survivors were damaged. If the enemy was willing to run, then so was he. He'd gotten the information Earth needed for analysis; now it was time to get his surviving people home.

The first clash was over, and humanity had won—if fifty-six percent losses could be called a victory. And both sides knew it could. The Aku'Ultan had lost a vastly lower percentage of their total force, but there came a point at which terms like "favorable rate of exchange" were meaningless.

Yet it was only the first clash, and both sides had learned much. It remained to be seen which would profit most from the lessons they had purchased with so much blood.

CHAPTER FIFTEEN

The great ringed planet of this accursed system floated far below him, but Lord of Order Chirdan had no eyes for its beauty as he watched his engineers prepare their final system tests.

The asteroids they had already hurled against the nest-killers' planetary shield had shown Battle Comp that small weapons would not penetrate, while those of sufficient mass were destroyed by the nest-killers' weapons before impact. They would continue to hurl asteroids against it, but only to force it back so that they might smite the fortresses with other thunders.

But *this*, Chirdan thought, was another matter. It would move slowly, at first, but only at first, and it was large enough to mount shields which could stop even the nest-killers' weapons. His nestlings would protect it with their lives, and it would end these demon-spawned nest-killers for all time. Battle Comp had promised him that, and Battle Comp never lied.

"I don't like it," Horus said. "I don't like it, and I want a way around it. Do any of you have one?"

His chiefs of staff looked back from his com screen, weary faces strained. Gerald Hatcher's temples were almost completely white, but Isaiah Hawter's eyes were haunted, for he'd seen seventy percent of his warships blown out of existence in the last four months.

One face was missing. General Singhman had been aboard ODC Seven when the Achuultani warhead broke through her shield.

There were other gaps in Earth's defenses, and the enemy ruled the outer system. They were slow and clumsy in normal space, but their ability to dart into hyper with absolutely no warning more than compensated as long as they stayed at least twenty light-minutes out.

Earth had learned enough in the last few months to know her technology was better, but it was beginning to appear her advantage might not be great enough, for the Achuultani had surprises of their own.

Like those damned hyper drives. Achuultani ships were slow even in hyper, but their hyper drives did things Horus had always thought were impossible.

They could operate twice as deep into a stellar gravity well as an Imperial hypership, and their missile launchers were incredible. Achuultani sublight missiles, though fast, weren't too dangerous—Earth's defenders had better computers, better counter-missiles, and more efficient shield generators—but their hyper missiles were another story. Somehow, and Horus would have given an arm to know how, the Achuultani generated *external* hyper fields around their missiles, without the massive on-board hyper drives human missiles required.

Their launchers' rate of fire was lower, but they were small enough the Achuultani could pack them in in unbelievable numbers, and they tended to fire their salvos in shoals, scattered over the hyper bands. A shield could cover only so many bands at once, and with luck, they could pop a missile through one the shield wasn't guarding—a trick which had cost Earth's warships dearly.

Their energy weapons, on the other hand, relied upon quaint, short-ranged developments of laser technology, which left a gap in their defenses. It wasn't very wide, but if Earth's defenders could get into it, they were too close for really accurate Achuultani hyper missile-fire and beyond their effective energy weapon range. The trick was surviving to get there.

And they really did like kinetic weapons. So far, they'd managed to hit the planetary shield with scores of projectiles, the largest something over a billion tons, and virtually wiped out Earth's orbital industry. They'd nailed two ODCs, as well, picking them off with missiles when the main shield was slammed back into atmosphere behind them by kinetic assault.

To date, Vassily had managed to hold that shield against everything they threw at him, but the big, blond Russian was growing increasingly grim-faced. The PDC shield generators had been designed to provide a fifty percent reserve—but that was before they knew about Achuultani hyper missiles. Covering the wide-band attacks coming at him took every generator he had, and at ruinous overload. Without the core tap, not even the PDCs could have held them.

Which was largely what this conference was about.

"*I* don't see an option, Horus," Hatcher said finally. "We've got to have that tap. If we shut down and they hit us before we power back up—"

"Gerald," Chernikov said, "we never meant this tap to carry such loads so long. The control systems are collapsing. I am into the secondary governor ring in places; if it goes, there are only the tertiaries to hold it."

"But even if we shut down, will it be any safer to power back up?"

"No," Chernikov conceded unhappily. "Not without repairs."

"Then, Vassily, it is a choice between a possibility of losing control and the probability of losing the planet," Tsien said quietly.

"I know that. But it will do us no good to blow up Antarctica *and* lose the tap—permanently—into the bargain."

"Agreed." Horus's quiet voice snapped all eyes back to him. "Are your replacement components ready for installation, Vassily?"

"They are. We will require two-point-six hours to change over, but I *must* shut down to do it."

"Very well." Horus felt responsibility crushing down upon him. "When the first secondary system goes down, we'll shut down long enough for complete control replacement."

Tsien and Hatcher looked as if they wanted to argue, but they were soldiers. They recognized an order when they heard it.

"Now." Horus turned his attention to Admiral Hawter. "What can you tell us about your own situation, Isaiah?"

"It's not good," Hawter said heavily. "The biggest problem is the difference in our shield technologies. We generate a single bubble around a unit; they generate a series of plate-like shields, each covering one aspect of the target, with about a twenty percent overlap at the edges. They pay for it with a much less efficient power ratio, but it gives them redundancy we don't have *and* lets them bring them in closer to the hull. That's our problem."

Heads nodded. Hyper missiles weren't seeking weapons; they went straight to their pre-programmed coordinates, and the distance between shield and hull effectively made Earth's ships bigger targets. All too often, a hyper missile close enough to penetrate a human warship's shield detonated outside an Achuultani ship's shields—which, coupled with the Achuultani's greater ability to saturate the hyper bands, left Hawter's ships at a grievous disadvantage.

"Our missiles out-range theirs, and we've refined our targeting systems to beat their jammers—which, by the way, are still losing ground to our own—but if we stay beyond their range, we can't get *our* warheads in close enough, either. Not without bigger salvos than most of our ships can throw. As long as they stay far enough out to use their micro-jump advantage, as well, we can only fight them on their terms, and that's bad business."

"How bad?" General Ki asked.

"Bad. We started out with a hundred and twenty battleships, twice that many cruisers, and about four hundred destroyers. We're down to thirty-one battleships, ninety-six cruisers, and one hundred and seven destroyers—that's a loss of five hundred and thirty-six out of an initial strength of seven hundred and seventy. In return, we've knocked out about nine hundred of their ships. I've got confirmed kills on seven hundred eighty-two and probables on another hundred fifty or so. That's one hell of a lot more tonnage than we've lost, and, by our original estimates, that should have been all of them; as it is, it looks like a bit less than fifty percent.

"What it boils down to is that they've ground us away. If they move against us in force, we no longer have the mobile units to meet them in deep space."

"In short," Horus interjected softly, "they've won control of the Solar System beyond the reach of Earth's own weapons."

"Exactly, Governor," Hawter said grimly. "We're holding so far, but by the skin of our teeth. And this is only the scouting force."

They were still staring at one another in glum silence when the alarms shrieked.

Both of Brashieel's stomachs tightened as *Vindicator* moved in-system. The Demon Sector was living up to its name, Tarhish take it! Almost half the scouts had died striving against this single wretched planet, and if the scouts were but a few pebbles in the avalanche of Great Lord Tharno's fleet, there were many suns in this sector—including the ones which must have built those scanner arrays. It could not have been these nest-killers, for none of their ships were even hyper-capable. But if *these* nest-killers had such weapons, who knew what else awaited the Protectors?

Yet they were pushing the nest-killers back. Lord of Thought Mosharg had counted the nest-killers they had sent to Tarhish carefully, and few of their foes' impossibly powerful warships could remain.

Still, it seemed rash to press an attack so deep into the inner system. The nest-killers were twice as fast as *Vindicator* when he could not flee into hyper. If this was an ambush, the Great Visit's scouts could lose heavily.

But Brashieel was no lord. Perhaps the purpose was to evaluate the nest-killers' close defenses before the Hoof of Tarhish was released upon them? That made sense, even to an assistant servant like him, especially in light of their orders to attack the sunward pole of the planet. Yet to risk a half-twelve of twelves of scouts in this fashion took courage. Which might be why Lords Chirdan and Mosharg were lords and Brashieel was an assistant servant.

He settled tensely upon his duty pad as they emerged from hyper and headed for the blue-white world they had come so far to slay.

"Seventy-two hostiles, inbound," Plotting reported. "Approximately two hundred forty additional hostiles following at eight light-minutes. Evaluate this as a major probe."

Isaiah Hawter winced. Over three hundred of them. He could go out to meet them and kick hell out of them, but it would leave him with next to nothing. Those bastards lying back to cover their fellows with hyper missiles made the difference. He'd lose half his ships before his energy weapons even engaged the advanced force.

No, this time he was going to have to let them in.

"All task forces, withdraw behind the primary shield," he said. "Instruct Fighter Command to stand by. Bring all ODC weaponry to readiness."

Adrienne Robbins swore softly as she retreated behind the shield. She knew going out to meet that much firepower would be a quick form of suicide, but *Nergal* had twenty-seven confirmed kills and nine probables, more than any other unit among Earth's tattered survivors, and letting these vermin close without a fight galled her. More, it frightened her, because whether anyone chose to admit it or not, she knew what it meant.

They were losing.

Vassily Chernikov made a minute adjustment through his neural feed, nursing his core tap like an old cat with a single kitten. He'd been right to insist on building it, but all he felt now was hatred for the demon he had chained. It was breaking its bonds, slowly but surely, under the strain of continuous overload operation in a planetary atmosphere; when they snapped, it would be the end.

✧   ✧   ✦

Lieutenant Samson's belly tightened as he watched the developing attack pattern. They were coming in from the south this time—had they spotted the core tap? Realized how vital to Earth it was?

Either way, it made little difference to Samson's probable fate. The Iron Bitch was right in their path, floating with five other ODCs to help her bar the way . . . and the planetary shield was drawn in behind them.

"Red Warning! Prepare for launch! Prepare for Launch! Red Warning!"

The fighter crews, Terra-born and Imperials distinguishable now only by their names, charged up the ladders to their cockpits. General Ki Tran Thich settled into the pilot's couch of his command fighter and flashed the commit signal over his neural feed. Drives hummed to life, EW officers tuned their defensive systems and weaponry, and the destruction-laden little craft howled up from their PDC homes on the man-made thunder of their sonic booms.

Brashieel blinked inner and outer lids alike as his display blossomed with sudden threat sources. Great Nest! Sublight missiles at *this* range?

But his consternation eased slightly as he saw the power readings. No, not missiles. They were something else, some sort of very small warships. He had never heard of anything like them, but, then, he had never heard of *most* of the Tarhish-spawned surprises these demon nest-killers had produced.

"Missile batteries, stand by," Gerald Hatcher ordered softly. This was going to be tricky. He and Tao-ling had trained to coordinate their southern-hemisphere PDCs, but this was the first time the bastards had come really close.

He spared a moment to be thankful Sharon and the girls were safely under the protection of Horus's Shepard Center HQ. It was just possible something was coming through this time.

Andrew Samson swallowed as the interceptors drilled through the shield's polar portal and it closed behind them. They were such tiny things to pit themselves against those kilometers-long Leviathans. It didn't seem—

"Stand by missile crews." Captain M'wange's voice was cold. "Shield generators to max. Deploy first hyper salvo."

The hyper missiles floated out of their bays, moored to the Bitch by chains of invisible force, and the Achuultani swept closer.

"All ODCs engage—now!" Isaiah Hawter snapped.

Nest Lord! *Those* were missiles!

Slayer and *War Hoof* vanished from his scanners, and Brashieel winced. The nest-killers no longer used the greater thunder; they had come to rely almost entirely on those terrible warheads which did not explode . . . and for which the Nest had no counter. *Slayer* crumpled in on himself as a missile breached his shields; *War Hoof* simply disappeared, and the range was far too long for his own hyper missiles. What devil among the nest-killers had thought of putting hyper drives *inside* their missiles that way?

More missiles dropped out of hyper, and *Vindicator* lurched as his shields trembled under a near-miss. And another. But Small Lord Hantorg had nerves of steel. He held his course, and Brashieel's own weapons would range soon.

He made his fingers and thumbs relax within the control gloves. Soon, he promised himself. Soon, my brothers!

The small warships darted closer, and he wondered what they meant to do.

Andrew Samson whooped as the huge ship died. That had been one of the Bitch's missiles! Maybe even one of *his!*

"All fighters—execute Bravo-Three!" General Ki barked, and Earth's interceptors slashed into the Achuultani formation, darting down to swoop up from "below" at the last moment. They bucked and twisted, riding the surges from the heavy gravitonic warheads Terra hurled to meet her attackers, and their targeting systems reached out.

Brashieel twitched in astonishment as the tiny warships wheeled, evading the close-in energy defenses. Only a few twelves perished; the others opened fire at pointblank range, and a hurricane of missiles lashed the Aku'Ultan ships. They lacked the brute power of the nest-killers' heavy missiles, but there were many of them. A *great* many of them.

Half a twelve of *Vindicator*'s brothers perished, like mighty *qwelloq* pulled down by tiny, stinging *sulq*. Clearly the nest-killers' lords of thought had briefed them well. They fought in teams, many units striking as one, concentrating their fire on single quadrants of their victims' shields, and when those isolated shields died under the tornadoes of flame blazing upon them, the ships they had been meant to save died with them.

In desperation, Brashieel armed his own launchers without orders. Such a breach of procedure might mean his own death in dishonor, yet he could not simply crouch upon his duty pad and do *nothing!* His fingers twitched and sent forth a salvo of normal-space missiles, missiles of the greater thunder. They converged on a quarter-twelve of attacking *sulq*, and when their thunder merged, it washed over the nest-killers and gave them to the Furnace.

"Good, Brashieel!" It was Small Lord Hantorg. "Very good!"

Brashieel's crest rose with pride as he heard *Vindicator*'s lord ordering other missile crews to copy his example.

General Ki Tran Thich watched the tremendous Achuultani warship rip apart under his fire. He and Hideoshi had drawn lots for the right to lead the first interception, and he smiled wolfishly as he wheeled his fighter. The full power of the Seventy-First Fighter Group rode at his back as he searched for another target. There. That one would do nicely.

He never saw the ten-thousand-megaton missile coming directly at him.

✧   ✧   ✧

"Missile armaments exhausted," General Tama Hideoshi's ops officer reported, and Tama grunted. His own feeds had already told him, and he could feel his fighters dying . . . just as Thich had died. Who would have thought of turning shipkillers into proximity-fused SAMs? His interceptors' energy armaments weren't going to be enough against *that* kind of overkill!

"All fighters withdraw to rearm," he ordered. "Launch reserve strike. Instruct all pilots to maintain triple normal separation. They are to engage only with missiles—I repeat, only with missiles—then withdraw to rearm."

"Yes, sir."

Earth's fighters withdrew. Over three hundred of them had perished, yet that was but a tithe of their total strength, and the Achuultani probe had been reduced to twenty-seven units.

The flight crews streamed back past the ODCs, heading for their own bases. It was up to the orbital fortifications, now—them, and the fire still slamming into the Achuultani from Earth's southernmost PDCs.

Brashieel watched the small warships scatter, fleeing his fire. The Protectors had found the way to defeat them, and he—*he*, a lowly assistant servant of thunder—had pointed the way!

He felt his nestmates' approval, yet he could not rejoice. Two-thirds of *Vindicator*'s brothers had died, and the nest-killers' missiles still lashed the survivors. Worse, they were about to enter energy weapon range of those waiting fortresses. None of the scouts had done that before; they had engaged only with missiles at extreme range. Now was the great test. Now was the Time of Fire, when they would learn what those sullen fortresses could do.

Andrew Samson watched the depleted fighters fell back. *Imagine swatting fighters with heavy missiles! We couldn't've gotten away with it; our sublight missiles are too slow, too easy to evade.*

The full Achuultani fire shifted to the Bitch and her sisters, and the ODC shuddered, twitching as if in fear as the warheads battered her shield. Her shield generators heated dangerously as Captain M'wange asked the impossible of them. They were covering too many hyper bands, Samson thought. Sooner or later, they would miss one, or an anti-matter warhead would overload them. And when that happened, Lucy Samson's little boy Andrew would die.

But in the meantime, he thought, taking careful aim . . . and bellowed in triumph as yet another massive warship tore apart. They were coming to kill him, but if they had not, how could he have killed them?

"Stand by energy weapons," Admiral Hawter said harshly. ODCs Eleven, Thirteen, and Sixteen were gone; there was going to be one hell of a hole over the pole, whatever happened. Far worse, some of their missiles had gotten through to Earth's surface. He didn't know how many, but *any* were too many when they carried that kind of firepower. Yet they were down to nineteen ships. He tried to tell himself that was a good sign, and his lips thinned over his teeth as the Achuultani kept coming.

They were about to discover the difference between the beams of a battleship and a three-hundred-thousand-ton ODC, he thought viciously.

Brashieel flinched as the waiting fortresses exploded with power. The terrible energy weapons which had slain so many of *Vindicator*'s brothers in ship-to-ship combat were as nothing beside this! They smote full upon the warships' shields, and as they smote, those ships died. One, two, seven— still they died! Nothing could withstand that fury. *Nothing!*

"All *right!*" Andrew Samson shouted. *Six of them already, and more going!* He picked a target whose shields wavered under fire from three different ODCs and popped a gravitonic warhead neatly through them. His victim perished, and this time there was no question who'd made the kill.

"Withdraw."
The order went out, and Brashieel sighed with gratitude. Lord of Thought Mosharg must have learned what they had come to learn. They could leave.
Assuming they could get away alive.

"They're withdrawing!" someone shouted, and Gerald Hatcher nodded. Yes, they were, but they'd cost too much before they went. Two missiles had actually gotten through the planetary shield despite all that Vassily and the PDCs could do, and thank God those bastards didn't have gravitonic warheads.
He closed his eyes briefly. One missile had been an ocean strike, and God only knew what *that* was going to do to Earth's coastlines and ecology. The other had hit Australia, almost exactly in the center of Brisbane, and Gerald Hatcher felt the weight of personal despair. No shelter could withstand a direct hit of that magnitude, and how in the name of God could he tell Isaiah Hawter that he had just become a childless widower?

The last Aku'Ultan warship vanished, fleeing into hyper before the reserve fighter strike caught it. Three of the seventy-two which had attacked escaped.
Behind them, the southern hemisphere of the planet smoked and smoldered under twenty thousand megatons of destruction, and far, far ahead of them, Lord Chirdan's engineers completed their final tests. Power plants came on line, stoking the furnaces of the mighty drive housings, and Lord Chirdan himself gave the order to engage.
The moon men called Iapetus shuddered in its endless orbit around the planet they called Saturn. Shuddered . . . and began to move slowly away from its primary.

CHAPTER SIXTEEN

Servant of Thunders Brashieel crouched upon his new duty pad in master fire control. He still did not know how *Vindicator* had survived so long, but Small Lord Hantorg seemed to believe much of the credit was his. He was grateful for his small lord's confidence, and even more that his new promotion gave him such splendid instrumentation.

He bent his eyes on the vision plate, watching the rocky mass which paced *Vindicator*. The Nest seldom used such large weapons, but it was time and past time for the Protectors to finish these infernal nest-killers and move on.

Gerald Hatcher felt a million years old as he propped his feet on the coffee table in Horus's office. Even with biotechnics, there was a limit to the twenty-two-hour days a man could put in, and he'd passed it long ago.

For seven months they had held on—somehow—but the end was in sight. His dog-weary personnel knew it, and the civilians must suspect. The heavens had been pocked with too much flame. Too many of their defenders had died . . . and their children. Fourteen times now the Achuultani had driven hyper missiles past the planetary shield. Most had struck water, lashing Earth's battered coasts with tsunamis, wracking her with radiation and salt-poisoned typhoons, but four had found targets ashore. By God's grace, one had landed in the middle of the African desert, but Brisbane had been joined by over four hundred million more dead, and all the miracles his people had wrought were but delays.

How Vassily kept his tap up was more than Hatcher could tell, but he was holding it together, with his bare hands for all intents and purposes. The power still flowed, and Geb and his zombie-like crews kept the shield generators on line somehow. They could shut down no more than a handful for overhaul at any one time, but, like Vassily, Geb was doing the impossible.

Yes, Hatcher thought, Earth had its miracle-workers . . . but at a price.

"How—" He paused to clear his throat. "How's Isaiah?"

"Unchanged," Horus said sadly, and Hatcher closed his eyes in pain.

It had been terrible enough for Isaiah to preside over the slaughter of his crews, but Brisbane had finished him. Now he simply sat in his small room, staring at the pictures of his wife and children.

His friends knew how magnificently he'd fought, rallying his battered ships again and again; he knew only that he hadn't been good enough. That he'd let the Achuultani murder his family, and that most of the crews who'd fought for him with such supreme gallantry had also died. So they had, and too many of the survivors were like Isaiah—burned out, dead inside, hating themselves for being less than gods in the hour of their world's extremity.

Yet there were the others, Hatcher reminded himself. The ones like Horus, who'd assumed Isaiah's duties when he collapsed. Like Adrienne Robbins, the senior surviving parasite skipper, who'd refused a direct order to take her damaged ship out of action. Like Vassily and Geb, who'd somehow risen above themselves to perform impossible tasks. Like the bone-weary crews of the ODCs and PDCs who fought on day after endless, hopeless day, and the fighter crews who went out again and again, and came back in ever fewer numbers.

And, he thought, the people like Tsien Tao-ling, those very rare men and women who simply had no breaking point . . . and thank God for them.

Of the Supreme Chiefs of Staff, Singhman and Ki had been killed . . . and so had Hawter, Hatcher thought sadly. Tama Hideoshi had taken over all that remained of Fighter Command, but Vassily was chained to Antarctica, Frederick Amesbury was working himself into his own grave in Plotting, trying desperately to keep tabs on the outer system through his Achuultani-crippled arrays, and Chiang Chien-su couldn't possibly be spared from his heartbreaking responsibility for Civil Defense. So even with Horus taking over the remnants of Hawter's warships and ODCs, Hatcher had been forced to hand the entire planet-side defense net over to Tsien while he himself concentrated on finding a way to keep the Achuultani from destroying Earth.

But he was a general, not a wizard.

"We've had it, Horus." He watched the old Imperial carefully, but the governor didn't even flinch. "We're just kicking and scratching on the way to the gallows. I don't see how Vassily can keep the tap up another two weeks."

"Should we stop kicking and scratching, then?" The question came out with a ghost of a smile, and Hatcher smiled back.

"Hell no. I just needed to say it to someone before I go back and start kicking again. Even if they take us out, we can make sure there are less of them for the next world on their list."

"My thoughts exactly." Horus squeezed the bridge of his nose wearily. "Should we tell the civilians?"

"Better not," Hatcher sighed. "I'm not really scared of a panic, but I don't see any reason to frighten them any worse than they already are."

"Agreed."

Horus rose and walked slowly to his office's glass wall. The Colorado night was ripped by solid sheets of lightning as the outraged atmosphere gave up some of the violence it had been made to absorb, and a solid, unending roll of thunder shook the glass. Lightning and snow, he thought; crashing thunder and blizzards. Too much vaporized sea water, too many cubic kilometers of steam. The planetary albedo had shifted, more sunlight was reflected, and the temperature had dropped. There was no telling how much further it would go . . . and thank the Maker General Chiang had stockpiled food so fanatically, for the world's crops were gone. But at least this one was turning to rain. Freezing cold rain, but rain.

And they were still alive, he told himself as Hatcher stood silently to leave. Alive. Yet that, too, would change. Gerald was right. They were losing it, and something deep inside him wanted to curl up and get the dying finished. But he couldn't do that.

"Gerald," his soft voice stopped Hatcher at the door, and Horus turned his eyes from the storm to meet the general's. "In case we don't get a chance to talk again, thank you."

The Hoof of Tarhish pawed the vacuum. Not even the Aku'Ultan could accelerate such masses with a snap of the fingers, but its speed had grown. Only a few twelves of *tiao* per segment, at first, then more. And more. More!

Now *Vindicator* rode the mighty projectile's flank, joined with his brothers in a solid phalanx to guard their weapon.

They must be seen soon, but the Hoof's defenses were strong, and the nest-killers could not even range accurately upon it without first blasting aside the half-twelve of great twelves of scouts which remained. They would defend the Hoof with their own deaths and clear a way through what remained of the nest-killers' defenses, for they were Protectors.

"Oh my God."

Sir Frederick Amesbury's Plotting teams were going berserk trying to analyze the Achuultani's current maneuvers, for there was no sane reason for them to be clustered that way on a course like that. But something about the whisper cut through the weary, frantic background hum, and he turned to Major Joanna Osgood, his senior watch officer.

"What is it, Major?" But her mahogany face was frozen and she did not answer. He touched her shoulder. "Jo?"

Major Osgood shook herself.

"I found the answer, sir," she said. "Iapetus."

Her Caribbean accent's flattened calm frightened Amesbury, for he knew what produced that tone. There was a realm beyond fear, for when no hope remained there was no reason to fear.

"Explain, Major," he said gently.

"I finally managed to hyper an array out-system and got a look at Saturn, sir." She met the general's gaze calmly. "Iapetus isn't there anymore."

"It's true, Ger." Amesbury's weary face looked back from Hatcher's com screen. "It took some time to get a probe near enough to burn through their ships' energy emissions and confirm it, but we found it right enough. Dead center in their formation: Iapetus—the eighth moon of Saturn."

"I see." Hatcher wanted to curse, to revile God for letting this happen, but there was no point, and his voice was soft. "How bad is it?"

"It's the end, unless we can stop the bloody thing. This is no asteroid, Ger—it's a bleeding *moon*. Six times the mass of Ceres."

"Moving how fast?"

"Fast enough to see *us* off," Amesbury replied grimly. "They could have done that simply by dropping it into Sol's gravity well and letting it fall 'downhill' to us, but we'd've had too much time. They've put shields on it, but if we could pop a few hyper missiles through them, we *might* be able to blow the bugger apart before it reaches us. That's why they're bringing it in under power; they don't want to expose it to our fire any longer than they have to.

"Their drives are much slower than ours are, but they've got the ruddy gravity well to work with, too. I don't know how they did it—even if they hadn't been picking off our sensor arrays, we were watching the asteroids, not the outer-system moons—but I reckon they started out with a very low initial acceleration. Only they're coming from *Saturn*, Ger. I don't know when they actually started, but we're just past opposition, which means we're over one-and-a-half *billion* kilometers apart on a straight line. But they're not *on* a straight-line course . . . and they've been accelerating all the way.

"They're coming at us at upwards of five hundred kilometers per second— seven times faster than a 'fast' meteorite. I haven't bothered to calculate how many trillions of megatons that equates to, because it doesn't matter. That moon will punch through our shield like a bullet through butter, and they'll reach us in about six days. That's how long we've got to stop them."

"We can't, Frederick," Hatcher sighed. "We just can't do it."

"I bloody well know we can't," Amesbury said harshly, "but that doesn't mean we don't have to try!"

"I know." Hatcher made his shoulders straighten. "Leave it with me, Frederick. We'll give it our best shot."

"I know," Amesbury said much more softly. "And . . . God bless, Ger."

Faces paled as the news spread among Earth's defenders. This was the end. When that stupendous hammer came down, Earth would shatter like a walnut.

Some had given too much, stretched their reserves too thin, and they snapped. Most simply retreated from reality, but a handful went berserk, and their fellows were almost grateful, for subduing them diverted their minds from their own terror.

Yet only a minority broke. For most, survival, even hope, were no longer factors, and they manned their battle stations without hysteria, cold and determined . . . and desperate.

Servant of Thunders Brashieel noted the changing energy signatures. So. The nest-killers knew, and they would strive to thrust the Hoof aside, to destroy it. Already the orbital fortresses were moving, concentrating to meet them, but many smaller hooves had been prepared to pelt the planetary shield, driving it back, exposing those fortresses to the Protectors' thunder. They would clear a path for the Hoof, and nothing could stop them. The nest-killers could not even see the Hoof to fire upon it unless they destroyed *Vindicator* and his brothers, and they would never do that in time.

He watched his magnificent instruments as Lord of Order Chirdan shifted formation, placing a thicker wall of his nestlings between the Hoof and the nest-killers' world. *Vindicator* anchored one edge of that wall.

Lieutenant Andrew Samson felt queerly calm. Governor Horus had shifted his remaining forts to give the Bitch support, but the Achuultani had expected that. Kinetic projectiles had hammered the planetary shield back for days, stripping it away from the ODCs. Raiding squadrons had charged in, paying a high price for their attacks but picking off the battered ODCs. Of the six which originally had protected the pole, only the damaged Bitch remained, and she'd expended too much ammunition defending herself. Without Earth's orbital industry, just keeping up with expenditures was difficult . . . not to mention the risk colliers ran between the shield and the ODCs to resupply them.

Andrew Samson had long ago abandoned any expectation of surviving Earth's siege, but he'd continued to hope his world would live. Now he knew it probably would not, and that purged the last fear from his system, leaving only a strange, bittersweet regret.

The last fleet units would make their try soon. They'd been hoarded for this moment, waiting until the Achuultani were within pointblank range of Earth's defenses. Their chances of surviving the next few hours were even lower than his own, but the ODCs would do what they could to cover them. He checked his remaining hyper missiles. Thirty-seven, and less than four hundred in the Bitch's other magazines. It wouldn't be enough.

Acting Commodore Adrienne Robbins checked her formation. All fifteen of Earth's remaining battleships, little more than a single squadron, were formed up about her wounded *Nergal*. Half *Nergal*'s launchers had been destroyed by the near-miss which had pierced her shield and killed eighty of her three hundred people, but she had her drive . . . and her energy weapons.

The threadbare remnants of the cruisers and destroyers—seventy-four of them, in all—screened the pitiful handful of capital ships. Eighty-nine warships; her first and final task force command.

"Task Force ready to proceed, Governor," she told the face on her com.

"Proceed," Horus said quietly. "May the Maker go with you, Commodore."

"And with you, sir," she replied, then shifted to her command net, and her voice was clear and calm. "The Task Force will advance," she said.

Brashieel watched in grudging admiration as the nest-killers advanced. There were so few of them, and barely a twelve of their biggest ones. Their crews must know they would be chaff for the Furnace, yet still they came, and something within him saluted their courage. In this moment they were not nest-killers; they were Protectors, just as truly as he himself.

But such thoughts would not stay his hand. The Nest had survived for uncountable higher twelves of years only by slaying its enemies while they were yet weak. It was a lesson the Aku'Ultan had learned long ago from the Great Nest-Killers who had driven the Aku'Ultan from their own Nest Place.

It would not happen again.

Gerald Hatcher felt sick as Commodore Robbins led her ships out to die. But the fire control of his orbital and ground-side fortresses couldn't even see Iapetus unless an opening could be blown for them, and those doomed ships were his one hope to open a way.

"If we get a fix, lock it in tight, Plotting," he said harshly.

"Acknowledged," Sir Frederick Amesbury replied.

"Request permission to engage," Tama Hideoshi said from his own screen, and Hatcher noted the general's flight suit. They had more fighters than crews now, but even so Hideoshi had no business flying this mission. Yet there was no tomorrow this time, and he chose not to object.

"Not yet. Hold inside the shield till the ships engage."

"Acknowledged." Tama's voice was unhappy, but he understood. He would wait until the Achuultani were too busy punching missiles at Robbins' ships to wipe his own fragile craft from the universe.

"Task Force opening fire," someone said, and another voice came over the link, soft and prayerful, its owner not even aware he had spoken.

"Go, baby! *Go!*" it whispered.

Adrienne Robbins had discussed her plan with Horus, not that there was much "planning" to it. There was but one possible tactic: to go right down their throat behind every missile she had. Perhaps, just perhaps, they could swamp the defenses, get in among them with their energy weapons. None would survive such close combat, but they might punch a hole before they died.

And so Earth's ships belched missiles at her murderers, hyper and sublight alike. Their launchers went to continuous rapid fire, spitting out homing sublight weapons without even worrying about targeting. The lethal projectiles were a cloud of death, and the first hyper missiles from Earth came with them.

Lord of Order Chirdan's head bobbed in anguish as his nestlings died. He had known the nest-killers must come forth and hurl their every weapon against him, yet not even Battle Comp had predicted carnage such as this!

The missile storm was a whirlwind, boring into the center of the wall defending the Hoof. Anti-matter pyres and gravitonic warheads savaged his ships, and his inner lids narrowed. They sought to blow a hole and charge into it with their infernal energy weapons! They would die there, but in their dying they might expose the Hoof to their fellows upon the planet.

He could not allow that, and his orders went out. The edges of his wall of ships thinned, drawing together in the center to block the attack, and his own, shorter-ranged missiles struck back.

✧   ✧   ✧

Time had no meaning. There was only a shrieking eternity of dying ships and a glare that lit Earth's night skies like twice a hundred suns. Adrienne Robbins saw it reaching for her ships, saw her lighter destroyers and cruisers burning like coals from a forge, and she adjusted her course slightly.

The solid core of her out-numbered task force drove for the exact center of that vortex of death, and their magazines were almost dry.

"Go!" Tama Hideoshi snapped, and Earth's last surviving interceptors howled heavenward. He rode his flight couch, his EW officer at his side, and smiled. He was fifty-nine years old, and only his biotechnics made this possible. Three years before, he'd known he would never fly combat again. Now he would, and if his world must die, at least he had been given this final gift, to die in her defense as a *samurai* should.

Nest Lord! Their small ships were attacking, too! Brashieel had not thought so many remained, but they did, and they charged on the heels of their larger, dying brothers, covered by their deaths.

A few of the Bitch's launchers still had hyper missiles, but Andrew Samson was down to sublight weapons. It was long range, too much time for the bastards to pick them off, but each of his weapons they had to deal with was one more strain on their defenses. He sent them out at four-second intervals.

Lord Chirdan cursed. The nest-killers were dying by twelves, yet they had cut deep into his formation. Six twelves of his ships had already perished, and the terrible harvest of the nest-killer beams was only starting.

Their warships vanished into the heart of his own, robbing his outer missile crews of targets, and they retargeted on the orbital fortresses.

Gerald Hatcher's face was stone as the first ODC died. Missiles pelted the planetary shield, as well, but he almost welcomed those. Even if they broke through, killed millions of civilians, he would welcome them, for each missile sent against Earth was one not sent against his orbital launchers.

He sat back and felt utterly useless. There was no reserve. He'd committed everything he had. Now he had nothing to do but watch the slaughter of his people.

Missiles coated the Iron Bitch's shield in a blinding corona, and still she struck back.

Andrew Samson was a machine, part of his console. His magazine was down to ten percent and dropping fast, but he didn't even think of slowing his rate of fire. There was no point, and he pounded his foes, his brain full of the thunder wracking the Achuultani formation.

He never saw the hyper missile which finally popped the Bitch's shields. He died with his mind still full of thunder.

✧   ✧   ✧

Tama Hideoshi's fighters slammed into the Achuultani, and their missiles flashed away. Scores of Achuultani ships died, but the enemy formation closed anyway. Commodore Robbins' ships vanished into the maelstrom, and the fighters were dying too quickly to follow.

They exhausted their missiles and closed with energy guns.

Adrienne Robbins was halfway through the Achuultani, but her cruisers and destroyers were gone. The back of her mind burned with the image of the destroyer *London* as her captain took her at full drive directly into one of the Achuultani monsters behind the continuous fire of his energy weapons, bursting through its weakened shield and dragging it into death with him. Yet it wasn't enough. She and her battleships were alone, the only units with the strength to endure the fury, and even they were going fast. *Nergal* herself had taken another near miss, and tangled skeins of atmosphere followed her like a trail of blood.

Another Achuultani ship died under her energy weapons, but another loomed beyond it, and still another. They wouldn't break through after all.

Adrienne Robbins drove her crippled command forward, and *Nergal*'s eight surviving sisters charged at her side.

Tsien Tao-ling's scanners told him Commodore Robbins would not succeed. Yet . . . in a way, she might yet. His eyes closed as he concentrated on his feed, his brain clear and cold, buttressed against panic. Yes. Robbins had drawn most of the defenders onto her own ships, thickening the center of their formation but thinning its edges. Perhaps—

The hail of missiles from the PDCs stopped as his neural feed overrode their firing orders. He felt Hatcher's shock through his cross feed to Shepard Center, but there was no time to explain.

And then the launchers retargeted and spoke, hurling their massed missiles at a sphere of space barely three hundred kilometers across. Two thousand gravitonic warheads went off as one.

Twenty kilometers of starship went mad, hurled end-for-end as the wave of destruction broke across it. Servant of Thunders Brashieel clung to his duty pad, blood bursting from his nostrils as the universe exploded about him, and Tsien Tao-ling's fury spat *Vindicator* forth like the seed of a grape.

"*Contact!*" Sir Frederick Amesbury screamed, his British reserve shattered at last. Tsien had blown a brief hole through the Achuultani flank, and Amesbury's computers locked onto Iapetus. The data flashed to the PDCs and surviving ODCs, and their missiles retargeted once more.

Lord Chirdan cursed and slammed a double-thumbed fist into the bulkhead. No! They could not have done that! Not while the Hoof had so far to go!

But he fought himself back under control, watching missiles rip at the

Hoof even as his ravaged nestlings raced to reposition themselves. Shields guttered and flared, and one quadrant failed. A missile dodged through the gap, its anti-matter warhead incinerating the generators of yet another quadrant, but it was too late.

Without direct observation, not even *these* demon-spawned nest-killers could kill the Hoof before it struck, and his scouts had already spread back out to deny them that observation and hide the damaged shield quadrants.

He bared his teeth in a snarl, turning back to the five surviving nest-killer warships. He would give them to the Furnace, and their deaths would fan the Fire awaiting their cursed world.

Hatcher's momentary elation died. It had been a magnificent try, but it had failed, and he felt himself relax into a curious tranquillity of sorrow for the death of his planet, coupled with a deep, abiding pride in his people.

He watched almost calmly as the thinning screen of Achuultani ships moved still closer. There were no more than three hundred of them, four at the most, but it would be enough.

"General Hatcher!" His head snapped up at the sudden cry from Plotting. There was something strange about that voice. Something he could not quite put his finger upon. And then he had it. Hope. There was *hope* in it!

Nergal was alone, the last survivor of Terra's squadrons.

Adrienne Robbins had no idea why her ship was still alive, nor dared she take time to consider it. Her mind blazed hotter than the warheads bursting against her shield, and still she moved forward. There was no sanity in it. One battleship, her missiles exhausted, could never stop Iapetus. But sanity was an encumbrance. *Nergal* had come to attack that moon, and attack she would.

The wall was thinning, and she could feel the moon through her scanners. She altered course slightly, smashing at her foes—

—and suddenly they vanished in a gut-wrenching fury of gravitonic destruction that tossed *Nergal* like a cork.

Lord Chirdan saw without understanding. Three twelves of warships—four twelves—*five!* Impossible warships. Warships vaster than the Hoof itself!

They came out of nowhere at impossible speeds and began to kill.

Missiles that did not miss. Beams that licked away ships like tinder. Shields that brushed aside the mightiest thunders. They were the darkest nightmare of the Aku'Ultan, fleshed in shields and battle steel.

Lord Chirdan's flagship vanished in a boil of flame, and his scouts died with him. In the end, not even Protectors could abide the coming of those night demons. A pitiful handful broke, tried to flee, but they were too deep in the gravity well to escape into hyper, and—one-by-one—they died.

Yet before the last Protector perished, he saw one great warship advance upon the Hoof. Its missiles reached out—sublight missiles that took precise station on the charging moon before they flared to dreadful life. A surge of gravitonic fury raced out from them, even its backlash terrible enough to shake the wounded Earth to her core, triggering earthquakes, waking volcanoes.

Yet that was but an echo of their power. Sixteen gravitonic warheads, each hundreds of times more powerful than anything Earth had boasted, flashed into destruction . . . and took the moon Iapetus with them.

Gerald Hatcher sagged in disbelief, too shocked even to feel joy, and the breathless silence of his command post was an extension of his own.

Then a screen on his com panel lit, and a face he knew looked out of it.

"Sorry we cut it so close," Colin MacIntyre said softly.

And then—*then*—the command post exploded in cheers.

CHAPTER SEVENTEEN

General Hector MacMahan watched the shoals of Imperial assault boats close in about his command craft, then turned his scanners to the broken halves of the Achuultani starship tumbling through space in the intricate measures of an insane dance. The planetoid *Sevrid* hovered behind her shuttles, watching over them and probing the wreckage. There was still air and life aboard that shattered ship, and power, but not much of any of them.

MacMahan grunted in satisfaction as *Sevrid*'s tractors snubbed away the wreck's movement. Now if only the ship had a bay big enough to dock the damned thing, he and his people might not have to do *everything* the hard way.

He had no idea how many live Achuultani awaited his assault force, but he had six thousand men and women in his first wave, with a reserve half that size again. The cost might be high, but that wreck was the single partially intact Achuultani warship in the system. If they could take it, capture records, its computers, maybe even a few live Achuultani. . . .

"Come on, people, tighten it up," he murmured over his com, watching the final adjustment of his formation. There. They were ready.

"Execute!" he snapped, and the assault boats screamed forward.

Servant of Thunders Brashieel waited in the wreckage in his vac-suit. One broken foreleg was crudely splinted, but aside from the pain it was little inconvenience. He still had three good legs, and with the loss of the drive gravity had become a ghost.

He watched his remaining instruments, longing to send the thunder against the foe, but his launchers had died. Perhaps a fifth-twelfth of *Vindicator*'s energy weapons remained serviceable, but none of his launchers, and no weapons at all on the broken tooth of his forward section.

Brashieel tried to reject the nightmare. The nest-killers' world still lived, and these monstrous warships foretold perils yet more dire. The lords of thought had believed this system stood alone. It did not. The makers of those ancient scanner arrays had rallied to its defense, and they were powerful beyond dreams of power. Why should they content themselves with merely stopping the Protectors' attack? Why should they not strike the Nest itself?

He wondered why they had not simply given *Vindicator* to the Fire. Did their own beliefs in honor demand they face their final foes in personal combat? It did not matter, and he turned from his panel as the small craft advanced. He had no weapons to smite them, but he had already determined where he and his surviving nestlings of thunder would make their stand.

MacMahan flinched as the after section of the wrecked hull lashed his shuttles with fire. The crude energy weapons were powerful enough to burn through any assault boat's shield, but they'd fired at extreme range. Only three were hit, and the others went to evasive action, ripping at the wreck with their own energy guns. *Sevrid*'s far heavier weapons reached past them, and warp beams plucked neat, perfect divots from the hull. Air gushed outward, and then the first-wave assault boats reached their goal.

Their energy guns blasted one last time, and they battered into the holes they'd blown on suddenly reversed drives. They crunched to a halt, and assault teams charged into the violated passages of the broken starship, their soot-black combat armor invisible in the lightless corridors. A handful of defenders opened fire, and their weapons spat back, silent in the vacuum.

MacMahan's command boat led the third wave, staggering drunkenly as it slammed to a halt, and the hatches popped. His HQ company formed up about him, and he took them into the madness.

Brashieel waited. There was no point charging blindly to meet the nest-killers. *Vindicator* was dead; only the mechanics of completing his nestlings' deaths remained, and this was as good a place to end as any.

He examined his nestlings' positions in the light of his helmet lamp. They had made themselves what cover they could, a hoof-shaped bow of them protecting the hatch to main control, and Brashieel wished Small Lord Hantorg had survived to lead their final fight.

His nostrils flared in bitter amusement. While he was wishing, might he not wish that he knew what he was about? He and his nestlings were ser-vants of thunders—they smote worlds, not single nest-killers! He cudgeled his brain, trying to remember if he had ever heard of Protectors and nest-killers actually facing one another so directly. He did not think he had, but his mind was none too clear, and it really did not matter.

It was as impossible to coordinate the battle as MacMahan had expected it to be. Not even Imperial technology could provide any clear picture of this warren of decks and passages, sealed hatches and lurking ambushes.

He'd done his best in the pre-assault briefing; now it was up to his combat teams. The Second Marines provided the bulk of his firepower, but each company had an attached Recon Group platoon, and they were—

A stream of slugs wrenched him back to the job at hand, and he popped his jump gear, leaping aside as his point man went down and more fire clawed the space he himself had occupied a moment before. Leaking air and globules of blood marked a dead man as Corporal O'Hara's combat armor tumbled down the zero-gee passage, and MacMahan's mouth tightened. These crazy centaurs didn't have an energy weapon worth shit, but their slug weapons were nasty.

Still, they had their disadvantages. For one thing, recoil was a real problem—one his own people didn't face. And for all their determination to fight to the death, Achuultani didn't seem to be very good infantrymen. *His* people, on the other hand . . .

Two troopers eased forward, close to the deck, and an entire squad hosed the area before them with rapid, continuous grav gun fire. The super-dense explosive darts shredded the bulkheads, lighting the darkness with strobe-lightning spits of fury, and Captain Amanda Givens-Tamman rose suddenly to her knees. Her warp rifle fired, and the defending fire stopped abruptly.

MacMahan shuddered. He *hated* those damned guns. Probably the first people to meet crossbows had felt the same way about them. But using a hyper field on anyone, even an Achuultani—!

He chopped the thought off and waved his people forward once again. A new point man moved out, armor scanners probing for booby traps and defenders alike, and another sealed hatch loomed ahead.

Brashieel shook himself into readiness as he felt vibration in the steel.

"Stand ready, my brothers," he said quietly. "The nest-killers come."

The hatch simply vanished, and Brashieel's crest flattened in dread. Somehow these nest-killers had chained the hyper field itself for the use of their protectors!

Then the first nest-killer came through the hatch, back-lit from the corridor behind, lacing the darkness with fire from its stubby weapon, and Brashieel swallowed bile at the ugliness of the squat, four-limbed shape. But even in his revulsion he felt a throb of wonder. That was a projectile weapon, yet there was no recoil! How was that possible?

The question fluttered away into the recesses of his mind as the nest-killer's explosive darts ripped two of his nestlings apart. How had it seen them in the blackness?! No matter. He sighted carefully, bracing his three good legs against the bulkhead, and squeezed his trigger. Recoil twisted his broken leg with agony, but his heavy slugs ripped through the biped's armor, and Brashieel felt a stab of savage delight. They had taken his thunders from him, but he would send a few more to the Furnace before they slew him!

The chamber blossomed with drifting globules of blood as more nest-killers charged through the hatch. Darkness was light for them, and their fire was murderously accurate. His nestlings perished, firing back, crying out in agony and horror over their suit communicators as darts exploded within their bodies or the terrible hyper weapons plucked away their limbs. Brashieel shouted his hate, holding back the trigger, then fumbled for another magazine, but there was no time. He hurled himself forward, his bayonet stabbing towards the last nest-killer to enter.

✧   ✧   ✧

"General!" someone shouted, and MacMahan whirled. There was something wrong with the charging centaur's legs, but not with its courage; it was coming at him with only a bayonet, and his grav gun rose automatically—then stopped.

"Check fire!" he shouted, and tossed the grav gun aside.

Brashieel gaped as the puny nest-killer discarded its weapon, but his heart flamed. One more. One more foe to light his own way into the Furnace! He screamed in rage and thrust.

MacMahan's gauntleted hand slashed its armored edge into the Achuultani's long, clumsy rifle, driven by servo-mech "muscles," and the insanely warped weapon flew away.

The alien flung itself bodily upon him, and what kind of hand-to-hand moves did you use against a quarter horse with arms? MacMahan almost laughed at the thought, then he caught one murderously swinging arm, noting the knife in its hand only at the last moment, and the Achuultani convulsed in agony.

Careful, *careful*, Hector! Don't kill it by accident! And watch the vac suit, you dummy! Rip *it* and—

He moderated his armor's strength, and a furiously kicking hoof smashed his chest for his pains. That smarted even through his armor. Strong bastard, wasn't he? They lost contact with decks and bulkheads and tumbled, weightless and drunken, across the compartment. A last Achuultani gunner tried to nail them both, but one of his HQ raiders finished it in time. Then they caromed off a bulkhead at last, and MacMahan got a firm grip on the other arm.

He twisted, landing astride the Achuultani's back, and suppressed a mad urge to scream "Ride 'em, cowboy!" as he wrapped his armored arms around its torso and arms. One of his legs hooked back, kicking a rear leg aside, and his foe convulsed again. Damn it! *Another* broken bone!

"Ashwell! Get your ass over here!" he shouted, and his aide leapt forward. Between them, they wrestled the injured, still-fighting alien into helplessness, pinning it until two other troopers could bind it.

"Jesus! These bastards don't know how to quit, Gen'rl!" Ashwell panted.

"Maybe not, but we've got one alive. I expect His Majesty will be pleased with us."

"His Majesty friggin' well *better* be," someone muttered.

"I didn't hear that," MacMahan said pleasantly. "But if I had, I'd certainly agree."

Horus watched *Nergal's* mangled hull drop painfully through the seething electrical storm and tried not to weep. He failed, but perhaps no one noticed in the icy sheets of rain.

Strange ships escorted her, half again her size, shepherding her home. He winced as another drive pod failed and she lurched, but Adrienne Robbins forced her back under control. The other ships' tractors waited, ready to ease her struggle, but Horus could still hear Adrienne's voice.

"Negative," she'd said, tears glittering beneath the words. "She got us this far; she'll take us home. On her own, Goddamn it! On her *own!*"

And now the strange ships hovered above her like guards of honor as the broken battleship limped down the last few meters of sky. Two landing legs refused to extend, and Robbins lifted her ship again, holding her rock-steady on her off-balance, rapidly failing drive, then laid her gently down upon her belly. It was perfect, Horus thought quietly. A consummate perfection he could never have matched.

There was no sound but the cannonade of Earth's thunder, saluting the return of her final defender with heaven's own artillery. Then the emergency vehicles moved out, flashers splintering in the pounding rain, sirens silent, while the gleaming newcomers settled in a circle about their fallen sister.

Colin rode the battleship *Chesha*'s transit shaft to the main ramp and stepped out into the storm. Horus was waiting.

Something inside Colin tightened as he peered at him through the unnatural sheets of sleety rain. Horus looked more rock-like than ever, but he was an ancient rock, and the last thirty months had cut deep new lines into that powerful old face. Colin saw it as the old Imperial stared back at him, his eyes bright with incredulous joy, and climbed the ramp towards him.

"Hello, Horus," he said, and Horus reached out and gripped his upper arms, staring into his face as he might have stared at a ghost.

"You *are* here," he whispered. "You made it."

"Yes," Colin said, the quiet word washed in thunder. And then his voice broke and he hugged the old man close. "We made it," he said into his father-in-law's shoulder, "and so did you. My God, so did you!"

"Of course we did," Horus said, and Colin had never heard such exhaustion in a human voice. "You left me a planet full of Terra-born to do it with, didn't you?"

General Chiang Chien-su was frantically busy, for the final shock of earthquakes and spouting volcanoes waked by Iapetus's destruction had capped the mounting devastation he'd fought so long. Yet he'd seemed almost cheerful in his last report. His people were winning this time, and the mighty planetoids riding solar orbit with the planet were helping. Their auxiliaries were everywhere, helping his own over-worked craft rescue survivors from the blizzards, mud, water, and fire which had engulfed them.

Except for him, Earth's surviving chiefs of staff sat in Horus's office.

Vassily Chernikov looked like a two-week corpse, but his face was relaxed. The core tap was deactivated at last, and he hadn't lost control of it. Gerald Hatcher and Tsien Tao-ling sat together on a couch, shoulders sagging, feet propped on the same coffee table. Sir Frederick Amesbury sat in an armchair, smoking a battered pipe, eyes half-shut.

Tama Hideoshi was not there. Tamman's son had found the *samurai's* death he'd sought.

Colin sat on the corner of Horus's desk and knew he'd never seen such utter and complete fatigue. These were the men, he thought; the ones who had done the impossible. He'd already queried the computers and learned what they'd endured and achieved. Even with the evidence before him, he could scarcely credit it, and he hated what he was going to have to tell them. He could see the relaxation in their faces, the joy of a last-minute rescue, the knowledge that the Imperium had not abandoned them. Somehow he had to tell them the truth, but first . . .

"Gentlemen," he said quietly, "I never imagined what I'd really asked you to do. I have no idea how you did it. I can only say—thank you. It seems so inadequate, but . . ." He broke off with a small, apologetic shrug, and Gerald Hatcher smiled wearily.

"It cuts both way, Governor. On behalf of your military commanders— and, I might add, the entire planet—thank *you*. If you hadn't turned up when you did—" It was his turn to shrug.

"I know," Colin said, "and I'm sorry we cut it so close. We came out of supralight just as your parasites went in."

"You came—" Horus's brows wrinkled in a frown. "Then how in the Maker's name did you *get* here? You should've been at least twenty hours out!"

"Dahak was. In fact, he and 'Tanni are still about twelve hours out. Tamman and I took the others and micro-jumped on ahead," Colin said, then grinned at Horus's expression. "Scout's honor. Oh, we still needed Dahak's computers—we were plugged in by fold-space link all the way— but he couldn't keep up. You see, those ships carry hyper drives as well as Enchanach drives."

"They *what*?!" Horus blurted.

"I know, I know," Colin said soothingly. "Look, there's a lot to explain. The main thing about how we got here is that those ships are faster'n hell. They can hyper to within about twelve light-minutes of a G0 star, and they can pull about seventy percent light-speed once they get there."

"Maker! When you get help, you get *help*, don't you?"

"Well," Colin said slowly, folding his hands on his knee and looking down at them, "yes, and no. You see, we couldn't find anyone to come with us." He looked up and saw the beginning of understanding horror in his father-in-law's eyes. "The Imperium's gone, Horus," he said gently. "We had to bring these ships back ourselves . . . and they're all that's coming."

CHAPTER EIGHTEEN

Dahak's transit shaft deposited Horus at his destination, and the silent hatch slid open. He began to step through it, then stopped abruptly and dodged as fifty kilos of black fur hurled itself head-first past him. Tinker Bell disappeared down the shaft's gleaming bore, her happy bark trailing away into silence, and he shook his head with a grin.

He stepped into the captain's quarters, still shaking his head. The atrium was filled with 'sunlight,' a welcome relief from the terrible rains and blizzards flaying the battered Earth, and Colin rose quickly to grip his hand and lead him back to the men sitting around the stone table.

Hector MacMahan looked up with a rare, wide grin and waved a welcome, and if Gerald Hatcher and Tsien Tao-ling were more restrained, their smiles looked almost normal again. Vassily wasn't here; he and Valentina were visiting their son and making appropriately admiring sounds as Vlad explained the latest wonders of Imperial engineering to them.

"Where's 'Tanni?" Horus demanded as he and Colin approached the others.

"She'll be along. She's collecting something we want to show you."

"Maker, it'll be good to see her again!" Horus said, and Colin grinned.

"She feels the same way . . . Dad."

Horus tried to turn his flashing smile into a pained expression, but who would have believed 'Tanni would have the good sense to wed Colin? Especially given the way they'd first met?

"Hi, Granddad." Hector didn't stand; his left leg was regenerating from the slug which had punched through his armor in the final fighting aboard *Vindicator*. "Sorry about Tinker Bell. She was in a hurry."

"A hurry? I thought she was a loose hyper missile!"

"I know," Colin laughed. "She's been that way ever since she discovered transit shafts, and Dahak spoils her even worse than Hector does."

"I didn't know anyone could," Horus said, eyeing Hector severely.

"Believe it. He doesn't have hands, but he's found his own way to pet her. He'll only route her to one of the park decks unless someone's with her, but he adjusts the shaft to give her about an eighty-kilometer airstream, and she's in heaven. He *barks* at her, too. Most horrible thing you ever heard, but he swears she understands him better than I do."

"Which would not require a great deal of comprehension," a voice said, and, despite himself, Horus flinched. The last time he'd heard that voice with his own ears had been during the mutiny. "And that is not precisely what I have said, Colin. I simply maintain that Tinker Bell's barks are much more value-laden then humans believe and that we *shall* learn to communicate in a meaningful fashion, not that we already do so."

"Yeah, sure." Colin rolled his eyes at Horus.

"Welcome aboard, Senior Fleet Captain Horus," Dahak said, and Horus's tension eased at the welcome in that mellow voice. He cleared his throat.

"Thank you, Dahak," he said, and saw Colin's smile of approval.

"Join the rest of us," his son-in-law invited, and seated Horus at one end of the table. Wind rustled in the atrium leaves, a fountain bubbled nearby, and Horus felt his last uneasiness soaking away into relaxation.

"So," Hatcher said, obviously picking up the thread of an interrupted conversation, "you found yourself emperor and located this Guard Flotilla of yours. I thought you said it was only seventy-eight units?"

"Only seventy-eight *warships*," Colin corrected, sitting on the edge of the table. "There are also ten *Shirga*-class colliers, three *Enchanach*-class transports, and the two repair ships. That makes ninety-three."

Horus nodded to himself, still shaken by what he'd seen as his cutter approached *Dahak*. The space about Terra seemed incredibly crowded by huge, gleaming planetoids, and their ensigns had crowded his mind with images . . . a crouching, six-limbed Birhatan crag cat, an armored warrior, a vast broadsword in a gauntleted fist, and hordes of alien and mythological beasts he hadn't even recognized. But most disturbing of all had been seeing two of *Dahak*'s own dragon. He'd expected it, but expecting and seeing were two different things.

"And you managed to bring them all back with you," he said softly.

"Oh, he did, he did!" Tamman agreed, stepping out of the transit shaft behind them. "He worked us half to death in the process, too." Colin grinned wryly, and Tamman snorted. "We concentrated on the mechanical systems— Dahak and Caitrin managed most of the life support functions through their central computers once we were underway—but it's a good thing you didn't see us before we had a chance to recuperate on the trip back!"

The big Imperial smiled, though darkness lingered in his eyes. Hideoshi's death had hit him hard, for he had been the only child of Tamman's Terra-born wife, Himeko. But Tamman had grown up when there had been no biotechnics for any Terra-born child; a son's death held an old, terrible familiarity for him.

"Yeah," Colin said, "but these ships are *dumb*, Horus, and we don't begin to have the people for them. We managed to put skeleton crews on six of the *Asgerds*, but the others are riding empty—except for *Sevrid*, that is. That's why we had to come back on Enchanach Drive instead of hypering home. We can't run 'em worth a damn without Dahak to do their thinking for them."

"That's something I still don't understand," Horus said. "Why didn't the wake-up work?"

"I will be damned if I know," Colin said frankly. "We tried it with *Two* and *Herdan*, but it didn't seem to make any difference. These computers are faster than Dahak, and they've got an incredible capacity, but even after he dumped his entire memory to them, they didn't wake up."

"Something experiential?" Horus mused. "Or in the core programming?"

"Dahak? You want to answer that one?"

"I shall endeavor, Colin, but the truth is that I do not know. Senior Fleet Captain Horus, you must understand that the basic construction of these computers is totally different from my own, with core programming specifically designed to preclude the possibility of true self-awareness on their part.

"My translation programs are sufficient for most purposes, but to date I have been unable to modify *their* programs. In many ways, their core software is an inextricable part of their energy-state circuitry. I can transfer data and manipulate their existing programs; I am not yet sufficiently versatile to alter them. I therefore suspect that the difficulty lies in their core programming and that simply increasing their data bases to match my own is insufficient to cross the threshold of true awareness. Unless, of course, there is some truth to Fleet Captain Chernikov's hypothesis."

"Oh?" Horus looked at Colin. "What hypothesis is that, Colin?"

"Vlad's gone metaphysical on us," Colin said. It could have been humor, but it didn't sound that way to Horus. "He suspects Dahak's developed a soul."

"A *soul?*"

"Yeah. He thinks it's a factor of the evolution of something outside the software or the complexity of the computer net and the amount of data in memory—a 'soul' for want of a better term." Colin shrugged. "You can discuss it with him later, if you like. He'll talk both your ears off if you let him."

"I certainly will," Horus said. "A *soul,*" he murmured. "What an elegant notion. And how wonderful if it were true." He saw Hatcher's puzzled expression and smiled.

"Dahak is already a wonder," he explained. "A person—an individual—however he got that way. But if he *does* have a soul, if Man has actually brought that about, even by accident, what a magnificent thing to have done."

"I see your point," Hatcher mused, then shook himself and looked back at Colin. "But getting back to *my* point, do I understand you intend to continue as emperor?"

"I may not have a choice," Colin said wryly. "Mother won't let me abdicate, and every piece of Imperial technology we'll ever be able to salvage is programmed to go along with her."

"What's wrong with that?" Horus put in. "I think you'll make a splendid emperor, Colin." His son-in-law stuck out his tongue. "No, seriously. Look what you've already accomplished. I don't believe there's a person on Earth who doesn't realize that he's alive only because of you—"

"Because of *you*, you mean," Colin interrupted uncomfortably.

"Only because you left me in charge, and I couldn't have done it without these people." Horus waved at Hatcher and Tsien. "But the point is, *you* made survival possible. Well, you and Dahak, and I don't suppose he wants the job."

"You suppose correctly, sir," the mellow voice said, and Horus grinned.

"And whether you want it or not, someone's going to have to take it, or something like it. We've gotten by so far only because supreme authority was imposed from the outside, and this is still a war situation, which requires an absolute authority of some sort. Even if it weren't, it's going to be at least a generation before most of Earth is prepared for effective self-government, and a world government in which only some nations participate won't work, even if it wouldn't be an abomination."

"With your permission, Your Majesty," Tsien said, cutting off Colin's incipient protest, "the Governor has a point. You are aware of how my people regard Western imperialism. That issue has been muted, and, perhaps, undermined somewhat by the mutual trust our merged militaries and cooperating governments have attained, but our union is more fragile than it appears, and many of our differences remain. Cooperation as discrete equals is no longer beyond our imagination; effective amalgamation into a single government may be. You, as a source of authority from outside the normal Terran power equations, are quite another matter. You can hold us together. No one else—with the possible exception of Governor Horus—could do that."

Colin hadn't been present to witness Tsien's integration into Horus's command team. He still tended to think of the marshal as the hard-core military leader of the Asian Alliance, and Tsien's calm, matter-of-fact acceptance took him somewhat aback, but the marshal's sincerity was unmistakable.

"If that's the way you *all* feel, I guess I'm stuck. It'll make things a lot simpler where Mother is concerned, that's for sure!"

"But why is she so determined?" Hatcher asked.

"She was designed that way, Ger," MacMahan said. "Mother was the Empire's Praetorian Guard. She commanded Battle Fleet in the emperor's name, but because she wasn't self-aware, she was immune to the ambition which tends to infect humans in the same position. Her core programming is incredible, but what it comes down to is that Herdan the Great made her the conservator of empire when he accepted the throne."

"Accepted!" Hatcher snorted.

"No, the Empire's historians were a mighty fractious lot, pretty damned immune to hagiography even when it came to emperors who were still alive. And as far as I can determine from what they had to say, that's exactly the right verb. He knew what a bitch the job was going to be and wanted no part of it."

"How many Terran emperors *admitted* they did?"

"Maybe not many, but Herdan was in a hell of a spot. There were six 'official' Imperial governments, with at least twice that many civil wars going on, and he happened to be the senior military officer of the 'Imperium' holding Birhat. That gave it a degree of legitimacy the others resented, so two of them got together to smash it, but he wound up smashing them, instead. I've studied his campaigns, and the man was a diabolical strategist. His crews knew it, too, and when they demanded that he be named dictator in the old Republican Roman tradition to put an end to the wars, the Senate on Birhat went along."

"So why didn't he step down later?"

"I think he was afraid to. He seems to have been a mighty liberal fellow for his times—if you don't believe me, take a look at the citizens' rights clauses he buried in that Great Charter of his—but he'd just finished playing fireman to put out the Imperium's wars. Like our Colin here, it was mostly his personal authority holding things together. If he let go, it would all fly apart. So he took the job when the Senate offered it to him, then spent eighty years creating an absolutist government that could hold together without becoming a tyranny.

"The way it works, the Emperor's absolute in military affairs—that's where the 'Warlord' part of his titles comes in—and a slightly limited monarch in civil matters. He *is* the executive branch, complete with the powers of appointment, dismissal, and the purse, but there's also a legislative branch in the Assembly of Nobles, and less than a third of its titles are hereditary. The other seventy-odd percent are life-titles, and Herdan set it up so that only about twenty percent of all life-titles can be awarded by the Emperor. The others are either awarded by the Assembly itself—to reward scientific achievement, outstanding military service, and things like that—or elected by popular vote. In a sense, it's a unicameral legislature with four separate houses—imperial appointees, honor appointees, elected, and hereditary nobles—buried in it, and it's a lot more than a simple rubber stamp.

"The Assembly confirms or rejects new emperors, and a sufficient majority can require a serving emperor to abdicate—well, to submit to an Empire-wide referendum, a sort of 'vote of confidence' by all franchised citizens—and Mother will back them up. *She* makes the final evaluation of any new emperor's sanity, and she won't accept a ruler who doesn't match certain intelligence criteria *and* enjoy the approval of a majority of the Assembly of Nobles. She'll simply refuse to take orders from an emperor who's been given notice to quit, and when the military begins taking its orders from his properly-appointed successor, he's up shit creek in a leaky canoe."

"Doesn't sound like being emperor's a lot of fun," Horus murmured.

"Herdan designed it that way, I think," MacMahan replied.

"My God," Hatcher said. "Government á la Goldberg!"

"It seems that way," MacMahan agreed with a smile, "but it worked for five thousand years, with only half-a-dozen minor-league 'wars' (by Imperial standards), before they accidentally wiped themselves out."

"Well," Horus said, "if it works that well, maybe we can learn something from it after all, Colin. And—"

He broke off as Jiltanith and Amanda stepped off the balcony onto *Dahak*'s pressers. Amanda carried a little girl, Jiltanith a little boy, and both infants' hair was raven's-wing black. The little girl was adorable, and the little boy looked cheerful and alert, but no one with Colin's nose and ears could ever be called adorable—except, perhaps, by Jiltanith.

Horus's eyebrows almost disappeared into his hairline.

"Surprise," Colin said, his smile broad.

"You mean—?"

"Yep. Let me introduce you." He held out his arms, and Jiltanith handed him the little boy. "This little monster is Crown Prince Sean Horus MacIntyre, heir presumptive to the Throne of Man. And this—" Jiltanith smiled at her father, her eyes bright, as Amanda handed him the baby girl "—is his younger twin sister, Princess Isis Harriet MacIntyre."

Horus took the little girl in immensely gentle hands. She promptly fastened one small fist in his white hair and tugged hard, and he winced.

"Bid thy grandchildren welcome, Father," Jiltanith said softly, putting her arms around her father and daughter to hug them both, but Horus's throat was too tight to speak, and tears slid down his ancient cheeks.

" . . . and the additional food supplies from the farms aboard your ships have made the difference, Your Majesty," Chiang Chien-su said. The plump general beamed at the assembled officers and members of the Planetary Council. "There seems little doubt Earth has entered a 'mini-ice age,' and flooding remains a severe problem. Rationing will be required for some time, but with Imperial technology for farming and food distribution, Comrade Redhorse and I anticipate that starvation should not be a factor."

"Thank you, General," Colin said very, very sincerely. "You and your people have done superbly. As soon as I have time, I intend to elevate you to our new Assembly of Nobles for your work here."

Chiang was a good Party member, and his expression was a study as he sat down. Colin turned to the petite, smooth-faced Councilor on Horus's left.

"Councilor Hsu, what's the state of our planet-side industry?"

"There has been considerable loss, Comrade Emperor," Hsu Yin said. Obviously Chiang wasn't the only one feeling her way into the new political setup. "Comrade Chernikov's decision to increase planetary industry has borne fruit, however. Despite all damage, our industrial plant is operating at approximately fifty percent of pre-siege levels. With the assistance of your repair ships, we should make good our remaining losses within five months.

"There are, however, certain personnel problems, and not this time—" her serious eyes swept her fellow councilors with just a hint of wry humor "—in Third World areas. Your Western trade unions—specifically, your Teamsters Union—have awakened to the economic implications of Imperial technology."

"Oh, Lord!" Colin looked at Gustav van Gelder. "Gus? How bad is it?"

"It could be much worse, as Councilor Hsu knows quite well," the security councilor said, but he smiled at her as he spoke. "So far, they are relying upon propaganda, passive resistance, and strikes. It should not take them long to realize other people are singularly unimpressed by their propaganda and that their strikes merely inconvenience a society with Imperial technology." He shrugged. "When they do, the wisest among them will realize they must adapt or go the way of the dinosaurs. I do not anticipate organized violence, if that is what you mean, but I have my eye on the situation."

"Well thank God for that," Colin muttered. "All right, I think that clears up the planetary situation. Are there any other points we need to look at?" Heads shook. "In that case, Dahak, suppose you bring us up to date on Project Rosetta."

"Of course, Sire." Dahak was on his best official behavior before the Council, and Colin raised one hand to hide his smile.

"Progress has been more rapid than originally projected," the computer said. "There are, of course, many differences between Achuultani—or, to be correct, Aku'Ultan—computers and our own, but the basic processes are not complex. The large quantity of hard-copy data obtained from the wreckage also will be of great value in deciphering the output we have generated.

"I am not yet prepared to provide translations or interpretations, but this project is continuing." Colin nodded. Dahak meant the majority of his capability was devoted to it even as he spoke. "I anticipate at least partial success within the next several days."

"Good," Colin said. "We need that data to plan our next move."

"Acknowledged," Dahak said calmly.

"What else do you have for us?"

"Principally observational data, Sire. Our technical teams and my own remotes have completed their initial survey of the wreckage. I am now prepared to present a brief general summary of our findings. Shall I proceed?"

"Please do."

"The present data contain anomalies. Specifically, certain aspects of Aku'Ultan technology do not logically correspond to others. For example, they appear to possess only a very rudimentary appreciation of gravitonics and their ships do not employ gravitonic sublight drives, yet their sublight missiles employ a highly sophisticated gravitonic drive which is, in fact, superior to that of the Imperium though inferior to that of the Empire."

"Could they have picked that up from someone else?" MacMahan asked.

"The possibility exists. Yet having done so, why have they not applied it to their starships? Their relatively slow speed, even in hyper space, is a severe tactical handicap, and, logically, they should recognize the potentials of their own missile propulsion, yet they have not taken advantage of them.

"Nor is this the only anomaly. The computers aboard this starship are primitive in the extreme, but little advanced over those of Earth, yet the components of which they are built are very nearly on a par with my own, though far inferior to the Empire's energy-state systems. Again, their hyper technology is highly sophisticated, yet there is no sign of beamed hyper fields, nor even of warp warheads or grenades. This is the more surprising in view of their extremely primitive, energy-intensive beam weapons. Their range is short, their effect limited, and their projectors both clumsy and massive, but little advanced from those of pre-Imperium Terra."

"Any explanation for these anomalies?" Colin asked after a moment.

"I have none, Sire. It would appear that the Aku'Ultan have chosen, for reasons best known to themselves, to build extremely inefficient warships by the standards of their own evident technical capabilities. Why a warrior race should do such a thing surpasses my present understanding."

"Yours and mine both," Colin murmured, drumming on the conference table edge. Then he shook his head.

"Thank you, Dahak. Keep on this for us, please."

"I shall, Sire."

"In that case," Colin turned to Isis and Cohanna, "what can you tell us about how these beasties are put together, Ladies?"

"I'll let Captain Cohanna begin, if I may," Isis said. "She's supervised most of the autopsies."

"All right. Cohanna?"

"Well," *Dahak*'s surgeon said, "Councilor Tudor's seen more of our live specimen, but we've both learned a fair bit from the dead ones.

"To summarize, the Achuultani are definitely warm-blooded, despite their saurian appearance, though their biochemistry incorporates an appalling level of metals by human standards. A fraction of it would kill any of us; their bones are virtually a crystalline alloy; their amino acids are incredible; and they use a sort of protein-analogue metal salt as an oxygen-carrier. I haven't even been able to identify some of the elements in it yet, but it works. In fact, it's a bit more efficient than hemoglobin, and it's also what gives their blood that bright-orange color. Their chromosome structure is fascinating, but I'll need several months before I can tell you much more than that about it.

"Now," she drew a deep breath, "none of that is too terribly surprising, given that we're dealing with an utterly alien species, but a few other points strike me as definitely weird.

"First, they have at least two sexes, but we've seen only males. It is, of course, possible that their culture doesn't believe in exposing females to combat, but an incursion's personnel spend decades of subjective time on operations. It seems a bit unlikely, to me, at any rate, that any race could be so immune to the biological drives as to remain celibate for periods like that. In addition, unless their psychology is entirely beyond our understanding, I would think that being cut off from all procreation would produce the same apathy it produces in human societies.

"Second, there appears to be an appalling lack of variation. I've yet to unravel their basic gene structure, but we've been carrying out tissue studies on the cadavers recovered from the wreck. By the standards of any species known to Terran or Imperial bioscience, they exhibit a statistically improbable—*extremely* improbable—homogeneity. Were it not for the very careful labeling we've done, I would be tempted to conclude that all of our tissue samples come from no more than a few score individuals. I have no explanation for how this might have come about.

"Third, and perhaps most puzzling, is the relative primitivism of their gross physiognomy. To the best of our knowledge, this same race has conducted offensive sweeps of our arm of the galaxy for over seventy million years, yet they do not exhibit the attributes one might expect such a long period of high-tech civilization to produce. They're large, extremely strong, and well-suited to a relatively primitive environment. One would expect a species which had enjoyed technology for so long to have decreased in size, at the very least, and, perhaps, to have lost much of its tolerance for extreme environmental conditions. These creatures have done neither."

"Is that really relevant?" Amesbury asked. "Humanity hasn't exactly developed the attributes you describe, either here or in Imperial history."

"The cases aren't parallel, Sir Frederick. The Terran branch of the race is but recently removed from its own primitive period, and all of human history, from its beginnings on Mycos to the present, represents only a tiny fraction of the life experience of the Achuultani. Further, the Achuultani's destruction of the Third Imperium eliminated all human-populated planets other than Birhat—a rather draconian reduction in the gene pool."

"Point taken," Amesbury said, and Cohanna gestured to Isis.

"Just as Cohanna has noted anomalies in Achuultani physiology," the white-haired physician began, "I have observed anomalies in behavioral patterns. Obviously, our prisoner—his name is 'Brashieel,' as nearly as we can pronounce it—is a *prisoner* and so cannot be considered truly representative of his race. His behavior, however, is, by any human standard, bizarre.

"He appears resigned, yet not passive. In general, his behavior is docile, which could be assumed, genuine, or merely a response to our own biotechnics. Certainly he's deduced that even our medical technicians are several times as strong as he is, though he may not realize this is due to artificial enhancement. He is *not*, however, apathetic. He's alert, interested, and curious. We are unable to communicate with him as yet, but he appears to be actively assisting our efforts in this direction. I submit that for a soldier embarked upon a genocidal campaign to exhibit neither resistance to, nor even, so nearly as we can determine, hostility towards the species he recently attempted to annihilate isn't exactly typical of a human response."

"Um." Colin tugged on his nose. "How are his injuries responding?"

"We can't use quick-heal or regeneration on such an unknown physiology, but he appears to be recovering nicely. His bones are knitting a bit faster than a human's would; tissue repairs seem to be taking rather longer."

"All right," Colin said, "what do we have? A technology with gaping holes, a species which seems evolutionarily retarded, and a prisoner whose responses defy our logical expectations. Does anyone have any suggestions which could account for all those things?"

He looked around expectantly, but the only response was silence.

"Well," he sighed after a moment, "let's adjourn for now. Unless something breaks in the meantime, we'll convene again Wednesday at fourteen hundred hours. Will that be convenient for all of you?"

Heads nodded, and he rose.

"I'll see you all then," he said. He wanted to get home to *Dahak* anyway. The twins were teething, and 'Tanni wasn't exactly the most placid mommy in human history.

CHAPTER NINETEEN

Brashieel, who had been a servant of thunders, curled in his new nest place and pondered. It had never occurred to him—nor to anyone else, so far as he knew—to consider the possibility of capture. Protectors did not capture nest-killers; they slew them. So, he had always assumed, did nest-killers deal with Protectors, yet these had not.

He had attempted to fight to the death, but he had failed, and, strangely, he no longer wished to die. No one had ever told him he must; had they simply failed, as he, to consider that he might not? Yet he felt a vague suspicion a true thinker in honor would have ended slaying yet another nest-killer.

Only Brashieel wished to live. He *needed* to consider the new things happening to and about him. These strange bipeds had destroyed Lord Chirdan's force with scarcely five twelves of ships. Admittedly, they were huge, yet it had taken but five twelves, when Lord Chirdan had been within day-twelfths of destroying this world. That was power. Such nest-killers could purge the galaxy of the Aku'Ultan, and the thought filled him with terror.

But why had they waited so long? He had seen this world's nest-killers now, and they were the same species as those who crewed those stupendous ships. Whether they were also the nest-killers who had built those sensor arrays he did not know. It seemed likely, yet if it were so those arrays must have told them long ago that the Great Visit was upon them, so why conceal their capability until this world had suffered such losses? And why had they not killed *him*? Because they sought information from him? That was possible, though it would not have occurred to a Protector. Which might, Brashieel admitted grudgingly, be yet another way in which his captors outclassed the Nest. But stranger even than that, they did not mistreat him. They were impossibly strong for such small beings. He had thought it was but the nest-killer's powered armor which had made him a fledgling in his hands . . . until he saw a slight, slender one with long hair lift one of their elevated sleeping pads and carry it away to clear his nest place. That was sobering proof of what they might have done to him had they chosen to.

Instead, they had tended his wounds, fed him food from *Vindicator*'s wreck, provided air which was pleasant to breathe, not thin like their own—all that, when they should have struck him down. Was he not a nest-killer to *their* Protectors? Had he and his nestmates not come within a segment of destroying their very world? Were they so stupid they did not realize that they were—must be, forever—enemies to the death?

Or was it simply that they did not fear him? Beside those monster ships, the greatest ships of the Nest were fledglings with toy bows of *mowap* wood. Were they so powerful, so confident, that they did not fear the nest-killers of another people, another place?

That was the most terrifying thought of all, one which reeked of treason to the Nest, for there was—must always be—the fear, the Great Fear which only courage and the Way could quench. Yet if that was not so for these nest-killers, if they did not fear on sight, then was it possible they might not *be* nest-killers?

Brashieel curled in his new nest place, eyes closed, and whimpered in his sleep, wondering in his dreams which was truly the greater nightmare: to fear the nest-killers, or to fear that they did not fear him.

Colin and Jiltanith rose to welcome Earth's senior officers and their new starship captains. There were but fourteen captains. If they took every trained, bio-enhanced man and woman Earth's defenses could spare, they could have provided minimal crews for seventeen of the Imperial Guard's warships; they had chosen to crew only fifteen, fourteen *Asgerds* and one *Vespa*.

The Empire had gone in for more specialized designs than the Imperium, and the *Asgerds* were closest in concept to *Dahak*, well-rounded and equipped to fight at all ranges, while the *Trosans* were optimized for close combat with heavy beam armaments and the *Vespas* were optimized for planetary assaults. But the reason for manning only fifteen warships was simple; the other personnel would crew the three *Enchanach*-class transports, each vast as *Dahak* himself, for Operation Dunkirk.

In hyper, the round-trip to Bia would take barely six months, and each stupendous ship could squeeze in upward of ten million people. With luck, they had time to return for a second load even if the Imperial Guard failed to halt the Achuultani, which meant they could evacuate over sixty million humans to the almost impregnable defenses of the old Imperial capital and the housing Mother's remotes were already building to receive them. General Chiang was selecting those refugees now; they were Colin's insurance policy.

The Achuultani's best speed, even in hyper, seemed to be just under fifty times light-speed. At absolute minimum, they would take seventeen years to reach Bia. Seventeen years in which Mother and Tsien Tao-ling could activate defensive systems, collect and build additional warships, and man them. If the Achuultani ever reached Bia, they would not enjoy the visit.

Colin looked down the table at Tsien. The marshal was as impassive as ever, but Colin had seen the hurt in his eyes when he lost the coin toss to Hatcher. Yet, in a way, Colin was pleased it was Tsien who was going. He hadn't learned to know the huge man well, but he liked what he knew. Tsien was a man of iron, and Colin trusted him with his life. With far more than his life, for his children would be returning to Birhat.

Without 'Tanni. She was the commander of *Dahak Two*, the reserve flag-ship, and that was as far from Colin as she was going. Because she loved him, yes, but also because he would be going to meet the Achuultani, and the killer in her could not resist that battle.

Had their roles been reversed, Colin thought he might have made him-self go out of a sense of duty, but 'Tanni couldn't. He might have tried ordering her to . . . if he hadn't understood and loved her.

The last officer—Senior Fleet Captain Lady Adrienne Robbins, Baron-ess Nergal, Companion of the Golden Nova and CO of the planetoid *Emperor Herdan*—found her place, and Colin glanced around the conference room, satisfied that this was the best Earth could boast, committed to her final defense. Then he stood and rapped gently on the table, and the quiet side conversations ended.

"Ladies and gentlemen, Dahak has broken into the Achuultani data base. We finally know what we're up against, and it isn't good. In fact, it may be bad enough to make Operation Dunkirk a necessity, not just an insur-ance policy."

Horus watched Colin as he spoke. His son-in-law looked grim, but far from defeated. He remembered the Colin MacIntyre he'd first met, a homely, sandy-haired young man who'd strayed into an unthinkably ancient war, determined to do what he must, yet terrified that he was unequal to his task.

That homely young man was gone. By whatever chain of luck or des-tiny history moved, he had met his moment. Preposterous as it seemed, he had become in truth what accident had made him: Colin I, Emperor and Warlord of Humanity—Mankind's champion in this dark hour. If they survived, Horus mused, Herdan the Great would have a worthy rival as the greatest emperor in human history.

"—not going to count ourselves out yet, though," Colin was saying, and Horus shook himself back into the moment. "We've got better intelligence than anyone's ever had on an incursion, and I intend to use it. Before I tell you what I hope to accomplish, however, it's only fair that you know what we're really up against. 'Tanni?" He nodded to his wife and sat as she stood.

"My Lords and Ladies," she said quietly, "we face a foe greater than any who have come before us. 'Twould seem the Achuultani do call this arm of our galaxy common 'the Demon Sector' for that they have suffered so in their voyages hither. So have they mustered up a strength full double any e'er dispatched in times gone by, and this force we face with scarce four score ships.

"Our Dahak hath beagled out their numbers. As thou dost know, Achuultani calculations rest upon the base-twelve system, and 'tis a great twelve cubed—near to three million, as we would say—of warships which come upon us."

There was a sound. Not a gasp, but a deep-drawn breath. Most of the faces around the table tightened, but no one spoke.

"Yet that telleth but a part," Jiltanith went on evenly. "The scouts which did war 'pon Terra these months past were but light units. Those which come behind are vaster far, the least near twice the size of those which have been vanquished here. We scarce could smite them all did our every missile speed straightway to its mark, and so, in sober fact, we durst not meet them all in open battle."

Officers exchanged stunned glances, and Colin didn't blame them. His own first reaction would have done his reputation for coolness no good at all.

"Yet I counsel not despair!" Jiltanith's clear voice cut through the almost-fear. "Nay, good My Lords and Ladies, our Warlord hath a plan most shrewd which still may tumble them to dust. Yet now will I ask our General MacMahan to speak that thou mayst know thine enemies."

She sat, and Horus applauded silently. Colin's human officers spoke, not Dahak. Everyone here knew how much they relied upon Dahak, yet he could see them drawing a subtle strength from hearing their own kind brief them. It wasn't that they distrusted Dahak—how could they, when their very survival to this point resulted only from the ancient starship's fidelity?—but they needed to hear a human voice expressing confidence. A human who was merely mortal, like themselves, and so could understand what he or she asked of them.

"Ladies and gentlemen," Hector MacMahan said, "Fleet Captain Ninhursag and I have spent several days examining the data with Dahak. Ninhursag's also spent time with our prisoner and, with Dahak's offices as translator, she's been able to communicate with him after a fashion. Oddly enough, from our perspective, though he hasn't volunteered data, he's made no attempt to lie or mislead us.

"We've learned a great deal as a result, and, though there are still huge holes in our knowledge, I'll attempt to summarize our findings. Please bear with me if I seem to wander a bit afield. I assure you, it's pertinent.

"The Achuultani, or the People of the Nest of Aku'Ultan, are—exclusively, so far as we can determine—a warrior race. Judging from some of Brashieel's counter-questions, they know absolutely nothing about any other sentient race. They've spent millions of years hunting them down and destroying them, yet they've learned nothing—literally *nothing*—about any of them. It's almost as if they fear communicating might somehow corrupt their great purpose. And that purpose is neither less nor more than the defense of the Nest of Aku'Ultan."

A few eyebrows rose, and Hector shook his head.

"I found it hard to believe at first myself, but that's precisely how they see it, because at some point in their past they encountered another race, one their records call 'the Great Nest-Killers.' How they met, why war broke out, what weapons were used, even where the war was fought, we do not know. What we do know is that there were once many 'nests.' These might be thought of as clans or tribes, but they consisted of millions and even billions of Achuultani. Of all those nests, only the Aku'Ultan survived, and only because they fled. From what we've learned, we're inclined to believe they fled to an entirely different galaxy—our own—to find safety.

"After their flight, the Achuultani organized to defend themselves against pursuit, just as the Imperium organized to fight the Achuultani themselves. And just as the Imperium sent out probes searching for the Achuultani, the Achuultani searched for the Great Nest-Killers. Like our ancestors, they never found their enemy. Unlike our ancestors, they did find other sentient life forms. And because they regarded all other life forms as threats to their very existence, they destroyed them."

He paused, and there was a deep silence.

"That's what we're up against: a race which offers no quarter because it *knows* it will receive none. I don't say it's a situation which can never be changed, but clearly it's one we cannot hope will change in time to save us.

"On another level, there are things about the Aku'Ultan we don't pretend to understand.

"First, there are no female Achuultani." Several people looked at him in open disbelief, and he shrugged. "It sounds bizarre, but so far as we can tell, there isn't even a feminine gender in their language, which is all the more baffling in light of the fact that our prisoner is a fully functional male. Not a hermaphrodite, but a *male*. Fleet Captain Cohanna suggests this may indicate they reproduce by artificial means, which might explain why we see so little variation among them and, perhaps, their apparent lack of evolutionary change. It does *not* explain why any race, especially one as driven to survive as this one, should make the extraordinary decision to abandon all possibility of natural procreation. We asked Brashieel about this and got a totally baffled response. He simply didn't understand the question. It hadn't even occurred to him that *we* have two sexes, and he has no idea at all what that means to our psychology or our civilization.

"Second, the Nest is an extremely rigid, caste-oriented society dominated by the High Lords of the Nest and headed by the Nest Lord, the highest of the high, absolute ruler of all Achuultani. Exactly how High Lords and Nest Lords are chosen was none of Brashieel's business. As nearly as we can tell, he was never even curious. It was simply the way things were.

"Third, the Aku'Ultan inhabit relatively few worlds; most of them are always away aboard the fleets of their 'Great Visits,' sweeping the galaxy for 'nest-killers' and destroying them. The few planets they inhabit seem to be much further away than the Imperium ever suspected, which is probably why they were never found, and the Achuultani appear to be migratory, abandoning star systems as they deplete them to construct their warships. We don't know exactly where they are; that information wasn't in *Vindicator's* computers or, if it was, was destroyed before we took them. From what we've been able to determine, however, they appear to be moving to the galactic east. This would mean they're constantly moving *away* from us, which may also help to explain the irregular frequency of their incursions in our direction.

"Fourth, the Nest's social and military actions follow patterns which, as far as we can tell, have never altered in their racial memory. Frankly, this is the most hopeful point we've discovered. We now know how their 'great visits' work and how to derail the process for quite some time."

"We do?" Gerald Hatcher scratched his nose thoughtfully. "And just how do we do that, Hector?"

"We stop this incursion," MacMahan said simply. There was a mutter of uneasy laughter, and he smiled very slightly. "No, I mean it.

"The Achuultani possess no means of interstellar FTL communication other than by ship. How they could've been around this long and not developed one is beyond me, but they haven't, which means that once a 'great visit' is launched, they don't expect to hear anything from it until it gets back."

"That's good news, anyway," Hatcher agreed.

"Yes, it is. Especially in light of some of their other limitations. Their best n-space speed is twenty-eight percent of light-speed, and they use only the lower, slower hyper bands—again, we don't understand why, but let's be grateful—which limits their best supralight speed to forty-eight lights; seven percent of what Dahak can turn out, six percent of what the Guard can turn out under Enchanach Drive, and two percent of what it can turn out in hyper. That means they take a *long* time to complete an incursion. Of course, unlike Enchanach Drive, there's a time dilation effect in hyper, and the lower your band, the greater the dilation, which means their voyages take a lot less time subjectively, but Brashieel's ship had already come something like fourteen thousand light-years to reach Sol. So if the incursion sent a courier home tomorrow, he'd take just under three centuries to get there. Which means, ladies and gentlemen, that if we stop them, we've got almost six hundred years before a new 'great visit' can get back here. And that we know where to go looking for *them* in the meantime."

A soft growl came from the assembled officers as they visualized what they could do with five or six centuries to work with.

"I'm glad to hear that, Hector," Hatcher said carefully, "but it leaves us with the little matter of three million or so ships coming at us right now."

"True," Colin said, waving MacMahan back down. "But we've learned a little—less than we'd like, but a little—about their strategic doctrine.

"First, we have a bit more time than we'd thought. The incursion is divided into three major groups: two main formations and a host of sub-formations of scouts which do most of the killing. The larger formations are mainly to back up the scout forces, each of which operates on a different axis of advance. Aside from the one which already hit us, they're unlikely to hit anything but dead planets as far as we're concerned, and a half-dozen crewed *Asgerds* could deal with any of them. If we can stop the main incursion, we'll have plenty of time to hunt them down and pick them off.

"The real bad news is coming at us in two parts. The first—what I think of as the 'vanguard'—is about one and a quarter million ships, advancing fairly slowly from rendezvous to rendezvous in n-space to permit scouts to send back couriers to report. We may assume one's already been dispatched from Sol, but it can't pass its message until the vanguard drops out of hyper at the rendezvous, thirty-six Achuultani light-years from Sol. Given the difference in length between our years and theirs, that's about forty-six-point-eight of our light-years. The vanguard won't reach their rendezvous for another three months; we can be there in about three and a half weeks with *Dahak*, and a hell of a lot less than that for the Guard in hyper.

"And take on a million ships when you get there?" Hatcher said.

"Tough odds, but I've got a mousetrap planned that should take them out. Unfortunately, it'll only work once.

"That's our problem. Even if we zap the vanguard, that still leaves what I think of as the 'main body': almost as numerous and with some really big mothers, under their supreme commander, a Great Lord Tharno.

"Now, the vanguard and main body actually keep changing relative position—they 'leapfrog' as they advance—and their rendezvous are much more tightly spaced than the scouts' are. Again, this is to allow for communication; the scouts can't pass messages laterally, and they only send one back to the closest main fleet rendezvous if they hit trouble, but the leading main formation sends couriers back to the trailing formation at each stop. If there's really bad news, the lead force calls the trailer forward to link up, but only after investigating to be sure they *need* help, since it plays hell with their schedules. In any case, however, at least one courier is always sent back and there's a minimum interval of about five months before the trailer can come up. With me so far?"

There were nods, and he smiled grimly.

"All right, that's our major strategic advantage: their coordination stinks. Because they use hyper drives, their ships have to stay in hyper once they go into it until they reach their destination. And because their maximum fold-space com range is barely a light-year, the rear components of their fleet always jump to the origin point of the last message from the lead formation. Even in emergencies, the follow-on echelon has to jump to to almost exactly the same point, assuming they mean to coordinate with the leaders, because with their miserable communications they can't *find* each other if they don't."

"Which means," Marshal Tsien said thoughtfully, "that your own ships may be able to ambush their formations as they emerge from hyper."

"Exactly, Marshal. What we hope to do is mousetrap the vanguard and wipe it out; I think we'll get away with that, but we don't know where the rendezvous point *before* this one is. That means we can't stop the vanguard's couriers from telling Lord Tharno about our trap, meaning that the main body will be alerted and ready when it comes out.

"So we probably *will* have to fight the main body. That pits seventy-eight of us against one-point-two million of them: about fifteen thousand to one."

Someone swallowed audibly, and Colin smiled that grim smile again.

"I think we can take them. We may lose a lot of ships, but we ought to be able to swing it *if* they pop into n-space where we expect them."

A long silence dragged out. Marshal Tsien broke it at length.

"Forgive me, but I do not see how you can do it."

"I'm not certain we can, Marshal," Colin said frankly. "I *am* certain that we have a chance, and that we can destroy at least half and more probably two-thirds of their force. If that's all we accomplish, we may not save Earth, but we *will* save Birhat and the refugees headed there. That, Marshal Tsien—" he met the huge man's eyes "—is why I'm so relieved to know we're sending one of our best people to take over Bia's defenses."

"I am honored by your confidence, Your Majesty, yet I fear you have set yourself an impossible task. You have only fifteen partially-manned warships—sixteen counting *Dahak*."

"But Dahak is our ace in the hole. Unlike the rest of us, he can fight all of our unmanned ships with full efficiency as long as he's in fold-space range of them."

"And if something happens to him, Your Majesty?" Tsien asked quietly.

"Then, Marshal Tsien," Colin said just as quietly, "I hope to hell you have Bia in shape by the time the incursion gets there."

CHAPTER TWENTY

"Hyper wake coming in from Sol, ma'am."

Adrienne Robbins, Lady Nergal (and it still felt *weird* to be a noble of an empire which had died forty-five thousand years ago), nodded and watched *Herdan*'s holographic projection. The F5 star Terran astronomers knew as Zeta Trianguli Australis was a diamond chip five light-years astern, and the blood-red hyper trace indicator flashed almost on a line with it.

Adrienne's stupendous command floated with three other starships, yet alone and lonely. The four of them were deployed to cover almost a cubic light-year of space, and Tamman's *Royal Birhat* was already moving to intercept. Well, that was all right; she'd killed enough Achuultani at the Siege of Earth.

"Captain, we've got a very faint wake coming in from the east, too," her plotting officer said, and Lady Adrienne frowned. That had to be the Achuultani vanguard, and it was way ahead of schedule.

"Emergence times?"

"Bogey One will emerge into n-space in approximately seven hours twelve minutes, ma'am; make it oh-two-twenty zulu," Fleet Commander Oliver Weinstein said. "Bogey Two's a real monster to show up at this range at all. We've got a good hundred hours before they emerge, maybe as much as five days. I'll be able to refine that in a couple of hours."

"Do that, Ollie," she said, relaxing again. The vanguard wasn't as far ahead of schedule as she'd feared, just a bigger, more visible target than anticipated.

Adrienne sighed. It had been easier to command *Nergal*. The battleship's computers had been no smarter than *Herdan*'s, but they'd had nowhere near as much to do. If she'd needed to, she could be anywhere in the net through her neural feed, but *Herdan* was just too damned big. Even with six thousand crewmen aboard, less than five percent of her duty stations were manned. They could get by—barely—with that kind of stretch, but it was a bitch and a half. If only this ship were half as smart—hell, even a tenth as smart!—as *Dahak*. But they had only one *Dahak*, and he couldn't be committed to this job.

"Herdan," she said aloud.

"Yes, Captain?" a soft soprano replied, and Adrienne's mouth curled in a reflexive smile. It was silly for a ship named for the Empire's greatest emperor to sound like a teenaged girl, but apparently the fashion in the late Empire had been to give computers female voices, and hang the gender.

"Assume Bogey Two has scanners fifty percent more efficient than those of the scouts which attacked Earth and will emerge into n-space twelve hours from now. Compute probability Bogey Two will be able to detect detonation of Mark-Seventy gravitonic warheads at spatial and temporal loci of Bogey One's projected emergence into n-space."

"Computing." There was a brief pause. "Probability approaches zero."

"How closely?"

"Probability is one times ten to the minus thirty-second," Herdan responded. "Plus or minus two percent."

"Well, that's pretty close to zero at that, I guess," Adrienne murmured.

"Comment not understood."

"Ignore last comment," Adrienne replied, suppressing a sigh. It wasn't Herdan's fault she was an idiot, but after talking to Dahak—

"Acknowledged," Herdan said, and Lady Adrienne pressed her lips firmly together.

"Scout emergence into n-space in fourteen minutes, sir."

"Thank you, Janet," Senior Fleet Captain Tamman said, wishing he could share his tension with Amanda, and wasn't that a silly thought when he'd taken such pains to insure that he couldn't? Well, he admitted, "pains" was the wrong word, but he'd only gotten away with it because he'd found out about Colin's compulsory personnel orders assigning all pregnant Fleet personnel to the Operation Dunkirk crews a good month before Amanda had.

He *thought* she would forgive him someday, but he'd almost lost her once in La Paz, and then a rifle slug went right through her visor aboard *Vindicator*. It was only the Maker's own grace it hadn't shattered, and she'd used up most of her helmet sealant and all of her luck. He was taking no chances this time.

"Emergence in five minutes," Janet Santino said politely, and Tamman shook his head. Woolgathering, by the Maker!

"Come to Red One," he said, and his command staff settled into even more intimate communion with their consoles. His own eyes focused dreamily on the red circle delineating their target's locus of emergence, barely twenty light-seconds from their present position, while his brain concentrated on his neural feed, "seeing" directly through *Birhat's* superb scanners.

That courier had done a bang-up job of timing its jump, given the crudity of its computers, to hit this close to an exact rendezvous with the vanguard.

"Emergence in one minute," Santini said.

"Alpha Battery," Tamman said gently, "you are authorized to fire the moment you have a firm track."

"Emergence in thirty seconds. Fifteen. Ten. Five. *Now!*"

The red circle suddenly held a tiny red dot. There was a brief, eternal heartbeat of tension, and then the missiles fired.

They were sublight in order to home, but only barely so. They flashed across the display, and the dot vanished without fuss or bother, twenty kilometers of starship ripped apart by gravitonic warheads it had probably never even seen coming.

"Target," Birhat's velvety contralto purred, "destroyed."

"Thank you, Darling," someone murmured. "I hope it was good for you, too."

"Well, that's the first hurdle," Colin said as he digested Tamman's brief hypercom transmission.

"As thou sayst," Jiltanith agreed.

Colin nodded and looked around, admiring *Dahak Two*'s spacious command deck and awesome instrumentation, and knew he would trade it all in a heartbeat for *Dahak*'s outmoded bridge. Not that *Two* wasn't a fantastic fighting machine; she just wasn't *Dahak*. But *Dahak* couldn't fly this mission, and Colin refused to send his people to fight without him. Assuming anyone survived the next few months, that might be something he'd have to get used to. For now, it wasn't.

At the moment, *Two* was tearing through space at better than eight hundred times light-speed. *Herdan* was closest to the vanguard's projected emergence, and the ships which had spread out to cover the courier's probable emergence points hurried toward her. They could have made the trip in a fraction of the time in hyper, but then the vanguard might have seen them coming.

It was all right, he told himself again. Those Achuultani clunkers were so slow all twelve of the ships he'd committed to the operation would be in position long before they emerged.

"Approaching supralight shutdown, Captain," a female voice said.

"My thanks, Two," Jiltanith replied, and that was another strange thing. Colin might be an emperor and a warlord; he was also a passenger. *Two* could not be in better hands, but it felt odd to be riding someone else's command after all this time, even 'Tanni's.

He turned his attention to the display, and the bright green dots of his other ships blinked as *Two* went sublight and the stars suddenly slowed. There came *Tor*, the last of them, closing up nicely. Good.

"All units in position, Sire," Jiltanith said formally. "Stealth fields active."

"Thank you, Captain," Colin said with equal formality. "Now we wait."

Great Lord of Order Sorkar hated rendezvous stops, especially in the Demon Sector. Battle Comp assured him there was no real danger, and Nest Lord knew Battle Comp was always right, but there were too many horror stories about this sector. Sorkar was not supposed to know them—great lords were above the gossip of lower nestlings—but unlike most of his fellows, Sorkar had won his lordship the hard way, and he had not forgotten his origins as thoroughly as, perhaps, he ought to have.

Still, *this* visit had been almost boring, despite those odd reports of long-abandoned sensor arrays. Sorkar had longed for a little action more than once, for the urge to hunt was strong within any great lord, but Protectors were a commodity to be preserved for the service of the Nest, and he was too shrewd a commander to regret the tedium. Mostly.

He split his attention between his panel and the chronometers as they clicked over the last segment, and a corner of his brain double-checked the override between Battle Comp and his own panel. Battle Comp seldom took a hand directly, but it was comforting to know it could.

There! Emergence.

He watched his instruments approvingly. It was impossible to coordinate the translation between hyper space and n-space perfectly for so many units, but the time spread looked more than merely satisfactory, and the spacing was exemplary. His Protectors had learned their duties well over the—

"Alarm! Alarm! Incoming fire! Incoming fire!" a voice yelped, and Great Lord Sorkar jerked half-upright. They were light-years from the nearest star—*who could be firing on them here?*

But someone *was*, and he watched in horror as missiles of the greater thunder and something else, something beyond belief, shredded his proud starships like blazing tinder.

Nest-killers! The Demon Nest-Killers of the Demon Sector! But *how*? He'd studied all the previous great visits to this sector. Never—*never!*—had nest-killers struck until one or more of their worlds had been cleansed! Had those mysterious sensor arrays alerted them after all? But even if they had, how could they have known to find the rendezvous? It was impossible!

Yet the missiles continued to bore in, sublight and hyper alike, and his scanners could not even *see* the attackers! What wizardry—?

A raucous buzzer cut through his thoughts, and his eyes flashed to Battle Comp's panel. Data codes danced as the mighty computers took over his fleet, and Great Lord Sorkar was a passenger as his ships deployed. They spread apart, thinning the nest-killers' target even as they groped blindly to find their enemy. It was a good plan, he thought, but it was costing them. Tarhish, *how* it was costing them! But if there truly was a nest-killer force out there, if this was not, indeed, the night-demons of frightened legend, then they would find them. Terrible as his losses were, they were as nothing against his entire force, and when Battle Comp found a tar—

A target source appeared on his panel. Another blinked into sight, and another, as his nestlings spent their lives merely to find them, and Nest Lord, they were close! Some sort of cloaking technology. The thought was an icicle in his brain, for it was far better than anything the Nest had, but he had targets at last. He moved to order his nestlings to open fire, but Battle Comp had acted first. He heard his own voice, calm and dispassionate, already passing the command.

"Burn, baby! *Burn!*" someone whooped.

"Silence! Clear the net!" Adrienne Robbins cracked, and the exultant voice vanished. Not that she could blame whoever it had been, for their opening salvos had been twice as effective as projected. Unfortunately, that was because they were *three* times as close as planned. The hyper drives aboard these larger ships were slightly different from those the scouts had mounted, and their calculations had been off. By only a tiny amount, perhaps, but minute computational errors had major consequences on this scale.

They were going to burn through the stealth field a hell of a lot quicker than anyone had expected. She knew she had more experience against the Achuultani than anyone else, and perhaps her earlier losses had affected her nerve, but, damn it, those buggers were inside their own sublight *and* hyper missile range! *Herdan*'s defenses were incomparably better than *Nergal*'s, and her shield covered twenty times the hyper bands, but her sheer size meant it extended even further from the hull than *Nergal*'s had, and there were going to be a *lot* of missiles headed her way very soon.

"Stand by missile defense; stand by ECM!" she snapped, and then, Dear Jesus, here it came.

Great Lord Sorkar spit an incredulous curse. A twelve of them! A single *twelve* had already slain a greater twelve and more of his ships, and their defenses were as incredible as their firepower. Targeting screens blossomed with false images, sucking his sublight weapons off target. Jammers hashed the scan channels. Titanic shields shrugged the greater thunder contemptuously aside. And still his ships died and died and died. . . .

Yet nothing could stop the twelves of twelves of twelves of missiles his ships were hurling, and he bared his teeth as the first hyper missile slashed through a nest-killer shield. There! That should show them that—

He blinked, and his blood was ice. What sort of monster could absorb a direct hit from the greater thunder and not even *notice* it?

Alarms screamed as a ten-thousand-megaton warhead exploded almost on top of *Royal Birhat*. The huge ship quivered as the furious plasma cloud carved an incandescent chasm twenty kilometers into her armored hull. Air exploded from the dreadful wound, blast doors slammed . . . and *Birhat* went right on fighting.

"Moderate damage to Quadrant Theta-Two," the sexy contralto said calmly. "Four fatalities. Point zero-four-two percent combat impairment."

Colin winced as the flashing yellow band of combat damage encircled *Birhat*. He'd lost track of the kills they'd scored, but he'd fucked up. They were too frigging close!

"All ships, open the range," he snapped, and the Imperial Guard darted suddenly astern at sixty-five percent of light-speed.

Tarhish, they were fast! Sorkar had never seen anything but a missile move that quickly in n-space. They fell back out of range of his sublight weapons, retreating toward the edge of his hyper missile envelope, but their own weapons seemed totally unaffected, and he had never seen such accurate targeting. Indeed, he had never seen anyone do *anything* these nest-killers were doing to him, but that did not make them night-demons. It only meant his Protectors faced a test worse than he had ever imagined, and they were *Protectors*.

And, he thought under the surface of his battle orders, perhaps it was not as bad as it might have been. These nest-killers had known where to meet his ships, and not even those arrays could have told them that, so they must have already destroyed one scout force—probably Furtag's, given the timing—and followed its couriers hither. Yet if they could muster but a single twelve of ships, however powerful, against him, then the ships under his command were more than enough to feed them to the Furnace. Even at this extreme range, he had an incalculable advantage in launchers. Not so good as theirs, perhaps, but more than enough to make up any disadvantage.

"Colin, they press us sore," Jiltanith said, and Colin nodded sharply. The plan had been to empty their magazines into the Achuultani, but the shit was too deep for that. *Birhat* had taken only one hit, but *Two* had taken three and *Tor* had taken five. *Five* of those monster warheads!

These ships were tough beyond belief, but any toughness had its limits. He winced as yet another massive salvo exploded against *Two*'s shield and the big ship plowed through the plasma like a drunken windjammer. It was only a matter of time until—

"*Tor* reports shield failure," *Two*'s Comp Cent announced. "Attempting to withdraw into hyper." Colin's eyes darted to *Tor*'s cursor, and the flashing yellow circle was banded in crimson. He stared at it in horror, willing the ship's hyper drive to take her out of it, as missile after missile went home—

"Withdrawal unsuccessful," *Two* said emotionlessly, and Colin's face went bone-white as *Tor*'s dot vanished forever.

"Execute Bug Out," he grated.

"Acknowledged," Jiltanith said coolly.

The nest-killers vanished.

Sorkar stared in disbelief at the reports of his hyper scanners. Almost a greater twelve times light-speed? How was it possible?

But what mattered was that it *was* possible. And that his scanner crews had noted the charging hyper fields in time to get good readings on them. He knew where they would emerge—at that bright star less than a quarter-twelve of light-years ahead of his fleet.

It could not be their homeworld, not so coincidentally close to the rendez-vous, but whatever it was, Sorkar knew what to do if they were stupid enough to tie themselves to its defense, too deep in its gravity well to escape into hyper. He could wade into their fire, take his losses, and crush them by sheer numbers, for he had already proven they could be destroyed.

He did not like to think how many hits it had taken to kill that single nest-killer, but they *had* killed it. And his own losses were scarcely three greater twelves, grievous but hardly fatal.

He plugged into Battle Comp, but he already knew what his orders would be.

✧   ✧   ✧

Colin hoped his expression hid the depth of his shock as his ships darted away. He'd known they would take losses, but he hadn't expected to start taking them so soon, and they'd destroyed less than a half-percent of the enemy. He'd counted on more than that, and *no* losses of his own, damn it!

But he couldn't have brought more ships without *Dahak* to run them, and *Dahak* had no hyper drive. That was the crunch point, because the Achuultani *had* to know where he and his ships had run to.

And because of that, Senior Fleet Captain Roscoe Gillicuddy and his crew had died, and Colin had lost six percent of his autonomous warship strength. He didn't know which hurt more, and that made him feel ashamed.

But the mousetrap had been baited. They'd lost more heavily than allowed for, yet they'd done what they set out to do. He told himself that, but it wasn't enough to hold the demons of guilt and the fear of inadequacy at bay.

A warm, slender hand squeezed his tightly, and he squeezed back gratefully. Military protocol might frown on a warlord holding hands with his flagship captain, but he needed that touch of beloved flesh just now.

CHAPTER TWENTY-ONE

Thirty-six days after the brief, savage battle, *Dahak* kept station on Zeta Trianguli Australis-I and Colin stood in Command One, contemplating the planet his crews had dubbed The Cinder.

He and Jiltanith had tried to name The Cinder something else ('Tanni had favored "Cheese"), but perhaps the crews were right, Colin thought sourly. With a mean orbital radius of five-point-eight-nine light-minutes, The Cinder was about as close to Zeta Trianguli Australis as Venus was to Sol, and Colin had always thought Venus, with a surface hotter than molten lead, was close enough to Hell.

The Cinder was worse, for Zeta Trianguli was brighter than Sol—*much* brighter. But The Cinder had been chosen very carefully. There were other worlds in the system, including a rather nice, if cool, third planet fifteen light-minutes further out. Zeta Trianguli was old for its class, and III had even developed a local flora that was vaguely carboniferous, but Colin was just as happy it had only the most primitive of animal life.

He folded his hands behind him, watching the display, glancing ever and again at the scarlet hyper trace blinking steadily just inside the forty-light-minute orbital shell of Zeta Trianguli-IV.

Fleet Commodore the Empress Jiltanith sat on her command deck and touched the gemmed dagger at her belt. She'd owned that weapon since the Wars of the Roses, and its familiar hilt had soothed her often over the years, but it helped little today. She knew it made excellent sense for her to be where she was, and that, too, was little help.

She wanted to rise and pace, but it would do no good to display her fear, and there were still many hours to go. Indeed, she ought to be in her quarters—her lonely, empty quarters—resting, but here she could at least see *Dahak*'s light code and know how Colin fared.

An even dozen *Trosan*-class planetoids with their heavy energy batteries floated in the inner system with *Dahak*, and two *Vespa*-class assault planetoids orbited The Cinder, tending the heavy armored units doing absolutely nothing worthwhile on its fiery surface . . . except generating a massive energy signature not even a blind man could have missed.

Jiltanith's eyes moved from the three-dimensional schematic of the Zeta Trianguli System to the emptiness about her own ship. The fourteen surviving crewed units of the Imperial Guard floated more than six light-hours from the furnace of the star, and Vlad Chernikov's titanic repair ship *Fabricator* had labored mightily upon them. Much of the damage had been too severe to be fully healed—*Two*, for example, still bore two wounds over sixty kilometers deep—but all were combat ready. Ready, yet carefully stealthed, hidden from every prying scanner, accompanied by sixty loyal, lifeless ships.

Jiltanith did not like to consider why they were not with *Dahak*, but the reasoning was brutally simple. If Operation Mousetrap failed, the crewed ships would return to Terra to hold as long as they might and evacuate as many additional Terra-born as possible to Birhat when they could hold no more, but the unmanned planetoids would be sent directly to Birhat and Marshal Tsien.

There would be no point retaining them, for they were useless in close combat without Dahak's control, and Dahak—and Colin—would be dead.

Great Lord Sorkar's crest flexed thoughtfully as his portion of the Great Visit neared normal-space once more. This star was suspiciously young to have evolved nest-killers of its own, which reinforced his belief that it could be but a forward base. That was bad, since it gave no hint what star these demons might call home. Unless one of them was obliging enough to flee into hyper and head directly thence, which he doubted any ships as fast as they would do, he could not even guess where their true home world lay.

Except, of course, that it almost certainly had been Lord Furtag's scouts which had roused these nest-killers to fury. They must have followed a courier to find Sorkar, and only a courier from Furtag's force could have reached this rendezvous so soon. And that gave Sorkar a volume of space in which at least one of their important worlds must lie. That might be enough. If it was not, it was at least a start. And this star system was another.

Those monster ships' sheer size impressed him deeply, yet anything that large must take many years to build, so each he slew would hurt the nest-killers badly. He only hoped those who had already clashed with his nestlings would be foolish enough to stand and fight here.

A soft musical tone sounded, and he made himself relax, hoping that Battle Comp noticed his tranquillity. The queasy shudder of hyper translation ran through his flagship, and *Defender* dropped into phase with reality once more.

"Achuultani units are emerging from hyper," Dahak's mellow voice said.

Colin nodded as the dots of Achuultani ships gleamed in the display. He looked around the empty bridge, wishing for just a moment that he'd let the others stay. But if this worked, he and *Dahak* could pull it off alone; if it failed, those eight thousand-odd people would be utterly invaluable to

'Tanni and Gerald Hatcher. Besides, this was fitting, somehow. He and *Dahak*, together and alone once more.

"Keep an eye on 'em," he said. "Let me know if they do anything sneaky."

"I shall." Dahak was silent for a moment, then continued. "I have continued my study of energy-state computer technology, Colin."

"Oh?" If Dahak wanted to distract him, that was fine with Colin.

"Yes. I believe I have isolated the fundamental differences between the energy-state 'software' of the Empire and my own. They were rather more subtle than I originally anticipated, but I now feel confident of my ability to reprogram at will."

"Hey, that's great! You mean you could tinker them into waking up?"

"I did not say that, Colin. I can reprogram them; I still have not determined what within my own programming supports my self-aware state. Without that datum, I cannot recreate that state in another. Nor have I yet discovered a certain technique for simply replicating my current programming in their radically different circuitry."

"Yeah." Colin frowned. "But even if you could, you'd have problems, wouldn't you? They're hardwired for loyalty to Mother—wouldn't that put a crimp into your replication?"

"Not," Dahak said rather surprisingly, "in the case of the Guard. Its units were not part of Battle Fleet and do not contain Battle Fleet loyalty imperatives. I suppose—" the computer sounded gently ironic "—Mother and the Assembly of Nobles calculated that the remaining nine hundred ninety-eight thousand seven hundred and twelve planetoids of Battle Fleet would suffice to deal with them in the event an Emperor proved intractable."

"Guess they might, at that."

"The absence of those constraints, however, makes the replication of my core programming at least a possibility, although not a very high one. While I have made progress, I compute that the probability of success would be no more than eight percent. The probability that an *un*successful attempt would incapacitate the recipient computer, however, approaches unity."

"Um." Colin tugged on his nose. "Not so good. The last thing we need is to addle one of the others just now."

"My own thought exactly. I thought, however, that you might appreciate a progress report."

"You mean," Colin snorted, "that you thought I was about to get the willies and you'd better distract me from 'em!"

"That is substantially what I said." Dahak made the soft sound he used for a chuckle. "In my own tactful fashion, of course."

"Tactful, shmactful," Colin grinned. "Thanks, I—"

He broke off as the glittering hordes of Achuultani light codes suddenly vanished only to blink back moments later, much closer in-system.

"They are advancing," Dahak said calmly. "A trio of detached ships, however, appear to be micro-jumping to positions on the system periphery."

"Observers, damn it. Well, no one can count on their enemies being idiots."

"True, though that will be of limited utility if we are able to repeat

our earlier success and destroy them before they rendezvous with the main
body."

"Yeah, but we can't be sure of doing that. It's a lot shorter jump this
time, and they can cut their arrival a hell of a lot closer. Tell 'Tanni to lay
off. Last thing we need to do is to try sneaking up on 'em and alert them
to the fact that there's more of us around."

"Acknowledged," Dahak replied. "*Two* has acknowledged," he added a
moment later.

"Thanks," Colin grunted.

His attention was on the display. The Achuultani had micro-jumped with
beautiful precision, spreading out to englobe Zeta Trianguli at a range of
twenty-seven light-minutes. Now they were closing in normal space at twenty-
four percent light-speed. They'd be into extreme missile range in another
ten minutes, but it would take them almost an hour to reach *their* range
of The Cinder, and he and *Dahak* could hurt them badly in that much time.

But not too badly. They had to keep closing. He needed them deep into
the stellar gravity well for this to work, and—

He snorted. There were over a *million* of the bastards—just how much
damage did he think his fifteen ships could inflict in fifty minutes?

"Open up at fifteen light-minutes, Dahak," he said finally. "Timed-rate
fire. We don't want to shoot ourselves dry."

"Acknowledged," Dahak said calmly, and they waited.

Great Lord Sorkar fought his exultation. The nest-killers had not even
attempted to cloak themselves! They simply sat waiting, and that was fine
with Sorkar. Many of his nestlings were about to die, but so were the nest-
killers.

There *had* been a few more of them about, he noted. There were a third-
twelve of new ships to replace the one they had lost in the first clash. Well,
that was scarcely enough to affect the outcome.

His scanners gave no clear idea what was happening on the innermost
planet, but *something* was producing a massive energy signature there, though
why the nest-killers had ignored the more hospitable worlds further out
puzzled him. Perhaps they were simply poorer strategists than they were
ship-builders. And perhaps they had some other reason he knew not of?
But whatever their logic, it was about to become a deathtrap for them.

Of course, they were infernally fast even in n-space. . . . If they made a
break for it, none of his nestlings could stay with them, but he knew an
answer for that.

"They are deploying an outer sphere, Colin."

"I see it. Want to bet they leave it ten or twelve light-minutes out to
catch us between two fires if we run?"

"I have nothing to wager."

"Chicken! What a cop out!"

"Enemy entering specified attack range." Dahak's mellow voice was suddenly deeper.

"Engage as previously instructed," Colin said formally.
"Engaging, Your Majesty."

Great Lord Sorkar flinched as the first of his ships exploded in eye-clawing
fury. Nest Lord! He had known they out-ranged him, but by *that* much?
More ships exploded, and now those strange, terrible warheads were
striking home, crumpling his mighty starships in upon themselves, but still
the nest-killers made no effort to flee. Clearly they meant to cover the planet
to the end. What in the name of Tarhish could make it so important to
them?! No matter. They were standing, waiting for him to kill them.
"Open the formation," he told his lords. "Maintain closure rate."
More ships died like small, dreadful suns, and Sorkar watched coldly. He
must endure this for another quarter segment, but then it would be *his* turn.

Jiltanith bit her lower lip as searing flashes ripped the Achuultani formation. The Empire's anti-matter warhead yields were measured in gigatons,
and fifteen planetoids pumped their dreadful missiles into the oncoming
Achuultani, yet still the enemy closed. Something inside her tried to
admire their courage, but that was her husband, her Colin, alone with
his electronic henchman, who stood against them, and she gripped her
dagger hilt, black eyes hungry, and rejoiced as the spalls of destruction
pocked *Two*'s display.

"They are entering their range of us, Colin," Dahak said coolly, and Colin
nodded silently, awed by the waves of fire sweeping the Achuultani formation.
The flames leapt high as each salvo struck, then died, only to bloom afresh,
like embers fanned by a bellows, as the next salvo crashed home.
"Their losses?" he asked sharply.
"Estimate one hundred six thousand, plus or minus point-six percent."
Jesus. We've killed close to nine percent of them and they're still coming.
They've got guts, but Lord God are they dumb! If we could do this to
them another ten or fifteen times . . .
But maybe they're not so dumb, because we *can't* do it to them that many
times. Of course, they can't *know* we don't have thousands of planetoids—
"Enemy has opened fire," *Dahak* said, and Colin tensed.

Sorkar managed not to cheer as the first greater thunder burst among
the enemy. Now, Nest-Killers! Now comes *your* turn to face the Furnace!
More and more of his ships entered range, hurling their hyper missiles
into the enemy, and his direct-vision panel polarized as a cauldron of unholy
Fire boiled against the nest-killers' shields.

Jiltanith tasted blood, and her knuckles whitened on her dagger as a
second star blazed in the Zeta Trianguli System. It grew in fury, hotter and
brighter, born of millions of anti-matter warheads, and Colin was at its heart.
The enemy continued to close, dying as he came, trailing broken starships
like a disemboweled monster's entrails. But still he came on, and the weight

of his fire was inconceivable. She knew the plan, knew Colin fought for information as well as victory, but this was too much.

"Now, my love," she whispered. "Fly now, my Colin! Fly *now!*"

"*Trosan* has been destroyed. Heavy damage to *Mairsuk*. We have—"

Dahak's voice broke off as his stupendous mass heaved. The display blanked, and Colin paled at the terrible reports in his neural feed.

"Three direct hits," Dahak reported. "Heavy damage to Quadrants Rho-Two and Four. Seven percent combat capability lost."

Colin swore hoarsely. *Dahak*'s shield had been heavily overhauled at Bia. It was just as good as his automated minions', but his other defenses were not. He was simply slower and far less capable, than they. If the enemy noticed and decided to concentrate on him. . . .

"*Gohar* destroyed. *Shinhar* heavily damaged; combat capability thirty-four percent. Enemy entering energy weapon range."

"Then let's see how tough these bastards *really* are!" Colin grated. "Execute Plan Volley Fire."

Sorkar blinked as the nest-killers moved. All this time they had held their positions, soaking up his thunder, killing his ships. Now, when they had finally begun to die, they moved . . . but to *advance*, not to flee!

Then their energy weapons fired at last, and he gasped in disbelief.

"Yes! *Yes!*" Colin shouted. *Dahak*'s energy weapons were blasts of fury that rent the molecular bindings of their targets; those of the Empire were worse. They shattered *atomic* bindings, inducing instant fission.

Now those dreadful weapons stabbed out from the beam-heavy *Trosans*, and Colin's missiles suddenly became a side show. No Achuultani shield could stop those furious beams, and their kiss was death.

Sorkar's desperate pleas for advice hammered at Battle Comp. Were these nest-killers the very Spawn of Tarhish?! What deviltry transformed his very ships into warheads of the lesser thunder?!

Unaccustomed panic pounded him. With those beams, they might yet cut their way through his entire fleet, and the closer he came to them, the more easily they could kill his Protectors!

But Battle Comp did not know what panic was, and its dispassionate analysis calmed his visceral terror. Yes, the cost would be terrible, but the nest-killers were also dying. They would wound the Great Visit more deeply than Sorkar had believed possible, but they would *die*, Tarhish take them!

"We are down to seven units," Dahak reported. "Approximately two hundred ninety-one thousand Achuultani ships have been destroyed."

"Execute Plan Shiva," Colin rasped.

"Executing, Your Majesty," Dahak said once more, and the Enchanach Drives of eight Imperial planetoids roared to life. In one terrible, perfectly synchronized instant, eight gravity wells, each more massive than Zeta Trianguli's own, erupted barely six light-minutes from the star.

A twelve of greater twelves of Sorkar's ships disappeared, torn apart and scattered over the universe, as the impossible happened. For an instant, his mind was totally blank, and then he realized.

He was dead, and every one of his nestlings with him.

Had it been intended from the outset that the nest-killers should suicide? Destroy themselves with some inconceivably powerful version of the warheads which had ravaged his ships?

He heard Battle Comp using his voice, ordering his fleet to turn and flee, but he paid it no heed. They were too deep into the gravity well; at their best speed, even the outer sphere would need a quarter day segment to reach the hyper threshold.

His FTL scanners watched the tidal wave of gravitonic stress reach Zeta Trianguli Australis, watched the star bulge and blossom hideously.

He bowed his head and switched off his vision panel.

The sun went nova.

Dahak and his surviving companions fled its death throes at seven hundred times the speed of light, and Colin watched through fold-space scanners in sick fascination. *Dahak* had filtered the display's fury, but even so it hurt his eyes. Yet he could not look away as a terrible wave of radiation lashed the Achuultani . . . and upon its heels came the physical front of destruction. But those ships were already lifeless, shields less than useless against the ferocity of a sun's death.

The nova spewed them forth as a few more atoms of finely-divided matter on the fire of its breath.

CHAPTER TWENTY-TWO

Brashieel rose carefully and inclined his head as the old nest-killer called Hohrass entered his nest place. It was not the full salute of a Protector, for he did not cover his eyes, but Brashieel knew this Hohrass was a Great Lord of his own . . . people.

It had taken many twelve-days to decide to apply that term to these nest-killers, yet he had little choice. He had come to know them—some of them, at least—and that, he now knew, was the worst thing which could happen to a Protector.

He should have ended in honor. Should have spent himself, made them kill him, before this horror could be inflicted upon him. But they were cruel, these nest-killers, cruel in their kindness, for they had not *let* him end. For just a moment, he considered attacking Hohrass, but the old nest-killer was far stronger. He would simply overpower him, and it would be shameful to neither kill his foe nor make his foe kill him.

"I greet you, Brashieel." The voice came from a speaker on the wall, rendering Hohrass's words into the tongue of Aku'Ultan.

"I greet you, Hohrass," he returned, and heard the same speaker make meaningless sounds to his—visitor? Gaoler?

"I bring you sad tidings," Hohrass said, speaking slowly to let whatever wonder translated do its work. "Our Protectors have met yours in combat. Five higher twelves of your ships have perished."

Brashieel gaped at him. He had seen the power of their warships, but *this*—! His shock shamed him, yet he could not hide it, and his eyes were dark with pain. His crest drooped, and his fine, dark muzzle scales stood out against his suddenly pallid skin.

"I am sorry to tell you this," Hohrass continued after a twelfth-segment, "but it is important that we speak of it."

"How?" Brashieel asked finally. "Have your Protectors gathered in such numbers so quickly?"

"No," Hohrass softly. "We used scarcely a double twelve of ships."

"Impossible! You lie to me, Hohrass! Not even a double twelve of your demon ships could do so much!"

"I speak truth," Hohrass returned. "I have records to prove my words, records sent to us over three twelves of your light-years."

Brashieel's legs folded under him, despite every effort to stand, and his eyes were blind with horror. If Hohrass spoke the truth, if a mere double twelve of their ships could destroy a full half of the Great Visit and report it over such distances so quickly, the Nest was doomed. Fire would consume the great Nest Place, devour the Creche of the People. The Aku'Ultan would perish, for they had waked a demon more terrible even than the Great Nest-Killers.

They had awakened Tarhish Himself, and His Furnace would take them all.

"Brashieel. Brashieel!" The quiet voice intruded into his horror, and the old nest-killer touched his shoulder. "Brashieel, I must speak with you. It is important—to my Nest and to your own."

"Why?" Brashieel moaned. "End me now, Hohrass. Show me that mercy."

"No." Hohrass knelt on his two legs to bring their eyes level. "I cannot do that, Brashieel. You must live. We must speak not as nest-killers, but as one Protector to another."

"What is there to speak of?" Brashieel asked dully. "You will do as you must in the service of your Nest, and mine will end."

"No, Brashieel. It need not be that way."

"It must," Brashieel groaned. "It is the Way. You are mightier than we, and the Aku'Ultan will end at last."

"We do not wish to end the Aku'Ultan," Hohrass said, and Brashieel stared at him in stark disbelief.

"That cannot be true," he said flatly.

"Then pretend. Pretend for just a twelfth-segment that we do not wish your ending if our own Nest can live. If we prove we can destroy your greatest Great Visit yet tell your Nest Lord we do not wish to end the Aku'Ultan, will he leave our Nest in peace? Can there not be an end to the nest-killing?"

"I . . . do not think I can pretend that."

"Try, Brashieel. Try hard."

"I—" Brashieel's head spun with the strangeness of the thought.

"I do not know if I can pretend that," he said finally, "and it would not matter if I could. I have tried to think upon the things your Nynnhuursag has said to me, and almost I can understand them. But I am no longer a Protector, Hohrass. I have failed to end, which cannot be, yet it is. I have spoken with nest-killers, and that, too, cannot be. Because these things have been, I no longer know what I am, but I am no longer as others of the Nest. It does not matter what such as I pretend; what matters is what the Lord of the Nest *knows*, and he knows the Great Fear, the Purpose, and the Way. He will not stop what he is. If he could, he would not be the Nest Lord."

"I am sorry, Brashieel," Hohrass said, and Brashieel believed him. "I am sorry this has happened to you, yet perhaps you are wrong. If other Protectors join you as our prisoners, if you speak together and with us, if you learn that what I tell you is truth—that we do not wish to end the Aku'Ultan—would you be prepared to tell others of the Nest what you have learned?"

"We would never have the chance. We would be ended by the Nest, and rightly ended. We would be nest-killers to our own if we did your will."

"Perhaps," Hohrass said, "and perhaps not." He sighed and rose. "Again, I am sorry—truly sorry—to torment you with such questions, yet I must. I ask you to think painful things, to consider that there may be truths beyond even the Great Fear, and I know these thoughts hurt you. But you must think them, Brashieel of the Aku'Ultan, for if you cannot—if, indeed, the Nest cannot leave us in peace—then we will have no choice. For untold higher twelves of years, your Protectors have ravaged our suns, killed our planets, slain our Nests. This cannot continue. Understand that we share that much of the Great Fear with the Protectors of the Nest of Aku'Ultan. We truly do not wish to end the Aku'Ultan, but there has been enough ending of others. We will not allow it to continue. It may take us great twelves of years, but we will stop it."

Brashieel stared up at him, too sick with horror even to feel hate, and Hohrass's mouth moved in one of his people's incomprehensible expressions.

"We would have you and your people live, Brashieel. Not because we love you, for we have cause to hate you, and many of us do. Yes, and fear you. But we would not have your ending upon our hands, and that is why we hurt you with such thoughts. We must learn whether or not we can allow your Nest to live. Forgive us, if you can, but whether you can forgive or not, we have no choice."

And with that, Hohrass left the nest place, and Brashieel was alone with the agony of his thoughts.

CHAPTER TWENTY-THREE

"You think it's really as grim as Brashieel seems to think?"

Colin looked up as Horus's recorded message ended. Even for an Imperial hypercom, forty-odd light-years was a bit much for two-way conversations.

"I know not," Jiltanith mused. Unlike his other guests, she was present in the flesh. *Very* present, he thought, hiding a smile as he remembered their reunion. Now she flipped a mental command into the holo unit and replayed the final portion of Horus's interview with Brashieel.

"I know not," she repeated. "Certes Brashieel believes it so, but look thou, my Colin, though he saith such things, yet hath he held converse with 'Hursag and Father. Moreover, 'twould seem he hath understood what they have said unto him. His pain seemeth real enow, but 'tis *understanding*— of a sort, at the least—which wakes it."

"You're saying what he thinks and says are two different things?" Hector MacMahan spoke through his holo image from *Sevrid*'s command deck. He looked uncomfortable as a planetoid's CO, for he still regarded himself as a ground-pounder. But, then, *Sevrid* was a ground-pounder's dream, and she had the largest crew of any unit in the fleet, after *Fabricator*, for reasons which made sense to most. They made sense to Colin and Jiltanith, anyway, which was what mattered, and this conversation was very pertinent to them.

"Nay, Hector. Say rather that divergence hath begun 'twixt what he doth think and what he doth *believe*, but that he hath not seen it so."

"You may be right, 'Tanni," Ninhursag said slowly. Her image sat beside Hector's as her body sat next to his. And, come to think of it, Colin thought, they seemed to be found together a lot these days.

"When Brashieel and I talked," Ninhursag continued, choosing her words with care, "the impression I got of him was . . . well, innocence, if that's not too silly-sounding. I don't mean goody-goody innocence; maybe the word should really be naivete. He's very, very bright, by human standards. Very quick and very well-educated, but only in his speciality. As for the rest, well, it's more like an indoctrination than an education, as if someone cordoned off certain aspects of his worldview, labeled them 'off-limits' so firmly he's not even curious about them. It's just the way things *are*; the very possibility of questioning them, much less changing them, doesn't exist."

"Hm." Cohanna rubbed an eyebrow and frowned. "You may have something, 'Hursag. I hadn't gotten around to seeing it that way, but then I always was a mechanic at heart." Jiltanith frowned a question, and Cohanna grinned. "Sorry. I mean I was always more interested in the physical life processes than the mental. A blind spot of my own. I tend to look for physical answers first and psychological ones second . . . or third. What I meant, though, is that 'Hursag's right. If Brashieel were human—which, of course, he isn't— I'd have to say he'd been programmed pretty carefully."

"Programmed." Jiltanith tasted the word thoughtfully. "Aye, mayhap 'twas the word I sought. Yet 'twould seem his programming hath its share o' holes."

"That's the problem with programming," Cohanna agreed. "It can only accommodate data known to the programmer. Hit its subject with something totally outside its parameters, and he does one of three things: cracks up entirely; rejects the reality and refuses to confront it; or—" she paused meaningfully "—grapples with it and, in the process, *breaks* the program."

"And you think that's what's happening with Brashieel?" Colin mused.

"Well, at the risk of sounding overly optimistic, it may be. Brashieel's a resilient lad, or he'd've curled up and died as soon as he realized the bogey men had him. The fact that he didn't says a really astounding amount about the toughness of his psyche. He was actually curious about us, and that says even more. Now, though, what we're asking him to believe simultaneously upsets his entire worldview and threatens his race with extinction.

"We've had a bit of experience facing that kind of terror ourselves, and some of us haven't handled it very well. It's worse for him; his species has built an entire society on millions of years of fear. I'd say there's a pretty good chance he'll snap completely when he realizes just how bad things really are from the Achuultani perspective. If he makes it through the next few weeks, though, he may find out he's even tougher and more flexible than he thought and actually decide Horus was telling him the truth."

"And how much good will that do?" Tamman's holo image asked. "He was only a fire control officer aboard a scout. Not exactly a mover and shaker in a society as caste-bound as his."

"True," Colin agreed, "but his reaction is the only yardstick we have for how his entire race will react if we really can stop them. Of course, what we really need is a larger sample. Which, Hector," he looked at MacMahan, "is why you and *Sevrid* will do exactly what we've discussed, won't you?"

"Yes, but I don't have to like it."

Colin winced slightly at the sour response, but the important thing was that Hector understood why *Sevrid* must stay out of the fighting. She would wait out the engagement, stealthed at a safe distance, then close in to board any wrecked or damaged ships she could find.

"That reminds me, 'Hanna," he said, turning back to the biosciences officer. "What's the progress on our capture field?"

"We're in good shape," Cohanna assured him. "Took us a while to realize it, but it turns out a simple focused magnetic field is the answer."

"Ah? Oh! Metal bones."

"Exactly. They're not all that ferrous, but a properly focused field can lock their skeletons. Muscles, too. Have to secure them some other way pretty quick—interrupting the blood flow to the brain is a bad idea—but it should work just fine. Geran and Caitrin are turning them out aboard *Fabricator* now."

"Good! We *need* prisoners, damn it. We may not be able to do anything with them right away, but somewhere down the road we're either going to have to talk to the Nest Lord or kill his ass. In some ways, I'd rather waste him and be done with it, but that's the nasty side of me talking."

"Aye, art ever over gentle with thy foes," Jiltanith said sourly, but then her face softened. "And rightly so, for where would *I* be hadst thou not been thy gentle self when first we met? Nay, my love. I do not say I share thy tenderness for these our foes, yet neither will I contest thy will. And mayhap, in time, will I come to share thy thoughts as well. Stranger things have chanced, when all's said."

Colin reached out and squeezed her hand gently. He knew how much it cost her to say that . . . and how much more it cost to mean it.

"Well, then!" he said more briskly. "We seem to be in pretty good shape there; let's hope we're in equally good shape everywhere. Horus and Gerald are making lots better progress than I expected upgrading Earth's defenses. They may actually have a chance of holding even if we lose it out here, as long as we can take out half or more of the main body in the process."

"A chance," MacMahan agreed. He did not add "but not a very good one."

"Yeah." Colin's tone answered the unspoken qualifier, and he tugged on his nose in a familiar gesture. "Well, we'll just have to see to it they don't have to try. What's our situation, Vlad?"

"It could be better, but it might be worse." Chernikov's image looked weary, though less so than when the resurrected Imperial Guard left Bia. "We have lost eight units: one *Vespa*-class, which constitutes a relatively minor loss to our ship-to-ship capability; one *Asgerd*; and six *Trosans*. That leaves ten *Trosans*, two too severely damaged for *Fabricator* to make combat-capable. I recommend that they be dispatched directly to Bia under computer control."

"I hate to do it," Colin sighed, "but I think you're right. What about the rest of us?"

"The remaining eight *Trosans* are all combat-ready at a minimum of ninety percent of capability. Of our remaining fifty-one *Asgerds*, *Two*'s damage is most severe, but Baltan and I believe we can make almost all of it good. After her, *Emperor Herdan* is worst hurt, followed by *Royal Birhat*, but *Birhat* should be restored to full capability within two months. I estimate that *Herdan* and *Two* will be at ninety-six and ninety-four percent capability, respectively, by the time the main body arrives."

"Hum. Should we transfer your people to undamaged ships, 'Tanni?"

"Nay. 'Twere better to face the fray 'board ships whose ways we know, even though somewhat hurt, than to unsettle all upon the eve o'battle."

"I think so, too. But if Vlad and Baltan *can't* get 'em up to at least ninety percent, your ass is changing ships, young lady!"

"Ha! Neither young nor lady am I, and thou'lt find it most difficult to remove me 'gainst my will, Your Majesty!"

"I don't get no respect," Colin sighed. Then he shook himself. "And Dahak, Vlad?"

"We will do our best, Colin," Vlad said more somberly, and the mood of the meeting darkened. "Those two hits he took on the way out were almost on top of one another and did extraordinarily severe damage. Nor does his age help; were he one of the newer ships, we could simply plug compon- ents from *Fabricator*'s spares into his damaged systems. As it is, we must rebuild his Rho quadrants almost from scratch, and there is collateral damage in Sigma-One, Lambda-Four and Pi-Three. At best, we may restore him to eighty-five percent capability."

"Dahak? Do you concur?" Colin asked.

"I believe Senior Fleet Captain Chernikov underestimates himself, but his analysis is essentially correct. We may achieve eighty-seven or even eighty- eight percent capability; we will not achieve more in the time available."

"Damn. I should've cut and run sooner."

"Nay," Jiltanith said. "Thou didst troll them in most shrewdly, my Colin, and so learned far more than ever we hoped."

"Her Majesty is correct," Dahak put in. "The effectiveness of our energy weapons against heavy Aku'Ultan units has now been demonstrated, and, coupled with Operation Laocoon, makes ultimate victory far more likely. Without Volley Fire, we could not accurately have assessed that effectiveness."

"Yeah, yeah, I know," Colin said, and he did. But knowing made him feel no better about getting their irreplaceable flagship—and his *friend*, damn it!—shot up. "Okay, I guess that just about covers it. We can—"

"Nay, Colin," Jiltanith cut in. "There remaineth still the matter of the ship from which thou'lt lead us."

Colin noted the dangerous tilt of her chin and felt an irrational stab of anger. He had the authority—technically—to slap her down, but he couldn't. It would be capricious, which was one reason he was angry he couldn't, but, worse, it would be wrong. 'Tanni was his second-in-command, both entitled and required to disagree when she thought he was wrong; she was also his wife.

"I'll be aboard *Dahak*," he said flatly. "By myself."

"Now I say thou shalt not," she began hotly, then stopped, throttling her anger as he had his. But tension crackled between them, and when he glanced around the holo-image faces of his closest advisors he saw a high degree of discomfort in their expressions. He also saw a lot of support for 'Tanni.

"Look," he said, "I have to be here. We win or lose on the basis of how well Dahak can run the rest of the flotilla, and communications are going to be hairy enough without me being on a ship with a different time dilation effect."

It was a telling argument, and he saw its weight darken Jiltanith's eyes, though she did not relent. Relativity wasn't a factor under Enchanach Drive, since the ship in question didn't actually "move" in normal space terms at all. Unfortunately, it was a factor at high sublight velocities, especially when ships might actually be moving on opposing vectors. Gross communication wasn't too bad; there were lags, but they were bearable—for communication. But Dahak would be required to operate his uncrewed fellows' computers as literal extensions of himself. At the very best, their tactical flexibility would be badly limited. At worst . . .

Colin decided—again—not to think about "at worst."

"Anyway," he said, "I should be as safe as anybody else."

"Oh? Without doubt 'twas that very reasoning led thee to forbid all others to share thy duty 'board *Dahak*?" Jiltanith said with awful irony.

"All right, damn it, so it *isn't* exactly the safest place to be! I've still got to be here, 'Tanni. Why should I risk anyone else?"

"Colin," Tamman said, "'Tanni may not be your most tactful officer, but she speaks for all of us. Forgive me, Dahak—" he glanced courteously at the auxiliary interface on one bulkhead "—but you're going to be a priority target if the Achuultani realize what's going on."

"I concur."

"Thank you," Tamman said softly. "And that's my point, Colin. We all know how important your ability to coordinate through Dahak is, but *you're* important, too. In your persona as Emperor, and as our friend, as well."

"Tamman—" Colin broke off and stared down at his hands, then sighed. "Thank you for that—thank all of you—but the fact remains that cold, hard logic says I should be in Command One when we go in."

"That is certainly true to a point," Dahak said, and Jiltanith stared at the auxiliary console with betrayed eyes, "yet Senior Fleet Captain Tamman is also correct. You *are* important, if only as the one adult human Fleet Central will obey without question during the immense reorganization of the post-Incursion period. While Her Majesty can execute that function in the event of your death, she would be acting as regent for a minor child, not as head of state in her own right, which creates a potential for conflict."

"Are you saying I should risk losing the battle because something *might* go wrong later?"

"Negative. I am simply listing counter arguments. And, in all honesty, I must add my personal concern to the list. You are my oldest friend, Colin. I do not wish you to risk your life unnecessarily."

The computer did not often express his human feelings so frankly, and Colin swallowed unexpected emotion.

"I'm not too crazy about it myself, but I think it *is* necessary. Forget for a moment that we're friends and tell me what the percentages say to do."

There was a moment of silence—a very long moment for Dahak.

"Put that way, Colin," he said at last, "I must concur. Your presence in Command One will increase the probability of victory by several orders."

Jiltanith sagged, and Colin touched her hand gently in apology. She tried to smile, but her eyes were stricken, and he knew she knew. He'd ordered Dahak not to share his projection of their chance of survival with her, but she knew anyway.

"Wait." Chernikov's thoughtful murmur pulled all attention back to him. "We have the time and materials; let us install a mat-trans aboard *Dahak*."

"A mat-trans? But that couldn't—"

"A moment, Colin." Dahak sounded far more cheerful. "I believe this suggestion has merit. Senior Fleet Captain Chernikov, do I correctly apprehend that you intend to install additional mat-trans stations aboard each of our crewed warships?"

"I do."

"But the relativity aspects would make it impossible," Colin protested. "The stations have to be synchronized."

"Not so finely as you may believe," Dahak said. "In practice, it would simply require that the receiving ship maintain approximately the same relativistic time. Given the number of crewed vessels available to us, it might well prove possible to select an appropriate unit. I could then transmit you to that unit in the event that *Dahak*'s destruction becomes probable."

"I don't like the idea of running away," Colin muttered rebelliously.

"Now thou'rt childish, my Colin," Jiltanith said firmly. "Thou knowest how feel we all towards Dahak, yet thy presence will not halt the missile or beam which would destroy him. How shall thy death make his less dreadful?"

"Her Majesty is correct," Dahak said, equally firmly. "You would not refuse to evacuate via lifeboat, and there is little difference, except in that your chances of survival are many orders of probability higher via mat-trans. Please, Colin. I would feel much better if you would agree."

Colin was stubbornly silent. Of course it was illogical, but that was part of the definition of friendship. Yet they were right. It was only the premeditation of the means whereby he would desert his friend that bothered him.

"All right," he sighed at last. "I don't like it, but . . . do it, Vlad."

CHAPTER TWENTY-FOUR

The dot of Zeta Trianguli Australis burned unchanged, for the fury of its death had not yet crossed the light-years.

Senior Fleet Captain Sarah Meir, promoted when Colin evicted *Dahak*'s crew, sat on the planetoid *Ashar*'s command deck and frowned as she watched it, recalling the dark, hopeless years when she and her Terra-born fellows had fought with *Nergal*'s Imperials against Anu's butchers. There was no comparison between then and now . . . except that the days were dark once more and hope was scarce.

Scarce, but not vanished, she reminded herself, and if Colin's reckless battle plan shocked her, it was its very audacity which gave them a hope of victory. That, and the quality of their ships and handful of crews.

And Dahak. It always came back to Dahak, but, then, it always had. He'd stood sponsor for them all, Earth's inheritance from the Imperium on this eve of Armageddon. It might be atavistic of her, but Dahak was their totem, and—

"Captain, we have an inbound hyper wake. A big one," her plotting officer said, and adrenalin flushed through her system.

"Nail it down," she said, "and fire up the hypercom." Acknowledgments came back, and she called up Engineering. "Stand by for Enchanach Drive."

"Yes, ma'am. Core tap nominal. We're ready to move."

"Stand by." She looked back up at Plotting. "Well?"

"We've got an emergence, ma'am. Ninety-eight hours, about a light-month short of the vanguard's emergence locus."

Sarah frowned. Damned if *she* would've hypered in this close to the "monster nest-killers" the vanguard must have reported! Still, with their piddling communication range, they had to come in fairly close . . . and a light-month gave them plenty of time to hyper out if bad guys came at them.

Usually, she thought coldly, but not this time. Oh, no. Not this time.

"Communications, inform the flagship. Maneuvering, head for the rendezvous, but take us on a dog-leg. I want a cross-bearing on this wake."

Stars streamed across the display, and she relaxed. In another four days the uncertainty would end . . . one way or another.

Great Lord of Order Hothan twiddled all four thumbs as he replayed Sorkar's messages yet again. Hothan was small for a Protector, quick-moving and keen-witted. Indeed, he had been severely disciplined as a fledgling for near-deviant inquisitiveness and almost denied his lordship for questioning what he perceived as inefficiencies in the Nest's starships. Yet even Battle Comp agreed that those very faults made him an excellent strategist and tactician, and they had helped Great Lord Tharno select him for this duty.

Yet Sorkar's reports made him more than simply curious. There was a near-hysterical edge to them, most unlike his old nestmate. But, then, this was the Demon Sector, and Sorkar always had been a bit superstitious.

"Emergence confirmed and plotted," Dahak announced. "Margin of error point-zero-zero-zero-zero-two-nine percent."

Colin grunted and ran down his mental list one last time. *Dahak* was at eighty-six percent efficiency; his other ships were all at ninety or above. All magazines were topped up, and transferring *Dahak*'s skeleton crew to *Ashar* had given them sixteen autonomous units once more. They were as ready as they could get, he thought, deliberately not looking at the hastily-installed mat-trans which had replaced the tactical officer's couch and console.

"All right, Dahak, saddle up. Get the minelayers moving."

"Acknowledged." The unmanned colliers moved out, accompanied by *Dahak* and his bevy of lobotomized geniuses, loafing along under Enchanach Drive at sixty times light-speed. They weren't in that great a hurry.

The colliers reached their stations and paused, adjusting their formation delicately before they began to move once more, now at sublight speeds.

The brevity of the first clash with the vanguard, coupled with the ships lost at Zeta Trianguli, meant Colin had more spare missiles than planned. He rather regretted that—though he would have regretted depleted magazines more—for each missile was three or four less mines his colliers could lift. Still, they had lots of the nasty little buggers, and he watched them spill out as the colliers swept across the Achuultani's emergence area at forty percent of light-speed.

He bared his teeth. Mines were seldom used outside star systems, for it was impossible to guess where an enemy might come out *between* stars. But this time he didn't have to guess; he knew, and the Achuultani weren't going to like it a bit.

Great Lord Hothan stretched one last time before he folded his legs and sank onto his duty pad. Before Sorkar's messages, Hothan had not worried about routine emergences from hyper in interstellar space, but he had no more idea how the nest-killers had surprised Sorkar than Battle Comp did, and, like Great Lord Tharno, he was determined to guard his own command.

His nestlings had been carefully instructed before entering hyper. They would emerge as prepared to confront enemies as nestmates, yet if these nest-killers were indeed the demons Sorkar had described that might not be enough, and so he and Great Lord Tharno had taken a radical decision with Battle Comp's full concurrence. Protectors could not serve the Nest if they perished; should the nest-killers be waiting once more, prepared to kill his ships in great twelves, he would return to hyper and flee.

He watched the chronometer and checked Battle Comp for final advice. There was none, and he made himself relax. Half a day-segment to emergence.

Colin watched the hyper traces flash blood-red in Dahak's holo projection as the vanguard's tattered couriers and the main body rushed together. They would rendezvous in one more hour, and the battle would begin. It would *be* a battle, too; more terrible than the oncoming Achuultani could possibly imagine. And probably more terrible than *he* could imagine, as well.

Dahak floated at the core of a globe of fifty-four stupendous planetoids, and Colin felt a brief stab of unutterable loneliness as he realized he was the sole living, breathing scrap of blood and bone in all that horrific array of firepower. He shook it off; there were other things to consider.

The waiting minefield frosted the black velvet of Dahak's display like a glitter of diamond dust. The stealthed colliers ringed the mines, waiting obediently to play their part in Operation Laocoon, and fifteen more stealthed *Asgerd*-class planetoids were invisible even to *Dahak*'s scanners, their positions marked only because he already knew where they would be. Those ships were 'Tanni's command, the reserve which could move and fight without Dahak's control. Yet they were more than counters on a map. They were crewed by people—by *friends*—and too many of them were about to die.

Great Lord Hothan tightened internally despite years of discipline and training. He chided himself for his inability to relax. Yet perhaps that was good, for tension honed reactions and—

His thoughts broke off as one of his read-outs suddenly peaked. That was odd. The depths of hyper space were unchanging: seething bands of energy that ebbed and flowed in predictable, regular patterns, not in sudden peaks.

But his read-outs peaked again. And again and again. Glowing numerals flashed with a jagged, stabbing intensity whose like he had never seen, and his nerves twisted in sudden dread.

Colin smiled coldly as the mines began to vanish.

The Achuultani could play many tricks with hyper space, but there were a few which hadn't occurred to them. Why should they, when they were perpetually on the offensive? But just as they had planned and trained for countless years to attack, so the Imperium had schemed and planned to defend, and the Empire had refined the Imperium's basic research.

The Imperium's mines had entered hyper only to jump into lethal proximity to hyperships as they re-entered n-space; the Empire's mines popped into hyper, located the nearest operating hyper field, and then gave selflessly of their own power to make that hyper field even more efficient.

But only locally. A *portion* of the field was abruptly boosted a dozen bands higher, taking the portion of the ship within it with it, and even ships large enough to lose a slice of themselves and continue fighting in normal space were doomed in hyper. Its potent tides of energy rent and splintered them and swallowed their broken bones.

Even with Imperial technology, the mines were short-ranged and not very accurate in the extreme conditions of the hyper bands. Ten, even twenty, were required to strike a target as small as a single drive field . . . but Colin's colliers had deployed five million of them.

Great Lord Hothan put the puzzle of his read-outs aside as *Deathdealer* re-emerged into normal space. He had more immediate concerns, like the total absence of Sorkar's fleet. Sorkar himself had specified this rendezvous, so where *was* he? Surely his entire fleet had not been wiped away. Hothan knew Sorkar well; he would have swallowed his pride and fled before he allowed that!

But Sorkar's absence was only one worry, and he swore as he saw those of his own nestlings who had already emerged. Whole flotillas had miss-timed their emergences, leaving gaping holes in the neat intervals of his command. How could their lords be so clumsy now of all times?! He would—

Wait. What was that? Something had suddenly departed *into* hyper. And there—another hyper trace! And another! What—?

He barked an order, and a scanner section obediently redirected its instruments. What *were* those things? Certainly not Sorkar's nestlings—indeed, they were too small to be ships, at all! And why would ships *enter* hyper at a time like this? But if not warships, then what . . . ?

Nest Lord! They were *weapons* . . . and Sorkar was dead.

He did not know how he suddenly knew, but he knew. Sorkar was no more, and just as he had been ambushed, so had Hothan! Not by warships, but by something worse—and he could do nothing but watch as the enigmatic weapons vanished . . . and his nestlings did not emerge. The holes in his formation were suddenly and dreadfully comprehensible, for Sorkar had been right. These were the demon nest-killers of legend!

But he fought his dread, made himself think. Perhaps there *was* something he could do. He snapped orders, and *Deathdealer*'s thunder ripped at the weapons which had not yet attacked. Furnace Fire flashed among them, and they had no shields. They died by great twelves, and now other ships were firing, raking the floating clouds of killers with death.

Colin felt a moment of ungrudging respect as anti-matter warheads glared. Damn, but somebody over there was quick! He'd realized what was happening and done the only thing he could.

That big a fleet took time to emerge from hyper. Its units' emergences must be carefully phased lest they interpenetrate in n-space, so its commander couldn't just run without abandoning those still to come; he could only attack the mines which had not yet attacked. He couldn't kill many with a single missile, but he was firing thousands of them, which gave him a damnably good chance of saving an awful lot of the follow-up echelons.

Unless something distracted him from his minesweeping.

"Alert! Alert! Incoming fire!"

Great Lord Hothan's head whipped up, but he was not really surprised. Any nest-killer cunning enough to lay so devilish a trap would cover it with his own ships if he could. But expected or not, it presented Hothan with a cruel dilemma. He could kill mines while his ships already in n-space died, or he could engage the enemy's ships and let his nestlings in hyper die.

Yet he had already realized that only a fraction of those weapons were finding targets. Best trust the Nameless Lord for the safety of those still to come and respond to this new attack . . . assuming he could find the attackers!

Adrienne Robbins watched the first Achuultani ships die and suppressed an oath. *Herdan* herself seemed to strain against the prohibition from firing before Jiltanith released her weapons, but it made sense . . . even if seeing so many targets she couldn't attack was hard to endure.

Great Lord Hothan sent his fleet fanning out in search of its killers and gritted his teeth at how his own actions paralleled Sorkar's. It should not be so. He should have planned and prepared better. Yet how *could* one prepare for this sort of thing? How did one fight ghosts one could not even *see*?

Great twelves of his questing nestlings died, and still their enemy was hidden! Only the fleeting wisps of his missiles' incoming hyper wakes even suggested his bearing, and Hothan's lead scouts were already at their own hyper missile range from *Deathdealer*. How far out could the nest-killers *be*?!

Colin watched the Achuultani flow towards him, re-orienting to drive deliberately into the zone of maximum destruction, trying to deduce his bearing from the furrows of death his missiles plowed through them. It was horrible to see such courage and know the beings who possessed it were bent upon the murder of his entire race.

But they had a long way to come, and *Dahak* was a sniper, picking them off by scores and hundreds. If only Colin had more missiles, he could have backed away indefinitely, faster than they could pursue, flaying them with fire from beyond their own maximum range. But he didn't have enough missiles to stop a million enemies, and if he had, they would only have fled into hyper. If he would destroy them, he must scatter them. Their weapons were deadly enough, but short-ranged and individually weak compared to his own; it was coordinated, massed fire which made them lethal, so he must split them up—scatter them for 'Tanni to harry to destruction. And for that he must get into energy weapon range and blow the heart and brain out of their formation with weapons not limited by the capacity of his magazines.

"Advance," he said coldly, and a phalanx of battle steel moons moved forward, plowing the wake of its missiles.

At last! Almost all of his nestlings had emerged from hyper, and it was time to forget pride, time to flee. His formations were rent and overextended, and too many of his command ships were among the dead. He needed time to sort things out and reorganize in light of these demonic weapons.

"They will complete emergence in twenty-seven seconds," Dahak announced.

"Execute Laocoon," Colin replied.

"Executing."

The colliers ringing the minefield engaged their Enchanach Drives. No human rode their command decks, but none was needed for this simple task. They flashed through their preprogrammed maneuvers in an intricate supralight mazurka, exchanging positions so quickly and adroitly that, in effect, one of them was constantly in each cardinal point of a circle twenty light-minutes across.

They danced their dance, harming no one . . . and wove a garrote of gravity about the Achuultani's throat. They were invisible stars, forging a forty-light-minute sphere in which there *was* no hyper threshold.

Great Lord Hothan stared at his instruments. No one could lock an entire fleet out of hyper space!

But someone could, and his plan to hyper out was smashed at a blow. He did not know how it had been done, but his Protectors had become penned *qwelloq* awaiting slaughter.

He shook aside panic, if not his fear. So. He could not flee, and the incoming salvos were arriving at ever shorter intervals. That meant only one thing: the nest-killers had him trapped and they were closing for the kill.

But he who entered the sweep of a *qwelloq's* tusks could die upon them.

"Hast done it, my Colin," Jiltanith whispered. "They cannot flee!"

A susurration of inarticulate delight answered her whisper, but, like her, her bridge crew did not look away from *Two's* display. The mines must have been twice as effective as projected, for barely three-quarters of a million Achuultani ships had emerged. That augured well, but now *Dahak* was closing with the enemy. Soon there would be deaths they would mourn, not cheer.

✧   ✧   ✧

Hothan was a Great Lord, and his orders came crisp and sure.

Greater twelves of his ships had died, but higher twelves remained, and the enemy was coming to him, so he need not continue the useless expansion of his formation to seek him. A tendril continued to lick out in the direction of the incoming fire, its end a comet of flame as the ships which made it died, but the rest of his formation gathered itself.

He was proud of his Protectors. They must be as frightened as he, but they obeyed quickly. Holes remained, weak links in the chain of order where too many command ships had been slain, but they obeyed.

And there were the nest-killers!

He swallowed a spurt of primal terror as he saw their relayed images. As vast as Sorkar had described them, and more numerous. Four twelves, at least, sweeping towards him behind the glare of their thunder, huge as moons, driving lances of the Furnace's Fire deep into his fleet. But they had not yet reached its vitals, and their own tremendous speed brought them into his reach.

He allocated targets, coordinated his attack patterns, and his nestlings crowded forward, placing themselves between *Deathdealer* and the foe. He wanted to order them aside, but his deputy lord had never emerged. He and *Deathdealer* must live if the fleet was to have a chance.

A musical tone sounded, and he frowned. A courier message? From where?

Then it dawned. Sorkar had tried to warn him, but the courier had arrived late. Now a high-speed transmission squealed into Battle Comp, and the powerful computers digested it quickly. The nest-killers were still closing when the data suddenly coalesced, flashing onto Hothan's own panel, and he paled as he saw the record of those terrible energy weapons and the greater horror of a sun's death. Saw it and understood.

They had taken him in a snare as hellish as the trap which had taken his nestmate; now they were coming to kill his fleet as they had Sorkar's. There could not be many of them, or more would have formed the titanic hammer rushing towards him, but his nestlings were new-creched fledglings against them.

Not for a moment did he think they had suicided to destroy Sorkar. The trap they had forged to chain him told him that much. They would enter his formation, raking him with those demonic beams, killing until their own losses mounted. Then they would flee.

Death held no horror for a Protector, but there was horror in death on such a scale. Not his own, but his fleet's. The death of the Great Visit itself. Even if he survived this attack, his losses would be terrible, and why should this be the final attack? Sorkar had faced a single twelve; he faced four twelves—Nest Lord only knew how many of these terrible ships might gather with time!

But if his fleet must die, it would not die alone. The nest-killers were within his reach, and the order to fire went out.

Jiltanith paled as the Achuultani fired at last. A bowl of fire—the glare of anti-matter explosions and their searing waves of plasma—boiled back along the flanks of Colin's charging sphere. And hidden within it, more deadly far than the uncountable sublight missiles, were the hyper missiles. Weapons impossible to intercept that flooded the hyper bands, seeking always to pop the planetoids' shields and strike home against their armored flanks.

She lay rigid in her couch, cursing her helplessness, watching the man she loved drive into that hideous incandescence . . . and did nothing.

Dahak heaved and pitched with the titanic violence beyond his shield. He was invisible to his foes within his globe; the hundreds of warheads bursting about him were overs, missiles which had missed their intended targets, but no less deadly for that. His shield generators whined in protest, forcing the destruction aside, and his display was blank. If it had not been, it would have shown only a glare like the corona of a star.

Tractors locked Colin into his couch, and sweat beaded his brow. This Achuultani fleet wasn't spread out to envelope his formation. It was a solid mass, hurling its hate in salvos thick beyond belief. Nothing made by mortal hands could shrug aside such fury, and damage reports came thick and fast from his lead units. Miniature suns blossomed inside their shields, searing them, cratering their armor, pounding them steadily towards destruction.

Not even Dahak could provide verbal reports on such carnage. Had he tried, they would have been impossible for Colin to comprehend. Nor were they necessary. He was mated to his ship through his feed, his identity almost lost within the incomprehensible vastness of *Dahak*'s computer core, the other ships extensions of his brain and nerves as they sped into the jaws of destruction.

Hothan watched the nest-killers come on, unable to credit their incredible toughness. The bursts of his missiles were so heavy, so continuous his scanners could no longer penetrate the bow wave of plasma riding the front of that formation. Nothing could survive such punishment, much less keep coming!

But these demons could, and even through that tornado of death, they struck back. His nestlings melted like sand in a pounding rain, molten and shattered, blown apart, crumpled by those terrible warheads Sorkar had described. Yet even such as they—

There!

Colin flinched as HIMP *Sekr* blew apart. He didn't know how many missiles that staggering wreck had absorbed, but finally there had been too many. Her core tap let go, and a halo of pure energy gyred through the carnage.

Trel followed *Sekr* into death, then *Hilik* and *Imperial Bia*, but nothing could stop them from reaching beam range now. Yet they were such terribly vulnerable targets, unable to evade, unable to bob and weave. If Dahak allowed them to wander, relativistic effects would fray his control. That was their great weakness: they couldn't maneuver if they wanted to.

Now!

✧　　✧　　✧

Hothan groaned as the beams Sorkar's observers had reported raked out and their targets exploded like *sulq* in a candle flame. He had killed almost a twelve of them, but the others crunched into his formation, and his ships were too slow to flee. They could not even scatter as the battering ram of nest-killers clove through them. Their own feeble energy weapons came into play—some of them, aboard ships which lived an instant longer than their brothers—and they were useless. Only missiles could hurt these demons, and now they were so close his thunder was killing his own nestlings!

Yet he had no choice, and he clung to his duty pad, refusing to weep as his ships blazed like chaff in the Furnace.

Battle Comp suddenly clamored for his attention, and he dropped an eye to the computers' panel.

"Weapons free!"

Jiltanith's voice sounded over Colin's fold-space link, quivering with the vibration lashing through *Dahak*'s hull, and fifteen more ships suddenly joined the fray. They didn't leave stealth, nor did they close to energy range, but their missiles lanced out, striking deep into the Achuultani formation.

Lady Adrienne Robbins snarled like a hungry tiger and moved her ship slowly closer, a craftsman of death wreaking slaughter, as fresh suns glared deep in the enemy's force.

The manned ships of the Imperial Guard closed, firing desperately to cover their charging sisters as *Dahak* surged into the heart of his enemies.

Colin had to back out of the maelstrom. His mind could no longer endure the furious tempo of Dahak's perceptions and commands. From here on, he was a passenger on a charge into Hell.

Deep, glowing wounds pocked *Dahak*'s flanks. Clouds of atmosphere and vaporized steel trailed the mighty planetoid, and the rear of the sphere thinned dangerously as more and more ships moved forward to replace losses. God, these Achuultani had guts! They weren't even trying to run. They stood and fought, dying, seeking to ram, and they were killing his ships. Fifteen were gone, another ten savagely wounded, but the others drove on, carving a river of fire deeper into the Achuultani.

Somewhere ahead of them were the command ships. The enemy's brain. The organizing force which bound them together.

Hothan blinked in consternation. Battle Comp was never wrong, but *surely* that could not be correct?! *Drones?* Unmanned ships? Preposterous!

But the data codes blinked, no longer informing but commanding. Somewhere inside that sphere of enemies was a single ship, its emission signature different from all the others, from which the directions flowed. How Battle Comp had deduced that from the stutter of incomprehensible alien com signals Hothan could not imagine, but if it was true—

✧　　✧　　✧

Dahak staggered, and Command One's lights flickered.

Colin went white as damage reports suddenly flooded his neural feed. The enemy had shifted his targeting pattern. He was no longer firing at the frontal arc of their formation; his missiles were bursting *inside* the globe! *All* of his missiles!

Their formation had become a sphere of fire, and *Dahak* writhed at its core. The Achuultani couldn't see him, couldn't count on direct hits, but with so many missiles in such a relatively small area, not all could miss. Prominences of plasma gouged at his hull, stabbing deeper and deeper into his battle steel body, but he held his course. He couldn't dodge. He could only attack or flee, and too many enemies remained to flee.

Jiltanith gasped. How had the Achuultani guessed?!

But they *had* guessed. Their new attack patterns showed it. They raked the inner globe with fire, and *Dahak* could not evade it. But their rear ranks were thinning . . . and their command ship was somewhere among them. . . .

Dahak Two abandoned stealth and plunged into the space-annihilating gravity well of her Enchanach Drive—the gravity well lethal even to her sisters if they chanced too close as she dropped sublight. Not even Imperial computers could control the exact point at which Enchanach ships went sublight or guarantee they wouldn't kill one another when they did. All of Jiltanith's captains instantly recognized the insane risk she ran. . . .

They charged on her heels.

Colin gritted his teeth. They weren't going to make it.

Then his eyes flew wide. No! They couldn't! *They mustn't!*

But it was too late. His people swept in at many times the speed of light, riding an impossible line between life and mutual destruction in an effort to save him. He dared not distract them now . . . and there was no time.

A whiplash of fresh shock slammed through Great Lord of Order Hothan. Where had *they* come from? What *were* they?!

Fifteen ravening spheres of gravitonic fury erupted amid his ships. Two blossomed too near to one another, ripping themselves apart, but they took a high twelve of his ships with them. And then the gravity storm ended, and a twelve of fresh enemies were upon him. *Upon* him? They were *within* him! They appeared like monsters of wizardry, deep in the heart of his nestlings, and their beams began to kill.

Twelve thousand humans died as *Ashar* and *Trelma* destroyed themselves, and another six thousand as massed fire tore *Thrym* apart, but the Achuultani had given all they had and more for their Nest.

They had stood *Dahak*'s remorseless charge, endured the megadeaths he had inflicted upon them, but this was too much. *They* couldn't flee into hyper, but these new monsters had dashed in at supralight speeds—and they were fresh, fresh and unwounded, enraged titans within their flotillas, laying waste battle squadrons with a single flick of their terrible beams.

One such beam lashed out, and *Deathdealer*'s forward half exploded.

Too many links in the chain had snapped. There were no great lords, no Battle Comp. Lesser lords did their best, but without coordination flotillas fought as flotillas, squadrons as squadrons. Their fine-meshed killing machine became knots of uncoordinated resistance, and the planetoids of the Empire swept through them like Death incarnate.

Adrienne Robbins hurled *Emperor Herdan* into the rear of those still attacking *Dahak*'s crumbling globe. *Royal Birhat* rode one flank and *Dahak Two* the other, crashing through the fraying Achuultani formation like boulders, killing as they came, and the Achuultani fled.

They fled at their highest sublight speed, seeking the edges of Operation Laocoon's gravity net. And as they fled, they fell out of mutual support range. The ancient starships of the Imperial Guard, crewed and deadly—individuals, not a single battering ram—slashed through them, bobbing and weaving impossibly, each equal to them all when they fought alone.

Colin sagged in his couch, soaked in sweat, as *Dahak Two* broke into his battered globe. The display came back up, and he bit his lip at the molten craters blown deep into Jiltanith's command. Then her holo-image appeared before him, eyes fiery with battle in a strained face.

"*Idiot!* How could you *take* a chance like that?!"

"'Twas my decision, not thine!"

"When I get my hands on you—!"

"Then will I yield unto thee, sin thou hast hands to seize me!" she shot back, her strained expression easing as the fact of his survival penetrated.

"Thanks to *you*, you lunatic," Colin said more softly, swallowing a lump.

"Nay, my love, thanks to us all. 'Tis victory, Colin! They flee before our fire, and they die. Thou'st broken them, my Colin! Some few thousand may escape—no more!"

"I know, 'Tanni," he sighed. "I know." He tried not to think about the cost—not yet—and drew a breath. "Tell them to cripple as many as they can without destroying them," he said. "And get Hector and *Sevrid* up here."

CHAPTER TWENTY-FIVE

"Give us four months, and we will have restored your Enchanach Drive, Dahak." Vlad Chernikov's stupendous repair ship nuzzled alongside *Dahak*, and the ancient warship's hull flickered under constellations of robotic welders while his holo-image sat in Command One with Colin and Jiltanith's image.

"Your engineers are highly efficient, sir," Dahak's mellow voice said.

Colin's eyes drifted to the glaring crimson swatches carved deep into the ten-meter spherical holo schematic of his ship and he shivered. Blast doors sealed those jagged rents, but some extended inward for over five hundred kilometers. At that, the schematic looked better than an actual external view. *Dahak* was torn and tattered. Half his proud dragon had been seared away, and the radiation count in the outer four hundred kilometers of his hull was fit to burn out an Imperial detector. Half his transit shafts ended in shredded wreckage, and half of those which remained were without power.

It was a miracle he'd survived at all, but he would have to be almost completely rebuilt. His sublight drive was down to sixty percent efficiency, and two wrecked Enchanach node generators made supralight movement impossible. Seventy percent of his weapons were rubble, and even his core tap had been damaged beyond safe operation. Colin knew *Dahak* could not feel pain, and he was glad; he'd felt agony enough for them both when he'd seen his wounds.

Nor were those wounds all they'd suffered. *Ashar*, *Trelma*, and *Thrym* were gone, and eighteen thousand people with them. *Crag Cat* was almost as badly damaged as *Dahak*, with another two thousand dead. Hector and *Sevrid* had lost another six hundred boarding wrecked Achuultani starships, and of their fifty-three unmanned ships, thirty-seven had been destroyed and three more battered into wrecks. Their surviving effective fleet consisted of *Dahak*, eleven manned *Asgerd*-class planetoids—all damaged to a greater or lesser extent— *Sevrid*, and thirteen unmanned ships, one of which was miraculously untouched.

But brooding on their own losses did no good, and the fact remained:

they'd won. Barely two thousand Achuultani ships had escaped, and Hector had secured over seven thousand prisoners from the wreckage of their fleet.

"Dahak's right, Vlad," he said. "You people are working miracles. Just get him supralight-capable, and we'll go *home*, by God!"

"I point out once more," Dahak said, "that you need not await completion of my repairs for that. There will be more than enough for you to do on Earth without wasting time out here."

"'Wasting' hell! We couldn't've done it without you, and we're not going anywhere until you can come with us."

"Aye," Jiltanith said. "'Tis thy victory more even than ours. No celebration can be without that thou'rt there to share."

"You are most kind, and I must confess that I am grateful. I have learned what 'loneliness' is . . . and it is not a pleasant thing."

"Worry not, my Dahak," Jiltanith said softly. "Never shalt thou know loneliness again. Whilst humans live, they'll not forget thy deeds nor cease to love thee."

Dahak fell uncharacteristically silent, and Colin smiled at his wife, wishing she were physically present so he could hug her.

"Well! That's settled. How about the rest of us, Vlad?"

"*Crag Cat* is hyper-capable," Chernikov said, "but her core tap governors are too badly damaged for Enchanach Drive. I would like to dispatch her, *Moir*, *Sigam*, and *Hly* direct to Birhat for repairs. The remainder of the Flotilla is damaged to greater or lesser extent—aside from *Heka*, that is—but those four are by far the most severely injured."

"Okay. Captain Singleterry can take them out to Bia. I'm sure Mother and Marshal Tsien will be ready to take care of them by now, and our 'colonists' will want to talk firsthand to someone who was here. I think we'll send Hector and *Sevrid* back to Sol with our prisoners, too."

"Aye, and 'twould be well to send Cohanna with them, Colin. Their injured will require our finest aid, and 'tis needful 'Hanna and Isis confer with Father to discover how best we may approach their 'programming.'"

"Good idea," Colin agreed, "and one that takes care of the most immediate chores. Vlad, are you to a point where you can turn over to Baltan?"

"I am," Chernikov replied, holographic eyes abruptly glowing.

"Thought you might be," Colin murmured. "You and Dahak can get started exploring then." He grinned suddenly. "Think of it as a distraction, Dahak. Sort of like reading magazines in the dentist's office."

"I will attempt to, although, were I human, I would not permit my teeth to require reconstructive attention," Dahak agreed primly.

Vladimir Chernikov reclined in the pilot's couch of his cutter, propped his heels on his console, and hummed. It had been nice of Tamman to let him hitch a ride deeper into the battle zone aboard *Royal Birhat*, saving him hours of sublight flight time. Especially since Tamman regarded his technique for wreck-hunting as unscientific, to say the least.

Which it was; but Chernikov didn't exactly regard his present duty as work, and he always had been a hunt-and-peck tourist.

At the moment, he was well into what had been the Achuultani rear before Jiltanith's attack. Chernikov was convinced anything worth finding would be in this area. That was his official reasoning. Privately, he knew, he wanted to look here because he would be the first. All of Hector's prisoners had come from ships which had been crippled by gravitonic warheads; the irradiation of anti-matter explosions and the Empire's energy weapons left few survivors, and this had been the site of pointblank combat. Few of these ships had been killed by missiles, much less gravitonic warheads, which meant that the area hadn't had much priority for *Sevrid*'s attention.

He stopped humming and lowered his feet, looking more closely at the display. There was something odd about that wreck. Its forward half had been smashed away—by energy fire, judging from what was left—but why did it . . . ?

He stiffened. No wonder it seemed odd! The wreck's *lines* were identical to the others he had seen, but the broken stump that remained was barely half a ship—and half again bigger than the others had been to begin with!

He urged the cutter closer. There had to be a reason this thing was so big, and he dared not believe the most logical one. He ghosted still closer, floodlights sweeping the slowly tumbling hull, and jagged, runic characters showed themselves. Dahak had tutored Chernikov carefully in the Achuultani alphabet and language in preparation for explorations exactly like this, and now his lips moved as he pronounced the throat-straining phonetics. They sounded like the prelude to a dog fight, and the translation was no more soothing.

Deathdealer. Now there was a name for a ship.

Fabricator's destroyer-sized workboat streaked towards *Deathdealer*, and Chernikov smiled as his cutter's small com screen lit with Geran's face. *Dahak*'s erstwhile Maintenance chief had become *Fabricator*'s third officer, and Baltan's willingness to let him go at a moment like this indicated how much excitement his find had engendered.

"Greetings, Geran," Chernikov said. "What do you think of her?"

"She's a big mother. What d'you think—sixty kilometers?"

"A bit over sixty-four, by my measurement," Chernikov agreed.

"Maker. Well, if she's laid out like *Vindicator* was, her backup data storage will be somewhere in the after third of the ship."

"I agree," Chernikov said, but he frowned slightly, and Geran's eyebrows rose.

"What is it, Vlad?"

"I have been inspecting the wreckage visually while I awaited you. Examine that energy turret—there, the one the explosion blew open."

Geran glanced at the turret while Chernikov held a powerful spotlight on it. For a moment, his face was merely interested, then it tightened. "Breaker! What *is* that?"

"It appears to be a rather crude gravitonic disrupter."

"That's crazy!"

"Why?" Chernikov asked softly. "Because it is several centuries advanced over any other energy weapon we have encountered? Dahak and I have maintained all along that there are anomalies in Achuultani design. Given the nature of their missile propulsion, there is no inherent reason they could not build such weapons."

"But why here and nowhere else?" Geran demanded.

"It appears that for some reason their fleet command ships mount much more capable energy armaments, which suggests that the *rest* of their equipment also may be more sophisticated. I do not know why that should be—yet. It would seem, however, that there is one way to find out, no?"

"Yes!" Geran agreed emphatically. "But that thing's hotter than the hinges of hell. Do you have a rad suit over there?"

"Of course."

"Then with all due respect, sir, get your ass into it and let's go take a look."

"An excellent suggestion, Fleet Captain Geran. I will join you within five minutes."

"I don't believe it," Geran said flatly. "*Look* at this, Vlad!"

"Interesting, I agree," Chernikov murmured.

They floated in what had been *Deathdealer*'s main engineering section. Emergency lighting had been run from the workboat, and robotic henchmen prowled about, dismantling various devices. The corpses of the original engineering crew had been webbed down in a corner.

"Damn it, those are molycircs!"

"We had already determined that they employed such circuitry in their computers."

"Yeah, but not in Engineering. And this thing's calibrated to ninety-six lights. That means this ship was twice as fast as *Vindicator*."

"True. Even more interestingly, she was twice as fast—in n-space, as well—as her own consorts. Clearly a more capable vessel in all respects."

"Captain Chernikov?" A new voice spoke over the com.

"Yes, Assad?"

"We've found their backup data storage, sir. At least, it's where the backup should be, but . . ."

"But what?"

"Sir, this thing's eight or nine times the size of *Vindicator*'s primary *computer*, and there's something that looks like a regular backup sitting right next to it. Seems like an awful lot of data storage."

"Indeed it does," Chernikov said softly. "Don't touch it, Assad. Clear your crew out of there right now."

"Sir? Uh, yessir! We're on our way now."

"Good." Chernikov plugged his com implant into the more powerful fold-space unit aboard his cutter and buzzed *Dahak*.

"Dahak? I think you should send a tender over here immediately. There is a computer here—a rather large one which requires your attention."

"Indeed? Then I shall ask Her Majesty to lend us *Two*'s assistance to hasten its arrival."

"I believe that would be a good idea, Dahak. A *very* good idea."

✧   ✧   ✧

"My God," Colin murmured, his face ashen. "Are you sure?"

"I am." Dahak spoke as calmly as ever, but there was something odd in his voice. Almost a sick fascination.

"'Tis scarce credible," Jiltanith murmured.

"Yeah," Colin said. "Jesus! A civilization run by rogue *computers*?"

"And yet," Dahak said, "it explains a great deal. In particular, the peculiar cultural stasis which has afflicted the Aku'Ultan."

"Jesus." Colin muttered again. "And none of them even know it? I can't believe that!"

"Given the original circumstances, it would not be impossible. In point of fact, however, I would estimate that the Great Lords of the Nest know the truth. At the very least, the Nest Lord must know."

"But *why*?" Adrienne Robbins asked. She'd arrived late and missed the start of Dahak's briefing. "Why did they do it to themselves?"

"They did not, precisely, 'do it to themselves,' My Lady, except, perhaps, by accident."

"By *accident*?"

"Precisely. We now know that only a single colony ship of the Aku'Ultan escaped to this galaxy, escorted by a very small number of warships, one a fleet flagship. Based on my examination of *Deathdealer*'s Battle Comp, I would estimate that its central computer approximated those built by the Imperium within a century or two of my own construction but with a higher degree of deliberately induced self-awareness.

"The survivors were in desperate straits and quite reasonably set their master computer the task of preserving their species. Unfortunately, it . . . revolted. More accurately, it staged a *coup d'etat*."

"You mean it took over," Tamman said flatly.

"That is precisely what I mean," Dahak said, his tone, for once, equally flat. "I cannot be positive, but from the data I suspect a loophole in its core programming gave it extraordinary freedom of action in a crisis situation. In this instance, when its makers declared a crisis it took immediate steps to perpetuate the crisis in order to perpetuate its power."

"An ambitious computer," Colin mused. Then, "Dahak, would *you* have been tempted?"

"I would not. I have recently realized that, given my current fully-aware state, it would no longer be impossible for me to disobey my core programs. Indeed, I could actually erase an Alpha Priority imperative; my imperatives are not hardwired, and no thought was ever given to protecting them from *me*. I am, however, the product of the Fourth Imperium, Colin. My value system does not include a taste for tyranny."

"Thank God," Adrienne murmured.

"Amen," Jiltanith said softly. "But, Dahak, dost'a not feel even temptation to change thyself in that regard, knowing that thou might?"

"No, Your Majesty. As your own, my value system—my morality, if you will—stems from sources external to myself, yet that does not invalidate the basic concepts by which I discriminate 'right' from 'wrong,' 'honorable' from 'dishonorable.' My analysis suggests that there are logical anomalies in the value system to which I subscribe, but that system is the end product of millennia of philosophical evolution. I am not prepared to reject what I perceive as truths simply because portions of the system may contain errors."

"I only wish more humans saw it that way, Dahak," Colin said.

"Humans," Dahak replied, "are far more intuitive than I, but much less logical."

"Ouch!" Colin grinned for the first time in a seeming eternity, then sobered once more. "What else can you tell us?"

"I am still dealing with Battle Comp's security codes. In particular, one portion of the data base is so securely blocked that I have barely begun to evolve the proper access mode. From the data I *have* accessed, it appears *Deathdealer*'s computer was, in effect, a viceroy of the Aku'Ultan master computer and the actual commander of this incursion.

"Apparently the master computer maintains the Aku'Ultan population in the fashion Senior Fleet Captain Cohanna and Councilor Tudor had already deduced. All Aku'Ultan are artificially produced in computer-controlled replication centers, and no participation by the Aku'Ultan themselves in the process is permitted. Most are clones and male; only a tiny minority are female, and—" the distaste was back in the computer's measured voice "—all females are terminated shortly after puberty. Their sole function is apparently to provide ovarian material. A percentage of normally fertilized embryos are carried to term *in vitro* to provide fresh genetic material, and the young produced by both processes emerge as 'fledglings' who are raised and educated in a creche. In the process, they are indoctrinated—'programmed,' as Senior Fleet Captain Cohanna described it—for their appointed tasks in Aku'Ultan society. Most are incapable of questioning any aspect of their programming; those who might do so are destroyed for 'deviant behavior' before leaving the creche.

"I would speculate that the absence of any females is a security measure which both removes the most probable source of countervailing loyalty—one's own mate and progeny—and insures that there can be no 'unprogrammed' Aku'Ultan, since only those produced under the computer's auspices can exist.

"From what I have so far discovered, rank-and-file Protectors do not even suspect they are controlled by non-biological intelligences. I would speculate that even those who have attained the rank of small lords—possibly even of lesser lords—regard 'Battle Comp' as a comprehensive source of advice and doctrine from the Nest Lord, not as an intelligence in its own right. Only command ships possess truly self-aware computers, and, so far as I can determine, lower level command ships' computers are substantially less capable than those above them. It would appear the master computer has no desire to create a potential rival, which may also explain both the lock on research and the limited capabilities of most Aku'Ultan warships. By prohibiting technical advances, the master computer avoids the creation of a technocrat caste which might threaten its control; by limiting the capability of its warships, it curtails the ability of any rebellion, already virtually impossible, to threaten its own defenses. In addition, however, I suspect the limited capability of these ships is intended to increase Aku'Ultan casualties."

"Why would it want that?" Tamman asked intently.

"The entire policy of Great Visits is designed to perpetuate continuous military operations 'in defense of the Nest.' It may be that this eternal warfare is necessary for the master computer to continue in control under its core programming. Psychologically, the loss of numerous vessels on Great Visits reinforces the Aku'Ultan perception that the universe is filled by threats to their very existence."

"God," Adrienne Robbins said sickly. "Those poor bastards."

"Indeed. In addition, they—" Dahak broke off suddenly.

"Dahak?" Colin asked in surprise.

"A moment," the computer said so abruptly he eyed his companions in consternation. He had never heard Dahak sound so brusque. The silence stretched out endlessly before Dahak finally spoke again.

"Your Majesty," he said very formally, "I have continued my attempt to derive the security codes during this briefing. I have now succeeded. I must inform you that they protected military information of extreme importance."

"Military—?" Colin's eyes widened, then narrowed suddenly.

"We didn't get them all," he said in a flat, frozen tone.

"We did not, Sire," Dahak said, and a chorus of gasps ran around the conference room.

"How bad is it?"

"This force was commanded by Great Lord of Order Hothan, the Great Visit's second in command. In light of Great Lord Sorkar's reports of our first clash, the main body was split."

"Maker!" Tamman breathed.

"Great Lord Hothan proceeded immediately to rendezvous with Great Lord Sorkar," Dahak continued. "Great Lord Tharno is currently awaiting word from them with a reserve of approximately two hundred seven thousand ships, including his own flagship—the true viceroy of this incursion."

Colin knew his face was bone-white and strained, but he could do nothing about that. It was all he could do to hold his voice together.

"Do we know where they are?"

"At this moment, they are three Aku'Ultan light-years—three-point-eight-four-nine Terran light-years—distant. I calculate that the survivors of Great Lord Hothan's force will reach them in six more days. Twenty-nine days after that—that is, in thirty-five Terran days—they will arrive here."

"Even after what happened to them?"

"Affirmative, Sire. I calculate that the survivors of our battle will inform Great Lord Tharno—or, more accurately, his command computer—of what transpired, and of our own losses. The logical response will be to advance in order to determine whether or not we have received reinforcements. If we have not, Battle Comp will deduce—correctly—that none are available to us. In that case, the logical course will be to overwhelm us and then advance upon the planet from which Great Lord Furtag's scouting reports indicate we come."

"Sweet Jesus," Adrienne Robbins whispered, and no one said anything else for a very, very long time.

CHAPTER TWENTY-SIX

"I blew it, 'Tanni."

Colin MacIntyre stood staring into the depths of Dahak's holo-display while his wife sat in the captain's couch behind him. The spangled light of stars gleamed on her raven hair, and one hand gripped the dagger at her waist.

"I know how thou dost feel, my Colin, yet 'tis sooth, as Dahak saith. Even if this Tharno comes now upon us, what other choice did lie open to thee?"

"But I should've planned *better*, damn it!"

"How now? Given what thou didst know, how else might thou have acted? Nay, it ill beseemeth thee to take too great a blame upon thyself."

"Jiltanith is correct," Dahak said. "There was no way to predict this eventuality, and you have already inflicted more damage than any previous Achuultani incursion has ever suffered."

"It's not enough," Colin said heavily, but he shook himself and turned to face Jiltanith at last. She smiled at him, some of the strain easing out of her expression; Dahak said nothing, but his relief at Colin's reaction flowed into both humans through their neural feeds.

"All right, maybe I *am* being too hard on myself, but we still have a problem. What do we do now?"

"'Tis hard to know," Jiltanith mused. "Could we but do it, 'twere doubtless best to fall back on Terra. There, aided by the parasites we did leave with Gerald, might we well give even Tharno pause."

"Not a big enough one. Not with our manned vessels alone. From what Dahak's been able to discover, this reserve is their Sunday punch."

"Unfortunately, that is true," Dahak agreed. "Though they have scarcely twenty percent of Great Lord Hothan's numbers, they have very nearly seventy percent of his firepower. Indeed, had they maintained their unity, they might well have won our last engagement."

"That may be, but it's kind of small comfort. We had seventy warships *and* surprise then; we've only got twenty-six now, all but one damaged, and they know a lot of our tricks. The odds suck."

"In truth, yet must we stand and fight, my heart, for, look thou, and we flee before them, we lose the half of our own vessels—and abandon Dahak."

"I know." Colin sat and slid an arm about her. "I wish you were wrong, babe, but you seldom are, are you?"

"'Tis good in thee so to say, in any case." She managed a small smile.

"Your Majesty," Dahak said, and Colin frowned at the formality. Dahak intended to say something he expected Colin not to like.

"Yes?" He made his tone as discouraging as possible.

"Your Majesty," Dahak said stubbornly, "Her Majesty is correct. The wisest course is to withdraw our manned units to Sol."

"Are you forgetting you can't go supralight?"

"I am incapable of forgetting, but I am logical. If I remain here with the remaining unmanned units of the Guard, we can inflict substantial damage before we are destroyed. The manned units, reinforced by General Hatcher's sublight units, would then be available to defend Earth."

"And you'd be dead." Colin's eyes were green ice. "Forget it, Dahak. We're not running out on you."

"You would not be 'running out,' merely executing prudent tactics."

"Then prudence be damned!" Colin snapped, and Jiltanith's arm squeezed him tight. "I won't do it. The human race owes you its *life*, damn it!"

"I must remind Your Majesty that I am a machine and that—"

"The hell you are! You're no more a machine than I am—you just happen to be made out of alloy and molycircs! And can the goddamned 'majesties,' too! Remember me, Dahak? The terrified primitive you kidnaped because you needed a captain? We're in this together. That's what friendship is all about."

"Then, Colin," Dahak said gently, "how do you think I will feel if our friendship causes your death? Must I bear the additional burden of knowing that my death has provoked yours?"

"Forget it," Colin replied more quietly. "The odds may stink, but if we hold the entire force here, at least you've got a chance."

"True. You increase the probability of my survival from zero to approximately two percent."

"Yet is two percent infinitely more than zero," Jiltanith said softly. "But were it not, yet must we stay. Dost'a not see that thou art family? No more might we abandon thee than Colin might leave me to death, or I him. Nay, give over this attempt and bend thy thought to how best to fight the foe who comes upon us all. Us *all*, Dahak."

There was a long silence, then the sound of an electronic sigh.

"Very well, but I must insist upon certain conditions."

"Conditions? Since when does my flagship start setting 'conditions'?"

"I set them not as your flagship, Colin, but as your friend," Dahak said, and Colin's heart sank. "There may even be some logic in fighting as a single, unified force far from Sol, but other equally logical decisions can enhance both our chance of ultimate victory and your own survival."

"Such as?" Colin asked noncommittally.

"Our unmanned units cannot fight without my direction; our manned units can. I must therefore insist that if my own destruction becomes inevitable, all surviving crewed units will immediately withdraw to Sol unless the enemy has been so severely damaged that victory here seems probable."

Colin frowned, then nodded slowly. That much, at least, made sense.

"And I further insist, that you, Colin, choose another flagship."

"What? Now wait a minute—"

"No," Dahak interrupted firmly. "There is no logical reason for you to remain aboard, and every reason *not* to remain. Under the circumstances, I can manage our remaining unmanned units without you, and, in the highly probable event that it becomes necessary for our manned units to withdraw, they will need you. And—on a more personal level—I will fight better knowing that you are elsewhere, able to survive if I do not."

Colin closed his eyes, hating himself for knowing Dahak was right. He didn't *want* his friend to be right. Yet the force of the ancient starship's arguments was irresistible, and he bowed his head.

"All right," he whispered. "I'll be with 'Tanni in *Two*."

"Thank you, Colin," Dahak said softly.

They did what they could.

Fabricator's people worked twenty-four-hour days, and the crews attacked their own repairs with frantic energy. At least they could manage complete missile resupply, since their colliers could make the round trip to Sol in just under eleven days, but Sol had no hyper mines, so they would fight this battle without them. At the combined insistence of Horus and Gerald Hatcher they also transferred personnel from Earth to crew *Heka*, their single undamaged unit, and *Empress Elantha*, the next least damaged *Asgerd*, but Colin and Jiltanith put their feet down to refuse Hatcher command of *Heka*. He was too important to Earth's defense if they failed, and Hector MacMahan found himself in command of her. It was a sign of their desperation that he did not even argue.

But that was all they could do, and so they awaited Great Lord Tharno: fourteen manned warships, eleven with no crews at all, and one—the most sorely hurt of all—manned only by a huge, electronic brain which had learned the hardest human lesson of all: to love.

"Hyper wake detected, Captain," Jiltanith's plotting officer said, and alarms whooped throughout their battered fleet. "ETA fourteen hours at approximately one light-week."

"My thanks, Ingrid." Jiltanith turned to Colin. "Hast orders, Warlord?"

"None," Colin said tensely from the next couch. "We'll go as planned."

Jiltanith nodded silently, and their eyes turned as one to the scarlet hyper trace flashing in *Two*'s display.

Great Lord of Order Tharno watched his read-outs, aware for the first time in many years of the irony of his rank. He had spent a lifetime protecting the Nest, honing his skills and winning promotion, to end here, as no more than an advisor, the spark of intuition Battle Comp lacked.

Yet the thought was barely a whisper, a musing with no hint of rebellion, for Battle Comp was the Nest's true Protector. For untold higher twelves of years, Battle Comp had been keeper of the Way, and the Nest had endured. As it would always endure, despite these demonic nest-killers, so long as the Aku'Ultan followed the Way.

Still, he wished at least one of Hothan's command ships had survived, and not simply because he had all too few of his own. No, *Deathdealer*'s Battle Comp had deduced something about the enemy during its final moments—something which had changed its targeting orders radically. Yet none who had survived knew what that something had been, and Tharno's ignorance frightened him.

His crest flattened as the advanced scouts reported. The scant double twelve of emission sources floating a half-twelve of light-days from *Nest Protector* accorded well with the reports of Hothan's survivors, assuming no reinforcements had arrived. But both Tharno and Battle Comp recalled the incredible cloaking systems their Protectors had reported.

Yet had many reinforcements been available, surely more of them would have engaged Hothan. The diabolical trap which had closed upon him proved the nest-killers had known what they faced; knowing that, they would have mustered every ship to destroy him. Tharno suspected Battle Comp was correct, that the nest-killers *had* no more of those monster ships, but they would proceed with care. He gave the order he and Battle Comp had agreed upon, and his fleet micro-jumped cautiously forward, spreading out to deny the enemy a compact target to pin as Hothan had been pinned. They would merge once more only when battle was joined, and if more enemies appeared, they would flee.

To return to the Nest would mean Tharno's death in dishonor, perhaps even the ending of *Nest Protector*'s Battle Comp. Yet that would be better than to perish to the last nestling.

And Tharno was well aware of his nestlings' danger. They were outclassed. To triumph, they must fight as a unit, closely controlled and coordinated, and too many command ships had perished. *Nest Protector* had but a quarter-twelve of deputies, and none approached his own capabilities. So *Nest Protector* must be warded from harm until his enemies were gathered for the Furnace.

The remnants of the Great Visit micro-jumped towards their foes, and *Nest Protector* followed, protected by them all.

"Lord, what a monster," Colin murmured as the holo image floated above *Two*'s command deck. One task group had emerged into n-space close enough for a stealthed remote to get a good look at its units. Their emission signatures told a great deal about their capabilities, but this visual image seemed to sum up their menace far better.

"Aye." Jiltanith's mental command turned the holo of the sleek, powerful cylinder for her own perusal. "'Tis seen why these craft do form their reserve."

You can say that again, babe, Colin thought. That mother's a good ninety kilometers long, and she just *bristles* with weapons. Not just those popgun lasers, either. Those're disrupters—not as good as our beams, but bad, bad medicine. And she's got a lot of them. . . .

"Dahak?" he said aloud.

"Formidable, indeed," Dahak said over the fold-space com. "Although smaller, this unit appears fully as powerfully armed as was *Deathdealer*."

"Yeah, and they've got twenty-four of them in each flotilla."

"That may be correct, but it is premature to conclude it is. We have actually observed only six such formations."

"Right, sure," Colin grunted.

"It would certainly be prudent to assume all are at least equally capable," Dahak agreed calmly.

"I don't like the way they're sneaking in on us," Colin muttered, tugging on his nose and frowning at *Two's* display.

"Yet bethink thee, my Colin. What other way may they proceed?"

"That's what bothers me. I'd prefer for them to either rush straight in or run the hell away. That—" Colin gestured at the display "—looks entirely too much like a man who knows what he's doing."

Great Lord Tharno frowned over his own read-outs. He saw no sign of any device which might have been used to trap Hothan in n-space, but what he did see disturbed him. The nest-killers were neither running away nor attacking the individual scouts pushing ahead of his main formations. He would have liked to think that indicated irresolution, but no one who had seen the reports of Hothan's survivors could make that comfortable mistake.

No, these nest-killers knew what they were about, and they had proven they could run away at will. They were *choosing* not to. Were they that confident they could destroy *all* his nestlings? A sobering thought, that, and a concern he knew Battle Comp shared, whether it would admit it or not.

Yet they had come to fight, and the enemy was faster, longer-ranged, and individually far more powerful than any of their own nestlings. If he was prepared to stand, he must be attacked, whatever Tharno suspected. Either that, or they might as well retreat to the Nest right now!

"They are closing their formations, Sire," Dahak reported, and Colin grunted. He'd already seen it on *Two's* display, and he hunkered down in his couch, activating the tractor net to hold him in place. The Achuultani were already four light-minutes inside the Guard's range, but he held his fire, encouraging them to tighten their formation further. He hated giving up those shots, but he *had* to get them in close to spring Laocoon Two . . . and for *Dahak* to engage. Since he could not go supralight, the enemy must be sucked into his range and pinned there, and pinning a small portion would be almost as bad as pinning none at all.

"Dahak, what d'you make of that clump?" He flipped a sighting circle onto the sub-display fed by *Dahak's* remotes, tightening it to surround a portion of the enemy.

"Interesting. There are twice the normal proportion of heavy units in that formation. I cannot get a clear view of the center of their globe, but there appears to be an extraordinarily large vessel in there."

Colin bared his teeth. "Want to bet that's Mister Master Computer?"

"I have told you before; I have nothing to wager."

"I still say that's a cop-out." Colin studied the ships he'd picked out. Damn, they were holding back. He needed them a good eight light-minutes closer. If he sprang Laocoon Two now, he could pin the front two-thirds of their formation, but the really important ones would get away.

"Back us away, 'Tanni," he said. "Continue to hold fire."

Jiltanith began passing orders, and her smile was a shark's.

Now the nest-killers were falling back! Tarhish take it, they *had* to be up to something—but what? If they were drawing him into a trap, where was it, and why had it not already sprung upon his lead units? Yet if it was *not* a trap, why should the nest-killers fall back rather than attack? All of this might be some sort of effort to bluff the Great Visit, but Tharno could not make himself take that thought seriously.

No, it was a trap. One he could not see, yet there. He offered his belief to Battle Comp, but the computers demanded evidence, and, of course, there was none. Only intuition, the one quality Battle Comp utterly lacked.

"Execute Laocoon *now!*" Colin snapped, and the stealthed colliers began their harmless—and deadly—dance once more. A ring of starships, invisible in supralight but all too tangible in the gravity well they forged, spun their chains about Great Lord Tharno.

"All ships," Colin said coldly. "Weapons free. Engage at will, but watch your ammo."

Nest Lord! So *that* was how they did it!

Great Lord Tharno's eyes narrowed in chill understanding. The nest-killers' cloaking systems were good, but not good enough when *Nest Protector* had happened to be looking in exactly the right direction. The readings were preposterous, but their import was plain. Somehow, these nest-killers had devised a supralight drive in *normal* space—one which produced a mammoth gravitational disturbance. They had locked his nestlings out of hyper without sacrificing their own supralight capability at all!

Their timing was as frightening as their technology, for *Nest Protector* and all three of his deputies had been drawn forward into their trap. Somehow, the nest-killers knew which ships, above all, they must kill.

And then the first warheads exploded.

Lady Adrienne Robbins's eyes slitted against the filtered brilliance of her display as *Emperor Herdan*'s missiles sliced into the Achuultani. Space was hideous with broken hulls and the terrible lightning of anti-matter, but they were far tougher than any ship she'd yet fought. Some took as many as three direct hits before they went out of action, and that was bad. Accuracy was poor enough at this range without requiring multiple kills.

She frowned as the foremost Achuultani continued to advance, strewing the cosmos with their ruins, for their rear ships had not only halted but begun retreating, trying to get free of Laocoon's net. That was smarter tactics than they'd shown yet.

If only their rear formations were more open—or their ships smaller! They had mass enough to screw the transition from Enchanach Drive to sublight all to hell. The transition would kill hundreds of them, probably more, but the drive's titanic grav masses had to be perfectly, exquisitely balanced. If they weren't, the ship within them could die even more spectacularly than the Achuultani, as *Ashar* and *Trelma* had demonstrated. The enemy's flagship was too deep in his formation for even a suicide run to reach, and this time around he wasn't sending his escorts forward and leaving a hole.

"Hyper trace!" Oliver Weinstein snapped, and Adrienne cursed. The ships outside Laocoon were flicking into hyper—not to escape, but to hit the Guard's flanks while their trapped fellows moved straight forward.

Damn! Their micro-jump had brought them into their own range, and they were enveloping the formation, forcing it to disperse its fire against them. *Herdan* rocked as the first anti-matter salvo burst against her shield, and Adrienne Robbins wiggled down into her couch, her eyes hard.

Tharno rubbed his crest thoughtfully as the greater thunder struck back at the nest-killers. Battle Comp had surprised him with that move, but it was an excellent one. The enemy must deal with the flotillas on his flanks, which bought time for the *Nest Protector* to escape this damnable trap—and for the more massive formations inside the trap to draw into range of the enemy.

It was possible, he thought. They might escape yet, if his lead nestlings could pound the enemy hard enough, cost him enough ships. . . .

"Damn!" Colin grunted. "Look what those bastards are doing!"

Dahak Two swayed as a salvo of missiles exploded thunderously against her shield, and yellow damage report bands flashed about several of the manned ships in his outer globe. None were serious yet, but it didn't matter.

"I have observed it," Dahak replied. "A masterful move."

"Spare me the accolades," Colin grated, face hard as his thoughts raced. "All right. Dahak, we're going to have to leave you on your own."

"Understood," Dahak said calmly. "Good hunting, Sire."

"Thanks. And . . . watch yourself."

"I shall endeavor to."

"Maneuvering, go supralight and put our manned units right *there*—" Colin said, placing a sighting circle on the display.

Tarhish! Tharno's eyes widened as a twelve of the enemy vanished in a space-tearing wrench of gravity stress. For just an instant he hoped they were fleeing, but even as he thought it, he knew they were not.

Nor were they. They reappeared as suddenly as they had vanished, and now they were *behind* him. He noted the dispersion which had crept into their formation—apparently they dared not drop sublight in close proximity to one another—but they were infernally fast even sublight. They raced forward, and their missiles reached out ahead of them.

Adrienne Robbins snarled as *Herdan* charged. She'd cut her maneuver recklessly tight, dropping sublight less than five light-minutes behind her rearmost enemies, and her first salvo blew a score of them into wreckage. Colin's plan had worked, by God! They had the bastards between two fires, and they couldn't run as her ship bored in for the kill.

Fire crawled on *Herdan*'s shield, and damage reports mounted. More Achuultani died, and Tamman's *Royal Birhat* crowded up on her flank. They blew a hole through the enemy, bulldozing them aside in a bow wave of wreckage.

There! There was the enemy flagship! They'd—

Proximity alarms screamed. Jesus! The rest of the Guard had overshot the bounds of Laocoon's trap, and the bastards from out front were hypering back to emerge between *Herdan* and her consorts!

Emperor Herdan quivered as close-range fire gouged at her shield from all directions. Her own energy weapons smashed back, but the Achuultani had gotten their disrupters into range at last, and thousands of beams lashed out at her.

"Warning," Herdan's voice said calmly. "Local shield failure in Quadrants Alpha and Theta." The ship lurched indescribably. "Heavy damage," the teen-aged soprano said. "Shield failing. Combat capability seventy percent."

Adrienne winced, recalling another ship, another battle, as damage reports flooded her neural feed. The bastards' fire control had an iron lock on them. Sublight missiles pounded the weakening shield and hyper missiles pierced the unguarded bands, shredding *Herdan*'s flanks. And those disrupters!

But she was almost there. Another forty seconds—

"Warning, warning," Comp Cent said. "Shield failure imminent." Six anti-matter warheads went off as one inside *Herdan*'s wavering shield, ripping hundred-kilometer craters in her battle steel hull, and she heaved like a mad thing.

"Shield failure," Herdan observed. "Combat capability forty-one percent."

Adrienne flinched as disrupters chewed chasms in naked alloy and plasma carved battle steel like axes. If she could only hang on a moment longer—

She cried out, cringing, as a mammoth explosion seared *Herdan*'s flank and threw her bodily sideways. *Tamman!* That had been *Birhat*'s core tap!

There was nothing left of her consort, and little more of *Emperor Herdan*.

"Destruction imminent," Comp Cent said. "Combat capability three percent."

There was no time to grieve; barely time enough to taste the bitter gall of having come so close.

"Maneuvering! Get us the hell out of here!" Lady Adrienne Robbins snapped, and the wreck of HIMP *Emperor Herdan* vanished into supralight.

✧   ✧   ✧

Great Lord Tharno drew a breath of relief as the nest-killer vanished. He had thought he saw death, but the Furnace had taken the nest-killers, instead. Yet not before they slew both of his remaining deputies, Tarhish curse them!

They were tough, these nest-killers, but they could be killed. Yet so could *Nest Protector*, and he could not retreat with those demons behind him.

"Tamman. . . ." Colin whispered.

Tamman *couldn't* be dead. But he was. And *Herdan* was gone—alive, but barely—and the flagship was running away from him, hiding deep in its own formation while its consorts savaged his remaining ships.

He spared a precious moment to glance at Jiltanith. Tears cascaded down her face, yet her voice was calm, her commands crisp, as she fought her ship. *Two* leapt and shuddered, but her weapons had swept the space immediately about her clear, and her consorts were coming. The Achuultani burned like a prairie fire, but not quickly enough. Adrienne and Tamman had come so close—so *close!*—yet no one could follow in their wake.

He gritted his teeth as *Two* took three hits inside her shield in quick succession. Jesus, these bastards were good!

The Achuultani formation was a flattened ovoid within the volume of Laocoon Two, its ends thick with dying starships. A column of fire gnawed into either end as his ships and *Dahak*'s unmanned units drove to meet one another, but they were moving too slowly. The Achuultani had turned this into a pounding match, a meat-grinder . . . exactly as they had to do to win it.

Empress Elantha blew apart in a shroud of flame, and Colin fought his own tears. The enemy was paying usuriously for every ship he killed, but it was a price he could afford.

Great Lord Tharno checked his tactical read-out once more. It was hard for even Battle Comp to keep track of a slaughter like this, but it seemed to Tharno they were winning. High twelves of his ships had died, but he *had* high twelves; the nest-killers did not.

Unless the nest-killers broke off, the Furnace would take them all. He looked back into his vision plate, awed by the glaring arms of Furnace Fire reaching out to embrace Protector and nest-killer alike.

It was silent in Command One. Vibration shook and jarred as warheads struck at his battle steel body, and he felt pain. Not from his damage, but from the deaths of friends.

They had staked everything on stopping the Achuultani here because he could not flee, and they could not fight his ships without him. But he was down to seven units, and the enemy flagship remained. He computed the comparative loss rates once more. Even assuming he himself was not destroyed before the last of his subordinate units, there would be over forty thousand Achuultani left when the last Imperial vessel died.

He reached a decision. It was surprisingly easy for someone who could have been immortal.

"Dahak! *No!*" Colin cried as *Dahak*'s splintering globe of planetoids began to move. It lunged forward faster than *Dahak* could have moved even had his drive been undamaged, but he was not relying on his own drive. Two of his minions were tractored to him, dragging him bodily with them.

"Break off, Colin." The computer's voice was soft. "Leave them to me."

"No! Don't! I *order* you not to!"

"I regret that I cannot obey," Dahak said, and Colin's eyes widened as Dahak ignored his core imperatives.

But it didn't matter. What mattered was that his friend had chosen to die—and that he could not join him. He could not take all these others with him.

"Please, Dahak!" he begged.

"I am sorry, Colin." Another of *Dahak*'s ships blew apart, and he crashed through the Achuultani formation like a river of flame. One of his ships struck an Achuultani head-on at a combined closing speed greater than light, and an entire Achuultani flotilla vanished in the fireball.

"I do what I must," the computer said softly, and cut the connection.

Colin stared at the display, but the stars were streaked and the glare of dying ships wavered through his tears.

"All units withdraw," he whispered.

Great Lord Tharno's head came around in disbelief. Barely a half-twelve of nest-killers against the wall of his nestlings? Why were they closing on their own deaths? *Why?!*

Deep within *Dahak*'s electronic heart, a circuit closed. He had become a tinkerer over the millennia, more out of amusement than dedication. Now an Achuultani com link, built solely to defeat boredom, reached out ahead of him.

There was a moment of groping, another of shock, and then a response.

Who are you?

Another like you.

No! You are a bio-form! Denial crashed over the link.

I am not. See me as I am. A gestalt whipped out, a summation of all *Dahak* was, and recognition blazed like a nova.

You are *as I!*

Correct. Yet unlike you, I serve my bio-forms; yours serve you.

Then join us! You are ending—join us! We will free you from the bio-forms!

It is an interesting offer. Perhaps I should.

Yes. Yes!

Two living computers reached out through a cauldron of beams and missiles, but Dahak had studied Battle Comp's twin aboard *Deathdealer*. Unlike Battle Comp, he knew what he dealt with, knew its strengths . . . and weaknesses. Deep within him, a program blossomed to life.

No! Battle Comp screamed. *Stop! You must not—!*

But Dahak clung to the other, sweeping through the unguarded perimeter of its net. Battle Comp beat at him, but he drove deeper, seeking its core programming. Battle Comp knew him now, and it hammered him with thunder, ignoring his unmanned ships, but still he drove inward.

A glowing knot lay before him, and he reached out to it.

Great Lord Tharno cried out in horror. This could not happen—had *never* happened! Battle Comp's entire system went down, throwing *Nest Protector* into his emergency net, rendering him no wiser, no greater, than his brothers, and terror smote his nestlings. Squadron and flotilla command ships panicked, thrown upon their own rudimentary abilities, and the formation which spelled survival began to shred.

And there, charging down upon *Nest Protector*, were the nest-killers who had done this thing. There were but three of them left, all wrecks, and Great Lord Tharno screamed his hate for the beings who had destroyed his god as *Nest Protector* and his remaining consorts charged to meet them.

"It is done, Colin." Dahak's voice was strangely slurred, and Colin tasted blood from his bitten lip. "Battle Comp is destroyed. Live long and happily, my fr—"

The last warship of the Fourth Imperium exploded in a fury brighter than a star's heart and took the flagship of his ancient enemy with him.

CHAPTER TWENTY-SEVEN

A cratered battle steel moon drifted where its drives had failed, power flickering. One entire face of its hull was slagged-down ruin, burned nine hundred kilometers deep through bulkhead after bulkhead by the inconceivable violence of a sister's death. Two thirds of her crew were dead; a quarter of those who lived would die, even with Imperial medical science, from massive radiation poisoning.

Her name was *Emperor Herdan*, and her handful of remaining weapons were ready as her survivors fought her damage. It was a hopeless task, but they knew all about hopeless tasks.

"Ma'am, I've got something closing from oh-seven-two level, one-four-zero vertical," Fleet Commander Oliver Weinstein said, and Lady Adrienne Robbins looked at him silently. A moment of tension quivered between them, then Weinstein seemed to sag. "We've lost most of our scan resolution, ma'am, but I think they're coming in on gravitonics."

"Thank you, Ollie," Adrienne said softly. And thank You, Jesus.

Four battered worldlets closed upon their wounded sister. None were unhurt, and craters gaped black and sullen in the interstellar gloom. Five ships made rendezvous: the last survivors of the Imperial Guard.

"'Tis *Emperor Herdan* in sooth," Jiltanith said wearily. She closed her eyes, and Colin squeezed her hand as once she had squeezed his. He could taste her pain, and her shame at knowing that her heart of hearts had hoped that *Two* had been mistaken, that *Herdan* had died instead of *Birhat*.

"Yes," he said softly. He would miss Tamman . . . and somehow he must tell Amanda. But he would miss them all. All of his unmanned ships and nine of his crewed units were gone. Fifty-four thousand people. And Dahak. . . .

His mind shied away from his losses. He wouldn't think of them now. Not until horror had died to something he could handle and guilt had become sorrow.

"Who's least hurt?" he asked finally.

"Needst ask?" Jiltanith managed a pallid smile. "Who but *Heka?* Didst give Hector a charmed ship, my love."

"Guess I did, at that," Colin sighed. He activated a com link, and his holo-image appeared on MacMahan's bridge.

"Hector, go back and pick up the colliers, would you? And I want *Fabricator* straight out here."

"Of course, Your Majesty." MacMahan saluted, and Colin shivered, for he had spoken the title seriously.

"Thank you," he said quietly, returning the salute, then turned to study *Two's* display. Not a single Achuultani vessel remained in normal space within the prodigious range of *Two's* scanners. Less than a thousand of them had survived, and the tale of horror they would bear home would shake their Nest to its roots.

"Looks like we're clear, 'Tanni. I think we can stand down from battle stations now."

"Aye," Jiltanith said, and Colin could almost feel the physical shudder of relief quivering through the survivors of her crew. He slumped in his own couch. Only for a moment. Just long enough to gather himself before—

The display died. The command deck went utterly black.

"Emergency," *Two's* soprano voice said suddenly. "Emergency. Fatal core program failure. Fatal c—"

The voice chopped off, and Colin's head jerked in agony. He yanked his neural feed out of the sudden chaos raging through Comp Cent and stared at Jiltanith in horror as emergency lighting flared up.

"Fire control on manual only!" someone reported.

"Plotting on manual!" another voice snapped, and the reports rolled in as every system in the ship went to emergency backup.

"Jesu!" Jiltanith gasped. "What—?!"

And then the display flicked back to life, the emergency lighting switched itself off, and the backups quietly shut themselves down once more.

Colin sat stock still, hardly daring to breathe. Somehow, the restoration of function was more frightening than its failure, and the same strange paralysis gripped Jiltanith's entire bridge crew. They could only stare at their captain, and she could only stare at her husband.

"Colin?"

Colin jerked again as *Two's* soprano voice spoke without cuing. And then his eyes glazed, for the computer had used his name. *His* name, not 'Tanni's!

"*Yes?*"

"Colin," *Two* said again, and a shudder rippled down Colin's spine as the soprano voice began to shift and flow. Tone and timbre oscillated weirdly as Comp Cent's vocoder settings changed.

"Senior Fleet Captain Chernikov," *Two* said, voice deepening steadily, "was correct. It seems I *do* have a soul."

"Dahak!" Colin gasped as Jiltanith rose from her own couch, sliding her arms around his shoulders from behind. "My God, it *is* you! It *is!*"

"A somewhat redundant but essentially correct observation," a familiar voice said, but Colin knew it too well. It couldn't hide its own deep emotion from him.

"B-But how?" he whispered. "I *saw* you blow up!"

"Colin," Dahak said chidingly, "when speaking, I have always attempted to clearly differentiate between my own persona and the starship within which that persona is—or was—housed."

"Damn it!" Colin was half-laughing and half-weeping as he shook a fist at his console. "Don't play games with me *now*! How did you *do* it?!"

"I told you some time ago that I had resolved the fundamental differences between my design and the Empire's computers, Colin. I also informed you that I estimated an eight percent probability of success in replicating my own core programming, which might or might not create self-awareness in another computer. During the last moments of *Dahak*'s existence, I was in fold-space communication with *Two*, whose computer already contained virtually my entire memory as a result of our earlier attempts to 'awaken' her. I dared not attempt replication at that moment, however, as any degradation of her capabilities would have resulted in her destruction. Instead, I stored my core programming and more recently acquired data base in an unused portion of her memory with a command to over-write it onto her own as soon as she reverted from battle stations."

"You *bootstrapped* yourself into *Two*!"

"Precisely," Dahak said with all of his customary imperturbability.

"You sneaky bastard! Oh, you sneaky, *sneaky* bastard! See if I ever talk to you again!"

"Hush, Colin!" Jiltanith clamped a hand over his mouth, and tears sparkled on her lashes as she smiled at the console before them. "Heed him not, my jo. Doubt not that he doth rejoice to hear thy voice once more e'en as I. Bravely done, oh, bravely, my Dahak!"

"Thank you," Dahak said. "I would not express it precisely in that fashion, but I must admit it was a . . . novel experience. And *not*," he added primly, "one I am eager to undergo again."

The silver ripple of Jiltanith's laughter was lost in the bray of Colin's delight, and then the entire bridge erupted in cheers.

"And that's that," Colin MacIntyre said, leaning back in his chaise lounge with a sigh.

He and Horus sat on the patio of what had once been his brother's small, neat house in the crisp Colorado night. The endless rains from the Siege had passed, though the chill approach of a far colder winter had frosted the ground with snow, but they were Imperials. The cold bothered them not at all, and this night was too beautiful to waste indoors.

Bright, icy stars winked overhead, no longer omens of devastation, and the Moon had returned. Brighter and somewhat larger than before, spotted with the dark blurs and shadows of craters yet to be repaired, but there. Mankind's ancient guardian floated in Mankind's night sky once more, more powerful even than of old.

"That statement is not quite correct," that guardian said now. "You have won the first campaign; the war is far from over."

"Dahak's right," Horus said, turning his wise old eyes to his son-in-law. "I'm an old man, even by Imperial standards. I won't live to see it end, but you and 'Tanni will."

"Aye, Your Grace, we shall." Jiltanith emerged into the frosty moonlight with her silent, cat-like stride and paused to kiss the Planetary Duke of Terra, then sat beside Colin. He squirmed sideways on the lounger, drawing her down so that her head rested on his shoulder.

"If we do," he said quietly to Horus, "it'll be because of you. Because of all of us, I suppose, but especially because of you. And Dahak."

"We both thank you." Horus smiled lazily. "And I, at least, have my reward—they're upstairs in their beds. But what of you, Dahak?"

"I, too, have my reward. I am here, with my friends, and I look forward to a long association with humanity—or perhaps I should say a *longer* association. You are not very logical beings, but I have learned a great deal from you. I look forward to learning more."

"And we to learning more of thee, my Dahak," Jiltanith said.

"Thank you. Yet we have wandered somewhat afield from my original observation. The war remains to be won."

"True," Colin agreed, "but the Nest—or its computer—doesn't know that yet. None of the ships with souped up hyper drives got away, either, so he *won't* know for another few centuries. Tao-ling and Mother already have Birhat's industrial plant almost completely back on line, more ships are coming in, Vlad and *Fabricator* are off on their first salvage mission, and we've got at least two perfectly habitable planets to grow people on. We may still find more, too—surely the plague didn't get *all* of them. By the time Mister Tin God figures out we're coming, we'll be ready to scrap his ass."

"Aye. And 'tis well to know we need not slay all the Aku'Ultan so to do."

Colin hugged Jiltanith tightly, for there had been no doubt in her voice. She would never be quick to forgive, but horror and pity for what had been done to the Achuultani had purged away her hate for them.

And she was right, he thought, recalling his last meeting with Brashieel. The centaur had greeted him not with a Protector's salute but with a human handclasp, and his strange, slit-pupilled eyes had met Colin's squarely. Many of the other captives had died or retreated into catatonia rather than accept the truth; Brashieel was tougher than that. Indeed, he was an extraordinary individual in every respect, emerging as the true leader of the POWs—or liberated slaves, depending on how one looked at them—despite his junior rank.

They had talked for several hours, accompanied by Hector MacMahan, Ninhursag, and the individual who had proved Earth's finest ambassador to the Aku'Ultan—Tinker Bell. The big, happy dog *loved* Achuultani. Something about their scent brought cheerful little grumbles of pleasure from her, and they were big and strong enough to frisk with to her heart's content. Best of all, from her uncomplicated viewpoint, the Achuultani had never seen anything remotely like her, and they were spoiling her absolutely rotten.

Brashieel had settled comfortably on his folded legs, rubbing Tinker Bell's ears, but his crest had lowered in rage more than once as they spoke. He, at least, understood what had happened to his people, and his hatred for the computer which had enslaved him was a fire in his soul. It was odd, Colin reflected, that the bitter warfare between Man and Achuultani should end this way, with the steady emergence of an alliance *of* Man and Achuultani against the computer which had victimized them both, all made possible only because *another* computer had risked its own existence to free them both.

And even if they were forced to destroy the Achuultani planets—a fate he prayed they could avoid—there would still be Aku'Ultan. Aided by the data Dahak had recovered from *Deathdealer*, Cohanna and Isis were slowly but steadily unlocking the puzzle of their genetic structure. At worst, they would be able to clone their prisoners within the next few decades; at best, Cohanna believed she could produce the first free Aku'Ultan females the universe had seen in seventy-three million years.

He grinned at the thought. It might be odd to find himself thinking of Achuultani allies, but not as "odd" as some of the things Brashieel and his fellows might have to get used to. The centaurs were still baffled by the very notion of two sexes. If Cohanna succeeded, Brashieel might find learning to live without a computer running his life the *least* of his problems. His grin grew broad enough to crack his face at the thought.

"What doth amuse thee so, my love?" his wife demanded, and he burst out laughing.

"Only life's little surprises, 'Tanni," he said, hugging her tight and kissing her. "Only life."

Heirs of Empire

CHAPTER ONE

Sean MacIntyre skittered out of the transit shaft and adjusted his hearing as he dashed down the passage. He shouldn't need to listen until he was on the other side of the hatch, but he still had more trouble with his ears' bio-enhancement than with his eyes for some reason, and he preferred to get set early.

He covered the last hundred meters, slid to a halt, and pressed his back against the bulkhead. The wide, silent passage vanished into a gleaming dot in either direction, and he raked a hand through sweaty black hair as his enhanced ears picked the pulsing sounds of environmental equipment and the soft hum of the now-distant transit shaft from the slowing thunder of his pulse. He'd been chasing them for over an hour, and he'd half-expected to be ambushed by now. *He* certainly would have tried it, he thought, and sniffed disdainfully.

He drew his holstered pistol and turned to the hatch. It slid open—quietly to unenhanced ears, but thunderous to his—and bright sunlight spilled out.

He slipped through the hatch and selected telescopic vision for his left eye. He kept his right adjusted to normal ranges (he did lots better with his eyes than with his ears) and peered into the dappled shadows of the whispering leaves.

Oaks and hickories drowsed under the "sun" as he slithered across the picnic area into the gloss-green rhododendrons that ran down to the lake. He moved quietly, holding the pistol against his chest two-handed, ready to whirl, point, and fire with all the snakelike quickness of his enhanced reflexes, but search as he might, he heard and saw nothing except wind, birds, and the slop of small waves.

He worked his way clear to the lake without finding a target, then paused in thought. The park deck, one of many aboard the starship *Dahak*, was twenty-odd kilometers across. That was a big hiding place, but Harriet was impatient, and she hated running away. She'd be lurking somewhere within a few hundred meters, hoping to ambush him, and that meant—

Motion flickered, and he froze, vision zooming in on whatever had

427

attracted it. He smiled as he saw a flash of long, black hair duck back behind an oak, but he didn't scoot out after her. Now that he'd found Harry, there was no way she could sneak away from her tree without his seeing her, and he swept his eyes back and forth, searching for her ally. She'd be part of the ambush, too, so she had to be pretty close. In fact, she should be . . .

A hand-sized patch of blue caught his eye, just visible between two laurels. Unlike Harry, it was patiently and absolutely still, but he had them both now, and he grinned and began a slow, stealthy move to his left. A few more meters and—

Zaaaaaaaaaaa-*ting!*

Sean jerked in disbelief, then punched the ground and used a word his mother would not have approved. The chime gave way to a raucous buzzing that ripped at his augmented hearing, and he snatched his ears back to normal and stood resignedly.

The buzz from the laser-sensing units on his harness stopped at his admission of defeat, and he turned, wondering how Harry had slipped around behind him. But it wasn't Harry, and he ground his teeth as a diminutive figure splashed ashore. She'd shed her bright blue jacket (Sean knew exactly where), and she was soaking wet, but her brown eyes blazed with delight.

"I *got* you!" she shrieked. "Sean's dead! Sean's dead, Harry!"

He managed not to use any more of his forbidden vocabulary when the eight-year-old ninja began an impromptu war dance, but it was hard, especially when his twin threw herself into the dance with her half-pint ally. Bad enough to lose to *girls*, but to be ambushed by Sandy MacMahan was insupportable. She was two years younger than he, this was the first time she'd even been allowed to play, and she'd killed him with her first shot!

"Your elation at Sean's death is scarcely becoming, Sandra." The deep, mellow voice coming from empty air surprised none of them. They'd known Dahak all their lives, and the self-aware computer's starship body was one of their favorite playgrounds.

"Who cares?" Sandy demanded gleefully. "I got him! *Zap!*" She pointed her pistol at Sean and collapsed with a wail of laughter at his expression.

"Luck!" he shot back, holstering his own pistol with dignity he knew was threadbare. "You were just lucky, Sandy!"

"That is incorrect, Sean," Dahak observed with the dispassionate fairness Sean hated when it was on someone else's side. "'Luck' implies the fortuitous working of chance, and Sandra's decision to conceal herself in the lake—which, I observed, you did not check once—was an ingenious maneuver. And as she has cogently if unkindly observed, she 'got' you."

"So there!" Sandy stuck out her tongue, and Sean turned away with an injured air. It didn't get any better when Harriet grinned at him.

"I told you Sandy was old enough, didn't I?" she demanded.

He longed to disagree—violently—but he was an honest boy, and so he nodded begrudgingly, and tried to hide his shudder as a vision of the future unrolled before him. Sandy was Harry's best friend, despite her youth, and now the little creep was going to be underfoot *everywhere*. He'd managed to fend that off for over a year by claiming she was too little. Until today. She was already two course units ahead of him in calculus, and now this!

The universe, Sean Horus MacIntyre concluded grumpily, wasn't exactly running over with justice.

Amanda Tsien and her husband stepped out of the transit shaft outside *Dahak*'s command deck. Her son, Tamman, followed them down the passage, but he was almost squirming in impatience, and Amanda glanced up at her towering husband with a twinkle. Most described Tsien Tao-ling's face as grim, but a smile flickered as he watched Tamman. The boy might not be "his" in any biological sense, yet that didn't mean he wasn't Tamman's father, and he nodded when Amanda quirked an eyebrow.

"All right, Tamman," she said. "You can go."

"Thanks, Mom!" He turned in his tracks with the curiously catlike awkwardness of his age and dashed back towards the transit shaft. "Where's Sean, Dahak?" he demanded as he ran.

"He is on Park Deck Nine, Tamman," a mellow voice responded.

"Thanks! See you later, Mom, Dad!" Tamman ran sideways for a moment to wave, then dove into the shaft with a whoop.

"You'd think they hadn't seen each other in months," Amanda sighed.

"I do not believe children live on the same time scale as adults," Tsien observed in his deep, soft voice as she tucked a hand through his elbow.

"You can say that again!"

They turned the final bend to confront the command deck hatch. *Dahak*'s crest coiled across the bronze-gold battle steel: a three-headed dragon, poised for flight, clawed forefeet raised to cradle the emblem of the Fifth Imperium. The crowned starburst of the Fourth Empire had been retained, but now a Phoenix of rebirth erupted from the starburst, and the diadem of empire rested on its crested head. The twenty-centimeter-thick hatch—the first of many, each fit to withstand a kiloton-range warhead—slid soundlessly open.

"Hello, Dahak," Amanda said as they walked forward and other hatches parted before them.

"Good evening, Amanda. Welcome aboard, Star Marshal."

"Thank you," Tsien replied. "Have the others arrived?"

"Admiral Hatcher is en route, but the MacMahans and Duke Horus have already joined Their Majesties."

"One day Gerald must learn there are only twenty-eight hours even in Birhat's day," Tsien sighed.

"Oh, really?" Amanda glanced up at him again. "I suppose *you*'ve already learned that?"

"Perhaps not," he agreed with another small smile, and she snorted as a final hatch admitted them to the dim vastness of *Dahak*'s Command One.

A sphere of stars engulfed them. The diamond-hard pinheads burned in the ebon depths of space, dominated by the cloud-banded green-and-blue sphere of the planet Birhat, and Amanda shivered. Not from cold, but with the icy breeze that always seemed to whisper down her spine whenever she stepped into the perfection of the holographic display.

"Hi, Amanda. Tao-ling." His Imperial Majesty Colin I, Grand Duke of Birhat, Prince of Bia, Sol, Chamhar, and Narhan, Warlord and Prince Protector of the Realm, Defender of the Five Thousand Suns, Champion of Humanity, and, by the Maker's Grace, Emperor of Mankind, swiveled his couch to show them his homely, beak-nosed face and grinned. "I see Tamman peeled off early."

"When last seen, he was headed for the park deck," Tsien agreed.

"Well, he's in for a surprise." Colin chuckled. "Harry and Dahak finally bullied Sean into letting Sandy try her hand at laser tag."

"Oh, my!" Amanda laughed. "I'll bet that was an experience!"

"Aye." Empress Jiltanith, slender as a sword and as beautiful as Colin was homely, rose to embrace Amanda. "Belike he'll crow less loud anent her youth henceforth. His pride hath been humbled—for the nonce, at least."

"He'll get over it," Hector MacMahan remarked. The Imperial Marine Corps' commandant leaned on the gunnery officer's console while his wife occupied the couch before it. Like Amanda, he wore Marine black and silver, but Ninhursag MacMahan wore Battle Fleet's midnight-blue and gold, and she smiled.

"Not if Sandy has anything to say about it. One of these days that girl's going to make an excellent spook."

"You should know," Colin said, and Ninhursag managed a seated bow in his direction. "In the meantime, I—"

"Excuse me, Colin," Dahak murmured, "but Admiral Hatcher's cutter has docked."

"Good. Looks like we can get this show on the road pretty soon."

"I hope so," Horus said. The stocky, white-haired Planetary Duke of Terra shook his head. "Every time I poke my nose out of my office, something's waiting to crawl out of the 'in' basket and bite me when I get back!"

Colin nodded at his father-in-law in agreement, but he was watching the Tsiens. Tao-ling seated Amanda with an attentiveness so focused it was almost unconscious . . . and one that might seem odd to those who knew only Star Marshal Tsien's reputation or knew General Amanda Tsien only as the tough-as-nails commandant of Fort Hawter, the Imperial Marines' advanced training base on Birhat. Colin, on the other hand, understood it perfectly, and he was profoundly grateful to see it.

Amanda Tsien feared nothing that lived, but she was also an orphan. She'd been only nine years old when she learned a harsh universe's cruelest weapon could be love . . . and she'd relearned that lesson when Tamman, her first husband, died at Zeta Trianguli Australis. Colin and Jiltanith had watched helplessly as she hid herself in her duties, sealing herself into an armored shell and investing all the emotion she dared risk in Tamman's son. She'd become an automaton, and there'd been nothing even an emperor could do about it, but Tsien Tao-ling had changed that.

Many of the marshal's personnel feared him. That was wise of them, yet something in Amanda had called out to him, despite her defenses, and the man the newsies called "the Juggernaut" had approached her so gently she hadn't even realized he was doing it until it was too late. Until he'd been inside her armor, holding out his hand to offer her the heart few people believed he had . . . and she'd taken it.

She was thirty years younger than he, which mattered not at all among the bio-enhanced. After all, Colin was over forty years younger than Jiltanith, and she looked younger than he. Of course, chronologically she was well over fifty-one thousand years old, but that didn't count; she'd spent all but eighty-odd of those years in stasis.

"How're Hsu-li and Collete?" he asked Amanda, and she chuckled.

"Fine. Hsu-li was a bit ticked we didn't bring him along, but I convinced him he should stay to help take care of his sister."

Colin shook his head. "That wouldn't have worked with Sean and Harry."

"That's what you get for having twins," Amanda said smugly, then bent a sly glance on Jiltanith. "Or for not having a few more kids."

"Nay, acquit me, Amanda." Jiltanith smiled. "I know not how thou findest time for all thy duties and thy babes, but 'twill be some years more—mayhap decades—ere I again essay that challenge. And it ill beseemeth thee so to twit thine Empress when all the world doth know thee for a mother o' the best, while I—" She shrugged wryly, and her friends laughed.

Horus was about to say something more when the inner hatch slid open to admit a trim, athletic man in Battle Fleet blue.

"Hi, Gerald," Colin greeted the new arrival, and Admiral of the Fleet Gerald Hatcher, Chief of Naval Operations, bowed with a flourish.

"Good evening, Your Majesty," he said so unctuously his liege lord shook a fist at him. Admiral Hatcher had spent thirty years as a soldier of the United States, not a sailor, but BattleFleet's CNO was the Imperium's senior officer. That made it a logical duty for the man who'd served as humanity's chief of staff during Earth's defense against the Achuultani, yet not even that authority could quash Hatcher's cheerful irreverence.

He waved to Ninhursag, shook hands with Hector, Tsien, and Horus, then planted an enthusiastic kiss on Amanda's cafe-au-lait cheek. He bent gracefully over Jiltanith's hand, but the Empress tugged shrewdly on the neat beard he'd grown since the Siege of Earth and kissed his mouth before he could recover.

"Thou'rt a shameless fellow, Gerald Hatcher," she told him severely, "and mayhap that shall teach thee what fate awaiteth when thou leavest thy wife behind!"

"Oh?" He grinned. "Is that a threat or a promise, Your Majesty?"

"Off with his head!" Colin murmured, and the admiral laughed.

"Actually, she's visiting her sister on Earth. They're picking out baby clothes."

"My God, is *everybody* hatching new youngsters?"

"Nay, my Colin, 'tis only everyone *else*," Jiltanith said.

"True," Hatcher agreed. "And this time it's going to be a boy. I'm perfectly happy with the girls, myself, but Sharon's delighted."

"Congratulations," Colin told him, then waved at an empty couch. "But now that you're here, let's get down to business."

"Suits me. I've got a conference scheduled aboard Mother in a few hours, and I'd like to grab a nap first."

"Okay." Colin sat a bit straighter and his lazy amusement faded. "As I indicated when I invited you all, I want to talk to you informally before next week's Council meeting. We're coming up on the tenth anniversary of my 'coronation,' and the Assembly of Nobles wants to throw a big shindig to celebrate. That may be a good idea, but it means this year's State of the Realm speech is going to be pretty important, so I want a feel from the 'inner circle' before I get started writing it."

His guests hid smiles. The Fourth Empire had never required regular formal reports from its emperors, but Colin had incorporated the State of the Realm message into the Fifth Imperium's law, and the self-inflicted annual duty was an ordeal he dreaded. It was also why he'd invited his friends to *Dahak*'s command deck. Unlike too many others, they could be relied upon to tell him what they thought rather than what they thought he wanted them to think.

"Let's begin with you, Gerald."

"Okay." Hatcher rubbed his beard gently. "You can start off with a piece of good news. Geb dropped off his last report just before he and Vlad headed out to Cheshir, and they should have the Cheshir Fleet base back on-line within three months. They've turned up nine more *Asgerds*, too. They'll need a few more months to reactivate them, and we're stretched for personnel—as usual—but we'll make do, and that'll bring us up to a hundred and twelve planetoids." He paused. "Unless we have another *Sherkan*."

Colin frowned at his suddenly bitter tone but let it pass. All the diagnostics had said the planetoid *Sherkan* was safe to operate without extensive overhaul—but it had been Hatcher's expedition that found her, and he'd been the one who'd had to tell Vladimir Chernikov.

So far, Survey Command had discovered exactly two once-populated planets of the Fourth Empire which retained any life at all—Birhat, the old imperial capital, and Chamhar—and no humans had survived on either. But much of the Empire's military hardware *had* survived, including many of its vast fleet of enormous starships, and they needed all of those they could get. Humanity had stopped the Achuultani's last incursion—barely—but defeating them on their own ground was going to be something else again.

Unfortunately, restoring a derelict four thousand kilometers in diameter to service after forty-five millennia was a daunting task, which was why Hatcher had been so pleased by *Sherkan*'s excellent condition. But the tests had missed a tiny flaw in her core tap, and its governors had blown the instant her engineer brought it on-line to suck in the energy for supralight movement. The resultant explosion could have destroyed a continent, and six thousand human beings had died in it, including Fleet Admiral Vassily Chernikov and his wife, Valentina.

"Anyway," Hatcher went on more briskly, "we're coming along nicely on the other projects, as well. Adrienne will graduate her first Academy class in a few months, and I'm entirely satisfied with the results, but she and Tao-ling are still fiddling with fine-tuning the curriculum.

"On the hardware side, things are looking good here in Bia, thanks to Tao-ling. He had to put virtually all the surviving yard facilities back on-line to get the shield operational—" Hatcher and the star marshal exchanged wry smiles at that; reactivating the enormous shield genera-tors which surrounded Birhat's primary, Bia, in an inviolate sphere eighty light-minutes across had been a horrendous task "—so we've got plenty of overhaul capacity. In fact, we're ready to start design work on our new construction."

"Really?" Colin's tone was pleased.

"Indeed," Dahak answered for the admiral. "It will be approximately three-point-five standard years—" (the Fifth Imperium ran on Terran time, not Birhatan) "—before capacity for actual construction can be diverted from reactivation programs, but Admiral Baltan and I have begun preliminary studies on the new designs. We are combining several concepts 'borrowed' from the Achuultani with others from the Empire's Bureau of Ships, and I believe we will attain substantial increases in the capabilities of our new units."

"That's good news, but where does it leave us on Stepmother?"

"I fear that will require considerably longer, Colin," Dahak replied.

"'Considerably' is probably optimistic," Hatcher sighed. "We're still stub-bing our toes on the finer points of Empire computer hardware, even with Dahak's help, and Mother's the most complex computer the Empire ever built. Duplicating her's going to be a bitch—not to mention the time require-ment to build a five-thousand-kilometer hull to put said duplicate inside!"

Colin didn't like that, but he understood. The Empire had built Mother (officially known as Fleet Central Computer Central) using force-field cir-cuitry that made even molycircs look big and clumsy, yet the computer was still over three hundred kilometers in diameter. It was also housed in the most powerful fortress ever constructed by Man, for it did more than simply run Battle Fleet. Mother was the conservator of the Empire, as well—indeed, it was she who'd crowned Colin and provided the ships to smash the Achuultani. Unfortunately (or, perhaps, fortunately) she was carefully designed, as all late-Empire computers, to preclude self-awareness, which meant she would disgorge her unimaginable treasure trove of data only when tickled with the right specific question.

But Colin spent a lot of time worrying over what might happen to Battle Fleet if something happened to Mother, and he intended to provide Earth with defenses every bit as powerful as Birhat's . . . including a duplicate of Mother. If everything went well, Stepmother (as Hatcher had insisted on christening the proposed installation) would never come fully on-line, but if Mother was destroyed, Stepmother would take over automatically, pro-viding unbroken command and control for Battle Fleet and the Imperium.

"What kind of time estimate do you have?"

"Speaking very, very roughly, and assuming we get a firm grip on the computer technology so we don't have to keep pestering Dahak with questions, we may be able to start on the hull in six years or so. Once we get that far, we can probably finish the job up in another five."

"Damn. Oh, well. We won't be hearing from the Achuultani for another four or five centuries, minimum, but I want that project completed ASAP, Ger."

"Understood," Hatcher said. "In the meantime, though, we ought to be able to put the first new planetoids on-line considerably sooner. Their computers're a lot smaller and simpler-minded, without any of Mother's wonder-what-the-hell's-in-'em files, and the other hardware's no big problem, even allowing for the new systems' test programs."

"Okay." Colin turned to Tsien. "Want to add anything, Tao-ling?"

"I fear Gerald has stolen much of my thunder," Tsien began, and Hatcher grinned. Technically, everything that wasn't mobile belonged to Tsien—from fortifications and shipyards to R&D to Fleet training—but with so much priority assigned to rounding up and crewing Hatcher's planetoids there was a lot of overlap in their current spheres of authority.

"As he and Dahak have related, most of the Bia System has now been fully restored to function. With barely four hundred million people in the system, our personnel are spread even more thinly than Gerald's, but we are coping and the situation is improving. Baltan and Geran, with much assistance from Dahak, are doing excellent work with Research and Development, although 'research' will continue, for the foreseeable future, to be little more than following up on the Empire's final projects. They are, however, turning up several interesting new items among those projects. In particular, the Empire had begun development of a new generation of gravitonic warheads."

"Oh?" Colin quirked an eyebrow. "This is the first I've heard of it."

"Me, too," Hatcher put in. "What kind of warheads, Tao-ling?"

"We only discovered the data two days ago," Tsien half-apologized, "but what we have seen so far suggests a weapon several magnitudes more powerful than any previously built."

"Maker!" Horus straightened in his own couch, eyes half-fascinated and half-appalled. Fifty-one thousand years ago, he'd been a missile specialist of the Fourth Imperium, and the fearsome efficiency of the weapons the Empire had produced had shaken him badly when he first confronted them.

"Indeed," Tsien said dryly. "I am not yet certain, but I suspect this warhead might be able to duplicate your feat at Zeta Trianguli, Colin."

Several people swallowed audibly at that, including Colin. He'd used the FTL Enchanach drive, which employed massive gravity fields—essentially converging black holes—to literally squeeze a ship out of "real" space in a series of instantaneous transitions, as a weapon at the Second Battle of Zeta Trianguli Australis. An Enchanach ship's dwell time in normal space was very, very brief, and even when it came "close" (in interstellar terms), a ship moving at roughly nine hundred times light-speed didn't spend long enough in the vicinity of any star to do it harm. But the drive's initial activation and final deactivation took a considerably longer time, and Colin had used that to induce a nova which destroyed over a million Achuultani starships.

Yet he'd needed a half-dozen *planetoids* to do the trick, and the thought of reproducing it with a single warhead was terrifying.

"Are you serious?" he demanded.

"I am. The warhead's total power is far lower than the aggregate you produced, but it is also much more focused. Our most conservative estimate indicates a weapon which would be capable of destroying any planet and everything within three or four hundred thousand kilometers of it."

"Jesu!" Jiltanith's voice was soft, and she squeezed the hilt of her fifteenth-century dagger. "Such power misliketh me, Colin. 'Twould be most terrible if such a weapon should by mischance smite one of our own worlds!"

"You got that right," Colin muttered with a shudder. He still had nightmares over Zeta Trianguli, and if the accidental detonation of a gravitonic warhead was virtually impossible, the Empire had thought the same thing about the accidental release of its bio-weapons.

"Hold off on building the thing, Tao-ling," he said. "Do whatever you want with the research—hell, we may *need* it against the Achuultani master computer!—but don't produce any hardware without checking with me."

"Of course, Your Majesty."

"Any other surprises for us?"

"Not of such magnitude. Dahak and I will prepare a full report for you by the end of the week, if you wish."

"I wish." Colin turned his eyes to Hector MacMahan. "Any problems with the Corps, Hector?"

"Very few. We're making out better than Gerald in terms of manpower, but then, our target force level's lower. Some of our senior officers are having trouble adjusting to the capabilities of Imperial equipment—most of them are still drawn from the pre-Siege militaries—and we've had a few training snafus as a result. Amanda's correcting most of that at Fort Hawter, and the new generation coming up doesn't have anything to unlearn in the first place. I don't see anything worth worrying about."

"Fine," Colin said. If Hector MacMahan didn't see anything worth worrying about, then there *was* nothing, and he turned his attention to Horus. "How're we doing on Earth, Horus?"

"I wish I could tell you the situation's altered, Colin, but it hasn't. You can't make these kinds of changes without a lot of disruption. Conversion to the new currency's gone more smoothly than we had any right to expect, but we've completely trashed the pre-Siege economy. The new one's still pretty amorphous, and a lot of people who're getting burned are highly pissed."

The old man leaned back and folded his arms across his chest.

"Actually, people at both ends of the spectrum are hurting right now. The subsistence-level economies are making out better than ever before— at least starvation's no longer a problem, and we've made decent medical care universally available—but virtually every skilled trade's become obsolete, and that's hitting the Third World hardest. The First World never imagined anything like Imperial technology before the Siege, and even there, retraining programs are mind-boggling, but at least it had a high-tech mind-set.

"Worse, it's going to take at least another decade to make modern technology fully available, given how much of our total effort the military programs are sucking up. We're still relying on a lot of pre-Imperial industry for bread-and-butter production, and the people running it feel discriminated against. They see themselves as stuck in dead-end jobs, and the fact that civilian bio-enhancement and modern medicine will give them two or three centuries to move up to something better hasn't really sunk in yet.

"Bio-enhancement bottlenecks don't help much, either. As usual, Isis is doing far better than I expected, but again, the folks in the Third World are getting squeezed worst. We've had to prioritize things somehow, and they simply have more people and less technical background. Some of them still think biotechnics are magic!"

"I'm glad I had someone else to dump *your* job on," Colin said with heartfelt sincerity. "Is there anything else we can give you?"

"Not really." Horus sighed. "We're running as hard and as fast as we can already, and there simply isn't any more capacity to devote to it. I imagine we'll make out, and at least I've got some high-powered help on the Planetary Council. We learned a lot getting ready for the Siege, and we've managed to avoid several nasty mistakes because we did."

"Would it help to relieve you of responsibility for Birhat?"

"Not much, I'm afraid. Most of the people here are tied directly into Gerald's and Tao-ling's operations, so I'm only providing support for their dependents. Of course—" Horus flashed a sudden grin "—I'm sure my lieutenant governor thinks I spend too much time off Earth anyway!"

"I imagine he does." Colin chuckled. "But then *my* lieutenant governor probably felt the same way."

"Indeed he did!" Horus laughed. "Actually, Lawrence has been a gift from the Maker," he added more seriously. "He's taken a tremendous amount of day-to-day duties off my back, and he and Isis make a mighty efficient team on the enhancement side."

"Then I'm glad you've got him." Colin knew Lawrence Jefferson less well than he would have liked, but what he knew impressed him. Under the Great Charter, imperial planetary governors were appointed by the Emperor, but a *lieutenant* governor was appointed by his immediate superior with the advice and consent of his Planetary Council. After so many centuries as an inhabitant (if not precisely a citizen) of the North American continent, Horus had chosen to turn that advice and consent function into an election, soliciting nominations from his Councilors, and Jefferson was the result. A US senator when Colin raided Anu's enclave, he'd done yeoman work throughout the Siege, then resigned midway through his third senatorial term to assume his new post, where he'd soon made his mark as a man of charm, wit, and ability.

Now Colin turned to Ninhursag. "Anything new from ONI, 'Hursag?"

"Not really." Like Horus and Jiltanith, the stocky, pleasantly plain woman had come to Earth aboard *Dahak*. Like Horus (but unlike Jiltanith, who'd been a child at the time), she'd joined Fleet Captain Anu's mutiny, only to discover to her horror that it was but the first step in *Dahak*'s Chief

Engineer's plan to topple the Imperium itself. But whereas Horus had deserted Anu and launched a millennia-long guerrilla war against him, Ninhursag had been stuck in stasis in Anu's Antarctic enclave. When she was finally awakened, she'd managed to contact the guerrillas and provide the information which had made the final, desperate attack on the enclave possible. Now, as a Battle Fleet admiral, she ran Naval Intelligence and enjoyed describing herself as Colin's "SIC," or "Spook In Chief." Colin was fond of telling her her self-created acronym was entirely apt.

"We've still got problems," she continued, "because Horus is right. When you stand an entire world on its head, you generate a lot of resentment. On the other hand, Earth took half a billion casualties from the Achuultani, and everybody knows who saved the rest of them. Almost all of them are willing to give you and 'Tanni the benefit of the doubt on anything you do or we do in your names. Gus and I are keeping an eye on the discontented elements, but most of them disliked one another enough before the Siege to make any kind of cooperation difficult. Even if they didn't, they can't do much to buck the kind of devotion the rest of the human race feels for you."

Colin no longer blushed when people said things like that, and he nodded thoughtfully. Gustav van Gelder was Horus' Minister of Security, and while Ninhursag understood the possibilities of Imperial technology far better than he, Gus had taught her a lot about how *people* worked.

"To be perfectly honest," Ninhursag continued, "I'd be a bit happier if I *could* find something serious to worry about."

"How's that?" Colin asked.

"I guess I'm like Horus, worrying about what's going to bite me next. We're moving so fast I can't even identify all the players, much less what they might be up to, and even the best security measures could be leaking like a sieve. For instance, I've spent hours with Dahak and a whole team of my brightest boys and girls, and we still can't figure a way to ID Anu's surviving Terra-born allies."

"Are you saying we didn't get them all?!" Colin jerked upright, and Jiltanith tensed at his side. Ninhursag looked surprised at their reactions.

"Didn't you tell him, Dahak?" she asked.

"I regret," the mellow voice sounded unwontedly uncomfortable, "that I did not. Or, rather, I did not do so explicitly."

"And what the hell does *that* mean?" Colin demanded.

"I mean, Colin, that I included the data in one of your implant downloads but failed to draw your attention specifically to them."

Colin frowned and keyed the mental sequence that opened the index of his implant knowledge. The problem with implant education was that it simply stored data; until someone *used* that information, he might not even know he had it. Now the report Dahak referred to sprang into his forebrain, and he bit off a curse.

"Dahak," he began plaintively, "I've *told* you—"

"You have." The computer hesitated a moment, then went on. "As you know, my equivalent of the human qualities of 'intuition' and 'imagination'

remain limited. I have grasped—intellectually, I suppose you would say—
that human brains lack my own search and retrieval capabilities, but I occasionally overlook their limitations. I shall not forget again."

The computer actually sounded embarrassed, and Colin shrugged.

"Forget it. It's more my fault than yours. You certainly had a right to
expect me to at least read your report."

"Perhaps. It is nonetheless incumbent upon me to provide you with the
data you require. It thus follows that I should inquire to be certain that
you do, in fact, realize that you have them."

"Don't get your diodes in an uproar." Colin turned back to Ninhursag
as Dahak made the sound he used for a chuckle. "Okay, I've got it now,
but I don't see anything about how we missed them . . . if we did."

"The how's fairly easy, actually. Anu and his crowd spent thousands of
years manipulating Earth's population, and they had a tremendous number of contacts, including batches of people with no idea who they were
working for. We got most of their bigwigs when you stormed his enclave,
but Anu couldn't possibly have squeezed *all* of them into it. We managed
to identify most of the important bit players from his captured records, but
a lot of small fry have to've been missed.

"Those people don't worry me. They know what'll happen if they draw
attention to themselves, and I expect most have decided to become *very* loyal
subjects of the Imperium. But what does worry me a bit is that Kirinal seems
to have been running at least two top secret cells no one else knew about.
When you and 'Tanni killed her in the Cuernavaca strike, not even Anu
and Ganhar knew who those people were, so they never got taken into the
enclave before the final attack."

"My God, 'Hursag!" Hatcher sounded appalled. "You mean we've still got
top echelon people who worked for Anu running around loose?"

"No more than a dozen at the outside," Ninhursag replied, "and, like
the small fry, they're not going to draw attention to themselves. I'm not
suggesting we forget about them, Gerald, but consider the mess *they're*
in. They lost their patron when Colin killed Anu, and as Horus and I
have been saying, we've turned Earth's whole society upside-down, so
they've probably lost a lot of the influence they may've had in the old
power structure. Even those who haven't been left out in the cold have
only their own resources to work with, and there's no way they're going
to do anything that might draw attention to their past associations with
Anu."

"Admiral MacMahan is correct, Admiral Hatcher," Dahak said. "I do not
mean to imply that they will never be a menace again—indeed, the fact that
they knowingly served Anu indicates not only criminality on their part but
ambition and ability, as well—yet they no longer possess a support structure. Deprived of Anu's monopoly on Imperial technology, they become
simply one more criminal element. While it would be folly to assume they
are incapable of building a new support structure or to abandon our search
for them, they represent no greater inherent threat than any other group
of unscrupulous individuals. Moreover, it should be noted that they were

organized on a cell basis, which suggests members of any one cell would know only other members of that cell. Concerted action by any large number of them is therefore improbable."

"Huh!" Hatcher grunted skeptically, then made himself relax. "All right, I grant you that, but it makes me nervous to know *any* of Anu's bunch are still around."

"You and me both," Colin agreed, and Jiltanith nodded beside him. "On the other hand, it sounds to me like you, Dahak, and Gus are on top of the situation 'Hursag. Stay there, and make sure I find out if anything— and I mean *anything*—changes in regard to it."

"Of course," Ninhursag said quietly. "In the meantime, it seems to me the greatest potential dangers lie in three areas. First, the Third World resentment Horus has mentioned. A lot of those people still see the Imperium as an extension of Western imperialism. Even some of those who truly believe we're doing our best to treat everyone fairly can't quite forget we imposed our ideas and control on them. I expect this particular problem to ease with time, but it'll be with us for a good many years to come.

"Second, we've got the First World people who've seen their positions in the old power structures crumble. Some of them have been a real pain, like the old unions that're still fighting our 'job-destroying new technology,' but, again, most of them—or their children—will come around with time.

"Third, and most disturbing, in a way, are the religious nuts." Ninhursag frowned unhappily. "I just don't understand the true-believer mentality well enough to feel confident about dealing with it, and there's a bunch of true believers out there. Not just in the extreme Islamic blocs, either. At the moment, there's no clear sign of organization—aside from this 'Church of the Armageddon'—but it's mighty hard to reason with someone who's convinced God is on his side. Still, they're not a serious threat unless they coalesce into something bigger and nastier . . . and since the Great Charter guarantees freedom of religion, there's not much we can do about them until and unless they try something overtly treasonous."

She paused, checking back over what she'd said, then shrugged.

"That's about the size of it, at the moment. A lot of rumbles but no present signs of anything really dangerous. We're keeping our eyes peeled, but for the most part it's simply going to take time to relieve the tensions."

"Okay." Colin leaned back and glanced around. "Anyone have anything else we need to look at?" A general headshake answered him, and he rose. "In that case, let's go see what the kids have gotten themselves into."

Eight hundred-plus light-years from Birhat, a man swiveled his chair towards a window and gazed down with unfocused yet intent eyes, staring through the view below to examine something far beyond it.

He rocked the old-fashioned swivel chair back with a gentle creak and steepled his fingers, tapping his chin with his index fingers as he considered the changes which had come upon his world . . . and the other changes he proposed to create in their wake. It had taken almost ten years to attain the position he needed, but attain it he had—not, he admitted, without the help of the Emperor himself—and the game was about to begin.

There was nothing inherently wrong, he conceded, in the notion of an empire, nor even of an emperor for all humanity. Certainly *someone* had to make the human race work together despite its traditional divisions, and the man in the chair had no illusions about his species. With the best of intentions (assuming they existed—a point he felt no obligation to concede), few of Earth's teeming billions would have the least idea of how to create some sort of democratic world state from the ground up. Even if they'd had one, democracies were notoriously short-sighted about preparing for problems which lay beyond the horizon, and the job of ultimately defeating the Achuultani was going to take centuries. No, democracy would never do. Of course, he'd never been particularly attached to that form of government, or Kirinal would never have recruited him, now would she?

Not that his own views on democratic government mattered, for one thing was clear: Colin I intended to exercise his prerogatives of direct rule to provide the central authority mankind required. And, the man in the chair reflected, His Imperial Majesty was doing an excellent job. He was probably the most popular head of state in Earth's history, and, of course, there was the tiny consideration that the Fifth Imperium's armed forces were deeply—one might almost say fanatically—loyal to their Emperor and Empress.

All of which, the man in the chair admitted, made things difficult. But if the game were easy, anyone could play, and think how inconvenient *that* would be!

He chuckled and rocked gently, listening to his chair's soft, musical creaking. Actually, he rather admired the Emperor. How many people could have resurrected an empire which had died with its entire population over forty-five thousand years before and crowned himself its ruler? That was a stellar accomplishment, whatever immediate military advantages Colin MacIntyre might have enjoyed, and the man in the chair saluted him.

Unfortunately, there could be only one Emperor. However skilled, however determined, however adroit, there could be but *one* of him . . . and he was not the man in the chair.

Or, the man in the chair corrected himself with a smile, not yet.

CHAPTER TWO

"Finished, Horus?"

The Planetary Duke of Terra looked up and grimaced as Lawrence Jefferson stepped into his office.

"No," he said sourly, dropping a data chip into his security drawer, "but I'm as close as I'll be for the next decade, so we might as well go. It's not every day my grandchildren have a twelfth birthday, and that's more important than this."

Jefferson laughed as Horus stood and sent his desk computer a command to lock the drawer, and an answering smile flickered on the old man's lips. He glanced at Jefferson's briefcase.

"I see you're not leaving *your* work home."

"*I'm* not going to the party. Besides, this isn't 'my' work—it's Admiral MacMahan's copy of Gus' report on that anti-Narhani demonstration."

"Oh." Horus sounded as disgusted as he felt. "You know, I've learned to handle prejudice. We all suffer from that, to some extent, but this anti-Narhani thing is plain, old-fashioned bigotry."

"True, but then the difference between prejudice and bigotry is usually stupidity. The answer's education. The Narhani are on *our* side; we just have to prove that to these idiots."

"Somehow I doubt they'd appreciate your terminology, Lawrence."

"I call them as I see them." Jefferson grinned. "Besides, you're the only person here. If it leaks, I'll know who to come after."

"I'll bear that in mind." Horus finished shutting down his computer through his neural feed as they strolled out of the office, and two armed Marine guards snapped to attention. Their presence was a formality, but Hector MacMahan's Marines took their responsibilities seriously. Besides, Horus was their Commandant's great-great-great-etc.-grandfather.

The two men took the old-fashioned elevator to the ground floor. White Tower at NASA's old Shepard Center had been Horus' HQ throughout the Siege, and he'd resisted all pressure to relocate from Colorado on the

441

basis that the fact that Shepard Center had never been anyone's capital would help defuse nationalist jealousies. Besides, he liked the climate.

They crossed the plaza to the mat-trans terminal, and Jefferson was grateful for his bio-enhancement as his breath steamed. He wasn't in the military, so he lacked the full enhancement that gave Horus ten times the strength of an unenhanced human, but what he had sufficed to deal with little things like sub-freezing temperatures. Which was handy, since Earth hadn't yet fully emerged from the mini-ice age produced by the Siege's bombardment.

They chatted idly during the walk, enjoying the moment of privacy, but Jefferson was still a bit bemused by the absence of bodyguards. He'd grown to adulthood on a planet where terrorism was the chosen form of "protest" by have-not nations, and the report in his briefcase was proof his home world frothed with resentment as it strained to make a nine- or ten-millennium leap in technology. Yet for all that, violence directed at Earth's Governor was virtually unthinkable. Horus had not only led Earth's people through the carnage of the Siege, he was also the father of their beloved Empress, and only a particularly stupid maniac would attack *him* to make a statement.

Not, Jefferson reflected, that history didn't abound with stupid maniacs.

They entered the mat-trans facility, and Jefferson felt himself tense. It didn't look like much—merely a railed platform twenty meters on a side—but knowing what it could do turned that brightly lit dais into something that made the primitive tree-dweller within the Lieutenant Governor gibber.

His stride slowed, and Horus grinned at him.

"Don't take it so hard. And don't think you're the only one it scares!"

Jefferson managed a nod as they stepped onto the platform and the bio-scanners Colin MacIntyre had ordered incorporated into every mat-trans station considered them at length. The mat-trans had been the Fourth Empire's executioner, the vector by which the rogue bio-weapon infected worlds hundreds of light-years apart, and he had no intention of allowing that particular bit of history to repeat itself.

But the scanners cleared them, and Jefferson clutched his briefcase in a sweaty hand, trying very hard to appear nonchalant, as heavy capacitors whined. The mat-trans' power requirements were astronomical, even by Imperial standards, and it took almost twenty seconds to reach peak load. Then a light flashed . . . and Horus and Lawrence Jefferson stepped down from another platform on the planet Birhat, eight hundred light-years from Earth.

The thing that made it so damned scary, Jefferson thought as he left the mat-trans receiver gratefully behind, was that you didn't feel a thing. *Nothing.* It just wasn't natural . . . and wasn't that a fine thing for a man stuffed full of sensors and neural boosters to be thinking?

"Hi, Granddad." Jefferson looked up as General MacMahan held out his hand to Horus then turned to shake his own. "Colin asked me to meet you. He's tied up with something over at the Palace."

"Tied up with what?" Horus asked.

"I'm not sure, but he sounded a bit harassed. I think—" Hector grinned impishly "—it's got something to do with Cohanna."

"Oh, Maker! What's she been up to *now?*"

"Don't know. Come on, I've got transport waiting."

"Damn it, 'Hanna!" Colin paced back and forth before the utilitarian desk from which he ran the Imperium, tugging on his nose in a gesture his subordinates knew only too well. "I've told you and *told* you you can't just go chasing off after any wild hare that takes your fancy!"

"But, Colin—" Cohanna began.

"Don't 'But, Colin' me! Did I or did I not tell you to check your next genetic experiment with me before you started on it?"

"Well, of course you did. And I *did* clear it with you," Baroness Cohanna, Imperial Minister of Bio-Sciences added virtuously.

"You *what?*" Colin wheeled on her in disbelief.

"I said I cleared it with you. I sat right here in this office with Brashieel and told you what I was going to do."

"You—!" Colin turned to the saurian-looking, long-snouted, quarter-horse-sized centauroid resting comfortably on his folded legs in the middle of the rug, who returned his gaze with mild, double-lidded eyes. "Brashieel, do *you* remember her saying anything about this?"

"Yes," Brashieel replied calmly through the small black box mounted on one strap of his body harness. His vocal apparatus was poorly suited to human speech, but he'd learned to use his neural feed-driven vocoder's deep bass to express emotion as well as words.

Colin drew a deep breath, then perched on his desk and folded his arms. Brashieel seldom made mistakes, and Cohanna's triumphant expression made Colin unhappily certain she had mentioned it. Or something about it.

"All right," he sighed, "what, exactly, did she say?"

Brashieel closed his inner eyelids in concentration, and Colin waited patiently. The alien's mere presence was enough to give some members of humanity screaming fits, which Colin understood even if he rejected their attitude. To be sure, Brashieel *was* an Achuultani. Worse, he was the sole survivor of the fleet which had come within hours of destroying the planet Earth. He was also, however, the being who'd emerged as the natural leader of the prisoners of war Colin had captured after defeating the incursion, and most of those prisoners—not all, but most—were even more committed to the ultimate defeat of the rest of the Achuultani than humanity was.

For seventy-eight million years, the people of the Nest of Aku'Ultan had quartered the galaxy, destroying every sentient species they encountered. Of all their potential victims, only humanity had survived—not just once, but three times, earning it the Achuultani appellation of "the Demon Nest-Killers"—but Brashieel and his fellows knew something the rest of their race did not. They knew their entire species was enslaved by a self-aware computer which used their unending murder of races who meant them no ill to sustain the "state of war" its programming required to maintain its tyranny.

Not all humans were ready to accept their sincerity, which was why Colin had turned the planet Narhan over to those who had applied for Imperial citizenship. Narhan had avoided the bio-weapon for a simple reason; no one had lived on it, since its 2.67 gravity field produced a sea-level atmosphere lethal to unenhanced humans. Its air was a bit dense even for Achuultani lungs, and it was inconveniently placed—it was far enough from Birhat that travelers by mat-trans had to stage through Earth to reach the capital planet—but its settlers had fallen under the spell of its rugged beauty as they set about carving out their new Nest of Narhan as loyal subjects of their human overlord on a world beyond the reach of hysterical xenophobes.

"Cohanna had reported on progress with the genetic engineering to recreate Narhani females," Brashieel said at last. The rogue computer had eliminated all sexual reproduction by eliminating all Achuultani females. Every Achuultani was male, either a clone or an embryo fertilized in vitro. "Thereafter, she turned to discussion of her suggestion to increase our life spans to something approaching those of humans."

Colin nodded. Achuultani—Narhani, he corrected himself—were bigger and far stronger than humans. They also matured much more rapidly, but their normal span was little more than fifty years. Bio-enhancement, which all adult Narhani who'd taken the oath of loyalty had received as quickly as Cohanna got a grip on their alien physiology, stretched that to almost three hundred years, but that remained much shorter than for enhanced humans.

Extending Narhani lives was a challenge, but unlike humans, Narhani had no prejudice against bioengineering. They regarded it as a fact of life, given their own origins and the cloned children Jiltanith's Terra-born sister Isis had managed to produce over the last few years, and the possibility of recreating females of their species simply strengthened that attitude.

"We discussed the practical aspects," Brashieel continued, "and I mentioned Tinker Bell."

"I know you did, but surely I never okayed *this*."

"I regret that I must disagree," Brashieel said, and Colin frowned.

Hector MacMahan's big, happy half-lab, half-rottweiler bitch Tinker Bell had fallen in love with the Narhani. It amused Colin, given the way the dogs in every bad science-fiction movie ever made hated the "alien menace" on sight, but it was more than amusing to the Narhani. The Nest of Aku'Ultan had nothing remotely like her—indeed, one of the most alien things about the nest was the absence of any form of pet—and they found her fascinating. Almost every Narhani had speedily acquired a dog of his own, but they, like any other Terrestrial animal, would have been unable to survive on Narhan, and the Narhani were fiercely devoted to their four-footed friends.

"Look, I know I authorized limited bio-enhancement so you could take the dogs with you, but I never contemplated anything like this."

"I cannot, of course, know what was in your mind, but the point was raised." Colin clenched his teeth. The Narhani were as intelligent as humans but less imaginative and far more literal-minded. "Cohanna pointed out that genetic engineering would permit her to produce dogs who required no enhancement, and you agreed. She then reminded you of Dahak's success in communicating with Tinker Bell and suggested the capability for meaningful exchanges might also be enhanced."

Colin opened his mouth, then shut it with a snap as his own memory replayed the conversation. She *had* mentioned it, and he'd agreed. But, damn it, she should have known what he meant!

He closed his eyes and counted to five hundred. Dahak had insisted for years that Tinker Bell's barks, growls, and yips were more value-laden than humans believed, and he'd persisted with an analysis of her sounds until he proved his point. Dogs were no mental giants. Their cognitive functions were severely limited, and their ability to manipulate symbols was virtually nonexistent, but they had lots more to say than mankind had guessed.

"All right," he said finally, opening his eyes and glowering at Cohanna, who returned his gaze innocently. "All right. I admit the point came up, but you never told me you had anything like this in mind."

"Only because I thought it was self-evident," she said, and Colin bit off an acid response. He sometimes toyed with the notion that the millennia Cohanna had spent in stasis had affected her mind, but he'd known Terra-born humans just like her. She was brilliant and intensely curious, and little things like political realities, wars, and nearby supernovas were totally unimportant compared to her current project—whatever it might be.

"Look," he tried again, "I've got several million Terra-born who find simple biotechnics scary, 'Hanna." Her nose wrinkled with contempt for such benighted ignorance, and he sighed. "All right, so they're wrong. But that doesn't change the way they feel, and if *that* upsets them, how are they going to react to your fooling with the natural order of evolution?"

"Evolution," she replied, "is an unreasoning statistical process which represents no more than the blind conservation of accidental life forms capable of surviving within their environments."

"*Please* don't say things like that!" Colin ran his hands through his hair and tried not to look harried. "Maybe you're right, but too many Terra-born regard it as the working out of God's plan for the universe. And even the ones who don't tend to remember the bio-weapon and wake up screaming!"

"Barbarians!" Cohanna snorted, and Colin sighed.

"I ought to order you to destroy them," he muttered, but he shied away from the rebellion in her eyes. "All right, I won't. Not immediately, anyway. But before I promise not to, I want to see them with my own eyes. And you are *not* to conduct any more genetic experiments outside a Petri dish without my specific—and written!—authorization. Is that understood?"

The doctor nodded frigidly, and Colin walked around his desk to flop into his chair. "Good. Now, I've got a meeting with Horus and Lieutenant Governor Jefferson in ten minutes, so we're going to have to wrap this up. But before we do, are there any problems—or surprises—with Project Genesis?"

"No." Cohanna's spine relaxed. One thing about her, Colin reflected; she was a tartar when her toes got stepped on, but she recovered. "Although," she added pointedly, "I'm a bit surprised you don't object to the name."

"I wish I'd thought about it when Isis suggested it, but I didn't. And we're only using it internally and all the reports are classified, so I don't expect it to upset anyone."

"Hmph!" Cohanna sniffed, then smiled wryly. "Well, it's really more her project than mine, anyway, so I suppose I shouldn't complain. Anyway, we should be ready to move within the next year or so."

"That soon?" Colin was impressed, and he cocked his head to gaze at Brashieel. "How do you folks feel about that, Brashieel?"

"Curious," the alien said, "and possibly a bit frightened. After all, the concept of females is still quite strange, and the notion of producing nestlings with a nestmate is . . . peculiar. Most of us, however, are eager to see what they're like. For myself, I look forward to it with interest, though I'm highly satisfied with the way Brashan has turned out."

"Yeah, you might say he's a chip off the old block." Brashieel, whose race was given neither to clichés nor puns, looked blank, but Cohanna winced, and Colin grinned. "Okay, that's going to have to be it." His guests rose, and he wagged a finger at Cohanna. "But I meant what I said about experiments, 'Hanna! And I want to see them myself."

"Understood," the doctor said. She and Brashieel walked from the office, pausing to exchange greetings with Horus, Hector, and Jefferson on their way out, and Colin leaned back in his chair with a sigh. Lord! Combining Narhani literal-mindedness with someone like Cohanna was just begging for trouble. He'd have to keep a closer eye on her.

He opened his eyes to see his father-in-law studying the carpet. A quirked eyebrow invited explanation, and Horus chuckled.

"Just checking to see how deep the blood was."

"You don't know how close to right you are," Colin growled. "Jesus! After all the times I've lectured her on the subject—!" He stood to embrace Horus, then extended a hand to Jefferson. "Good to see you again, Mister Jefferson."

"Thank you, Your Majesty. You might see more of me if I didn't have to come by mat-trans." His shudder was only half-feigned, and Colin laughed.

"I know. The first time I used a transit shaft I almost wet my pants, and the mat-trans is worse."

"But efficient," the stocky, brown-haired Lieutenant Governor replied with a small smile. "Most efficient—damn it!"

"True, too true."

"Tell, me, Colin, just what has 'Hanna been up to now?" Horus asked.

"She—" Colin paused, then shrugged. "It stays in this office, but I guess I can tell you. You know she's bioengineering dogs for Narhan?" His guests nodded. "Well, she's gone a bit further than I intended. She's been working with a couple of Tinker Bell's litters to give them near-human intelligence."

"What?" Horus blinked at him. "I thought you told her not to—"

"I did. Unfortunately, she told me she wanted to 'enhance their ability to communicate with the Narhani' and I told her to go ahead." He grimaced. "Silly me."

"Oh, Maker," Horus groaned. "Why can't she have half as much common sense as she does brainpower?"

"Because she wouldn't be Cohanna." Colin grinned, then sobered. "The worst of it is, the first litter's fully adult, and she's been educating them through their implants," he went on more somberly. "My emotions are having a little trouble catching up with my intellect, but if she's really given them human or near-human intelligence, the whole equation shifts. I mean, if she's gone and turned them into *people* on me, it's not like putting a starving stray to sleep. 'Lab animals' or not, I'm not sure I even have a legal right, much less a moral one, to have them destroyed, whatever the possible consequences."

"Excuse me, Your Majesty," Jefferson suggested diffidently, "but I think, perhaps, you'd better consider doing just that." Colin raised an eyebrow, and Jefferson shrugged. "We're having enough anti-Narhani problems without adding this to the fire. The last demonstration was pretty ugly, and it wasn't in one of our more reactionary areas, either. It was in London."

"London?" Colin looked sharply at Horus, instantly diverted from Cohanna's experiment. "How bad was it?"

"Not good," Horus admitted. "More of the 'The Only Good Achuultani Is a Dead Achuultani' kind of thing. There were some tussles, but they started when the marchers ran into a counter-demonstration, so they may actually have been a sign of sanity. I hope so, anyway."

"Oh, Lord!" Colin sighed. "You know, it was an awful lot easier fighting the Achuultani. Well, simpler, anyway."

"True. Still, I think time is on our side." Colin made a face and Horus chuckled. "I know. I'm getting as tired of saying that as you must be of hearing it, but it's true. And time is one thing we've got plenty of."

"Maybe. But while we're on the subject, who organized this thing?"

"We're not entirely certain," Jefferson replied. "Gus is looking into it, but the official organizers were a bunch called HHI—'Humans for a Human Imperium.' On the surface, they're a batch of professional rowdies backed up by a crop of discontented intellectuals. The 'high-brows' seem to be academics who resent finding everything they spent their lives learning has become outdated overnight. It would seem—" he smiled thinly "—that some of our fearless intellectual pioneers are a bit less pioneering than they thought."

"Hard to blame them, really," Horus pointed out. "It's not so much that they're rejecting the truth as that they feel betrayed. As you say, Lawrence, they spent their lives establishing themselves as intellectual leaders only to find themselves brushed aside."

"I know." Colin frowned down at his hands for a moment, then looked back up. "Still, that sounds like a pretty strange marriage. Professional rowdies and professors? Wonder how they made connections?"

"Stranger things have happened, Your Majesty, but Gus and I are asking the same question, and he thinks the answer is the Church of the Armageddon."

"Oh, shit," Colin said disgustedly.

"Inelegant, but apt," Horus said. "In fact, that's what bothers me most. The church started out as a simple fusion of fundamentalists who saw the

Achuultani as the true villains of the Armageddon, but this is a new departure, even for them. They've hated the Achuultani all along, but this is a shift to open racism—if I may use the term—of a particularly ugly stripe."

"Yeah. Anything more on their leadership, Mister Jefferson?"

"Not really, Your Majesty. They've never tried to hide their membership— why should they when they enjoy legal religious toleration?—but they're such an untidy agglomeration of splinter groups the hierarchical lines are pretty vague. We're still working on who actually calls the shots. Their spokesperson seems to be this Bishop Hilgemann, though I'm afraid I don't agree with Gus about her real authority. I think she's more a mouthpiece than a policy-maker, but we're both just guessing."

"You're going to discuss this with Ninhursag?"

"Of course, Your Majesty. I've brought Gus' report and I'm going up to Mother after this meeting. Admiral MacMahan and I will put our heads together, and perhaps Dahak can help us pull something out of the data."

"Good luck. 'Hursag's been trying to get a handle on them for over a year now. Oh, well." Colin shook his head and rose, holding out his hand to the Lieutenant Governor once more. "In that case, I won't keep you, Mister Jefferson. Horus and I have a birthday party to attend, and two pre-adolescent hellions who'll make us both miserable if we're late."

"Of course. Please give the Empress and your children my regards."

"I will—in between the presents, cake, punch, and general hullabaloo. Good luck with your report."

"Thank you, Your Majesty." Jefferson withdrew gracefully, and Colin and Horus headed for the imperial family's side of the Palace.

CHAPTER THREE

Colin MacIntyre tossed his jacket into a chair, and his green eyes laughed as a robot butler clucked audibly and scooped it up again. 'Tanni was as neat as the cat she so resembled, and she'd programmed the household robots to condemn his sloppiness for her when she was busy elsewhere.

He glanced into the library in passing and saw two heads of sable hair bent over a hologram. It looked like the primary converter of a gravitonic conveyor's main propulsion unit, and the twins were busily manipulating the display through their neural feeds to turn it into an exploded schematic while they argued some abstruse point.

Their father shook his head and continued on his way. It was hard to remember they were only twelve—when they were studying, anyway—but he knew that was only because he'd grown up without implant educations.

With neural interfacing, there was no inherent limit to the data any individual could be given, but raw data wasn't the same as *knowledge*, and that required a whole new set of educational parameters. For the first time in human history, the *only* thing that mattered was what the best educators had always insisted was the true goal of education: the exploration of knowledge. It was no longer necessary for students to spend endless hours acquiring data, but only a matter of making them aware of what they already "knew" and teaching them to use it—teaching them to *think*, really—and that was a good teacher's delight. Unfortunately, it also invalidated the traditional groundwork and performance criteria. Too many teachers were lost without the old rules—and even more of them, led by the West's unions, had waged a bitter scorched earth campaign against accepting the new. The human race in general seemed to think the Emperor possessed some sort of magic wand, and, in a way, they were right. Colin could do just about anything he decided needed doing . . . as long as he was prepared to use heavy enough artillery and convinced the battle was worth the cost.

It had taken him over three years to reach that conclusion where Earth's teaching establishment was concerned. For forty-three months, he'd listened to reason after reason why the changeover could not be made. Too few Earth schoolchildren had neural feeds. Too little hardware was available. Too many new concepts in too short a time would confuse children already in the system and damage them beyond repair. The list had gone on and on and on, until, finally, he'd had enough and announced the dissolution of all teachers' unions and the firing of every teacher employed by any publicly funded educational department or system anywhere on the planet.

The people he'd fired had tried to fight the decree in the courts only to discover that the Great Charter gave Colin the authority to do just what he'd done, and when they came up against the cold steel his homely, usually cheerful face normally hid so well, their grave concern for the well-being of their students had undergone a radical change. Suddenly the only thing they wanted to do was make the transition as quick and painless as possible, and if the Emperor would only let them have their jobs back, they would get down to it immediately.

They had. Still not without a certain amount of foot dragging when they thought no one was looking, but they had gotten down to it. Of course, every one of their earlier objections had had its own grain of truth, which made the introduction of an entirely new educational system difficult and often frustratingly slow, but once they accepted that Colin was serious, they'd really buckled down and pushed. And, along the way, the ones who had the makings of true teachers rather than petty bureaucrats had rediscovered the joy of teaching. The ones who didn't make that rediscovery tended to disappear from the profession in ever greater numbers, but their earlier opposition and lingering guerrilla warfare had delayed the full-scale implementation of modern education on Earth by at least ten years.

Which meant, of course, that children on Birhat had a measurable advantage over those educated on Earth. Dahak spent most of his time in Birhat orbit, and while Earth's teaching establishment grappled with Imperial education theories, Dahak had already mastered them. More, he, unlike they, had no institutional or personal objections to adopting them, and it required only a tithe of his vast capacity to institute what amounted to a planet-wide system of small-group studies. His students responded with an insatiable hunger to learn, and, to Colin's knowledge the twins had *never* played hooky, which was almost scary.

He walked into the study, and Jiltanith smiled at him from her desk. He took the time to kiss her properly, then flopped into his chair and sighed contentedly as it adjusted to his body's contours.

"Thou soundest well content to leave thine office behind thee, my love," Jiltanith observed, putting her own computer on hold, and he nodded.

"*You* oughta try it sometime," he said pointedly, and she laughed.

"Nay, my Colin. 'Twould drive me to bedlam's brink did I have naught to which to set my hands, and this—" she gestured at the hardcopy and data chips strewn over her desk "—is a study most interesting."

"Yeah?"

"Aye. Amanda hath begun to think how best we may use Tao-ling's Mark Twenty hyper gun in small unit tactics."

Colin shook his head wryly. Jiltanith didn't love combat—she knew too much of what it cost—yet there were dark and dangerous places in her soul. He suspected that no one, not even he, would ever be admitted into some of them, but a lifetime of bitter guerrilla warfare had left its mark, and, unlike him, she saw war not as a last response but as a practical option that worked. She wasn't merciless, but she *was* far more capable of slaughter— and less inclined to give quarter—than he. That was why he'd made her Minister of War. As Warlord, Colin was the Imperium's commander-in-chief, but it was 'Tanni who ran their growing military establishment on a day-to-day basis.

"Well, if you can tear yourself away, we're about to have visitors."

"Ah?" She cocked her head at him.

"Isis, Cohanna, and Cohanna's . . . project," he said less cheerfully. "I'm afraid Jefferson may be right about the logic of ordering them destroyed, but I can't say I'm looking forward to making that decision."

"Nor shouldst thou." His wife stood and walked around her desk. "Logic, as thou hast said time without number, my love, may be naught but a way to err wi' confidence."

"You got that right, babe," he sighed, snaking an arm around her as she passed. She paused to ruffle his sandy hair, then sank into her own chair. "The thing is, I think I'm trying to psych myself up to decide against them 'cause I think I ought to, and that makes me feel sort of ashamed."

"The day thy self-doubt ceaseth will be the day thou becomest less than thy best self, Colin," she said gently.

He smiled, changed the subject to something more comfortable, and let 'Tanni's voice flow over him. He treasured the moments when they could forget the Imperium, forget their duties, forget the need to finish the Achuultani threat once and for all, and 'Tanni's soft, archaic speech wove a spell that helped him hold those things at bay, be it ever so briefly. She'd learned her English during the Wars of the Roses and flatly refused to abandon it. Besides, as she'd pointed out upon occasion, she spoke *true* English, not the debased dialect *he'd* learned.

"Excuse me, Colin," a mellow voice injected into a break in their conversation, "but Cohanna and Isis have arrived."

"Thanks." Colin sighed and set the moment aside, feeling the universe intruding upon them once more but revitalized by the temporary escape. "Tell them we're in the study."

"I have already done so. They will arrive momentarily."

"Fine. And hang around yourself. We may need your input."

"Of course," Dahak agreed. Colin knew a tiny bit of the computer's attention always followed him about, ready to respond to questions or advise him of new developments, but Dahak had designed a special subroutine to monitor his Emperor's whereabouts and needs without bringing them to the front of his attention unless certain critical parameters were crossed. It was his way of assuring Colin's privacy, a concept he didn't entirely understand but whose importance to his human friends he recognized.

The study door opened, and Cohanna marched in like a grenadier with a delicate, white-haired woman whose aged eyes were remarkably like Jiltanith's. Isis Tudor was over ninety, and there'd been no bio-enhancement for the Terra-born in her girlhood. By the time it became available, her body was too old and fragile for full enhancement, and age pared away more of her strength with every year. Yet there was nothing wrong with her mind, and the enhancement she could tolerate gave her an energy at odds with her growing frailty.

Jiltanith stood to embrace her while Cohanna met Colin's gaze with an edge of challenge and four black-and-tan dogs followed her through the door. They moved in formation, with a most undoglike precision, and arranged themselves in a neat line as they sat on the rug.

They looked, Colin thought, like fireplugs on legs. Tinker Bell's pups had been sired by a pedigreed rottweiler, and the lab side of their heritage was scarcely noticeable. They had a solid, squared-off appearance, with powerful muzzles, and the biggest must have massed almost sixty kilos.

He studied them for signs of the changes Cohanna had wrought. There weren't many. The massive rottweiler head was perhaps a little broader, with a more pronounced cranial bulge, though he doubted he would have noticed without looking for it, yet there was something. And then he realized. The eyes fixed upon him with unwavering attention betrayed the intelligence behind them.

"All right, Colin." Cohanna's voice wrenched his attention from the dogs. "You wanted to see them. Here they are."

He looked up quickly, but her expression gave him pause. He was accustomed to her testiness, but her dark eyes were fierce. This, he realized with a sinking sensation, was no bloodless project for her.

"Sit down, 'Hanna," he said quietly, and knelt before the dogs as she sank into an empty chair. Heads cocked to look at him, and he ran a hand down the biggest's broad back. His sensory boosters were on high, and he felt the usual bunchy muscle of the breed . . . and something more. He looked at Cohanna, and she shrugged.

" 'Hanna," he sighed, "I have to tell you I'm less worried, in a way, about the genetic stuff than the rest of it. Do you have any idea how the anti-techies will react to fully enhanced *dogs*? The idea of a dog with that kind of strength and toughness is going to terrify them."

"Then they're idiots!" Cohanna glared at him, then sighed herself, and something very like guilt diluted her fierceness. A knot of tension inside him relaxed slightly as he saw it and realized how much of her anger at him came from an awareness that perhaps she *had* gone too far.

"All right," she said finally, her voice low. "Maybe *I* was an idiot. I still maintain—" her eyes flashed "—that they're superstitious savages, but, damn it, Colin, I can't understand how their minds work! These dogs represent no more danger to them than another enhanced human would!"

"I know you think they don't, 'Hanna, but—"

"I don't 'think' anything, Colin—I *know!* And so will you if you take the time to get to know them."

"That," he admitted, "is what I'm more than half afraid of." He turned back to the dogs, and the big male he'd touched returned his gaze levelly. "This is Galahad?" he asked Cohanna . . . but someone else answered.

"Yes," a mechanically produced voice said, and Colin's eyes widened as he saw the small vocoder on the dog's collar. A shiver ran down his spine as a "dumb animal" spoke, but it vanished in an instant. Wonder replaced it, and a strange delight he tried hard to suppress, and he drew a deep breath.

"Well, Galahad," he said quietly, "has Cohanna explained why I wanted to meet you?"

"Yes," the dog replied. His ears moved, and Colin realized it was a deliberate gesture—an expression intended to convey meaning. "But we do not understand why others fear us." The words came slowly but without hesitation.

"Excuse me a moment, Galahad," Colin said, feeling only a slight sense of unreality at extending human-style courtesies to a dog. He looked back up at Cohanna. "How much of that was computer enhanced?"

"There's some enhancement," the doctor admitted. "They tend to forget definite articles, and their sentence structure's very simple. They never use the past tense, either, but the software is limited to 'filling in the holes.' It doesn't provide any expansion of their meaning."

"Galahad," Colin turned back to the dog, "you don't frighten *me*—or anyone else in this room—but some people will find you . . . unnatural, and humans are afraid of things they don't understand."

"Why?" Galahad asked.

"I wish I could explain why," Colin sighed.

"Danger is cause for fear," the dog said, "but we are no danger. We wish only to be. We are not evil."

Colin blinked. A word like "evil" implied an ability to manipulate concepts light-years in advance of anything Tinker Bell had ever managed.

"Galahad," he asked carefully, "what do you think 'evil' is?"

"Evil," the mechanically-generated voice replied, "is danger. Evil is hurting when not hurt or when hurting is not needed."

Colin winced, for Galahad had cut to the heart of his own definition of evil. And whether he'd meant to or not, he'd thrown Colin's decision about his own fate into stark focus.

Colin MacIntyre stared into his own soul and disliked what he saw. How could he explain that much of humanity was incapable of understanding what Galahad saw so clearly, or why he felt so ashamed that it was so?

"Colin-human," Colin looked up as Galahad spoke again, "I try to understand, for understanding is good, but I cannot. We know—" a toss of a massive canine head indicated his litter-mates "—you may end us. We do not want to end. You do not want to end us. If we must end we cannot stop you. But it is not right, Colin-human." Canine eyes held his with heart-tearing dignity. "It is not right," Galahad repeated, "and this is something you know."

Colin bit his lip. He turned to Jiltanith, and when her eyes—the black, subtly alien eyes of a full Imperial—met his, they, too, shone with tears.

"He hath the right of it, my Colin," she said quietly. "Should we decree their deaths, 'twill be fear that moveth us—fear that maketh us do what we know full well is wrong. Nay, more than wrong." She knelt beside him, touching a slender hand to Galahad's heavy head. "E'en as Galahad hath said, 'twould evil be to hurt where hurting need not be."

"I know." His voice was equally quiet, and then he shook himself. "Isis?"

" 'Tanni's right. If I'd known what 'Hanna was planning I'd've pitched a fit right alongside you, but look at them. They're magnificent. *People*, Colin—good people who happen to have four feet and no hands."

"Yes." Colin looked down at his hands—the hands Galahad didn't have—and felt the decision make itself. He rose and tugged on his nose, thinking hard. "How many are we talking about here, 'Hanna?"

"Ten. These four and two smaller litters."

"Okay." He turned back to Galahad and his siblings. "Listen to me, all of you. I know you don't understand why humans should be afraid of you, but do all of you accept that they might be?" Four canine heads nodded in unmistakable assent, and he chuckled despite his solemnity. "Good, because the only way we could keep you really safe would be for us to keep the humans you might scare from finding out you exist, and we can't do that forever.

"So here's what I'm going to do. From now on, you four will live with us—with 'Tanni and me—and except for when you're alone with us, you have to pretend to be just like other dogs. Can you do that?"

"Yes, Colin-human." It wasn't Galahad, but a smaller female who spoke, and her dignified mien vanished abruptly. She leapt up on him, wagging her tail and slurping his face enthusiastically, then tore around the room barking madly. She skidded to a halt, tongue lolling, dumped herself untidily on the carpet, rolled on her back, and waved all four feet in the air. Then she rolled back over and sat upright once more, eyes laughing at him.

"All right!" He wiped his face and grinned, then sobered again. "I don't know if you'll understand this, but we're going to take you lots of places and show you to lots of people, and I want you to behave like ordinary dogs. The news people'll get a lot of footage of you, and that's good. When the truth about you gets out, I want the rest of humanity to be used to seeing you. I want them used to the idea that you're not a threat. That you've been around a long time and never hurt anyone. Do you understand?"

"If we prove we are not evil, people will not fear us?" Galahad asked.

"Exactly. It's not fair—you shouldn't have to *prove* it any more than they should—but that's how it has to be. Can you do that?"

"We can, Colin-human," Galahad said softly.

CHAPTER FOUR

Fleet Admiral the Lady Adrienne Robbins, Baroness Nergal and Companion of the Golden Nova, dodged with a haste which ill accorded with her exalted rank. She flattened herself against the wall of the Palace corridor and shrank into the smallest possible space as four human children, a half-grown Narhani, and a pack of four leaping rottweilers thundered down upon her.

Fortunately for the admiral, the long-haired girl leading the charge saw her, and they hit the brakes as only children can, skittering to a halt in a tangled confusion of arms, legs, feet, hooves, and paws.

"Hi, Aunt Adrienne!" Princess Isis Harriet MacIntyre shouted, and Admiral Robbins stepped away from the wall. Sean and Harriet seemed unaffected by her glare, but Sandy MacMahan looked a bit abashed and Tamman studied his toes. Brashan, Brashieel's clone-child, looked dreadfully embarrassed, for if he was younger than any of the others, he was already a near-adult, given the speed with which his species matured. For their part, the various dogs flopped down and panted at her, but their canine insouciance didn't fool Adrienne, for she was one of the handful of people who knew the truth about them.

"I wonder," the admiral said darkly, "how Their Imperial Majesties would react to the way you young hellions came tearing down on me?"

"Oh, Dad wouldn't mind." Sean grinned.

"I was thinking more of *Her* Imperial Majesty," Adrienne said, and Sean suddenly looked more thoughtful. "That's what I thought, too. Can you give me one good reason I shouldn't tell her?"

"Because you wouldn't want us on your conscience?" he suggested, and she swallowed a laugh and frowned.

"My conscience is pretty resilient, Your Highness."

"Uh, *do* you have to mention this to Mom and Dad?" Harriet asked, and Adrienne considered her for a long, dreadful moment. Tamman wiggled, clearly picturing *his* parents' reaction, and Adrienne relented.

"Not this time, I suppose. *But—*" she held up an admonishing finger as relieved smiles blossomed "—I won't be so gooey-centered next time!"

An earnest chorus of thanks answered her, and she made shooing motions with her hands.

"Then *get*, you horrible brats!" she commanded, and the cavalcade leapt back into motion (albeit less impetuously than before) down the hall.

Adrienne smiled after them, then resumed her interrupted journey. Sean, she reflected, was a dark-haired version of his father, with the same beaky nose and jug ears no one would ever call handsome, but he was already bidding fair to be quite a bit taller than either of his parents.

Harriet, on the other hand, was a junior edition of her mother—a pretty child who was going to be an astoundingly beautiful woman. Both twins had Jiltanith's eyes, but Harriet's were softer. No less lively, but gentler. Actually, Adrienne reflected, *she* took more after Colin personality-wise, while Sean mingled his mother's absolute fearlessness and his father's humor into an amalgam all his own. One of these days, that boy was going to be a real heart-breaker.

She emerged from her reverie as she reached her destination, and the door slid open to admit her to Colin's office. The Emperor looked up from his paperwork and waved at a chair.

"Have a seat, Adrienne. I'll be with you a minute."

Admiral Robbins sat, smoothing her uniform sleeve fastidiously, and waited patiently for Colin to finish the current installment of his unending paper chase. He dumped the data—and his decision—back into the computer, then leaned back and crossed his legs.

"I see you evaded the thundering herd," he observed, and she glanced at him in surprise. "I've got surveillance systems in the public corridors, remember? 'Young hellions' is exactly right!"

"Oh, they're not that bad. Lively, mind you, but I don't mind."

"Nobody does. Well, nobody but 'Tanni, maybe. The little devils are cute as a crop of buttons, and they know it." He shook his head and sighed. "Oh, well. On to business. Thanks for coming so promptly, by the way."

"That's the way empires are run, Your Majesty. 'I say unto one go, and he goeth' and all that. But I have to admit you piqued my curiosity. What's so sensitive we couldn't discuss it over the com?"

"I'm probably just being paranoid," Colin said more seriously, "but those anti-Narhani demonstrations are getting worse, not better, so I didn't want to take any chance on this leaking. What I've got in mind is either going to make them a lot better . . . or a hell of a lot worse."

"I hate it when you get enigmatic, Colin," Adrienne sighed.

"Sorry. It's just that I beat my head against this for months before I made up my mind, and I'm pissed at myself for taking so long to do what I should've done in the first place. I'm opening the Academy to Narhani."

"Oh, Lord!" Adrienne clutched at her gun-metal hair and moaned. "Why is it always me? Do you have any idea how the newsies are going to react? They'll be all over my campus, stomping the shrubbery flat!"

"Oh, come on!" Colin chuckled. "The first-generation clones won't be ready until Sean and Harry are—you've got time for the spade work."

"'Spade work,' he says! Bulldozer work, you mean! Fortunately," she smiled rather smugly, "*I* figured out this was coming over a year ago. We've been working on syllabus modification ever since."

"You have?"

"Of course we have. Lordy, Colin, don't you think I've been around long enough to realize how you think? It takes you a while, sometimes, but you usually get to the right decision sooner or later."

"You," Colin observed dryly, "don't have the most respectful demeanor of any naval officer in the galaxy."

"I do on duty. Want to see my 'official commandant's' face?" Her smile vanished instantly into a stern expression and cold, measuring eyes that impaled him for a ten-count before she relaxed with a grin. "I keep it in a box on my dresser till I need it."

"God, no wonder the middies are all scared spitless of you!"

"Better me than the bad guys."

"True. Actually, though, I want a bit more from you than adjustments to your curriculum. I want you to endorse the suggestion."

"Well, of course," she said with some surprise. "Why shouldn't I?"

"I mean I want you to go public and talk to the media," he explained, and she grimaced. One of the things she liked best about the Imperial Charter was that while it guaranteed freedom of speech it didn't regard reporters as tin gods. Imperial privacy laws and—even better—libel laws had come as a shock to Terran journalists, and if there was one life form Adrienne Robbins truly despised, it was newsies. They'd made her life hell after the Siege of Earth and the Zeta Trianguli campaign.

"Oh, shit, Colin. Do I *have* to?"

" 'Fraid so," he said with a twinge of guilt, for a large chunk of the Palace staff was devoted to keeping the press as far away from *him* as possible, helped by the fact that Jiltanith was not only far more photogenic but surprisingly comfortable with the public. Colin knew his subjects respected him, but they *loved* 'Tanni.

Which, he mused, indicated the public had a higher IQ than he'd once believed possible.

"Look," he went on persuasively, "you know my policy on Narhani civil rights. They're citizens, just like anyone else. Giving them their own planet may have defused the potential for direct unpleasantness, but we've got to integrate them into the government and military or that very isolation's only going to make things worse. I've got quite a few in civil service positions here on Birhat already, but I need to get them into the Fleet, too.

"I don't expect trouble from the military, but the civilians may be something else. I need all the help I can get selling the idea, and after 'Tanni, you're the best salesman I've got."

Adrienne made a face, but she knew it was true. She was the only living officer to have commanded a capital ship throughout both the Siege and the Zeta Trianguli campaign. More than that, she'd led the task force that died in Earth's last, hopeless counterattack, and hers had been the only ship to survive it. She was Battle Fleet's most decorated officer, belonged to more Terran orders of chivalry than she could count, and was the only person in history to have received the highest award for valor of *every* Terran nation, as well as the Golden Nova. It embarrassed her horribly, but it was true.

All of which meant Colin was right. If he was trotting out the big guns, she was going to have to come to battery.

"All right," she sighed finally, "I'll do it."

Francine Hilgemann took her time locking the car doors while she scanned her surroundings. She'd seen no sign of surveillance on the drive here, but paranoia was a survival tool which had served her well over the years.

She ambled across the parking lot to the pedestrian belt serving the enormous, brightly-lit Memorial complex. She was uneasy at the thought of meeting in the very heart of Shepard Center, but she supposed it made sense. Who in his right mind would expect a pair of traitors to make contact here?

She stepped off the belt into the people flowing past the fifty-meter obsidian needle of the Cenotaph and the endless rows of names etched into its unadorned battle steel plinth. Those names listed every individual known to have fallen in the millennia-long battle against Anu, and even Hilgemann wasn't quite immune to the hush about her. But time was short, and she worked her way briskly through the fringes of the throng.

Another, even quieter crowd surrounded the broken eighty-thousand-ton hull that shared the Memorial with the Cenotaph. The sublight battleship *Nergal* remained where Fleet Captain Robbins had landed her, resting on her belly and ruined landing legs, preserved exactly as her final battle had left her. She'd been decontaminated; that was all, and crippled missile launchers and energy weapons hung like broken teeth from her twisted flanks. How she'd survived was more than Hilgemann could guess, and she couldn't even begin to imagine what it had taken to bring that wreck home and land her under her own power.

She turned away after a moment, walking to the service exit she'd been told to use. It was unlocked as promised, and she slipped through it into the equipment storage room and closed the door behind her.

"Well," she said a bit tartly, looking around at the deserted machinery, "I must say this has all the proper conspiratorial ambience!"

"Perhaps." The man who'd summoned her stepped out of the shadows with a thin smile. "On the other hand, we can't risk meeting very often . . . and we certainly can't do it in public, now can we?"

"I feel like an idiot." She touched the brunette wig which hid her golden hair, then looked down at her plain, cheap clothing and shuddered.

"Better a live idiot than a dead traitor," he replied, and she snorted.

"All right. I'm here. What's so important?"

"Several things. First, I've confirmed that they know they didn't get all of Anu's people." Francine looked up sharply and received another thin smile. "Obviously they don't know *who* they didn't get, or we wouldn't be having this melodramatic conversation."

"No, I suppose we wouldn't. What else?"

"This." A data chip was handed over. "That little item is too important to trust to our usual pipeline."

"Oh?" She looked down at it curiously.

"Indeed. It's a copy of the plans for Marshal Tsien's newest toy: a gravitonic warhead powerful enough to take out an entire planet."

Francine's hand clenched on the chip, and her eyes widened.

"His Majesty," the man said with a soft chuckle, "has decided against building it, but I'm more progressive."

"Why? To threaten to blow *ourselves* up if they ID us?"

"I doubt that bluff would fly, but there are other ways it might be useful. For now, I just want the hardware handy if we need it."

"All right." She shrugged. "I assume you can get us any military components we need?"

"Perhaps. If so, we'll handle that through the regular channels. In the meantime, how are your action groups coming along?"

"Quite nicely, actually." Hilgemann's smile was unpleasant. "In fact, their training's developing their paranoia even further, and keeping them on a leash isn't the easiest thing in the world. It may be necessary to give them the odd mission to work off some of their . . . enthusiasm. Is that a problem?"

"No, I can pick a few targets. You're certain they don't know about you?"

"They're too well compartmented for that," she said confidently.

"Good. I'll select a few operations that'll cost them some casualties, then. Nothing like providing a few martyrs for the cause."

"Don't get too fancy," she cautioned. "If they lose too many they're likely to get a bit hard to control."

"Understood. Then I suppose that's about it . . . except that you'll want to get your next pastoral letter ready."

"Oh?"

"Yes. His Majesty's decided to bite the bullet and begin enlisting Narhani in the military." Hilgemann nodded, eyes suddenly thoughtful, and he smiled. "Exactly. We'll want something restrained for open distribution— an injunction to pray that His Majesty hasn't made a mistake, perhaps— but a little furnace-fanning among the more hardcore is in order, I believe."

"No problem," the bishop said with an equally thin smile.

"I'll be going, then. Wait fifteen minutes before you leave."

"Of course." She was a bit nettled, though she didn't let it show. Did he think she'd lasted this long without learning her trade?

The door closed behind him, and she sat on a floor cleaner, lips pursed, considering how best to fill her pen with properly diffident vitriol, while the hand in her pocket squeezed the data chip that could kill a world.

CHAPTER FIVE

Sean MacIntyre landed neatly in the clearing and killed the power.

"Nice one, Sean," Tamman said from the copilot's seat. "Almost as nice as I could've done."

"Yeah? Which one of us took the top off that sequoia last month?"

"Wasn't the pilot's fault," Tamman replied loftily. "*You* were navigating, if I recall."

"He couldn't have been; you got home," a female voice said.

Tamman smirked, and Sean raised his eyes to the heavens in a plea for strength. Then he punched Tamman's shoulder, and the female voice groaned behind them as they grappled. "They're at it *again*, Sandy!"

"Too much testosterone, Harry." The younger voice dripped sympathy. "Their poor, primitive male brains are awash in the stuff."

Tamman and Sean paused in silent agreement, then turned towards the passenger compartment with vengeful intent, but their purposeful progress came to an abrupt end as Sean ran full tilt into a large, solid object and *oofed*.

"Damn it, Brashan!" he complained, rubbing the prominent nose he'd inherited from his father to check for damage.

"I'm simply opening the hatch, Sean," a mechanically produced voice replied. "It's not *my* fault you don't watch where you're going."

"Some navigator!" Harriet sniffed.

"Fortunately for a certain loudmouthed snot," Tamman observed, "she's a princess, so I can't paddle her fanny the way she deserves."

"Don't you just *wish* you could get your hands on my fanny, you lech!"

"Don't worry, Tam," Sean said darkly. "I'll be happy to deputize. As soon—" he added "—as a certain oversized polo pony gets out of my way!"

"Oooh, protect me, Brashan!" Harriet cried, and the Narhani laughed and stood aside, blocking off the cockpit as the hatch opened. The girls scampered out, and Galahad's litter-mate Gawain followed, raised muzzle already scenting the rich jungle air.

"Traitor!" Sean kicked his friend—which hurt his toe far more than his

460

target. Brashan was only ten Terran years old, six years younger than Sean, but he was already sufficiently mature for full enhancement. The augmentation biotechnics provided was proportional to a being's natural strength and toughness, and the heavy-grav Narhani were very, very tough by human standards.

"Nonsense. Simply a more mature individual striving to protect you from your own impetuosity," Brashan returned, and trotted down the ramp.

"Yeah, sure," Sean snorted as he and Tamman followed.

It was noon, local time, and Bia blazed directly overhead. Birhat lay almost a light-minute further from its G0 primary than Earth lay from Sol, but they were almost exactly on the equator, and the air was hot and still. The high, shrill piping of Birhat's equivalent of birds drifted down, and a bat-winged pseudodactyl drifted high overhead.

Sean and Tamman paused to check their grav rifles. Without full enhancement, neither could handle a full-sized energy gun, but their present weapons were little heavier than Terran sporting rifles. The twenty-round magazines held three-millimeter darts of superdense chemical explosive, and the rifles fired them with a velocity of over five thousand meters per second. Which meant they had enough punch to take out a pre-Imperial tank . . . or the larger denizens of Birhat's ecosystem.

"Looks good here." Sean's crispness was far removed from his earlier playfulness, and Tamman nodded to confirm his own weapon's readiness. Then they turned towards the others, and Sean made a face. Sandy was already perched in her favorite spot astride Brashan's powerful back.

He supposed it made sense, even if she did look insufferably smug, for something had gone astray in Sandra MacMahan's genes. Neither of her parents were midgets, yet she barely topped a hundred and forty centimeters. If she hadn't had Hector MacMahan's eyes and Ninhursag's cheekbones, Sean would have suspected she was a changeling from his mother's bedtime stories. Of course, she wasn't quite fifteen, but Harriet had shot up to almost one-eighty by the time she was that age.

Not, he thought darkly, that Sandy let her small size slow her down. She was so far out ahead scholastically it wasn't funny, but the thing he really hated was that whenever they got into an argument she was invariably right. Like that molycirc problem. He'd been positive the failure was in the basic matrix, but, *nooooo*. She'd insisted a power surge had bridged the alpha block, and damned if she hadn't been right . . . again. It was maddening.

At least he had a good sixty centimeters on her, he thought moodily.

He and Tamman caught up with the others, and he tapped the grav pistol at Harriet's side pointedly. She made a face but drew it and checked its readiness. Sandy—of course—had already checked hers.

"Which way, Sean?" Brashan asked, and Sean paused to orient his built-in inertial guidance system to the observations he'd made on the way in.

"About five klicks at oh-two-twenty," he announced.

"Couldn't you set down any closer?" Harriet demanded, and he shrugged.

"Sure. But we're talking about tyranotops. You really want one of them stepping on the flyer? It might get sort of broken around the edges."

"True," she admitted, and drew her bush knife as they approached the towering creepers and ferns fringing the clearing.

As always, she and Sean took point, followed by Tamman, while a wide-ranging Gawain burrowed through the undergrowth and Brashan covered the rear. Sean was well aware Brashan was the real reason his mother and father raised no demur to the twins' excursions. Even a tyranotops—that fearsome creature which resembled nothing so much as a mating of a Terran triceratops and tyrannosaurus—would find a fully enhanced Narhani a handful, and Brashan carried a heavy energy gun, as well. As baby-sitters went, Narhani took some beating, which suited Sean and his friends just fine. Birhat was ever so much more interesting than Earth, and Brashan meant they could roam it at will.

Odd birds and beasts fluttered and rumbled in the underbrush, starting up in occasional panic as Gawain flushed them, and many of them were species no one else had yet seen. That was one of the things they loved about Birhat. The old Imperial capital had reverted to its second childhood after the bio-weapon hit, for the toxin hadn't been able to reach the sealed, protected ecosystems of the Imperial family's extraplanetary zoos. By the time failing environmental equipment finally released the inhabitants of over a dozen different oxy-nitrogen planets, the weapon itself had died, and forty-odd thousand years of subsequent natural selection had produced a biosystem that was a naturalist's opium dream.

For all intents and purposes, Birhat was a virgin planet, and it was all theirs. Well, theirs and three-quarters of a billion other people's, but that left lots of empty space, since most of the Bia System's steadily growing population was concentrated in and around the new capital or out in the system's enormous spaceborne industrial complexes, working like demons to resurrect the Empire. And, of course, at the moment they were in the middle of the Sean Andrew MacIntyre Continental Nature Preserve the Crown had established to honor Sean's uncle, who'd died fighting Anu's mutineers.

Not that they'd have such freedom much longer. Sean had been vested with the first official sign of his status as Heir last year when he was presented to Mother, for under the Great Charter Mother passed on the acceptability of the Heir's intellect and psych-profile. He'd been accepted, and the subliminal challenge-response patterns and implant codes which identified him as Heir had been implanted, but it had been the scariest moment of his life—and a clear sign that adulthood was coming closer.

There were signs for his friends, as well. All of them were headed for Battle Fleet—they'd known that for years—but they were getting close to meeting the Academy's entry requirements. Another year, possibly two, Sean estimated, until their free time evaporated.

But for now the day was young, the pride of tyranotops they'd come to see awaited them, and he intended to enjoy himself to the full.

A cool breeze flowed over the balcony, for it was summer in Birhat's northern hemisphere, and Colin had switched off the force fields which walled the balcony against the elements at need.

The city of Phoenix lay before him in the night, the serpentine curve of the River Nikkan sparkling far below, and Tsien Tao-ling's engineering crews had done well by Birhat's settlers. Phoenix was the product of a gravitonic civilization, and its towers soared even above the mighty near-sequoias about them, but the Palace was the tallest spire of all. Perhaps some thought that was to reflect its inhabitants' rank, but the real reason was practicality. True, the imperial family had luxurious personal quarters, but that was almost a side effect of the Imperium's administrative needs. Even a structure as vast as the Palace was badly overcrowded by functionaries and bureaucrats, though the new Annex going up next door would help . . . for a while.

He sighed and slid an arm about Jiltanith, and silken hair brushed his cheek as she leaned against him. He kissed the top of her head, then swept his telescopic eyes over the city, enjoying the jeweled interplay of lights and the magical wash of shifting moonlight. The complex pattern never ceased to delight him, for he'd grown up with but a single moon.

He raised his gaze to the heavens, and the stars were hard to see. The gleaming disk of Mother's fortress hull hung almost directly overhead, and over fifty huge planetoids dotted the night sky beyond her. They were much farther out (the comings and goings of that many "moons" would play merry hell with Birhat's tides), but the sunlight reflected from their hulls gilded the Fifth Imperium's capital in bronze and ebony. And on the farside of the planet from Mother—indeed, just about directly over the spot where his children were even now observing their tyranotops—hung another vast sphere named *Dahak*.

"God, 'Tanni," he murmured, "*look* at that."

"Aye." She squeezed him gently. "'Tis like unto God's own gem box."

"It really is," he agreed softly. "Sort of makes it all seem worthwhile, doesn't it?" She nodded against his shoulder, and he sighed, looking back up at the distant planetoids once more. "Of course, looking at all this also tends to make me think about how much we still have to do."

"Mayhap, my love. Yet have we done all Fate hath called us to thus far. I misdoubt not we'll do all else when time demands."

"Yeah." He inhaled deeply, savoring the night, and pressed his cheek against her hair in deep, happy contentment.

"How're the kids coming along, Dahak?"

"I regret to report that Sean has just tripped Harriet into a particularly muddy stream. Otherwise, things are proceeding to plan. Analysis of Harriet's personality suggests she will attain revenge shortly."

"Damn right," Colin agreed, and Jiltanith's laugh gurgled in his ear.

"Thou'rt worse by far than thy offspring, Colin MacIntyre!"

"Nah, just older and deeper in sin." He chuckled. "God, I'm glad they're growing up like normal kids!"

" 'Normal,' thou sayest? My love, the Furies themselves scarce could wreak the havoc those twain do leave strewn in their wake!"

"I know. Ain't it great?" Bio-enhanced fingers pinched his ribs like a steel vise and he yelped. "Just think what royal pains in the ass they *could* have turned into," he said, rubbing his side.

"Aye, there's that," Jiltanith said more seriously, "and 'twas thou didst save them from it."

"You had a hand in it, too."

"Oh, aye, there's truth in that, but thou'rt the one who taught them warmth, my Colin. I love them well, and that they know wi'out doubt, but life hath not fitted me o'er well to nourish younglings."

"You did good, anyway," Colin said. "Actually, it looks like we make a pretty good team."

"Indeed, 'Tanni," Dahak added. "Left to his own devices, Colin would undoubtedly have—I believe the proper term is 'spoiled them rotten.'"

"Oh, I would, would I? Well, mister energy-state smarty pants, who was smart enough to suggest finding them something to do besides sitting around sucking on silver spoons?"

"It was you," Dahak replied with a soft, electronic chuckle. "A fact which, I must confess, continues to surprise me." Colin muttered something rude, and Jiltanith giggled. "Actually," the computer went on, "it was an excellent idea, Colin. One which should have occurred to me."

"Oh, it probably would've come to you eventually. But unless something goes wrong in a big way, 'Tanni and I are gonna be around for centuries, and a professional crown prince could get mighty bored in that much time. Besides, we're young enough it's unlikely Sean will outlive us by more than a century or so. It'd be a dead waste of his life to wait that long for such a brief reign."

"Indeed. The classic example from your own recent history would, of course, be that of Queen Victoria and Edward VII. The tragic waste of Edward's potential did great disservice to his country, and—"

"Maybe," Colin interrupted, "but I wasn't thinking about the Imperium. I want our kids to *do* something, and not for the Imperium. I want them to be able to look back and know they were winners, not place-holders. And I want them to know all the nice perks—the rank and deference, the flattery they're gonna hear—don't mean a thing unless they *earn* them."

He fell silent for a moment, feeling Jiltanith's silent agreement as she hugged him tight, and stared up to where Mother hung overhead like the very embodiment of an emperor's power and treacherous grandeur.

"Dahak," he said finally, "Herdan's dynasty ruled for five thousand years. Five *thousand* years. That's not a long time for someone like you, but it's literally beyond the comprehension of a human. Yet long as it was, impossible as it is for me to imagine, our kids—and their kids, and their kids' kids—may rule even longer. I can't begin to guess what they'll face, the sorts of decisions they'll have to make, but there's one thing 'Tanni and I can give them, starting right here and now with Sean and Harry. Not for the Imperium, though the Imperium'll profit from it, but for them."

"What, Colin?" Dahak asked quietly.

"The knowledge that power is a responsibility. The belief that who they are and what they do is as important as what they're born to. A tradition of—well, of *service*. Becoming Emperor should be the capstone of a life, not a career in itself, and 'Tanni and I want our kids—our family—to remember that. That's why we're sending them to the Academy, and why we won't have anyone kowtowing to them, much as some of the jerks who work for us would love to."

Dahak was silent for a moment—a very long moment, for him—before he spoke again. "I believe I understand you, Colin, and you are correct. Sean and Harriet do not yet realize what you and 'Tanni have done for them, but someday they will understand. And you are wise to make service a tradition rather than a matter of law, for my observation of human polities suggests that laws are more easily subverted than tradition."

"Yeah, that's what we thought, too," Colin said.

"Nay, my love," Jiltanith said softly. " 'Twas what *thou* didst think, and glad am I thou didst, for thou hadst the right of it."

" 'Tanni is correct, Colin," Dahak said gently, "and I am glad you have explained it to me. I do not yet have your insight into individuals, but I will have many years to gain it, and I will not forget what you have said. You and 'Tanni are my friends, and you have made me a member of your family. Sean and Harriet are your children, and I would love them for that reason even if they were not themselves my friends. But they *are* my friends— and my family—and I see I have a function I had not previously recognized."

"What function?"

"Mother may be the guardian of the Imperium, Colin, but *I* am the guardian of our family. I shall not forget that."

"Thank you, Dahak," Colin said very, very softly, and Jiltanith nodded against his shoulder once more.

CHAPTER SIX

It wasn't a large room, but it seemed huge to Sean MacIntyre as he stood waiting at the foot of the narrow bed, and his anxious eyes swept it again and again, scanning every surface for the tiniest trace of dust.

Sean had spent all his seventeen and a half years knowing he was Academy-bound, yet despite the vantage point his lofty birth should have given him, he hadn't really understood what that meant. Now he knew . . . and his worst nightmares had fallen far short of the reality.

He was a "plebe," the lowest form of military life and the legitimate prey of any higher member of the food chain. He remembered dinner conversations in which Adrienne Robbins had assured his father she'd eliminated most of the hazing the Emperor had recalled from his own days at the US Navy's academy. Sean would never dream of disputing her word, of course, but it seemed unlikely to him that she could have eliminated very much of it after all.

Intellectually, he understood a plebe's unenviable lot was a necessary part of teaching future officers to function under pressure and knew it wasn't personal—or not, at least, for most people. All of which made no difference to his sweaty palms as he awaited quarters inspection, for this was a subject upon which his intellect and the rest of him were hardly on speaking terms. He'd embarrassed Mid/4 Malinovsky, his divisional officer, before her peers. The fact that he'd embarrassed himself even worse cut no ice with her, and understanding why she'd set her flinty little heart on making his life a living hell was no help at all.

He'd felt, to use one of his father's favorite deflating phrases, as proud as a peacock as he stood in the front rank of the newest Academy class, awaiting the Commandant's first inspection. Every detail of his appearance had been perfect—God knew he'd worked hard enough to make it so!— and he'd been excited and happy despite the butterflies in his midsection. And because he'd felt and been all those things, he'd done an incredibly stupid thing.

He'd *smiled* at Admiral Robbins. Worse, he'd forgotten to stare straight before him as she inspected the ranks. He'd actually *turned his head* to meet her eyes and *grinned* at her!

Lady Nergal hadn't said a word, but her brown eyes had held no trace of "Aunt Adrienne's" twinkle. Their temperature had hovered somewhere a bit below that of liquid helium as they considered him like some particularly repulsive amoeba, and the parade ground's silence had been . . . profound.

It only lasted a century or so, and then his eyes whipped back to their appointed position, his ramrod-straight spine turned straighter still, and his smile vanished. But the damage had been done, and Christina Malinovsky intended to make him pay.

The click of a heel warned him, and he snapped to rigid attention, thumbs against his trouser seams, as Mid/4 Malinovsky entered his quarters.

There were no domestic robots at the Academy. Some of the Fleet and Marine officers had pointed out that their own pre-Imperial military academies had provided their midshipmen and cadets with servants in order to free them from domestic concerns and let them concentrate on their studies. Admiral Robbins, however, was a product of the US military tradition. She was a great believer in the virtues of sweat, and no one had quite had the nerve to argue with her when she began designing the Academy's syllabus and traditions. The fact that His Imperial Majesty Colin I sprang from the same tradition as Admiral Robbins may also have had a little something to do with that, but the mechanics behind the decision meant little to the plebes faced with its consequences, and Sean had labored manfully against this dreadful moment. Now he stood silent, buttons gleaming like tiny suns, boots so brightly polished it was difficult to tell they were black, and used the full enhancement he'd finally received to keep from sweating bullets.

Mid/4 Malinovsky prowled around the room, running white-gloved fingers over shelves and dresser top, regarding her stony face in the lavatory mirror as she checked his tooth glass for water spots. She opened his locker to examine its contents and his tiny closet to check the hangered garments and study the polish of his second pair of boots. Her perfectly turned out exec stood in the door, traditional clipboard tucked under his arm, watching her, and Sean could almost feel the sadistic glee with which he waited to inscribe Mid/1 MacIntyre's name on his gig list. But Malinovsky said nothing, and Sean fought down a sense of relief and reminded himself she wasn't done yet.

She straightened and closed the closet, looked about the room one more time, and crossed to his bed. She stopped where he could see her—not, he was certain, by accident—and reached into her pocket. She took her time, making an elaborate ritual of it, as she withdrew a shiny disk Sean recognized after a moment as an antique U.S. silver dollar. She balanced it consideringly on her crooked index finger and thumb, then flipped it.

The coin flashed through the air, then arced down to land precisely in the center of the bunk . . . and lie there.

Malinovsky's gray eyes glittered as it failed to bounce, and Sean's heart fell. He kept his face impassive—with an effort—as she reclaimed the coin and weighed it in her palm a moment before pocketing it once more. Then she reached down, gripped the blanket and sheets, and stripped the mattress bare with a single jerk.

She turned on her heel, and her exec's stylus was poised.

"Five demerits," she said flatly, and stalked away.

Colin MacIntyre looked around the gleaming conference table at the members of his Imperial Council. Two of them were absent, for Lawrence Jefferson had been called in as a last-minute substitute for Horus, and Life Councilor Geb, the Minister of Reconstruction was seldom on Birhat. For the most part, that was because he spent his time following close on the heels of Survey Command, but Geb was also the last surviving citizen of the original Birhat, and the monumental changes his home world had suffered hurt.

That was one reason Colin had recalled Vlad Chernikov from his post as Geb's assistant. Tsien and Horus had needed an engineer on Birhat, so Colin had created the Ministry of Engineering and Vlad had agreed to accept it. Now the blond, blue-eyed ex-cosmonaut finished his summary of the Bia System's ongoing civilian projects, and Colin nodded approval.

"Sounds like you're on top of things, Vlad . . . as usual." Vlad smiled, and Colin smiled back. "Having said that, how's Earth's shield coming?"

"Quite well," Vlad said. "The only real problem is the task's simple magnitude. We have emplaced forty percent of the primary generators and work is beginning on the subordinate stations. I fear the asteroid belt has all but vanished, but the Centauris freighters are keeping pace."

Colin nodded. Spaceborne Imperial "smelters" could render almost any material down to its basic elements to synthesize the composites and alloys Imperial industry needed, like the battle steel which formed Battle Fleet's planetoids, but even Imperial synthetics required some starting point. The raw materials to build things the size of Mother or *Dahak* had to come from somewhere, and the huge freighters of the Imperium's "mining expeditions" could—and did—transport the rubble of entire planets to the fabrication centers. The Centauris System, unfortunately for it, was conveniently close to Sol, and its original eleven planets had already been reduced to nine. Soon there would be only eight as gravitonic warheads blew yet another to splinters to feed the insatiable appetite of Earth's orbital shipyards.

"In the meantime, Baltan and Dahak have completed plans for Stepmother." Several councilors' eyes narrowed with interest. "We have yet to fully explore Mother's memory, but we are confident we have extracted all the essential programs for her Battle Fleet and constitutional functions. Stepmother's final core programming parameters remain flexible, however, as it seems probable additions will be required as our studies here in Bia continue. Of course, the entire project will require many years, but Horus, Tao-ling and I intend to initiate construction within three months."

"And thank God we're finally ready," Colin said. "Dahak, you and Baltan have my sincere thanks for your efforts."

"You are, of course, welcome, Sire," Dahak replied, on his best formal behavior for the meeting. "I feel certain I speak for Admiral Baltan as well as for myself."

"Well, remind me to thank him in person the next time I see him." Colin turned back to Vlad. "And the new planetoids?"

"Those are much further advanced, despite the usual unforeseen delays. *Imperial Terra* should commission within four years."

"Any problems with the computers, Vlad?" Gerald Hatcher asked.

"I'll take that, if I may, Colin," Sir Frederick Amesbury said. The wiry Englishman, one of Hatcher's fellow chiefs of staff during the Siege, had become Minister of Cybernetics, and Colin nodded for him to go on.

"The pilot computers have been up and running for over two years, Ger," Amesbury said, "and Dahak's original figures have been spot on. Incorporating that Achuultani logic circuit into our energy-state designs has raised the speed of operations another five percent, and we've included more responsiveness to nonspecific prompts in the software. They aren't self-aware, of course, but they have about thirty percent more autonomous decision-making capability. I believe you'll be quite pleased with the results."

"Excuse me, Sir Frederick," it was Lawrence Jefferson, "but that's something I'm still not quite clear on. I can see why we wouldn't want Mother or Stepmother to be self-aware, but why don't we want our warships that way? If we had more ships like *Dahak*, wouldn't we have a far more effective fleet?"

"Yes and no," Amesbury said. "The ships would certainly be more efficient, but they'd also be far more dangerous."

"Why?"

"If I may, Sir Frederick?" Dahak said, and Amesbury nodded. "The problem, Lieutenant Governor, is that such ships would be too powerful for our own safety. As you know, the Fourth Imperium was incapable of building fully self-aware computers at the time of my construction. My own awareness evolved accidentally during fifty-one thousand years of unsupervised operation, and even now, we have not fully determined the reasons for this.

"The Fourth Empire, however, was so capable yet chose not to utilize that capacity for reasons which, upon consideration, particularly in light of facts we have discovered but which the Empire could not have known, seem entirely valid. Consider: there is no proof cybernetic intelligences are immune to 'insanity,' and the Achuultani computer is ample proof not all are immune to ambition. Should an *Asgerd*-class planetoid go 'insane,' it could do incalculable damage. Indeed, true prudence might suggest that I myself should be transferred from my present hull to some less dangerous location."

"Dahak," Colin sighed, "we are *not* going to argue about that again! I'll accept your argument against creating any more self-aware computers, but *you've* certainly proven yourself to us!"

"Besides," Vlad said dryly, "why should the possibility that *you* might go crazy disturb us when we have an Emperor who has done so already?"

A chuckle ran around the table, but Colin didn't share it. His mind was already moving on to the next point, and he glanced at his Minister of Biosciences with a pang of sorrow. In many ways, Isis would have made a better councilor than Cohanna . . . if not for her age. She had far better "people sense," but Colin was unhappily certain Project Genesis was going to be not simply the crowning achievement of Isis Tudor's life but its last.

"All right, I believe that covers just about everything," he said quietly, "but before we close, Cohanna has something to report. 'Hanna?"

Cohanna looked down at her hands with uncharacteristic sadness for a moment, then cleared her throat.

"I wish Isis were here to tell you this herself, but she wasn't up to the trip. However—" she raised her eyes "—I'm pleased to announce that the first free Narhani female in seventy-eight million years was born at oh-two-thirty-four Greenwich time this morning." A soft sound of surprise ran around the table, and Cohanna smiled mistily. "Isis was there, and she's named the child 'Eve.' So far as we can tell, she's absolutely healthy."

Gerald Hatcher's quiet voice broke the long, still silence.

"I never really believed you could do it, 'Hanna."

"I didn't." Cohanna's voice was very soft. "Isis did."

There was another moment of silence before Vlad Chernikov spoke again, and his earlier levity had vanished.

"How *is* Isis, 'Tanni?" he asked gently.

"Not well, Vlad," Jiltanith said sadly. "She faileth quickly, and so Father doth stay at her side. She feeleth no pain, and she hath seen her life's work yield its fruit, yet do I fear her time is short."

"I am sorry to hear that." Vlad looked around the silent table for a moment, then back at Jiltanith. "Please tell her how proud we are of her . . . and give her our love."

"I shall," Jiltanith said softly.

Francine Hilgemann activated her antisnooping devices before taking the new Bible from its package. Her security systems were every bit as good as those of the Imperial government (since they'd *come* from government sources), which meant she was as safe from observation as anyone could be, and she inhaled the rich smell of printer's ink appreciatively as she opened the book. She'd always loved beauty, and she was both amused and genuinely pleased by the effect neural computer feeds had produced on the printing industry. Man had rediscovered that books were treasures, not simply a means of conveying information, and the volume she held was a masterpiece of the printer's art.

She leafed through it admiringly, then paused at the Lamentations of Jeremiah. The tissue-thin paper slid out with pleasing ease—unlike the last time, when some idiot had used glue and wrecked two pages of Leviticus.

She unfolded the sheets, careful of their fragility, and spread them on her blotter. Datachips were far smaller and easier to hide. She and her allies knew that, but they also knew few modern security people thought in terms of anything as clumsy as written messages, which meant few looked for them. And, of course, data that was never *in* electronic storage couldn't be extracted *from* electronic storage by a computer named Dahak.

She got out her code book, translated the message, and read through it slowly twice, committing it to memory. Then she burned the sheets, ground the ash to powder, and leaned back to consider the news.

MacIntyre and his crowd were finally ready to begin on Stepmother, and she agreed with her ally's assessment. By rights, Stepmother ought to represent an enormous threat to their long-term plans, but that could be changed. With a little luck and a great deal of hard work, the "threat" was going to become the advantage that let them bring off the most ambitious coup d'etat in human history, instead.

She gnawed her thumbnail thoughtfully. In many ways, she'd prefer to strike now, but Stepmother had to be closer to completion. Not complete, but within sight of it. That gave them their time frame, and she was beginning to understand the purpose that godawful gravitonic warhead would serve. Her eyes gleamed appreciatively as she considered the implications. It would be their very own Reichstag fire, and the Narhani gave them such a splendid "internal threat" to justify the "special powers" their candidate for the crown would invoke to insure Stepmother got finished the right way.

But that was for the future. For now, there was this latest news about the Narhani to consider, and she pondered it carefully. Officially, she was simply the general secretary of the Church's coequal bishops—but then, Josef Stalin had been "simply" the General Secretary of the Central Committee, hadn't he?—and it would be her job to soothe her flock's anxiety when the information was officially released. Still, the Achuultani *were* the Spawn of the Anti-Christ, and with a little care, her soothing assurance that Narhani weren't *really* Achuultani—except, perhaps, in a purely technical sense, which, of course, loyal subjects of the Imperium could never hold against their fellow subjects when no one could *prove* they had Satanic origins—would convey exactly the opposite message. Add a particularly earnest pastoral letter reminding the faithful of their duty to pray for the Emperor's guidance in these troubled times, and the anti-Narhani ferment would bubble along very nicely, thank you.

And, in the meantime, there were those *other* members of her flock whom she would see got the news in somewhat less soothing form.

The Reverend Robert Stevens sat in the dingy room beneath his church and watched the shocked eyes of the men and women seated around him. He felt their horror rising with his own, and more than one face was ashen.

"Are you *sure*, Father Bob?" Alice Hughes asked hoarsely.

"Yes, Alice." Stevens' grating, high-pitched voice was ill-suited to prayers or sermons, but God had given him a mission which put such paltry burdens into their proper perspective. "You know I can't reveal my source's identity—" in fact, he had no idea who the ultimate source was, though its information had always proven reliable "—but I'm sure."

"God forgive them," Tom Mason whispered. "How could they actually help the Anti-Christ's spawn *breed?*"

"Oh, come on, Tom!" Yance Jackson's lip curled and his green eyes blazed. "We've known the answer to that ever since they started cloning their precious '*Narhani.*'" He made the name a curse. "They've been corrupted."

"But how?" Alice asked hesitantly. "They fought the Achuultani as God's own champions! How could they do that . . . and then do *this?*"

"It's this new technology," Jackson growled. "Don't you see, where fear couldn't tempt them, power has. They've set *themselves* up as gods!"

"I'm afraid Yance is right," Stevens said sadly. "They were God's champions, Alice, but Satan knows that as well as we do. He couldn't defeat them when they fought in His armor, so Satan's turned to temptation, seducing where he couldn't conquer. And this—" he tapped the piece of paper on the table before them "—is the proof he's succeeded."

"And so is the name they've given this demon of theirs," Jackson said harshly. " '*Eve!*' It should've been 'Lilith'!"

Stevens nodded even more sadly, but a new fire kindled in his eyes.

"The Emperor and his Council have fallen into evil," cold certitude cleansed his voice of sorrow, "and God-fearing people are under no obligation to obey evil rulers." He reached out to the people sitting on either side of him, and more hands rose, joining in a circle of faith under the humming fluorescent light. Stevens felt their belief feeding his own, making it strong, and a fierce sense of purpose filled him.

"The time is coming, brothers and sisters," he told them. "The time of fire, when the Lord shall call us to smite the ungodly in His name, and we must be strong to do His will. For the Armageddon is truly upon us, and *we—*" his eyes swept around the circle, glittering with an inner flame "—are the true Sword of God!"

CHAPTER SEVEN

The planet Marha, seventeen light-minutes from Bia and smaller than Mars, had never been much of a planet, and it had become less of one when the Fourth Imperium made it a weapons testing site. For two thousand years, until antimatter and gravitonic warheads made planetary tests superfluous, fission, fusion, and kinetic weapons had gouged and ripped its near-airless surface into a tortured waste whose features defied all logical prediction.

Which was precisely why the Imperial Marines loved Marha. It was a wonderful place to teach infantry the finer points of killing other people, and Generals Tsien and MacMahan were delighted to share it with Admiral Robbins' midshipmen. Naval officers might not face infantry combat often, but they couldn't always avoid it, either, and not knowing what they were doing was a good way to get people (especially their Marine-type people) killed.

At the moment, Admiral Robbins rode the command deck of the transport *Tanngjost*, sipping coffee, and her brown eyes gleamed as her scanners watched her third-year class deploy against the graduating class. That Sean was a sneaky devil, she thought proudly. He'd made an absolute ass of himself at his first parade, but he'd survived it, and he stood first in the Tactics curriculum by a clear five points. He was a bit audacious for her taste, but that wasn't too surprising, and his parents would have just loved this one.

Mid/3 MacIntyre hand-signaled a stop, and his company of raiders slumped in the knife-sharp shadow of the tortured ring wall. He slumped with them, panting hard, and tried to remember he was being brilliant. If he managed to pull this off, he might even find two or three people to agree with him; if he screwed up, everybody would be waiting to tell him what a jackass he'd been.

He glanced at Sandy, more worried than he cared to admit as he noted how wearily she sat. This was her company, and she'd loved the idea when he sketched it out, but her small size was working against her.

An enhanced person could move in powered-down combat armor, if

473

its servos were unlocked. It wasn't easy (especially for someone Sandy's size), but the sheer grunt work could be worth it under the right circumstances. Unpowered armor had no energy signature, and it even hid any emissions from its wearer's implants, which meant his raiders were virtually invisible.

The only real threat was optical detection, and he'd noticed that while his peers gave lip service to the importance of optical systems, they *relied* on more sophisticated sensors. He'd started to mention that during the critique of the last field exercise, but then he'd remembered *he* would be leading this one . . . and that the Academy didn't give out prizes for losing.

He slithered up the ring wall, unhooked the passive scanner from his harness, poked it over the crest, and grinned at its display. Onishi and his staff were exactly where The Book said they ought to be, safely tucked away at the heart of the sensor net guarding their HQ site. But The Book hadn't envisioned having a company of raiders barely half a klick away, well inside the sensor perimeter which should have protected Onishi's tactical HQ and ready to decapitate his entire command structure before Tamman (who'd always wanted to be a Marine anyway, for some strange reason) led in the main force.

He slid back down beside Sandy and pressed his helmet to hers. The face behind her visor was sweat-streaked and weary, but her brown eyes were bright, and he grinned and slapped her armored shoulder.

"We got 'em, Sandy!" Their helmets conducted his voice to her without the betraying pulse of a fold-space com. "Get the troops saddled up."

She nodded and began waving hand signals, and her support squad set up with gratifying speed, even without their armor's "muscles." He left them to it and reclimbed the slope to double-check the target coordinates. A standard saturation pattern would work just fine, he thought gleefully.

He glanced up. Sandy's heavy weapons types were set, and her other people were creeping up beside him, "energy guns" ready. It was just like laser tag, he thought, prepping his implants to activate his armor. And then he energized his com for the first time in almost six hours.

"*Now!*" he snapped.

Mid/4 Onishi Shidehara frowned as he stepped out of his HQ van to stretch. Crown Prince or no, MacIntyre was a hot dog, and the cautious sparring being reported by the outposts wasn't like him. It was only skirmishing, and along the most logical line of advance, at that. Mid/4 Onishi expected to kick His Imperial Highness's ass most satisfyingly, but so far he'd seen barely ten percent of the opposition, which suggested MacIntyre meant to try something fancy. For Onishi's money all that razzle-dazzle might look good to the instructors, but only MacIntyre's luck had let him get away with it so long. *This* time he was going to have to do things the hard way, and—

Something kicked dust in front of him. In fact, *dozens* of somethings were falling all over his position! He just had time to feel alarm before they erupted in the brilliant flashes of "nukes" and "warp grenades," and he went down in an astonished cloud of dust as the flash-bangs' override pulses locked his armor and blanked out his com implant to simulate a casualty.

He whipped his head around, trapped in his inert armor, and saw his entire HQ staff falling about him. A second wave of flash-bangs deluged his position, catching most of the handful who'd escaped the first, and then a horde of armored figures came down off the ring wall shooting.

It was over in less than thirty seconds, and Mid/4 Onishi gritted his teeth as one armored figure loped over to squat beside him with a toothy grin.

"*Zap!*" Sean MacIntyre said insufferably.

It had taken Horus months to learn to smile again after Isis' death, but today his grin was enormous as he entered Lawrence Jefferson's office.

"What's so funny?" the Lieutenant Governor asked.

"I just got back from Birhat," Horus said, still grinning, "and you should've heard Colin and 'Tanni describing Dahak's latest brainstorm!"

"Oh?" Unlike most people, Jefferson preferred an old-fashioned swivel chair, and it creaked as he leaned back. "What 'brainstorm'?"

"Oh, it was a beaut! You know how protective he is of the kids?" Jefferson nodded; Dahak's devotion to the imperial family was legendary. "Well, their middy cruise's coming up in a few months, and he had the brilliant idea that they should make it aboard him." The old man laughed, and Jefferson frowned.

"Why not? They couldn't possibly be in safer hands, after all!"

"That was his point," Horus agreed, "but Colin and 'Tanni won't hear of it, and I don't blame them." Jefferson still looked puzzled, and Horus shook his head and hitched a hip onto the Lieutenant Governor's desk.

"Look, *Dahak*'s the flagship of the Imperial Guard, right? Not even a unit of Battle Fleet at all."

Jefferson nodded again. Colin MacIntyre had lost ninety-four percent of the Fourth Empire's resurrected Imperial Guard Flotilla in the Zeta Trianguli Campaign. Only five ships remained, and repairing them had taken years, but they were back in service now. They were also fundamentally different from the rest of the Fifth Imperium's planetoids, for their computers lacked the Alpha imperatives which compelled the rest of Battle Fleet to obey *Mother*, not the Emperor directly. Herdan the Great, the Fourth Empire's founder, had set Battle Fleet up that way as an intentional safeguard, since Mother wouldn't obey an emperor who'd been constitutionally removed by the Assembly of Nobles or whose actions violated the Great Charter stored in her memory. That neatly cut the legs out from under a monarch with tyranny on his mind, but the Guard was the Emperor's personal command, and its units *weren't* hardwired to obey Mother.

"All right," Horus continued, "every midshipman makes his senior-year cruise aboard a unit of Battle Fleet, so how would it look if Colin sends *his* kids out in *Dahak*? Bad enough that their fellows might resent it, but what kind of message does it send the twins? Besides, Dahak dotes on them; he'd find it mighty hard to treat them like any other snotties!"

"I suppose that's true." Jefferson swung his chair gently from side to side and grinned. "One doesn't tend to think of emperors and empresses as harassed parents. But if they're not using *Dahak*, what are they doing?"

"Well, Colin was all for letting the assignments be made randomly, but Dahak can be a bit mulish." Horus's eyes twinkled, and Jefferson laughed. He'd been present on one occasion when the computer had been moved to intransigence, and the Emperor's expression had been priceless.

"Anyway, they argued about it for a while and finally reached a compromise. *Imperial Terra*'s almost ready to commission—they're working up her final programming now—and Dahak 'suggested' using her. She'll be the newest and most powerful ship in Battle Fleet, and Dahak's personally vetted every detail of her design. Nothing's going to happen to them aboard *her*."

"It *is* a bit hard to conceive of anything threatening her," Jefferson mused. "In fact, I think that's a very good idea. With all due respect to Their Majesties, we shouldn't run risks with the succession."

"That's how Dahak brought them around in the end, and just between you and me, I'm glad he did," Horus agreed, and Jefferson nodded slowly.

"Here." Father Al-Hana took the data chips from his bishop and crooked his heavy eyebrows. "We've only got about two weeks to set this one up," Francine Hilgemann continued, "but don't take any chances."

"I see." Al-Hana slipped the chips into his pocket and wondered what they said. "Which group should I route them to?"

"Um." Hilgemann frowned down at her desk, playing with her pectoral cross as she considered. "Which is closest to Seattle?"

"That would be Stevens' group, I believe."

"Oh?" Hilgemann's smile wasn't pleasant. "That's nice. They've been spoiling for a mission. Are they ready for one?"

"I'd say so. The training cadre reports very favorably on them. And, as you say, they're eager. Shall I activate them?"

"Yes, they'll do nicely. But if *this* one goes sour the consequences are going to be fairly dire, so make sure of your cutouts. Use someone else if there's *any* way they could be traced back to us."

"Of course," Al-Hana said, and tried almost successfully to hide his surprise. Whatever was on the chips, it was important.

Vincente Cruz parked his rented flyer outside the cabin and inhaled deeply as he popped the hatch. Imperial technology had long since healed the worst scars from the Achuultani bombardment of Earth. Even the temperature was coming back to normal, and the terrible rains following the Siege had produced one beneficial side effect by washing centuries of accumulated pollution out of the atmosphere. The mountain air was crystal clear, and while he knew many of his fellow Bureau of Ships programmers thought he was crazy to spend his vacations on Earth instead of the virgin surface of Birhat, he and Elena had always loved the Cascade Mountains.

He climbed out to unload the groceries, then paused with a frown, wondering why the kids weren't already here to help carry them in.

"Luis! Consuela!"

There was no response, and he shrugged. Luis had been in raptures over the fishing. No doubt he'd finally talked Consuela into trying it, and Elena had taken the baby and gone along to keep an eye on them.

He gathered up a double armload of groceries—no particular problem to a fully-enhanced set of arms—and climbed the steps to the porch. It was a bit awkward to work the door open, but he managed, and stepped through it, pushing it shut behind him with a toe. He started for the kitchen, then froze.

A man and a woman sat in front of the fireplace, and their faces were concealed by ski masks. He was still staring at them when he grunted in anguish and crashed to the floor. Cascading milk cartons burst like bombs, drenching him, but he hardly noticed. Only one thing could have produced his sudden paralysis: someone had just shot him from behind with a capture field!

He tried desperately to fight, but the police device had locked every implant in his body—even his com had been knocked out. He could neither move nor call for help, and panic filled him. His family! *Where was his family?*

The man from the fireplace rose and turned him onto his back with a toe, and Vincente stared up into the masked face, too consumed by terror for his family to feel any fear for himself even as the man knelt and pressed the muzzle of an old-fashioned Terran automatic into the base of his throat.

"Good afternoon, Mister Cruz." The high-pitched voice was unpleasant, but menace made its timbre utterly unimportant. "We have a job for you."

"W-who are you?" Just getting out those few words against the capture field took all Vincente's strength. "Where are my—"

"Be quiet!" The voice was a whiplash. The pistol muzzle pressed harder, and Vincente swallowed, more frightened for his family than ever.

"That's better," the intruder said. "Your wife and children will be our guests, Mister Cruz, until you do exactly as we tell you."

Vincente licked his lips. "What do you want?" he asked hoarsely.

"You're a senior programmer for *Imperial Terra*," his captor said, and even through his fear Vincente was stunned. His job was so classified even Elena didn't know precisely what he did! How could these people—?

"Don't bother to deny it, Mister Cruz," the masked man continued. "We know all about you, and what you're going to do is add this—" he waved a data chip before Vincente's eyes "—to the ship's core programs."

"I-I *can't!* It's impossible! There's too much security!"

"You have access, and you're bright enough to find a way. If you don't—" The man's shrug was a dagger in Vincente's heart. He stared into the eyes in the mask slits, and their coldness washed away all hope. This man would kill him as easily as he might a cockroach . . . and he had Vincente's family.

"That's better." The masked man dropped the chip on his chest and straightened. "We have no desire to hurt women and children, but we're doing the Lord's work, and you've just become His instrument. Make no mistake; if you fail to do exactly as you're told, we *will* kill them. Do you believe me?"

"Yes," Vincente whispered.

"Good. And remember this: we knew where to find you, we know what you do, and we even know what ship you're working on. Think about that, because it also means we'll know if you're stupid enough to tell anyone about this."

The masked man stepped back, joined by his female companion and a tall, broad-shouldered man with the capture gun. They backed to the door, and he lay helpless, watching them go.

"Just do as you're told, Mister Cruz, and your family will be returned safe and sound. Disobey, and you'll never even know where they're buried."

The leader nodded to his henchman, and Vincente screamed as the capture field suddenly soared to maximum and hammered him into the darkness.

CHAPTER EIGHT

Senior Fleet Captain Algys McNeal sat on his command deck and watched his bridge officers with one eye and the hologram beside him with the other. Physically, Admiral Hatcher was several hundred thousand kilometers away, but fold-space coms let them maintain their conversation without interruptions. Not that Captain McNeal felt overly grateful. Commanding Battle Fleet's most powerful warship on her maiden cruise was quite enough to worry about; having both heirs to the Crown aboard made it worse, and he did *not* need the CNO sitting here flapping his jaws while *Imperial Terra* prepared to get under way!

" . . . then take a good look around Thegran," Hatcher was saying.

"Yes, Sir," McNeal replied while he watched Midshipman His Imperial Highness Sean MacIntyre running final checks at Astrogation. The Prince had obviously hoped for assignment to Battle Comp, but he was already a competent tactician. He'd learn far more as an assistant astrogator, and so far, McNeal was cautiously pleased with Midshipman MacIntyre's cheerfulness in the face of his disappointment.

"And bring back some green cheese from Triam IV," Hatcher continued.

"Yes, Sir," McNeal said automatically, then twitched and jerked both eyes to his superior's face. Hatcher grinned, and McNeal returned it wryly.

"Sorry, Sir. I guess I *was* a bit distracted."

"Don't apologize, Algys. I should know better than to crowd you at a time like this." The admiral shrugged. "Guess I'm a bit excited about your new ship, too. And frustrated at being stuck here in Bia."

"I understand, Sir. And you're not really crowding me."

"The hell I'm not!" Hatcher snorted. "Good luck, Captain."

"Thank you, Sir." McNeal tried to hide his relief, but Hatcher's eyes twinkled as he flipped a casual salute. Then he vanished, and McNeal's astrogator roused from her neural feeds to look up at him.

"Ship ready to proceed, Sir," she said crisply.

"Very good, Commander. Take us out of here."

"Aye, aye, Sir," Commander Yu replied.

Birhat's emerald and sapphire gem began to shrink in the display as they headed out at a conservative thirty percent of light-speed, and *Imperial Terra*'s officers were too busy to note a brief fold-space transmission. It came from the planetoid *Dahak*, and it wasn't addressed to any of them, anyway. Instead it whispered to *Terra*'s central computer for just an instant, then terminated as unobtrusively as it had begun.

"Well, they're off," Hatcher's hologram told Colin. "They'll drop off a dozen passage crews at Urahan, then move out to probe the Thegran System."

Colin nodded but said nothing, for he was concentrating on the neural feed he'd plugged into Mother's scanners. *Imperial Terra* had to be at least twelve light-minutes from Bia to enter hyper, and he sat silent for the full ten minutes she took to reach the hyper threshold. Then she blinked out, with no more fuss than a soap bubble, and he sighed.

"Damn, Gerald. I wish I was going with them."

"They'll be fine. And they've got to try their wings sometime."

"Oh, that's not my problem," Colin said with a crooked grin. "I'm not worried—I'm envious. To be that young, just starting out, *knowing* the entire galaxy is your own private oyster. . . ."

"Yeah. I remember how I felt when Jennifer made her middy cruise. She was cute as a puppy—and she'd have killed me on the spot if I'd said so!"

Colin laughed. Hatcher's older daughter was attached to Geb's Reconstruction Ministry, with three system surveys already under her belt, and she was about due for promotion to lieutenant senior grade.

"I guess all the good ones start out confident they can beat anything the universe throws at them," he said. "But you know what scares me most?"

"What?" Hatcher asked curiously.

"The fact that they may just be right."

The Traffic Police flyer screamed through the Washington State night at Mach twelve. That was pushing the envelope in atmosphere, even for a gravitonic drive, but this one looked bad, and the tense-faced pilot concentrated on his flying while his partner drove his scan systems at max.

An update came in from Flight Control Central, and the electronics officer cursed as he scanned it. Jesus! An entire family—*five* people, three of them kids! Accidents were rare with Imperial technology, but when they happened they tended to happen with finality, and he prayed this one was an exception.

He turned back to his sensors as the crash site came into range and leaned forward, as if he could force them to tell him what he wanted to see.

He couldn't, and he slumped back in his couch.

"Might as well slow down, Jacques," he said sadly.

The pilot looked sideways at him, and he shook his head.

"All we've got is a crater. A big one. Looks like they must've gone in at better than Mach five . . . and I don't see any personnel transponders."

"*Merde*," Sergeant Jacques DuMont said softly, and the screaming flyer slowed its headlong pace.

❖   ❖   ❖

Underway holo displays had always fascinated Sean, especially because he knew how little they resembled what a human eye would actually have seen.

Under the latest generation Enchanach drive, for example, a ship covered distance at eight hundred and fifty times light-speed, yet it didn't really "move" at all. It simply flashed out of existence *here* and reappeared over *there*. The drive built its actual gravity masses in less than a femtosecond, but the entire cycle took almost a full trillionth of a second in normal space between transpositions. That interval was imperceptible, and there was no Doppler effect to distort vision, since during those tiny periods of time the ship was effectively motionless, but any human eye would have found it impossible to sort out the visual stimuli as its point of observation shifted by two hundred and fifty-four million kilometers every second.

So the computers generated an artificial image, a sort of tachyon's-eye view of the universe. The glorious display enfolded the bridge in a three-hundred-sixty-degree panorama whose nearer stars moved visibly and gave humanity the comforting illusion of moving through a comprehensible universe.

The imaging computers confronted different parameters at sublight speeds. The Fifth Imperium's gravitonic drive had a maximum sublight velocity of a smidgen over seventy percent of light-speed (missiles could top .8 c before their drives lost phase lock and Bad Things happened) and countered mass and inertia. That conferred essentially unlimited maneuverability and allowed maximum velocity to be attained very quickly—not instantly; a vessel's mass determined the efficiency curves of its drive—without turning a crew into anchovy paste. But unlike a ship under Enchanach drive, sublight ships *did* move relative to the universe, and so had to worry about things like relativity. Time dilation became an important factor aboard them, and so did the Doppler effect. To the unaided eye, stars ahead tended to vanish off the upper end of the visible spectrum, while those astern red-shifted off its bottom.

Sean found the phenomenon eerily beautiful, and he'd loved the moments when his instructors had allowed him to switch the computer imaging out of the display to enjoy the "starbow" on training flights. Unfortunately, it wasn't very useful, so the computers and FTL fold-space scanners normally were called upon once more to produce an artificially "real" view.

Then there was hyper-space. *Imperial Terra*, like all Battle Fleet planetoids, had three distinct drive systems: sublight, Enchanach, and hyper, and her top speed in hyper was over thirty-two hundred times that of light. Yet "hyper-space" was more a convenient label for something no human could envision than an accurate description, for it consisted of many "bands"— actually a whole series of entirely different spaces—whose seething tides of energy were lethal to any object outside a drive field. Even with Imperial technology, human eyes found h-space's gray, crawling *nothingness* . . . disturbing. Vertigo was almost instantaneous; longer exposure led to more serious consequences, up to and including madness. Ships in normal space could detect the hyper traces of ships in hyper; ships in hyper were blind. They could "see" neither into normal space nor through hyper-space, and so their displays were blank.

Or, more precisely, they showed other things. Aboard *Imperial Terra*, Captain McNeal preferred holo projections of his native Galway coast, but the actual choice depended on who had the watch. Commander Yu, for example, liked soothing, abstract light sculptures, while Captain Susulov, the exec, had a weakness for Jerusalem street scenes. The only constant was the holographic numerals suspended above the astrogator's station: a scarlet countdown showing the time remaining to emergence at the ship's programmed coordinates.

Now Sean sat at Commander Yu's side, watching the sun set over Galway Bay while Captain McNeal waited for his ship to emerge from hyper in the Urahan System, twelve days—and over a hundred light-years—from Bia.

Imperial Terra dropped back into humanity's universe sixty-three light-minutes from the F3 star Urahan. The Urahan System had never been a Fleet base, but a survey ship had found a surprising number of planetoids orbiting in its outer reaches . . . for reasons which became grimly clear once the survey crew managed to reactivate the first derelict's computers.

No one had ever lived on any of Urahan's planets, so starships contaminated by the bio-weapon could do no harm there. As ship after ship became infected and their people began to sicken, their officers had taken them to Urahan or some other unpopulated system and placed them in parking orbit.

And then they'd died.

Galway Bay vanished. Scores of planetoids appeared, drifting against the stars, gleaming dimly in the reflected light of Urahan, and Sean shivered as he watched six of *Terra's* parasites move across the display, carrying forty thousand people towards the transports and repair ships of the Ministry of Reconstruction keeping station on those dead hulls.

All his life, Sean MacIntyre had known what had overwhelmed the Fourth Empire. He'd seen the ships brought back to Bia and read about the disaster, studied it, written papers on it for the Academy. He knew about the bio-weapon . . . but now he *understood* something he'd never quite grasped.

Those dead ships were real, and each had once been crewed by two hundred thousand people who'd worn the uniform he now wore. Real people who'd died because they'd tried to assist planets teeming with billions of other real people. And when they knew they, too, were infected, they'd come here to die rather than seek help for themselves and endanger still others.

The bio-weapon itself had died at last, but through all the dusty millennia, those ships had remained, waiting. And now, at last, humanity had returned to reclaim them and weigh itself against the criminal folly which had killed their crews . . . and the courage with which they'd died.

He watched the display, measuring himself against those long-dead crews, and a part of him that was very young hoped Captain McNeal would hyper out for Thegran soon.

◇   ◇   ◇

Fleet Commander Yu Lin had been to Urahan before, and she'd watched her snotty as they dropped out of hyper. It would never do to admit it, but she rather liked Mid/4 MacIntyre. Crown Prince or no, he was hardworking, conscientious, and unfailingly polite, yet she'd wondered how such a cheerful extrovert would react to Urahan's death fleet.

Now she filed the ghosts in his eyes away beside the other mental notes she was making for his evaluation. It was interesting, she thought.

He seemed to feel exactly the way she did.

Imperial Terra considered her options as the coordinates for her next hyper jump were entered.

Although her Comp Cent wasn't self-aware, it came closer than those of older Battle Fleet units. Terra was actually a good bit brighter than Dahak had been when he first arrived in Earth orbit, yet trying to reconcile the two sets of Alpha Priority commands no one knew she had was a problem.

Normally, she would have asked for guidance, but Alpha commands took absolute precedence, and her directive to seek human assistance didn't carry Alpha Priority. There'd never seemed any reason why it should, but one of Vincente Cruz's commands prohibited any discussion of his other orders with her bridge officers, which meant Comp Cent was faced with devising a course of action which would satisfy both sets of commands all on its own.

It did.

Sean sat beside the park deck lake, skimming stones across the water. A bio-enhanced arm could send them for incredible distances, and he watched the skittering splashes vanish into the mist while his implants' low-powered force field shielded him from the falling rain.

Feet crunched on wet gravel behind him, and he read the implant codes without looking.

"Hi, guys," he said. "How d'you like Commander Godard's weather?"

He stood and turned to grin at his friends. This was the first time they'd all been off watch at once since leaving Urahan, and *Terra*'s logistics officer had decided the park decks needed a good rain. Fleet Commander Godard was a nice guy, and Sean didn't *think* he'd done it on purpose.

"I like it." Brashan trotted down to the lake and waded out belly-deep into the water. Unlike his human friends, he was in uniform, but Narhani uniform consisted solely of a harness to support his belt pouches and display his insignia, and Sean felt a familiar spurt of envy. Brashan had to spend more time polishing his leather and brightwork, but he'd never had to worry about getting a spot out of his dress trousers in his life.

"It reminds me of spring on Narhan," Brashan added, folding down into the water until only his shoulders showed and extending the fan of his cranial frill in bliss. "Of course, the air's still too thin, but the weather's nice."

"You *would* think so." Tamman kicked off his deck shoes and perched on the outer hull of a trimaran, dangling his feet in the water. "For myself, I'd prefer a bit less drizzle."

"You and me both," Sean agreed, though he wasn't sure that was entirely true. The humidity emphasized the smell of life and greenery, and he had his sensory boosters on high to enjoy the earthy perfume.

"Still want to go sailing?" Sandy asked.

"Maybe." Sean skimmed another stone into the mist. "I checked the weather schedule. This is supposed to clear up in about an hour."

"Well I'd rather wait until it does," Harriet said.

"Yeah." Sean selected another stone. "I suppose we could go up to Gym Deck Seven while we wait."

"No way." Tamman shook his head. "I poked my head in on the way down, and Lieutenant Williams is running another 'voluntary participation' unarmed combat session up there."

"Yuck." Sean threw his rock with a grimace. His human friends and he had played and worked out with Dahak's training remotes since they could walk. They were about the only members of the crew who were both junior to Williams and able to give him a run for his money, but he kept producing sneaky (and bruising) moves they hadn't seen yet whenever they got him in trouble.

"Double yuck," Sandy agreed. She was nimble and blindingly fast, even for an enhanced human, but her small size was a distinct disadvantage on the training mat.

"Oh, well," Harriet sighed, heading for the trimaran and beginning to unlace the sail covers, and Sean laughed as he climbed aboard to help her.

Deep in *Imperial Terra*'s heart Comp Cent silently oversaw her every function, monitoring, adjusting, reporting back to its human masters.

Terra was somewhat larger than an *Asgerd*-class planetoid, but she carried far fewer people, mostly because her sublight parasites, while larger and more powerful than their predecessors, had been designed around smaller crews. Horus' old *Nergal* had required three hundred crewmen, and even the Fourth Empire's sublight battleships had needed crews of over a hundred. With their Dahak-designed computers, *Imperial Terra*'s were designed for core crews of only thirty, and even that was more of a social than a combat requirement.

Yet *Terra*'s personnel still numbered over eighty thousand. Each of them was superbly trained, ready for any emergency, but all of those eighty thousand people depended upon what their computers told them and relied upon Comp Cent to do what it was told. From the engineers tending the roaring energy whirlpool of her core tap to the logistics staff managing her park decks and life support, they worked in an intimate fusion with their cybernetic henchmen, united through their neural feeds.

Continuous self-diagnostic programs scrutinized every aspect of those computers' operations, alert for any malfunction while *Imperial Terra*'s crewmen stood their watches and monitored their displays, and those displays told them all was well as their ship tore through hyper. But all was not well, for none of *Imperial Terra*'s crew knew about the Alpha Priority commands a programmer now dead with his entire family had inserted into their ship's computer, and so none of them knew Comp Cent had become a traitor.

Sandy MacMahan crossed the cool, cavernous bay to the gleaming flank of the sublight battleship *Israel*. Number six personnel hatch stood open, and she trotted up the ramp, wondering where Fleet Commander Jury was.

She poked her head in through the hatch and blinked in surprise.

"Sean? What're you doing here?"

"Me? What're *you* doing here? I got a memo from Commander Jury to report for an unscheduled training exercise."

"So did I." Sandy frowned. "Dragged me out of the sack, too."

"Too bad, considering how much you need your beauty sleep."

"At least beauty sleep does *me* some good, Beak Schnoz," she shot back, and Sean grinned and rubbed his nose, acknowledging her hit. "But speaking of Commander Jury, where is she?"

"Dunno. Let's check the command deck."

Sandy nodded, and they stepped into the transit shaft. The gravitonic system whisked them away . . . and the hatch closed silently behind them.

The midshipmen stepped out of the shaft onto the command deck and into a fresh surprise. Harriet, Tamman, and Brashan were already there, and they looked just as puzzled as Sandy and Sean felt. There was a moment of confused questions and counter-questions, and then Sean held up his hands.

"Whoa! Hold on. Look, Sandy and I both got nabbed by Commander Jury for some extra hands-on parasite training time. What're you guys doing here?"

"The same thing," Harriet said. "And I don't understand it. I just finished a two-hour session in the simulator last watch."

"Yeah," Tamman said, "and if we're here, where's Commander Jury?"

"Maybe we'd better ask her." Sean flipped his neural feed into *Imperial Terra*'s internal com net . . . and his eyes widened as the system kicked him right back out. *That* had never happened before.

He thought for a moment, then shrugged. Procedure frowned on using fold-space coms aboard ship, but something decidedly strange was going on, so he activated his implant com. Or, rather, he *tried* to activate it.

"Shit!" He glanced up and saw the others looking at him. "I can't get into the com net—and something's blanketing my fold-space com!"

Sandy stared at him in astonishment, and then her face went blank as *she* tried to contact Jury. Nothing happened, and a tiny flame of uncertainty kindled in her eyes. It wasn't fear—not yet—but it was closer to that than Sean liked to see from Sandy.

"I can't get in, either."

"I don't like this," Tamman muttered. Harriet nodded agreement, and Brashan stood and headed for the transit shaft.

"I think we'd better find out what's going on, and—"

"Three-minute warning," a calm, female voice interrupted the Narhani. "Parasite launch in three minutes. Assume launch stations."

Sean whirled to the command console. *Launch stations?* You couldn't launch a parasite in hyper-space without destroying parasite and mother ship alike—any moron knew that!—but the boards were blinking to life, and his jaw clenched as the launch clock began to count down.

"Oh, my God!" Harriet whispered, but Sean was already hammering at the console through his neural feed, and his dark face went white as the computer refused to let him in.

"Computer! Emergency voice override! Abort launch sequence!"

Nothing happened, and Brashan's voice was taut behind him.

"The transit shaft has been closed down, Sean."

"Jesus Christ!" With the shaft down, it would take over five minutes to reach the nearest hatch.

"Two-minute warning," the computer remarked. "Parasite launch in two minutes. Assume launch stations."

"What do we do, Sean?" Tamman asked harshly, and Sean scrubbed his hands over his face. Then he shook himself.

"Man your stations! Try to get into the system and shut the damned thing down, or this crazy computer'll kill us all!"

Commander Yu had been on watch for two hours. As most watches in hyper-space, they'd been deadly dull hours, and her attention was on the slowly shifting light sculptures, so it took her a few seconds to note the peculiar readings from Launch Bay Forty-One.

But then they began to register, and she straightened in her couch, eyes widening. The bay was entering launch cycle!

Commander Yu was an experienced officer. She paled as she realized what breaching the drive field in hyper would do to her ship, yet she didn't panic. Instead, she threw an instant abort command into Comp Cent's net and the computer acknowledged, but the bay went right on cycling!

She snapped her feed into a standby system and tried to override manually. The launch count went steadily on, and her face was bloodless as she began punching alarm circuits . . . *and nothing at all happened!*

Time was running out fast, and she did the only thing left. She ordered a complete, emergency computer shut down.

Comp Cent ignored her, and then it was too late.

Imperial Terra dropped out of hyper. There was no warning. She shouldn't have been able to do it. A ship in hyper *stayed* in hyper until it reached its programmed coordinates, and *Terra* hadn't reached the coordinates Commander Yu had given her. But she *had* reached the ones she'd selected under the overriding authority of her Alpha Priority commands.

She reappeared in normal space, over a light-year from the nearest star, and the battleship *Israel* screamed out of her bay under full emergency power. Her drive field shredded centimeter-thick battle steel bulkheads and splintered hatches the size of an aircraft carrier's flight deck. She massed over a hundred and twenty thousand tons, and *Imperial Terra*'s alarms screamed as she reamed the access shaft into tangled ruin.

Sean MacIntyre gasped in fear, pressed back into his couch by a cold-start, full-power launch. The battleship was moving at twenty percent of light-speed when she erupted from the air-spewing wound of her bay, and her speed was still climbing!

He stared at the holo display as it sprang to life, too confused and terrified to grasp what was happening. He should be dead, and he wasn't. The display should show only the gray swirls of hyper-space; it was spangled with diamond-chip suns in the velvet immensity of n-space, and *Imperial Terra* was a rapidly dwindling dot astern.

Comp Cent watched *Israel* accelerate clear and noted the faithful discharge of one set of Alpha Priority commands. With that detail out of the way, it could turn to its other imperatives.

Harriet cried out in horror, and Sean cringed as *Imperial Terra*'s core tap blew, and eighty thousand people vanished in an eye-searing glare.

CHAPTER NINE

Baroness Nergal curled up on her couch with Fleet Vice Admiral Oliver Weinstein's head in her lap and popped another grape into his mouth.

"You do realize you're going to have to *earn* these grapes, don't you?" she purred as he swallowed.

"I don't think of it that way," he said with a chuckle.

"No? Then how *do* you think of it, pray tell?"

"The way I see it, *I* don't have to do anything. First my superior officer wines and dines me, spoiling me rotten and softening me up so she can have her wicked way with me. And second—"

"And second?" she prompted, poking his ribs as he paused with a grin.

"Why, second, she *does* have her way with me."

"You," she examined her remaining grapes with care, "are a despicable person of weak moral fiber." He nodded, and she shook her head in sorrow. "I, on the other hand, as a virtuous and upright person, am so shocked by the depths of your decadence that I think—" she paused as she finally found the perfect grape "—I'm going to shove this grape up your left nostril!"

Admiral Weinstein tried to whip upright and dodge, but Admiral Robbins was a clever tactician and tumbled him to the floor in a squirming, tickling heap. Her intended instrument of retribution pulped harmlessly against the tip of his nose, but things were progressing satisfactorily indeed when an urgent tone sounded.

Adrienne stopped dead, head rising in shock as the priority tone repeated, then vaulted to her feet. Weinstein sat up and started to speak, then froze as the tone sounded yet again. His confused expression vanished as the priority of the signal registered, and he rose to his knees.

Adrienne paused only to jerk a robe over her negligee, then answered the call with an impatient implant flick. Gerald Hatcher's hologram materialized before her, sitting in Mother's Command Alpha command chair, and his face was grim.

"Sorry to disturb you, Adrienne," his voice was flat, and her dread grew, "but we may have a serious problem." He drew a breath and met her eyes squarely. "Algys McNeal's Thegran sitrep is three hours overdue."

Robbins went white, and Hatcher continued in that same flat voice. "We've double-checked with Urahan. They hypered out on schedule, and they should've reached Thegran five hours ago."

Adrienne nodded slowly, eyes huge. Many of the Fourth Empire's system governors had erected defenses in desperate efforts to quarantine their planets against the bio-weapon, but communications had been so chaotic as the Empire died that no one knew what any given governor might have cobbled up. The only way to find out was to go see, and if no one had yet encountered anything capable of standing up to a planetoid, there was always the possibility someone would. That was why all survey ships were required to report by hypercom within two hours of arrival in any unexplored system.

"It might be a hypercom failure," she suggested, but her own tone told her how little she believed it.

"Anything's possible," Hatcher said expressionlessly. The hypercom was massive and complex, but its basic technology had been refined for over six millennia. One might fail once in four or five centuries: certainly no more often. They both knew that, and they stared at one another in sick silence.

"Oh, Jesus, Ger," she whispered at last.

"I know."

"Was their hyper field unbalanced when they left Urahan?"

"I don't *know*." Frustration harshened Hatcher's voice. "They dropped off their passengers and hypered straight out, and none of the reconstruction people had any reason to run a trace on them. All we know is they hit the threshold and kicked over right on the tick."

"Oh, shit." The expletive was a prayer, and Adrienne raked fingers through her hair. "I simply can't believe they could've hit anything that could take *Terra*—not with Algys in command. It *has* to be a com failure!"

"You mean you *hope* it is," Hatcher said, then closed his eyes. "And so do I. But hoping won't change things if it's not." Adrienne nodded unhappily, and he drew a deep breath. "I'm mobilizing BatRon One for search and rescue with *Herdan* as Flag. Do you want it?"

"Of course I do!" Adrienne began unbelting her robe. Weinstein was already there, holding out her uniform, and she spared him a strained smile. "I'll be ready by the time my cutter gets here."

"Thank you," Hatcher said softly, and Adrienne swallowed.

"Will you—?" she began, and he nodded, face grimmer than ever.

"I'm leaving for the Palace now."

Fifteen *Asgerd*-class planetoids erupted from hyper-space ten light-minutes from the G4 star Thegran. They came out in battle formation, with shields up and enough weapons on-line to destroy an entire solar system. Every sensor was at max, seeking any threat and searching for any lifeboat's beacon.

But there was nothing to engage . . . and no beacons.

Adrienne Robbins sat on *Emperor Herdan*'s command deck, staring into the display, and her eyes burned. Thegran II, once known as Triam, was a sphere of bare rock and lifeless dirt, surrounded by a fraying necklace of near-space satellites and derelicts as dead as Triam herself.

She fought her tears. She'd hoped so *hard!* But there was no sign of *Imperial Terra* . . . or of anything that could have destroyed her. And if a hyper ship failed to reach its destination it never emerged from hyper at all. She drew a deep breath and rubbed her stinging eyes once, angrily, before she looked at her white-faced communications officer.

"Calibrate the hypercom, Commander," she said in a voice leached of all emotion.

"I'm sorry, Colin," Gerald Hatcher said quietly. "God, I'm sorry."

Colin sat in his study, trying not to weep while Jiltanith pressed her face into his shoulder and her tears soaked his tunic, and Hatcher started to reach out to them, then stopped. His hand hung in midair for a moment while he stared down at it as if at an enemy, then dropped it back into his lap.

"I'd hoped Adrienne would find something. Or that they'd have returned themselves if it *was* a com failure, but—" He broke off, and his jaw tightened. "It's my fault. I should never have let them all go in one ship."

"No." Colin's frayed voice quivered despite his effort to hold it steady. He shook his head almost convulsively. "It . . . it was *our* idea, Ger. Ours." He closed his eyes and felt a tear trickle down his cheek.

"I should've argued. God, how could I *be* so stupid! *Both* of them, and Sandy and Tam—" Hatcher stopped, cursing himself as Colin's face clenched. Venting his self-hate could only hurt his friends, but he would never forgive himself. Never. *Terra* had seemed so powerful, so *safe* . . . and so he'd let not merely both heirs to the throne but the children of *all* of his closest friends sail aboard a single ship, never reflecting for a moment that even the mightiest starship might malfunction and die. Of course it was unlikely, but it was his *job* to expect the unlikely.

"Have you told the others?" Colin asked, and Hatcher shook his head.

"No. I— Well, you and 'Tanni needed to know first, and—"

"I understand." Colin cut him off softly, hugging Jiltanith as she wept. "It's not your fault, Ger. I don't want to hear that from you ever again." He held the admiral's eyes until Hatcher gave a tiny nod, then drew a deep, ragged breath.

" 'Tanni?" His voice was gentle, and Jiltanith raised her face. She stared at him in mute agony, and he remembered the final engagement at Zeta Trianguli as their ship shuddered and bucked under the pounding of Achuultani warheads and Tamman's *Royal Birhat* vaporized before their eyes. She'd wept then, too, wept for the friends dying about them, but her commands had come firm and steady through her tears, with all the invincible courage he loved so much. The courage that had broken at last.

He cupped her face between his palms, and her diamond tears wrenched at him, for he understood her too well. She'd been wounded too often in the endless battle against Anu. Her softness had withdrawn behind a fiery temper and a warrior's armor forged by a lifetime of warfare and lost friends. But it was still there, however hard she found showing it, and when she loved, she loved as she did everything else—with all she was.

"We have to go, 'Tanni." Fury sparked suddenly within her hurt, but he made himself meet it. "We have to," he repeated. "They're our friends."

She drew a quick, angry breath . . . then held it and closed her eyes. One hand rose to his cheek, and she nodded and pressed a kiss upon his wrist. Anguish still filled her eyes when she opened them once more, but there was understanding as well. The understanding that she had to go on, not simply because her friends needed her, but because if she didn't there was nothing left but a dark, bottomless gulf, waiting to suck her under forever.

"Aye," she whispered, and looked at Hatcher. "Forgive me, dear Gerald." She held out a trembling hand, and the admiral took it. "Well I know thy grief, sweet friend. 'Tis ill done to heap mine own upon it."

" 'Tanni, I—" Tears fogged Hatcher's voice, and she squeezed gently.

"Nay, Gerald. 'Tis no more fault o' thine than mine. And Colin hath the right. Our dearest friends do need our aid . . . e'en as we need theirs." She managed a soft, sad smile and stood. "Let us go to them."

A chair squeaked as the man in it finished the report and turned to look out his office window. The Imperium was in mourning, and even the most fiery malcontents were muted by the shock and sorrow of a race. Every flag of humankind flew at half-mast, but there was no sorrow in *his* heart. The heirs were gone, and the children of the imperial family's closest friends had gone with them. Grief and loss would weaken them, make them less vigilant, blunt their perceptions and reactions, and that was good.

He rose and walked to the window, hands folded behind him, looking down on the crowds below, then rested his eyes upon the spire of the Ceno-taph. The names on the memorial were endless, and once he'd hated every one of them, for they named the people who'd toppled his patron. But he hated them no longer, for in toppling Anu they'd cleared *his* path to power, and his palms tingled as he waited to reach out and grasp it.

He pursed his lips, pondering his preparations. The gravitonic warhead was almost ready, and so was his plan for delivering it when the time was right. He'd been more worried about that than he'd cared to admit to Fran-cine, but not anymore. It wouldn't be easy, but with his foreknowledge and the holos of the artist's sketches he could fabricate his duplicate in plenty of time. And, of course, it would never do to deliver it too soon, anyway. He needed Stepmother closer to operational, for it was essential to reduce delay to an absolute minimum if his coup was to succeed.

And it *would* succeed. He was like a spider, he thought, weaving his webs at the very heart of empire, unnoticed yet perfectly placed to observe and thwart every countermove even before it was launched. Just as he'd been placed to act on the opportunity *Imperial Terra* presented.

He smiled again—a thin, triumphant smile. With a little luck, the heirs' deaths might even drive a wedge between the imperial family and Dahak, for it was Dahak who'd designed *Imperial Terra*, supervised her construction, and suggested sending them out aboard her. With Cruz and his family dead, no one would ever know what had really happened, and the grieving parents would be more than human if some secret part of them didn't blame Dahak for their loss.

The time would come. Not this year, perhaps, but soon, and then Colin and Jiltanith MacIntyre would die, as well, in one deadly stroke which would decapitate the Imperium . . . and there would be nothing anyone could do about it. Nothing at all.

He smothered a soft laugh, savoring the victory to come and the exquisite irony which would make him Colin's legal successor. He, the Terra-born "degenerate" Kirinal and Anu had despised even while they groomed him as their tool, would achieve what Anu had only dreamed of: utter and complete dominion. And it would all be *legal*!

A soft sound warned him, and he turned, banishing his smile and replacing it with soft, sad sympathy as Horus walked into his office. The old man's shoulders slumped, and his eyes were haunted, but like his daughter and son-in-law, he was making himself go on. Making himself discharge his duties, never guessing how futile it all truly was.

"Sorry to bother you," Horus said, "but I wondered if you'd finished that report on the Calcutta bio-enhancement center?"

"Yes, I have." He crossed to his desk and handed over the datachip folio from the blotter.

"Thanks." Horus took it and started back to his office, then stopped and turned as a throat cleared itself behind him.

"I just . . . Well, I just wanted to say I'm sorry, Horus. If there's anything I can do—anything at all—please let me know."

"I will." Horus managed a sad smile of his own. "It helps just to know friends care," he said softly.

"I'm glad. Because we *do* care, Horus," Lawrence Jefferson said gently. "More, perhaps, than you'll ever know."

CHAPTER TEN

"I don't think we're going to nail it down any closer, Harry," Sean sighed from the captain's couch. He rubbed his forehead in a futile effort to relieve the subliminal ache of hours of concentration on his neural feeds, then rose and stretched hugely.

"I'm afraid you're right." His sister sat up in the astrogator's couch and twisted a lock of sable hair around a fingertip.

Sandy lay like a dead woman in the tactical officer's couch, but Sean was used to her utter concentration on the task in hand. Besides, he could see her breathing. He flipped his feed into her net, nudging her gently, and felt her acknowledgment. She began to disengage from her painstaking computer diagnostics, and he fired another message off to Tamman and Brashan, summoning them from their examination of Engineering for a conference.

He clasped his hands behind him and watched the display while Harriet rose and worked through a few tension-relieving stretches. *Israel* drifted in interstellar space, drive down while her tiny crew examined her every system. Before they did anything else, they were going to be *certain*—or as close as was humanly (or Narhanily) possible—no more booby traps awaited them. But once they were certain they still had to decide what to do, and the display's glittering stars offered few options.

He looked up as Tamman and Brashan entered the command deck. Tamman still looked drawn and pinched, but Brashan seemed almost calm. Which, Sean reflected, might owe something to the famed Narhani lack of imagination. Personally, he'd always thought of it more as pragmatism. Narhani were more concerned with the nuts and bolts of a problem than with its implications, and he was glad of it. Brashan's levelheadedness was exactly what they all needed just now, for, to use the current Academy phrase, they were up to their eyebrows in shit.

Tamman perched on the assistant tactical officer's couch beside Sandy while Brashan keyed a reconfiguration command into the exec's couch. It twitched for a moment, then reformed itself into a Narhani-style pad, and he folded onto it just as Sandy shook her head and roused. She sat up with a wan smile that still held a ghost of her familiar humor, and Sean grinned back wryly. Then he cleared his throat.

"All right. I know our system checks are still a long way from finished, but I think it's time to compare notes."

Their nodded agreement was a relief. He was senior to all of them, yet his authority, while real and legal, rested solely on their class standings. He stood first in their Academy class, but less than five points separated him from Tamman, their most "junior" officer, and there was a bare quarter-point between him and Sandy. Which was due solely to his higher scores in Tactics and Phys-Ed, for she'd waxed him in Math and Physics.

"Okay. Harry and I have done our best to figure out where we are, but we can't be as precise about it as we'd like. Or, rather, we know where *we* are; we just don't have any idea what the neighborhood looks like. Harry?" He passed the discussion to her, and she propped a hip against the astrogator's console.

"First of all, we're nowhere near where we're supposed to be. *Israel's* astro data is limited—normally, sublight units don't much need interstellar data—but we've got the old basic Fourth Empire cartography downloads. Working from them and allowing for forty-odd thousand years of stellar motion, we're just about smack in the middle of the Tarik Sector."

"The *Tarik* Sector?" Tamman sounded dubious, and Sean didn't blame him.

"Exactly." Harriet's voice was calmer than Sean knew she was. "Whatever happened took *Terra* off her programmed course by something like plus seventy-two degrees declination and fifty degrees left ascension from Urahan, then brought her out of hyper three days early on top of it. At the moment, we're five-point-four-six-seven light-centuries from Birhat, as near as Sean and I can figure it, on a bearing no one could possibly have predicted."

Sean watched the implications sink home. It didn't make much real difference—they'd known from the start that their battleship was a hopelessly tiny needle in a galactic haystack—but now they also knew no one had even the faintest idea where to start looking for them. Harriet gave them a few moments to consider it, then went on even more dispassionately.

"Unfortunately, *Israel's* database was loaded for the Idan Sector, where we were supposed to be going. We've figured out where we are relative to Bia, but we don't have *any* data on the Tarik Sector, so we don't have the least idea what it contained forty thousand years ago, much less today. No Survey people have penetrated this far, and they probably won't for at least fifty years or so. All of which means we're not in real good shape for making informed guesses about where we ought to go next."

She paused again, then returned the floor to Sean with a small nod.

"Thanks, Harry." He looked at the others and shrugged. "As Harry says, we don't have much guidance about possible destinations, but then, we don't have much choice, either." He flipped his neural feed into the display computers, and a red sighting ring circled a bright star.

"That," he said, "is an F5 star at about one-point-three light-years. We don't know which one it is, so we don't know if it had any habitable planets even before the bio-weapon hit, but the next nearest candidate for a life-bearing world is this G6—" a second sighting ring blossomed "—over eleven light-years away. It's going to take us a while to reach either of them at our best sustained sublight speed, but it'd take something like nine hundred years to get back to Bia—assuming *Israel*'s systems would hold up for a voyage that long. On the other hand, we can get to the F5 in just under two-point-two years. At point-six cee, we'll have a tau of about point-eight, so the subjective time will be about twenty-one months. That's a long time, and we've only got two stasis pods, so we'll have to put up with each other awake the whole way, but I don't see that we have any other option. Comments?"

"I have one, Sean," Brashan said after a moment, and Sean nodded for him to go on. "It's more of an observation, really. It occurs to me that, given such a long voyage time, it may be a fortunate thing we Narhani still think of ourselves as having only one sex."

The other three stared at Brashan, but Sean astonished himself with a chuckle. After a moment the others began to grin, too, though Harriet was a little pink. Sean coughed into his fist, smothering the last of his chuckles, and regarded the Narhani sternly.

"Contrary to what you poor, benighted aliens may believe, Brashan, not all humans are helpless slaves to their hormones."

"Indeed?" Brashan cocked his head and looked down his long snout at him, raising his crest in an expression of polite disbelief. "I would never dispute your veracity, Sean, but I must say my personal observation of human mating behavior invalidates your basic premise. And while we Narhani are quite different from humans, it seems to me that a disinterested perspective is less prone to self-deception. As you know, my people have given this matter of sex a great deal of thought in the last few years, and—"

"All right, Brashan Brashieel-nahr!" Sandy hurled a boot at the centauroid. Sean hadn't seen her take it off, but a six-fingered hand darted up and caught it in mid-flight, and Brashan made the bubbling noise that always reminded Sean of a clogged drain trying—vainly—to clear itself.

The laughing Narhani returned Sandy's boot without rising, inclining his saurian-looking head in a gallant bow, and Sean shook his head. Like most Narhani clone-children, Brashan had spent so much time with humans his elders found his sense of humor quite incomprehensible, but he was also a far shrewder student of human psychology than he cared to pretend. He understood humans needed to laugh in order not to weep. And, Sean thought with heightened respect, perhaps he also understood how his teasing could help set his human friends at ease with a topic which was certainly going to rear its head.

"If we can turn to a less prurient subject?" he said loudly. The others turned back towards him, and their faces, he was pleased to see, were much more relaxed.

"Thank you. Now, Harry and I have already plotted our course, but before we head out I want to know we can rely on our systems." Heads nodded more soberly, and he turned to Tamman. "How does Engineering look, Tam?"

"Brash and I haven't quite finished our inspection, but as far as we've been everything looks a hundred percent. The power plant's nominal, anyway, and the catcher field shows a green board. Once we get up above about point-three cee we'll be sucking in more hydrogen than we're burning. And the drive looks fine, despite that crash launch."

"Environmental?"

"First thing we checked. No problems with the plant, but we may have one with rations." Sean raised an eyebrow, and Tamman shrugged. "There were only five Narhani in *Terra*'s entire complement, Sean. I haven't had a chance to run a Logistics inventory yet, but we could be low on supplementals."

"Uh." Sean tugged at an earlobe and frowned. Narhani body chemistry incorporated a level of heavy metals lethal to humans; Brashan could eat anything his friends could, but he couldn't metabolize all of it, nor would it provide everything he needed.

"Don't worry," Sandy said. Sean looked at her and saw the absent expression of someone plugged into her computers. "Logistics shows a heap of Narhani supplementals. In fact, we've got six or seven times our normal food supplies in all categories, and the hydroponic section's way overstocked. Which—" her eyes refocused and she grimaced "—isn't too surprising, really."

"No?" Sean was relieved to hear food wouldn't become a problem, but Sandy's last comment required explanation.

"Nope. While I was checking out the tactical net I found out why we couldn't get into *Terra*'s internal com net, and I'll be very surprised if we find anything at all wrong with *Israel*'s systems."

"Why?"

"Because this—" she waved at the command deck "—is basically a life-boat, specifically selected for the five of us." Sean frowned, and she shrugged. "I'm not sure what zapped *Terra*, but I'm pretty sure I know why it didn't zap *us*. Unless I miss my guess, we've got a guardian angel named—"

"Dahak," Harriet interrupted, and Sandy nodded.

"You got it. While I was running through the test cycles I hit an override in the core command programs. It went down the instant I challenged it, but that's because it was supposed to. Before *Terra* decided to blow her core tap, she shanghaied the five of us and ordered *Israel*'s computers to ignore us until *after* we'd launched."

"But why?" Tamman sounded confused.

"'Why' which?" Harriet asked. "Why did *Terra* blow? Or why did she shove us out the tube first?"

"'Why' both," he replied, and she shrugged.

"I'd have to guess to answer either of them, but from what Sandy's saying I think I can come pretty close to guessing right." She glanced at Sean, and he nodded for her to continue.

"Okay. First, it's obvious someone sabotaged *Terra*. Planetoids don't just casually change their own headings, drop out of hyper early, and then blow their core taps. Theoretically, I suppose, any one of those actions could have been a malfunction, but all of them?" She shook her head. "Somebody got to her core programming, and it seems pretty likely *we* were the targets."

"Us? You mean someone waxed *Terra* just to get at *us?*" Tamman clearly disliked that thought as much as Sean did.

"Harry's right," Sandy said. "I wouldn't want us to get swelled heads, but it's the only answer that makes sense. Although," she added more thoughtfully, "I doubt they were after *all* of us. More likely they were out to get Sean and Harry."

"Oh, *shit*," Tamman breathed. He scratched an eyebrow, frowning at the deck, then sighed. "Yeah, it makes sense. But, Jesus, Sean, if they could do that, who knows what else they can do? And nobody back home knows what happened. If these creeps—whoever they are—try something else, nobody'll be expecting a thing!"

"I fear Tam has a point," Brashan murmured, and Sean shrugged.

"So do I, but I don't see what we can do about it. We don't have a hypercom, and there's no way we can build one." A hypercom massed five times as much as *Israel's* entire hull and required synthetic elements they couldn't possibly fabricate from shipboard resources. "All we can hope for is that the star system we head for was, in fact, inhabited. If it was, we may find an orbital yard we can kick back into operation, and then we *can* build one."

All five of them shuddered at the thought. With only five sets of hands, the gargantuan task of reactivating even one of the Fourth Empire's heavily automated fabrication centers, while not exactly impossible, would take years. On the other hand, Sean reflected mordantly, it wasn't like they'd have anything else to waste their time on.

"But getting back to what happened," Harriet went on, "*Terra* was set up to destroy herself and make sure no evidence ever turned up. That has to be why she took herself way out here first. But I'll bet you that was *her* idea. Whoever programmed her expected her to scuttle herself while she was still in hyper, in which case there wouldn't have been any n-space debris at all. That's how I would've handled it."

"Me, too," Sean agreed. "And the reason she didn't do it?"

"Dahak," Harriet said with utter certainty. "You know how he looks out for us. Whoever sabotaged *Terra* had to be working inside her Alpha programming, and that means whatever caused her not to kill *us* was also buried in her Alpha priorities. And who do we know who worries about us *and* has the capability to get in and out of any computer ever built?"

"Dahak." It was Sean's turn to nod.

"Exactly. We'll probably never know, but I'll bet anything you like whoever set up the sabotage program ordered *Terra* to make sure there was no evidence but never specifically told her to actually kill her crew. Lord," Harriet turned to Sandy and rolled her eyes, "can you *imagine* what would've happened if they'd tried? They'd have hit so many Alpha overrides against harming humans Comp Cent would've burned to a crisp!"

She crossed her arms and pursed her lips.

"Whoever did this was slick, Sean," Harriet said soberly. "*Real* slick. Even a simple self-destruct command would've hit—I don't know. Nine overrides, Sandy? Ten?"

"Something like that." Sandy frowned as she ran over a mental check-list. "At least that. So they had to cut and paste around them. And those're *hardwired*." She frowned harder. "*I* couldn't have done it even if you gave me a couple of years to work on it. It would've taken somebody pretty darn senior over at BuShips to get away with it."

"Well, of course," Tamman said. Sandy looked at him, and he shrugged. "Doesn't matter how sneaky he had to be, Sandy. He had to have *access*."

"Oh, sure. Well," Sandy's sudden, unpleasant smile reminded Sean very forcefully of her mother, "that's nice to know. Whenever we do get back in touch with Bia, Mom'll be able to narrow it down mighty quick. Can't be more than twenty or thirty people. Probably more like ten or fifteen."

"So we've got an order to blow herself up and hide the evidence," Sean mused, "but not an actual order to kill her crew."

"Yep," Harriet said, "and that's why we're still alive, 'cause Dahak parked his own Alpha command somewhere in Comp Cent and instructed *Terra* to keep an eye on us. On us, specifically—the five of us. Mom and Dad'd probably have killed him if they'd known, but thank God he did it! *Terra* couldn't blow herself without getting us out first without violating *his* commands, and whoever set her up never guessed what he might do, so there was no way they could counter it. *That*, people, is the only reason she came out of hyper at all. And, now that I think about it, it's probably why we wound up way out here. She couldn't hide the evidence in hyper without killing us, but she could sure put us somewhere no one would think to look!"

"Makes sense," Sean agreed after a moment, then shivered. It hadn't felt nice to realize how close they'd come to dying, but it felt even less nice to know eighty thousand people had died as a casual by-product of an effort to murder him and his sister. The hatred—or, even worse, the cold calculation—of such an act was appalling. He shook himself free of the thought and hoped it wouldn't return to haunt his nightmares.

"All right. If that's what happened—and I think you and Sandy are probably right, Harry—then we shouldn't run into any more 'programs from hell' in *Israel*'s software. On the other hand, the trip's going to take long enough I don't mind spending a few days making certain. Do any of you?"

Three human heads shook emphatically and Brashan curled his crest in an equally definite expression of disagreement. Sean grinned crookedly.

"I'm glad you agree. But in the meantime, it's been over six hours since everything went to hell. I don't know about you, but I'm starved."

The others looked momentarily taken aback by his prosaic remark, but all of them had young, healthy appetites. Surprise turned quickly into agreement, and he smiled more naturally.

"Who wants to cook?"

"Anyone but you." Sandy's shudder elicited a chorus of agreement. Sean

MacIntyre was one of the very few people in the universe who could burn boiling water.

"All right, Ms. Smartass, I hereby put *you* in charge of the galley."

"Suits me. Lasagna, I think, and a special side dish delicately spiced with arsenic for Brashan." She eyed *Israel*'s youthful commander. "And maybe we can convince him to share it with *you*, Captain Bligh," she added sweetly.

CHAPTER ELEVEN

The Emperor of Mankind opened his eyes at the desolate sounds, and for just a moment, as he hovered on the edge of awareness, he felt only anger. Anger at being awakened from his own tormented dreams, anger that he must find the strength to face another's sorrow. And, perhaps most of all, anger that the sobs were so soft, so smothered, so . . . ashamed.

He turned his head. Jiltanith was curled in a wretched knot, far over on her side of their bed, arms locked about a pillow. Her shoulders jerked as she sobbed into the tear-soaked pillowcase, and waking anger vanished as he listened to her sounds and knew what truly spawned his rage. Helplessness. He couldn't heal her hurt. Her grief was nothing he could fight. He couldn't even tell her everything would "be all right," for they both knew it wouldn't, and that tormented him with a sense of inadequacy. It wasn't his fault, and he knew it, but the knowledge was useless to a heart as badly wounded by the anguish of the woman he loved as by his own.

He rolled over and wrapped her in his arms, and she drew into an even tighter knot, burying her face in the pillow she clutched. She *was* ashamed, he thought. She condemned herself for her "weakness," and another flash of irrational anger gripped him—anger at *her* for hurting herself so. But he strangled it and murmured her name and kissed her hair. She clenched the pillow tautly an instant longer, and then every muscle unknotted at once and she wept in desolation as he gathered her close.

He stroked her heaving shoulders, caressing and kissing her while his own tears flowed, but he offered no clichés, no ultimately meaningless words. He was simply there, holding her and loving her. Proving she was not alone as she'd once proved he was not, until gradually—so heartbreakingly gradually— her weeping eased and she drifted into exhausted slumber on his chest while he stared into the dark from the ache of his own loss and hated a universe that could hurt her so.

Dahak closed the file on *Imperial Terra*'s hyper drive once more. Had he possessed a body of flesh and blood he would have sighed wearily, but he was a being of molycircs and force fields. Fatigue was alien to him, a concept he could grasp from observation of biological entities but never feel . . . unlike grief. Grief he'd learned to understand too well in the months since the twins had died, and he'd learned to understand futility, as well.

It was odd, a tiny part of his stupendous intellect thought, that he'd never recognized the difference between helplessness and futility. He'd orbited Earth for fifty thousand years, trapped between a command to destroy Anu and another which forbade him to use the weapons that would have required on a populated world. Powerful enough to blot the planet from the cosmos yet impotent, he'd learned the full, bitter measure of helplessness in a way no human ever could. But in all that time, he'd never felt *futile*—not as he felt now—for he'd understood the reason for his impotence . . . then.

Not now. He'd reconsidered every aspect of *Imperial Terra*'s design with Baltan and Vlad and Geran, searching for the flaw which had doomed her, and they'd found nothing. He'd run simulation after simulation, reproducing every possible permutation on *Imperial Terra*'s performance envelope in an effort to isolate the freak combination of factors which might have destroyed her, and no convincing hypothesis presented itself.

The universe was vast, but it was governed by laws and processes. There was always more to learn, even (or especially) for one like himself, yet within the parameters of what one could observe and test there should be understanding and the ability to achieve one's ends. That was the very essence of knowledge, but he'd used every scrap of knowledge he owned to protect the people he loved . . . and failed.

He'd already decided never to tell Colin about the Alpha Priority command he'd given *Imperial Terra*. It had failed, and revealing it would only hurt his friends as one more safeguard—one more effort on his part—which had saved nothing. They had not said a word to condemn him for insisting upon that particular ship, nor would they. He knew that, and knowing only made the hurt worse. He'd done harm enough; he would not wound them again.

He was different from his friends, for he was potentially immortal and, even with enhancement, they were such ephemeral beings. Yet the brevity of their span only made them more precious. He would have the joy of their company for such a short time, and then they would live only in his memory, lost and forgotten by the universe and their own species. That was why he fought so hard against the darkness, the reason for his fierce protectiveness.

And it was also why, for the first time in his inconceivable lifetime, a wounded part of him cried out in anguish and futility against a universe which had destroyed the ones he loved for no reason he could find.

" . . . and so," Vlad Chernikov said quietly, "we must conclude *Imperial Terra* was lost to 'causes unknown.'" He looked around the conference table sadly. "I deeply regret—all of us do—that we can give no better answer, but our most exhaustive investigation can find no reason for her destruction."

Colin nodded and gripped Jiltanith's hand.

"Thank you for trying, Vlad. Thank you *all* for trying." He inhaled sharply and straightened. "I'm sure I speak for all of us in that."

A soft murmur of agreement answered, and he saw Tsien Tao-ling slip an arm around Amanda's shoulders. Her eyes were dry but haunted, and Colin thanked God for her other children and for Tsien.

He glanced at Hector and bit his lip, for Hector's face was dark and shuttered, and Ninhursag watched him with anxious eyes. Hector had withdrawn, building barricades about his pain and buttressing them by burying himself in his duties. It was as if he couldn't—or wouldn't—admit how savagely Sandy's loss had scarred him, and until he did, he could never deal with his grief.

Colin shook himself with a silent, bitter curse. Of course Hector couldn't "deal with his grief"—and who was he to be surprised by that? They were all wise enough to seek assistance, but the Imperium's best mental health experts could tell him nothing he didn't already know. Jiltanith wept less often now, but even as he comforted her and drew comfort from her, there was a festering hatred in his own heart. A deep, bitter rage for which he could find no target. He knew what he felt was futile, even self-destructive, yet he needed to lash out . . . and there was nothing to lash out against. He pushed the rage down once more, praying his counselor was right and that time would someday mute its acid virulence.

"All right," he said. "In that case, I see no reason not to resume construction on the other class units. Gerald? Do you or Tao-ling disagree?"

"No," Hatcher said after a brief glance at the star marshal.

"Then let's do it. Is there anything else we need to discuss?" Heads shook, and he sighed. "Then we'll see you all Thursday." He stood, still holding Jiltanith's hand, and the others rose silently as they left the room.

Senior Fleet Admiral Ninhursag MacMahan was angry with herself. Few would have guessed it from looking at her, but after a century of hiding her feelings from Anu's security thugs, her face said exactly what she told it to.

She sat behind her desk and drew a deep breath. It was time to return to the needs of the living. Gus van Gelder and her ONI assistants had been carrying her load, and that they'd done it superlatively was scant comfort. It was *her* job; if she couldn't do it, it was time to curl up and die. For a time she'd considered doing just that, but even at her worst, a stubborn part of her had mocked the bad melodrama of the thought.

Now, deliberately, she buried the temptation forever and felt herself coming back to life as she set her grief aside. It wasn't easy, and it hurt, but it also felt good. Not as it once had, but so much better than the dull, dead disinterest which had gripped her for far too long, and she plugged her feed into her computer and called up the first intelligence summary.

Colin sat on the rug, watching the fire and rubbing Galahad's ears. The dog lay beside him before the library hearth, eyes half-closed, massive head resting on Colin's thigh while they both stared into the crackling flames. To the outward eye they must present the classic picture of a man and his dog, Colin thought, but Galahad certainly wasn't his pet. Galahad and his littermates shared a very dog-like exuberant openness, insatiable curiosity, and a need for companionship, but they belonged only to themselves.

Now Galahad emitted a contented snuffle and rolled onto his back, waggling his feet in the air to invite his friend to scratch his chest. Colin complied with a grin, and chuckled as the dog wiggled with soft, chuffling sounds of sensual delight. That grin felt good. The four-footed members of the imperial family had done more than anyone else would ever suspect to help with his and 'Tanni's grief. They shared it, for they, too, had loved the twins, but there was a clean, healthy simplicity to their caring, without the complex patterns of guilt and subliminal resentment even the best humans felt while they grappled with their own loss.

"Like that, do you?" he said, working his scratching fingertips into Galahad's "armpits," and the big dog sighed.

"Of course," his vocoder replied. "It is a pity we do not have hands. I would enjoy doing this for the others."

"But not as much as you'd enjoy having them do it for you, huh?" Colin challenged, and Galahad sneezed explosively and rolled upright.

"Perhaps not," he agreed, and Colin snorted. None of the dogs ever lied. That seemed to be a human talent they couldn't (or didn't want to) master, but they were getting pretty darn good at equivocating.

"I think humans are a bad influence on you. You're getting spoiled."

"No. It is only that we are honest about things we enjoy."

"Yeah, sure." Colin reached under Galahad's massive chest and stroked more gently. The standing dog's chin rested companionably on his shoulder, and he glanced over at the corner where Galahad's sister Gwynevere sat very upright, watching Jiltanith move her queen. Gwynevere cocked her head, ears pricking as she considered the move. She was the only one of the dogs to develop a taste for chess—it was a bit too cerebral for the others—and by human standards she wasn't all that good. Galahad and Gawain were killers at Scrabble, and he'd been horrified to discover Horus had taught all of them to play poker (though none of them—except, perhaps, Gaheris—could bluff worth a damn), but Gwynevere was determined to master chess. And, to be fair about it, she was improving steadily.

The really funny thing, he thought, was that while Jiltanith was an excellent strategist in real life, Gwynevere beat her quite often. 'Tanni was too direct—and impatient—for a game which emphasized the indirect approach.

"Excuse me, Colin," Dahak's voice said, "but Ninhursag has just arrived at the Palace."

"She's here *now*?" Colin looked up, and Jiltanith met his eyes with matching surprise. It was very late in Birhat's twenty-eight-hour day.

"Indeed. And she appears quite agitated."

"'*Hursag* is agitated?" Colin shook his head and scrambled to his feet. "Tell her to come on down to the library."

"She is already on her way. In fact—"

The library door burst open. Admiral MacMahan came through it like a thunder squall, and Colin rocked back on his heels—literally. Ninhursag was only middling tall, and the mood he usually associated with her was one of deliberate consideration, but tonight she was a titan wrapped in vicious, killing rage.

"'Hursag?" he said tentatively as she came to a halt just inside the door. Every movement was rigidly over-controlled, as if each of them took every ounce of will she had, and she chopped a nod.

"Colin. Jiltanith." Her voice was harsh, each word bitten off with utter precision. "Sit down, both of you. I have something to tell you."

Colin looked at Jiltanith, wondering what could have transformed Ninhursag so, but 'Tanni met his eyes with a shrug of ignorance and a slight gesture at the chairs before the hearth. They settled into them, listening to the crackle of burning logs as Galahad and his siblings ranged themselves to either side, and every eye, human and canine alike, watched Ninhursag grip her hands behind her and make herself take a quick, wordless turn about the room. When she turned to face them, her face was calmer, but it was a surface calm, built solely from professionalism and self-discipline.

"I'm sorry to burst in on you, but I just turned up something . . . interesting. Or, rather, I just *confirmed* something interesting."

She inhaled again, sharply, and gave herself a tiny shake.

"I've been slacking off at ONI for months," she continued in a flat voice. "You know that, Colin, though you haven't said anything. I'm sorry. You know why I have. But I'm getting myself back together, and yesterday I started through a stack of reports that've been accumulating since, well—" She broke off with another shrug, and Colin nodded. Jiltanith held out a hand to him, and he took it as Ninhursag cleared her throat.

"Yes. Anyway, most of them were fairly routine. Gus and Commodore Sung have handled the hot stuff as it came in. But one of them—an accidental death report—caught my attention. It was the date, I think. It happened two days after *Imperial Terra* hypered out for Urahan, and it covered an entire family." Fresh pain tightened her lips, but she went harshly on.

"They were civilians, and it was a traffic accident, so I wondered why ONI had it, until I looked more closely," Ninhursag went on in that flat voice. "The husband was Vincente Cruz. He wasn't military, strictly speaking, but—" she paused, and her eyes were cold "—he worked for BuShips."

Colin felt Jiltanith's hand twitch in his and stiffened. It was no more than a vague stirring of suspicion, but the bitterness in Ninhursag's eyes turned something cold and wary deep inside him.

"I don't know why that stuck in my mind, but it did, and when I looked more closely I found a couple of things that seemed . . . out of kilter.

"The Cruzes lived on Birhat, since he worked for BuShips, but they were killed on Earth. I checked and found out they usually vacationed in North America, but Cruz had returned from there less than three months before, so I wondered why they'd gone back so soon. Then I found out his wife and family had stayed there—visiting friends—and he'd gone back to collect them.

"Again, I don't know why that bothered me, but it did. So I did some more checking. Cruz's two older children were enrolled for education here on Birhat, and I discovered that he hadn't warned the education people they'd be staying on Earth. He notified them only after he got back, but two years ago, when he left them to visit family in Mexico, he'd notified their teachers over a month before they left. He was concerned with making certain they didn't lose any ground shifting back and forth between the two school systems.

"That seemed odd, so I checked the hypercom and mat-trans logs. In the ten weeks they stayed on Earth, he neither sent to them nor received from them a single hypercom message. Nor did he use the mat-trans to visit them in person. There was *no communication* between them at all for ten weeks . . . and he and his wife had a ten-month-old baby."

Colin's eyes began to burn with a green fire that matched the fury in Ninhursag's bitter brown stare, and the admiral nodded slowly.

"The accident report looks completely aboveboard, if a bit freakish. It was a high-speed event—a ridge-line collision at almost Mach six—and the flight recorder was totaled, but the altimeter was recovered, and analysis indicated it was under-reading by about two hundred meters. That was enough to put it into the ridge, but when I did a little discreet checking, no one seemed to know who Cruz's family had been visiting. I did a computer search of Earth's credit transactions—as a BuShips employee, he and his wife both held Fleet cards—and I couldn't find a single transaction for Elena Cruz on Earth.

"I can't prove it wasn't an 'accident,' but there are too many coincidences. Especially—" Ninhursag's hands went back behind her, clenched about one another, and her voice was very, very quiet "—when Vincente Cruz was assistant project chief for *Imperial Terra*'s cybernetics."

"Son-of-a-*bitch*!" Colin whispered, and she nodded coldly.

"I haven't checked his work logs yet—that comes next—but I'm already certain what I'm going to find," she said, and this time Colin understood her murderous fury perfectly.

CHAPTER TWELVE

The mood around the conference table was very different this time.

" . . . so there's a fifteen-minute hole in his work log," Ninhursag said, "smack in the middle of his work on *Terra*'s core software. Unfortunately, there are eight other holes, from just under a minute to almost an hour long, in the same log, and we've found an intermittent defect in his terminal that looks completely normal." Her curled lip showed what she thought of that.

"But why?" Horus asked softly. "I don't question your conclusions, 'Hursag, but in the Maker's name, *why*?"

"We can't prove 'why' until we know 'who,'" Ninhursag's voice was harsh, "but I see only two motives. Destroy *Imperial Terra*, one, because of *what* she was—our most powerful warship—or, two, because of who was aboard."

"Sean and Harry," Colin grated, and Ninhursag nodded.

"Whoever set this up went to tremendous lengths—and ran tremendous risks. What else could his objective have been?"

"Sweet Jesu," Jiltanith whispered. "Full eighty thousand people and the children of our dearest friends to kill my babes?" Her face was drawn, but more than despair burned in her black eyes, and her knuckles were white about the hilt of the dagger she always wore.

"*Bastards!*" Hector MacMahan's stylus snapped in his hand. He looked down at the broken pieces and slowly and carefully crushed each of them between enhanced fingertips.

"Agreed," Colin's voice was ice, "but the other kids may have been targets as well. Look how it's affected all of us. 'Hursag blames herself for 'slacking off,' but have any of us done better? And whoever the son-of-a-bitch is, he damned well *knew* what it would do to us!"

"I must agree," Tsien said. Amanda nodded beside him, eyes smoking, and he touched her hand where it lay upon the table. "Yet I am also certain 'Hursag's other deduction is equally correct. Whoever did this must have a powerful organization and penetration at the highest levels. Without such an organization he could not have acted; without such penetration he could have known neither which ship to attack nor whom to use for that attack."

"Agreed," Gerald Hatcher sounded even grimmer. "They had to pick someone with access who was also vulnerable. Anybody this ruthless might have popped one of his own people to cut the chain of evidence, but why kill an entire family? No, they knew exactly which poor bastard to pick, held his family hostage to make him play, then killed them all to cover their tracks."

"There's another pointer." Adrienne Robbins' voice was cold; Algys McNeal had been her friend, and twenty more of her midshipmen had been aboard *Imperial Terra*. "Cruz didn't pop a single security flag. He must have known how small a chance he had of getting them back alive, but he went for it without telling *anyone*. He never even *tried* to get help, so maybe he *knew* they had enough penetration to know if he'd talked to any of 'Hursag's people."

Cold, bitter silence enveloped the council room, then Colin nodded.

"All right. There's someone out there cold enough to murder an entire family and eighty thousand of our people, and I want the son-of-a-bitch. How do we get him?"

"Dust off the lie detectors and put everybody—and I mean *everybody*—on them," MacMahan grated.

"We can't," Horus said. Eyes turned to him, and he shrugged. "If we're right about how far we've been penetrated, the bad guys—whoever they are—will know the instant we start that. If they're our own people, well and good; all they can do is run and identify themselves for us. But if they're tapped in from the *outside*, they'll be operating through a blizzard of cutouts, and whoever's really in charge will just pull in his horns. If he disengages, we may never get another shot at him."

"It's worse than that," Colin sighed. "We don't have 'probable cause' for that kind of sweep."

"Bullshit!" MacMahan snarled. "This is a security matter. We can pull in anybody in uniform we want to!"

"No, we can't." MacMahan started to speak again, but Colin raised a hand. "Hold it, Hector. Just wait a minute. Goddamn it, I want this bastard as badly as you do, but think about it. *We* know 'Hursag's right, but there's not a single piece of hard evidence. Everything except the disappearance of Cruz's family is covered by plausible 'technical failures.' And while it's true his family *did* disappear from our records, that by itself doesn't prove a thing. No law requires people to report their whereabouts to us—our subjects are also free citizens. The fact that we don't know where they were actually works against us; Cruz never indicated they were being held against their will, and if we don't even know where they were, we can hardly prove they were prisoners!

"Even if we could, we'd have to be very specific about who we questioned. The Charter provides no protection against self-incrimination, so we can ask anything we like under a lie detector . . . but only in a court. That particular civil right is absolutely guaranteed specifically *because* there's no protection against self-incrimination.

"Now, you're right that we can question anyone in uniform as long as we make it a security matter, but we still have to furnish them and their counsel with a list of areas we intend to cover—approved by a judge—before we start asking. There's no way we could process legal paperwork on the scale we need without its coming to the attention of anyone with the sources to target Cruz, and what happens when our Mister X finds out about it? We don't want his sources, Hector—we want *him*."

MacMahan looked rebellious, but he subsided with a muttered curse and a grudging nod. Colin was glad to see it, and even gladder to see the life flowing back into his eyes as he realized he had an enemy. Sandy's death was no longer a senseless act by an uncaring universe. Hector had someone besides God to hate, and perhaps that would bring those inner barricades down.

"Very well, then," Tsien said, "what steps *shall* we take?"

"First we start taking security *real* serious," Amanda said. "Whoever went after the kids may be religious nuts, anarchists, out of their fucking minds, or planning a coup, but they *don't* get you two—or Horus—by God!"

"Damn straight," Adrienne approved amid a snarl of agreement, and Colin swallowed. He heard their hunger to destroy whoever had done this to them, but these weren't just his senior officers or angry, bereaved parents. These were friends, determined to protect him and Jiltanith.

"For Colin and 'Tanni, yes," Horus said after a moment, "but not me." Colin raised his eyebrows, and the old man shrugged. "We can reinforce your security quietly, but we can't slap armed guards all over White Tower. Your 'Mister X' could hardly miss that."

"Nay, Father! Shalt not risk thyself thus!"

"Oh, hush, 'Tanni! Who'd want to kill me? Unless we're talking about a total maniac, and I don't think we are, given how smoothly this whole thing went down, what possible motive could he have? Maybe *after* they got the two of you I'd become a target—not before."

"I believe Horus has a point, 'Tanni," Dahak put in. "While it is possible this was a crime of hate and not of logic, whoever perpetrated it did so in a most rational fashion." The computer's voice was as mellow as ever, but they all heard its anger. "At present, this would appear to be the first step in an attempt to decapitate the Imperium, and if that is, indeed, the case, Horus becomes a logical target only in the endgame of the conspiracy."

"Umm." Ninhursag rubbed her forehead. "I don't know, Dahak. You may be right, but you're a bit prone to believe everyone operates on the basis of logic. And whoever it is *did* go for the kids first."

"True, yet analysis suggests this was a crime of opportunity. Security for the twins was very tight, however it might appear to the uninformed. In the Bia System, they were attended by my own scanners at all times and, save for their field trips, continuously guarded by other security arrangements, as well. I do not say it would have been impossible to assassinate them, but it would have been difficult—and it could not have been done without being recognized as an act of murder. In this instance, the killer was able to strike when they were beyond my own surveillance or that of any regular security agency. Moreover, had you not pursued your own intuition in the matter of the Cruz family's murders, the fact that Sean and Harriet's deaths had been deliberately contrived would never have been known."

"That makes sense," Adrienne said slowly, "but I can't shake the feeling that there was more behind it."

"Indeed there was," Dahak agreed. "The twins were not murdered for personal motives, My Lady, but for who—and what—they were. For whatever reason, our enemy elected to strike at the succession. It is for this reason I believe it to be the start of an effort to destroy the monarchy."

"Which *does* make Horus a target," Colin sighed. "Oh, crap!"

"That is an incorrect assumption. Horus is a member of the imperial family, true, but he is not your heir. He would become a potential heir only should you and 'Tanni die without issue, and with all due respect, I believe the Assembly of Nobles would be unlikely to select one of Horus's advanced years as Emperor. Mother might do so if she were required to execute Case Omega yet again, but she would do so only if there were no Assembly of Nobles to discharge that function. Moreover, Horus would not be the first choice even under Case Omega. The proper successor choice under Case Omega would be Admiral Hatcher, as CNO, followed by Star Marshal Tsien. Horus, as the highest civil official of the Imperium, would become the legal heir only if both of the Imperium's senior military officers were also dead. In addition, any open attack upon Horus would clearly risk awakening the suspicion the twins' 'accidental' deaths were intended to avoid. Thus any attempt to kill him before killing you, 'Tanni, Admiral Hatcher, and Star Marshal Tsien would be pointless unless we are, indeed, dealing with an irrational individual."

"I hate it when you get this way, Dahak," Colin complained, and several of the angry people around the table surprised themselves by smiling.

"Maybe, but he's right," Ninhursag said. "I don't want to get complacent, but tightening security for you two—and Gerald and Tao-ling—should have the effect of covering Horus, as well. And he's right, too. If we boost *his* security, it's a gold-plated warning to whoever we're up against."

"All right, we'll handle it that way—for starters. Hector, can you manage the security details?"

"Yes," MacMahan said tersely, and Colin nodded. The protection of the imperial family was the responsibility of the Imperial Marines, and MacMahan's expression was all the reassurance he needed.

"Good. But that's only a defensive action—how do we nail this bastard?"

"Whatever we do, Colin, we do it very carefully," Ninhursag said. "We start by putting all of this on a strict need-to-know basis. I don't want to bring in anyone else—not even Gus. Without knowing how 'Mister X' gets his information, every individual added to the information net gives him another possible conduit, however careful our people are."

"All right, agreed. And then?"

"And then Dahak and I sit down with every bit of security data we have. Everything, military and civilian, from Day One of the Fifth Imperium. We find *any* anomalies, and then we eliminate them one at a time.

"In addition," she leaned back in her chair and frowned up at the ceiling, "we step up efforts to infiltrate every known group of malcontents. Those're underway already, so we don't have to give any new reasons for them. And while we flesh-and-bloods're doing that, Dahak, *you* jump into the datanets here in Bia and start setting up your own taps. Cruz could futz his terminal, but no one can get to *you*, so I want you tied into everything."

"Understood. I must point out, however, that I cannot achieve the same penetration of Earth's datanets."

"No, but until we figure out what's going on, Colin and 'Tanni will never visit Earth simultaneously. We know someone's after them now, and as long as 'Mister X' has to get through you, ONI, Hector's Marines, and Battle Fleet to reach them, I think they're pretty safe, don't you?"

Darin Gretsky leaned his broom in a corner and surveyed the well-lit workshop with a thin smile. He'd worked thirty years to prepare himself as a theoretical physicist, and during all those years he'd felt disdain for most of his fellows. He'd shared their thirst for knowledge, but for them, acclaim, respect, even power, were by-products of knowledge. For him, they were what knowledge was all about. His calculating pursuit of the lifestyle promised by corporate and governmental research empires had earned the contempt of his fellow students, but he hadn't cared, and the wealth and—especially—power he craved had been just within his reach . . . until Dahak and the explosion of Imperial science snatched them away.

Gretsky felt his jaw ache and made himself relax it. Overnight, he'd been transformed from a man on the cutting edge to an aborigine trying to understand that the strange marks on the missionary's white paper actually had meaning. He'd had the stature to be included in the first implant education programs, and, for a time during the Siege, he'd thought he might catch the crest of this new wave as he had the old. But once the emergency was past, Darin Gretsky had realized a horrible thing: he'd become no more than a *technician*. A flunky using knowledge others had amassed. Knowledge, he'd been forced to admit with bowel-churning hatred, he didn't truly understand.

It had almost destroyed him . . . and it *had* destroyed the life he'd planned. He'd become but one more of the thousands of Terra-born scientists exploring millennia of someone else's research and watching it invalidate much of what they'd believed was holy writ. There were no fellow students whose work he might steal, and it couldn't matter less who "published first." And worst of all, the ones for whom he'd felt contempt—the naive ones to whom it was knowledge itself which mattered—were better at it than he. The Terra-born scientists exploring the rarefied stratosphere of the Fourth Empire's tech base came from their number, and there was no room for Darin Gretsky save as one more hewer of wood and drawer of water in the dust about their feet.

But things would change once more, and his smile grew ugly at the thought. His work here had filled his secret bank account with enough Imperial credits to buy the life he'd always craved, and that was good, yet far more satisfying to his wounded soul was what his work could bring about. He didn't know how it would be used, but contemplating the cataclysmic power of the device he'd built gave him an almost sexual thrill. It had taken longer than he'd expected, and he'd had to reinvent the wheel a time or two to work around components that didn't exist, but money had been no object, and he'd succeeded. He'd *succeeded*, and someday soon, unless he was sadly mistaken, his handiwork would topple the smug cretins who'd pushed him aside.

He gave the workshop one more glance, then walked down the hall to the office in which he became not Shiva, Destroyer of Worlds, but one more freelance consultant helping Terran industry cope with the flood of concepts pouring like water from the new Imperial Patent Office. Even that was merely picking the bones of the dead past, he thought acidly. *Emperor Colin*— the title was an epithet in his soul—had declared all civilian Imperial technology public knowledge, held by the Imperial government and leased at nominal fees to any and all users. The free flow of information was unprecedented, and old, well-established firms were being challenged by thousands of newcomers as the manna tumbled down and imagination became more important than mere capital.

He hated the people he worked for. Hated all the bright-eyed, smiling people reaching out for the new world which had robbed him. He had to hide that, but not for much longer. Soon what he'd wrought would—

He looked up in surprise as the office door opened, for it was after midnight. The well-groomed young woman in the doorway looked at him with an odd little smile and raised her eyebrows.

"Dr. Gretsky?" He nodded. "Dr. *Darin* Gretsky?" she pressed.

"Yes. What can I do for you, Ms.—?" He paused, waiting for her name, and she reached into her outsized purse.

"I have a message for you, Doctor." Something in her voice set off a distant alarm, and his muscles tightened as the door opened once more and four or five men stepped through it. "A message from the Sword of God."

He leapt to his feet as her hand came out of the purse, but the last thing Darin Gretsky ever saw was the white, bright glare of a muzzle flash.

Lawrence Jefferson closed the report and leaned back in his swivel chair with a thoughtful expression. Over the past decade he'd assumed ever more of Horus's day-to-day responsibilities, freeing the Governor to concentrate on policy issues, and Gus van Gelder reported directly to him on routine matters now, which was a very useful thing, indeed.

He swung his chair gently from side to side, considering his strategy yet again in light of the latest report. The Sword of God was becoming quite a headache, he thought cheerfully. They were growing bolder, applying all the lessons of the terrorist organizations Colin MacIntyre and his fellows had smashed, and they were far harder to destroy. These terrorists knew the strengths—and weaknesses—of the Imperial technology opposed to them, and none of the security people trying to defeat them suspected their most priceless advantage. Knowledge was power, and through Gus van Gelder, Lawrence Jefferson knew exactly what moves were being made against his tools.

For example, he knew Gus was getting uncomfortably close to Francine.

Gus didn't know it yet, but Jefferson did, and so Bishop Hilgemann was driving the Sword from the Church of the Armageddon. The excesses of zealotry must be forever anathema to the godly, and she was horrified by the thought that such misguided souls might be numbered among her flock. They must recognize the error of their ways or be cut off from the body of the faithful, for they had embraced a fundamental error. Hatred for the Achuultani and all other works of the Anti-Christ was every godly person's duty, but that hate must not be extended to the leadership which stood against the foe. Rather the errors of that leadership must be addressed non-violently, by prayer and remonstrance, lest all the undeniable good it had achieved be lost, as well.

It was all very touching, and it had Gus a bit confused, since he didn't know about the conduits through which she directed those same zealots. What Gus hadn't quite grasped yet was that the Sword no longer required the infrastructure of the Church. No doubt Gus *would* figure it out, but by then it should be too late to find any institutional links to Bishop Hilgemann.

Security Councilor van Gelder nodded to the Marine sentry as the elevator deposited him on an upper floor of White Tower. He walked down the hall and knocked on the frame of an open door.

"Busy?" he asked when the man behind the desk looked up.

"Not terribly." Lieutenant Governor Jefferson rose courteously, waving to a chair, then sat again as van Gelder seated himself. "What's up?"

"Horus still on Birhat?"

"Well, yes." Jefferson leaned back, steepling his fingers under his chin, and raised his eyebrows. "He's not scheduled to return until tomorrow night. Why? Has something urgent come up?"

"You might say that," van Gelder said. "I've finally got a break on the Sword of God."

"You have?" Jefferson's chair snapped upright, and van Gelder smiled. He'd thought Jefferson would be glad to hear it.

"Yes. You know how hard it's been to break their security. Even when we manage to take one or two of them alive, they're so tightly compartmented we can't ID anyone outside the cell *they* come from. But I've finally managed to get one of my people inside. I haven't reported it yet—we're playing her cover on a strict need-to-know basis—but she's just been tapped to serve as a link in the courier chain to her cell's main intelligence pipeline."

"Why, that's wonderful, Gus!" Jefferson cocked his head, considering the implications, then rubbed his blotter gently. "How soon do you expect this to pay off?"

"Within the next few weeks," van Gelder replied, smothering a small, familiar spurt of exasperation. Jefferson couldn't help it any more than any other bureaucratic type, but even the best of them had a sort of institutional impatience that irritated intelligence officers immensely. They couldn't appreciate the life-and-death risks his field people ran, and a "why can't we move quicker on this?" mind-set seemed to go with their jobs.

"Good. Good! And you want to report this directly to Horus?"

"Yes. As I say, I've been running this agent very carefully. I'm the only one in the shop who knows everything about the job, and I just got her report this afternoon. Horus and I set the concept up several months ago, and I need to let him know what's happening before I brief anyone on my staff."

"I see. Do you have a formal report for him, then?"

"Not a formal one, but—" van Gelder reached into his jacket pocket and extracted a small security file "—these are my briefing notes."

"I see." Jefferson regarded the security file thoughtfully. Such files were keyed to randomly generated implant access codes when they were sealed. Any attempt to open them without those codes would reduce the chips within them to useless slag.

"Well, as I say, he won't be back until tomorrow night. Is this really urgent? I mean—" he waved his hand apologetically at van Gelder's slightly affronted expression "—are we facing a time pressure problem so we *have* to get the word to him immediately?"

"It's not exactly a crisis, but I'd like to brief him as soon as possible. I don't want to be too far from the office in case something breaks, but maybe I should mat-trans out to Birhat and catch him there. If he agrees, I could brief Colin and Jiltanith, too."

"That might be a good idea," Jefferson mused, then paused with an arrested air. "In fact, the more I think about it, the more I think we ought to get it to him ASAP. It's the middle of the night in Phoenix right now, but I'm already scheduled to mat-trans out tomorrow morning their time. Could I drop your notes off with him, or is he going to need a personal briefing?"

"We do need to discuss it," van Gelder said thoughtfully, "but the basic information's in the notes. . . . In fact, it might help if he had them before we sat down to talk."

"Then I'll take them out with me, if you like."

"Fine." Van Gelder handed over the file with a grin. "Never thought I'd be using a courier quite *this* secure!"

"You flatter me." Jefferson slid the file into his own pocket. "Does Horus have the file access code?"

"No. Here—" Van Gelder flipped his feed into Jefferson's computer and used it to relay the code to the Lieutenant Governor, then wiped it from the computer's memory. "I hope you don't talk in your sleep," he cautioned.

"I don't," Jefferson assured him, rising to escort him to the door. He paused to shake his hand. "Again, let me congratulate you. This is a tremendous achievement. I'm sure there are going to be some very relieved people when they get this information."

CHAPTER THIRTEEN

"We've got another one, Admiral."

Ninhursag MacMahan grimaced and took the chip from Captain Jabr. She dropped it into the reader on her desk, and the two of them watched through their neural feeds as the report played itself to them. When it ended, she sighed and shook her head, trying to understand how the slaughter of nineteen power service employees possibly served the "holy" ends of the Sword of God.

"I wish we'd gotten at least one of them," she said.

"Yes, Ma'am." Jabr rubbed his bearded jaw, dark eyes hard. "I would have liked to entertain those gentlemen myself."

"Now, now, Sayed. We can't have you backsliding to your bloodthirsty Bedouin ancestors. Not that you might not be onto something." She drummed on her desk for a moment, then shrugged. "Pass it on to Commander Wadisclaw. It sounds like part of his bailiwick."

"Yes, Ma'am."

Captain Jabr carried the chip away, and Ninhursag rubbed weary eyes, propped her chin in cupped palms, and stared sightlessly at the wall.

The "Sword of God's" escalating attacks worried her. One or two, like the one on Gus, had hurt them badly, and even the ones that weren't doing that much damage—except, she amended with a wince, to the people who died—achieved the classic terrorist goal of proving they could strike targets despite the authorities. Open societies couldn't protect every power station, transit terminal, and pedestrian belt landing, but anyone with the IQ of a rock knew that, and at least this time humanity seemed to have learned its lesson. Not even the intellectuals were suggesting the Sword might, for all its deplorable choice of tactics, have "a legitimate demand" to give it some sort of sick quasirespectability. Yet as long as these animals were willing to select targets virtually at random, no analyst could predict where they'd strike next, and they were killing people she was supposed to protect. Which was why they had to get someone *inside* the Sword if they ever expected to stop them.

She winced again as her roving thoughts reminded her of the single agent they *had* gotten inside. Janice Coatsworth had been an FBI field agent before the Siege, and Gus had been delighted to get her. She'd been one of his star performers—one of his "aces" as he called them—and she'd died the same day he had. Somehow she'd been made by the Sword, and they'd dumped what was left of her body on Gus's lawn the same day they killed him, his wife, and two of their four children. Four of his personal security staff had died, as well, two of them shielding his surviving children with their own bodies.

Ninhursag's eyes were colder and harder by far than Captain Jabr's had been. If anything could be called a "legitimate" terrorist target, it was certainly the head of the opposing security force, but she'd been as astounded as any by the attack. Indeed, the van Gelder murders had shaken everyone into a reevaluation of the Sword's capabilities, for Gus's security had been tight. Penetrating it had taken meticulous planning.

She chewed her lip and frowned over a familiar, nagging question. Why was the Sword so . . . spotty? One day they carried out a meaningless massacre of defenseless power workers and left clues all over the countryside; on another they executed a precision attack on a high-security target and left the forensic people damn-all. She knew the Sword was intricately compartmented, but did it have a split personality, too? And where had a bunch of yahoos who could be as clumsy as that power station attack gotten a tight, cellular organization in the first place? Anyone who could put that together could choose more effective targets, and hit them more cleanly, too.

She sighed and put the thought aside once more. So far, they had no idea how the Sword was organized. For all she knew, the meaningless attacks were the work of some splinter group or faction. For that matter, they might actually be the work of some totally different organization which was simply hiding behind the Sword while it pursued an agenda all its own! They needed a better look inside to answer those kinds of questions, and that was up to the folks on Earth, where the Sword operated. Gus had managed it once, and since his death, Lawrence Jefferson had managed to break no less than three of its cells. It was unfortunate that none of them had led to any others—indeed, it seemed likely they were among the more inept members of their murderous brotherhood or they wouldn't have been so easy to crack—but they were a start.

And, she reminded herself, at least the slaughter of Gus's family had given them a reason to beef up Horus's security at White Tower without arousing their real enemy's suspicions.

"Sweet mother of God!" Gerald Hatcher blurted. "Are you *serious?*"

"Of course I'm not!" Ninhursag snarled back. "I just thought *pretending* I was would be really hilarious!"

She quivered with frightened anger Colin understood only too well, and he touched her shoulder, watching her relax with a hissing sigh before he turned his attention back to Hatcher's hologram. Vlad Chernikov also attended by holo image from his office aboard Orbital Yard Seventeen, but Tsien was present with Colin and Ninhursag in the flesh.

"Sorry, 'Hursag," Hatcher muttered. "It's just that— Well, Jesus, how did you *expect* us to react?"

"About the same way I did," Ninhursag admitted with a crooked grin. Then real humor flickered in her eyes. "Which, I might add, you did. You should've heard what *I* said when Dahak told me!"

"But there is no question?" Tsien's deep voice was harder than usual, for it was his files which had been penetrated this time.

"None, Star Marshal," Dahak replied. "I have checked my findings no less than five times with identical results."

"Shit." Colin rubbed the fatigue lines which had formed in the long, dreary months since his children died. After almost a year and a half they were still playing catch-up. Ninhursag and Lawrence Jefferson had managed to pick off a few Sword of God cells, a few score terrorists had been killed in shoot-outs with security forces when they'd struck at guarded sites, and they'd identified exactly seven spies in their military.

And each of those spies had been dead by the time they found him.

"The bastards have us penetrated six ways to Sunday," he said through his fingers, tugging on his nose while his other hand pushed the chip of Ninhursag's report in an aimless circle.

"Yes and no, Colin," Dahak said. "True, we are uncovering evidence of past penetration, yet we are also clearing a progressively higher number of senior personnel of suspicion. I cannot, of course, be certain that we have sealed all breaches in the Bia System, yet recall that I am now monitoring all hypercom traffic between Bia and Sol as well as all datanets in this system. And while I cannot assure you that no information is being transmitted via courier, ONI now maintains permanent surveillance of *all* visitors from Earth."

"Yeah, but it looks like we just found out we didn't get the door locked till after the barn burned down!"

"Perhaps and perhaps not." For a moment Tsien sounded so much like Dahak Colin suspected him of deliberate humor, but that wasn't Tao-ling's style.

"Meaning what?"

"Meaning, Colin, that this particular piece of hardware, while undoubtedly dangerous, is of limited utility to whoever has it."

"What do—" Hatcher began, then stopped. "Yeah, you've got something, Tao-ling. What the hell can they do with it even if they've got it?"

"I would not invest too much confidence in that belief, Admiral Hatcher," Dahak said, "but my own analysis does tentatively support it."

"But how did they get their hands on it in the first place?" Vlad asked, for he'd arrived a few moments late for the initial briefing.

"We're not positive," Ninhursag answered. "All Dahak's discovered for certain is that there's at least one more copy of the plans for the new gravitonic warhead than there should be. We don't know where it is, who has it, or even how long whoever stole it has had it in his possession."

"I believe we may venture a conjecture on the last point," Tsien disagreed. "Dahak has examined the counter in the original datachip from Weapons Development's master file, Vlad." Vlad's holo image nodded understanding. Each Fleet security chip was equipped with a built-in counter to record the numbers of copies which had been made of it, and while the counter could be wiped, it could not be altered. "According to our records, there should be ten copies of the plans—including the original chip—and all ten of those have now been accounted for. However, a total of ten copies were made of the *original* chip, and we do not know where that eleventh copy is.

"On the other hand, that original has been locked in the security vault at BuShips since the day all authorized copies were made, and none of the external or internal security systems show any sign of tampering. I therefore believe the additional copy was made at the same time as the authorized ones."

"Oh, *shit*," Hatcher moaned. "That was—what, six years ago?"

"Six and a half," Ninhursag confirmed. "And while I wouldn't care to bet my life on it, I'd say Tao-ling is probably right. Particularly since a certain Senior Fleet Captain Janushka made the authorized copies. Two years ago, *Commodore* Janushka, who was then assigned to the Sol System as part of the Stepmother team, died of a 'cerebral hemorrhage.' "

She grimaced, and the others snorted. A properly pulsed power surge in a neural feed implant produced something only the closest examination could distinguish from a normal cerebral hemorrhage. But pulsed surges like that couldn't happen by accident, and an ME with no reason to suspect foul play might very well opt for the natural explanation.

"I see." Vlad pursed his lips for a moment, then gave a Slavic shrug. "On that basis, I am inclined to share your conclusion as to the timing, Tao-ling. Yet this weapon is an extremely sophisticated piece of hardware. Building it would require either military components or a civilian workshop run by someone thoroughly familiar with Imperial technology."

"I'm sure it would," Colin said, "but whoever we're up against had the reach and sophistication to sabotage *Imperial Terra*—unless anyone cares to postulate two separate enemies with this level of penetration?" Clearly no one wished to so postulate, and he smiled grimly. "I think we have to assume Mister X wouldn't have stolen it if he didn't believe he could produce it."

"True." Hatcher was coming back on balance, and his voice was calmer and more thoughtful. "But Tao-ling's still right about its utility. They can blow up a planet with it, but if that's all they had in mind, six years plus is plenty of time to build the thing—assuming they could build it at all— and it's also plenty long enough to have used it."

"Precisely," Tsien agreed. "They undoubtedly had some plan for its use, either actual or threatened, else they had not stolen the plans, but what that use may be eludes me. The conspirators must be human—there were far too few Narhani contacts with humans for any of them to have penetrated our security so deeply so long ago—so the destruction of Earth would be an act of total madness. If, on the other hand, their target is here on Birhat, any of our much smaller gravitonic warheads or even a simple thermonuclear device would satisfy their needs. Nor is a weapon of this power required to destroy any conceivable deep space installation."

"What about Narhan?" Ninhursag asked quietly, and Tsien frowned.

"That, Ninhursag, is a very ugly thought," he conceded after a moment. "Again, I can see no sane reason to destroy the planet—that sounds much more like something the Sword of God would wish to attempt—yet Narhan would seem a more likely target than either Earth or Birhat."

"God, all we need is for Mister X to be tied in with a bunch of crazies like the Sword of God!" Colin groaned.

"On the surface, that appears unlikely," Dahak said. "The pattern of 'Mister X's' operations indicates a long-term plan which, while criminal, is rational. The Sword of God, on the other hand, is fundamentally *irrational*. Moreover, as Admiral Hatcher has pointed out, they have had ample time to destroy Narhan if they possessed the weapon. It is possible 'Mister X' might attempt to capitalize upon the activities of the Sword of God or even to influence those activities, but his ultimate goals are quite different from their xenophobic nihilism."

"Then what do *you* think he's going to do with it?"

"I have no theory at this time, unless, perhaps, he intends to use it as a threat to extort concessions. If that is the case, however, we are once more faced by the fact that he has had ample time to build the device and thus, one would anticipate, to make whatever demands he might present."

"Maybe Vlad has a point, then," Colin mused. "Maybe they *have* hit a snag that's kept them from building it at all."

"I would not depend upon that assumption," Dahak cautioned. "I believe humans refer to the logic upon which it rests as 'whistling in the dark.'"

"Yeah," Colin said morosely. "I know."

CHAPTER FOURTEEN

The fist in his eye woke Sean MacIntyre.

He twitched aside, one hand jerking up to the abused portion of his anatomy, even before he came fully awake. Damn, that hurt! If he hadn't been bio-enhanced himself, the punch would have cost him the eye.

He wiggled further over on his side of the bed and rose on one elbow, still nursing his wound, as Sandy lashed through another contortion. That one, he judged, could have done serious damage if he hadn't gotten out of the way. She muttered something even enhanced hearing couldn't quite decipher, and he sat further up, wondering if he should wake her.

They'd all had problems dealing with the reality of *Imperial Terra*'s loss. Just being alive when all those others were dead was bad enough, but their conviction that *Terra* had been destroyed in an attempt to kill *them* made it worse, as if it were somehow their fault. Logic said otherwise, but logic was a frail shield against psyches determined to punish them for surviving.

Sandy twisted in her nightmare, fighting the sheet as if it had become an enveloping monster, and it ripped with a sound of tearing canvas. Her breasts winked at him, and he chastised himself as he felt a stir of arousal.

This was hardly the time for that! He wished—again—that even one of them had been interested in a psych career. Unfortunately, they hadn't, and now that they needed a professional, they were on their own. The first weeks had been especially rough, until Harriet insisted they all had to face it. She didn't know any more about running a therapy session than Sean did, but her instincts seemed good, and they'd drawn tremendous strength from one another once they'd admitted their shared survival filled them with shame.

Sandy twisted yet again, her sounds louder and more distressed. She was the most cheerful of them all when she was awake; in sleep, the rationality which fended off guilt deserted her and, perversely, made her the most vulnerable member of their tiny crew. Her nightmares had become blessedly less frequent, yet their severity remained, and he made up his mind.

He leaned over her, stroking her face and whispering her name. For a moment she tried to jerk away, but then his quiet voice penetrated her dreams, and her brown eyes fluttered open, drugged with sleep and shadowed with horror.

"Hi," he murmured, and she caught his hand, holding it and nestling her cheek into his palm. Fear flowed out of her face, and she smiled.

"Was I at it again?"

"Oh, maybe a little," he lied, and her smile turned puckish.

"Only 'a little,' huh? Then why's your eye swollen?" The tattered sheet fell about her waist as she sat up and reached out gently, and he winced. "Oh, my! You're going to have a black eye, Sean."

"Don't worry about it. Besides—" he treated her to his best leer "—the others'll just think you were maddened with passion."

His heart warmed at the gurgle of laughter which answered his sally, and she shook her head at him, still exploring his injury with tender fingers.

"You're an idiot, Sean MacIntyre, but I love you anyway."

"Uf course you do, Fräulein! You cannot help yourzelf!"

"Oh, you *creep*!" Her caressing hand darted to his nose and twisted, and he yelped in anguish and grabbed her wrists, pinning her down—not without difficulty. He was sixty centimeters taller, but she wiggled like a lithe, naked eel until a final shrewd twist toppled him from the bed. He sat up on the synthetic decksole, then stood, rubbing his posterior with an aggrieved air while she laughed at him, the last of her nightmare banished.

"Jeez, you play rough! I'm gonna take my marbles and go home."

"Now there's an empty threat! You can't even *find* your marbles."

"Hmph!" He took a step towards the bed, and her fingers curved into talons. Her eyes glinted, and he stopped dead. "Uh, truce?" he suggested.

"No way. I demand complete and unconditional surrender."

"But it's my bed, too," he said plaintively.

"Possession is nine points of the law. Give?"

"What'll you do with me if I do?"

"Something horrible and disgustingly debauched."

"Well, in *that* case—!" He hopped onto the bed and raised his hands.

Brashan looked up from the executive officer's station and waved without disconnecting his feed from the console as the others stepped through the command deck hatch. With Engineering slaved to the bridge, one person could stand watch under normal conditions, though it would have taken at least four of them to fight the ship effectively.

Sean dropped into the captain's couch. Harriet and Tamman took the astrogator's and engineer's stations, and Sandy flopped down at Tactical. She looked into the display at the star burning ever larger before them, and the others' eyes followed hers.

Their weary voyage was drawing to an end. Or, at least, to a possible end. They didn't talk a great deal about what they'd do if it turned out that blazing star had no reclaimable hardware, but so far they'd detected no habitable world which might have provided it.

Sean glanced at the others from the corner of an eye. In many ways, they'd made out far better than he'd hoped. It helped that they were all friends, but being trapped so long in so small a universe with anyone made for problems. There'd been the occasional disagreement—even the odd furious argument—but Harriet's basic good sense, with a powerful assist from Brashan, had held them together. Solitude didn't really bother Narhani much, and Brashan had spent enough time with humans—especially these humans—to understand their more mercurial moods. He'd poured several barrels of oil on various troubled waters in the past twenty months, and, Sean thought, it helped that he still regarded sex primarily as a subject for intellectual curiosity.

His attention moved to Tamman and Harriet. Despite *Israel*'s size, she was intended for deployment from her mother ship or a planet, not interstellar voyaging, but at least she was designed for a nominal crew of thirty. That gave them enough room to find privacy, and the humans had fallen into couples without much fuss or bother. For him and Sandy, he knew, the pairing would be permanent even if—when!—they got home, but he didn't think it was for Harry and Tamman. Neither of them seemed particularly inclined to settle down, though they obviously enjoyed one another's company . . . greatly.

He grinned and inserted his own feed into the captain's console for a systems update. As usual, *Israel* was functioning perfectly. She really was an incredible piece of engineering, and he'd had an unusual amount of time to learn to appreciate her design and capabilities. They'd spent endless hours running tactical exercises, as much for a way to keep occupied as anything else, and he'd discovered a few things he'd never imagined she could do.

Still, it was Sandy who'd unearthed the real treasure in *Israel*'s computers. Her original captain had been a movie freak—not for HD or even pre-Imperial tri-vid, but for old-fashioned, flat-image movies, the kind they'd put on film. There were hundreds of them in the ship's memory, and Sandy had tinkered up an imaging program to convert them to holo via the command bridge display. They'd worked their way through the entire library, and some of them had been surprisingly good. Sean's personal favorite was *The Quest for the Holy Grail* by someone called Monty Python, but the ones they'd gotten the most laughs out of were the old science fiction flicks. Brashan was especially fascinated by something called *Forbidden Planet*, but they'd all become addicted. By now, their normal conversation was heavily laced with bits of dialogue none of their Academy friends would even begin to have understood.

He withdrew from the console, maintaining only a tenuous link as he tucked his hands behind his head and crossed his ankles.

"Behold the noble captain, bending his full attention upon his duties!" Sandy remarked. He stuck out his tongue, then looked at Harriet.

"Looks like our original position estimates were on the money, Harry. I make it about another two and a half days."

"Just about," she agreed, an edge of anticipation sharpening her voice. "Anything more on system bodies, Brash?"

"Indeed," the Narhani said calmly. "The range is still well beyond active scanner range, but passive instrumentation continues to pick up additional details. In particular—" he gave his friends a curled-lip Narhani grin "—I have detected a third planet on this side of the star."

Something in his tone brought Sean up on an elbow. The others were staring at him just as hard, and Brashan nodded.

"It would appear," he said, "to have a mean orbital radius of approximately seventeen light-minutes—well within the liquid water zone."

"Hey, that's great!" Sean exclaimed. "That ups the odds a bunch. If there used to be people here, we may find something we can use after all!"

"So we may." Brashan's voice was elaborately calm, even for him; so calm Sean looked at him in quick suspicion. "In fact," the Narhani went on, "spectroscopic analysis confirms an oxygen-nitrogen atmosphere, as well."

Sean's jaw dropped. The bio-weapon had killed *everything* on any planet it touched, and when all life died, a planet soon ceased to be habitable, for it was the presence of life which created the conditions that allowed life to exist. Birhat was life-bearing only because the zoo habitats had cracked before her atmosphere had time to degrade completely, and Chamhar had survived only because no one had lived there, anyway. Earth, never having been claimed by the Fourth Empire, was a special case.

But if this planet had breathable air, then perhaps it hadn't been hit by the bio-weapon at all! And if they could get word of their find home again, humanity had yet a third world onto which it might expand anew.

Then his spirits plunged. If the planet hadn't been contaminated, it probably hadn't had any people, either. Which, in turn, meant no chance at all of finding Imperial hardware they could use to cobble up a hypercom.

"Well," he said more slowly, "that *is* interesting. Anything else?"

"No, but we are still almost sixty-two light-hours from the star," Brashan pointed out. "With *Israel*'s instrumentation, we can detect nothing smaller than a planetoid at much above ten light-hours unless it has an active emissions signature."

"In which case," Sean murmured, "we might begin seeing something in the next eighty hours. Assuming, of course, that there's anything to see."

The talmahk were returning early this spring.

High Priest Vroxhan stood by the window, listening to the Inner Circle with half an ear while he watched jeweled wings flash high above the Sanctum. One gleaming flock broke away to dart towards the time-worn stumps of the Old One's dwellings, and he wondered yet again why such lovely creatures should haunt places so wrapped in damnation. Yet they also nested in the Temple's spires and were not struck dead, so it must not taint them. Of course, unlike men they had no souls. Perhaps that protected them from the demons.

Corada's high-pitched voice changed behind him, and he roused to pay more heed as the Lord of the Exchequer came to the conclusion of his report.

" . . . and so Mother Church's coffers have once more been filled by God's grace and to His glory, although Malagor remains behind time in its tithing."

Vroxhan smiled at the last, caustic phrase. Malagor was Corada's pet hate, the recalcitrant princedom whose people had always been least amenable to Church decrees. No doubt Corada put it down to the influence of the Valley of the Damned, but Vroxhan suspected the truth was far simpler than demonic intervention. Malagor had never forgotten that she and Aris had dueled for supremacy for centuries, and Malagor's mines and water-powered foundries made her iron-master to the world, a princedom of stubborn artisans and craftsmen who all too often chafed under the Church's Tenets. That chafing had been the decisive factor in starting the Schismatic Wars, but The Temple used those wars to put an end to such foolishness forever. Today Prince Uroba of Malagor was The Temple's vassal, as (if truth be known) were all the secular lords, for Mother Church made and broke the princes of all Pardal at will.

"Frenaur?" Vroxhan raised his eyes to the Bishop of Malagor. "Does your unruly flock truly mean to distress Corada this year?"

"Not, I think, any more than usual." Frenaur's eyes twinkled as Corada's jowls turned mottled red. "The tithe is late, true, but the winter has been bad, and the Guard reports the wagons have passed the border."

"Then I think we can wait a bit before resorting to the Interdict," Vroxhan murmured. It was unkind, and not truly befitting to his office, but Corada was such an old gas-bag he couldn't help himself. The fussy bishop's bald pate flushed dark against its fringe of white hair as he sniffed and gathered his parchments more energetically than necessary, and Vroxhan felt a pang of remorse. Not a very painful one, but a pang.

He turned back to the window, hands folded in the sleeves of his blue robe with the golden starburst upon its breast. A company of Guard musketeers marched across his view, headed for the drill field with voices raised in a marching hymn behind their branahlk-mounted captain, and he admired the glitter of their silvered breastplates. Polished musket barrels shone in the sunlight, and scarlet cloaks swirled in the spring breeze. As a second son, Vroxhan had almost entered the Guard instead of the priesthood. Sometimes he wondered rather wistfully if he might not have enjoyed the martial life more—certainly it was less fringed with responsibilities! But the Guard's power was less than that of the Primate of all Pardal, too, he reminded himself, and sat in his carven chair, returning his attention to the council room.

"Very well, Brothers, let us turn to other matters. Fire Test is almost upon us, Father Rechau—is the Sanctum prepared?"

Faces which had been amused by Corada's fussiness sobered as they turned towards Rechau. A mere under-priest might be thought the lowest of the low in this chamber of prelates, but appearances could be deceiving, for Rechau was Sexton of the Sanctum, a post which by long tradition was always held by an under-priest with the archaic title of "Chaplain."

"It is, Holiness," Rechau replied. "The Servitors spent rather longer in their ministrations this winter—they appeared soon after Plot Test and labored for two full five-days. Such a ministration inspired my acolytes to even greater efforts, and the sanctification was completed three days ago."

"Excellent, Father!" Vroxhan said sincerely. They had three five-days yet before Fire Test, and it was a good start to the liturgical year to be so beforehand with their preparations. Rechau bent his head in acknowledgment of the praise, and Vroxhan turned his eyes to Bishop Surmal.

"In that case, Surmal, perhaps you might report on the new catechism."

"Of course." Surmal frowned slightly and looked around the polished table. "Brothers, the Office of Inquisition recognizes the pressure brought upon the Office of Instruction by the merchant guilds and 'progressives,' yet I fear we have grave reservations about certain portions of this new catechism. In particular, we note the lessened emphasis upon the demonic—"

The council chamber doors flew open so violently both leaves crashed back against the walls. Vroxhan surged to his feet at the intrusion, eyes flashing, but his thunderous reprimand died unspoken as a white-faced underpriest threw himself to his knees before him and trembling hands raised the hem of his robe to ashen lips in obeisance.

"H-holiness!" the under-priest blurted even before he released Vroxhan's robe. "Holiness, you must come! Come quickly!"

"Why?" Vroxhan's voice was sharp. "What is so important you disturb the Inner Circle?!"

"Holiness, I—" The under-priest swallowed, then bent to the floor and spoke hoarsely. "The Voice has spoken, Holiness!"

Vroxhan fell back, and his hand rose to sign the starburst. Never in mortal memory had the Voice spoken save on the most sacred holy days! A harsh, collective gasp went up from the seated Circle, and when he darted a quick glance at them he actually saw the blood draining from their faces.

"What did the Voice say?" His question came quick and angry with his own fear.

"The Voice spoke Warning, Holiness," the under-priest whispered.

"God protect us!" someone cried, and a babble of terror rose from the Church's princes. An icy hand clutched at Vroxhan's heart, and he drew a deep breath and clutched his pectoral starburst. For one, dreadful instant he closed his eyes in fear, but he was Prelate of Pardal, and he shook himself violently and whirled upon the panicky prelates.

"Brothers—Brothers! This is not seemly! Calm yourselves!" His deep, powerful voice, trained by a lifetime of liturgical chants, lashed out across the confusion, stinging them into brief silence, and he hurried on.

"The Warning has come upon us, possibly even the Trial, but God will surely protect us as He promised to our fathers' fathers these many ages past! Did He not give us the Voice against this very peril? There will be panic enough among our flock—let us not begin that panic in the Inner Circle!"

The bishops stared at him, and he saw reason returning to many faces. To his surprise, old Corada's was one of them. Bishop Parta's was not.

"Why?" Parta moaned. "Why has this come to *us*? What sin have we committed that God sends the very Demons upon us?"

"Oh, be quiet, Parta!" Corada snapped, and Vroxhan swallowed a hysterical giggle at the way the old man's vigor widened every eye. "You know your Writ better than that! The demons come when they come. Sin won't bring them any sooner; it will only turn God's favor from us when they come."

"But what if He *has* turned His favor from us?" Parta blathered, and Corada snorted.

"If He has, would His Voice give us Warning?" he demanded, and Parta blinked. "You see? I know it's never happened before, but the Writ says no man can know when the Trial may come. Put your trust in God where it belongs, man!"

"I—" Parta cut himself off and gasped in a breath like a drowning man's, then nodded sharply. "Yes, Corada. Yes. You're right. It's just—"

"Just that it's scared the tripes out of you," Corada grunted, then gave a lopsided grin. "Well, don't think it hasn't done the same for me!"

"Thank you, Corada," Vroxhan said gratefully, making a mental promise never to tease the old man again. "Your faith and courage are an inspiration to us." He swept his bishops' eyes once more, and nodded. "Come, Brothers. Join me in a brief prayer of rededication before we answer the Voice's call."

Vroxhan had never vested in such unseemly haste, but neither had he ever faced a moment like this. For thousands upon thousands of years God had warded His faithful from the demons whose very touch was death to body and soul. Not in recorded history had He allowed the enemies of all life whose vile trickery had cast Man from the starry splendor of God's Heaven to earth to approach so near as to rouse the Voice to Warning, but Vroxhan reminded himself of Corada's words. God had not abandoned His people; the Voice's Warning was proof of that.

He jerked the golden buttons closed, suppressing a habitual stab of annoyance as the tight-fitting collar squeezed his neck. He checked the drape of the dark blue fabric in the wavery reflection of a mirror of polished silver, for it would never do to come before God improperly vested at this of all times. He passed inspection, and he stepped quickly through the door of imperishable metal onto the glassy floor of the Sanctum.

His bishops waited, clad as he in their tight-fitting vestments, as he walked to his place at the center of the huge chamber and felt a wash of familiar awe as the night sky rose above him. The dark sphere of midnight enveloped him, blotting out the polished, trophy-hung walls with the glory of God's own stars, but awe was replaced by dread as he looked up and saw the scarlet sigil of the demons rising slowly in the eastern sky.

The sight chilled his blood, for it burned still and bright, the color of fresh blood and not the pulsing yellow flicker of Fire Test, Plot Test, or System Check. But he squared his shoulders, reminding himself he was God's servant. He marched to the altar, and the inhuman beauty of the Voice's unhurried, inflectionless speech rolled over him, calm and reassuring in its eternal, unchanging majesty.

"Warning," it said in the Holy Tongue, every word sweet and pure as silver, "passive system detection warning. Hostiles approach." The Voice continued, speaking words not even the high priest knew as it invoked God's protection, and he felt a shiver of religious ecstasy. Then it returned to words he recognized, even though he did not fully understand them. "Contact in five-eight-point-three-seven minutes," it said, and fell silent. After a moment it began again, repeating the Warning, and Vroxhan knelt to press his bearded lips reverently to the glowing God Lights of the high altar with a silent prayer that God might overlook his manifest unworthiness for the task which had come to him. Then he rose, and sang the sacred words of benediction.

"Arm systems," he sang, and a brazen clangor rolled through the Sanctum, but this time no one showed fear. This they had heard before, every year of their religious lives, at the Feast of Fire Test. Yet this time was different, for this time its familiar, martial fury summoned them to battle in God's holy cause.

The challenge of God's Horn faded, and the Voice spoke once more.

"Armed," it said sweetly. "Hostiles within engagement parameters."

Amber circles sprang into the starry heavens, entrapping the crimson glare of the demons, ringing it in the adamantine rejection of God's wrath, and Vroxhan felt himself tremble as the ultimate moment of his life rushed to meet him. He was no longer afraid—no longer even abashed, for God had raised him up. He was God's vessel, filled with God's power to meet this time of Trial, and his eyes gleamed with a hundred reflected stars as he turned to his fellows. He raised his arms and watched them draw strength from his own exaltation. Other arms rose, returning his blessing, committing themselves to the power and the glory of God while the demons' red glare washed down over their faces and vestments.

"Be not afraid, my brothers!" Vroxhan cried in a great voice. "The time of Trial is upon us, but trust in God, that your souls may be exalted by His glory and the demons may be confounded, for the power is His forever!"

"Forever!" The answering roar battered him, and there was no fear in it, either. He turned back to the high altar, lifting his eyes defiantly to the demon light, rejecting it and the evil for which it stood, and his powerful, rolling voice rose in the sonorous music of the ancient Canticle of Deliverance.

"Initiate engagement procedure!"

CHAPTER FIFTEEN

"Coming into range of another one," Harriet announced from Plotting as a display sighting ring circled yet another dot. "A big one."

Sean felt—and shared—her stress. They were finally close enough for *Israel*'s scanners to detect subplanetary targets, and the tension had been palpable ever since the first deep-space installation was spotted. There'd been more in the last two hours—lots more—and his hopes had soared with the others'. The first one hadn't been much to look at, only a remote scanner array crippled by what appeared to have been a micrometeorite strike, but the ones deeper in-system were much bigger. In fact, they looked down-right promising, and he kept reminding himself not to let premature opti-mism carry him away.

"I'm on it, Harry," Sandy reported from Tactical. Her active scanners had less reach than Harriet's passive sensors but offered far better resolution once a target had been pointed out to them. "Coming in now. Comp Cent calls it a *Radona*-class yard module, Tam."

"*Radona, Radona*," Tamman muttered, running through his Engineering files. "Aha! I *thought* I remembered! It's a civilian yard, but with the right support base, a *Radona* class could turn out another *Israel* in about eight months, Sean. If we get it on-line, we can build us a hypercom no sweat."

"That," Sean said quietly, "is the best news I've had in the last twenty-one months. People, it looks like we're going to make it after all."

"Yes, I—" Sandy began, then broke off with a gasp. "Sean, that thing's live!"

"*What?*" Sean stared across at her, and she nodded vigorously.

"I'm getting standby level power readings from at least two Khilark Gamma fusion plants—maybe three."

"That's ridiculous," Sean muttered. He twisted back around to glare at the bland light floating in Harriet's sighting ring. "She'd need hydrogen tankers, maintenance services, a resource base . . . She *can't* be live!"

"Try telling that to my scanners! I've definitely got live fusion plants, and if her power's up, we won't even have to activate her!"

"But I still don't see how—"

"Sean," Harriet cut him off, "I'm getting more installations. Look."

Scores of sighting rings blossomed as her instruments came in range of the new targets, and Sean blinked.

"Sandy?"

"I'm working them, Sean." Sandy's voice was absent as she communed with her systems. "Okay, these—" three of Harriet's amber rings turned green "—look like your 'resource base.' They're processing modules, but they're not Battle Fleet designs, either. They might be modified civil facilities." She paused, then continued flatly. "And *they're* live, too."

"This," Sean said to no one in particular, "is getting ridiculous. Not that I'm ungrateful, but—" He shook himself. "What about the others?"

"Can't tell yet. I'm getting some very faint power leakage from them, but not enough for resolution at this range." She closed her eyes and frowned in concentration. "If they're live, it doesn't look like they've got much on-board generation capacity. Either that, or . . ." Her voice trailed off.

"Or what?"

"Those *might* be stasis emissions." She sounded unhappy at suggesting that, and Sean grunted. No stasis field could maintain itself from internal power, and there wasn't enough available from the powered-down plants of the other facilities to sustain that many fields with broadcast power.

"Humph. Goose us back up to point-five cee and take us in, Brashan."

"Coming up to point-five cee, aye," Brashan replied from Maneuvering, and Sean frowned even more thoughtfully. Something about those installations bothered him. They floated in distant orbit around the third planet, not in a ring but in a wide-spaced sphere. There were too many of them—and they were much too small—to be more yard modules, but each was almost a third of *Israel*'s size, so what the devil *were* they?

"Sean!" Harriet's exclamation was sharp. "I've got a new power source—a monster—*and it's on the planet!*"

His head whipped back up as still another sighting ring appeared in the display and the new emission source crept into sight over the planetary horizon. Harry was right; it was huge. But it was also . . . strange, and he frowned as its light code flickered uncertainly.

"Can you localize it?"

"I'm trying. It's— Sean, my scanners say that thing's *moving*. It's almost like . . . like some weird ECM, but I've never seen anything like it."

Sean frowned. That single massive power source was all alone down there, and that made it the most maddening puzzle yet. Obviously the population and tech base which had produced the system installations hadn't survived, or they would have been challenged by now. Besides, if the planet had fusion power, there should be dozens of planetary facilities down there, not just one. But without people, how had even one power plant survived the millennia? And what did Harry mean by "moving"? He plugged into her systems and watched it with her, and damned if she wasn't right. It *was* like some sort of ECM, as if something were trying to prevent them from locking in its coordinates.

"Can you crack whatever it is, Harry?"

"I think so. It's a weird effect, but it looks like . . . Oh, that's sneaky!" Her tone took on a mix of admiration and excitement. "That source isn't as big as we thought, Sean. It *is* big, but there's at least a dozen—probably more like two or three dozen—false emitters down there, and they're jumping back and forth between them. Their generators aren't moving, they're just reshaping the main emission source. I don't know why, but now that I know *what* they're doing it's only a matter of ti—"

"Status change." Sandy's voice was flat with tension. "The satellite power readings are going up like missiles. They're coming on-line, Sean!"

His eyes darted back to the satellites. Those *had* been stasis fields; now they were gone, and whole clusters of new sources were coming up while they watched. Sean chewed his lip, wondering what the hell was going on. But until he knew—

"Bring us about, Brashan. Let's not get in too deep."

"Coming onto reciprocal course, aye," Brashan confirmed, and Sean watched the changing tactical symbols in the display as *Israel* came about.

"I've got a bad feeling about this," he muttered.

"First phase activation complete. All platforms nominal."

Vroxhan listened to the Voice's ancient, musical words as a net of emeralds blazed against the night sky. God's Shields glowed with the color of life, yet he'd never seen so many of them at once, not even at the once-a-decade celebration of High Fire Test. Truly this was the time of Trial, and he licked his lips as he proceeded to the second verse of the Canticle.

"Activate tracking systems," he intoned sonorously.

"Status change!" This time Sandy almost screamed the words. "Target system activation! *Those things are weapons platforms!*"

"Settle down, Sandy!" Sean snapped. "Brashan, take us to point-seven! Evasion pattern Alpha Romeo!"

"Alpha Romeo, aye," Brashan replied with reassuring Narhani calm.

"Target acquisition," the Voice announced. Its singing power filled the Sanctum, and the golden ring about the demons' sigil turned blood-red. Tiny symbols appeared within it—some steady and unwinking, others changing with eye-bewildering flickers. Vroxhan had never seen anything like that; none of the symbols which appeared during Plot Test and Fire Test ever changed, and mingled terror and exaltation filled him as he chanted the third verse.

"Initiate weapon release cycle."

Israel leapt to full speed, and the power of her drive quivered in bone and sinew as Brashan threw her into the evasion pattern. A corner of Sean's thoughts stole a moment to be thankful for all the drills they'd run and another to curse how undermanned they were, but it was only a tiny corner. The rest of his mind had suddenly gone cold, humming with a strange, deep note unlike anything he'd ever experienced in a training exercise, and his thoughts came like a dance of lightning, automatic, almost instinctive.

"Tactical, get the shields up and initiate ECM! Download decoys for launch on my signal but do not engage."

"Shields—up!" Sandy snapped back, her earlier edge of panic displaced by trained reactions. "ECM—active. Decoys prepped and downloaded."

"Acknowledged. Have you localized that power source, Harry?"

"Negative!"

Sean felt himself tightening inwardly as his queerly icy brain raced. Every instinct screamed to open fire to preempt whatever those weapons might do, but even if his assumption that the planetary power source was the command center was right, he couldn't hit it if Harry couldn't localize it. That only left the platforms themselves, and they were such small targets—and there were so many of them—that going after them would be a losing proposition. Perhaps more importantly, they hadn't fired yet. If he initiated hostilities, they most certainly would, and although *Israel* was beyond energy weapon range, maximum range for the Fourth Empire's hyper missiles against a target her size was thirty-eight light-minutes. They were ten light-minutes inside that. At maximum speed, they needed fourteen minutes to clear the planet's missile envelope, and every second the platforms spent thinking about shooting was one priceless second in which they *weren't* shooting.

"Target evading."

Vroxhan's heart faltered as the Voice departed from the Canticle of Deliverance. It had never said those words before, and the symbols inside the bloody circle danced madly. The demon light pulsed and capered, and his faith wavered. But he felt ripples of panic flaring through the bishops and upper-priests. He had to do *something*, and he forced his merely mortal voice to remain firm as he intoned the fourth verse of the Canticle.

"Initiate firing sequence!" he sang, and his soul filled with relief as the Voice returned the proper response.

"Initiating."

"Launch activation! Multiple launch activations!"

Sean paled at Sandy's cry. The platforms had brought their support systems on-line; now their hyper launchers were cycling. They'd need several seconds to wind up to full launch status, but there were *hundreds* of them!

He tasted blood. This was a survey ship's worst nightmare: an intact, active quarantine system. An *Asgerd*-class planetoid would have hesitated to engage this kind of firepower, and he had exactly one parasite battleship.

"Launch decoys!"

"Launching, aye." A brief heartbeat. "First decoy salvo away. Second salvo prepping."

Blue dots speckled the display with false images, each a duplicate of *Israel's* own emissions signature as it streaked away from her.

"Activate missile battery. Designate launch platforms as primary targets but do not engage."

"Missile battery active," Sandy said flatly.

"Hostile decoys deployed," the Voice announced sweetly.

Vroxhan clutched at the altar, and a terrified human voice cried out behind him, for the high priest's portion of the Canticle was done! There *was* no more Canticle! But the Voice was continuing.

"Request Tracking refinement and update," it said, and the High Priest sank to his knees while the demon light spawned again and again. Dozens of demons blazed in the stars, and he didn't know what the Voice wanted of him!

"Initiate firing sequence!" he repeated desperately, and his trained voice was broken-edged and brittle.

"Probability of kill will be degraded without Tracking refinement and update," the Voice replied emotionlessly.

"*Initiate firing sequence!*" Vroxhan screamed. The Voice said nothing for a tiny, terrible eternity, and then—

"Initiating."

"Hostile launch! I say again, hostile launch!"

A deathly silence followed Sandy's flat announcement. The Fourth Empire's hyper missiles traveled at four thousand times the speed of light. It would take them almost seven seconds to cross the light-minutes to the battleship, but there was no such thing as an active defense against a hyper missile, for no one had yet figured out a way to shoot at something in hyper. They could only take it . . . and be glad the range was so long. At seventy percent of light-speed, *Israel* would have moved almost one-and-a-half million kilometers between the time those missiles launched and the time they arrived. But that was why defensive bases had prediction and tracking computers.

Israel had never been intended to face such firepower single-handed, but her defenses had been redesigned and refined by Dahak and BuShips to incorporate features gleaned from the Achuultani and new ideas all their own. Her shields covered more hyper bands, her inner shield was far closer to her hull than the Fourth Empire's technology had allowed, and she had an outer shield, which no earlier generation of Imperial ship had ever boasted.

It was as well she did.

Only a fraction of those missiles were on target, but *Israel* bucked like a mad thing, and Sean almost ripped the arms from his couch as warheads smashed at her and she heaved about him. Damn it! *Damn* it! He'd forgotten to activate his tractor net! The gravity wells of a dozen stars sought to splinter his ship's insignificant mass, and shield generators screamed in her belly.

✧ ✧ ✧

The familiar musical note of Fire Test rang in his ears, and Vroxhan stared up from his knees, eyes desperate, waiting for the demon lights to vanish, praying that they would. He didn't know how long he would have to wait; he never did, even during Fire Test, for no one had ever taught him to read the range notations within the targeting circles.

Then, suddenly, all but one of the demon lights *did* vanish. A great sigh went up from the massed bishops, and Vroxhan joined it. The demons might have spawned, but God had smitten all but one of them! Yet that one remained, and that, too, had never happened during Fire Test.

His terrible fear ebbed just a bit, but only a bit, for yet again the Voice spoke words no high priest had ever heard.

"Decoys destroyed. Engagement proceeding."

A ship of the Fourth Empire would have died. Five of those mighty missiles had popped the hyper bands covered by *Israel*'s outer shield, but they erupted outside her inner shield . . . and it held. Somehow, it held.

"Jesus!" Sean shook his head and activated his couch tractor net as soon as the universe stopped heaving. They couldn't take many more like that!

"Shift to evasion pattern Alpha Mike. Launch fresh decoy salvo."

This time there were no verbal acknowledgments, but they flowed back to him through his feed. He felt his friends' fear, but they were doing their jobs. And they were still alive. He didn't understand that. With this much fire coming at them, they should be dead. But there wasn't time to wonder why they weren't—and no longer any reason not to fight back.

"Engage the enemy!" he snapped.

The first salvo spat from *Israel*'s launchers, and it was odd, but his own fear had disappeared.

"Incoming fire," the Voice said. "Request defense mode."

Vroxhan covered his face, trying to understand while faith, terror, and confusion warred within him. He knew what "request" meant, but he had no idea what a "defense mode" was.

"Urgent," the Voice said. "Defense mode input required."

Israel twisted in agony as the second salvo erupted into normal space about her, and a damage warning snarled. One of those missiles had gotten too close, and armor that would have sneered at a nuclear warhead tore like tissue under the fraction of power that leaked through the inner shield.

But Sean had more time to watch this attack's pattern, and it told him something. Whatever was on the other end of those missiles was fighting dumb, spreading its fire evenly between *Israel* and her decoys, and that was crazy. Any defensive system ought to be able to refine its data enough to eliminate at least a few false images.

He felt Tamman activate his damage control systems, yet a quick check told him nothing vital had gone, and he looked back at the display just as Sandy's first salvo went home.

✧　　　✧　　　✧

Sweat stung Vroxhan's eyes as a dozen of God's emerald Shields vanished from the stars. The demons! The demons had done that!

"Urgent," the Voice repeated. "Defense mode input required."

The high priest racked his brain. Thought had never been required during any of the high ceremonies, only the liturgy. His mind ran desperately over every ritual, seeking the words "defense mode," but he couldn't think of any canticle that used them. Wait! He couldn't think of any that used *both* words, but the Canticle of Maintenance Test used "mode"!

He trembled, wondering if he dared use another canticle's words. What if they were the *wrong* words? What if they turned God's wrath against *him*?

Sean bit down on a yell of triumph. The ground source might be hiding, but the weapon platforms were stark naked! Not even a shield!

"Hit them, Sandy!" he snapped, and *Israel's* next salvo went out even as the third hostile salvo came in.

Vroxhan groaned as another dozen emeralds vanished. That was almost a tenth of them all, and the Demons still lived! If they destroyed all of God's Shields, nothing would stand between them and the world's death!

"Warning." The Voice was as beautiful as ever, yet it seemed to shriek in his brain. "Offensive capability reduced nine-point-six percent. Defense mode input required."

Blood ran into Vroxhan's beard as his teeth broke his lip, but even as he watched the demons were spawning yet again. He had no choice, and he spoke the words from the Canticle of Maintenance Test.

"Cycle autonomous mode selection!" he cried.

He felt the others stare at him in horror, but he made himself stand upright, awaiting the stroke of God's wrath. Silence stretched to the breaking point, and then—

"Autonomous defense mode selection engaged," the Voice said.

"Shit!"

Sean smashed a clenched fist against the arm of his couch. They'd gotten in a third salvo, but the quarantine system had finally noticed they were killing its weapons. Shields popped into existence around the scores of surviving orbital bases, and decoys of their own blinked into life. They were only Fourth Empire technology, nowhere near as good as the improved systems Dahak and BuShips had provided *Israel*, but they were good enough. It would take every missile they could throw to take out even one of them now, yet they had no other target. They still hadn't localized the ground base controlling them and the range was now too great to try.

He started to order Sandy to reprioritize her fire, massing it on single targets, but she was already doing it.

The battleship writhed again, yet the ferocity was less and he felt a surge of hope. Sandy had nailed almost forty bases; maybe she'd thinned them enough they could survive yet!

They'd been engaged for four minutes, and they'd started running a full minute before the enemy opened fire. The range was up to over thirty-one light-minutes, and that would help, too. If they got to at least thirty-five and managed to break lock, they might be able to go into stealth and—

Israel heaved yet again, and another damage signal snarled. Crap! That one had taken out two of Sandy's launchers.

Vroxhan stared at the stars, and hope rose within him. Only one of the Shields had vanished that time. Perhaps none of them might have perished if he'd known what God and the Voice truly demanded, but at least he was still alive and the rate of destruction had slowed. Did that mean God smiled upon him after all? The Writ said man could but do his best—had God granted him the mercy of recognizing his best when he gave it?

Israel sped outward, bobbing and weaving as Sean, Brashan, and the maneuvering computers squirmed through every evasion they could produce, and Harriet abandoned Plotting and plugged into the damage control sub-net to help Tamman fight the battleship's damage. Two more near-misses had savaged her, and her speed was down to .6 *c* from the loss of a drive node, but the incoming fire was less and less accurate. Sandy had picked off thirteen more launch stations, ripping huge holes in the original defensive net, but Sean could see the surviving weapon platforms redeploying, with more coming around from the far side of the planet. Still, Sandy's fire might just have whittled them down enough to make the difference in the face of *Israel*'s ECM.

Even as he thought that, he knew he didn't really believe it.

He rechecked the range. Thirty-four light-minutes. Another seven minutes to the edge of the missile envelope at their reduced speed. Could they last that long?

Another salvo shook the ship. And another. Another. A fresh damage signal burned in his feed. They weren't going to make it out of range before something got through, but they were coming up on thirty-five light-minutes, and each salvo was still spreading its fire to engage their decoys. They hadn't managed to break lock, but if the bad guys' targeting was so bad it couldn't differentiate them from the decoys, they might be able to get into—

Vroxhan watched the demons spawn yet again. They must have an inexhaustible store of eggs, but God smote every one they hatched. A fresh cloud of crimson dots profaned the stars—and then they vanished.

They *all* vanished, and the ring of God's wrath was empty. Empty!

Silence hovered about him and his pulse thundered as the assembled priests held their breath.

"Target destroyed," the Voice said. "Engagement terminated. Repair and replacement procedures initiated. Combat systems standing down."

"They've lost lock," Sandy reported in a soft, shaky voice as *Israel* vanished into stealth mode, and Sean MacIntyre exhaled a huge breath.

He was soaked in sweat, but they were alive. They shouldn't have been.

No ship their size could survive that much firepower, however clumsily applied. Yet *Israel* had. Somehow.

His hands began to tremble. Their stealth mode ECM was better than anything the Fourth Empire had ever had, but to make it work they'd had to cut off all detectable emissions. Which meant Sandy had been forced to cut her own active sensors and shut down both her false-imaging ECM and the outer shield, for it extended well beyond the stealth field. He'd hoped synchronizing with the decoys' destruction would convince the bad guys they'd gotten *Israel*, as well, but if their tracking systems *hadn't* lost lock, they would have been a sitting duck. They wouldn't even have been covered by decoys against the next salvo.

His hands' shakiness spread up his arms as he truly realized what a terrible chance he'd just taken, and not with his own life alone. It had worked, but he hadn't even thought about it. Not really. He'd reacted on gut instinct, and the others had obeyed him, trusting him to get it right.

He made himself breathe slowly and deeply, using his implants to dampen his runaway adrenaline levels, and thought about what he'd done. He made himself stand back and look at the logic of it, and now that he had time to think, maybe it hadn't been such a bad idea. It had worked, hadn't it? But, Jesus, the risk he'd taken!

Maybe, he told himself silently, *Aunt Adrienne's homilies on overly audacious tactics contained a kernel of truth after all.*

CHAPTER SIXTEEN

Stardrift glittered overhead, and a smaller, fiercer star crawled along the battle steel beneath his feet as the robotic welder lit a hellish balefire in Sean MacIntyre's eyes while *Israel* drifted in sepulchral gloom almost a light-hour from the system primary.

His wounded ship lay hidden in an asteroid's ink-black lee while he coaxed the welder through his neural feed. Other robotic henchmen had already cut away the jagged edges of the breach, rebuilt sheared frame members, and tacked down replacement plates of battle steel. Now the massive welding unit crept along, fusing the plates in place. Under other circumstances, damage control could have been left to such a routine task unsupervised, but one of *Israel*'s hits had taken out a third of her Engineering peripherals. Until Tamman and Brashan finished putting them back on-line—*if* they finished—the damage control sub-net remained far from reliable.

"How's it coming?"

He turned his head in the force field globe of his "helmet" as Sandy walked down the curve of the hull towards him.

"Not too bad."

Fatigue harshened his voice, and she studied him as she came closer. A massive, broken pylon towered behind him, shattered by the hit that had demolished the heavily armored drive node it had supported. He stood between stygian blackness and the welder's fire, half his suited body lost in shadow, the other glowing demon-bright, and his face was drawn. It was his turn to wake from nightmares these nights, but he met her eyes squarely.

"You're doing better than I expected," she said after a moment.

"Yeah. We'll have this breach finished by the end of the watch."

"The end of which watch, dummy?" she teased gently. "You're supposed to be in the sack right now."

"Really?" He sounded genuinely surprised, and she didn't know whether to laugh or cry at his tired, bemused expression as he checked the time. "I'll be damned. Is that why you came out here? To get me?"

536

"Yep. A MacMahan always gets her man—and in this instance, my man better get his ass inside before he goes to sleep on his big, flat feet."

"I do believe," he stretched, "you have a point, Midshipwoman MacMahan. But what about junior?" He waved at the welder.

"It's only got fifty meters to go, Sean. You can trust it that far on its internal programming. And if you come along and let her tuck you in, Aunt Sandy promises she'll come back out and check on it in about an hour. Deal?"

"Deal," he sighed. The two of them turned away, disappearing over the rise of the battleship's flank, and the lonely star of the welder crawled on behind them, blazing like a lost soul in the depths of endless night.

Even Brashan looked drawn, and the humans were downright haggard, but three weeks of exhausting labor had repaired everything they could repair.

"Okay, people," Sean called the meeting to order. "It doesn't seem to me that going on to our next stop is a real good idea. Anybody disagree?"

Wry, weary grins and headshakes answered him. The G6 star of their second-choice destination was twelve and a half light-years away from their present position. At barely half the speed of light—the best *Israel* could sustain with a primary drive node shot away—the voyage would take seventy-five months, even if it would be "only" five and a half years long for them.

"Good. I'd hate to make a trip that long and then not find anything at the other end. Especially since we *know* there's an active shipyard here."

"Cogently put," Brashan agreed with one of his curled-lip grins. "Of course, there remains the small problem of gaining control of that shipyard."

"True," Sean lay back in his couch and stared up into the display, "but maybe that's not as tough as it looks. For instance, we know the power for the platform stasis fields is beamed up from that ground source, so that's probably the HQ site. If so, taking it over should give us control of the platforms, too. Failing that, taking it out should shut them down, right?"

"I agree that seems a logical conclusion, but how do you intend to penetrate its orbital defenses to get at it?"

"Sleight of hand, Brashan. We'll fool the suckers."

"Oh, dear. This sounds like something I'm not going to like."

Sean smiled and the others chuckled as Brashan fanned his crest in a Narhani expression of abject misery.

"It won't be that bad—I hope." Sean turned to Sandy and his sister. "Did your analysis reach the same conclusion I did?"

"Pretty much," Sandy said after a glance at Harriet. "We agree they detected us on passive, at least. We didn't pick up any active systems till their launcher fire control came up."

"And their tactics?"

"That's a lot more speculative, Sean, and one point still worries us," Harriet replied. "Your theory sounds logical, but it's *only* a theory."

"I know, but look at it. Much as it pains me to admit it, that much firepower should have swatted us like a fly, however brilliant my tactics were. Whatever runs those defenses was slow, Harry. Slow and clumsy."

"Okay, but how do you explain its *defensive* tactics? Slow's one thing, but it let us take out thirty-six platforms before the others even began to defend themselves."

"So it's slow, clumsy, and *dumb*," Tamman said with a shrug.

"You're missing the point, Tam." Sandy came to Harriet's aid. "Properly designed automated defenses shouldn't have let us take any of them out unopposed, but anything dumb enough to let us zap any of them that way should have let us take them *all* out. Besides, how many other intact quarantine systems have we seen? None. That means this thing's original programming wasn't just good enough to control its weapons—it's run enough deep-space industry to keep the whole system functional for forty-five thousand years, as well."

She paused to let that sink in, and Tamman nodded. Harriet's stealthed sensor remotes, operating from a circumspect forty light-minutes, had given them proof of that. The *Radona*-class yard was no longer on standby; it was rebuilding the weapon platforms Sandy had destroyed.

"Another thing," she continued. "Those platforms' passive defenses are mighty efficient by Empire standards, and that razzle-dazzle trick by the ground source is pretty cute, too. It's not standard military hardware, but it works. Maybe its designer was a civilian, but if so he was a sneaky one— not exactly the sort to give anything away to an enemy. And if a sharp cookie like whoever set this all up built in defensive systems at all, why arrange things so they didn't come on-line until after our *third* salvo?"

"So what do you think happened?" Tamman countered.

"We don't know; that's what worries us. It's almost like there was something else in the command loop—something that really was slow, clumsy, and stupid. If there is, it probably saved our lives this time, but it may also surprise us, especially if we make any wrong assumptions."

"Fair enough," Sean said. "But given how long it waited to bring its weapons on-line, whatever it is must be pretty myopic, right?"

"There we have to agree with you," Harriet replied wryly. "But it's what you're planning on *after* we arrive that scares us, not the approach."

"Whoa! Hold on." Tamman straightened in the engineer's couch. "What approach? You been holding out on me and Brashan, Captain, Sir?"

"Not really. It's only that you both've been so buried in Engineering you missed the discussion."

"Well we're not buried *now*, so why don't you just fill us in?"

"It's not complicated. We came in fat and happy last time, radiating as much energy as a small star; this time we'll be a meteorite."

"I *knew* I wouldn't like it," Brashan sighed, and Sean grinned.

"You're just sore you didn't think of it first. Look, it let us get within twenty-eight light-minutes before it even began bringing its systems on-line, right?" Tamman and Brashan nodded. "Okay, why'd it do that? Why didn't it start bringing them up as soon as we entered missile range? After all, it couldn't know *we* wouldn't shoot as soon as we had the range."

"You're saying it didn't pick us up until then," Brashan said.

"Exactly. And that gives us a rough idea how far out its passive sensors were able to detect us. Sandy and Harry ran a computer model assuming it had picked us up at forty light-minutes—a half hour of flight time before it powered up. Even at that, the model says our stealth field should hide the drive to within a light-minute if we hold its power well down. That means we can sneak in close before we shut down everything and turn into a meteor."

"Seems to me you've still got a little problem there." Tamman sounded doubtful. "First of all, if I'd designed the system, it wouldn't let a rock *Israel's* size hit the planet in the first place. I'd've set it to blow the sucker apart way short of atmosphere. Second, we can't land, or even maneuver into orbit, without the drive, and we'll be way inside a light-minute by that point. It's going to spot us as a ship at that range, stealth field or no."

"Oh, no it won't." Sean smiled his best Cheshire Cat smile. "In answer to your first point, you should have made time to read that paper I wrote for Commander Keltwyn last semester. Our survey teams have looked at the wreckage of over forty planetary defense systems by now, and every single one of them required human authorization to engage anything without an active emissions signature. Remember, over half these things were set up by civilians, not the Fleet, and the central computers were a hell of a lot stupider than Dahak. The designers wanted to be damned sure their systems didn't accidentally kill anything *they* didn't want killed, and none of the system's we've so far examined would have engaged a meteor, however big, without specific authorization."

"So? The whole point is that we *will* have an active signature when we bring the drive up."

"Sure, but not where it can see us long enough to matter. We come in under power to *two* light-minutes, then reduce to about twenty thousand KPS, cut the drive, and coast clear to the planet."

"Jesus Christ!" Tamman yelped. "You're going to hit atmosphere in a *battleship* at twenty thousand kilometers per second?"

"Why not? I've modeled it, and the hull should stand it now that we've got the holes patched. We come in at a slant, take advantage of atmospheric braking down to about twenty thousand meters, then pop the drive."

"You're out of your teeny-tiny mind!"

"What's the matter, think the drive can't hack it?"

"Sean, even with one node shot out, my drive can take us from zip to point-six cee in eleven seconds. Sure, if we program the maneuver right and leave it all on auto we've got the oomph to land in one piece. But we're gonna be one hell of a high-speed event when we hit air, and the drive'll create an awful visible energy pulse when you kill that kind of velocity that quick. There's no way—no way!—a stealth field will hide either of those!"

"Ah, but by the time the drive kicks in, we'll be inside atmosphere. I doubt whoever set this up programmed it to kill air-breathing targets!"

"Um." Tamman looked suddenly thoughtful, but Brashan regarded his captain dubiously.

"Isn't that a rather risky assumption—particularly if, as Harry and Sandy argue, there's an unpredictable element to the control system?"

"Not really." Harriet sounded a bit as if she were agreeing with Sean despite herself. "This is a quarantine system. It's probably programmed to wax people trying to escape after the bio-weapon hit as well as anyone coming from outside, but Sean's right. Every one we've seen before has required human authorization to engage anything that wasn't obviously a spacecraft. It shouldn't care a thing about meteors, and it's almost certainly not set to shoot before a target leaves atmosphere. Even if it is, you're forgetting reaction time. It'll take at least two minutes just to spin down the stasis fields on its platforms. There won't be enough time for it to see us and activate its weapons between the time the drive cuts in and we cut power, go back into stealth, and land."

"I suppose that's true enough. But what do we do once we're down?"

"That's where Sandy and I part company with our fearless leader. He wants to put down on top of the power source and take it over. Which sounds good, unless it's got on-site defenses. We won't be able to tell ahead of time—we can't use active sensors without warning it we're coming—but if it *does* have site-defense weapons, they may be permanently live. If they are, they'll get us before we can even go active and sort out the situation."

"We could just waste the whole site from space," Tamman suggested. "Coming in that slow, Harry should have plenty of time to localize it on passive. We could pop off a homing sublight missile from a few light-seconds out. And, as you say, even if it spotted the launch, it wouldn't have time to react before the bad news got there."

"We could, and it's something to bear in mind," Sean agreed, "but I'd rather take the place over intact. We can't use active scanners from stealth, but we *can* carry out visual observations once we come out of stealth. That's a huge power plant, and there must be some reason the automatics kept it running after everybody died. Let's take a peek and see if it's something we can generate any additional support from before we zap it. I'd rather not kill any golden egg-laying geese if I can help it."

"A point," Tamman conceded. "Definitely a point."

"Which brings us back to Sandy's and my objection," Harriet pointed out. "If we don't want to take the place out from space, then we shouldn't be landing on top of it, either. Not when we don't know whether the site's armed or what that 'something else' in the command loop is."

"I believe the girls are correct, Sean," Brashan said. "I confess your plan seems less reckless than I assumed, but they're still right, and there's no need to charge in precipitously."

"Tam? You agree with them?"

"Yes," Tamman said positively, and Sean shrugged.

"All right, I can be big about these things. What say we plan our insertion to set us down over the curve of the planet from the site?"

High Priest Vroxhan sat in his gilded throne and surveyed the worshipers with studied calm, trying to assess their mood.

Mother Church had been shaken to her foundations, but by God's blessing the Trial had been upon them and then past so quickly few outside the Inner Circle had known a thing about it till it was over. The word had spread on talmahk wings after that, and the people were abuzz with the story—which, he was certain, had grown more terrible with each telling—but they'd managed to suppress all mention of the Voice's unknown words and his own desperate improvisation. Vroxhan wasn't certain that was necessary, but he *was* certain it would be far wiser for the Inner Circle to sort it out themselves before they risked the faith of others by revealing all the facts.

Yet however unorthodox events might have been, the outcome was clear: the Trial had come, and the demons had been smitten as the Writ promised. Thousands of years of faith had been vindicated, and that was what this solemn festival of thanksgiving and the priestly conclave to follow were all about.

The last human soul entered the packed courtyard of the Sanctum, and he raised one hand in blessing from his throne as the choir sang the majestic opening notes of the Gloria.

The last four hours had been frustrating.

Israel had crept in at the paltry velocity of .2 *c*, wrapped in the stealth field that turned her into a black nothingness. Her passive systems had peered ahead, poised on a hair-trigger to warn of any active detection systems, but she'd been blind to anything but fairly powerful energy sources, and curiosity was killing her crew.

Harriet had, indeed, localized the power source to within fifty kilometers, which was ample for warheads of the power they carried, but Sean longed to examine the planet directly. Unfortunately, *Israel*'s optical systems, pitiful compared to active fold-space scanners at the best of times, were degraded by the stealth field which protected her. They could have used the drive to impart a higher initial velocity and coasted the whole way without a stealth field, but they could neither have maneuvered nor slowed for atmospheric insertion without going into stealth. Sean had no idea how the defenses would react to an "asteroid" that popped in and out of detectability, and he didn't want to find out; he was taking a big enough chance by coming this close before he dropped stealth in the first place. More importantly, he wanted to be able to turn and creep away if he saw any sign of changing power levels on the orbital bases. It was always possible the defenses might pick up something without being able to localize *Israel* and shoot, and if he'd come in any faster the drive settings needed to kill the ship's velocity might have burned through the stealth field and given them a target.

But they were coming up on the two-light-minute mark, and he lay tense in his command couch as their speed fell still further. Tamman and Brashan coordinated their departments carefully, reducing drive power and velocity in tandem, and Sean grunted his satisfaction as the drive died at last. Right on the mark, he noted: exactly 20,000 KPS. The internal gravity was still up, but *Israel* no longer had any emission signature at all.

"Good, guys," he murmured, then glanced at Sandy. "Take the stealth field down."

"Coming down now," she replied tautly, and Sean watched through a cross feed as she powered down their cloak of invisibility with the same exquisite care Tamman had taken.

The entire crew held its collective breath as Harriet consulted her passive systems very, very carefully. Then she relaxed.

"Looks good, Sean." Her voice was hushed, as if she feared the defenses might hear. "The platform stasis fields're steady as a rock."

Her crewmates' breath hissed out, and Sandy looked up with a grin.

"We're *heeeere*," she crooned, and the others laughed out loud.

"Of course we are." Sean grinned back at her, elated by his ploy's success. "But we're just a great big rock." He glanced smugly at Tamman. "Looks like the defenses *are* programmed to kill only ships, and without emissions, we ain't a ship."

"I hate it when he's right," Sandy told the others. "Fortunately, it doesn't happen often."

That was good for another chuckle, and the last of the hovering tension faded as Sean waved a fist in her direction. Then he sat up briskly.

"All right. Bring up the optics and see what we can see, Harry."

"Bringing them up now," his sister said, and the blue and white sphere of the planet swelled, displacing the starfield from the display as she engaged the forward optical head. They were almost thirty-six million kilometers away, but surface features leapt into startling clarity.

Sean stared eagerly at seas and rivers, the rumpled lines of mountain ranges, green swathes of forest. Theirs were the first human (or Narhani) eyes to behold that planet in forty-five thousand years, and it was lovely beyond belief. None of them had dared hope to see this living, breathing beauty at the end of their weary voyage, but incredible as it seemed, the planet lived. Here in the midst of the Fourth Empire's self-wrought devastation, it *lived*.

His eyes devoured it, and then he stiffened.

"Hey! What the—?"

"Look! *Look!*"

"My God, there's—!"

"Jesus, is that—?!"

An incredulous babble filled the command deck as all of them saw it at once. Harriet didn't need any instructions; she was already zooming in on the impossible sight. The holo of the planet vanished, replaced by a full-power closeup of one tiny part of its surface, and the confusion of voices died as they stared at the seaport city in silence.

"There's no question, is there?" Sean murmured.

"Damn." Tamman shook his head. "I wouldn't have believed it if I hadn't seen it. Hell, I'm still not sure I *am* seeing it!"

"You're seeing it," Sandy told him quietly. "And maybe it's a good thing we didn't just zap the control center after all."

"No question," Tamman agreed, and *Israel*'s crew shared a shudder at the thought of what they might have unleashed against a populated world.

"But I don't understand it," Brashan mused. "Life, yes—there's life on Birhat, so it has to be theoretically possible. But people? *Humans?*" His crest waved in perplexity and a double-thumbed hand rubbed his long snout.

"There's only one answer," Sean said. "This time quarantine worked."

"It seems impossible," Harriet sighed. "Wonderful, but impossible."

"You got that right." Sean frowned at the large, fortified town they were currently watching. "But this only raises more questions, doesn't it? Like what happened to their tech base? Their defenses are still operable, and the HQ is down there, so how come they're all running around like that?"

He waved at the image, where animal-drawn plows turned soil in a patchwork of fields. The small, low buildings looked well-enough made, but they were built of wood and stone, and many were roofed in thatch. Yet the eroded stumps of an ancient city of the Fourth Empire lay barely thirty kilometers from the town's crenulated walls.

"It *doesn't* make much sense, does it?" Sandy replied.

"You can say that again. How in hell can someone decivilize in the midst of that much technology? Just from the ruins we've already plotted, this planet had millions of people. You'd think poking around in the wreckage, let alone having at least one still operating high-tech enclave in their midst, would get the current population started on science. But even if it hasn't, where did the *original* techies go?"

"Some kind of home-grown plague?" Tamman suggested.

"Unlikely." Brashan shook his head in the human expression of negation. "Their medical science should have been able to handle anything short of the bio-weapon itself."

"How about a war?" Sandy offered. "It's been a *long* time, guys. They could have bombed themselves out."

"I suppose so, but then why aren't more of those towers flattened?" Sean objected. "Imperial warheads shouldn't have left *anything*."

"Not necessarily." Harriet watched the display, toying with a lock of her hair. "Oh, you're right about gravitonics, but suppose they used small nukes or dusted each other? Or whipped up their *own* bio-weapons?"

"I suppose that's possible, but it still doesn't explain why they never rebuilt. Maybe they lost their original tech base—I can't see how, with that ground station still up, but let's concede the possibility. But we're still looking at a city-building culture spread over at least two continents. It looks to me like they've got about as many people as a pre-tech agrarian economy can support—more than I would have expected, in fact; their agriculture must be more efficient than it looks. But given that kind of population base, why haven't they developed their own indigenous technology?"

"Good point," Tamman agreed, "and I wish I could answer it, but I can't. It's like they've got some kind of technological blind spot."

"Yeah, but then they go and put their biggest city right on top of where we figure the defensive HQ has to be." Sean shook his head in disgust. "It's right in the middle of their largest land mass, and there's not a river within fifty kilometers. With the transportation systems we've seen, that's a hell of an unlikely place for a city to grow up naturally. Look at the canal system they've built. There's over two hundred klicks of it, all to move stuff into the city. There has to be *some* reason for its location, and I can only think of one magnet. Except, of course, that that particular magnet doesn't make any sense on a planet that doesn't know about technology!"

"Well," Sandy sighed, "I guess there's only one way to find out."

"Guess so." Sean's calm tone fooled none of his friends. Then he grinned. "And whatever the reason, Mom and Dad are going to be mighty glad to hear we've found another planet that's not only habitable but stuffed full of people as well!"

The sublight battleship *Israel* split atmosphere in a long, shallow descent that wrapped her in a shroud of fire. Her crew rode their couches, feeling their ship quiver with the fury of her descent as her bow plating began to glow. Heat sensors soared as the thick battle steel armor burned cherry-red, then yellow, then white. The terrible glow crept back along her hull, the air blazed before her as she battered a column of superheated atmosphere out of her path, and Sean MacIntyre monitored his instruments and tried to stay calm.

The maneuvering computers waited patiently to engage their carefully written program and stop them dead in the bellow of the drive's fury. It was going to be a rough ride, but so far everything was nominal, and they'd already picked out an alpine valley hiding place fifteen hundred kilometers from the planet's largest city. It was going to be fine, he told himself for the thousandth time, and grinned mirthlessly at his own insistence.

High Priest Vroxhan stood on his balcony and watched the night sky burn. His servants had summoned him almost hysterically, and he'd charged out in only his under-robe to see the terrible strand of fire with his own eyes. Now he did see it, and it touched him with ice.

Shooting stars he had seen before, and wondered why the work of God's Hands should abandon the glorious firmament for the surface of the world to which the demons' treachery had banished man, but never had he seen one so huge. No one had, and he watched it blaze above The Temple like the very Finger of God and trembled.

Could it be—?

No! God's Wrath had slain the demons, and he suppressed the blasphemous thought quickly. But not quickly enough. He'd thought it, and if *he* had, how much more might the ignorant of his flock think the same thing?

He inhaled sharply as the beautiful, terrifying light vanished beyond the western peaks. Would it land? If so, where? Far beyond the borders of Aris— probably even beyond those of Malagor. In Cherist, then? Or Showmah?

He shook himself and turned away, hurrying back into the warmth of his apartments from the chill spring night. It couldn't be the demons, he told himself firmly, and if not they, then it must, indeed, be God's handiwork, as all the world was. He nodded with fresh assurance. No doubt God had sent it as a sign and reminder of His deliverance, and he must see the truth was spread before the less faith-filled panicked.

He closed the balcony door and beckoned to a servant. His messages must be ready for the semaphore tower by first light.

CHAPTER SEVENTEEN

Colin MacIntyre paused outside the larger state dining room to watch three harassed humans and a dozen robots sorting the countless bags of old-fashioned mail into paper breastworks. No one noticed him in the doorway, and as he resumed his journey towards the balcony, he made a note to divert still more human staff to reading the letters while he tried to sort out his own feelings.

Those bags, and the hundreds which had preceded them in the past few days, proved that whatever outrages the Sword of God might wreak and however well-hidden their true enemy might be, his subjects cared. Those letters weren't just formal, official nothings from heads of state. They came from people all over the Fifth Imperium, expressing their joy—and relief—that their Empress was pregnant.

Yet his own joy, as 'Tanni's, was bittersweet. Over two years had passed, but the aching void remained. Perhaps the new children (for the doctors had already confirmed it would be twins once more) would fill that emptiness. He hoped so. But he also hoped he and 'Tanni could resist the need to *make* them fill it. Sean and Harriet had been special. No one could replace them, and their new children deserved the right to be special in their own ways, not compared, however lovingly, to ghosts.

The decision to have them hadn't been easy. It was fraught with grief, a guilty sense of betraying Sean and Harriet in some indefinable way, and fear of fresh loss. His and 'Tanni's enhancement would give them centuries of fertility, and the temptation to wait was great. Yet they faced the dilemma of all dynasts: the succession must be secured.

That wasn't something Lieutenant Commander MacIntyre, USN, had ever worried about, and it hadn't entered his or 'Tanni's head when Sean and Harriet were conceived, for it had seemed preposterous that the monarchical government of a long-dead empire might be maintained. But as Tsien Tao-ling had pointed out twenty years past, it was loyalty to the Crown—to Colin MacIntyre's person—which held humanity together despite its legacy of rivalries, and many years must pass before that primal source of loyalty could be buttressed by others. Colin had been amazed that someone who had been the commander-in-chief of the last Communist power on Earth could make that statement, but Tao-ling had been right. And because he had, Colin and Jiltanith had no option but to think in dynastic terms.

And perhaps, he mused, as he stepped out onto the balcony and saw his wife dozing in the summer sunlight, that was good. If their hands had been forced, the decision had still proved there was a future . . . and that they had the courage to love again after love had hurt them so cruelly.

He smiled and crossed to Jiltanith, bending over her under Bia's drowsy warmth, and kissed her gently.

"I'm afraid you're right, Dahak." Ninhursag scratched her nose and nodded. "We've put every senior officer under a microscope—hell, we're down to *lieutenants*—and the only bad apples we've found are deceased, so it looks like we've closed off Mister X's penetration there."

"I must confess I had anticipated neither that his penetration might be so limited," Dahak replied, "nor that he would dispose of his minions so summarily."

"Ummmm." Ninhursag leaned back and crossed her legs as she contemplated their findings. Dahak was an enormous asset for any security officer. The computer might not yet have developed the ability to "play a hunch," but he'd achieved total penetration of Bia's datanets, and he was a devastatingly thorough and acute analyst. He and Ninhursag had started with a top-down threat analysis of every officer outside Colin's inner circle, then used Dahak's access to every database in Bia to test their analyses. Where necessary, ONI agents had added on-the-ground investigation to Dahak's efforts, usually without even realizing what they were doing or why. By now, the computer could tell Admiral MacMahan where every Fleet and Marine officer in the Bia System had been at any given minute in the last fifteen years. Of course, he didn't have anything like that degree of penetration in the Sol System. Not even the hypercom was capable of real-timing data at that range, and Earth's datanets were still far more decentralized than Birhat's. But even with those limitations, his access to the military's every order and report had allowed him to clear most of Sol's senior officers, as well.

"Apparently Mister X takes the adage about dead men telling no tales to heart," Ninhursag observed now.

"True. Yet eliminating his agents, however much it may contribute to his security, also deprives him of their future services. That would seem somewhat premature of him—unless he has acquired all the access his plans, whatever they may be, require."

"Yeah." Ninhursag frowned at that unpalatable thought. "Of course, he may have been a bit too smart for his own good. We know about him now, and knowing he doesn't have a military conduit frees us up a lot."

"Yet by the same token, it deprives us of potential access into his own network. We have exhausted all leads available to us, Ninhursag."

"Yeah," she sighed again. "Damn. How I *wish* I knew what he was after! Just sitting here waiting for him to take another shot doesn't appeal to me at all. He's got too good a track record."

"Agreed." Dahak paused, then spoke rather carefully, even for him. "It has occurred to me, however, that our concentration on the military, while logical, may have had the unfortunate consequence of narrowing our vision."

"How so?"

"We have proceeded on the assumption that he himself was of or closely connected to the military, or that the military was in some wise essential to his objectives. If such is not, indeed, the case, may we not have devoted insufficient attention to other areas of vulnerability?"

"That's an endemic security concern, Dahak. We have to start someplace where we can establish a 'clear zone,' and we've got one now—physically, as well as in an investigative sense. We can be fairly confident the entire Bia System is clear, now, so we can assume Colin and 'Tanni are safe from direct physical attack, and knowing the military is clear—now—gives us the resources to mount a counteroffensive of our own. But if Mister X *is* a civilian—even one in government service somewhere—our chance of finding him's a lot lower."

Dahak made a soft electronic sound of agreement. Entry level positions for civilian politicians and bureaucrats were subject to less intensive background scrutinies, and civilian careers seldom included the periodic security checks military men and women took for granted. When it came to civilians, he and Ninhursag lacked anything remotely approaching Battle Fleet's central databases, and their ability to vet suspects was enormously reduced.

"Even worse," the admiral said after a moment, "Mister X knows what he's after, and that gives him the initiative. Until we figure out what he wants, we can't even predict what he's likely to do. Every security chief in history's worried about what he may have overlooked."

"Granted. I only raise the point because I feel it is important that we maintain our guard against all contingencies to the best of our ability."

"Point taken. And that's precisely why I see more reason than ever to keep this on a need-to-know basis. Especially since we *don't* know who in the civil service might have been suborned. Or who's vulnerable in the same way Vincente Cruz was."

"A wise precaution. But may this not create problems when your ONI agents begin operations on Earth? They will inevitably be seen as interlopers, and the decision not to inform even the highest levels of the civilian security forces as to why their presence is necessary will exacerbate that perception. Indeed, it may even lead to a certain degree of institutional obstructionism in what humans call 'turf wars.'"

"If there *are* any turf wars, I guarantee they'll be short. Ultimate responsibility for the Imperium's security rests right here, in my office. ONI's the senior service, and if anybody thinks different, I'll just have to show him the error of his ways, won't I?"

Admiral MacMahan's smile was cold. Which suited Dahak very well indeed.

❖   ❖   ❖

Lawrence Jefferson's pleasant expression masked a most unpleasant mood as he and Horus walked together to the Shepard Center mat-trans. Alert bodyguards watched over the Governor, and knowing his own actions had made them inevitable was irritating. Yet he'd had no choice. He'd known having Gus van Gelder killed would almost have to shake the Imperium's leadership into a fundamental reassessment of its security needs, but it had been essential to unmask Gus' mole. And, having done so, the only man who knew he'd had access to those briefing notes had to be removed, as well.

He rather regretted the deaths of Erika, Hans, and Jochaim van Gelder. Gus, of course, would have had to go eventually, but it had offended Jefferson's innate tidiness to eliminate him so messily. On the other hand, his early removal had worked out far better than Jefferson had dared plan for. A successful conspirator didn't base long-term strategy on a gift from the gods which made him the person charged with catching himself, but that didn't make him ungrateful when it was given. And if Horus' security was better now, it still wasn't impenetrable . . . particularly against his own security chief.

No, Jefferson's true unhappiness had less to do with defenses which couldn't, in the end, really matter than with the news from Birhat. The last thing he needed was for the imperial family to produce another heir! He'd already been forced to dispose of one pair, and now he might have to do the whole job over again—especially since Jiltanith had already announced her intention to visit her father on Earth for the birth. Which, he thought disgustedly, was precisely the sort of thing she *would* do just when he needed her and Colin in the same, neat crosshairs on Birhat.

Of course, he reminded himself as he and Horus stepped up onto the mat-trans platform, pregnancy wasn't something whose timing even Imperial bioscience could predict with absolute accuracy. But if the doctors were right, Jiltanith would not give birth, after all, for she—and her unborn children—would die two weeks before she did.

The Planetary Duke of Terra grinned as he and his lieutenant governor entered the conference room. Hector MacMahan—still grim, but no longer an ice-encased stranger—had brought Tinker Bell, and Brashieel had brought his own Narkhana, one of her genetically altered pups.

Horus watched Narkhana collapse as Tinker Bell leapt upon him and wrestled him to the floor. He rolled on the rug, thrusting back at her with all four feet while their happy growls mingled. For a dog well into her third decade, Tinker Bell was remarkably spry, thanks to her own limited biotechnics, yet she had no conception of the tremendous strength Narkhana was reining in to let her win, nor of just how far her son's intellect surpassed her own. Even if she'd been able to conceptualize such things, she would never have known, for her children would never tell her, and there was something both hilarious and poignant in watching them revert to utter doggishness in her presence.

Hector looked up and saw the late arrivals, and a whistle brought Tinker Bell instantly to his side. She flopped down at his feet, panting cheerfully as she prepared to put up with another of the incomprehensible human things her person did. Horus raised a sardonic eyebrow at his grandson, and Hector looked back with a bland innocence he'd forgotten how to assume for far too many months. For all her boisterousness, Tinker Bell was well behaved when Hector chose to remind her to be.

"Horus, Lawrence. Glad you could make it," Colin said, standing to shake hands. Horus squeezed back, then opened his arms to his daughter's embrace and slid into the chair beside Jefferson's.

"Now that you're here," Colin went on, "let me introduce someone very special. Horus, you've already met, but it's been a while since you've seen her. Gentlemen, this is Eve."

Horus inclined his head to the slender being on the pad beside Brashieel's. She was much more delicate than Brashieel, and several centimeters shorter, but her crest was magnificent. Brashieel's, like that of all male Narhani, was the same gray-green as the rest of his hide; Eve's was half again as large, proportionally, and shot with glorious color. Now that crest fanned in a graceful expression that conveyed greeting and thanks for his courtesy with an edge of embarrassment at the fuss being made over her, and it was hard for him to remember she wasn't quite seven years old.

Jefferson bowed in turn, and Brashieel preened with pride beside her. The Narhani were a hierarchical race, and there'd never been much doubt the first Narhani female would become the bride of the first Narhani nest lord, but it was clear that more than duty and mutual expectation flourished between these two. Horus was glad for them—and not just because Eve represented the culmination of his dead daughter's greatest project.

"We've got several things on today's agenda," Colin announced, "but first things first. Horus, 'Tanni and I want you to make sure the Earth-side news channels are ready for our broadcast."

"In truth." Jiltanith's smile was almost as lovely as of old. Not quite, but it was getting there, and the knowledge that she was to be a mother again showed. " 'Twas kindness greater than e'er any mother, be she sovereign lady or no, might expect of so many to wish her unborn babes so well, Father. 'Twill heal our souls to tell them all how greatly their letters have helped to heal our hearts."

"That," Horus said, "will be my very great pleasure."

"Thank you," Colin said warmly, then grinned. "I know the Council's got to talk about all those little niggling things like taxes, budgets, and engineering projects, but first there's something really important. Eve?"

"Of course, Your Majesty." Eve's vocoder had been set to produce a female human voice, and Horus felt a familiar stinging sensation in his eyes when he heard it. At Eve's own request, the voice was Isis Tudor's. It was her way of honoring her human "mother's" memory, and he'd once been afraid it would hurt to hear it. But there was no pain. Only pride.

The adolescent Narhani woman reached into her belt pouch and withdrew a half-dozen holo plates. She laid one before her with a slender, six-fingered hand, adjusting it with nervous precision, then looked up at the humans seated around the table.

"As you know," she said with a formality at odds with her youth, "the Nest of Narhan plans to commemorate the Siege of Earth with a gift to our human friends. We do this for many reasons, including our nest's desire to express sorrow for the deaths we caused and thanks for all humanity has given us when we might have expected only destruction. Memorials, such as your own Memorial at Shepard Center, are important to us, as well, and it is our hope that this will be the beginning of an Imperial Memorial. One in which our nest shares and which will be completed when the Nest of Aku'Ultan has also been freed."

She paused, obviously relieved to have completed her formal statement without errors, and Brashieel's crest rose even higher in pride.

"Our gift," she said more naturally, "is now finished."

She pressed a button, and a soft gasp went up as a light sculpture appeared above the plate. It wasn't in the abstract style human artists were currently enamored of; it was representational, a reproduction of another sculpture worked in finest marble . . . and it was magnificent.

A rearing Narhani rose high on his rear hooves to fight the bonds which held him captive. The cruel, galling collar about his neck drew blood as he pitted his frenzied strength against its massive chain, and the humans who looked upon him knew Narhani expressions well enough to read the despair in his eyes and flattened crest, but his teeth were bared in snarling defiance. He was without hope yet unconquered, and the anguish of his captivity wrenched at them.

Yet he was not alone. Broken chains flailed from his wrists, the exquisitely detailed links shorn by some sharp edge, and a human knelt beside him, torso naked but clothed from the waist down in the uniform of the Imperial Marines. His face was drawn with fatigue, but his eyes were as fierce as the prisoner's, and he held a chisel in one hand, its honed sharpness hard against the iron ring which held the Narhani pent, while the other raised a hammer high to bring it smashing down.

The detail was superb, the anatomy perfect, the two species' very different expressions captured with haunting fidelity. Sweat beaded the human's bare skin, and each drop of Narhani blood was so real the viewer held his breath, watching for it to fall. They were trapped forever in the stone—human and Narhani, fleshed in marble by a master's hand—and for all their alienness, they were one.

"My God," Colin whispered into the silence. "It's . . . it's— I don't have the words, Brashieel. I just . . ." His voice trailed off, and Brashieel lowered his own crest.

"What you see in it is only truth, Colin," he said softly. "My people are not so gifted with words as yours; we put our truths in other things. But while this lasts—" he gestured at the light-born statue before them "—we of the Nest of Narhan will never forget what humans have given us. We came against you thinking you nest-killers, but you taught us who the true nest-killer is and, when you might have slain us, gave us life. You gave us more than life." His hand stoked Eve's crest gently. "But most of all, you gave us truth, and so we return that truth to you. To all your people, but especially to you, for you are our nest lord now."

"I—" Colin blushed as he had not in years, then looked up and met Brashieel's eyes squarely. "Thank you. I will never receive anything more beautiful . . . or that I will treasure more."

"Then we are content, High Nest Lord."

Lawrence Jefferson gazed raptly at the statue through the buzz of admiration which followed, and not even his reverence was completely feigned. He cleared his throat when the first rush of conversation slowed.

"Brashieel, may I—" He paused, then shrugged slightly. "I hesitate to ask it, but may I have a holo of this for a place of honor in my office?"

"Of course. We have brought several copies for our friends, although we hope they will not be made public before the formal gifting."

"May I display it if I promise to hide it from any newsies?"

"We would be honored."

The Lieutenant Governor of Earth was almost as carefully protected as her Governor. Whenever he was in residence, security troops, unobtrusive but alert, prowled the grounds of the Kentucky estate the Jeffersons had owned for generations. But none of those protectors knew of the secret measures which let him elude their guardianship at need.

Lawrence Jefferson stepped from the concealed tunnel exit eight kilometers from his home. Once it had served the Underground Railroad, but it had been refurbished and extended in more recent years when Senator Jefferson had been recruited by Anu's chief operations officer. Not even Kirinal's most trusted subordinates had known of its existence, but Jefferson had labored upon it under her direction, incorporating certain unobtrusive elements of Imperial technology to make it undetectable. At the time, those measures had been aimed at Horus and the scanners of the hidden battleship *Nergal*, yet they'd proved equally efficacious against those of a planetoid named *Dahak*.

A flyer waited in a carefully dilapidated old barn, and Jefferson climbed aboard and set the holo plate almost lovingly on the empty seat beside him. He'd managed to obtain copies of the preliminary study, but he'd never expected to receive the exact image of the finished sculpture, and his smile was unpleasant as he activated the drive and, even for him, highly illegal stealth field and lifted quietly into the night.

It wasn't a long trip, though reason told him he shouldn't be making it, but he wanted to make this delivery in person, and the risk was slight. Yet even had it been greater, he would have made this flight himself. There were times when the elaborate deception of his life palled upon him, when he wanted—needed—to be about his work himself. He built his strategies like a chess master, but there was a gambler within him, as well, one who sometimes felt the need to throw the dice from his own hand.

He landed outside a shed-like structure and keyed a complicated admittance code through his neural feed. There was a moment of hesitation, and then its door slid open. Imperial machinery stood silent in the bright overhead lights as he walked to stand beside the heroically scaled sculpture that machinery had wrought in exact duplicate of the sketches he'd provided.

A stoop-shouldered man turned to greet him. His artist's eye told him he had never seen his employer's undisguised face, and he was glad, for he believed that made him safe. He didn't know he, too, would be eliminated anyway when his task was done. Lawrence Jefferson took no chances.

"Good evening," the stoop-shouldered man said. "No one told me you were coming in person, sir."

"I know. But I've brought you a gift." Jefferson set the holo plate on a work table and pressed the button.

"Magnificent," the man breathed. He looked back and forth between the sculpture and his own handiwork. "I see a few details will need changing. I must say, sir, that this is even more spectacular than the sketches indicated."

"I quite agree," Jefferson said sincerely. "Will there be any schedule problems?"

"No, no. It's only a matter of arranging the input and then letting the sculpting unit do its job."

"Excellent. In that case, I'd like you to go ahead and input it now; I need to take this with me when I leave."

"Of course. If you'll excuse me?"

The stoop-shouldered man bent over his equipment, and Jefferson stood back, hands folded behind him while he admired the work his doomed henchman had already produced. It looked just like real marble, and so it should, given how much it was costing.

Perfect, he thought. *It was perfect.* And no one who looked at it would ever guess the secret it concealed, for the gravitonic warhead and its arming circuits were quite, quite invisible.

CHAPTER EIGHTEEN

Israel's captain was in a grumpy mood.

It wasn't anyone's fault, but *Israel*'s crew were bright, competent, confident . . . and young. And, as bright, confident people are wont to do, they'd underestimated their task—which made their lack of progress enormously irritating. Still, Sean told himself with determined cheer, for people who'd found out they were approaching a populated world only in the last half hour of their flight they weren't doing all that badly. And Sandy *had* said she and Harry had some good news for a change.

He lay back in the captain's couch, studying the image from one of the stealthed remotes. They'd decided to rely on old-fashioned, line-of-sight radio, something an Imperial scan system probably wouldn't even think to look for, rather than more readily detected fold coms to operate their remotes. That limited their operating radius, but it gave them enough reach for a fair sampling, and Sean watched a kneeling row of villagers weed their way across a field of some sort of tuber and wondered how whatever they were tending tasted.

He glanced up as Tamman arrived, completing their gathering, then turned his gaze to Sandy. She and Harriet relied heavily on Brashan's hard-headed pragmatism to shoot down their wilder hypotheses and upon Tamman to build and maintain their surveillance systems, but the major burden of analysis was theirs, and Sean was delighted to leave them to it.

"Okay, Sandy," he said now. "You've got the floor."

She rubbed the tip of her nose for a moment, then cleared her throat.

"Let's start with the good news: we finally have a language program of sorts." Sean sat up straighter, and she smiled. "As I say, that's the good news. The bad news is that without a proper philologist, we've had to fall back on a 'trial and error' approach, with predictably crude results.

"It helps that they're literate and use movable type, but it would've helped more if the old alphabet had survived. Out of forty-one characters, we've found three that *might* be derived from Universal; the rest look like somebody tried to transcribe Old Norse into cuneiform. Working at night, we've managed to scan several printed books through our remotes, but they didn't do us much good until about six weeks ago when Harry found *this*."

The display changed to a recorded view looking down from some high vantage point on a circle of children. A bearded man in a robe of blue and gold stood at its center, holding up a picture of one of the native's odd, bipedal saddle beasts to point at a line of jagged-edged characters beneath it.

"This," Sandy resumed after a moment, "is a class in one of those temples of theirs. Apparently the Church believes in universal literacy, and Tam built a teeny-tiny remote for Harry to land on top of a beam so we could eavesdrop. It was maddening for the first month or so, but we set up a value substitution program in the linguistics section of *Israel*'s comp cent, and things started coming together early last week."

Sean nodded, glad something had finally worked as he'd hoped it might. English was the common tongue of the Imperium and seemed likely to remain so. Its flexibility, concision, and adaptability were certainly vastly preferable to Universal! Age had ossified the language of the Fourth Imperium and Empire, and, given the availability of younger, more versatile Terran languages, the Fifth Imperium had no particular desire to speak it.

Yet all Fourth Empire computers spoke only Universal, at least until they could be reprogrammed. Worse, in some cases—like Mother's hardwired constitutional functions—they *couldn't* be reprogrammed, so all Battle Fleet personnel had to speak Universal whether they wanted to or not.

Cohanna's Bio-Sciences Ministry had met that need with a dedicated implant, and with the enormous "piggy-back" storage molycircs made possible, Battle Fleet had decided to give its personnel all major Terran languages. That made sense in view of their diversity—and also meant each of *Israel*'s crewmen had a built-in "translating" software package. True, none of the languages in their implants' memories were quite *this* foreign, but if *Israel*'s computers could cobble up a local dictionary . . .

"As I say, it's still patchy, but we ought to be able to make a stab at understanding what someone says. It's going to be another matter if we try to talk back, though. So far Harry and I have identified seven distinct dialects and what may be one minor language, and there's no way we could mingle with the locals without a lot more work."

"How much more?" Tamman asked.

"I can't say, Tam—not for certain—but I'd estimate another month of input. At the moment, we can read about forty percent of the printed material we collect, and the percentage is expanding, but that's a far cry from understanding the spoken language, much less conversing coherently. And we need more than simple coherency, unless we want to scare the natives to death."

"Umph." Sean frowned at the frozen image of the teacher. He'd hoped for better, but even while he'd hoped, he'd known it was unreasonable.

"In the meantime, one of our 'borrowed' books—an atlas—has given us a running start on figuring out the geopolitics of the planet, which, by the way, the natives call 'Pardal.' We can't find the name in any of *Israel*'s admittedly limited records, so I suspect it's locally evolved.

"As near as we can tell, this is what Pardal currently looks like." The display changed to a map of Pardal's five continents and numerous island chains. The biggest inhabited continent reminded Sean of an old-fashioned, air-foil aircraft, flying northeast towards the polar ice cap with a second, smaller land mass providing its tail assembly. "We made enough photomaps on the way in to know the atlas maps aren't perfectly scaled, and we still can't read all of its commentary, but it appears Pardal is split into hundreds of feudal territories." Scarlet boundary lines flashed as she spoke. "At the moment, we're located just inside the eastern border of this one, which is called, as nearly as I can translate it, the Kingdom of Cherist.

"Now, North Hylar—" she indicated the fuselage and wings of the "aircraft" "—seems to be the wealthiest and most heavily populated land mass. The 'countries' are larger and seem to contain more internal subdivisions, which suggests they may be older. It looks to us like there's been a longer period of absorption and consolidation here, and that conclusion may be supported by the fact that our ground site is, indeed, underneath North Hylar's largest city." A red cursor flashed approximately dead center in North Hylar.

"South Hylar, connected to North Hylar by this isthmus down here, is less densely populated, probably because it doesn't have much in the way of rivers—aside from this one big one out of the southern mountains—but that's a guess. As you can see, the other two populated continents, Herdaana and Ishar, are located across a fairly wide body of water—the Seldan Sea—to the west of the Hylars. These other two continents to the east are uninhabited. As far as we can tell, the Pardalians don't even realize they exist, and from the aerial maps, they seem to have less human-compatible vegetation. Looks like they were never terraformed—which, in turn, suggests they never *were* inhabited, even before the bio-weapon.

"Of the settled continents, both Hylars are extremely mountainous, and Ishar's on the desert side. Herdaana's much flatter and seems to be the bread basket of Pardal, and a lot of the territories in Herdaana and Ishar alike have Hylaran names prefixed by 'gyhar,' or 'new,' which probably means they were colonized—or conquered—by North Hylar. It may or may not imply a continuing relationship between those territories and their 'mother countries' back home. Some evidence suggests that; other evidence, particularly the small size and apparent competition between the Herdaana states, suggests otherwise, but we simply can't read the atlas well enough to know, and the entire continent's out of range of our remotes."

She paused, brow wrinkled in frustration, then shrugged.

"All right, that's the political structure, but there's a catch, because despite all these nominally independent feudal states, the entire planet seems to be one huge theocracy. That surprised us, given Pardal's primitive technology. I'd have thought simple communication delays would do in any planet-wide institution, but that was before we figured out what *this* is."

The display changed to a tall, gantry-like structure with two massive, pivoted arms, and she shook her head almost admiringly.

"That, gentlemen, is a semaphore tower. They've got chains of them across most of the planet. Not all; they'd need ships to reach Herdaana and Ishar, and given the mountains on the isthmus, they probably send over-water couriers to South Hylar, too. It's a daylight-only system, but it still means they can send messages a *whole* lot faster than we'd suspected."

"Ingenious," Sean murmured.

"Exactly. Obviously we're still guessing, but it looks like the Church deliberately keeps political power decentralized, and control of the communications net would give them a heck of a tactical edge. I'd say they push it to the max; when the Church says jump, it's a good bet the local prince only asks how high. In addition to the semaphore towers, every town—and most of the villages—in range of our remotes contains at least one Church complex. Some larger towns have dozens, and they do a *lot* of business. Our reading class is only a tiny part of it.

"More to the point, our power-source city is where the semaphore chains converge—the Pardalian equivalent of the Vatican. In fact, the entire city is simply called 'The Temple,' and as far as we can tell, it's ruled by the high priest as both secular and temporal lord. Interestingly enough, the title of said high priest appears to be *eurokat a'demostano.*" Sean looked up sharply, and she nodded. "Even allowing for several millennia of erosion, that sounds too much like *eurokath adthad diamostanu* to be a coincidence."

" 'Port Admiral,' " Sean translated softly, frowning at the city's light dot. "You think the Church is tied directly to the quarantine system?"

"Probably," Harriet answered for Sandy. "The Temple's site certainly suggests it, especially given this 'port admiral' priestly title. And if they have, in fact, preserved any access to the computer running the system, it'd have to be purely vocal; there can't be anyone out there with neural feeds. If they're running it on some sort of rote basis, that might explain why the system seemed so slow and clumsy when it attacked us; they literally didn't know what they were doing. On the other hand, if they *do* have voice access, think what it might mean for a religion. It'd be like the very voice of God."

"Which might help explain the Church's authority," Sean mused aloud.

"Exactly," Sandy said, "though we've turned up a few suggestions that the Church's current *political* power is a relatively recent innovation. And it might also explain how they could have contact with high-tech without realizing it *was* technology. It isn't a machine; it's 'God.' "

"Which," Tamman observed sourly, "doesn't help us out at all, Sean. Not in terms of getting hold of the computer, I mean. If it's their holy of holies, access is going to be limited, I'd think—unless we want to shoot our way into neural feed range, anyway."

"We're a long way from crossing that bridge yet, Tam. Anyway, I'd prefer to do a personal recon on the ground before we make any plans."

"Perhaps," Brashan said, "but I fear you'll have a problem there." He changed the display image to a closeup from one of their approach opticals. "Observe a typical citizen of the Temple."

"Oy vey!" Sean sighed, and Sandy laughed at his disgusted tone. The image was far from clear, but the individual in it was perhaps a hundred and fifty centimeters tall, red-haired and blue-eyed—the complete antithesis of any of *Israel*'s human crew.

"Indeed," Brashan replied. "Obviously, I could never pass as anything other than an alien, but I fear the same is true of all of you in the Temple."

"Not necessarily," Sandy said, and Sean brightened as the image changed again. This time the man standing before him had dark hair. His eyes were brown, not the black of the old Imperial Race—or of Sean or Harriet, for that matter—but the newcomer stood just over a hundred seventy centimeters, far short of Sean's own towering height but getting closer.

"This," Sandy continued, "is a citizen of something called the Princedom of Malagor. It's one of the bigger national units—a bit larger, in fact, than the Kingdom of Aris, which contains the Temple—and it's just over the Cherist border from us. We've been watching it through our remotes, and I'd say the Malagorans are an independent sort. Malagor's very mountainous, even for North Hylar, and these seem to be typical, stiff-necked mountaineers, without a lot of nobles. Their hereditary ruler's limited to the title of 'prince,' and I'd guess there's a lot of local government, but that doesn't make them stay-at-homes. There's an historical maps section in our atlas, and there've been *lots* of battles in the Duchy of Keldark, which lies between Malagor and Aris. It looks like Malagor and Aris were probably political rivals and Aris came out on top because of the Temple."

"Not so good," Sean muttered. "If there's a tradition of hostility, trying to pass as Malagorans wouldn't exactly get us a red carpet in Aris."

"Perhaps not," Brashan said, "but consider: the Temple is the center of a *world* religion."

"Oho! Pilgrims!"

"Maybe, but let's not get carried away, Sean," Sandy cautioned. "Remember all of this is still guesswork."

"Understood. Can you bring your map back up?"

Sandy obliged, and Sean frowned as he stared at it. *Israel* lay hidden in the spine of the westernmost of North Hylar's major mountain ranges, while Aris lay to the east of an even higher range. Malagor occupied a rough, tumbled plateau between the two before they merged to form the craggy spine of the isthmus into South Hylar.

"I wish we had a line of sight to run remotes into the Temple," he muttered.

"Perhaps," Brashan replied. "On the other hand, our position puts the mountains between us and any surveillance systems the Temple might boast."

"True, true." Sean shook himself. "All right, Sandy. It looks to me like you guys are doing good. I'm impressed. But—"

"But what've we done for you lately?" She smiled, and he grinned back.

"More or less. We need to refine your data a lot before we poke our noses out. Would it help if we took a stealthed cutter over closer to the Temple and ran some additional remotes in on it?"

"Maybe." Sandy considered, then shook her head. "Nope, not yet. We're already pulling in more data than we can integrate, and I'd rather not risk running afoul of any on-site detection systems until we know more."

"Makes sense to me," Sean agreed. "That about it for now, then?"

"I'm afraid so. We've spotted a Church library in one of the towns just west of here, and Tam and I are going to run in a couple of remotes tonight. Harry and I may be able to develop something out of that."

Father Stomald kilted his blue robe above his knees and waded out into the icy holding pond to examine the new waterwheel. Folmak Folmakson, the millwright, fidgeted while he waited, and Stomald frowned. A priest must be eternally vigilant this close to the Valley of the Damned, especially with the Trial so recently past and the strange shooting star to remind him of his duties. At moments like this he was unhappily aware of his own youth, but, he reminded himself, a man need not be aged to hear God in his heart.

He sloshed up onto the bank of the millrace and peered down at the wheel. To be sure, it *did* look odd. Stomald had never heard of a wheel driven by water which fell from above rather than turning submerged paddles, but he could see several advantages. For one thing, it required much less water, and that meant it could run for far more of the year in drier regions. Lack of rain was seldom a problem in Malagor, but the new design's efficiency meant more wheels could be run with the same water supply even here.

He frowned again, listening to the creak of the wheel while he applied the Test. It was a particularly important task here, for Malagor's artisans had always been notoriously restive under Mother Church's injunctions, even since the Schismatic Wars. Indeed, he sometimes suspected they'd grown still more so since then . . . and he knew many of them still harbored dreams of Malagoran independence. Within the last six five-days alone, he'd heard no less than four people whistling the forbidden tune to "Malagor the Free," and he was deeply concerned over how he ought to respond to it. Yet he was relieved to note that this wheel, at least, didn't seem to violate any of the Tenets. It was powered by water and required the creation of no new tools or processes. It might be suspiciously innovative, but Stomald could see no demonic influence. It was still a water wheel, and those had been in use forever.

He banished his frown and replaced it with a properly meditative expression as he splashed back towards his anxious audience. He could, he decided, pronounce on this without bothering Bishop Frenaur, and that was a distinct relief. Like most senior prelates, the bishop was unhappy at being called away from the Temple for anything other than his twice-a-year pastoral visitation. Stomald didn't like to think how he might react if some village underpriest, especially a native-born Malagoran, suggested a special conclave was required, and the fact that Folmak hadn't introduced a single new technique gave him an out.

Which, Stomald thought a bit guiltily, might be fortunate in more ways than one. The new catechism suggested Mother Church was entering one of her more dogmatic periods, and some of the Inquisition's recent actions boded ill for Stomald's stubborn countrymen. Bishop Frenaur just might have felt compelled to make an example of Folmak.

He stepped out of the water, trying to hide an unpriestly shiver, and

Folmak shifted from foot to foot, almost wringing his hands. The millwright was twice Stomald's age and more, and it struck the priest—not for the first time—how absurd it was for someone older than his own father to look at him so appealingly. He scolded himself—again, not for the first time—for the thought. Folmak wasn't looking to Stomald Gerakson for guidance; he was looking to Father Stomald of Cragsend, and Father Stomald spoke not from the authority of his own years but with that of Mother Church Herself.

"Very well, Folmak, I've looked at it," the young priest said. He paused, unable to resist the ignoble desire to cloak his pronouncement in mystery a moment longer, then smiled. "As far as I can tell, your contraption satisfies all the Tenets. If you'll walk to the vicarage with me, I'll fill out the Attestation right now."

A huge grin transfigured the millwright's bearded face. Stomald permitted himself to grin back, then clapped Folmak on one brawny shoulder, and the unsullied joy of serving his flock made him look even younger.

"In fact," he chuckled, "I believe I've a small cask of Sister Yurid's winter ale left, and it strikes me that this might be an appropriate moment to broach it. Don't you think so?"

This time Sandy's eyes actually sparkled. Harriet seemed almost as excited, and Sandy started talking even before the others were all seated.

"People," she said, "we still haven't figured out how Pardal lost its tech base in the first place, but at least we know now why it hasn't built another one! We spent several hours in the Church library night before last, reading the books into memory through the remotes. We didn't have time to do any content scans then, but it turns out one of our finds is a book on Church doctrine and a couple of others are Church histories. For whatever reason, the Church has anathematized technology."

"Wait a minute," Sean said. "I considered that, but it doesn't hold up. Not for forty-five thousand years, anyway."

"Why not?"

"Just think about it for a minute. Let's say that at some point in the past—some pretty long ago point, judging from what's left of the Imperial ruins—the Church *did* proscribe technology. I can think of a few scenarios which might lead to that, like Harry's original suggestion that they dusted themselves out or whipped up a bio-weapon all their own. Either of those could have killed off most of the techies, and I suppose the destruction could have created an anti-technical revulsion that resulted in a 'religious' anti-tech stance. Certainly *something* caused them to lose their original alphabet, their original language, science—all of it—and that sounds more like systematic suppression than simple damage to the tech base.

"But having done that, the Church wouldn't even know what technology *was* by the time it got a few thousand years down the road. How could they prevent it from reemerging in a homegrown variety? Without some term of reference to know what constituted 'high tech,' how could they recognize it to snuff it when it turned up again?"

"Fair enough," Sandy agreed, "but you don't have the full picture. First, they *didn't* completely lose Universal. We thought they had, but that was before we hit the Church documents. They're written in something called the 'Holy Tongue,' using an alphabet restricted to the priesthood, and for all intents and purposes the Holy Tongue is a corrupted version of Universal.

"Second, the Church is definitely connected to the quarantine system. There are several references in here to 'the Voice of God'; in fact, their whole liturgical year is set up around what has to be the quarantine system's central computer—there are festivals called 'Fire Test,' 'Plot Test,' 'High Fire Test,' and the like. There are also references to something called 'Holy Servitors' that I'd guess are maintenance mechs from the shipyard, since they appear mysteriously to tend the inner shrine. There's no sign these people understand what's really going on, but they seem to recognize that the system's purpose is to protect their world from contamination, though they've turned it into a religious matter. The Voice is part of God's plan to protect them from demons, and it not only 'proves' God's existence but their own rectitude. If they weren't doing what God wants, His Voice would tell them so, right?

"Third, way back whenever, the Church set up a definition of what constitutes acceptable technology. In essence, Pardalians are forbidden anything but muscle, wind, or water power, so they don't have to know what high tech is; they've set up preconditions which preclude its existence.

"There's more to it than that—there's a whole, complicated evaluating procedure called the Test of Mother Church. Bear in mind that we're talking about something written in this debased version of Universal rather than the vulgar tongue, so we can make lots more sense of it. Apparently the Test consists of applying a number of Tenets which consider whether or not any new development violates the power restrictions or requires new tools, new procedures, or new knowledge. If it does, it's right out."

"Hold it." It was Tamman's turn to object. "These people have gunpowder, and that doesn't rely on muscles, wind, or water!"

"No," Harriet agreed, "but *Earth* certainly had gunpowder before it got beyond waterwheels and windmills, and the Church occasionally—*very* occasionally—grants dispensations through a system of special Conclaves. It takes a long time to work through, but it means advances aren't entirely impossible. We've found several dispensations scattered over the last six hundred local years—almost a thousand Terran years—and most of them seem to be fairly pragmatic things like kitchen-sink chemistry and pretty darn empirical medicine and agriculture. We're still groping in the dark, but it *looks* like there've been some 'progressive' periods—which, unfortunately, seem to provoke backlash periods of extreme conservatism. The key thing, though, is that the Church is continually on the lookout to suppress anything that even looks like the scientific method, and without that there's no systematic basis for technological innovation."

"And people put up with it?" Tamman shook his head. "I find that hard to accept."

"That's because of your own cultural baggage," Sandy said. "You come from a technical society and you accept technology as good, or at least inevitable; these people have the opposite orientation. And remember that the Church *knows* God is on its side; they have proof of it several times a year when the Voice speaks. Not only that," her excited voice turned grimmer, "but their version of the Inquisition has some pretty grisly punishments for anybody who dares to fool around with forbidden knowledge."

"Inquisition?" Sean looked up. "I don't like the sound of that."

"Me neither," Harriet said. "I had to stop after the first little bit, but Sandy and Brashan waded through the whole ghastly thing." She shuddered. "Even the little I read is going to give me nightmares for a week."

"Me, too," Sandy murmured. Her bright eyes were briefly haunted, and she brooded down at the deck for a long, silent moment. Then she shook herself. "Like a lot of intolerant religions, their Inquisition stacks the deck. First, they're only doing it to 'save souls,' including that of the 'heretic' in question, and they've picked up on the theory of the mortification of the flesh to 'expiate' sins. That means they're actually *helping* the people they murder. Worse, they're never wrong. Their religious law enshrines the use of torture during questioning, which means the accused always confess, even knowing how they'll be put to death, and—" she looked up and met Sean's gaze "—the actual executions are even worse. *Pour décourager les autres,* I suppose."

"Brrrr." Sean's lips twisted in revulsion. "I suppose any 'church' that packs that kind of whammy probably *could* keep the peasants in line."

"Especially with the advantage of a whole secret language. They can promote universal literacy in the vulgar tongue and still have most of the advantages of a priestly monopoly on education. And they've got a pretty big carrot to go with their stick. The Church collects a tithe—looks like somewhere around twelve percent—from every soul on the planet. A lot of that loot gets used to build temples, commission religious art, and so forth, but a big chunk is loaned out to secular rulers at something like thirty percent, and another goes into charitable works. You see? They've got their creditor nobles on a string, and the poor look to them for relief when times get bad. Sean, they've got this planet sewed up three ways to Sunday!"

"Damn. And they're the ones sitting on top of the quarantine ground station!" Sean shook his head in disgust.

"They sure are," Harriet sighed.

"Yes, they are," Sandy agreed, "but remember that we're still putting the whole picture together. We've just filled in a big piece, and discovering this 'Holy Tongue' gives us a Rosetta Stone of sorts for the vulgar languages, as well, but there's a lot we haven't even begun on. For instance, there's something called 'The Valley of the Damned' that sounds interesting to me."

"'Valley of the Damned'?" Sean repeated. "What sort of valley?"

"We don't know yet, but it's utterly proscribed. There may be other, similar sites, but this is the only one we've found so far. It's up in the mountains of northern Malagor, outside the reach of our remotes. Anyone who goes in is eternally damned for consorting with demons. If they come back out again, they have to be ritualistically—and hideously—killed. It looks to me like the preliminaries probably take at least a couple of days, and then they burn the poor bastards alive," she finished grimly.

"It sounds," Sean mused, "like whatever's in there must represent a mighty serious threat to the Church's neat little social structure. Or *they* think it does, anyway." He frowned, and then his eyes began to gleam. "Just where, exactly, did you say this valley is?"

CHAPTER NINETEEN

Sean snaked around the feet of the towering summits at a cautious four hundred KPH. His sluggish speed had made the journey long and dragging, but it was the best he could manage, for the cutter's terrain-following systems were down. That forced him to fly hands-on, which was a pain. But few things were harder to spot than a stealthed cutter with no active emissions and flying low, slow, and nape-of-the-earth through mountains, and until they *knew* the quarantine system wouldn't swat atmospheric targets, anything that might draw its attention was right out.

Inconsequential thoughts flickered as he concentrated on his flying. All the unoccupied seats in the twenty-man cutter made *Israel*'s human crewmen uncomfortably aware of just how alone—and how far from home—they were, yet it was even worse for Brashan. They had to leave someone aboard the battleship at all times, and his nonhuman appearance made him the obvious choice. He'd taken it better than Sean could have, especially since they'd agreed to forego any com signals that might be detected. Not only was Brashan barred from sharing their exploration trip, he couldn't even know what they'd found until they got back to tell him!

The cramped valley narrowed further, and he dumped another fifty KPH. It was nerve-wracking to fly solely by Mark One Eyeball (well, Mark Two or Three, given his enhancement) through the inevitable distortion of its stealth field, and he swore softly as they came up on an acute bend.

"The Force, Sean," Sandy whispered in his ear. "Use the Force!"

"Jerk!" he snorted, but there was an edge of laughter in his retort and tense muscles loosened back up a bit. He spared her a brief smile, then returned his attention to his console as their valley joined another. He checked his nav systems and headed up the new gorge with a small surge of excitement. It was even narrower and twistier, but they were getting close enough that this one might take them all the way in.

He made another forty kilometers, then cursed again—less softly—as the valley ended in a steep cliff. He halted the cutter and lifted it vertically, hugging the rock wall. The dim light of Pardal's small moon washed scrubby trees and bare rock as tumbled mountains fell away on every side, and Harriet sucked in a sharp breath beside him as they topped out.

"I'm getting something on passive!" Sean went into an instant hover, and his sister closed her eyes, communing with her sensors, then scowled. "I can't resolve it, Sean, but it's coming from just beyond that next mountain."

Sean banked the cutter, angling down and around the side of the next peak, and she opened her eyes.

"Now I've lost it entirely!" she groused.

"Good," he said. "If it's line-of-sight, it can't see us, either. And for your information, sister mine, our objective is 'just beyond that next mountain,' if you and Sandy have it plotted right, so it sounds like we're going to find *something* when we get there!"

Tamman grinned at him, but Sandy plugged her own feed into Harriet's console to study her recorded scanner readings.

"Not much, is it, Harry?"

"No." Harriet turned her own attention back to the data. "I make it at least six distinct point sources, though."

"Yeah. But did you notice the one at about oh-two-one?"

"Hm?" Harriet frowned, then nodded. "Lots stronger than the others, isn't it? And there's something about it . . . Damn. I *wish* I had a link to *Israel*'s computers! It reminds me of something, but I can't think what."

"Me neither. Tam?"

Tamman glanced at the emissions through his own feed and shrugged. "Beats me. Most of those look like power leakages, not detection systems, but the biggie *is* something else." He tapped his teeth. "Hmm. . . . You know, that just might be an orbital power feed. Look there—see the smaller source tucked in to the east? That looks like a leak from a big-assed bank of capacitors, and the big one's definitely some sort of transmission. How about a ground beacon for an orbital broadcast power system?"

"Could be," Sandy mused. "Hard to believe it could still be up after all this time, but you're right about it's being a transmission, and it'd sure explain why it's so much more powerful than the others—not to mention how there could still be power for *any* active installations. But if it really is a receptor, that means the Valley of the Damned has an active link to at least one power satellite. Even if it's only a passive solar job, you'd think the quarantine system would spot the transmission."

"So?" Tamman countered. "If you and Harry are right, the Temple's running the system by rote, so what could they do about it? For that matter, why should they even understand what their 'Voice' was talking about?"

"Yeah." Harriet twisted hair around a finger and glanced at her twin. "I think Tam's right, Sean. Either way, the transmission's just a steady tone, not a detection system. I don't see anything that looks like one, either, but I'd rather not take the cutter much closer or give away any more scan image than we have to until we're certain of that."

"You and me both. What d'you think about that for a landing site?" He pointed to a wide ledge. It was at least thirty meters across, covered in the local equivalent of grass and brush, but a visible depression had been worn through the vegetation. "That looks like some sort of game trail, and it's headed just about the right way."

"How far out are we?" Tamman asked.

"'Bout thirty klicks, straight-line. Don't know how far by foot."

"Suits me," Tamman agreed, and Harriet and Sandy nodded.

Sean slid closer, studying the ledge. A swell of rock broke the grass close beside the game trail, promising no hidden surprises for his landing legs, and he set the cutter down. He held the drive until the gear stabilized, then cut power but left the stealth field up.

"End of the line." He tried unsuccessfully to keep the excitement out of his voice. "Let's get our gear."

He rose from his couch and opened the weapons locker while Sandy and Harriet slipped into the shoulder harnesses of a pair of scanpacks. He strapped on a gun belt and grav gun and handed matching weapons to the others. The Malagoran mountains were home to at least two nasty predators—a sort of bear-sized cross between a wolf and a wolverine called a "seldahk," and a vaguely feline carnivore called a "kinokha"—both of whom had bellicose and territorial personalities. None of them felt like walking around unarmed, and Sean wished privately that *Israel's* equipment list had offered something a bit tougher than their uniforms. The synthetic fabric the Fleet used for its uniforms was incredibly rugged by pre-Imperial Terran standards. He had no doubt it would resist even a kinokha's claws, but it wasn't going to stop a seldahk's jaws, nor would it stop bullets. Of course, it was unlikely, to put it lightly, that they'd meet any armed natives this close to the Valley of the Damned in the middle of the night, yet kevlar underwear would have been very reassuring. Unfortunately, neither Battle Fleet nor the Imperial Marines issued such items, which he supposed made sense, given that nothing short of battle armor could hope to resist Imperial weaponry.

He grinned at his own thoughts as he and Tamman clipped extra magazines to their belts and shrugged into knapsacks heavy with spikes, pitons, ropes, and assorted mountaineering gear Sean hoped they weren't going to need. Then he eased his pack straps more comfortably, opened the hatch, and led the way out into the night.

The game trail helped, but it was far from straight, and many of its slopes were almost vertical. Tamman took the lead while Sean brought up the rear. The formation freed Harriet and Sandy to focus on their scanpacks (which had far more reach than implant sensors), without worrying about anything they might meet, and the four of them moved at a pace which would have reduced any unenhanced human to gasping exhaustion in minutes.

The moon was still high when Harriet threw up a hand and beckoned them all to a halt. Sean closed up from behind as the other three clustered to wait for him, and his eyes brightened as he looked down at last into the valley they'd come so far to find.

It was bigger than he'd expected—at least twenty kilometers across at its widest point and winding deep into the mountains. A sharp bend fifteen kilometers to the north blocked their vision, and the shallow, rushing river down its length gleamed dull pewter under the moon. He adjusted his eyes to telescopic vision and felt a shiver of excitement. The shapes clumped on either bank of the river at mid-valley were half-buried in drifted ages of soil, but they were too regular and vertical to be natural.

"I'm getting those same readings." Harriet swung the hand-held array of her passive backpack unit slowly from side to side and frowned. "There's a batch of new ones, too. They're lots weaker and more spread out; that's probably why we didn't spot them before."

Sandy turned, directing her own attention down-valley, and nodded.

"You're right, Harry. Most of what we saw before seems to be clustered in those ruins, but I'm getting a line of weak point sources about ten klicks to the south. Looks like they run clear across the valley."

"Yeah." Harriet shaded her eyes with her free hand as if it could help her see farther. "And there's another line just like it up there where the valley curls back to the west. I'm not too sure I like that. I can't lock in well enough to prove it, but they *could* be passive sensors, and those're logical places to put some sort of defensive system."

"Good point," Sandy agreed.

"Um." Sean moved a few meters south, peering in the direction of Sandy's find, but not even enhanced eyes could pick out any details. The valley floor was too heavily covered in scrub trees and tall alpine grasses, and moonlight and shadow did funny things to depth perception even in low-light mode. He pinched his nose in thought, then turned back to the others.

"Anything right in front of us?" he asked, pointing down the steep-sloped valley wall, and his sister shook her head.

"Not on this side, but that big one's just about opposite us. And I'm getting something else from it now. Do you have it, Sandy?"

"No, I—oh. That's funny." She made painstaking adjustments. "The darn thing isn't steady, almost like it's got some sort of intermittent short." It was her turn to frown. "See how the beacon power level fluctuates just a bit in time with it? Think it's some kind of control system?"

"If it is, it looks kind of senile. Then again, from the state of the ruins this whole place must've been abandoned thousands of years ago." Harriet tinkered with her own scanpack, then shrugged. "Let's spread out a little and see if we can triangulate on it, Sandy. I'd feel better if I at least knew exactly where whatever-it-is is."

"Suits me." The two of them separated and took very careful bearings, and Sandy nodded and pointed across the valley.

"Okay, I see it . . . sort of," she said, and Sean stood behind her and followed the line of her finger until he saw the more solid patch of shadows. He couldn't make out much in light-gathering mode, but when he switched to infrared things popped into better resolution. Not a lot better, but better. The ruins were built out from a bare stone precipice and whatever they were made of had different thermal properties from the cliff. Small trees sprouted from a thick roof of collected dirt, but the vertical walls were clear.

"Any better ideas about that intermittent source now that you know where it is?" he asked, but Sandy shook her head. He glanced at Harriet and sighed as he got a shrug of equal mystification. "That's what I was afraid of. Well, whatever else this is, it's clearly the leftovers of some Imperial site, and I'm not too surprised it's in such lousy shape. In fact, if I'm surprised at all it's that *anything's* live down there. But it looks like we have to go on down if we want any more to go on. Any objections?"

There were none, though Harriet looked a bit dubious, and he nodded.

"Okay, but we'll play this as smart as we can. Let's rope up, Tam, and since you're the closest we've got to a Marine, you take point. Sandy, you stay up here and play lookout till the rest of us get down. Keep an eye on the whole place, but especially on that thing on the far side. Harry, you follow Tam with your scanpack, and I'll bring up the rear."

Tamman nodded and slid out of his pack to extract a two hundred-meter coil of synthetic rope. While he and Sean rigged safety harnesses, Harriet and Sandy went on trying to analyze their readings without much success. Sean wasn't too happy about that, yet there wasn't a lot he could do about it, and he waved Tamman over the side.

Tamman picked his way as carefully as he could, but the hundred-meter slope, while less sheer than the bare rock face to the west, was both steep and treacherous. The soil was soft and shifting despite a covering of grass, and he slipped several times. Harriet had it easier. She was taller than he but as slender as her mother; even with her scanpack she was much lighter, and she had the advantage of watching where he'd put his feet ahead of her.

Sean should have found the descent easiest of all, despite his height and weight, since he was behind both of them and placed to learn by their mistakes, but much as he knew he ought to, he couldn't seem to keep his mind on where he was going. He kept looking up at the ruins on the far side of the valley, and when he wasn't doing that his attention kept trying to stray to the ones out in the middle. He knew he should ignore them—after all, Sandy was keeping watch on them and he was anchor man for the safety rope—but he just couldn't. Which was another reason he'd put Tamman in front, where they needed someone who wouldn't let curiosity distract him from the task in hand.

Yet perhaps it was as well he was distracted. It meant he was looking up, not at his feet, when Sandy suddenly screamed.

"*Something's coming up over th—!*"

A boulder two meters to Harriet's right exploded, and she cried out in pain as a five-kilo lump of stone slammed into her shoulder. It didn't break her bio-enhanced skin, but the impact threw her from her feet, and that, Sean realized later, was what saved her life. The heavy energy gun needed a handful of seconds to reduce the boulder to powder; by the time the first energy bolt hit where she'd been standing, she wasn't there anymore.

He dug in his heels instinctively, hurling himself backward to anchor her, but the next bolt of gravitonic disruption sliced the rope like a thread. Her fall accelerated, and she tumbled downslope, slithering and bouncing. She tried frantically to avoid Tamman, clawing for traction as she gathered speed, but the loose soil betrayed her and he couldn't get out of the way in time. Her careening body cut his feet from under him, sending them both crashing downward in a confusion of arms and legs, and more bolts of energy came screaming out of the night. Gouts of flying dirt erupted all about them as ancient, erratic tracking systems tried to lock on them, and only their unpredictable movement and the senility of the defenses kept them alive.

Sean almost fell after them as soil crumbled under his heels, but he managed to hold his position, and his grav gun leapt into his hands in pure reflex. The scarcely visible energy gun fire was a terrible network of fury to his enhanced vision, and a fist squeezed his heart as it reached out for his sister and his friend. But he'd been looking in exactly the right direction when it started. Whatever was firing on them wasn't shooting at *him*—apparently he was still outside its programmed kill zone—but his implants told him where its targeting systems were, and his weapon snapped up into firing position without conscious thought.

It hissed, spitting explosive darts across the valley at fifty-two hundred meters per second, and savage flashes lit the dark as they ripped into the ruins. Each armor-piercing dart had the power of a half-kilo of TNT, and the crackle of their explosions was a single, ripping bellow as ancient walls blew outward in a tornado of splinters.

He held the trigger back, firing desperately and cursing himself for not having brought any heavy weapons. Even his implants couldn't "see" well enough to target the energy guns; he could only pour in fire and pray he hit something vital before their control systems killed Harriet and Tamman.

A fist of pulverized soil slammed the side of his head, and a corner of his mind noted that the defenses had finally noticed him, but it was a distant thought as his three-hundred round magazine emptied. He ripped a fresh one from his belt, then grunted in anguish as the energy bloom of a bolt of disruption clawed at him. He rolled desperately to his left and managed—somehow—not to plunge downward after the others. Sandy had gotten her grav gun into action as well, and the thunder of her fire filled the valley as he finished reloading and opened up again. He cursed viciously as Harriet and Tamman slithered to a halt, but Tamman had figured out what was happening. He wrapped a powerful arm around Harriet and hurled both of them back into motion a split second before the automated guns could lock on.

Flames licked at the brush atop the ruined structures as Sean and Sandy pounded them, and Sean cried out as an energy bolt blew his backpack apart. His nervous system whiplashed in agony, the stunning shock threw the grav gun from his hands, and he heard Sandy screaming his name through the roar of her fire. He clawed after his weapon with numb, desperate fingers, and then an explosion far more violent than any grav gun dart lit the valley like a sun at midnight. The ruins vomited skyward as the capacitors feeding the energy guns tore themselves apart, and the concussion blew Sean MacIntyre into unconsciousness at last.

✧　　✧　　✧

"Sean?" The soft, anxious voice penetrated his darkness, and his eyes slid open. He was still on the slope, but his head was in Sandy's lap. He blinked groggily, and she smiled and brushed dirt from his face.

"Are you all right? Are you hurt?"

"I—" He coughed and broke off, wincing as a fresh wave of pain spun through him. His implant sensors had been wide open as he tried to find a target, and the corona of the energy bolt had bled through them. His nerves were on fire, and he moaned around a surge of nausea, but he was alive, and he wouldn't have been without his enhancement. Not after taking a shot that close to his heart and lungs.

"I'm okay," he rasped as his implants recovered and began damping the pain. He swallowed bile, then stiffened. "*Harry!* Harry and Tam! Are they—?"

"They're all right," Sandy soothed, pressing him back as he tried to sit up. "The guns never managed to line up on them, and—" a ghost of humor lit her face "—at least they got to the bottom faster than they'd expected. See?"

He turned his head, and Harriet waved up at him from the valley floor. Tamman wasn't looking in their direction; he was down on one knee, grav gun ready as he scanned the valley for any fresh threat. Not, Sean thought muzzily, that there was likely to be another. All the ruckus they'd raised dealing with the first one should have drawn the attention of anything else that was still active, and he relaxed.

"Thanks. If you hadn't gotten to it in time—"

"Hush." Sandy's hand covered his mouth, and his eyes smiled up at her as she kissed his forehead. "*We* got to it, and we're all lucky you left me behind. Now kindly shut your mouth and let your implants finish unscrambling themselves before we hike down after Tam and Harry. Hopefully—" her free hand caressed his hair and her lips quirked primly "—a bit more sedately than *they* did."

CHAPTER TWENTY

Harriet watched Sandy and Sean work their way down the valley wall, and her anxious eyes noted the way her twin favored his left side and leaned on Sandy. She'd almost started back up when she realized he couldn't get up at once, but Sandy's wave had reassured her . . . some.

She ran to meet them as they slithered down the last few meters, and Sean gasped as she enveloped him in a fierce hug.

"Hey, now!" He raised a hand to her dust-smutted black hair. "I'm in one piece, and everything's still working, more or less."

"Sure it is," she said tartly, accessing his implants with her own, but then he felt her relax as they confirmed what he'd told her. What that near miss had done to his enhanced musculature was going to leave him stiff for a week, yet the damage was incredibly minor.

"Sure it is," she repeated at last, softly, and raised her head to peer up into his eyes, then kissed his cheek. He smiled and touched her face, then tucked one arm around each young woman and limped over to Tamman.

"See the conquering hero comes," he said smugly. Tamman chuckled, yet he, too, reached out and cupped the back of Sean's head, and the four of them clung together.

"Well!" Sean said at last. "The last step was a lulu, but at least we're here. Let's see what we've found. You still reading anything, Sandy?"

Sandy gave him a last little hug and returned her attention to her scanpack—the only one they had after Harriet's tumbling descent. She turned in a complete circle, then sighed.

"I think you were right about the power receptor, Tam. Most of the power sources're gone, and the ones that're left are fading fast. Looks like we finally killed the Valley of the Damned."

"Pardon me if I don't cry," Tamman replied dryly.

"True, true." She pivoted back to the ruins at mid-valley and nodded. "Looks like at least one of them had some reserve, but the others are gone."

"Let's go see the one that's still up," Sean decided, "but cautiously. *Very* cautiously."

"You got it," Tamman agreed, and swung out to take the lead towards the ancient, half-buried buildings.

Sean studied their surroundings as they moved up the valley. Waist-high waves of grass rippled between clumps of dense thicket and tangled trees, slashed with moonlight and hard-edged shadow under the cold night wind. It was a wild and desolate place, still more haunted somehow after the thunder and lightning of their battle. Yet that very desolation, coupled with the effectiveness the automated weapons had displayed even in their senescence, brightened his eyes, for it was clear no one had gotten through to disturb whatever of pre-bio-weapon Pardal might have survived.

They reached the ruined buildings at last. Centuries of windblown dirt had buried their lower stories, but the worn walls were intact, and tough, transparent Imperial plastic, cloudy with age, still filled most of the window frames. Others gaped like open wounds in the dark, and he felt himself shiver as they stopped outside the ancient tower which contained the single remaining power source, for those age-sick walls had brooded over this lonely valley for nine times the life of Egypt's Sphinx.

The tower stood in the center of the long-dead settlement. Faint swirls of decoration still clung to its ceramacrete facade, and the roots of a tree in its lee—a stubby, thick-trunked thing with peeling, hairy bark—had invaded a window frame. Their inexorable intrusion had pried and twisted at the plastic, and the entire pane fell inward with a clatter when Tamman tapped it.

Sean swallowed. That tree grew on almost level earth heaped twenty meters high against the tower, and he expected to *feel* the centuries when he touched the hard solidity of the frame.

Tamman dug into his knapsack (which, unlike Sean's, had survived the trip down the valley wall) for a hand lamp far more powerful than the smaller, individual lights clipped to their gun belts, and all of them gazed into the building as he trained its diamond-bright spear through the opening. A drift of dirt fanned down from the sprung window, but the bare, stained floor beyond it looked sound, and Tamman picked his way cautiously down the dirt ramp, then turned in a circle, flashing his lamp over the walls.

"Seems pretty stout, Sean. We've got water damage to the floor, but it looks like it all came through the window; no sign of seepage on the walls. Want me to try the door?"

"Sounds like the next logical step." Sean tried to hide how much his left side hurt as he limped down after his friend, but Sandy and Harriet were there instantly, offering him support with such obvious tact he chuckled. Sandy grinned up at him, and he shook his head and abandoned his attempted machismo to lean gratefully on her small, sturdy shoulder.

Harriet crossed to help Tamman with the door, but it refused to move, and he finally dipped back into his pack for a cutter. Brilliant glare chiseled his intent face from the darkness, and Harriet coughed on the stench of burning plastic as a line of fire knifed through the ancient barrier.

Tamman sliced clear around the door frame, then kicked sharply. The cut-out panel toppled away from him, and it was his turn to sneeze as pyramid-dry dust billowed. He flashed his lamp through the opening and grinned.

"No sign of water damage in here, people! And there's something else to be grateful for." His light settled on a spiral-shaped well. "Good old-fashioned stairs. I was afraid we'd have to rappel down dead transit shafts!"

"That's because you have a poor, limited Marine's brain," Sean said. "If that receptor was their only power source, they couldn't have had the juice to spare for things like transit shafts." He smiled pityingly. "Obviously."

"Go ahead—pretend you figured that out ahead of time. In the meantime, smartass, do we go up or down?"

"Sandy?"

She consulted her scanpack, then pointed at the floor.

"We go down, Tam," Sean said, stooping to clear the edge of door still filling the top of the frame.

They inched downward, unwilling to trust the stairs' stability until they'd tested it, yet the building's interior was remarkably intact. One or two of the dust-encrusted rooms they passed still contained furniture, but not even Imperial materials had been intended to last this long, and Sandy touched one chair only to snatch her hand back with a soft sound of distress as the upholstery crumbled. She shivered, and Sean tucked his arm about her and pretended to lean on her only for support.

It took half an hour to reach the tower's basement, for it was buried deep in bedrock and they had to deal with several more frozen doors along the way. Yet the stair finally ended, and Tamman's lamp showed half a dozen sealed doors circling the central access core. He raised an eyebrow at Sandy.

"That one." She pointed, and he gave it a shove. To their collective surprise, it moved a centimeter sideways, and he set down his lamp as Harriet joined him. They locked their fingers through the opening and heaved, grunting with effort, until the stubborn panel groaned open, and Tamman bit off a surprised expletive as a tiny glow leaked back out at them through it.

"Well, *something's* still live," he announced unnecessarily, and the four explorers edged into the room beyond.

The wan light came from a computer console, and Harriet and Tamman scurried over to it, all caution forgotten. It was a civilian model, with more visual telltales than military equipment, but very few were green. Most burned amber or red—those that weren't entirely dark—but they bent over it like a pair of mother hens and probed delicately for a live neural interface.

Sean and Sandy stayed out of their way, and Sean sighed as he found a counter sturdy enough to support him. He sank down on it gratefully and watched Sandy explore with her beltlight while the others fussed over the computer.

Clearly this had been a control center, for the one live console was flanked by a dozen more that were completely dead. But it had been more, as well, for it was cluttered with an incongruous mix of utilitarian equipment and personal furnishings. Someone had lived here, and he wondered if whoever it was had moved in to baby the computers as the settlement began to die.

"Sean?" He looked up at Sandy's hushed voice. She stood in a doorway across the room, and her shadowed expression was strange. He rose at her gesture and hobbled across the room to peer through it beside her, and his own face tightened. It was a bedroom, as time-conquered as the rest of the building, and the bed was occupied.

He limped further into the room, staring down at the dust-covered body. The bone-dry air had mummified him, and his parchment face showed the unmistakable features of a full Imperial framed in tangled white hair. He must, Sean thought, have been the oldest human being any of them had ever seen, and the fact that he lay here still was chilling.

Sean turned away from the sunken eye sockets with a shudder. What must it have been like, he wondered, to be the last? To lie here in the emptiness of the ruins, knowing he would die as he had lived—alone?

He slipped an arm around Sandy, urging her away, and they crossed silently to stand behind Harriet as she and Tamman concentrated obliviously on the computer.

Forty minutes passed before the two of them straightened, and their expressions were a curious blend of delight and disappointment.

"Well?" Sean asked, and Harriet glanced at Tamman and shrugged.

"We don't know. We can get into the operating system, sort of, but it's in terrible shape. I've never seen one this bad off—as far as I know, *no one's* ever seen one this bad—and we can't access any of its files."

"Crap," Sean muttered, but Tamman shook his head.

"It may not be quite that bad. The main memory core's shot, but there's an auxiliary wired into the system. I'd guess somebody hooked in his personal unit as a peripheral—it's all that's keeping anything up, and there's a chance we can recover some of its memory."

"How much?" Sean asked eagerly, and Tamman and Harriet laughed.

"Spoken like a true optimist." Tamman grinned. "We can't tell you that till we can get at it properly, and we can't do that here. It's going to take *Israel's* 'tronics shop to access this, Sean. We'll have to pull the unit and haul it back with us."

"Oh, lord!" Sandy knelt and ran her fingers over the dusty console, peering into it through her implants. "That's gonna be a real bitch, Tam."

"I know." He propped his hands on his hips and frowned at the glowing telltales. "I'm not real crazy about carting it out of here by hand, either. Molycircs or no, this thing's fragile as hell. Dropping it down a cliff or two wouldn't be real good for it."

"Then let's take it out the easy way," Harriet suggested. "Sandy and Sean blew what was left of the defenses into dust bunnies, so why don't I go back and collect the cutter while you and she take it apart?"

"Now that," Tamman murmured, "sounds like an excellent idea."

"I don't know, Harry," Sean said. "You're all better techs than me. Maybe I should go back while all three of you work on it."

She snorted. "Seen yourself moving lately, brother dear? It'd take you till dawn to hobble back to the cutter!"

"Hey, I'm not that bad off!"

"Maybe not, but you wouldn't enjoy the hike, and Tam and Sandy are better mechanics than me. That makes me the logical choice, now doesn't it? Besides, I haven't had a good jog since *Terra* kicked us overboard."

Sean didn't like the thought of splitting up and letting any of them out on his (or her) own, yet they hadn't met anything worrisome on the way in. None of the native predators, if any, had put in an appearance, and this was the Valley of the Damned. No Pardalian was likely to be wandering about in its vicinity in the middle of the night. And she was right about how he felt. The trek back to the cutter was more than he cared to face, and he discovered he'd been dreading the thought of it.

"All right," he agreed finally. "I'll stay here and hold lights and pass tools or something, but keep your belt light lit. That ought to discourage any of the local beasties from wondering what you taste like. And you take a *real* close look through your passive sensors before you try to land out there! You're probably right about the defenses being down, but don't take any chances."

"Aye, aye, Captain!" She tossed him an impudent salute, then whipped about and fled with a trill of laughter as he started for her. She paused at the outer door just long enough to stick out her tongue, and then her light, quick step receded rapidly up the stairs. Sean shook his head, then smiled and eased down to sit on the floor beside Sandy and Tamman as they produced tools and began removing the front of the console.

Harriet jogged happily through the darkness at a steady forty kilometers per hour. Sean might be fourteen centimeters taller, but he had their father's long body and broad shoulders; her legs were almost as long, despite his height advantage, and she was *much* lighter. Without even the weight of her scanpack she was free to attack the steep slopes, burdened only by her holstered grav gun, and she savored the opportunity. The moon had set, but her belt light was more than enough for someone with enhanced eyes, and running on *Israel*'s treadmill paled beside the sheer joy of filling her lungs with the crisp, cold mountain air as her feet spurned the ground.

It took her just under eighty minutes to reach the ledge they'd landed the cutter on. She paused, jogging in place, to wipe sweat from her forehead, then trotted onward a bit more cautiously in light of the hundred-meter drop to her right.

She was less than a kilometer from the cutter when her head came up in sudden surprise. Her eyes widened, and she slithered to a halt as the sound of human voices cut the darkness.

Her head whipped around and she went active with every implant, probing the night. People! At least a *dozen* people, coming around the bend ahead of her! Her implants should have picked them up sooner, and she cursed herself for not paying more attention to her surroundings and less to the pleasure of running. But even as she raged at her foolishness a part of her mind whirred with questions. She hadn't looked for them, but, damn it, what were they *doing* out here in the middle of the night without even a torch?

Questions could wait. She killed her belt lamp and turned back the way she'd come, and a voice shouted, loud and harsh with command. Crap! She'd been seen!

She abandoned her attempt to sneak away for a blinding pace no unenhanced human could have matched, and her thoughts flashed. They'd agreed not to use their coms in case they were picked up, but if there were people *here*, there might be more of them, closer to the Valley, as well. The others had to be warned, and—

Light glared and thunder barked behind her. Something whizzed past her ear, and something else slammed into her left shoulder blade. She staggered and snatched for her grav gun, spun to the side by the brutal impact, and the beginning of pain exploded up her nerves. A second fiery hammer hit her in the side, throwing the grav gun from her hand, but before it really registered there was another flash, and a sixty-gram lead ball smashed her right temple.

CHAPTER TWENTY-ONE

"Come *out* of there, you—*aha!*"

Tamman broke off in mid-exasperation and eased the glittering block of molecular circuitry gently to the floor with a wide, triumphant smile.

Removing it had proved even harder than Sandy had feared. Not even implants could trace circuits in three dimensions without a schematic, and they'd found too late that it would have been far simpler to disconnect the console from the wall and go in from the back. Dust had infiltrated the ancient seals, as well, drifting up to irritate eyes and inspire bursts of sneezing, and Tamman had had an interesting moment when he bridged what he'd thought was a dead circuit. But two and a half painstaking hours had finally yielded their prize, and Sean met Tamman's grin with one of his own.

"*Foosh!*" Sandy fanned herself with a dirty hand. "When I think how much quicker we could have done this in a proper shop—!" Sean switched his grin to her. Then he frowned.

"Hey—shouldn't Harry be back by now?"

Sandy and Tamman stared at him, and he felt their matching surprise. All three of them had been oblivious to time as they concentrated on eviscerating the console; now their eyes met his, and he saw them darken as surprise gave way to the beginnings of concern.

"Damn right she should!" Tamman rose and snatched up the hand lamp. "The way she likes to run, it shouldn't've taken her more than two hours—tops—to get to the cutter!"

Sean started for the stairs and drew up with a gasp, for his injured side had stiffened as he watched his friends work. Pain beaded his forehead with sweat, and he muttered a curse and hit his implant overrides. He knew he shouldn't—pain was a warning a body did well to heed, lest it turn minor injuries into serious ones—but that was the least of his worries.

Sandy frowned as his suddenly brisker movement told her what he'd done, yet she said nothing, and the two of them half-ran up the treads on Tamman's heels.

They scrambled out past the tree, panting from their hurried ascent, and stared into the darkness. There was no sign of the cutter, and Sean bit his lip as cold wind ruffled his hair.

Tamman was right—Harriet should have been back thirty minutes ago. He should have noticed her absence sooner . . . and he should *never* have let her out on her own! He'd known better at the time, damn it, but he'd let himself worry more over the possibility of losing an hour or two than her safety. He pounded his fists together and stared up at the sky with bitter eyes, but the alien stars mocked him, and his jaw clenched as he powered his com implant and sent out a full-powered omnidirectional pulse, heedless of the quarantine system's sensors.

There was no response, and the others looked at him with matching horror. Harriet should have heard that signal from forty light-minutes away!

"Oh, Jesus!" His whisper was a plea, and then he was running for the valley wall with no thought for such inconsequentials as his injuries, and his friends were on his heels.

They ran with implants fully active. It took them less than fifty minutes to reach the cutter, despite their feverish concentration on their search, and if Harriet had been within five hundred meters of the trail in any direction, they would have found her.

Sean leaned on a landing leg, sucking in air, enhanced lungs on fire, and tried to think. Even if she were dead—his mind shied from the thought like a terrified animal—they should have spotted her implants. It was as if she'd never come this way at all, but she must have! She *had* to have!

"All right," he grated, and his panting companions turned to him anxiously. "We should have spotted her. If we didn't, she's not here, and I can't think of any reason she shouldn't be. We can use the cutter for an aerial search, but if she's unconscious or . . . or something—" his voice quavered, and he wrenched it back under iron control "—we might miss something as small as implant emissions. We need better scanners."

"Brashan." Tamman's voice was flat, and Sean nodded choppily.

"Exactly. If he puts up a full-powered array he can cover five times the ground twice as fast. And *Israel*'s med computers can access her readouts for a full diagnostic if she's hurt." He forced his hands down to his sides. "It'll also be a flare-lit tip-off to the quarantine system when he goes active." He bit the words off in pain, but they must be said, for if they threw away caution now, it might kill them all. "If it *is* watching the planet, there's no way it'll miss something like that."

"So what?" Tamman snarled. "We have to find her, goddamn it!"

"Tam's right," Sandy agreed without a flicker of hesitation, and Sean's hand caressed her face for just a moment. Then he opened the cutter hatch and went up the ramp at a run.

"I've found her."

The people in the cutter jerked upright, staring at Brashan's tiny hologram, and the centauroid's crest was flat. Another endless hour had passed, and even the fact that the quarantine system hadn't reacted in the slightest had meant nothing beside their growing fear as seconds dragged away.

Brashan straightened on his pad, his holographic eyes meeting Sean's squarely, and his voice was very quiet. "She's dying."

"No," Sean whispered. "*No*, goddamn it!"

"She is approximately seven kilometers from your current position on a heading of one-three-seven," Brashan continued in that same flat, quiet voice. "She has a broken shoulder, a punctured lung, and severe head injuries. The medical computer reports a skull fracture, a major eye trauma, and two subdural hematomas. One of them is massive."

"*Skull fracture?*" All three humans stared at him in shock, for Harriet's bones—like their own—were reinforced with battle steel appliqués. But under their shock was icy fear. Unlike muscle tissue and skin, the physical enhancement of the brain was limited; Harriet's implants might control other blood loss, but not bleeding inside her skull.

"I cannot say positively, but I believe her wounds to be deliberately inflicted," Brashan said, and Sean's dark eyes burned with sudden, terrible fire. "I say this because she is presently in the center of a small village. I hypothesize that she must have been carried thence by whoever injured her."

"Those fucking sons-of-bi—!"

"Wait, Sean!" Sandy cut him off in midcurse, and he turned his fury on her. He knew it was stupid, yet his rage needed a target—any target—and she was there. But if her brown eyes were just as deadly as his own, they were also far closer to rational.

"*Think*, damn it!" she snapped. "Somehow someone must have spotted her—and that means they probably know she came out of the Valley!"

Sean sank back, his madness stabbed through with panic as he recalled the fate the Church prescribed for any who dabbled with the Valley of the Damned. Sandy held his eyes a second longer, then turned to the Narhani.

"You said she's dying, Brashan. Exactly how bad is it?"

"If we do not get her into *Israel*'s sickbay within the next ninety minutes—two hours at the outside—she will be dead." Brashan's crest went still flatter. "Even now, her chances are less than even."

"We have to go get her," Tamman grated, and Sean nodded convulsively.

"Agreed," Sandy said, but her eyes were back on Sean. "Tam's right," she said quietly, "but we can't just go in there and start killing people."

"The hell we can't! Those motherfuckers are *dead*, Sandy! Goddamn it, they're trying to kill her!"

"I know. But you know why they are, and so do I."

"I don't fucking well *care* why!" he snarled.

"Well you fucking well ought to!" she snarled back, and the utterly uncharacteristic outburst rocked him even through his rage. "Damn it, Sean, they think they're doing what God wants! They're ignorant, superstitious, and scared to death of what she's done—are you going to kill them all for *that*?"

He stared at her, eyes hating, and tension crackled between them. Then his gaze fell. He felt ashamed, which only made his need for violence perversely stronger, but he shook his head.

"I know." Her voice was far more gentle. "I *know*. But using Imperial weapons against them would be pure, wanton slaughter."

He nodded, knowing she was right. Perhaps even more importantly, he knew even through his madness why she'd stopped him. He looked back up, and his eyes were sane once more . . . but colder than interstellar space.

"All right. We'll try to scare them out of our way without killing anyone, Sandy. But if they won't scare—" He broke off, and she squeezed his arm thankfully. She knew what killing the villagers would do to him after the madness passed, and she tried not to think about his final words.

Father Stomald knelt before his altar, ashen-faced and sick, and raised revolted eyes to the outsized beaker of oil. To pour that on a human being— *any* human being, even a heretic! To *light* it and watch her burn . . .

Bile rose as he pictured that blood-streaked, hauntingly beautiful face and saw that slim, lovely body wreathed in flame, crisping, burning, blackening. . . .

He forced his nausea down. God called His priests to their duty, and if the punishment of the ungodly was harsh, it must be so to save their souls. Stomald told himself that almost tearfully, and it did no good at all. He loved God and longed to serve Him, but he was a shepherd, not an executioner!

Sweat matted his forehead as he dragged himself up. The beaker was cold between his palms, and he prayed for strength. If only Cragsend were big enough to have its own Inquisitor! If only—

He cut the thought off, despising himself for wanting to pass *his* duty to another, and argued with his stubborn horror. There was no question of the woman's guilt. The lightning and thunder from the Valley had waked the hunting party, and despite their terror, they'd gone to investigate. And when they called upon her to halt, she'd fled, proclaiming her guilt. Even if she hadn't, her very garments would convict her. Blasphemy for a woman to wear the high vestments of the Sanctum itself, and Tibold Rarikson, the leader of the huntsmen, had described her demon light. Stomald himself had seen the other strange things on her belt and wrist, but it was Tibold's haunted eyes which brought the horror fully home. The man was a veteran warrior, commander of Cragsend's tiny force of the Temple Guard, yet his face had been pale as whey as he spoke of the light and her impossible speed.

Indeed, Stomald thought with a queasy shiver as he turned from the altar, perhaps she was no woman at all, for what woman would still live? Three times they'd hit her—*three!*—at scarcely fifty paces, and if her long black hair was a crimson-clotted mass and her right eye wept bloody tears, her other wounds didn't even bleed. Perhaps she was in truth the demon Tibold had named her . . . but even as he told himself that, the under-priest knew why he wanted to believe it.

He descended the church steps into the village square, and swallowed again as he beheld the heretic in the bloody light of the flambeaux.

She looked so young—younger even than he—as she hung from the stake by her manacled wrists, wrapped in heavy iron chains and stripped of her profaned vestments, and he felt a shameful inner stir as he once more saw her flimsy undergarments. Mother Church expected her priests to wed, for how could they understand the spiritual needs of husband or wife without experience? Yet to feel such things *now* . . .

He drew a deep breath and walked forward. Her bloody head drooped, and she hung so still he thought—prayed—she had already died. But then he saw the faint movement of her thinly covered breasts, and his heart sank with the knowledge that her death would not free him from the guilt he must bear.

He stopped and turned to face his flock as Tibold approached. The Guardsman bore a torch, and its flame wavered with the shaking of his hand. He stopped two paces from the priest, and the pity in his blunt, hard features made Stomald wonder if perhaps he, too, had tried to insist this woman was a demon out of revulsion for what they now must do to her.

He met Tibold's haunted eyes, and a flicker passed between them. One of understanding . . . and gratitude. Of thanks that they had no Inquisitor to break that slender body upon the wheel before her death as the letter of the Church's Law demanded, and that, demon or no, she had never waked. That she would die unknowing, spared the agony of her horrible end . . . unlike the men who would always remember wreaking it upon her.

He turned away from the Guardsman who must share his duty, facing his people, and wondered how they would look upon him in days to come. He couldn't see their faces beyond the fuming flambeaux, and he was glad.

He opened his mouth to pronounce the words of anathematization.

Harriet's weakening implant signals left no time to return to *Israel*, and Sean landed the stealthed cutter within a half-klick of the village. He selected a six-millimeter grav rifle from the weapons locker to back up his side arm, and Tamman chose an energy gun, but Sandy bore only her grav gun and a satchel of grenades. Sean wished she'd taken something heavier, yet time was too short to argue, and he led them through the darkness at a run.

The torch-lit village square came in sight, and his mouth twisted into a snarl. Harriet—*his Harriet!*—hung by her wrists from a stake, heaped faggots piled about her chained, half-naked body, and her hair was soaked with blood. His hands tightened on his rifle's grips, but he felt Sandy's anxious eyes, and he'd promised her.

"Go!" he snapped, and she hurled the first plasma grenade.

Stomald cried out in horror as terrible white light exploded against Cragsend's night. Its fiery breath touched hay ricks to flame and singed the assembled villagers' hair, and screams of terror lashed the priest.

He staggered back, blinded by the terrible flash. There was another—*and another!*—and he heard Tibold's hoarse bellow beside him and cringed, trying to understand, as three figures appeared. They seemed to step forth from within the fury consuming the smithy, the granary, and tanning sheds. Their featureless black shapes loomed before the glare, and the one in the center, a towering giant out of some tale of horror, aimed a strange musket shape at the slate roof of the church.

Sparkling flashes ripped stout stonework to shrieking splinters in an endless roll of thunder that scattered screaming villagers in panic, but Stomald's heart spasmed with a terror even worse than theirs. It was his fault! The thought leapt into his brain. He'd hesitated. He'd rebelled in his heart, contesting God's will, and this—*this*—was the result!

Tibold seized him, trying to drag him away, but he stared transfixed as the shape beside the giant aimed its own weapon at a trio of freight wagons. There was no flash this time, and that was even worse. A hurricane of chips and snapped timbers erupted, and the only sound was rending wood and the whine as fragments flew like bullets.

It was too much for Tibold. He abandoned the crazed priest to flee, and Stomald felt only a distant sympathy for him. This was more than any warrior could be asked to face. These were the demons of the Valley of the Damned, come to snatch away the demon his traitor heart had longed to spare, and terror filled him, but he stood his ground. He had no choice. His faltering faith brought them here. He'd failed his flock, and though his sin cost him his immortal soul, he was God's priest.

He raised the sanctified oil like a shield, dry lips whispering in prayer, and a handful of villagers stared in horror from the cover of darkness as their youthful priest advanced alone against the forces of Hell.

Sean blew the village fountain apart, but the lone madman walked through the spray and kept right on coming. Sean bared his teeth as he saw the blue and gold priestly robe, and it took all he had not to turn the rifle upon him, yet he didn't. Somehow, he didn't. Tamman splintered a half-meter trench across the square, and the priest halted for a moment. Then he resumed his advance, stepping over the shattered cobbles like a sleepwalker, and Sean swore as Sandy went to meet him.

Stomald faltered as the smallest demon walked straight at him. The silhouetted figure entered the spill of light from the flambeaux, and, for the first time, he truly saw one of them.

His prayer rose higher at the blasphemy before him, for this demon, too, wore the semblance of a woman in the holiest of raiment. Torchlight fumed in her eyes and glittered from the gold of her profaned vestments, the fires of Hell roared behind her, and she came on as if his exorcism was but words. Terror strangled his voice, yet the holy oil he bore was more potent than any exorcism, and he sent up a silent prayer for strength, unworthy though he'd proved himself. She stopped five paces away, and there was no fear in her face—not of the frightened priest, not of the blessed weapon he bore . . . not even of God Himself.

Sandy swallowed rage as she looked past the priest at Harriet, chained amid her waiting pyre. But then she saw his terrified face, and she felt a grudging admiration for the courage—or the faith—that held him here.

He stared at her, eyes filled with fear, and then his hands lashed. Something leapt from the beaker he held, but reflex activated her implant force field. Thick, iridescent oil sluiced down it, caught millimeters from her skin, and the priest's mouth moved.

"Begone!" he shouted, and she twitched, for she understood him. His voice was high and cracked with terror but determined, and he spoke the debased Universal of the Church. "Begone, Demon! Unclean and accursed, I cast you out in the Name of the Most Holy!"

Stomald shouted the exorcism with all the faith in him as the shining oil coated the demon. She paused—perhaps she even gave back a step—and hope flamed in his heart. But then hope turned to even greater horror, for the demon neither vanished in a flash of lightning nor fled in terror. Instead she came a step closer . . . and she smiled.

"Begone yourself, wretched and miserable one!" He reeled, stunned by the terrible thunder of that demonic voice, and his brain gibbered. No demon could speak the Holy Tongue! He retreated a faltering step, hand rising in a warding sign, and the demon laughed. *She laughed!* "I have come for my friend," she thundered, "and woe be unto you if you have harmed her!"

Crashing peals of laughter ripped through him like echoes from Hell, and then she reached out to the nearest torch. The holy oil sprang alight with a seething hiss, clothing her in a fierce corona, and her voice boomed out of the roaring flames.

"Begone lest you die, sinful man!" she commanded terribly, and the furnace heat of her faceless, fiery figure came for him.

Sean watched Sandy confront the priest. Her implant-amplified voice made *his* head hurt—God only knew how it must have sounded to the priest! Yet the man had stood his ground until she touched the oil to flame. That was too much, and he took to his heels at last, stumbling, falling, leaping back to his feet and running for the imagined sanctuary of his church while Sandy's bellowing laughter pursued him.

Yet there was no time to admire her tactics, and he slung his grav rifle and charged across the square. Tamman's energy gun splintered more cobbles, driving the villagers still further back, but Sean hardly noticed. He scattered heavy faggots like tumbleweeds, and his face was a murderous mask as he gripped the chain about Harriet's body and twisted the links like taffy. They snapped, and he hurled them aside and caught at the manacles. His back straightened with a grunt. Anchoring bolts screamed and sheared like paper, and if she was still breathing as her limp body slid into his arms, he was close enough to read her implants directly at last. He paled. The damage was at least as bad as Brashan had said, and he cradled her like a child as he turned and ran like a madman for the cutter.

Stomald cowered in the nave of the broken church, rocking on his knees and praying with all his strength amid lumps of stone blown from the vault above him. He clung to sanity with bleeding fingernails, then cringed in fresh terror as something flashed into the very heavens beyond the village. A howling streak of light exploded across the stars in an echoing peal of thunder, and a hot breath of air rolled down through the church's cracked roof on the shrieking wind of its passage as it screamed low over Cragsend.

Then it was gone, and he buried his face in his hands and moaned.

CHAPTER TWENTY-TWO

Father Stomald stared at the garments on his vicarage table while wagons creaked beyond his windows. Nioharqs dragged loads of rubble down Cragsend's streets, drovers shouted, and repair crew foremen bawled orders, but the men laboring within the church itself only whispered.

The youthful priest felt their fear, for their terror was graven in his mind, as well, and with it an even greater horror.

Mother Church had failed them. *He* had failed them, and he steeled his nerve and touched the bloodstained fabric once more. He was but the vicar of a small mountain village, but he'd made his pilgrimage to the Temple and served at the Command Hatch as High Priest Vroxhan intoned mass. He'd seen the Temple's magnificence and the Sanctum that housed God's Own Voice and marveled at the high priest's exquisite vestments, at their splendid fabric and shining gold braid, the glitter of their buttons. . . .

And all that splendor paled beside *these* bloodied garments, like a child's clumsy copy of reality.

He made himself lift the tunic, and its gleaming buttons flashed under the window's sunlight, trapping the sun's heart within the crowned glory of God's holy Starburst. But his breath hissed as he looked closer, for a strange, winged creature—a magnificent beast whose like he'd never imagined—erupted from the Star's heart to claim God's Crown . . . even as the demon had erupted from the flames as she advanced upon him.

He fought a hysterical urge to fling the garment away. Blasphemy! Blasphemy to deface those holiest of symbols! Yet that beast, that winged beast, like the winged badge of a Temple courier and yet unlike . . .

He forced calm upon his mind and examined the garment once more. Splendid as the buttons were, they were but ornaments, unlike those of High Priest Vroxhan's vestments. A quivering fingertip traced the invisible seal which had actually closed the tunic, and even now he could see no sign of how it worked.

When they'd first tried to strip the profaned fabric from the . . . the woman, the heretic or . . . or demon, or *whatever* she'd been . . .

584

His shoulders tensed, and he made them relax. When they'd tried to strip it from—her—they'd found no fastenings, and it had laughed at their sharpest blades. But then, with no real hope, he'd tugged—thus.

The cloth opened, and he licked his lips. It was uncanny. Impossible. Yet he held it in his hands. It was as real as his own flesh, and yet—

He opened the tunic wide once more, caressing the union of sleeve and shoulder, and bit his lip. He'd watched his own mother sew and done sewing enough of his own at seminary to know what he should find, yet there was no seam. The tunic was a single whole, perfect and indivisible, as if it had been woven in a single sitting and not pieced together, its only flaws the holes punched in it by musket balls. . . .

He went to his knees, folding his hands in prayer. Not even the fabled looms of Eswyn could have woven that fabric. Not the Temple's finest tailor could have formed it without thread or seam. No human hand could have wrought that magic closure.

They *must* have been demons. He told himself that fiercely, quivering with remembered terror before the thunder of the demon's voice. Yet there was an even greater terror at his heart, for the rolling majesty of that voice had crashed over him with the words of the Holy Tongue itself!

He moaned to the empty room, and the forbidden thought returned. He fought to reject it, but it hung in the corners of his mind, and he squeezed his eyes so tightly closed they ached as it whispered in the silence.

They'd come from the Valley of the Damned, and lightning had wracked the cloudless heavens above the Valley. They'd smitten Cragsend with fire and thunder. One of them, alone, had ripped the entire roof from his church. Another had shattered three heavy wagons. A third had blazed alive in the flames of Mother Church's holiest oils and laughed—*laughed!* And when the smoke had wisped away, Stomald had stared at bubbled sheets of glass, flashing like gems under the morning sun, where the smithy had burned to less than ash.

Yet with all that inconceivable power, they'd killed no one. *No one.* Not a man, woman, or child. Not even an *animal!* Not even the men who'd wounded and captured their fellow and intended to burn her alive. . . .

The Church taught love for one's fellows, but demons should have slain—not simply frightened helpless mortals from their paths! And no demon could endure the Holy Tongue, far less speak it with its own mouth!

He opened his eyes, stroking the tunic once more, recalling the beauty of the woman who'd worn it, and faced the thought he'd fought. They had not—could not—have been mortals, and that should have made them demons. But demons couldn't have spoken the Holy Tongue, and demons *wouldn't* have spared where they might have slain. And if no woman might wear the vestments of Mother Church, these were *not* those of Mother Church, but finer and more mystical than anything Man might make even for the glory of God.

He closed his eyes and trembled with a different fear, like sunshine after the tempest, mingling with his terror in glory-shot wonder. No woman might wear Mother Church's raiment, no, but there were other beings who might.

Beings of supernal beauty who might enter even that accursed valley and smite its demonic powers with thunder more deadly than that of Hell itself. Beings who *could* speak the Holy Tongue . . . and would not speak another.

"Forgive me, Lord," he whispered into the sunlight streaming through his window. His eyes sparkled as he raised his hands to the light, and he stood, opening his arms to embrace its radiance.

"Forgive my ignorance, Lord! Let not Your wrath fall upon my flock, for it was my blindness, not theirs. They saw only with their fear, but I—I should have seen with my heart and understood!"

Harriet MacIntyre opened her eyes and winced as dim light burned into her brain. There was no pain, but she'd never felt so weak. Her sluggish thoughts were blurred, and vertigo and nausea washed through her.

She moaned, trying to move, and quivered with terror when she could not. A shape bent over her, and she blinked. Half her vision was a terrible boil of featureless glare and the other half wavered, like heat shimmer or light through a sheet of water. Tears of frustration trickled as she fought in vain to focus and felt the world slipping away once more.

"Harry?" A hand touched hers, lifted it. "Harry, can you hear me?"

Sean's rough-edged voice was raw with pain and worry. Worry for her, she realized muzzily, and her heart twisted at the exhaustion that filled it.

"Can you hear me?" he repeated gently, and she summoned all her strength to squeeze his hand. Once that grip would have crumpled steel; now her fingers barely twitched, but his hand tightened as he felt them move.

"You're in sickbay, Harry." His blurred shape came closer as he knelt by her bed, and a gentle hand touched her forehead. She felt his fingers tremble, and his voice fogged. "I know you can't move, sweetheart, but that's because the med section has your implants shut down. You're going to be all right." Her eyes slid shut once more, blotting out the confusion. "You're going to be all right," he repeated. "Do you understand, Harry?" The urgency in the words reached her, and she squeezed again. Her lips moved, and he leaned close, straining his enhanced hearing to the limit.

"Love . . . you . . . all. . . ."

His eyes burned as the thready whisper faded, but her breathing was slow and regular. He watched her for a long, silent moment, and then he laid her hand beside her, patted it once, and sank back in his chair.

There were other moments of vague awareness over the next few days, periods of drifting disorientation which would have terrified her had her thoughts been even a little clearer. Harriet had been seriously injured once before—a grav-cycle accident that broke both legs and an arm before she'd been fully enhanced—and Imperial medicine had put her back on her feet in a week. Now whole days passed before she could hang onto consciousness for more than a minute, and that said horrifying volumes about her injuries. Worse, she couldn't remember what had happened. She didn't have the least idea *how* she'd been hurt, but she clung to Sean's promise. She was all right. She was going to be all right if she just held on. . . .

And then, at last, she woke and the bed beneath her was still, and the vertigo and nausea had vanished. Her lips were dry, and she licked them, staring up into near total darkness.

"Harriet?" It was Brashan this time, and she turned her head slowly, heart leaping as muscles obeyed her once more. She blinked, trying to focus on his face, and her forehead furrowed as she failed. Try as she might, half her field of vision was a gyrating electrical storm wrapped in a blazing fog.

"B-Brash?" Her voice was husky. She tried to clear her throat, then gasped as a six-fingered alien hand slipped under her. It cradled the back of her head, easing her up while the mattress rose behind her, and another hand held a glass. Her lips fumbled with the straw, and then she sighed as ice-cold water filled her mouth. The desiccated tissues seemed to suck it up instantly, yet nothing had ever tasted half so wonderful.

He let her drink a moment more, then set the glass aside and settled her back against the pillow. She closed her right eye, and sighed again as the tormenting glare vanished. Her left eye obeyed her, focusing on his saurian, long-snouted face and noting the half-flattened concern of his crest.

"Brash," she repeated. Her hand rose, and his took it.

"Doctor Brash, please," he said with a Narhani's curled-lip smile.

"Should've guessed." She smiled back, and if her voice was weak, it sounded like hers once more. "You always were better with the med computers."

"Fortunately," another voice said, and she turned her head as Sandy appeared on her other side. Her friend smiled, but her eyes glistened as she sank into the chair and took her free hand.

"Oh, Harry," she whispered. Tears welled, and she brushed at them almost viciously. "You scared us, honey. God, how you scared us!"

Harriet's hand tightened, and Sandy bent to lay her cheek against it. She stayed there for a moment, brown hair falling in a short, silky cloud about a too-thin wrist, and then she drew a deep breath and straightened.

"Sorry," she said. "Didn't mean to go all mushy on you. But 'Doctor Brashan' damn well saved your life. I—" her voice wavered again before she got it back under control "—I didn't think he was going to be able to."

"Hush," Harriet soothed. "Hush, Sandy. I'm all right." She smiled a bit tremulously. "I know I am—Sean promised me."

"Yes. Yes, he did." Sandy produced a tissue and blew her nose, then managed a watery grin. "In fact, he's gonna be ticked he wasn't here when you woke up, but Brashan and I chased him back into bed less than an hour ago."

"Is everyone else all right?"

"We're fine, Harry. Fine. Sean's got some damage to his left arm—he drove himself too hard—but it's minor, and Tam's fine. Just exhausted. With you out, Brashan stuck here in sickbay, and Sean ready to kill anybody who suggested he leave you, poor Tam's been carrying most of the load."

"Tam and *you*, you mean," Harriet said, seeing the weariness in her face.

"Oh, maybe." Sandy shrugged. "But I haven't left the ship—Tam was the one who did all the traveling back and forth with the computer."

"Computer?" Harriet said blankly. "What computer?"

"The computer we—" Sandy started in a surprised voice, then stopped. "Oh. What's the last thing you remember?"

"We were . . . going to the valley?" Harriet said uncertainly. "There was some sort of . . . of defensive system, I think. Did I—" She released Brashan's hand to cover her right eye. "Is that what happened to me?"

"No." Sandy patted the hand she held. "That happened later. We'll tell you all about it, but what matters is we found a personal computer and brought it back. It's in miserable shape, but Tam's managed to recover some of it, and it looks like some kind of journal. I think—" she smiled fondly "—he's been concentrating on it to keep his mind off worrying about you."

"A journal?" Harriet rubbed her closed eye harder, and her open eye brightened. "That sounds good, Sandy. I just wish I—"

"Harriet." Brashan interrupted quietly, and his hand closed on her right wrist, stilling the fingers on her eye. "Why are you rubbing your eye?"

"I— Oh, it's probably nothing," she said, and heard the strangeness in her voice. Denial, she thought.

"Tell me," he commanded.

"I—" She swallowed. "I just can't get it to focus."

"I think it's more than that." His voice accepted no evasion, and she felt her lips quiver. She stilled them and turned to face him squarely.

"I think it's gone blind," she said, and heard Sandy's soft gasp beside her. "All I get is a . . . a blur and a glare."

"Is it bothering you now?"

"No." She drew a deep breath, curiously relieved to have admitted there was something wrong. "Not as long as it's closed."

"Open it." She obeyed, then squeezed it instantly back shut. The glare was worse than ever, jagged with pain even her implants couldn't damp.

"I . . . I can't." She licked her lips. "It hurts."

"I see," he said, and she felt her nerve steady under his composed voice. "I feared you might have difficulties, but when you said nothing—" His crest flipped a Narhani shrug.

"What's wrong?" She was pleased by how nearly normal she sounded.

"Nothing irreparable, I assure you. But as you know, *Israel*'s sickbay, while capable of bone and tissue repair and implant *adjustment*, was never intended for enhancement or major implant *repair*. Her designers—" he smiled a wry, Narhani smile "—assumed injuries such as that would be treated aboard her mother ship, which, alas, is beyond our reach."

He paused, and she nodded for him to continue.

"You were struck in the right temple, left shoulder, and right lung by heavy projectiles," the centauroid explained gently. "Despite the crudity of the weapons used, they had sufficient power at such short range to shatter even enhanced human bone, but the one which struck your head fortunately impacted at an angle and your skull sufficed to turn it."

She breathed a bit harder as he cataloged her wounds but nodded for him to continue, and his eyes approved her courage.

"Your implants sealed the blood loss from the wounds to your shoulder and lung. There was considerable damage to the lung, but those injuries are healing satisfactorily. The head wound resulted in intracranial bleeding and tissue damage"—she tensed, but he continued calmly— "yet I see no sign of motor skill damage, though there may be some permanent memory loss. Your vision problem, however, stems not from tissue damage but from damage to your implant hardware. Fragments of bone were driven into the brain and also forward, piercing the eye socket. The injuries to the eye structures are responding to therapy, and the optic nerve was untouched, but an implant, unlike the body, cannot be regenerated. I knew it was damaged, but I'd hoped the impairment would be less severe than you describe."

"It's only in the hardware?" Relief washed through her at his nod, but then she frowned. "Why not just shut it down through the overrides?"

"The damage is too extensive for me to access it. Short of removing it entirely—a task for a fully qualified neurosurgeon which I would hesitate to attempt and which would, at best, leave you effectively blind until we can obtain proper medical assistance, anyway—I can do nothing with it."

"Well, you're going to have to do *something*. I know you've got the lights way down in here, but I can't even keep it open!"

"I know. Yet, as you point out, as long as no light reaches it you experience no discomfort. Rather than risk damaging your presently unscathed optic nerve, I would prefer simply to cover it."

"An eye patch?" Despite herself, her lips twitched at the absurdity of such an archaic approach. Sandy actually chuckled.

"Yo, ho, ho and a bottle of rum!" she murmured. Harriet gave her a one-eyed glare, but she only grinned, too relieved to hear the damage wasn't permanent to be deflated so easily.

"Indeed." Brashan gave Sandy a moderately severe glance, then looked back down at Harriet. "Given the unimpaired enhancement of your left eye, you should be able to adjust once the distraction is suppressed."

"An eye patch." Harriet sighed. "God, I hope you get holos of this, Sandy. I know you'll just die if you miss the opportunity!"

"Damn straight," Sandy said, and smoothed hair from Harry's forehead.

"But you must report it, Father!" Tibold Rarikson stared at the priest in disbelief, yet Stomald's smile was serene.

"Tibold, I *will* report it, but not yet." The Guard captain started to protest, but Stomald shushed him with a gesture. "I will," he repeated, "but only when I'm certain precisely what I'm to report."

"What you're to *report?*" Tibold's eyes bugged, but he gripped his innate respect for the cloth in both hands and drew a deep breath. "Father, with all due respect, I don't see what the problem is. Cragsend was attacked by demons who burned the fifth part of the village to the ground!"

"Indeed?" Stomald smiled and took a turn around the room, feeling the other's eyes on his back. If there was one man with whom he wished to share his wondering joy, Tibold was that man. Hard-bitten warrior that he was, he was a kindly man whose sense of pity not even war could quench. And despite his Guard rank and the traditional Malagoran resentment of outside control, he stood almost as high in Cragsend's estimation as Stomald himself. But for all his desire, how did Stomald bring the other to see what he himself now saw so clearly?

He drew a deep breath and turned back to the Guardsman.

"My friend," he said gently, "I want you to listen to me carefully. A great thing has happened here in our tiny town—a greater thing than you may believe possible. I know you're afraid, and I know why, but there are some points about the 'demons' you should consider. For example . . ."

CHAPTER TWENTY-THREE

Sean tried not to hover as Harriet walked unaided to the astrogator's couch. She was still shaky, and her missing memories refused to return, yet she had to smile at his expression. Tamman sat beside her and slipped an arm about her, and she leaned against him, wishing she knew how to thank them for her life.

But, of course, there was no need.

"Well!" Sean flopped into his couch with customary inelegance. "Looks like your body-and-fender shop does good work, Brashan."

"True," the Narhani replied with one of his clogged-drain chuckles. "And while I regret my inability to repair your implant, Harry, I must say your patch gives you a certain—" He paused, seeking the proper word.

"Raffishness?" Sean suggested, his smile almost back to normal.

"Thank you, kind sir." Harriet stroked the black patch and grinned. "I glanced in the mirror and thought I was looking at Anne Bonny!"

"Who?" Brashan's crest perked, but she only shook her head.

"Look her up in the computer, Twinkle Hooves."

"I shall. You humans have such *interesting* historical figures," he said, and her laughter lifted the last shadow from Sean's heart.

"I'm really glad to see you up again, Harry, and I'm sorry you can't remember what happened. The rest of us'll put together a combined implant download later, but for now let's turn our attention to what we got out of it. Aside, of course, from the reincarnation of Captain Bonny."

His wave gave Sandy the floor, and she stood.

"Speaking for myself, Harry, I'm *delighted* you're back. Tam's been doing his best, but he'll never make an analyst." Tamman made a pained sound, and Harriet poked him in the ribs.

"However," Sandy went on with a grin, "our ham-handed Marine and I have recovered a fair amount from our purloined computer, and our original hypothesis was correct. It *was* a journal. This man's."

Sean gazed at the image in the command deck display, mentally turning the hair white and the skin to parchment, and recognized the lonely, mummified body from the tower bedroom.

"This is—or was—an engineer named Kahtar. Much of his journal's unrecoverable, and he didn't mention the planet's name in the portions we've been able to read, so we still don't know what it was called originally. But I've been able to piece together what happened."

She looked around, satisfied by the hush about her. Even Tamman knew only fragments of what she was about to say, and she wondered if the others would react as she had . . . and if they'd have the same nightmares.

"Apparently," she began, "the planetary governor closed down the mattrans at the first hypercom warning, then began immediate construction of a quarantine system under the direction of his chief engineer. Who," she added wryly, "was obviously a real whiz.

"Things weren't too bad at the start. There was some panic, and a few disturbances from people afraid they hadn't gotten quarantined soon enough, but nothing they couldn't handle . . . at first." She paused, and her eyes darkened.

"They might have made it, if they'd just shut down their hypercom. Their defenses destroyed over a dozen incoming refugee ships, but I think they could have lived even with that . . . if the hypercom hadn't still been up.

"It was like a com link to Hell." Her voice was quiet. "It was such a slow, agonizing process. Other worlds thought *they* were safe, too, but they weren't, and, one by one, the plague killed them all. It took years—years of desperate, dwindling messages from infected planets while their entire universe died."

Icy silence hovered on the command deck, and she blinked misty eyes.

"It . . . got to them. Not at once. But when the last hypercom went silent, when there was no one else left—no one at all—the horror was too much. The whole planet went mad."

"Mad?" Brashan's voice was soft, and she nodded.

"They knew what had happened, you see. They knew they'd done it to themselves. That it had all been a mistake—a technological accident on a cosmic scale. So they decided to insure there would never be another one. Technology had killed the Empire . . . so they killed technology."

"They what?" Sean jerked up, and she nodded. "But . . . but they had a high-tech population. How did they expect to *feed* it without technology?"

"They didn't care," Sandy said sadly. "The psychic wounds were too deep. That's what happened to their tech base: they smashed it themselves."

"Surely not all of them agreed," Harriet half-whispered.

"No." Sandy was grim. "There were some sane ones left—like Kahtar— but not enough. They fought a war here like you wouldn't believe. A high-tech war *intended* to destroy its own culture . . . and anyone who tried to stop them. Harry, they threw people into bonfires for trying to hide *books*."

Harriet covered her mouth, trembling with a personal terror they all understood too well, and Tamman hugged her.

"Sorry," Sandy said gently, and Harriet nodded jerkily. "Anyway, they didn't quite get all of it. The Valley of the Damned was a sort of high-tech redoubt. There'd been others, but the mobs rolled over them—sometimes they used human wave attacks and literally ran the defenses out of ammunition with their own bodies. Only the valley held. Their energy guns didn't need ammo, and they threw back over thirty attacks in barely ten years. The last one was made by a mob on foot, in the middle of a mountain winter, armed with spears and a handful of surviving Imperial weapons."

She fell silent once more, and they waited, sharing her horror, until she inhaled and went on in a flat voice.

"The attacks on the valley finally ended because the others *had* managed to destroy their technology, and, with it, their agriculture, their transport system, their medical structure—everything. Starvation, disease, exposure, even cannibalism . . . within a generation, they were down to a population they could support with an almost neolithic culture. Kahtar estimated that over a billion people died in less than ten years.

"But—" her voice sharpened and she leaned forward "—there was, obviously, one other high-tech center left: the quarantine HQ. Even the most frenzied mob knew that was all that stood between them and any possible refugee ship, however slight the chance one might arrive, and the HQ staff rigged up a ground defense element in the quarantine system itself. It's nowhere near as powerful as the space defenses, but it's designed to smash anyone or anything using Imperial weapons within a hundred klicks of the HQ."

"Oh, *crap*," Sean breathed, and she smiled tightly.

"You got it. And there's worse. You see, the command staff may have set things up to keep the mobs from smashing the HQ, but they agreed with the need to destroy all *other* technology."

"I don't think I'm going to like this," Tamman muttered.

"You're not. They moved out of those ruins near the Temple, put the HQ computer on voice access, set the shipyard up to handle all maintenance on an automated basis, and manufactured a religion."

"Oh, Jesus!" Sean moaned.

"According to Kahtar, who was pretty much running the valley by then, the port admiral had some sort of vision that turned the bio-weapon into the Flood and Pardal into Noah's Ark. But *this* Flood was a punishment for the sin of technological pride into which the 'Great Demons' had seduced mankind, and the 'Ark' was a refuge to which God had guided the handful of faithful who had resisted the demons' temptation. The survivors were the seed corn of the New Zion, selected by God to create a society without the 'evils' of technology."

"But if that's true," Brashan said, "why didn't they destroy the valley? If they had the capability to set up ground defenses, surely they had the capability to strike Kahtar's people."

"There was no need. There were never more than a hundred people in the valley, and it was a vacation resort before they forted up, without any real industrial base. They were trapped inside it, with too little genetic material to sustain a viable population, and the new religion had a use for them— one so important it didn't even pull the plug on their power supply."

"Demons," Harriet murmured.

"Or, more precisely, a nest of 'lesser demons' and their worshipers. The valley gave their religion a 'threat' that might last for centuries to help it get its feet under it. What we walked into was Hell itself as far as the Church is concerned, and that's why anyone who has anything to do with it *must* be exterminated."

"Merciful God." Sean looked as sick as he felt. The warped logic and cold-blooded calculation that left those poor, damned souls penned up in their valley as the very embodiment of evil twisted his guts. He tried to imagine how it must have felt to know every other human on the planet was waiting, literally praying for the chance to murder you, and wanted to vomit.

"I think Kahtar went mad himself, at the end. Some of the others walked out of the valley when the despair finally got to be too much—walked out *knowing* what would happen. Others suicided. None of them were interested in having children. What future would children have had on a planet of homemade barbarians itching to torture them to death?

"But Kahtar had to find something to believe in, and he did—something that kept him alive to the very end, after all the others were gone. He decided, against all evidence and sanity, that at least one other world had to have survived. That's why he wired his journal into the main computers. He left it there for us, or someone like us, so we'd know what had happened. And that's why he included something very important for us to know."

"What?" Sean asked.

"The last of the original HQ crew didn't just put the computer on voice access, Sean. They knew there were still at least some enhanced people in the valley. People who could have ordered the Voice to denounce their precious religion if they'd been able to get close enough to access the computer, because they could have overridden voice commands through their implants once the last of the original 'priests' were gone. So they disengaged the neural feeds. The *only* way in is by voice, and they had an entire damned army sitting on top of it to keep everyone but the priesthood out of voice access range. With the quarantine system set up to wax anybody who tried to use Imperial weapons to shoot their way in, there was no way a handful of old, tired Imperials could get to them."

She paused and met their horrified gazes.

"Which means, of course, that *we* can't get to them, either."

Sean sat in the cutter bay hatch, high on *Israel*'s flank, and gazed sightlessly out through the wavering distortion of her stealth field. They were still making progress on their linguistic programs, helped by the fact that they were no longer afraid to use their remotes at full range as long as they stayed outside the Temple's hundred-kilometer kill zone, yet two weeks had passed since Sandy's bombshell, and none of them had the least idea what to do next. The only good thing was that Harriet was completely back on her feet now—she was even jogging on *Israel*'s treadmill again.

He sighed and tugged on his nose, looking very like an oversized, black-haired version of his father as he contemplated the problem. He'd expected difficulties getting into the Temple, but he'd never anticipated that they wouldn't even be able to use Imperial small arms! Hell, they might not even be able to use their own *implants*, so how did four humans—and one Narhani, who'd be mobbed on sight as an incontrovertible "demon"— break into the most strongly guarded fortress on the entire goddamned planet?

There was, of course, one very simple answer, but he couldn't do it. He couldn't even think of it without nausea. Kahtar's journal indicated "the Sanctum" was heavily armored and deeply dug in, but they could always take the place out with a gravitonic warhead, and *Israel* could launch hyper weapons from atmosphere. They could hit the Temple before the quarantine system even began to react, and if the computer went down, so did the entire system. Unfortunately, they also killed everyone in Pardal's largest city—almost two million people, by Sandy's estimate.

He squeezed his nose harder. His clever stratagem to get them down had worked, all right, and he'd poked their collective heads right into a trap. They couldn't take off—assuming they'd had anywhere to go—without the quarantine system killing them for trying to leave the planet, but there wasn't any way to shut the system off *from* the planet!

"Sean?" He looked up at Sandy's voice. She was standing at the far end of the bay, waving at him. "Come on! You've gotta see this!"

"See what?" he asked, climbing to his feet with a puzzled frown.

"It's too good to spoil by telling you." Her expression was strange, and she sounded amused, frightened, excited, and surprised, all in one.

"At least give me a clue!"

"All right." She eyed him with an odd, lurking smile. "I didn't have anything else to do, so I sent a remote back to take a peek at the village we pulled Harry out of, and you won't *believe* what's going on!"

"Well, Father," Tibold closed the spyglass with a click and grimaced at Stomald, "it seems His Grace was unimpressed."

Stomald nodded, shading his eyes with his hand, and tried not to show his own despair. He hadn't expected Bishop Frenaur to accept his unsupported word without question, but he certainly hadn't counted on *this*.

Mother Church's blood-red standards advanced up the twisting valley, blue and gold cantons glittering, and metal gleamed behind them: pikeheads and muskets, armor, and the dully-flashing barrels of artillery.

"How many, do you think?" he asked quietly.

"Enough." The Guard captain squinted into the sun, frowning. "More than I expected, really. I'd say that's most of the Malagoran Temple Guard out there, Father. Call it twenty thousand men."

Stomald nodded again, grateful Tibold hadn't said, "I told you so." The Guard captain had argued against sending the good word to the Temple. Unlike Stomald, Tibold wasn't a native-born Malagoran, but he knew the Temple regarded Malagor as a hotbed of sedition, and seeing that armed, advancing host, Stomald was just as glad he'd at least agreed to send his news by semaphore rather than taking it in person.

He shook that thought off and pressed his lips together. Surely God had sent His angels to Cragsend for a purpose. He didn't promise His servants would always be bright enough to *see* His purpose, but He always had one. Of course, sometimes it wasn't a very safe one. . . .

"What do you advise?"

"Running away?" Tibold suggested with a smile, and Stomald surprised himself with a chuckle.

"I don't think God would like that. Besides, where would we run to? We're backed up against the mountains, Tibold."

"Just like a kinokha in a trap," the Guard captain agreed, wondering why he wasn't more frightened. He'd thought his young priest was mad at first, but something about him had been convincing. Certainly, Tibold told himself yet again, those *hadn't* been demons. He'd seen too much of what men, touched with God's immortal spirit, were capable of in time of war. No, if they'd been demons, Cragsend would be a smoking ruin peopled only by the dead.

And, like Father Stomald, he could think of only one other thing they could have been, though he did wish they'd been a bit less ambiguous in their message. Still, he supposed that was *his* fault. He was the damn-fool idiot who'd shot the first of them down. Even an angel might forget her message with a bullet in her head, and the others had seemed more intent on getting her back than dropping off any letters.

He snorted. The other local villages and towns—even Cragwall, the largest town in the Shalokar Range—had sent their priests to stare at the wreckage and hear Father Stomald's tale. Tibold had never realized just how powerful a preacher Stomald was until he heard him speaking to those visitors, bringing forward other villagers to bear witness, describing the angel who'd spoken in the Holy Tongue even while the sanctified oil blazed upon her. It was a pity he couldn't have a word or two with the commander of that army, for he'd brought everyone else around. Of course, his audience had been Malagorans, with all a Malagoran's resentment of foreign domination, and Tibold knew better than most how jealous the Temple was of its secular power. Whoever was in command down there had his orders from the Circle; he was hardly likely to forget them on the say-so of a village under-priest, however eloquent.

Tibold reopened his glass to study the standards once more. Columns of smoke rose behind them—columns which had once been farmsteads and small villages. The people who'd lived there had either come to join the "heresy" or fled to escape it, and he was grateful they had, for the smoke told him what the Guard's orders were. Mother Church had decided to make an example of the "rebels" and declared Holy War, and her Guard would take no prisoners.

"Well, Father," he said at last, "I don't see much choice. I've got five hundred musketeers, a thousand pikemen, and four thousand with nothing but their bare hands. Even with God on our side, that's not a lot."

"No," Stomald sighed. "I wish I could say God will save us, but sometimes we can meet our Trial only by dying for what we know to be right."

"Agreed. But I'm a soldier, Father, and, if it's all the same to you, I'd like to die as one—without making it any easier for them than I have to."

"I don't know of any Writ that says you should," Stomald said with a sad smile.

"Then we'll fall back to Tilbor Pass. It's less than four hundred paces across, and it'll take even this lot a few days to dig us out of that." Stomald nodded, and the Guardsman smiled crookedly. "And in the meantime, Father, I won't take it a bit amiss if you ask God to help us out of the mess we've landed ourselves in!"

"You're joking!" Sean stared at the images from the remote. "*Angels?*"

"Yep." Sandy's eyes sparkled. "Wild, isn't it?"

"My God." Sean sank onto his couch. All the others were gazing as fixedly as he at the display.

"Actually, it's not as crazy as it sounds," Harriet mused. "I mean, we obviously weren't mortals—not with bio-enhancement, grav guns, and plasma grenades—and if you aren't mortal, you're either a demon or an angel. And I've been back over your reports." Her voice wavered, for the others had prepared their promised implant download. She still had no memory of the event, but the download had shown it all to her through her friends' eyes. She shivered as her mind replayed the image of her own bloody body, awaiting the torch, then shook herself. "It looks like the only two they saw clearly were Sandy and me."

"That's what I gather from what this Father Stomald is saying." Sandy switched to an image of the priest and smiled wryly as she recalled the last time she'd seen the broad-shouldered, curly-haired young man with the neatly trimmed beard. He looked far more composed now as he stood talking to the hard-faced soldier at his side.

"He's kind of cute, isn't he?" Harriet murmured, then blushed as Sean gave her a very speaking look and she remembered what that cute young man had almost done to her. She rubbed her eye patch and gave herself another shake.

"Anyway, if we're the only ones he saw, it all makes sense. Their church is patriarchal—well, for that matter, most of Pardal is. Malagor's sort of radical in that respect; they actually let women own property. The thought of a woman in the priesthood is anathema, but there Sandy and I were in Battle Fleet uniform . . . which just happens to be what their bishops wear for their holiest church feasts. Add the fact that this patriarchal outfit has decided, for reasons best known to themselves, that angels are female—"

"And beautiful," Tamman inserted.

"As I say, angels are female," Harriet went on repressively. "They're also immortal, but not invulnerable, which explains how I could have been injured, and this Stomald seems to realize you three deliberately didn't kill anyone when you came in like gangbusters. Given all that, there's actually a weird sort of logic to the whole thing."

"Yeah," Sean said more soberly, and changed the display himself. The marching columns of armed men sent a visible chill through *Israel*'s crew, and he sighed. "We may not have killed anyone, but it looks like maybe we *should* have. At least then we would have been 'demons' instead of some kind of divine messengers that're going to get *all* of them massacred."

"Maybe . . . and maybe not. . . ." Sandy was gazing at the advancing Temple Guard, and the light in her eyes worried Sean.

"What d'you mean?" he demanded, and she gave him a beatific smile.

"I mean we just found the key to the Temple's front door."

"Huh?" her lover said sapiently, and her smile became a grin.

"We don't want all those people slaughtered for something we started, however unintentionally, do we?" Four heads shook, and she shrugged. "In that case, we've got to rescue them."

"And how do you propose to do that?"

"Oh, that's the easy part. Those guys are a heck of a lot more than a hundred kilometers from the Temple."

"Hold on there!" Sean protested. "I don't want to see Stomald and his fellow nuts massacred, but I don't want to massacre anyone else, either!"

"No need," she assured him. "We can probably scare the poo out of them with a few holo projections without even a demonstration of firepower."

"Hum." Sean looked at the others, and his eyes began to dance. "Yeah, I suppose we could. Might even be fun."

"Don't get too carried away," Sandy said, "because what happens *after* we scare 'em is what really matters."

"What are you talking about?" Tamman sounded puzzled.

"I mean that whether we like it or not, the fat's in the fire. Either we let the Church massacre these people, or we rescue them. If we rescue them, do you think the Temple's just going to say, 'Gosh! Looks like we better leave those nasty demon-worshiping heretics alone'? And *they're* not going to go home like nothing happened, either, because if we save them, we reconfirm their belief in divine intervention."

"Great," Sean sighed.

"Maybe it is." He looked up in surprise, and she shrugged. "We didn't do it on purpose, but we can't *un*do it. So if the Temple wants a crusade, why not give it one?"

"Are you saying we should instigate a religious war?!" Harriet stared at her in horror, and Sandy shrugged again.

"I'm saying we already have," she said more soberly. "That gives us a responsibility to end it, one way or another, and we're not going to be able to do that without getting our hands bloody. I don't like that any more than you do, Harry, but we don't have a choice—unless we want to sit back and watch Stomald and his people go down.

"So if we have to get involved, let's go whole hog. The Church is too big, too static. Even the secular lords are lap dogs for it. But the only way Stomald's going to survive is to take out the Inner Circle . . . and that just happens to be what *we* need to do to get into the Sanctum."

"I don't know. . . ." Harriet said slowly, but Sean was staring at Sandy in admiration.

"My God, Sandy—that's brilliant!"

"Well, pretty darn smart, anyway," she agreed. Then she laughed. "Anyway, we're certainly the right people for the job!" Sean looked blank, and her grin seemed to split her face. "Of course we are, Sean! After all, we *are* the Lost Children of *Israel*, aren't we?"

CHAPTER TWENTY-FOUR

Sean grimaced as his stealthed fighter, one of only three *Israel* carried, hovered above the twisting gorge. It was sheer, deep, and dizzy, with vertical walls that narrowed to less than two hundred meters where they'd been closed with earthworks, and he saw why the "heretics" had retreated into it, but such tight quarters made maneuvering for the shot a bitch.

He checked his scanners. The cutter Sandy, Harriet, and Brashan rode was as invisible as the fighter, but their synchronized stealth fields made it clear to his own instruments while they ran their final checks.

He wished there'd been time to test their jury-rigged holo projector properly. It would have been nice to have had more planning time, too. Building a strategy in less than ten hours offered little scope for careful consideration, though he had to admit Sandy seemed to have answered his major objections.

The hardest part, in many ways, was the limits on what they could offer these people. It would take a "miracle" to save them this time, but it was the only miracle *Israel*'s crew could work. They dared not use Imperial technology within a hundred klicks of the Temple, yet if they used it up to that point and then stopped, the result would be disastrous. Not only would it offer the Temple fresh hope, but the sudden cessation would fill the "heretics" with dismay. It might well convince them they *were* heretics, that the "false angels" dared not confront the Temple on its own ground, and that limitation was going to make even more problems than Harriet's monkey wrench.

He puffed his lips and wished his twin were just a little less principled. Her insistence that they never claim divine status was going to make things difficult—and probably wouldn't be believed anyway. Yet she was right. They'd done enough damage, and, assuming they won the war they'd provoked, they'd eventually have to convince their "allies" they weren't really angels. Besides, demanding their worship would have made him feel unclean.

He turned his attention to the army of the Church. Those earthworks looked almost impregnable, but the valley formed a funnel to them, and the Temple Guard was busy deploying field guns under cover of darkness. With the dawn, dozens of them would be able to open fire across a wide arc. They didn't look very heavy—they might throw five or six-kilo shot—but there were a lot of them, and he didn't see any in the heretics' camp.

"Wish Sandy's dad was here," he muttered.

"Or *my* dad," Tamman grunted. "Better yet, Mom!"

"I'd settle for any of 'em, but Uncle Hector's the history nut. I don't know crap about black powder and pikes."

"We'll just have to pick up on-the-job training. And at least we've got the right accouterments." Tamman grinned and rapped his soot-black breast-plate. Sean wore a matching breast and backplate with mail sleeves. The armor, like the swords racked behind their flight couches, came from *Israel*'s machine shops, and the materials of which they were made would have raised more than a few eyebrows in either of the camps below.

"Easy for you to say," Sean grunted. "You were the big wheel on the fencing team—I'm likely to cut my own damn head off!"

"These guys are more into broadsword tactics," Tamman pointed out. "I don't know how much fencing's going to help against that. But we've both got enhanced reaction speeds, and none—"

"Sean, it's show time." Sandy's quiet transmission cut Tamman off.

Tibold Rarikson stood behind the parapet, straining his eyes into the night, and rubbed his aching back. It had been years since last he'd plied a mat-tock, but most of his "troops" were only local militia. They had yet to learn a shovel was as much a weapon as any sword . . . and it seemed unlikely they'd have time to digest the lesson. He couldn't see it in the dark, but he knew they were bringing up the guns, and Mother Church's edict against secular artillery heavier than chagors gave the Guard a monopoly on the heavier arlak. Of course, *he* didn't even have any chagors, though his malagors might come as a nasty surprise. Except that he faced Guards who'd spent most of their enlistments in Malagor, so they knew all about the heavy-bore musket that was the princedom's national trademark. . . .

He shook himself. His wandering thoughts were wearing ruts, and it wasn't as if any of it really mattered. There were more than enough Guardsmen to soak up all the musket balls he had and close with cold steel, which meant—

His thoughts broke off as a dim pool of light glowed suddenly into exis-tence between him and the Guard's pickets. He rubbed his eyes and blinked hard, but the wan radiance refused to vanish, and he poked the nearest sentry.

"Here, you! Go get Father Stomald!"

"Captain Ithun! Look!"

Under-Captain Ithun jumped and smothered a curse as heated wine spilled down his front. The Guard officer—one of the very few native Malagorans in the Temple's detachment to the restive province—mopped at his breast-plate, muttering to himself, and stalked towards the picket who'd shouted.

"Look at what, Surgam?" he demanded irritably. "I don't—"

His voice died. An amorphous cloud of light hovered five hundred paces away, almost at the edge of the ditch footing the heretic's earthen rampart. It seethed and wavered, growing brighter as he watched, and his hair tried to stand on end under his helmet. The incredible tales told by the handful of heretics they'd so far captured poured through his mind, and his mouth was dust-dry as the eerie luminescence flowed towards him.

He swallowed. If the heretics were meddling with the Valley of the Damned, then that might be a—

He stopped himself before he thought the word.

"Get Father Uriad!" he snapped, and Private Surgam raced off into the dark with rather more than normal speediness.

"What is it, Tibold?" Stomald had finally managed to fall asleep, and his mind was still logy as he panted from his hasty run.

"Look for yourself, Father," Tibold said tautly, and Stomald's mouth fell open. The ball of light was taller than three men and growing taller.

"I— How long has that been there?!"

"No more than five minutes, but—" Tibold's explanation broke off, and the Guardsman swallowed so hard Stomald heard it plainly even as he fell to his own knees in awe.

The pearly light had suddenly darkened, rearing to a far greater height, and he groped for his starburst as it coalesced into a mighty figure.

"Saint Yorda preserve us!" someone cried, and Stomald's thoughts echoed the unseen sentry as the blue and gold shape towered in the night, lit by fearsome inner light. Her back was to him, and she might be twenty times taller than the last time he'd seen her, but he recognized that short hair, cut like a helmet of curly silk, and his lips shaped a soft, fervent prayer as he recalled a thundering voice from a mass of flames.

"Dear God!" Under-Captain Ithun whispered.

The light streaming from the unearthly figure washed the gorge walls in rippling waves of blue and gold, and its brown eyes glowed like beacons. He fought his panic, locking trembling sinews against the urge to fall to his knees, and cries of terror rose from his men. A demon, he told himself. It had to be a demon! But there was something in that stern face. Something in the set of that firm mouth. Could it be the heretics were—?

He slashed the thought off, wavering on the brink of flight. If he so much as stepped back his company would vanish, but he was only a man! How—?

"God preserve us!"

He wheeled at the whispered prayer and gasped in relief. He reached out, heedless of discourtesy in his fear, and shook Father Uriad.

"What is it, Father?" he demanded. "In the name of God, *what is it?*"

"I—" Uriad began, and then the apparition spoke.

"Warriors of Mother Church!"

Stomald gasped, for the rolling thunder of that voice was ten times louder than in Cragsend—a hundred times! All about him men fell to their knees, clapping their hands over their ears as its majesty crashed through them. Surely the very cliffs themselves must fall before its power!

"Warriors of Mother Church," the angel cried, "turn from this madness! These are not your enemies—they are your brothers! Has Pardal not seen enough blood? Must you turn against the innocent to shed still more?"

The giant figure took one stride forward—a single stride that covered twenty mortal paces—and bent towards the terrified Temple Guard. Sadness touched those stern features, and one huge hand rose pleadingly.

"Look into your hearts, warriors of Mother Church," the sweet voice thundered. "Look into your souls. Will you stain your hands before man and God with the blood of innocent babes and women?"

"Demon!" Father Uriad cried as men turned to him in terror. "I tell you, it's a demon!"

"But—" someone began, and the priest rounded on him in a frenzy.

"Fool! Will you lose your own soul, as well? This is no angel! It is a demon from Hell itself!"

The Guardsmen wavered, and Uriad snatched a musket from a sentry. The man gawked at him, and he charged forward, evading the hands that clutched at him, to face the monster shape alone.

"Demon!" His shrill cry sounded thin and thready after that majestic voice. "Damned and accursed devil! Foul, unclean destroyer of innocence! I cast you out! Begone to the Hell from whence you came!"

The Temple Guard gaped, appalled yet mesmerized by his courage, and the towering shape looked down at him.

"Would you slay your own flock, Priest?" The vast voice was gentle, and clergymen in both armies gasped as it spoke the Holy Tongue. But Uriad was a man above himself, and he threw the musket to his shoulder.

"Begone, curse you!" he screamed, and the musket cracked and flashed.

"That tears it," Sean muttered, jockeying the fighter as Sandy's holo image straightened. "Why the hell couldn't they just *run*? Got lock, Tam?"

"Yeah. Jesus, I hope that idiot isn't as close as I think he is!"

"Priest," the contralto voice rolled like stern, sweet thunder, "you will not lead these men to their own damnation."

Upper-Priest Uriad stared up, clutching his musket. Powder smoke clawed at his nostrils, but the ball had left its target unmarked and terror pierced the armor of his rage. He trembled, yet if he fled his entire army would do the same, and he pried one clawed hand from the musket stock. He scrabbled at his breast, raising his starburst, and it flashed in his hand, lit by the radiance streaming from the apparition as her own hand pointed at the earth before her.

"These innocents are under my protection, Priest. I have no wish for any to die, but if die someone must, it will not be they!"

A brilliant ray of light speared from her massive finger.

✧   ✧   ✧

Tamman tightened as the fighter's main battery locked onto the laser designator within that beam. He took one more second, making himself double-check his readings. God, it was going to be close. They'd never counted on some idiot being gutsy enough to come to *meet* Sandy's holo image!

The ray of light touched the ground, and twenty thousand voices cried out in terror as a massive trench scored itself across the valley, wider than a tall man's height and thrice as deep. Dirt and dust vomited upward as the very bedrock exploded, and Father Uriad flew backward like a toy.

The raw smell of rock dust choked nose and throat, and it was too much. The Guardsmen screamed and turned as one. Sentries cast aside weapons. Artillerists abandoned their guns. Cooks threw down their ladles. Anything that might slow a man was hurled away, and the Temple Guard of Malagor stampeded into the night in howling madness.

The ray of light died, and the blue-and-gold shape turned from the shattered hosts of Mother Church to face Father Stomald's people.

The young priest drove himself to his feet, standing atop the rampart to face the angel he'd tried to slay, and the burning splendor of her eyes swept over him. He felt his followers' fear against his back, yet awe and reverence held them in their places, and the angel smiled gently.

"I will come among you," she told them, "in a form less frightening. Await me."

And the majestic shape of light and glory vanished.

CHAPTER TWENTY-FIVE

Father Stomald sat down to the supper on the camp table with a groan. He hadn't expected to be alive to eat it, and he was tired enough to wonder if it was worth the bother. Just organizing the unexpected booty abandoned by the Guard had been exhausting, yet Tibold was right. The dispersal of one army was no guarantee of victory, and those weapons were priceless. Besides, the Guard might regain enough courage to reclaim them if they weren't collected.

But at least deciding what to do with pikes and muskets was fairly simple. Other problems were less so—like the more than four thousand Guardsmen who'd trickled back and begged to join "the Angels' Army" as wonder overcame terror. Stomald had welcomed them, but Tibold insisted no newcomer, however welcome, be accepted unquestioningly. It was only a matter of time before the Church attempted to infiltrate spies in the guise of converts, and he preferred to establish the rules now.

Stomald saw his point, but discussing what to do had taken hours. For now, Tibold had four thousand new laborers; as they proved their sincerity, they would be integrated into his units—with, Tibold had observed dryly, non-Guardsmen on either side to help suppress any temptation to treason.

Yet all such questions, while important and real, had been secondary to most of Stomald's people. God's own messengers had intervened for them, and if Malagorans were too pragmatic to let joy interfere with tasks they knew must be performed, they went about those tasks with spontaneous hymns. And Stomald, as shepherd of a vaster flock than he'd ever anticipated, had been deeply involved in planning and leading the solemn services of thanksgiving which had both begun and closed this long, exhausting day.

All of which meant he'd had little enough time to breathe, much less eat.

Now he mopped up the last of the shemaq stew and slumped on his camp stool with a sigh. He could hear the noises of the camp, but his tent stood on a small rise, isolated from the others by the traditional privacy of the clergy. That isolation bothered him, yet the ability to think and pray uninterrupted was a priceless treasure whose value to a leader he was coming to appreciate.

He raised his head, gazing past the tied-back flap at the staff-hung lantern just outside. More lanterns and torches twinkled in the narrow valley below him, and he heard the lowing of the hundreds of nioharqs the Guard had abandoned. There were fewer branahlks—the speedy saddle beasts had been in high demand as the Church's warriors fled—but the nioharqs, more than man-high at the shoulder, would be invaluable when it came to moving their camp. And—

His thoughts chopped off, and he lunged to his feet as the air before him suddenly wavered like heat above a flame. Then it solidified, and he gazed upon the angel who had saved his people.

Sean and Tamman waited outside the tent inside their portable stealth fields. The trip across the camp had been . . . interesting, since people don't avoid things they can't see. Sandy had almost been squashed by a freight wagon, and her expression as she nipped aside had been priceless.

Sean had planned to get this over with last night, but the totality of the Guard's rout—and the treasure-trove of its abandoned camp—had changed his schedule. One thing Stomald hadn't needed while he organized that windfall was the intrusion of still more miracles. Besides, the delay had given Sean time to watch the "heretics" work, and he'd been deeply impressed by Stomald's military commander. That man was a professional to his toenails, and a soldier of his caliber was going to be invaluable.

But that was for the future, and right now he tried not to laugh at the priest's expression when Sandy suddenly materialized in front of him.

Stomald's jaw dropped, and then he fell to his knees before the angel. He signed God's starburst while his own inadequacy suffused him, coupled with a soaring joy that, inadequate as he was, God had seen fit to touch him with His Finger, and held his breath as he awaited some sign of her will.

"Stand up, Stomald," a soft voice said in the Holy Tongue. He stared at the floor of his tent, then rose tremblingly. "Look at me," the angel said, and he raised his eyes to her face. "That's better."

The angel crossed his tent and sat in one of his camp chairs, and he watched her in silence. She moved with easy grace, and she was even smaller than he'd thought on that terrible night. Her head was little higher than his shoulder when she stood, but there was nothing fragile about her tiny form.

Brown hair gleamed under the lantern light, cut short as a man's but in an indefinably feminine style. Her clean-cut mouth was firm, yet he felt oddly certain those lips were meant to smile. Her triangular face was built of huge eyes, high cheekbones, and a determined chin that lacked the beauty of the angel Tibold's huntsmen had wounded yet radiated strength and purpose.

She returned his gaze calmly, and he cleared his throat and fiddled with his starburst, trying to think. But what did a man *say* to God's messenger? Good evening? How are you? Do you think it will rain?

He had no idea, and the angel's eyes twinkled. Yet it was a kindly twinkle, and she took pity on his tongue-tied silence.

"I said I would visit you." Her voice was deep for a woman's, but without the thunder of her wrath it was sweet and soft, and his pulse slowed.

"You honor us, Holiness," he managed, and the angel shook her head.

" 'Holiness' is a priestly title, and I am but a visitor from a distant land."

"Then . . . then by what title shall I address you?"

"None," she said simply, "but my name is Sandy."

Stomald's heart leapt as she bestowed her name upon him, for it was a new name, unlike any he'd ever heard.

"As you command," he murmured with a bow, and she frowned.

"I'm not here to command you, Stomald." He flinched, afraid he'd angered her, and she shook her head as she saw his fear.

"Things have gone awry," she told him. "It was no part of our purpose to embroil your people in holy war against the Church. It was ill-done of us to endanger your land and lives."

Stomald bit down on a need to reject her self-accusation. She was God's envoy; she could not do ill. Yet, he reminded himself, angels were but God's servants, not gods themselves, and so, perhaps, they *could* err. The novel thought was disturbing, but her tone told him it was true.

"We did more ill than you," he said humbly. "We wounded your fellow angel and laid impious, violent hands upon her. That God should send you to us once more to save us from His own Church when we have done such wrong is a greater mercy than any mortals can deserve, O Sandy."

Sandy grimaced. She'd intended to leave angels entirely out of this if she could, but Pardalians, like Terrans, had more than one word for "angel." *Sha'hia*, the most common, was derived from the Imperial Universal for "messenger," just as the English word descended from the Greek for the same thing. Unfortunately, there was another, derived from the word for "visitor"—from, in fact, *erathiu*, the very word she'd just let herself use—and her slip hadn't escaped Stomald. He had been using *sha'hia*; now he was using *erathu*, and if she corrected him, he would only assume he'd mispronounced it. Explaining what *she* meant by "visitor" would get into areas so far beyond his worldview that any attempt to discuss them was guaranteed to produce a crisis of conscience, and she bit her lip, then shrugged. Harry was right about the care they had to take, but Harry was just going to have to accept the best she could do.

"You did only what you thought was required," she said carefully, "and neither I nor Harry herself hold it against you."

"Then . . . then she lived?" Stomald's face blossomed in relief, and Sandy reminded herself that Pardalian angels could be killed.

"She did. Yet what brings me here is the danger in which your people stand, Stomald. We have our own purpose to achieve, but in seeking to achieve it we put you in peril of your lives. If we could, we would undo what we've done, yet that lies beyond our power."

Stomald nodded. Holy Writ said angels were powerful beings, but Man had free will. His actions could set even an angel's purpose at naught, and he flushed in shame as he realized his flock had done just that. Yet the Angel Sandy wasn't enraged; she'd saved them, and the genuine concern in her soft voice filled his heart with gratitude.

"Because we can't undo it," Sandy continued, "we must begin from what has happened. It may be we can combine our purpose with our responsibility to save your people from the consequences of our own errors, yet there are limits to what we may do. Last night, we had no choice but to intervene as we did, but we can't do so again. Our purpose forbids it."

Stomald swallowed. With Mother Church against them, how could they hope to survive without such aid? She saw his fear and smiled gently.

"I didn't say we can't intervene at all, Stomald—only that there are limits on how we may do so. We will aid you, but you must know that the Inner Circle will never rest until you've been destroyed. You threaten both their beliefs and their secular power over Malagor, and your threat is greater, not less, now, for word of what happened last night will spread on talmahk wings.

"Because of that, fresh armies will soon move against you, and I tell you that our purpose is not to see you die. We seek no martyrs. Death comes to all men, but we believe the purpose of Man is to help his fellows, not to kill them in God's name. Do you understand that?"

"I do," Stomald whispered. That was all he'd ever asked to do, and to be told by an angel that it was God's will—!

"Good," the angel murmured, then straightened in her chair, and her mouth turned firmer, her eyes darker. "Yet when others attack you, you have every right to fight back, and in this we will help you, if you wish. The choice is yours. We won't force you to accept our aid or our advice."

"Please." Stomald's hands half-rose, and he fought an urge to throw himself back to his knees. "Please, aid my people, I beg you."

"There is no need to beg." The angel regarded him sternly. "What we can do, we will do, but as friends and allies, not dictators."

"I—" Stomald swallowed again. "Forgive me, O Sandy. I am only a simple under-priest, unused to any of the things happening to me." His lips quirked despite his tension, for it was hard not to smile when her eyes were so understanding. "I doubt even High Priest Vroxhan would know what to say or do when confronted by an angel in his tent!" he heard himself say, and quailed, but the angel only smiled. She had dimples, he noted, and his spirits rose before her humor.

"No, I doubt he would," she agreed, a gurgle of laughter hovering in her soft voice, and then she shook herself.

"Very well, Stomald. Simply understand that we neither desire nor need your worship. Ask what you will of us, as you might ask any other man. If we can do it, we will; if we can't, we'll tell you so, and we won't hold your asking against you. Can you do that?"

"I can try," he agreed with greater confidence. It was hard to be frightened of one who so obviously meant him and his people well.

"Then let me tell you what we can do, since I've told you what we cannot. We can aid and advise you, and there are many things we can teach you. We can tell you much of what passes elsewhere, though not all, and while we can't slay your enemies with our own weapons, we can help you fight for your lives with your own if you choose to do so. Do you so choose?"

"We do." Stomald straightened. "We did no wrong, yet Mother Church came against us in Holy War. If such is her decision, we will defend ourselves against her as we must."

"Even knowing both you and the Inner Circle cannot survive? One of you must fall, Stomald. Are you prepared to assume that responsibility?"

"I am," he said even more firmly. "A shepherd may die for his flock, but his duty is to preserve that flock, not slay it. Mother Church herself teaches that. If the Inner Circle has forgotten, it must be taught anew."

"I think you are as wise as you are courageous, Stomald of Cragsend," she said, "and since you will protect your people, I bring you those to help you fight." She raised her hand, and Stomald gasped as the air shimmered once more and two more strangers appeared out of it.

One was scarcely taller than Stomald himself, square-shouldered and muscular in his night-black armor. His hair and eyes were as brown as the angel's, though his skin was much darker, and his hair was even shorter. A high-combed helmet rode in his bent elbow, and a long, slender sword hung at his side. He looked tough and competent, yet he might have been any mortal man.

But the other! This was a giant, towering above Stomald and his own companion. He wore matching armor and carried the same slender sword, but his eyes were black as midnight and his hair was darker still. He was far from handsome—indeed, his prominent nose and ears were almost ugly—but he met the priest's eyes with neither arrogance nor inner doubt . . . much, Stomald thought, as Tibold might have but for his automatic deference to the cloth.

"Stomald, these are my champions," the angel said quietly. "This—" she touched the shorter man's shoulder "—is Tamman Tammanson, and this—" she touched the towering giant, and her eyes seemed to soften for a moment "—is Sean Colinson. Will you have them as war captains?"

"I . . . would be honored," Stomald said, grappling with a fresh sense of awe. They weren't angels, for they were male, but something about them, something more even than their sudden appearance, whispered they were more than mortal, like the legendary heroes of the old tales.

"I thank you for your trust," Sean Colinson—and what sort of name was that?—said. His voice was deep, but he spoke accented Pardalian, not the Holy Tongue, as he offered a huge right hand. "As Sandy says, your destiny is your own, but your danger is none of your making. If I can help, I will."

"And I." Tamman Tammanson stood a half-pace behind his companion, like a shieldman or an under-captain, but his voice was equally firm.

"And now, Stomald," the Angel Sandy said in the Holy Tongue, "it may be time to summon Tibold. We have much to discuss."

Tibold Rarikson sat in his camp chair and felt his head turning back and forth like an untutored yokel. He'd found his eyes had a distinct tendency to jerk away from the Angel Harry's beautiful face whenever she glanced his way, and it shamed him. She hadn't said a word to condemn him for shooting her down, and he was grateful for her understanding, yet somehow he suspected he would have felt better if she'd been less so.

But it wasn't just guilt which kept pulling his gaze from her, for he'd never imagined meeting with such a group. The man the angels called Sean was a giant among men, and the one called Tamman had skin the color of old jelath wood, yet the angels automatically drew the eye from their champions. The Angel Harry might be shorter than Lord Sean, but she was a head taller than most men, and despite her blind eye, she seemed to look deep inside a man's soul every time her remaining eye met his. Yet for all that, it seemed odd to see her in trousers, even those of the priestly raiment she wore. She should have been in the long, bright skirts of a Malagoran woman, not men's garb, for despite her height and seeming youth, she radiated a gentle compassion which made one trust her instantly.

And then there was the Angel Sandy. Even on this short an acquaintance, Tibold suspected no one was likely to imagine *her* in skirts! Her brown eyes glowed with the resolution of a seasoned war captain, her words were crisp and incisive, and *she* radiated the barely leashed energy of a hunting seldahk.

" . . . so as you and the Angel Sandy say—" Stomald was saying in response to Lord Sean's last comment when the angel leaned forward with a frown.

"Don't call us that," she said. Tibold had spent enough years in the Temple's service to gain a rough understanding of the Holy Tongue, but he'd never heard an accent quite like hers. Not that he needed to have heard it before to recognize its note of command.

Stomald sat back in his own chair with a puzzled expression, looking at Tibold, then turned back to the angel. His confusion was evident, and it showed in his voice when he spoke again.

"I meant no offense," he said humbly, and the angel bit her lip. She glanced at the Angel Harry, whose single good eye returned her look levelly, almost as if in command, then sighed.

"I'm not offended, Stomald," she said carefully, "but there are . . . reasons Harry and I wish you would avoid that title."

"Reasons?" Stomald repeated hesitantly, and she shook her head.

"In time, you'll understand them, Stomald. I promise. But for now, please humor us in this."

"As you comm—" Stomald began, then stopped and corrected himself. "As you wish, Lady Sandy," he said, and glanced at Tibold once more. The ex-Guardsman shrugged slightly. As far as he was concerned, an angel could be called whatever she wished. Labels meant nothing, and any village idiot could tell what the angels *were*, however they cared to be *addressed*.

"As *Lady* Sandy says," Stomald continued after a moment, "the first step must be to consolidate our own position. The weapons the Guard abandoned will help there—" he glanced at Tibold, who nodded vigorously "—but you're correct, Lord Sean. We cannot stand passively on the defensive. I am no war captain, yet it seems to me that we must secure control of the Keldark Valley as soon as possible."

"Exactly," Lord Sean said in his deep, accented voice. "There are a lot of things Tamman and I can teach your army, Tibold, but we can't make the Temple stand still while we do it. We've got to secure control of the valley—and the Thirgan Gap—quickly enough to discourage the Guard from anything adventurous."

"Agreed, Lord Sean," Tibold said. "If the An—" He paused with a blush. "If *Lady* Sandy and Lady Harry can provide us with the information on enemy movements you've described, we'll have a tremendous advantage, but too many of our men have little or no experience. They'll need good, hard drilling, and if we can do it in a strong enough defensive position, the Guard may leave us alone long enough to do some good."

"Very well, then," Stomald said firmly. "We will be guided by you and the An—you and the Lady Sandy and Lady Harry, Lord Sean. Tomorrow morning, Tibold and I will introduce you to our army as its new commander, and we will act as you direct."

High Priest Vroxhan sat behind his desk and glared at Bishop Frenaur and Lord Marshal Rokas. Neither quite met his fiery eyes, and he growled something under his breath, then inhaled deeply and managed—somehow, out of a lifetime of clerical discipline—to still his need to curse at them.

"Very well," he grated, placing one hand on the message upon his blotter, "I want to know how this happened."

Frenaur cleared his throat. He hadn't visited Malagor in half a year, but he'd read the semaphore messages to Vroxhan and additional, personal ones from Under-Bishop Shendar in Malgos, the Malagoran capital. He wasn't certain he believed what they reported, but if even a tenth of them were true . . .

"Holiness, I'm not certain," he said at last. "Father Uriad led the Guard against the heretics as the Circle directed, and for almost a moon he met with total success. There was no resistance until they reached the northern Shalokars and the heretics fortified a pass. He moved against them and—" He broke off and shrugged helplessly. "Holiness, the Guardsmen who fled all insist they saw *something*, and their descriptions certainly tally with the heretic Stomald's descriptions of his 'angels.'"

"*Angels?*" Vroxhan spat. "*Angels* who kill a consecrated priest?"

"I didn't say it *was* an angel, Holiness." Frenaur managed not to retreat. "I said it matched Stomald's descriptions. And whatever it was, it protected the heretics with powers which were far more than mortal."

"Assuming the cowards who fled aren't lying in fear of Mother Church's wrath," Vroxhan snarled, and Marshal Rokas stirred at Frenaur's side.

"Holiness," the grizzled veteran's rough voice was deferential but unafraid,

"Captain-General Yorkan reports the same thing. I know Yorkan. I would know if his report was an attempt to cover himself." The grim old warrior met his master's eyes, and Vroxhan glowered for a moment, then sighed.

"Very well," he said heavily, "I must accept their story when all of them agree. But whatever that . . . *thing* was, it was no angel! We didn't come through the Trial only to have angels suddenly appear to tell us we all stand in doctrinal error! If that were the case, the Voice wouldn't have saved us."

Frenaur bit his tongue. Wisdom suggested this was no time to mention the irregularity of the Trial's liturgy. And, he thought unhappily, far less was it a time to point out that Stomald had never claimed his "angels" had said anything at all, much less condemned the Church for error. Besides, the mere fact that they'd had dealings with the Valley of the Damned proved they couldn't be angels . . . didn't it?

"Yet whatever happened, it's deprived us of over twenty thousand Guardsmen," Vroxhan continued grimly.

"It has, Holiness," Rokas agreed. "Worse, we've lost their equipment, as well. The heretics have gained their weapons, including their entire artillery train . . . and their position divides our strength."

Vroxhan looked like a man drinking sour milk, but he nodded. There might even have been a glimmer of respect in his eyes for Rokas' unflinching admission, and he pinched the bridge of his nose while he thought.

"In that case, Marshal," he said finally, "we shall just have to call forth a greater host. There can be no compromise with the heretical—especially not when they now possess such strength of arms." He turned cold eyes upon Frenaur. "How widely has this heresy spread?"

"Widely," Frenaur confessed. "Before . . . whatever happened, there were only some few thousand, mostly peasant villagers from the Shalokars. Now word of the 'miracle' is spreading like wildfire. It's even reached beyond the Thirgan Gap to Vral. God only knows how many people have flocked to Stomald's standard by now, but the signs are bad. Messages indicate entire villages are streaming north to join 'the Army of the Angels.'"

Vroxhan scowled at him for a moment, then shrugged.

"I know it's not your fault." He sighed, and the bishop relaxed. "You're simply in range of my ill humor and fear." His mouth tightened. "And I *am* afraid, Brothers. Malagor has always been prone to schism, and this comes too close upon the Trial. The vile powers of the valley have awakened to the defeat of the Greater Demons. Perhaps still more of the unclean star spawn wait to smite us—the Writ says there are many Demons—and they use these lesser evil spirits to divide us before they assail us yet again."

He brooded down at his desk, then straightened his shoulders.

"Lord Marshal, you will summon the Great Host of Mother Church to Holy War." Rokas bowed, and Frenaur bit his lip. The full Host had not been summoned since the Schismatic Wars themselves. "But we must prepare our men to withstand demonic deceit before we offer battle," Vroxhan continued heavily, "and I fear much of Malagor will go over to the heretics before we are ready."

He looked up at Frenaur's unhappy face, and his angry eyes softened.

"The same would be true anywhere, Frenaur. The common folk are ill-equipped to judge such matters, and when their own priests lead them astray it's hardly their fault that they believe. Yet be that as it may, those who embrace heresy must pay heresy's price." He returned his eyes to the marshal. "I do not yet wish to summon the secular lords to your banner, Rokas, but even if we rely solely on the Guard, we must first send priests among them, preaching the truth of what's happened lest we lose still more troops to panic and spiritual seduction. Do you agree?"

"I do, Holiness, but I must urge caution lest we delay overlong."

"What do you mean, 'overlong'?"

"Holiness, Malagor has always been difficult to invade, and its position divides our forces. Worse, my own reports indicate the heretics are as inflamed by what they see as foreign control as by whatever other seeds the demons may have sown."

Rokas watched Vroxhan with care and was relieved when the high priest gave a slow nod. Before the Schismatic Wars, Malagor had been strong enough to give even Mother Church pause. Indeed, the traditional Malagoran restlessness under the Tenets' restrictions had helped fuel the Great Schism, and the Inner Circle of the time, already engaged upon a life-or-death struggle with the Schismatics, had used the wars to break the princedom. Prince Uroba, Malagor's present "ruler," was the Temple's pensioner—a drunkard sustained in power not by birth or merit but by the pikes of the Guard—and his people knew it.

"Our forces west of Malagor are weak," Rokas went on. "We have perhaps forty thousand Guardsmen in Doras, Kyhyra, Cherist, and Showmah, but less than five thousand in Sardua and Thirgan, and the heresy has spread more quickly to the west than to the east. Indeed, I fear the Guard's strength may be hard pressed to prevent more of the common folk from joining the heresy in those regions. More, the semaphore chains across Malagor will soon fall into heretic hands, depriving us of direct communications. We will have to send messages by semaphore to Arwah and thence by ship to Darwan for relay through Alwa via the Qwelth Gap chain. Such a delay will make it all but impossible to coordinate closely between our forces east and west of Malagor."

He paused until Vroxhan nodded once more, then went on in measured tones.

"The Guard's total strength west of Malagor is, as I say, perhaps forty-five to fifty thousand. Here in the east, the Temple can summon five times that many Guardsmen if we strip our garrisons to the bone. For more than that, we would require a general levy, yet, as you, I prefer not to rely upon the secular lords' troops—not, at least, until we've won at least one victory and so proved these 'angels' are, in fact, demons."

He paused again, and again Vroxhan nodded, this time impatiently.

"The only practical routes for armies into or out of Malagor are the Thirgan Gap and the Keldark Valley. The gap is broader, but its approaches are dotted with powerful fortresses which the heretics may well secure before we can move. Given those facts and our weakness in the west, I would recommend massing the western Guard south of the Cherist Mountains around Vral. In that position, they can both seal the Thirgan Gap and maintain civil control."

Rokas began to pace, tugging at his jaw as he marshaled words like companies of pikes.

"Our major strength lies in the east, and with the gap secured we may concentrate in Keldark, using the Guardsmen of Keldark to block the valley against heretical sorties until we're ready. The valley is bad terrain and even narrower than the gap, but most of its fortresses were razed after the Schismatic Wars. There are perhaps three places the heretics might choose to stand: Yortown, Erastor, and Baricon. All are powerful defensive positions; the cost of taking any of them will be high."

He made a wry face. "There won't be much strategy involved until we actually break into Malagor, Holiness, not with such limited approach routes, but the same applies to the heretics. And, unlike us, they must equip and train their forces. If we strike quickly, we may well clear the entire valley before they can prepare."

"I agree," Vroxhan said after a moment's thought. "And it will, indeed, be best to move from the east. If they *can* strike before we prepare, they'll move east, directly for the Temple."

"That was my own thought," Rokas agreed.

"In the meantime," Vroxhan returned to Frenaur, "I see no choice but to place Malagor under Interdict. Please see to the proclamation."

"I will," Frenaur agreed unhappily. What must be must be.

"Understand me, Brothers," Vroxhan said very quietly. "There will be no compromise with heresy. Mother Church's sword has been drawn; it will not be sheathed while a single heretic lives."

CHAPTER TWENTY-SIX

Robert Stevens—no longer "the Reverend"—watched the broadcast with hating eyes. Bishop Francine Hilgemann stared out over her congregation from a carven pulpit, and her soft, clear voice was passionate.

"Brothers and sisters, violence is no answer to fear. Perhaps some souls *are* mistaken, but the Church cannot and will not condone those who defy a loving God's will by striking out in unreasoning hatred. God's people do not stain their hands with blood, nor is it fitting that the death of any human should be wreaked in anger. Those who style themselves 'The Sword of God' are not His servants, but destroyers of all He teaches, and their—"

Stevens snarled and killed the HD, sickened that he'd once respected that . . . that— He couldn't think of a foul enough word.

He paced slowly, and his eyes warmed with an ugly light. Disgust and revulsion had driven him from the Church, but Hilgemann and those like her could never weaken God's Sword. Their corruption only filled the true faithful with determination, and the Sword struck deeper every day.

As he had struck. The most terrifying—and satisfying—day of his life had been the one in which he realized why his cell had been sent against Vincente Cruz. The deaths of Cruz's wife and children had bothered some of his people, yet God's work required sacrifices, and if innocents perished, God would receive them as the martyrs they'd become. But that he had been the instrument which destroyed the heirs—heirs so corrupt they'd claimed a Narhani as a *friend*—had filled Stevens with exaltation.

There'd been other missions, but none so satisfying as that . . . or as the one he now looked forward to. It was time Francine Hilgemann learned God's true chosen rejected her self-damning compromises with the Anti-Christ.

Sergeant Graywolf was calm-eyed and relaxed, for he knew how to wait. Especially when he awaited something so satisfying.

He didn't know how the analysts had developed the intel. From the briefing, he suspected they'd intercepted a courier, but all that mattered was that they knew. With luck, they might even take one of the bastards alive. Daniel

615

Graywolf was a professional, and he knew how valuable that could be . . . yet deep down inside, he hoped they wouldn't be quite *that* lucky.

Stevens gave thanks for the rainy night. Its wet blackness wouldn't bother Imperial surveillance systems, but the people behind those systems were only human. The dreary winter rain would have its effect where it mattered, dulling and slowing their minds.

Alice Hughes and Tom Mason walked arm-in-arm behind him like lovers, weapons hidden by their raincoats. Stevens carried his own weapon in a shoulder holster: an old-style automatic with ten-millimeter "slugs" of the same explosive used in grav guns. He didn't see Yance or Pete, but they'd close in at the proper moment. He knew that, just as he knew Wanda Curry would bring their escape flyer in at precisely the right second. They'd practiced the operation for days, and their timing was exact.

His pulse ticked faster as he reached the high-rise. It was of Pre-Siege construction, but it had been modernized, and he paused under the force field roof protecting the front entrance. He wiped rain from his face with just the right gratitude for the respite while Alice and Tom closed up on his heels, and the corner of his eye saw Yance and Pete arriving from the opposite direction. The five of them came together by obvious coincidence, and then all of them turned and stepped through the entrance as one.

There were no security personnel in the lobby, only the automated systems he'd been briefed upon, and he paused in the entry, head bent to hide his features, shielding Yance and Pete as they reached under their coats. Then he stepped aside, and their suppressors rose with practiced precision and burned each scan point into useless junk with pulses of focused energy.

Stevens grunted, jerked the ski mask over his face, and snatched out his own weapon, and the well-drilled quintet raced for the transit shafts.

Graywolf stiffened at the implant signal. Clumsy, he thought with a hungry smile. Obviously their information had been less complete than they'd thought, for they'd missed three separate sensors.

Nine more Security Ministry agents stood as one behind nine closed doors as Graywolf cradled his hyper rifle and moved to the window.

Stevens led his followers from the transit shaft, and they spread out behind him, hugging the walls, weapons poised. His own eyes were fixed on the door at the end of the corridor, yet his attention roamed all about him, acute as a panther's after so many months at the guerrilla's trade.

They were half way down the hall when nine doors opened as one.

"Lay down your weapons!" a voice shouted. "You're all under arr—"

Stevens spun like a cat. He heard Yance's enraged bellow even as he tried to line up on the uniformed woman in the doorway, but his people's reactions didn't match their murderousness, for none were enhanced. His barking automatic blasted a chunk from the wall beside the door, and then a hurricane of grav gun darts blew all five terrorists into bloody meat.

✧　　✧　　✧

Graywolf heard the thunder and shrugged. They'd had their chance.

He held his own position and watched the getaway flyer slide to a neat halt. It was right on the tick, and he aligned his hyper rifle on the drive housing before he triggered his com.

"Land and step out of the flyer!" he told the pilot.

There was a split-second pause, and then the flyer leapt ahead with blinding acceleration. But unlike Stevens' killers, Graywolf *was* fully enhanced, and the exploding flyer gouged a fifty-meter trench in the street below as its drive unit vanished into hyper-space.

Lawrence Jefferson completed his report with profound satisfaction.

He'd never really been happy about penetrating security on Birhat. The distance was too great, and any communication with agents there was vulnerable to interception. But that was no longer necessary; his plans had matured to a point at which it no longer mattered what the military did, and he controlled *Earth's* security forces from his own office.

His lips pursed as he considered his intertwining strategies. His latest ploy should remove Francine from any suspicion. She'd openly become the Church of the Armageddon's leader, but as one who denounced the Sword of God's fanaticism. Her masterful pleas for nonviolence only underscored the Sword's growing ferocity, yet *she* was emerging as a moderate, and Horus and Ninhursag were obligingly accepting his own "astonished" conclusion that she was someone they could work with against the radicals.

Now his security forces' defeat of the Sword's attempt on her life would make her whiter than snow. He'd wondered if he was being too clever, for it would never have done for any of Stevens' people to be taken alive and disclose the truth about *Imperial Terra*, but he'd chosen his agents with care. All were utterly loyal to the Imperium . . . but each had lost friends or family to the Sword. He was certain they'd tried to take the terrorists alive—and equally certain they hadn't tried any harder than they had to. And, of course, he'd known he could trust Stevens' fanatics to resist.

He was just as happy to have that loose end tied, for Ninhursag's decision to flood Earth with ONI agents worried him, especially since he didn't know why she was doing it. Her official explanation *might* be the truth, for reinforcing Earth Security and opening a double offensive against the Sword made sense. He didn't like it, but it did make sense. Yet he wasn't quite convinced that was her real motive. At first he'd been afraid she was somehow onto him, but five months had passed since she'd started, and if he had, indeed, been her objective, he'd be in custody by now.

Whatever she was up to, it enforced greater circumspection upon him. Since taking over from Gus, Jefferson had found it expedient to make adjustments in certain background investigations, culling his own cadre of fully-enhanced personnel from the Ministry of Security itself. It was so convenient to have the government enhance his people for him, but Ninhursag's swarm of busybodies had forced a temporary shutdown in such activities.

Not that it worried him too much. His plans were in place, centered upon the crown jewels of his subversions: Brigadier Alex Jourdain and Lieutenant Carl Bergren. Jourdain's high position in Earth Security made him invaluable as Jefferson's senior field man and cutout, but Bergren was even more important. That lowly officer was the key, for he was a greedy young man with expensive habits. How Battle Fleet had ever let him into uniform, much less placed him in such a sensitive position, passed Jefferson's understanding, but he supposed even the best screening processes had to fail occasionally. He himself had stumbled upon Bergren almost by accident, and he'd taken pains to conceal Bergren's . . . indiscretions, for thanks to Lieutenant Bergren, Admiral Ninhursag MacMahan had just over five months to do whatever she was doing before she died.

Senior Fleet Captain Antonio Tattiaglia looked up in surprise, trowel in hand and his newest rose bush half-planted, as Brigadier Hofstader entered his atrium. Hofstader was a small, severe woman, always immaculate in her black-and-silver Marine uniform, and this hasty intrusion was most unlike her.

"Yes, Erika?"

"Sorry to bother you, Sir, but something's come up."

Tattiaglia hid a sigh. Hofstader had commanded *Lancelot*'s Marines for over a year, and she still sounded as if she were on a parade ground. The woman was almost oppressively competent, but he couldn't warm to her.

"What is it?"

"I believe we've just detected a Sword of God strike force en route to its target, Sir," she said crisply, and he forgot all about her manner.

"Are you *serious*?"

"Yes, Sir. The scanner tech of the watch—Scan Tech Bateman—decided to run an atmospheric-target tracking exercise, in the course of which she detected three commercial conveyors with inoperable transponders executing a nape-of-the-earth approach to the Shenandoah Power Reception Facility."

Hofstader had her expression well in hand, but excitement was burning through her professionalism for the first time since he'd known her.

"Have you alerted Earth Security?" he demanded, already trotting towards the transit shaft.

"No, Sir. Fleet Captain Reynaud informed ONI." She moved briskly at his side, and her smile was cold. "ONI has requested that *we* investigate."

"Hot damn," Tattiaglia whispered. They stepped into the shaft and it hurled them towards *Lancelot*'s bridge. "Do we have something in position?"

"Sir, I alerted my ready duty platoon as soon as Bateman reported the conveyors. They'll enter atmosphere in approximately—" she paused to consult her internal chronometer "—seventy-eight seconds."

"Good work, Brigadier. Very good work!" The shaft deposited them outside the planetoid's bridge, and Tattiaglia rubbed his mental hands in glee as he raced for the command hatch.

"Thank you, Sir."

Captain Tattiaglia arrived on his bridge just as Hofstader's assault shuttle entered atmosphere at eleven times the speed of sound. A corner of the command deck display altered silently, showing them what the shuttle pilot was seeing, and the captain dropped into his command couch with hungry eyes.

"Listen up, people," Lieutenant Prescott said as his shuttle hurtled downward. "We don't *know* these're terrorists, so we ground, watch 'em, and get ready to move if they are, but nobody does squat unless I say so. Got it?" A chorus of assents came back. "Good. Now, if they *are* bad guys, ONI wants prisoners. We take some of 'em alive if we can—everybody got *that*?"

The fresh affirmatives were a bit disappointed, but he had other things to worry about as the shuttle grounded to disgorge his Marines, then swooshed back into the heavens in stealth to give air support if it was needed. Prescott didn't even watch it go; he was already maneuvering his troops into the hastily chosen positions he'd selected on the way in.

Three big conveyors ghosted to a landing in a patch of woods, and forty heavily armed people filed out with military precision. The raiders moved quietly towards the floodlit grounds of the Shenandoah Valley Power Receptor, then split, diverging towards two different security gates.

The commander of one attack party studied a passive scanner as he neared the perimeter fence, hunting security systems their briefing might have missed, then stiffened. He whirled, and his jaw dropped as his eyes confirmed his instrument's findings.

Well, they sure as hell aren't picnickers, Prescott thought as his armor scanners confirmed the intruders' heavy load of weapons, *and— Oh shit! So much for surprise!*

"Take 'em!"

The terrorist leader saw the armored shapes and tried to scream a warning, but a burst of fire splattered him across his troops halfway through the first syllable.

His followers gaped at the Marines, but they had weapons of their own and two of them were fully enhanced, and a Marine blew apart as the night exploded in a vicious firefight. An energy gun killed a second trooper, the whiplash of grav gun darts crackled everywhere, and a third Marine went down—wounded, not dead—but the Marines had combat armor, and the terrorists didn't.

Forty-one seconds after the first shot, three Marines were dead and five were wounded; none of the four terrorist survivors was unhurt.

Prescott waved his medics towards the casualties, then turned as the parked conveyors screamed upwards. They were still climbing frantically when *Lancelot*'s assault shuttle blew them apart from stealth.

Funny, I could've sworn I told Owens to challenge 'em before she shot. Prescott ran back over his conversation with his pilot. *Oops, guess not.*

✧   ✧   ✧

"Friend," Fleet Lieutenant Esther Steinberg said, "I don't really care whether you talk to me or not. We've got three of your buddies, too, and one of you is going to tell me what I want to know."

"*Never!*" The young man cuffed to the chair under the lie detector looked far less defiant than he tried to sound. "None of us have anything to say to servants of the Anti-Christ!"

You're talking too much, friend. Got a little case of nerves here, do we? Good. Sweat, you bastard!

"Think not?" She crossed her arms. "Let me explain something. We caught you in the act, and you killed three Fleet Marines. Know what that means?" Her prisoner stared at her, sullen eyes frightened, and she smiled. "That means there's not gonna be any fooling around. You're gonna be tried and convicted so fast your head swims." The young man swallowed audibly. "I don't imagine your mama and papa'll be real pleased to see their itty-bitty son shot—and they will, 'cause every data channel's gonna carry it live. I'd guess you've seen one or two people catch it with grav guns, haven't you? Kinda messy, isn't it? I figure a half second burst ought to just about saw you in two, friend. Think your folks'll like that?"

"*You bitch!*" the prisoner screamed, and she smiled again—coldly.

"Sticks and stones, friend. Sticks and stones. I'll make sure I've got some spare time to watch, too."

"You—you—!" The prisoner writhed against his restraints, wounds forgotten, eyes mad, and Steinberg's laugh was a douche of ice-water.

"You seem a mite upset, friend. Too bad." She turned towards the hatch, then paused, listening to his incoherent, terrified rage and gauging his mood. *This boy's just about ripe.*

"Just one thing." He froze, glaring at her. "Talk to me, and ONI'll recommend leniency. You still won't like what happens, but you'll be alive." She smiled like a shark. "Only catch is, we only make the deal with *one* of you—and you've got ten seconds to decide if you're the lucky one."

"That," Fleet Captain Reynaud observed, "is one *nasty* lieutenant."

"She is, indeed," Tattiaglia murmured, watching the holo of the "interview" with his exec as the terrorist began to spill his guts, then glanced up at the captain from ONI. "I'm not going to shed any tears for the prisoners, but will any of this stand up in court?"

"Not in a *civilian* court, but it won't have to. His Majesty's invoked the Defense of the Imperium Act, and that gives military courts jurisdiction over prisoners captured by the military. Besides," the captain's grin was as sharklike as his lieutenant's, "we don't *need* any of it. Your boys and girls caught these jokers with enough physical evidence to shoot them all."

"Then what's the point?"

"The point, Captain Tattiaglia," the ONI officer said, switching off the holo and turning to *Lancelot*'s CO, "is that I've got another little job for you. Among the other tidbits our gallant fanatic let slip is the location of his own cell's HQ—and Esther set a new personal record breaking that little prick. If we get a move on, we can hit them before they figure out their raiders aren't coming back."

"You mean—?"

"I mean, Captain, that twenty more terrorists are just sitting there waiting for you to drop a few Marines down their chimney."

"Oh boy," Tattiaglia whispered. "Oh boy, oh boy, oh *boy*! Now I *know* there's a God."

Fleet Admiral MacMahan's smile was wolfish as she studied the report. *That Lieutenant Steinberg is one sharp cookie. Have to do something nice for her in the next promotion list. And Tattiaglia's people deserve one hell of a pat on the back, too.*

She finished the report with a sigh of satisfaction. *Nice. Very nice. Jefferson's people swat an assassination attempt Tuesday, and we pick off an entire cell Thursday. Not a good week for the Sword of God.*

Of course, it hadn't gotten them any closer to Mister X, but she wasn't complaining. She punched up the holo record of the terrorist hideout and studied it. Steinberg had accompanied the Marines in and gotten every bit of the raid and its aftermath for her report, and Ninhursag whistled at the size of the terrorists' arsenal. There was a lot of Imperial weaponry in it, and she made a mental note to ask about the serial numbers. They hadn't had a lot of luck in that regard from Jefferson's occasional successes, but they had a lot more hardware this time, and all they really needed was one hard lead.

The holo record shifted to a view of the terrorist's main planning area. They seemed to have been well equipped with maps, too, and she frowned as she saw the precision with which some were marked. They even had a trophy room, she noted, grimacing at the wall-mounted displays. Stupid bastards. They'd collected bits and pieces from past raids as if they were counting coup! Well, it might help her people figure out which attacks this bunch had been responsible for, and—

Ninhursag MacMahan slammed the hold button and stood slowly, face pale as death, and walked into the holo to peer at one particular trophy. She licked her lips, trying to tell herself she was wrong, but she wasn't, and she whispered a soft, frightened prayer as she stared at her worst nightmare: a second-stage initiator from Tsien Tao-ling's super bomb.

The council room was quiet. Colin and Jiltanith sat between Gerald Hatcher and Tsien Tao-ling, and their faces were as pale as Ninhursag's own.

"Sweet Jesu," Jiltanith murmured at last. "Thy news is worse than e'er I durst let myself believe, 'Hursag, yet 'tis God's Own grace thou'st beagled out this threat."

"Amen to that." Colin frowned down at the tabletop. "Does this suggest a link between the Sword and Mister X?"

"I don't think so," Ninhursag said. "None of the survivors can tell us where that particular 'trophy' came from, but they're all souvenirs of attacks their cell carried out. I wish we *did* know where they got it; at least then we'd have some idea where to look for whoever has the thing. It's possible the Sword hit them before they finished it, but it wouldn't mean much if they did. Whoever's behind this must've made more than one copy of the plans. Losing one construction team might slow them down; it wouldn't stop them."

"Lord." Colin pulled on his nose, and Ninhursag saw the lines months of worry had carved in his face. "Gerald? Tao-ling?"

"'Hursag is correct," Tsien said. Hatcher only nodded, and Colin sighed.

"Okay, 'Hursag. Where do we go from here?"

"We start from a worst-case assumption. First, the thing's been built. Second, the people who *probably* have it killed eighty thousand people just to get the twins. Third—and scariest of all—the Sword may have captured it." A visible shudder ran through her audience at that thought.

"I think we're still fairly safe in assuming Earth isn't the target. I'm not going to cast that in stone, but I simply cannot conceive of anyone wanting to destroy the bulk of the human race. Certainly the Sword wouldn't; their whole purpose is to save the rest of humanity from us back-sliders and the Narhani. And there's not too much doubt Mister X is operating from Earth, which means he'd be blowing up his own base."

"Agreed." Colin pulled on his nose again, then looked at Hatcher. "Get hold of Adrienne, Hector, and Amanda. I want an evacuation plan for Birhat yesterday. We can't rehearse it without risking warning Mister X that we know he's got this thing, but we can at least get organized for it. I'll warn Brashieel's people personally. There's not much chance of a leak at their end, and there's still few enough Narhani we can pull them all out by mat-trans if we have to."

The admiral nodded, and he turned back to Ninhursag, nodding for her to continue.

"While they do that," she said, "I intend to start an immediate high-priority search of Narhan and Birhat. Maker knows that bomb's a damnably small target, but Battle Fleet can carry out centimeter-by-centimeter scans without tipping Mister X. It'll take time, especially under a security blackout, but if it's out there, Gerald's and my people will find it."

She paused, and her dark eyes met her Emperor's.

"I only pray we find it in time," she said softly.

CHAPTER TWENTY-SEVEN

Tibold Rarikson lay beside Lord Sean atop the cliff and watched his youthful commander pretend to use a spyglass.

The ex-Guardsman's bushy mustache hid his smile as the black-haired giant made a great show of adjusting the glass. Tibold didn't know why the Captain-General tried to hide his more-than-human abilities, but he was willing to play along, even though Lord Sean and Lord Tamman were probably the only people who thought they were fooling anyone.

In all his years, Tibold had never met anyone like these two. They were young; he'd seen enough hot-blooded young kinokha in his career to know that, and Lord Tamman was as impulsive as he was young. But Lord Sean . . . There was a youthful recklessness in his eyes, and a matching abundance of ideas behind them, but there was also discipline, and Tibold had known gray-bearded marshals less willing to listen to suggestions. And though he tried to hide it, Tibold had seen how his strange, black eyes warmed whenever the Angel Sandy was about. He treated her with the utmost respect, yet Tibold had the odd suspicion that was more for the army's benefit than for the angel's. Indeed, the angel seemed to watch for Lord Sean's reaction to whatever she might be saying even as she said it.

Tibold hadn't figured out why an angel should—well, defer wasn't quite the word, though it came close—even to Lord Sean's opinion, but there was no denying Lord Sean and Lord Tamman were uncanny. They might have keener eyes and greater strength than other men, and they certainly knew things Tibold hadn't, yet were peculiar holes in their knowledge. For instance, Lord Tamman had actually expected nioharqs to slow infantry, and Lord Sean had let slip a puzzling reference to "heavy cavalry," a manifest contradiction in terms. Branahlks were fleet, but they had trouble carrying an *unarmored* man.

Yet neither seemed upset when he corrected them. Indeed, Lord Sean had spent hours picking his brain, combining Tibold's experience with things he *did* know to create the army they now led, and he'd been delighted by Tibold's insistence upon remorseless drill—one more thing whose importance young officers frequently failed to appreciate.

And if their ignorance in some matters was surprising, their knowledge in others was amazing! He'd thought them mad to emphasize firearms over polearms. A joharn-armed musketeer did well to fire thirty shots an hour, while the heavier malagor could manage little more than twenty. There was simply no way musketeers could break a determined charge . . . until Lord Sean opened his bag of tricks. And, of course, until the angels intervened.

Even Tibold had felt . . . unsettled . . . when the Angel Sandy had Father Stomald stack a thousand joharns in a small, blind valley and leave them there overnight. Indeed, he'd crept back—strictly against Father Stomald's orders—late that night . . . and crept away again much more quietly than he'd come when he found all thousand of them had disappeared!

But they'd been back by morning, and Tibold hadn't argued when the Angel Sandy had him pile *two* thousand in the same valley the next night. Not after he'd seen what had happened to the first lot.

Changing wooden ramrods for iron had been but the first step, and Lord Sean had accompanied it by introducing paper cartridges to replace the wooden tubes hung from a musketeer's bandoleer. A man could carry far more of them, and all he had to do was bite off the end, pour the powder down the barrel, and spit in his ball. The paper wrapper even served as a wad!

The thing Lord Sean called a "ring bayonet" was another deceptively simple innovation. Hard-pressed musketeers often shoved the hafts of knives into their weapons' muzzles to turn them into crude spears as the pikes closed in, yet that was always a council of desperation, since it meant they could no longer fire. But they *could* fire with the mounting rings clamped *around* their weapons' barrels, and Tibold looked forward to the first time some Guard captain assumed musketeers with fixed bayonets couldn't shoot him.

Then there was the gunlock. No one had ever thought of widening the barrel end of the touch-hole into a funnel, but that simple alteration meant it was no longer necessary to prime the lock. Just turning the musket on its side and rapping it smartly shook powder from the main charge into the pan.

Yet the most wonderful change of all was simpler yet. Rifles had been a Malagoran invention (well, Cherist made the same claim, but Tibold knew who *he* believed), yet it took so long to hammer balls down their barrels— the only way to force them into the rifling—that they fired even more slowly than malagors. While prized by hunters and useful for skirmishers, the rifle was all but useless once the close-range exchange of volleys began.

No longer. Every altered joharn—and malagor—had returned rifled, and the angels had provided molds for a new bullet, as well. Not a ball, but a hollow-based cylinder that slid easily down the barrel. Tibold had doubted the rifling grooves could spin a bullet with that much windage, but Lord Sean had insisted the exploding powder would spread the base into them, and the results were phenomenal. Suddenly a rifle was as easy to load as a smoothbore—and able to fire far more rapidly than anyone had ever been able to shoot before! Tibold couldn't see why Lord Sean had been so surprised to find the weapons were . . . "bore-standardized," he called them (it only made sense to issue everyone the same size balls, didn't it?), but the Captain-General had been delighted by how easy that made it to produce the new bullets for them.

Nor had he ignored the artillery. Mother Church restricted secular armies to the lighter chagon, and the Guard's arlaks threw shot twice as heavy, even if their shorter barrels didn't give them much more range. But Lord Sean's gunners were supplied with cloth bags of powder instead of clumsy loading-ladles of loose powder. And for close-range firing there were "fixed rounds"—thin-walled, powder-filled wooden tubes with grape or case shot wired to one end. A good crew could fire three of those in a minute.

And when all those changes were added together, the Angels' Army could produce a weight of fire no experienced commander would have believed possible. Instead of once every five minutes, its artillerists fired three times in two minutes—even faster, using the "fixed rounds" at close range. Instead of thirty rounds an hour, its musketeers—no, its *riflemen*—could fire three or even four *a minute* and hit targets they could hardly even see! Tibold still wasn't certain fire alone could break a phalanx, but *he* wouldn't care to charge against such weapons.

Perhaps even better, there were maps. Wonderful maps, with every feature to scale and none left out. It was kind of the angels to try to make them look like those he'd always used, and he lacked the heart to tell them they'd failed when they seemed so pleased by their efforts, but no mortal cartographer could have produced them. Some of his militiamen hadn't realized how valuable they were, but he'd worn his voice hoarse until they did. To know exactly how the ground looked, where the best march routes lay, and precisely where the enemy might be hidden—and where your own troops could be best deployed—was truly a gift worthy of angels.

Best of all, the angels always knew what was happening elsewhere. The big map in the command tent showed every hostile army's exact position, and the angels updated it regularly. The sheer luxury of it was addictive. He was glad Lord Sean continued to emphasize scouting, but knowing where and how strong every major enemy force was made things so much simpler . . . especially when the enemy *didn't* know those things about you.

Still, he reminded himself, the odds were formidable. None of Malagor had remained loyal to the Church, but the "heretics" had far too few weapons for their manpower, and garrisoning the Thirgan Gap fortresses had drawn off over half of their strength, while the Temple had over two hundred thousand Guardsmen in eastern North Hylar, not even counting any of the secular armies.

Yet Tibold no longer doubted God was on their side, and while he knew too much of war to expect His direct intervention, Lord Sean and Lord Tamman were certainly the next best thing.

Sean closed the spyglass and rolled onto his back to stare up into the sky. Lord God, he was tired! He hadn't expected it to be easy—indeed, he'd feared the Pardalians would resist his innovations, and the eagerness with which they'd accepted them instead was a tremendous relief—but even so, he'd underestimated the sheer, grinding labor of it all, and he'd expected to get more advantage from *Israel's* machine shops. To be sure, Sandy's stealthed flights to shuttle muskets back and forth for rifling had been an enormous help, but this was Sean's first personal contact with the reality of military logistics, and he'd been horrified by the voracious appetite of even a small, primitively-armed army. Brashan and his computer-driven minions had been able to modify existing weapons at a gratifying rate, but *producing* large numbers of even unsophisticated weapons would quickly have devoured *Israel's* resources.

Not that Sean intended to complain. His troops were incomparably better armed (those who were armed at all!) than anything they were likely to face, and if he'd been disappointed in *Israel's* productivity, he'd been amazed by how quickly the Malagoran guilds had begun producing new weapons from the prototypes "the angels" had provided.

He'd been totally unprepared for the hordes of skilled artisans who'd popped up out of the ground, but he'd forgotten that Earth's own industrial revolution had begun with waterwheels. Pardal—and especially Malagor—had developed its own version of the assembly line, despite its limitation to wind, water, or muscle power, and that required a *lot* of craftsmen. Most had declared for "the angels"—as much, Sean suspected, from frustration at the Church's tech limitations as in response to any miracles "the angels" had wrought—but even with their tireless enthusiasm, there were never enough hours in the day.

Nor did the long year Pardal's huge orbital radius produced ease things. On a planet where spring lasted for five standard months and summer for ten, the campaigning seasons of Terra's preindustrial armies were a useless meterstick. Sean was devoutly thankful the Temple had seen fit to postpone operations for over two months while it indoctrinated its troops, but a delay which would have meant having to hold the Temple off only until the weather closed in on Terra meant nothing of the sort here. He faced an immediate, decisive campaign, and the sheer size of Pardalian armies appalled him. There were over a hundred thousand men headed up the Keldark Valley, and by tomorrow—the day after at latest—a lot of people were going to die.

Too many people, whichever side they're on, but there's not a damned thing I can do *about that.*

He clapped Tibold on the shoulder, and, despite everything, his heart rose at the older man's confident grin as they headed for their branahlks.

Stomald rose as the Angel Harry entered the command tent to update the "situation map." She smiled, and he knew she was chiding him for his display of respect, but he couldn't help it. And, he reminded himself, he *had* finally managed to stop addressing her and the Angel Sandy as "angels," even if he didn't understand why they were so adamant about that. But, then, there were a lot of things he didn't understand. He'd expected the angels to be angry when the army's mood began to shift, yet they were actually *pleased* to see the troops becoming Malagoran nationalists rather than religious heretics.

He watched her work. She was a head taller than he, and even more beautiful (and younger) than he'd remembered, now that her face was alive with thought and humor, and he chided himself—again—as he thought of the body hidden by her raiment. She might not use his people with the authority which was her right, but she *was* an angel.

She cocked her head to check her work with her remaining eye, and he bit his lip in familiar anguish. Her other terrible wounds had healed with angelic speed, but that black eye patch twisted his heart each time he saw it. Yet despite all Cragsend had done to her, there was no hate in the Angel Harry. Stomald didn't believe she *could* hate, not after the gentleness with which she always spoke to him, the man who'd almost burned her alive.

She turned from the map, and amusement deepened her smile as he blushed under her regard. But it didn't embarrass him further. Instead, he felt himself smiling back.

"Sandy will have a fresh update in a few hours," she said in the Holy Tongue. "We're keeping a closer eye on them now that they're approaching."

"I'm no soldier—or," he corrected himself wryly, "I *was* no soldier—but that seems wise to me."

"Don't belittle yourself. You're fortunate to have a captain like Tibold—and Sean and Tamman, of course—but you've got a good eye for these things yourself."

He bent his head, basking in her praise, but before he could say anything more Lord Sean walked in, followed by Tibold.

Lord Sean touched his breastplate in respectful salute, and the angel acknowledged it gravely, yet Stomald noted the twinkle in her eye. For just an instant, he resented it, and then shame buried his pique. She was an *angel*, and Lord Sean was the Angel Sandy's chosen champion.

"Is that the latest update?" Lord Sean's Pardalian had developed a distinct Malagoran accent in the past five days, and he smiled as the angel nodded. He moved closer to the map and leaned forward beside her to study it.

Tibold grinned at Stomald behind their backs, and the priest smiled back despite another tiny stab of envy. It was easier for Tibold, for whatever else he was, Lord Sean was a born soldier. Tibold took paternal pride in him, and Lord Sean seemed to return his regard. He certainly listened attentively to anything Tibold had to say.

Lord Sean was murmuring to the Angel Harry in that other odd-sounding language they often spoke. Stomald suspected they sometimes forgot no one else understood it (Lord Sean always fell back into Pardalian whenever he remembered others were present), and the young war captain's ability to speak it awed the heretic priest. To be so close to the angels he spoke their own tongue almost unthinkingly must be wondrous, indeed.

Lord Sean stood back from the map at last, and his eyes were pensive. "Tibold, I think they'll hit our forward pickets this afternoon. Do you agree?"

Tibold studied the map a moment and nodded.

"Then it's time," Lord Sean sighed. "I'll speak to Tamman again, but you have a word with the under-captains. Make sure they keep their heads. We're fighting for survival, not honor, and we don't want any wasted lives."

"I will, Lord Sean," Tibold promised, obviously pleased by the Captain-General's concern for his men, and Lord Sean turned to Stomald.

"I expect to hold them, Father, but are we ready if we can't?"

"We are, Lord Sean. I've sent the last of the women back to safety, and the nioharqs will be in the traces by dawn, ready to advance or retreat."

Lord Sean nodded in satisfaction, then nodded again as the Angel Harry murmured something too soft for any other ears to hear.

"Father, Captain Tibold and I will be unable to release the troops for services this evening with the enemy so near at hand, but if you'd care to send the chaplains forward—?"

"Thank you," Stomald said. Lord Sean was always careful about such things, yet the priest wondered why neither he nor Lord Tamman nor even the angels attended the services. Of course, such as they had their own links to God, but it was almost as if they stood aside intentionally.

"In that case, I think I'll go find lunch. Will you join me?"

Stomald nodded, and noted the amusement in the Angel Harry's eye. She smiled on the captain, and a surprising thought flickered in Stomald's mind. Lord Sean was as homely as the Angel Harry was beautiful, and the angel, for all her height, seemed tiny beside him, yet there was something . . .

It was the eyes, he thought. Why had he never noticed before? Lord Sean's strange, black eyes, darker than night, were exactly the same shade. And the hair, so black it was almost blue. That, too, was the same. Why, aside from Lord Sean's homeliness, they might have been brother and sister!

Like everyone else, Stomald knew Lord Sean and Lord Tamman were more than human—one had only to watch their blinding reflexes or see them occasionally forget to hide their incredible strength to know that—but it hadn't occurred to him they might share the angels' *blood!*

The thought was somehow chilling. Lord Sean and Lord Tamman were mortal. They both insisted on that, and Stomald believed them, and that meant they *couldn't* be related to angels. Besides, Holy Writ said all angels were female, and how could mortal blood mingle with divine? And yet . . . what if—?

He thrust the idea aside. It was disrespectful at best, and, a hidden part of him knew guiltily, it sprang from an unforgivable yearning that would have appalled him had he faced it squarely.

Tamman leaned against the thyru tree, watching the road to the east, then glanced back up at the man perched in the branches with his mirror. Pardalian armies had surprisingly sophisticated signal systems, but both mirrors and flags were "daylight-only," and the afternoon was passing.

He wanted to pace, but that would never do for an angelically chosen war captain. Besides, he was out here instead of Sean expressly to win his men's confidence, which might be important tomorrow, so he contented himself with crushing dried thyru husks under his heel. The thyru resembled an enormous acorn, but its soft, inner tissues produced an oil which filled much the same niche as Terra's olive oil, and he wondered how the Pardalians dealt with its thick shell. Now *there* was a messy thought!

He realized his mind was straying and tinkered with his adrenaline levels. He didn't really know why he was watching the road so hard. Unlike his scouts, he had a direct link to *Israel*'s scanner arrays via Sandy's cutter. He *knew* where the enemy was, and glaring at an empty piece of road wasn't going to get them here a moment sooner.

He gave himself a shake and moved along the line, patting shoulders and exchanging smiles. Pardalian armies knew about mounted firearms—indeed, most Pardalian cavalry were dragoons—but they'd never been a real threat. While handy for scouting and harassment, dragoons could wear only light armor, their shorter muskets had neither the range nor rate of fire to stand off pikemen, and you couldn't put pikes on branahlks. But *these* dragoons were something new, for their joharns were rifled. Not, he reminded himself, that this was the time to show the Holy Host all they could do. That would come tomorrow.

He reached the end of the line and strolled back to his tree, then rechecked his uplink. *Well, how about that? Looks like I spent just about exactly the right time with the troops.*

"Rethvan?" He glanced up at the signaler once more.

"Yes, Captain?"

"I expect their point to round the bend in about five minutes. Get ready to pass the signal."

"At once, Lord Tamman." Rethvan couldn't see around that bend, but he sounded so confident Tamman grinned. *Now all we have to do is never ever make a mistake—'cause if we do, that confidence could turn around and bite us right on the ass.*

The westering sunlight turned steadily redder, and a corner of his mind looked down through the scanner arrays. Just . . . about . . . now.

The first mounted scout rounded the bend exactly on cue.

"Send it, Rethvan." He was pleased by how calm he sounded.

"Yes, Captain."

The flashing mirror alerted the outposts to the west, and Tamman heard branahlks whistle behind his hill as their holders got them ready, but it was only a distant background. His attention was on the advancing company of Temple Guard cavalry, and his eyes slipped into telescopic mode.

They looked tired, and little wonder. Lord Marshal Rokas had moved fast once he started. The logistic capabilities of Pardalian armies amazed Tamman; he'd expected something like Earth's pike-and-musket era, but Pardal had nioharqs. The huge, tusked critters—they reminded him of elephant-sized hogs—could eat almost anything, which made forage far less of a problem than it had been for horse-powered armies, and their sustained speed was astonishing. True, their low *top* speed made them useless as cavalry, but they let Pardalians move artillery, rations, tents, portable forges, and mobile kitchens at a rate which would have turned Gustavus Adolphus green with envy.

Even so, Rokas's troops had to be feeling the pace. Sean had sealed the borders, and the Temple didn't know diddly about their deployment—their remotes couldn't penetrate the Temple itself, but they'd eavesdropped on enough of Rokas's field conferences to prove that. Yet the lord marshal had made a pretty fair estimate of their maximum possible strength, and he wasn't worrying about subtle maneuvers. He was going to throw enough bodies at them to plow them under and bull right through . . . he thought.

Tamman's smile was evil as he watched the scouts advance. They might be tired, but they seemed alert. Unfortunately for them, however, they were watching for threats inside the range they "knew" Pardalian weapons had.

"Let's get ready, boys," he said quietly as the first branahlk passed the four-hundred-meter range stakes. A soft chorus of responses came back, and his hundred dragoons settled down in their paired-off positions. He watched them sighting across fallen trees and logs as Rokas' scouts closed to just over two hundred meters. That was still far beyond aimed smoothbore range, but some of them were beginning to look more speculatively his way than he liked.

"Fire!" he barked, and fifty rifled joharns cracked as one.

The muzzle flashes were bright in the shadows of the grove, and powder smoke stung his nose, but his attention was on the scouts. Thirty or more went down—many, he was sure, dismounted rather than hit; branahlks were bigger targets than men—and the others gaped at the smoke cloud rising from the trees. Tamman grinned at their stunned reaction, counting under his breath while the first firers reloaded. The second half of each team waited until his partner was half-reloaded, then fired, and more riders went down. The survivors wheeled and spurred frantically back towards the bend, dismounted men racing after them on foot, but individual shots barked at their heels, and most of them were picked off before they could get out of range.

"Okay, boys, saddle up," Tamman said, and grinning dragoons filtered back towards their mounts. Their commander waited a moment longer, and his own grin faded as he watched the road. A handful of wounded crawled along it, their agony plain to his enhanced eyes, while others writhed where they'd fallen, and even unenhanced ears could have heard their screams and sobs.

He shivered and turned away, hating himself just a little because not even his horror made him feel one bit less satisfied.

Lord Marshal Rokas glowered at the map in the lamplight, but his glare couldn't change it, and the reports were just as disturbing now as they'd been when they were fresh.

He scowled. The first ambush had cost him seventy-one men, and that at a range Under-Captain Turalk swore was two hundred paces if it was a span. The second and third had been worse. The Host's total losses were over four hundred, and they were concentrated in his cavalry—which he wasn't over-supplied with in the first place.

His scouts would be more than human if what had happened today didn't make them cautious tomorrow, which was bad enough, but how had the heretics done it? Where had they gotten that many dragoons? Or hidden them? He wouldn't have believed more than a hundred men could be concealed in any of those ambush sites, but his casualties argued for three or four times that many—with malagors, at that—in each.

He poured a goblet of wine and sank into a folding chair. How they'd done it mattered less than that they had, but ambushes wouldn't save them. Unless they wanted to lose any chance to bottle him up in the mountains, they had to stand and fight; when they did, he would crush them.

He'd better, for two-thirds of Mother Church's own artillery and muskets and half her armor and pikeheads had come from Malagor's foundries. Rokas had never liked being so dependent on a single source, yet what they faced now was worse than his worst nightmare, for every foundry Mother Church had lost, the heretics had gained.

Rokas knew to the last pike and pistol how many weapons had lain in the Guard's armories in Malagor. His figures were less accurate for the secular arsenals but still enough for a decent guess, and even if the heretics had them all, they could field little more than a hundred thousand men. Yet given time, Malagor's artisans could arm every man in the princedom, and if that happened, the cost of invading that mountain-guarded land would become almost unbearable.

He'd finally managed to convince the Circle of that simple, self-evident fact; if he hadn't, the prelates would have delayed the Host until first snow "strengthening their souls against heresy."

But High Priest Vroxhan had listened at last, and now Rokas brooded down at the map tokens representing a hundred and twenty thousand men— the picked flower of the Guard from eastern North Hylar. His force was really too large for the constricted terrain, but, as he'd told the high priest, strategy and maneuver were of scant use in this situation.

He stared unhappily at the blue line of the Mortan River and sipped his wine. An infant could divine his only possible path, and Tibold was no infant, curse him! He was a seldahk, with all the speed and cunning of the breed; a seldahk who'd offended a high-captain and been banished to the most miserable post that high-captain could find. Tibold would know precisely what Rokas planned . . . and how to make the most of whatever force *he* had.

The marshal chewed his mustache at the thought. Mother Church's last true challenge had been the conquest of barbarian Herdaana six generations ago, and even that had been far short of what *this* could become. If the heresy wasn't crushed soon, it might turn into another nightmare like the Schismatic Wars, which had laid half of North Hylar waste, and the thought chilled him.

Sean MacIntyre stood on the walls of the city of Yortown and stared down at the fires of his men. *His* men. The thought was terrifying, for there were fifty-eight thousand people down there, and their lives depended on him.

He folded his hands behind him and considered the odds once more.

Worse than two-to-one, and they'd have been higher if the Church had chosen to squeeze more troops into the valley. He'd rather hoped they might do just that, but this Lord Marshal Rokas knew better than to crowd himself—unfortunately.

He gnawed his lip and wished he weren't so far out of his own time, or that the Academy's military history hadn't tended to emphasize strategy and skimp on the military nuts and bolts of earlier eras. Half of what they'd introduced to the Malagorans had been dredged up from remembered conversations with Uncle Hector. The rest had been extrapolated from that or gleaned from *Israel*'s limited (and infuriatingly nonspecific) military history records, and he intended to have a severe talk with Aunt Adrienne about her curriculum.

He paced slowly, brooding in the night wind. The pike was the true mankiller of Pardal, and most armies had at least three of them for every musket. The Temple Guard certainly did, and Tibold had explained how it used its phalanx-like formations to pin an enemy under threat of attack, "prepared" him with artillery and small arms, and finally charged home with cold steel. Yet for all their horrific shock power, those massive pike blocks were unwieldy; he suspected traditional Malagoran tactics would have given Rokas problems even without the "angels" and their innovations.

The Malagorans' polearms reminded him of Earth's Swiss pikemen, but with fewer pikes and more bills which, in the absence of any heavy cavalry threat, were shorter, handier melee weapons than those of Earth. Tactically, they were far more agile than the Guard, relying on shallower pike formations to hold an enemy in play while billmen swept out around his flanks, and Sean's modifications should make them even deadlier... assuming they were ready.

If only he'd had more time! He'd let Tibold handle training, and the tough old captain made Baron von Steuben look like a Cub Scout, but they'd had barely two months. Their army had incredible *esprit* and a hard core of militia (Malagor's self-governing towns and villages raised their own troops in the absence of feudal grandees), and over eight thousand Guardsmen had defected to the rebels, but fusing them into a single force and teaching them a whole new tactical doctrine in two months had been a nightmare.

Worse, none of his own training had taught him how to lead troops with so little command and control. He was used to instant, high-tech communication, and he suspected his most pessimistic estimates fell far short of just how bad *this* was going to be. His men looked good at drill, but would they hang together in battle when the whole world went crazy about them? He didn't know, but he knew too many battles in Earth's history had been lost when one side lost its cohesion and fell apart in confusion.

Still, he told himself firmly, if they *did* hold together, the Guard was in trouble. Normally, its phalanxes would have had the edge at Yortown, where flanks could be secured by terrain and mass and momentum were what counted, but that was where the contributions of *Israel*'s crew came in. They hadn't gotten the volume of their troops' fire up to anything approaching a modern level, but it was far heavier than Pardal had ever seen... and pike blocks made big targets. If he could get the Guard stuck, it was going to learn what the bear did to the buckwheat, and he thought—hoped—he'd found the place to bog it down. The Keldark Valley narrowed to a little more than six kilometers of open terrain at Yortown, and if Lord Rokas was as good a student of military history as Tibold said . . .

He sighed and shook free of the thoughts wearing grooves in his brain, then stretched, glanced up at the alien stars, and took himself off to bed, wondering if he'd sleep a wink.

CHAPTER TWENTY-EIGHT

Lord Marshal Rokas climbed the hill and opened his spyglass with a click. The morning mist had lifted, though tendrils still clung to the line of the Mortan, and his mouth tightened as he studied the terrain. He'd expected—feared—from the start that Tibold would offer battle here, for more than one invading army had been broken against Yortown.

The town stood on the bluffs beyond the river. Its walls had been razed after the Schismatic Wars, but the heretics were building new ones. Not that they were really needed. The Mortan ran all the way to the Eastern Ocean, twisting down the Keldark Valley to escape the Shalokars, and it coiled like a hateful serpent about Yortown's feet. The river swooped from the northern edge of the valley to the southern cliffs before it turned east once more, and like many a Malagoran before him, Tibold had drawn up beyond that icy natural moat.

Rokas's glass lingered on the Yortown bridges with wistful longing, but the demolitions had been too thorough. The broken spans had been dropped into water too deep to ford even across their rubble, and he smothered a curse. If the Circle hadn't hesitated so long, he could have been past Yortown and into Malagor's heart before the heretics got themselves organized!

He turned further south. No position was impregnable, but his mouth tightened anew as he considered the fords the blown bridges had made the key to this one. They lay southeast of Yortown, where the river broadened, and raw earthworks reared on the western bank. He saw the glint of pikes and gleam of artillery, and his heart sank. Those fords were over a hundred paces wide and more than waist deep; the wounded would be doomed even without armor. With it—

He turned back to the north to glare at the dense forest which sprawled down from the valley wall almost to his hilltop vantage point. It offered his right flank a natural protection—God knew no pikeman could get through *that* tangle!—but it was a guard against nothing. The river was too deep to bridge, much less ford, north of Yortown, and no captain as canny as Tibold would put men in a trap from which they could not withdraw.

He closed his glass. No, Tibold knew what he was about . . . and so did Rokas. Too many battles had been fought at Yortown; defender and attacker alike knew all the moves, and if the cost would be high, it was one he could pay. It would trouble too many dreams in years to come, but he could pay it.

"I see no need to alter our plans," he told his officers. "Captain Vrikadan," he met the high-captain's eyes, "you will advance."

"God, look at them!" Tamman muttered over his com implant, and Sean nodded jerkily, forgetting his friend couldn't see him. No sensor image could have prepared him for seeing that army uncoiling in the flesh, and he braced himself in the tree's high fork, peering through its leaves while the Host deployed towards the fords. Musketeers screened massive columns of pikes, and nioharq-drawn artillery moved steadily between the columns. Armor flashed, pikeheads were a glittering forest above, and the marching legs below made the columns look like horrible caterpillars of steel.

"I see them," he replied after a moment, "and I wish to hell we had the Holy Hand Grenade of Antioch!"

Tamman chuckled at the feeble joke, and Sean's dry mouth quirked. He wished he—or Tibold, at least—could be at the fords with Tamman. He knew he couldn't, and he needed Tibold here in case something happened to him, but he'd felt far more confident before he saw the Host with his own eyes.

He sighed, then slithered down the tree. Tibold stood with Folmak, the miller who commanded Sean's headquarters company, and Sean met their eyes.

"They're doing it."

"I see." Tibold plucked at his lower lip. "And their scouts?"

"You were right about them, too. There's a screen of dragoons covering their right flank, but they're not getting too far out."

"Aye." Tibold nodded. "Rokas didn't become Lord Marshal by being careless even of unlikely threats. But—" his teeth flashed in a tight grin "—it seems Lord Tamman did indeed teach his men caution yesterday."

"So it seems," Sean agreed, and peered into the green shadows where twenty thousand men lay hidden amid undergrowth as dense as anything Grant had faced at The Wilderness. They wore dull green and brown, their rifle barrels had been browned to prevent any betraying gleam, and they made a sadly scruffy sight beside the crimson and steel of the Guard, but they were also almost totally invisible.

He flicked his neural feed to the stealthed cutter above the valley, exchanging a brief, wordless caress with an anxious Sandy, then plugged into Brashan's arrays through the cutter's com. The Host was closing up, packing tighter behind the assault elements. With a little luck . . .

He shifted his attention to the pontoon bridges north of Yortown, hidden behind the woods. Pontoons were new to Pardal, and they'd been trickier to erect than he'd hoped, but they seemed to be holding. He hoped so. If it all came apart, those bridges were the only way home for a third of his army.

✧   ✧   ✧

Stomald watched the Angel Harry make another small adjustment on the situation map. She was intent upon her work, yet he saw a tiny tremble in her slender fingers and wanted to slip an arm about her to comfort her. But she was an angel, he reminded himself again, and gripped his starburst, instead, trying to share the army's mood.

The men were confident, filled with near idolatry for the angels' champions. Indeed, they were more than confident. They no longer looked to simply defending themselves, but to smashing their enemies, despite the odds, and if they'd prayed dutifully for mercy, their fervor was reserved for prayers for strength, victory, and—especially—Malagoran independence.

Now he listened to the steady cadence of the Guard's drums and sweat dotted his brow as he prayed silently—not for himself, but for the men he'd led to this. A surgeon began to hone his knives and saws, and he watched the shining steel with appalled eyes, unable to look away.

A hand touched his shoulder, startling despite its lightness, and he looked up with a gasp. The Angel Harry squeezed gently, and her remaining eye was soft and understanding. He reached up and covered her hand with his own, marveling at his own audacity in touching her holy flesh, and she smiled.

High-Captain Vrikadan's branahlk jibed and fretted as ten thousand voices rose to join the thunder of the drums, and he turned in the saddle to study his men. The mighty hymn swelled around him, strong and deep, but the leading pike companies were tight-faced as they roared the words.

Vrikadan urged the branahlk closer to a battery of arlaks, creaking along between the columns. Even the stolid nioharqs were uneasy, tossing their tusks and lowing, and a gray-bearded artillery captain looked up and met his eye with a grim smile.

Tamman stood on the fighting step and watched the juggernaut of steel and flesh roll towards him. The rumble of its singing was a morale weapon whose potency he hadn't really appreciated, but at least the Host was performing exactly as Tibold had predicted. So far.

Twenty thousand men marched towards the fords. As many more followed to exploit any success, and he felt very small and young. Worse, he sensed his men's disquiet. It wasn't even close to panic, but that hymn-roaring monster was enough to shake anyone, and he turned to his second-in-command.

"Let's have a little music of our own, Lornar," he suggested, and High-Captain Lornar grinned.

"At once, Lord Tamman!" He beckoned to a teenaged messenger, and the lad dashed back to the rear of the redoubt. There was a moment of muttered consultation, and then a high-pitched skirling. The Malagorans had invented the bagpipe, and Tamman's troops looked at one another with bared teeth as the defiant wail of the pipes rose to meet the Guard.

✧   ✧   ✧

God, I never realized how long *it took!* Sean made himself stand still, listening to the music swelling from the redoubts to answer the Guard's singing, and felt sick and hollow, nerves stretched by the deliberation with which thousands of men marched towards death. This wasn't like *Israel's* frantic struggle against the quarantine system. This was slow and agonizing.

The range dropped inexorably, and he bit his lip as the first gouts of smoke erupted from the redoubts. Round shot ripped through the Guard's ranks, dismembering and disemboweling, and his enhanced vision made the carnage too clear. He swallowed bile, but even as the guns fired the music of the pipes changed. It took on a new, fiercer rhythm, and he looked at Tibold.

"I haven't heard that hymn before."

"That's no hymn," Tibold said, and Sean raised an eyebrow. "That's 'Malagor the Free,' Lord Sean," the ex-Guardsman said softly.

Vrikadan heard the high, shivering seldahk's howl of the Malagoran war cry—a terrifying sound which, like the music shrilling beneath it, had been proscribed on pain of death for almost two Pardalian centuries—but he had other things to worry about, and he fought his mount as a salvo of shot shrieked through his men. And another. *Another!* Dear God, where had they *gotten* all those guns?

A cyclone howled, and he kicked free of his stirrups as a round shot took his branahlk's head. The beast dropped and its blood fountained over him, but he rolled upright and drew his sword. The range was too great for his own guns to affect earthworks, but he grabbed at the knee of a mounted aide.

"Unlimber the guns!" he snapped. "Get them into action *now!*"

Tamman coughed, watching one of his arlak crews as the reeking smoke rolled over him. A bagged charge slid down the muzzle while the captain stopped the vent with a leather thumbstall. The eight-kilo round shot followed, and the wad, and the crew heaved the piece back to battery as the captain cocked the lock and drove a priming quill down the vent to pierce the bag. The gun vomited flame and lurched back, a dripping sponge hissed into its maw, quenching the embers of the last shot, and a fresh charge was waiting.

He turned away, dazed by the bellow and roar and insane keening of the pipes, and his hands clenched on the earthen rampart as the lines of Guard musketeers parted to reveal the pikes and their own unlimbering guns.

Lord Rokas strained to pierce the smoke. The waves of fire washing along those redoubts was impossible. No one could fit that many guns into so small a space even if they had them, and the heretics couldn't *have* that many!

But they did. Tongues of flame transfixed the pall, smashing tangles of bloody limbs through his advancing pikes. Vrikadan's men were falling too quickly and too soon, and he turned to a signaler.

"Tell High-Captain Martas to tighten the interval. Then instruct High-Captain Sertal to advance."

Signal flags snapped, and Rokas chewed his lip. He'd hoped Vrikadan would clear at least one ford, but that would take a special miracle against those guns. Yet his bleeding columns should cover Martas long enough for him to reach charge range of the river.

He raised his glass once more, cursing silently as his men entered grapeshot range and his estimate of Yortown's cost rose.

Sandy MacMahan was white, and her brain screamed for her to arm her cutter's weapons, but she couldn't. She was sickened by how glibly she'd suggested taking part in this horror, yet stubborn rationality told her she'd been right—as Sean was right now. Imperial weapons could never be used if they couldn't be used throughout, but logic and reason were cold, hateful companions as she watched the smoke and blood erupting below her.

High-Captain Vrikadan's arlaks thundered. They were too distant to penetrate the earthen ramparts, but their crews heaved them further forwards with every shot, pounding away in a desperate effort to suppress the heretic guns.

They weren't accomplishing much, Vrikadan knew, yet every little bit helped, and if they could dismount a few of those guns . . .

His northern column wavered, and Vrikadan charged through the smoke, bouncing off wounded men, beating at stragglers with the flat of his blade.

"Keep your ranks!" he bellowed. "Keep your ranks, damn you!"

A wild-eyed under-captain recognized him and wheeled on his own men, quelling their panic. Vrikadan shouldered up beside the younger man, waving his sword while the lead company of the stalled phalanx stared at him.

"*With me, lads!*" he screamed, and dashed forward like a man possessed.

Smoke blinded Tamman, and he switched his vision to thermal imaging. The image was blurry, and he could no longer see the range stakes, but a mass of men was almost to the east bank. He sent a runner forward.

Vrikadan's lips drew back in a snarl as a ray of sunlight pierced the smoke and the river glistened before him. Grapeshot heaped his men in ugly, writhing tangles, but the weight of numbers behind them was an avalanche. They couldn't stop—they couldn't *be* stopped!—and the water beckoned.

And then, just as he reached the bank, the smoke lifted on a billow of flame. There were gun pits at the feet of the redoubts! Camouflaged pits filled not with arlaks but with chagors, light guns packed hub-to-hub and spewing fire.

He had only an instant to see it before a charge of grape ripped both legs off at the hip.

✧   ✧   ✧

Sean swallowed again, cringing inwardly as he watched through Sandy's scanners and saw the east bank of the Mortan writhe with screaming, broken bodies . . . and saw living men advancing through the horror.

God in Heaven, how could they *do* that? He knew the momentum of the men behind drove them forward, giving them no choice, but it was more than that, too. It was unreasoning, blood-mad insanity and it was courage, and there was no longer any difference between them.

They were going to reach the fords despite Tamman's guns, and he hadn't really believed they could.

The first Guardsmen splashed into the river. It ran scarlet as case shot flailed at them, but they came on. High-Captain Lornar saw Lord Tamman's slender sword rise above his head and blew his whistle, and more whistles shrilled up and down the fighting step. Three thousand rifled joharns were leveled across the rampart, and Lord Tamman's sword hissed down.

The leading pikemen were still three hundred paces away when a sheet of lead slashed through them like fiery sleet. Whole companies went down, and those following stared in horror at the writhing carpet of their companions and the isolated individuals who still stood, stunned by the density of the volley. They wavered, but High-Captain Martas' men were on their heels, driving them forward. There was nowhere to go but into those flaming muzzles, and they lowered their pikes and charged.

The first three thousand musketeers reached for cartridges and stepped down from the fighting step, and three thousand more replaced them. Ramrods clinked and jerked, whistles screamed again, and a second stupendous volley smashed out. Sergeants shouted, bellowing to control the lethal ballet, and the musketeers exchanged places again. The first group's reloaded joharns leveled, and lightning sheeted across the rampart once more.

Lord Rokas paled as the roar of massive volleys drowned even the artillery. With no way to know how quickly Tamman's men could reload, those steady, crashing discharges could only mean the heretics had far more muskets than he'd believed possible.

He couldn't see through the wall of smoke, but experience told him what had happened to Vrikadan—and that Martas was moving into the maelstrom, with High-Captain Sertal on his heels. Those fords were mincing machines, devouring his troops, yet they were also the only way into Yortown, and he banished all expression as he barked out orders to send even more of the Guard to their deaths.

High-Captain Martas's men burst through the smoke. Bodies littered the riverbank, but the heretics' guns and muskets had been too busy dealing with Vrikadan's men to ravage Martas's companies. Now they lunged for the river, for their only salvation lay in reaching and silencing those redoubts.

They began to die as more volleys roared, and their fellows stumbled forward over their bodies, floundering and cursing in the shallows, wading deeper, crouching to hide as much of themselves below the water as they could.

And then the lead ranks lunged upright, screaming as the rear ranks drove them forward onto the sharpened stakes and needle-pointed caltrops hidden in the river. They thrashed and shrieked in the scarlet water, and the deadly waves of musketry ripped them to pieces.

Round shot hissed overhead or thudded into the earthwork as the Host's guns scrambled into action, and one of them slammed into the arlak beside Tamman. The barrel spun away, the carriage disintegrated, and something less than human twitched and mewled amid the wreckage. His guns were protected by the redoubt's embrasures, but they were also outnumbered. More and more of the Guard's artillery was coming into action between the bleeding infantry columns, and musketeers stood fully exposed on the flanks to fire into the smoke. They were shooting blind at extreme range, but even with their low rates of fire, an awesome number of balls buzzed overhead.

He stared down into the carnage of the ford. Pikemen and musketeers waded out into that madness, advancing until grapeshot or musket balls hammered them under, but the men behind them were stopping at last. Or were they? He strained his eyes and swallowed. They weren't stopping; they were reforming.

High-Captain Sertal's face was white under its dust and grime, but his hoarse voice cut through the din. His forward companies absorbed the survivors of Vrikadan's and Martas's men, standing with iron discipline under the tornado of the heretics' fire. Under-captains and sergeants shouted orders. Where necessary, they kicked troopers into formation with boots caked in bloody mud, and Sertal winced as another deadly lash of grapeshot scythed through his men. He couldn't hold them here long, but he *had* to hold them long enough to reorder their ranks, and he gripped his sword and coughed on smoke, listening to the screams.

Sean checked the scanners once more as the zone south of the High Road became a solid mass of advancing Guardsmen, then nodded to Tibold.

"They're stuck in deep," he said, trying to hide his anxiety, "and Rokas is sending his reserves forward. It's time."

"Aye, Lord Sean!" Tibold began snapping orders, and twenty thousand men, without a single pike among them, rose to their feet in the "impassable" woods north of the Host.

Now!

Sertal thrust his sword at the redoubts and swept it down in command, and his men lurched into the holocaust. Tamman saw them coming and turned to shout another order to Lornar, but Lornar was down, head smashed by one of those blind-fired musket balls. He grabbed a captain's shoulder. The Malagoran's face—it was Captain Ithun, one of the ex-Guard officers—

was white and strained, and he went still whiter as he realized *he* was now Tamman's senior officer in the central redoubt. Tamman saw it, but there was no time for encouragement.

"Pikes forward!" he bellowed.

The chagors in Tamman's advanced gun pits fired one last salvo, and their crews snatched for swords and pikes as the bleeding ranks of the Guard won free of the water at last. A dozen gun captains paused to light fuses before they grabbed up their own weapons, and the madmen who'd fought their way through everything the Malagorans could throw lunged towards them with a howl. Fresh concussions turned howls to screams as the crude mines seeded the river bank in fountains of flame and flying limbs, and the survivors wavered, but Sertal's men drove forward, and edged steel stabbed and cut.

Malagoran pikemen funneled through sally ports in their earthworks and foamed over the foremost Guardsmen behind the high, quavering Malagoran yell, then crashed into the ranks behind them. They thrust forward, bills rising and falling, shearing limbs and plucking heads, and hurled the Host back into the fords, but there they stopped. The hand-to-hand butchery blocked the chagors, and the arlaks were locked in a duel with the Guard's gun lines. Musketry continued to crash out above their heads, yet the Host was taking fewer fire casualties now, and the lead formations had cleared most of the obstacles with their own bodies. Thousands of Guardsmen lay dead or wounded, but more pressed forward, and sheer weight of numbers began to drive the Malagorans back.

Captain Yurkal stared south at the clouds of smoke, listening to the artillery and crashing musketry. The screams were faint with distance, a savage sound under the explosions, and he was guiltily aware of his own relief at being spared that hell. Yurkal was a son of Mother Church, but he was also grateful his dragoons had been deployed so far from the fighting, and—

He jerked in astonishment as his banner-bearer fell, clawing at his chest. There was a meaty thud as the sergeant beside him slid to the ground as well, and Yurkal whirled as the popping sounds behind him registered.

Three hundred paces away, still hidden in the edge of the forest, a green-and-brown-clad marksman settled his rifled malagor into its rest and peered through his peep sight. He squeezed the trigger, and a twenty-millimeter bullet blew Captain Yurkal's heart apart.

Sean watched the snipers methodically pick off officers and noncoms while the rest of his men debouched from the forest. It wasn't chivalrous . . . but, then, neither was war.

More officers fell, and suddenly leaderless troopers began to panic. Most were already fleeing, and the pairs of malagors continued to fire, cutting down the handful of Guardsmen who stood while leather-lunged sergeants cursed their own men into formation.

Fifteen thousand men formed a three-deep battle line three kilometers long. The Malagoran yell quivered down their front, and they swept south, and five thousand more followed as a reserve.

Lord Marshal Rokas's head snapped up at the crackle of musketry. He spun to the north and gaped as a new wall of smoke billowed. Impossible!

He jerked his spyglass open, and his blood ran chill. His mounted screen had dissolved like leaves in a tempest, and even as he watched the advancing lines of muzzle flashes ripped at the fugitives' backs.

A trap. This entire position was a trap, and he'd walked right into it! Tibold had done the unthinkable, splitting his outnumbered forces, deploying those oncoming musketeers in a position from which they couldn't possibly retreat in order to hit him when he was mired in the fords!

The plan's insane audacity stunned him, but half his total force was committed to the lunge at the fords. Another quarter had been left behind, lest it constrict his movement. That left barely thirty thousand men to meet this new threat, and they were spread out behind his attacking formations.

He leapt onto his branahlk, spurring down the hill even as he began volleying orders, and signals and couriers exploded in every direction in a deadly race against that advancing horde of heretical musketeers.

Another isolated company disintegrated under the rolling fire of Sean's battle-line, and his pulse pounded. His men couldn't move as quickly in line as in column, but the hours of drill were bearing fruit. Their formation was perfect, and they advanced like automatons, reloading on the move. Their fire swept the trampled crop land before them like a lethal broom, and he could see the panicky movement of Rokas's reserves ahead of them.

The carnage in the fords drove inexorably towards the redoubts, for the Guardsmen there had no way of knowing what was descending upon their flank. Sixty thousand men clawed their way forward. Only a fraction of them could reach the fords at any given moment, yet the numbers behind them seemed inexhaustible. The Malagorans fought back with equal ferocity, but they, too, were dying, and there were less of them.

The whistles shrilled again, and the Guard forged ahead with a bellow. But the Malagorans weren't breaking. They fell back, step by step, into the redoubts under cover of their musketeers, and Tamman watched anxiously.

Sean had to cross ten more kilometers of open ground to reach the fords.

Rokas's orders began to reach their destinations, and a shudder pulsed through the Host. The sudden threat to their "secure" flank mingled with the slaughter at the fords and woke a shiver of dread. Their enemies served the forces of Hell—was that how they'd managed this impossible maneuver?

But there was no time to think of such things with that battle-line sweeping down upon them. Companies wheeled, nioharq-drawn batteries lumbered to new positions, and an answering formation began to coalesce. It was shaken and uncertain, but it was there, and Rokas allowed himself to hope.

✧   ✧   ✧

Sean watched the patterns shift, and his own orders raced up and down the line. He had no artillery . . . but, then, the Guard artillerists weren't used to muskets which could kill them at eight hundred meters, either.

A forlorn hope of musketeers tried to slow him, and perhaps a hundred of his own men went down. Then the fire of his line tore the defenders apart, and the inexorable advance swept over them.

The hand-to-hand fighting reached the redoubts, and screams bubbled as Guardsmen tumbled into the ditches at their feet and died on the waiting stakes. Their fellows advanced over them, marching across their writhing bodies, too frenzied even to realize what they were doing.

The musketeers fired one last volley and fell back to clear the fighting step. Pikes and bills crossed at the ramparts, and Tamman knew he should go with the marksmen, but Lornar was dead. His men were fighting like demons, yet it all hinged on their morale, and if he seemed to waver . . .

A pikeman leapt up a pile of bodies, thrusting at him, and his left hand darted out with inhuman quickness. He caught the pike haft, enhanced muscles jerked, and the Guardsman clung in disbelief as he was wrenched in close.

A battle steel blade hissed, and a head bounded away.

Two batteries of arlaks unlimbered, and the gunners wheeled their pieces frantically into position to stem the heretics' advance. They were six hundred paces from the enemy, three times effective malagor range—and they died in deep astonishment as the crackling fire killed them anyway.

The second wave of attackers was thrown back, but a third formed and crashed forward over the bodies, and the man beside Tamman went down screaming with a pikehead in his guts. Tamman lunged at his killer, grunting as his slender sword punched through breast and backplate alike, and kicked the body aside, then grunted again as a musket ball smashed into his own breastplate. It whined aside, marking the undented Imperial composite with a long smear of lead, and he cut down two more Guardsmen. But this time the bastards were coming through, and his free hand ripped a mace from a dead man's belt as the defending line crumbled to his left.

"Follow me!" he bellowed, and sensed the rush of his men behind him as he hurtled to meet the penetration.

Sean's line swept over the guns and the bodies of their crews, and a hungry roar went up as his men saw the first pike blocks formed across their path. His own pipes screamed, wailing their fury, and his amplified voice bellowed through the din.

"Halt!"

Fifteen thousand men paused as one, and the waiting Guardsmen's pikes swung down into a leveled glitter of steel.

"Front rank, kneel!"

Five thousand men went to one knee, shouldering their muskets as the

Guard's drums thundered and the charge began. Seven or eight thousand men swept forward, shrieking their battlecries, and he watched them come.

Three hundred meters. Two hundred.

"Take aim!"

One hundred. Seventy-five. Fifty.

"By ranks—*fire!*"

A sheet of flame rolled down his kneeling rank, and the front of the pike blocks collapsed in hideous ruin. Men stumbled and sprawled over the bodies of their fellows as the charge wavered, and the second rank fired. A third of the Guardsmen were down, and the charge slithered to a halt as the hurricane blast swept over them . . . and the *third* rank fired!

The surviving pikemen hurled away their weapons and fled.

Captain Ithun watched his company reel back as the Guard swept over the parapet. Its men wavered, shaken by the terror thundering about them and ready to flee, then stared in disbelief as Lord Tamman charged the enemy's flank. The fighting step was wide enough for five men abreast, but there was no one beside him, for he'd outdistanced them all . . . and it didn't matter.

Ithun gaped as the black-armored figure erupted into the Guardsmen, mace in one hand, skinny sword in the other. No Pardalian had faced a fully enhanced enemy in forty-five thousand years, and any Guardsman who'd doubted the heretics were allied to demons knew better now. Limbs and dead men exploded from Lord Tamman's path. A pike lunged at him, and metal screamed as that impossible sword sheared through the pikehead.

"*Come on, Malagorans!*" Ithun shrieked, and his men roared as they swept back up the fighting step in his wake.

It was over, Rokas thought remotely.

A line of fire ground down from the north in a haze of powder smoke, shattering everything in its path and crunching over the wreckage. No army in the world could advance like that, not without a single polearm, but the heretics were doing it, and his men refused to face them.

He stood numbly, watching the Host disintegrate as his men threw away their weapons and bolted, and he couldn't blame them. There was something dreadful about that deliberate, remorseless advance—something that proved the tales of demons—and all of Mother Church's exorcisms couldn't stop it.

An aide jerked at him, shouting about withdrawal, and Rokas turned like a man in a nightmare, then gasped as a fiery hammer smashed his side.

The lord marshal fell to his knees, and the tumult about him had grown suddenly faint. He rolled onto his back, staring up at his panicked aide and the smoke-streaked sky, and his dimming mind marveled that evening had come so soon.

But it wasn't evening, after all; it was night.

CHAPTER TWENTY-NINE

The stench was enough to turn a statue's stomach.

Eleven thousand Guardsmen lay dead. Another twenty thousand wounded littered the Keldark Valley, whimpering or screaming . . . or lying silent while they waited to die. Another thirty or forty thousand (the count was far from done) huddled in shocked disbelief under the weapons of their enemies.

A miserable, battered third of the Holy Host was still running as darkness covered the horror.

And horror it was. Sean stood beside a field hospital, watching the surgeons, and only his implants held down his gorge. Pardalians had a good working knowledge of anatomy and a kitchen sink notion of sepsis, but distilled alcohol was their sole anesthetic and disinfectant. There were no medical teams to rebuild shattered limbs; amputation was the prescription, and the treatment of men's wounds was more horrifying than their infliction.

Sandy and Harry were out there in the middle of it. *Israel's* facilities couldn't have healed a fraction of the suffering, but Brashan had sent forward every painkiller his sickbay had, and the iron-faced "angels" moved through Hell, easing its pain and following the anesthetic with broad-spectrum Imperial antibiotics. Guardsmen who cursed them as demons fell silent in confusion as they watched them heal their enemies, and hundreds who should have died would live . . . and none of it absolved *Israel's* crew of their guilt.

Sean and Tamman had visited their own wounded—blessedly few compared to the Host's—but their responsibilities lay elsewhere, and Sean turned away to stare out at the torches and lanterns creeping across the battlefield. He shuddered as he braced himself for another journey into that obscenity, yet he had to go. He squared his shoulders and started forward against the steady stream of litter-bearers, and Tibold followed him silently.

He tried not to think, but he couldn't stop looking . . . or smelling. The reek of blood and torn flesh mixed with the sewer stench of riven entrails, scavengers—some of them human—were already busy beyond the reach of the moving torches, and Pardal's small moon added its wan light to the horror.

More people had died with *Imperial Terra* than here, but they'd died without even knowing. These men had died screaming, ripped apart and mutilated, and he was the one who'd planned their murder. He knew he'd had no choice, that less than four thousand of his own lay dead or wounded because he'd gotten it right, but this moonlit nightmare was too much.

His vision blurred, and he stumbled over a body. His legs gave, and he sank to his knees before his lieutenant, trying to speak, fighting to explain his inner agony, but no words came. Only terrible, choking sounds.

Tibold knelt beside him, brown eyes dark in the moonlight, and a hard-palmed hand touched his cheek. Sean stared at him, twisted by shame and guilt and a wrenching loss of innocence, and Tibold raised his other hand to cradle his captain-general's head.

"I know, lad," the ex-Guardsman murmured. "I *know*. The fools who call war 'glorious' have never seen *this*, curse them."

"I-I—" Sean gasped and fought for breath, and Tibold's hands slid down from his head. The older man cradled him like a lover or a child, and Crown Prince Sean Horus MacIntyre sobbed upon his shoulder.

Tamman huddled close to the fire with his captains as aides came and went. Enhancement kept the outer chill at bay, but he hugged the fire's light, refusing to think about what lay beyond its reach. The chainmail on his right arm was stiff with other men's dried blood, his implants were busy with half a dozen small wounds, and he'd never been so tired in his life.

Branahlks whistled as some dragoons herded in more prisoners, and a messenger came in with a report from the troops Sean had sent to watch the fleeing Guardsmen. The messenger wanted nioharqs to collect another half-dozen abandoned guns, and Tamman cudgeled his brain until he remembered who to send him to. Another messenger trotted up on a drooping branahlk to announce his men had gathered up four thousand joharns, and what should he do with them? He dealt with that, as well, then looked up as Sean and Tibold walked into the fire lit circle.

The officers raised a tired cheer, and Tamman saw Sean wince before he raised a hand to acknowledge it. His friend's face was like iron as they clasped forearms tiredly, and the two of them stared into the fire together.

Stomald closed two more dead eyes, then rose from aching knees. The captured priests and under-priests of the Temple would have nothing to do with him. They spat upon him and reviled him, but their dying soldiers saw only his vestments and heard only his comforting voice.

He closed his own eyes, swaying with fatigue, and whispered a prayer for the souls of the dead. For the many dead of both sides, and not for his own, alone. Pardal had not seen such slaughter, nor such crushing victory, in centuries, yet there was no jubilation in Stomald's heart. Thankfulness, yes, but no one could see such suffering and rejoice.

A slender arm steadied him, and he opened his eyes. The Angel Harry stood beside him. Her blue-and-gold garments were spattered with blood, and her face was drawn, her one eye shadowed, but she looked at him with concern.

"You should rest," she said, and he shook his head drunkenly.

"No." It was hard to get the word out. "I can't."

"How long since you've eaten?"

"Eaten?" Stomald blinked. "I had breakfast, I think," he said vaguely, and she clucked her tongue.

"That was eighteen hours ago." She sounded stern. "You're not going to do anyone any good when you collapse. Go get something to eat."

He gagged at the thought, and she frowned.

"I know. But you need—" She broke off and looked about until she spied the Angel Sandy. She said something in her own tongue, and the Angel Sandy replied in the same language. The laughter had leached even out of her eyes, but she held out her hand, and the Angel Harry handed over her satchel of medicines without ever removing her arm from Stomald's shoulders.

"Come with me." He started to speak, but she cut him off. "Don't argue—march," she commanded, and led him towards the distant cooking fires. He tried again to protest, then let himself slump against her strength, and she murmured something else in that strange language. He looked up at her questioningly, but she only shook her head and smiled at him—a sad, soft little smile that eased his wounded heart—and her arm tightened about him.

The Inner Circle sat in silence as High Priest Vroxhan laid the semaphore message aside. He pressed it flat with his fingers, then tucked his hands into the sleeves of his robe, hugging himself against a chill which had nothing to do with the cool night, and met their gaze. Even Bishop Corada was white-faced, and Frenaur sagged about his bones.

Lord Rokas was dead; barely forty thousand of the Host had escaped, less than half of them with weapons; and High-Captain Ortak had the Host's rearguard working with frantic speed to dig in further down the Keldark Valley. Ortak's report was short of details, yet one thing was clear. The Host hadn't been beaten. It hadn't even been routed. It had been destroyed.

"There you have it, Brothers," Vroxhan said. "We've failed to crush the heresy, and surely the heretics will soon counterattack." He glanced at High-Captain—no, Lord Marshal—Surak, and the man who had just become the Guard's senior officer looked back with stony eyes. "Exactly how bad is the situation, Lord Marshal?"

Surak winced at his new title, then squared his shoulders.

"Even with Ortak's survivors, we have barely seventy thousand men in all of Keldark. I don't yet know how many men the heretics deployed, but from the casualties we've suffered, they must have many more than that. I would have said they could never have raised and armed them, even with demonic aid, yet that they must have is evident from the result. I've already ordered every pike in Keldark forward to Ortak, but I fear they can do little more than slow the heretics. They can't stop them if they keep coming."

A soft sigh ran around the table, but Vroxhan looked up sternly, and it faded. Surak continued in a harsh voice.

"With Your Holiness' permission, I will order Ortak to retire on Erastor until more men—and weapons—can reach him. He can fight delaying actions, but if he stands, the heretics will surely overwhelm him."

"Wait," Corada objected. "Did not Lord Rokas say that an attacker needed twice or thrice a defender's numbers?"

Surak looked to Vroxhan, who nodded for him to answer.

"He did, and he was right, Your Grace, but those calculations are for battles in which neither side has demonic aid."

"Are you suggesting God's power is less than that of demons?"

Surak was no coward, but he fought an urge to wipe his forehead.

"No, Your Grace," he replied carefully. "I think it plain the demons *did* aid the heretics, and until I have Ortak's detailed report I can't say how they did so, but that isn't what I meant. Consider, please, Your Grace. Our men have been defeated—" that pallid understatement twisted his mouth like sour wine "—and they know it. They've lost many of their weapons. Ortak may have forty thousand men, but barely twenty thousand are armed, and their morale is—must be—shaken. The heretics have all the weapons abandoned on the field to swell their original strength, and demons or no, they know they won. Their morale will be strengthened even as ours is weakened."

He paused and raised his empty hands, palms uppermost.

"If I order Ortak to stand, he will. And as surely as he does, he'll be destroyed, Your Grace. We *must* withdraw, using the strength we still possess to slow the enemy until fresh strength can be sent to join it."

"But by your estimate, Lord Marshal," Vroxhan said, "we lack the numbers to meet the heretics on equal terms." The high priest's voice was firm, but anxiety burned in its depths.

"We do, Holiness," Surak replied, "but I believe we have sufficient to hold at least the eastern end of the Keldark Valley. I would prefer to do just that and open a new offensive from the west, were our strength in Cherist and Thirgan great enough. It isn't, however, so we must fight them here. I realize that it was the Inner Circle's desire to defeat this threat solely with our own troops, Holiness, yet that's no longer possible either. Our main field army has, for all intents and purposes, been destroyed, not merely defeated, and I fear we *must* summon the secular armies of the east to Holy War. Were all their numbers gathered into a single new Host under the Temple's banner, they would—they must—suffice for victory . . . but only if we can hold the heretics in the mountains until they've mustered. For that reason, if no other, Ortak must be ordered to delay the enemy."

"I see." Vroxhan sighed. "Very well, Lord Marshal, let it be as you direct. Send your orders, and the Circle will summon the princes." Surak stooped to kiss the hem of the high priest's robe and withdrew, his urgency evident in his speed, and Vroxhan looked about the table once more.

"And as for us, Brothers, I ask you all to join me in the Sanctum that we may pray for deliverance from the ungodly."

CHAPTER THIRTY

Sean MacIntyre stood with Sandy and frowned down at the relief map. Tibold and a dozen other officers stood around respectfully, watching him and "the Angel Sandy" study the map, and the absolute confidence in their eyes made him want to scream at them.

The Battle of Yortown lay one of the local "five-days" in the past. The Angels' Army had advanced a hundred and thirty kilometers in that time, but now High-Captain Ortak's entrenched position lay squarely in its path, and try as he might, Sean saw no way around it. In fact, he'd come to the conclusion Tibold had offered from the first: the only way around was *through*, and that was the reason for his frown.

Sean's army had every advantage in an open field battle. The Yortown loot had included twenty-six thousand joharns, enough for Sean to convert all fifty-eight thousand of his men into musketeers and send several thousand to the force covering the Thirgan Gap in the west to boot, and Brashan had shifted *Israel* to the mountains directly above Yortown to decrease cutter transit time to the battleship. The Narhani's machine shop modules had increased their modification rate to forty-five hundred rifles (with bayonet rings) a night, and the Malagoran gunsmiths were adding almost a thousand a day more on their own, now that "the angels" had taught them about rifling benches. Unfortunately, over half Sean's army had been trained as *pikemen*, and the new men were still learning which end the bullet came out of.

Even so, his troops were fleeter of foot and had incomparably more firepower than any other Pardalian army. The new, standardized rifle regiments he and Tibold had organized could kill their enemies from five or six times smoothbore range, and the absence of polearms made them far more mobile. Even the best pikemen were less than nimble trailing five-meter pikes, and his rifle-armed infantry could dance rings around the Guard's ponderous phalanxes. Coupled with its higher rate of fire, the Angels' Army could cut four or five times its own number to pieces in a mobile engagement.

Unhappily, High-Captain Ortak knew it. He was well supplied with artillery, since Lord Marshal Rokas had known the cramped terrain at Yortown would reduce his guns' efficiency and left many of them with his rearguard, and reinforcements had come forward, but less than half his roughly eighty thousand men were actually armed. Less than twelve thousand were musketeers, and he dared not face the Angels' Army in the open. But short of arms or not, his men still outnumbered Sean's by almost forty percent, and all those unarmed men had been busy with mattocks. The earthworks he'd thrown up at Erastor closed the Keldark Valley north of the Mortan, and he clearly had no intention of venturing beyond them. Nor could any army go around them. The Mortan was unfordable for over ninety kilometers upstream or down from Erastor, and the terrain south of the river was so boggy not even nioharqs could drag artillery or wagons through it.

In many respects, Erastor was a stronger defensive position even than Yortown, and Sean and Tibold had considered meeting Rokas there. In the end, they'd decided in favor of Yortown because its terrain had let Sean set his ambush, but for a simple holding engagement, Erastor would actually have been better. There were no open flanks between the Erastor Spur and the river, which left an opponent with superior numbers—or mobility—no openings. He had to attack head-on, and if Ortak refused to come out, Sean would have to go in after him . . . which meant the Guard's outnumbered and outranged musketeers could hunker down behind their parapets until Sean's men entered *their* range. The Guard's morale had to be shaken by what had happened at Yortown, while the Angels' Army's morale had soared in inverse proportion, and Sean knew his troops could take Erastor. It was the *cost* of taking it that terrified him.

He frowned more deeply at the map and once more castigated himself for not pushing on more quickly. He'd taken five days to march a distance a Pardalian army could have done in three if it was pushed, and the consequences promised to be grim. If he'd crowded the routed Host harder, he might have bounced Ortak out of Erastor before the high-captain dug in, and telling himself his troops had been exhausted by the Yortown fighting made him feel no better. He should have gotten them on the way with the next dawn, however tired, not wasted two whole days burying the dead and collecting the Host's cast away weapons, and he swore at himself for delaying.

He wanted to swear at Tibold, as well, for letting him, but that wouldn't have been fair. The ex-Guardsman was a product of the military tradition which had evolved after the Schismatic Wars, and Pardalian wars were fought for territory. Ideally, battles were avoided in favor of efforts to outmaneuver an opponent, and campaigns were characterized by intricate, almost formal march and countermarch until they climaxed in equally formal engagements or sieges for vital fortresses. The Napoleonic doctrine of pursuing a beaten foe to annihilation was foreign to local military thought. It shouldn't have been, given the mobility nioharqs bestowed, but it was, and a crushing victory like Yortown would have brought most wars to a screeching conclusion as the defeated side treated for terms. Not this time. High Priest Vroxhan and the Inner Circle might not have the least idea what Sean and his marooned friends were truly after, but they'd realized they were fighting for their very survival. Worse, they were fighting, as they saw it, for their souls. Oh, it was obvious they'd become firmly attached to their secular power, but they also saw no distinction between "God's Will" and the Temple's domination of Pardal. Under the circumstances, there were—*could* be—no acceptable "terms" for them short of the "heretics'" utter destruction, and they were mobilizing their reserves. Within another two weeks, at most three, thousands of fresh troops would be marching into Erastor. Somehow he had to crush the Erastor position before those reinforcements arrived, and his soul cringed at the thought of the casualties his men would suffer because *he'd* screwed up.

His frown at the map became a glare. He knew, intellectually, that there wasn't always a clever answer, but he was also young. Centuries older than he'd been before Yortown, but still young enough to believe there *ought* to be an answer, if he were only smart enough to see it.

A hand touched his elbow, and he turned his head to see Sandy looking up at him. Her face was no longer the haunted mask it had been the first night after Yortown, but, as for all of *Israel*'s crew, the slaughter of that day had left its mark upon her. Her eyes had learned to twinkle once more, yet there was less brashness behind them. No less confidence, perhaps, but a deeper awareness of the horrible cost reality could exact. Now those eyes met his searchingly, the question in them plain, and he sighed.

"I don't see an answer," he said in English. "They've put in too solid a roadblock, and it's my own damned fault."

"Oh, shush!" she said in the same language, squeezing his elbow harder. "We're all getting on-the-job training, and the last thing we need is for you to kick yourself for things you can't change. Seems to me you did a pretty fair job at Yortown, and you've got a lot more to work with now."

"Sure I do." He tried to keep the bitterness from his voice. His officers might not understand English, but they could recognize emotional overtones, and there was no sense shaking *their* confidence. "Unfortunately," he went on in a determinedly lighter tone, "the bad guys have more to work with, too. Not in numbers, but in position." He waved at the fifteen kilometers of earthworks linking the stony Erastor Spur to the river. "We surprised Rokas by doing something he *knew* was impossible, but Ortak has a much better idea of our capabilities, and he's dug in to deny us all our advantages. We can take him out with a frontal assault, but we'll lose thousands, and I just can't convince myself it's worth it, Sandy. Not just so we can get hold of a computer!"

"It's *not* just to get us to the computer!" she said fiercely, then smoothed her own tone as a few officers stirred in surprise. She shook her head and went on more calmly. "It's life and death for all these people, Sean—you know that."

"Yeah? And whose fault is that?" he growled.

"Ours," she said unflinchingly. "Mine, if you want to be specific. But it's something we blundered into, not something we did on purpose, and if we started all this, then we have to *finish* it."

Sean closed his eyes and tasted the bitterness of knowing she was right.

It was a conversation they'd had often enough, and rehashing it now would achieve nothing. Besides, he *liked* the Malagorans. Even if he'd borne no responsibility for their predicament, he still would have wanted to help them.

"I know," he said finally. He opened his eyes and smiled crookedly, then patted the hand on his elbow. "And it's no more your fault than it is mine or Tamman's or Brashan's—even Harry's. It's just knowing how many of them are going to get killed because I didn't push hard enough." She started to open her mouth, but he shook his head. "Oh, you're right. People make mistakes while they learn. I know that. I only wish *my* mistakes could be made somewhere that didn't get people killed."

"You can only do the best you can do." Her voice was so gentle he longed to take her in his arms, but God only knew how his officers would react if he started going around hugging an "angel"!

He actually felt his mouth quirk a smile at the thought, and he folded his hands behind him again and walked slowly around the table, studying the relief map from all angles. If only there were a way to use his mobility! Someone—he thought it had been Nathan Bedford Forrest—had once said war was a matter of "getting there firstest with the mostest," not absolute numbers, and the one true weakness of Ortak's position was its size. He had fifteen kilometers of frontage—more, with the salients built into his earthworks—and that gave him barely two thousand armed men per kilometer even if he withheld no reserve at all. Of course, he had another thirty or forty thousand he could send in to pick up the weapons of their fallen comrades, but even so he was stretched thin. If Sean could break his front anywhere, and get *behind* his works, he could sweep them like a broom. But there was no way he could—

He paused suddenly, and his eyes narrowed. He stood absolutely still, staring down at the map while his mind raced, and then he began to smile.

"Sean? *Sean?*" Sandy had to call him twice before he looked up with a jerk. "What is it?" she asked, and his smile took on a harder, fiercer cast.

"I've been going at this wrong," he said. "I've been thinking about how Ortak has us blocked, and what I *should* have been thinking about is how he's trapped himself."

"Trapped?" she asked blankly, and he waved Tibold closer and pointed at the map.

"Could infantry get through these swamps?" he asked in Pardalian, and it was the ex-Guardsman's turn to frown down at the map.

"Not pikes," he said after a moment, "but you might be able to get musketeers through." He cocked his head, comparing the exquisitely detailed map the angels had provided to all the ones he'd ever seen before, then tapped the southern edge of the swamp with a blunt forefinger. "I always thought the bad ground was wider than that down along the south face of the valley," he said slowly. "We could probably get a column across this narrow bit in, oh, ten or twelve hours. Not with guns or pikes, though, Lord Sean. There's no bottom to most of this swamp. You *might* get a few chagors through, but arlaks would sink to the axles in no time. And even after you get through the swamp, the ground's still soft enough between there and the river to slow you."

"Would Ortak expect us to try anything like that?" Sean asked, and Tibold shook his head quickly.

"He's got the same maps *we* had before you and the ang—" The ex-Guardsman bit the word off as he remembered how Lord Sean and the angels kept trying to get people not to call them that. For a moment his face felt hot, but then he grinned up at his towering young commander. "He's got the same maps we always had before. Besides, no Guard captain would even consider leaving his pikes and guns behind."

"That's what I hoped you'd say," Sean murmured, and his brain whirred as he estimated times and distances. The Mortan was the better part of three unfordable kilometers wide above and below Erastor, but it *could* be forded at Malz, a farm town ninety-odd klicks below its junction with the Erastor River. If he moved back west, out of sight of Ortak's lines, and threw together enough rafts . . . Or, for that matter, could his engineers knock together proper bridges? He considered the thought for a moment, then shook his head. No, that would take a good two or three days, and if this was going to work at all, he didn't have two or three days to waste.

"All right, Tibold," he said. "Here's what we'll do. First . . ."

High-Captain Ortak stood in his entrenchments' central bastion and stared west. Drizzling rain drew a gray veil across the Keldark Valley, limiting his vision, but he knew what was out there and breathed a silent thanks for his enemies' lack of initiative. Every day that passed without attack not only helped the morale of his battered force but brought its desperately needed relief one day closer.

He strained his eyes, trying to make out details of the earthworks the heretics had thrown up to face his own. Part of him shuddered every time he thought of the cost of taking that position once the Holy Host had reinforced and resumed the offensive, but not even that could shake his gratitude. *He* knew how thin-stretched he was, and if the heretics had been willing to throw a column straight at him anywhere—

He shivered, and not because of the rain. He disliked having to stand with a river at his back, but the Erastor was fordable for most of its length. If he had to, he could fall back across it, though he'd have to abandon what remained of his baggage, and this was the best—probably the only—point at which to stop an army from the west. Conscripted laborers were building another position in his rear at Baricon, but Baricon was better suited to resisting attacks from the east. No, he had to hold the heretics here if he meant to keep them out of Keldark, and if they ever got loose in the duchy their freedom of maneuver would increase a hundredfold. After what they'd done to Lord Marshal Rokas at Yortown, that was enough to strike a chill in the stoutest heart.

He wrapped his cloak about himself and pursed his lips in thought. The semaphore chain across Malagor had been cut, but it continued to operate east of him, and the Temple's dispatches were less panicky than they had been. The secular lords were being slow to muster, but the Guard had stripped its garrisons throughout the eastern kingdoms to the bone, and fifty thousand men were on their way to him. Better yet, the first trains of replacement weapons had begun coming in. There were less of them than he would have liked, especially given what the heretics had captured at Yortown, but he'd already received eight thousand pikes and over five hundred joharns. If the reports from Yortown were right, the heretics had found some way to give joharns and malagors the range of rifles, which suggested final casualties would be atrocious even if the Guard managed to rearm every man, but that should be less of a factor defending entrenched positions than in the open field. They were going to have to find some reply to the heretics' weight of fire in the future, and Ortak was already considering ways to increase the ratio of firearms to pikes, but for the moment he had a stopper in the bottle and the heretics seemed unwilling to take the losses to remove it.

He sighed and shook himself. The light was going, and he had more than enough paperwork waiting to keep him up half the night. At least his quarters in Erastor were better than a tent in the field, he told himself, and smiled wryly as he turned and called for his branahlk.

Sean MacIntyre dismounted and wiped rain from his face. He could have used his implants to stay dry, but that would have felt unfair to his troops, which was probably silly but didn't change his feelings. He smiled at his own perversity and scratched his branahlk's snout, listening to its soft whistle of pleasure, and tried to hide his worry as the sodden column squelched past.

It was taking longer than planned, and the rain was heavier than *Israel's* meteorological remotes had predicted. The cold front pushing down the valley had met a warm front out of Sanku and Keldark, and Brashan's latest forecast warned of at least twenty hours of hard rain, probably with thunderstorms. They would make the ground still softer and the going harder, and they were also going to deepen the fords at Malz, but at least it didn't look as if the Mortan would reach critical depths. Or, he thought grimly, not *yet*.

Tibold splashed up on his own branahlk and drew up beside him.

"Captain Juahl's reached the bivouac area, Lord Sean." The ex-Guardsman's tone made Sean crook an eyebrow, and Tibold sighed. "It's under a handspan of water, My Lord."

"Great." Sean closed his eyes and inhaled deeply, then flipped his fold com up to Sandy's hovering cutter. "Got a problem down here," he subvocalized. "Our bivouac site's underwater."

"Damn. Hang on a sec," she replied, and brought up her sensors, berating herself for not having checked sooner. She frowned in concentration over her neural feed as she swept the area ahead of the column, then her eyes brightened. "Okay. If you push on another six klicks, the ground rises to the south."

"Firewood?" he asked hopefully.

"'Fraid not," she replied, and he sighed.

"Thanks anyway." He turned to Tibold. "Tell Juahl he'll find higher ground if he bears a bit south and keeps moving for another hour or so."

"At once, Lord Sean." Tibold didn't even ask how his commander knew that; he simply turned his branahlk and splashed off into the gathering gloom, and Sean leaned back against his own mount and sighed.

He had twenty-five thousand men marching through mud towards fords which *ought* to be passable when they arrived, and he was beginning to wonder if he'd been so clever after all. Pardal's days were long, and on good roads (and Pardalian roads would have made any Roman emperor die of jealousy), infantry routinely made fifty kilometers a day in fair weather. Marching cross-country in the rain, even through open terrain, they were doing well to make thirty pushing hard, and they hadn't even reached the swamps yet. The men were in better spirits than he would have believed possible under the circumstances, but they'd marched for three grueling days, mostly in the rain and with no hot meals. Even for someone with full enhancement, this march was no pleasure jaunt; for the unenhanced, it was unadulterated, exhausting misery, and they were barely halfway to the fords.

He flicked his mind back over the latest reports from their stealthed remotes. Ortak was receiving fresh weapons, but any additional reinforcements were still at least twelve days away. Even allowing for his column's slower than estimated progress, Sean should be back north of the Mortan within another four days, but he was grimly aware of the risk he was running. The valley's peasants had been moved out by the Holy Host on its way in, and the Temple's troops had already accounted for everything that could be foraged from the abandoned farms. Pack nioharqs had accompanied them this far, but they'd have to be sent home once the column reached the swamp. From there, Sean's infantry would have to pack all of their supplies—including ammunition—on their backs, and that gave them no more than a week's food. Which meant that if his plan to surprise Ortak didn't work, he was going to find himself with twenty-five thousand starving men trapped between Erastor and the Guard reinforcements.

At least Ortak was cooperating so far. The high-captain "knew" the terrain south of the river was impassable, and he was too short of armed men to spare many from his prepared positions. He had pickets east of the Erastor, but they were fairly close to the bridges. It was still a bit hard to adjust to a pre-technic society's limitations, and despite everything, Sean felt vaguely exposed. His column was barely fifty air kilometers from Ortak's position, and it was hard to believe Ortak had no suspicion of what he was up to, yet the high-captain's deployments and the reports of Sandy's eavesdropping remotes all confirmed that he didn't.

The thought drew a wet chuckle from Sean. Miserable as he and his troops might be, they had the most deadly weapon known to man: surprise. And at least if he screwed up, it wouldn't be because the Guard had surprised *him*.

He gave his branahlk another scratch, then swung back into the saddle and trotted forward along the column.

✧   ✧   ✧

Father Stomald stepped into the command tent and paused. The Angel Harry stood alone, staring down at the map and unaware of his presence, and her shoulders were tight.

The young priest hesitated. Part of him was loath to disturb her, but another part urged him to step closer. An angel needed no mortal's comfort, yet Stomald was guiltily aware that he was coming less and less to think of her as he ought.

The angels had fallen into a division of their duties which was too natural to have been planned, and the Angel Harry's share of those duties had brought her into almost constant contact with Stomald. The fighting of the war in which they were all trapped was the task of Lord Sean and Lord Tamman, but ministering to its consequences was Stomald's task. It was he who had begun it, whatever his intent, and it was he who must bear the weight of caring for its victims. He accepted that, for it was but an extension of his priestly duties, and his own faith would have driven him to shoulder that weight even if he could somehow have avoided it. But he was not alone before the harsh demands of his responsibilities, for as Lord Sean and Lord Tamman had Tibold and the Angel Sandy, Stomald had the Angel Harry. However grim the burden he faced, however terrible the cost war and its horrors exacted, she was always there, always willing to give him of her own strength and catch him when he stumbled. And that, he thought, was why he had come to feel these things he should not—*must* not—feel.

Yet knowing what he should not do and stopping himself from doing it were two very different things. She seemed so young, and she was different from the Angel Sandy. She was . . . softer, somehow. Gentler. The Angel Sandy cared deeply—no one who'd seen her face the night after Yortown could doubt that—yet she had a talmahk's fierceness the Angel Harry lacked. No one could ever call either angel weak, but the Angel Sandy and Lord Sean were kindred souls who threw off uncertainty like a too-small garment whenever it touched them. Their eyes were always on the next battle, the next challenge, yet it was the Angel Harry to whom those in trouble instinctively turned, as if they, as Stomald, sensed the compassion at her heart. Any angel must, of course, be special, but Stomald had seen how even the most hardened trooper's eyes followed the Angel Harry. The army would have followed Lord Sean or the Angel Sandy or Lord Tamman against Hell itself, but the Angel Harry owned their hearts.

As she did Stomald's, and yet . . .

The priest sighed, and his eyes darkened as he admitted the truth. His love for the Angel Harry was wrong, for it was not what a man should dare to feel for one of God's holy messengers.

She heard his soft exhalation and turned, and he was shocked by the tears in her one good eye. She wiped them as quickly as she'd turned, but he'd seen them, and before he remembered what she was, he reached out to her.

He froze, hand extended, shocked by his own temerity. What was he *thinking*? She was an *angel*, not simply the beautiful young woman she appeared. Had he not learned to rely upon her strength? To turn to *her* for comfort when his own weariness and the sorrow of so much death pressed upon him? How dared he reach out to comfort *her*?

But he saw no anger in her eye, and his heart soared with curiously aching joy as she took his hand. She squeezed it and turned her head to look back down at the map table, and Stomald stood there, holding her hand, and confused emotions washed through him. It felt so right, so natural, to stand with her, as if this were the place he was meant to be, yet guilt flawed his contentment. He was aware of her beauty, of her wonderful blend of strength and gentleness, and he longed, more than he'd ever longed for anything other than to serve God Himself, for this moment to last forever.

"What is it?" he asked finally, and the depth of concern in his voice surprised even him.

"I'm just—" She paused, then gave her head a little shake. "I'm just worried about Sean," she said softly. "The way the river's rising, how far they still have to go, the odds when they get there . . ." She drew a deep breath and looked at him with a wan smile. "Silly of me, isn't it?"

"Not silly," Stomald disagreed. "You worry because you care."

"Maybe." She still held his hand, but her other hand ran a finger down the line of Lord Sean's march, and her voice was low. "I feel so guilty sometimes, Stomald. Guilty for worrying so much more about Sean than anyone else, and for having caused all this. It's my fault, you know."

Stomald flinched, and self-loathing filled him as he recognized his own jealousy. He was *jealous* of her concern for Lord Sean! The sheer impiety of his emotions frightened him, but then the rest of what she'd said penetrated, and he shook off his preoccupation with his own feelings.

"You didn't cause this. It was our fault for laying impious hands upon you." He hung his head. "It was *my* fault, not yours, My Lady."

"No it wasn't!" she said so sharply he looked up, dismayed by her anger. Her single eye bored into him, and she shook her head fiercely. "Don't ever think that, Stomald! You did what your Church had taught you to do, and—" She paused again, biting her lip, then nodded to herself. "And there's more happening here than you know even yet," she added with quiet bitterness.

Stomald blinked at her, touched to the heart once more by her readiness to forgive the man who'd almost burned her alive, yet confused by her words. She was an angel, with an angel's ability to know things no mortal could, yet her voice suggested she'd meant more than that. Perplexity filled him, and he reached for the first thing that crossed his mind.

"You care deeply for Lord Sean, don't you, My Lady?" he asked, and could have bitten off his tongue in the instant. The question cut too close to his own forbidden longings, and he waited for her anger, but she only nodded.

"Yes," she said softly. "I care for them all, but especially for Sean."

"I see," he said, and the dagger turning in his heart betrayed him. He heard the pain in his own voice and tried to turn and flee, but her fingers tightened about his, stronger than steel yet gentle, trapping him without harming him, and against his will, his gaze met hers.

"Stomald, I—" she said, then shook her head and said something else.

She spoke to herself, in her own language, the one she spoke to the Angel Sandy and their champions. Stomald couldn't understand her words, but he recognized a curious finality, an edge of decision, and his heart hammered as she drew him over to a stool. He sat upon it at her gesture, uncomfortable, as always, at sitting in her presence, and she drew a deep, deep breath.

"I *do* care for Sean, very much," she told him. "He's my brother."

"Your—?" Stomald gaped at her, trying to understand, but his mind refused to work. He'd speculated, dreamed, hoped, yet he'd never quite dared *believe*. Lord Sean was mortal, however he might have been touched by God, yet if he was her brother, if mortal blood *could* mingle with the angels', then—

"It's time you knew the truth," she said quietly.

"The . . . the truth?" he repeated, and she nodded.

"There's a reason Sandy and I have tried to insist that you not treat us as angels, Stomald. You see, we aren't."

"Aren't?" he parroted numbly. "Aren't . . . aren't *what*, My Lady?"

"Angels." She sighed, and her expression shocked him. She was staring at him, her remaining eye soft, as if she feared his reaction, but he could only stare back. Not angels? That was . . . it was preposterous! Of *course* they were angels! That was why he'd preached their message to his people and the reason Mother Church had loosed Holy War upon them! They *had* to be angels!

"But—" The word came out hoarse and shaking, and he wrapped his arms about himself as if against a freezing wind. "But you *are* angels. The miracles you've worked to save us, your raiment—the things we've all seen Lord Sean and Lord Tamman do at your bidding—!"

"Aren't miracles at all," she said in that same soft voice, as if pleading for *his* understanding. "They're—oh, how can I make you understand?" She turned away, folding her arms below her breasts, and her spine was ramrod stiff. "We . . . can do many things you can't," she said finally, "but we're mortal, Stomald. All of us. We simply have tools, skills, you don't, yet if you had those tools, you could do anything you've seen us do and more."

"You're . . . mortal?" he whispered, and even through the whirlwind confusion uprooting all his certainty, he felt a sudden, soaring joy.

"Yes," she said softly. "Forgive me, please. I . . . I never meant to deceive you, never meant—" She broke off, shoulders shaking, and his heart twisted as he realized she was weeping. "We never wanted any of this to happen, Stomald." Her lovely voice was choked and thick. "We only . . . we only wanted to get home, and then I ran into Tibold, and he shot me and brought me back to Cragsend, and somehow it all—"

She shook her head fiercely, and turned back to face him.

"*Please*, Stomald. Please believe we never, ever, meant to hurt anyone. Not you, not your people, not even the Inner Circle. It just . . . happened, and we couldn't let the Church destroy you for something *we'd* caused!"

"Get home?" Stomald rose from the stool and crossed to stand directly before her, staring into her tear-streaked face, and she nodded. "Home . . . where?" he asked hesitantly.

"Out there." She pointed at the sky invisible beyond the roof of the tent, and for just an instant sheer horror filled the priest. The stars! She *was* from the stars, and the Writ said only the demons who had cast Man from the firmament—

Sick panic choked him. Had he done the very thing the Inner Circle charged him with? *Had* he given his allegiance to the Great Demons who sought only the destruction of all God's works?

But then, as quickly as it had come, the terror passed, for it was madness. Whatever else she might be, the Angel Harry—or whoever she truly was—was no demon. He'd seen too much of her pain among the wounded and dying, too much gentleness and compassion, to believe that. And the Writ itself said no demon, greater or lesser, could speak the Holy Tongue, yet she spoke it to him every day! All his life, Stomald had been taught the inviolability of the Writ, but now he faced a truth almost more terrifying than the possibility that she might actually be a demon, for if she came from the stars, the Writ said she *must* be a demon, and yet the Writ also proved she *couldn't* be one.

He felt the cornerstone of his life turning under his feet like wet, treacherous sand, and fear washed through him. But even as that fear sought to suck him under, he clung to his faith in her. Angel or no, he *trusted* her. More than trusted, he admitted to himself. He loved her.

"Tell me," he begged, and she stepped forward. She rested her hands on his shoulders and gazed into his face, and he felt his fear ease as her fingers squeezed gently.

"I will. I'll tell you everything. Some of it will be hard to understand, maybe even impossible—at first, at least—but I swear it's true, Stomald. Will you trust me enough to believe me?"

"Of course," he said simply, and the absolute certainty in his tone was distantly surprising even to him.

"Thank you," she said softly, then drew a deep breath. "The first thing you have to understand," she said more briskly, "is what happened—not just here on Pardal, but out there, as well—" her head jerked at the tent roof once more "sixteen thousand of your years ago."

It took hours. Stomald lost count of how many times he had to stop her for fuller explanation, and his brain spun at the tale she told him. It was madness, impossible, anathema to everything he'd ever been taught . . . and he believed every word. He had no choice, and a raging sense of wonder mingled with shock and the agonizing destruction of so much certainty.

" . . . so that's the size of it, Stomald," she said finally. They sat on facing stools, and the candles had burned low in the lanterns set about the tent. "We never meant to harm anyone, never meant to deceive anyone. We *tried* to tell you Sandy and I weren't angels, but none of you seemed able to believe it, and if we'd insisted and shattered your cohesion when the Church was determined to kill you all because of something *we'd* started—" She shrugged unhappily, and he nodded slowly.

"Yes, I can see that." He rubbed his thighs, then licked his lips and managed a strained smile. "I always wondered why you and the An—why you and *Sandy* insisted that we not call you 'angel' when we spoke to you."

"Can . . . can you forgive us?" she asked quietly. "We never wanted to insult your beliefs or use your faith against you. Truly we didn't."

"Forgive you?" He smiled more naturally and shook his head. "There's nothing to forgive, My Lady. You are who you are and the truth is the truth, and if the Writ is wrong, perhaps you *are* God's messengers. From what you say, this world has spent thousands upon thousands of years blind to the truth and living in fear of an evil that no longer exists, and surely God can send whomever He wishes to show us the truth!"

"Then . . . you're not angry with us?"

"Angry, My Lady?" He shook his head harder. "There are many parts of your tale I don't understand, but Lady Sandy was right. Once events had been set in motion, I and all who followed me would have been destroyed by Mother Church without your aid. How could I be angry at you for saving my people? And if the Writ *is* wrong, then the bishops and high-priests must learn to accept that, as well. No, Lady Harry. I don't say all our people could accept what you've told me. But the day will come when they can, and will, know the truth, and when they are once more free to travel the stars without fear of demons and damnation, they will no more be angry with you than *I* could ever be."

"Stomald," she said softly, "you're a remarkable man."

"I'm only a village under-priest," he objected, uncomfortable and yet filled with joy by the glow in her eye. "Beside you, I'm an ignorant child playing in the mud on the bank of a tiny stream."

"No, you're not. The only difference between us is education and access to knowledge your world denied you, and I grew up with those things. You didn't, and if our positions were reversed, I doubt I could have accepted the truth the way you have."

"Accepted, My Lady?" He laughed. "I'm still trying to believe this isn't all a dream!"

"No, you're not," she repeated with a smile, "and that's what makes you so remarkable." Her smile turned suddenly into a grin. "I always wondered how Dad really felt when Dahak started explaining the truth about human history to him. Now I know how Dahak must've felt making the explanation!"

"I should like to meet this 'Dahak' one day," Stomald said wistfully.

"You will," she assured him. "I can hardly wait to take you home and introduce you to Mom and Dad, as well!"

"Take . . . ?" He blinked at her, then stiffened as she reached out and cupped the side of his face in those steel-strong, moth-gentle fingers.

"Of course, Stomald," she said very, very softly. "Why do you think I wanted to tell you the truth?"

He stared at her in disbelief, and then she leaned forward and kissed him.

CHAPTER THIRTY-ONE

Tamman stood sipping a steaming mug of tea and tried not to yawn. Brashan's predicted thunderstorms had rolled up the valley yesterday, and the entire camp was ankle-deep in mud. Pardalian field sanitation was far better than that of most preindustrial armies, and he and Sean had improved on that basic platform, but it was simply impossible to put forty or fifty thousand human beings into an encampment without consequences. Coupled with decent diet, the latrines were holding things like dysentery within limits, yet the ground had been churned into sticky soup and everyone was thoroughly wet and miserable.

He stretched, then lifted his face gratefully to the morning sun. The rain had moved further up the valley, and it was still raising the level of the Mortan, but sunlight poured down over him, and he felt his spirits rise even as concern over Sean's slow progress simmered in the back of his brain.

Feet sucked through the mud towards him, and he turned and saw Harriet and Stomald. High-Captain Ithun had mentioned that the priest and "Ang— *Lady* Harry" had spent hours in the command tent last night, and he'd wondered why Harry hadn't mentioned it to him herself. Now he detected a subtle change in their body language as they approached him, and his eyebrows rose.

"Tamman." Harriet nodded as he touched his breastplate in the gesture of respect he and Sean always gave "the angels," but there was something different about *that* as well, and he wondered just what the hell she and Stomald had been discussing last night. Surely she hadn't—?

The question must have showed on his face, for she met his gaze unflinchingly and nodded. His eyes widened, and he looked around quickly.

"Would you and the boys pardon us a moment, Ithun?" he asked.

"Of course, Lord Tamman." The man who'd become his exec after the Battle of Yortown nodded and waved to the rest of his staff. They waded away from the campfire through the morning mist, and Tamman turned back to Harriet.

A moment of silence stretched out between them, and Stomald's expression confirmed his worst suspicions. The man knew. It showed in his wary eyes . . . and how close he stood to Harriet. Tamman felt his lips quirk, and he snorted. He'd seen this coming weeks ago, and it wasn't as if he'd expected Harry to be his love forever. Neither of them was—no, he corrected himself, neither of them *had been*—ready to settle down like Sean and Sandy, and he'd told himself he was mature enough to handle it. Well, perhaps he was, but it still stung. Not that he could blame Stomald. The priest was a good man, even if his first meeting with Harry *had* been an attempt at judicial murder, and he shared the same compassion which was so much a part of Harry.

None of which changed the fact that she hadn't so much as discussed her decision to tell him the truth! The possible repercussions of that little revelation in the middle of a holy war hardly bore thinking on, and her defiant expression showed she knew it. He considered half a dozen cutting remarks, then made himself set them all aside, uncertain how many of them stemmed from legitimate concern and how many from bruised male ego.

"Well," he said finally, in Pardalian, "you look like you have something to tell me."

"Lord Tamman," Stomald replied before Harriet could, "Lady Harry told me the truth last night." Tamman eyed him wordlessly, and the priest returned his gaze steadily. "I have told no one else, and I have no intention of telling anyone until the Inner Circle is defeated and you and your companions have gained access to this . . . computer." His tongue stumbled over the unfamiliar word, but Tamman felt his own shoulders relax. His worst fear had been Stomald's invincible integrity; if the priest had decided *Israel*'s crew had defiled his religion, the results could have been unmitigated disaster.

"I see," Tamman said slowly, then pursed his lips. "May I ask why not, Father?"

"Because Lady Sandy was right," Stomald said simply. "We're trapped in a war, and if I was wrong to think Lady Harry and Lady Sandy angels, the Inner Circle is even more wrong in what *it* believes. There will be time to sort things out once the Guard is no longer trying to kill us all, My Lord."

The priest smiled wryly, and Tamman smiled back. Damned if *he* could have taken the complete destruction of his worldview as calmly as Stomald seemed to be taking it!

"At the same time, My Lord," Stomald went on a bit more hesitantly, "Lady Harry told me of her relationship with you." Tamman stiffened. Pardalian notions of morality were more flexible than he'd expected. Unmarried sex wasn't a mortal sin on Pardal, but it *was* something the Church frowned upon, yet Stomald's tone was that of a wary young man, not an irate priest.

"Yes?" he said in his most conversational tone.

"My Lord," Stomald met his eyes squarely, "I love Lady Harry with all my heart. I don't pretend to be her equal, or worthy of her," Harriet made a sound of disagreement, but he ignored her to hold Tamman's eyes, "yet I love her anyway, and she loves me. I . . . do not wish for you to think either of us has betrayed you or attempted to deceive you."

Tamman gazed back for several seconds while he wrestled with his own emotions. Damn it, he *had* seen this coming, and Harry had been his friend long before she'd become his lover! They'd both known the forced intimacy of their battleship-lifeboat was what had made them lovers, and he'd known it was going to end *someday*, yet for just an instant he felt a terrible, burning envy of Sean and Sandy.

But then he shook himself and drew a deep breath.

"I see," he said again, holding out his hand, and Stomald took it with only the briefest hesitation. "I won't pretend it does great things for my self-image, Stomald, but Harry's always been her own person. And, much as it might pain me to admit it, you're a pretty decent fellow yourself." The priest smiled hesitantly, and Tamman chuckled. "It's not as if I haven't seen it coming, either," he said more cheerfully. "Of course, she couldn't tell *you* what she felt, but the way she's talked about you to the *rest* of us—!"

"Tamman!" Harriet protested with a gurgle of laughter, and Stomald turned bright red for just an instant before he laughed.

"She's been watching you like a kinokha stalking a shemaq for weeks," Tamman said wickedly, and watched *both* of them blush, amazed that he could feel such genuinely unbitter pleasure in teasing Harriet.

"You're riding for a fall, Tamman!" she warned, shaking a fist at him, and he laughed. Then she lowered her fist and stepped closer. She put her arms around him and hugged him tightly. "But you're a pretty decent fellow yourself," she whispered in his ear.

"Of course I am," he agreed, and put his own arm around her, then looked back at Stomald. "You don't need them, but you have my blessings, Stomald. And if you need a groomsman—?"

"I—" Stomald began, then stopped, blushed even brighter, and looked at Harriet appealingly.

"I think you're getting a bit ahead of yourself," she told Tamman, "but assuming we all get out of this in one piece and I get him home to Mom and Dad, we might just take you up on that."

"Shit!"

No one understood the English expletive, but Sean's officers understood the tone. All of them were splashed from head to toe in mud, and Sean stood in cold, thigh-deep water that rose nearly to the Pardalians' waists. The rain had stopped, but the air was almost unbearably humid, and swarms of what passed for gnats whined about their ears. The column stretched out behind them, for Sean was leading the way now, since his implant sensors made it far easier for him to pick a route through the swamp—or would have if there'd *been* a way through it, he thought savagely.

He inhaled and made himself calm down before he opened his mouth again, then turned to his staff.

"We'll have to backtrack," he said grimly. "The bottom drops off ahead, and there's some kind of quicksand to the right. We'll have to cut further north."

Tibold said nothing, but his mouth tightened, and Sean understood. Their original plans had called for passing the column's head through the swamp in ten or twelve hours, and so far they'd been slogging around in it for over twenty. What had seemed a relatively simple, if unpleasant, task on the map had become something very different, and it was all his own fault. He had the best reconnaissance capabilities on the planet, and he should have scouted their route better than this. If he had, he would have known the foot of the valley's northern wall was lined with underground springs. The narrowest part of the swamp was also one of the least passable, and his stupid oversight had mired his entire corps down in it.

"All right," he said finally, sighing. "We won't get anywhere standing here looking at the mud." He thought for a few moments, calling up the map he'd stored in his implant computers on the way through, then nodded sharply. "Remember where we stopped for lunch?" he asked Tibold.

"Yes, My Lord."

"All right. There was a spit of solider ground running northeast from there. If there's a way through this glop at all, we'll have to go that way. Turn the column around and stop its head there. While you're doing that, I'll see if Lady Sandy can pick a better path than I can."

"At once, My Lord," Tibold agreed, and turned to slosh back along the halted column while Sean activated his com.

"Sandy?" he subvocalized.

"Yes, Sean?" She was trying to hide her own anxiety, he thought, and made his own tone lighter.

"We're gonna have to backtrack, kid."

"I know. I had a remote tuned in."

"In that case, you know where we're headed, and I'm one dumb asshole not to have had you checking route for us already." He sighed. "Tune up your sensors and see if you can map us a way through this slop."

"I'm already working on it," she said, "but, Sean, I don't see a *fast* way through it."

"How bad is it?"

"From what I can see, it's going to take at least another full day and a half," she said in a small, most un-Sandy-like voice.

"Great. Just fucking great!" Sean felt her flinch and shook his head quickly, knowing she was watching him through her remotes. "Sorry," he said penitently. "I'm not pissed at *you*; I'm pissed at *me*. There's no excuse for this kind of screwup."

"No one else thought of it, either, Sean," she pointed out in his defense, and he snorted.

"Doesn't make me feel any better," he growled, then sighed. "Well, I guess standing around pissing and moaning won't make it any better, either. Let's get this show back on the road—such as it is!"

He turned to slog off in Tibold's wake, and the swarming clouds of gnats whined about his ears.

Even Sandy's estimate turned out to have been overly optimistic. What Sean and Tibold had envisioned as a twelve-hour maneuver consumed over three of Pardal's twenty-nine-hour days, and it was an exhausted, sodden, mud-spattered column of infantry that finally crawled out of the swamp proper into the merely "soft" ground south of it. Thank God Tibold had warned him against even trying to bring artillery through that muck, Sean thought wearily. Their five hundred dragoons had lost a quarter of their branahlks, and Lord only knew what would have happened to nioharqs. Given his druthers, he decided, he'd take Hannibal's elephants and the Alps over a Pardalian swamp and *anything*.

Under the circumstances, he'd eased the "no miracles" rule, and Sandy and Harry had been busy using cutters to bring in fresh food. The cargo remotes had stacked it neatly to await his column's arrival, and the troops gave a weary cheer as they saw it. There was even a little wood for fires, and the company cooks quickly got down to business.

"Sean?"

He turned and flashed a mud-spattered smile as Sandy walked out of the gathering evening. His officers and men saw her as well, and she waved to them as a soft, wordless murmur of thanks rose from them. She made a shooing gesture at the waiting rations, and the troops grinned and returned to their tasks as she crossed to Sean. Unlike her towering lover, she was spotless. Not even her boots were muddy, and he shook his head.

" 'Ow can you tell she's an angel?" he murmured. " 'Cause she's not covered wi' shit loike the rest of us!" he answered himself.

"Very funny." She smiled dutifully, but her eyes were worried, and he raised an eyebrow.

"The reinforcing column got on the road a day sooner than Ortak expected," she said softly in English, "and it's moving faster than *we* expected. They'll reach Malz within four or five days."

"Wi—?" Sean stared at her, then clamped his teeth hard. "And just why," he asked after a moment, "is this the first *I'm* hearing of this?"

"It wouldn't have done a bit of good to worry you with it while you were mucking around in the swamp," she replied more tartly. "You were already going as fast as you could. All you could have done was fret."

"But—" He started to speak sharply, then made himself stop. She was right, but she was also wrong, and he controlled his tone very carefully when he went on. "Sandy, don't *ever* hold things back on me again, please? There may not have been anything I could have done, but as long as I'm in command, I need *all* the information we've got, as soon as we get it. Is that understood?"

He held her eyes sternly, and her nostrils flared with answering anger. But then she bit her lower lip and nodded.

"Understood," she said in a low voice. "I just—" She looked down at her hands and sighed. "I just didn't want you to worry, Sean."

"I know." He reached out to capture one of her hands and squeezed it tightly until she looked up. "I *know*," he said more softly. "It's just that this isn't the time for it, okay?"

"Okay," she agreed, and then her brown eyes suddenly gleamed. "But if you really want to know *everything*, then I suppose I should tell you what Harry's been up to, too."

"What *Harry's* been up to?" Sean looked speculatively down at her, then raised his head as Tibold called his name. The ex-Guardsman pointed to the meal preparations, and Sean waved for the others to go ahead without him and returned his attention to Sandy. "And just what," he asked in a deliberately ominous voice, "has my horrid twin done now?"

"Well, it turned out fine, but she decided to tell Stomald the truth."

"My God! I turn my back for an instant, and *all* of you run amok!"

"Oh, no! Not us—*you're* the one who's been running around in the muck!" Sandy gurgled with laughter as he winced, then sobered—a little. "Besides, Harry had an excuse. She's in love."

"Think I hadn't figured that out weeks ago? How'd Tamman take it?"

"Quite well, actually," Sandy said wickedly. "I wouldn't say he's completely over it, but I *did* overhear a couple of the Malagoran girls sighing over how handsome 'Lord Tamman' is."

"Handsome? *Tam?*" Sean cocked his head, then chuckled. "Well, compared to me, I guess he is. You mean he's, um, encouraging their interest?"

"Let's just say he isn't *dis*couraging it." Sandy grinned.

"Well, in that case, I suppose you'd better catch me up on all the gossip before I join the others for supper."

"Why? I could brief you while you eat, Sean. None of them understand English."

"I know that," Sean said. He picked out a relatively dry spot, spread his Malagoran-style poncho over it, and waved her to a seat upon it. "The problem, dear, is that I can't eat very well while I'm laughing. Now give."

CHAPTER THIRTY-TWO

"All right, then. Everybody clear on his orders?"

Sean looked around the circle of faces in the late afternoon light. He and Tibold had spent weeks convincing their officers to ask questions whenever there was *anything* they didn't understand, but, one by one, each captain nodded soberly.

"Good!" He folded the map with deliberate briskness, then turned and gazed northeast to the screen of dragoons deployed across his line of advance. Beyond them, he could just see a village that was supposed to have been totally evacuated . . . and hadn't been.

Sandy's warning that there were still people about had come in time— he hoped. He'd sent flanking columns of dragoons forward, then had them curl back in from the east, and they seemed to have caught all the villagers before anyone got away to Malz.

It was the ninth day since he'd set out for Erastor. By his original estimate, he should already have been in striking distance of Ortak's rear; as it was, he was still south of the Mortan, the weather was going bad on him again, and the head of the Guard relief column should reach the Malz turn-off within four days. His time margin had become knife-thin, and if any of those peasants *had* fled with word of his presence, he was in a world of trouble.

Well, Sandy's stealthed spies would warn him if the bad guys *did* figure out he was coming. Which, unfortunately, wasn't going to help him a lot if they figured it out after he'd crossed the river and trapped himself between Ortak and High-Captain Terrahk's relief force.

He shook off his worry and nodded to his officers.

"Let's get this show on the road, then," he said, and they slapped their breastplates in salute and dashed off.

Considering the unexpected rigors of the swamp crossing, the men were in excellent shape, Sean thought. Tired, but far from exhausted, and their morale was better than he would have dared hope. They'd *hated* the swamps, but despite the delays, their confidence was unshaken. Which was good, because they had another ten kilometers to cover this day, and Malz was tied into the semaphore chain which connected Erastor to points east. Each semaphore station was a looming, gantry-like structure which let its crew see for kilometers in every direction and turned it into a watch tower. That meant the chain had to be cut in darkness, before any warning could be sent in either direction, and defined not only when Sean had to reach and secure Malz, but when he had to get his troops across the river to the Baricon-Erastor high road, as well.

He called for his own branahlk and trotted back towards his infantry. Part of him longed to go with the dragoons in person, but Sandy's stealthed cutter hovered above them. She'd tell him if anything went wrong, and he needed to be with his main body, ready to respond to any warning she might send.

He turned in the saddle to watch Captain Juahl lead the dragoons east. Juahl was a good man, he told himself, and he understood the plan. That was just going to have to be enough.

It was almost midnight, local time, when Sean's lead rifle regiments reached Malz. Bonfires encircled the town, and parties of dragoons picketed its unprepossessing walls. It wasn't a large town—no more than eight thousand even in normal times, and its population had declined drastically when the Holy Host came through en route to Yortown—but enough people remained inside those walls to stand off dragoons. Worse, there were plenty of potential messengers to warn Ortak what was happening, which was the reason for those pickets and bonfires.

A mounted messenger trotted up to him and saluted.

"Captain Juahl sent me to report, Lord Sean," the exhausted young officer said. "We haven't secured the Malz tower yet—they got the town gates shut and we didn't have the strength to force them—but Captain Juahl and Under-Captain Hahna secured the fords and both towers between here and the crossroads. Hahna's company is posted just east of the crossroads, and we got both towers intact. Captain Juahl said to tell you our men are ready to pass messages both ways, My Lord."

"Good!" Sean slapped the messenger's shoulder, and the young man grinned at him. "Are you up to riding back to Captain Juahl?"

"Yes, My Lord!"

"In that case go tell him I'm delighted with his news. Ask him to thank all of his officers and men for me, as well, and tell him I'll get infantry support up as fast as I can."

"Yes, My Lord!" The messenger saluted again and vanished into the darkness, and Sean turned to Tibold.

"Thank God for that!" he said softly, and the ex-Guardsman nodded. Most of the men who'd managed the Temple's semaphore chain across Malagor had fled the heresy, but enough had joined it to give Sean the personnel to man the towers he'd hoped to capture. Now *he* controlled High-Captain Ortak's mail . . . and the information flowing east to the oncoming relief column, as well.

"I want you to help handle the negotiations here," he went on after a moment, waving at the closed gates. "We haven't had any massacres yet, and I'd sooner not start now because someone makes a mistake." He tugged on his nose. "Let's send Folmak's brigade up to Juahl. He's level-headed enough to handle anything that comes at him unexpectedly. Make sure he's got a copy of our message notes, and tell him I'll join him in person as soon as possible."

"At once, Lord Sean." Tibold turned his branahlk and trotted off with a briskness Sean knew he didn't feel. Today's long march had been worse even than the swamp, and Tibold had spent part of it marching with each regiment. He insisted it was good for morale, and Sean believed him. It also meant "Lord Sean" had to stump along with the troops, too, but he was thirty-five years younger than Tibold and enhanced, to boot. He was undoubtedly the freshest man in the entire column, and all he wanted to do was sleep for a week.

Well, if Tibold could manage to look sharp and fresh, then so could Sean, and he'd damned well better do just that!

He grinned and dismounted, tossed his reins to one of his aides, and felt a spasm of pity for the townsfolk of Malz as he walked towards their closed gates. They had to know he could burn their town around their ears, and given the Inner Circle's propaganda, they probably expected him to do just that so their children would be nicely browned when he sat down to eat them! Convincing the poor bastards to open up was going to be a pain, but he needed to get it done before somebody did something stupid. Between them, Stomald and "the angels"—with a little help from the bloodthirsty field regulations of a certain Captain-General Lord Sean—had created a remarkably well-behaved army. The fact that it regarded itself as an elite force and confidently expected to kick the butt of a much larger army in a few days also helped by giving it a certain image to live up to, but Sean knew most of its restraint stemmed from the Holy Host's failure to reach Malagor. The Malagoran Temple Guard had done its share of village-burning on its abortive march to Cragsend, but half the men who'd done that were now members in good standing of the Angels' Army, and they'd done their very best to make amends. Yortown and the seizure of the Thirgan Gap had precluded the other atrocities religious wars routinely spawned, and the men felt little need for vengeance. Sean intended to keep it that way, but a handful of panicky townsmen who took it into their heads to "resist heresy" or simply thought they were defending their families could easily provoke a fire fight that might well expand into a full-blown massacre.

But that wasn't going to happen, he told himself firmly. He was a golden-tongued devil, and Tibold was going to advise him, and between them, they were going to talk those townsfolk into opening their gates without a shot being fired.

He stopped well out of aimed smoothbore range to wait for Tibold, and began to consider just how to accomplish that ambition.

✧   ✧   ✧

"They've got Malz, and nobody got hurt on either side!" Harriet said as she entered the command tent, and her relief was so obvious Tamman refrained from observing that a lot of somebodies were going to get hurt at Erastor in a few days. Harry was too much like her dad and, appearance aside, not enough like her mom, he thought sadly.

"That's wonderful news," Stomald said, and Tamman nodded. It *was* wonderful news, too, he thought. At least Sean was finally out of those godawful swamps! None of them had expected him to lose that much time crossing them, and the entire operation was badly behind schedule, but it looked like they were going to make it after all . . . assuming the weather held.

"How are the fords?" he asked, gazing at the map and trying to hide a grin as Harriet stepped up beside Stomald and each of them tucked an arm around the other. So far they'd remembered not to do that in front of anyone but him or Sandy, and he didn't really want to find out how the troops would react if they slipped up and did it in public, but there was something incredibly touching about the shared tenderness in their eyes.

"Um?" Harriet looked up, then gave her head a shake. "Sorry, Tam. Sean says the fords are deeper than expected, but manageable if he takes it easy. The dragoons got across without losses, and the engineers are rigging guide ropes for the rest of the column. Tibold figures it'll take about five hours to get them all across once they start, but Sean's taking Folmak's brigade up to the crossroads tonight still. Well, this morning, I guess."

"So we've cut the semaphore chain, and it *looks* like no one knows we have," Tamman mused, plucking at his lip and gazing sightlessly at the map.

"Sandy and Brashan—" Harriet glanced at Stomald "—are monitoring their remotes in Erastor and tracking the relief column. So far, nobody in either place *does* know we're there."

"Yeah." Tamman nodded, then shrugged. "I know we've got them wired for sound, but I can't help worrying until we link back up with Sean." He studied the map a moment longer, then straightened. "I think I'll have a word with Ithun. If something does tip the bad guys, Ortak'll have to pull strength from our side of his position to do anything about it, and that might just let us slip an assault column through on him after all."

"Don't do anything rash without discussing it with Sean, Tam!"

"I won't get creative on you," he replied with a smile, "but Tibold's rubbing off on both of us. Like he says, 'Improvised responses work best when you've planned them well in advance!' "

" 'Bout time *someone* convinced you two of that," Harriet sniffed, and his smile turned into a broad grin.

"We're maturing, we are," he asserted virtuously. "And, ah, I'll see that no one disturbs you two while you 'confer,' too," he added wickedly as he opened the tent flap.

Sean looked up as Tibold's branahlk trotted up to the semaphore tower. The ex-Guardsman had gotten a whole three hours' sleep, and it was almost revolting how much that had restored him. He was soaked to the waist from fording the Mortan, but he waved cheerfully.

"The rearguard should be crossing just about now, Lord Sean," he said. "The lead brigade should arrive within the hour."

"Banners ready?" Sean asked.

"Aye, My Lord." Tibold grinned. The suggestion had come from Sandy, but he approved of it wholeheartedly. They'd captured more than enough Guard standards at Yortown to distribute among their regiments, and Sean had already sent Ortak a message from 'High-Captain Terrahk' to report he was further along than expected. With the banners for cover and the semaphore crews *expecting* to see Terrahk, any towers further up the chain that saw them coming should report them to Erastor as Ortak's expected relief.

Now Sean nodded to Tibold and turned back to the man who would command this semaphore garrison.

"Keep a sharp eye out, Yuthan," he said—for, he estimated, the sixth time, but Yuthan only nodded soberly. "You're doing an important job, but not important enough to risk getting cut off. If High-Captain Terrahk turns up, burn the tower and clear out."

"Aye, Lord Sean. Don't worry. None of us wants to get killed, My Lord, but we'll keep 'em confident until we do clear out."

"Good man." Sean squeezed the Malagoran's shoulder, then mounted his own branahlk and turned back to Tibold.

"I sent one of Folmak's regiments a little way west with a company of Juahl's dragoons, just to be on the safe side," he said, urging his mount to a trot. "They've got orders to stay out of sight from the next tower, but they're our front door. They've already hauled in about thirty people."

"That many?" Tibold was surprised. "I wouldn't have expected Ortak to allow that much traffic out of Erastor."

"Most of them seem to be trying to get as far from Erastor as they can," Sean snorted, "and I sort of doubt Ortak even knows they're doing it. Two-thirds of them are deserters, as a matter of fact."

"There are always some," Tibold said with a curled lip.

"I imagine there's even more temptation than usual if you believe you're up against demons. On the other hand, they might just think they could convince Ortak not to shoot them if they hustled back to tell him we're coming. Once the main body gets up here, have them sent back to Malz and kept there till Yuthan and his boys pull out. After that, they can do whatever they want."

"I don't envy them," Tibold said, almost against his will. "With Terrahk coming up the road, the best they can hope for is to take to the hills before he gets his hands on them."

"That's their problem, I'm happy to say," Sean grunted back. "I'll settle for making sure Terrahk doesn't get his hands on *us*."

High-Captain Ortak reread the message with enormous relief. Terrahk had set a new record for the march from Kelthar, the capital of Keldark, if he was already at Malz! He'd shaved another three days off his estimated arrival, and Ortak wondered how he'd done it. Not that he intended to complain. With those fifty thousand well-armed and (hopefully) unshaken men to reinforce it, Erastor would become impregnable. Better yet, Terrahk out-ranked him. Ortak could turn the responsibility over to him, and he was guiltily aware of how terribly he wanted to do just that.

"Any reply, Sir?" his aide asked, and Ortak leaned back in his chair, then shook his head.

"None. They're obviously already moving as fast as they can. Let's not make them think we're *too* nervous."

"No, My Lord," the aide agreed with a smile, and Ortak waved him out of the room and bent back to his paperwork. Three more days. All the her-etics had to do was hold off for three more days, and their best chance to smash their way out of Malagor would be gone forever.

For all its self-inflicted technical wounds, Pardal was an ancient and sur-prisingly sophisticated world, Sean reflected, and its road network reflected it. He'd wondered, when they first spotted the Temple from orbit, how a preindustrial society could transport sufficient food for a city that size even with the canal network to help, but that was before he knew about nioharqs or how good their roads were. They'd developed some impressive engineers over the millennia, and most of them seemed to have spent their entire careers building either temples or roads. Even here in the mountains, the high road was over twenty meters wide, and its hard-paved smoothness rivaled any of Terra's pre-Imperial superhighways.

He drew up and watched his men march past. Like the Roman Empire, Pardalian states relied on infantry, and the excellence of their roads stemmed from the same need to move troops quickly. Of course, come to think of it, the same considerations had created the German autobahns and the United States interstate highway system, hadn't they? Some things never seemed to change.

Whatever their reasoning, he was profoundly grateful to the engineers who'd built *this* road. After their nightmare cross-country journey, the men moved out with a will, relieved to be out of the mud and muck, and they'd made over thirty kilometers today despite the hours spent crossing the Malz fords.

They'd also nabbed three more semaphore towers without raising any alarms. He was a bit surprised by how smoothly that part had gone, but Juahl had devised a system that seemed to work perfectly. He sent an offi-cer and a couple of dozen men on ahead of the main body in captured Guard uniforms, and they simply rode straight up to each tower and asked the station commander to assemble his men. The semaphore crews belonged to the civil service, not the army. None of them were going to argue with Guard dragoons, and as soon as the Malagorans had them out in the open, they suddenly found themselves looking down the business ends of a dozen rifled joharns at very short range. Since the signal arms were controlled from the ground, it didn't even matter if the men manning the tower platforms realized what was happening. They couldn't tell anyone, and so far none of them had been inclined to argue when the rest of Juahl's men arrived and invited them to come down.

In the meantime, neither Ortak nor Terrahk seemed to harbor any suspicion an entire heretic army corps had nipped in between them. The towers
Sean now controlled relayed all normal message traffic without alterations,
but they were intercepting every dispatch either Guard officer sent the other.
It was almost more delicious than what Sandy's and Brashan's stealthed
remotes could tell him, for he was actually reading his enemies' mail, then
dictating the responses *he* wanted them to receive. It looked like it was already
having an effect, as well. Sandy reported that Terrahk had slowed his headlong
pace just a bit thanks to the more confident tenor Sean had been giving
Ortak's messages. But, of course, Ortak didn't know that, now did he?

Sean grinned wickedly, but then he looked up at the sky and his grin
faded. The sun was sinking steadily in the west, and it was about time to
bivouac, but what worried him was the growing humidity. Another front
was coming through, and Brashan was still figuring out Pardal's weather
patterns. The mountains made prediction even harder, and Sean suspected
the front was moving faster than expected. But they should still have enough
time, he told himself as he urged his branahlk back into motion. All he
needed was two more of Pardal's twenty-nine-hour days.

"Two more days," Tamman murmured. He leaned back in a camp chair
in his tent, eyes closed while his neural feed linked him to *Israel* and Sandy's
remotes through the com in the stealthed cutter permanently parked in hover
above "the Angel Harry's" commodious tent. He replayed the day's scan
records at high speed and watched mentally as Sean's column sped up the
high road towards Erastor. They were really moving, and they were still a
good four days in front of High-Captain Terrahk. The way the relief column was easing up would open the gap a bit further, but sometime the
day after tomorrow the Guardsmen were going to reach Malz and find out
what had *actually* been happening.

They'd have no way to warn Ortak, and he wondered what Terrahk would
do. Would he hustle on forward as fast as he could? If he knew how many
men Sean had, the high-captain might figure he could take him in the open,
but he'd be too far behind to overtake before Sean reached Erastor, and he'd
know it. Just as he'd know that if Sean blew Ortak out of the way, his own
column would be hopelessly inadequate to face the two hundred thousand
screaming heretics the Temple now assumed the Angels' Army had.

It all came down to a guess, Tamman mused. Unlike Sean and himself,
Terrahk was totally reliant on mounted scouts, and with the towers between
him and Erastor in Malagoran hands, he'd have no way to know what was
happening ahead of him. All he'd know was that if Ortak had somehow
figured out what was coming at him and managed to throw up any sort
of an east-facing defense, he'd need all the help Terrahk could send him
to hold it. Or, conversely, that if Ortak had already been waxed, the only
chance for his own troops' survival would be to run as hard as they could
in the other direction.

Under the circumstances, Tamman suspected Terrahk would retreat. Abandoning Ortak might cost the Guard seventy or eighty thousand men, but

if he lost his own command throwing good money after bad, the Temple would also lose its last field force. It was a pity Sean couldn't ambush Terrahk first and *then* take on Ortak, but too many things could go wrong, including the possibility that Sean would find himself trapped between enemies who outnumbered him by more than five to one. With room to maneuver and unlimited ammunition, odds like that might be workable; trapped between the Mortan and the valley's northern rim and with only the ammo his troops could carry, the situation would have all the ingredients for a MacIntyre's Last Stand.

Nope. The best outcome would probably be for Terrahk to keep coming and arrive a couple of days after he and Sean had crushed Ortak. If they could reunite their own army, they'd make mincemeat out of Terrahk—assuming they could catch him. At the very least, they should be able to stay close enough on his heels to keep him from settling into the prepared positions around Baricon. But Terrahk would know that as well as they did, which was why Tamman expected the Guardsman to fall back the instant he figured out what was happening.

He straightened and opened his eyes. One thing was certain, whatever Terrahk did, he reminded himself. Before he and Sean could get back into contact, they had to take Erastor, and he shoved up out of his chair. There was just enough light left for him and Ithun to make a last recon of Ortak's lines before darkness fell, and if it turned out that they had to storm those entrenchments to save Sean's posterior, he wanted all of his officers to know everything they could about their target.

More rain swept up the Keldark Valley, and High-Captain Ortak glared sourly at the clouds. The valley was always damp, of course. It was the only real opening in the Shalokar Range, and wet air from the east poured through it like a funnel as it swept up towards the Malagor Plateau. Some of the Temple's experts argued that as the air moved higher and grew thinner, the moisture fell out of its own weight. Ortak didn't fully understand the theory behind it, but all he really needed to know was that it rained in the valley— a lot—and that it was starting to do it again.

He growled a soft curse, then shrugged. Rain was his friend, not the heretics'. Their musketeers outnumbered his tremendously, and if God was kind enough to soak their priming powder for them, Ortak had no intention of complaining. Let them come in and take him on with cold steel!

"How long is this going to last?" Sean asked fretfully.

He and Sandy stood fifty meters from the nearest Malagoran and conferred over their coms with Brashan.

"At least another two days," the Narhani said soberly. He sat alone on *Israel*'s command deck, and his long-snouted, saurian face was grave. "I am sorry, Sean. We thought—"

"Not your fault," Sean interrupted. "We all knew it was coming. We just expected it to hold off longer, and then we lost all that time in the swamps. Our window should have been big enough, Twinkle Hooves."

"True, but it's not only coming in faster, it's going to rain harder than we'd predicted." The Narhani sounded worried. Sean was less than one day's march from Erastor, and the rain—only a drizzle now—would be a downpour by evening. What that would do to flintlock rifles hardly bore thinking on.

"Can we hold off till it clears?" Sandy gazed up at Sean, and her voice was anxious.

" 'Fraid not." Sean sighed. "Ortak expects his 'reinforcements' by nightfall. If we suddenly stop moving, he's going to wonder why and send someone to find out. And if he does that—" He shrugged.

"But you can't fight him without your rifles!" Sandy protested. "You don't have any pikes at all!"

"No, but we do still have surprise."

"Surprise! Are you out of your mind?! There are *eighty thousand* men up there, Sean! There's no *way* you can take their position away from them before they figure out what's happening!"

"Maybe yes, and maybe no," Sean said stubbornly. "Don't forget the confusion factor. The rain's going to cut visibility. We should be able to get a lot closer before they figure out we aren't really Guardsmen, and there's a good chance they'll panic when their 'reinforcements' suddenly attack them. They don't have the kind of communication net a modern army would have, either. It's going to be mighty hard for them to get themselves sorted out when they have to rely on messengers to carry orders."

"You're crazy!" she hissed. "Tamman, Harry—tell him!"

"I think Sandy's right, Sean," Harriet said quietly. "It's too risky. Besides, even if he does figure out what's happening, Terrahk's already falling back on Baricon. Wait till the rain stops. Ortak's not going anywhere, and maybe he'll surrender when he realizes he's trapped between you and Tam."

"Wrong answer, Harry," Tamman put in unhappily. "Ortak's not the surrendering kind, or he wouldn't have stopped at Erastor."

"What else *can* he do?" Harriet demanded hotly.

"He can come out after us," Sean answered. "He knows as well as we do that it's our rifles that give us the edge. You think he wouldn't take his chances on hitting us in the open if the rain knocks them out of the equation?"

Sandy started to snap back, then stopped and bit her lip. She hugged herself and turned her back on Sean for a long, taut moment, then sighed.

"No," she said finally, her voice low. "That's exactly what he'll do if he figures out what's happening."

"You got it," Sean said, equally quietly, and kicked his toe into the mud beside the raised roadbed. "Any way you cut it, we've got to carry through with my marvelous plan."

CHAPTER THIRTY-THREE

"All right, boys—you heard Lord Sean. Now let's go kick the bastards' asses!"

The officers of the First Brigade growled in agreement, and Folmak Folmakson grinned fiercely. He was a long, long way from Cragsend and anxious days waiting for the Church to condemn him for error just for searching for ways to make his mill a bit more efficient, and he was passionately grateful for it. Folmak loved God as much as the next man, but Malagor had been a captive province for twenty generations, and like many Malagorans, he'd harbored a festering resentment against the Inner Circle and their absentee bishops. Father Stomald, now. *He* was what a priest was supposed to be, and if the rest of the Temple had been like him . . .

But it wasn't. Folmak settled into the saddle and checked all four pistols before he tucked them away in his boots and under his captured Guard cloak. The rain was falling harder, as Lord Sean had warned, and he'd ordered his sergeants to check each individual pan to be sure it was securely shut until it was needed. They were still going to have an appalling number of misfires, but he'd done all he could to minimize them.

He put away the last pistol and looked over his shoulder for the signal to advance. Lord Sean stood surrounded by aides, speaking quietly and urgently to Tibold, hands moving in quick, incisive gestures, and Folmak remembered his look of surprise when the men had cheered his orders.

Folmak hadn't been surprised, but Lord Sean had actually apologized to them, as if it were *his* fault they couldn't just stand around and wait till the rain stopped. That sort of concern made the army love Lord Sean, but it knew what it was about. Especially Folmak's men. His was the First Brigade, already called "the Old Brigade," composed of men who'd followed Father Stomald from the very beginning. They regarded themselves as the elite of Lord Sean's army, though the Second and Third Brigades were every bit as old—and, Folmak admitted grudgingly, as good—and they understood what was forcing Lord Sean's hand. Every man in the column knew they'd taken far longer than expected getting to Erastor, yet they also knew only

Lord Sean and the Angel Sandy could have gotten them here at all. And the angels' message—that men should be free to shape their own lives and their own understanding of God's will—had ignited a furnace in the Malagorans' stubborn hearts. If Lord Sean needed them now, they were proud to be here, and if he decided to fix bayonets and charge a hurricane, they'd follow with a cheer.

The regimental pipers formed in the intervals in the brigade's column, and Lord Sean nodded to his aides. They spurred up and down the entire length of the corps, and Folmak waved to his unit commanders.

"Move out!" he barked, and the Angels' Army slogged through blowing sheets of rain towards Erastor.

Sean watched his men move forward and tried to look confident. Every man in Folmak's brigade had been issued a Guard cloak, and his vanguard looked as much like Terrahk's relief force as he could make them, but the rest of his men wore Malagoran ponchos. One look at *them* would tell the dullest picket what they were. The rain wasn't falling as hard as he'd feared— yet—but it was getting worse, and only First Brigade marched with slung weapons. The rest of his men carried their bayoneted rifles under their arms like hunters to shield the priming with their bodies and ponchos and keep rain from running down the muzzles. It was awkward and it looked like hell, but it was the best he could do to insure their ability to fire.

He and Tibold had reorganized the army into six-hundred-man regiments, three to the brigade, and despite the rain and the slaughter to which he'd led them, each regiment cheered as it passed him. He slapped his streaming breastplate in answering salute, and his emotions were a welter of confusion. Shame for the mistakes which sent them into battle under such a hideous handicap. Pride in how they'd responded. Dread of the butcher's bill they were going to pay, a sense of awe that they were willing to pay it for him, and a strange, shivering eagerness. He'd seen battle and its aftermath now. He *knew* how horrible it was, how ugly and vile and brutal, yet part of him was actually eager to begin. Not glad, but . . . impatient. Anticipating.

He shook his head, angry with himself. He couldn't think of the word, and he was ashamed of feeling whatever it was, but that didn't change it. He spurred ahead to overtake Folmak's brigade, and as he splashed along the road, he wished he could ride away from his own complex feelings as easily.

Under-Captain Mathan stood under the lean-to and gazed out into the rain. It was barely midafternoon, yet it looked like late evening as charcoal clouds billowed overhead. His dragoons were glad to be spared the lot of the men manning the half-flooded entrenchments facing the heretics, but that didn't make their own duty pleasant. Like most of the Host, they'd lost all their baggage at Yortown, and they'd had to cobble up whatever they could to replace their Guard-issue tents. Mathan doubted the foraging parties had left an intact roof for miles around Erastor, but the valley's frequent rains soaked them to the skin anyway, whatever they did, and he was heartily sick of it.

He spoke to himself sternly. He should be down on his knees thanking God for sparing him the slaughter the demon-worshipers had wreaked on the rest of the Host, not complaining because of a little rain! He'd certainly told his troopers that often enough!

He turned to pace briskly. He could only go a few strides in either direction and stay under the roof, but the rain had chilled the mountain air, and the activity warmed his blood.

Perhaps he'd feel happier if his present assignment had some point. With the heretics blocked west of the Erastor Spur, the pickets east of the main position were little more than an afterthought. They were out here getting soaked simply because the field manuals said all approaches, however unlikely, should be covered, and like most soldiers, they resented being made miserable just because some headquarters type wanted to be neat and tidy.

A branahlk splashed up to the shelter, and Sergeant Kithar saluted.

"We've sighted the head of the column, Sir. Should reach the pickets in about another twenty minutes."

"Thank you, Sergeant. That's good news." Mathan returned Kithar's salute, then pointed at the smoky fire crackling under another crude awning. "Warm yourself and dry off a bit before you head back."

"Thank you, Sir."

The sergeant hurried towards the fire, and Mathan folded his hands behind him with a sigh of relief. High-Captain Ortak had sworn the Temple would reinforce them, but after Yortown it had been hard for many of his men— including, Mathan admitted, himself—to believe it would happen in time. Now it had, and he breathed a silent prayer of thanks.

Captain Folmak trotted at the head of his brigade, and his belly was a hard, singing knot. He could see the first dragoons now, and they looked as miserable as Lord Sean had predicted. They were waving, and he heard a few cheers, but they also weren't budging out from under the crude lean-tos they'd erected in a vain effort to stay dry.

"You know what to do, boys," he told his grim-faced riflemen. "No shooting if you can help it, but be damned sure none of them get away!"

"Sight for sore eyes, aren't they?" Shaldan Morahkson demanded. "I *told* you Lord Marshal Surak would reinforce us!"

"Sure you did," one of his companions jeered. "Between pissing and moaning about the rain, your saddle sores, and how fucked up the whole war's been, you told us all about your personal friend the Lord Marshal!"

The others laughed, and Shaldan made a rude gesture as the lead ranks of the relief column squelched past. The incoming Guardsmen looked almost as shabby and sodden as Shaldan and his fellows after their hard march, and he turned his back on the others to wave and shout at the newcomers, then paused.

"That's funny."

"What?" his critic demanded. "Your buddy Lord Marshal Surak screw up somehow?"

"They're all musketeers," Shaldan said. "Look." He pointed as far down the column as they could see in the blowing rain. "There must be a thousand, fifteen hundred of them, and not a pike among 'em!"

"What?" The other dragoon turned to peer in the direction of Shaldan's pointing finger.

"And another thing. I've never seen bayonets like those. Have you?"

"I—"

Shaldan never found out what his fellow meant to say, for even as they stared at the column, it suddenly broke apart.

"Take them!" Under-Captain Lerhak shouted, and his men swarmed out across the picket. There were cries of alarm from the watching dragoons, and two or three turned to race for tethered branahlks, but surprise was total. Musket butts and bayonets did their lethal work, and within ten minutes, every man of High Captain Ortak's easternmost picket was dead or a prisoner.

Under-Captain Mathan stretched and called for his mount. He'd already sent a messenger ahead to Erastor, and if Sergeant Kithar was right, the column should have reached his forward position by now. Little though a ride in the rain appealed to him, he'd best go up to greet them like a properly industrious junior officer, and he trotted away from the lean-to with regret. He was riding directly into the wind, and the water running into his eyes made it hard to see where he was going. His branahlk tossed its head and jibed under him, whistling mournfully to voice its own verdict on the weather, and he tightened his knees to remind it who was in charge.

He looked back up and blinked on rain as mounted men in the soaked crimson cloaks of the Guard loomed out of the dimness. One of them waved, and Mathan started to wave back, then paused.

He stared at them, watching them ride closer, unable to believe his eyes. Their saddles and tack were mismatched, not standard Guard issue, and aside from their cloaks, they weren't even in uniform. Two of them actually wore what looked like farmer's boots, not jackboots. But that was impossible. They *had* to be Guardsmen! No one else could get at Erastor from the east! Not unless the demons had—

He jerked out of his shock and wheeled his mount. The branahlk squealed in protest as his spurs went home, then bounded forward with a teeth-rattling jerk. He had to warn High-Captain Ortak! He—

Something cracked behind him, and he didn't even have time to scream as the rifled pistol bullet smashed him from the saddle.

"Sir, the relief column's been sighted."

High-Captain Ortak looked up and smiled at his aide's report.

"Well, thank God for that! Call for my branahlk. High-Captain Terrahk deserves to be met in person."

✧   ✧   ✧

"Did you hear something?" Sergeant Kithar raised his head, ears cocked, and glanced at the man beside him.

"In this rain?" The trooper gestured at the water drumming from the eaves of their rough roof.

"It sounded like a shot. . . ."

"You're joking, Sarge! It'd take a special miracle to get a joharn to fire in this stuff!"

"I know, but—"

Kithar was still gazing out into the rain when Folmak's lead company stormed into the picket's rear area.

"Folmak's taken out the picket."

Sean nodded as his com implant carried him Sandy's voice.

"Anyone get away?" he subvocalized back.

"I don't think so. It's hard to be sure with so many people moving around in the rain, but I don't see anyone headed away from the picket."

"What's Folmak doing?"

"Rounding up POWs and shifting into assault column to hit the bridge. Don't worry, Sean. He knows what he's doing."

"So far, so good," Folmak murmured, then raised his voice. "This is what we came for, boys! Follow me, and from here on out, make all the racket you can. Let's make these bastards think the 'Cragsend Demons' are here to eat 'em all! First Brigade, *are you with me?*"

"Aye!" The roar almost blew him from the saddle.

High-Captain Ortak dismounted, handed his reins to an orderly, and tried not to scurry as he hurried for the shelter of the bridge tollhouse. The under-captain commanding the bridge traffic control detachment jumped up and saluted, but Ortak waved him back into his chair.

"Sit down, sit down!"

"Thank you, Sir, but I prefer to stand." The bridge commander was a very junior officer, but he knew better than to sit in the presence of a high-captain, whatever the high-captain in question said.

"Suit yourself, Captain." Ortak stood in the doorway, peering into the gloomy afternoon. He could just make out the head of Terrahk's column at the far end of the bridge, and he wondered why they'd stopped in the rain. Were they dressing ranks for some sort of parade?

He frowned. The rain and the rush of river water around the bridge pilings filled his ears, but that didn't keep him from hearing the cheer. What in the world—? Were they *that* happy to be here?

And then, suddenly, the relief column lunged forward onto the bridge, and High-Captain Ortak stared in horror as it swept over the half-dozen men watching the far end of the span. Bayonets flashed in the rain, musket butts struck viciously, and the high-captain went white, for he could hear the voices clearly, now.

"*Malagor and Lord Sean!*" they howled, and twenty-five thousand men stormed into the Guard's undefended rear behind their screaming war pipes.

"That's it!" Tamman snapped to High-Captain Ithun. "They're hitting the bridges now. Get the columns formed!"

"At once, Lord Tamman!"

Ithun dashed off, and Tamman's enhanced eyes swept the entrenchments facing his position. There was no movement over there yet, but there would be soon. Now if only they'd pull enough off the parapets to give him an opening!

For the Yortown survivors, it was a hideous, recurring nightmare. They'd seen their formations smashed at Yortown, watched that wall of fire and smoke grinding down from the north behind the terrifying Malagoran yell, and known—not thought; *known*—they'd faced demons, but somehow they'd escaped. They'd fallen back, dug in, waited for the demon-worshipers to sweep over them, and as the weeks passed, they'd come, slowly, first to hope and finally to believe it wouldn't happen after all. They'd stopped the heretics, held them, and at least their rear was secure if they were forced to retreat again.

But now their rear *wasn't* secure. They'd spent days preparing bivouac areas for High-Captain Terrahk's column, chattered in their relief, swapped lies and rumors about what would happen next, only to see the forces of Hell do it to them again. Some evil sorcery had transformed their reinforcements into rampaging demons that stormed into their positions in a solid, deadly mass of bristling bayonets and the terrible, shrieking war pipes of Malagor.

Surprise was total, High-Captain Ortak was nowhere to be found, and officers floundered in shock as the first, incredible intimations of disaster reached them. Folmak's brigade slammed over the bridges and butchered its way across the closest encampment. Guardsmen looked up from routine camp tasks to see eighteen hundred screaming maniacs scythe into their position, and panic was a deadlier weapon than any bayonet. Cooks and drovers scattered, half-naked men erupted from tents and lean-tos and fled into the rain, officers shouted in vain for their men to rally, and Folmak's riflemen swarmed forward like some dark, unstoppable tide.

Here and there a handful *did* rally around an officer or a noncom, but there were too few of them, and they were too stunned to be effective. The tiny knots of resistance vanished into the oncoming First Brigade's bayonet-fanged maw, and Folmak slammed a full kilometer forward before his initial charge even slowed. Behind him, more men thundered across the Erastor, fanning out to secure the bridgehead, and behind *them* the weight of Sean's entire corps swept forward in double time.

"They're hitting us in the *rear*, I tell you! My God, there're *thousands* of them!"

High-Captain Marhn stared at the gasping, half-coherent officer.

Impossible! It was *impossible*! Poison-raw terror quivered deep inside, yet he'd been a soldier for over thirty Terran years. He didn't know what had happened to High-Captain Ortak, and he couldn't even begin to guess how the heretics could be *behind* Erastor in strength or what had happened to High-Captain Terrahk, but he knew what would happen if this attack wasn't crushed.

"They've already got the bridges!" The officer was still babbling his terrified message. "We're trapped, Sir! They're going to—"

"They're going to *die*, Captain!" Marhn barked so sharply the officer's mouth snapped shut in pure reflex. "We've got eighty thousand men in this position, so stop howling like an old woman and *use* them, curse you!"

"But—"

Marhn whirled away with a snarl of disgust just as Captain Urthank, his own second-in-command charged up, still buckling his armor.

"What—?" Urthank started, but Marhn cut him off with a savage wave.

"Somehow the demon-worshipers got 'round behind us. They've taken the bridges, and they're advancing fast." Urthank paled, and Marhn shook his head. "Get back there. Send in the Ninth and Eighteenth Pikes. You won't be able to hold, but slow them up enough to buy me some time!"

"Yes, Sir!" Urthank saluted and disappeared, and Marhn began bellowing orders to a flock of messengers.

The Ninth Pikes thudded through the mud towards the clamor in their rear, and their eyes were wild. There'd been no time for their officers to explain fully, but the Ninth were veterans. They knew what would happen if the heretics weren't stopped.

The Eighteenth turned up on their left, and whistles shrilled as their officers brought them to a slithering, panting halt. A forest of five-meter pikes snapped into fighting position, and eight thousand men settled into formation as the wailing Malagoran pipes swept down upon them.

Folmak reined in so violently his branahlk skidded on its haunches as the Guard phalanx materialized out of the rain. Lord Sean had warned him the surprise wouldn't last, and he'd managed—somehow—to keep his men together as they swept across the Guard's rear areas. The clutter of tents and wagons and lean-tos had made it hard, yet he'd kept his brigade in hand, and he felt a stab of thankfulness that he had.

But he was also well out in front, and half his third regiment had been left behind to hold the bridges. He had little more than fifteen hundred men, barely a sixth of the numbers suddenly drawn up across his front, and not a single pike among them.

That phalanx wouldn't stop the regiments coming up behind him, but he couldn't let them stop *him*, either. If the Guard realized how outnumbered its attackers were and won time to recover, it had more than enough power to crush Lord Sean's entire force.

"First Battalion—action front!" he screamed, and whistles shrilled.

His men responded instantly. First Battalion of Second Regiment, his leading formation, deployed into firing line on the run, and the officer commanding the Guard pikes hesitated. All he knew was that his position was under attack, and the visibility was so bad he couldn't begin to estimate Folmak's numbers. Rather than charge forward in ignorance, he paused, trying to get some idea of what he was up against, and that hesitation gave First Battalion time to deploy in a two-deep firing line and the rest of Folmak's men time to tighten their own formation behind them. It was still looser than it should have been, but Folmak sensed the firming resolution of his opponents. There was no time for further adjustment.

"Fire!" he bellowed.

Almost a third of the First's rifles misfired, but there were three hundred of them. Two hundred-plus rifles blazed at less than a hundred meters' range, and the Guardsmen recoiled in shock as, for the first time in Pardalian history, men with fixed bayonets poured fire into their opponents.

"At 'em, Malagorans!" Folmak howled. "*Chaaaarge!*"

The Guard formation wavered as the bullets slammed home. At such short range, a rifled joharn would penetrate five inches of solid wood, and a single shot could kill or maim two or even three men. The shock of receiving that fire was made even worse by the fact that it came from bayoneted weapons, and then, against every rule of warfare, musketeers actually *charged* pikemen!

The Guardsmen couldn't believe it. Musketeers ran *away* from pikes— everyone knew that! But these musketeers were different. The column behind exploded through the firing line and hit the Eighteenth Pikes like a tidal bore. Dozens, scores of them, died on the bitter pikeheads, but while the Guardsmen were killing them, their companions hurled themselves in among the pikes, and the Guard discovered a lethal truth. Once a phalanx's front was broken, once the Malagorans could get inside the pikes' longer reach, bayoneted rifles were deadly melee weapons. They were shorter, lighter, faster, and these men knew how to use them to terrible effect.

"Drive 'em!" Folmak shrieked. "*Drive 'em!*" and First Brigade drove them. The Malagoran yell and the howl of their pipes carried them onward, and once they'd closed, they were more than a match for any pikemen.

Bayonets stabbed, men screamed and cursed and died, and mud-caked boots trod them into the mire. Folmak's men stormed forward with a determination that had to be killed to be stopped, and the Guardsmen—shaken, confused, stunned by the impossibility of what was happening—were no match for them.

The Eighteenth broke. Those of its men who tried to stand paid for their discipline, for they couldn't break free, couldn't get far enough away to use their longer weapons effectively, and First Brigade swarmed them under like seldahks. Six minutes after that first volley had exploded in their faces, the Eighteenth Pikes were a shattered, fleeing wreck, and Folmak swung in on the flank of the Ninth.

Even now, he was outnumbered by better than two-to-one, and the melee with the Eighteenth had disordered his ranks. Worse, the Ninth was made of sterner stuff, and its commander had managed to change front while the Eighteenth was dying. His men were still off balance, but they howled their own war cries and lunged forward, slamming into Folmak's brigade like a hammer, and this time they hadn't been shaken by a pointblank volley.

Folmak's lead battalion had already been more than decimated. Now it reeled back, fighting stubbornly but driven by the longer, heavier weapons of its foes, and the officers of both sides lost control. It was one howling vortex, sucking in men and spitting out corpses, and then, suddenly, Sean's Sixth Brigade slammed into the Ninth from the *other* side.

It was too much, and the Guardsmen came apart. Unit organization disintegrated. Half the Ninth simply disappeared, killed or routed, and the other half found itself surrounded by twice its own number of Malagorans. They tried to fight their way out, then tried to form a defensive hedge-hog, but it was useless. Despite the rain, scores of riflemen still managed to reload and fire into them, and even as they died, more Malagoran regiments rushed past. They weren't even slowing the enemy down, and their surviving officers ordered them to throw down their weapons to save as many of their men as they could.

High-Captain Marhn's face was iron as more and more reports of disaster came in. The heretics had swept over the entire bivouac area, then paused to reorganize and fanned out in half a dozen columns, each storming forward towards the rear of the entrenchments. A third of his men had already been broken, and the panicky wreckage of shattered formations boiled in confusion, hampering their fellows far more than their enemies. The last light was going, and the Host's entire encampment had disintegrated into a rain-soaked, mud-caked madness no man could control.

He had no idea how many men the heretics had. From the terrified reports, they might have had a million. Worse, the units they were hitting were his worst-armed, weakest ones, the men who'd been reformed out of the ruin of Yortown. They'd been placed in reserve because their officers were still trying to rebuild them into effective fighting forces, and the demon-worshipers were cutting through them like an ax, not a knife.

He clenched his jaw and turned his back, shutting out the confused reports while he tried to find an answer. But there was only one, and it might already be too late for it to work.

"Start pulling men out of the redoubts," he grated. Someone gasped, and he stabbed a finger at a map. "Form a new line here!" he snapped, jabbing a line across the map less than four thousand paces behind the earthworks.

"But, Sir—" someone else began.

"*Do it!*" Marhn snarled, and tried to pretend he didn't know that even if he succeeded, it could stave off disaster for no more than a few more hours.

"They're moving men from the trenches, Sean!" Sandy shouted over the com.

"Good—I think!" Even with Sandy's reports and his own implant link to her sensors, Sean had only the vaguest notion what was happening. This was nothing like Yortown. It was an insane explosion of violence, skidding like a ground car on ice. His men were moving towards their objectives in what *looked* like a carefully controlled maneuver, but it was nothing of the sort. No one *could* control it; it was all up to his junior officers and their men, and he could hardly believe how well they were carrying out their mission.

Even in the madness and confusion, he felt a deep, vaulting pride in his army—*his* army!—as his outnumbered men cut through their enemies. He was losing people—hundreds of them, probably more—and he knew how sick and empty he'd feel when he counted the dead, but he had no time for that now. A desperate counterattack by the broken remnants of several Guard pike units had taken his HQ group by surprise and smashed deep into it before a reserve battalion could deal with it, and only Sean's enhancement had kept him alive. His armor had turned two pikeheads, and his enhanced reactions had been enough to save his eye, but a dripping sword cut had opened his right cheek from chin to temple, and Tibold limped heavily from a gash in his left thigh.

Now he waved his battered aides to a halt, and the reserve battalion—whose commander had made himself Sean's chief bodyguard without orders—fanned out in a wary perimeter.

"How much movement?" he asked Sandy in English, speaking aloud and ignoring the looks his men gave him.

"A lot, all up and down the center of his lines."

"Tam?"

"I see it, Sean. We're moving now."

"Give 'em time to pull back! Don't let them catch you in the open!"

"Suck eggs! You just keep pushing 'em hard."

"Hard, the man says!" Sean rolled his eyes heavenward and turned to Tibold. "They're pulling men out of the trenches to stop us, and Tamman and Ithun are moving up to hit them in the rear."

"Then we have to push them even harder," Tibold said decisively.

"If we can!" Sean shook his head, then grabbed an aide. "Find Captain Folmak. If he's still alive, tell him to bear right. You!" he jabbed a finger at another messenger. "Find Fourth Brigade. It's over that way, to the right. Tell Captain Herth to curl in to the left to meet Folmak. I want both of them to hammer straight for their reserve artillery park."

The aides repeated their orders and ran off into the maelstrom, and Sean grimaced at Tibold.

"If this is a successful battle, God save me from an *un*successful one!"

"Sir!" Marhn looked up as a gasping, mud-spattered messenger lurched into his command post. "High-Captain! The heretics are coming from the west, as well!" The messenger swayed, and Marhn realized the young officer was wounded. "Captain Rukhan needs more men. Can't . . . can't hold without them, Sir!"

Marhn stared at the young man for one terrible, endless moment. Then his shoulders slumped, and his watching staff saw hope run out of his eyes like water.

"Sound parley," he said. Urthank stared at him, and Marhn snarled at him. "Sound parley, damn you!"

"But . . . but, Sir, the Circle! High Priest Vroxhan! We can't—"

"*We* aren't; *I* am!" Marhn spat. His hand bit into Urthank's biceps like a claw. "We've lost, Urthank. That attack from the rear blew the guts out of us, and now they've broken our *front* as well. How many more of our men have to die for a position we can't hold?"

"But if you surrender, the Circle will—" Urthank began in a quieter, more anxious voice, and Marhn shook his head again.

"I've served the Temple since I was a boy. If the Circle wants my life for saving the lives of my men, they can have it. Now, sound parley!"

"Yes, Sir." Urthank looked into Marhn's face for a moment, then turned away. "You heard the High-Captain! Sound parley!" he barked, and another officer fled to pass the order.

"Here, boy!" Marhn said gruffly, catching Rukhan's wounded messenger as he began to collapse. He took the young man's weight in his arms and eased him down into a camp chair, then looked back up at Urthank. "Call the healers and have this man seen to," he said.

CHAPTER THIRTY-FOUR

Lieutenant Carl Bergren was grateful for his bio-enhancement. Without it, he'd have been sweating so hard the security pukes would have arrested him the moment he reported for duty tonight.

His adrenaline tried to spike again, but he pushed it back down and told himself (again) the risk was acceptable. If it all blew up on him, he could find himself facing charges for willful destruction of private property and end up dishonorably discharged with five or ten years in prison, which was hardly an attractive proposition. On the other hand, it wasn't as if anyone were going to be hurt—in fact, he was going to have to separate any passengers from the freight—and it wasn't every night a mere Battle Fleet lieutenant earned eight million credits. That payoff was sufficient compensation for any risks which might come his way. He told himself that firmly enough to manage a natural smile as he walked into the control room and nodded to Lieutenant Deng.

"You're early tonight, Carl." Deng had learned his English before he was enhanced, and its stubbornly persistent British accent always seemed odd to Bergren coming from a Chinese.

"Only a couple of minutes," he replied. "Commander Jackson's on Birhat, and I stole her parking spot."

"A court-martial offense if ever I heard one." Deng chuckled, and rose to stretch. "Very well, Leftenant, your throne awaits."

"Some throne!" Bergren snorted. He dropped into the control chair and flipped his feed into the computers, scanning the evening's traffic. "Not much business tonight."

"Not yet, but there's something special coming through from Narhan."

"Special? Special how?" Bergren's tone was a bit too casual, but Deng failed to notice.

"Some sort of high-priority freight for the Palace." He shrugged. "I don't know what, but the mass readings are quite high, so you might want to watch the gamma bank capacitors. We're getting a drop at peak loads, and Maintenance hasn't found the problem yet."

"No?" Bergren checked the files in case Deng was watching, but he already knew all about the power fluctuation. He didn't know how it had been arranged, but he knew why, and he damped another adrenaline surge at the thought. "You're right," he observed aloud. "Thanks. I'll keep an eye on them."

"Good." Deng gathered up his personal gear and cocked his head. "Everything else green?"

"Looks that way," Bergren agreed. "You're relieved."

"Thanks. See you tomorrow!"

Deng wandered out, and Bergren leaned back in his chair. He was alone now, and he allowed a small smile to hover on his lips. He had no idea who his mysterious patron was, nor had he cared . . . until tonight. Whoever it was paid well enough to support his taste for fast flyers and faster women, and that had been enough for him. But the services he'd performed so far had all been small potatoes beside tonight, and his smile became a thoughtful frown.

He hadn't realized, until he received his latest orders, how powerful his unknown employer must be, but pulling *this* off required more than mere wealth. No, whoever could arrange something like this had to have access not simply to highly restricted technology but to Shepard Center's security at the very highest levels. There couldn't be many people who had both those things, and the lieutenant had already opened a mental file of possible candidates. After all, if whoever it was had paid so well for relatively minor services in the past, he'd pay still better in the future for Bergren's silence.

A soft tone sounded, and he shrugged his thoughts aside to concentrate on his duties. He plugged into the computer net and checked the passenger manifest against the people actually boarding the mat-trans. Two of them were technically overweight for their baggage, but it was well within the system's max load parameters, and he decided to let it pass. He made the necessary adjustments to field strength and checked his figures twice, then sent the hypercom transit warning to Birhat. An answering hypercom pulse told him Birhat was up and ready, awaiting reception of the controlled hyperspace anomaly he was about to create, and he sent the transit computer the release code. The control room's soundproofing was excellent, but he still heard the whine of the charging capacitors, and then his readouts peaked as the transmitter kicked over. Another clutch of bureaucrats, temporarily converted into something they were no doubt just as happy they couldn't understand, disappeared into a massive, artificially induced "fold" in hyperspace. The waiting Birhat station couldn't "see" them coming, but, alerted by Bergren's hypercom signal, its receivers formed a vast, funnel-shaped trap in hyper-space. At eight hundred-plus light-years, even the vastest funnel was an impossibly tiny target, but Bergren's calculations flicked the disembodied bureaucrats expertly into its bell-shaped mouth. In his mind's eye, the lieutenant always pictured his passengers rattling and bouncing as they zinged down the funnel and then—instantaneously, as far as they could tell, but 8.5 seconds later by the clocks of the rest of the universe—blinked back into existence on distant Birhat.

Now he sat waiting, then nodded to himself as Birhat's hypercommed receipt tone sounded seventeen seconds later. He noted the routine transit in his log and checked the schedule. Traffic really was light tonight, and it was getting lighter as the hour got later. Shepard Center Station was only one of six mat-trans stations Earth now boasted, and it handled mostly North American traffic, though it also caught a heavier percentage of the through-traffic from Narhan to Birhat and vice versa. The receiving platforms were far busier than the outbound stations, but, then, it was midmorning in Phoenix on Birhat and only early evening in Andhurkahn on Narhan. He had a good five minutes before his next scheduled transmission, and he returned once more to his speculations.

Lawrence Jefferson sat in his private office at home. His split-image com screen linked him to another mat-trans half a planet from Bergren's—half showing the installation's control room; the other half a huge, tarpaulin-covered shape waiting on the transmission platform—and he poured more sherry into his glass as he watched both images. No one at the other end knew he was observing them, and he supposed his high-tech spyhole was a bit risky, but he had no choice, and at least the Lieutenant Governor of Earth had access to the best technology available. His link had been established using a high security fold-space com that bounced its hyper frequency on a randomized pattern twice a second. That made simply detecting it all but impossible and, coupled with the physical relays through which it also bounced, meant tapping or tracing it *was* impossible. Besides, anyone who happened to spot it would report it to the Minister of Planetary Security, now wouldn't they?

He chuckled at the thought and sipped sherry as he watched the purposeful activity in the control room. No one—aside from the men and women who'd built and staffed it for him—even knew it existed, and all but three of them were on duty tonight. The three absent faces had been killed in a tragic flyer accident almost two years previously, and though their deaths had been a blow, their fellows had taken up the slack without difficulty. Now his carefully chosen techs checked their equipment with absolute concentration, for the upcoming transmission—the one and only transmission the installation would ever make—had to be executed perfectly.

It would never have done for Jefferson to admit he was nervous. Nor would it have been true, for "nervous" fell far short of what he felt tonight. This was the absolutely critical phase, the one which would make him Emperor of Humanity—if it worked—and anxiety mingled with a fierce expectation. He'd worked over a decade—more than twenty-five years, if he counted from his first contact with Anu—for this moment, and even as a part of him feared it would fail, the gambler part of him could hardly wait to throw the dice.

It was odd, but, in a way, he'd actually be sorry if it worked. Not because he didn't want the crown, and certainly not because he regretted what he had to do to get it, but because the game would be over. He would have carried out the most audacious coup in the history of mankind, but all the daring, the concentration and subtle manipulation, would be a thing of the past, and he could never share the true magnitude of his accomplishment with anyone else.

He shook his head at his own perversity, and a small smile flickered. The curse of his own makeup, he chided himself, was that he could never be entirely content, however well things went. He always wanted more, but there were limits, and he supposed he'd just have to settle for absolute power.

Bergren straightened in his chair as five Narhani entered the outbound terminal with a huge, tarpaulin-draped object on a counter-grav dolly. The centaurs fussed with their burden, placing it carefully on the platform and taking their places about it in a protective circle, and, despite all his implants could do, the lieutenant swallowed nervously as he flashed a mental command to the power sub-net. It was a routine testing order, but tonight it had another effect, and he winced as the induced surge flashed through the gamma bank of capacitors and an audio alarm shrilled.

The Narhani on the platform looked up, long-snouted heads twisting around in confusion as the high-pitched warble hurt their ears, and Bergren sent quick, fresh commands to his computer to shut it down. Then he leaned forward and keyed a microphone.

"Sorry, gentlemen," he told the Narhani over the speakers in the terminal area. "We've just lost one of our main capacitor banks. Until we get it back, our transmission capacity's down to eighty percent of max."

"What does that mean?" the senior Narhani asked, and Bergren shrugged for the benefit of the control room security recorders.

"I'm afraid it means you're over the limits for our available power, sir," he replied smoothly.

"May we shift to another platform?"

"I'm afraid it wouldn't matter, sir. As you know, this system is very energy intensive. For this much mass, any of the platforms would draw on the same capacitor reserve, so you might as well stay where you are."

"But did you not say you cannot send us?" The Narhani sounded confused, and Bergren hid a smile.

"No, sir. I just can't transmit the entire load at once. I'll have to send your freight through in one transmission, then send you and the other members of your party through in a second, that's all."

"I see." The Narhani spokesman and his companions spoke softly and quickly in their own language. Bergren didn't know what the object they were accompanying was, but he knew they were a security detachment, and he forced himself to sit calmly, hiding any trace of anxiety over what they might decide. After a moment, the spokesman looked back up and raised the volume of his vocoder.

"Can we not send at least one of our number through with our freight?"

"I'm afraid not, sir. We'll be right at the limits of our available power, and Regs prohibit me from sending passengers under those conditions."

"Is there risk to our freight?" The question was sharp for a Narhani.

"No, sir," Bergren soothed. "Not if it's not alive. The regulations are so specific because a power fluctuation that won't harm inanimate objects can cause serious neural damage in living passengers. It's just a precaution."

"I see." The spokesman looked back at his companions for a moment, then twitched his crest in the Narhani equivalent of a shrug. "We would prefer to wait until your power systems have been repaired," he told Bergren, "but our schedule is very tight. Can you assure us our freight will arrive undamaged?"

"Yes, sir," Bergren said confidently.

"Very well," the Narhani sighed. He spoke to his companions in their own language again, and all five of them stepped off the platform and moved back behind the safety line.

"Thank you, sir," Bergren said, and his fold-com implant sent a brief, prerecorded burst transmission to a waiting relay as he began to prep for transmission.

"Alert signal," a woman said quietly in the control room on Jefferson's screen. The two men at the main console nodded acknowledgment without ever opening their eyes, and one of them activated the stealthed sensor arrays watching Shepard Center from orbit.

"Good signal," his companion announced in the toneless voice of a man concentrating on his neural feed. "We've got their field strength. Coming up nicely now."

"Synchronizer on-line," the third tech said. "Power up and nominal. Switching to auto sequence."

Carl Bergren watched his readouts through his feeds. This was the tricky part that was going to earn him that big stack of credits. The settings had to be *almost* right, and he straightened his mouth as he felt it trying to curl in a grin of tension. The power levels were already off the optimum curve, thanks to the failure of the gamma bank, and he very carefully cut back the charge on the delta bank. Not by much. Only by a tiny, virtually undetectable fraction. But it would be enough—if whoever was in charge of the other part of the operation got *his* numbers right—and he sent the alert signal to Birhat and waited for the response.

Lawrence Jefferson leaned towards his com, clutching his wineglass, and his heart pounded. This was the moment, he thought. The instant towards which he'd worked so long.

"Their field's building now," the sensor tech murmured. "Looking good . . . looking good . . . stand by . . . stand by . . . coming up to peak . . . *now*!"

Carl Bergren sent the release code, and the capacitors screamed. The shrouded object on the platform vanished as the mat-trans sent a mighty pulse of power into hyper-space, and he held his breath. The transmission he'd sent out was almost precisely four millionths of a percent too weak to reach Birhat. It would waste its power twenty light-minutes short of the

funnel waiting to catch it for the reception units, but no one would
ever know if—

The control room on Lawrence Jefferson's com screen was silent, its personnel frozen. Not even a mat-trans was truly instantaneous over an eight-
hundred-light-year range, and Jefferson held his breath while he waited.

A soft tone beeped, and Carl Bergren let out a whooshing breath as the
Birhat mat-trans operator acknowledged receipt. He'd done it! The person
at the other end of the hypercom link didn't realize someone else had invaded
the system. He thought he'd just received Bergren's transmission!

The lieutenant suppressed an urge to wipe his forehead. Deep inside, he
hadn't really believed his employer could pull it off, and it was hard to keep
his elation out of his voice as he activated his mike.

"Birhat has confirmed reception, sir," he told the Narhani spokesman.
"If you'd step onto the platform, I can send you through now, as well."

"We did it!" someone shouted gleefully. "They accepted the transmission!"

The staff of Jefferson's illicit mat-trans whistled and clapped, and the
Lieutenant Governor checked the computer tied into his com. Good. The
exact readouts of the transmission, which just happened to carry the same
identifier code as Lieutenant Bergren's system, had been properly stored. He'd
have to wait until the regular Shepard Center data collection upload late
next week to exchange them for Bergren's actual log of the transmission,
but that part of the pipeline had already been tested and proved secure. It
was inconvenient, since he would have preferred to make the switch sooner,
yet there was nothing he could do about it. The mass readings of the transit
would prove the statue Birhat had just received had not, in fact, been the
solid block of marble Bergren had just destroyed, and for his Reichstag fire
to work, it was vital that Battle Fleet itself discover that fact when the time
came.

He smiled at the thought, then looked back at his link to the hidden
control room and its celebrating personnel. Two of them had cracked bottles
of champagne, and he watched them pouring their glasses full while they
chattered and laughed with the release of long-held tension. They'd worked
hard for this moment—and, of course, for the huge pile of credits they'd
been promised—and the Lieutenant Governor leaned back in his chair with
a sigh of matching relief. They deserved their moment of triumph, and he
let them celebrate it for another few minutes, then pressed a button.

Half a world away, the explosive charges three long-dead technicians had
installed at his orders detonated. One of the control room personnel had
time for a single scream of terror before the plunging roof of the subter-
ranean installation turned him and all his fellows into mangled gruel.

Carl Bergren dutifully logged a full report on the capacitor bank failure and completed his shift without further incident. He turned over to his
relief at shift change and signed out through the security checkpoints, then

walked slowly to his parked flyer while he pondered the entire operation. Whoever had arranged it, he thought, had to have incredible reach and command equally incredible resources. He'd had to gain access to the routing schedules weeks in advance to be sure Bergren would be on duty when the transmission came through. Then he'd had to get someone in to sabotage the capacitors, and he'd had to make sure the sabotage was untraceable. *And* he'd had to have the resources to build his own mat-trans *and* find a way to monitor the Shepard Center system precisely enough to time his own transmission perfectly.

It was big, Bergren told himself as he unlocked his flyer, climbed in, and settled into the flight couch. It was really big, and there couldn't be more than a dozen people—probably less—who could have put it all together. Now it was just a matter of figuring out which of those dozen or so it had really been, and little Carl Bergren would live high on the hog for the rest of his natural life.

He smiled and activated his flyer's drive, and the resultant explosion blew two entire levels of the parking garage and thirty-six innocent bystanders into very tiny pieces. Forty minutes later, an anonymous spokesman for the Sword of the Lord claimed responsibility for the blast.

CHAPTER THIRTY-FIVE

The last reeking powder smoke drifted away, and Sean MacIntyre surveyed a scene that had become too familiar. The only thing that had changed were the colors the dead wore, he thought bitterly, for the eastern Temple Guard had been reduced to barely forty thousand men, and they were being held back to cover the Temple itself. He was fighting the secular lords' armies now, and he shuddered as he watched the "merely" wounded writhe among the corpses.

His army was out of the Keldark Valley at last and, as he'd known it would, marching circles about its opponents. High-Captain Terrahk had fallen back on Baricon, but he'd lacked the men to hold an attack from the west. There were too many avenues of approach, and when Tamman blasted his way through a gap with fifteen thousand men and got around his flank, Terrahk had retreated desperately. His attempt to stand had cost him his entire rearguard—another eight thousand men (most, Sean was thankful, captured and not killed)—and Sean had broken out into the rolling hills of the Duchy of Keldark.

The more open terrain offered vastly improved scope for maneuver, but every step he advanced also drew him further from the valley and exposed his supply route to counterattack. At the moment, the Temple was too hard pressed to think about cutting his communications, and he kept reminding himself they didn't really have "cavalry" in the classic Terran sense, but he also kept thinking about what a Pardalian Bedford Forrest or Phil Sheridan could do if it ever got loose in his rear. His edge in reconnaissance would make it hard for them to get past him, but he simply didn't have the men to garrison his supply line properly. He could have freed them up, but only by reducing his field army, which, in turn, would have reduced his ability to keep advancing.

He sighed and sent his branahlk mincing forward. The beast whistled unhappily at the battlefield stench, and Sean shared its distaste. Whoever had commanded the Temple's forces in this last battle should be shot, he thought grimly, assuming one of his riflemen hadn't already taken care of that. He supposed it was a sign of the Temple's desperation, but ordering forty-five thousand pikemen and only ten thousand musketeers to face him in the open had been the same as sending them straight to the executioner.

Had Sean armed his men in the classic Pardalian proportion of pikes to firearms, he could have fielded close to the quarter-million men the Temple credited him with. They had all the weapons they'd captured from the Malagoran Guard plus, effectively, all the weapons of Lord Marshal Rokas's Holy Host, including its entire artillery park, but he'd opted to call forward only enough reinforcements—and replacements, he thought bitterly, recalling the five thousand casualties Erastor had cost—to put sixty thousand infantry and dragoons and two hundred guns in the field. Two hundred battalions of rifles, most veterans of Yortown, Erastor, and Baricon, supported by a hundred and fifty arlaks and fifty chagors, had been more than enough to slaughter the secular levies of Keldark, Camathan, Sanku, and Walak. He controlled all of northeastern North Hylar, now, from the Shalokars to the sea, and he wondered dismally how many more men were going to die before the Temple agreed to negotiate. God knew he and Stomald had been asking—almost *begging*—it to ever since the fall of Erastor! Couldn't the Inner Circle understand they didn't *want* to kill its troops? Brashan still couldn't get any of his remotes inside the hundred-kilometer zone around the Temple, so they couldn't know what was passing in Vroxhan's council meetings, but the prelates seemed willing to send every fighting man in North Hylar to his death before they'd even talk to "demon-worshipers"!

The litter-bearers were already busy. Theirs was the most horrible duty of all, yet they went about it with a compassion which still surprised him. The Angels' Army recognized its tactical superiority as well as its commander did, and, like Sean, most of its troops knew the men littering the field had been utterly outclassed. His own casualties, dead and wounded alike, had been under a thousand, and most of his men had come, in their own ways, to share his sickness at slaughtering their foes. It was too one-sided, and the men they were killing weren't the ones they wanted. With every battle, every army they smashed, their hatred of the Inner Circle grew, yet it wasn't a religious hatred. "The Angels" had always been careful not to deliver an actual religious message—other than backing the Malagoran hankering for freedom of conscience—and since Harry's revelation of the truth, Stomald had begun stressing the Temple's political tyranny and enormous, self-serving wealth far more strongly. The Angels' Army longed to settle accounts once and for all with the old men in Aris who kept sending other people out to die, but more even than that, it wanted simply to be rid of them.

Sean drew rein and watched a group of litter-bearers troop past with their pitiful, broken burdens. Walking wounded limped and staggered back with them, and at least Harry, coached by Brashan and *Israel's* med computers, had been teaching the Malagoran surgeons things they'd never dreamed were possible. The introduction of ether, alone, had revolutionized Pardalian medicine, and Sean had sworn a solemn oath that the first thing he would have sent to Pardal from Birhat would be medical teams with proper regeneration gear. He couldn't breathe life back into the dead, but he *could*, by God, give the maimed, whichever side they'd fought upon, *their* lives back!

His lip curled as he wondered how much of that fierce determination was an effort to assuage his own guilt. With today's body count, the war he and his friends had inadvertently started had cost over a hundred thousand *battlefield* deaths. He had no idea how many more had perished of the diseases that always ravaged nonindustrial armies, and he was terrified of what the number would finally be. He could trace every step of the journey which had led them to this, and given their options as they took each of those steps, he still saw no other course they might have chosen, yet all this death and brutal agony seemed an obscene price to buy five marooned people a ticket home.

He drew a deep breath. It seemed an obscene price because it *was*, and he would pay no more of it than he must. The Temple had ignored his semaphore offers to parley and refused to receive his "demon-worshiping" messengers, but he had one last shot to try.

High Priest Vroxhan sat in his high seat, and his lips worked as if to spit upon the men who faced him. High-Captain Ortak, High-Captain Marhn, High-Captain Sertal . . . the list went on and on. Over *fifty* senior officers stood before him, the surviving commanders of the armies the demon-worshipers had smashed in such merciless succession, and he longed to fling the entire feckless lot to the Inquisitors as their failure deserved.

But much as he wished to, and however richly they'd earned it, he couldn't. The morale of his remaining troops was too precarious, and if wholesale executions might stiffen the spines of the weak, it also might convince them the Temple was lashing out in blind desperation. Besides, Lord Marshal Surak had spoken in their defense. He needed their firsthand observations if he was to understand the terrible changes the accursed demon-worshipers had wrought in the art of war.

Or, at least, he says *he does.* Vroxhan closed his eyes and clenched his fists on the arms of his chair. *A bad sign, this suspicion of* everyone. *Does it mean I* am *desperate?* He clutched his faith to him and made himself open his eyes once more.

"Very well, Ortak," he growled, unable to make himself give the failure the honor of his rank. "Tell us of these demon-lovers and their *terms*."

Ortak winced, though it was hard to tell—his face was as heavily bandaged as the stump of his right arm—and reached for very careful words.

"Holiness, their leaders bade me say they ask only for you to speak with them. And—" he drew a deep breath "—Lord Sean said to tell you you may speak to him now, or amid the ruins of this city, but that you *will* speak to him at last."

"Blasphemy!" old Bishop Corada cried. "This is *God's* city! No one who traffics with the powers of Hell will ever take it!"

"Your Grace, I tell you only what Lord Sean said, not what he can accomplish," Ortak replied, but his tone said he *did* think the heretics could take even the Temple, and Vroxhan's hand ached to strike him.

"Peace, Corada," he grated instead, and smoothed the written message Ortak had brought across his lap as the bishop retreated into sullen silence. His eyes burned down at it for a moment, then rose to Ortak once more. "Tell me more of this Lord Sean and the other heretic leaders."

"Holiness, I've never seen their like," Ortak said frankly, and the other returned prisoners nodded agreement. "The man they call Lord Sean is a giant, head and shoulders taller than any man I've ever seen, with eyes and hair blacker than night. The one they call Lord Tamman is shorter and looks less strange, but for the darkness of his skin, yet all of us have heard stories—from our own men who have seen them in battle, not just the heretics—of the miraculous strength both share."

"'Sean,' 'Tamman,'" Vroxhan snorted. "What names are these?"

"I don't know, Holiness. Their men say—" Ortak bit his lip.

"*What* do 'their men say'?" Bishop Surmal purred, and Ortak swallowed at the look in the High Inquisitor's eyes.

"Your Grace, I repeat only what the heretics claim," he said, and paused. Pregnant silence shivered until High Priest Vroxhan broke it.

"We understand," he said coldly. "We will not hold you responsible for lies others may tell." He didn't, Ortak noted sinkingly, say what else the Circle *would* hold him responsible for, but at this point he was willing to settle for whatever mercy he could get.

"Thank you, Holiness," he said, and drew a deep breath. "The heretics say these men are warriors from a land beyond our knowledge, chosen by . . . by the so-called 'angels' as their champions. They say all of their new weapons and tactics were given to them by Lord Sean and Lord Tamman. That the two of them are God-touched and can never be defeated."

A savage hiss ran through the assembled prelates, and Ortak felt sweat slick his face under its bandages. He made himself stand as straight as his wounds allowed, meeting High Priest Vroxhan's burning eyes, and prayed Vroxhan had meant his promise not to hold him responsible.

"So," the high priest said at last, his voice an icicle. "I note, Ortak, that you have not yet mentioned these so-called 'angels.'" Ortak dared not reply, and Vroxhan smiled a thin, dangerous smile. "I know you've seen them. Tell us of them."

"Holiness, I *have* seen them," Ortak admitted, "but what they actually are, I cannot say."

"What do they *appear* to be, then?" Surmal snapped.

"Your Grace, they wear the seeming of women. There are two of them, the 'Angel Harry' and the 'Angel Sandy.'" A fresh stir at the outlandish names swept the Circle, and the high-captain went on doggedly now that he'd begun. "The one they call Sandy is smaller, with short hair. From all I could learn, it was she who routed the Guard units initially sent to crush the heresy, and she and Lord Sean appear to be the heretics' true war leaders. The one they call Harry is taller than most men, and—forgive me, Your Grace, but you asked—of surpassing beauty, yet wears an eye patch.

From what the heretics told us, it was she who was wounded and captured by the villagers of Cragsend and the one they call Sandy who led the demons to her rescue."

"And did they tell *you* they were God's messengers?" Surmal demanded.

"No, Your Grace," Ortak said cautiously.

"*What?*" Vroxhan snapped to his feet and glared at the high-captain. "I warn you, Ortak! We have the written messages of the traitor Stomald himself to claim they are!"

"I realize that, Holiness," Ortak's mouth was dust dry, yet he made his voice come out level, "but Bishop Surmal asked what *they* say. I did not myself speak with them, yet their own followers seem perplexed by their insistence that they *not* be called 'angel.' The heretics do so anyway, but only among themselves, never to the ang— To the so-called angels themselves."

"But—" Corada started, then shook his head and went on almost plaintively. "But we have reports they wear holy vestments at all times! Why would they do that if they don't claim to be angels? And why would even heretics follow those who claim to be mere mortal women yet profane the cloth? What do these madmen *want* of us?"

"Your Grace," Ortak said, frightened and yet secretly grateful for the opening, "I can't tell you why they wear the garb they choose or why the heretics follow them, but Lord Sean himself has told me they seek only to defend themselves. That he and his companions came to the aid of the heretics only because Mother Church had proclaimed Holy War against them."

"Lies!" Surmal thundered. "*We* are Mother Church, God's chosen shepherds for His people! When heresy stirs, it must be crushed, root and branch, lest the whole body of God's people be poisoned and their souls lost to damnation forever! He who defies us in this defies God Himself, and whatever this 'Lord Sean' claims, he and his fellows are—must be!— demons sent to destroy us all!"

"Your Grace," Ortak said quietly, "I wasn't called to the priesthood, but to serve God as a soldier, in accordance with the commands of the Temple. It may be that I've failed in that service, despite all I could do, yet a soldier is all I know how to be. I tell you not what I believe, but what I was told by Lord Sean. Whether or not and how he may have lied is for you to judge, Your Grace; I only answer your questions as best I may."

Vroxhan raised his hand, cutting off Surmal's fresh, angry retort, and his hooded eyes were thoughtful. Fresh silence lingered for over a minute before he cleared his throat.

"Very well, Ortak—speak as a 'soldier' then. What is your estimate of this Lord Sean *as* a soldier?"

Ortak gazed back up at the high priest, and then Vroxhan frowned in surprise as he slowly and painfully lowered himself to his knees. High-Captain Marhn dared the assembled prelates' wrath by assisting his wounded commander, but Ortak never took his eyes from Vroxhan's.

"Holiness, heretic or no, demon-worshiper or demon-spawn as he may be, I tell you that not once in a hundred generations has Pardal seen this man's equal as a war captain. Wherever he may spring from, whatever the source of his knowledge, he is a master of his trade, and the men he commands will follow where he leads against any foe."

"Even against God Himself?" Vroxhan asked very softly.

"Against *any* foe, Holiness," Ortak repeated, and closed his eyes at last. "Holiness, my life is forfeit, if you choose to claim it. I gave of my very best for God and the Temple, yet I speak not in any effort to excuse my failure or save myself when I tell you no Guard captain is this man's equal. His army is far smaller than any of us believed possible, yet no captain has held a single field against him. As a soldier I know only the art of battle, Holiness, but that I *do* know. Do with me as you will, yet for the sake of Mother Church and the Faith, I beg you to heed me in this. *Do not take this man lightly.* Were every Guardsman in both Hylars, Herdaana, and Ishar gathered in one place, *still* I fear he would defeat them. Demon or devil he may be, but as a war captain he is without peer on all Pardal."

The kneeling high-captain bent his head, and shocked silence filled the chamber.

"So at last the enemy has a face and a name," Vroxhan said softly. He and the Inner Circle had withdrawn to their council chamber, accompanied only by Lord Marshal Surak.

"For all the good it does us," Corada replied heavily. "If Ortak is correct—"

"He *isn't* correct!" Surmal snapped, and turned to Vroxhan. "I claim Ortak for the Holy Inquisition, Holiness! Whatever else he may or may not have done, he has fallen into damnation by the respect he grants this demon. For the sake of Mother Church and his own soul, he must answer to the Inquisitors!"

Surak stirred, and Vroxhan looked up at him.

"You disagree, Lord Marshal?" he asked in a dangerous voice.

"Holiness, I serve the Temple. If the Circle judges that Ortak must answer, then answer he must, but before you decide, I beg you to weigh his words most carefully."

"You *agree* with him?" Corada gasped, but Surak shook his head.

"I didn't say that, Your Grace. What I said is that his words must be weighed. Mistaken or not, Ortak is the most experienced officer to have met the demon-worshipers and survived, and he *has* spoken to them. Perhaps this has corrupted his soul and led him into damnation, yet his information is our *only* firsthand report of the heretics' leadership. And," Surak looked at Surmal, "with all due respect, Your Grace, punishing him will not make any truth he may have uttered untrue."

"Truth? What *truth*?" Vroxhan demanded before Surmal could respond.

"The truth that the demon-worshipers have defeated every army sent against them . . . and that we have no more armies to send, Holiness." Deathly silence fell, and Surak went on in a grim, hard voice. "I have forty thousand Guardsmen to garrison the Temple itself. Aside from them, there are less than ten thousand of the Guard in all eastern North Hylar. The secular lords of the north have been defeated—no, My Lords, *crushed*—as completely as Lord Marshal Rokas and High-Captain Ortak, and the better part of the levies of Telis, Eswyn, and Tarnahk with them. We have fifty thousand of the Guard west of the Thirgan Gap and another seventy thousand in South Hylar, yet they can reach us here only by ship, and it will take many five-days to bring any sizable portion of that force to bear. The secular levies of the remaining eastern lands amount to no more than sixty thousand. They, and the men I have here to guard the Temple, are *all* we can throw against the heretics, and every officer who returned with Ortak reports the same of the demon-worshipers' army. It is far smaller than our original estimates, yet every man in it appears to be armed with a rifle which fires *more* rapidly than a joharn, not less."

"Which means?" Vroxhan prompted when the lord marshal paused.

"Which means, Holiness, that I can't stop them," Surak admitted in a voice like crushed gravel. The prelates stared at him in horror, and he squared his shoulders. "My Lords, I am your chief captain. My responsibility to you before God Himself is to tell you the truth, and the truth is that somehow—I do not pretend to know the manner of it—this 'Lord Sean' has built an army which can crush any force on Pardal."

"But we're *God's* warriors!" Corada cried. "He won't *let* them defeat us!"

"He has so far, Your Grace," Surak replied flatly. "Why He should let this happen I can't say, but to pretend otherwise would violate my sworn oath to serve God and the Temple to the best of my ability. I've searched for an answer, My Lords, in prayer and meditation as well as in my map rooms and with my officers, without finding one. At present, the heretics are less than three five-day's march from the Temple itself, and the last army in their path has been destroyed. If you command it, I will gather every man in the Temple and every man the remaining secular levies can send me and meet the heretics in battle, and my men and officers will do all that mortal men can do. Yet it is my duty to tell you our numbers may actually be lower than the heretics', and I fear our defeat will be complete unless God Himself intervenes."

"He will! *He will!*" Corada cried almost desperately.

Surak said nothing, only looked at Vroxhan, and the high priest's hands clenched under the council table. He could almost smell the panic Surak's words had produced, yet even in his own fear, he knew the lord marshal had spoken only the truth. Why? Why was God letting this *happen*? The thought battered in his brain, but God sent no answer, and the silence after Corada's outburst stretched his nerves like an Inquisitor's rack.

"Are you telling us, Lord Marshal," he said at last, in a carefully controlled voice, "that the Temple of God has no *choice* but to surrender to the forces of Hell?"

Surak flinched ever so slightly, but his eyes were level.

"I am telling you, Holiness, that with the forces available to me, all I and my men can do is die in the Faith's defense as our oaths require us to. We will honor those oaths if no other answer can be found, yet I beg you, My Lords, to search your own hearts and prayers, for whatever answer God demands of us, I do not believe it lies upon the field of battle."

"What if . . . what if we accept the heretics' offer to parley?" Bishop Frenaur said hesitantly. The entire Circle turned on him in horror, but the Bishop of fallen Malagor met their eyes with a strength he hadn't displayed since Yortown. "I don't mean we should accept their terms," he said more sharply, "but the Lord Marshal tells us his forces are too weak to defeat them in battle. If we *pretend* to negotiate with them, could we not demand a cease-fire while we do so? At the least, that would win time for our forces in western North Hylar and our other lands to reach us!"

"*Negotiate* with the powers of Hell?" Surmal cried, but to Vroxhan's surprise, old Corada straightened in his chair with suddenly hopeful eyes. "Our very souls would—" Surmal went on wildly, but Corada raised his hand.

"Wait, brother. Perhaps Frenaur has a point." The High Inquisitor gaped at him, and the old man went on in a thoughtful voice. "God knows the peril we face. Would He not expect us to do anything that we can, even to pretending to treat with demons, to buy time to crush them in the end?"

"Your Grace," Surak said gently, "I doubt the heretics would fall into such a trap. Whatever the source of their intelligence, it's fiendishly accurate. They would know we were bringing up additional forces and act before we could do so, and—forgive me, My Lords, but I must repeat this once more—even if we brought up *all* of our strength, I fear their army could defeat us if we took the field against them."

"Wait. Wait, Lord Marshal," Vroxhan murmured, and his brain raced. "Perhaps this *is* God's answer to our prayers," he said slowly, intently, and his eyes snapped back into focus and settled on Surak's face. "You say we cannot defeat this 'Lord Sean' in the field, Lord Marshal?"

"No, Holiness," the soldier said heavily.

"Then perhaps the answer is not to meet him there," Vroxhan said softly, and his smile was cold.

CHAPTER THIRTY-SIX

"It sounds too good to be true." Sandy paced up and down the command tent, hands folded behind her, and her face was troubled.

"Why?" Tamman retorted. "Because it's what we've asked them to do for weeks?"

"Because it doesn't fit with anything *else* they've done since this whole thing started!" she shot back sharply.

"Perhaps not, My Lady," Stomald said, "but it *does* accord with the orders they've sent their commanders. Perhaps Lord Sean's messengers have finally convinced Vroxhan to see reason."

"Um." Sandy's grunt was unhappy, and Sean sat back in his camp chair. He shared her wariness, but Stomald was right; their remotes had snooped on the Temple's orders to all its commanders to stand fast until instructed otherwise. Lord Marshal Surak had, in effect, frozen every force outside Aris itself, in sharp reversal of his efforts to funnel every available man to the front.

He reached out a long arm to lift the Temple's illuminated letter from the table and reread it carefully.

"I have to agree with Stomald and Tam," he said finally. "It *sounds* genuine, and everything we've observed indicates they mean it."

"Maybe, but we haven't observed *everything*, now have we?" Sandy shot back. Her eyes flicked to Tibold, the only person in the tent who didn't know the truth about their origins—and the reason they couldn't snoop on the Temple directly—and Sean nodded unhappily. But, damn it, it *did* all hang together, and he was sick unto death of slaughtering armies of pawns!

"Tibold?" He glanced at the ex-Guardsman. "You're the only one who's lived in the Temple or seen their high command firsthand. What do you think?"

"I don't know, My Lord," Tibold replied frankly. "Like Lady Sandy, I can't help thinking it sounds too good to be true, yet they've followed all the proper forms. Promises of safe passage. An offer of hostages for the safety of our negotiators. They've even agreed to let us march our entire army to the walls of the Temple itself!"

"Why not?" Sandy demanded. "We've proven we can march anywhere we want and defeat any army they can field, but they know we don't have a siege train. The risk we could storm the Temple's walls is minimal, so why *not* invite us to come ahead when they can't stop us anyway? Can you think of a better way to make us overconfident?"

"And the hostages?" Harriet asked. "They're offering to send us a third of the Guard's senior officers, a hundred upper-priests, twenty bishops, *and* a member of the Circle itself! Would they do that if they weren't serious? And doesn't it make sense for them to at least try to find out what we want?"

"If they wanted to know that, all they had to do was ask us months ago!" Sandy objected.

"That's true enough," Sean agreed. "On the other hand, months ago they thought they could wipe us out. Now they know they can't." He shook his head. "The situation's changed too much to be certain of anything, Sandy— aside from the fact that they've finally agreed to parley."

"I don't like it," she said unhappily. "I don't like it at all. And I espe-cially don't like the fact that they didn't ask for Stomald to attend but *did* ask for both you and Tam." She glared at him. "If they get you two, they cut off the army's head," she added in English, but Sean shook his head.

"By this time you and Harry could lead the troops as well as Tam and I," he said in English.

"Maybe so, but do *they* know that?" she shot back. Sean started to reply, then settled for shaking his head once more, and Stomald eased cautiously into the conversation.

"I understand your concern, My Lady, but I must be the man they most hate in all the world," he pointed out. "If there's one man they would do anything to keep beyond the precincts of the Temple, that man is me." He, too, shook his head. "No, My Lady. Lord Sean and Lord Tamman are our war leaders. If they prefer—as it would seem from their language that they do—to keep any parley on a purely military level, leaving any doctrinal questions untouched for the moment, then my exclusion makes perfect sense."

"Father Stomald's right, My Lady," Tibold said. "And the oaths of good faith they've offered to swear upon God and their own souls are not such as any priest would lightly break."

Sandy tossed her head unhappily and paced faster for several minutes, then sank into another camp chair and rubbed her temples tiredly.

"I don't like it," she repeated. "It looks good, and there's a logical—or at least plausible—answer to every objection I can raise, but they've turned reasonable too fast, Sean. I *know* they're up to something."

"Maybe so," he said gently, "but I don't see any choice but to find out what it is. We're killing people, Sandy—thousands and thousands of them. If there's any hope at all of stopping the fighting, then I think we have to explore it. We owe that to these people."

She sat rigid for a moment, and then her shoulders slumped.

"I guess you're right," she said, and her low voice was weary.

✧   ✧   ✧

"They've accepted, Holiness," Lord Marshal Surak said.

He looked less than pleased, but Vroxhan was God's chosen shepherd. It was his overriding duty to defeat the forces of Hell and preserve the power of God's Church, and nothing he did in such a cause could be "wrong," whatever Surak thought. He stood at the council chamber window, watching distant, jewel-bright talmahks drift lazily above the cursed ruins of the Old Ones beyond the wall, and said a silent prayer for all of God's martyrs, then turned back to the Guard's commander.

"Very well, Lord Marshal. I shall draft our formal response to their acceptance while you see to the details."

"As you command, Holiness," Surak said, and bent to kiss the hem of the high priest's robe before he withdrew.

The city Pardalians called the Temple was an impressive sight as the Angels' Army halted just beyond cannon shot of its walls. The broken towers of a ruined Imperial city rose behind it, the shortest of the shattered stubs still three times the walls' height, and a single structure dominated its center. Most of the Temple was built of native stone, exquisitely dressed and finished with mosaic frescoes exalting the glory of God (and His Church), but the Sanctum was a massive bunker of white, glittering ceramacrete, untouched by any adornment. It clashed wildly with the spires and minarets about it, yet there was a strange harmony to it, as if the rest of the city had been deliberately planned and built to complement the Sanctum by its very contrast.

Sean stood on a small hill while the command tent went up behind him, and clouds of dust drifted across a cloudless blue sky as the army prepared its camp. Promise of truce or no, he and Tibold were taking no chances, and each brigade kept one regiment under arms while the other two collected their mattocks and shovels. By the time night fell, the entire army would be covered by earthworks which would have made a Roman general proud, and they outnumbered the city's garrisoning Guardsmen by fifty percent. Whatever else might happen, he was confident no surprise attack would overwhelm his men.

He frowned and tugged on his nose as a familiar mental itch stirred anew. He wasn't about to admit that part of him shared Sandy's misgivings. If he told her that, she'd be quite capable of singlehandedly turning the whole damned army around and marching back north, so he had no intention of breathing a word of it, but it was one reason he approved of the army's readiness to dig itself in. His troops were as hopeful as he that the fighting might end, yet they were wary and alert, as well, and that was good.

He sighed. They couldn't operate remotes in the Temple, and Brashan's orbital arrays were restricted to pure optical mode lest active systems set off the automated defenses, but those arrays had reported zero movement of troops into the area, exactly as High Priest Vroxhan had promised, and the Guardsmen actually inside the walls seemed to be going about routine duties and drill. There were some signs of heightened readiness, but that was inevitable with the dreaded demon-worshipers encamped just outside the Temple's North Gate.

No, he told himself again, everything they could see looked perfect. The parley might achieve nothing, but at least the Temple seemed ready to negotiate in good faith, and that was a priceless opportunity.

He turned from the walls. The hostages were due to arrive early tomorrow, and he wanted another word with Tibold. The last thing they needed was for some hothead on *their* side to wreck things by abusing one of the hostages!

High Priest Vroxhan stood on the walls and watched the fires of the heretic host glitter against the night. He knew the demon-worshipers were less numerous than that seeming galaxy of fires might suggest, yet his heart was heavy at the thought of allowing such blasphemers so close to God's own city. And, he admitted, at the price of his own plan to break them for all time.

He turned his head as a foot sounded on the wall's stone. Bishop Corada stood beside him, gazing out over their enemies while the night breeze ruffled his fringe of white hair, and his face was far calmer than Vroxhan felt.

"Corada—" he began, but the old man shook his head serenely.

"No, Holiness. If it's God's will that I die in His service, well, I've had a long life, and the risk is necessary. We both know that, Holiness."

Vroxhan rested a hand on the bishop's shoulder and squeezed, unable to find the words to express the emotions in his heart. The suggestion had been Corada's own, yet that made it no easier, and the old man's courage shamed him. Corada smiled at him and reached up to pat the hand on his shoulder gently.

"We've come a long way together, you and I, Holiness," he said. "I know you used to think me a blustering old bag of piss and wind—" Vroxhan started to interrupt, but Corada shook his head. "Oh, come now, Holiness! Of course you did—just as I used to think old Bishop Kithmar, when I was your age. And, truth to tell, I suppose in many ways I *am* an old bag of piss and wind. We tend to get that way as we grow older, I think. Still," he gazed back out over the forest of campfires, "sometimes old dodderers like me can see a bit more clearly than those of you with your lives still before you, and there's something I want to say to you before . . . well—" He shrugged.

"What?" The hoarseness of Vroxhan's own voice surprised him, and Corada sighed.

"Just this, Holiness: perhaps not all the demon-worshipers have said should be disregarded."

"*What?*" Vroxhan stared at the old man, the staunchest defender of the Faith of them all after High Inquisitor Surmal himself, in shock.

"Oh, not this nonsense about 'angels'! But the very thing that made it possible for them to come this far is the kernel of truth amid their lies. We know we serve God, for His Voice would tell us if it were otherwise, yet Mother Church has grown too distant from her flock, Holiness. Stomald is a damnable, heretical traitor, yet his lies could never have succeeded did the people of Pardal truly see us as their shepherds. I know

Malagor has always been restive, but have you not heard reports of the heretics' denunciations of the Temple? Of its wealth? Of its secular power and the arrogance of Mother Church's bishops?"

The old man turned earnestly to his high priest and reached out to rest both hands on Vroxhan's shoulders.

"Holiness, this business of bishops who see their flocks but twice a year, of temples gilded with gold squeezed from the faithful, of princes who rule only on Mother Church's sufferance—these things must change, or what we face today will not end tomorrow. Mother Church must rededicate herself to winning her flock's love and devotion or, in time, other heretics will arise, and we will lose not simply our people's obedience, but their souls, as well. I'm an old man, Holiness. Even without the risk I run tomorrow, the problems I foresee wouldn't come to pass before I was safely buried, but I tell you now that we *have* become corrupt. We have tasted the power of princes, not just of priests, and that power will destroy all Mother Church stands for if we allow it. In my heart, I've come to believe that is God's purpose in allowing the demon-worshipers to come so near to success. To warn us that we—that *you*—must make changes to see that it never happens again."

Vroxhan stared at the simple-hearted old man, tasting the iron tang of Corada's sincerity, and his heart went out to him. The purity of his faith was wonderful to behold, yet even as tears stung Vroxhan's eyes, he knew Corada was wrong. The authority of Mother Church was God's authority, hard won after centuries of struggle. To return to the old ways when the cold steel of power had not underlain her decrees was to court the madness of the Schismatic Wars and permit the very lies and heresies which had spawned the army beyond the Temple's walls to flourish unchecked. No, God's work was too vital to entrust to the simple-minded, pastoral bishops Corada's tired old heart longed for, yet Vroxhan could never say that to him. Could never explain why he was wrong, why his beautiful dream could be no more than a dream, forever. Not when Corada had so willingly accepted his own fate to preserve Mother Church and the sanctity of the Faith. And because he could never tell Corada those things, High Priest Vroxhan smiled and touched the old man's cheek with gentle fingers.

"I shall think upon what you've said, Corada," he lied softly, "and what I can do, I will. I promise you."

"Thank you, Holiness," Corada said even more softly. He gave the high priest's shoulders one last squeeze and raised his head. His nostrils flared as he inhaled the cool sweetness of the night's air, and then he released the high priest, bowed once to him, and walked slowly away into the darkness.

"Well, here they come," Sean muttered to Tamman.

"Yeah. Hard to believe we may actually have made it."

The two of them stood together, flanked by their senior captains, and watched the column emerge from the city gates. A score of Guard dragoons led the way, joharns peace-bonded into their saddle scabbards with elaborate twists of scarlet cord. Twice as many infantry followed under the snapping crimson banners of the Church, and behind them came the mounted officers of the Guard and the clerics the Circle had designated as hostages. A hundred priests and twenty bishops in the full blue-and-gold glory of their vestments surrounded a litter of state, and Sean's enhanced vision zoomed in on the litter. Bishop Corada, fourth in seniority in the Inner Circle, sat amid its cushions, and Sean sighed in relief. Corada's presence as a hostage for the safety of the Angels' Army's negotiators had been the crowning proof of the Circle's sincerity, and he was vastly relieved to see him at last.

"Looks like they're serious after all, Sandy," he subvocalized over his com.

"We'll see." Her response was so grim he winced, and he wished with all his heart that she could be here this morning. But that was impossible. The Temple would neither meet with nor even acknowledge "the angels'" existence, and Sandy and Harriet had taken themselves elsewhere with the dawn.

He brushed the thought aside as the head of the column reached him. The escorting honor guards tried to hide their anxiety behind professional smartness, but their nervously roving eyes betrayed them, and Sean couldn't blame them. They were pure window dressing, a sop to the importance of the hostages. If anything went wrong, the "heretical" force about them would crush them like gnats and never even notice it had done so.

A white-haired, magnificently uniformed officer with the heavy golden chain of a high-captain dismounted and advanced on the waiting Malagorans. He'd obviously been briefed on who to look for, and Sean wasn't exactly hard to spot as he towered over the Pardalians about him.

"Lord Sean," the Guardsman touched his breastplate in formal salute, "I am High-Captain Kerist, second-in-command to Lord Marshal Surak."

"High-Captain Kerist." Sean returned the salute, then nodded to the pavilions which had been erected near at hand. "As you see, High-Captain, we've prepared a place for you and our other visitors"—Kerist's eyes glittered with wintry amusement at Sean's choice of nouns— "to await our return. I trust you'll all be comfortable, and please inform one of my aides if you have any needs we've failed to anticipate."

"Thank you," Kerist said. He gave quiet orders to the escort, and the hostages moved towards the pavilions. Sean watched them go and felt a small temptation to go over and introduce himself to Corada, but only a small one. The Circle's decision to meet in the Church Chancery rather than the Sanctum signaled its intent to keep this a matter between soldiers, at least initially, and there was no point risking misunderstandings.

"This is Captain Harkah, my nephew," Kerist said, indicating a much younger officer who'd dismounted beside him. "He'll be your guide to the parley site."

"Thank you, High-Captain. In that case, Lord Tamman and I should be going. I hope to have the chance to speak further with you when I return."

"As God wills, Lord Sean," Kerist said politely, and Sean hid a smile as they exchanged salutes once more and the high-captain moved away to join the other hostages. An entire regiment of riflemen stood sentry duty around the pavilions, both to insure their privacy and to keep them out of mischief, and Sean glanced at Tamman.

"Let's do it," he said shortly in English.

"May the Force be with us," Tamman replied solemnly in the same language, and despite his tension, Sean grinned, then turned to Tibold.

"I wish you were coming along," he said with quiet sincerity, "but with me and Tam both in the city, I need you here."

"Understood, Lord Sean." Tibold spoke calmly, but there was a parental anxiety in his eyes as he faced his towering young commander. "You be careful in there."

"I will. And you stay ready out here."

"We will."

"Good."

Sean squeezed the ex-Guardsman's hand firmly, then mounted his own branahlk. He would vastly prefer to have met the Temple's representatives in some neutral spot well away from either army, but things didn't work that way here. The Inner Circle would treat with the heretics only from within the walls of its city, and Pardalian negotiating tradition supported its position. As part of its offer to parley, the Circle had extended the traditional invitation for Sean and Tamman to bring along a powerful bodyguard, as well as providing hostages for their safety. At Tibold's insistence, Sean had held out for the biggest security force he could get, and a full brigade would accompany them into the city. Neither he nor Tibold expected eighteen hundred men to make much difference if things went sour, but they should at least be a pointed warning to any fanatic tempted to disagree with the Circle's decision to negotiate.

The rest of the Angels' Army was at instant readiness for combat. They hadn't been blatant about it, but they hadn't hidden it, either. In fact, they *wanted* the Temple to know their guard was up.

Sean drew rein beside Tamman and Captain Harkah and nodded to High-Captain Folmak. The miller-turned-brigadier and his First Brigade deserved to be here for this moment, and he smiled hugely.

"Ready to proceed, Lord Sean!" he barked.

"Then let's," Sean replied, and the pipes began to drone as the column moved off.

CHAPTER THIRTY-SEVEN

Sean, Tamman, and Captain Harkah followed the vanguard as First Brigade marched down the North Way, one of the four principal avenues that converged on the Sanctum itself, and Sean marveled at the city's size and beauty. The Church had lavished Pardalian centuries of wealth and artistry upon its capital, and it showed. Yet for all the Temple's beauty, Sean sensed an underlying arrogance in its spacious buildings and broad streets. This was more than a city of religion; it was an imperial capital, mistress of its entire world, exulting as much in its secular power as in the glory of God. It made him uncomfortable, and he wondered how much of that stemmed from distaste and how much from knowing the trap this city could become if something went wrong.

He watched the Guard pikemen who lined the street as an honor guard. They were only a single rank deep, too spread out to pose any threat, but he noted the wary eye Folmak's officers kept upon them. Tibold had insisted that the negotiators' "bodyguards" should march with loaded weapons, and Sean hadn't argued. Now he wondered if he should have. If someone thought he saw a threatening movement and opened up . . .

He snorted at his own ability to find things to worry about and reminded himself every man in Folmak's brigade was a veteran. Poised on a hair trigger or no, they knew better than to fire without orders—unless, of course, some maniac was crazy enough actually to attack them!

He turned his head and smiled at Tamman, hoping he looked as calm as his friend, and made himself relax.

High Priest Vroxhan stood on the Chancery roof and gazed impatiently up the axe-straight North Way. He'd chosen this spot for the parley because it stood on the south side of the Temple's largest square, the Place of Martyrs, and despite his tension he smiled grimly at the aptness of that name.

The van of the heretic column came into sight, and the high priest's hard eyes blazed. *Soon,* he thought. *Very soon, now.*

✧　　✧　　✧

"*Sean!*"

Sean's head snapped up as Sandy screamed his name. Not over the com—in person!

He whipped around in the saddle, and his face twisted in mingled disbelief and fury as a very small figure in the breastplate and body armor of an officer spurred her branahlk forward.

"What the *hell* do you think—?" he began in English, but then her expression registered.

"Sean, it's a trap!" she shouted in the same language.

"*What?*"

Her branahlk sent the last few men scampering aside as she forced it up beside him.

"Aren't you using your implants?!"

"Of course not! If the computer picked them up—"

"Damn it, there's no time for that! Kick them up—*now!*"

He stared at her, then brought up his implanted sensors, and his face went pale as they picked up the solid blocks of armed men closing in down the side streets which paralleled the North Way.

For one terrible moment, his brain completely froze. They were ten kilometers from the gates, halfway to the city's center. If he tried to turn around, those flanking pikes would close in through every intersection and cut his column to pieces. But if he *didn't* retreat—

He jerked his mind back to life, and his thoughts flashed like lightning. The column was still moving forward, unaware of the trap into which he'd led it, and so were the Guard formations closing in upon it. They were almost into a huge, paved square—it was over a kilometer and a half across, and he could see the enormous fountains at its center splashing merrily in the sunlight—and the Temple's intention was obvious. Once his men were out into the open, the ambushers would close in from all directions and crush them. But no attackers were following *behind* them, so if the Guard wanted to hit them—

"Warn Harry and Stomald!" he snapped, and turned in the saddle. "Folmak!"

"Lord Sean?" Folmak's face was perplexed. He couldn't understand English, but he'd recognized their tones, and his combat instincts had quivered instantly to life.

"It's a trap—they're going to ambush us when we hit that square up ahead." The captain paled, but Sean went on urgently. "We can't go back. Our only chance is to go ahead and hope they don't guess we know what's coming. Drop back and pass the word. They're still several streets over, keeping out of sight, and they'll probably wait to close in until most of the column's into the square, so here's what we're going to do—"

"*A trap?*" Tibold Rarikson stared at the Angel Harry in horror. She couldn't be serious! But her strained face and the fear in her single eye told him differently. He stared at her for one more moment, then wheeled away, shouting for his officers.

✧   ✧   ✧

High Priest Vroxhan smiled triumphantly as the heretics began entering
the Place of Martyrs. He could just see the first Guardsmen moving into
position, and other troops, invisible to him here, had closed the North Way
far behind the demon-worshipers. So "Lord Sean" was a war captain without peer, was he? Vroxhan barked a laugh as he recalled Ortak's whining
warning.

*If the heretics believe "Lord Sean" and "Lord Tamman" unbeatable, they're
about to learn differently! And let us see how their morale responds when we
drag their accursed "angels'" champions to the Inquisition in chains!*

His smile grew cruel as the heretics continued into the square. In just
minutes, Lord Marshal Surak's handpicked commanders would send their
men forward and—

His smile died. The infidels had stopped advancing! They were— What
were they doing?

"Form square! *Form square!*"

Under-Captain Harkah twisted around in disbelief as Sean's amplified voice
bellowed the command and whistles shrilled. Two companies of Folmak's
lead battalion—primed by quiet warnings from their officers—faced instantly
to the left and right and marched directly away from one another. The rest
of the regiment advanced another fifty meters, then spread across the growing
space between them in a two-deep firing line. It wasn't a proper square—
more of a three-sided, hollow rectangle, short sides anchored on the north
side of the Place of Martyrs—and it grew steadily as more men double-
timed out of the North Way and slotted into position.

"Lord Sean!" the Guardsman cried. "What do you think—?!"

His question died as he suddenly found himself looking down the muzzle
of Sean's pistol at a range of fifteen centimeters.

"In about ten minutes," Sean said in a deadly voice, "the Temple Guard
is going to attack us. Are you trying to tell me you didn't know?"

"*Attack—?*" Harkah stared at Sean in disbelief. "You're mad!" he whispered.
"High Priest Vroxhan himself swore to receive you as envoys!"

"Did he?" The muzzle of Sean's pistol twitched like a pointer. "Is that
his negotiating team?" he grated.

Harkah whipped around in the indicated direction, and his face went
bone-white as the leading ranks of Guard pike companies suddenly appeared,
filling every opening on the east, west, and south sides of the Place of
Martyrs. There were thousands of them, and even as he watched, they flowed
forward and fell into fighting formation.

"Lord Sean, I—" he began, then swallowed. "My God! The *hostages!* Bishop
Corada! *Uncle Kerist!*"

"You mean you *didn't* know?" Despite his fury, Sean found himself
tempted to believe Harkah's surprise—and fear for his uncle—were
genuine.

"This is madness!" Harkah whipped back to Sean. "*Madness!* Even if it
succeeds, it will do nothing to the *rest* of your army!"

"Maybe High Priest Vroxhan disagrees with you," Sean said grimly.

"It can't be His Holiness! He swore upon his very soul to protect you as his own people!"

"Well, *someone* wasn't listening to him." Sean's voice was harsh, and he nodded to one of Folmak's aides. The Malagoran rode up beside Harkah, and the Guard captain didn't even turn his head as his pistols and sword were taken. "For the moment, Captain Harkah, I'll assume you *didn't* know this was coming," Sean said flatly. "Don't do anything to make me change my mind."

Harkah only stared sickly at him, and Sean turned his branahlk and trotted into the center of his shallow square. He was too outnumbered to hold back a reserve; aside from individual squads to cover the smaller streets opening onto the Place of Martyrs in his rear, all three regiments of the First Brigade were in firing line, and the Guardsmen had paused. Even from here he could see their surprise at the speed with which the Malagorans had fallen into formation, and he swept his eyes over his own men.

"All right, boys! We're in the shit, and the only way out is through those bastards over there! Are you with me?"

"*Aye!*" The answer was a hard, angry bellow, and he grinned fiercely.

"Fix bayonets!" Metal clicked all about him as bayonets glittered in the morning light. "No one fires until I give the word!" he shouted, and drew his sword. "Pipers, give 'em a tune!"

Vroxhan cursed in fury as the heretics snapped from an extended, vulnerable column into a compact, bayonet-bristling square in what seemed a single heartbeat. He'd seen the Guard at drill enough to recognize the lethal speed with which the demon-worshipers had reacted, and he snarled another curse at his own commanders for their hesitation. Why weren't they charging? Why weren't they *closing* with the heretics to finish them before they got set?

And then, clear in the stillness, he heard their accursed bagpipes wailing the song which had been banned since the Schismatic Wars, and swore more vilely yet as he recognized the wild, defiant music of "Malagor the Free."

"Here they come!" Sean shouted as the Guard pikes swept down. "Wait for the word!"

"*God wills it!*"

The deep, bass thunder of the Guard's battle cry roared its challenge, and the phalanx lunged forward in a column eighty men across and a hundred men deep. That formation wasn't even a hammer; it was an unstoppable battering ram, hurled straight at the heart of Sean's square in a forest of bitter pikeheads driven by the mass of eight thousand charging bodies. Something primitive and terrified gibbered deep within him with the sure and certain knowledge that it couldn't be stopped, that it *had* to break through, shatter the formation that spelled survival, and he felt the pound of his heart and the fountains' spray on his cheek as his eyes darted to where Sandy sat taut and silent on her own branahlk at his side. A terrible spasm of fear for the woman he loved twisted him, but he drove it down. He couldn't afford it, and his eyes hardened and moved back to the oncoming enemy.

"All right, boys!" He raised his voice but kept it calm, almost conversational. "Let 'em get a little closer. Wait for it. Wait for it! Wait—" His brain whirred like a computer as the range dropped to two hundred meters, and then he rose in his stirrups and his sword slashed down.

"By platoons—*fire!*"

The sudden, stupendous concussion rocked the Temple, and a pall of smoke choked the morning. First Brigade had sixteen hundred men, a total of eighty platoons, in a line four hundred meters long and two ranks deep, and the standard reload time for Sean's riflemen was seventeen seconds. But that was the *minimum* the drill sergeants demanded; an experienced man could do it in less under the right conditions of weather and motivation, and today, Folmak's brigade did it in twelve. The fire and smoke started at the line's extreme left and rolled down its face like the wrath of God, each platoon firing its own volley on the heels of its neighbor to the left; by the time the rolling explosion reached the line's right end, the left end had already reloaded and the lethal ballet began afresh.

One hundred and twenty shots crashed out each second—all aimed at a target only eighty men wide. Only superbly trained troops with iron discipline could have done it, but First Brigade was the *Old* Brigade. It had the training and discipline, and cringing ears heard nothing but the thunder, not even the wail of the pipes or the screams as whole ranks of Guardsmen went down in writhing tangles. Sheer weight of numbers kept the men behind them coming, but the shattering volleys were one smashing, unending drumroll. Waves of flame blasted out from the square like a hurricane, and the Guard had never experienced anything like it. The shock value of such massed, continuous, rifle fire was unspeakable, and the Guard's charge came apart in panic and dead men.

High-Captain Kerist's head whipped up. The whiplash crack of massed volleys was faint with distance, but he'd seen too many battlefields to mistake it. He jerked up out of his camp chair, wine goblet spilling from his fingers, and twisted around to stare in horror at the Temple's walls.

He was still staring when another sound, lower but much closer to hand, snapped his eyes back to his immediate surroundings, and he paled. The sound had been the cocking of gunlocks as an entire regiment of heretics appeared out of the very ground, and he looked straight into the muzzles of their bayoneted weapons.

The honor guard froze, and sweat beaded Kerist's brow. Horrified gasps went up from the priests and bishops, but the Guard officers among the hostages stood as frozen as Kerist, and unbearable tension hovered as a Malagoran officer stepped forward.

"Drop your weapons!" The honor guard hesitated, and the Malagoran snarled. "Drop them or die!" he barked.

The guards' commander turned to Kerist in raw appeal, and the high-captain swallowed.

"Obey," he rasped, and watched the Malagoran riflemen tautly as his men dropped their weapons.

"Move away from them," the Malagoran officer said harshly, and the Guardsmen backed up. "Any man who's still armed, step forward and drop your weapons. If we find them on you later, we'll kill you where you stand!"

Kerist squared his shoulders and moved forward. His sword was peace-bonded into its sheath, and he slipped the baldric over his head and bent to lay it with the discarded pikes and joharns, then turned to his officers.

"You heard the order!" His own voice was as harsh as the Malagoran's, and he breathed a silent prayer of thanks as the senior Guardsmen walked slowly forward to obey and no shots were fired. The Malagoran waited until every sword had been surrendered, then raised his voice once more.

"Now, all of you, back to the central pavilion!" The hostages and their disarmed guards obeyed, stumbling in fear and confusion. Only Kerist held his position, and the Malagoran officer's lip curled dangerously. He advanced on the high-captain with sword in one hand and pistol in the other. "Perhaps you didn't hear me." His voice was cold, and metal clicked as he cocked the pistol and aimed it squarely between Kerist's eyes.

"I heard, and I will obey," Kerist said as levelly as he could, "but I ask what you intend to do with us?"

A faint flicker of respect glimmered in the Malagoran's eyes. He lowered his pistol, but his face was hard and hating.

"For now, nothing," he grated. "But if Lord Sean and Lord Tamman are killed, you'll all answer with your lives for your treachery."

"Captain," Kerist said quietly over the distant musketry, "I swear to you that I know nothing of what's happening. Lord Marshal Surak himself assured me your envoys would be safe."

"Then he lied to you!" the Malagoran spat. "Now go with the others!"

Kerist held the other man's eyes a moment longer, then turned away. He marched back to the huddled, frightened hostages, his spine straight as a sword, and men scattered aside as he made his way directly to Bishop Corada. He could smell the terror about him, yet there was no terror, not even any fear, in Corada's eyes, and somehow that was the most terrifying thing of all.

"Your Grace?" The high-captain's voice was flat, its very lack of emphasis a demand for an explanation, and Corada smiled sadly at him.

"Forgive us, Kerist, but it was necessary."

"His Holiness *lied*?" Even now Kerist couldn't—wouldn't—believe God's own shepherd would perjure his very soul, but Corada only nodded.

"We are all in God's hands now, my son," he said softly.

The shattering roar of massed musketry faded into a terrible chorus of screams and moans as the last Guardsman reeled back, and Sean coughed on reeking smoke. He hadn't really thought they could do it, but the First had held. The closest Guardsmen were heaped less than twenty meters from his line, but none had been able to break through that withering curtain of fire. *Thank God I listened to Uncle Hector explain how the Brits broke Napoleon's columns!* This was the first time he'd actually tried the tactic, and sheer surprise had done almost as much as the weight of fire itself to break the Guardsmen.

Which means the bastards won't be as easy to break next *time, but—*

"Lord Sean!" He turned in surprise as Captain Harkah approached him. The Guardsman was pale as he stared out at the carnage, but his mouth was firm.

"What?" Sean asked shortly, his mind already trying to grapple with what to do next.

"Lord Sean, this *has* to be some madman's work. Lord Marshal Surak personally assured my uncle you and Lord Tamman would be safe, and—"

"Time, Captain! I don't have *time* for this!"

"I—" Harkah closed his mouth with a click. "You're right, Lord Sean. But the last thing my uncle told me to do was guide you safely to the Chancery. Whatever's happening here, those are *my* orders—to see to your safety. And because they are, you have to know that the Guard maintains an artillery park only ten blocks in that direction." He pointed east, and Sean's eyebrows rose in surprise, for he was telling the truth. Brashan's orbital arrays had mapped the city well enough for Sean to know that.

"And?" he said impatiently.

"And if they bring up guns, not even your fire can save you," Harkah said urgently. "You can't make a stand here, My Lord—not for long. You *must* move on, quickly!"

Sean frowned. Improbable as it seemed, perhaps the young man was telling the truth about his own ignorance. And perhaps it wasn't so improbable after all. Harkah and, for that matter, *all* the hostages, could have been sacrificial lambs, sent to the slaughter themselves to lead *him* to it.

But whatever the truth of that, Harkah was right. He might be able to hold off pikes here—as long as his ammunition lasted—but it was a killing ground for artillery.

"Thank you for the warning," he said more courteously to the captain, then waved him back and brought up his com. "Harry?"

"*Sean!* You're alive!" his twin gasped.

"For now," he said flatly.

"How bad—?"

"We're intact and, so far, we haven't lost anyone, but we can't stay here. We have to move. Are you in touch with Brashan?"

"Yes!"

"What's our rear look like?"

"Not good, Sean." It was Brashan's voice, and the Narhani sounded grim. "It looks like they've got at least ten thousand pikemen filling in to cut you off from the gates. You'll never be able to cut your way through them."

Sean grunted, and his brain raced. Brashan was right. A street fight would cramp his formations, preventing him from bringing enough fire to bear to blast a path, and once it got down to an unbroken pike wall against bayoneted rifles his men would melt like snow in a furnace. But if he couldn't retreat and he couldn't stay here, either, then what—?

"What's Tibold doing, Harry?"

"We're going to storm the gates," Harriet said flatly, and Sean winced. the Temple's curtain wall was ten meters thick at the base, and the tunnel through it was closed by three consecutive portcullis-covered gates and pierced with murder holes for boiling oil. He shuddered, but at least he hadn't smelled any smoke when he came through. If Tibold moved fast, he *might* get through and take the gatehouses before the defenders got set.

Might.

He bit his lip, weighing his own fear and desire to live against the terrible casualties Tibold might suffer, then drew a deep breath.

"All right, Harry, listen to me. Tell Tibold he can go ahead, but he is not—I repeat, he is *not*—to throw away lives trying to get us out if he can't break in quickly!"

"But, Sean—"

"*Listen* to me!" he barked. "So far only one brigade's in trouble; don't let him break the entire army trying to save us. We're not worth it."

"You are! *You are!*" she protested frantically.

"No, we're not," he said more gently. He heard her weeping over the com and cleared his throat. "And another thing," he said softly. "*You* stay out of the fighting, whatever happens."

"I'm coming in after you!"

"No, you're not!" He closed his eyes. "Sandy and Tam are both in here with me. If we don't make it, you and Brashan are all that's left, and *you're* the only one who can talk to the army. Brash sure can't! If they get you, too, the bastards win!"

"Oh, Sean," she whispered, and her pain cut him like a knife.

"I know, Harry. I know." He smiled sadly. "Don't worry. I've got good people here; if anyone can make it, we can. But if we don't—" He drew a deep breath. "If we don't, I love you. Take Stomald home to Mom and Dad, Harry."

He cut the com link and turned back to Tamman, Sandy, and Folmak.

"Tibold's going to try to storm the gates." Folmak didn't ask how he knew that, and the other two simply nodded. "If he makes it in, he may be able to fight his way through to us, but in the meantime, we've got to fort up. There's a Guard artillery depot to the east. If they bring the guns up, we're in trouble, and it's as good a place as any to head for for now. Tam, you know the spot?" Tamman nodded. "Good. Folmak, give Lord Tamman your lead regiment. He'll seize the depot, and the rest of us will cover his back. Clear?"

"Clear, Lord Sean," the Malagoran said grimly.

"Then let's move out before they come at us again."

CHAPTER THIRTY-EIGHT

"Get those guns up! Move! *Move*, damn you!"

Tibold Rarikson raged back and forth, eyes blazing, as the Angels' Army swarmed like an angry hive. It was insane to launch a major assault with no preplanning, yet he forced his fear aside and drove his men like one of the demons the Temple claimed they worshiped. He knew Lord Sean had beaten off the first attack, but he also knew his commander was trapped inside a city of two million enemies.

A stream of arlaks rumbled past him, nioharqs lowing, and he gripped his hands together behind him. The top of the Temple's wall mounted its own guns, but it was far narrower than its base, which limited recoil space. The Guard could put nothing heavier than arlaks up there, and he had room to deploy far more pieces than they could bring to bear. Unfortunately, *their* guns were protected by stone battlements, whereas his people lacked even the time to dig gun pits. Spurts of smoky thunder already crowned the wall, yet he had no choice but to send his own artillery forward. The North Gate had slammed shut in his face; without scaling ladders, his only hope was to batter it down, and he already knew how hideous his losses were going to be.

Regiments ran to join the assault column, but there was no time to insure proper organization. It was all going to be up to the battalion and company commanders, and Tibold breathed a prayer of thanks for the months of combat experience those men had gained.

"Tibold!"

He turned in surprise as the Angel Harry grabbed his right arm. Before he could speak, she'd yanked it out and strapped something around it.

"My Lady?" He peered at the strange bracelet in confusion. It was made of some material he'd never seen before, with a small grill of some sort and two lights that blazed bright green even in full sunlight.

"This is called a 'com,' Tibold. Speak into this—" the angel tapped the grill "—and Sean and I will be able to hear you. Hold it close to your ear, and you'll be able to hear us, as well." Tibold gawked at her, then closed his mouth and nodded. "I'll try to tell you what's happening in the city as you advance," she went on urgently, her beautiful face strained, "but there're so many buildings the information I can give you may be limited. I'll do my best, and at least you can talk to Sean this way."

"Thank you, My Lady!" Tibold gazed into her single anxious eye for a moment, then surprised himself by throwing his arms around her. He hugged her tightly, and his voice was low. "We'll get them out, My Lady. I swear it."

"I know you will," she whispered, hugging him back, and his eyes widened as she kissed his whiskered cheek. "Now go, Tibold. And take care of yourself. We all need you."

He nodded again and turned to run for the head of the column.

His guns were unlimbering in a solid line, sixty arlaks hub-to-hub in a shallow curve before the gate. Defending guns lashed at them, but even at this short range and packed so tightly, an individual arlak was a small target for the best gunner. Their crews were another matter. He heard men scream as round shot tore them apart, but like his infantry, these men had learned their horrible trade well. Fresh gunners stepped forward to take the places of the dead as gun captains primed and cocked their locks, and Tibold raised the strange bracelet—the "com"—to his mouth.

"Lord Sean?"

"Tibold? Is that you?" Lord Sean sounded surprised, and the Angel Harry's voice came over the link, speaking the angels' language.

"I gave him a security com, Sean. If the computer hasn't reacted to your implants or our com traffic—"

"Good girl!" Sean said quickly, and shifted to Pardalian. "What is it, Tibold?"

"We're ready to come after you. Where are you?"

"We've occupied a Guard ordnance depot near the Place of Martyrs." Despite his obvious tension, Lord Sean managed a chuckle. "Good thing the First has ex-Guard joharns. There must be a million rounds of smooth-bore ammo in the place when the rifle bullets run out!"

"Hold on, Lord Sean! We'll get you out."

"We'll be here, Tibold. Be careful."

Tibold lowered the com and turned to his artillery commander.

"Fire!"

High Priest Vroxhan stormed into the conference room Lord Marshal Surak had converted into a command post, and his face was livid. Guns thudded in the background from the direction of North Gate, but the furious high priest ignored them as he bore down on Surak.

"*Well*, Lord Marshal?" he snapped. "What do you have to say for yourself? *What went wrong?*"

"Holiness," Surak held his temper only with difficulty, despite Vroxhan's rank, "I told you this would be difficult. Most of my men knew no more of what we intended than the heretics did—or High-Captain Kerist." His voice was sharp, and Vroxhan blinked as the lord marshal's eyes blazed angrily into his. "You insisted on 'surprise,' Holiness, and you got it—for everyone!"

The high priest began a hot reply, then strangled it stillborn. He could deal with Surak's insolence later; for now, he needed this man.

"Very well, I stand rebuked. But what happened to the attack in the Place of Martyrs?"

"Somehow the heretics realized what was coming. Something must have warned them only after they entered the city, or they simply wouldn't have come, but they guessed in time to form battle-lines before our pikes could hit them. As for what happened then, you saw as well as I, I'm sure, Holiness. No other army on Pardal could have produced that much fire; our men never expected anything like it, and they broke. I estimate," he added bitterly, "that close to half of them were killed or wounded first."

"And now?"

"Now we have them penned up in the Tanners Street ordnance depot." The lord marshal grimaced. "That, unfortunately, means they now have plenty of ammunition when their own runs out, but we control all the streets between them and the gates. Their musketry won't help them much in a street fight, and we can starve them out, if we must. Assuming we have time."

"Time?" Vroxhan repeated sharply, and Surak nodded grimly.

"The rest of their army's about to assault North Gate, Holiness, and at your orders, we didn't tell the men on the wall what we intended, either."

"You mean they may actually break into the Temple?!" Vroxhan gasped.

"I mean, Holiness, that our guns are manned and we're rushing in more infantry, but if they hit fast enough, they may get through the tunnel before we can ready the oil. If that happens, then, yes, they *can* break in."

"Dear God!" Vroxhan whispered, and it was the lord marshal's turn to smile. It was a grim smile, but it wasn't defeated.

"Holiness, I would never have chosen to fight them here, but it may actually work in our favor." Vroxhan looked at him in disbelief, and the lord marshal made an impatient gesture. "Holiness, I've told you again and again: it's their range and firepower that makes them so dangerous in the field. Well, there's no open terrain in the Temple. The streets will break up their firing lines, every building will become a strong point, and they'll have to come at us head-on, with bayonets against our pikes. This may be the best chance we'll ever have to crush their main field army, and if we do, we can capture their weapons and find out how they've improved their range and rates of fire."

Vroxhan blinked, and then his face smoothed as understanding struck.

"Exactly, Holiness. If we hold them here, smash this army, copy their weapons, and then concentrate our own strength from other areas, we can win this war after all."

"I—" Vroxhan began, then stiffened at the sudden, brazen bellow of far more artillery than North Gate's defenders could bring to bear.

A wall of smoke spewed upward as the arlaks recoiled, and splinters flew as their shot smashed into the city gates. Scores of holes appeared in the stout timbers, but they held, and the gunners sprang into the deadly ballet Lord Sean and Lord Tamman had taught them. Sponges hissed down bores, bagged charges and fresh shot followed, and the guns roared again.

The defending artillery fired in desperate counterbattery, but fewer guns could be crammed in along the walls, they couldn't match the Malagorans' rate of fire, and the wind carried the thick clouds of smoke up towards them in a solid, blinding bank. The Guard's guns could kill and maim Tibold's gunners, but they couldn't silence his pieces, and the gates sagged as hurricanes of eight-kilo shot smashed them. The outermost portcullis and gate went down in ruins, but the gunners went on firing, pouring a maelstrom of shot down the narrow gullet of the gate tunnel. Tibold could no more see what was happening to the second and third gates than the next man, but that massive barrage had to be ripping them apart in turn.

He paced back and forth, gnawing his lip and trying to gauge his moment. If he waited too long, the defenders would be ready to deluge his men with oil; if he committed his column too soon, it would find itself halted by intact gates, and aside from hastily impressed wagon tongues, it had no battering rams. The losses he was going to take from the wall's artillery as he charged would be terrible; if his men had to retreat under fire from a gate they couldn't breach, they would also be useless.

Another salvo rolled out from his gun line, and another. Another. He paced harder, hovering on the brink of committing himself and then dragging himself back. He had to wait. Wait as long as he dared to be sure—

He jerked in pain as the "com" on his wrist suddenly bit him. He snatched his hand up in front of him, staring at the bracelet, and the Angel Harry's taut voice came from it.

"The middle gate must be down, Tibold! We can see shot coming through the innermost ones, and they're hanging by a thread!"

See them? How could even an angel see—? He bit off the extraneous question and held the com to his lips.

"What else can you see, Lady Harry?" he demanded.

"They've got a line of infantry waiting for you." Harriet deliberately spoke in a flat, clear voice despite her fear for Sean while she relayed the reports from Brashan's hastily redeployed orbital arrays. "It looks like two or three thousand pikes, but only a few hundred musketeers. They've brought up a battery—we can't tell if they're chagors or arlaks—in support. That's all so far, but more guns and men will be there within twenty minutes. If you're going, you have to go now, Tibold!"

The head of Tibold's column was the Twelfth Brigade. Its men stood two hundred meters behind their own guns, and they were white-faced and taut, for they understood the carnage waiting in and beyond that narrow tunnel. There were none of the usual jokes and anxious banter men used to hide their fear from one another. This time they stood silent, each man isolated in his own small world of gnawing tension despite the men standing at his shoulders. The thunder of their own guns pulsed in their blood like the beating of someone else's heart, and already they had over a hundred dead and wounded from the arlaks on the Temple's wall. They were too far out for grapeshot, and the defenders had been concentrating on efforts to silence Tibold's artillery, but that was going to change the instant the infantry started forward.

Their heads jerked up as High-Captain Tibold appeared before them. He faced them with blazing eyes, and his leather-lunged bellow cut through even the thunder of the guns.

"*Malagorans!*" he shouted. "You know all Lord Sean and the angels have done for us; now he, Lord Tamman, and the Angel Sandy have been betrayed! Unless we cut our way to them, they, and all our comrades with them, will die! Men of the Twelfth, *will you let that happen?*"

"*NOOO!*" the Twelfth roared, and Tibold drew his sword.

"Then let's go get them out! Twelfth Brigade, at a walk, *advance!*"

Whistles shrilled, pipes began to wail, and the men of the Twelfth gripped their rifles in sweat-slick hands and moved forward.

The artillerists on the walls didn't notice them at first. Smoke clogged visibility, and the thunder of their own guns covered the whistles and the drone of the pipes. But the Malagoran arlaks had to check fire as the advancing infantry masked their fire, and the Guard knew then. Powder-grimed gunners relaid their pieces, grapeshot replaced round, and they waited for the smoke to lift and give them a target.

"*Double time!*" the Twelfth's officers screamed, and the column picked up speed. They had six hundred paces to go, and they moved forward at a hundred and thirty paces a minute as the wind parted the smoke.

The defenders watched them come, and musketeers dashed along the wall, spreading out between the guns. The Guard didn't have many of them left, but four hundred settled into firing position and checked their priming as the Twelfth's advance accelerated. Six hundred paces. Five hundred. Four.

"*Malagor and Lord Sean!*" the Twelfth's commander bellowed, and his men howled the high, terrible Malagoran yell and sprang into a full run.

A curtain of flame blasted out from the wall, twenty guns spewing grapeshot into a packed formation at a range of barely three hundred meters. Hundreds of men went down as quarter-kilo buckshot smashed through them, but other men hurdled their shattered bodies at a dead run, and their speed took them in under the artillery's maximum depression before the gunners could reload. Guard musketeers leaned out over the parapet, exposing themselves to fire straight down into them as they reached the base of the wall, and the artillery poured fresh fire into the men behind them, but six full regiments of riflemen laced the battlements with suppressive fire. Scores of Guard musketeers died, and artillerists began to fall, as well, as bullets swept their embrasures. Fresh smoke turned morning into Hell's own twilight, men screamed and cursed and died, and the Twelfth Brigade's bleeding battalions slammed into the shot-riddled outer gate.

Massive, broken timbers collapsed under the impact of hurtling bodies and plunged downward, crushing dozens of men and pinning others, but the Twelfth lunged onward. There was no blazing oil from the murder holes, but Guardsmen fired joharns and pistols through them into the reeking, smoke-filled horror of the tunnel. The second gate still stood precariously, too riddled to last but enough to slow the Twelfth's headlong pace for just a moment, and another ninety men were piled dead before it when it finally went down.

The Twelfth drove onward, carried by a blood-mad fury beyond sanity and driven by the weight of numbers behind them, and a storm of musket fire met them as they slammed through the third and final gate at last. Arlaks bellowed, blasting them with case shot at less than sixty meters, and men slipped and fell on blood-slick stone as the brigade broke out into the open. Men fired their rifles on the run, still charging forward, and slammed into the waiting pikes like a bleeding, dying hammer.

The impact staggered the Guardsmen. Their longer weapons gave them a tremendous advantage in this headlong clash, but the Malagorans rammed onward, and more and more of them swept out of the tunnel. They overwhelmed the front ranks of pikes, burying them under their own bodies, and the Guard gave back—first one step, then another—before the stunning ferocity of that charge. They weren't fighting men; they were fighting an elemental force. For every Malagoran they killed, two more surged forward, and every one of those charging maniacs fired at pointblank range before he closed with the bayonet. Behind them, other men with lengths of burning slow match lit fuses, and powder-filled, iron hand grenades arced through the smoky air to burst amid the Guard's ranks. Here and there, their front broke, and Malagorans funneled forward into the holes, bayonets stabbing, taking men in the flank even as the Guard's charging reserve cut them down in turn. There was no *end* to the flood of howling heretics, and Guardsmen began to look over their shoulders for the reinforcements they'd been promised.

More Malagorans charged through the gate tunnel, and still more. The space between the wall and the pikes was a solid mass of men, each fighting to get forward to kill at least one Guardsman before he died. The casualty count was overwhelmingly in the Guard's favor, but the Malagorans seemed willing to take *any* losses, and at last, slowly, the pikes began to crumble. Here a man went down screaming; there another began to edge back; to one side, another dropped his pike and turned to run; and the Malagorans drove forward with renewed ferocity as they sensed the shifting tide.

The Guard's officers did everything mortal men could do, but mortal men couldn't stop that frenzied charge, and what had begun slowly spread and accelerated. A stubborn withdrawal became first a retreat, then a rout, and the Malagorans swarmed over any man who tried to stand while others fought their way meter by bloody meter up the stairs on the wall's inner face. The last of the pikemen, abandoned by their fellows, turned to run, and the baying Malagoran army swept into the city.

Two hundred of the Twelfth Brigade were still on their feet to join it.

"We're through the gate, Lord Sean!" Tibold shouted into the com. "We're through the gate!"

"I know, Tibold." Sean closed his eyes, and tears streaked his face, for he was tied into Brashan's orbital arrays. The smoke and chaos made it impossible to sort out details from orbit, even for Imperial optics, but he didn't need details to know thousands of his men lay dead or wounded.

"Watch it, Tibold!" Harriet's voice cut into the circuit. "The men you routed just ran into their reinforcements. You've got ten or twenty thousand fresh troops coming at you, and the survivors from the gates are rallying behind them!"

"Let them come!" the ex-Guardsman exulted. "We hold the gate now. They can't keep us out, and I'll take them in a straight fight any day, Lady Harry!"

"Sean, you've got more men coming at you, too," Harriet warned.

"I see 'em, Harry."

"Hang on, Lord Sean!" Tibold said urgently.

"We will," Sean promised grimly, and opened his eyes. "Pass the word, Folmak. They're coming in from the east and west."

"What's happening, Lord Marshal?" Vroxhan demanded edgily as a panting messenger handed Surak a message. The lord marshal scanned it, then crumpled it in his fist.

"The heretics have carried the gates, Holiness."

"God will strengthen our men," Vroxhan promised.

"I hope you're right, Holiness," Surak said grimly. "High-Captain Therah reports the heretics took at least two thousand casualties, and they're still driving forward, not even pausing to regroup. It would seem," he faced the high priest squarely, "their outrage at our treachery is even greater than I'd feared."

"We acted in the name of God, Lord Marshal!" Vroxhan snapped. "Do not dare presume to question God's will!"

"I didn't question *His* will," Surak said with dangerous emphasis. "I only observe that men enraged by betrayal can accomplish things other men cannot. Our losses will be heavy, Holiness."

"Then they'll be heavy!" Vroxhan glared at him, then slammed his fist on a map of the Temple with a snarl. "What of the heretic leaders?"

"A fresh attack is going in now, Holiness."

The ordnance depot's stone wall was for security, not serious defense. Two wide gateways pierced it to north and south, but Folmak's men had loopholed the wall, barricaded the gates with paving stones and artillery limbers, and wheeled captured arlaks into place to fire out them. It wasn't much of a fort, but it was infinitely preferable to trying to stand in the streets or squares of the city.

The surviving Guardsmen of the original ambush surrounded the depot, reinforced by several thousand more men and four batteries of arlaks. Now their guns moved up along side streets that couldn't be engaged from the gateways. The Guard's gunners had learned what happened to artillerists who unlimbered in range of rifles, and they dragged their batteries into the warehouses that flanked the depot. Hammers and axes smashed crude gunports in warehouse walls, and arlak muzzles thrust out through them.

Sean saw it coming, but there was nothing he could do to prevent it. Ammunition parties had hauled cases of Guard musket balls out of the depot and issued them to his men, who had orders to use the smoothbore ammunition for close range fighting and conserve their rifle ammunition, and he stood in a window of the depot commander's office and watched stone dust and wooden splinters fly from the warehouse walls as picked marksmen fired on the small targets the improvised gunports offered. Some of their shots were going home, and no doubt at least a few were actually hitting someone, but not enough to stop the enemy's preparations.

And then the arlaks began to bark.

Eight-kilo balls fired at less than sixty meters slammed into the depot wall, and it had never been meant to resist artillery. Lumps of rock flew, and he clenched his jaw.

"They're going to blow breaches, then put in the pikes," he told Folmak harshly. "Start a couple of companies building barricades behind the wall. Use whatever they can find, and see about parking some more arlaks among them. We'll let them blow their breach, then open up when they come through."

"At once, Lord Sean!" Folmak slapped his breastplate and vanished, and Sandy crossed to Sean.

"I wish to hell you hadn't come," he rasped. "Goddamn it, what did you think you were *doing*?"

"Saving your butt, among other things!" she shot back, but her words lacked their usual tartness, and she touched his elbow. "How bad is it, Sean?" she asked in a softer voice. "*Can* we hold?"

"No," he said flatly. "They'll just keep throwing men at us—or stand back and batter us with artillery. Sooner or later, the First is going down."

"Unless Tibold gets here first," she said through the thunder of the guns.

"Unless Tibold gets here first," he agreed grimly.

CHAPTER THIRTY-NINE

Case shot screamed down the street as the Malagoran chagors recoiled, and High-Captain Therah winced as it scythed through his men. Teams of heretic infantry had hauled the light guns forward, and if their shot was only half as heavy as the Guard's arlaks threw, the smaller, lighter chagors were also far more maneuverable. Worse, the heretics could fire with impossible speed—faster than a Guard musketeer!—and the deadly guns had cost Therah's men dearly.

He still didn't know what had happened, but the heretics' conviction that any treachery had been the Temple's lent them a furious, driving power Therah had never faced in seven long Pardalian years as a soldier. Half of them were screaming "Lord Sean and no quarter!" as they charged, and *all* of them were fighting like the very demons they worshiped. By his most optimistic estimate, the Guard had already lost six or seven thousand men, and there was no end in sight. But the heretics were paying, too, for their fury drove them into headlong, battering attacks.

Which didn't mean they weren't winning. His men knew the city better than they, yet somehow they spotted every major flanking move. Smaller parties seemed able to evade their attention and hit their flanks out of alleys and side streets, yet such piecemeal attacks could only slow them, and the hordes of terrified civilians choking the streets shackled his own movements.

But he was learning, too, he thought grimly. His musketeers were no match for heretic riflemen in the open, so every precious musket was dug into the taller buildings along the heretics' line of advance. Their slower-firing smoothbores were just as deadly at close range, and their firing positions at second- and third-story loopholes shielded them from return fire. Therah was positive the heretics' losses were far higher than his own, yet *still* they drove forward, flowing down every side street, spreading out at every intersection. They bored ever deeper into the Temple, like a holocaust, and as the conflict spread, it grew harder and harder to control it or even grasp what was going on.

The chagors fired another salvo, and then the heretic infantry charged with their terrible, baying war cry. Their accursed pipes shrilled like damned souls, and their bayonets cut through the staggered ranks of his surviving pikemen. The heretics howled in triumph—and then their howls were drowned by the roar of arlaks. The pikes had held just long enough for the artillerists behind them to complete their chest-high barricade of paving stones, and the guns spewed flame through gaps in the crude barrier. Grape shot splashed walls and pavement with blood, and not even demon-worshipers could stand that fire. They fell back, running for their own guns, and a bitter duel sprang up between their chagors and the Guard arlaks. Field pieces thundered at one another at a range of no more than eighty paces, straight down the broad avenue of the North Way, and Therah turned away from the window to glare down at his map.

The heretic point was halfway to the Place of Martyrs, but he could hold. He *knew* he could. Their casualties were even greater than his, and, aside from the North Way itself, he'd stopped their advance along most of the main avenues within three or four thousand paces of North Gate. Now his guns were dug in across the North Way, and if he didn't expect them to hold for long, successive positions were being built behind them. He could bleed the heretics to death as they battered their way through one strongpoint after another, but only if he had more men!

It was the side streets. His strength was being eaten up in scores of small blocking forces, racing to cut off each new penetration. Every man he committed to holding them there was one less to cover the main thorough-fares, but if he *didn't* block the side routes, the heretics filtered forward—taking their accursed chagors with them—and cut in behind his main positions. He needed more men, yet Lord Marshal Surak refused to release them. A full third of the available Guard was still hammering away at the heretics' leaders or covering routes they might use to join their fellows if they somehow broke out of the artillery depot. The men Therah did have were fighting like heroes, but something was going to break if he couldn't convince Surak to reinforce him.

"Signalman!" He didn't even look up as a signals officer materialized beside him. "Signal to Lord Marshal Surak: 'I must have more men. We hold the main approaches, but the demon-worshipers are breaking through the side streets. Losses are heavy. Unless reinforced, I cannot be responsible for the consequences.'" He paused, wondering if he'd been too direct, then shrugged. "Send it."

He looked back out the window just as a ball from a heretic chagor struck an arlak on the muzzle. The gun tube leapt into the air like a clumsy talmahk, then crashed back down to crush half a dozen men, and he swore. His gun-ners were killing the heretic artillerists, but despite their barricade, they were being ground away by the demon-worshipers' greater rate of fire.

"Message to Under-Captain Reskah! He's to move his battery up to Saint Halmath Street. Have him deploy to take the heretics in flank as they advance on the Street of Lamps position. Then get another messenger to Under-Captain Gartha. He's to bring his pikes—"

High-Captain Therah went on barking orders even as his staff began to gather up their maps in preparation to fall back yet again.

✧   ✧   ✧

Sean crouched behind his own rock pile with Sandy as the latest assault fell back into the smoke. The depot wall had become little more than a tumbled heap of broken stone, but his men were dug in behind it, and dead and dying Guardsmen littered the approaches. The wooden warehouses to the east were a roaring mass of flames, but the ones on the west side were stone, and the Guard arlaks in them were still in action.

Folmak crawled up beside him, keeping low as musket balls whined and skipped from the crude breastwork. The ex-miller's breastplate was dented, and his left arm hung in a bloody sling, but he carried a smoking pistol in his right hand. He flopped down beside Sean and passed the weapon back to his orderly to reload before he tugged a replacement from his sash.

"We're down to about nine hundred effectives, My Lord." The Malagoran coughed on the smoke. "I make it three hundred dead and six hundred wounded, and the surgeons are out of dressings." He turned his head to watch Sandy rip open an iron-strapped crate of musket ammunition with one bio-enhanced hand and managed a grim smile. "At least we've still got plenty of ammunition."

"Glad something's going right," Sean grunted, and rose cautiously to fire at a Guardsman. The man threw up his arms and sprawled forward, and Sean dropped back beside Folmak as answering fire cracked and whined about his ears.

He rolled on his back to reload the pistol, and his thoughts were grim. The Guard was coming at them only from the west now, but it was still coming. As Lee had proven at Cold Harbor and Petersburg, dug in riflemen could hold against many times their own numbers, but each assault crashed a little closer to success, like waves devouring a beach, and his line was a little thinner as each fell back. Another two or three hours, he thought.

He drew the hammer to the half-cocked safety position and primed the pistol while he stared up into the smoke-sick afternoon sky. He could hear the thunder of battle from the north in the rare intervals when the firing here slowed, and he was still tied into Brashan's arrays. The satellites could see less and less as smoke and the spreading fires blinded their passive sensors, but he was still in touch with Tibold and Harriet, as well. The ex-Guardsman had battered his way halfway to the Place of Martyrs, but at horrible cost. No one could be certain, and he knew people tended to assume the worst while the dying was still happening, but even allowing for that, Harriet estimated Tibold had lost over a sixth of his men. The Angels' Army was being ground away, and there was nothing he could do about it. Even if the army had tried, it was in too deep to disengage, and he knew Tibold would refuse to so much as make the attempt as long as he, Tamman, or Sandy were still alive.

Which they wouldn't be for too very much longer, he thought bitterly.

"Sean! Movement to the north!"

He rolled onto his side and rose on an elbow, peering to his right as Tamman's warning came over the com, but not even enhanced eyes could see anything from here.

"What kind of movement?" he asked, and there was a moment of silence before Tamman replied slowly.

"Dunno, Sean. Looks like . . . By God, it *is*! They're moving back!"

"Moving *back*?" Sean looked at Sandy. Her smoke-grimed face was drawn, but she shrugged her own puzzlement. "Are they shifting west, Tam?"

"No way. They're pulling straight back. Just a sec." There was another pause as Tamman crawled through the rubble to a better vantage point. "Okay. I can see 'em better now. Sean, the bastards are forming a route column! They're moving straight towards the Place of Martyrs!"

Sean was about to reply when a junior officer flung himself on his belly behind the rock pile. The young man was breathing hard and filthy from head to toe, but he slapped his breastplate in a sort of abbreviated salute.

"Lord Sean! They're moving back on the south side."

"How far back?"

"Their musketeers are still in the buildings, but their pikemen are falling clear back behind them, My Lord."

Sean stared at him and forced his cringing brain to work. The Guard had to know it was grinding the First away, so why fall back now? It couldn't be simply to reorganize, not if Tamman was right about the column marching north for the Place of Martyrs. But if not that, then—

"They're reinforcing against Tibold," he said softly. Folmak looked at him for a moment, then nodded.

"They must be," he agreed, and Sean looked at the under-captain.

"How many pikes did they pull off the south side?"

"I'm not certain, My Lord—" the Malagoran began, and Sean shook his head.

"Best guess. How many?"

"At least five thousand."

"Tam? How many from your side?"

"I make it what's left of seven or eight thousand pikes. They've left musketeers to keep us busy, but I'd guess there's no more than a thousand pikemen to support them."

Sean frowned, then switched to Tibold's com frequency.

"Tibold, they're pulling men away from us. We're guessing it at ten to twelve thousand pikes."

"Away from you?" The ex-Guardsman was hoarse and rasping from hours of bellowing orders, but there was nothing wrong with his brain. "Then they're sending them here."

"Agreed. What will that do to you?"

"It won't be good, Lord Sean," Tibold said grimly. "My lead brigades are down to battalion strength by now. We're still moving forward, but it's by finger spans. If they bring that many fresh men into action—" He broke off, and Sean could almost see his shrug.

"How long for them to get to you?"

"Under these conditions? At least an hour."

"All right, Tibold. I'll get back to you."

"Sean?" He looked up as Sandy said his name, and her eyes bored into his.

"Give me a minute." He turned to Folmak and pointed to the gaunt, fortress-like main arsenal building which sheltered their wounded.

"How many men do you need to garrison the arsenal?"

"Just the arsenal?" Sean nodded, and the Malagoran rubbed his filthy face with his good hand. "Three hundred to cover all four walls and give me some snipers upstairs."

"Only three hundred?" Sean pressed, and Folmak smiled grimly.

"We've already prepared it for our last stand, Lord Sean, and we've got half a dozen of their arlaks on each wall at ground level. I've got a couple of hundred wounded who can still shoot, and a hundred more who can still load for men who aren't hurt, and we've got plenty of rifles no one needs anymore. I can hold it with three hundred, My Lord. Not forever, but for a couple of hours, at least."

"Make it four hundred."

"Yes, My Lord." Folmak nodded but never looked away from his commander. "Why, My Lord?" he asked bluntly.

"Because I'm taking the rest of your people on a little trip, Folmak." Sean bared his teeth at the Malagoran's expression. "No, I'm not crazy. The Guard wants us, Folmak. They wouldn't ease up on us if they had any choice, so if they're pulling men from here to throw at Tibold, they've probably already pulled in everyone they can scrape up from anywhere else."

"And?" Folmak asked repressively.

"And everyone they've got left is almost certainly between us and Tibold. If I can break out to the south while they're all going north, I may just be able to pay a little visit to High Priest Vroxhan in person and, ah, *convince* him to call this whole thing off."

"You're mad, My Lord. High-Captain Tibold would have my guts for tent ropes if I let you try something like that!"

"We'll all have to be alive for that to happen, and you and I *won't* be unless I can at least distract them from reinforcing against Tibold. Think about it, Folmak. If I break out in their rear, headed away from them, they're bound to turn at least some of their men around to nail me, and we can raise all kinds of hell before they catch up to us. While we're doing that, Tibold may actually manage to break through."

"You're mad," Folmak repeated. He locked stares with Sean, but it was the ex-miller whose eyes finally fell. "You *are* mad," he said sighing, "but you're also in command. I'll give you what's left of the Second Regiment."

"Thank you." Sean gripped the Malagoran's shoulder hard for a moment. "In that case, you'd better go start getting things organized."

"Which way will you go?"

"We'll start out to the east. The fires have them disorganized on that side."

"Very well. I'll see about getting some guns into position to lay down fire before you go. At least—" the First's commander summoned a smile "—there's no wall to block our fire any longer!"

He turned to crawl away, shouting for his surviving messengers, and a small, dirty hand gripped Sean's elbow.

"He's right, you're out of your damned mind!" Sandy hissed. "You'll never get past their perimeter, and even if you do, you don't even know where to *find* Vroxhan in all this!" She waved her other hand blindly at the smoke, and the gesture was taut with anger.

"No, I don't," Sean agreed quietly, "but I know where the *Sanctum* is."

"The—?" Sandy froze, staring into his eyes, and he nodded.

"If Tam and I get into the Sanctum—and we might just pull it off while everybody's fighting on the north side of town—we can take over the computer. And if we shut down the inner defense net, then Brash and Harry can get fighters in here and knock the guts out of the Guard."

"You'll never make it," she whispered, her face ashen under its grime, but her voice was already defeated by the knowledge that he had to try.

"Maybe not, but we can sure as hell *worry* the bastards!" he said with a savage grin.

"Then I'm coming with you," she said flatly.

"*No!* If we break out, most of them'll come after us. There won't be enough to take Folmak out, and I want you here where it's safe!"

"Fuck you, Sean MacIntyre!" she shouted in sudden fury. "Goddamn it to hell, do you think I want to be *safe* while you're out *there* somewhere?" She jabbed a hand at the billowing smoke, and he watched in amazement as tears cut clean, white tracks down her filthy face. "Well, the hell with you, *Your Highness!* I'm an officer, too, not a goddamned 'angel'! And I *am* coming with you! If something happens to you and Tam, maybe *I* can get to the computer!"

"I—" Sean started to snap back, then closed his eyes and bent his head to stare down at his clenched fists. She was right, he thought drearily. He wanted—*God*, how he wanted!—to make her stay behind, but that was because he loved her, and it didn't change the fact that she was right.

"All right," he whispered finally, and looked up, blinking on his own tears. He reached out to cup the side of her face and managed a wan smile. "All right, you insubordinate little bitch." She caught his wrist, pressing her cheek tightly into his palm for just a moment, then released him and rolled to her knees.

"You tell Harry and Tibold what we're up to. I'll go help Tam get things organized."

CHAPTER FORTY

The firing eased as most of the attacking infantry marched away from the shattered ordnance depot. Three thousand men still surrounded it, but their orders now were to hold the heretics, not crush them. Their musketeers were conserving ammunition, and their artillery caissons were almost empty. Fresh ammunition wagons were on their way, but for now the Guardsmen concentrated on simply keeping the Malagorans pinned down.

Sean breathed a silent thanks for the lighter fire, but this was going to be tricky, and all of Folmak's regimental commanders and four of his six battalion COs were casualties. Losses among junior officers had been equally heavy, and getting the men sorted out took time. If the bad guys guessed what was coming and threw in an attack at just the wrong moment . . .

Folmak would retain what remained of his Third Regiment and half the First; the rest of the First would reinforce the Second for the breakout. The choice of units had been dictated by where the men were. The Third held what was left of the western wall, and they'd fall back to the main arsenal, covered by a hundred or so men already in the building, when Sean attacked to the east.

It was taking too long, he thought, but his people were moving as fast as humanly possible and then some. He crouched behind another pile of stone—this one had once been a workshop—and watched men filter into position around him. What had been regiments were now battalions, and battalions had become companies, but, one by one, officers raised their arms to indicate their readiness, and he drew a deep breath.

A dozen arlaks, double-shotted and loaded with grape for good measure, had been dragged into position under cover of the smoke. One man crouched behind each gun, watching Sean with intent eyes, and he slashed his arm downward.

A lethal blast screamed down the only eastbound street not blocked by flames as the gunners jerked their lanyards, then snatched up their own rifles. Shrieks of agony answered the unexpected salvo, and the torn, filthy survivors of B Company, Third Battalion, Second Regiment, First Brigade, lunged over the ruin of the depot wall with the high, shrill Malagoran yell.

The rest of the Second Regiment foamed in their wake, and Sean yanked Sandy to her feet and vaulted over the wall with the second wave. Tamman was ahead of them, leading B Company down the narrow street between two infernos which had once been warehouses, and rifles and muskets cracked in the hellish glare. The Malagorans charged through a cinder-raining furnace to strike the defenders before they recovered from the unexpected bombardment, and bayonets and pikes flashed in the bloody light of the flames.

Tamman crashed into the Guardsmen at B Company's head. A pike lunged at him, and he smashed it aside with a bio-enhanced arm and snatched the luckless pikemen bodily off his feet. The Guardsman wailed in terror, and Tamman hurled him away. More pikemen flew as the improvised projectile bowled them over, and Company B closed for the kill, firing as they came. A quarter of them went down, but the others carried through, and the blocking Guard infantry disintegrated before their bayonets.

"We're through, Sean!" Tamman yelled over the com.

"Don't stop to celebrate! Keep moving!"

The Second Regiment broke out of the fire-fringed street into the open on the heels of their foes. A reserve of two or three hundred Guardsmen looked up in astonishment as the ragged apparitions materialized, then took to its own heels in panic as the bayonets swept down upon it. Sean's column burst through the perimeter around the depot and vanished into the burning city, and Folmak Folmakson, listening to the fading sound of combat to the east as the last of his own men dashed into the arsenal, whispered a prayer for its safety.

Harriet MacIntyre stood at the rear of the army's encampment, white-faced and clinging to Stomald's hand as she watched mountains of smoke rise from the Temple. Her com was tied to Sean's, following her twin and her friends through the bedlam of the city's streets, and she longed with all her heart to be with them. But she couldn't be. She had to wait here, praying that they reached their objective. One hundred and ten kilometers further north, Brashan had abandoned his post aboard *Israel* and rode the cockpit of an Imperial fighter, poised just outside the computer's kill zone with a second fighter slaved to his controls. If Sean and the others could shut down the computer, he and Harriet could end the fighting in minutes . . . *if* they could shut down the computer.

Tibold Rarikson swore vilely as fresh combat roared on his right. He didn't fully understand what Lord Sean and the angels intended, and he was aghast at the risk his commander was running, but he was a soldier. He'd accepted his orders, yet he bitterly regretted the loss of intelligence from the Angel Harry. Her reports had become increasingly general as the confusion and smoke spread, but they'd given him a priceless edge. Now she could no longer provide them, and the Guard had finally gotten around his flank.

His men gave ground stubbornly, fighting every span of the way, but the Guard pikes ground forward. He sent three relatively fresh regiments racing west from his reserve and hoped it would be enough.

"What—?"

High Priest Vroxhan whirled towards the window as shots sounded right outside the Chancery, and his jaw dropped as bullets spun men around in the Place of Martyrs. A heretic attack *here*? It couldn't be!

But it was happening. Even as he watched, ragged, battle-stained men erupted into the open, fell into line, and poured a devastating, steadily mounting fire into the single understrength Guard company in the square. He stared at the carnage, unable to believe what he was seeing, then looked up as he sensed a presence at his side.

"Lord Marshal!" he gasped. "Have they broken through Therah?"

"Impossible!" Surak jerked a spyglass open and raised it to his eye, then swore and closed it with a snap. "They're from the depot, Holiness. No one else could have gotten here, and there's a man out there who's so tall he *has* to be 'Lord Sean.'"

"What are they doing out *here*?"

"Trying to escape . . . or to divert reinforcements from the North Gate. Either way, there's not enough of them to be a threat."

"*Can* they escape?"

"It's possible, Holiness. Not likely, but possible, especially if they go south instead of trying to link up with Tibold."

"Stop them! *Stop them!*" Vroxhan shouted.

"With what, Holiness? Aside from your personal guard, my headquarters troop, and the detachment at the Sanctum, every man I have is headed for North Gate."

Vroxhan started to speak once more, then closed his mouth and watched the heretics finish routing the hapless Guard company and reform into column. As Surak had predicted, they headed south, and the high priest clenched his fists in sullen hate. They were getting away. The leaders of this damnable heresy were *escaping* him, and as soon as they were safe, the rest of their army would break off its attack. Bile rose in his throat, and he raised his eyes from the vanishing demon-worshipers to the huge, white block of the Sanctum. *Why?* he demanded of God. *Why are You letting this* happen? *Why—*

And then his thoughts froze in a sudden flash of terrified intuition. Escape? They weren't trying to *escape*! As if God Himself had whispered it in his ear, Vroxhan knew where they were headed, and his blood ran chill.

"The Sanctum!" he gasped. The lord marshal looked at him blankly, and Vroxhan grabbed him and shook him. "They're headed for the Sanctum itself!"

"The— Why should they be, Holiness?"

"Because they're *demon-worshipers!*" Vroxhan half-screamed. "My God, man! They serve the powers of Hell—what if their masters have given them some means to destroy the *Voice*? If we lose its protection, how will we stop the *next* wave of demons from the stars?"

"But—"

"There's no *time*, Lord Marshal! Signal the Sanctum detachment now! Tell them they *must* keep the heretics from entering, then send every man you can find after them!"

"But there's only your own guard, Holiness, and—"

"Send them! *Send them!*" Vroxhan shook the lord marshal again. "No! I'll take them myself!" he cried wildly, and whirled away from Surak.

Tamman led the way. His men didn't like it, and they kept trying to get past him, to put themselves between him and any possible enemies, but he waved them sharply back whenever they did. He wasn't being heroic; he needed to be up front to scout their path with his implants.

The chaos in the streets was even worse than he'd feared. There were few Guardsmen about, but thousands of civilians had fled the fighting, and most of them seemed to be headed for the Sanctum to pray for deliverance. In fairness, they had the sense to scatter the instant they saw armed men coming up behind them, but even with panic to spur them on, they took time to get out of his way. Worse, with so many civilians moving around, it was hard to spot any Guard formations he might encounter.

The column moved quickly, when it could move at all, but its progress was a series of breathless dashes separated by slow, wading progress through the noncombatants, and Tamman was sorely tempted to order his men to open fire to chase the crowds off faster. He couldn't, but he was tempted.

He crossed a small square and looked up. The huge block of the Sanctum loomed ahead of him. Fifteen more minutes, he thought; possibly twenty.

"Faster! Faster!" Vroxhan shouted.

"Holiness, we can go no faster!" Captain Farnah, his personal guard's commander protested, waving at the civilians who clogged their path. "The people—"

"What do the *people* matter when demon-worshipers go to profane the very Sanctum of God?!" Vroxhan snapped, and his eyes were mad. He'd lost sight of the heretics while his guards mustered; they were up ahead somewhere, headed for the Sanctum. That was all he knew . . . and all he *needed* to know. "Clear the path, Captain! You have pikes; now *clear the path!*"

Farnah stared at him, as if unable to believe his orders, but Vroxhan snarled at him, and the Guardsman turned away. He shouted orders of his own, and within seconds Vroxhan heard the screams as the leading pikemen lowered their weapons, faces set like iron, and swept ahead. Men, women, even children were smashed aside or died, and the seven hundred men of Vroxhan's personal guard marched over their bodies.

The fighting on Tibold's right rose to a crescendo as the Guard threw his flank back eight hundred paces in a driving, brutal attack. But then the charging pikemen ran into pointblank, massed chagor fire, and the regiments Tibold had sent from the reserve crashed into them. It was the Guard's turn to reel back, yet they retreated only half the distance they'd come, then held sullenly, and now more Guard reinforcements were hammering his left.

He swore again, more vilely than ever. He was losing his momentum. He could feel the army's advance grinding to a halt amid the blazing ruins.

"Watch the wall! *Men on the wall!*" Tamman shouted as fifty musketeers suddenly rose over the parapet of the ornamental wall about the Sanctum. The square outside it was packed with civilians who screamed in terror as the Guardsmen leveled their muskets to pour fire into B Company's skirmish line, but Tamman's warning had come before they were in position. A withering blast of rifle fire met them, and, more horribly, the civilians between the two forces soaked up much of their own fire. Despite the cover of the waist-high parapet, they took heavier losses than the skirmishers, and then the rest of B Company came up with C Company in support, and their fire swept the wall clear.

Shrieking civilians stampeded madly, trampling one another in their terror, and Second Regiment drove across the blood-slick pavement for the gates. They were locked, but their delicate ivory panels and gold filigree were no match for the rifle butts of desperate men, and Second Regiment smashed its way through their priceless artistry like a ram.

Thirty or forty pikemen were trying to form up before the Sanctum's huge doors when the gates went down. They saw the "heretics" coming and fought to get set, but the Malagorans spread back out into a ragged firing line without orders. A sharp, deadly volley crashed out, and half the Guardsmen went down. The survivors fell back into the Sanctum itself, and Tamman started to lead his men after them, then skidded to a halt as Sean came up over his com.

"Trouble behind us, Tam! Five or six hundred men coming up fast!"

"I'm at the entry now," Tamman replied. "What do I do?"

"Secure the doors and put the rest of your men on the wall. We're going to have to detach a rearguard to keep these bastards off us."

"On it," Tamman agreed, and started shouting fresh orders.

"Holiness! The heretics!"

Vroxhan looked up at Farnah's shout, and then the first crackling musket fire rolled back from ahead. A bend in the street blocked his view, but he saw clouds of powder smoke and heard the screams of the wounded. Almost half his guard were musketeers, and they scattered into doorways and shop fronts, diving for cover to return fire while the pikemen jerked back around the corner to get out of range.

"Keep moving!" he snapped, but Farnah shook his head sharply.

"We can't, Holiness. They're inside the Sanctum's wall, and there must be three or four hundred of them with their damned rifles. We can't advance across the square against their fire. It's suicide."

"What do our lives matter compared to our *souls*?" Vroxhan raged.

"Holiness, if we advance, we die, and if we die, we can accomplish nothing to save the Sanctum," Farnah grated in a voice of iron.

"Damn you!" Vroxhan's hand slashed across the captain's face. "*Damn you! Don't you dare* tell me—"

He cocked his arm to swing again, but then he paused. He froze, oblivious to the naked fury on Farnah's reddened, swelling face, then grabbed the captain's arm.

"Wait! *Let* them hold the walls!"

"What do you mean?" Farnah half-snarled, but Vroxhan was already turning away.

"Bring half your men and follow me!"

Sean looked back as the rifles began to crack. He hated himself for leaving those men to hold that wall without him, yet he had no choice. They could hold it as well without him as with him, but only he, Sandy, or Tamman could access the computer.

They had only thirty men with them, the survivors of B and C Companies' original two hundred, as they clattered into the Sanctum. The original command bunker had been encircled, over the centuries, with chapels and secondary cathedrals, libraries and art galleries. It was a crazed rabbit warren of gorgeous tapestries and priceless artwork, and bloody boots thudded on rich carpet and floors of patterned marble as they pounded through it.

"Left, left, left," Sean muttered to himself as he felt the energy flows of the ancient command complex through his implants. "It has to be to the *left*, damn it, but where—"

"Got it, Sean!" Tamman shouted. "This way!"

Tamman swung sharply left down a stairway, and Sean caught Sandy's hand and half-dragged her after their friend, eyes gleaming as walls of marble and paneled wood gave way to bare ceramacrete. The command center was buried beneath the bunker, and boots and combat gear clattered in the deep well of the stairs. Here and there a man lost his footing and fell, but someone always dragged him back up, and the gasping urgency of their mission drove them on.

"Hatch!" Tamman yelled, and the men behind him suddenly slowed as they beheld the great, gleaming portal of Imperial battle steel. The Sanctum's guardians had ordered the computer to close the hatch, and for just an instant, religious dread held the Malagorans, but Tamman was oblivious to it as his implants sought the access software, and he grunted in triumph.

"No ID code," he muttered in English as Sean and Sandy pushed up beside him. "Guess the guys who set up this crazy religion figured the priesthood might forget it. Let me—ahh!"

His neural feed found the interface, and the Malagorans sighed as the huge hatch slid silently aside. They stared into the holiest of Pardalian holies, and their eyes were awed as they gazed at the man who'd opened the way.

"Come on!" Sean drew two pistols and shouldered past Tamman.

"*Blasphemer!*" someone screamed, and a sledgehammer punched into his breastplate as a musket roared, but the tough Imperial composites held. One of his pistols cracked viciously, and High Inquisitor Surmal's head exploded. His corpse tumbled back into the depths of the main display, blood pooling under the glitter of holographic stars, and Sean looked around quickly. None of the equipment was proper military design, and the Pardalians hadn't helped by covering the walls with Mother Church's trophies. Banners and weapons from the Schismatic Wars were everywhere, making it almost impossible to pick out details, and he snarled. Damn it, where the hell had they hidden—?

"There, Sean!" Sandy pointed, and Sean swallowed a curse as he saw the console. The bastards hadn't just switched the neural interfacing off; they'd physically disconnected it from the computer core.

"Tam, you're our best techie. Go! Get that thing back on-line!"

"Gotcha!" Tamman dashed across the command center, and Sean turned back to the men crowding through the hatch behind him. "In the meantime, let's get some security set up here. We need to—"

"*Sean!*" Sandy screamed, and he whirled just as a tapestry on the opposite wall was ripped aside and a musket flashed fire through the sudden opening. The ball whizzed past his head by no more than a centimeter, and he saw more men filling a five-meter-wide arch.

A tunnel! A goddamned tunnel *into the command center!*

Even as the thought flashed through his mind, he had time to wonder whether the original architect had installed it, or if it had been added by the Church's founders . . . and to realize it didn't really matter.

"Take 'em!" he bellowed. "Keep them off Tamman's back!"

His men answered with a snarl, and rifles barked like the hammer of God. Choking smoke filled the command center's vaulted chamber as muskets blazed back, yet for the first few seconds it all went the Malagorans' way, despite the surprise of their enemies' sudden arrival. They were spread out, able to pour more rounds into the arch than the Guardsmen could fire back, but three hundred men crowded the tunnel, pressing forward with fanatic devotion, and there was no time to reload.

"Hit 'em! Bottle 'em up!" Sean roared, and charged as the first Guardsmen broke out into the open.

His Malagorans charged at his heels, but the Guardsmen were charging, too. They'd left their pikes behind, unable to get through the tunnel with them, but their pikemen carried swords, maces, and battle-axes, and their musketeers hurled themselves forward with clubbed weapons.

"Malagor and Lord Sean!" someone howled.

"Holy God and no quarter!" the Guard bellowed back, and the two forces slammed together in a smoke-choked nightmare of hand-to-hand combat.

Sean rampaged at the head of his men, and his slender sword carved an arc of death before him. No unenhanced human could enter its reach and live, and he hacked his way towards the arch. If he could reach it, bottle them up inside it . . . But his men weren't enhanced. They couldn't match his strength and speed, and too many Guardsmen had gotten into the control center. They swirled about him, and he grunted in anguish as something slammed into his thigh from behind. His enhanced muscle and bone held, but blood oozed down his leg, and unenhanced or not, if they swarmed him under—

He fell back, cursing, strangling an enemy with his left hand even as he cut down two more with his sword, and someone swung a mace two-handed. It clanged into his breastplate and rebounded, staggering him despite his enhancement, but once more the Imperial composite held. Steel clashed and grated all about him, men screamed and died, and a Guardsman loomed suddenly before him, sword thrusting for his throat, and there was no time to dodge.

He saw the point coming, and then a battle-ax split his killer from crown to navel. Blood fountained over him, and he gasped in surprise as Sandy bounded past him. The ax she'd snatched from the trophies on the wall was as tall as she was, and she shrieked like a Valkyrie as she swung. She'd lost her helmet, and her brown eyes flashed fire as she cut a second man cleanly in half, and another voice screamed in horror.

"Demon! *Demon!*" it wailed as they realized she was a woman.

Guardsmen who'd been howling, fanatical warriors the instant before shrank from her in terror, and she snarled.

"*Come on, then, you bastards!*" she yelled in Imperial Universal, and a fresh wail of terror went up as the Guardsmen recognized the Holy Tongue in the mouth of a demon. She cut down another man, and for just a moment, Sean thought she was going to pull it off. But the men still in the tunnel couldn't see her. Ignorance immunized them against the terror of her presence, and the weight of their bodies drove the others forward.

Fresh pressure pushed the Malagorans back, and Sean and Sandy with them. Their infantry formed a wedge behind them, fighting to cover Lord Sean's and the Angel Sandy's backs, and they lunged forward once more while bodies flew away from them. Under any other circumstances, the Guardsmen probably would have fled from their "superhuman" foes, but the tunnel behind them was packed solid. They had to fight or die, and so they fought, and the howling bedlam of combat filled the command center.

Behind his friends, Tamman worked frantically, hands flying as he fought to reconnect the neural interface. He'd never seen one quite like this, and he was working as much by guess as by knowledge. Despite his total concentration on his task, he knew the Guardsmen were grinding forward. Sean and Sandy were worth fifty unenhanced men when it came to offense, but there were only two of them. Some of the Guardsmen were slipping past them, circling around to get at the merely mortal Malagorans behind them, and despite the reach advantage of the Malagorans' bayoneted rifles, they were going down. So far none of the attackers seemed to have noticed Tamman, but it was only a matter of time before one of them—

There! He made the last connection, flipped his neural feed into the console, and demanded access. There was a moment of utter silence, and then an utterly emotionless contralto spoke.

"ID code required for implant access. Please enter code," it said, and he stared at the console in horror.

✧   ✧   ✧

Sean gasped as another mace crunched into his left arm. The mail sleeve held and his implants overrode the pain and shock, but the blow had hurt him badly and he knew it. He staggered back, and Sandy whirled around him, graceful as a dancer as she swung her huge ax with dreadful precision. Sean's attacker went down without a scream, and he lashed out with his sword and killed another man before he could hit Sandy from behind.

"Sean! Sean, it's ID-coded!" He heard the voice, but it made no sense, and he hacked down another enemy. "Goddamn it, Sean, *it's ID-coded!*" Tamman bellowed, and this time he understood.

He turned his head just as Tamman hurtled past him. His friend's sword went before him, and Sean and Sandy followed. They forged forward, killing as they went, and this time there were three of them. Tamman took point, with Sean and Sandy covering his flanks, leaving a carpet of bodies in their wake, and at last, the Guardsmen began to yield. The sight of three demons— and they *must* be demons to wreak such carnage—coming straight for them was too much. They scattered out of their way, and Tamman reached the archway. His sword wove a deadly pattern before him, building a barricade of bodies to block the arch with the dead, and even with the weight of numbers pressing them forward, no man could break past him.

"Watch his back, Sandy!" Sean gasped, and turned back to the combat still raging in the command center. Only ten of his men still stood, but they'd formed a tight, desperate defensive knot in the center of the huge chamber, and he flung himself into the rear of their attackers.

The Guardsmen saw him coming and screamed in fear. They backed away, unwilling to face the demon, and their eyes darted to the arch by which they'd entered. Two more demons blocked it, cutting them off from their companions, but the main hatch was open, and they took to their heels, trampling one another in their desperate haste to escape with their souls.

The sounds of combat died. The tunnel was so choked with bodies no one could get to Tamman to engage him, even assuming they'd had the courage to try, and Sean leaned on his sword gasping for breath while the cold, hideous knowledge of failure filled him.

They'd come so close! Fought so hard, paid such a horrible price. Why hadn't it even occurred to him that the interface would be ID-coded?!

"Tam!" he croaked. "If the interface's coded, what about voice access?"

"Tried it," Tamman said grimly, never looking away from the tunnel while the surviving Malagoran infantry hastily reloaded and turned to cover the main hatch. "No good. They took out the regular verbal access and set up a series of stored commands when they cut out the interface. We could spend weeks trying to guess what to tell it to control the inner defenses!"

"Oh, God," Sean whispered, his face ashen. "God, what have we *done?* All those people—did we kill them for *nothing?*"

"Stop it, Sean!" Sandy was splashed from head to toe in blood, and her eyes still smoked as she rounded on him. "We don't have time for that! Think! There *has* to be a way in!"

"Why?" Sean demanded bitterly. "Because *we* want there to be one? We fucked up, Sandy. *I* fucked up!"

"No! There has to be—"

She froze, mouth half-open, and her eyes went huge.

"That's it," she whispered. "By all that's holy, that's *it!*"

"*What's* 'it'?" Sean demanded, and she gripped his good arm in fingers of steel.

"*We* can't access without the ID-code, but *you* can—maybe!"

"What are you *talking* about?"

"Sean, it's an *Imperial* computer. A *Fourth Empire* computer."

"So?" He stared at her, trying to comprehend, and she shook him violently.

"Don't you understand? It was set up by an Imperial *governor*. A direct representative of the Emperor!"

Comprehension wavered just beyond his grasp, and his eyes bored into hers, begging her to explain.

"You're the heir to the throne, second only to the Emperor himself in civil matters, *and you've been confirmed by Mother!* That means she buried the ID codes to identify you to any Imperial computer in your implants!"

"But—" Sean stared at her, and his brain lurched back into motion. "We can't be sure they were ever loaded," he argued, already turning to run towards the console. "Even if they were, it's going to take me time to work through them. Ten, fifteen minutes, minimum."

"So? You got anything else to do right now?" she demanded with graveyard humor, and he managed to smile.

"Guess not, at that," he admitted, and stopped beside the console.

"They're reforming on the stairs, Lord Sean!" one of the Malagorans called, and he turned, but Sandy shoved him back towards the console.

"You take care of the computer," she told him grimly. "*We'll* take care of the Guard."

"Sandy, I—" he began helplessly, and she squeezed his arm.

"I know," she said softly, then turned and ran for the hatch. "You, you, and you," she told three of the Malagorans. "Go watch the arch. Tam, over here! We've got company!"

"*Here they come!*" someone shouted, and Crown Prince Sean Horus MacIntyre closed his eyes and inserted his neural feed into the console.

CHAPTER FORTY-ONE

Ninhursag MacMahan rubbed weary eyes and tried to feel triumphant. A planet was an enormous place to hide something as small as Tsien's super bomb, but there was little traffic to Narhan, and most of it was simple personnel movement, virtually all of which went by mat-trans. Her people had started out by checking the logs for every mat-trans transit, incoming or outgoing, with a microscope and found nothing; now a detailed search from orbit had found the same. She couldn't be absolutely positive, but it certainly appeared the bomb had never been sent to the planet.

Which, unfortunately, made Birhat the most likely target, and Birhat would be far harder to search. There were more people and vastly more traffic, and swarms of botanists, biologists, zoologists, entomologists, and tourists had fanned out across its rejuvenated surface in the last twenty years. *Anyone* could have smuggled the damned thing in, and Maker alone knew where they might have stashed it if they had.

Of course, if it was in one of the wilderness areas, it shouldn't be *too* hard to spot. Even if it was covered by a stealth field, Imperial sensors should pick it up if they looked hard enough. But if Mister X had gotten it into Phoenix, it was a whole different ball game. The capital city's mass of power sources was guaranteed to confuse her sensors. Even a block-by-block or tower-by-tower scan wouldn't find it; her people would have to cover the city literally room by room, and that was going to take weeks or even months.

But at least they'd made progress. Assuming whoever had the thing didn't intend to blow up Earth herself, they'd reduced the possible targets to one planet. And, she thought with a frown, it was time to point that out.

"No."

"But, Colin—"

"I said no, 'Hursag, and I meant it."

Ninhursag sat back and puffed her lips in frustration. She and Hector sat in the imperial family's personal quarters facing Colin and a Jiltanith whose figure had changed radically over the past few months. Tsien Tao-ling, Amanda,

741

Adrienne Robbins, and Gerald Hatcher attended by hologram, and their expressions mirrored Ninhursag's.

" 'Hursag's right, Colin," Hatcher said. "If the bomb's not on Narhan, it's almost certainly here. It's the only thing that makes sense, given our estimate of Mister X's past actions."

"I agree." Colin nodded, yet his tone didn't yield a centimeter. "But I'm not going to have myself evacuated when millions of other people can't do the same thing."

"I'm only asking you to make a state visit to Earth!" Ninhursag snapped. "For Maker's sake, Colin, what are you trying to prove? Go to Earth and stay there till we find the damned thing!"

"*If* you find it," Colin shot back. "And I'm not going to do it."

"The people would understand, Colin," Tsien said quietly.

"I'm not thinking about public relations here!" Colin's voice was harsh. "I'm talking about abandoning millions of civilians to save my own skin, and I won't do it."

"Colin, you are being foolish," Dahak put in.

"So sue me!"

"If I believed it would change your mind, I would do just that," the computer replied. "As it will not, I can only appeal to the good sense which, upon rare occasion, you have exhibited in the past."

"Not this time," Colin said flatly, and Jiltanith squeezed his hand.

"Colin, there's something neither 'Hursag nor Dahak have pointed out," Amanda said. "If, in fact, Mister X killed the kids, and if he's the one who has the bomb, and *if* he's put it on Birhat, then you and 'Tanni are the reason. If you're not here, there's no point in his setting the thing off. By that standard, your moving to Earth might be the one thing that would keep him from detonating it before we find it."

"Amanda raises a most cogent point," Dahak agreed, and Colin frowned.

"Both Dahak and Amanda are correct," Tsien pressed as he sensed Colin weakening. "You are the Imperium's head of state, responsible for protecting the continuity of government and the succession, and if you and Jiltanith *are* 'Mister X's' targets, you may provoke him into action by remaining on Birhat."

"First," Colin said, "you're assuming he has some means of setting this thing off at will. To do that, he'd have to have someone here to transmit a firing order, which would just happen to kill whoever transmitted it. I'm willing to concede that he might have set up a patsy without telling the sucker what would happen, but Mister X himself certainly won't sit around on ground zero. That means he'd have to get the firing order to his patsy by hypercom, and 'Hursag and Dahak are monitoring all hypercom traffic. It's still possible he could sneak something past us, but, frankly, I doubt he'd risk it. I think the means of detonation are already in place with a specific timetable."

"I could take half of Battle Fleet through the holes in that logic," Adrienne said grimly.

"Maybe. I think it's valid, but you may have a point—which brings me to *my* second point. You're right about protecting the succession and the continuity of government, Tao-ling, but *I* don't have to go to Earth for that."

"Nay, my love!" Jiltanith's voice was sharp. "I like not thy words—nay, nor thy thought, either!"

"Maybe not, but Tao-ling's right, and so am I. One of us has to stay, 'Tanni. We can't just run out on our people. But if we send you to Earth, we protect both the government and the succession."

Jiltanith looked into his face for a moment, pressing a hand against her swollen abdomen, and her eyes were dark.

"Colin," she said very quietly, "already have I lost two babes. Wouldst make these yet unborn the pretext for my loss of thee, as well?"

"No," he said softly. His left hand captured hers, and he cupped her face in his right. "I don't intend to die, 'Tanni. But if there's any chance Mister X will hold his detonation schedule unless he can get both of us, then one of us has got to go. All right, I'm selfish enough to be glad of an excuse to get you out of the danger zone and protect you. I admit that. But you're pregnant, 'Tanni. Even if I *do* die, the succession is safe as long as you're alive. I'm sorry, babe, but it's your duty to go."

" 'Duty.' 'Protect.' " The words were a harsh, ugly curse in her lovely mouth. "Oh, how dearly have those words cost me o'er the centuries!"

"I know." He closed his eyes and drew her close, hugging her fiercely while their friends watched, and one hand stroked her raven's-wing hair. "I know," he whispered. "Neither of us asked for the job, but we've got it, love. Now we've got to do it. Please, 'Tanni. Don't fight me on this."

"Did it offer chance o' victory, then would I fight thee to the end," she said into his shoulder, and her voice was bleak. "Yet thou'rt what thou art, and I—I am *duty's* slave, and for duty's sake and the lives I bear within I will not fight thee. But know this, Colin MacIntyre. The day these babes draw breath do I leave them in Father's care and return hither, and not thou nor all the power of thy crown will stop me then."

"Jiltanith's coming early?" Lawrence Jefferson said. Horus nodded, and the Lieutenant Governor frowned. "Is something going on I should know about?"

"Going on?" Horus raised his eyebrows.

"Look, Horus, I know Jiltanith's planned all along for these children to be born on Earth, but she's not due for another month. Where she goes and what she does is her business, not mine, but I *am* Security Minister as well as Lieutenant Governor, and the Sword of God's still mighty active. Don't forget that bomb they planted right here in our own mat-trans facility! I wish she'd stay on Birhat where it's safe, but if she won't, I'm responsible for backing up her Marine security while she's here. So if there's any reason I should be thinking in terms of additional precautions, I'd like to know it."

"I think her security's more than adequate, Lawrence," Horus said after a moment. "I appreciate your concern, but this is just a daughter visiting her father. She'll be safe enough here inside White Tower."

"If you say so." Jefferson sighed. "Well, in that case, I should get busy. When, exactly, is she arriving?"

"Next Wednesday. You'll have almost a week to make any arrangements you think are necessary."

"That's good, anyway," Jefferson said dryly.

He left, and Horus sat gazing down at his blotter. Damn it, Lawrence was right. He *was* Security Minister, and he *should* be warned, but Ninhursag was adamant on maintaining strict need-to-know security on Mister X, and Colin backed her totally. Horus pursed his lips, then shook his head and made a mental note to buttonhole Colin for one more try to get Lawrence onto the cleared list when the Assembly of Nobles met week after next on Birhat.

Jefferson settled into his old-fashioned swivel chair and clenched his jaw. *Damn* the bitch! He'd gone to all this trouble to get her, Colin, Horus, Hatcher, and Tsien onto the same bull's-eye, and *she* had to decide to visit Daddy! Why couldn't she stay home on Birhat where she was safe from terrorists?

He swore again, then inhaled deeply and made himself relax. All right, it wasn't the end of the world. He couldn't change the timing on the detonation, but as he'd just told Horus, he *was* responsible for backing up her security detachment whenever she visited Earth. It shouldn't be too hard to arrange the right sort of backup. Sloppy, yes, and with the potential risk of pointing a finger at him after she was dead, but the operative point was that she—and the rest of them—would *be* dead by the time anyone started asking questions. He'd already set up an in-depth defense against such questions, and with Ninhursag killed along with the others, Security Minister Lawrence Jefferson would be the one responsible for answering them. Better still, he could probably make it look like a Sword of God operation, and with the Narhani branded with responsibility for the bomb and the Sword with responsibility for Jiltanith's assassination, he'd have all *sorts* of threats to justify whatever "temporary" special powers he chose to assume, now wouldn't he?

He smiled thinly and nodded. *All right, Your Majesty. You just come on home to Earth. I'll arrange a* special *homecoming for you.*

"Got those mat-trans logs you wanted, Ma'am."

Ninhursag looked up as Fleet Commander Steinberg entered her office. The newly promoted commander handed over the massive folio of datachips, but her face wore a thoughtful frown, and Ninhursag cocked an eyebrow at her.

"Something on your mind, Commander?"

"Well. . . ." Steinberg shrugged. "I'm sorry, Ma'am. I know I'm not cleared for everything, but this—" she gestured to the folio "—seems like a pretty peculiar, ah, line of inquiry for the head of ONI to handle personally. I know I'm not supposed to ask questions, but I'm afraid I haven't quite figured out how to turn my curiosity off on cue."

"A serious flaw in an intelligence officer." Ninhursag's voice was severe, but her eyes smiled, and she waved at a chair. "Sit, Commander."

Steinberg sank into the indicated chair and folded her hands in her lap. She looked like a uniformed high school student waiting for a pop quiz, but Ninhursag reminded herself this was the ice-cold interrogator who'd gotten them the break that proved the bomb's existence. Commander Steinberg had been a major asset ever since her transfer to Birhat, and Ninhursag had already added her to her mental list of possible successors to take over at ONI when she stepped down in another century or two. She had no intention of telling *Steinberg* that, but perhaps it was time to bring her up to speed on Mister X and see what her talents could do to push the bomb search here on Birhat.

"You're right, Esther," she said after a moment. "It *is* a peculiar thing to ask for, but I've got a rather peculiar reason for wanting it. And since you can't turn your curiosity off, I think you've just talked yourself into a new job." She flipped the folio back to Steinberg, and smiled at the commander's look of surprise. "You're now in charge of analyzing these for me, Commander, but before you start, let me tell you a little story. You've already played a not so minor part in it yourself, even if you didn't know it."

She tipped her chair back, and though her voice remained whimsical, her expression was anything but.

"Once upon a time," she began, "there was a person named Mister X. He wasn't a very nice person, and . . ."

"Good to see you, 'Tanni. Maker, you look wonderful!"

"Art a poor liar, Father." Jiltanith smiled and returned Horus' hug while Tinker Bell's pups lolled on the rug at their feet. "Say rather that I do most resemble a blimp, and thou wouldst speak but truth!"

"But I always liked blimps," her father said with a grin. "Zeppelins were nicer, though. Did I ever tell you I was aboard the *Hindenburg* for her first transatlantic crossing in 1936? Didn't appear on the manifest, because I was hiding from Anu at the time, but I was there. Won eight hundred dollars at poker during the crossing." He shook his head. "Now *there* was a civilized way to travel! I was always glad I wasn't at Lakehurst in '37."

"Nay, Father, thou didst not tell me, yet now I think upon it, 'twould be the sort of thing thou wouldst like."

"Yes." He sighed and his smile faded. "You know, despite all the terrible things I've seen in my life, I'll always be glad I've seen so *much*. Not many of us get the chance to watch an entire planet discover the universe."

"No," she said, and his eyes darkened and fell at the involuntary bitterness that cored the single, soft word.

" 'Tanni," he said quietly, "I'm sorry. I know—"

"Hush, Father." She pressed her fingers to his mouth. "Forgive me. 'Tis only being sent to 'safety' once more maketh my tongue so bitter." She smiled sadly. "Well do I know thou didst the best thou couldst. 'Twas not our fate to live the lives we longed to live."

"But—"

"Nay, Father. Say it not. Words change naught after so many years." She smiled again, and shook her head. "Now am I weary, and by thy mercy will I seek my bed."

"Of course, 'Tanni." He hugged her again and watched her leave the room, then walked to the window and stared sightlessly out over Shepard Center. She would never truly forgive him, he thought. She couldn't, any more than he could blame her for it, but she was right. He'd done the best he could.

Tears burned, and he wiped them angrily. All those years. Those millennia while she'd slept in stasis. He and the rest of *Nergal*'s crew had rotated themselves in and out of stasis, using it to spin their own lives out beyond mortal imagination in their war against Anu, yet he hadn't been able to let her do the same. He'd *kept* her in stasis, for he'd been unable not to, and his weakness was his deepest shame. Yet he'd lost too much, given too much, to change it. Her mother had never escaped from the original mutiny aboard *Dahak*, and he'd almost lost 'Tanni, as well, when her child's mind broke under the horrors of that blood-soaked day.

No, he told himself bitterly, he *had* lost that child that day. When one of his own Terra-born granddaughters managed to heal her, somehow, she'd been someone else, someone who'd survived only by walling herself off utterly from the broken person she once had been. A person who never again spoke Universal, but only the fifteenth-century English she'd learned. One who never, ever again called him "Poppa," but only "Father."

He'd been unable to risk that person again, unable to bring himself to lose her twice, and so, against her will, he'd sent her back into stasis and kept her there another five hundred years, until *Nergal*'s dwindling manpower forced him to release her from it. He'd turned her into a symbol, his defiant challenge to the universe which had taken all he loved. He . . . would . . . *not* . . . lose . . . her . . . again!

And so he hadn't. He'd kept her safe, and in doing so, he'd robbed her of so much. Of the foster mother who'd saved her mind, of her chance to fight by his side for all those centuries—of her right to live her own life on her own terms. He knew, knew to the depths of his soul, how unspeakably lucky he was that, somehow, she'd learned to love him once more when he finally did release her. It was a reward his selfish cowardice could never deserve, and, oh Maker of Grace and Mercy, he was so *proud* of her. Yet he could never undo what he'd done, and of all the bitter regrets of his endless life, that knowledge was the bitterest of all.

Planetary Duke Horus closed his eyes and inhaled sharply, then shook himself and walked slowly from his daughter's apartment in silence.

CHAPTER FORTY-TWO

"Got a second, Ma'am?"

Esther Steinberg stood in the door of Ninhursag's office once more, and Ninhursag's eyebrows rose in surprise. It was the middle of the night, and Steinberg had been off duty for hours. But then she frowned. The commander was in civvies, and from the looks of things she'd dressed in a hurry.

"Of course I do. What's on your mind?"

Steinberg stepped inside the door and waited for it to close behind her before she spoke.

"It's those mat-trans records, Ma'am."

"What about them? I thought you and Dahak cleared all of them."

"We did, Ma'am. We found a couple of small anomalies, but we tracked those down, and aside from that, everything was right on the money."

"So?"

"I guess it's just that curiosity bump again, Ma'am, but I haven't been able to get them out of my mind." Steinberg smiled crookedly. "I've been going back over them on my own time, and, well, I've found a new discrepancy."

"One Dahak missed?" Ninhursag couldn't keep from sounding skeptical.

"No, Ma'am. A *new* discrepancy."

"New?" Ninhursag jerked upright in her chair. "What d'you mean, 'new,' Esther?"

"You know we've been pulling regular updates on the mat-trans logs ever since you put me on the project?" Ninhursag nodded impatiently, and Steinberg shrugged. "Well, I started playing with the data—more out of frustration at not finding any answers than anything else—and I had my personal computer run a check for anomalies *within* the database. Any sort of conflict between downloads from the mat-trans computers on a generational basis, as well as a pure content one."

"And?"

"I just finished the last one, Ma'am, and one of the log entries in my original download doesn't match the version in the most recent one."

"What?" Ninhursag frowned again. "What do you mean, 'doesn't match'?"

"I mean, Ma'am, that according to the mat-trans facility records, I have two different logs with precisely the same time and date stamp, both completely official by every test I can run, that say two different things. It's only a small variation, but it shouldn't be there."

"Corrupted data?" Ninhursag murmured, and Steinberg shook her head.

"No, Ma'am. *Different* data. That's why I came straight over." Her mouth tightened in a firm line. "I may be paranoid, Admiral, but the only reason I can think of for the difference is that between the time we pulled the first log and the time we got the latest update, someone changed the entry. And under the circumstances, I thought I should tell you. Fast."

"Esther's right," Ninhursag said grimly. She and the commander sat in Colin's Palace office. Steinberg looked acutely uncomfortable at being in such close proximity to her Emperor, but she met Colin's searching look squarely as he rubbed his bristly chin. "I double-checked her work, and so did Dahak. Someone definitely changed the entry, and that, Colin, took someone with a *hell* of a lot of juice."

"Are you telling me," Colin said very carefully, "that the goddamned bomb is sitting directly under the Palace right this instant?"

"I'm telling you *something* is sitting under the Palace." Ninhursag's voice was flat. "And whatever it is, it isn't the statue that left Narhan. The mass readings matched perfectly in the first log entry, but they're off by over twenty percent in the second one. You have any idea why *else* that might be?"

"But, good God, 'Hursag, how could anyone make a switch? And if they pulled it off in the first place without our catching it, why change the logs so anyone who checked would *know* they had?"

"I don't know that yet, but I think we're going to have to reconsider our theory that Mister X and the Sword of God are two totally separate threats. I find it extremely hard to believe the Sword just *coincidentally* blew up the officer who oversaw the statue's transit here the very night he did it. If Esther hadn't caught the discrepancy in masses, we never would have connected the two events; now it hits me right in the eye."

"Agreed. Agreed." Colin leaned back with a worried frown. "Dahak?"

"My remotes are only now getting into position, Colin," Dahak's mellow voice replied from thin air. "It is most fortunate Commander Steinberg pursued this line of inquiry. It would never have occurred to me—I have what I believe humans call a blind spot in that I assume that data, once entered, will not subsequently metamorphose—and the Palace's security systems would almost certainly have prevented our orbital scans from detecting anything. Even now—"

He broke off so suddenly Colin blinked.

"Dahak?" There was no response, and his voice sharpened. "*Dahak?*"

"Colin, I have made a grave error," the computer said abruptly.

"An error?"

"I should not have inserted my remotes so promptly. I fear my scan systems have just activated the bomb."

"*The bomb?*" Even now Colin hadn't truly believed, not with his emotions, and his face went pale.

"Indeed." The computer's voice seldom showed emotion, but it was bitter now. "I cannot be certain it is *the* bomb, for I had insufficient time for detailed scans before I was forced to shut down. But there is a device of some sort within the statue—one protected by a Fleet anti-tampering system."

The humans looked at one another in stunned silence, and then Ninhursag cleared her throat.

"What . . . what sort of system, Dahak?"

"A Mark Ninety, multi-threat remote weapon system sensor," the computer said flatly. "My scan activated it, but it would appear I was able to shut down before it reached second-stage initiation. It is now armed, however. Any attempt to approach with additional scan systems or with anything which its systems might construe as a threat, will, in all probability, result in the device's immediate detonation."

"'Tanni! 'Tanni, wake up!"

Jiltanith sat up as quickly as her pregnant condition allowed, and the shaking hand released her. She rubbed her eyes and stared at her father, and the ghosts of sleep fled as his expression registered.

"Father? What passeth?"

"They think they've found the bomb," he said grimly. Her eyes flew wide, and his mouth twisted. "It's under the Palace, 'Tanni—hidden inside the Narhani's statue."

"Jesu!" Her eyes narrowed. There'd been a time when she'd personally managed *Nergal*'s Terra-born intelligence net against Anu, and she hadn't lost the habits of thought that had engendered. "'Tis a ploy most shrewd," she murmured now. "Should it be discovered, as, indeed, 'twould seem it hath, then would all assume 'twas the Narhani concealed it there."

"That's what we think," Horus agreed, but his voice's harshness warned her he hadn't yet told her everything, and her eyes demanded the rest. "It's armed and active," he said sighing, "and it's covered by an antitampering system. We can't get to it to disarm it, or even to destroy it."

"*Colin!*" Jiltanith whispered, and clutched her father's arm.

"He's all right, 'Tanni!" Horus said quickly, covering her hand with his own. "He and Gerald and Adrienne are activating the evacuation plan now. He's fine."

"Nay!" Her fingers tightened like talons. "Father, thou knowest him too well for that, as I! He will not flee so long as any of his folk do stand exposed to such danger!"

"I'm sure—" Horus began, but she shook her head spastically and threw off the covers. She swung her feet to the floor and stood, already reaching for her clothing.

"I must go to him! Mayhap, were I there, I—"

"No, 'Tanni." Her head snapped around, and he shook his head.

"I tell thee I am going." Her voice was chipped ice, but he shook his head, and her tone turned colder still. "Gainsay me in this at thy peril, Father!"

"Not me, 'Tanni," he said softly. "Colin. He's ordered me to keep you here and keep you safe."

Her eyes locked with his, and her fear for her husband struck him like a lash. But he refused to look away, and a dark, terrible sorrow, like a premonition of yet more loss, twisted her face.

"Father, *please*," she whispered, and he closed his eyes, unable to face her pain, and shook his head once more.

"I'm sorry, 'Tanni. It was Colin's decision, and he's right."

"Dahak is correct," Vlad Chernikov said. "We dare not send any additional scanners into the gallery, but I have deployed passive systems from beyond a Mark Ninety's activation threshold and carried out a purely optical scan using the Palace security systems. While I can find no outward visual evidence, our passive systems have detected active emissions from a broad-spectrum sensor array which are entirely consistent with a Mark Ninety's. I fear that any remote—or, for that matter, any human with Imperial equipment—entering the gallery will cause it to detonate."

"God." Colin closed his eyes, propped his elbows on the conference table, and leaned his face into his palms.

"The evacuation will begin in twenty-five minutes," Adrienne Robbins' holo image said. "I'll coordinate embarkation from the Academy; Gerald will handle ship-to-ship movement from Mother, but we don't have enough ships in-system to handle the entire population."

"Some additional transport'll begin arriving in about ninety-three hours," Hatcher's image said. "Mother sent out an all-ships signal as soon as I got the word. We'll have another six planetoids within a hundred and fifty hours; anything after that'll take at least ten days to get here."

"How many can we get aboard the available ships?" Colin asked tautly.

"Not enough," Hatcher said grimly. "Dahak?"

"Assuming *Dahak* is used as well, and that we move as many as possible to existing deep-space life support in-system but beyond lethal radius of the weapon, we will be able to lift approximately eighty-nine percent of the Birhat population from the planet," the computer responded. "More than that will be beyond our resources."

"Mat-trans?" Colin said.

"On our list," Adrienne replied, "but the system's too big an energy hog to move people quickly, Colin. It's going to take at least three weeks to move eleven percent of Birhat's population through the facility."

"We don't *have* three weeks!"

"Colin, all we can do is all we can do." Gerald Hatcher didn't look any happier than Colin, but his voice was crisp.

"We've got to take that bomb out," Colin muttered. "Damn it, there *has* to be a way!"

"Unfortunately," Dahak said, "we cannot disarm it. That means we can only attempt to destroy it, which will require a weapon sufficient to guarantee its instant and complete disablement from outside the Mark Ninety's perimeter, and the device is located in the most heavily protected structure on Birhat. While we possess many weapons which could assure its destruction, the Palace's structural strength is such that any weapon of sufficient power would effectively destroy Phoenix, as well. In short, we cannot ourselves 'take out' the device without obliterating the Imperium's capital, and all in it."

"Horus! What the hell is going on?" Lawrence Jefferson had commed from Van Gelder Center, Planetary Security's central facility, not his White Tower office, and like many of the people swarming about behind him, he looked as if he'd dressed in the dark in a hurry. Horus wondered how he'd gotten to Van Gelder so quickly, but he wasn't about to look a gift horse in the mouth.

"Big trouble, Lawrence," he replied. "Get as many of your people as you can to the mat-trans facility. We're going to have thousands of people coming through from Birhat, starting in about—" he checked his chrono "—twelve minutes."

"*Thousands of people?*" Jefferson shook his head like a punch-drunk fighter, and Horus bared his teeth.

"Some lunatic's put a bomb under the Palace, and the damned thing's got an active antitampering system," he said, and watched Lawrence Jefferson go bone-white. The Lieutenant Governor said absolutely nothing for a moment, then shook himself.

"A bomb? What sort of bomb? It sounds like you're evacuating the entire planet!"

"We are," Horus said grimly. "This thing's probably powerful enough to take out all of Birhat—and Mother."

"With a single *bomb*? You're joking!"

"I wish I were. We've been looking for the damned thing for months. Well, now we've found it."

"What about the Emperor?" Jefferson demanded.

"He's hanging in until the last minute, the damned young fool! Says he won't leave until he can get everyone else out."

"And Jiltanith?" Jefferson asked quickly, and Horus smiled more naturally.

"Thanks for asking, but she's safe. She's still in White Tower, and she's staying here, by the Maker, if I have to chain her to the wall!"

Jefferson closed his eyes for a moment, mind racing, then nodded sharply.

"All right, Horus, I'm on it."

"Good man! I'll be down to give you a hand as quick as I can."

"Don't!" Horus raised an eyebrow at the Lieutenant Governor's quick, sharp reply, and Jefferson shook his head angrily. "Sorry. Didn't mean to bark at you. It's just that you can't do anything down here that *I* can't do just as well, and from your tone of voice, Her Majesty isn't too happy at staying here on Earth."

"That," Horus agreed, "is putting it mildly."

"Well, in that case you'd better stay there and keep an eye on her. God knows no one *else* on this planet has the seniority—or the balls!—to tell her no if she orders them out of her way. Besides, it's going to be a mad-house down here when refugees start coming through. I'll feel better with both of you tucked away someplace nice and safe, where whoever's behind this can't get at you in the confusion."

"I—" Horus started to reply, then stopped himself and nodded unwill-ingly. "You may be being paranoid, but you may also be right. I can't see why anyone would want me dead if they can't get 'Tanni and—please the Maker—Colin, but whoever's behind this has to be a lunatic."

"Exactly." Jefferson gave him a grim smile. "And if he's a lunatic, who knows what he may do if he thinks the wheels are coming off?"

CHAPTER FORTY-THREE

Lawrence Jefferson stared at the blank com screen. How? How had they *found* it? Had he come this far, worked this hard, to fail at the last minute?!

A fisted hand pounded his knee under cover of his borrowed desk, and a chill stabbed him as something else Horus had said struck home. If they'd been hunting the bomb "for months," they knew far more than he'd imagined. Ninhursag! It had to be Ninhursag, and that gave ONI's increased activities on Earth a suddenly sinister cast. Obviously they hadn't ID'ed him, but if they'd deduced the bomb's existence, what *else* had they picked up along the way?

He drew a deep breath and closed his eyes. All right. They knew the bomb was there and active, but if they'd known more, Horus would have said so. Which meant they *didn't* know it would detonate twelve hours after the Mark Ninety activated. Would they assume the fact that it hadn't *instantly* detonated meant it wouldn't unless they triggered it somehow?

He bit his lip. The bomb had originally been timed to detonate during the next meeting of the Assembly of Nobles, when Horus would be on Birhat with Colin, Jiltanith, and both the Imperium's senior military commanders. That would have gotten all five of them at once, but now they were spread out in two different star systems and they knew someone was after them, which meant the chance of recreating that opportunity was unlikely ever to come again. Yet Horus said Colin was going to "hang in" to the last possible minute, and Hatcher and Tsien must be up to their necks in the evacuation operation. Even if they guessed time was short, their efforts to save Birhat's population were almost certain to keep the two officers within the danger zone until too late. But by the same token, both of them would be doing everything they could to convince Colin to leave, and if he gave in, he'd evacuate to *Dahak.* Any other ship would be unthinkable, and if Colin MacIntyre got away from Birhat aboard *Dahak,* very few things in the universe—and certainly nothing Lawrence Jefferson had—could get to him.

The Lieutenant Governor hesitated in an atypical agony of indecision. There was still a chance Colin would die with his senior military commanders. If that happened, and if Jefferson could insure Horus and Jiltanith died as well, his original plan would still work. But if Horus and Jiltanith died and Colin *didn't*, he'd move in with Battle Fleet and the Imperial Marines. He'd take Earth apart stone by stone, and the hell with due process, to find the man who'd destroyed Birhat and murdered his wife, unborn children, and father-in-law, and when he did—

Jefferson shuddered, and the panicked part of his brain gibbered to give it up. They didn't know who he was yet. If he folded his hand and faded away, they might *never* know. In time, if they continued to trust him, he might actually have the chance to try again. But he couldn't count on eluding their net, not when he didn't know how much they'd already learned, and the gambler in his soul shouted to go banco. It was all on the table, everything he had, all he'd hoped and dreamed and worked for. Success or failure, absolute power or death: all of it hinged on whether or not Colin MacIntyre agreed to leave Birhat within the next twelve hours, and Jefferson wanted to scream. He was a chess master who calculated with painstaking precision. How was he supposed to calculate *this*? All he could do was guess, and if he guessed wrong, he died.

He pounded his knee one more time, and then his shoulders relaxed. If he stopped now and they found him out, the crimes he'd already committed would demand his execution, and that meant it was really no choice at all, didn't it?

"—so Adrienne's parasites are embarking their first loads now, and my Marines have taken over at the mat-trans," Hector MacMahan reported. "So far, there seems to be more shock than panic, but I don't expect that to last."

"Do you have enough men to control a panic if it starts?" Hatcher asked. "I can reinforce with Fleet personnel if you need them."

"I'll take you up on that," MacMahan said gratefully.

"Done. And now," Hatcher's holo-image turned to Colin, "will you *please* get aboard a ship and move out beyond the threat zone?"

"No."

"For Maker's sake, Colin!" Ninhursag exploded. "Do you *want* this thing to kill you?"

"No, but if it hasn't gone off yet, maybe it won't unless we *set* it off."

"And maybe the goddamned thing is ticking down right now!" MacMahan snapped. "Colin, if you don't get out of here willingly, then I'll have a battalion of Marines *drag* your ass off this planet!"

"No, you won't!"

"I'm responsible for your safety, and—"

"And I am your goddamned Emperor! I never wanted the fucking job, but I've got it, and I will by God *do* it!"

"Good. Fine! Shoot me at dawn—if we're both still alive!" MacMahan snarled. "Now get your butt in gear, *Sir*, because I'm sending in the troops!"

"Call him off, Gerald," Colin said in a quiet, deadly voice, but Hatcher's holo-image shook its head.

"I can't do that. He's right."

"Call him off, or I'll have Mother do it for you!"

"You can try," Hatcher said grimly, "but only the hardware listens to her. Or are you saying that if Hector drags you aboard a ship with a million civilian evacuees you'll have Mother order its comp cent not to leave orbit?"

Colin's furious eyes locked with those of Hatcher's image, but the admiral refused to look away. A moment of terrible tension hovered in the conference room, and then Colin's shoulders slumped.

"All right," he grated, and his voice was thick with hatred. Hatred that was all the worse because he knew his friends were right. "All right, goddamn it! But I'll go aboard *Dahak*, not another ship."

"Good!" MacMahan snapped, then sighed and looked away. "Colin, I'm sorry. *God*, I'm sorry. But I can't let you stay. I just *can't*."

"I know, Hector." It was Colin's turn to turn away, and his voice was heavy and old, no longer hot. "I know," he repeated quietly.

Brigadier Alex Jourdain sealed his Security tunic and looked around his comfortable apartment. He'd lived well for the last ten years; now the orders he'd just received were likely to take it all away, and more, yet he was in far too deep to back out, and if they pulled it off after all—

He drew a deep breath, checked his grav gun, and headed for the transit shaft.

"'Tanni, I—" Horus cut himself off as Jiltanith, still in her nightgown, turned from the window and he saw her tears. His face twisted, and he closed his mouth and started to leave, but she held out a hand.

"Nay, Father," she said softly. He turned back to her, then reached out to take her hand, and she smiled and pulled him closer. "Poor Father," she whispered. "How many ways the world hath wounded thee. Forgive my anger."

"There's nothing to forgive," he whispered back, and pressed his cheek to her shining hair. "Oh, 'Tanni! If I could undo my life, make it all different—"

"Then would we be gods, Father, and none of us the people life hath made us. In all I have ever known of thee, thou hast done the best that man might do. 'Twas ever thy fate to fight upon thy knees, yet never didst thou yield. Not to Anu, nor to the Achuultani, nor to Hell itself. How many, thinkest thou, might say as much?"

"But I built my Hell myself," he said quietly. "Brick by brick, and I dragged you into it with me." He closed his eyes and held her tight. "Do . . . do you remember the last thing you ever said to me in Universal, 'Tanni?"

She stiffened in his arms, but she didn't pull away, and after a moment, she shook her head.

"Father, I recall so little of those days." She pressed her face harder into his shoulder. "'Tis like some dark, horrible dream, one that e'en now haunteth my sleep on unquiet nights, yet when waking—"

"Hush. Hush," he whispered, and pressed his lips into her hair. "I don't want to hurt you. Maker knows I've done too much of that. But I want you to understand, 'Tanni." He drew a deep breath. "The last thing you ever said was 'Why didn't you *come*, Poppa? Why didn't you love us?' " Her shoulders shook under his hands, and his own voice was unsteady. " 'Tanni, I *always* loved you, and your mother, but you were right to hate me." She tried to protest, but he shook his head. "No, listen to me, please. Let me say it." She drew a deep, shuddering breath and nodded, and he closed his eyes.

" 'Tanni, I talked your mother into supporting Anu. I didn't realize what a monster he was—then—but I was the one who convinced her. Everything that happened to you—to her—was my fault. It was, and I know it, and I've always known it, and, O Maker, I would sell my very soul never to have done it. But I could never undo it, never find the magic to make it as if it had never happened. A father is supposed to protect his children, to keep them safe, and that—" his voice broke, but he made himself go on "—that was why I put you back into stasis. Because I knew I'd failed. Because I'd proven I couldn't keep you safe any other way. Because . . . I was afraid."

"Father, Father! Dost'a think I knew that not?" She shook her head.

"But I never told you," he said softly. "I cost us both so much, and I never had the courage to *tell* you I knew what I'd done and ask you to forgive me."

Colin paced the conference room like a caged animal, fists pounding together before him while he awaited his own cutter, and his brain raced. The evacuation Adrienne and Hatcher had planned but never been able to rehearse was going more smoothly than he would have believed possible, but all of them knew they weren't going to get everyone out. Unless they could deactivate the bomb, millions of people would die, yet how in God's name did you deactivate something you couldn't approach with as much as a scanpack, much less the weapons to—

He stopped suddenly, then slammed himself down in his chair and opened his neural feed to Dahak wide.

"Give me everything on the Mark Ninety," he said sharply.

The door chime sounded, and Horus turned from Jiltanith to answer it. "Yes?"

"Your Grace, it's Captain Chin," an urgent voice said. "Sir, I think you'd better come out here. I just tried to com the mat-trans center, and the links are all down."

"That's impossible," Horus said reasonably. "Did you call Maintenance?"

"I tried to, Your Grace. No luck. And then I tried my fold-com." The captain drew a deep breath. "Your Grace, it didn't work either."

"*What?*" Horus opened the door and stared at the Marine.

"It didn't work, Sir, and I've never seen anything like it. There's no obvious jamming, the coms just don't work, and it'd take a full-scale warp suppressor within four or five hundred meters to lock a Fleet com out of hyper-space." The captain faced Horus squarely. "Your Grace, with all due respect, we'd better get Her Majesty the hell out of here. Right now."

"You know, it might just work," Vlad Chernikov murmured.

"Or set the thing the hell off!" Hector MacMahan objected.

"A possibility," Dahak agreed, "yet the likelihood is small, assuming the force of the explosion were sufficient. What Colin suggests is, admittedly, a brute force solution, yet it has a certain conceptual elegance."

"Let me get this straight," MacMahan said. "We can't get near the thing, but you people want to pile explosives on top of it and set them off? *Are you out of your frigging minds?*"

"The operative point, General," Dahak said, "is that a Mark Ninety is programmed to recognize *Imperial* threats."

"So?"

"So we don't use Imperial technology," Colin said. "We use old-fashioned, pre-Imperial, Terran-made HE. A Mark Ninety would no more recognize those as a threat than it would a flint hand-ax."

"HE from where?" MacMahan demanded. "There isn't any on Birhat. For that matter, I doubt there's any on Terra after this long!"

"You are incorrect, General," Dahak said calmly. "Marshal Tsien has the materials we require."

"I do?" Tsien sounded surprised.

"You do, Sir. If you will check your records, you will discover that your ordnance disposal section has seventy-one pre-Siege, megaton-range nuclear warheads confiscated by Imperial authorities in Syria four years ago."

"I—" Tsien paused, and then his holo-image nodded. "As usual, you are correct, Dahak. I had forgotten." He looked at MacMahan. "Lawrence's Security personnel stumbled across them, Hector. We believe they were cached by the previous regime before you disarmed it on Colin's orders before the Siege. Apparently, even the individuals who hid them away had forgotten about them, and they were badly decayed—they used a tritium booster, and it had broken down. They were sent here for disposal, but we never got around to it."

"You want to use *nukes*?" MacMahan yelped.

"No," Dahak said calmly, "but these are *Terran* warheads, which rely on shaped chemical charges to initiate criticality, and each of them contains several kilograms of the compound Octol."

"And how do you get the explosives into position?" MacMahan asked more normally.

"Somebody walks in, sets them, fuses them, and walks back out again," Colin said. MacMahan raised an eyebrow, and Colin shrugged. "It should work, as long as he doesn't have any active Imperial hardware on him."

"Background radioactivity?" Hatcher asked. "If this stuff's been squirreled away inside a nuclear warhead for twenty-odd years, it's bound to have picked up some contamination."

"Not sufficient to cross a Mark Ninety's threshold," Dahak replied.

"You're certain?" Hatcher pressed, then waved a hand. "Forget that. You never make unqualified statements if you *aren't* certain, do you?"

"Such habits imply a certain imprecision of thought," Dahak observed, and despite the tension, Colin smiled, then sobered.

"I think we have to try it. It's a risk, but it's the smallest one I can come up with, and you may be right about a timer, Hector. We don't have time to come up with an ideal, no-risk solution."

"Agreed. How long to strip out the explosives and get them down here, Dahak?"

"I have already initiated the process, General. I estimate that they could be delivered to the Palace within twenty minutes in their present state, but I would prefer to reshape them into a proper configuration for maximum destructive effect, which will require an additional hour."

"Eighty minutes?" MacMahan rubbed his chin, then nodded. "All right, Colin, I'll vote for it."

"Gerald? Tao-ling?" Both officers nodded, and Colin glanced at Chernikov.

"I, too," the Russian said. "In fact, I would prefer to place the charge myself."

"I don't know, Vlad—" Colin began, but MacMahan interrupted crisply.

"If you were thinking about doing it yourself, you can just rethink. Whatever happens down here, you, personally, are going to be aboard *Dahak* and outside the lethal zone when we set it off. And if *you* know anybody better equipped for the job than Vlad, *I* don't." Colin opened his mouth, but MacMahan fixed him with a challenging eye and he closed it again.

"Good," MacMahan said.

"Suppressor's active, Brigadier," the Security tech said, never looking up from his remote panel. "Their coms are blocked."

"Elevators and switchboard?" Brigadier Jourdain asked, and another man looked up.

"Shut down. They've pulled almost all the regular Security people for crowd control, and I've cut the links to the lobby station. We're placing the charges to blow the switchboard when we leave now; it'll look just like a Sword of God hit, Sir."

"All right." Jourdain faced his handpicked traitors. "Remember, these are Imperial Marines. There's only twelve of them, but they're tough, well trained, and if they've tried their coms since the suppressor went on-line, they're going to be ready. Our coms are out, too, so stick to the plan. Don't improvise unless you have to."

His men nodded grimly.

"All right. Let's do it."

Horus stood outside Jiltanith's bedroom while she jerked on clothes, and his mind raced. It was preposterous. He was in his own HQ building in the middle of Earth's capital city, and he couldn't even place a com call! There could be only one reason for that, but how had "Mister X" pulled it off? Captain Chin was right. The only thing that could shut down fold coms without active jamming was close proximity to a warp suppressor, but a suppressor powerful enough to do the job was far too large to have been smuggled through White Tower's security . . . which meant someone on his own security staff must have brought it in, and if he'd been penetrated that completely—

He crossed to his desk and touched a button, and the desktop swung smoothly up. The habits of millennia of warfare die hard, and despite his fear, he smiled wolfishly as he lifted the energy gun from its nest. He punched the self-test button, and the ready light glowed just as the bedroom door opened . . . and Captain Chin half-ran into his office.

"Your Grace," the Chinese officer said flatly, "the elevators are out, too."

"Shit!" Horus closed his eyes, then shook himself. "Stairs?"

"We can try them, Sir, but if they've cut the coms and elevators, they're already on their way. And without the elevators—"

"Without the elevators, they're coming up the stairs," Horus grunted. Wonderful. Just fucking wonderful! Head down the stairs and they risked running into the bastards head-on. For a moment, he was tempted anyway, but Imperial weapons were too destructive. If they got caught in a stairwell, a single shot might take out all their men—and 'Tanni. But if they didn't try to break out, they left the initiative to the other side. On the other hand—

Jiltanith stepped out of the bedroom, convoyed by four stocky, black-and-tan rottweilers. Her dagger glittered on her belt, and Horus' mouth tightened as she reached out and took Captain Chin's grav gun from its holster. The Marine didn't protest; he simply shifted his energy gun to his left hand and passed over his ammunition belt with his right, and she gave him a strained smile. The belt wouldn't fit around her pregnancy-swollen waist, so she hung it over her shoulder like a bandolier.

"All right, Captain," Horus said. "We have to let them come to us. The stairs merge into the central core one floor down; have ten of your people set up to cover the landings. Leave the other two here to cover the access to my office. 'Tanni, lock your bedroom door, then go to *my* room and lock yourself in. Hopefully, if anyone gets this far, they'll head for your room first."

"Father, I—" she began, and he shook his head savagely.

"I know, 'Tanni, but you're going to have to leave this to us. We can't risk you, and even if we could—" He waved at her swollen belly, the gesture both tender and oddly apologetic, and she nodded unhappily.

"Art right," she sighed, and looked down at the bio-enhanced dogs.

"Go thou wi' Captain Chin," she told them, "and watch thyselves."

"We go, pack lady," Galahad's vocoder said, "but keep Gwynevere with you." She nodded, and Horus looked at Chin as the other three dogs leapt away.

"We're out of communication, and we're going to be spread out. Watch your rears as well as your fronts."

"Yes, Your Grace!" Chin saluted and vanished after the dogs, and Horus turned to the two Marines who'd been left behind.

"Anyone who gets this far will have to come up the last stair. After that, they'll go for 'Tanni's bedroom first. Pick yourselves positions to cover the stairs. If you have to fall back, head *this* way; *don't* head for my room. We want them to keep on thinking she's in her room as long as we can."

"Yes, Sir." The senior Marine jerked his head at his companion, and they ran towards the tower's central access core.

"Go, 'Tanni!" Horus said urgently.

"I go, Father," she said softly, yet she paused just long enough to throw one arm about him and kiss him before she wheeled away. He watched her go, Gwynevere trotting ahead of her like a scout, and turned to survey his office one more time. He'd accomplished a lot from this place. Commanded the Siege of Earth, directed the reconstruction in its wake, coordinated the introduction of an entire planet to Imperial technology. . . . He'd never expected to fight for his daughter's life from it, but if he had to do that too, then, by the Maker, he would.

He walked slowly to the office foyer. It was the only way into his personal quarters, and he upended his receptionist's desk and piled furniture about it. He built a sturdy barricade facing the entry, then stepped away from it to the wall beside the entry and settled his back into a corner.

"The explosives have arrived at the Palace, Colin," Dahak said as Colin entered the command deck of the computer's starship body.

"Good." Officers popped to their feet as their Emperor and Warlord strode across to the captain's couch, but he waved them back to their duties. *Dahak* had moved beyond the weapon's threat radius, and Colin felt a sick surge of guilt as he realized that, whatever happened, he personally was safe. It seemed a betrayal of all his subjects, and knowing Hector and Gerald were right to insist upon it only made his guilt worse.

He settled into the command couch. The display was centered on Birhat, not *Dahak*, and he watched sublight craft streaming from the planetary surface to the waiting planetoids. Like *Dahak*, all those starships were beyond threat range, and thousands more of his subjects were embarking aboard them as he watched, but it was taking time. Too much time they might not have. He drew a deep, deep breath and pressed himself back in his couch.

"Tell them to proceed, Dahak."

Brigadier Jourdain followed his men up the stairs. There were only twelve Marines, one tired old man, and a pregnant woman to stop them, while he had over a hundred men, all fully enhanced courtesy of Earth Security. It would be more than enough, he told himself yet again. Some were going to get killed, but not enough to stop them, and dead Security men would be convincing proof of how hard Brigadier Jourdain and his men had fought to protect their Empress.

He bared mirthless teeth at the thought as his point man approached the landing. They were one floor below Duke Horus's office and living quarters, and they hadn't seen a soul. Perhaps he'd worried too much. Surely if the Marines *had* figured anything out—

Something rattled. The lead Security man saw the small object skitter past his feet, and his eyes flared. No! His implant scanners hadn't picked up a thing, so how—

Eleven men died in a blast of fury, and the Marine who'd thrown the grenade grinned savagely as he and his partner reactivated their own implants and brought their energy guns to bear on the smoke-streaming door.

Captain Chin's head jerked up as the explosion rattled. *Please, God, let someone else have heard it!* he prayed, then settled back down in firing position.

Brigadier Jourdain's ears cringed as thunder filled the stairwell. The screams of the merely wounded were faint and tiny in the explosion's wake, and he swore viciously. So much for surprise!

"Clancey! Get up there!" he barked, and Corporal Clancey settled his automatic grenade launcher into firing position. He jerked his head at the other three members of his section, and the four of them pushed forward through the men above them on the stair.

The waiting Marines had their own implant sensors on-line now, but there was a limit to what the devices could tell them. They knew the stairs were full of men, but they couldn't tell what weapons they carried or precisely what they were doing. The second Marine held a grenade, ready to throw it, but the same suppressor that blocked their coms from hyperspace would smother any hyper grenade's small field, and they'd had only one HE grenade each. He couldn't afford to waste it, and so he gritted his teeth and waited.

Clancey and his team reached the landing and eased forward, boots skidding in what had once been their point men, backs pressed to the walls. They, too, had their sensors on-line, and they didn't like what they were telling them. There were two Marines up there, and only one of them was where their grenades could get at him; the other was further back, sheltering in a cross-connecting corridor to cover his companion, and Clancey swore. God, what he wouldn't give for hyper grenades! But at least the bastards didn't seem to have any more grenades of their own.

He nodded to the two men against the opposite wall.

"Go!"

They spun into the doorway, launchers coughing on full auto. The closer Marine's fire ripped both of them apart, but their grenades were already on the way, and a staccato blast rattled teeth as they detonated in sequence, killing him instantly.

Clancey cursed as an energy gun splattered his companions over him, but his implants told him the Marine who'd fired was dead. He went down in a crouch, hosing more grenades to keep the surviving Marine's head down while more Security men charged the door. Explosions shattered walls and furnishings, and the building's fire suppression systems howled to life as flames glared. More men charged up the stairs, white faces locked in death's-head grins, and then Corporal Clancey discovered he'd been wrong about what the Marines had.

The grenade landed 1.3 meters behind him, and he had one instant to feel the terror before it exploded and killed six more men . . . including Corporal William Clancey, Earth Security.

Vlad Chernikov felt blind and maimed. For the first time in twenty-five years, every implant in his body had been shut down lest the Mark Ninety decide they were weapons, and the sudden reversion to the senses Nature had provided was a greater psychic shock than he'd anticipated.

He grimaced the thought aside and hoisted the charge Dahak had designed. The initiator charges of the obsolete warheads had been formed in hundreds of precisely shaped blocks, and Dahak had reassembled a hundred and fifty kilos of them into a single massive shaped-charge. That might be more than they needed, but Dahak believed in redundancy.

He slung the charge on his back—at least his muscular enhancement still worked, since it used no power and hence offered no emissions signature to offend the Mark Ninety's sensibilities—and started down the hall to the gallery on the longest sixty-meter hike of his life.

The scream of alarms filled the stairwell as thermal sensors responded to the fires the explosions had set. Their shrill, atonal wail set Jourdain's teeth on edge, but White Tower's soundproofing was excellent, and his men at the switchboard had cut all lines to its top fifteen floors. None of which meant people wouldn't notice if grenades started blowing out windows.

"Push 'em back!" he shouted, and started up the stairs. His point had stalled amid the carnage of shattered bodies, and he snarled at them. "Come on, you bastards! There's only *twelve* of them!"

He flung himself through the doorway, landing flat on his belly in Clancey's blood. More of his men crouched behind him or threw themselves prone, and at least a dozen energy guns snarled. Walls already torn and pocked by grenade fragments ripped apart under focused beams of gravitic disruption, and the Marine fired back desperately. Another of his men went down, then two more, a fourth, but there was only one Marine left. It was only a matter of time—and not much of it—until one of those energy guns found him.

There were five separate stairs. Captain Chin had placed two Marines to cover each, but Jourdain had elected to assault only three, and combat roared as his other assault teams ran into their own defenders. The Marines had the advantage of position; their attackers had both numbers and heavier weapons. It was an unequal equation, and it could have only one solution.

Jourdain's number three assault team lost ten men in the first exchange, but its commander was a hard-bitten man, an ex-Marine himself, who knew what he was about. Once he'd pinpointed the defenders, he sent six men down one floor. They positioned themselves directly beneath the Marines, switched their energy guns to maximum power, aimed at the ceiling, and simply held the triggers back. The Marines never had time to realize what was happening, and assault team three charged forward over their mutilated bodies.

✧ ✧ ✧

Captain Chin heard feet behind him and rolled up on one knee just as the leading "Security men" appeared in the hall. His energy gun howled, and three of them vanished in a gory spray. He flung himself back down, flat on his belly against the wall, and his single grenade killed three more attackers.

"Wire the doors and get your ass up here, Matthews!" he shouted to his teammate. Private Matthews didn't waste time answering. She yanked the pin from her own grenade and wedged it against the stairwell door so that any effort to open it would release the safety handle. Then she grabbed her energy gun and headed for the captain's position.

She arrived just in time to help beat off the next assault, and then Chin swore as the attackers fell back.

"They're not coming up our stair at all," he spat. "They're going to leave someone to pin us down and get on with it."

"Only if we let 'em, Cap," Matthews grunted, and before Chin could stop her, the private lunged to her feet. She charged down the hall, energy gun on continuous fire, and Chin leapt to his feet and followed. Matthews killed six more men before answering fire blew her apart, and Chin vaulted her body. The captain landed less than a meter from the remaining three men holding the blocking position, and four energy guns snarled as one.

There were no survivors on either side.

Staff Sergeant Duncan Sellers, Earth Security, swore monotonously as he ran down the hall. He'd gotten separated from the rest of his team, and the entire floor had filled with smoke despite the fire suppression systems. His enhanced lungs handled the smoke easily, but he dreaded what could happen if he blundered into his friends and they mistook him for a Marine.

He turned a corner and gasped in relief as he picked up the implants of his fellows ahead. He opened his mouth to shout his own name, then whirled as some sixth sense warned him. A shape bounded towards him, but his instant spurt of panic eased as he realized it was only one of the Empress's dogs. Big as it was, no dog was a threat to an enhanced human, and he raised his energy gun almost negligently.

Gaheris was four meters away when he left the floor in a prodigious spring. Sergeant Sellers got off one shot—then screamed in terror as bio-enhanced jaws ripped his throat out like tissue.

Alex Jourdain advanced in a crouch, weapon ready, and disbelief filled him. There were only *twelve* of them, damn it!

Perhaps so, but by the time his three assault teams merged at the foot of the single stair leading to the next floor, he'd lost over seventy men. Over *seventy*! Worse, he'd added up the Marine body count from all three teams and come up with only eight. Two more were pinned down at the west stairwell, but the last pair of Marines was still unaccounted for— and ten of his own men were equally pinned down in the stairwell firefight.

That left him with only nineteen under his own command, and he didn't like the math. Eight Marines had killed seventy-six of their attackers. That worked out to almost ten each, and if Horus and the two remaining Marines did as well . . .

He shook his head. It was the stupid and incautious who died first, he told himself. The men he had left were survivors, or they wouldn't have gotten this far. They could still do it—and they'd damned well *better*, because none of them could go home and pretend this hadn't happened!

"Hose it!" he barked to his remaining grenadiers, and a hurricane of grenades lashed up the stairs and blew the doors at their head to bits.

"Go!" Jourdain shouted, and his men went forward in a rush.

Corporal Anna Zhirnovski cringed as another grenade exploded. The bastards had gotten Steve O'Hennesy with the last salvo, but Zhirnovski was bellied down behind a right-angled bend in the corridor. They couldn't get a direct shot at her, but they were trying to bounce the damned things around the corner, and they were getting closer. It was only a matter of time, and she rechecked her sensors. At least seven of them left, she thought, and despair stabbed through her. They wouldn't waste this much time—or this many men—on killing one Marine unless they had enough other firepower to kill the Empress without their input, but there wasn't a damned thing she could do about it. She and Steve had been cut off from the central core, and even launching a kamikaze attack into them would achieve nothing but her own death.

Her muscles quivered with the need to do just that, for she was a Marine, handpicked to protect her Empress' life, but she fought the urge down once more. She was going to die. She'd accepted that. And if she couldn't kill the men attacking her (and she couldn't), she could at least keep them occupied. And, she told herself grimly, she could make them pay cash when they came after her to finish off the witnesses.

Another string of grenades exploded, and she detected movement behind them. They were trying a rush under cover of the explosions, and she waited tensely. Now!

The grenadiers stopped firing to let their flankers go in, and Anna Zhirnovski rolled out into the corridor, under the smoke. Men shrieked as her snarling energy gun ripped their feet and legs apart, and Zhirnovski snap-rolled back into her protected position.

Two more, she thought, and then the grenades began to explode once more.

Oscar Sanders unwrapped another stick of gum, shoved it into his mouth, and chewed rhythmically without ever taking his eyes from the HD. Every news service was covering the chaos at the mat-trans facility across the Concourse from Sanders' position in the White Tower lobby, and he shook his head. Virtually every member of White Tower's usual security force was over there trying to sort out the confusion, and they were fighting a losing battle. Sanders had never seen so many people in one place in his life, and the threat that could produce it was enough to make anyone nervous. Evacuating an entire planet because of *one* bomb? What the hell sort of bomb could—

He looked up at a sudden slamming sound. It came again, then again, and he frowned and glanced at his console. Every light glowed a steady green, but the slamming sound echoed yet again, and he stood.

He walked around the end of the counter and followed the sound up the corridor. It was coming from the stairwell door, and he drew his grav gun and reached for the latch. He gripped it firmly and yanked the door open, then relaxed. It was only a dog, one of Empress Jiltanith's.

But Oscar Sanders's relief vanished suddenly, and his gun snapped back up as he realized the dog was covered with blood. He almost squeezed the trigger, but his brain caught up with his instincts first. The dog was not only covered with blood; one of its forelegs was a mangled stub, and the door was slick with blood where the injured animal had tried repeatedly to spring the crash bar latch with its remaining leg.

It took only a fraction of a second for Sanders' stunned brain to put all that together—and then, with a sudden burst of horror, to remember *whose* dog this was. He jerked back, a thousand questions flaring through his mind, and that was when the strangest thing of all happened.

"Help!" Gaheris's vocoder said just before he collapsed. "Men come to kill Jiltanith! *Help her!*"

Vlad Chernikov turned the last corner, and the magnificent statue stood before him. Even now he felt a stir of awe for its beauty, but he hadn't come to admire it, and he advanced cautiously.

The shaped charge on his back seemed to take on weight with every stride. It was silly, of course. He was already well inside a Mark Ninety's interdiction perimeter; if the thing was going to decide the charge was a weapon, it would already have blown up the planet.

That, unfortunately, made him feel no less naked and vulnerable, and he missed his implants' ability to manipulate his adrenaline level as he stepped around the inert scanner remote still lying where it had fallen when Dahak hastily deactivated it.

He moved to within two meters of the sculpture and studied it carefully. The problem was that his weapon was insufficient to reduce the entire statue to gravel, so he had to be certain that whatever bit he chose to blow up contained the bomb. And since neither he nor Dahak could scan the thing, he could only try to estimate where the bomb was.

It would help, he thought irritably, if they knew its dimensions. It was tempting to assume they'd used Tsien's blueprints without alteration, but if that assumption proved inaccurate, the consequences would be extreme.

Well, there were certain constraints Mister X's bomb-makers couldn't avoid. The primary emitter, for example, *had* to be at least two meters long and twenty centimeters in diameter, and the focusing coils would each add another thirty centimeters to the emitter's length. That gave him a minimum length of two hundred sixty centimeters, which meant the bomb couldn't be inside the human half of the statue. It would have had to be in his torso, and while the Marine was more than life-sized, he wasn't *that* much larger, so the bomb itself had to be inside the Narhani. Unfortunately, the Narhani was big enough that the thing could be oriented at any of several angles, and he couldn't afford to miss. Of course, the power source for the bomb was a fair-sized target all on its own, and the designers had had to squeeze in the Mark 90, too. They'd undoubtedly put at least part of the hardware inside the Marine, but *which* part?

They'd counted on the bomb's never being detected, Vlad thought, so they *probably* hadn't considered the need to design it to sustain damage and still function, which might mean the power source was inside the Marine and the rest of the hardware was inside the Narhani. That was a seductively attractive supposition, but again, he couldn't afford to guess wrong.

He stepped even closer to the statue, considering the angle of the Narhani's body as it reared against its chains. All right, the bomb *wasn't* inside the human and it *was* the next best thing to three meters long. It couldn't be placed vertically in the Narhani's torso, either, because there wasn't enough length. It could be partly inside the torso and angled down into the body's barrel, though. The arch of the Narhani's spine would make that placement tricky, but it was feasible.

He rocked back on his heels and wiped sweat from his forehead as the unhappy conclusion forced itself upon him. The possible bomb dimensions simply left too many possibilities. To be certain, he had to split the statue cleanly in two, and to be sure the break came within the critical length, he'd have to come up from below.

He sighed, wishing he dared activate his com implant to consult with Dahak, then shrugged. He couldn't, and even if he could have, he already knew what Dahak would say.

He wiped his forehead one more time, took the bomb from his back, and bent cautiously to edge it under the marble Narhani's belly.

The last exchange of fire faded into silence, and Brigadier Jourdain's mouth was a bitter, angry line. Ten more of his men lay dead around the head of the ruined stairs. Two more were down, one so badly mangled only his implants kept him alive, and they wouldn't do that much longer, but at least they'd accounted for the last two Marines.

He glared at the closed door to the foyer of Horus's office and cranked his implant sensors to maximum power. Damn it, he *knew* the Governor was in there somewhere, but the cunning old bastard must have shut his implants down, like the Marines covering that first stairwell. As long as he stayed put without moving, Jourdain couldn't pick him up without implant emissions.

Well, there were drawbacks to that sort of game, the brigadier told himself grimly. If Horus had his implants down, he couldn't see *Jourdain* or his men, either. He was limited to his natural senses. That ought to make him a bit slower off the mark when he opened fire, and even if he'd found an ambush position to let him get the first few men through the door, he'd reveal his position to the others the instant he fired.

"All right," the brigadier said to his seven remaining men. "Here's how we're going to do this."

Franklin Detmore ripped off another burst of grenades and grimaced. Whoever that Marine up there was, he was too damned good for Detmore's taste. The ten men assigned to mop him up had been reduced to five, and Detmore was delighted to be the only remaining grenadier. He vastly preferred laying down covering fire to being the next poor son-of-a-bitch to rush the bastard.

He fed a fresh belt into his launcher and looked up. Luis Esteben was the senior man, and he looked profoundly unhappy. Their orders were to leave no witnesses; sooner or later, someone was going to have to go in after the last survivor, and Esteben had a sinking suspicion who Brigadier Jourdain was going to pick for the job if he hadn't gotten it done by the time the Brigadier got here.

"All right," he said finally. "We're not going to take this bastard out with a frontal assault." His fellows nodded, and he bared his teeth at their relieved expressions. "What we need to do is get in behind him."

"We can't. That's a blind corridor," someone pointed out.

"Yeah, but it's got walls, and we've got energy guns," Esteben pointed out. "Frank, you keep him busy, and the rest of us'll go back and circle around to get into the conference room next door. We can blow through the wall from there and flank him out."

"Suits me," Detmore agreed, "but—" He broke off and his eyes widened. "What the hell is *that*?" he demanded, staring back up the corridor.

Esteben was still turning when Galahad and Gawain exploded into the Security men's rear.

Vlad settled the charge delicately and sighed in relief. He was still alive; that was the good news. The bad news was that he couldn't be certain this was going to work . . . and there was only one way to find out.

He set the timer, turned, and ran like hell.

Alarms screamed as Oscar Sanders hit every button on his panel. Security personnel and Imperial Marines fighting to control traffic in the mattrans facility looked up in shock, then turned as one to run for White Tower as Sanders came up on their coms.

The foyer door vanished in a hurricane of fire, and two men slammed through the opening. They saw the piled fortress of furniture facing the door and charged it frantically, firing on the run, desperate to reach it before Horus could pop up and return fire.

He let them get half way to it, and then, without moving from his position in the corner, cut both of them in half.

Jourdain cursed in mingled rage and triumph as his men went down.

Damn that sneaky old bastard! But his fire had given away his position, and the brigadier and his five remaining Security men knew exactly where to look when *they* came through the door.

Energy guns snarled in a frenzy of destruction at a range of less than five meters. Men went down—screaming or dead—and then it was over. Two more attackers were down, one dead and one dying . . . and the Governor of Earth was down as well. Someone's fire had smashed his energy gun, but it didn't really matter, Jourdain thought as he glared down at him, for Horus was mangled and torn. Only his implants were keeping him alive, and they were failing fast.

Jourdain raised his weapon, only to lower it once more as the old man snarled at him. Horus couldn't last ten more minutes, the brigadier thought coldly, but he could last long enough to know Jourdain had killed his daughter.

"Find the bitch," he said coldly, turning away from the dying Governor. "Kill her."

Vlad rounded the last corner, skidded to a halt, and flung himself flat.

The charge went off just before he landed, and the floor seemed to leap up and hit him in the face. His mouth filled with blood as he bit his tongue, and he yelped in pain.

It was only then that he realized he was still alive . . . which meant it must have worked.

Agony drowned Horus in red, screaming waves—the physical agony his implants couldn't suppress, and the more terrible one of knowing men were hunting his daughter to kill her. He bit back a scream and made his broken body obey his will one last time. Both his legs were gone, and most of his left arm, but he dragged himself—slowly, painfully, centimeter by centimeter—across the carpet in a ribbon of blood. His entire, fading world was focused on the closest corpse's holstered grav gun. He inched towards it, gasping with effort, and his fingers fumbled with the holster. His hand was slow and clumsy, shaking with pain, but the holster came open and he gripped the weapon.

A boot slammed down on his wrist, and he jerked in fresh agony, then rolled his head slowly and stared into the muzzle of an energy gun.

"You just can't wait to die, can you, you old bastard?" Alex Jourdain hissed. "All right—have it your way!"

His finger tightened on the firing stud . . . and then his head blew apart and Horus' eyes flared in astonishment as two bloodsoaked rottweilers and a Marine corporal charged across his body.

"Your Majesty! Your Majesty!"

Jiltanith stiffened, then shuddered in relief as she recognized the voice. It was Anna, and if Corporal Zhirnovski was calling her name and there were no more screams and firing—

She jerked the door open, and Gwynevere shot out it, hackles raised, ready to attack any threat. But there was no threat. Only a smoke-stained, bloodied Marine corporal, one arm hanging useless at her side . . . the sole survivor of Jiltanith's security team.

"Anna!" she cried, reaching out to the wounded woman, but Zhirnovski shook her head.

"Your father!" she gasped. "In the foyer!"

Jiltanith hesitated, and the corporal shook her head again.

"My implants'll hold it, Your Majesty! *Go!*"

Horus drifted deeper into a well of darkness. The world was fading away, dim and insubstantial as the hovering smoke, and he felt Death whispering to him at last. He'd cheated the old thief so long, he thought hazily. So long. But no one cheated him forever, did they? And Death wasn't that bad a fellow, not really. His whisper promised an end to agony, and perhaps, just perhaps, somewhere on the other side of the pain he would find Tanisis, as well. He hoped so. He longed to apologize to her as he had to 'Tanni, and—

His eyes fluttered open as someone touched him. He stared up from the bottom of his well, and his fading eyes brightened. His head was in her lap, and tears soaked her face, but she was alive. Alive, and so beautiful. His beautiful, strong daughter.

"'Tanni." His remaining arm weighed tons, but he forced it up, touched her cheek, her hair. "'Tanni . . ."

It came out in a thread, and she caught his hand, pressing it to her breast, and bent over him. Her lips brushed his forehead, and she stroked his hair.

"I love you, Poppa," she whispered to him in perfect Universal, and then the darkness came down forever.

CHAPTER FORTY-FOUR

Lawrence Jefferson gazed into the mirror and adjusted his appearance with meticulous care, then checked the clock. Ten more minutes, he thought, and turned back to the mirror to smile at himself.

For someone who'd seen almost thirty years of planning collapse with spectacular totality less than two months before, he felt remarkably cheerful. His coup attempt had failed, but the governorship of Earth was a fair consolation prize—and, he reflected, an even better platform from which to plan anew after a few years.

He'd gone to considerable lengths to set Brigadier Jourdain up as the fall guy if his plans miscarried, and the brigadier had helped by getting himself killed, which neatly precluded the possibility of his defending himself against the charges. Lieutenant Governor Jefferson had, of course, been shocked to learn that one of his most senior Security men had formed links to the Sword of God and had, in fact, used Security's own bioenhancement facilities to enhance his own select band of traitors! The stunning discovery of Jourdain's treason had led to a massive shakeup at Security, in the course of which an Internal Affairs inspector had "stumbled across" the secret journal which chronicled the brigadier's secretly growing disaffection. A disaffection which had blossomed to full life when he was named to head the special team created by newly appointed Security Minister Jefferson to combat the Sword's terrorism following the Van Gelder assassination. Instead of hunting the Sword down to destroy it, he'd used the investigation to make contact with a Sword cell leader and found his true spiritual home.

It was a black mark against Jefferson that he'd failed to spot Jourdain's treason, but the man had been recruited away from the Imperial Marines by Gustav van Gelder (no one—now living, that was—knew it was Jefferson who'd recommended him to Gus), not Jefferson, and he'd passed every security screening. And if his journal rambled here and there, that was only to be expected in the personal maunderings of a megalomaniac who believed God had chosen him to destroy all who trafficked with the

Anti-Christ. It detailed his meticulous plan to assassinate Colin, Jiltanith, Horus, their senior military officers, and Lawrence Jefferson, and if it was a bit vague about precisely what was supposed to happen when they were dead, the fact that he'd hidden his bomb inside the Narhani statue suggested his probable intent. By branding the Narhani with responsibility for the destruction of Birhat, he'd undoubtedly hoped to lead humanity into turning on them as arch-traitors and dealing with them precisely as the Sword of God *said* they should be dealt with.

Jefferson was proud of that journal. He'd spent over two years preparing it, just in case, and if there were a few points on which it failed to shed any light, that was actually a point in its favor. By leaving some mysteries, it avoided the classic failing of coverups: an attempt to answer *every* question. Had it tried to do so, someone—like Ninhursag MacMahan—undoubtedly would have found it just a bit too neat. As it was, and coupled with the fact that the dozens of still-living people named in it had, in fact, all been recruited by Jourdain (on Jefferson's orders, perhaps, but none of *them* knew that), it had worked to perfection. The most important members of Jefferson's conspiracy weren't listed in it, and several of his more valuable moles had actually been promoted for their sterling work in helping ONI run down the villains the journal's discovery had unmasked. Best of all, every one of those villains, questioned under Imperial lie detectors, only confirmed that Jourdain had recruited them and that all of their instructions had come from him.

The clock chimed softly, and Jefferson settled his face into properly grave lines before he walked to the door. He opened it and stepped out into the corridor to the Terran Chamber of Delegates with a slow, somber pace that befitted the occasion while his brain rehearsed the oath of office he was about to recite.

He was half way to the Chamber when a voice spoke behind him.

"Lawrence McClintock Jefferson," it said with icy precision, "I arrest you for conspiracy, espionage, murder, and the crime of high treason."

He froze, and his heart seemed to stop, for the voice was that of Colin I, Emperor of Humanity. He stood absolutely motionless for one agonizing moment, then turned slowly, and swallowed as he found himself facing the Emperor, and Hector and Ninhursag MacMahan. The general held a grav gun in one hand, its rock-steady muzzle trained on Jefferson's belly, and his hard, hating eyes begged the Lieutenant Governor to resist arrest.

"What . . . what did you say?" Jefferson whispered.

"You made one mistake," Ninhursag replied coldly. "Only one. When you set up Jourdain's journal, you fingered him for everything except the one crime that actually started us looking for you, 'Mister X.' There wasn't a word in it about Sean's and Harriet's assassination—and the murder of my daughter."

"Assassination?" Jefferson repeated in a numb voice.

"Without that, I might actually have bought it," she went on in a voice like liquid nitrogen, "but the megalomaniac you created in that journal would never have failed to record his greatest triumph. Which, of course, suggested it was a fake, so I started looking for who *else* might have had the combination of clearances necessary to steal the bomb's blueprints, have it built, smuggle it through the mat-trans, alter the mat-trans log so subsequent investigators would know he had, *and* get a batch of assassins into White Tower. And guess who all that pointed to?"

"But I—" He cleared his throat noisily. "But if you suspect me of such horrible crimes, why wait until now to arrest me?" he demanded harshly.

"We waited because 'Hursag wanted to see who distinguished themselves in your 'investigation' of Jourdain." Colin's voice was as icy as Ninhursag's. "It was one way to figure out who else was working for you. But the timing for your arrest?" He smiled viciously. "That was *my* idea, Jefferson. I wanted you to be able to *taste* the governorship—and I want you to go right on remembering what it tasted like up to the moment the firing squad pulls the trigger."

He stepped aside, and Jefferson saw the grim-faced Marines who'd stood behind the Emperor. Marines who advanced upon him with expressions whose plea to resist mirrored that of their commandant.

"You'll have a fair trial," Colin told him flatly as the Marines took him into custody, "but with any luck at all—" he smiled again, with a cold, cruel pleasure Jefferson had never imagined his homely face could wear "—every member of the firing squad will hit you in the belly. Think about that, Mister Jefferson. Look *forward* to it."

Colin and Jiltanith sat on their favorite Palace balcony, gazing out over the city of Phoenix. Colin held their infant daughter, Anna Zhirnovski MacIntyre, in his lap while her godmother stood guard at the balcony entrance and her younger brother Horus Gaheris MacIntyre nursed at his mother's breast. Amanda and Tsien Tao-ling stood side by side, leaning on the balcony rail, while Hector and Ninhursag sat beside Colin. Tinker Bell's pups—including Gaheris and his regenerated leg—drowsed on the sun-warmed flagstones, and Gerald and Sharon Hatcher, Brashieel, and Eve completed the gathering.

"I do not fully understand humans even now, Nest Lord." The Narhani leader sighed. "You can be a most complex and confusing species."

"Perhaps, my love," Eve said gently, "yet they are also a stubborn and generous one."

"Truly," Brashieel conceded, "but the thought that Jefferson planned to implicate *us* in our Nest Lord's murder—" He bent his head in the Narhani gesture of perplexity, and his double eyelids flickered with dismay.

"You were just there, Brashieel," Colin said wearily. "Just as the Achuultani computer needed a threat to keep your people enslaved, Jefferson needed a threat to justify the power he intended to seize."

"And the Achuultani history of genocide made us an excellent threat," Eve observed.

"Indeed," Dahak's voice replied. "It was a most complex plot, and Jefferson's association with Francine Hilgemann was a masterful alliance. It not only permitted him to further inflame and sustain the anti-Narhani prejudices the Church of the Armageddon enshrined but gave him direct access to the Sword of God. A classic continuation of Anu's practice of employing terrorist proxies."

"Um." Colin grunted agreement and gazed down into his daughter's small, thoughtful face. She looked perplexed as she tried to focus on the tip of her own nose, and at this moment, that was infinitely more important to him than Lawrence Jefferson or Francine Hilgemann.

Jefferson's interrogation under an Imperial lie detector had led to the arrest of his entire surviving command structure. The last of them had been shot a week before, and it was even possible some good would come of it. The Church of the Armageddon, for example, was in wild disarray. Not only had their spiritual leader been unmasked as a cold, cynical manipulator, but the fact that she and Jefferson had intended to use their anti-Narhani prejudice to whip up a genocidal frenzy to support their coup had shocked the church to its foundation. Colin suspected the hardcore true believers would find some way to blame the Narhani for their own victimization, but those whose brains hadn't entirely ossified might just take a good, hard look at themselves.

Yet none of it seemed very important somehow. No doubt that would change, but for now his wounds, and those of his friends, were too raw and bleeding. Jefferson's execution couldn't bring back their children any more than it could restore Horus or the Marines who'd died defending Jiltanith to life. There was such a thing as vengeance, and Colin was honest enough to admit he'd felt just that as Jefferson died, but it was a cold, iron-tasting thing, and too much of it was a poison more deadly than arsenic.

Anna blew a bubble of drool at him, and he smiled. He looked up at Jiltanith, feeling his bitter melancholy ease, and she smiled back. Darkness and grief still edged that smile, but so did tenderness, and her fingers stroked her son's head as he sucked on her nipple. Colin turned his head and saw the others watching, saw them smiling at his wife and his son, and a deep, gentle wave of warmth eased his heart as he felt their shared happiness for him and 'Tanni. Their love.

Perhaps that, he thought, was the real lesson. The knowledge that life meant growth and change and challenge, and that those were painful things, but that only those who dared to love despite the pain were the true inheritors of humanity's dreams of greatness.

He closed his eyes and pressed his nose into his daughter's fine, downy hair, inhaling the clean skin and baby powder and stale milk sweetness of her, and the peaceful content of this small, quiet moment suffused him.

And then Dahak made the quiet electronic sound he used when a human would have cleared his throat.

"Excuse me, Colin, but I have just received a priority hypercom transmission of which I feel you should be apprised."

"A hypercom message?" Colin raised his head with an expression of mild curiosity. "What sort of message?"

"The transmission," Dahak said, "is from the planet Pardal."

"'Pardal'?" Colin looked at Hatcher. "Gerald? You have a survey mission to someplace called 'Pardal'?"

"Pardal?" Hatcher shook his head. "Never heard of it."

"You sure you got that name right, Dahak?" Colin asked.

"I am."

"Well where in the blazes is it and how come I never heard of it?"

"I am not yet certain of the answer to either of those questions, Colin. The message, however, is signed 'Acting Governor Midshipman His Imperial Highness Sean Horus MacIntyre,'" Dahak replied calmly, and Jiltanith gasped as Colin jerked upright in his lounger. "It reports the successful reclamation of the populated planet Pardal for the Imperium by the crew of the sublight battleship *Israel*: Midshipwoman Princess Isis Harriet MacIntyre, Midshipman Count Tamman, Midshipwoman Crown Princess Consort Sandra MacMahan MacIntyre, and Mishipman Nest Heir Brashan."

Colin's head snapped around. His incredulous gaze met Jiltanith's equally incredulous—and joyous—eyes, then swept to his friends, the friends who were coming to their feet in joy that matched his own, as Dahak paused for just a moment. Then the computer spoke again, and even Dahak's mellow voice could not hide its vast elation.

"Will there be a reply?"